With love to my sons
Nathaniel and Joseph

זכור

Foreword

The Winds of War *is fiction, and all the characters and adventures involving the Henry family are imaginary. But the history of the war in this romance is offered as accurate; the statistics, as reliable; the words and acts of the great personages, as either historical, or derived from accounts of their words and deeds in similar situations. No work of this scope can be free of error, but readers will discern, it is hoped, an arduous effort to give a true and full picture of a great world battle.*

World Empire Lost, the military treatise by "Armin von Roon," *is of course an invention from start to finish. Still, General von Roon's book is offered as a professional German view of the other side of the hill, reliable within the limits peculiar to that self-justifying military literature.*

Industrialized armed force, the curse that now presses so heavily and so ominously on us all, came to full flower in the Second World War. The effort to free ourselves of it begins with the effort to understand how it came to haunt us, and how it was that men of good will gave—and still give—their lives to it. The theme and aim of The Winds of War *can be found in a few words by the French Jew, Julien Benda:*

> Peace, if it ever exists, will not be based on the fear of war, but on the love of peace. It will not be the abstaining from an act, but the coming of a state of mind. In this sense the most insignificant writer can serve peace, where the most powerful tribunals can do nothing.

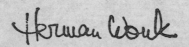

PART ONE

Natalie

1

COMMANDER Victor Henry rode a taxicab home from the Navy Building on Constitution Avenue, in a gusty gray March rainstorm that matched his mood. In his War Plans cubbyhole that afternoon, he had received an unexpected word from on high which, to his seasoned appraisal, had probably blown a well-planned career to rags. Now he had to consult his wife about an urgent decision; yet he did not altogether trust her opinions.

At forty-five, Rhoda Henry remained a singularly attractive woman, but she was rather a crab. This colored her judgment, and it was a fault he found hard to forgive her. She had married him with her eyes open. During an incandescent courtship, they had talked frankly about the military life. Rhoda Grover had declared that all the drawbacks—the separations, the lack of a real place to live and of a normal family existence, the long slow climb through a system, the need to be humble to other men's wives when the men were a notch higher—that none of these things would trouble her, because she loved him, and because the Navy was a career of honor. So she had said in 1915, when the World War was on, and uniforms had a glow. This was 1939, and she had long since forgotten those words.

He had warned her that the climb would be hard. Victor Henry was not of a Navy family. On every rung of the slippery career ladder, the sons and grandsons of admirals had been jostling him. Yet everyone in the Navy who knew Pug Henry called him a comer. Until now his rise had been steady.

The letter that first got him into the Naval Academy, written to his congressman while in high school, can be

3

adduced here to characterize the man. He showed his form early.

May 5th, 1910

Dear Sir:

You have sent me three kind answers to three letters I have sent you, from my freshman year onward, reporting my progress in Sonoma County High School. So I hope that you will remember my name, and my ambition to obtain appointment to the Naval Academy.

Now I am about to complete my senior year. It may seem conceited to list my achievements, but I am sure you will understand why I do so. I am captain of the football team this year, playing fullback, and I am also on the boxing team.

I have been elected to the Arista Society. In mathematics, history, and the sciences, I am a candidate for prizes. My English and foreign language (German) marks are not on that level. However, I am secretary of the small Russian-speaking club of our school. Its nine members come from local families whose ancestors were settled in Fort Ross long ago by the Czar. My best chum was in the club, so I joined and learned some Russian. I mention this to show that my language ability is not deficient.

My life aim is to serve as an officer in the United States Navy. I can't actually explain this, since my family has no seafaring background. My father is an engineer in the redwood lumbering business. I have never liked lumbering, but have always been interested in ships and big guns. I have gone to San Francisco and San Diego often just to visit the naval ships there. Out of my savings I have bought and studied about two dozen books on marine engineering and sea warfare.

I realize you have only one appointment to make, and there must be many applicants in our district. If one is found more deserving than I am, I will enlist in the Navy and work up from the ranks. However, I have seriously tried for your consideration, and trust that I have earned it.

Respectfully yours
Victor Henry

With much the same directness, Henry had won his wife five years later, though she was a couple of inches taller than he, and though her prosperous parents had looked for a better match than a squat Navy fullback from California, of no means or family. Courting Rhoda, he had come out of his single-minded shell of ambition to show much tenderness, humor, considerateness, and dash. After a month or two Rhoda had lost any inclination to say no. Mundane details like height differences had faded from sight.

Still, over the long pull it may not be too good for a pretty woman to look down at her husband. Tall men tend to make plays for her, regarding the couple as slightly comic. Though a very proper woman, Rhoda had a weakness for this sort of thing—up to a point short of trouble —and even coyly provoked it. Henry's reputation as a bleak hard-fibered individual discouraged the men from ever getting out of hand. He was very much Rhoda's master. Still, this physical detail was a continuing nag.

The real shadow on this couple was that Commander Henry thought Rhoda had welshed on their courtship understanding. She did what had to be done as a Navy wife, but she was free, loud, and frequent in her complaints. She could crab for months on end in a place she disliked, such as Manila. Wherever she was, she tended to fret about the heat, or the cold, or the rain, or the dry spell, or servants, or taxi drivers, or shop clerks, or seamstresses, or hairdressers. To hear Rhoda Henry's daily chatter, her life passed in combat with an incompetent world and a malignant climate. It was only female talk, and not in the least uncommon. But talk, not sex, constitutes most of the intercourse between a man and his wife. Henry detested idle whining. More and more, silence was the response he had come to use. It dampened the noise.

On the other hand, Rhoda was two things he thought a wife should be: a seductive woman, and an adroit homemaker. In all their married years, there had been few times when he had not desired her; and in all those years, for all their moving about, wherever they landed, Rhoda had provided a house or an apartment where the coffee was hot, the food appetizing, the rooms well furnished and always clean, the beds properly made, and fresh flowers in sight. She had fetching little ways, and when her spirits were good she could be very sweet and agreeable. Most women, from the little Victor Henry knew of the sex, were

vain clacking slatterns, with less to redeem them than
Rhoda had. His long-standing opinion was that, for all her
drawbacks, he had a good wife, as wives went. That was
a closed question.

But heading home after a day's work, he never knew
ahead of time whether he would encounter Rhoda the
charmer or Rhoda the crab. At a crucial moment like this,
it could make a great difference. In her down moods, her
judgments were snappish and often silly.

Coming into the house, he heard her singing in the
glassed-in heated porch off the living room where they
usually had drinks before dinner. He found her arranging
tall stalks of orange gladiolus in an oxblood vase from
Manila. She was wearing a beige silky dress cinched in
by a black patent-leather belt with a large silver buckle.
Her dark hair fell in waves behind her ears; this was a
fashion in 1939 even for mature women. Her welcoming
glance was affectionate and gay. Just to see her so made
him feel better, and this had been going on all his life.

"Oh, HI there. Why on EARTH didn't you warn me Kip
Tollever was coming? He sent these, and LUCKILY he
called too. I was slopping around this house like a SCRUB-
WOMAN." Rhoda in casual talk used the swooping high
notes of smart Washington women. She had a dulcet, rather
husky voice, and these zoomed words of hers gave what
she said enormous emphasis and some illusion of sparkle.
"He said he might be slightly late. Let's have a short one,
Pug, okay? The fixings are all there. I'm PARCHED."

Henry walked to the wheeled bar and began to mix
martinis. "I asked Kip to stop by so I could talk to him.
It's not a social visit."

"Oh? Am I supposed to make myself scarce?" She gave
him a sweet smile.

"No, no."

"Good. I like Kip. Why, I was flabbergasted to hear
his voice. I thought he was still stuck in Berlin."

"He's been detached."

"So he told me. Who relieved him, do you know?"

"Nobody has. The assistant attaché for air took over
temporarily." Victor Henry handed her a cocktail. He sank
in a brown wicker armchair, put his feet up on the ottoman, and drank, gloom enveloping him again.

Rhoda was used to her husband's silences. She had taken in his bad humor at a glance. Victor Henry held himself very straight except in moments of trial and tension. Then he tended to fall into a crouch, as though he were still playing football. He had entered the room hunched, and even in the armchair, with his feet up, his shoulders were bent. Dark straight hair hung down his forehead. At forty-nine, he had almost no gray hairs, and his charcoal slacks, brown sports jacket, and red bow tie were clothes for a younger man. It was his small vanity, when not in uniform, to dress youthfully; an athletic body helped him carry it off. Rhoda saw in the lines around his greenish brown eyes that he was tired and deeply worried. Possibly from long years of peering out to sea, Henry's eyes were permanently marked with what looked like laugh lines. Strangers mistook him for a genial man.

"Got a dividend there?" he said at last.

She poured the watery drink for him.

"Thanks. Say, incidentally, you know that memorandum on the battleships that I wrote?"

"Oh, yes. Was there a backlash? You were concerned, I know."

"I got called down to the CNO's office."

"My God. To see Preble?"

"Preble himself. I hadn't seen him since the old days on the *California*. He's gotten fat."

Henry told her about his talk with the Chief of Naval Operations. Rhoda's face took on a hard, sullen, puzzled look. "Oh, I see. *That's* why you asked Kip over."

"Exactly. What do you think about my taking this attaché job?"

"Since when do you have any choice?"

"He gave me the impression that I did. That if I didn't want it, I'd go to a battlewagon next, as an exec."

"Good Lord. Pug, that's more like it!"

"You'd prefer that I go back to sea?"

"I'd prefer? What difference has that ever made?"

"All the same. I'd like to hear what you'd prefer."

Rhoda hesitated, sizing him up with a slanted glance. "Well—naturally I'd adore going to Germany. It would be much more fun for me than sitting here alone while you steam around Hawaii in the *New Mexico* or whatever. It's the loveliest country in Europe. The people are so friendly. German was my major, you know, aeons ago."

"I know," Victor Henry said, smiling, if faintly and wryly, for the first time since arriving home. "You were very good at German." Some of the early hot moments of their honeymoon had occurred while they stumbled through Heine's love poetry aloud together.

Rhoda returned an arch glance redolent of married sex. "Well, all right, you. All I mean is, if you must leave Washington—I suppose the Nazis are kind of ugly and ridiculous. But Madge Knudsen went there for the Olympics. She keeps saying it's still wonderful, and so cheap, with those tourist marks they give you."

"Yes, no doubt we'd have a gay whirl. The question is, Rhoda, whether this isn't a total disaster. Two shore assignments in a row, you understand, at this stage—"

"Oh, Pug, you'll get your four stripes. I know you will. And you'll get your battleship command too, in due course. My God, with your gunnery pennants, your letter of commendation—Pug, suppose CNO's right? Maybe a war is about to pop over there. Then it would be an important job, wouldn't it?"

"That's just sales talk." Pug got up and helped himself to cheese. "He says the President wants top men in Berlin now as military attachés. Well, okay, I'll believe that. He also says it won't hurt my career. That's what I can't believe. First thing any selection board looks for—or will ever look for—in a man's record is blue water, and lots of it."

"Pug, are you sure Kip won't stay to dinner? There's plenty of food. Warren's going to New York."

"No, Kip's on his way to a party at the German embassy. And why the hell is Warren going to New York? He's been home all of three days."

"Ask him," Rhoda said.

The slam of the front door and the quick firm steps were unmistakable Warren sounds. He entered the porch greeting them with a wave of two squash rackets in a fist. "Hi."

In an old gray sweater and slacks, his tanned lean face glowing from the exercise, his hair tousled, a cigarette slanting from his thin mouth, he looked much like the lad who, on graduating from the Academy, had vanished from their lives. Pug was still not used to the way Warren had filled out on shipboard food. The boyish weediness was changing into a tall solid look. A sprinkle of premature gray in his dark hair had startled his parents on his return. Victor Henry envied Warren the deep sunburn which bespoke a destroyer bridge, tennis, green Oahu hills, and above all, duty at sea thousands of miles from Constitution Avenue. He said, "You're off to New York, I hear."

"Yes, Dad. Is that okay? My exec just blew into town. We're going up there to see some shows. He's a real Idaho farmer. Never been to New York."

Commander Henry made a grouchy sound. It was no bad thing for Warren to be friendly with his executive officer. What bothered the father was thoughts of a woman who might be waiting in New York. A top student at the Academy, Warren had almost ruined his record with excessive frenching-out. He had ended with a bad back attributed by himself to a wrestling injury; by other reports, to an escapade involving an older woman and a midnight car crash. The parents had never raised the topic of the woman, partly from bashfulness—they were both prudish churchgoers, ill at ease with such a topic—and partly from a strong sense that they would get nowhere with Warren.

The door chimes rang. A gray-headed houseman in a white coat passed through the living room. Rhoda stood up, touching her hair and sliding slim hands over her silk-clad hips. "Remember Kip Tollever, Warren? That's probably Kip."

"Why, sure. That tall lieutenant commander who lived next door in Manila. Where's he stationed now?"

"He's just finished a tour as naval attaché in Berlin," Victor Henry said.

Warren made a comic grimace, and dropped his voice. "Jehosephat, Dad. How did he ever get stuck with *that?* Cookie pusher in an embassy!"

Rhoda looked at her husband, whose face remained impassive.

"Commander Tollever, ma'am," said the houseman at the doorway.

"Hello, Rhoda!" Tollever marched in with long arms outstretched, in a flawlessly cut evening uniform: blue mess jacket with medals and gold buttons, a black tie, a stiff snowy shirt. "My lord, woman! You look ten years younger than you did in the Philippines."

"Oh, you," she said, eyes gleaming, as he lightly kissed her cheek.

"Hi, Pug." Smoothing one manicured hand over heavy wavy hair just turning gray, Tollever stared at the son. "Now for crying out loud, which boy is this?"

Warren held out his hand. "Hello, sir. Guess."

"Aha. It's Warren. Byron had a different grin. And red hair, come to think of it."

"Right you are, sir."

"Rusty Traynor told me you're serving in the *Monaghan*. What's Byron doing?"

Rhoda chirruped after a slight silence, "Oh, Byron's our romantic dreamer, Kip. He's studying fine arts in Italy. And you should see Madeline! All grown up."

Warren said, "Excuse me, sir," and went out.

"Fine arts! Italy!" One heavy eyebrow went up in Tollever's gaunt handsome face, and his cobalt-blue eyes widened. "Well, that is romantic. Say, Pug, since when do you indulge?" Tollever inquired, accepting a martini and seeing Henry refill his own glass.

"Why, hell, Kip, I was drinking in Manila. Plenty."

"Were you? I forget. I just remember what a roaring teetotaller you were in the Academy. No tobacco either."

"Well, I fell from grace long ago."

Victor Henry had started to drink and smoke on the death of an infant girl, and had not returned to the abstinences his strict Methodist father had taught him. It was a topic he did not enjoy exploring.

With a slight smile, Tollever said, "Do you play cards on Sunday now, too?"

"No, I still hold to that bit of foolishness."

"Don't call it foolishness, Pug."

Commander Tollever began to talk about the post of naval attaché in Berlin. "You'll love Germany," were his first words on the topic. "And so will Rhoda. You'd be crazy not to grab the chance."

Resting his elbows on the arms of his chair, legs neatly crossed, he clipped out his words with all the old articulate crispness; still one of the handsomest men in Pug's class and one of the unluckiest. Two years out of the Academy, while officer of the deck of a destroyer, Tollever had rammed a submarine at night in a rainsquall, during a fleet exercise. The submarine had surfaced without warning a hundred yards in front of him. It had scarcely been his fault, nobody had been hurt, and the general court-martial had merely given him a letter of reprimand. But that letter had festered in his promotion jacket, sapping his career. He drank two martinis in about fifteen minutes, as he talked.

When Victor Henry probed a bit about the Nazis and how to deal with them, Kip Tollever sat up very erect, his curled fingers stiffened as he gestured, and his tone grew firm. The National Socialists were *in,* he said, and the other German parties were out, just as in the United States the Democrats were in and the Republicans out. That was the one way to look at it. The Germans admired the United States, and desperately wanted our friendship. Pug would find the latch off, and the channels of information open, if he simply treated these people as human beings. The press coverage of the new Germany was distorted. When Pug got to know the newspapermen, he would understand why—disgruntled pinkos and drunks, most of them.

"Hitler's a damned remarkable man," said Tollever, poised on his elbows, one scrubbed hand to his chin, one negligently dangling, his face flushed bright pink. "I'm not saying that he, or Göring, or any of that bunch, wouldn't murder their own grandmothers to increase their power or to advance the interests of Germany. But that's politics in Europe nowadays. We Americans are far too naïve. The Soviet Union is the one big reality Europe lives with, Pug —that Slav horde, seething in the east. We can hardly picture that feeling, but for them it's political bedrock. The Communist International is not playing mah-jongg, you know, those Bolos are out to rule Europe by fraud or force or both. Hitler isn't about to let them. That's the root of the matter. The Germans do things in politics that we wouldn't—like this stuff with the Jews—but that's just a passing phase, and anyway, it's not your business. Remember that. Your job is military information. You can get a hell of a lot of that from these people. They're proud of what they're accomplishing, and not at all bashful about showing off, and I mean they'll give you the real dope."

Rhoda asked questions about the Jews, as Pug Henry mixed more martinis. Tollever assured her that the newspaper stories were exaggerated. The worst thing had been the so-called Crystal Night when Nazi toughs had smashed department store windows and set fire to some synagogues. Even that the Jews had brought on themselves, by murdering a German embassy official in Paris. As an embassy official himself, Tollever said, he took rather a dim view of that! He and his wife had gone to the theatre that very night, and on the way home had seen a lot of broken glass along the Kurfürstendamm, and the glow of a couple of distant fires. The account in *Time* had made it seem that Germany was ablaze from end to end, and that the Jews were being slaughtered en masse. There had been conflicting reports, but so far as he knew not one of them had really been physically harmed. A big fine had been put on them for the death of the official, a billion marks or something. Hitler did believe in strong medicine. "Now as to the President's recalling our ambassador, that was a superfluous gesture, utterly superfluous," Tollever said. "It only made things worse for the Jews, and it completely fouled up our embassy's workings. There's just no common sense here in Washington about Germany."

Drinking two more martinis, the erect warrior began dissolving into a gossipy, slouched Navy insider, reminiscing about parties, weekends, hunting trips, and the like; about the potato soup he had drunk with Luftwaffe officers in the dawn, while recovering from a drinking bout after a Party rally; about the famous actors and politicians who had befriended him. Great fun and high living went with an attaché's job, he chuckled, if one played one's cards right. Moreover, you were *supposed* to do those things, so as to dig up information. It was dream duty. A man was entitled to get whatever he could out of the Navy! He had sat in a front seat, watching history unfold, and he had had a glorious time besides. "I tell you, you'll love it, Pug. It's the most interesting post in Europe nowadays. The Nazis are a mixed crowd, actually. Some are brilliant, but between you and me, some are pretty crude and vulgar. The professional military crowd sort of looks down on them. But hell, how do we feel about our own politicians? Hitler's in the saddle and nobody's arguing about *that*. He is boss man, and I kid you not. So lay off that topic and you'll do fine, because really you can't beat these people for hospitality. In a way they're a lot like us, you know, more so than the French or even the Limeys. They'll turn themselves inside out for an American naval officer." A strange smile, rueful and somewhat beaten, appeared on his face as he glanced from Rhoda to Pug. "Especially a man like you. They'll know all about you long before you get there. Now if this is off the reservation say so, but how on earth did a gunnery redhot like you come up for this job?"

"Stuck my neck out," Pug growled. "You know the work I did on the magnetic torpedo exploder, when I was at BuOrd—"

"Hell, yes. And the letter of commendation you got? I sure do."

"Well, I've watched torpedo developments since. Part of my job in War Plans is monitoring the latest intelligence on armor and armaments. The Japs are making some mighty healthy torpedoes, Kip. I got out the old slide rule one night and ran the figures, and the way I read them our battlewagons are falling below the safety margin. I wrote a report recommending that the blisters be thickened and raised on the *Maryland* and *New Mexico* classes. Today CNO called me down to his office. My report's turned into a hot potato. BuShips and BuOrd are blaming each other, memos are flying like fur, the blisters are going to be thickened and raised, and—"

"And by God, Pug, you've got yourself another letter of commendation. Well done!" Tollever's brilliant blue eyes glistened, and he wet his lips.

"I've got myself orders to Berlin," Victor Henry said. "Unless I can talk my way out of it. CNO says the White House has decided it's a crucial post now."

"It is, Pug, it is."

"Well, maybe so, but hell's bells, Kip, you're wonderful at that sort of thing. I'm not. I'm a grease monkey. I don't belong there. I had the misfortune to call attention to myself, that's all, when the boss man was looking for someone. And I happen to know some German. Now I'm in a crack."

Tollever glanced at his watch. "Well, don't pass this up. That's my advice to you as an old friend. Hitler is very, very important, and something's going to blow in Europe. I'm overdue at the embassy."

Victor Henry walked him outside to his shiny gray Mercedes. Tollever's gait was shaky, but he spoke with calm clarity. "Pug, if you do go, call me. I'll give you a book full of phone numbers of the right men to talk to. In fact—" A twisted grin came and went on his face. "No, the numbers of the little fräuleins would be wasted on you, wouldn't they? Well, I've always admired the hell out of you." He clapped Henry's shoulder. "God, I'm looking forward to this party! I haven't drunk a decent glass of Moselle since I left Berlin."

Reentering the house, Victor Henry almost stumbled over a suitcase and a hatbox. His daughter stood at the foyer mirror in a green wool suit, putting on a close-fitting hat. Rhoda was watching her, and Warren waited, trench coat slung on his shoulder, holding his old pigskin valise. "What's this, Madeline? Where are *you* going?"

She smiled at him, opening wide dark eyes. "Oh, didn't Mom tell you? Warren's taking me to New York."

Pug looked dourly at Rhoda, who said, "Anything wrong with that, dear? Warren's lined up extra tickets for the shows. She loves the theatre and there's precious little in Washington."

"But has college closed down? Is this the Easter vacation?"

The daughter said, "I'm caught up in my work. It's only for two days, and I don't have any tests."

"And where would you stay?"

Warren put in, "There's this Hotel Barbizon for women."

"I don't like this," Victor Henry said.

Madeline glanced at him with melting appeal. Nineteen and slight, with Rhoda's skin and a pert figure, she oddly resembled her father, in the deep-set brown eyes and the determined air. She tried wrinkling her small nose at him. Often that made him laugh, and won her point. This time his face did not change. Madeline glanced at her mother and then at Warren for support, but it was not forthcoming. A little smile curved Madeline's mouth, more ominous perhaps than a rebellious tantrum; a smile of indulgence. She took off her hat. "Well, okay! That's that. Warren, I hope you can get rid of those extra tickets. When's dinner?"

"Any time," Rhoda said.

Warren donned his trench coat and picked up the suitcase. "Say, incidentally, Dad, did I mention that a couple of months ago my exec put in for flight training? I sent in one of the forms too, just for the hell of it. Well, Chet was snooping around BuNav today. It seems we both have a chance."

"Flight training?" Rhoda looked unhappy. "You mean you're becoming a carrier pilot? Just like that? Without consulting your father?"

"Why, Mom, it's just something else to qualify in. I think it makes sense. Doesn't it, sir?"

Commander Henry said, "Yes, indeed. The future of this here Navy might just belong to the brown shoes."

"I don't know about that, but Pensacola ought to be interesting, if I don't bilge out the first week. Back Friday. Sorry, Madeline."

She said, "Nice try. Have fun."

He kissed his mother, and left.

Pug Henry consumed vichyssoise, London broil, and strawberry tart in grim abstracted silence. Kip Tollever's enthusiasm for the mediocre spying job had only deepened Henry's distaste. Madeline's itch to avoid schoolwork was a steady annoyance. But topping all was Warren's casually dropped news; Pug was both proud and alarmed. Carrier aviation was the riskiest duty in the Navy, though officers even his own age were now applying for Pensacola, so as to get into the flattops. A devoted battleship man, Henry wondered all through the meal whether Warren hadn't hit on something, whether a request for flight training might not be a respectable if desperate way to dodge Berlin.

Madeline kept a cheerful face, making talk with her mother about the student radio station at George Washington University, her main interest there. The houseman, an old Irishman who also did the gardening in warm weather, walked softly in the candlelit dining room, furnished with Rhoda's family antiques. Rhoda contributed money to the household costs so that they could live in this style in Washington, among her old friends. While Victor Henry did not like it, he had not argued. A commander's salary was modest, and Rhoda was used to this better life.

Madeline excused herself early, kissing her father on the forehead. The sombre quiet during dessert was unbroken except by the hushed footfalls of the manservant. Rhoda said nothing, waiting out her husband's mood. When he cleared his throat and said it might be nice to have brandy and coffee on the porch, she smiled pleasantly. "Yes, let's, Pug."

The houseman set the silver tray there, turning up the red flickering light in the artificial fireplace. She waited until her husband was settled in his favorite chair, drinking coffee and sipping brandy. Then she said, "By the bye, there's a letter from Byron."

"What? He actually remembered we're alive? Is he all right?"

They had not heard from him in months. Henry had had many a nightmare of his son dead in an Italian ditch in a smoking automobile, or otherwise killed or injured. But since the last letter he had not mentioned Byron.

"He's all right. He's in Siena. He's given up his studies in Florence. Says he got bored with fine arts."

"I couldn't be less surprised. Siena. That's still Italy, isn't it?"

"Yes, near Florence. In the Tuscan hills. He goes on and on about the Tuscan hills. He seems to be interested in a girl."

"A girl, eh? What kind of girl? Eyetalian?"

"No, no. A New York girl. Natalie Jastrow. He says she has a famous uncle."

"I see. And who's her uncle?"

"He's an author. He lives in Siena. Dr. Aaron Jastrow. He once taught history at Yale, Briny says."

"Where's the letter?"

"On the telephone table."

He returned in a few minutes with the letter, and with a thick book in a black dust jacket, marked with a white crucifix and a blue Star of David. "That's who the uncle is."

"Oh, yes. *A Jew's Jesus*. That thing. Some club sent it. Did you ever read it?"

"I read it twice. It's excellent." Henry scanned his son's letter in yellow lamplight. "Well. This business is kind of far along."

"She does sound attractive," Rhoda said. "But he's had other nine-day wonders."

Commander Henry tossed the letter on the coffee table and poured more brandy for himself. "I'll read it through later. Longest letter he's ever written. Is there anything important in it?"

"He wants to stay on in Italy."

"Indeed? How does he propose to live?"

"He has some kind of research job with Dr. Jastrow. The girl works there, too. He thinks he can get by on what he earns, plus the few dollars from my mother's trust."

"Really?" Henry peered at her. "If Byron Henry is talking about supporting himself, that's the biggest news about him since you had him." He drank his coffee and brandy, and stood up, retrieving the letter with a swipe of his hand.

"Now *don't* take on, Pug. Byron's a strange fish, but there's a lot of brains underneath."

"I have some work to do."

Henry went to his den and smoked a cigar, reading Byron's letter twice through with care. The den was a converted maid's room. On the ground floor a large handsome study looked out on the garden through french windows. That room in theory was his. It was so attractive that Rhoda sometimes liked to receive visitors there, and was given to nagging at her husband when he left papers and books around. After a few months of this Henry had put bookshelves, a cot, and a tiny secondhand desk in the narrow maid's room, had moved into it, and was content enough with this small space. He had done with less in a destroyer cabin.

When the cigar was burned out, Henry went to his old portable typewriter. With his hands on the keys he paused, contemplating three pictures in a leather frame on the desk: Warren, in uniform and bristle-headed, a stern boyish candidate for flag rank; Madeline, at seventeen much, much younger than she seemed now; Byron, in the center, with the defiant large mouth, the half-closed analytic eyes, the thick full hair, the somewhat sloping face peculiarly mingling softness and obstinate will. Byron owed his looks to neither parent. He was his strange self.

Dear Briny:

Your mother and I have your long letter. I intend to take it seriously. Your mother prefers to pooh-pooh it, but I don't think you've written such a letter before, or described a girl in quite such terms. I'm glad you're well, and gainfully employed. That's good news. I never could take that fine arts business seriously.

Now about Natalie Jastrow. In this miserable day and age, especially with what is going on in Germany, I have to start by protesting that I have nothing against Jewish people. I've encountered them very little, since few of them enter the Navy. In my Academy class there were four, which was very unusual back in 1911. One of them has stayed the course, Hank Goldfarb, and he is a damned good officer.

Here in Washington there is quite a bit of prejudice against Jews. They've made themselves felt in business lately, doing somewhat too well. The other day one of your mother's friends told me a joke. I wasn't amused, possibly because of my own Glasgow great-grandfather. The three shortest books in the Library of Congress are *A History of Scotch Charities, Virginity in France,* and *A Study of Jewish Business Ethics.* Ha ha ha. This may be a far cry from Hitler's propaganda, but the person who told me this joke is a fine lawyer and a good Christian.

You'd better give some hard thought to the long pull that a marriage is. I know I'm jumping the gun, but now is the time to reflect, before you're too involved. Never, never forget one thing. *The girl you marry, and the woman you must make a life with, are two different people.*

Women have a way of living in the present. Before marriage she's out to win you. Afterward you're just one of the many factors in her life. In a way you're secondary, because she *has* you, whereas everything else is in flux—children household, new clothes, social ties. If these other factors are disagreeable to her, she will make you unhappy.

In a marriage with a girl like Natalie Jastrow, the other factors would all tend to bother her perpetually, from the mixed-breed children to the tiny social slights. These might get to be like the Chinese water-drop torture. If so, you'd both gradually grow bitter and miserable, and by then you'd be tied together by children. This could end up as hell on earth.

Now I'm just telling you what I think. Maybe I'm old-fashioned, or stupid, and out of touch. It doesn't matter to me that this girl is Jewish, though there would be grave questions about the children's faith, since I feel you're a pretty good Christian, somewhat more so than Warren at the moment. I'm impressed by what you say about her brains, which her being the niece of Aaron Jastrow sure bears out. *A Jew's Jesus* is a remarkable work. If I thought she could make you happy and give you some direction in life I'd welcome her, and take pleasure in personally punching in the nose anybody who upset her. But I think this might become a second career for me.

Now, I'm reconciled to letting you go your own way. You know that. It's hard for me to write a letter like this. I feel like a fool, elaborating the obvious, expressing truths that I find distasteful, and above all intruding on your personal feelings. But that's okay. You sent us your letter. I take it to mean that you wanted an answer. This is the best I can do. If you want to write me off as a bigot, that's all right with me.

I'll show this letter to your mother, who will no doubt disapprove of it, so I'll be forwarding it without her endorsement. Maybe she'll add something of her own.

Warren is home. He has put in for flight training and may get it.

Love,
Dad

Rhoda liked to sleep late, but her husband woke her the following morning at eight o'clock, handing her his letter to Byron and a cup of hot coffee. She sat up with grouchy abrupt gestures, read the letter through as she sipped, and passed it back to him without a word.

"Do you want to add anything?"

"No." Her face was set. She had worked her eyebrows a bit over Pug's passage on women and marriage.

"Don't you approve of it?"

"Letters like that don't change things," Rhoda said with deep sure female contempt.

"Shouldn't I send it?"

"I don't care."

He put the envelope in his breast pocket. "I see Admiral Preble at ten o'clock this morning. Have you had any second thoughts?"

"Pug, will you please do exactly as you choose?" Rhoda said, in a pained bored tone. She sank down into the bedclothes as he left.

The Chief of Naval Operations did not appear surprised when Pug said he would take the post. At dawn Henry had awakened with an overmastering sense that he could not duck the assignment, and with this, he had stopped thinking about it. Preble told him to get ready in a hurry. His orders to Berlin were already cut.

2

BYRON HENRY's encounter with Natalie Jastrow two months earlier had been much in character. He had drifted into it.

Unlike his father, Byron had always been directionless. Growing up, he had dodged the Sea Scouts, Severn Academy, and anything else pointing to a naval career. Yet he had no ideas for any other career. His marks were usually poor, and he developed early a remarkable capacity for doing absolutely nothing. In fits of resolve he had shown himself able to win a few A's, or put together a radio set that worked, or rescue an old car from a junkyard and make it run, or repair a collapsed oil heater. In this knack for machinery he took after his father and grandfather.

But he became bored with such tinkering. He did too poorly in mathematics to think of engineering.

He might have been an athlete. He was agile, and sturdier than he looked, but he disliked the regimens and teamwork of school athletics, and he loved cigarettes and beer, though the gallons of beer he drank did not add a millimeter to his waistline. At Columbia College (where he was admitted because he charmed an interviewer, scored well on the intelligence test, and wasn't a New Yorker) he barely avoided expulsion for bad grades. What he enjoyed was taking his ease at his fraternity house, or playing cards and pool, or reading old novels over and over, or talking about girls and fooling with them. He did find in fencing a sport suited to his independent temper and his wiry body. Had he trained more he might have been an intercollegiate finalist at the epée. But it was a bore to train, and it interfered with his idleness.

In his junior year he elected a course in fine arts, which athletes took because, so the report ran, nobody ever failed it. However, at mid-semester, Byron Henry managed to fail. He had done no work and cut half the classes. Still, the F startled him. He went to see the professor and told him so. The professor, a mild bald little lover of the Italian Renaissance, with green spectacles and hairy ears, took a liking to him. A couple of remarks Byron made on Leonardo and Botticelli showed that, in the few sessions he had attended, he had learned something, unlike the rest of the hulking somnolent class. They became friends. It was the first intellectual friendship in Byron Henry's life. He became an enthusiast for the Renaissance, slavishly echoing the professor's ideas, and he finished college in a blaze of B pluses, cured of beer guzzling and afire to teach fine arts. One year of graduate work at the University of Florence for a Master of Arts degree; that had been the plan.

But a few months in Florence cooled Byron. One rainy November night, in his squalid rented room overlooking the muddy Arno, sick of the smells of garlic and bad plumbing, and of living alone among foreigners, he wrote his friend that Italian painting was garish, saccharine, and boring with its everlasting madonnas, babes, saints, halos, crucifixions, resurrections, green dead Saviors, flying bearded Jehovahs, and the rest; that he much preferred moderns like Miró and Klee; and that anyway, painting was just interior decoration, which didn't really interest him. He scrawled several pages in this cornered-rat vein, mailed them off, and then went vagabonding around Europe, forsaking his classes and his hope of a graduate degree.

When he got back to Florence, he found a cheering letter from the professor.

. . . I don't know what will become of you. Obviously art was a false lead. I think it did you good to get hot on some subject. If you can only shake off your lethargy and find something that truly engages you, you may yet go far. I am an old traffic cop, and standing here on my corner I have seen many Chevrolets and Fords go by. It's not hard for me to recognize the occasional Cadillac. Only this one seems badly stalled.

I've written about you to Dr. Aaron Jastrow, who lives outside Siena. You know of him. He wrote *A Jew's Jesus*, made a pot of money, and got off the miserable academic treadmill. We used to be friends at Yale, and he was very good indeed at bringing out the best in young men. Go and talk to him, and give him my regards.

That was how Byron happened to call on Dr. Jastrow. He took a bus to Siena, a three-hour run up a rutted scary mountain road. Twice before he had visited the bizarre little town, all red towers and battlements and narrow crooked streets, set around a gaudy zebra-striped cathedral, on a hilltop amid rolling green and brown Tuscan vineyards. Its main claim to fame, aside from the quasi-Byzantine church art he had studied there, was a peculiar annual horse race called the Palio, which he had heard about but never seen.

At first glance, the girl at the wheel of the old blue convertible made no strong impression on him: an oval face, dark enough so that he first took her for an Italian, dark hair, enormous sunglasses, a pink sweater over an open white shirt. Beside her sat a blond man covering a yawn with a long white hand.

"Hi! Byron Henry?"

"Yes."

"Hop in the back. I'm Natalie Jastrow. This is Leslie Slote. He works in our embassy in Paris, and he's visiting my uncle."

Byron did not much impress the girl either. What Natalie Jastrow saw through the dark glasses was a slender lounger, obviously American, with red glints in his heavy brown hair; he was propped against the wall of the Hotel Continental in the sun, smoking a cigarette, his legs loosely crossed. The light gray jacket, dark slacks, and maroon tie were faintly dandyish. The forehead under the hair was wide, the long slanting jaws narrow, the face pallid. He looked like what he was—a collegiate drone, a rather handsome one. Natalie had brushed these off by the dozen in earlier years.

As they wound through narrow canyons of crooked ancient red-brown houses and drove out into the countryside, Byron idly asked Slote about his embassy work. The Foreign Service man told him he was posted in the political section and was studying Russian and Polish, hoping for an assignment to Moscow or Warsaw. Sitting in the car, Slote appeared very tall; later Byron saw that he himself was taller than Slote; the Foreign Service officer had a long trunk but medium-size legs. Slote's thick blond hair grew to a peak over a high forehead and narrow pinkish face; the light blue eyes behind rimless glasses were alert and penetrating, and his thin lips were compressed as though with habitual resolve. All the time they drove, he held a large black pipe in his hand or in his mouth, not smoking it. It occurred to Byron that the Foreign Service might be a pleasant career, offering travel, adventure, and encounters with important people. But when Slote mentioned that he was a Rhodes Scholar, Byron decided not to pursue the topic.

Jastrow lived in a yellow stucco villa on a steep hillside, with a fine view of the cathedral and Siena's red towers and tile roofs. It was a drive of about twenty minutes from town. Byron hurried after the girl and Slote through a terraced flowering garden full of black-stained plaster statues.

"Well, there you are!" The voice was high, authoritative, and impatient, with a faint foreign note in the pronouncing of the *r*'s.

Two sights struck Byron as they entered a long beamed

living room: a painting of a red-robed Saint Francis with arms outstretched, on a background of gold, taking up a good part of one wall, and far down the long sitting room on a red silk couch, a bearded little man in a light gray suit, who looked at his watch, stood, and came toward them coughing.

"This is Byron Henry, Aaron," the girl said.

Jastrow took Byron's hand in two dry little paws and peered up at him with prominent wavering eyes. Jastrow's head was large, his shoulders slight; he had aging freckled skin, light straight hair, and a heavy nose reddened by a cold. The neatly trimmed beard was all gray. "Columbia '38, is it?"

"Yes, sir."

"Well, well, come along." He went off down the room, buttoning the flapping folds of his double-breasted suit. "Come here, Byron." Plucking the stopper out of a heavy crystal decanter, he carefully poured amber wine into four glasses. "Come Leslie, Natalie. We don't take wine during the day, Byron, but this is an occasion." He held up his glass. "To Mr. Byron Henry, eminent hater of the Italian Renaissance."

Byron laughed. "Is that what Dr. Milano wrote? I'll drink to that."

Jastrow took one sip, put down his glass, and looked at his watch. Seeing the professor wanted to get at his lunch, Byron tossed off the sherry like a shot of rye. Jastrow exclaimed with a delighted smile, "Ah! One, two, three. Good lad. Come along, Natalie. Leslie, take your glass to the table."

It was a spare lunch: nothing but vegetables with white rice, then cheese and fruit. The service was on fine old china, maroon and gold. A small, gray-headed Italian woman passed the food. The tall dining room windows stood open to the garden, the view of Siena, and a flood of pale sunshine. Gusts of cool air came in as they ate.

When they first sat, the girl said, "What have you got against the Italian Renaissance, Byron?"

"That's a long story."

"Tell us," said Jastrow in a classroom voice, laying a thumb across his smiling mouth.

Byron hesitated. Jastrow and the Rhodes Scholar made

him uneasy. The girl disconcerted him more. Removing her sunglasses, she had disclosed big slanted dark eyes, gleaming with bold intelligence. She had a soft large mouth, painted a bit too orange, in a bony face. Natalie was regarding him with a satiric look, as though she had already concluded that he was a fool; and Byron was not fool enough to miss that.

"Maybe I've had too much of it," he said. "I started out fascinated. I'm ending up snowed under and bored. I realize much of the art is brilliant, but there's a lot of over-rated garbage amid the works of genius. My main objection is that I can't take the mixture of paganism and Christianity. I don't believe David looked like Apollo, or Moses like Jupiter, or Mary like every Renaissance artist's mistress with a borrowed baby on her lap. Maybe they couldn't help showing Bible Jews as local Italians or pseudo-Greeks, but—" Byron dried up for a moment, seeing his listeners' amused looks. "Look, I'm not saying any of this is important criticism. I guess it just shows I got into the wrong field. But what has any of it to do with Christianity? That's what sticks in my craw. Supposing Christ came back to earth and visited the Uffizi, or Saint Peter's? The Christ of your book, Dr. Jastrow, the poor idealistic Jewish preacher from the back hills? That's the Lord I grew up with. My father's a religious man; we had to read a chapter of the Bible every morning at home. Why, Christ wouldn't even suspect the stuff related to himself and his teachings."

Natalie Jastrow was regarding him with an almost motherly smile. He said brusquely to her, "Okay. You asked me what I had against the Italian Renaissance. I've told you."

"Well, it's a point of view," she said.

Eyes twinkling behind his glasses, Slote lit his pipe, and said between puffs, "Don't fold up, Byron, there are others who have taken your position. A good name for it is Protestantism."

"Byron's main point is accurate." Dr. Jastrow sounded kindly, dancing his little fingers together. "The Italian Renaissance was a great blossoming of art and ideas, Byron, that occurred when paganism and the Hebrew spirit—in its Christian expression—briefly fertilized instead of fighting each other. It was a hybrid growth, true, but some hybrids are stronger than either parent, you know. Witness the mule."

"Yes, sir," said Byron, "and mules are sterile."

Amused surprise flashed on Natalie Jastrow's face, and her enormous dark eyes flickered to Leslie Slote, and back to Byron.

"Well said. Just so." Jastrow nodded in a pleased way. "The Renaissance indeed couldn't reproduce itself, and it died off, while the pagan and Hebrew spirits went their separate immortal ways. But that mule's bones are now one of mankind's richest deposits of cultural achievement, Byron, whatever your momentary disgust from overexposure."

Byron shrugged. Leslie Slote said, "Is your father a clergyman?"

"His father's a naval officer," said Jastrow.

"Really? What branch?"

Byron said, "Well, right now he's in War Plans."

"My goodness! *War* Plans?" Dr. Jastrow pretended a comic flutter. "I didn't know that. Is it as ominous as it sounds?"

"Sir, every country draws up theoretical war plans in peacetime."

"Does your father think a war is imminent?"

"I got my last letter from him in November. He said nothing about a war."

The other three exchanged odd glances. Slote said, "Would he, in casual correspondence?"

"He might have asked me to come home. He didn't."

"Interesting," said Dr. Jastrow, with a little complacent grin at Slote, rubbing his tiny hands.

"As a matter of fact, I think there's going to be a war," Byron said. This caused a silence of a second or two, and more glances.

Jastrow said, "Really? Why?"

"Well, I just toured Germany. You see nothing but uniforms, parades, drills, brass bands. Anywhere you drive you end up passing army trucks full of troops, and railroad cars loaded with artillery and tanks. Trains sometimes a couple of miles long."

"But, Byron, it was with just such displays that Hitler

won Austria and the Sudetenland," said Jastrow, "and he never fired a shot."

Natalie said to Byron, "Leslie thinks my uncle should go home. We've had a running argument for three days."

"I see."

Jastrow was peeling a pear with elderly deliberate gestures, using an ivory-handled knife. "Yes, Byron, I'm being mulish." The use of the word was accidental, for he grinned and added, "Being a hybrid of sorts myself, I guess. This is a comfortable house, it's the only home I have now, and my work is going well. Moving would cost me half a year. If I tried to sell the house, I couldn't find an Italian to offer me five cents on the dollar. They've been dealing for many centuries with foreigners who've had to cut and run. They'd skin me alive. I was aware of all this when I bought the villa. I expect to end my days here."

"Not this fall at the hands of the Nazis, I trust," Slote said.

"Oh, hell, Slote," Natalie broke in, slicing a flat hand downward through the air. "Since when does the Foreign Service have such a distinguished record for foresight? Since Munich? Since Austria? Since the Rhineland? Weren't you surprised every time?"

Byron listened with interest to this exchange. The others seemed to have forgotten he was at the table.

"Hitler has been making irrational moves with catastrophic possibilities," Slote retorted. "Anybody can pull a gun in the street and shoot four people down before the cops come and stop him. Until now that's been Hitler's so-called foreign policy brilliance in a nutshell. The surprise of an outlaw running wild. That game's played out. The others are aroused now. They'll stop him over Poland."

Jastrow ate a piece of pear, and began to talk in a rhythmic, mellifluous way, something between meditating aloud and lecturing in a classroom. "Leslie, if Hitler were the Kaiser, or a man like Charles the Twelfth, I admit I'd be worried. But he's far more competent than you think. Fortunately the old ruling class is destroyed. They unleashed the World War with their dry-rotted incompetence, those preening, posturing, sleek royalties and politicians of 1914, those bemedalled womanizers and sodomites out of Proust. They never dreamed that the old manners, the old paperwork, the old protocol, were done for, and that industrialized warfare would shatter the old system like a boot kicked through a dollhouse. So they went to the trash heap, and new leadership came up out of the sewers, where realism runs and change often starts. The early Christians haunted the sewers and catacombs of Rome, you know," Jastrow said to Byron Henry, clearly relishing a fresh audience.

"Yes, sir, I learned about that."

"Of course you did. Well. Hitler's a vagabond, Mussolini's a vagabond, and Stalin's a jailbird. These are new, tough, able, and clever men, straight up from the sewers. Lenin, another jailbird, was the great originator. He made it all up. Leslie, you realize- -the Jesuitical secret party, the coarse slogans for the masses and the contempt for their intelligence and memory, the fanatic language, the strident dogmas, the Moslem religiosity in politics, the crude pageantry, the total cynicism of tactics, it's all Leninism. Hitler is a Leninist, Mussolini is a Leninist. The talk of anti-communism and pro-communism is for fools and children."

"Oh, for Pete's *sake*, Aaron—"

"Just a moment, now! Lenin was all prudence and caution in foreign affairs, and *that* is my whole point. Glory, and honor, and all those tinselly illusions of the old system that led to wars, were to Lenin the merest eyewash. So it is to Hitler. He has never moved when he couldn't get away with it. The outlaw running wild with a gun is the exact effect he wishes to create. I'm surprised that you're taken in. He is really a very, very prudent man. If he can make it in Poland without war, he'll do it. Otherwise he'll not move. Not now. Perhaps in ten years, when he's built Germany up enough. I shall be very content to live another ten years."

Slote pulled at his moustache with lean nervous fingers. "You really lose me, Aaron. Can you be serious? Hitler a Leninist! That's a coffeehouse paradox, and you know it. The Russian Revolution is a radical change in history. The abolition of private property has created a new world. You may like it or detest it, but it's new. Hitler's socialism was a sham to get a mob of gangsters into power. He's frozen the German economy just as it was, smashed the labor unions, lengthened the working hours, cut the pay, and kept all the old rich crowd on top, the Krupps and Thyssens, the men who gave him the money to run for office. The big Nazis live like barons, like sultans. The concentration camps are for anybody who still wants the socialist part of National Socialism. Don't you know that? The 1934 purge was nothing but a showdown between the socialist element of the Nazi Party, and the army generals and rich conservatives. Hitler shot his old Party friends like partridges. That you rely on this man's prudence for your safety, and for Natalie's, strikes me as grotesque."

"Does it?" Jastrow glanced at his watch and sighed. "I'm sorry. I'm impressed with Hitler's ability to use socialist prattle when necessary, and then discard it. He uses doctrines as he uses money, to get things done. They're expendable. He uses racism because that's the pure distillate of German romantic egotism, just as Lenin used utopian Marxism because it appealed to Russia's messianic streak. Hitler means to hammer out a united Europe. If a nonsense jumble of racist bunkum, socialist promises, brass bands, parades, uniforms, and weepy songs is what welds Germans into a blunt instrument, he gives them that. The Germans are stolid, clever, brutal, and docile, and they will vigorously execute any command barked at them with a loud enough voice. He understands them, and he may just succeed. A unified Europe must come. The medieval jigsaw of nations is obsolete. The balance of power is dangerous foolishness in the industrial age. It must all be thrown out. Somebody has to be ruthless enough to do it, since the peoples with their ancient hatreds will never do it themselves. It's only Napoleon's original vision, but he was a century ahead of his time. The old crowd was still strong enough to catch him and put him in a cage to die. But there's nobody to cage Hitler."

Byron blurted, "Dr. Jastrow, when I was in Germany I saw the signs on park benches and in trolley cars about the Jews. I saw burnt-out synagogues."

"Yes?"

They all looked at him. He went on, "I'm surprised you talk as calmly about Hitler as you do. Being Jewish, I mean."

Dr. Jastrow smiled a slow, acid smile, showing little yellowish teeth with one gold crown. He stroked his beard and spoke deliberately, the classroom note strong. "Well! Your surprise doesn't surprise me. Young people—young Americans especially—aren't aware that the tolerance for Jews in Europe is only fifty to a hundred years old and that it's never gone deep. It didn't touch Poland, where I was born. Even in the West—what about the Dreyfus case? No, no. In that respect Hitler represents only a return to normalcy for Europe, after the brief glow of liberalism. The hostility simply moved from the Church to the anti-Semitic parties, because the French Revolution changed Europe from a religious to a political continent. If Hitler does win out, the Jews will fall back to the second-class status they always had under the kings and the popes. Well, we survived seventeen centuries of that. We have a lot of wisdom and doctrine for coping with it."

Slote shook his head. "You love to spin such talk, I know, but I wish you would do it on the next boat home."

"But I'm quite serious, Leslie," Jastrow said with a faintly puckish smile. "You rang wild alarms when Mussolini passed the anti-Jewish laws. They proved a joke."

"They're on the books, if the Germans ever press him to use them."

"The Italians loathe and fear the Germans to a man. Even if by some mischance there is a war, Italy won't fight. Siena may well be as safe a place as any."

"I doubt that Natalie's parents think so."

"She can go home tomorrow. Perhaps she finds Siena slightly more attractive than Miami Beach."

"I'm thinking of going," the girl said. "But not because I'm afraid of war or of Hitler. There are things that bother me more."

"I daresay," Jastrow said.

Slote's face turned astonishingly red. His pipe lay smoking on an ashtray, and he was playing with a yellow pencil he had taken from a pocket, turning it in one fist. The pencil stopped turning.

Jastrow stood. "Byron, come along."

They left the girl and the scarlet-faced man at the table, glowering at each other.

Books filled the shelves of a small wood-panelled library, and stood in piles on the desk and on the floor. Over a white marble fireplace a stiff Sienese madonna and child hung, blue and pink on gold; a tiny painting in a large ornate gilded frame. "Berenson says it's a Duccio," Jastrow observed, with a little wave at the painting, "and that's good enough for me. It's not authenticated. Now then. You sit there, in the light, so that I can see you. Just put those magazines on the floor. Good. Is that a comfortable chair? Fine." He sighed and laid a thumb against his lower lip. "Now, Byron, why didn't you go to the Naval Academy? Aren't you proud of your father?"

Byron sat up in his chair. "I think my father may be Chief of Naval Operations one day."

"Isn't he worth emulating?"

"My brother Warren's doing that. I'm just not interested."

"Dr. Milano wrote that you took a naval reserve course and obtained a commission."

"It made my father feel good."

"And you've had no second thoughts about the Navy? It's not too late yet."

Byron shook his head, smiling. Jastrow lit a cigarette, studying Byron's face. The young man said, "Do you really like living in Italy, sir?"

"Well, I was ordered to a warm climate. I did first visit Florida, Arizona, southern California, and the French Riviera." The professor spoke these place-names with an irony that wrote them off, one by one, as ridiculous or disagreeable. "Italy is beautiful, quiet, and cheap."

"You don't mind making your home in a Fascist country?"

Jastrow's smile was indulgent. "There are good and bad things in all political systems."

"How did you ever come to write *A Jew's Jesus,* sir? Did you write it here?"

"Oh, no, but it got me here." Jastrow spoke somewhat smugly. "I was using the Bible in a course on ancient history, you see. And as a boy in Poland I'd been a Talmud scholar, so in teaching the New Testament I tended to stress the rabbinic sources that Jesus and Paul used. This novelty seemed to fascinate Yale juniors. I cobbled up a book, with the working title *Talmudic Themes in Early Christianity,* and then at the last minute I thought of *A*

Jew's Jesus. The Book-of-the-Month Club selected it."
Jastrow made a soft gesture with both hands all around the
room, smiling. "And here I am. The club payment bought
this place. Now then, Byron, what are your plans? Are
you going to return to the United States?"

"I don't know. I couldn't be more up in the air."

"Do you want a job?"

Byron was taken aback. "Well, I guess maybe I do, sir."

Jastrow ambled to his desk and searched through a pile
of books, taking off his glasses and holding the titles very
close to his face. "I had a fine researcher, a boy from
Yale, but his parents called him home, afraid of a war—ah,
here we are. Can I interest you, for twenty dollars a week,
in the Emperor Constantine? This is a good general biog-
raphy to start with."

"Sir, I've flunked more history courses—"

"I see. You don't want the job."

The young man took the thick book and turned it dubiously in his hands. "No. I'll try it. Thank you."

"Oh, you will, will you? When you say you have no
aptitude? Why?"

"Well, for the money, and to be around you." This was
true enough, though it omitted a third good reason: Natalie
Jastrow.

Jastrow looked stern, and then burst out laughing. "We'll
give it a try."

.   .   .

The letter his parents received from him some time later
about the girl—which elicited Victor Henry's strong answer—was unintentionally misleading. There was a love
affair going on, but Natalie's lover was Leslie Slote. His
letters came two or three times a week: long fat white
Foreign Service envelopes, addressed in an elongated stiff
hand, in brown ink, with stamps stuck over the government
frank. Byron hated the sight of them.

He was spending hours every day with her in the huge
second-floor room that was Jastrow's main library. Her
desk was there. She answered letters, typed manuscripts,
and with the Italian woman managed the household. Byron
worked at the long library table, reading up on Constantine,

checking facts, and drawing maps of the emperor's military campaigns. Whenever he raised his eyes he saw the smooth face bent over the desk, the shapely bones highlighted by sunshine, or on dark days by a lamp. There was also the ever-present view of her long pretty legs in a sheen of silk. Natalie dressed in dun wool, and was all business with him; she used almost no paint once Slote left, combed her hair back in a heavy bun, and talked to Byron with offhand dryness. Still, his infatuation took quick root and grew rankly.

She was the first American girl he had spoken to in months; and they were thrown together for many hours every day, just the two of them in the book-lined room. This was reason enough for him to feel attracted to her. But she impressed him, too. Natalie Jastrow talked to her famous uncle as to a mental equal. Her range of knowledge and ideas humiliated Byron, and yet there was nothing bookish about her. Girls in his experience were light-weights, fools for a smile and a bit of flattery. They had doted on him at college, and in Florence too. Byron was something of an Adonis, indolent and not hotly interested; and unlike Warren, he had absorbed some of his father's straitlaced ideas. He thought Natalie was a dark jewel of intellect and loveliness, blazing away all unnoticed here in the Italian back hills. As for her indifference to him, it seemed in order. He had no thought of trying to break it down.

He did things he had never done before. He stole a little pale blue handkerchief of hers and sat at night in his hotel room in town, sniffing it. Once he ate half a cake she had left on her desk, because it bore the mark of her teeth. When she missed the cake, he calmly lied about it. Altogether he was in a bad way. Natalie Jastrow seemed to sense nothing of this. Byron had a hard shell of inscrutability, grown in boyhood to protect his laziness and school failures from his exacting father.

They chatted a lot, of course, and sometimes drove out in the hills for a picnic lunch, when she would slightly warm to him over a bottle of wine, treating him more like a younger brother. He soon got at the main facts of her romance. She had gone to the Sorbonne for graduate work in sociology. Jastrow had written about her to Slote, a former pupil. A fulminating love affair had ensued, and Natalie had stormily quit Paris, and lived for a while with her parents in Florida. Then she had come back to Europe to work for her uncle; also, Byron surmised, to be near Slote for another try. The Rhodes Scholar had now received orders to Warsaw, and Natalie was planning to visit him there in July while Jastrow took his summer holiday in the Greek islands.

On one of their picnics, as he poured the last of the wine into her glass, Byron ventured a direct probe. "Natalie, do you like your job?"

She sat on a blanket, hugging her legs in a heavy checked skirt, looking out over a valley of brown wintry vineyards. With an arch questioning look, cocking her head, she said, "Oh, it's a job. Why?"

"It seems to me you're wasting away here."

"Well, I'll tell you, Byron. You do peculiar things when you're in love." His response to this was a dull unfocussed expression. She went on: "That's one thing. Besides, frankly, I think Aaron's rather wonderful. Don't you? Horribly crotchety and self-preoccupied and all that, but this Constantine book is good. My father is a warm, clever, good-hearted man, but he's the president of his temple and he manufactures sweaters. Aaron's a famous author, and he's my uncle. I suppose I bask in his glory. What's wrong with that? And I certainly enjoy typing the new pages, just watching the way his mind works. It's an excellent mind, and his style is admirable." She gave him another quizzical look. "Now why *you're* doing this, I'm far less sure."

"Me?" Byron said. "I'm broke."

Early in March Jastrow accepted an offer from an American magazine for an article about the upcoming Palio races. It meant he would have to put off his trip to Greece, for the race was run in July and again in August; but the fee was too absurdly fat, he said, to decline. If Natalie would watch the races and do the research, he told her, he would give her half the money. Natalie jumped at this, not perceiving—so Byron thought—that her uncle was trying to stop, or at least delay, her trip to Warsaw. Jastrow had once flatly said that Natalie's pursuit of Slote was unlady-like conduct and bad tactics. Byron had gathered that Slote

did not want to marry Natalie, and he could see why. For
a Foreign Service man, a Jewish wife at this time would be
disastrous; though Byron thought that in Slote's place he
would cheerfully give up the Foreign Service for her.

Natalie wrote to Slote that same day, postponing her
visit until after the August Palio. Watching her bang out
the letter, Byron tried to keep joy off his face. She might
go, he was thinking, and then again she might not! Maybe
a war would come along meantime and stop her. Byron
hoped that Hitler, if he was going to invade Poland, would
do it soon.

When she finished, he went to the same typewriter and
rattled off the famous letter to his parents. He intended to
write one sheet, and wrote seven. It was his first letter to
them in months. He had no idea that he was picturing himself as an infatuated young man. He was, he thought, just
describing his job, his employer, and the charming girl he
worked with. And so Pug Henry got needlessly worked up,
and wrote the solemn reply, which startled and amused
Byron when it came; for he was no more thinking of marrying Natalie Jastrow than of turning Mohammedan. He
was just head over ears in love, with a young woman as
near as his hand and as remote as a star; and for the
moment it was enough to be where she was. He wrote again
to set his father straight, but this letter arrived in Washington after the Henrys had left for Germany.

3

IN all her years as a Navy wife, Rhoda had never become
reconciled to packing and moving. She could do it well
enough, compiling long lists, remembering tiny details,
waking in the middle of the night to scrawl notes, but she

became a termagant. The angry voice rang in the house from dawn to midnight. Pug spent the days in the Office of Naval Intelligence, boning up on Germany, and ate most of his meals at the Army and Navy Club. Still, on the short notice given her, Rhoda accomplished everything: stored the furniture, closed the house and put it up for rent, paid the bills, packed her clothes and Pug's heavy double wardrobe of civilian dress and uniforms, and moved Madeline to the home of her sister.

The gold letters B R E M E N stretched across the curved black stern of the steamship, high over the cobbled waterfront street. Above the letters, an immense red flag rippled in the cool fishy breeze off the Hudson, showing at its center a big black swastika circled in white.

"Glory be, it all really exists," Madeline said to Warren as she got out of the taxicab.

"What really exists?" Warren said.

"Oh, this whole Hitler business. The Nazis, the *Sieg Heils,* the book-burnings—when you read about it in the papers, it all seems too ridiculous and crazy to be real. But there's the swastika."

Victor Henry glanced up at the Nazi flag, wrinkling his whole face. Rhoda was briskly giving the porter orders about the luggage. "I had to get special permission to ride this bucket. Let's hope the German language practice proves to be worth it. Come aboard with us and have a look at the ship."

In a first-class stateroom panelled in gloomy carved wood, they sat making melancholy small talk amid piled suitcases and trunks, until Rhoda restlessly jumped up and took Warren with her for a walk around the *Bremen.* Madeline chose the moment to jolt her father with the news that she wanted to drop out of college. The prospect of living with her dull aunt and duller uncle and twin cousins for two years was unbearable, she said.

"But what can you do? Two years of college, and you keep failing courses," Victor Henry said. "You can't just lie around and read *Vogue* till you get married."

"I'd find a job, Dad. I can work. I'm just bored at school. I hate studying. I always have. I'm not like you, or Warren. I'm more like Byron, I guess. I can't help it."

"I never liked studying," Commander Henry returned. "Nobody does. You do what you must, and get it done."

Perched on the edge of a deep armchair, the girl said with her most winning smile, "Please! Let me take just one year off. I'll prove I can do it. There are lots of jobs for girls at the radio networks in New York. If I don't make good, I promise I'll trot back to college, and—"

"What! New York? Nineteen, and alone in New York? Are you nuts?"

"Let me just try it this summer."

"No. You'll go with Aunt Augusta to Newport, the way it's been planned. You've always enjoyed Newport."

"For a week, yes. A whole summer will be a perishing bore."

"That's where you'll go. In the fall I'll expect regular letters from you, reporting improved performance in college."

Madeline, slumping back in the armchair, bit noisily into an apple from a heaping bon voyage basket of fresh fruit, sent by Kip Tollever. Staring straight ahead, except for brief mutinous glares at her father, she gnawed at the apple until her mother and brother returned. Pug did his best to ignore the glares, reading a book on German steel-making. He did not like parting from his daughter on such terms, but her proposal seemed to him unthinkable.

The *Bremen* sailed at noon. As Warren and Madeline left the pier, a band thumped out a merry German waltz. They took a taxi uptown, saying little to each other. Henry had set the uncommunicative pattern of the family; the children, after romping and chattering through their early years, had from adolescence onward lived separate, largely undiscussed lives. Warren dropped Madeline at Radio City, not inquiring what she intended to do there. They agreed to meet for dinner, go to a show, and take a midnight train to Washington.

Madeline poked here and there in the huge lobby of the RCA building, gawking at the Sert murals and ceiling paintings. She found herself at the bank of elevators for NBC entertainers and employees. Many of these people, she noticed, showed no pass to the uniformed page, but smiled, waved, or just walked busily past the roped entrance. She sailed past too, trying to look twenty-five and employed. Squinting at her, the page held out an arresting hand. She dived into a crowded elevator.

For an hour she wandered the inner halls of the broadcasting company, relishing the thick maroon carpets, the immense round black pillars, the passing trucks of spotlights and broadcast equipment, the flashing red lights outside of studios, the pretty girls and handsome young men hurrying in and out of doors. She came on the employment office and hung outside, peering through the open double doors like a child at a candy counter. Then she left, and spent the day shopping in department stores.

As for Warren, the taxi took him a few blocks further uptown. In Rumpelmayer's, he met a good-looking woman of thirty or so with large sad eyes, a cloud of ash-blonde hair, and a clever soulful way of talking about novels, paintings, and music, subjects which did not greatly interest him. His majors had been history and the sciences. After an early lunch, he spent the day with her in a hotel bedroom. That did interest him.

When he dined with his sister that evening, Madeline helped herself to a cigarette from his pack on the table, and lit and smoked it inexpertly. Her defiant, self-satisfied, somewhat pathetic air made Warren laugh. "When the cat's away, hey?" he said.

"Oh, I've been smoking for years," Madeline said.

* * *

The three blasts of the ship's born, the pier girders moving outside the porthole, the band far below crashing out "The Star-Spangled Banner," touched a spring in Rhoda. She turned to her husband with a smile such as he had not seen on her face for weeks, threw her arms around him, and gave him an aroused kiss, opening her soft familiar lips.

"Well! We made it, Pug, didn't we? Off to Deutschland. Second honeymon and all THAT! Mmm!"

This mild pulse of sex in his hitherto preoccupied and cross wife was like a birthday present to the monogamous Pug. It augured well for the crossing, and possibly for the entire sojourn in Berlin. He pulled her close.

"Well!" Rhoda broke free, with a husky laugh and shiny

eyes. "Not so fast, young fellow. I want a drink, that's what I want, and I don't care if the sun isn't over the yardarm. And I know just what I want. Champagne cocktail, or two, or three."

"Sure. Let's have it right here. I'll order a bottle."

"Nothing doing, Pug. This will be a nice long crossing. We're getting out of here and going to the bar."

The ship was clearing the dock and hooting tugs were turning it south, as the deck started to vibrate underfoot. A crowd of tired-looking jocund voyagers already filled the bar, making a great noise.

"I thought there was a war scare," Rhoda said. "Nobody here seems to be worried."

They found two stools at the bar. Rhoda said, holding up her champagne cocktail, "Well, to whom?"

"The kids," Pug said.

"Ah, yes. Our abandoned nestlings. All right, to the kids." As she polished off the champagne, Rhoda talked excitedly about the fine accommodations of the *Bremen*. She felt very adventurous, she said, sailing on a German ship these days. "Pug, I wonder if there are any Nazis right here in this bar?" she prattled.

The fat red-faced man sitting next to Rhoda shifted his glance to her. He wore a feathered green hat and he was drinking from a stein.

"Let's take a walk on deck," Pug said. "See the Statue of Liberty."

"No, sir. I want another drink. I've seen the Statue of Liberty."

Pug made a slight peremptory move of a thumb, and Rhoda got off the stool. When anything touched his Navy work, Pug could treat her like a deckhand. He held open a door for her, and in a whipping wind they walked to the stern, where gulls swooped and screeched, and passengers clustered at the rails, watching the Manhattan buildings drift past in brown haze.

Pug said quietly, leaning on a patch of clear rail, "Look, unless we're in the open air like this, you can assume anything we say on this ship will be recorded, one way or another. At the bar, at the table, or even in our stateroom. Have you thought of that?"

"Well, sort of, but—in our stateroom too! Really?"

Pug nodded.

Rhoda looked thoughtful, then burst out laughing. "You mean—you don't mean day and night? Pug? Always?"

"That's what this job is. If they didn't do it, they'd be sloppy. The Germans aren't a sloppy people."

Her mouth curled in female amusement. "Well, then, mister, keep your DISTANCE on this boat, that's all I can say."

"It'll be no different in Berlin."

"Won't we have our own house?"

He shrugged. "Kip says you get used to it and don't think about it. I mean the loss of privacy. You're just a fish in a glass bowl and that's that. You can never stop thinking about what you say or do, however."

"Honestly!" A peculiar look, half-vexed, half-titillated, was on her face. "I can't imagine why I didn't think of that. Well! They say love will find a way, but—oh hell. It really couldn't be less important, could it? Can I have my other drink?"

An engraved card, slid under their cabin door shortly before dinner, invited them to the captain's table. They debated whether Pug should wear a uniform, and decided against it. The guess turned out to be correct. A German submarine officer at the table, a man as short and as taciturn as Victor Henry, wore a brown business suit. The captain, a paunchy stiff man in gold-buttoned blue, heavily joshed the ladies in slow English or clear German, blue eyes twinkling in his weathered fat face. Now and then he flicked a finger, and a steward in full dress jumped to his side. The captain would crackle a few words, and off the steward would bustle with a terrified face, gesturing at the waiters, long tailcoat flapping. The food was abundant and exquisite, the bowl of white and purple orchids spectacular. The parade of wines worried Pug, for when Rhoda was excited she could drink too much. But she ate heartily, drank normally, and delighted the captain by bantering with him in fluent German.

The submarine man's wife sat on Henry's left, a blonde in green low-cut chiffon that lavishly showed big creamy breasts. Pug surprised her into warm laughter by asking if she had ever worked in films. At his right sat a small

English girl in gray tweed, the daughter of Alistair Tudsbury. Tudsbury was the only real celebrity at the table, a British broadcaster and correspondent, about six feet two, with a big belly, a huge brown moustache, bulging eyes, a heavy veined nose, thick glasses, bearish eyebrows, booming voice, and an enormous appetite. He had arrived at the table laughing, and laughed at whatever was said to him, and at almost everything he said himself. He was a very ugly man, and his clothes did little to mitigate the ugliness: a rust-brown fuzzy suit, a tattersall shirt and a copious green bow tie. He smoked cigarettes, tiny in his sausage-fat fingers; one expected a pipe or a long black cigar, but the cigarette was always smoldering in his hand, except when he was plying a knife and fork.

For all the forced badinage, it was an awkward meal. Nobody mentioned politics, war, or the Nazis. Even books and plays were risky. In long silences, the slow-rolling ship squeaked and groaned. Victor Henry and the submariner exchanged several appraising glances, but no words. Pug tried once or twice to amuse Tudsbury's daughter at his right, eliciting only a shy smile. Over the dessert, turning away from the blonde—who kept telling him how good his stumbling German was—he made one more effort. "I suppose you're on vacation from school?"

"Well, sort of permanently. I'm twenty-eight."

"You are? Hm! Sorry. I thought you were about in my daughter's class. She's nineteen." The Tudsbury girl said nothing, so he kept talking. "I hope you took my stupidity as a compliment. Don't women like to be thought younger than they are?"

"Oh, many people make that mistake, Commander. It comes of my travelling with my father. His eyes aren't very good. I help him with his work."

"That must be interesting."

"Depending on the subject matter. Nowadays it's sort of a broken record. Will the little tramp go, or won't he?"

She took a sip of wine. Commander Henry was brought up short. The "little tramp" was Charlie Chaplin, of course, and by ready transfer, Hitler. She was saying that Tudsbury's one topic was whether Hitler would start a war. By not dropping her voice, by using a phrase which a German ear would be unlikely to catch, by keeping her face placid, she had managed not only to touch the forbidden subject, but to express a world of contempt, at the captain's table on the *Bremen,* for the dictator of Germany.

.   .   .

Half a dozen early-morning walkers were swinging along, looking preoccupied and virtuous, when Pug Henry came out on the cool sunlit deck, after a happy night of second honeymooning. He had calculated that five turns would make a mile, and he meant to do fifteen or twenty turns. Rounding the bow to the port side he saw, far down the long deck, the Tudsbury girl coming toward him, pumping her arms and rolling her hips. She wore the same gray suit. "Good morning." They passed each other with nods and smiles, then on the other side of the ship repeated this ritual. At the third encounter he said, reversing his direction, "Let me join you."

"Oh, thank you, yes. I feel stupid, preparing to smile forty feet away."

"Doesn't your father like to walk before breakfast?"

"He hates all forms of exercise. He's strong as a bull and nothing he does makes much difference. Anyway, right now poor Talky has a touch of gout. It's his curse."

"Talky?"

Pamela Tudsbury laughed. "His middle name is Talcott. Since schoolboy days, he's been 'Talky' to his friends. Guess why!" She was moving quite fast. In flat shoes she was very short. She glanced up at him. "Commander, where's your wife? Also not a walker?"

"Late sleeper. Not that she'll walk to the corner drugstore if she can drive or hail a cab. Well, what does your father really think? Will the little tramp go?"

She laughed, a keen look brightening her eyes, evidently pleased that he remembered. "He's come out boldly to the effect that time will tell."

"What do you think?"

"Me? I just type what *he* thinks. On a special portable with oversize print." She gestured at three deep-breathing German matrons in tailored suits marching by. "I know that I feel queer sailing on a ship of theirs."

"Didn't your father just publish a book? I seem to remember reviews."

"Yes. Just a paste-up of his broadcasts, really."

"I'd like to read it. Writers awe me. I have a tough time putting one word down after another."

"I saw a copy in the ship's library. He sent me there to check," she said, with a grin that reminded him of Madeline, catching him in self-importance or pretense. He wished Warren could meet this girl or one like her. Last night he had not paid her much mind, with the busty, half-naked, talkative blonde there. But now, especially with the fresh coloring of the morning sea air, he thought she had an English lady's face, a heart-shaped face from a Gainsborough or a Romney: thin lips, expressive green-gray eyes set wide apart, fine straight nose, heavy brown hair. The skin of her hands and face was pearl-smooth. Just the girl for Warren, pretty and keen.

"You're going around again? I get off here," she said, stopping at a double door. "If you do read his book, Commander Henry, carry it under your arm. He'll fall in love with you. It'll make his trip."

"How can he care? Why, he's famous."

"He cares. God, how they care." With a clumsy little wave, she went inside.

After breakfasting alone, Pug went to the library. Nobody was there but a boyish steward. The shelves held many German volumes on the World War. Pug glanced at one titled *U-boats: 1914–18,* and settled into a leather armchair to scan the discussion of American destroyer tactics. Soon he heard the scratch of a pen. At a small desk almost within his reach, the German submarine man sat with his bristly head bent, writing. Pug had not seen him come in.

Grobke smiled, and pointed his pen at the U-boat book. "Recalling old times?"

"Well, I was in destroyers."

"And I was down below. Maybe this is not the first time our paths cross." Grobke spoke English with a slight, not unpleasant Teutonic accent.

"Possibly not."

When Pug put the U-boat volume on the shelf and took down the Tudsbury book, Grobke remarked, "Perhaps we could have a drink before dinner and compare notes on the Atlantic in 1918?"

"I'd enjoy that."

Pug intended to read Tudsbury in a deck chair for a while and then go below to work. He had brought weighty books on German industry, politics, and history, and meant to grind through the lot on the way to his post. Intelligence manuals and handbooks were all right, but he was a digger. He liked to search out the extra detail in the extra-discouraging-looking fat volume. Surprising things were recorded, but patient alert eyes were in perpetual short supply.

The bow wave was boiling away, a V of white foam on the blue sunlit sea, and the *Bremen* was rolling like a battleship. Wind from the northwest, Pug estimated, glancing up at the thin smoke from the stacks, and at the sea; wind speed fifteen knots, ship's speed eighteen, number four sea on the port quarter, rain and high winds far ahead under the cumulo-nimbus. Nostalgia swept over him. Four years since he had served at sea; eleven since he had had a command! He stood by the forward rail, leaning against a lifeboat davit, sniffing the sea air. Four unmistakable Jews walked by in jolly conversation, two middle-aged couples in fine sports clothes. They went out of sight around the deckhouse. He was still looking after them when he heard Tudsbury blare, "Hello there, Commander. I hear you were out walking my Pam at the crack of dawn."

"Hello. Did you see those people who just went by?"

"Yes. There's no understanding Jews. I say, is that *my* book? How touching. How far have you got?"

"I just drew it from the library."

Tudsbury's moustache drooped sadly. "What! You didn't buy it? Damn all libraries. Now you'll read it and I won't gain a penny by it." He bellowed a laugh and rested one green-stockinged leg on the rail. He was wearing a baggy pepper-and-salt golfing outfit and a green tam o'shanter. "It's a bad book, really a fake, but it's selling in your country, luckily for me. If you didn't happen to hear my drivelling on the air in the past year or two, there are a couple of interesting paragraphs. Footnotes to history. My thing on Hitler's entry into Vienna is actually not too awful. Quite a time we're living in, Commander."

He talked about the German take-over of Austria, sounding much as he did on the air: positive, informed, full of scorn for democratic politicians, and cheerfully ominous. Tudsbury's special note was that the world would very likely go up in flames, but that it might prove a good show. "Can you picture the bizarre and horrible triumph that we let him get away with, dear fellow? I saw it all. Something straight out of Plutarch, that was! A zero of a man, with no schooling, of no known family—at twenty a dropped-out student, a drifter and a failure—five years a dirty, seedy tramp in a Vienna doss house—did you know that, Henry? Do you know that for five years this Führer was what you call a Bowery bum, sharing a vile room with other assorted flotsam, eating in soup kitchens, and not because there was a depression—Vienna was fat and prosperous then—but because he was a dreamy, lazy, incompetent misfit? That house painter story is hogwash. He sold a few hand-painted postcards, but to the age of twenty-six he was a sidewalk-wandering vagrant, and then for four years a soldier in the German army, a lance corporal, a messenger-runner, a low job for a man of even minimum intelligence, and at thirty he was lying broke, discharged, and gassed in an army hospital. That is the background of the Führer.

"And then—" The ship's horn blasted, drowning out Tudsbury's voice, which was beginning to roll in his broadcasting style. He winced, laughed, and went on: "And then, what happened? Why, then this same ugly, sickly, uncouth, prejudiced, benighted, half-mad little wretch leaped out of his hospital bed, and went careering in ten years straight to the top of a German nation thirsting for a return match. The man was a foreigner, Henry! He was an Austrian. They had to fake up a citizenship proceeding for him, so he could run against Hindenburg! And I myself watched this man ride in triumph through the streets of Vienna, where he had sold postcards and gone hungry, the sole heir to the combined thrones of the Hapsburgs and the Hohenzollerns." Victor Henry smiled, and Tudsbury's impassioned popeyed stare gave way to a loud guffaw. "A-hawr, hawr, hawr! I suppose it *is* rather funny when you think about it. But this grotesque fantasy happens to be the central truth of our age."

Henry was smiling because much of this tirade was in Tudsbury's book, almost word for word. "Well, it's the old story of the stitch in time," he said. "Your politicos could have got the weird little bastard with no trouble early on, but they didn't. Now they have problems. Incidentally, where are you headed? Berlin, too?"

Tudsbury nodded. "Our Berlin man's prostate chose an awkward time to act up. A-hawr-hawr! Dr. Goebbels said I could come along and fill in. Amazement! I've been *persona non grata* in the Third Reich since Munich. No doubt I'll be kicked out on my big arse in a few weeks. For some reason the Jerries are being kind to Englishmen this month. Probably so we'll hold still while they roll over the Poles. And we will, we will. The Tories are all polite gray worms. Aristocratic funks, Lloyd George called them. Except for Churchill, who's quite out of it."

■   ●   ■

The American commander and the U-boat man took to meeting in the bar each evening before dinner. Henry figured that it was his job to pump Grobke, as it might well be the German's to work on him. Grobke was a thorough professional, an engineering expert, and a real seafarer. He talked freely about the machinery in the present U-boats, and even confessed to problems with torpedoes, a topic Henry was well versed in, though he discussed it cautiously. In Grobke's harassed disdain for politicians, he seemed like any American naval man. A satiric look came on his face when he spoke of the Nazis, and he said things that caused his wife, when she was with them, to give him warning glances.

Alistair Tudsbury said to Pug one evening, as they sat on a couch in the main saloon watching the dancing, "You've been fraternizing with Jerry."

"In the line of business. I doubt Grobke's a Nazi."

"Oh, those U-boat fellows are all right, as much as any Germans are."

"You don't like the Germans."

"Well. Let's talk about *that* after you've been there a month. Assuming I haven't been booted out."

"Of course I don't blame you. They gave your people hell."

"No worse than we gave them. We won, you know." After a pause he said, "My eyes were spoiled at Amiens, when we broke through with the tanks. I commanded a tank battalion, and was gassed. It was worth it, all in all, to see Jerry on the run. It was a long time coming."

The captain of the *Bremen,* at the moment, was dancing with Rhoda. He had long capering legs, strange in a stout man. Rhoda was radiating enjoyment. Pug was glad of this. Night after night she had been dancing with a very tall young officer, a blond-eagle type, all clicking bows and glittering blue eyes, who held her a bit too close. Pug had said something about it, and Rhoda had countered with a brief snarl about his spending the trip with his nose in books, and he had let it drop. She was being so complaisant, on the whole, that he only wanted to keep things so.

The captain brought her back. Pamela Tudsbury returned from a listless effort to follow the flailing prances of an American college boy. She said, "I shall get myself a cane and a white wig. They look so shattered if I refuse, but I really can hardly dance, and as for the Lindy Hop—"

The music struck up again, and Rhoda's tall young officer approached in spotless white and gold. An irritated look crossed Pug's face. The captain saw it, and under the loud music, as the officer drew near, he muttered half a dozen words. The young man stopped, faded back, and darted out of the saloon. Pug never saw him again.

Rhoda, smiling and about to rise, was baffled by the young German's peculiar exit.

"Dance, Rhoda?" Pug got to his feet.

"What?" she said crossly. "No, thanks."

Pug extended a hand to the Tudsbury girl. "Pamela?"

She hesitated. "You don't do the Lindy Hop?" Pug burst out laughing. "Well, one never knows with Americans."

She danced in a heavy, inexperienced way. Pug liked her gentle manner, her helpless smile when she trod on his foot. "You can't be enjoying this," she said.

"I am. Do you think you'll be going back to the United States?"

"If Father gets thrown out of Germany, which seems inevitable, I suppose we will. Why?"

"I have a son about your age with quite a fine record, and unlike me, tall and very handsome."

Pamela made a face. "A Navy man? Never. A girl in every port."

At the captain's table, on the last night, there were white orchids at every lady's place; and under these, white gold compacts. Champagne went round, and the topic of international politics finally surfaced. Everybody agreed that in this day and age war was a silly, wasteful way of settling differences, especially among advanced nations like England, France, and Germany. "We're all of the same stock, all north Europeans," Tudsbury said. "It's a sad thing when brothers fall out."

The captain nodded happily. "Exactly what I say. If we could only stick together, there would never be another war. The Bolsheviks would never move against so much power. And who else wants war?" All through the saloon people were wearing paper hats and tossing streamers, and Pug observed that the four Jews, whose table was not far away, were having as gay a time as everybody else, under the polite ministrations of smiling German waiters. The captain followed Henry's glance, and a genial superior grin relaxed his stern fat face. "You see, Commander? They are as welcome aboard the *Bremen* as anybody else, and get the same service. The exaggerations on that subject are fantastic." He turned to Tudsbury. "Between us, aren't you journalists a wee bit responsible for making matters worse?"

"Well, Captain," Tudsbury said, "journalism always looks for a theme, you know. One of the novel things about your government, to people outside Germany, is its policy toward the Jews. And so it keeps turning up."

"Tudsbury is not entirely wrong, Captain," Grobke broke in, draining his wineglass. "Outsiders think of nothing but the Jews nowadays when Germany is mentioned. That policy has been mishandled. I've said so many times. That and plenty of other things." He turned to Henry. "Still, they're so unimportant, Victor, compared to what the Führer has achieved: Germany has come back to life. That's God's truth. The people have work, they have food and houses, and they have spirit. What Hitler has done for our youth alone is just incredible." (The captain's eyes lit up and he emphatically nodded, exclaiming, *"Ja, ja!"*) "Under Weimar they were rioting, they were becoming Communists, they were going in for sex perversions and drugs, it was just horrible. Now they're working, or training, or *serving,* all of them. They're happy! My crews are happy. You can't imagine what navy morale was like under the Republic—I tell you what." He struck the table. "You come visit our squadron, at the sub base in Swinemünde. You do that! You're a man that can look at a navy yard or a ship's crew and see what's going on! It'll open your eyes. Will you?"

Henry took a moment to reply, with everybody at the table turning expectantly to him. An invitation like this, if accepted, made mandatory a similar offer to the German naval attaché in Washington. Did the Navy want to trade glimpses of submarine bases with the Nazi regime? The decision was beyond Pug's power. He had to report the invitation to Washington and act on the dictated answer.

He said, "I'd like that. Perhaps we can work it out."

"Say yes. Forget the formalities!" Grobke waved both arms in the air. "It's a personal invitation from me to you, from one seaman to another. The U-boat command gets damn small budgets, and we're pretty independent chaps. You can visit us with no strings. I'll see to that."

"This invitation wouldn't include me, would it?" Tudsbury said.

Grobke hesitated, then laughed. "Why not? Come along, Tudsbury. The more the British know about what we've got, the less likely anybody is to make a hasty mistake."

"Well, here may be an important little step for peace," said the captain, "transacted at my table! I feel honored, and we will have more champagne on it at once."

And so the diners at the captain's table on the *Bremen* all drank to peace a few minutes before midnight, as the great liner slowed, approaching the shore lights of Nazi Germany.

.   .   .   .

In bright sunshine, the *Bremen* moved like a train between low green banks of a wide river. Pug was at the rail of the sun deck, taking his old pleasure in the sight of land after a voyage. Rhoda was below in her usual fit of the snarls and the snaps. When they travelled together, Rhoda in deep martyrdom did the packing. Pug was an old hand at packing for himself, but Rhoda claimed she could never find anything he put away.

"Oh, yes, the country is charming to look at," said Tudsbury, who had sauntered up and commenced a discourse on the scenery. "You'll see many a pretty north German town between Bremerhaven and Berlin. The heavy half-timbered kind of thing, that looks so much like English Tudor. The fact is Germany and England have strong resemblances and links. You know of course that the Kaiser was Queen Victoria's grandson, that our royal family for a long time spoke only German? And yet on the whole the Jerries are stranger to us than Eskimos." He boomed a laugh and went on, sweeping a fat hand toward the shore: "Yes, here the Germans sit at the heart of Europe, Henry, these perplexing first cousins of ours, simmering and grumbling away, and every now and then they spill over in all directions, with a hideous roar. Out they pour from these lovely little towns, these fairy-tale landscapes, these clean handsome cities—wait till you see Cologne, Nuremberg, Munich, even Berlin and Hamburg—out they bubble, I say, these polite blue-eyed music lovers, ravening for blood. It gets a bit unnerving. And now here's Hitler, bringing them to a boil again. You Americans may have to lend more of a hand than you did last time. We're fairly worn out with them, you know, we and the French."

It had not escaped Henry that Tudsbury's talk, one way or another, usually came back to the theme of the United States fighting Germany.

"That might not be in the cards, Tudsbury. We've got the Japanese on our hands. They're carving up China, and they've got a first-class fighting navy, growing every month. If they make the Pacific a Japanese lake and proceed to do what they want on the Asian mainland, the world will be theirs in fifty years."

Tudsbury said, sticking his tongue out of a corner of his smiling mouth, "The Yellow Peril."

"It's a question of facts and numbers," Henry said. "How many people are there in all of Europe? Couple of hundred million? Japan is now well on the way to ruling one billion people. They're as industrious as the Germans or more so. They came out of paper houses and silk kimonos in a couple of generations to defeat Russia. They're amazing. Compared to what faces us in Asia, this Hitler business strikes us as just more of the same old runty cat-and-dog fight in the back yard."

Tudsbury peered at him, with a reluctant nod. "Possibly you underestimate the Germans."

"Maybe you overestimate them. Why the devil didn't you and the French go in when they occupied the Rhineland? They broke a treaty. You could have walked in there at that point and hung Hitler, with not much more trouble than raiding a girls' dormitory."

"Ah, the wisdom of hindsight," Tudsbury said. "Don't ask me to defend our politicians. It's been a radical breakdown, a total failure of sense and nerve. I was talking and writing in 1936 the way you are now. At Munich I was close to suicide. I covered the whole thing. Czechoslovakia! A huge chain of strong fortifications, jutting deep into Germany's gut. Fifty crack divisions, spoiling for a scrap. The second biggest arms factory in the world. Russia and even France ready at last to stand up and fight. All this, six short months ago! And an Englishman, an *Englishman,* goes crawling across Europe to Hitler and hands him Czechoslovakia!" Tudsbury laughed mechanically and puffed at a cigarette made ragged by the breeze. "I don't know. Maybe democracy isn't for the industrial age. If it's to survive, I think the Americans will have to put up the show."

"Why? Why do you keep saying that? On paper you and the French still have the Germans badly licked. Don't you realize that? Manpower, firepower, steel, oil, coal, industrial plant, any way you add it up. They've got a small temporary lead in the air, but they've also got the Soviet Union at their backs. It's not the walkover it was last year and two years ago, but you still figure to win."

"Alas, they've got the leadership."

A strong hand clapped Henry's shoulder, and a voice tinged with irony said, *"Heil Hitler!"* Ernst Grobke stood there in a worn, creased navy uniform; with it he had put on a severe face and an erect posture. "Well, gentlemen, here we are. Victor, in case I don't see you again in the confusion, where do I get in touch with you? The embassy?"

"Sure. Office of the Naval Attaché."

"Ah!" said Tudsbury. "Our little trip to Swinemünde! So glad you haven't forgotten."

"I'll do my best to include you," said Grobke coldly. He shook hands with both of them, bowing and clicking his heels, and he left.

"Come and say good-bye to Pamela," Tudsbury said. "She's below, packing."

"I'll do that." Pug walked down the deck with the correspondent, who limped on a cane. "I have notions of matching her up with a son of mine."

"Oh, have you?" Tudsbury gave him a waggish glance through his thick spectacles. "I warn you, she's a handful."

"What? Why, I've never met a gentler or pleasanter girl."

"Still waters," said Tudsbury. "I warn you."

4

THE Henrys had only just arrived in Berlin when they were invited to meet Hitler. It was a rare piece of luck, the embassy people told them. Chancellery receptions big enough to include military attachés were none too common. The Führer was staying away from Berlin in order to damp down the war talk, but a visit of the Bulgarian prime minister had brought him back to the capital.

While Commander Henry studied the protocol of Nazi receptions in moments snatched from his piled-up office work, Rhoda flew into a two-day frenzy over her clothing, and over her hair, which she asserted had been ruined forever by the imbecile hairdresser of the Adlon Hotel (Pug thought the hair looked more or less the same as always). She had brought no dresses in the least suitable for a formal afternoon reception in the spring. *Why* hadn't somebody *warned* her? Three hours before the event Rhoda was still whirling in an embassy car from one Berlin dress shop to another. She burst into their hotel room clad in a pink silk suit with gold buttons and a gold net blouse. "How's this?" she barked. "Sally Forrest says Hitler likes pink."

"Perfect!" Her husband thought the suit was terrible, and decidedly big on Rhoda, but it was no time for truth-telling. "Gad, where did you ever find it?"

Outside the hotel, long vertical red banners of almost transparent cheesecloth, with the black swastika in a white circle at their center, were swaying all along the breezy street, alternated with gaudy Bulgarian flags. The way to the chancellery was lined with more flags, a river of fluttering red, interspersed with dozens of Nazi standards in the style of Roman legion emblems—long poles topped by stylized gilt eagles perching on wreathed swastikas—and underneath, in place of the Roman SPQR, the letters NSDAP.

"What on earth does NSDAP stand for?" Rhoda said, peering out of the window of the embassy car at the multitudinous gilded poles.

"National Socialist German Workers Party," said Pug.

"Is that the name of the Nazis? How funny. Sounds sort of Commie when you spell it all out."

Pug said, "Sure. Hitler got in on a red-hot radical program."

"Did he? I never knew that. I thought he was against all that stuff. Well, it couldn't be more confusing, I mean European politics, but I do think all this is terribly exciting. Makes Washington seem dull and tame, doesn't it?"

When Victor Henry first came into Hitler's new chancellery, he was incongruously reminded of Radio City Music Hall in New York. The opulent stretch of carpet, the long line of waiting people, the high ceiling, the great expanses of shiny marble, the inordinate length and height of the huge space, the gaudily uniformed men ushering the guests along, all added up to much the same theatrical, vulgar, strained effort to be grand; but this was the seat of a major government, not a movie house. It seemed peculiar. An officer in blue took his name, and the slow-moving line carried the couple toward the Führer, far down the hall. The SS guards were alike as chorus boys with their black-and-silver uniforms, black boots, square shoulders, blond waved hair, white teeth, bronzed skin, and blue eyes. Some shepherded the guests with careful smiles, others stood along the walls, blank-faced and stiff.

Hitler was no taller than Henry himself; a small man with a prison haircut, leaning forward and bowing as he shook hands, his head to one side, hair falling on his fore-head. This was Henry's flash impression, as he caught his first full-length look at the Führer beside the burly much-medalled Bulgarian, but in another moment it changed. Hitler had a remarkable smile. His downcurved mouth was rigid and tense, his eyes sternly self-confident. but when he smiled this fanatic look vanished; the whole face bright-ened up, showing a strong hint of humor, and a curious, almost boyish, shyness. Sometimes he held a guest's hand and conversed. When he was particularly amused he laughed and made an odd sudden move with his right knee: he lifted it and jerked it a little inward.

His greeting to the two American couples ahead of the Henrys was casual. He did not smile, and his restless eyes wandered away from them and back again as he shook hands.

A protocol officer in a sky-blue, gold-crusted foreign service uniform intoned in German:

"The naval attaché to the embassy of the United States of America, Commander Victor Henry!"

The hand of the Führer was dry, rough, and it seemed a bit swollen. The clasp was firm as he scanned Henry's face. Seen this close the deep-sunk eyes were pale blue, puffy, and somewhat glassy. Hitler appeared fatigued; his pasty face had streaks of sunburn on his forehead, nose, and cheekbones, as though he had been persuaded to leave his desk in Berchtesgaden and come outside for a few hours. To be looking into this famous face with its hanging hair, thrusting nose, zealot's remote eyes, and small moustache was the strangest sensation of Henry's life.

Hitler said, *"Willkommen in Deutschland,"* and dropped his hand.

Surprised that Hitler should be aware of his recent arrival, Pug stammered, *"Danke, Herr Reichskanzler."*

"Frau Henry!"

Rhoda, her eyes gleaming, shook hands with Adolf Hitler. He said, in German, "I hope you are comfortable in Berlin." His voice was low, almost folksy; another surprise to Henry, who had only heard him shouting hoarsely on the radio or in the newsreels.

"Well, Herr Reichskanzler, to tell the truth I've just begun looking for a house," Rhoda said breathlessly, too overcome to make a polite reply and move on.

"You will have no difficulty." Hitler's eyes softened and warmed at her clear German speech. Evidently he found Rhoda pretty. He kept her hand, faintly smiling.

"But there are so many charming neighborhoods in Berlin that I'm bewildered. That's the real problem."

This pleased or amused Hitler. He laughed, kicked his knee inward, and turning to an aide behind him, said a few words. The aide bowed. Hitler held out his hand to the next guest. The Henrys moved on to the Bulgarian.

The reception did not last long. Colonel Forrest, the military attaché, a fat Army Air officer from Idaho who had been in Germany for two years, introduced the Henrys to foreign attachés and Nazi leaders, including Goebbels and Ribbentrop, who looked just like their newsreel pictures, but oddly diminished. These two, with their perfunctory fast handshakes, made Henry feel like the small fry he was; Hitler had not done that. Pug kept trying to watch Hitler. The Führer wore black trousers, a gray double-breasted coat with an eagle emblem on one arm, and a small Iron Cross on his left breast. By American styles the clothes were cut much too full. This gave the leader of Germany the appearance of wearing secondhand, ill-fitting garments. Hitler from moment to moment looked restless, tired, or bored, or else he flashed into winning charm. He was seldom still. He shifted his feet, turned his head here and there, clasped his hands before him, folded them, gestured with them, spoke absently to most people and intensely to a few, and every so often did the little knee kick. Once Pug saw him eating small iced cakes from a plate, shoving them toward his mouth with snatching greedy fingers while he talked to a bemedalled visitor.

Shortly thereafter he left, and the gathering started to disperse.

It was drizzling outside; the massed red flags were drooping, and from the helmets of the erect guards water ran unheeded down their faces. The women clustered in the entrance while Pug, Colonel Forrest, and the chargé d'affaires went out to hail the embassy cars. The chargé, a tall moustached man with a pale clever face full of wrinkles, and a weary air, ran the embassy. After the Crystal Night, President Roosevelt had recalled the ambassador, and had not yet sent him back. Everybody in the embassy disliked this policy. It cut the Americans off from some official channels, and hampered their ability to conduct business, even the business of interceding for Jews. The staff thought the President had made a political gesture toward the New York Jews that, in Germany, seemed ineffectual and laughable.

The chargé said to Henry, "Well, what did you think of the Führer?"

"I was impressed. He knew I'd just arrived."

"Really? Well, now you've seen German thoroughness. Somebody checked, and briefed him."

"But he remembered. In that long line."

The chargé smiled. "Politician's memory."

Colonel Forrest rubbed his broad flat nose, smashed years ago in a plane crash, and said to the chargé: "The Führer had quite a chat with Mrs. Henry. What was it about, Pug?"

"Nothing. Just a word or two about house-hunting."

"You have a beautiful wife," the chargé said. "Hitler likes pretty women. And that's quite a striking suit she's wearing. They say Hitler likes pink."

*   *   *

Two days later, Henry was working at the embassy at a morning pile of mail, in an office not unlike his old cubicle in War Plans—small, crowded with steel files, and piled with technical books and reports. This one had a window, and the view of Hitler's chancellery slightly jarred him each morning when he got there. His yeoman buzzed from a tiny anteroom smelling of mimeograph ink, cigarette smoke, and overbrewed coffee, like yeomen's anterooms everywhere.

"Mrs. Henry, sir."

It was early for Rhoda to be up. She said grumpily that a man named Knödler, a renting agent for furnished homes, had sent his card to their hotel room, with a note saying he had been advised they were looking for a house. He was waiting in the lobby for an answer.

"Well, what can you lose?" Henry said. "Go and look at his houses."

"It seems so odd. You don't suppose *Hitler* sent him?"

Pug laughed. "Maybe his aide did."

Rhoda called back at three-thirty in the afternoon. He had just returned from lunch. "Yes?" he yawned. "What now?" The long heavy wine-bibbing meal of the diplomats was still too much for him.

"There's this wonderful house in the Grunewald section, right on a lake. It even has a tennis court! The price is ridiculously cheap, it doesn't come to a hundred dollars a month. Can you come right away and look at it?"

Pug went. It was a heavily built gray stone mansion roofed in red tile, set amid tall old trees on a smooth lawn sloping to the water's edge. The tennis court was in back, beside a formal garden with flower beds in bloom around a marble fountain swarming with large goldfish. Inside the house were Oriental carpets, large gilt-framed old paintings, a walnut dining table with sixteen blue silk-upholstered chairs, and a long living room cluttered with elegant French pieces. The place had five upstairs bedrooms and three marbled baths.

The agent, a plump matter-of-fact man of thirty or so, with straight brown hair and rimless glasses, might have been an American real estate broker. Indeed he said that his brother was a realtor in Chicago and that he had once worked in his office. Pug asked him why the price was so low. The agent cheerfully explained in good English that the owner, Herr Rosenthal, was a Jewish manufacturer, and that the house was vacant because of a new ruling affecting Jews. So he badly needed a tenant.

"What's this new ruling?" Henry asked.

"I'm not too clear on it. Something related to their owning real estate." Knödler spoke in an entirely offhand tone, as though he were discussing a zoning regulation in Chicago.

"Does this man know you're offering the house to us, and at what price?" Pug said.

"Naturally."

"When can I meet him?"

"Any time you say."

Next day Pug used his lunch hour for an appointment with the owner. After introducing them in the doorway of the house, the agent went and sat in his car. Herr Rosenthal, a gray-headed, paunchy, highly dignified individual, clad in a dark suit of excellent English cut, invited Henry inside.

"It's a beautiful house," Henry said in German.

Rosenthal glanced around with wistful affection, gestured to a chair, and sat down. "Thank you. We're fond of it, and have spent a lot of time and money on it."

"Mrs. Henry and I feel awkward about leasing the place."

"Why?" The Jew looked surprised. "You're desirable tenants. If a lower rent would help—"

"Good lord, no! It's an incredibly low rent. But will you actually receive the money?"

"Of course. Who else? It's my house." Rosenthal spoke firmly and proudly. "With the agent's commission deducted, and certain municipal fees, I'll receive every penny."

Pug pointed a thumb at the front door. "Knödler told me that some new ruling compels you to rent it."

"That won't affect you as tenant, I assure you. Are you thinking of a two-year lease? I myself would prefer that."

"But what's this ruling?"

Though they were alone in an unoccupied house, Rosenthal glanced over one shoulder and then the other, and dropped his voice. "Well—it's an emergency decree, you understand; I am sure it will eventually be cancelled. In fact I have been assured of that by people in high places. Meantime this property can be placed under a trusteeship and sold at any time without my consent. However, if there's a tenant in residence with diplomatic immunity, that can't be done." Rosenthal smiled. "Hence the modest rent, Herr Commandant! You see, I'm not hiding anything."

"May I ask you a question? Why don't you sell out and leave Germany?"

The Jew blinked. His face remained debonair and imposing. "My family has a business here more than one hundred years old. We refine sugar. My children are at school in England, but my wife and I are comfortable enough in Berlin. We are both native Berliners." He sighed, looked around at the snug rosewood-panelled library in which they sat, and went on: "Things are not as bad as they were in 1938. That was the worst. If there is no war, they'll improve quickly. I've been told this seriously by some high officials. Old friends of mine." Rosenthal hesitated and added, "The Führer has done remarkable things for the country. It would be foolish to deny that. I have lived through other bad times. I was shot through a lung in Belgium in 1914. A man goes through a lot in a lifetime." He spread his hands in a graceful resigned gesture.

Victor Henry said, "Well, Mrs. Henry loves the house, but I don't want to take advantage of anybody's misfortune."

"You'll be doing just the opposite. You know that now. Two years?"

"How about one year, with an option to renew?"

At once Rosenthal stood and held out his hand. Henry rose and shook it. "We should have a drink on it perhaps," said Rosenthal, "but we emptied the liquor closet when we left. Liquor doesn't last long in a vacant house."

It felt odd the first night, sleeping in the Rosenthals' broad soft bed with its exquisite French petit-point footboard and headboard. But within a few days, the Henrys were at home in the mansion and busy with a new life. From an employment agency suggested by the agent came a maid, a cook, and a houseman-chauffeur, all first-rate servants, and—Henry assumed—all planted informers. He checked the electric wiring of the house for listening devices. The German equipment and circuits were strange to him, and he found nothing. Still, he and Rhoda walked on the lawn to discuss touchy matters.

A whirling couple of weeks passed. They saw Hitler once more at an opera gala, this time at a distance, up in a crimson damask-lined box. His white tie and tails were again too big, emphasizing his Charlie Chaplin air of a dressed-up vagrant, despite his severe stiff saluting and the cheers and applause of beautiful women and important-looking men, all stretching their necks to stare worshipfully.

At two receptions arranged for the Henrys, one at the home of the chargé and one at Colonel Forrest's house, they met many foreign diplomats and prominent German industrialists, artists, politicians, and military men. Rhoda made a quick hit. Notwithstanding her panic before the chancellery reception, she had brought a large costly wardrobe. She sparkled in her new clothes. Her German kept improving. She liked Berlin and its people. The Germans sensed this and warmed to her, though some embassy people who detested the regime were taken aback by her cordiality to Nazis. Pug was something of a bear at these parties, standing silent unless spoken to. But Rhoda's success covered for him.

Rhoda was not blind to the Nazi abuses. After her first walk in the Tiergarten, she refused to go back. It was far more clean, pretty, and charming than any American public park, she admitted, but the signs on the benches, JUDEN VERBOTEN, were nauseating. Seeing similar signs in restaurant windows, she would recoil and demand to go elsewhere. When Pug told her of his interview with Rosenthal, she had a deep attack of the blues: she wanted to forgo the house and even talked of getting out of Germany. "Why, imagine! Renting out that beautiful house for a song, just to keep it from being sold over his head—to some fat Nazi, no doubt, lying in wait to pick it off cheap. How horrible." But she agreed that they had better take it. They had to live somewhere, and the house was divine.

Day by day, she reacted less to such things, seeing how commonplace they were in Berlin, and how much taken for granted. When Sally Forrest, who loathed the Nazis, took her to lunch at a restaurant where a window placard announced that Jews were not served, it seemed silly to protest. Soon she ate in such places without a second thought. In time, the Tiergarten became her favorite place for a Sunday stroll. But she insisted that anti-Semitism was a blot on an otherwise exciting, lovely land. She would say so to prominent Nazis. Some stiffened, others tolerantly smirked. A few hinted that the problem would straighten out in time.

"I'm an American to the bone, going back six generations," she would say, "and I'll never see eye to eye with you on this business of the Jews. It's absolutely awful."

Most Germans seemed resigned to this independent, outspoken manner of American women and the way their husbands tolerated it; they regarded it as a national oddity.

Victor Henry stayed off the Jewish topic. Nazi Germany was a big, not readily digestible lump of new life. Most foreigners were strongly for or against the Nazis. The correspondents, as Kip Tollever had observed, hated them to a man. Within the embassy views varied. According to some, Hitler was the greatest menace to America since 1776. He would stop at nothing less than world rule, and the day he was strong enough, he would attack the United States. Others saw him as a benefactor, the only bulwark in Europe against communism. The democracies had shown themselves impotent against the spread of Bolshevist parties, they said. Hitler fought totalitarian fire with hotter and stronger fire.

These judgments, either way, stood on slender bases of knowledge. Pressing his new acquaintances for facts, Victor Henry got vehement opinions and gestures. Statistics abounded in sheaves of analyses and reports, but too much of this stuff also came down to guesses, propaganda, and questionable paid intelligence. He tried to study German history late at night and found it a muddy tangle going back more than a thousand years. In it he could find no pattern and no guide at all to the problems of 1939. Just to figure out where the Nazis had come from, and what the secret was of Hitler's hold on the Germans, seemed a task beyond him and beyond anybody he talked to; even the outlandish question of German anti-Semitism had a dozen different explanations, depending on which of any twelve Foreign Service men you asked. Commander Henry decided that he would grope uselessly if he tried to fathom these major matters in a hurry. Military capacity was something he knew about; it was a narrow but decisive aspect of Hitler's Third Empire. Was Nazi Germany as strong as the ever-marching columns in the streets, and the throngs of uniforms in cafés, suggested? Was it all a show, no more substantial than the transparent red cheesecloth of the towering swastika banners? Deciding to take nothing for granted and to marshal facts for himself, Victor Henry dug into the job of penetrating this one puzzle.

Meanwhile Rhoda adapted merrily to diplomatic life. As she got used to her staff and to Berlin customs, her dinner parties increased in size. She invited the Grobkes to a big one that included the chargé d'affaires, a French film actress, the conductor of the Berlin Philharmonic Orchestra, and a dour, stout German general named Armin von Roon, with a peculiarly hooked nose and an exceedingly stiff carriage. Rhoda knew none of these people well. General von Roon, for instance, she had met at Colonel Forrest's house; and because someone had told her that he stood high in the Wehrmacht and was considered brilliant, she had made up to him. She had a gift for charming in a momentary encounter. She always looked elegant, she could be amusing or sexy without forcing either note, and she made one feel that it would be pleasant to know her better. People tended to accept her invitations.

The company was above the level of Grobke and his wife. They were dazzled and flattered, and the presence of Roon all but froze them with awe. Grobke whispered to Victor Henry at one point that Roon was the real brain in Supreme Headquarters. So Pug tried to talk to Roon about the war, and found that he spoke astonishingly good English. But he would utter only frosty generalities, which made the attaché think the better of him, though it yielded nothing to report.

Before the evening was out Grobke, full of wine and brandy, took Victor Henry aside and told him that the captain of the Swinemünde navy yard was making stupid difficulties, but that he was going to push the visit through, "and I'll get your English friend in too, God damn it. I said I would and I will. These shore-based bastards just live to create trouble."

The Henrys received one cheerless letter from Madeline, written when she arrived in Newport for the summer. Warren, as usual, did not write at all. Early in July the letter Byron had written his father at last caught up with him:

Dear Dad:

I received your letter and it threw me. I guess I gave you the wrong impression about this girl Natalie Jastrow. It's fun to work with her, but she's older than I am, and she was a junior Phi Bete at Radcliffe. Her best boyfriend is a Rhodes Scholar. I'm not in that league. However, I appreciate your good advice. She is really excellent company, and talking to her improves my mind. That should please you.

Dr. Jastrow has me researching the Emperor Constantine's military campaigns. I took the job for the money, but I'm enjoying it. That whole period, when the world balance tips from paganism to Christianity, is really worth knowing, Dad. It has some parallels to our own day. I think you'll like Dr. Jastrow's new book. He's just a scholar and wouldn't know a torpedo boat from a medium tank, yet he has a way of grasping an ancient campaign and describing it so anybody can understand it and sort of picture what those times were like.

Siena's going to be overrun with tourists for the Palio, a goofy horse race they put on every year. The nags run around the town square, and they say all hell usually breaks loose. Warren will make a great flier. Well, I guess that's about it. Love to all.

Byron

5

SINCE the fourteenth century—so Byron had learned—nothing much had happened in Siena besides the Palios. A rich city-state of the Middle Ages, the military rival of Florence, Siena in 1348 had been isolated by the Black Death, and frozen in its present form as by a spell. A few art lovers now drifted here to admire the fourteenth-century paintings and architecture. The world at large flocked to Siena twice a year to watch the mad horse races, and otherwise let the bypassed town, a living scene out of an old tapestry, molder in the Tuscan sunshine.

In nine years of living just outside Siena, Aaron Jastrow had never attended a Palio. When Byron asked why, Jastrow held forth on the cruel public games of Roman times, the forerunners of all these burlesque races of the Middle Ages. The Palio had happened to survive in mountain-locked Siena, he said, like a dinosaur in the Lost World. "Some medieval towns raced donkeys or buffaloes," he said. "In papal Rome, they raced Jews. I'm not exactly afraid I'll be pressed into service if a horse should break its leg. I'm just not very interested." Moreover, his friend the archbishop had told him long ago that elderly people avoided the Palio, because of the risk of being jostled or trampled.

But now there was the article to write. Jastrow obtained tickets for both runnings, and sent Byron and Natalie to do research in the town while he read books on the subject.

They first learned that the race was a contest among Siena's neighborhoods or parishes. Each district, called a *contrada,* comprised a few square blocks of old houses. All of Siena contained but two and a half square miles and some thirty thousand people. But these little wards—there were seventeen, and ten competed each year—took themselves, their boundaries, their loyalties, their colors, their emblems, with inconceivable seriousness. They bore curious names like Oca, Bruco, Torre, Tartuca, Nicchio (Goose, Caterpillar, Tower, Tortoise, Seashell). Each ward had its flag, its anthems, its separate churches, and even a sort of capital hall.

Byron and Natalie spent days walking through the hilly angular streets. When an occasional old omnibus snorted by, they had to flatten against the high red-brown walls for their lives; there were no sidewalks, and the somnolent, deserted streets were hardly wider than the bus. Maps in hand, the pair visited the tiny districts one by one, trying to pin down the background of the Palio. They found out about alliances and hatreds going back hundreds of years. Panther was friendly to Giraffe, Tortoise loathed Snail, and so forth, in a tangle of emotions, very real and current.

They came to realize too that the famous race itself was

just a crooked farce, and that everybody knew it. The *contrade* owned no horses. A few days before each race, animals from the nearby countryside were brought into town, and the competing districts drew lots for them. The same stolid durable nags came back year after year, shuffling from one neighborhood to another by the luck of the draw.

What then made a race of it? Bribing the jockeys, doping the animals, conspiring to block the best horses or injure their riders: only such devices turned the Palio into a murky contest of a sort. The largest, richest neighborhoods therefore tended to win; but the outcome was unpredictable, because a poor, small district might put on a desperate surge. It might squander funds in bribes, pledge future alliances, swear to future treacheries, just to win a banner to bear off to its hall. For that was what the "Palio" itself was: a banner painted with a picture of the Virgin. Like all medieval races, this one was run on sacred days; it was a *manifestazione* in honor of the Virgin. Hence her portrait graced the prize, and faded Palios by the dozens hung in the *contrada* halls.

After a while, even Jastrow became interested too, in an ironic way. The crookedness, he said, was obviously the soul of the thing; old European skulduggery, bribes and counterbribes, doublecross and triplecross, sudden reversals of old alliances, secret temporary patching up of ancient enmities, convoluted chicanery in the dark—all leading at last to the horse race, when all the shadowy corruption was put to explosive proof in red sunset light.

"Why, this article will write itself," he said cheerfully one day at lunch. "These Sienese have evolved willy-nilly a grotesque little parody of European nationalism. The archbishop told me that a woman from the Panther neighborhood who marries a Caterpillar or a Tower man will go back to have her babies in a house on a Panther street to make sure they'll be Panthers. Patriotism! And of course, the insane explosion every summer is the key. All this obsolete mummery—Snails, Giraffes, what have you—would have died out centuries ago, except for the lovely colorful outbursts of excitement, treachery, and violence in the races. The Palio is war."

"You ought to go over to town, sir," Byron said.

"They're laying the track. Hundreds of truckloads of this golden-red earth, all around the Piazza del Campo."

"Yes," Natalie said, "the way they're decorating up the streets is quite amazing. And wherever you look the flag-wavers are practicing—"

"I'm taking off two whole workdays for the races themselves. That's plenty," Jastrow said severely.

.   .   .

"You know what?" Byron said. "This whole thing is utterly idiotic."

Natalie looked at him with startled, excited eyes, touching a handkerchief to her sweaty forehead. It was the day of the first Palio, and they stood on the balcony of the archbishop's palace, watching the parade. The great façade of the cathedral gave a bit of shade at one end of the balcony, where Jastrow in his big yellow Panama hat and white suit stood talking with the archbishop. Byron and Natalie were crowded among privileged onlookers at the other end, in the hot sun. Even in her sleeveless light pink linen dress, the girl was perspiring, and a seersucker jacket and silk tie were making Byron acutely uncomfortable.

Below, the Caterpillar marchers in green and yellow costumes—puffed sleeves and trunks, colored hose, feathered hats—were leaving the thronged cathedral square, waving great banners to cheers and applause from the crowd; and the red-and-black Owl company was coming in, repeating the same flag stunts: intertwining whorls, two flags flung pole and all in the air crisscrossing, flag-wavers leaping over each other's poles while keeping their banners in fluid motion.

"Idiotic?" Natalie said. "I was just deciding it's rather magical."

"What is? They do the same things over and over. We've been here for hours. There's still the Porcupine, the Eagle, the Giraffe, and the Forest to come and show off with their flags. I'm roasting."

"Ah, Byron, it's the liquid flow of color, don't you see, and the *faces* of these young men. So help me, these people look more natural in medieval togs than in their workaday clothes. Don't they? Look at those long straight noses, those deep-set sad big eyes! Maybe they're really a remnant of the Etruscans, as they claim."

"Six months of work," Byron said. "Special buildings and churches for Unicorns. Porcupines, and Giraffes. Thousands of costumes, a whole week of nothing but ceremonies, general marching hither and yon, trumpeting and drumming and trial runs, and all for one crooked race of decrepit nags. In honor of the Virgin, no less."

"Oh, beautiful," Natalie exclaimed, as two Owl flags flew high in the air in crossing arcs, and the wavers caught them and whirled red-and-black arabesques to the applause of the crowd.

Byron went on, mopping his face, "I was in the Goose church today. They brought the horse right inside, up to the very altar to be blessed. I didn't believe the books, but I saw it happen. The priest laid a crucifix on its nose. The horse had more sense than the people. He didn't misbehave, but I guess that finished the Palio for me."

Natalie glanced at him, amused. "Poor Briny. Italian Christianity really troubles your soul, doesn't it? Leslie was right, you're simply a Protestant."

"Does a horse belong in a church?" Byron said.

The sun was low when the parade ended. In the short walk from the cathedral to the Piazza del Campo, Jastrow grew nervous. A thick crowd jostled down the narrow street, all in good humor, but shouting, gesturing, and hurrying between the high red-brown stone walls of the old palazzos. More than once the little professor stumbled and tottered. He clung to Byron's arm. "Do you mind? I've always had a slight fear of crowds. People mean no harm, but somehow they don't notice me." They halted in a crush at a low arch and slowly squeezed through.

"Good gracious," Jastrow said, as they emerged on the earth of the race track. "The piazza's transformed!"

"They've been working on it for weeks," Byron said. "I told you."

Siena's main piazza was one of the sights of Italy. The forgotten town planners of the Middle Ages had designed a memorably beautiful open space, hemmed in by a semicircular sweep of reddish palazzos and the imposing, almost straight façade of the fourteenth-century town hall; all overarched by the blue sky of Tuscany, and pierced heaven-

ward by the red stone bell tower of the town hall, more
than three hundred fifty feet high. All year round the vast
shell-shaped space was empty except for market stalls and
scattered foot traffic; and the ancient buildings that ringed
it seemed abandoned or asleep.

Today, in the golden light of a late afternoon sun, it was
a sea for people, surging and roaring inside a ring of
wooden barriers. Between these barriers and the palazzo
walls lay a track of earth, and against the walls were steep
banks of temporary benches. Faces crowded at every
window of every building around the piazza; flags and
rich hangings decorated the palazzos. The benches were
jammed; all the roofs were jammed; the great central space
looked full, and yet from half a dozen narrow streets more
people were streaming across the track and jamming themselves in. The parade was now going around the track of
earth, and all the *contrade* at once were doing the flag
whorls, the flings, the arabesques to continuous plaudits of
the throng and the cacophonous blare of many brass bands.

Byron led the way to their seats, still holding Jastrow's
thin arm. "Well, hasn't the archibishop done us proud!"
said the professor, as they settled on a narrow, splintery
plank, directly below the judges' stand. "One couldn't have
a better view of the thing." He laughed without reason,
obviously feeling better out of the press of bodies.

"See the mattresses?" said Natalie gaily. "There they are,
down at the corners."

"Oh, yes. My lord, what an extraordinary business."

The noise of the crowd rose into a general cheer. A
wooden cart, drawn by four white Tuscan oxen with giant
curved horns, was entering the track surrounded by
marchers in rich costume. On a tall pole in the cart swayed
the Palio. "Why, it's an Assumption," said Jastrow, peering
through small binoculars at the narrow painted cloth.
"Naïve, but not bad at all."

Around the piazza the cart slowly rolled, with helmeted
policemen behind it driving the crowd from the track,
while sweepers cleared up papers and trash. By now the
paved square was one dense mass of white shirts, colored
dresses, and dark heads, bringing out the half-moon shape
of the track, and its danger. The red palazzos sloped downward to the town hall, where a straight street sliced off the

broad curve. Heavy mattresses padded the outer barriers
at these sharply cut corners. Even at the trial runs, Byron
and Natalie had seen horses thud against the mattresses
and knock their jockeys senseless.

The sunset light on the façade of the Palazzo Pubblico,
the town hall, was deepening to a blood color. The rest of
the piazza was in shadow, and a heavy bell was tolling in
the tower. From the town hall a long fanfare sounded. The
crowd fell quiet. Trumpets struck up the old Palio march
that had been echoing all week in Siena's streets. Out of the
palazzo courtyard trotted the caparisoned racehorses with
their flamboyantly costumed jockeys.

Natalie Jastrow's fingers slid into Byron's and clasped
them, and for a moment she put her cheek, cool, bony,
and yet soft, against his. "Idiotic, Briny?" she murmured.

He was too delighted with the contact to answer.

The starting line was directly in front of them, and behind them, above the judges' stand, the Palio hung on its
pole, stirring in a cool breeze blowing across the great
amphitheatre. An ancient contraption of wood and rope
controlled the start. To line up the dancing, overwrought
animals inside the ropes proved almost impossible. The
harried creatures capered in and out, they turned, reared,
stumbled, and broke away twice in false starts. At last the
ten horses went thudding off in a pack, with the jockeys
clubbing wildly at the creatures and at each other. A yell
rose above the steady roar, as two horses went down at
the first set of mattresses. After that Byron lost track of
the race. While he watched an unconscious jockey being
dragged off the dirt, another wild yell of the crowd told
of more mishaps, which he couldn't see. The pack came
racing by in a club-waving dirt-flying jumble, strung out
over five or six lengths. A riderless horse galloped well up
among them, dripping foam, its reins dangling.

"Can a riderless horse win?" Jastrow shouted at Byron.

A man in the row below him turned up a fat warty red
face with pointed moustaches and popping yellow eyes.
"*Si, si.* Riderless is *scosso.* meestair, *scosso. Viva Bruco!
Scosso!*"

When the pack came past the judges' box a second
time, the riderless horse was clearly in the lead, and Byron
could see its Caterpillar colors and emblems.

"*Scosso!*" the warty red face turned and bellowed happily at Dr. Jastrow, exhaling heavy odors of garlic and wine, and two fists waved at him. "See, meestair? Whoo! *Bruco!* Cater-peel-air, meestair!"

"Yes, indeed, just so," said Jastrow, shrinking a bit against Byron.

The noise in the piazza swelled to a general mad scream as the horses went round for the third and last time, with the surviving jockeys frantically beating their nags to make them overtake the riderless Bruco horse. They came past the finish in a shower of dirt, a maze of bobbing, straining heads and flailing jockeys' arms. The riderless horse, its eyes rolling redly, was still barely in front.

"*Bruco!*" screamed the warty man, leaping a couple of feet in the air. "*Scosso! Scosso!* Ha ha!" He turned to Jastrow with a maniacal laugh, and vividly gestured that the horse was drugged by pumping a huge imaginary hypodermic needle into his arm. "*Bravissimo! WHOO!*" He clattered down the narrow aisle to the track, ran on to the dirt, and vanished in the swarm boiling out of the seats and over the barriers. The track was full on the instant with people milling, yelling, waving arms, jumping and embracing in ecstasy, shaking fists, clutching their heads, beating their breasts. Here and there in the mob were the bobbing plumed heads of the horses. On the track before the judges' stand, a dozen white-shirted young men were beating an unhelmeted jockey, on his knees in the dirt, holding up both arms in a plea for mercy. The jockey's face was welling bright blood.

"My Lord, what's going on there?" Jastrow quavered.

"Somebody failed to doublecross," Byron said, "or else he triplecrossed."

"I suppose"—Jastrow put a trembling hand to his beard—"this is the part the archbishop warned us about. Perhaps we had better leave, and—"

Byron slammed an arm across his chest. "*Not now.* Sit right where you are, sir, and don't move. You too, Natalie."

A squad of young men, with yellow-and-green Caterpillar scarves around their necks, came driving through the mob straight for the judges' stand. They trampled up the benches past Jastrow, led by a pallid youngster streaming blood from his forehead. Byron held two protecting arms in front of the girl and Jastrow as the bloody-faced one seized the pole. The whole squad roared, cheered, and came thundering back down the benches with the banner.

"Now!" Byron took the hands of the other two. "Come."

The excited Sienese, as well as the tourists, were prudently making way for the triumphant Caterpillars. Moving right behind them, with one arm around the girl and another around Jastrow, Byron got through the archway into the main lower street of the town. But here the mob eddied in behind the Palio and its triumphant escort and engulfed them, crushing uphill toward the cathedral.

"Oh, Lord," Natalie said. "We're in for it now. Hang on to Aaron."

"Dear me, I'm afraid I didn't bargain for this," gasped Jastrow, fumbling at his hat and his glasses with one free hand. The other was pinned in Byron's grip. "My feet are scarcely touching the ground, Byron."

"That's okay. Don't fight them, sir, just go along. At the first side street this jam will ease up. Take it easy—"

A convulsive, panicky surge of the crowd at this moment tore the professor out of Byron's grasp. Behind them sounded the clatter of hoofs on stone, wild neighs and whinnies, and shouts of alarm. The crowd melted around Byron and Natalie, fleeing from a plunging horse. It was the winner, the Caterpillar animal. A brawny young man in green and yellow, his wig awry and sliding, was desperately trying to control the animal, but as it reared again, a flailing front hoof caught him full in the face. He fell bloodied to the ground, and the horse was free. It danced, reared, and screamed, plunging forward, and the crowd shrank away. As Byron pulled Natalie into a doorway out of the retreating mob, Aaron Jastrow emerged in the clear street without his glasses, stumbled, and fell in the horse's path.

Without a word to Natalie, Byron ran out into the street and snatched Jastrow's big yellow hat off his head. He waved the hat in the horse's face, crouching, watching the hoofs. The creature neighed wildly, shied against a palazzo wall, stumbled and lost its footing, then recovered and reared, flailing its forelegs at Byron, who waved the hat again, staying watchfully just out of range. The horse pranced about on two legs, rolling bloodshot mad eyes, foaming at the mouth. Half a dozen men in Caterpillar costumes now came running up the street, and four of them seized the reins, dragged the horse down, and began to quiet him. The others picked up their injured comrade.

People from the crowd darted out and helped Jastrow get up. Natalie ran to his side. Men surrounded Byron, slapping his shoulder and shouting in Italian as he made his way to Jastrow. "Here's your hat, sir."

"Oh, thank you, Byron. My glasses, you haven't seen them, have you? I suppose they're shattered. Well, I have another pair at the villa." The professor was blinking blindly, but he acted rather excited and cheerful. "Goodness, what a commotion. What happened? I was pushed down, I guess. I heard a horse clattering about, but I couldn't see a thing."

"He's all right," Natalie said to Byron, with a look straight into his eyes such as she had never before given him. "Thanks."

"Dr. Jastrow, if you're not too shaken up," Byron said, taking his arm again, "we should go to the Caterpillar church for the thanksgiving service."

"Oh, not at all," Jastrow laughed. The moment of action seemed to have cleared his nerves. "In for a penny, in for a pound. I find all this rather exhilarating. On we go. Just hang on to me a little better, Byron. You were a bit derelict there for a minute."

⁕   ⁕   ⁕

A week or so later, Natalie and Byron were at work in the library, with a summer thunderstorm beating outside at the darkened windows. Byron, happening to look up from a map when lightning flashed, saw Natalie staring at him, her face sombre in the lamplight.

"Byron, have you ever been to Warsaw?"

"No. Why?"

"Would you like to come there with me?"

With great willpower, choking back his joy, Byron summoned up the opaque dull look with which he had resisted twenty years of his father's probings: "What would be the point?"

"Well, it's probably worth seeing, don't you think? Slote even says it's rather old-world and gay. The thing is, Aaron's getting difficult about my trip. You know that. I could just tell him to go to hell, but I'd rather not."

Byron had heard the discussions. In the aftermath of the Palio, on learning how close he had come to getting injured or killed, Jastrow was having a spell of nerves. The American consul in Florence had come up after the Palio for a visit; following that, Jastrow's glum mood had worsened. He kept insisting that the Foreign Service was getting worried over the Polish situation, and that Natalie's proposed trip was now too risky.

Byron said, "Would my going make a difference?"

"Yes. You know what Aaron calls you behind your back now? *That golden lad.* He can't get over what you did at the Palio."

"You exaggerated it."

"I did not. You showed striking presence of mind. I was impressed, and so was Aaron when he found out. The horse might have killed him. If I can tell him you're coming, I bet he'll stop grumbling."

"Your friend Slote might take a dim view of my showing up with you."

Natalie said with a grim little smile, "I'll handle Leslie Slote. All right?"

"I'll think about it," Byron said.

"If you need money, I'll be glad to lend you some."

"Oh, I've got money. As a matter of fact, Natalie, there's not all that much to think about. I guess I'll come along. With Jastrow off in Greece, this will be a dismal place."

"Bless your heart." She gave him a delighted smile. "We'll have fun. I'll see to that."

"What happens after Warsaw?" Byron said. "Will you come back here?"

"I guess so, if the consul doesn't persuade Aaron to go home meantime. He's really working on him. And you, Briny?"

"Well, maybe I will too," Byron said. "I'm at loose ends."

That night at dinner, when he heard the news, Dr. Jastrow ordered up a bottle of champagne. "Byron, I can't tell you what a load you've taken off my mind! This headstrong girl doesn't know how wild and backward Poland is. I do. From what my relatives write me, it hasn't improved one iota since I left there forty-five years ago. And the situation really is unstable. The villain with the moustache is making nasty noises, and we must look for the worst. However, there's bound to be some warning. My mind is much more at ease now. You're a capable young man."

"You talk as though I were some kind of idiot," Natalie said, sipping champagne.

"You are a girl. It's something you have trouble remembering. You were that way as a child, climbing trees and fighting boys. Well, I'll be here alone, then. But I won't mind that."

"Won't you be in Greece, sir?" Byron said.

"I'm not so sure." Jastrow smiled at their puzzled looks. "It's some clumsiness about my passport. I let it lapse, and not being native-born, but naturalized through my father's naturalization, it turns out there's a bit of red tape involved in renewing it. Especially since I haven't been back in nine years. The problem may or may not be unravelled by the end of August. If it isn't, I'll just take the trip next spring."

"That's something you should certainly straighten out," Byron said.

"Oh, of course. These things used to be simple, the consul says. But since the flood of refugees from Hitler began, the rules have tightened up. Well, Briny, so you and Natalie will be off to Warsaw in a few weeks! I couldn't be more pleased, and I'm sure she can use a chaperone."

"Go climb a tree, Aaron," Natalie said, turning pink, and her uncle laughed at her, his first wholehearted laugh in a week.

"I hope you'll manage to meet my cousin Berel," Jastrow said to Byron. "I haven't seen him since I left Poland, but we've usually exchanged three or four letters a year. Presence of mind has always been his strong point, too."

6

PAMELA drove Commander Henry and her father to Swinemünde. The train would have been faster, but Henry wanted to see the countryside and the small towns, and the Englishman was more than agreeable. One could almost get to like Germans, he said, if one stayed out of the cities. Pug was appalled at the girl's driving. She chauffeured the rented Mercedes around Berlin in docile conformity to the lights and the speed laws, but once on the autobahn she rocketed the needle to one hundred fifty kilometers an hour. Tudsbury chatted over the wind roar, paying little attention to the scenery blurring past.

He now thought there might be no war. The British were dealing seriously at last with the Russians about a military alliance. They were starting to turn out airplanes so much faster that regaining air parity, which they had lost in 1936, was in sight. Their pledge to Poland showed Hitler that this time Chamberlain meant business. The Nazi Party in Danzig had quieted down. Mussolini had flatly told Hitler (so Tudsbury's inside information had it) that he was not ready to fight. The correspondent foresaw a respite of two or three years, during which the alarmed democracies would rearm faster than the Germans possibly could. The cornered dictator would eventually either fall, or start a war and be crushed, or very likely get assassinated.

"I can't understand why somebody hasn't shot him long ago, the way he shows himself. He bears a charm," Tudsbury shouted, as the car careered out on the two-lane road to pass a long line of thundering trucks full of new gray-painted army tanks. Pug Henry clutched at an armrest, for another truck was approaching head on, swelling

75

like a balloon; it went by in a howl and a screech half a
second after Pamela whisked into her own lane between
two trucks, brushing hair off her forehead with one relaxed
little hand. "But the charm is based on success. It may
lapse once he stops moving ahead. He's murdered a lot of
people on the way up. They all have relatives."

Commander Grobke came to meet them at the base gate
in a small car, which Tudsbury could barely squeeze into.
Pamela roared off to a hotel, and Grobke took the two
men for a long tour, by car and on foot, through the
Swinemünde yard. It was a gray afternoon, with low black
clouds threatening rain. The dank east wind off the Baltic
felt pleasantly cool after the sultriness of Berlin. The flat,
sandy, bleak seacoast base was much like New London,
Victor Henry thought. If one ignored flags and signs, in
fact, the naval facilities of big powers were hard to tell
apart. They were all in the same business, imitating the
British navy, which had first brought the industrial age to
war at sea. The low black U-boats tied in clusters to the
long piers or resting on blocks in dry docks; the smell of
tar, hot metal, and seawater; the slow clank and screech
of overhead cranes; the blaze of welding torches, the rattle
of riveters; the flat or curved sections of steel, painted with
yellow or red primer, swinging through the air; the gigantic
open sheds; the mounds of piping, cables, timbers, and oil
drums; the swarms of grease-blackened cheerful men in
dirty coveralls, goggles, and hard hats; the half-finished
hulls propped with timbers on rails slanting into dirty
water—he might have been in Japan, France, Italy, or the
United States. The differences that counted, the crucial
numbers and performance characteristics, were not discernible.

He could see that the Germans were not changing the
classic double hull of a submarine, and that, like the
Americans, they were doing more welding. He would have
liked to apply his pocket tape measure to a steel pressure
hull section. The plate seemed thinner than in American
submarines. If this were so, U-boats could probably not
dive quite as deep, unless the Germans had developed a
remarkably strong new alloy. But on such a visit one used
one's eye, not a camera or a tape measure.

A low sun broke out under the gray clouds, and the car

cast an elongated shadow when Grobke stopped near the entrance gate at a dry dock where a U-boat rested on blocks. From one side of the dock a gangway with rails, and from the other a precarious long plank, slanted down to the submarine's deck.

"Well, that's the tour," said Grobke. "This is my flagship. Since I cannot have you aboard, Tudsbury, much as I would like to, I suppose we all part company here."

Henry picked up his cue from the German's smile. 'Look, let's not stand on ceremony. If I can come aboard, I'll come and Tudsbury won't."

"Good God, yes," said the Englishman. "I've no business here anyway."

The U-boat commander spread his hands. "I don't want to drive a wedge in Anglo-American friendship."

A whistle blasted as they spoke, and workmen came trooping off the boats and docks, and out of the sheds. The road to the gate was soon thronged with them. They came boiling out of the U-boat, up the gangway. "The old navy yard hazard," Henry said. "Run for your life at five o'clock, or they'll trample you to death."

Grobke laughed. "All civilians are the same."

Tudsbury said, "Well, in my next broadcast I'll have to say that the U-boat command is humming like damn all. I hope they'll take notice in London."

"Just tell them what you saw." Grobke shook his hand through the car window. "We want to be friends. We know you have the greatest navy in the world. These silly little boats can do a lot of damage for their size, that's all. One of my officers will drive you to your hotel."

Since workmen were jamming the gangway, Grobke grinned at Henry, and pointed a thumb toward the plank on the other side of the dock. Pug nodded. The German with a gesture invited him to go first. It was a very long drop, something like seventy feet, to the greasy puddles in the concrete dock. Pug made his way around the rim and walked down the shaky paint-spotted plank, trying to look easier than he felt. Stolid eyes of side boys in white watched from below. As he set foot on deck, they snapped to attention. Grobke stepped off the rattling plank with a laugh. "Well done, for two old blokes."

U-46 looked much like an American submarine, but the

cleanliness, polish, and order were unusual. A United States
ship in dry dock, with civilian workmen aboard, soon became squalid and dirty. No doubt Grobke had ordered a
cleanup for the American visitor, which Pug appreciated
being himself a spit-and-polish tyrant. Even so, he had to
admire the German display. The diesels looked as though
they had never turned over, their red paint and brass fittings were unsullied by a grease spot, and the batteries
seemed fresh from the factory. The sailors were starched
pretty fellows, almost a crew for a nautical musical comedy.
As for the U-boat design, when you took the essential
spaces and machines of a war vessel and stuffed them
into the sausage casing of one long tube, the result was
the same in any country: change the instrument legends to
English, move the captain's cabin from port to starboard,
add two feet to the wardroom, alter a few valve installations, and you were in the *Grayling*.

"Smells pretty good," he said, as they passed the tiny
galley, where cooks in white were preparing dinner and
somehow managing to perspire neatly.

Grobke looked at him over his shoulder. "You wouldn't
care to eat aboard? It's awfully cramped, but these chaps
don't eat too badly."

Pug had a dinner appointment with the Tudsburys, but
he said at once, "I'd be delighted."

So he dined elbow to elbow with the captain and officers
of the U-boat in the narrow wardroom. He enjoyed it. He
was more at home here than in his silk-walled dining
room in Berlin. The four young officers were thin-lipped,
ruddy, blond, shy; like Americans in their features, but
with a different look around the eyes, more intense and
wary. They sat silent at first, but soon warmed to the
American's compliments about the boat, and the joking of
Grobke, who got into an excellent mood over the food and
wine. Stories passed about the stupidity and laziness of
navy yard workmen. One of Pug's best yarns, an incident
of crossed-up toilet plumbing on the *West Virginia,* brought
uproarious laughter. He had noticed before the German
taste for bathroom humor. The officers told tales, which
they considered comic, of their early training: first about
the cleaning of latrines, then of electric shocks to which
they had had to submit without flinching while their reac-

tions were filmed; exposure to cold and heat past the point
of collapse; knee bends until they dropped; the "Valley
of Death" cross-country run up and down hillsides, wearing seventy-pound loads and gas masks. An officer emerged
the better, they said, from such ordeals. Only Grobke
disagreed. That Prussian sadism was old-fashioned, he asserted. In war at sea, initiative was more important than
the blind submission that the ordeals implanted. "The
Americans have the right idea," he said, either because he
sensed that Pug was shocked, or out of maverick conviction. They feasted on cabbage soup, boiled fresh salmon,
roast pork, potato dumplings, and gooseberry *torten*. Obviously Grobke had ordered up this banquet on the chance
that Pug might stay.

Streaks of red sunset showed through the black rain
clouds when Henry and Grobke left the submarine. On the
dock some crewmen, naked except for trunks, were wrestling inside a cheering circle, on gray mats laid over the
crane tracks. Henry had seen everywhere this love of young
Germans for hard horseplay. They were like healthy pups,
and these U-boat men looked stronger and healthier than
American sailors.

"So, Henry, I suppose you join your English friend
now?"

"Not if you have any better ideas."

The German slapped him on the shoulder. "Good!
Come along."

They drove out through the gate. "Damn quiet after five
o'clock," said Pug.

"Oh, yes. Dead. Always."

Pug lit a cigarette. "I understand the British are working
two and three shifts now in their yards."

Grobke gave him an odd look. "I guess they make up
for lost time."

A couple of miles from the base, amid green fields near
the water, they drove into rows of wooden cottages. "Here's
where my daughter lives," Grobke said, ringing a doorbell.
A fresh-faced young blonde woman opened the door. Three
children, recognizing Grobke's ring, ran and pounced on
the paper-wrapped hard candies he handed out. The husband was at sea on maneuvers. On an upright piano in the

tiny parlor stood his picture: young, long-jawed, blond, stern. "It's good Paul is at sea," Grobke said. "He thinks I spoil the kids," and he proceeded to toss them and romp with them until they lost their bashfulness in the presence of the American, and ran around laughing and shrieking. The mother tried to press coffee and cake on the guests, but Grobke stopped her.

"The commander is busy. I just wanted to see the children. Now we go."

As they got into the car, looking back at a window where three little faces peered out at him, he said: "It's not much of a house. Not like your mansion in the Grunewald! It's just a cracker box. The German pay scale isn't like the American. I thought you'd be interested to see how they live. He's a good U-boat officer and they're happy. He'll have a command in two years. Right away, if there's war. But there won't be war. Not now."

"I hope not."

"I *know*. There is *not* going to be war over Poland—So? Back to Swinemünde?"

"I guess so."

As they drove into the small coastal town, Pug said, "Say, I could stand a beer. How about you? Is there a good place?"

"*Now* you're talking! There's nothing fancy, not in this boring town, but I can take you where the officers hang out. Isn't Tudsbury expecting you?"

"He'll survive."

"Yes. Englishmen are good at that." Grobke laughed with transparent pleasure at keeping the American naval attaché from the famous correspondent.

Young men in turtleneck sweaters and rough jackets sat at long tables in the dark, smoky, timbered cellar, bellowing a song to concertina accompaniment played by a strolling fat man in a leather apron. "Jesus Christ, I have drunk a lot of beer in this place, Henry," said Grobke. They sat at a small side table under an amber lamp. Pug showed him pictures of Warren, Byron, and Madeline. After a couple of beers, he told of his worry over Warren's involvement with an older woman. Grobke chuckled. "Well, the things I did when I was a young buck! The main thing is, he'll be an aviator. Not as good as a submariner, but the next best thing, ha ha! He looks like a smart lad. He'll settle down."

Pug joined in a song he recognized. He had no ear and sang badly off-key. This struck Grobke as hilarious. "I swear to God, Victor," he said, wiping his eyes after a fit of laughter, "could anything be crazier than all this talk of war? I tell you, if you left it to the navy fellows on both sides it could never happen. We're all decent fellows, we understand each other, we all want the same things out of life. It's the politicians. Hitler is a great man and Roosevelt is a great man, but they've both been getting some damn lousy advice. But there's one good thing. Adolf Hitler is smarter than all the politicians. There's *not* going to be any war over Poland." He drained his thick glass stein and banged it to attract a passing barmaid. *"Geben Sie gut Acht auf den Osten,"* he said, winking and dropping his voice. "Watch the east! There's something doing in the east."

The barmaid clacked on the table two foaming steins from clusters in her hands. Grobke drank and passed the back of his hand over his mouth. "Suppose I tell you that I heard the Führer *himself* address the senior U-boat command and tell them there would be no war? You want to report that back to Washington? Go ahead, it happens to be true. You think he'll start a war against England with seventy-four operational U-boats? When we have three hundred, that'll be a different story, and then England will think twice about making trouble. And in eighteen months, that's exactly what we'll have. Meantime *watch the east.*"

"Watch the east?" Victor Henry said in a wondering tone.

"Aha, you're a little curious? I have a brother in the foreign ministry. *Watch the east!* We're not going to be fighting, Henry, not this year, I promise you. So what the hell? We live one year at a time, no? Come on, I have a tin ear like you, but we'll sing!"

*   *   *

Victor Henry sat with his old portable typewriter on his knees, in the rosewood-panelled library. The magnificent antique desk was too high for comfortable typing; and anyway, the machine scratched the red leather top. It was not yet four in the morning, but the stars were gone, blue day showed in the garden, and birds sang. White paper, yellow paper, and carbons lay raggedly around him. The room was cloudy with smoke. He had been typing since midnight. He stopped, yawning. In the kitchen he found a cold chicken breast, which he ate with a glass of milk while he heated a third pot of coffee. He returned to the library, gathered up the top pages of his report to the Office of Naval Intelligence, and began reading.

COMBAT READINESS OF NAZI GERMANY
An Appraisal

Nazi Germany is a very peculiar country. The contradictions strike the observer as soon as he arrives. The old Germany is still here, the medieval buildings, the quaint country costumes, the clean big cities, the order, the good nature, the neatness, the "thoroughness," the beautiful scenery, the fine-looking people, especially the children. However, there is an extra layer of something new and different: the Nazi regime. It's all over the face of this old country like a rash. How deep it goes is a serious question. The Nazis have certainly put up a highly patriotic, colorful, and warlike façade. The swastika flags, new buildings, marching battalions, Hitler Youth, torchlight parades and such are all very striking. But what is behind the façade? Is there a strong potential for war-making, or is it mainly political propaganda and bluff?

This report gives the first impressions of an officer who has been in Germany four weeks, and has been digging for facts.

It is common knowledge that since 1933 Germany has been frankly and even boastfully rearming. Even before the Hitler regime, however, the army surreptitiously armed and trained in violation of the Versailles Treaty, with Bolshevik help. Once the Nazis took power, though the Russian contact was dropped, the rearming speeded up and became open. Nevertheless, twenty years ago this nation was disarmed. Seven years ago it was still helpless compared to the Allies. The question is, to what extent has that gap been closed by Hitler? Building a modern combat force is a big-scale industrial process. It takes material, manpower, and time, no matter what vaunting claims political leaders make.

Two preliminary and interesting conclusions emerge from the facts this observer has been able to gather.

(1) Nazi Germany has not closed the gap sufficiently to embark on a war with England and France.

(2) The regime is not making an all-out effort to close the gap.

The next five pages contained ten-year figures—contradicting many intelligence reports he had read—of German factory production, of the expansion of industry, and of the output of machines and materials. He drew heavily on his own reading and inquiries. He presented comparisons of French, British, and German gross national products and of strength on land, sea, and in the air, during this decade. These numbers indicated—as he marshalled them—that Germany remained inferior in every aspect of war-making, except for her air force; and that she was not pushing her industrial plant very hard to catch up. Contrary to popular opinion all over the world, there was no feverish piling of arms. This emerged by a comparison of plant capacity and output figures. He described in passing the desolate peace that fell over the Swinemünde navy yard at the usual quitting time. There was not even a second shift for constructing U-boats, the key to German sea warfare. He argued that the edge in the air would rapidly melt away with the present British speedup in making airplanes and buying them from the United States. As to land war, the swarming uniforms in the city streets were quite a show; but the figures proved that France alone could put a larger, longer trained, and better equipped army in the field.

On a U-boat, passing through the squadron's tiny flag office, he had seen scrawled on the outside of a mimeographed report some figures and abbreviations that he thought meant: *operational, 51—at sea, 6; in port, 40; overhaul, 5.* These figures met the intelligence evaluations of the British and the French. Grobke had claimed seventy-four operational boats, a predictable overestimate when talking big to a foreign intelligence officer. But even exaggerating, Grobke had not gone as high as a hundred. Fifty U-boats were almost certainly the undersea strength of Nazi Germany, give or take five, with perhaps only thirteen

under construction. In 1918 alone Germany had lost more
than a hundred U-boats.

Then came the crucial paragraph, which he had typed
with many pauses, and which he anxiously read over and
over.

What follows gets into prognostication, and so may be
judged frivolous or journalistic. However, the impression that
this observer has formed points so strongly to a single possibility, that it seems necessary to record the judgment. All
the evidence indicates to me that Adolf Hitler is at this time
negotiating a military alliance with the Soviet Union.

Arguing in support of his idea, Victor Henry alluded to
the Rapallo Treaty of 1922, when the Bolsheviks and the
Germans had stunned a European economic conference by
suddenly going off and making a separate deal of broad
scope. He pointed out that the present German ambassador
in Moscow, Schulenburg, was a Rapallo man. Litvinov,
Russia's Jewish pro-Western foreign minister, had recently
fallen. Hitler in two speeches had left out his usual attacks
on Bolshevism. A Russo-German trade agreement had been
in the news, but suddenly the papers had dropped all mention of it. He cited, too, the remark of a man high in the
U-boat command, *"Watch the east. Something's happening
in the east. I have a brother in the foreign ministry."* And
he cited Hitler's pledge to the U-boat officers that there
would be no war over Poland.

None of this, he acknowledged, added up to hard intelligence, nor did it impress the professionals at the embassy.
There were always, they said, rumors of theatrical surprises. They insisted on sticking to basic facts. The Nazi
movement was built on fear and hate of Bolshevism and a
pledge to destroy it. The whole theme of *Mein Kampf* was
conquest of "living room" for Germany in the southeast
provinces of Russia. A military reconciliation between the
two systems was unthinkable. Hitler would never propose
it. If he did, Stalin, assuming that it was a trick, would
never accept it. The words Henry had encountered most
often were "fantasy" and "melodrama."

He maintained, nevertheless, that the move not only
made sense, but was inevitable. Hitler was far out on a

limb in his threats against Poland. A dictator could not back down. Yet his combat readiness for a world war was marginal. Probably to avoid alarming the people, he had not even put his country on a war production basis, contrary to all the lurid blustering propaganda of "cannon instead of butter." Despite this tough talk of Nazi politicians and newspapers, the man in the street did not want a war, and Hitler knew that. A Russian alliance was a way out of the dilemma. If Russia gave the Germans a free hand in Poland, the English guarantee would become meaningless. Neither the French nor the British could possibly come to Poland's aid in time to avert a quick conquest. Therefore the Poles would not fight. They would yield the city of Danzig and the extraterritorial road across the Polish corridor, which was all Hitler was demanding. Maybe later, as in the case of Czechoslovakia, he would move in and take the rest of Poland, but not now.

Victor Henry argued that the sudden reversal of alliances was an old European stratagem, especially characteristic of German and Russian diplomacy. He cited many instances, fresh from his heavy history reading. He pointed out that Hitler himself had come to power in the first place through a sharp reversal of political lines, a deal with his worst enemy, Franz von Papen.

Fully clothed, he fell asleep on the red leather couch, with the report and two carbon copies tucked inside his shirt, after shredding the sheets of carbon paper into the wastebasket. His slumber was restless and brief. When his eyes popped wide open again, the sun was sending weak red rays through the treetops. He showered, dressed, read the report again, and walked five miles from the Grunewald to the Wilhelmstrasse, turning the document over in his mind. Compared to Tollever's reports, which he had studied, it was a presumptuous discussion of grand strategy, far beyond his competence and his position: the sort of "Drew Pearson column" against which the Chief of Naval Operations himself had warned him. On the other hand, it seemed to him factual. He had already sent in a number of technical reports like Kip's papers. He intended to write one on Swinemünde. *Combat Readiness of Nazi Germany* was a jump into the dark.

In War College seminars, instructors had poked rude fun at "global masterminding" by officers below flag rank. The question was, now that the paper was written, should he send it or forget it? Pug Henry had written and later destroyed many such documents. He had a continuing tendency to reach beyond routine. The result could be good or disastrous. His unsolicited memorandum on the battleship blisters had knocked him out of overdue sea duty and landed him in Berlin. That report, at least, had been within his professional sphere as an ordnance man. In diplomacy and grand strategy he was a naïve newcomer. Colonel Forrest knew Germany well and he had waved aside Henry's suggestion as nonsense. Pug had ventured to talk to the chargé d'affaires, whose only comment had been a subtle smile.

A Foreign Service courier was flying to England at 10 A.M., to board the New York–bound *Queen Mary*. The document could be on CNO's desk in a week.

Henry arrived at the embassy still undecided, with not much more than a half hour in which to make up his mind. Except for Rhoda, there was nobody whose advice he could ask. Rhoda liked to sleep late. If he called her now he would probably wake her, and even then he could scarcely describe the report on the German telephone. But would Rhoda in any case offer a judgment worth having? He thought not. It was up to him—the courier, or the burn basket.

He sat at his desk in the high-ceilinged, cluttered office, sipping coffee, looking out across Hermann Göring Strasse at Hitler's monumental new chancellery of pink marble. The sentry guards were changing: eight helmeted black-clad heavy SS men marching up, eight others marching away to a drum and fife. Through the open windows he heard the ritual orders in shrill German, the squeal of the fife, the scraping tramp of the big black boots.

Victor Henry decided that his job was intelligence, and that for better or worse this report told truly what he had seen so far in Nazi Germany. He hunted up the courier and gave him the document for urgent delivery to the Office of Naval Intelligence.

*   *   *

Admiral Preble read *Combat Readiness of Nazi Germany* a week later, and sent one page of extracts to the President. The Nazi-Soviet pact broke on the world on the twenty-second of August, as one of the most stunning surprises in all history. On the twenty-fourth Preble received the page back in an envelope from the White House. The President had scrawled at the bottom, in strong thick pen strokes in black ink:

> *Let me have V. Henry's service record.*
> FDR

7

THE announcement of the pact shrieked at Byron and Natalie from the news placards in the Rome airport. They had set out from Siena before dawn in an old Renault, and while the whole world was chattering about the astounding news, they had innocently driven down along the Apennines in golden Italian sunlight, amid old mountain towns, wild airy gorges, and green valleys where peasants worked their fields. With Natalie Jastrow at his side for a three-week journey that was only starting, Byron was in the highest of spirits, until he saw the bulletins.

He had never found a European airport so busy or so noisy. Gesticulating travellers were besieging the reservation desks, nearly everybody was either walking fast or running, and sweaty porters wheeling heaps of luggage were snarling at passengers and at each other. The loudspeaker never stopped its thunderous echoing drivel. At the first kiosk, he bought a sheaf of papers. The Italian papers shrilled that this great diplomatic coup by the Axis had ended the war danger. The headlines of the Paris and London newspapers were big, black, and frightened. The German press giggled coarse delight in tall red block letters. The front page of a Swiss newspaper caricatured Hitler and Göring in Russian blouses and fur hats, squatting and kicking out their boots, to the music of a concertina played by Stalin in an SS uniform. Across a Belgian front page, the stark headline was

1914

In a crowded, buzzing airport restaurant, while they ate a hasty lunch of cannelloni and cold white wine, Natalie astonished him by talking of going on. To proceed into a country that might soon be invaded by Germans struck Byron as almost mad.

But Natalie argued that the tourists milling in the airport were mere sheep. If a sudden political change could panic them, they had no right to be in Europe. She had stayed in Paris through the Munich crisis. Half of her American friends had fled, and later had straggled back— those who had not felt too silly. There was always less danger than most people thought. Even in a war, an American passport spelled safety. She wanted to see Poland. She wanted to see Leslie Slote and had given him her promise. She would be in and out of Poland in three weeks. The world wasn't going to end in three weeks.

It did not cheer Byron to perceive how much she really wanted to rejoin Slote. Since the Palio, he had hoped that she was warming to himself. The girl had been downright affectionate during the second Palio, which they had watched without Jastrow, and at one point in the evening —when they were well into a third bottle of Soave at dinner after the race—she had remarked that it was too bad he wasn't a few years older, and a Jew. "My mother would take to you, Briny," she had said. "My troubles would be over. You have good manners. You must have lovely parents. Leslie Slote is nothing but an ambitious, self-centered dog. I'm not even sure he loves me. He and I just fell in a hole."

But now she was on her way to her lover, and a political

explosion that had staggered Europe made no difference to her.

By now he knew something of her rash streak. Climbing on mountainsides or ruins, Natalie Jastrow took unladylike chances. She leaped gaps, she teetered along narrow ledges, she scrambled up bare rocks, careless alike of her modesty and her neck. She was a strong, surefooted girl, and a little too pleased with herself about it.

He sat slouched in his chair, contemplating her across the red and white checked cloth, the dirty dishes, the empty wineglasses. The Alitalia plane was departing for Zagreb on the first leg of their flight in little more than an hour. She stared back, her lips pushed out in a wry pout. Her dark gray travelling suit was sharply tailored over her pretty bosom. She wore a black crushable hat and a white shirt. Her ringless fingers beat on the cloth. "Look," she said, "I can well understand that for you it's no longer a gay excursion. So I'll go on by myself."

"I suggest you telephone Slote first. Ask him if you should come."

Natalie drummed her fingers. "Nonsense, I'll never get a call through to Warsaw today."

"Try."

"All right," she snapped. "Where are the damned telephones?"

The long-distance office was mobbed. Two switchboard girls were shouting, plugging, unplugging, scrawling, waving their hands, and wiping sweat from their brows. Byron cut through the crowd, pulling Natalie by the hand. When she gave the operator a number in Warsaw, the girl's sad huge brown eyes widened. "Signorina—Warsaw? Why don't you ask me to ring President Roosevelt? It's twelve hours' delay to Warsaw."

"That's the number of the American embassy there," Byron said, smiling at her, "and it's life and death."

He had an odd thin-lipped smile, half-melancholy, half-gay, and the Italian girl warmed to it as to an offered bunch of violets. "American embassy? I can try."

She plugged, rang, argued in German and Italian, made faces at the mouthpiece, and argued some more. "Urgent, emergency," she kept shouting. This went on for ten minutes or more, while Byron smoked and Natalie paced and kept looking at her watch. With a surprised look, the operator all at once nodded violently, pointing to a booth. Natalie stayed inside a long time, and came out red-faced and scowling. "We were cut off before we finished. I'm choking to death. Let's get some air." Byron brought her out into the terminal. "He got angry with me. He told me I was insane. The diplomats are burning their papers. . . . It was an awfully good connection. He might have been around the corner."

"I'm sorry, Natalie, but it's what I expected."

"He said I should get the hell out of Italy and go straight home, with or without Aaron. Is that what you'd have told me?" She turned on him. "I'm so *hot!* Buy me a lemonade or something."

They sat at a little table outside an airport café. She said, "Let's see the plane tickets."

"I'm sure we can get refunds." He handed her the envelope.

She extracted her ticket and gave the envelope back. "You get a refund. They burned papers before Munich too. England and France will fold up now just the way they did then. Imagine a world war over Danzig! Who the hell knows where Danzig is? Who cares?"

"Natalie, that embassy will be swamped. You won't see much of him."

"Well, if he's too busy for me, I'll do my sightseeing alone. My family lived in Warsaw for years. I still have relatives there. I want to see it. I'm on my way and I'm not turning back." The girl looked in her pocketbook mirror and jammed her hat further down on her head. "It must be about time for me to check in."

He held out his hand. "Give me the ticket. I'll check both of us in while you have your lemonade."

She brightened, but looked suspicious. "Are you sure you want to go? You needn't, honestly. I'm releasing you. Don't come. I don't want you. Tell Aaron I said that."

"Oh shut up, Natalie. Let's have the ticket."

She gave him a playful smile, clutching the green and yellow ticket to her bosom. "Well! Listen to Briny Henry being masterful. The thing is, darling, if anything does go wrong, I don't ever want to feel I dragged you into trouble."

This was the first time Natalie Jastrow had—however

casually—used a term of endearment to him. Byron stood up and pulled the ticket from her gloved hand.

●   ●   ●

The scheduled eight-hour trip lasted a day and a half. No connections worked. Their baggage vanished. They spent the night on benches in the Budapest terminal. At Warsaw, they were the only foreigners arriving at the small field in the nearly empty, rusty, shabby LOT plane, which turned right around and took off jam-packed with people fleeing Poland. Disconsolate travellers crowded the fence and watched it go.

A beefy young Pole in an olive uniform, speaking broken French, asked the two Americans many hostile questions and seemed to regard them as spies or lunatics. He confiscated their passports, muttered with other officials, told them to wait, and disappeared. They were famished, but the throng of refugees in the canteen, mostly Germans, sitting on luggage, squatting on the floor, or crowding every bench and chair, had long since eaten up all the food. Byron pounced on a couple of seats vacated for a moment. Bottles of warm Polish beer stood in the center of the table, with an opener and some glasses, so they drank warm beer and paid the waiter who came swooping down. Then Byron found a telephone and talked the waiter into calling the embassy. Slote was shocked to hear his voice. He appeared at the airport within the hour, chewing nervously on his cold pipe, in a shiny blue Chevrolet that prompted stares. Out came not only the passports, with various entry documents badly printed in purple ink on crude paper, but their luggage too, mysteriously rescued from the Balkans. They piled into the embassy car and set off for the city.

Natalie looked trim and pert after a last grooming in the ladies' lounge—the size of a telephone booth, she said, with one cold water tap, and no seat on the single toilet bowl. "Does this continue, Leslie?" she said. "I mean, this is the airport of the capital of Poland! The further east we've come, the smaller the airports have gotten, the more loused-up the schedules, the worse the airplanes, the surlier the officials, the cruder the johns, and the rougher the toilet paper. I'm not sure my bottom would survive a trip to Russia."

"Well, eastern Europe is another world, Natalie. And you're seeing it at a bad time. This little airport's usually deserted and half asleep. However"—he jabbed the stem of his pipe toward her—"if you choose to go on a pleasure trip during a time of general mobilization—"

"Here it comes, Briny," she said, her eyes full of dark amusement.

Slote reached a caressing hand, with a large blue-gemmed college ring, to her face. The easy intimate gesture hurt Byron's eyes, signalling the end of his exclusive (if unheated) possession of the girl's company. He slumped glumly in the back seat. "I'm thrilled to see you, darling, though you're stark mad," Slote said. "Things are looking much better tonight. England finally signed her guarantee to Poland, just today. The betting was that the pact with Russia would make her crawfish. Nothing of the sort. There's reliable word from Sweden that Hitler's calling off his invasion. The English knocked his breath out, that's unmistakable."

"Where are you putting us? A place with bathtubs, I hope."

"It's no problem. In the past three days the hotels have emptied. The Europeiski has some luxurious rooms, quite Western, really, and at Eastern prices. Don't figure on staying long. The situation can still turn sour overnight."

"I thought maybe a week," Natalie said. "Then Byron and I can fly or drive down to Cracow and visit Medzice, and then fly on back to Rome."

"Great bloody Christ, what are you talking about? Medzice! Just forget it, Natalie!"

"Why should I? Uncle Aaron said I should visit the family in Medzice. That's where we're all from. My gosh, this is flat country. Flat as a table."

They were driving through fields of sweet-smelling ripe grain, interspersed with pastures where cows and horses grazed. Far, far ahead on the level plain, the buildings of Warsaw dimly rose.

"Exactly, and that's Poland's curse. It's a soccer field, a hundred thousand square miles in size. Fine for invasions. Even the low mountains along the south have nice wide

easy passes. Half a million German soldiers are in
Czechoslovakia at this moment, poised at the Jablunka
pass, forty miles from Medzice. Now do you understand?"
Natalie made a face at him.

Warsaw was much calmer than Rome. In lamplit twilight, well-dressed crowds, heavily sprinkled with uniforms,
were happily promenading on the broad avenues, eating
ice cream, smoking, chatting. The green parks were
thronged with jocund children. Bright red buses went by
with side placards advertising a movie; the name SHIRLEY
TEMPLE stood out from Polish words. Splashy billboards
touted German toothpastes, radios, and hair tonic. The
long rows of four-story gray or brown buildings, the
boulevards running into great squares flamboyant with
statues, bordered by baroque official buildings or palaces,
the electric signs beginning to flash and dance—all this
made Byron think of Paris and London. It was strange to
find such a metropolis at the end of the primitive air
journey. The Europeiski Hotel had a lobby as ornate as
any he had seen, with a massive brown-and-white marble
staircase jutting down to the front door.

Natalie went up in the elevator. Slote detained Byron
by touching his arm, then lit his pipe with harried flaming
puffs. To Byron, seeing him after a lapse of many months,
the Foreign Service man appeared impossibly old for
Natalie: bespectacled, baggy-eyed, with marked lines in
his lean sallow cheeks. A double-breasted chalk-striped
dark suit emphasized his stodgy mature air, and he appeared shorter than Byron remembered.

"I wish I had time to buy you a drink," Slote said. "I'd
like to talk to you. This Cracow trip is dangerous nonsense. I'm going to get you air reservations out of here
as soon as I can. They must be booked solid for a week,
but the embassy has some pull. If it takes both of us to
put her bodily on a plane back to Rome, it's got to be
done. Don't tell her tonight, though. She'll become un-
manageable."

"Okay. You know her better than I do."

Slote shook his head, laughing. "I wonder, at this point.
I ought to be deeply touched by this cuckoo visit—and I
am, of course I am—but Natalie Jastrow is too much for

almost anybody. See you at dinner. The embassy's a mad-house. If I can't get away, I'll telephone."

Byron sat for a while in his cavernous gloomy room with tall windows facing the Bristol Hotel, wondering what the hell he was doing in Poland. He picked up the antique ivory-handled telephone, and with some haggling in German managed to get connected to Natalie's room.

"Hello. Are you in the bathtub yet?"

"Well, I'm glad you can't see me. What's up?"

"I'm beat. You have dinner with Slote. I'm going to bed."

"Stop that rubbish. You're dining with us, Briny. You come and fetch me at nine, do you hear? Leslie has booked me into Paderewski's suite, or something. It's fantastic. I've got a full-length mirror here, held up by two big brown wooden angels."

.   .   .

"This way," Slote said. "Our table's ready."

An orchestra in gold-frogged red coats was thumping old jazz tunes in the main dining room of the Bristol, which for size, silk hangings, white linen, gilt-and-crystal chandeliers, obsequiousness of waiters, fine dress of the thronging customers, and ineptness on the dance floor, might have been in any first-class hotel in Europe. Certainly there was no trace of a war scare.

"Sorry I'm late. It's the Jews," Slote apologized when they sat down. "They're storming the embassy. We've all become visa officers, right on up to Biddle. Christ knows I don't blame them. If they can show a relative, a friend, a letter, anything, we process them. A New York telephone book, today in Warsaw, is worth a hundred zlotys, that's about twenty dollars."

"That puzzled me," Natalie said. "I understood Warsaw was full of Jews. I've seen very few so far."

"Oh, they're here, all right. A third of this city's Jewish." At this point a tailcoated, bowing headwaiter brought a menu, and Slote had a long colloquy with him in Polish. Natalie listened with an admiring, envious look.

"Les, was it very hard to learn? One day I'll try," she said as the waiter left. "My folks used to talk Polish when they didn't want me to understand. I'm haunted by a sense of being back in my childhood, and yet this is such a foreign place! It's all very singular."

They ate amazingly good smoked salmon, a strange egg dish, and tough roast meat. Slote kept tossing off brown Polish vodka in a thimble-size glass, while the others drank good French wine.

"Leslie, you're going to be stone drunk." Natalie sounded more jovial than disapproving.

"There's so little in every glass," Slote said, pouring more from the bottle. "I've had a very hard day. Even without you turning up, you fool."

They smiled at each other. Byron wished he had gone to bed. Slote looked at him and with a polite effort resumed talking. "Hm, yes. It's a historical puzzle, really, how three and a half million Jews came to settle in Poland. It's such an anarchic country. You'd think they'd have chosen a more stable place. I have a theory. I sort of wonder what Aaron would make of it."

"What's your theory about us Polish Jews, Leslie?" Natalie said with a grin.

"That the anarchy was the inducement. Imagine a government of nearly a thousand barons, any one of whom could veto any legislation. That's the way they stumbled along here for centuries. No wonder Poland kept getting partitioned! Well, as long as the Jews could work things out with each individual nobleman they could at least live and farm and work. No royal oppression to fear."

"Not bad," said Natalie. "But in point of fact, didn't the Polish kings welcome them in with special protective laws? When Spain expelled them and the Holy Church was having one of its bad spasms of hounding and massacring the Jews? That's as I recall it."

"I haven't studied the thing," Slote said, "but the Poles eventually took to doing that too."

"That's why I was born on Long Island," said Natalie. "My grandfather got out, and a good thing."

"What military shape are the Poles in?" Byron asked Slote. "Will they give Hitler a fight, if it comes to that?"

"A fight?" Slote sucked on his pipe, looking up into the air. His tone turned measured and professional. "Why, ask any one of them, and he'll probably tell you they'll defeat the Germans. After all, they defeated them in 1410! These are strange people, Byron. They can be brilliant, talking about politics and history, yet they don't give a damn that Germany is now an industrial giant, while Poland remains all farms and Jews and castles and mazurkas. Maybe they're right. Maybe the Polish fighting spirit will scatter the stupid unwilling cattle of Hitler. That's the talk. There are supposed to be two and a half million Poles in uniform, more men than Hitler's got. A highly questionable figure, but in this country, any statistics—"

"Say, isn't that 'Stardust'?" Natalie put in. "It sounds a bit like 'Stardust.' Dance with me."

Byron thought Slote looked more like her uncle than her sweetheart, steering her clumsily around the floor. But Natalie's clinging attitude, closed eyes, and touching cheek weren't the ways of a niece. They exchanged a few laughing words, then Natalie said something that made Slote look serious and shake his head. They argued as they danced.

"I'll find him without you," Natalie was saying as they came back to the table.

"I didn't say I wouldn't help you find him. I said if you're going to talk to him about going to Medzice—"

"Just forget it. Forget I mentioned it."

Natalie glowered at the meat on her plate. Slote took two more shots of vodka. To lighten the atmosphere, Byron asked Slote about the workings of the embassy. Looking relieved, Slote turned on the measured voice. The alcohol hadn't blurred his brain; it made him talkative. He sketched the organization and said that he was in the political section, but that since his arrival, he had been preoccupied with the flood of emigrants, as had everybody else.

"Were you fellows surprised by the pact?"

"Naturally. Even the Poles were struck dumb, and in their history they've seen everything. But nobody can predict Hitler. That's his genius, if you want to call it that. He does have an instinct for the breathtaking."

The cloud was clearing from Natalie's face. "Leslie, why did Stalin go along?"

"Honey, that's perfectly simple. Hitler offered him a piece of cake on a gold platter, and he simply said, 'Yes, thank you!' Stalin's completely turned the tables on England and France now. They froze him out of Munich. In effect, they handed Czechoslovakia to Hitler and said, 'Here, boy, leave us alone and go smash Russia.' Now Stalin's done a Munich in reverse. 'No, no, *here,* boy, take *Poland,* and go and smash the West.' " With little rapid puffs of blue smoke, clearly enjoying the chance to expound, Slote went on, "Lord, how the British have been asking for this! An alliance with Russia was their one chance to stop Germany. They had years in which to do it. All of Stalin's fear of Germany and the Nazis was on their side. And what did they do? Dawdle, fuss, flirt with Hitler, and give away Czechoslovakia. Finally, finally, they sent some minor politicians on a slow boat to see Stalin. When Hitler decided to gamble on this alliance, he shot his foreign minister to Moscow on a special plane, with powers to sign a deal. And that's why we're within inches of a world war."

"Is it going to come?" Natalie asked.

"Why, I thought you and Aaron were the authorities for the view that it won't."

"I'm not ready to panic. It just seems to me that Hitler will get what he wants, as usual."

Slote's face turned pinched and sombre. He pulled at the pipe, sucking in his pallid cheeks. "No. The Poles now have the signed British guarantee. Very gallant, very irrational, very belated, and probably futile. To that extent we're back in 1914. Poland can plunge the world in by standing firm. It's all up to Hitler. If he wants to arm some more first, the crisis will subside, and that seems to be in the wind at the moment. But for all we know, he's already given the order to march. That's why I'm being such a pill about Medzice. Down there, in the next two weeks, you have a fifty-fifty chance of being captured by German soldiers. I do think that's a bit risky, dear."

* * *

After dinner Slote drove them to another part of town: street after street of old brick houses of three and four stories, with shops everywhere at ground level. Here indeed were Jews by the thousands, strolling on the sidewalks through narrow cobbled streets, looking out of windows, sitting in shop doorways. On the street corners knots of bearded men argued with loud voices and sweeping gestures, as on Manhattan's Lower East Side. Many of the men wore kaftans, or else the boots, blouses, and caps of the countryside. There were men in ankle-length black coats and black hats, and a few youngsters in army uniform. There were some prosperous people, too, smooth-shaven men wearing bowlers and well-groomed women looking much like the Warsaw Gentiles around the Europeiski. Children darted about at their street games, boys in caps and short trousers and girls in neat colored frocks, and their mothers gossiped as they watched them.

"I thought you said they were all storming the embassy," Byron remarked to Slote.

"There are three hundred and fifty thousand of them, Byron. Maybe one in a hundred has foresight. That puts three or four thousand hammering at our doors. The rest believe what they want to believe, and vaguely hope for the best. The government keeps telling everybody there won't be a war."

Natalie was looking around with an absent, pleased expression at the horse-drawn wagons and handcarts in the streets, and at an old trolley car clanking by. "My parents described all this to me when I was a child," she said. "It seems not to have changed." People stopped and looked after the embassy car as it passed. Once Slote halted to ask directions. The Jews came clustering around, but gave only vague cautious answers in Polish. "Let me try," Natalie said, and she began to talk Yiddish, causing an astonished outbreak of laughter, followed by a burst of warm, friendly talk. A chubby boy in a ragged cap volunteered to run ahead of the car and show the way. They set off after him.

"Well done," Slote said.

"I can hack out Yiddish after a fashion, if I must," Natalie said. "Aaron's a master of it, though he never utters a Yiddish word."

Natalie and Slote got out at a gray brick apartment building with tall narrow windows, an ornate iron door, and window boxes of blooming geraniums. It overlooked a small green park, where Jews congregated on the benches and around a gushing fountain in noisy numbers. Curious children ran from the park to ring Byron in the American car. Under their merry stares, as they freely discussed him and the machine, Byron felt somewhat like an ape behind glass. The faces of the Jewish children were full of life and mischief, but they offered no discourtesy, and some gave him shy smiles. He wished he had gifts for them. He took his fountain pen from his pocket, and through the open window offered it to a black-haired girl in a lilac dress with white lace cuffs and collar. The girl hung back, blinking wary dark brown eyes. The other children encouraged her with shouts and giggles. At last she took the pen, her little cool fingers brushing his hand for a moment, and ran lightly away.

"Well, wouldn't you know. He's not there," Natalie said, returning to the car with Slote a few minutes later. "Gone to Medzice for his son's wedding, with the whole family. Just my luck. Aaron told me he deals in mushrooms, but can that be such a good business? He's evidently well off."

"Unusually so." Slote was starting the car. "This must be the best apartment house around here."

The little girl in lilac reappeared, leading her parents, the father in a knee-length gray frock coat and a wide-brimmed gray hat, the mother kerchiefed, wearing a German-tailored brown suit, and carrying a baby in a pink blanket.

"He's thanking you," Slote said to Byron, as the father gravely spoke in Polish through the window, holding the fountain pen, "and he says it's much too expensive, and please take it back."

"Tell him the American fell in love with his daughter. She's the most beautiful girl in the world, and she must keep it."

The father and mother laughed when Slote translated. The little girl shrank against her mother's skirt and shot Byron an ardent look. The mother undid from her lapel a gold brooch with purple stones, and pressed it on Natalie, who tried to decline it, speaking in Yiddish. Again this caused surprise and a cascade of jocund talk, the upshot of which was that she had to keep the brooch.

The little girl kept the pen, and they drove off to shouted farewells.

"Well, I wasn't on a looting expedition," Natalie said. "Here, Byron. It's beautiful. Give it to your girlfriend, or your sister, or your mother."

"Keep it, it's yours," he said rudely. "I could consider staying in Warsaw and waiting for that girl to grow up."

"Not with those parents," Slote said. "She's for a rabbi."

"Steer clear of Jewish girls anyway, they're bad joss," Natalie said.

"Amen," said Slote.

Natalie was pinning the brooch on her jacket. "I guess I'll see Berel in Medzice, then. Too bad, Aaron said he was very clever, and could show me things in Warsaw that nobody else could. They used to study the Talmud together, though Berel was much younger."

At the mention of Medzice, Slote despairingly shook his head.

8

NATALIE telephoned Byron in his room at seven o'clock one morning, after they had stayed up till well past three, touring nightclubs with Slote; dismal Polish imitations of Paris dives. In a nervously merry mood, she had pushed them on from one club to another, ignoring Slote's show of collapsing fatigue.

"Hi, Briny, are you dead?" From her chipper note, she might have had ten hours' sleep. "This is playing sort of dirty, but I have two seats on the plane to Cracow, and it leaves at eleven. I bought them yesterday. If you'd rather sleep and just stay here, okay. I'll be back in a couple of days."

Half awake, Byron said, "What? Slote's got us on the plane to Rome tomorrow, Natalie, and those reservations were mighty hard to come by."

"I know. I'll leave him a note. Maybe I'll phone him from the airport. If you come, we won't have to return to Warsaw at all. We'll go straight on to Rome from Cracow, Saturday or Sunday, after I visit my family."

"Have you got reservations from there?"

"No. But Cracow's a hub. There are half a dozen ways to get out. We'll buy our tickets—plane or train or bus— as soon as we arrive there. Well? Byron! Have you fallen back asleep?"

"I'm thinking." Byron was weighing the advantage of leaving Warsaw and Slote, against these harebrained travel arrangements. The war crisis seemed to be abating. The Poles in the nightclubs had acted gay and carefree, though Slote had remarked on the absence of foreigners, especially Germans. The streets were as calm as ever, and there were no visible preparations for war. Byron had taken to gauging the state of the crisis by the tone of Radio Warsaw. He now knew a few key words and phrases about the crisis, and much could sometimes be surmised from the shaky or relieved accents of the newscasters. In the United States, announcers in a time of crisis tended to use sonorous doom-filled voices, to thrill their listeners. The Polish broadcasters, nearer the action, were less bent on being dramatic. In the past day or two they had not sounded quite so worried.

He said, "Have you heard any news?"

"I just got BBC on shortwave. Same bulletins as last night. Henderson's talking to Hitler."

"Natalie, this would be a damned wild excursion."

"Why? I'll probably never have another chance to see where my parents were born. I'm here now. Leslie himself said last night that the worst seems to be over, that they've agreed to negotiate. Anyway, you don't have to come. I mean that. It'll be a bore for you, slogging around in the Polish countryside."

"Well, I'll have breakfast with you."

Byron packed fast. The more time he spent with Natalie Jastrow the more she puzzled him. Her relationship with Leslie Slote now baffled him too. If they were spending time in bed together—and he had to assume that this was part of her purpose in coming to Warsaw, if not all of it—they were finding odd hurried occasions for this, or taking pains to mislead him. Night after night Slote had said his farewells in the hotel lobby. She treated Slote, when they were together, with the loving warmth of a fiancée, yet when Byron tried to withdraw from their company—for dinner, for a concert or the theatre, even for a tour of the embassy—she made him come along. It had crossed his mind, of course, that she might be using him—perhaps had even asked him along to Warsaw—to provoke Slote. If so, the tactic was failing. The Foreign Service man was cordial to Byron and appeared to take his tagging along entirely for granted. But it was hard to tell anything about Slote, except that he was weary, swamped with work, and very concerned about Natalie's presence in Poland.

There had been more to her persistence in the journey— that was becoming clear to Byron—than desire for her lover. The Jewish streets of Warsaw fascinated her. No matter where they started an evening, they ended in those narrow byways. She had even dragged Byron (Slote had begged off) to a performance of O'Neill's *Ah, Wilderness!* at a little Yiddish theatre in a back alley, with a stage not twenty feet wide and a ragged curtain. For him it was a bizarre and tedious experience. But the mixture of apple-pie American characters and stylized Jewish emoting in that shabby hall had much amused and moved her. "That was me, I guess," she had said, coming out of the theatre into the warm night, in the muddy alley bordered with sagging half-timbered houses. "That exact strange mixture. I never quite understood that, and I'm still sorting it out. It's disconcerting but exciting. Like seeing myself for the first time in a home movie." Evidently this same fascination was drawing her to Medzice.

She was waiting for him in the restaurant. Somewhere she had bought a Polish dress, a bright flowery print with an open neck, and she had combed her heavy hair forward covering much of her forehead in an outdated American style, as the Warsaw women did.

"Will I get by? I'm so bored with all these stares, as though I had horns."

"So long as you've got your passport handy, okay. Don't go too native."

"Oh sure, and there's always this." At her feet was a blue suede sack with drawstrings. "Suit, shirt, hat, stockings, girdle. I can go into a ladies' room anytime and emerge a complete *Amerikanka,* full of indignation and waving dollars. Are you coming? No, of course."

"Yes. My bag's in the lobby."

"Honestly? You're as goofy as I am, Briny." She looked at him from under her eyebrows, with a slow blink of her dark eyes, and Byron thought of the little ghetto girl in the lilac dress. "Tell me, don't you like Slote a little better now?"

"I don't dislike him. I'm sorry for him at the moment, he's certainly in over his head." The waitress put down plates of food. He said, "Well, you ordered for both of us. Fine. There's nothing like this Polish ham."

She said, "I'm even beginning to feel slightly guilty here, eating ham. Imagine!" Natalie cut and ate the thick pink meat with no visible remorse.

"I don't know anything about your religion," Byron said.

"Neither do I, and it's hardly my religion. I dropped it before I was eleven years old—temple, Hebrew classes, everything. It grieved my father: he's a Zionist, an officer in the temple, and all that. But our rabbi was such a boring dunce, Briny! And my father simply couldn't answer my questions. He's not an intellectual like Aaron, he's a businessman. When I was eleven I'd read more books than he had."

"But he just allowed you to drop it?" Byron said. "Like that? My father wouldn't have, that's for sure."

"Possibly military men are different," Natalie said with a skeptical smile. "Most fathers can't do much with daughters. Anyway, I was an only child, and very good, on the whole. I just wouldn't keep up flummery that made no sense to me. Well!" She set her knife and fork down. "Coffee and then on to Medzice. Correct?"

"I'm with you."

A rickety taxi, with thick surgical tape crisscrossing the cracked yellow windows, brought them to the airport. The lone aircraft on the sunny field looked so rusty and patched that Byron thought it might be a wreck; but as they arrived, people came out on the grass and began boarding it.

"I don't know," Byron said as he paid the cab driver. "Do you suppose it will leave the ground? Maybe we should have this fellow wait." Natalie laughed and went to telephone Slote; but he was not in his apartment, nor at the embassy. The terminal was still crowded with Germans, though so few seemed left in Warsaw. Only Poles, and a few Jews, boarded the Cracow plane and took the awkward iron seats.

The plane did leave the ground, with bumps and shudders that slightly parted the metal floor plates, affording a view underfoot of green fields and admitting a jet of warm air that billowed Natalie's skirt. She tucked it under her thighs and fell asleep. After a half hour or so the plane dived, slamming down to a stop near a barn in an open field, amid tall grass and wild flowers. Byron thought it was a forced landing, but several passengers took their valises and got off. Another hop of about an hour brought them to Cracow, the plane passing from green flatlands to low mountains, part forested, part farmed, all checkered with fields of yellow, black, and purple.

The Cracow terminal was a wooden hut inside a wire fence. Byron was glad to leave the plane, which reeked of hot iron and gasoline, and to walk out on a sunny, breezy field as fragrant as a flower garden. On either side of the tarred landing strip, kerchiefed peasant women were mowing hay in the sunshine. There were no taxis in sight, and only one mud-caked green bus. Some passengers, met by their relatives, climbed into heavy horse-drawn wagons and went creaking off.

"Any idea how we get to Cracow?" Byron said.

"That bus must go there," Natalie said.

A brown-bearded Jew standing alone and erect at the gate, in a long dark coat and a wide flat dark hat, drew near, touching his hat with his hand. "You excuse? Americans? Jastrow?"

Natalie regarded him dubiously. "Why, yes. You're not Berel?"

"Yes, yes. Jochanan Berel Jastrow." He broke into a

broad smile. "You excuse, poor English. Speak you Dytsche? *Français?*"

"*Français, un peu,*" and she switched into French. "How did you know we'd be on this plane? Well! Byron, this is Uncle Aaron's cousin, my father's cousin. Byron Henry is a good friend of mine, Berel."

The two men shook hands, and the Jew smoothed his long gray-flecked brown beard, scanning Byron's face. Berel Jastrow had a broad nose, heavy eyebrows, and surprisingly blue deep-set eyes with an almost Tartar slant. His glance was incisive. Byron felt that Jastrow classed him in a second or two as a Gentile, though probably a friendly one. "*Enchanté,*" Jastrow said.

He led them to a rust-pitted car on the other side of the shed. The driver was a scrawny man in a light sweater and a skullcap, with a little bright red beard. After a parley in Yiddish they set off. Natalie explained to Byron that they were going straight to Medzice. The Jastrow family was agog to see her, and Cracow was twenty miles the other way. They regarded it as a wonderful omen that the American cousin was falling on them from the skies the day before the wedding. Natalie had telegraphed to Jochanan Jastrow, Medzice, saying she expected to arrive today. But she had not mentioned the plane, scarcely expecting that the wire would reach him.

"*Mais pourquoi pas? La Pologne n'est pas l'Afrique,*" Berel interjected, brightly following Natalie's English. "*C'est un pays tout à fait moderne et civilisé.*"

Byron found it decidedly peculiar to hear clear good French spoken by this figure out of a ghetto painting or play. Jastrow told him he would arrange for their return to Rome the day after tomorrow; he had good connections in Cracow, and getting train or air tickets would be no problem at all.

Swerving to avoid the worst holes, the car bounced along a bad tar road. They drove through tiny villages of straw-thatched log houses, painted with strips of blue between the logs. The driver had to maneuver around pigs, chickens, and cattle wandering in the road. Many of the houses were weathered gray, sagging, or toppling; some had no windows; but nearly all had new, or freshly varnished, doors. Close to each village, on a rise of ground, stood a church of wood. In the sun-flooded fields women and men toiled with hand implements or horse-drawn plows. The car passed massive wagons of hand-hewn wood pulled by muscular, resigned horses, and driven by muscular, resigned women and men, their sex indistinguishable except for marks like kerchiefs and beards. No tractor or automobile or any other machine appeared along the way until they came to Oswiecim, a medium-sized railroad town of brick buildings and wide streets, cut in two by a muddy river. Here the car stopped in the main square at the telephone exchange, and Natalie got out with Berel to phone Slote.

Byron strolled around the square in the hot sun, attracting covert looks from the townspeople. He bought ice cream, and the shopgirl took his money without a word. Oswiecim was nothing like Warsaw: a flat town of low drab buildings, with an air of back-country dislike of strangers. Byron was glad to leave it. Natalie told him as they drove out into level green fields, on a dirt road along the river, that Slote, furious and alarmed, had said uncomplimentary things about Byron's intelligence, though she had tried to take all the blame on herself. "I think he's got a case of nerves," she said. "You don't suppose he's afraid of the Germans?"

"Look, it was an unceremonious way to leave him."

She said, with an odd little glance at Byron, "It wasn't all that unceremonious. We were together till dawn, you know, talking. He ought to be tired of me."

"What? I saw you turn in at three."

"Oh, yes, but then he rang me from the lobby, said he was too exhausted to sleep, or something, and I came down and we went out again."

"I see. You must be really beat."

"Strangely enough I feel wonderful. The nap on the plane, and now all this sweet country air! Poland *smells* delicious. I never read that in a book."

"Poland a foist-class country," Berel spoke up in English, stroking his beard. "Strong pipple. Hitler a big bluff. No war."

Byron's stay in Medzice remained in his memory forever after as something like a trip to the moon. Though the usual church stood on the usuall knoll, the villagers were almost all Jews. Medzice was a cluster of houses on crooked narrow dirt or cobbled streets, some log, some plastered, a few of brick, sloping down toward a flat green meadow and the winding river. About a mile beyond the town, a roofless great house in the style of a French château lay ruined on the riverbank. The noble family was extinct, the house was a casualty of the World War, but the village survived.

The Jastrows and their relatives seemed to comprise half of Medzice. They swarmed on Natalie and Byron and marched them joyously from home to home. The dark interiors were all much the same: tiny rooms, enormous stoves, heavy polished Victorian furniture, lace curtains, each house seething underfoot with children ranging from crawlers to adolescents. Wine, cake, tea, hard candies, vodka, and fish appeared on table after table. There was no polite way to refuse. After a while Byron was physically uncomfortable, because there was never a toilet pause. In all the hours that this was going on, he never understood a word that anybody said. It seemed to him that all the Jews talked continuously and simultaneously. Natalie chattered away with these bearded men in dark blouses, breeches, and heavy boots, these unpainted work-worn women in plain dresses that reached their ankles. They all appeared enthralled by her. Outside each house a crowd gathered, joining the conversation through the windows. The visit of the two Americans was obviously one of the grandest events in Medzice since the war.

What a world! No sidewalks, no shops, no movie houses, no garages, no cars, no bicycles, no streetlights, no hydrants, no billboards; not a sound, not a sight to connect the town with the twentieth century, except a string of telegraph poles stretching along the river. Yet Natalie Jastrow was only one generation removed from this place. Dr. Aaron Jastrow, the author of *A Jew's Jesus,* the full professor of history at Yale, the urbane friend of the archbishop of Siena, had lived here until his fifteenth year, and had looked like one of these pale, skinny, studious boys in big black skullcaps and ear curls! Byron could not imagine what these people made of him, but they were fully as cordial to him as to Natalie, substituting smiles and gestures for the talk with which they flooded her.

(The next day Natalie told him that she had identified him as her protector, an American naval officer sent along by Uncle Aaron. They had accepted this without question, since anything Americans did was equally unlikely and shocking and marvellous.)

The sleeping arrangements that night were as novel as everything else. Byron was quartered at the home of the rabbi. This was the outcome of a tremendous argument in which half the population participated, including at one point the village priest, a brown-bearded man who, except for his bare head and black robe, rather resembled Berel, and whose sudden appearance on the scene sobered everybody. The parleying language shifted to Polish, then to German, which Byron well understood. The priest wanted to extend his hospitality to the Gentile American. Berel managed, with a timely word of help in German from Byron, to deflect this offer. When the priest left, both Berel and Byron became the center of jubilant triumph, and the American was borne off to the rabbi's brick house by an escort of singing, hand-clapping yeshiva boys, led by the bridegroom himself, a pale lad of eighteen or so with a wispy goatee.

Here the rabbi and his wife tried to give him their own bed, but since it was obviously exactly that, the only large bed in the house, a black four-poster piled with huge pillows, Byron wouldn't have it. This caused another grand parley in Yiddish. The house had a second bedroom containing two beds, and a plank and mattress stretched across two chairs. In this room there were already five tittering girls, who, as the discussion went on, began blushing and roaring with laughter. The idea seemed to be to put Byron into one of those beds. Evidently no decent solution could be hammered out. He ended up sleeping on the floor of the main room, a sort of parlor and dining room combined, lined with giant leather-bound books. The rabbi gave him a feather mattress to lie on, and as six of the boys from the Cracow yeshiva shared the floor with him on similar mattresses, he did not feel ill-treated. Indeed he slept better on the floor of the rabbi's house in Medzice than he had in Warsaw's Europeiski Hotel. He found the feather mattress lulling.

He spent much of the next day walking with Natalie

around the town and in the fields and along the river, past an old cemetery to the ruined great house. The preparations for the wedding were going forward, so today the family let the visitors amuse themselves. The muddy narrow streets of Medzice—it had rained hard during the night, and the rattling on the rabbi's roof had increased Byron's sense of snugness—were filled with an autumnal fragrance of hay and ripening fruit, made more tangy by the smells of the free-roaming ducks, chickens, goats, and calves. Some of the fowl were encountering tragedy, happily strutting in the morning sunshine one moment, and the next swooped down upon by laughing children and carried off squawking and flapping to be slaughtered. In the fields beyond the outlying houses and barns—mostly one-room log structures with heavy yellow thatch roofs —cows and horses grazed in tall waving grass spotted with wild flowers. Water bugs skated on the surface of the slow-moving brown river. Fish jumped and splashed, but nobody was fishing.

Natalie told him she had stayed up half the night talking to the family. Most of what she had heard was news to her. Her father had tended to reminisce more about Warsaw than about his birthplace, and as a child she had been bored by the little she had heard, since she had only wanted to be a true-blue American. In the village, Uncle Aaron and her father were the legendary ones who had made an American success. Aaron Jastrow was variously thought to be a great surgeon, an astronomer, and a cancer specialist; "professor" had ambiguous meanings in Polish and Yiddish. Nobody but Berel knew that he had written a famous book about Jesus, and Natalie gathered that Aaron's cousin was at some pains to keep the achievement quiet. Berel (this was a familiar name for Jochanan, his real name) was the local success. He had begun trading in mushrooms while still a student in Cracow, had branched into other exports, and had prospered enough to move his family to Warsaw; but he had sent his son back to the Cracow yeshiva, and had found the boy a bride in Medzice among the second cousins. The numerous Jastrows, like the rest of the villagers, lived by farming and by selling dairy products in the markets of Oswiecim and Cracow.

Clambering around the ruined great house, Natalie went exploring out of sight, broke through some rotten flooring, and fell ten or twelve feet. Byron heard the splintering noise, her shriek, and the thud. He hurried to find her. She lay sprawled like a broken doll, her skirt up around her gartered white thighs. She had landed on dirt and thick grass; whatever the floor here had been, probably parquet or marble, nothing was left of it. Byron pulled down her skirt and lifted her to a sitting position. She was conscious but stunned, and greenish pale. In a minute or two her color returned, and life and amusement flowed back into her eyes. She shook her head. "Ye gods, I really saw stars, Byron. I thought I'd broken my silly neck." She put her head on his shoulder. "Glory, what a scare. I'm all right, help me up."

She limped; her left knee bothered her, she said. She took his arm with an abashed grin and leaned on him. Byron had tried to keep her from climbing the decayed staircase, and the grin was her only apology, but it was enough. He was worried by the injury, and still angry over her casual disclosure that she had been with Slote until dawn the day before. However, to have this girl leaning on him, in a sunlit orchard full of apple scent by a river, seemed to Byron almost all the pleasure he wanted in the world. Just holding her like this was sweeter than any delight any other girl had ever given him. Whatever it was that made a girl desirable—the enigmatic look in the eyes, the soft curve of a cheek, the shape of a mouth, the sudden charm of a smile, the swell of breasts and hips under a dress, the smoothness of skin—Natalie Jastrow for Byron was all composed of these lovely glints, all incandescent with them. That she stemmed from the strange Jews of Medzice, that she was, by all evidence, the mistress of a dour man ten years older than himself, that she was only a solid and human girl—indeed very heavy, leaning on him and limping—with a stubborn streak and some unattractive, almost coarse tomboy bravado: all these drawbacks just made her Natalie Jastrow, instead of the perfect girl he had been dreaming about since his twelfth year. The perfect girl had in fact been a blonde, and something of a sex fiend, like the dream girls of most boys. She was gone now, and this prickly Jewish brunette held her place. And here they were alone on a riverbank in south Poland, in golden sunshine, a mile from any house, amid apple trees laden with ripe fruit.

"This will be slow work, getting back," she said.

"I can try to carry you."

"What, a horse like me? You'd rupture yourself. I'm fine if I keep my weight off it. It's just such a bore."

"I'm not bored," said Byron.

They passed an old abandoned scow half full of water. "Let's use this," he said, tipping it to empty it out.

Natalie appreciatively watched him heave up the scow unaided. "No oars," she said.

"We can float downstream."

He guided the scow with a long rough plank that lay in it, using the plank as a rudder and as a pole. The river was very sluggish, almost oily, calm and brown. Natalie sat on the bow edge of the scow, facing Byron, her shoes in the seeping water. She said as they floated past the cemetery, "That's where all my ancestors are, I guess. The ones that aren't buried in Palestine."

"Or Egypt or Mesopotamia," Byron said.

Natalie shuddered. "I don't know. It's a godforsaken place, Briny."

"Medzice?"

"Poland. I'm glad Grandma and Grandpa got the hell out of here."

He banked the scow near the village. She climbed out and walked slowly, not limping. There was no doctor here, she said, and she didn't want to generate a crisis around the injured American cousin. She would have her knee taped in Cracow tomorrow. None of the villagers noticed anything the matter with her.

Byron tried to find out the war crisis news. There was one working radio in Medzice, and several broken-down ones. The priest had the working radio. The rabbi told Byron, in Yiddish tortured into a barely comprehensible kind of German, that the last broadcast from Warsaw had been encouraging: the Prime Minister of England had gone to his country home for the weekend, and the crisis seemed to be passing. "Henderson, Henderson," the rabbi said. "Henderson talked to Hitler." And he winked shrewdly, rubbing one hand over the other to pantomime a money deal.

The wedding made Byron wish over and over that he were a writer and could record it; a Jew, and could comprehend it. The mixture of solemnity and boisterousness baffled him. In his training, decorousness was the essence of a wedding, except for the shoes-and-rice moment at the very end, but the Medzice Jews—though arrayed in their best, the women in velvet dresses and the men in black satin coats or formal city clothes—did not seem to know what decorum was. They crowded, they chattered, they burst into song; they surrounded the veiled, silent, seated bride and discussed her vehemently; they danced, they marched here and there in the houses and in the streets, performing strange little rites; one and then another stood on a chair to speak or to sing and the guests wildly laughed and wildly cried. The pallid bridegroom, in a white robe and a black hat, looked on the verge of fainting. Byron accidentally learned, by offering him a plate of cakes at the long men's table where the American visitor sat in a place of honor beside the groom, that the weedy boy had been fasting for twenty-four hours, and still was, while everybody around him continuously ate and drank with vast appetite.

Byron, eating and drinking with the rest, and feeling very good indeed, was not sure for hours whether the marriage ceremony had or had not taken place. But near midnight a sudden gravity fell on the guests. In a courtyard, with the bright moon and a blaze of stars overhead, in a series of stern and impressive acts—including solemn incantations over silver goblets of wine and the lighting of long tapers—the bride and groom were brought together for a ring ceremony and a kiss, much as in a Christian union, under a hand-held canopy of purple velvet. Then the groom ground a wineglass to bits under his heel, and jubilation broke out that made everything before it seem staid and pale.

Byron almost became the hero of the evening by putting on a black skullcap and dancing with the yeshiva boys, since there was no dancing with the girls. All the guests gathered to clap and cheer, Natalie in the forefront, her face ablaze with fun. Her knee healed or forgotten, she joined in the girls' dances; and so she danced, and Byron danced, inside the house and outside, far into the morning hours. Byron scarcely remembered leaving the bride's home and falling asleep on the feather mattress on the floor of the rabbi's house.

But there he was when a hand shook him and he opened his eyes. Berel Jastrow was bending over him, and it took Byron a moment or two to recall where he was and who this man was, with the clever, anxious blue eyes and the long gray-streaked brown beard. All around him the yeshiva boys were sitting up and rubbing their eyes, or dressing. The girls were hurrying here and there in their nightclothes. It was hot, and the sun was shining into the room from a clear blue sky.

"Yes? What is it?" he said.

"Der Deutsch," the Jew said. *"Les Allemands."*

"Huh? What?"

"De Chormans."

Byron sat up, his voice faltering. "Oh, the Germans? What about them?"

"Dey comink."

*   *   *

... in for the little lunch, and to the dance, and they
danced inside the house and on the deck, and the morning
hours went away... triumphant among the bones
... and falling asleep on the ... or markers on the
floor of the little house.

But there is one more sad thing that must be told ...
... this. As I drew ... leaning over him, and to try to
draw ... nigh, as two to reach where he was and with
this arm was, and he drew ... blue eyes ... to the
... grey-tinged ... hair beneath. All undone ...
... he swore aloud his ... rob wit ...
... freeing. He is ... hung on it, the ... before he ...
... it was hot and no sound was hung into the
room from a cross bird sky.

"Look? No! No," he said.

"The Brunelle," she cry, and "Let Mianda?"

"Not what."

"Be Charming."

"Come on to ..." voice flurrying. "Oh! The Come, at ...
what all of them?"

"He! Oh! ..."

World Empire Lost

by General Armin von Roon

(adapted from his *Land, Sea, and Air Operations of World War II*)

English Translation by

VICTOR HENRY

9

Translator's Foreword

BY VICTOR HENRY

I never expected to translate a German military work. For years, like many flag officers, I planned to write up my own experiences in World War II; and in the end, like most of them, I decided against it. It was said of the late Fleet Admiral Ernest King that, if it had been up to him, he would have issued a single communiqué about the Pacific war: "We won." My war memoirs boil down more or less to this: "I served."

Upon retiring from the Navy, I became a consultant to a marine engineering firm. On my last business trip to Germany, in 1965, I noticed in the windows of bookstores, wherever I went, stacks of a small book called *World Empire Lost*, by General Armin von Roon. I distinctly recalled General von Roon, from my days of service in Berlin as naval attaché to the American embassy. I had met him, and chatted with him; and he came to one of my wife's frequent dinner parties. He was then on the Armed Forces Operation Staff. He had a distant, forbidding manner, a pudgy figure, and a large beaked nose, almost Semitic, that must have given him some grief. But of course, as his name indicates, he was of simon-pure Prussian descent. He was obviously brilliant, and I always wanted to know him better, but did not get the opportunity. I little thought then how well I would come to know him one day through his book!

Out of curiosity I bought a copy of *World Empire Lost*, and found it so absorbing that I visited the publisher's office in Munich, to learn who had printed it in America. I then discovered that the work had not yet been translated into English. On my return to the States, I induced the publishers of this volume to acquire the English-language rights. I was planning to retire from business, and I thought that translating the book might ease the pain of putting myself out to pasture.

World Empire Lost is an abstract from a huge two-volume operational analysis of the war, written by General von Roon in prison. He called it *Land, Sea, and Air Operations of World War II,* and he had plenty of time to write it; for at Nuremberg he got twenty years, for complicity in war crimes on the eastern front. This exhaustive technical work is not available in an English translation, and I doubt that it will be.

Roon prefaced his account of each major campaign with a summary of the strategic and political background. These brief sketches, pulled out and compiled by the publisher after his death, constitute *World Empire Lost.* (I doubt that the general would have approved of that melodramatic title.) *World Empire Lost* is, therefore, not solid military history, but rather a sort of publisher's stunt. It runs together Roon's sweeping assertions about world politics in one short volume, and omits the meticulous military analysis that backed them. However, I believe the result is readable, interesting, and valuable.

The remarkable thing about the book is its relative honesty. Nearly all the German military literature glosses over the killing of the Jews, the responsibility for the war, and Hitler's hold on the army and the people. About all these sticky questions, Roon writes with calm frankness. He planned to withhold his work from publication (and did) until he was safely dead and buried; so, unlike most German military writers, he was not trying either to save his neck or placate the victors. The result is a revelation of how the Germans really felt, and may well still feel, about Hitler's war.

Here then is a German general levelling, insofar as he can do so. Roon was an able writer, much influenced by the best French and British military authors, especially de Gaulle and Churchill. His German is more readable than that of most of his countrymen who write on military matters. I hope I have at least partly conveyed this in translation. My own style, formed in a lifetime of writing U.S. Navy reports, has inevitably crept in here and there, but I trust no substantial distortion has resulted.

This author, to my mind, portrays the Germans under Hitler as they were: a remarkably tough and effective fighting nation, not a horde of stupid sadists or comic bunglers, as popular entertainment now tends to caricature them. For six years these people battled almost the whole world to a standstill, and they also committed unprecedented crimes. The stake they were gambling for was, in Shakespeare's expressive phrase, nothing less than "the great globe itself." What was going on in their minds seems to me of importance. That is why I have translated Roon.

His version of events, while professional and well informed, can scarcely be taken at face value. He was a German through and through. On the whole I have let General von Roon describe the war his own way. I could not, however, translate certain passages without challenging them; hence my occasional comments.

Roon starts on his first page, for instance, exactly as Adolf Hitler started all his speeches: by denouncing the Versailles Treaty as an injustice imposed on an honorable and trusting Germany by the cruel Allies. He does not mention the historical catch to that. German writers seldom do. In 1917 Lenin overthrew the Kerensky government and sued for a separate peace on the eastern front. The Treaty of Brest-Litovsk, dictated by the Germans over a year *before* the Treaty of Versailles, deprived Russia of a territory much larger than France and England combined, of almost sixty million inhabitants, and of almost all her heavy industry. It was far harsher than the Versailles Treaty.

I used to bring up this little fact during my Berlin service, whenever Versailles was mentioned. My German friends were invariably puzzled by the comparison. They thought it made no sense at all. The Treaty of Versailles had happened to *them*; Brest-Litovsk had happened to the other fellow. In this reaction they were sincere. I cannot explain this national quirk of the Germans, but it should never be forgotten in reading *World Empire Lost*.

Oakton, Virginia   Victor Henry
27 May, 1966

Case White

The Responsibility for Hitler

In writing this book, I have only one aim: to defend the honor of the German soldier.

To trace the rise of Adolf Hitler, our leader in World War II, is not necessary here. No story of the twentieth century is better known. When the victorious Allies in 1919 created the crazy Treaty of Versailles, they also created Hitler. Germany in 1918, relying on the Fourteen Points of the American President Wilson, honorably laid down arms. The Allies treated the Fourteen Points as a scrap of paper, and wrote a treaty that partitioned Germany and made an economic and political madhouse of Europe.

In thus outwitting the naïve American President and butchering up the map, the British and French politicians probably imagined they would paralyze the German nation forever. The cynical policy boomeranged. Winston Churchill himself has called the Versailles settlement a "sad and complicated idiocy." The oppression of Versailles built up in the vigorous German people a volcanic resentment; it burst forth, and Adolf Hitler rode to power on the crest of the eruption. The Nazi Party, a strange alliance of radicals and conservatives, of wealthy men and down-and-outers, was united only on the ideal of a resurgent Germany, and unfortunately on the old middle-European political slogan of discontent—anti-Semitism. A riffraff of vulgar agitators, philosophic idealists, fanatics, opportunists, bullies, and adventurers, some of them extremely able and energetic, swept into power with Hitler. We of the General Staff for the most part watched these turbid political events with distaste and foreboding.

Our loyalty was to the state, however it was governed, but we feared a wave of weakening social change.

It is fair to say that Hitler surprised us. Swiftly, without bloodshed, this brilliant and inspiring politician repaired one injustice of Versailles after another. His methods were direct and strong. The Weimar regime had tried other methods, and had met only with contempt from Britain and France. Hitler's methods worked. Inside Germany, he was equally strict and harsh when needed. Here too the methods worked, and if historians now call his regime a terror, one must concede that it was then a popular terror. Hitler brought prosperity and he rearmed us. He was a man with a mission. His burning belief in himself and in his mission swayed the German masses. Though he usurped much power, the masses would probably have granted it all to him freely anyway.

Case Red

Naturally, the swift renascence of Germany under Hitler created anger and dismay among the Allies. France, war-weary, luxury-loving, and rotted by socialism, was reluctant to take effective action. England was another matter. England still ruled the world with her global navy, her international money system, her alliances, and her empire on five continents. In ascending to mastery of Europe, and upsetting the balance of power, Germany was once more challenging her for world rule. This was the confrontation of the Great War again. Nothing could avert this showdown, for Germany early in the twentieth century had passed England in both population and industrial plant. In this sense Churchill correctly calls the Second World War a continuation of the first one, and both conflicts together "another Thirty Years' War."

We of the German General Staff knew that at some point in Hitler's spectacular normalizing of Europe, England would intervene. The only questions were, when, and under what circumstances? Already in 1937 we had prepared a plan for a two-front war against England and Poland: *Fall Rot* ("Case Red"). We kept updating it as Adolf Hitler scored one bloodless victory after another, and our strategic situation and armed strength improved by leaps while Britain and France contented themselves with feeble scolding protests. We began to hope that the forceful Führer might actually bring his new order to Europe without bloodshed, by default of the perpetrators of Versailles. Had this occurred, he could have launched his grand crusade against the Soviet Union for living space in the east—the aim of his life—as a one-front war. History would have followed a different course.

But on March 31, 1939, a day that the world should not forget, all this changed. The British Prime Minister Chamberlain suddenly gave Poland an unconditional guarantee of military assistance! His pretext was anger at Hitler for breaking his promise not to occupy the weak fragment of Czechoslovakia, left after the Munich partition—the deal which Chamberlain himself had engineered. Hitler's promises, like those of all politicians, were merely contingent and tactical, of course. It was asinine of Chamberlain to think otherwise, if he did.

Whatever the motive for the Polish guarantee, it was a piece of suicidal stupidity. It stiffened the corrupt Polish army oligarchy to stand fast on the just German grievances involving Danzig and the Polish Corridor. It placed in the hands of these backward militarists the lever to start another world war. Otherwise it had no meaning, because in the event, England was unable to give Poland actual military help. With Russian participation the guarantee might have made sense; in fact it might have stopped Hitler in his tracks, because he feared above all things, as the General Staff also did, a two-front war. But the British gentlemen-politicians disdained the Bolsheviks, and Poland in any case utterly refused to consider admitting Russian protective troops. So foolishness and weakness joined hands to trigger the catastrophe.

For Chamberlain's defiant move, like the weak pawing of a cornered rabbit, only spurred the Führer to greater boldness. Like lightning, down came the word to our staff to prepare an operation order for an attack on Poland in the fall. Working day and night, with Case Red as a basis, we prepared the plan. On April 5 it went to the Führer under a new code name: *Fall Weiss*—"Case White."

Historic Ironies

Case White, the plan for smashing Poland, shaped itself on a few major and classic geographical facts.

Poland is a plain: a larger Belgium with few natural obstacles and no real boundaries. The Carpathian Mountains to the south are breached by the Jablunka pass, affording ready access from Czechoslovakia to Cracow and the Vistula. The rivers Vistula, Narew, and San present problems, but in the summer and early autumn the water levels are low and the rivers are in many places fordable by motor vehicles and horses.

Poland is itself a political freak, reflecting its formless geography. It has no permanent shape, no continuity of regime or national purpose. It has several times disappeared from the map of Europe, divided up as provinces of stronger and abler powers. Today it is again little more than a Russian province. At Yalta the Allied leaders moved the entire crude geographical parallelogram called "Poland" about two hundred kilometers to the west, to the Oder-Neisse Line. This was done at the expense of Germany, of course, giving to Poland cities, territories, and populations which had been German from time immemorial, and causing the tragic uprooting and resettling of millions of people. Such is war: to the victor, the spoils; to the defeated, the costs. The Second World War began over the question of Polish territorial integrity, but Poland has not recovered, and will never recover, its 1939 borders. It has lost that part of its territory which, through the deal between Hitler and Stalin, was absorbed into the Soviet Union. England went to war with us over the question of these borders, dragging in France and eventually the United States. At Yalta, England and the United States endorsed forever Hitler's gift of Polish territory to the Soviets. Such are the ironies of history.

The Polish strategic situation in 1939 was poor. The entire land could be regarded as a weak salient into Germany and German-occupied territory, flanked by East Prussia to the north and Czechoslovakia to the south, and wholly flat and open to a thrust from Germany to the west. To the rear, in the east, the Soviet Union stood poised, newly linked to Germany through the nonaggression pact engineered by Ribbentrop.

The Fatal Pact

Insufficient attention is paid to the plain fact that this treaty, hailed at the time as a masterstroke, all but lost Germany the Second World War before a shot was fired. The alliance with Bolshevism (however temporary and tactical) was certainly a repudiation of the Dictator's ideals, running counter to the German national spirit; but this might have been allowable had the tactical advantage proved real. In politics, as in war, only success matters. But the contrary was the case.

This pact handed Stalin the Baltic states and about half of Poland, allowing the Slav horde to march two hundred kilometers nearer Germany. Two years later we paid the price. In December 1941, the gigantic drive of our Army Group Center toward Moscow—the greatest armed march in world history—was halted forty kilometers from its goal, with advance patrols penetrating within sight of the Kremlin towers. Had the German forces jumped off from a line two hundred kilometers nearer Moscow, they would have engulfed the Russian capital, deposed Stalin, and won the campaign before the first flake of snow fell on the Smolensk road. England certainly would have made peace then, and we would have won the war.

Regarded as a triumph of daring diplomacy even by our enemies, this treaty contained between its lines the two words, *finis Germaniae*. Seldom in history has there been such a political *coup de théâtre*. Seldom has one so disastrously backfired. Yet we of the Staff who ventured to express doubts at the time, or merely to convey with our eyes our mutual dismay at the news, were very much in the minority.

No member of the armed forces, including Hitler's own chief of staff, Keitel, and the chief of operations, Jodl, knew of the secret protocol yielding half of Poland to the Bolsheviks. It was only when Stalin angrily telephoned Ribbentrop in the third week of the campaign, bitterly complaining about the advance of our Fourteenth Army into the southeast oil area, that the Wehrmacht received its specific chop lines, and retreated before the Russians, who airily rolled in without shedding a drop of their own, or of Polish, blood.

It was I who received at Supreme Headquarters the staggering telephone call from our military attaché in Moscow around midnight of September 16, informing me that the Russians were marching into Poland in accordance with a secret agreement Hitler had made in August. I immediately telephoned General Jodl with the news that the Russians were on the move. His response, in a tremulous voice most uncharacteristic of Alfred Jodl, was "Against whom?" So completely was the army in the dark.

In the last few days of August, as Case White preparations speeded up, Hitler tried to cash in on Ribbentrop's big political surprise with a comedy of peace negotiations. In the spring, in a calmer mood, he had stated with his usual prescience that the Western powers would not again permit a bloodless victory, that this time there would be battle. We had prepared Case White with feelings varying from misgivings to a sense of doom, because our combat readiness was much below par for a major conflict. We were so low on tanks, to cite just one key item, that even for Case White we had to deploy large numbers of Czech tanks of limited value; and the navy had only about fifty submarines ready for action. Worst of all, the Führer was far from ordering full wartime production, even then, for he knew it would be an unpopular move. All in all we were going out on very thin ice.

The staff placed no hope in the peace talks. Hitler, however, while going through his planned histrionics with Henderson, apparently got carried away by his own playacting and the constant assurances of Ribbentrop; he began to believe that England might be bluffed once more and might present us with another Munich. At Supreme Headquarters, in the first days of September, nobody could fail to notice that when the Western declarations of war came through, the Führer was surprised and shaken. But there was nothing to do at that point but execute Case White.

Strategy

The plan called for simultaneous flank attacks from the north and the south, aimed to cut off the Corridor and proceed to Warsaw. The Poles elected to stand all along their indefensible border, thus inviting quick fragmenting, encirclement, and reduction. They should have prepared their main defenses along the lines Vistula-Narew-Bug. This would have prolonged hostilities, and encouraged the British and French to attack our weak holding force in the west. This could have been devastating. Adventurous authoritarian leadership had exposed the German people to a bad risk. However, the gods smiled on us at the time, the Poles proved as inept in their strategic dispositions as they were brave in the field, and the French sat in their camps and fortresses, scarcely firing a shot.

Nowadays German commentators write of the "miracle" of the French static defense in September 1939, which made the Polish blitzkrieg possible. It is hard to see where the "miracle" lay. French military thinking was defensive and positional, because such thinking had triumphed in 1918. They had an obsession with the theoretical ten-to-one advantage of the defense in mechanized warfare. There is no doubt that in September France could have sent millions of well-trained soldiers, with more armored divisions than the Wehrmacht had in Poland, crashing out of the Maginot fortresses, or via the northern plain through Belgium and Holland, into our paper-thin western formations, and rolled to Berlin. But the will was not there. Adolf Hitler's political and military gamble on this vital point proved brilliant. Of all his opponents, he throughout best understood and anticipated the French.

Victory

The Polish breakthrough phase took approximately four days. Complete tactical surprise was achieved because the hypocritical Polish politicians, though wholly aware of the danger, kept giving their people false assurances. The Polish air force of almost a thousand planes was destroyed on the ground. Thereafter the Lutwaffe freely roamed the skies. Polish ground resistance was moderate to heavy, and our commanders in the field had to admire the bold cavalry dashes against tank formations. Perhaps the legend is true that the Polish horsemen were told by their government that our tanks were papier-mâché dummies! In that case, they were soon sadly disabused. The contrast between the possibilities of mechanized warfare and classic military tactics was never more strikingly demonstrated than in these ineffectual charges of the Polish horsemen against iron tanks.

Nevertheless, the Wehrmacht too was operating with but a thin knife-edge of fully motorized armored divisions. Our important ground advances were made by infantry masses on foot, exploiting the breakdown of communications, the panic, and the disarray of battle lines created by the narrow panzer thrusts. And while the Luftwaffe played a strong support role, it was the horse-drawn artillery massed outside Warsaw, and not the air bombardment, that in the end knocked out the city's capacity to resist and brought the eventual surrender. This heavy reliance on horses betrayed our serious lack of combat readiness for world war.

By September 21 the city was ringed by Wehrmacht forces; and the news from outside was of Polish soldiers being taken prisoner in the hundreds of thousands, of one pocket after another being liquidated, of a total collapse of the front, of a national government pusillanimously fleeing to Rumania. Yet it was not until September 27 that the city, under a round-the-clock rain of shells and bombs, without food, water, or light, with many of its buildings in ruins, with disease spreading, finally gave up its vain hopes of last-minute deliverance from the West, and surrendered.

Observations

From first to last, the Führer and his propagandists played down the Polish campaign as a local police action, a "special task" of the Wehrmacht. Hitler personally cancelled many sections of Case White dealing with rationing, troop mobilization, and transport, with one aim in mind: to soften the impact on the German people. This political meddling represented a considerable setback to operations, and precious months passed before the damage was righted. I may say here, that due to similar Party and Führer interference, which never ceased, the war effort was never, by professional standards, organized fully or properly.

The shabby farce enacted at our radio station at Gleiwitz near the Polish border on the night of August 31—the pretense that Polish soldiers had crossed over to attack the station and been repulsed, the dressing of condemned political prisoners in Polish uniforms and the scattering of their bullet-riddled bodies near the station, as an excuse for starting the invasion—none of this trivial humbug was known to the Wehrmacht. We were irrevocably on the march toward Poland seventy-two hours earlier. I myself did not learn of the incident until the Nuremberg trials; I was too busy at the time with serious matters.* Himmler was probably responsible.

Poland in 1939 was a backward and ill-informed dictatorship of reactionary colonels and politicians with fantastic territorial aims, a government extremely brutal to minorities (especially the Ukrainians and the Jews) and unjust and mendacious to its own people; a government that pounced like a hyena on Czechoslovakia at the Munich crisis and tore a province from that country in its hardest hour; a government that clumsily played a double game with Germany and the Soviet Union for twenty years; and to the last tried to talk and act like a major military power when it was in fact as weak as a kitten. It was to support this reactionary, bluffing, bigoted dictatorship that the democracies embarked on the Second World War. That government quickly and ignominiously fell to pieces and disappeared forever. But the war went on, and its starting point was soon all but forgotten. Some day, however, sober historians must again give the proper emphasis to these absurd paradoxes that governed the provoking of the world's biggest war.

The final absurdity of this inept start to a terrible global struggle was that Czechoslovakia, betrayed by England in 1938, did not fight, and in the whole war period lost less than one hundred thousand people. Poland, supported by England in 1939, fought and lost almost six million dead (though about half of these were Jews). Both countries ended up as Communist puppets under the heel of the Soviet Union. Which government then was the wiser, and which people the more fortunate? When great powers fall out, small powers do well to bow to the storm wind, in whichever direction it blows strongest. That was what the Poles forgot.

_____

TRANSLATOR'S NOTE: *The reader will have to grow used to the German habit of blaming other countries for getting themselves invaded by Germans. This note recurs throughout*

* The veracity of this statement is questionable.—V.H.

General von Roon's book, as through most of their military literature. Officers raised under the General Staff system apparently lost the power to think in other terms. Roon's discussion of the Polish government and the British guarantee are the telling passages in his preliminary sketch of Case White.—V.H.

*   *   *

10

GERMAN ARMY ATTACKS POLAND;
CITIES BOMBED, PORT BLOCKADED;
DANZIG IS ACCEPTED INTO THE REICH

THE *New York Times*, raising its voice to suit the occasion in its eight-column once-in-a-generation italic headlines, topped the sprawl of newspapers on the desk under Hugh Cleveland's stocking feet. The other papers had headlines far larger and blacker than the *Times*'s genteel bellow. Tilted back in his shirt-sleeves in a swivel chair, a telephone cradled between his head and left shoulder, Cleveland was making quick red crayon marks on a sheaf of yellow typing paper and sipping coffee as he talked. Eight years in the broadcasting business had made him deft at such juggling. Though he looked the picture of busy contentment, his voice was angry. His morning show, called *Who's in Town*, featured interviews with celebrities passing through New York. The war crisis, suddenly roaring into the Columbia Broadcasting System, had snatched off Cleveland's secretary to the newsroom for emergency service, and he was protesting to the personnel office, or trying to. He still could not get through to the manager.

A short girl in a flat black straw hat appeared in the open doorway. Behind her, in the big central offices of CBS News, the hubbub over the war news was still rising. Secretaries were rattling at typewriters or scampering with papers, messenger boys ran with coffee and sandwiches, knots of men in shirt-sleeves gathered at the chattering teletypes, and everybody appeared to be either shouting, or smoking, or both.

"Mr. Cleveland?" The girl's voice was sweet but shaky. Her awed round eyes made her look about sixteen.

Cleveland put his hand on the mouthpiece of his telephone. "Yes?"

"The personnel office sent me up to you."

"You? How old are you?"

"Twenty."

Cleveland appeared skeptical, but he hung up the telephone. "What's your name?"

"Madeline Henry."

Cleveland sighed. "Well, okay, Madeline. If you're in the pool, you must know the ropes. So take off that cartwheel and get started, okay? First get me another cup of coffee and a chicken sandwich, please. Then there's tomorrow's script"—he rapped the yellow sheets—"to be typed over."

Madeline could bluff no further. She was in New York to buy clothes. The outbreak of the war had prompted her to walk into CBS to see if extra girls were needed. In the employment office a harried woman wearing yellow paper cuffs had thrust a slip at her, after a few questions about her schooling, and sent her up to Cleveland. "Talk to him. If he likes you, we may take you on. He's screaming for a girl and we've got nobody to spare."

Stepping just inside the door and planting her legs apart, taking off her hat and clutching it, Madeline confessed that nobody had hired her yet; that she was visiting New York, lived in Washington, had to go back to school, detested the thought of it, feared her father too much to do anything else, and had just walked into CBS on an impulse. He listened, smiling and surveying her with eyes half-closed. She wore a sleeveless red cotton frock and she had excellent color from a sailing weekend.

"Well, Madeline, what does it add up to? Do you want the job or not?"

"I was thinking—could I come back in a week or so?"

His pleasant look faded. He picked up the telephone. "Get me Personnel again. Yes, you come back sometime, Madeline."

She said, "I'll fetch you your coffee and sandwich right now. I can do that. I'll type your script today, too. Couldn't I work for you for three weeks? I don't have to go back to school until the twenty-second. My father will kill me when he finds out, but I don't care."

"Where's your father? In Washington?"

"He's in Berlin. He's the naval attaché there."

"What?" Hugh Cleveland hung up the telephone and took his feet off the desk. "Your father is our naval attaché in Nazi Germany?"

"That's right."

"Imagine that. So! You're a Navy junior." He threw a five-dollar bill on the desk. "All right. Get me the sandwich, Madeline, please. White meat, lettuce, pepper, mayonnaise. Black coffee. Then we'll talk some more. Buy yourself a sandwich too."

"Yes, Mr. Cleveland."

Holding the bill, Madeline rushed into the outer hall and stood there dazed. Having heard the *Who's in Town* program a few times, she had at once recognized Cleveland's peculiarly warm rich voice; a real broadcaster, with his own program, and all at once she was working for him. That was wartime for you! A girl swishing by with a bag of food told her where to buy sandwiches. But twenty chattering girls swarmed at the takeout counter of the luncheonette off the lobby. She went out on Madison Avenue and stood blinking in the warm sunshine. The New York scene was normal. Crowds marched on the sidewalks; cars and buses streamed both ways in a stench of fumes; people carried packages into and out of stores and looked in windows. The only novelty was that the news vendors with fresh stacks of afternoon papers were crying war. Madeline ran to the big drugstore across the street, where the soda fountain was jammed with secretaries and shoppers, talking and laughing over bowls of chili or soup. The usual sort of people were wandering through the aisles, buying toothpaste, lotions, aspirin, candy, and cheap clocks. A fat old blonde woman in an apron and cap quickly made up her sandwiches.

"Well, honey, who's going to win the war?" she said sociably as she peppered the chicken.

"Let's just hope Hitler doesn't," Madeline said.

"Yes, isn't he something? *Sieg Heil!* Ha, ha. *I* think the man's crazy. I've always said so, and this proves it." She handed Madeline the sandwiches. "Well, honey, so long as we keep out of it, what do we care who wins?"

Madeline bought an evening paper that offered gigantic headlines but no fresh news. Just to scan such a dramatic front page was novel fun. Though the war was happening so far away, Madeline felt a springtime quickening in her veins. A scent of freedom, of new action, rose from the headlines. The President had announced at once, very firmly, that America was staying out of it. But things were going to be mighty different from now on. That was inevitable! All her thoughts were about the letter she would write to her father, if only she could get this job.

Cleveland, feet on his desk again, a flirtatious smirk on his face, was telephoning. He nodded at Madeline and—as he went on coaxing some girl, in his warmly rumbling voice, to meet him at Toots Shor's restaurant—he wolfed the sandwich.

"Why don't you eat the other one?" Madeline said. "I'm not hungry."

"Are you sure? I don't want to rob you." He hung up and unwrapped her sandwich. "Ordinarily I don't eat much during the day, but with all this war talk—" He took a great bite and went on talking. "Thanks. I swear I'm as hungry as I get at funerals. Ever notice how famished you get at a funeral, Madeline? It's the sheer delight of being alive, I guess, while this other poor joker's just been buried in a dirty hole. Now listen, you want to work for me for three weeks, is that it? That'll be fine. It'll give me a chance to look over what's around in Personnel." He flourished a brown envelope at her. "Now then. Gary Cooper is at the St. Regis, Room 641. This is a sample *Who's in Town* script. Take it to him. We may get him for Thursday."

"Gary COOPER? You mean the MOVIE star?" Madeline in astonishment zoomed words like her mother.

"Who else? He may ask you questions about the show and about me. So listen and get this rundown in your head. We work without an audience in a little studio, very relaxed. It's a room with armchairs, books, and a rug, really nice, like a library in a home. It's the same room Mrs. Roosevelt uses for her show. We can do the script in extra big type, if he needs that. He can take five minutes or fifteen. The whole show runs an hour and a half. I started this show in Los Angeles back in '34 and did it there for three years. I called it *Over the Coffee* then. Maybe he heard it. Of course he may be too busy to go into all that. Anyway, act as though you've been with the show for a while."

Too dazzled and excited to talk, Madeline held out her hand for the envelope. Cleveland gave it to her, saying, "All set? Anchors aweigh. For Christ's sake, don't ask him for his autograph. Telephone me if there's any holdup. Don't fail to reappear."

Madeline blurted, "You must have had some very stupid girls working for you," and hurried out.

A maid opened the door of the hotel suite where Gary Cooper, in a gray suit, sat eating lunch at a wheeled table. The star rose, immensely tall and slim, smiling down at Madeline. He put on black-rimmed glasses, glanced over the script as he drank coffee, and asked questions. He was all business, the farthest thing from a bashful cowboy; he had the manner of an admiral. When she mentioned the *Over the Coffee* show he brightened. "Yes, I remember that." Almost at once, it seemed, she was out on the sunny street again, overwrought, thrilled to her bones. *"England mobilizes! Hitler smashes into Poland!"* the news vendor at the corner hoarsely chanted.

"Bless your little heart," Cleveland said as she came into the office. He was banging rapidly at a typewriter. "Cooper just called. He likes the idea and he's in." Ripping the yellow sheet out of the machine, he clipped it with others. "He remarked on what a nice girl you were. What did you say to him?"

"Hardly anything."

"Well, you did a good job. I'm off to interview him now. There's tomorrow's script. Do a smooth copy of the red-checked pages, then get the whole thing to mimeo instanter. Room 309A." Cleveland stepped into his shoes, straightened his tie, and threw on a rust-colored sports jacket. He scratched his heavy blond hair, and grinned at her, raising thick humorously arched eyebrows. She felt she would do anything for him. He was charming, she decided, rather than actually handsome. There was something infectiously jovial about him, a spark of devilish amusement in his lively blue eyes. She was a bit disappointed to see, when he stood up, that though he could not be more than thirty-one or so, his stomach bulged. But it didn't matter.

He paused at the door. "Do you mind working nights? You'll get paid overtime. If you come back here around eight-thirty tonight, you'll find Thursday's rough on my desk, with the Cooper spot."

"Mr. Cleveland, I haven't been hired yet."

"You have been. I just talked to Mrs. Hennessy. After you get that script to mimeo, go down and fill out your papers."

Madeline toiled for five hours to finish the script. She turned it in, messy though her work was, hoping it would not end her radio career then and there. At the employment office she learned she was starting at thirty-five dollars a week. It seemed a fortune. She took her aching back to the drugstore, made a quick dinner of a chocolate drink and a bacon and tomato sandwich, and walked back to CBS. Over the tall black Madison Avenue buildings, checkered with gold-lit windows, a misty full moon floated in a sunset sky. This day when Hitler's war began was turning out the most delightful in Madeline Henry's life.

On Cleveland's desk the interview with Gary Cooper now lay, a mass of crude typing, quick scrawls and red crayon cuts. The note clipped to it said: *Try to copy it all over tonight. See you around ten.* Madeline groaned; she was terribly tired.

She put in a call to Warren at the bachelor officers' quarters of the Pensacola flying school. He wasn't there, but an operator with a Southern accent like a vaudeville imitation offered to track him down. In the smoky newsroom, girls kept crisscrossing with long teletype strips or paper cups of coffee, men were talking loud and fast, and the typewriter din never stopped. Through the open door Madeline heard contradictory rumors: Poland was already collapsing, Hitler was on his way to Warsaw, Mussolini was flying to Berlin, the French were pressing England for another Munich deal, Hitler was offering to visit Chamberlain.

The telephone rang at ten o'clock and there was Warren

on the line, with music and laughter in the background. He was at the beach club, he said, at a moonlight dance on a terrace lined with palm trees. He had just met a marvellous girl, the daughter of a congressman. Madeline told him about the CBS job, and he seemed amused and impressed.

"Say, I've heard *Who's in Town,*" he said. "This fellow Hugh Cleveland has an interesting voice. What's he like?"

"Oh, very nice. Do you think it's all right? Will Dad be furious?"

"Matty, you'll be back at school in three weeks, before he even knows about it. Where will you stay? . . . Oh, yes, that's an all-women hotel, I know *that* one. Ha! Little Madeline on the town."

"You don't object?"

"Me? Why, I think it's fine. Just be a good girl, and all that. What's the word at CBS, Madeline? Is the war on? The scuttlebutt down here is that England is chickening out."

"Nothing but rumors here too, a dozen an hour. Is your date really the daughter of a congressman?"

"You bet, and she is a dish."

"Tough life you're leading. How's the flying coming?"

"I ground-looped on my second solo landing, but don't write Dad that. I'm doing better now. It's great."

"Good, you're still here," Cleveland said, walking into the office a few minutes after this conversation. With him was a tall beauty in a black straw hat much wider than Madeline's, and a gray silk dress. Her gardenia perfume was too strong for the small office. Cleveland glanced at Madeline's typed pages. "Need a little practice, eh?"

"I warm up as I go along." Her voice trembled. She cleared her throat.

"Let's hope so. Now look, do you by any chance know of an admiral named Preble? Is he some high mucky-muck?"

"Preble? Do you mean *Stewart* Preble?"

"Stewart Preble, exactly. Who is he?"

"Why, he's the Chief of Naval Operations."

"That's a big job, eh?"

Madeline was used to civilian ignorance of the armed

forces, but this shocked her. "Mr. Cleveland, there's no-body higher in the United States Navy."

"Fine. Then he's our boy. I just found out he's at the Warwick. We keep tabs on the big hotels, Madeline. Now let's get off a letter to him." He leaned on the edge of the desk and started to dictate. The yawning beauty crossed glorious legs, lit a cigarette, and leafed the *Hollywood Reporter*. Madeline desperately tried to keep up, but had to plead with him to go slower.

"Don't you know shorthand?"

"I can learn it quickly enough."

Cleveland glanced at his watch and at the beauty, who drooped her eyelids contemptuously at Madeline. Madeline felt like a worm. Cleveland rumpled his hair and shook his head. "Look, you know these Navy characters. Write him a letter, that's all. Invite him to come on the Thursday morning show. Mention Gary Cooper, if you want to. Sign my name, and take it over to the Warwick. Can you do that?"

"Certainly."

"Fine. Wendy and I want to catch a ten o'clock movie. She plays a bit in it. Say, this Preble fellow, does he know your father? How about that, Wendy? This kid's father is our Navy attaché in Berlin."

Wendy yawned.

Madeline said coldly, "Admiral Preble knows my father."

"Well, how about mentioning that, then?" He gave her his persuasive impish smile. "I'd really like to get him, Madeline. Admirals and generals are usually crappy guests. Too cautious and stiff to say anything interesting. But there's a war on, so for the moment, they're hot. See you in the morning. I go on at nine, you know, so get here not later than eight."

* * *

As he had told Madeline, Warren was dancing away this first night of the war in moonlight, with a congress-man's pretty daughter.

The moon floats out in space, some thirty diameters of the earth away, shining on the just and the unjust as the

cloud cover allows. It had lent dim but helpful light to the
columns of young Germans in gray uniforms, miles and
miles long, trudging across the Polish border. Now Europe
had rolled into the sun, giving the Germans better illumination to get on with the work, and the same moon was
bathing the Gulf of Mexico, and the terrace of Pensacola's
Harbor View Club. The German General Staff had carefully planned on the moonlight, but the silver glow fell on
Warren Henry and Janice Lacouture by a pleasant chance.

Everyone said it was the best club dance in years. The
big headlines, the excited radio broadcasts, had created a
pleasurable stir in flat quiet Pensacola. The student aviators
felt more important and the girls found them more glamorous; war was in the air, and however remote the combat,
these were warriors. The talk about the German attack
soon gave way to homier topics, however: the horse show,
the new base commander, recent flying accidents, recent
romances. Der Führer, for these happy people, remained
the queer hoarse German of the newsreels, with the wild
gestures and the funny moustache, who had managed to
start up a European mess, but who could scarcely menace
the United States just yet.

Lieutenant (junior grade) Henry took a different view.
The invasion really interested him, and that was how he
first caught the interest of Janice Lacouture. At the Academy he had excelled on the subject of the World War.
They sat in a far corner of the terrace in the moonlight
soon after they met, and instead of talking aviation or
making a pass at her, this student pilot told her about the
Schlieffen Plan to capture Paris, and the way von Moltke
had fatally tampered with it; about the feat of German
railroading that had made the Tannenberg victory possible; about the strategic parallels of 1914 and 1939. He
had begun with the usual aviator chitchat, which after years
of Pensacola dating stupefied Janice. But once they began
on the war and she allowed her own knowledge of history
and politics to show, he turned serious. It had been an
exciting talk, the sort in which lovers sometimes discover
each other without speaking a romantic word.

Despite the big Lacouture nose, a mark of French ancestry, and rather irregular front teeth, Janice was one of
the belles of Pensacola. Her mouth, skin, and hazel eyes

were lovely; her figure so striking that all men automatically stared at her as at a fire. She was tall, blonde, with a soft purring voice, and a very lively manner. Her family owned the largest house in the club estates. The Lacoutures were solidly rich, from two generations in the timbering that had destroyed the Gulf pine forests for hundreds of miles, and turned northern Florida into a sandy insect-swarming waste. Her father was a wonder in somnolent and self-satisfied Pensacola, the first Lacouture who had ever bestirred himself in politics.

In Washington Janice had grown up farseeing and sober. She had majored in economics and American history at George Washington University, and she was about to start law school. She wanted to marry a public man; a congressman, a senator, a governor; with luck, why not a future President? This was hard on the young men who fell for her beauty and chic. Janice was out for big game, and she had acquired a reputation for frostiness which amused her. The last thing she had expected was to meet anybody worth knowing during her enforced summer in Pensacola. And of all people, a naval aviator! Nevertheless there was something different about Warren Henry. He was oddly appealing, with those penetrating eyes, bony ramshackle frame, gray-sprinkled hair, and easy smile, with its hint of shrewdness and immorality. He acted as though he knew women far too well for an Annapolis honor student. This did not trouble her; it added tang to Warren.

They stopped talking after a while and danced close-hugged in the moonlight. The Pensacola onlookers began inquiring about the background of the lieutenant junior grade with the scar; for Warren's ground loop had given him a forehead wound requiring nine stitches. The naval aviators told each other with envy who the Lacouture girl was.

When Warren returned to the bachelor officers' quarters he found two telephone messages from Mrs. Tarrasch. This was his Baltimore divorcée; the woman of thirty for whom he had risked expulsion from the Academy; the woman with whom he had spent the afternoon in bed the day his parents had sailed off to Germany. In his third Academy year, he had come upon her as the lady hostess in a tea-room. Responding to a bold remark, she had agreed to see him after the restaurant closed. She was a clever little woman, with a hard-luck story about two beastly husbands; she was a reader, a lover of the arts, and hungrily passionate. Warren had grown attached to her, and had briefly even thought of marrying her, when she had once roused his jealousy by going off with an older man for a weekend. Byron had talked him out of that, rendering him the greatest service in the power of a brother. Helene Tarrasch wasn't a bad woman, simply a lonely one. If young officer candidates are to be kept by law from marrying, then the lively ones will find one or another Mrs. Tarrasch. Warren's worst mistake had been asking her to come to Pensacola, but he had been three years at sea. Now she was installed at the San Carlos Hotel as the receptionist in the main dining room.

But how obsolete she suddenly was! Not only because of Janice Lacouture; Hitler's invasion of Poland had given the future a shape. Warren believed the United States would be at war within a year. The prospect glittered. He might get killed. But he was going to fly in this war and if God allowed, he was going to get a good war record. Warren believed in God, but thought he must be much more broad-minded than the preachers made him out. A Being who could create something as marvellous as sex was not likely to be priggish about it; Warren was fond of saying that God had clearly given a man balls not for beauty but for use. Sitting in his bleakly furnished room with the old-fashioned high ceiling, trying to ignore his room-mate's snores, Lieutenant Henry looked out of the window at the quiet moonlit lawn in front of the BOQ and allowed his mind to run to golden postwar fantasies.

Politics attracted him. His avid history study had taught him that politicians were the leaders, military men only the mechanics, of war. Warren had closely observed politicians visiting the Academy and the fleet. Some were impressive men like his father, but more were glad-handers with worried eyes, phony smiles, and soft bellies. His father's ambition, he knew, was flag rank in the Navy. Warren wanted that, but why not dream of more? Janice Lacouture had brains. She had everything. A single day had transformed Warren Henry's life. In the morning the war had opened up the future; in the evening the perfect partner for that future had come out of nowhere.

He did a strange thing. He walked to the window, and looking out at the moon, he whispered a prayer. His youthful marching to church with his father had taken that much hold. "Let me have her, and let me pass this course and be a good naval aviator. I don't ask you to let me live, I know that's up to me, and the numbers, but if I do live and get through the war, then"—he smiled at the dark star-splashed sky—"well, then we'll see. All right?" Warren was charming God.

He went to bed without telephoning Mrs. Tarrasch. She was always ready for a call from him. But now she seemed to him like somebody he had known in high school.

. . . .

Shortly before six in the morning a ring from the embassy woke Victor Henry. The chargé was summoning an urgent staff meeting on the outbreak of the war.

Rhoda muttered and turned, throwing a naked white arm over her eyes. From a crack in the curtains a narrow sunbeam crossed the bed and dust motes danced in the wan light as Pug threw back the covers. Hitler was having good weather for the kickoff, Pug sleepily thought; just the bastard's luck! The invasion news was no great surprise. Since the Nazi-Soviet pact, the Polish crisis had been skidding downhill. At the big Argentine embassy supper the night before, everybody had noticed the absence of German military men and Foreign Office people, and had talked of war. One American correspondent had told Pug flatly that the invasion was on for three o'clock in the morning; *that* man had had the dope! The world had crossed a red line in time, and Victor Henry jumped out of bed to go to work in a new era. It wasn't his war, the one he had been training for all his life; not yet. But he was fairly sure it would be. Despite the absence of surprise, he was excited and moved.

In the library he switched on the radio, which seemed to take a long time to warm up, and opened the french windows. Birds sang in the sunny garden, whence a mild breeze, passing through a red-flowering shrub at the window, brought in a heavy sweet odor. The radio hummed and crackled and an announcer came on, not sounding much different than any Berlin announcer had during the past week, when the air had been full of the "incredible atrocities" perpetrated against Germans in Poland: rape, murder, disembowelling of pregnant women, cutting off of children's hands and feet. In fact, after this long diet of gruesome bosh, the news that the war had started seemed almost tame. The voice was just as strident, just as full of righteousness, describing the Führer's decision to march, as it had been in denouncing the atrocities.

The account of a Polish attack at Gleiwitz to capture a German radio station—the outrage which, according to the broadcast, had sent the Wehrmacht rolling two million strong into Poland "in self-defense"—was narrated with the same matter-of-fact briskness as the report of the plunge of the Germans across Polish soil, and of the surprise collapse of the Polish border divisions. Obviously an invasion of this magnitude had been laid on for a month or more and had been surging irreversibly toward Poland for days; the Polish "attack" was a silly hoax for childish minds. Victor Henry was getting used to Berlin Radio's foggy mixture of facts and lies, but the contempt of the Nazis for the intelligence of the Germans could still surprise him. The propaganda had certainly achieved one aim—to muffle the impact of the new war.

Rhoda came yawning in, tying her negligee, and cocking her head at the radio. "Well! So he really went and did it. Isn't that something!"

"Sorry it woke you. I tried to keep it low."

"Oh, the telephone woke me. Was it the embassy?" Pug nodded. "I thought so. Well, I guess I should be up for this. We're not going to get in it, are we?"

"Most unlikely. I'm not even sure England and France will go to bat."

"How about the children, Pug?"

"Well, Warren and Madeline are no problem. The word is that Italy won't fight, so Byron should be okay, too."

Rhoda sighed, and yawned. "Hitler's a very strange person. I've decided that. What a way to act! I liked his handshake, sort of direct and manly like an American's, and that charming bashful little smile. But he had strange eyes,

you know? Remote, and sort of veiled. Say, what happens
to our dinner for that tycoon from Colorado? What's his
name? Will that be off?"

"Dr. Kirby. He may not get here now, Rhoda."

"Dear, please find out. I have guests coming, and extra
help and food, you know."

"I'll do my best."

Rhoda said slowly, "World War Two . . . You know,
Time has been writing about 'World War Two' for months.
It always seemed so unreal, somehow. Now here it is, but
it still has a funny ring."

"You'll soon get used to it."

"Oh, no doubt. It's on now. I'm supposed to have lunch
with Sally Forrest. I'd better find out if that's still on. What
a mess! And my hair appointment—oh, no, that's tomorrow. Or is it? I don't function this time of the morning."

Because of the early meeting, Pug gave up his cherished
five-mile morning walk to the embassy, and drove there.
Berlin was, if anything, quieter than usual. There was a
Sunday morning look to the tree-lined avenues in mid-city,
a slackening of auto traffic, a scarcity of people on the
sidewalks. All the shops were open. Small trucks with
machine guns at the ready, manned by helmeted soldiers,
stood at some intersections, and along the walls of public
buildings workmen were piling sandbags. But it was all a
desultory business. The coffee shops were full of break-
fasters, and in the Tiergarten the early morning strollers—
nannies, children, elderly people—were out as usual for
the fine weather, with the vendors of toy balloons and ice
cream. Loudspeakers everywhere were blatting the news,
and an unusual number of airplanes went humming across
the sky. The Berliners kept looking at the sky and then at
each other with cynical sad grins. He remembered pictures
of the happy cheering Berliners crowding Unter den Linden at the start of the last war. Clearly the Germans were
going into this one in a different mood.

The embassy was a maelstrom of scared tourists and
would-be refugees, mainly old Jews. In the chargé's large
quiet office the staff meeting was sombre and short. No
special instructions from Washington had yet come in.
Mimeographed sheets of wartime regulations were passed

around. The chargé urged on everyone special care to preserve a correct tone of neutrality. If England and France came in, the embassy would probably look out for their people caught in Germany; a lot of lives might depend on appropriate American conduct at this touchy moment toward the truculent Germans. After the meeting Victor Henry attacked an in-tray stuffed with paper in his office, telling his yeoman to try to track down Dr. Palmer Kirby, the electrical engineer from Colorado who bore a "very important" designation from the Bureau of Ordnance.

Alistair Tudsbury telephoned. "Hullo! Would you like to hear the bad man explain all to the Reichstag? I can get you in to the press box. This is my last story from Berlin. I have my marching papers and should have left days ago, but got a medical delay. I owe you something for that glimpse of Swinemünde."

"You don't owe me anything, but I'll sure come."

"Good. He speaks at three. Pam will call for you at two. We're packing up like mad. I hope we don't get interned. It's this German food that's given me the gout."

The yeoman came in and laid a telegram on the desk.

"Tudsbury, can't I take you and Pamela to lunch?"

"No, no. No time. Many thanks. After this little unpleasantness, maybe. In 1949 or thereabouts."

Pug laughed. "Ten years? You're a pessimist."

He opened the telegram, and got a bad shock. DO YOU KNOW WHEREABOUTS YOUR SON BYRON AND MY NIECE NATALIE PLEASE WIRE OR CALL. It was signed: AARON JASTROW, with an address and telephone number in Siena.

Pug rang for the yeoman and handed him the telegram. "Try to get through to Siena, to this man. Also wire him: NO KNOWLEDGE. PLEASE WIRE LAST KNOWN WHEREABOUTS."

"Aye aye, sir."

He decided not to tell Rhoda. Trying to go back to work he found himself unable to comprehend the substance of simple letters. He gave up, and looked out of the window at the Berliners going their ways in bright sunshine. Open trucks full of soldiers in gray were snorting along the street in a long procession. The soldiers looked bored. A small silver blimp came floating across the clear blue sky, towing a sign advertising Odol toothpaste. He swallowed his worry as best he could, and attacked his in-basket again.

The telephone rang as he was leaving the office for lunch. He heard multilingual jabber and then a cultured American voice with a faint accent, "Commander Henry? Aaron Jastrow. It's very good of you to call."

"Dr. Jastrow, I thought I'd better tell you immediately that I don't know where Byron and your niece are. I had no idea they weren't in Siena with you."

"Well, I hesitated to wire you, but I thought you could help locate them. Two weeks ago they went to Warsaw."

"Warsaw!"

"Yes, to visit a friend in our embassy there."

"I'll get on it right away. Our embassy, you said?"

"Yes. The second secretary, Leslie Slote, is a former pupil of mine, a brilliant fellow. I imagine he and Natalie will get married one day." Pug scrawled the name. Jastrow coughed. "Excuse me. It was a risky trip to make, I guess, but they did set out before the pact. She's twenty-seven and has quite a will of her own. Byron volunteered to go with her. That's really why I refuse to worry. He's a very capable young man."

Victor Henry, dazed by the news, still found pleasure in this good word for Byron. Over the years he had not heard many. "Thanks. I'll wire you when I find out something. And if you get any word, let me know."

Jastrow coughed again. "Sorry. I have a touch of bronchitis. I remember the last war so well, Commander! It really wasn't long ago, was it? All this is giving me a strange, terribly sad feeling. Almost despairing. I hope we'll meet one day. It would give me pleasure to know Byron's father. He worships you."

The long table in Horcher's restaurant was a listening post, an information exchange, and a clearing house for little diplomatic deals. Today, the cheery clink of silverware in the crowded restaurant, the smell of roast meats, the loud animated talk, were much the same; but at this special table there were changes. Several attachés had put on their uniforms. The Pole—a big cheerful purple-faced man with great moustaches, who usually outdrank everybody—was gone. The Englishman was missing. The French attaché, in heavy gold braid, gloomed in his usual place.

The comical Dane, senior among them, white-haired and fat, still wore his white linen suit; but he was stiff and quiet. The talk was constrained. Warsaw Radio claimed the Germans were being thrown back, but nobody could confirm that. On the contrary, the flashes from their capitals echoed German boasts: victory everywhere, hundreds of Polish planes smashed on the ground, whole armies surrounded. Pug ate little and left early.

Pamela Tudsbury leaned against the iron grillwork in front of the embassy, near the line of sad-looking Jews that stretched around the block. She wore the gray suit of their morning walk on the *Bremen*. "Well," he said, as they walked side by side, "so the little tramp went."

She gave him a surprised, flattered look. "Didn't he ever! Here's our car. Directly after the speech we're off. We're flying to Copenhagen at six, and lucky to have the seats. They're like diamonds."

She drove the car in nervous zigzags through side streets, to get around a long convoy of tanks on a main boulevard.

"Well, I'm sorry to see you and your dad go," Pug said. "I'll sure miss your fireball style at the wheel. Where to next?"

"My guess is back to the USA. The governor's well liked there, and it'll be the number one spot, actually, with Berlin shut down."

"Pamela, don't you have a young man in London, or several, who object to your being so much on the move?" The girl—that was how he thought of her, which showed his own age—looked flushed and sparkling-eyed. The driving gestures of her small white hands were swift, sharp, and well controlled. She diffused an agreeably light peppery scent, like carnations.

"Oh, not at the moment, Commander. And the governor does need me since his eyes have got so bad. I like to travel, so I'm happy enough to—bless my soul. Look to your left. Don't be obvious about it."

Beside them, halted at the traffic light, Hermann Göring sat at the wheel of an open red two-seater, looking imperious and enormous. He wore a tan double-breasted business suit, with the flaring lapels that all his clothes displayed. The broad brim of his Panama hat was snapped down to the side and back, in an out-of-date, somewhat gangsterish American style. The fat man's swollen be-ringed fingers drummed the steering wheel, and he chewed at his very long upper lip.

The light changed. As the red car darted forward, the policeman saluted, and Göring laughed and waved his hand.

"How easy it would have been to shoot him," Pamela said.

Pug said, "The Nazis puzzle me. Their security precautions are mighty loose. Even around Hitler. After all, they've murdered a lot of people."

"The Germans adore them. The governor got in trouble over one of his broadcasts from a Party Day in Nuremberg. He said anybody could kill Hitler, and the free way he moved around showed how solidly the Germans were for him. Somehow this annoyed them."

"Pamela, I have a son I hope you'll meet when you're Stateside." He told her about Warren.

The girl listened with a crooked smile. "You've already mentioned him. Sounds too tall for me. What's he actually like? Is he like you?"

"Not in the least. He's personable, sharp as a tack, and very attractive to the ladies."

"Indeed. Don't you have another son?"

"Yes. I have another son." He hesitated, and then he briefly told Pamela what he had not yet told his wife—that Byron was somewhere in Poland in the path of the German invasion, accompanying a Jewish girl in love with another man. Pug said Byron had a cat's way of getting out of trouble, but he expected to owe a few more gray hairs to his son before this episode was over.

"He sounds like the one I might enjoy meeting."

"He's too young for you."

"Well, maybe not. I never do hit it quite right. There's the governor." Tudsbury stood on a corner, waving. His handshake was violent. He wore tweed far too heavy for the weather, and a green velour hat.

"Hello there, my dear fellow! Come along. Pam, be back at this corner at four and wait, won't you? This won't be one of his three-hour harangues. The bad man hasn't had much sleep lately."

A young German in a business suit met them, clicked

his heels at Pug, and took them past SS men, along corridors and up staircases, to the crowded little press balcony of the Kroll Opera House, which the Nazis used for Reichstag meetings. The stylized gold eagle perched on a wreathed swastika behind the podium, with gold rays shooting out to cover the whole wall, had a colossal look in photographs, but before one's eyes it was just garish and vulgar—a backdrop well suited to an opera house. This air of theatrical impermanence, of hastily contrived show, was a Nazi trademark. The new Reichstag, still under construction, was dully massive, to suit Hitler's taste, and the heavy Doric colonnades were obviously of stone, but the building made Pug think of a cardboard film setting.

Like most Americans, he could not yet take the Nazis, or indeed the Germans, very seriously. He thought they worked with fantastic industry at kidding themselves. Germany was an unstable old-new country, with heavy baroque charm in some places, and Pittsburgh-like splotches of heavy industry in others; and with a surface smear of huffing, puffing political pageantry that strove to instill terror and came out funny. So it struck him. Individually the Germans were remarkably like Americans; he thought it curious that both peoples had the eagle for their national emblem. The Germans were the same sort of businesslike go-getters: direct, roughly humorous, and usually reliable and able. Commander Henry felt more at home with them, in these points, than with the slower British or the devious talkative French. But in a mass they seemed to become ugly gullible strangers with a truculent streak; and if one talked politics to an individual German he tended to turn into such a stranger, a sneering belligerent Mr. Hyde. They were a baffling lot. In a demoralized Europe, Pug knew, the German hordes of marching men, well drilled and well equipped, could do a lot of damage; and they had slapped together a big air force in a hurry. He could well believe that they were now rolling over the Poles.

The deputies were streaming to their seats. Most of them wore uniforms, confusing in their variety of color and braid, alike mainly in the belts and boots. It was easy to pick out the military men by their professional bearing. The uniformed Party officials looked like any other politicians—jovial, relaxed, mostly grizzled or bald—stuffed into splashy costumes; and they obviously took Teutonic pleasure in the strut and the pomp, however uncomfortable jackboots might be on their flat feet, and gun belts on their bulging paunches. But today these professional Nazis, for all their warlike masquerade, looked less jaunty than usual. A subdued atmosphere pervaded the chamber.

Göring appeared. Victor Henry had heard of the fat man's quick costume changes; now he saw one. In a sky-blue heavily medalled uniform with flaring buff lapels, Göring crossed the stage and stood with feet spread apart, hands on belted hips, talking gravely with a deferential knot of generals and Party men. After a while he took his place in the Speaker's chair. Then Hitler simply walked in, holding the manuscript of his speech in a red leather folder. There was no heavy theatricalism, as in his Party rally entrances. All the deputies stood and applauded, and the guards came to attention. He sat in a front platform row among the generals and cabinet men, crossing and uncrossing his legs during Göring's brief solemn introduction.

Henry thought the Führer spoke badly. He was gray with fatigue. The speech rehashed the iniquity of the Versailles Treaty, the mistreatment of Germany by the other powers, his unending efforts for peace, and the bloody belligerence of the Poles. It was almost all in the first person and it was full of strange pessimism. He spoke of falling in battle and of the men who were to succeed him, Göring and Hess. He shouted that 1918 would not recur, that this time Germany would triumph or go down fighting. He was extremely hoarse. He took awhile to work up to the flamboyant gestures; but at last he was doing them all. Tudsbury whispered to Henry once, "Damn good handwork today," but Pug thought it was absurd vaudeville.

Nevertheless this time Hitler impressed him. Badly as he was performing, the man was a blast of willpower. All the Germans sat with the round eyes and tense faces of children watching a magician. The proud cynical face of Göring, as he sat perched above and behind Hitler, wore exactly the same rapt, awestruck look.

But the Führer himself was a bit rattled, Pug thought, by the gravity of what he was saying. The speech sounded like the hasty product of a few sleepless hours, intensely personal, probably all the truer for being produced under such pressure. This whining, blustering "I—I—I" apologia must be one of the oddest state documents in the history of warfare.

The Führer's face remained a comic one to Pug's American eyes: the long straight thrusting nose, a right triangle of flesh sticking out of a white jowly face, under a falling lock of black hair, over the clown moustache. He wore a field-gray coat today—his "old soldier's coat," he said in his speech—and it was a decidedly poor fit. But the puffy glaring eyes, the taut downcurved mouth, the commanding arm sweeps, were formidable. This queer upstart from the Vienna gutters had really done it, Henry thought. He had climbed to the combined thrones, in Tudsbury's phrase, of the Hohenzollerns and the Holy Roman Emperors, to try to reverse the outcome of the last war; and now he was giving the word. The little tramp was going! Pug kept thinking of Byron, somewhere in Poland, a speck of unimportance in this big show.

When they emerged on the street in balmy sunshine, Tudsbury said, "Well, what did you think?"

"I don't think he's quite big enough."

Tudsbury stopped in his tracks and peered at him. "Let me tell you, he's big. That's the mistake we've all made over here for much too long."

"He has to lick the world," Pug said. "What'll he do it with?"

"Eighty million armed and ravening Germans."

"That's just talk. You and the French have him outmanned and outgunned."

"The French," Tudsbury said. He added in a pleasanter tone, "There comes Pam. Let us drive you back to the embassy."

"I'll walk."

The car stopped under a waving red swastika banner. Tudsbury shook hands, blinking at Henry through glasses like bottle bottoms.

"We'll put up a show, Henry, but we may need help. Stopping this fellow will be a job. And you know it must be done."

"Tell them that in Washington."

"Don't you think I will? You tell them, too."

Henry said through the car window, "Good-bye, Pam. Happy landings."

She put out a cold white hand, with a melancholy smile. "I hope you'll see your son soon. I have a feeling you will." The Mercedes drove off. Lighting a cigarette, Pug caught on his hand the faint carnation scent.

A big lean man in a pepper-and-salt suit, with a soft hat on his knees, was sitting in Henry's outer office. Henry did not realize how big he was until he stood up; he was six feet three or so, and he stooped and looked a little ashamed of his height, like many overgrown men. "Commander Henry? I'm Palmer Kirby," he said. "If you're busy just throw me out."

"Not at all. Welcome. How'd you get here?"

"Well, it took some doing. I had to dodge around through Belgium and Norway. Some planes are flying, some aren't." Kirby had an awkward manner, and somewhat rustic western speech. His pale face was pitted, as though he had once been a bad acne sufferer. He had a long nose and a large loose mouth; altogether an ugly man, with clever wrinkled eyes and a sad look.

The yeoman said, "Commander, sir, couple of priority messages on your desk."

"Very well. Come in, Dr. Kirby." Pug sized him up with relief as a serious fellow out to get a job done; not the troublesome sort who wanted women, a good time, and an introduction to high-placed Nazis. A dinner and some industrial contacts would take care of Palmer Kirby.

WARSAW
9 . 1 . 39.
BYRON HENRY NATALIE JASTROW SCHEDULED LEAVE CRACOW TODAY FOR BUCHAREST AND ROME AM ENDEAVORING CONFIRM DEPARTURE. SLOTE.

This dispatch, in teletyped strips on a gray department blank, gave Henry an evil qualm. In the afternoon bulletins, Berlin Radio was claiming a victorious thrust toward Cracow after a violent air bombardment. The other message, a slip of the chargé d'affaires' office stationery, was an unsigned scrawled sentence: *Please see me at once.*

Kirby said he would be glad to wait. Victor Henry walked down the hall to the richly furnished suite of the ambassador where the chargé had held the staff meeting.

The chargé looked at him over his half-moon glasses and waved at an armchair. "So you were at the Reichstag, eh? I heard part of it. How did it strike you?"

"The man's punch-drunk."

The chargé looked surprised and thoughtful. "That's an odd reaction. It's true he's had quite a week. Incredible stamina, though. He undoubtedly wrote every word of that harangue. Rather effective, I thought. What was the mood there?"

"Not happy."

"No, they have their misgivings this time around, don't they? Strange atmosphere in this city." The chargé took off his glasses and leaned back in his large, leather-covered chair, resting the back of his head on interlaced fingers. "You're wanted in Washington."

"Sec Nav?" Pug blurted.

"No. State Department, German desk. You're to proceed to Washington by fastest available transportation, civilian or military, highest priority, prepared to stay not more than one week in Washington, and then to return to your post here. No other instructions. Nothing in writing. That's it."

For twenty-five years Victor Henry had not made a move like this without papers from the Navy Department, orders stencilled and mimeographed with a whole sheaf of copies to be left at stops on the way. Even his vacations had been "leaves" ordered by the Navy. The State Department had no jurisdiction over him. Still, an attaché had a queer shadowy status. His mind moved at once to executing the assignment. "If I have nothing in writing, how do I get air priorities?"

"You'll get them. How soon can you go?"

Commander Henry stared at the chargé, and then tried a smile. The chargé smiled back. Henry said, "This is somewhat unusual."

"You sent in an intelligence report, I'm given to understand, on the combat readiness of Nazi Germany?"

"I did."

"That may have something to do with it. In any case, the idea seems to be that you pack a toothbrush and leave."

"You mean today? Tonight?"

"Yes."

Pug stood. "Right. What's the late word on England and France?"

"Chamberlain's addressing Parliament tonight. My guess is the war will be on before you get back."

"Maybe it'll be over."

"In Poland, possibly." The chargé smiled, and seemed taken aback when Henry failed to be amused.

The commander found Dr. Kirby, long legs sprawled, reading a German industrial journal and smoking a pipe, which, with black-rimmed glasses, much enhanced his professorial look. "I'll have to turn you over to Colonel Forrest, our military attaché, Dr. Kirby," he said. "Sorry the Navy can't do the courtesies. I'll be leaving town for a week."

"Right."

"Can you give me an idea of what you're after?"

Dr. Kirby took from his breast pocket a typewritten sheet.

"Well, no problem here," Pug said, scanning it. "I know most of these people. I imagine Colonel Forrest does, too. Now, Mrs. Henry has a dinner laid on for you, Thursday evening. As a matter of fact"—Henry tapped the sheet— "Dr. Witten will be one of the guests."

"Won't your wife prefer to call it off? I'm not really much on dinner parties."

"Neither am I, but a German's a different person in his office than he is at a table after a few glasses of wine. Not a setup, you understand, but different. So dinners are useful."

Kirby smiled, uncovering large yellow teeth and quite changing his expression to a humorous, coarse, tough look. He flourished the trade journal. "They don't seem to be setups, any way you look at them."

"Yes and no. I've just come from the Reichstag. They've sure been a setup for this character Hitler. Well, let me take you across the hall to Colonel Forrest. It may be he and Sally will host the dinner. We'll see."

Driving home through the quiet Berlin streets Pug

thought less about the summons to Washington than of the immediate problem—Rhoda and how to handle her, and whether to disclose that Byron was missing. The trip to the United States might well prove a waste of time; to speculate on the reason for it was silly. He had been on such expeditions before. Somebody high up wanted certain answers in a hurry—answers that perhaps did not exist— and started burning up the wires. Once he had flown three thousand miles during a fleet exercise only to find, on his arrival aboard the "Blue" flagship in Mindanao, that his services were no longer required, because the battle problem had moved past the gunnery scoring.

She was not at home. By the time she got back, he was strapping shut his suitcases. "NOW what on earth?" she said breezily. Her hair was whirled and curled. They had been invited to an opera party that evening.

"Come out in the garden."

He told her, when they were well away from the house, about the strange Washington summons.

"Oh, lord. For how long?"

"Not more than a week. If the Clippers keep flying, I should be back by the fifteenth."

"When do you go? First thing tomorrow?"

"Well, by luck, they've got me on a plane to Rotterdam at eight tonight."

"Tonight!" Vexation distorted Rhoda's face. "You mean we don't even get to go to the opera? Oh, damn. And what about that Kirby fellow? Is that on or off? How can I entertain a person I haven't even met? What an aggravating mess!"

Pug said the Forrests would be co-hosting the Kirby dinner, and that the opera might not be on.

"On? Of course it's on. I saw Frau Witten at the hairdresser's. They're planning a marvellous supper, but naturally I won't be there. I'm not going to the opera unescorted. Oh, hell. And suppose England and France declare war? How about that, hey? That's going to be just peachy, me stranded alone in Berlin in the middle of a world war!"

"Rhoda, I'll get back in any case via Lisbon or Copenhagen. Don't worry. I'd like you to go ahead with the Kirby thing. BuOrd wants the red carpet out for him."

They were sitting on a marble bench beside the little fountain, where fat red fish disported in the late sunshine. Rhoda looked around at the close-clipped lawn, and said in a calmer tone, "All right. I've been planning cocktails out here. Those musicians who played at Peggy's tea are coming. It'll be nice at that. Sorry you'll miss it."

"Bill Forrest said nobody in this world puts on dinners like you."

Rhoda laughed. "Oh, well. A week goes by fast. Berlin's interesting now." A pair of black-and-yellow birds darted past them, swooped to a nearby tree, and perched carolling. "Honestly, though, would you believe there's a war on?"

"It's just starting."

"I know. Well, you'll see Madeline, anyway. And be sure to telephone Warren, that rascal never writes. I'm glad Byron's up in the Italian hills. *He'll* be all right, unless he shows up married to that Jewish girl. But he won't. Byron seems much crazier than he is." She put her hand in her husband's. "Inherits it from his mother, no doubt. Sorry I threw my little fit, dear. You know me."

Clasping her hand tight, Victor Henry decided not to upset Rhoda further with the news of Byron's disappearance. She could do nothing about it, after all, but fret vainly; and he guessed that whatever pickle Byron was in, he would get himself out of it. That had been the boy's history.

Pug flew off on schedule that evening to Rotterdam. Tempelhof Airport was transformed. The shops were dark. All the ticket counters save Lufthansa were shut down. On the field, the usual traffic of European airliners had vanished, and squat Luftwaffe interceptors stood in grim shadowy rows. But from the air, Berlin still blazed with all its electric lights, as in peacetime. He was pleased that Rhoda had decided to dress up and go to *Der Rosenkavalier,* since Frau Witten had found a tall handsome Luftwaffe colonel to escort her.

11

BYRON was changing a tire by the roadside when he was strafed. He and Natalie were out of Cracow and heading for Warsaw in the rust-pitted Fiat taxi, together with Berel Jastrow, the bridal couple, the bearded little driver, and his inconveniently fat wife.

Cracow on the morning of the invasion had smoked and flamed here and there, but the picturesque city had not been much damaged by the first German bombardment. Byron and Natalie had had a good if hurried look at its splendid churches and castles and its magnificent old square like Saint Mark's in Venice, as they drove around in cheery sunshine trying to find a way out. The populace was not in panic. The Germans were more than fifty miles away. Still, crowds moved briskly in the streets, and the railroad station was mobbed. Berel Jastrow somehow obtained two tickets to Warsaw. Byron and Natalie would not use them, hard as Berel tried to persuade them to, so he shipped off his wife and twelve-year-old daughter. Then he adroitly took them to one office after another, through little streets and unused doors and gates, seeking to send them safely away. He seemed to know everybody, and he went at the job with assurance, but he couldn't get Byron and Natalie out. Air traffic was finished. The Rumanian border was reported closed. Trains were still departing at unpredictable times, eastward toward Russia and north to Warsaw, with people hanging from windows and clinging to the locomotives. Otherwise there were the roads.

The bearded taxi driver Yankel and his wife, poor relatives of Berel, were willing to go anywhere. Berel had managed to get him an official paper, exempting the cab from being commandeered; but Yankel had small faith that it would work for long. The wife insisted on driving to her flat first, picking up all the food she had, her bedding, and her kitchenware, and roping them onto the car top. Berel thought the Americans should head for their embassy in Warsaw, three hundred kilometers away, rather than chance a dash to the border in the path of the German army. So this odd party set forth: seven of them jammed in an ancient rusty Fiat, with mattresses flapping on the roof, and copper pots rhythmically banging.

They stopped at night in a town where Jastrow knew some Jews. They ate well, slept on the floor, and were off again at dawn. They found the narrow tarred roads filling with people on foot and horse-drawn wagons laden with children, furniture, squawking geese, and the like. Some peasants drove along donkeys piled with household goods, or a few mooing cows. Marching soldiers now and then forced the car off the road. A troop of cavalry trotted by on gigantic dappled horses. The dusty riders chatted as they rode, strapping fellows with helmets and sabres glittering in the morning sun. They laughed, flashing white teeth, twirling their moustaches, glancing down with good-humored disdain at the straggling refugees. One company of foot soldiers went by singing. The clear weather, the smell of the ripening corn, made the travellers feel good, though the sun as it climbed got too hot. There were no combatants in sight on the long black straight road through yellow fields when a lone airplane dived from the sky, following the line of the road and making a hard stuttering noise. It flew so low that Byron could see the painted numbers, the black crosses, the swastika, the clumsy fixed wheels. The bullets fell on people, horses, and the household goods and children in the carts. Byron felt a burning and stinging in one ear. He was not aware of toppling into the dirt.

He heard a child crying, opened his eyes, and sat up. The blood on his clothes surprised him—big bright red stains; and he felt a warm trickle on his face. Natalie kneeled beside him, sponging his head with a sodden red handkerchief. He remembered the airplane. Across the road the crying girl clutched a man's leg, looking down at a woman lying in the road. Between sobs she screamed a few Polish words over and over. The man, a blond barefoot Pole in ragged clothes, was patting the child's head.

"What's that, what's she saying?"

"Are you all right, Byron? How do you feel?"

"Sort of dizzy. What's that little girl saying?"

Natalie looked strange. Her nose seemed pinched and long, her hair was in disorder, her face was livid and dirty, and her lipstick was cracked. She had a little of Byron's blood smeared on her forehead. "I don't know. She's hysterical."

Berel stood beside Natalie, stroking his beard. He said in French, "She keeps saying, 'Mama looks so ugly.'"

Byron got to his feet, propping one hand against the car's hot fender. His knees felt watery. "I think I'm okay. What does the wound look like?"

Natalie said, "I don't know, your hair is so thick. But it's bleeding a lot. We'd better get you to a hospital and have it stitched."

The driver, hastily tightening the bolts of the jacked-up wheel, smiled at Byron. Sweat rolled off his pallid nose and forehead into his beard. His wife and the bridal couple stood in the shade of the car, a look of shock on their faces, gazing at the sky, at the road, and at the crying girl. All down the road, wounded horses were plunging and screaming, and fowls from overturned carts were scampering helter-skelter, chased by children making a great noise. People were bending over the wounded or lifting them into carts, with much excited shouting in Polish. The sun burned down white-hot from a clear sky.

Byron walked uncertainly to the crying girl, followed by Natalie and Jastrow. The mother lay on her back. She had caught a bullet straight in the face. The big red hole was an especially bad sight because her fixed eyes were undamaged. Berel spoke to the father, who had a stupid, gentle face and a bushy yellow moustache. The man shrugged, holding the little girl close. Yankel's wife came and offered a red apple to the child, whose sobbing almost at once died away. She took the apple and bit it. The man sat by his dead wife, folding his dusty bare feet, and began to mutter, crossing himself, his shoes dangling around his neck.

Natalie helped Byron, who was very dizzy, into the car.

They drove on; Jastrow said there was a good-sized town three miles away, where they could tell the authorities about the wounded on the highway. The bride, who out of her wedding clothes was just a freckled girl with thick glasses, started to cry, and cried all the way to the town, repulsing her wan-faced husband and burying her face in the huge bosom of the driver's wife.

The town was undamaged, and the hospital, a small brown brick building beside a church, was quiet and cool inside. Several nurses and nuns went off in a truck after Jastrow told his story. Byron was led to a white-painted room full of surgical equipment and buzzing flies. A fat old doctor in a white jacket and patched canvas trousers sewed up his head. The shaving of the hair around the wound hurt worse than the actual stitching. He suggested to Natalie, when he came out, that she get her knee taped, for she was limping again.

"Oh, hell," Natalie said. "Let's go. We can still reach Warsaw tonight, Yankel says. I'll get it fixed there."

What with the tablespoon of pain-killer the doctor had given him, general weariness, and the aftermath of shock, Byron dozed. He did not know how much time had passed when he woke. On a broad cobbled square near a red brick railway station, two soldiers, rifles in hand, had halted the car. The station and a freight train were on fire; flame and black smoke billowed from their windows. Several buildings around the square were smashed or damaged; two were in flames. People were crowding around shops, passing out merchandise, carrying it off. Byron realized with surprise that this was looting. Across the square, men were pumping water at the burning railroad station from horse-drawn fire engines, such as Byron had not seen except in old silent movies. A crowd was watching all this as it would any peacetime excitement.

"What is it?" Byron said.

One of the soldiers, a big young blond fellow with a square red face marred by boils, walked around to the driver's window. A conversation ensued in Polish between the soldier, Yankel, and Jastrow. The soldier kept smiling with peculiar unpleasant gentleness, as though at children he disliked. His scrawny companion came and looked through the yellow glass, coughing continually over a cigarette. He spoke to the big one, addressing him repeatedly as Casimir. Byron knew by now that *Zhid* was a Polish epithet for "Jew"; *Zhid* was occurring often in this talk. Casimir addressed the driver again, and once reached in and gave his beard a caress, and then a yank, apparently displeased with his answers.

Jastrow muttered something to Natalie in Yiddish, glancing at Byron.

"What is it?" Byron said.

Natalie murmured, "There are good Poles and bad Poles, he says. These are bad."

Casimir gestured with his gun for everybody to get out. Jastrow said to Byron, "Dey take our automobile."

Byron had a rotten headache. His ear had been nicked by the bullet, and this raw patch burned and throbbed, hurting him more than the stitched head wound. He had vague cramps, having eaten old scraps and drunk dirty water in the past two days, and he was still doped by the medicine. He had seldom felt worse. "I'll try talking to Redface, he seems to be in charge," he said, and he got out of the car.

"Look," he said, approaching the soldiers, "I'm an American naval officer, and I'm returning to the embassy in Warsaw, where they're expecting us. This American girl"—he indicated Natalie—"is my fiancée, and we've been visiting her family. These people are her family."

The soldiers wrinkled their faces at the sound of English, and at the sight of Byron's thick blood-stained bandage. "*Amerikanetz?*" the big one said.

Jastrow, at the car window, translated Byron's words.

Casimir scratched his chin, looking Byron up and down. The condescending smile made its reappearance. He spoke to Jastrow, who translated shakily into French, "He says no American Navy officer would ever marry a Jew. He doesn't believe you."

"Tell him if we're not in Warsaw by tonight the American ambassador will take action to find us. And if he's in doubt let's go to a telephone and call the embassy."

"Passport," Casimir said to Byron, after Jastrow translated. Byron produced it. The soldier peered at the green cover, the English words, the photograph, and at Byron's face. He spoke to his coughing companion and started to walk off, beckoning to Byron.

"Briny, don't go away," Natalie said.

"I'll be back. Keep everybody quiet."

The smaller soldier leaned against the car fender and lit another cigarette, hacking horribly and grinning at Natalie.

Byron followed Casimir down a side street, into a two-story stone building festooned outside with official bulletins and placards. They walked past rooms full of files, counters, and desks to a frosted glass door at the end of the hall. Casimir went inside, and after about ten minutes poked his head out and beckoned to the American.

A pudgy man in a gray uniform, smoking a cigarette in an amber holder, sat behind the big desk at the window; an officer, to judge by his colored tabs and brass ornaments. The passport was open before the man. He sipped tea from a glass as he glanced at it, and tea dripped on Byron's picture. In the narrow grimy room, metal files and bookshelves were shoved in a corner, with dirty legal tomes tumbled about.

The officer asked him if he spoke German. That was the language they used, though both were bad at it. He made Byron tell his story again and asked him how an American naval officer happened to be mixed up with Jews, and how he came to be wandering around Poland in wartime. When his cigarette was consumed to the last quarter inch, he lit another. He queried Byron hard about the head injury, and smiled sourly, raising his eyebrows at the account of strafing on the highway. Even if this were all true, he commented, Byron had been acting foolishly and could easily get himself shot. He wrote down Byron's answers with a scratchy pen, in long silent pauses between the questions; then clipped the scrawled sheets to the passport, and dropped them into a wire basket full of papers.

"Come back tomorrow afternoon at five o'clock."

"I can't. I'm expected in Warsaw tonight."

The officer shrugged.

Byron wished his temples would stop throbbing. It was hard to think, especially in German, and his vision was blurry, too. "May I ask who you are, and by what right you take my passport, and by what right this soldier tried to take our car?"

The unpleasant smile that Casimir had displayed—Casimir stood by the desk all through the interview with a wooden look—now appeared on the officer's face. "Never mind who I am. We have to make sure who you are."

"Then telephone the American embassy and ask for Leslie Slote, the political secretary. That won't take long."

The officer drank off his cold tea and began signing papers with a mutter in Polish to Casimir, who took Byron's arm, pushed him out of the room, and led him back to the car.

The station and freight cars were pouring steamy white smoke, and a smell of wet burned wood filled the street. The looting was over. Policemen stood in front of the wrecked shops. The faces of the three women looked out tensely through the yellowed car glass at Byron. Casimir spoke to his companion, who caused the bride to shrink from the window by knocking on the glass and winking at her; then they went off.

Byron told Natalie what had happened and she recounted it in Yiddish to the others. Jastrow said they could stay the night in the home of a friend in this town. When Byron got in behind the wheel, Yankel seemed glad to retire to the back seat beside his wife.

Following Berel's directions, Byron maneuvered to a crossroad. A large arrow pointing left, down a road through fields stacked with corn sheaves, read: WARSAW, 95 KM. Jastrow told him to turn right, along a road which led past small houses toward an unpainted wooden church. Byron, however, shifted gears and swooped left, driving out into the fields. "That's a bad outfit back there," he said to Natalie. "We'd better keep going."

Natalie exclaimed, "Byron, stop, don't be crazy! You *can't* drive around among these people without your passport."

"Ask Berel what he thinks."

There was colloquy in Yiddish. "He says it's much too dangerous for you. Go back."

"Why? If we run into any trouble, I'll say I lost the passport in a bombardment. I've got this hole in my head." Byron had the accelerator pressed to the floor, and the overloaded bumping old Fiat was doing its best speed, about thirty miles an hour. Overhead the pots were making a great din, and Byron had to shout. "Ask him if it isn't safest for you and for the rest to get the hell out of here."

He felt a touch on his shoulder and glanced around. Berel Jastrow's bearded face was fatigued and ashen, and he was nodding.

It took them two days to go the ninety-five kilometers. While it was happening it seemed to Byron a saga that he would be telling his grandchildren, if he lived through it. But so much happened afterward to him that his five-day drive from Cracow to Warsaw soon became a garbled fading memory. The breakdown of the water pump that halted them for half a day on a deserted back road in a forest, until Byron, tinkering with it in a daze of illness, to his astonishment got it to work; the leak in the gas tank that compelled them to take great risks to buy more; the disappearance of the hysterical bride from the hayfield where they spent one night, and the long search for her (she had wandered to another farm, and fallen asleep in a barn); the two blood-caked boys they found asleep by the roadside, who had a confused story of falling out of a truck and who rode the last thirty kilometers to Warsaw sitting on wooden slats on the sizzling hood of the Fiat—all this dimmed. But he always remembered how ungodly sick to the stomach he was, and the horrible embarrassment of his frequent excursions into the bushes; Natalie's unshakable good cheer as she got hungrier, dirtier, and wearier; and above all, never to be forgotten, he remembered the hole in his breast pocket where the passport had been, which seemed to throb more than the gashes in his ear and his scalp, because he now knew that there were Polish officers capable of ordering him taken out and shot, and soldiers capable of doing it. Following Jastrow's directions, he wound and doubled on stony, muddy roads to avoid towns, though it lengthened the journey and played hell with the disintegrating car.

They arrived in the outskirts of Warsaw in the chill dawn, crawling among hundreds of horse-drawn wagons. All across the stubbled fields, women, children, and bent graybeards were digging trenches and putting up tank barriers of tangled iron girders. The buildings cluttered against the pink northeast horizon looked like the heavenly

Jerusalem. The driver's immense wife, squeezed against Natalie for days and nights in an intimacy the girl had never known with another human being, smelling more and more like an overheated cow, embraced Natalie and kissed and hugged her. It took three more hours before the groaning, clanking car reached the embassy. The two boys jumped off the hood and ran away down a side street. "Go ahead, go in quickly," the mushroom dealer said to Natalie in Yiddish, stepping out of the car to kiss her. "Come and see me later if you can."

When Byron said good-bye, Berel Jastrow would not let his hand go. He clasped it in both his hands, looking earnestly into the young man's face. *"Merci. Mille fois merci.* Tousand times tank you. America save Poland, yes, Byron? Save de vorld."

Byron laughed. "That's a big order, but I'll pass it on, Berel."

"What did he say?" Berel asked Natalie, still holding Byron's hand. When she told him Berel laughed too, and then astonished Byron by giving him a bear hug and a brief scratchy kiss.

A lone marine stood watch at the closed gates. Gray sandbags lined the yellow stucco walls, ugly X-shaped wooden braces disfigured the windows, and on the red tile roof an enormous American flag had been painted. All this was strange, but strangest was the absence of the long line of people. Nobody but the marine stood outside. The United States embassy was no longer a haven or an escape hatch.

The guard's clean-scraped pink suspicious face brightened when he heard them talk. "Yes, ma'am, Mr. Slote sure is here. He's in charge now." He pulled a telephone from a metal box fastened on the gate, regarding them curiously. Natalie put her hands to her tumbled hair, Byron rubbed his heavy growth of red bristles, and they both laughed. Slote came running down the broad stairway under the embassy medallion. "Hello! God, am I ever glad to see you two!" He threw an arm around Natalie and kissed her cheek, staring the while at Byron's dirty blood-stained head bandage. "What the devil? Are you all right?"

"I'm fine. What's the news? Are the French and British fighting?"

"Have you been that out of touch? They declared war Sunday, after fussing at Hitler for three days to be nice and back his army out of Poland. I'm not aware that they've done anything since but drop leaflets."

Over a wonderful breakfast of ham and eggs, the first hot food they had eaten in days, they described their journey. Byron could feel his racked insides taking a happy grip on this solid boyhood fare and calming down. He and Natalie ate from trays on the ambassador's broad desk. Washington had ordered the ambassador and most of the staff out of Poland when the air bombing began; as the only bachelor on the number three level, Slote had been picked to stay. The diplomat was appalled at Byron's tale of abandoning his passport. "Ye gods, man, in a country at war! It's a marvel you weren't caught and jailed or shot. That you're a German agent would be far more plausible than the real reason you've been wandering around. You two are an incredible pair. Incredibly lucky, too."

"And incredibly filthy," Natalie said. "What do we do now?"

"Well, you're just in it, my love. There's no getting out of Poland at the moment. The Germans are overrunning the countryside, bombing and blasting. We have to find you places to stay in Warsaw until, well, until the situation clarifies itself one way or another. Meantime you'll have to dodge bombs like the rest of us." Slote shook his head at Byron. "Your father's been worrying about you. I'll have to cable him. We still have communication via Stockholm. He'll let A.J. know that Natalie's at least found and alive."

"I am dying for a bath," Natalie said.

Slote scratched his head, then took keys from his pocket and slid them across the desk. "I've moved in here. Take my apartment. It's on the ground floor, which is the safest, and there's a good deep cellar. When I was there last the water was still running and we had electricity."

"What about Byron?"

Byron said, "I'll go to the Methodist House."

"It's been hit," Slote said. "We had to get everybody out, day before yesterday."

"Do you mind," Natalie said, "if he stays with me?"

Both men showed surprise and embarrassment, and Byron said, "I think my mother would object."

"Oh, for crying out loud, Byron. With all the running into the bushes you and I have been doing and whatnot, I don't know what secrets we have from each other." She turned to Slote. "He's like a loyal kid brother, sort of."

"Don't you believe her," Byron said wearily. "I'm a hot-blooded beast. Is there a YMCA?"

"Look, I don't mind," Slote said, with obvious lack of enthusiasm. "There's a sofa in the sitting room. It's up to Natalie."

She scooped up the keys. "I intend to bathe and then sleep for several days—between bombings. How will we ever get out of Poland, Leslie?"

Slote shrugged, cleared his throat, and laughed. "Who knows? Hitler says if the Poles don't surrender, Warsaw will be levelled. The Poles claim they've thrown the Wehrmacht back and are advancing into Germany. It's probably nonsense. Stockholm Radio says the Nazis have broken through everywhere and will surround Warsaw in a week. The Swedes and the Swiss here are trying to negotiate a safe-conduct for foreign neutrals through the German lines. That's how we'll all probably leave. Till that comes through, the safest place in Poland is right here."

"Well then, we did the sensible thing, coming to Warsaw," Natalie said.

"You're the soul of prudence altogether, Natalie."

As the trolleybus wound off into the smaller residential streets, Byron and Natalie saw more damage than they had in Cracow—burned-out or smashed houses, bomb holes in the pavement, an occasional rubble-filled street roped off—but by and large Warsaw looked much as it had in peacetime, less than a week ago, though now seemingly in a bygone age. The threatened German obliteration was not yet happening, if it ever would. The other passengers paid no attention to Byron's bandage or growth of beard. Several of them were bandaged and most of the men were bristly. A thick human smell choked the car.

Natalie said when they got off, "Ah—*air!* No doubt we smell just like that, or worse. I must bathe at once or I'll go mad. Somehow on the road I didn't care. Now I can't stand myself another minute."

Slivers of sunlight through the closed shutters made Slote's flat an oasis of peaceful half-gloom. Books lining the sitting room gave it a dusty library smell. Natalie flipped switches, obviously quite at home in the place. "Want to wash up first?" she said. "Once I get in that tub there'll be no moving me for hours. There's only cold water. I'm going to boil up some hot. But I don't know. Maybe you should find a hospital, first thing, and get your head examined."

After the phrase was out of her mouth, it struck them both as funny. They laughed and laughed and couldn't stop laughing. "Well, while we still both stink," Natalie gasped, "come here." She threw her arms around him and kissed him. "You damned fool, abandoning your passport to protect some dopey Jews."

"My head's all right," Byron said. The touch of the girl's mouth on his was like birdsong, like flowers, exhausted and filthy though they both were. "I'll clean up while you boil your water."

As he shaved she kept coming into the bathroom emptying steaming kettles into the cracked yellow tub, humming a polonaise of Chopin. The music had introduced the noon news broadcast, in which Byron had understood only a few place-names: towns and cities more than halfway in from the western and southern borders toward Warsaw.

"My God, how pale you are, Briny," she said, inspecting his clean-shaven face, nicked here and there by the cold-water shave, "and how young! I keep forgetting. You're just a boy."

"Oh, don't exaggerate. I've already flunked out of graduate school," Byron said. "Isn't that a mature thing to do?"

"Get out of here. I'm diving into that tub."

An unmistakable wailing scream sounded outside about half an hour later. Byron, on the sofa, dozing over an old issue of *Time,* snapped awake and took binoculars from his suitcase. Scarlet-faced and dripping, Natalie emerged from the bathroom, swathed in Slote's white terry-cloth robe. "Do we have to go to the cellar?"

"I'll have a look."

The street was deserted: no cars, no people. Byron scanned the heavens from the doorway with his naked eye, and after a moment saw the airplanes. Sailing forth from a white cloud, they moved slowly across the sky through a scattering of black puffs. He heard grumbling muffled thumps far away, like thunder without reverberations. As he stepped out on the sidewalk, binoculars to his eyes, a whistle shrieked. Down the street a little man in a white helmet and white armband was waving angrily at him. He dropped back into the doorway, and found the planes with the glasses: black machines, bigger than the one that had wounded him, with a different thick shape but painted with the same crosses and swastikas. The fuselages were very long; in the rainbow-rimmed field of the glasses they looked a bit like small flying freight cars.

Natalie was combing her hair by candlelight at a hallway mirror. The electricity was off. "Well? Is that bombing?"

"It's bombing. They're not headed this way, the planes I saw."

"Well, I don't think I'd better get back in the tub."

The thumps became louder. They sat on the sofa, smoking cigarettes and looking at each other.

Natalie said in a shaky voice, "It's sort of like a summer electric storm coming toward you. I didn't picture it like this."

A distant whistling noise became louder, and a sudden crash jarred the room. Glass broke somewhere, a lot of glass. The girl uttered a small shriek, but sat still and straight. Two more close explosions came, one right after the other. Through the shutters harsh noises echoed from the street: shouts and screams, and the grumble of falling brick walls.

"Briny, shall we run for the cellar?"

"Better sit tight."

"Okay."

That was the worst of it. The thumps went on for a

while, some distant and faint, some closer; but there were no more explosions that could be felt in the air, in the floor, in the teeth. They died off. In the street outside bells clanged, running feet trampled on the cobblestones, men yelled. Byron pulled aside curtains, opened a window, and blinked in the strong sunshine at the sight of two smashed burning houses down the street. People were milling around scattered chunks of masonry and flaming wreckage, carrying pails of water into the tall thick red flames.

Natalie stood beside him, gnawing her lips. "Those horrible German bastards. Oh my God, Briny, look. Look!" Men were starting to carry limp figures out of the clouds of smoke. One tall man in a black rubber coat held a child dangling in each arm. "Can't we help? Can't we do something?"

"There must be volunteer squads, Natalie, that neutrals can work in. Nursing, rescue, cleanup. I'll find out."

"I can't watch this." She turned away. Barefoot, a couple of inches lower without her heels, wrapped in the oversize robe, the eyes in her upturned unpainted face shiny with tears, Natalie Jastrow looked younger and much less formidable than usual. "It was so close. They may kill both of us."

"We probably should dive for the cellar next time we hear the siren. Now we know."

"I got you into it. That keeps eating at me. Your parents in Berlin must be sick with worry about you, and—"

"My people are Navy. It's all in the day's work. As for me, I'm having fun."

"Fun?" She scowled at him. "What the devil? Don't talk like a child."

"Natalie, I've never had a more exciting time, that's all. I don't believe I'm going to get killed. I wouldn't have missed this for anything."

"Byron, hundreds of people have probably died out there in the last half hour! Didn't you see the kids they pulled out of the building?"

"I saw them. Look, all I meant was—" Byron hesitated because what he had meant was that he was having fun.

"It's just such a stupid, callous thing to say. Something a German might say." She hitched the robe around her closer. "Fun! Leslie thinks *I'm* screwy. You're really peculiar."

With an unfriendly headshake at him, she stalked to the bathroom.

12

COMING back to Washington from Berlin jolted Pug, as had his return in 1931 from Manila to a country sunk in the Great Depression. This time what struck him was not change, but the absence of it. After the blaring pageantry and war fevers of Nazi Germany, it was a bit like coming out of a theatre showing a technicolor movie into a gray quiet street. Even Rotterdam and Lisbon had been agog with war reverberations. Here, where the Capitol dome and the Washington Monument shimmered in ninety-degree heat, people were plodding apathetically about their business. The roaring invasion of Poland, already looking like one of the historic conquests of all time, was as remote from this city as a volcanic eruption on Mars.

He sat in the dining room of the Army and Navy Club, breakfasting on kippers and scrambled eggs. His arrival the day before had proved a puzzling letdown. The man in the German section of the State Department to whom he had reported—a very minor personage, to judge by his small office, shoddy furniture, and lack of a window—had told him to expect a call in the morning; nothing more.

"Well, well, our cookie-pushing friend!"

"Where's your striped pants, Pug?"

Grinning down at him were three classmates: Digger Brown, Paul Munson, and Harry Warendorf. Though Pug had not encountered any one of them for years, they joined him and began exchanging jokes and gossip as though they saw each other every day. He looked at them with interest, and they at him, for gain of fat and loss of hair. Munson had learned to fly way back in 1921, and now he was air operations officer of the *Saratoga*. Digger Brown, Pug's old room-mate, had an assured if pasty look. Well he might, the first officer of the class to make exec of a battleship! Warendorf, the brain of the three, was a hard-luck man like Tollever. Following orders of his commodore, he had piled a destroyer on the rocks off the California coast in a fog, with half a dozen others. He had fallen into minesweepers, and there he was still.

Under the rough banter about his pink-tea job, they were curious and respectful. They asked remarkably naïve questions about the European war. All of them assumed that the Nazis were twice as strong in the field as they were and that the Allies were all but impotent. It struck Pug again how little Americans knew of Europe, for all the flood of lurid newspaper and magazine stories about the Nazis; and how little most men ever knew beyond their constricted specialties.

"Why the hell are the Germans running away with it in Poland, Pug, if all this is so?" Warendorf said. They had been listening, attentive but unconvinced, to his estimate of the opposed forces.

"That's anybody's guess. I'd say surprise, superior matériel on the spot, concentration of force, better field leadership, better political leadership, better training, a professional war plan, and probably a lot of interior rot, confusion, and treason behind the Polish lines. Also the French and British seem to be sitting on their duffs through the best strategic opportunity against Hitler they'll ever have. You can't win a game if you don't get out on the field."

A page boy called him to the telephone. Briskly, an unfamiliar voice said, "Commander Henry? Welcome to these peaceful shores. I'm Carton. Captain Russell Carton. I think we were briefly at the War College together, fighting the Japs on a linoleum checkerboard floor."

"That's right, Captain, 1937. The Japs beat hell out of us, as I recall." Pug did his best to suppress the astonishment in his tones. Russell Carton was the name of President Roosevelt's naval aide.

The voice chuckled. "I hope you've forgotten that I was the admiral who blew the engagement. When shall I pick you up? Our appointment's at noon."

"How far do we have to go?"

"Just around the corner. The White House. You're seeing the President. . . . Hello? Are you there?"

"Yes, sir. Seeing the President, you said. Do I get a briefing on this?"

"Not that I know of. Wear dress whites. Suppose I pick you up at eleven-thirty."

"Aye aye, sir."

He went back to his table and ordered more coffee. The others asked no questions. He kept his face blank, but it was hard to fool these old friends. They knew it was odd that he was back from Berlin so soon. They probably guessed that he had received a startling call. That didn't matter. Munson said, "Pug, don't you have a boy in Pensacola? I'm flying down there day after tomorrow to drop some pearls of wisdom about carrier landings. Come along."

"If I can, Paul. I'll call you."

Pug was sorry when they left. The shoptalk about a combat exercise they were planning had brought back the smell of machinery, of sea air, of coffee on the bridge. Their gossip of recent promotions and assignments, their excitement over the quickening world events and the improving chances for action and glory—this was his element, and he had been out of it too long. He got a haircut, brilliantly shined his own shoes, put a fresh white cover on his cap, donned his whites and ribbons, and sat in the lobby for an eternally long forty-five minutes, puzzling over the imminent encounter with Franklin Roosevelt, and dreading it. He had met him before.

A sailor came through the revolving door and called his name. He rode the few blocks to the White House in a gray Navy Chevrolet, dazedly trying to keep up chitchat with Captain Carton, a beefy man with a crushing handgrip on whose right shoulder blue-and-gold "loafer's loops" blazed. This marked him as a presidential aide, to those who knew; otherwise staff aiguillettes belonged on the left shoulder. Pug kept step with the captain through the broad public rooms of the White House, along corridors, up staircases. "Here we are," Carton said, leading him into a small room. "Wait a moment." The moment lasted twenty-seven minutes. Pug Henry looked at old sea-battle engravings on the wall, and out of the window; he paced, sat in a heavy brown leather chair, and paced again.

He was wondering whether the President would remember him, and hoping he wouldn't. In 1918, as a very cocky Assistant Secretary of the Navy, Franklin Roosevelt had crossed to Europe on a destroyer. The wardroom officers, including Ensign Henry, had snickered at the enormously tall, very handsome young man with the famous family name, who made a great show of using nautical terms and bounding up ladders like a sea dog, while dressed in outlandish costumes that he kept changing. He was a charmer, the officers agreed, but a lightweight, almost a phony, spoiled by an easy rich man's life. He wore pince-nez glasses in imitation of his great relative, President Teddy Roosevelt, and he also imitated his booming manly manner; but a prissy Harvard accent made this heartiness somewhat ridiculous.

One morning Ensign Henry had done his usual workout on the forecastle, churning up a good sweat. Because there was a water shortage, he had hosed himself down from a saltwater riser on the well deck. Unfortunately the ship was pitching steeply. The hose had gotten away from him and spouted down into the hatchway to the wardroom, just as Roosevelt was coming topside in a gold-buttoned blazer, white flannel trousers, and straw hat. The costume had been wrecked, and Pug had endured a fierce chewing out by his captain and the dripping Assistant Secretary of the Navy.

A door opened. "All right. Come on in, Pug," Captain Carton said.

The President waved at him from behind the desk. "Hello there! Glad to see you!" The warm commanding aristocratic voice, so recognizable from radio broadcasts, jarred Pug with its very familiarity. He got a confused impression of a grand beautiful curved yellow room cluttered with books and pictures. A gray-faced man in a gray suit slouched in an armchair near the President. Franklin Roosevelt held out a hand: "Drop your bonnet on the desk, Commander, and have a chair. How about some lunch? I'm just having a bite." A tray with half-eaten scrambled eggs, toast, and coffee stood on a little serving table by the President's swivel chair. He was in shirt-sleeves and wore no tie. Pug had not seen him, except in newsreels and photographs, in more than twenty years. His high coloring was unchanged, and he was the same towering man, gone gray-headed, much older and very much heavier; and though he had the unmistakable lordly look of a person in great office, a trace remained in the upthrust big jaw of the youthful conceit that had made the ensigns on the *Davey* snicker. His eyes were sunken, but very bright and keen.

"Thank you, Mr. President. I've eaten."

"By the way, this is the Secretary of Commerce, Harry Hopkins."

The gray-faced man gave Henry a brief winning smile, with a light tired gesture that made a handshake unnecessary.

The President looked archly at Victor Henry, his big heavy head cocked to one side. "Well, Pug, have you learned yet how to hang onto a saltwater hose at sea?"

"Oh, gawd, sir." Pug put a hand to his face in mock despair. "I've heard about your memory, but I hoped you'd forgotten *that*."

"Ha, ha, ha!" The President threw his head back. "Harry, this young fellow absolutely ruined the best blue serge blazer and straw hat I ever owned, back in 1918. Thought I'd forget that, did you? Not on your life. Now that I'm Commander-in-Chief of the United States Navy, Pug Henry, what have you got to say for yourself?"

"Mr. President, the quality of mercy is mightiest in the mightiest."

"Oh, ho! Very good. *Very* good. Quick thinking, Pug." He glanced at Hopkins. "Ha, ha, ha! I'm a Shakespeare lover myself. Well said. You're forgiven."

Roosevelt's face turned serious. He glanced at Captain Carton, who still stood at attention near the desk. The aide made a smiling excuse and left the room. The President ate a forkful of eggs and poured himself coffee. "What's going on over there in Germany, Pug?"

How to field such a facetious question? Victor Henry

took the President's tone. "I guess there's a war on of sorts, sir."

"Of sorts? Seems to me a fairly honest-to-goodness war. Tell me about it from your end."

Victor Henry described as well as he could the peculiar atmosphere in Berlin, the playing down of the war by the Nazis, the taciturn calm of the Berliners. He mentioned the blimp towing a toothpaste advertisement over the German capital on the first day of the war—the President grunted at that and glanced toward Hopkins—and the pictures in the latest *Berliner Illustrierte Zeitung* which he had picked up in Lisbon, showing happy German crowds basking at the seashore and frolicking in folk dances on village greens. The President kept looking at Hopkins, who had what Victor Henry thought of as a banana face: long, meager, and curved. Hopkins appeared sick, possibly feverish, but his eyes were thoughtful and electrically alive.

Roosevelt said, "Do you suppose he'll offer peace when he finishes with Poland? Especially if he's as unprepared as you say?"

"What would he have to lose, Mr. President? The way things look now, it might work."

The President shook his head. "You don't know the British. Not that they're any better prepared."

"I'll admit I don't, sir."

For the first time, Hopkins spoke, in a soft voice. "How well do you know the Germans?"

"Not at all well, Mr. Secretary. They're hard people to make out. But in the end there's only one thing you have to know about the Germans."

"Yes? What's that?"

"How to lick them."

The President laughed, the hearty guffaw of a man who loved life and welcomed any chance to laugh. "A warmonger, eh? Are you suggesting, Pug, that we ought to get into it?"

"Negative in the strongest terms, Mr. President. Not unless and until we have to."

"Oh, we'll have to," Roosevelt said, hunching over to sip coffee.

This struck Victor Henry as the most amazing indiscre-

tion he had heard in his lifetime. He could hardly believe
the big man in shirt-sleeves had said the words. The newspapers and magazines were full of the President's ringing
declarations that America would stay out of the war.
Roosevelt went blandly on with a compliment about
Combat Readiness of Nazi Germany, which he said he
had read with great interest. His next questions showed
that he had retained little of the analysis. His grasp of the
important strategic facts about Germany was not much
better than Harry Warendorf's or Digger Brown's, and his
queries were like theirs, even to the inevitable "What's
Hitler really like? Have you talked to him?" Pug described
Hitler's war speech in the Reichstag. Franklin Roosevelt
exhibited a lively interest in this, asking how Hitler used
his voice and hands, and what he did when he paused.

"I'm told," Roosevelt said, "that they type his speeches
on a special machine with perfectly enormous letters, so
he won't have to wear glasses."

"I wouldn't know about that, sir."

"Yes, I got that from a pretty reliable source. 'Führer
type,' they call it." Roosevelt sighed, turned his chair away
from the food, and lit a cigarette. "There's no substitute
for being in a place yourself, Pug, seeing it with your own
eyes, getting the feel. That's what's missing in this job."

"Well, Mr. President, in the end it all boils down to cold
facts and figures."

"True, but too often all *that* depends on who writes the
reports. Now that was a fine report of yours. How did
you really foresee he'd make a pact with Stalin? Everybody here was stupefied."

"I guess mathematically somebody somewhere was
bound to make that wild guess, Mr. President. It happened to be me."

"No, no. That was a well-reasoned report. Actually, we
did have some warning here, Pug. There was a leak in
one German embassy—never mind where—and our State
Department had predictions of that pact. Trouble was,
nobody here was much inclined to believe them." He
looked at Hopkins, with a touch of mischief. "That's
always the problem with intelligence, isn't it, Pug? All
kinds of strange information will come in, but then—"

The President all of a sudden appeared to run out of

conversation. He looked tired, bored, and withdrawn, puffing at a cigarette in a long holder. Victor Henry would have been glad to leave, but he thought the President should dismiss him. He was feeling a bit firmer about the meeting now. Franklin Roosevelt had the manner, after all, of a fleet commander relaxing over lunch, and Pug was used to the imperious ways of admirals. Apparently he had crossed the Atlantic in wartime to kill an off-hour for the President.

Hopkins glanced at his watch. "Mr. President, the Secretary and Senator Pittman will be on their way over now."

"Already? The embargo business? Well, Pug." Henry jumped up, and took his cap. "Thank you for coming by. This has been grand. Now if there's anything else you think I should know, just anything that strikes you as significant or interesting, how about dropping me a line? I'll be glad to hear from you. I mean that."

At this grotesque proposal for bypassing the chain of command, which ran counter to Henry's quarter century of naval training and experience, he could only blink and nod. The President caught his expression. "Nothing official, of course," he said quickly. "Whatever you do, don't send me more reports! But now that we've gotten acquainted again, why not stay in touch? I liked that thing you wrote. I could just see that submarine base emptying out at five o'clock. It said an awful lot about Nazi Germany. Sometimes one little thing like that—or what a loaf of bread costs, or the jokes people are repeating, or like that advertising blimp over Berlin—such things can sometimes suggest more than a report umpteen pages long. Of course, one needs the official reports, too. But I get enough of those, heaven knows!"

Franklin Roosevelt gave Commander Henry the hard look of a boss who has issued an order and wants to know if it's understood.

"Yes, Mr. President," Henry said.

"And, oh, by the way, here's a suggestion that's just come to my desk, Pug, for helping the Allies. Of course we're absolutely neutral in this foreign war, but still—" The President broke into a sly grin. His tired eyes sparkled as he glanced here and there on his cluttered desk, and took up a paper. "Here we are. We offer to buy the *Queen Mary* and the *Normandie,* and we use them for evacuating Americans from Europe. There are thousands stranded, as you know. What do you think? It would give the Allies a pile of much needed dollars, and we'd have the ships. They're fine luxury liners. How about it?"

Victor Henry looked from Hopkins to the President. Evidently this was a serious question. They were both waiting for his answer. "Mr. President, I'd say those ships are major war assets and they'd be insane to sell them. They're magnificent troop transports. They're the fastest vessels for their tonnage of anything afloat, they can out-run any submarine at cruising speed, they hardly have to zigzag they're so fast, and with the interiors stripped their carrying capacity is gigantic."

The President said dryly to Hopkins, "Is that what the Navy replied?"

"I'd have to check, Mr. President. I think their response went mainly to the question of where the money'd come from."

Franklin Roosevelt cocked his head thoughtfully, and smiling at Victor Henry, held out a long arm for a handshake. "Do you know why I didn't make more of a fuss about those clothes? Because your skipper said you were one of the best ensigns he'd ever seen. Keep in touch, now."

"Aye aye, sir."

"Well, how did it go?" The President's aide was smoking a cigar in the anteroom. He rose, knocking off the ash.

"All right, I suppose."

"It must have. You were scheduled for ten minutes. You were in there almost forty."

"Forty! It went fast. What now?"

"How do you mean?"

"I don't have very specific instructions. Do I go straight back to Berlin, or what?"

"What did the President say?"

"It was a pretty definite good-bye, I thought."

Captain Carton smiled. "Well, I guess you're all through. Maybe you should check in with CNO. You're not scheduled here again." He reached into a breast pocket. "One more thing. This came to my office a little while ago, from the State Department."

It was an official dispatch envelope. Henry ripped it open and read the flimsy pink message form:

FORWARDED X BYRON HENRY SAFE WELL WARSAW
X AWAITING EVACUATION ALL NEUTRALS NOW UNDER
NEGOTIATION GERMAN GOVERNMENT X SLOTE

. . .

Victor Henry disappointed Hugh Cleveland when he walked into the broadcaster's office; just a squat, broad-shouldered, ordinary-looking man of about fifty, in a brown suit and a red bow tie, standing at the receptionist's desk. The genial, somewhat watchful look on his weathered face was not sophisticated at all. As Cleveland sized up people—having interviewed streams of them—this might be a professional ballplayer turned manager, a lumberman, maybe an engineer; apple-pie American, fairly intelligent, far from formidable. But he knew Madeline feared and admired her father, and day by day he was thinking more highly of the young girl's judgment, so he took a respectful tone.

"Commander Henry? It's a pleasure. I'm Hugh Cleveland."

"Hello. Hope I'm not busting in on anything. I thought I'd just drop by and have a look-see."

"Glad you did. Madeline's timing the script. Come this way." They walked along the cork floor of a corridor walled with green soundproofing slabs. "She was amazed. Thought you were in Germany."

"For the moment I'm here."

In a swishing charcoal pleated skirt and gray blouse, Madeline came scampering out of a door marked NO ADMITTANCE, and kissed him. "Gosh, Dad, what a surprise. Is everything all right?"

"Everything's dandy." He narrowed his eyes at her. She looked a lot more mature, and brilliantly excited. He said, "If you're busy, I can leave, and talk to you later."

Cleveland put in, "No, no, Commander. Please come in and watch. I'm about to interview Edna May Pelham."

"Oh? *The General's Lady?* I read it on the plane. Pretty good yarn."

In the small studio, decorated like a library with fake wood panelling and fake books, Cleveland said to the sharp-faced, white-haired authoress, "Here's another admirer of the book, Miss Pelham. Commander Henry is the American naval attaché in Berlin."

"You don't say! Hi there." The woman waved her pince-nez at him. "Are we going to stay out of this idiotic war, Commander?"

"I hope so."

"So do I. My hopes would be considerably higher if that man in the White House would drop dead."

Pug sat to one side in an armchair while they read through the script. The authoress, passing vinegary judgments on current literature, said that one famous author was obscene, another sloppy, a third superficial. His mind wandered to his meeting yesterday with "that man in the White House." It seemed to him that he had been summoned on a haphazard impulse; that he had spent a couple of thousand dollars of public money on a round trip from Germany for pointless small talk over scrambled eggs. The morning paper showed that yesterday had been a crowded, portentous day for the President. The leading story, spread over many columns, was *Roosevelt Proclaims Limited National Emergency.* Three other headlines on the front page began *FDR* or *President;* he had reorganized two major government boards; he had lifted the sugar quota; he had met with congressional leaders on revision of the Neutrality Act. All these things had been done by the ruddy man in shirt-sleeves who never moved from behind his desk, but whose manner was so bouncy you forgot he was helpless in his chair. Pug wanted to believe that he himself might have said one thing, made one comment, that by illuminating the President's mind had justified the whole trip. But he could not. His comments on Germany, like his original report, had rolled off the President, who mainly had sparked at details of Hitler's oratorical technique and touches of local Berlin color. The President's request for gossipy letters still struck him as devious, if not pointless. In the first few minutes Victor Henry had been attracted by President Roosevelt's warmth and good humor, by his remarkable memory and his ready laughter. But thinking back on it all, Commander Henry wasn't sure the President would have behaved much differently to a man who had come to the office to shine his shoes.

"Fourteen minutes and twenty seconds, Mr. Cleveland." Madeline's speaker-distorted voice roused him.

"That's fine. Ready to record, Miss Pelham?"

"No. All this about Hemingway is far too kind. I'd like about half an hour with this script. And I'd like some strong tea, with lemon."

"Yes, ma'am. Hear that, Madeline? Get it."

Cleveland invited the naval officer to his office, where Pug accepted a cigar. The young broadcaster displeased him by hitching a leg over the arm of his chair. Pug had used considerable severity to cure Byron of that habit. "Sir, you can be proud of Madeline. She's an unusual girl."

"Unusual in what way?"

"Well, let's see. She understands things the first time you tell them to her. Or if she doesn't, she asks questions. If you send her to fetch something or do something, she fetches it or she does it. She never has a long story about it. I haven't heard her whine yet. She isn't afraid of people. She can talk straight to anybody without being fresh. She's *reliable*. Are reliable people common in the Navy? In this business they're about as common as giant pandas. Especially girls. I've had my share of lemons here. I understand that you want her to go back to school, and that she'll have to quit next week. I'm very sorry about that."

"The girl's nineteen."

"She's better than women of twenty-five and thirty who've worked for me." Cleveland smiled. This easy-mannered fellow had an infectious grin and an automatic warmth, Pug thought, that in a trivial way was like the President's. Some people had it, some didn't. He himself had none of it. In the Navy the quality was not overly admired. The name for it was "grease." Men who possessed it had a way of climbing fast; they also had a way of relying upon it, till they got too greasy and slipped.

"I wish she'd show some of these 4.0 qualities at school. I don't appreciate the idea of a nineteen-year-old girl loose in New York."

"Well, sir, I don't mean to argue with you, but Washington's no convent either. It's a question of upbringing and character. Madeline is a superior, trustworthy girl."

Pug uttered a noncommittal grunt.

"Sir, how about coming on our show? We'd be honored to have you."

"As a guest? You're kidding. I'm nobody."

"America's naval attaché in Nazi Germany is certainly somebody. You could strike a blow for preparedness, or a two-ocean Navy. We just had Admiral Preble on the show."

"Yes, I know. That's how I found out what my little girl's doing these days."

"Would you consider it, sir?"

"Not on your life." The sudden frost in Pug's tone rose not only from the desire to be final, but the suspicion that the praise of Madeline had been a way of greasing him.

"No harm in asking, I hope," Cleveland grinned, running a hand through his heavy blond hair. He had a pink barbershop sunburn and looked well in a collegiate jacket and slacks, though Victor Henry thought his argyle socks were too much. He did not like Cleveland, but he could see that Madeline would relish working for such a Broadwayish fellow.

Later Madeline showed her father around the studios. Certain corridors were like passageways in the bowels of a ship, all jammed with electronic gear and thousands of bunched colored wires. These interested Pug. He would have enjoyed seeing the controlling diagrams and learning how radio amusement was pumped out of this nerve center all over the country. The performing studios, with their giant cardboard settings of aspirin bottles, toothpaste tubes, and gasoline pumps, their blinking red lights, posturing singers, giggling audiences, grimacing and prancing funny men, not only seemed tawdry and silly in themselves, but doubly so with Poland under attack. Here, at the heart of the American communications machine, the Hitler war seemed to mean little more than a skirmish among Zulus.

"Madeline, what attracts you in all this balderdash?"

They were leaving the rehearsal of a comedy program, where the star, wearing a fireman's hat, was spraying the bandleader, the girl singer, and the audience with seltzer bottles.

"That man may not amuse you, Dad, but millions of people are mad for him. He makes fifteen thousand dollars a week."

"That's kind of obscene right there. It's more than a rear admiral makes in a year."

"Dad, in two weeks I've met the most marvellous people. I met Gary Cooper. Just today I spent two hours with Miss Pelham. Do you know that I had lunch with the Chief of Naval Operations? Me?"

"So I heard. What's this fellow Cleveland like?"

"He's brilliant."

"Is he married?"

"He has a wife and three children."

"When does your school start?"

"Dad, do I have to go back?"

"When did we discuss any other plan?"

"I'll be so miserable. I feel as though I've joined the Navy. I want to stay in."

He cut her off with a cold look.

They went back to her little partitioned cubicle outside Cleveland's office. Smoking one cigarette and then another, Pug silently sat in an armchair and watched her work. He noted her neat files, her checkoff lists, her crisp manner on the telephone, her little handmade wall chart of guests invited or scheduled in September, and of celebrities due in New York. He noted how absorbed she was. In their walk around CBS she had asked only perfunctory questions about the family and none on Germany; she hadn't even asked him what Hitler was really like.

He cleared his throat. "Say, incidentally, Madeline, I'm going out to the Brooklyn Navy Yard to have dinner aboard the *Colorado*. Digger Brown's the executive officer. You know, Freddy Brown's father. Like to come along? What's the matter? Why the face?"

Madeline sighed. "Oh, I'll come, Dad. After all, I see you so seldom. I'll meet you at five or so—"

"Got something else planned?"

"Well, I didn't know you were about to fall out of the sky. I was going to dinner and the theatre with the kids."

"What kids?"

"You know. Just kids I've met at CBS. A couple of writers, musicians, an actress, some other new girls like me. There are eight of us, sort of a gang."

"I daresay there'll be some bright-eyed ensigns in the junior mess."

"Yes, exactly. Ensigns."

"Look, I don't want to drag you anywhere."

"It's just that you'll end up talking to Commander Brown, Dad, and I'll spend another evening with ensigns. Can't we have breakfast tomorrow? I'll come to your hotel."

"That'll be fine. These kids of yours, I'd think the young men would be these show business fellows, pretty flimsy characters."

"Honestly, you're wrong. They're serious and intelligent."

"I think it's damn peculiar that you've fallen into this. It's the furthest thing from your mother's interests or mine."

Madeline looked aslant at him. "Oh? Didn't Mother ever tell you that she wanted to be an actress? That she spent a whole summer as a dancer in a travelling musical show?"

"Sure. She was seventeen. It was an escapade."

"Yes? Well, once when we were up in an attic, it must have been at the Nag's Head house, she came on the parasol she had used in her solo dance. An old crinkled orange paper parasol. Well, right there in that dirty attic Mama kicked off her shoes, opened the parasol, picked up her skirt, and did the whole dance for me. And she sang a song. 'Ching-ching-challa-wa China Girl.' I must have been twelve, but I still remember. She kicked clear to the ceiling, Mama did. God, was I ever shocked."

"Oh, yes, 'Ching-ching-challa-wa China Girl'!" said Pug. "She did it for me too, long long ago. Before we were married, in fact. Well, I'm off to the *Colorado*. Tomorrow after breakfast I fly down to Pensacola to see Warren. Next day I return to Berlin, if I can firm up my air tickets."

She left her desk and put her arms around him. She smelled sweet and alluring, and her face shone with youth, health, and happiness. "Please, Dad. Let me work. Please."

"I'll write or cable you from Berlin. I'll have to discuss it with Ching-ching-challa-wa China Girl."

*   *   *

The harbor smell in the Brooklyn Navy Yard, the destroyers nesting in a row with red truck lights burning, the *Colorado* lit up from stem to stern, its great main battery guns askew for boresighting—these things gave Victor Henry the sense of peace that other men get by retiring to their dens with a cigar and a drink.

If he had a home in the world, it was a battleship. Put together at different times and places of different steel plates and machines, embodied in many forms under many names, a battleship was always one thing: the strongest kind of warship afloat. This meant a thousand ever-changing specifications of size, design, propulsion, armor, armament, interior communication, interior supply systems; a thousand rituals and disciplines binding the crew, from the captain to the youngest striker, into one dependable corporate will and intelligence. In this sense there had been battleships in the days of Phoenicia and Rome, and there would always be battleships—a living peak of human knowledge and craft, a floating engineering structure dedicated to one aim: the control of the sea. It was the only thing to which Victor Henry had ever given himself whole; more than to his family, much more than to the sprawling abstraction called the Navy. He was a battleship man.

With other top men, he had gone to a battleship straight from the Academy in 1913. He had served time in smaller ships, too. But he was marked *battleship,* and he had kept coming back to them. His shining service achievement was winning the "meatball pennant," the fleet gunnery competition, two years in a row as gunnery officer of the *West Virginia.* His improvised system for speeding sixteen-inch shells from the magazines to the turrets had become standard Navy doctrine. All he wanted in this life was to be executive officer of a battleship, then a captain, then an admiral with a BatDiv flag. He could see no further. He thought a BatDiv flag was as fine a thing as being a president, a king, or a pope. And he reflected, as he followed the erect quick-marching gangway messenger down the spotless white passageway to the senior officers' mess, that every month he spent in Berlin was cutting the ground from under his hopes.

Digger Brown had been exec of the *Colorado* only six weeks. Sitting at the head of the table, Digger was making too many jokes, Pug thought, so as to put himself at ease with the ship's lieutenant commanders and two-stripers. That was all right. Digger was a big fellow and could turn on impressive anger at will. Pug's style was more of a monotone. His own sense of humor, such as it was, went to jabbing ironies. As an executive officer—if he ever achieved it—he planned to be taciturn and short. They would call him a dull sour son of a bitch. One had plenty of time to warm up and make friends, but the job had to be done right from the hour one reported aboard. It was a sad fact of life that everybody, himself included, jumped to it when the boss was a son of a bitch, especially a knowledgeable son of a bitch. In the *West Virginia* he had been a hated man until that first meatball pennant had broken out at the yardarm. Thereafter he had been the ship's most popular officer.

The immediate target of Digger's raillery was his communications officer, a lean morose-looking Southerner. Recently the *Colorado* had received a new powerful voice radio transmitter which bounced waves off the Heaviside layer at a shallow angle. If atmospheric conditions were right, one could talk directly to a ship in European waters. Digger had chatted with his brother, the engineering officer in the *Marblehead*, now anchored off Lisbon. The communications officer had since been romancing an old girlfriend in Barcelona via the *Marblehead* radio room. Digger had found this out three days ago, and was still milking it for jokes.

Pug said, "Say, how well did this thing work, Digger? Could you understand Tom?"

"Oh, five by five. Amazing."

"D'you suppose I could talk to Rhoda in Berlin?" It occurred to Pug that this was a chance to tell her about Madeline, and perhaps reach a decision.

The communications officer, glad of an opportunity to stop the baiting, said at once, "Captain, I know we can raise *Marblehead* tonight. It ought to be simple to patch in the long-distance line from Lisbon to Berlin."

"It'll be what—two or three o'clock in the morning there?" Brown said.

"Two, sir."

"Want to break in on Rhoda's beauty sleep, Pug?"

"I think so."

The lieutenant carefully rolled his napkin in a monogrammed ring, and left.

The talk turned to Germany and the war. These battleship officers, like most people, were callowly inclined to admire and overestimate the Nazi war machine. One fresh-faced lieutenant said that he hoped the Navy was doing more work on landing craft than he'd been able to read about. If we got into the war, he said, landing would be almost the whole Navy problem, because Germany would probably control the entire coastline of Europe by then.

Digger Brown brought his guest to the executive officer's quarters for coffee, ordering around his Filipino steward and lolling on the handsome blue leather couch with casual pride of office. They gossipped about their classmates: a couple of juicy divorces, a premature death, a brilliant leader turned alcoholic. Digger bemoaned his burdens as a battleship exec. His captain had gotten where he was with sheer luck, charm, and a marvellous wife—that was all; his ship-handling was going to give Digger a heart attack. The ship was slack from top to bottom; he had made himself unpopular by instituting a stiff program of drills; and so forth. Pug thought that for an old friend Digger was showing off too much. He mentioned that he had come back from Berlin to talk to the President. Digger's face changed. "I'm not surprised," he said. "Remember that phone call you had at the Army and Navy Club? I told the fellows, I bet that's from the White House. You're flying high, fella."

Having taken the wind out of Digger's sails, Victor Henry was content to say nothing more. Digger waited, stuffed his pipe, lit it, then said, "What's Roosevelt really like, Pug?"

Henry said something banal about the President's charm and magnetism.

There was a knock on the door and the communications officer came in. "We raised the *Marblehead,* no strain, sir. It took all this time to get through to Berlin. What was that number again?" Pug told him. "Yes, sir, that checks. The number doesn't answer."

The eyes of Digger Brown and Victor Henry met for a moment. Brown said, "At two in the morning? Better try again. Sounds like a foul-up."

"We put it through three times, sir."

"She might have gone out of town," Henry said. "Don't bother anymore. Thanks."

The lieutenant left. Digger puffed thoughtfully at his pipe.

"Also, she cuts off the phone in the bedroom at night," Henry said. "I forgot that. She may not hear the ringing in the library if the door's closed."

"Oh, I see," Digger said. He puffed again, and neither said anything for a while.

"Well. Guess I'll make tracks." Victor Henry stood up.

The executive officer accompanied him to the gangway, looking proudly around at the vast main deck, the towering guns, the flawlessly uniformed watch. "Shipshape enough topside," he said. "That's the least I demand. Well, good luck on the firing line, Pug. Give my love to Rhoda."

"If she's still there, I will."

They both laughed.

* * *

"Hello, Dad!" When Paul Munson's plane landed, Warren was waiting at the Pensacola airfield in a helmet and flying jacket. The son's handgrip, quick and firm, expressed all Warren's pride in what he was doing. His deeply tanned face radiated exaltation.

"Say, where do you get this outdoors glow?" Pug said. He deliberately ignored the scar on his son's forehead. "I thought they'd make you sweat in ground school here. I expected you to look like something from under a rock."

Warren laughed. "Well, I had a couple of chances to go deep-sea fishing out in the Gulf. I tan fast."

Driving his father to the BOQ, he never stopped talking. The flight school was in a buzz, he said. The day after

Hitler invaded Poland, Washington had ordered the number of students tripled, and the year-long course cut to six months. The school was "telescoping the syllabus." In the old course a man qualified in big slow patrol planes, then in scout planes, and then, if he were good enough, went on into Squadron Five for fighter training. Now the pilots would be put on patrol, scout, or fighter tracks at once, and would stay in them. The lists would be posted in the morning. He was dying to make Squadron Five. Warren got all this out before he remembered to ask his father about the family.

"Ye gods, Briny's in *Warsaw?* Why, the Germans are bombing the hell out of that town."

"I know," Pug said. "I stopped worrying about Byron long ago. He'll crawl out of the rubble with somebody's gold watch."

"What's he doing there?"

"Chased a girl there."

"Really? Bully for him. What kind of girl?"

"A Jewish Phi Bete from Radcliffe."

"You're kidding. *Briny?*"

"That's right."

With an eloquent look, surprised and ruefully impressed, Warren changed the subject.

The audience at Paul Munson's lecture was surprisingly big. There must have been more than two hundred student aviators in khaki, youngsters with crew cuts and rugged clever faces, jammed into a small lecture hall. Like most naval men, Paul was a bumbling speaker, but the students sat on the edges of their chairs, because he was telling them how to avoid killing themselves. With slides and diagrams, with much technical jargon and an occasional heavy bloodthirsty joke, he described the worst hazards of carrier landings, the life-or-death last moments of the approach, the procedure after cracking up, and such cheerful matters. The students laughed at the jokes about their own possible deaths. The strong male smell of a locker room rose from the packed bodies. Pug's eye fell on Warren, sitting in a row across the aisle from him, erect and attentive, just one more close-cropped head in the crowd. He thought of Byron in Warsaw under the German bombs. It was going to be a tough ten years, he thought, for men with grown sons.

Warren told him after the lecture that Congressman Isaac Lacouture, the man who had taken him deep-sea fishing, had invited them to dinner at the beach club. Lacouture was president of the club, and before running for Congress had been chairman of the Gulf Lumber and Paper Company, the biggest firm in Pensacola. "He's anxious to meet you," Warren said as they walked back to the BOQ.

"Why?"

"He's very interested in the war and in Germany. His opinions are kind of strong."

"Why has he taken such a shine to you?"

"Well, sir, this daughter of his, Janice, and I have sort of hit it off." With an easy knowing grin, Warren parted from him in the lobby.

At his first sight of Janice Lacouture, Victor Henry decided against talking to Warren about Pamela Tudsbury. What chance had the slight English girl in her mousy suits against this magnetic blonde whose long legs dazzled at every turn and flip of her skirt, this assured radiant tall American girl with the princess-like air, and the lovely face only slightly marred by crooked teeth? She was another, early Rhoda, swathed in cloudy pink, all composed of sweet scent, sexual allure, and girlish grace. The slang was changed, the skirt hem higher. This girl looked and acted brainier. She greeted Pug with just enough deference to acknowledge that he was Warren's father, and just enough sparkle to hint that he was no old fud for all that, but an attractive man himself. A girl who could do that in half a minute of talk, with a flash of the eyes and a smile, was a powerhouse, and so much, thought Pug, for his inept matchmaking notions.

A stiff wind was blowing from the water. Waves broke over the club terrace and splattered heavy spray on the glass wall of the dining room, making the candlelit Lacouture dinner seem the cosier. Victor Henry never did get it clear who all the ten people at table were, though one was the beribboned commandant of the naval air station. The person who mattered, it was soon obvious, was Congressman Isaac Lacouture, a small man with thick white hair, a florid face, and a way of half sticking out his tongue when he smiled, with an air of sly profundity.

"How long are you going to be here, Commander Henry?" Lacouture called down the long table, as green-coated waiters passed two large baked fish on silver platters. "You might like to come out and spend a day fishing, if the weatherman will turn off this willawa. Your boy caught these two kingfish with me."

Pug said that he had to return to New York in the morning to get his plane for Lisbon.

Lacouture said, "Well, at that I suppose I'll be hurrying up to Washington myself for this special session. Say, how about that? What do *you* think of revising the Neutrality Act? How bad is the situation, actually? You should know."

"Congressman, I think Poland's going to fall fast, if you call that bad."

"Oh, hell, the Allies are counting on that! The European mind works in subtle ways. The President has sort of a European mind himself, you know. That mixture of Dutch and English is really the key to understanding him." Lacouture smiled, protruding his tongue. "I've done a lot of business with the Dutch, they're very big in the hardwoods trade, and I tell you they are tricky boys. The gloomier things look in the next few weeks, why, the easier it'll be for Roosevelt to jam anything he wants through Congress. Right?"

"Have you talked to Hitler, Commander Henry? What is he really like?" said Mrs. Lacouture, a thin faded woman, with a placating smile and a sweet tone that suggested her social life consisted mainly of softening her husband's impact, or trying to.

Lacouture said as though she had addressed him, "Oh, this Hitler is some kind of moonstruck demagogue. We all know that. But for years the Allies could have cleaned up him and his Nazis with ease, yet they just sat there. So it's their mess, not ours. Any day now we'll be hearing about the Germans raping nuns and boiling soldiers' corpses down for soap. British intelligence started both those yarns in 1916, you know. We've got the documentary evidence on that. How about it, Commander Henry? You've been living among the Germans. Are they really these savage Huns the New York papers make them out to be?"

All the faces at the table turned to Pug. "The Germans aren't easy to understand," he said slowly. "My wife likes them more than I do. I don't admire their treatment of Jews."

Congressman Lacouture held up two large hands. "Unpardonable! The New York press is quite understandable on that basis."

Warren said firmly from the middle of the table, "I don't see how the President's revision would weaken our neutrality, sir. Cash and carry simply means anybody can come and buy stuff who has the ships to haul it off and the money to pay for it. Anybody, Hitler included."

Lacouture smiled at him. "The administration would be proud of you, my boy. That's the line. Except we all know that the Allies have the ships and the money, and the Germans have neither. So this would put our factories into the war on the Allied side."

"But nobody ever stopped Hitler from building a merchant marine," Warren promptly came back. "Piling up tanks, subs, and dive bombers instead was his idea. All aggressive weapons. Isn't that his tough luck?"

"Warren's absolutely right," Janice said.

Lacouture sat back in his chair, staring at his daughter, who smiled back impudently.

"What both of you kids don't or won't understand," Lacouture said, "is that this proposal is the camel's nose under the tent flap. Of course it *seems* fair. Of *course* it does. That's the beauty of the package. That's the Roosevelt mind at work. But let's not be children. He isn't calling a special session to help Nazi Germany! He thinks he's got a mission to save the world from Hitler. He's been talking this way since 1937. He's cracked on the subject. Now I say Adolf Hitler's neither the foul fiend nor the Antichrist. That's all poppycock. He's just another European politician, a little more dirty and extreme than the rest. The way for us to save the world is to stay *out* of it. The citadel of sanity!" He rapped out the phrase and looked around the table, as though half expecting applause. "That's what we have to be. The Atlantic and Pacific are our walls. Broad, stout walls. The citadel of sanity! If we get in it we'll go bankrupt like the others and lose a couple of million of our finest young men. The whole world will sink into barbarism or communism, which aren't so very different. The Russians will be the only winners."

A small bald man with a hearing aid, seated across the table from Pug, said, "Damn right."

Lacouture inclined his head at him. "You and I realize that, Ralph, but it's amazing how few intelligent people do, as yet. The citadel of sanity. Ready to pick up the pieces when it's over and rebuild a decent world. That's the goal. I'm going back to Washington to fight like an alligator for it, believe you me. I'll be marked mud among a lot of my Democratic colleagues, but on this one I go my own way."

When dinner ended, Janice and Warren left the club together, not waiting for coffee, and not troubling to explain. The girl smiled roguishly, waved a hand, and disappeared in a whirl of silky legs and pink chiffon. Warren halted long enough to make an early morning tennis date with his father. Victor Henry found himself isolated with Lacouture over rich cigars, coffee, and brandy in a corner of a lounge, in red leather armchairs. The congressman rambled about the charms of life in Pensacola—the duck-hunting, the game-fishing, the year-round good weather, and the swiftly advancing prosperity. The war would make it a real boomtown, he said, between the expansion of the Navy air base and the spurt in the lumber trade. "Creosoted telephone poles. You take that one item, Commander. Our company's had some unbelievable orders, just in the last week, from North Africa, Japan, and France. The whole world's stringing wires all of a sudden. It's an indication."

He tried to persuade Henry to stay over one day. A ship carrying mahogany was due in from Dutch Guiana at noon. It would dump the logs in the harbor, and lumber mill workers would lash them into rafts and tow them up the bayou. "It's quite a sight," he said.

"Well, I've got this chance to fly back to New York with an old buddy. I'd better go."

"And from there to Berlin, via Lisbon?"

"That's the plan."

"Not much chance of our paths crossing then, in the

near future," Lacouture said. "Your wife's a Grover, isn't she? Hamilton Grover up in Washington is a friend of mine; we have lunch at the Metropolitan Club about once a month." Pug nodded. Hamilton Grover was the wealthiest of the cousins, rather beyond Rhoda's orbit.

"And you're a Henry. Not one of those Virginia Henrys that go back to old Patrick?"

Henry laughed, shaking his head. "I doubt it. I'm from California."

"Yes, so Warren told me. I mean originally."

"Well, my great-grandfather came west before the gold rush. We're not sure from where. My grandfather died young and we never got the story straight."

"You're probably Scotch-Irish."

"Well, no, sort of mixed. My grandmother was French and English."

"That so? We've got some French in our family ourselves. Not a bad thing, hey? Gives the men that certain touch in *l'amour*." Lacouture uttered a hearty coarse laugh, the get-together noise of American men. "Quite a boy, your Warren."

"Well, thanks. Your girl is beyond words."

Lacouture sighed deeply. "A girl's a problem. Warren tells me you have one, so you know. They'll fool you every time. We weren't as lucky as you, we have no boys. All Warren wants to do is fly airplanes the rest of his life for the Navy, right?"

"Well, those wings of gold look awfully big to him now, Congressman."

Lacouture puffed at his cigar. "I liked the way he talked up at dinner. Of course he's naïve about foreign affairs. You learn a lot about the outside world in the lumber business." Lacouture swirled the large brandy snifter. "No doubt you're glad to see Warren carrying on the Navy tradition. Wouldn't want to see him shift over into business, or anything like that." The congressman smiled, showing his tongue, and good but crooked teeth like his daughter's.

"Warren goes his own way, Congressman."

"I'm not so sure. He thinks the world of his dad."

The talk was getting awkward for Victor Henry. He had married a girl much better off than himself, and he had doubts about such a course in life. Nor did he especially like Janice Lacouture. Once the incandescence died down, she would be as tough as her father, who was already and openly weighing the notion of swallowing Warren. He said, "Well, until the war ends he's in, and that's that."

"Of course. But that may not be for long, you know. If we can just stay out, it'll be over in a year or so. Maybe less. As soon as the Allies are positive they can't suck us in, they'll make the best deal they can get. They'd be nuts to try anything else. Well, I've enjoyed visiting with you, Commander. What the hell? No sense trying to anticipate what the kids nowadays will do anyway. Is there? It's a different world than when you and I grew up."

"That's for sure."

Next morning, promptly at six-thirty, Warren appeared in his father's room. Not saying much, and rubbing his bloodshot and baggy eyes, he drank the orange juice and coffee brought by the steward. A strong wind still blew outside, and he and his father wore sweaters as they volleyed and began to play. Pug ran up three games. The balls soared erratically here and there.

"Have a good time last night?" Pug called, as Warren knocked one flying over the fence, and the wind bore it up on the roof of a nearby cottage.

Warren laughed, stripped his sweater off, and won the next five games, regaining his fast drive and his mid-court smash. The father was a plugging, solid player with an iron backhand, but he had to conserve his breath.

"Goddamn it, Warren, if you've got a point won, win it," he gasped. The son had passed up an easy kill to hit the ball where Pug could reach it.

"The wind took it, Dad."

"The hell it did."

Now Pug threw off his sweater, answered several of his son's smashes, caught his second wind, and drew even. "Whew! I've got to quit. Ground school," Warren called, mopping his face with a towel. "You've really kept your game up, Dad."

"Well, in Berlin we lucked into a house with a court. You've played better."

Warren came to the net. He was pouring sweat, his

eyes were clear, and he looked eager and happy. "You had more sleep."

"Quite a girl, that Janice."

"She's got a head on her shoulders, Dad. She knows a hell of a lot of history." The father gave him a quizzical look. They both burst out laughing. "All the same it's true. She does know history."

"What did you cover last night? The Hundred Years' War?" Warren guffawed, swishing his racket sharply. Pug said, "Her father figures to make a lumberman of you."

"He's a kidder. I'll ship out in March, and probably that'll be that."

Outside the ground school building, a wooden bulletin board was almost hidden by students clustering around in noisy excitement. Warren said, "Assignments," and dove among them. In a moment his arm in a white sweater thrust above the heads. "Eeyow!" Warren exulted all the way back to the BOQ; he was in Squadron Five, and some of the hottest student pilots had not made it. He had done *something* right, despite his one ground loop! His father listened, smiling and nodding, remembering the day at Annapolis when he had drawn his first battleship duty.

He said at last, "You told your mother in Washington that it's just something else to qualify in."

The son looked a bit abashed, then laughed. "I hadn't flown then, Dad. There's nothing like flying. It's hard to talk about, but there's absolutely nothing like it. Nothing!"

"Well, we both have to get cleaned up. Guess we'd better say good-bye here." They stood in the square dingy lobby of the BOQ.

Warren glanced at his watch. "Gosh, already? I guess so. Say, write me about Briny from Berlin, will you? As soon as you get some real dope."

"Good enough."

"And don't worry about Madeline, Dad. She'll be fine in New York."

"I haven't decided to let her stay in New York."

"Why sure, I know." Warren's grin was disingenuous. He obviously thought his father had already lost that point.

They shook hands. Then Warren did something that

embarrassed them both. He threw an arm around his father's shoulder. "I feel mixed up. I'm damn sorry to see you go, and I've never been happier in my life."

"Take it easy," Pug said. "That girl's fine, but the hell with the lumber business. The Navy needs officers."

Paul Munson, recovering from a hard night's drinking with some old friends on the Pensacola staff, said little until his plane finished its climb and levelled off, heading northeast over Georgia. "By the way," he shouted above the engine roar into his face mike, "how'd your boy do in those squadron assignments?"

Pug held up five fingers."

Munson slapped his shoulder. "Outstanding. My boy washed out of there last year. It's a tough school. Don't you have another boy? What about him?"

"Naval ROTC."

"Oh? Guess they'll call him up any day. Think he'll fly?"

Victor Henry looked out of the window at the green fields, and a wandering brown river far below.

"He'll never work that hard."

13

FROM the German viewpoint, the invasion of Poland was proceeding merrily. The arrows and the pins on the military maps were closing in day by day, from all directions, on Warsaw and Byron Henry.

All over Poland, lines of helmeted dusty Germans, miles and miles of them, walked along or rode in trucks, cars, or on horses. Tanks and motorized guns clanked with them, or rattled nearby on railroad cars. It was all going slowly and tediously, and on the whole peacefully. This outdoors mass adventure, though not precisely a picnic—ten thousand Germans were killed along the way—was far from wholly disagreeable. After each day's advance the horde ate in the fields or on the roadside, and camped under the stars or tented in black rain, peeved at the discomforts but enjoying good simple things: hard exercise, fresh air, food, drink, grumbling, jokes, comradeship, and sweet sleep.

The Poles, of course, kept shooting at them. This had been planned for. The Germans returned the fire, laying down studied bombardments according to grids on maps. Howitzers flamed with satisfying roars and recoils, everybody moved fast and worked up a sweat, officers shouted orders and encouragement, some fellows got killed or hurt but most did not, trees burned, village houses crumbled, and after a while the shooting died off and the invasion trudged ahead.

The front was a moving political edge; the Germans were forcing their national will on the Poles. As at a weather front, the squall line of violence was at the edge of change. The thin destructive squall churned across the flat green landscape, leaving a streaked mess behind. Even so, even in this combat zone there was mostly peace right there at the line. For every hour of firing there were many hours of camping, machine repairing, and trudging through green fields and scorched villages. But this ceased to be so when the wavering line of the front took the form of a circle shrinking in toward the city of Warsaw. As the target narrowed, the firing grew hotter, more frequent, and more concentrated.

The invaders were a new generation of German soldiers who had never faced hostile bullets, though some of their senior officers had fought in the last war. At any one place where the invasion jumped off, there were only a few hundred scared young Germans crossing a border and expecting to get shot at. But they were backed by swarms of more armed youths, marching along German roads toward Poland on a neat schedule, and that was reassuring to know. Pulling down the Polish border barriers in the gray dawn light, overpowering the few guards, setting foot on the foreign roads they had been watching through field glasses—all that was exhilarating. But once the Polish border garrisons opened fire there was much halting, panicking, running away, and stalled confusion. Luckily for the Germans, the Poles were even more panicked and confused, with the added disability of acting on the spur of the moment. World War II started in a messy amateurish style. But the Germans, however terrorized each individual may have been, were at least moving according to plan. They had more guns at key points, more ammunition, and a clearer idea of where and when to fire. They had, in fact, achieved surprise.

If two men are standing and amiably chatting, and one suddenly punches the other's belly and kicks his groin, the chances are that even if the other recovers to defend himself, he will be badly beaten up, because the first man has achieved surprise. There is no book on the military art that does not urge the advantage of this. It may not seem quite decent, but that is no concern of the military art. Possibly the Poles should not have been surprised, in view of the Germans' open threats and preparations, but they were. Their political leaders probably hoped the German menaces were bluster. Their generals probably thought their own armies were ready. A lot of wrong guessing goes with the start of a war.

The German plan for conquering Poland, Case White, provided the scenario for what ensued. They had many such plans, like Case Green, the invasion of Czechoslovakia (which they never had to use), and Case Yellow, the attack on France. Color-coded master plans for smashing other countries, far in advance of any quarrel with them, were a modern military innovation of the Germans. All advanced nations came to imitate this doctrine. The United States, for instance, by 1939 had a Plan Orange for fighting Japan, and even a Plan Red for fighting England; and it finally entered the war under Plan Rainbow Five.

Historians still argue, and will long argue, the genesis of the German General Staff, which originated this new line of conduct in human affairs. Some say the German genius produced the General Staff as a reflex of the humiliations inflicted by Napoleon; others assert that a flat country with many hostile borders, in an industrial age, had to develop such schemes to survive. In any case, it was certainly the Germans who first mastered industrial warfare and taught it to the nations: total war—the advance marshalling of railroads, factories, modern communications, and the entire population of a land into one centrally controlled system for destroying its neighbors, should the need or impulse arise.

This German system was well tested in the First World War, in which, geographically, they quit while they were well ahead. When they asked for an armistice, after four years of battling bigger forces on many fronts, they stood everywhere deep in foreign territory; only their big 1918 attack had failed, and their resources were running low. Thereafter, despite their surrender and through all political changes, they continued to work up their "Cases." Twenty-one years later, Case White paid off, quickly frightening a nation of forty million, with an army of a million and a half or more, into obeying the Germans. That, according to Napoleon, is the whole of war—to frighten the foe into doing your will.

The Germans invading Poland made mistakes, they sometimes broke and ran under fire, they disobeyed orders, they refused to advance against tough positions, they misreported gains, and exaggerated reports of the fire they were facing, to excuse retreat. They were ordinary young men. But there were good leaders and stout fellows among them, and the Germans are an obedient, strong-willed people. The Poles did all these wrong things too, and the weight of fire, surprise, numbers, and Case White was all with the Germans. So the invasion went well.

Soon the new companies of tanks—the panzers that became so famous—began to risk long trips into enemy ground far ahead of the front. This was a classic military blunder. The foe closes in behind a company that has ventured too far ahead of its line, pinches it off, and wipes it out. This was precisely what the Russians did several years later to the famous panzers, whereupon their fame dimmed. But now they were a surprise. In their debut against a scared, ill-organized, smaller and weaker foe, on level country in perfect weather, they shone. They proceeded slowly, at only five or ten miles an hour, more like moving lines of large iron bugs than the dashing red arrows of the maps in popular books and magazines. But they looked scary to the Polish soldiers and civilians, and indeed they were lethal enough, these green machines crawling down the roads, out of the forests, and over the ripe grain, firing big shells. From the pellucid September sky, slow clumsy little planes called Stukas kept diving and shooting at soldiers, or children, or animals, or women, whoever happened to be on the roads, to add to the bloodshed and horrid noise. The tanks and Stukas killed many Poles and scared immense masses of them into quitting what looked like a useless fight.

This was the blitzkrieg, the lightning war. It was halted at Warsaw. The fact was not much stressed at the time. The Germans had to inflict on the city an old-fashioned, horse-drawn, Napoleonic bombardment, while the panzer machines limped into the repair shops, low on gasoline and breaking down in large numbers. They had done their work. The Polish armies had been sliced and frightened into fragments. Allied and American newspapers were writing terrified accounts of blitzkrieg, "the new form of warfare."

But the panzers arrived at Warsaw on the ninth of September. On the tenth the German supreme commander was writing in his battle diary that the war was over. On the seventeenth Warsaw still stood. All available Luftwaffe airplanes were making unopposed runs over the city, dumping bombs and hurrying back to Germany for more bombs. Horses were dragging more and more howitzers from Prussia and Pomerania to ring the city and fire shells inside. And still Radio Warsaw played the *Polonaise*.

*

Leslie Slote, heading the American embassy's skeleton staff in Warsaw, was an able and exceptionally clever man, but at the moment he was in the wrong job, because he was a coward. He did not look or act like one. At Yale he had been on the track team, and this token of manliness—which he had carefully selected, knowing the Rhodes requirements—together with his work on the college newspaper, his Phi Beta Kappa key, and his friendships with certain useful professors, had won him the scholarship hands down. He had been one of the few popular Americans at Oxford; in the Foreign Service they talked of him as an outstanding officer in his age group. Well aware of his problem, he would never have gone knowingly into a situation requiring physical courage. He had thought much about this hole in his makeup, and he had theories about it, centered on an oversolicitous mother and some childhood accidents. The theories didn't change anything, but they served to contain the weakness in his own mind as a misfortune like a polio limp, rather than as a blight which could corrode his self-respect. Slote had a high regard for himself, his powers, and his future. Bad luck had now put him in a spot where all his broad political knowledge, all his gifts of analysis, humor, and foreign tongues were of little avail compared to the simple capacity to be brave. That, he lacked.

He hid the lack with an inner struggle that was showing at the surface only in absentmindedness, continuous headaches, irritability, and a tendency to laugh for no reason. When the ambassador had asked him to stay on, he had burst out laughing. Since the first word that the Germans were coming, and especially since the first air bombs had fallen on Warsaw, he had been in a black panic, hungering for word that he and the other Americans could leave. He had bandages on several fingers where he had bitten his nails raw. And then the ambassador had asked him to stay on in this horror! The shrill laugh had welled up out of him. With a quizzical look the ambassador had let it pass. Most of the people in Warsaw had reacted well to the air attacks, swinging over to almost lighthearted determination and stoicism, once the first bombs failed to kill them. But for Slote the hell went on and on. Every sounding of an air raid alarm all but deprived him of the ability to think. Down into the thick-walled embassy cellar he would dart with everybody else, ahead of most, and invariably he would stay down until the all clear sounded. In a way, being in charge was a help. It looked proper for him to move out of his apartment into the embassy, to stay there, and to set an example of strict compliance with air raid rules. Nobody guessed his trouble.

Dawn of September the seventeenth found him at the big desk, a smoking pipe clenched in his teeth, carefully redrafting his latest dispatch to the State Department on the condition of the embassy and of the hundred or so

Americans trapped in Warsaw. He was trying to retain all the urgency and gravity of the message, while editing out traces of his private hysteria. It was a hairline to walk, the more so as no replies were coming in to any of these dispatches, and he could not tell whether the American government had any idea of the plight of its nationals in the Polish capital.

"Come in," he called to a knock at the door.

"It's broad daylight outside," Byron Henry said hoarsely as he walked in. "Shall I open the curtains?"

"Anything going on out there?" Slote rubbed his eyes.

"Nothing unusual."

"Okay, let's have some daylight," Slote laughed. They both pulled back the heavy black curtains, admitting pallid sunshine in broken patterns through the diagonally crossed timbers in the windows. "What about the water, Byron?"

"I brought it."

With the curtains open, one could hear the dull far-off thumps of German artillery. Slote would have preferred to leave the curtains closed for a while longer, shutting out these daytime noises of gray, broken, burning Warsaw. The quiet of the black-curtained room lit by a desk lamp might be illusory, a false conjuring up of peaceful student days, but he found it comforting. He peered between the timbers. "Such smoke! Are there that many fires?"

"God, yes. The sky was terrific until the dawn came up. Didn't you see it? All red and smoky wherever you looked. Dante's Inferno. And these big orange star shells popping all over, way high up, and slowly floating down. Quite a sight! Over on Walewskaya they're still trying to put out two huge fires with shovels and sand. It's the water problem that's going to lick them, more than anything."

"They should have accepted the German offer yesterday," Slote said. "They'd have had at least half a city left. There's no future in this. How on earth did you fetch the water? Did you manage to find some gasoline, after all?"

Byron shook his head, yawned, and dropped on the long brown leather couch. His sweater and slacks were covered with brick dust and soot, his long shaggy hair was in a tangle, and his eyes glowed dully in purple rings. "Not a chance. From now on we can forget about the truck. I saw fire engines stalled in the middle of the street. Gasoline's finished in this town. I just scouted around till I found a cart and a horse. It took me most of the night." He grinned at Slote, his lower lip pulled in with exhaustion. "The Government of the United States owes me one hundred seventy-five dollars. The hardest part was getting the boiler off the truck and onto the cart. But this peasant who sold me the cart helped me. It was part of the deal. A little sawed-off fellow with a beard, but strong. Jesus!"

"You'll get paid, of course. Talk to Ben."

"Can I stretch out here for a minute?"

"Don't you want breakfast?"

"I'm not sure I have the energy to chew. I just need a half hour or so. It's quiet in here. That cellar is a mad-house." Byron put up his feet and collapsed on the leather cushions, a meager long dirty figure. "There's no water at the opera house corner anymore," he said, closing his eyes. "I had to go clear over to the pumping station. It's a slow horse and it sure doesn't like pulling an iron boiler full of sloshing water."

"Thank you, Byron. You're being a great help."

"Me and Gunga Din. 'You may talk of gin and beer,' " Byron mumbled into his elbow, " 'when you're quartered safe out 'ere'—where's Natalie? At the hospital?"

"I daresay."

Byron fell asleep. The telephone rang harshly, but he didn't stir. The mayor's office was calling; Mayor Star-zynski was on his way to the embassy to discuss with the American chargé a sudden development of the highest urgency. Excited, Slote phoned the marine sentry at the gate to admit the mayor. This must be news: safe-conduct for foreigners out of Warsaw, or perhaps imminent sur-render! Nothing but surrender made sense now. He thought of waking Byron and asking him to leave the office, but decided to wait. The mayor might not arrive for a while. This grimy kid needed sleep.

Water had become a problem all through Warsaw; and in the embassy, with seventy people under one roof and more coming, it was—or might have been—an alarming, a disastrous problem. But from the day the water main had broken, Byron Henry had started supplying water, though nobody had asked him to. While Slote had been on the telephone to the mayor's office—twenty times on that first wretched day—demanding immediate water delivery for the Americans in his charge and swift repair of the main, Byron had gone out in the embassy's Ford pickup truck, and had retrieved from the cellar of a bombed-out house a rusty broken little boiler. Somewhere he had obtained soldering tools to patch it up, and now he was using it as a makeshift tank to bring water to the embassy. What would have happened otherwise there was no telling. The main was still broken, mains were broken everywhere now, and the city government was overburdened supplying just the hospitals and the fire fighters from tank trucks.

Day after day, as a matter of course, Byron fetched water, through bombardment and air attack, joking about his own terror, and often arriving much filthier than he was now, having dived into some rubble pile at the "whiffling" sound of a howitzer shell sailing through the air. Slote had never heard this "whiffling," as many people described it, and never wanted to. Despite these scares, Byron Henry actually seemed to be enjoying himself in the siege. This state of mind Slote regarded as stupider than his own, and not particularly admirable. His fear at least was rational. Natalie had told him of Byron's remark that he was having fun. The boy was a neurotic, Slote thought; the excessively bland good nature was a mask. But his water-carrying was an undeniable blessing.

Slote was also grateful to Henry, in an obscurer way, for keeping Natalie Jastrow occupied when she wasn't at the hospital. Natalie was the one person in Warsaw capable of penetrating to his secret fear. So far he was sure she had not, simply through not being around him enough. The girl's presence in Warsaw, a haunting burden, gave him pangs of hatred for her. As it was, she plagued him with guilt and anxiety by existing, by not vanishing from the earth. He had a wild physical craving for this dark-haired strong-willed Jewess, but he didn't want to marry her. A smooth hand at managing romantic liaisons, he had never before come up against such an iron girl. She had broken off their sexual relations in Paris and had never resumed them; she had told him half a dozen times to let her alone and forget her—the one thing he could not do. Why in the devil's name, then, had she thrust herself on him in this evil hour, in this holocaust, in a city shuddering under bombs and shells, where he was saddled with the heaviest responsibility of his life and yet felt befogged and castrated by fear? He dreaded exposure of his fear to Natalie more than anything, except getting hurt. He thought now that if they escaped with their lives, he would summon his willpower to cut this dragging business off. She might have the power to set him in a blaze, but she was impossibly obstinate and exotic, totally wrong for his career and for him. Meantime he owed this dirty slumbering youth thanks for keeping her out of his way.

Mayor Starzynski arrived shortly in an old limousine, a thickset moustached man wearing a green knitted vest with his unpressed floppy black suit. His shoes were caked with red mud. He had a flushed, excited, almost happy air, this man at the head of a perishing city, whose broadcasts were doing more than anything else to keep Warsaw fighting. He could hardly be sleeping two hours a night. The whole burden of the city was on him. Everybody from the diplomatic corps to the firemen on the streets and the hospital doctors were bypassing the slovenly municipal bureaucracy and appealing straight to the mayor for their needs. Yet he looked fresh and combative, the hero of the hour, and also the target of all the bitter jokes. The new heavy bombs dropped by the German planes in recent days were "Starzynski cabbages," the antitank steel spikes were "Starzynski toothpicks."

"Who is that?" the mayor said, pointing a fat thumb at the couch.

"Just a boy. Dead to the world. He doesn't understand Polish. I can send him out."

"Never mind, never mind." Starzynski waved both hands high and sat in the chair to which Slote gestured. He rested his thick hands on his knees and blew out a long breath, looked around at the large well-furnished room, and ran his fingers along the polished desk. "Well. You seem in good condition here. Is there anything we can do for you? Are your people all right?"

"We're fine. We're consumed with admiration for the Varsovians."

"Yes? The Germans have a bone in their throat, eh? We drove them back in the north last night. Berlin Radio

says it's over. We'll see." The mayor was red with pride.
"Our forces are only twelve miles away this morning from
a join-up with the Modlin garrison! Then the world will
see something! We'll have a battle line again, not a siege."

"That's wonderful news, Your Honor." Slote ran his
fingers caressingly over the warm bowl of his pipe, and
tried to smile with a gladness he did not feel.

"Yes, but the other news is not so good." The mayor
paused, looked Slote in the face, and said dramatically,
"The Russians have marched. The Soviet Union invaded
our country at dawn. They are pouring over the border by
the millions! Their excuse is that they want to protect their
nationals in Poland from the Germans. It's a crude disgusting lie, of course, but the Russians never change. They
have already taken Tarnopol and Baranowicze, and Rowne
will fall in an hour, if it hasn't already fallen. We have no
forces in the east. We have been sacrificing everything to
hold off the Germans in the west, waiting for the Allies to
march. And now the Russians are coming. There is nothing to oppose them between the border and Warsaw."

Slote burst out laughing.

The mayor stared at him, eyes bulging. "What is the
matter, sir? Don't you believe me? I tell you the Russians
have pounced on Poland from the rear in her agony. It is a
historic treachery. I have a message for your President!"
He pulled a paper from his breast pocket, unfolded it, and
slapped it on the desk before Slote. "If you have suggestions on the phrasing they will be welcome, but the highest
speed is now a matter of life and death."

Slote could scarcely translate mentally the Polish words
on the gray official paper. All he could think of was the
Soviet tanks and soldiers approaching Warsaw. He could
see the crawling machines and the Slavic faces. Perhaps
they were coming to claim their part of the evil bargain,
nothing more. Perhaps they would engage the Germans in
battle and turn Warsaw into Armageddon. Perhaps they
would bring up the famed Russian artillery and help the
Germans pulverize the Polish capital twice as fast. This
news seemed to him the authentic end of the world, and he
was not aware of laughing. He peered at the paper swimming before his eyes. "I understand the situation is extraordinary," he managed to say, surprising himself with his

own reasonable glibness, "but a communication from the head of a municipality to a head of government is awkward. An approach from President Moscicki, or Marshal Smidgly-Rydz, somebody in the national government, might prove more fruitful."

"But sir, our national government has crossed the border into Rumania. They are probably under house arrest by now, and the Germans will have them by the neck before the week is out. There's only Warsaw, but we are unafraid and we are fighting on. We want to know what we can hope for."

Slote got hold of himself and scanned the dispatch: familiar, pathetic rhetoric of appeal, like all the messages from Radio Warsaw to France and England during the past weeks. In fact the mayor was talking very much in his broadcasting style. "I'm not sure how fast I can get this out, sir. Lately I've been encountering twelve-hour delays and more via Stockholm."

"I guarantee you immediate transmission. You can send this in plain language. Let the whole world know," the mayor shouted, waving a fist, "that the people of Warsaw are fighting on despite the Russian treachery, and that we are calling on the great American President for a word of hope. If he speaks the Allies will listen. They'll march before it's too late. The Germans can still be smashed from behind. All their power is in Poland. The Allies can roar to Berlin in two weeks. Let the President only speak, and they will march!"

"We can encode it very rapidly, Your Honor. I think that's more prudent. We'll be ready to transmit in half an hour."

In a more businesslike tone Starzynski said, "Call my office, and we will arrange direct voice communication for you with Stockholm or Berne." He stood up and glanced around the room. "A peaceful oasis. The Luftwaffe respects the American flag. Very wise of them. How soundly the boy sleeps."

"He's exhausted. Mr. Mayor, how about the evacuation of neutrals? Did you discuss that with the Germans yesterday?"

"It was not the moment. They came under a flag of truce to ask for our surrender. General Dzuma wouldn't accept the message. The German officers wouldn't discuss any other subject. They said they would reduce us to rubble!" The mayor's voice rose to broadcasting pitch. "They're dropping leaflets all over the city this morning with the same threat, but where are the 'swarms of airplanes' and the 'hurricanes of shells' they talk about? The Germans are already throwing at us everything they've got. They have nothing to add but words. They've been doing their worst for two weeks, and here we are still! Let President Roosevelt only speak out, and civilization can still see a historic victory on the Vistula." His voice dropped; the exalted glow left his face. "I did mention the problem of the neutrals. Their emissary indicated that something would be worked out soon." The mayor gave Slote a cool look and added, with a smile that twisted his moustache, "We don't expect you to stay on and share our fate."

"You understand that we have nineteen women here," Slote said, feeling under the weight of this smile a need to apologize.

"Men, women, what's the difference? You're neutral." The mayor held out his hand. "Please send the message. I must broadcast it eventually. I want to give your great President the courtesy of a period for private consideration of his reply."

Slote grasped his hand. "We Americans here are awed by the stand of Warsaw, of that I can assure you. We will never forget it, and when we get home we will tell the story."

The mayor seemed moved. "Yes? The Germans are not supermen, you see. Warsaw has already taught that to the world. Some Germans are personally fine people, but as a nation they are swine. It is a matter of deep national immaturity and feelings of inferiority. A very complex question. They have the machines, the railroads, the factories, but we are not afraid of them. All we ask is a chance to keep fighting them."

"I will certainly convey that to my government."

"We need help. I am going from here to dig a trench." The mayor theatrically showed his blistered palms, and left.

Slote scrawled at his desk for several minutes, then summoned a coding clerk.

"Byron, wake up!" He shook Byron's shoulder, smearing his hand with brick dust. "Come on, get up. All hell is breaking loose." Byron turned over and opened dull eyes. "The Russians are coming. God knows when they'll be here. They invaded Poland this morning. Go and call Natalie."

With an elastic movement, Byron came erect and awake. "The Russians? Holy cow. This thing's getting interesting."

"*Interesting?* Byron, look, Warsaw will probably become the no-man's-land between the German and Russian armies. The city can be blown to atoms! Get Natalie and tell her she's to come here and stay here. Working in a belligerent's hospital is damned questionable anyway, and now—" Slote walked to the door, putting a fist holding the pipe distractedly to his head. "What a mess. So much to do."

Byron yawned and rose. "But what's the rush? How far is the Russian border from here, two or three hundred kilometers? Their army can't possibly get to Warsaw for a week."

Slote laughed. It had not occurred to him that the Russian armies needed several days to advance three hundred kilometers, but it was true, and very obvious. He took out his pouch and packed the pipe slowly to calm himself, saying, "Of course, but the point is, this development changes everything. There's never any predicting what the Russians or the Germans will do next. There may be dogfights over Warsaw today. The Germans may decide on half an hour's notice to let the neutrals out of here."

"Well, I'll try to get her, but you know Natalie."

"Please tell Natalie it's not a message from me," Slote said in a tight ragged tone, his hand on the doorknob, his head pounding, "but an official notice from the United States Government. We can no longer be responsible for the safety of anybody outside the four walls of this building. If we suddenly get packed out of here under a flag of truce—and it can happen any time—and she isn't around, I can't delay five minutes. We'll go, and she'll be the only foreigner left in Warsaw, and if by some freak she survives the bombs and the Nazis she can write a book. Tell her that, will you?" He closed the door hard.

By now Byron knew the route to the hospital well. It went through a part of the town which the Germans had been pounding hard. Sooty heaps of rubble pockmarked the way; there were craters in the streets, broken sewer pipes, torn cable conduits, downed telephone poles, uprooted trees, and endless piles of broken glass, masonry, wood, and rubbish. Children played on the heaps and in the ruined buildings. Women were washing clothes in the open, or cooking over pale fires of splintered wood in the bright sunshine. Work gangs were digging in the fallen houses, clearing twisted wires from the street, and shovelling and bulldozing debris. Almost everybody appeared cheerful and matter-of-fact; that was the remarkable thing, though Byron was getting used to it. He passed no funerals or other traces of the dead. Leaping, climbing, laughing in the destroyed houses, the children seemed to be finding war an amusing novelty, and school was evidently out. Here and there black-shawled women sat with bowed heads on chairs or stones. Some bared breasts to sucking babies. Many people with blank faces wandered amid the rubble and stared, or fumbled to find things. No fires were burning. The destruction was capricious. One block would be undamaged; the next half razed, as though an airplane had dumped all its bombs at once. Over jagged slanting half-walls, rooms like stage settings hung in the air, their different wallpapers or paint colorfully and pathetically exposed. Byron saw a broken piano hanging half out of one room.

He made his way through the entrance hall of the hospital. Here Warsaw's surprisingly cheerful air gave way to a pitiful and disgusting scene. Wounded people were piled and crowded helter-skelter along the marble floor awaiting help; mostly in rags, all dirty, green-pale, groaning or crying or in a faint, men and women. Poles and Jews, blood-smeared, unbandaged, with clothing ripped, with faces torn open, with arms and legs gashed, with an occasional red stump of limb blown away and terrible white bone showing. The children were piled separately in a big anteroom, where a sad chorus of wailing and screaming rose, mingled with some incongruous laughter. Byron hurried past the open door and down the curving stone staircase, into a long low basement area much warmer than the floor above; here the stink of faultily burning oilstoves was even stronger than the smells of medicine.

"Is he crazy?" Natalie exclaimed. "How can I leave? I just came on duty. Look!" She swept her arm around at the women in the jammed-together beds, moaning and shrieking in Polish, at others sitting up dolefully on beds or low stools, with fat white breasts and brown nipples bared to infants, at the three pallid sweating doctors moving from bed to bed, at the hastening nurses, some in soiled blood-stained white dresses like herself, with hair bound in white cloths, some in dark gray nun's habits. "There are five of us down here and we counted eighty-two women this morning! It's the only maternity ward left in Warsaw now. The Germans bombed out Saint Catherine's last night. They say it was unspeakably horrible, pregnant women running around on fire, newborn babies burning up—"

"The point is, Natalie, with the Russians coming—"

"I heard you! They're hundreds of miles away, aren't they? Go away, Briny, I have to work."

A stoop-shouldered doctor with a big nose, a square red beard, and sad filmed eyes was walking past. He asked Natalie in German what the problem was, and she told him.

"Go, by all means go," he said, in an exhausted voice. "Don't be foolish, you must leave with the other Americans. If the embassy sends for you, you must obey."

"Oh, the embassy! Nobody says we're leaving yet. This young man can come and fetch me in five minutes if they do."

"No, no, that's a risk you can't take. You're not a Pole, you're not supposed to risk your life. And you're Jewish, you're Jewish." The doctor put his hand to her head and pulled off the white cloth. Her loose hair fell thick, curling, dark. "You must go home."

Tears ran out of Natalie's eyes and down her face. "The woman with the twins is hemorrhaging. Did you see her yet? And the baby with the bad foot—" she gestured jerkily at a bed nearby.

"They're all on the list. Go back to the embassy right away. Thank you. You've helped us. Have a safe journey." The doctor shuffled away.

She turned on Byron. "Leslie Slote is a selfish bastard. He just doesn't want to have me on his mind. One thing less to think about." Suddenly she raised her skirt to her hips. The gesture gave Byron a shocking little thrill, though in point of fact the heavy gray bloomers coming down to her knees were considerably less sexy than the white skirt. She must have gotten those gruesome bloomers from the nuns, he thought. "Here," she said, pulling a thick wallet from her bloomers and dropping the skirt. "I'll go back to the goddamn embassy. But just in case, I want you to go and find Berel, and give him this. It's all my American money. Will you do that for me?"

"Sure."

"Tell me, Briny," Natalie said, "are you still having fun?"

He looked around at the noisy, crowded, evil-smelling ward, where the Polish women were helplessly bringing new life into a city which was being dynamited to death by the Germans, going through unpostponable birth pangs with the best care the dying city could give them. "More fun than a barrel of monkeys. Be careful going back to the embassy, will you? There's a big burning church on Franzuski, and they've got the street blocked off. Go around by the museum."

"All right. You'll probably find Berel in that gray building, you know, where the Jewish council works. He's on the food committee or something."

"I guess I'll find him."

Byron came out in a back alley where two men were loading dead people from the hospital onto a two-wheeled cart, much like the one he had bought to carry the water. Bodies lay on the cobblestones, and one man wearing a red-smeared white oilcloth apron was taking them up one by one in his arms and thrusting them at the other man, who stacked them in the cart—large rigid horrors with open mouths and fixed eyes—like dead fish in a market. The man tossed up the light body of a scrawny old woman, whose gray pubic hair showed through the pink rag still hanging on her.

Hurrying down Marshal Pilsudski Boulevard toward the Jewish section he heard the thumping of heavy guns, and nearby explosions like the blasting at a building site. Byron muttered routine curses at the Germans. He had spent a week in Germany after defecting from the University of Florence. They had seemed odd, but no more so than the

Italians; foreigners, but human enough, with a boisterous sense of fun and very polite manners. Yet here they were, surrounding the Polish capital, pounding it with explosives and flying steel, breaking the water mains, killing the children, turning living people into stiff glassy-eyed dead stacked garbage to be carted away and disposed of. It was really the most amazing outrage. To call it "war" was not to make it any more understandable.

This peculiar and horrible state of affairs in which he accidentally found himself was nevertheless far more colorful and interesting than "peace," as Byron remembered it. Delivering water to the United States embassy was the most satisfying thing he had done in his life. He loved the job. He was willing to be killed doing it. But the odds were all with him. This was the novel thing he was finding out. Most of the people in Warsaw were still alive and unhurt and going about their business. The city was far from destroyed or even half-destroyed. As he made his way to Nareiskaya district he passed through many a block of brown three-story houses which stood undamaged, peaceful, and quiet, looking exactly as they had before the German attack.

But in the Jewish quarter itself there were no such undamaged blocks. It was one broad smoky ruin. Clearly the Germans were raining extra shells and bombs on this district—a pointless course, since the Jews of Warsaw could not compel the surrender of the city. Such a deluge of fire and explosion concentrated on the city's vitals— power, water, transport, bridges—instead of on the Jews, could break Warsaw much faster. The bombardment of the Nareiskaya was an irrational wasteful assault by a powerful army against sad unarmed paupers.

The JUDEN VERBOTEN signs Byron had seen on park benches in Germany had been too bizarre to seem real. This bombardment of the Nareiskaya district first drove home to him the queer fact that the Germans really had murder in their hearts for these people. Trolley cars lay on their sides, burned out. Swollen dead horses stank in the streets, in clouds of fat black flies that sometimes settled stickily on Byron's hands and face. There were dead cats and dogs, too, and a lot of dead rats scattered in the gutter. He saw only one human body, an old man crumpled in a doorway. He had noticed before how quick the Jews were to remove their dead, and how they treated the corpses with respect, covering the loaded carts with cloths and following them in silent mournful straggles through the streets.

But despite the smashing up of the houses, the continuing fires, the smoke, the rubble, this quarter still abounded in eager crowded life. On one corner, outside a ruined schoolhouse, boys in skullcaps sat with their bearded teacher on the sidewalk, chanting over enormous books; some of the boys were not much larger than the books. Kiosks were still festooned with dozens of different newspapers and journals printed in heavy Hebrew lettering. He heard someone in a house practicing on a violin. The vendors of wilted vegetables and spotted stunted fruit, of tinned food and old clothes, stood along the sidewalks or pushed their creaky handcarts amid crowds of people. Work gangs were clearing rubble from bombed houses off the streets and the sidewalks. There were plenty of hands for the work. Byron wondered at this, for in the past weeks Jewish men and boys—perhaps because they were so recognizable—had seemed to erupt all over Warsaw, digging trenches, fighting fires, repairing mains. One bent old graybeard in skullcap and kaftan, wielding a shovel in a trench, gave a Jewish look to a whole work force. Nevertheless they did appear to be pitching in everywhere.

Berel Jastrow was not in the council building. Wandering through crowded, dark, dingy corridors lit only by flickering thick candles, Byron chanced on a man whom he had once seen conferring with Berel, a little, neat, bearded Jew with a glass eye that gave him a walleyed stare. Talking a mishmash of German and Yiddish, the man conveyed that Berel was inspecting the community kitchens. Byron set out to hunt him down, and came on him in a huge Romanesque synagogue of gray stone, undamaged except for a broken stone Star of David in a round glassless window. Jastrow stood in a low hot anteroom where people were lined up for a strong-smelling stew ladled out by kerchiefed perspiring women from tubs on wood-burning stoves.

"The Russians!" Berel stroked his beard. "This is definite?"

"Your mayor came to the embassy with the news."

"Let us go outside."

They talked out in the street, well away from the food queue. The raggedly dressed people in line stared at them and tried to hear the conversation, even cupping hands to ears. "I must report this to the central committee," Berel said. "It may be good news. Who knows? Suppose the two robbers cut each other's throats? Such things have happened. The Russians could be messengers of God."

He was taken aback when Byron offered him Natalie's wallet. "But what is she thinking?" he said. "I have money. I have dollars. She may need that herself. She isn't out of Warsaw yet."

Byron was embarrassed. It had not occurred to him that Jastrow might be offended, but now the reaction seemed natural. He said the Americans expected to leave Warsaw soon under a flag of truce.

"So. We won't see you or Natalie again?"

"Possibly not."

"Ah. Well, if the Germans let all you Americans out together, she should be safe. She told me an American passport says nothing about religion. Tell her I thank her, and I'll put the money in the food fund. Tell her—*Vorsicht!*"

A shell whistled down and exploded some distance away, making Byron's ears ache. Berel spoke hurriedly. "So, they are coming back to this neighborhood again. They shell by a system, the Germans. Yesterday was Yom Kippur, and all day the shells fell on us, they never stopped. Now, you will be seeing Arele?" He smiled wryly at Byron's blank look. "Dr. Aaron Jastrow," he said, mimicking English pronunciation.

"I guess so."

"Tell him," Berel said, *"Lekh lekha.* Can you remember that? It's two simple Hebrew words. *Lekh lekha."*

"Lekh lekha," Byron said.

"Very good. You're a fine Hebrew student."

"What does it mean?"

"Get out." Berel gave a worn white card to Byron. "Now, will you do me a favor? This is a man in New Jersey, an importer. He sent a bank draft in August for a large shipment of mushrooms. It came too late. I destroyed

the draft, so there's no problem, but—what are you smiling at?"

"Well, you have so much to worry about. And yet you think of this."

Jastrow shrugged. "This is my business. The Germans, they'll either come in, or they won't. After all, they're not lions and tigers. They're people. They'll take our money. It'll be a very bad time, but a war always ends. Listen, if the Russians come they'll take our money, too. So"—he held out his hand to Byron—"so, God bless you, and—"

Byron heard the noise of a shell very close, the unmistakable sloppy whir and whistle. It went splintering through the synagogue roof. The stunning explosion came a second or two later, giving him a chance to clap his hands to his ears and fall to the ground. Strangely, it did not blow out the front wall, and this was what saved the people on the line. Fragments of the roof went flying through the air, raining in a clatter on the street and on nearby buildings. Then, even as he and Jastrow stood, they saw the whole façade of the synagogue come sliding down like a descending curtain, disintegrating as it went with a rumble and a gathering crash. By now the queue of people had run out of danger. White dust boiled up, and through this cloud, which the breeze thinned at once, Byron could see the marble pillars and carved wooden doors of the holy ark untouched on the far wall, looking naked and out of place in the pale smoky sunshine.

Berel slapped him sharply on the shoulder. "Go, go! Don't stay here. Go now. I have to help."

Jewish men and boys were already groping into the new ruin, where many little fires were flickering. Little as he knew of Judaism, Byron understood that they meant to save the scrolls.

"All right, I'm going back to Natalie."

"Good. Thank you, thank you. A safe journey to both of you."

Byron left at a trot. The uncovering of the holy ark to the sunshine had shocked him like a piece of powerful music. Jogging back through the Jewish quarter of Warsaw, he saw these smashed rows of gray and brown houses, these cobbled streets and dirt alleys, these shabby courtyards and mews hung with drying laundry, these crowds of orderly Jews in beards and broad hats, these dark-eyed cheerful children playing under the bombs, these dogged tired street vendors with their carts and baskets, these kiosks laden with newspapers, magazines, feuilletons, and paperbound books, this smoke-filtered sunshine, these overturned trolleys, these dead horses—he saw all this in superbright detail, each picture printing itself on his mind as though he were a painter.

Without surprise or fear, he noticed thick V's of German planes coming out of the north. The sight had grown ordinary. He continued to trot, a little faster, through the emptying shell-pitted streets toward the embassy. People around him glanced at the sky and took shelter. The first waves were Stukas, diving down and spitting out black smoke, and Byron heard the irritated answering rattle of the weak rooftop machine guns of the Poles. One plane dove toward the street where he was running. He jumped into a doorway. Bullets went chattering down along the cobblestones, with a great whing-whang of ricochets. He watched the plane zoom away, then he trotted on, muttering the usual obscenities about the Germans.

Byron was developing a sense of invulnerability to the worst the Germans could do. To him they were contemptible bungling butchers. He was sure that the United States was going to rise in its wrath in short order, cross the Atlantic and knock the hell out of them, if the British and the French really proved too decayed or too scared to do it. The events around him must be making gigantic headlines in America, he thought. He would have been stupefied to know that the Polish war, its outcome clear, was already slipping to the back pages of United States papers, and that people were ignoring even the supposed "great debate" in the Senate over revising the Neutrality Act, because of the tight National League pennant race.

He loped through the embassy gate very much out of breath. The marine sentry gave him a salute and a familiar grin. Inside, in the big dining room darkened by window braces and blackout curtains, some fifty or so Americans caught in Warsaw were lunching at long trestle tables lit by oil lamps, making a loud clatter. Slote sat with Natalie, a small dark man named Mark Hartley, and some others at the ambassador's polished dining table. Panting from the long run, Byron told Natalie about his meeting with Berel. He did not mention the destroyed synagogue.

"Thanks, Briny! God help them all. Sit down and eat something. We have marvellous breaded veal cutlets, by some miracle."

Slote said, "Did you come here through the streets during this air attack?"

"He has duck feathers for brains," Natalie said, giving Byron an affectionate look.

"Byron is all right," Hartley said. He was a fourth at bridge with Natalie, Byron, and Slote, when they whiled away long night hours in the cellar. Mark Hartley's name had once been Marvin Horowitz, and he liked to joke about the change. He was a New Yorker in the importing business.

Byron took an empty seat beside Natalie and helped himself to a cutlet. It had a rather gamy, sticky taste, but after a week of canned sprats and sausages it seemed delicious, and he was famished. He downed it and forked another onto his plate. Slote smiled at him, and glanced around with satisfaction at the Americans happily consuming the cutlets. "By the way, does anybody here object to eating horsemeat?"

"I most certainly do," said Natalie.

"Well, that's too bad. You've just eaten it."

Natalie said, "Aagh!" and choked into her napkin. "My God. Horse! I could kill you. Why didn't you warn me?"

"You need nourishment. We all do. There's no telling what's going to become of us, and I had the chance to buy up this lot and I did. You've been dining on one of the great breeds of Poland. The mayor ordered the slaughter of a thousand of them yesterday. We were lucky to get a share."

Mark Hartley took another cutlet from the platter. Natalie said, "Mark! How can you? Horse!"

He shrugged. "We got to eat. I've eaten worse meat in kosher restaurants."

"Well, I don't claim to be religious, but I draw the line at horses. I'd as soon eat a dog."

Byron pushed away his plate. The awareness of horse-flesh heavy in his stomach, the gluey taste of horse in his mouth, the remembered smell of fly-blown dead horses on the Jewish streets, blended in his consciousness as one thing—war.

14

FOUR days later, early in the morning Natalie came scampering out into the embassy back yard, hair and skirt flying, and pounced on Byron, who was burning passport blanks and visa application files. The embassy had hundreds of the maroon passport booklets, which went up slowly and smokily; in German hands they could be used for smuggling spies and saboteurs into the United States. The stacks and stacks of visa requests, because they identified Jews, were also high on the burn-list. Byron had given up riffling through the files for the American currency often clipped to application forms. His job was to reduce the stuff to ashes as fast as he could; he was burning money and didn't care.

"Hurry. Come with me." Natalie's voice had a cheerful, excited ring.

"Where?"

"Just come."

In a chauffeured black limousine at the front gate, Slote sat next to a plump, pink, gray-headed man. "Hi there, Byron!" Slote too sounded surprisingly cheerful. "This is the Swedish ambassador. Byron Henry's father is our naval attaché in Berlin, Ambassador. It might be well to take him along, don't you think?"

The ambassador rubbed the side of his bulbous nose with a small neat hand, and gave Byron a wise look.

"Very much so. Yes indeed. And he should perhaps take notes."

"Just what I thought. Hop in, Byron."

A blood transfusion could not have changed Slote more. Byron had talked to him an hour earlier; the familiar gray, dour, slumped Slote, who had been glooming around the embassy, taking medicines, snapping short answers, and spending hours locked in his office. Ever since a bomb had fallen on the building next door, killing ten Poles, Slote had been like that. Byron figured the responsibility was wearing the chargé down. But now his face had color, his eyes were bright, and the very plume of blue smoke from his pipe looked jaunty.

As Byron got into the back seat, Natalie blurted to the ambassador, "Can I come along? Byron and I are travelling together."

With an annoyed grimace, Slote shook his head. The ambassador looked her up and down, with masculine amusement. Natalie wore a green silk dress and an old pink sweater, an atrocious getup pulled from her suitcase without thought. It made her look vulgarly sexy. "But, my dear, wouldn't you be frightened?"

"Of what?"

"The sound of guns. We're going to inspect the safe-conduct exit route." The ambassador's slow British speech was almost perfect. His small pink hand, resting on the open window, was manicured to a gleam, siege or no siege. "We may come rather close to the front."

"I've heard guns."

The ambassador smiled at Byron. "Well, shall we have your friend along?" He moved to make room for her beside him as he spoke. Slote said nothing, but gnawed his pipe in an annoyed way.

The car started off on a rough, zigzag ride toward the river. Warsaw had been crumpling in the past four days. A strong wind was blowing away the smoke, and beautiful morning sunshine gave a mocking peaceful look to the streets. But smashed buildings met the eye everywhere. Thousands of windows had been blown out and patched with bright yellow plywood. Warsaw was becoming a place of smoke, broken masonry, and yellow patches. The sidewalks and gutters were broken and cratered, and spiky tank traps and barricades cluttered main intersections. Glowering nervous soldiers at these intersections stopped the car with raised machine guns, their fingers at the triggers. Few other people were in sight. Far off, cannon drummed and thumped. Each time that a soldier lowered his gun and waved them on, Slote laughed boisterously.

"What I find so incredible," he said, as they came to a long stone bridge over the Vistula, crowded with carts, trucks, and bicycles, "is that this thing is still standing at all. Haven't the Germans been bombarding it for two weeks?"

"Well, you see, they are just not quite as devastating as they would have us believe," the Swedish ambassador said. "Nor as accurate."

The car drove out on the bridge, over the broad brown river serenely flowing between Warsaw and its eastern suburb, Praha, a place of low houses and green woods. Behind them in the sunshine, under a soft smoky blue sky, Warsaw at this distance looked surprisingly unharmed: a broad metropolis with wide avenues, baroque church domes, tall factory chimneys, and many climbing columns of black smoke. It might almost have been a manufacturing city on a busy day in peacetime, except for the yellow fires billowing up here and there, the flashes like summer lightning all around the horizon, and the distant whumping of the artillery. Several busloads of singing and joking soldiers went past the car. Some waved at Natalie and shouted. Many soldiers were also heading the same way on bicycles.

"Where are they all going?" Natalie said.

"Why, to the front," said the ambassador. "It's quite a war. They leave their guns and go home for lunch or dinner, or perhaps to sleep with their wives, and then they take a bus to the front again and shoot at the Germans. Madrid was rather like this when I was there during the Civil War."

"How far do we go?" Slote said. Here over the river the gun booms from Praha were louder.

The ambassador pursed his lips. "I'm not sure. We have to look for a schoolhouse with a stone goose in the front yard, a hundred yards or so past a wayside shrine."

On the other side of the river, they found a scene of ruin. Broken houses, burned tree trunks, and fallen trees lined the narrow tarred road, which was so torn up by shell-fire that the car had to detour time and again on dirt tracks. A camouflaged heavy Polish gun in the woods suddenly went off as the limousine bumped along one of these paths. The driver swerved and brushed a tree, the passengers leaped in their seats. "My God!" Slote said. The car steadied up and drove on through the wooded flat land of Praha. They passed a house with its roof ablaze, and the family outside dolefully watching. Loud explosions went off around them, two or three a minute. Sometimes they saw flames from gun mouths in the woods, though the guns themselves were invisible. Sometimes through the trees they could observe Polish gun crews feverishly moving about. It was all novel and exciting, at least to Byron, and they seemed to be enjoying this wartime sightseeing in perfect safety, despite the unpleasant bumping along grass and dirt to avoid the shell holes. But then a German shell burst near the car, throwing up a geyser of dirt which rattled and tinkled on the limousine roof.

Slote said, "Christ Almighty! We're at the front right now!"

"Yes, the schoolhouse must be right past that next curve," the ambassador said. But past the curve they saw only four log houses around a dirt courtyard, where several pigs trotted here and there, bewildered by the gun noise. Beyond, the straight tar road continued into leafy woods and smoke, and visibility ceased.

Slote said, "Please stop the car."

The ambassador glanced over his shoulder at him, rubbed his nose with a pink hand, and spoke to the driver. The car pulled to the side of the road.

"I didn't in the least understand from you," Slote said, gesturing with the pipe clutched in a fist, "that we were going into the actual zone of fire. Are you sure that we haven't missed a turn, and that we aren't behind the German lines right now?"

The ambassador pushed out his lips. "I don't believe we've come more than three miles from the bridge."

Slote burst out laughing, and jerked the pipe at Natalie

and Byron. "These young people are my responsibility. I can't expose them in this way."

Two loads of soldiers came along in lumbering old street buses with route numbers still displayed in front and faded movie advertisements on their sides. The soldiers were singing, and some waved out of the window at the halted limousine, or gave good-humored yells in Polish.

"Clearly we're not yet behind the German lines," said the ambassador.

"Nevertheless we'll have to take these civilians back to Warsaw," Slote said. "I'm sorry, you and I misunderstood each other."

Natalie exclaimed, "But why? There's no reason on earth to take us back. I'm perfectly all right."

"I'm afraid there isn't time." The ambassador deliberately scratched his eyebrow. "The cease-fire will probably come within the hour. As soon as we get back, I'll have to start assembling my party."

"So will I. But it's up to the Poles and the Germans, after all, to ensure that the neutrals cross the lines safely."

The ambassador glanced at his watch. "Colonel Rakowski asked that we come out and view the route ahead of time. I really do think we'd better go on." Two heavy guns went off in the woods—*RRUMPH! RRUMPH!*—one to the left, one to the right. The chauffeur whirred the ignition.

"Just a moment!" The driver turned around and looked at Slote, who had gone dead pale, his mouth working. "Ambassador, I must insist that you at least take us back to the bridge first. Perhaps there we can hitch a ride on a truck or bus."

"But my dear sir, you should see the route, too. Our parties may get separated later in the woods."

A peculiar feeling knotted Byron's stomach. The ambassador's faultless manners did not obscure what was happening, and Slote represented the United States. He said, "Leslie, I think you're dead right about Natalie. Why not take her into one of those log houses and wait? I can go on with the ambassador and get the information, if you like."

The ambassador at once said cheerfully, "Excellent

idea! We can go and return in ten or fifteen minutes, I'm sure."

Slote opened the car door and got out. "Come on, Natalie. We'll wait in the one with the green blinds, Ambassador. I saw a woman at the windows."

Natalie stayed in her seat, looking from Slote to the ambassador, her mouth pulled down unpleasantly. The ambassador said to her in a stiff European tone, "My dear, please do as you are told."

Jumping out, she slammed the door and ran toward the house. Slote hurried after her, shouting. The limousine shot forward in a rattle of pebbles. The haze ahead thinned as they drove into it. About half a mile further along they came upon the shrine, a luridly colored wooden Jesus on a gilt cross in a sheltering frame; and not far beyond that was the schoolhouse. Several soldiers, smoking and talking, lounged in front of it around a stone goose bordered with red flowers. Byron thought that if Leslie Slote could have held on only three or four more minutes, he would have been all right. That one bad moment in the limousine, when the dirt hit the roof, had been unlucky for him.

Colonel Rakowski hailed the Swedish ambassador with a shout and a hug. He seemed in unrealistically good spirits, Byron thought, and indeed all the staff officers looked too chipper, considering the bad news that shrieked from the military map of the front on the wall: a crude thick red crayon circle, completely ringing Warsaw. On the other walls of the schoolhouse, bright kindergarten pictures hung. Rakowski, an enormous man with pointed blond moustaches, and a big nose empurpled by good living, led the visitors out a back door, and along a leaf-carpeted path to a concrete gun emplacement, where grimy, whiskered men stripped to the waist were piling shells. Motioning the visitors to come on up the colonel climbed the shallow cement slope and mounted the sandbags. Byron followed the ambassador. A forested plain lay before them, dipping toward the east, with a scattering of houses and farms, and three widely separated church spires. Puffs of smoke out there, Byron realized, came from German artillery.

Panting from the little climb, the ambassador and the officer talked volubly, gesturing at the church spires. The ambassador scrawled notes and translated bits to Byron. On the terms of the cease-fire, he said, the neutral refugees would cross unescorted from the Polish to the German lines, heading for the farthest church, where Wehrmacht trucks would meet them. Colonel Rakowski feared that some refugees might wander on the poorly marked dirt roads, head for the wrong church, and find themselves between two fires when the truce—for which the Germans were granting only two hours—was ended. So he had asked the Swedish ambassador to come out and study the route beforehand.

"He says," the ambassador observed to Byron, closing his notebook, "that the best view is from that observation tower. You can make out the different roads, all the way to the Kantorovicz church."

Byron looked at the spindly wooden tower erected close by in the school's play yard. A narrow ladder led to a square metal-shielded platform, where he could see the helmet of a soldier. "Well, I'll go up, okay? Maybe I can make a sketch."

"The colonel says the tower has been drawing quite a bit of fire."

Byron managed a grin.

With a paternal smile, the ambassador handed him the notebook and pen. Byron trotted to the ladder and went up, shaking the frail tower as he climbed. Here was a perfect view of the terrain. He could see all the roads, all the turnoffs of the brown zigzags across no-man's-land, to the far church. The soldier on watch glanced away from his binoculars to gawk, as the young American in an open shirt and loose gray sweater sketched the roads in the ambassador's notebook, struggling with the pages as they flapped in the wind, marking all the wrong turns with X's, and crudely picturing the three churches in relation to the route. The soldier nodded when Byron showed him the sketch, and slapped his shoulder. "Ho kay," he said, with a grin of pride at his mastery of Americanese.

Natalie leaned in the open doorway of the cottage, arms folded, as the limousine drew up. She hurried to the car, followed in a moment by Slote, who first said good-bye at the door to a kerchiefed old woman in heavy boots. As the car drove back toward Warsaw, the ambassador re-counted their visit to the front, including Byron's venture up the tower. Meantime Byron worked on the notebook in his lap.

"Think four copies is enough?" he said to the ambassador.

"Plenty, I should think. Thank you." The ambassador took the notebook. "We may have time to run off some mimeograph copies. Very well done."

Natalie clasped Byron's hand and pulled it to her lap. She was sitting between him and Slote. She pressed his fingers, looking seriously at him, her dark eyes half-closed. Through her light green dress, he felt the flesh of her thigh on the back of his hand, and the ridge of a garter. Slote repeatedly glanced at the two hands clasped in the girl's lap as he calmly smoked, looked out of the window, and chatted with the ambassador about assembling and trans-porting the refugees. A muscle in Slote's jaw kept moving under the skin of his white face.

In the embassy all was scurry and noise. The mayor's office had just sent word that the cease-fire was definite now for one o'clock. Polish army trucks would take the Americans to the departure point, and each person could bring one suitcase. The rush was on. The Americans still living outside the embassy were being summoned by tele-phone. A smell of burning paper filled the building, and fragments of black ash floated in the corridors.

Mark Hartley occupied the cot next to Byron's in the cellar, and Byron found him sitting hunched beside a strapped-up suitcase, head in hands, a dead cigar protrud-ing from his fingers. "Ready to go, Mark?"

Hartley uncovered a drawn face, the eyes frightened and bulging. "Horowitz is the name, Byron. Marvin Horowitz."

"Nonsense, how will they know that?" Byron pulled from under the cot his old torn bag with the sprung hard-ware.

Hartley shook his head. "I don't know what's wrong with me. I must be crazy. I never once pictured that any-thing like this would happen. I don't know what I thought. Maybe that Roosevelt would fly us out in Army planes. Something like that. I've never been so goddamned scared in my life. We're going to the Germans. The Germans."

"Put that in your bag," Byron said, tossing a worn black book to him as he packed. "And cheer up. You're an American. That's all. An American named Hartley."

"With a Horowitz face and a Horowitz nose. What's this? The New Testament? What's this for?"

Byron took the book, which had a gold cross stamped on the binding, and carefully tore out the flyleaf with his own name written on it. "Make a good Christian of you. Here, put it away. Don't sit around and worry. Go help Rowlandson burn papers."

"I wish I had my own Bible or prayer book," Hartley said dully, unstrapping his bag. "I haven't been inside a synagogue since my bar mitzvah. An old smelly Hebrew teacher made me memorize a lot of gibberish. I did it to please my mother, but that was the end. I never went back once. Now I wish I remembered the prayers. Any prayers." He glanced around at the bustling cellar. "So help me, this hole looks to me now like home sweet home. I'd give anything if I could just stay here. Do you think we'll ever play bridge again one day, the four of us? In New York, maybe?"

"Sooner than you think."

"From your mouth in God's ears. That's what my mother used to say."

The army trucks came snorting and rattling up to the embassy at half past eleven; loose wobbly old machines so caked with mud and rust that their gray paint was scarcely discernible. At their arrival, more than a hundred Americans milling inside the fence on the lawn, set up a cheer and began singing "California Here I Come" and such ditties. The Poles of the staff, mostly girl secretaries, were sadly passing out coffee and cake.

"They make me feel ashamed," Natalie said to Byron. Two of the Polish girls bearing trays had just gone by with fixed forced smiles and glistening eyes.

"What's the alternative?" Byron, famished, bit into the coarse gray cake and made a face. It tasted of raw dough and paper ashes.

"There's no alternative."

Byron said, "Mark Hartley is scared stiff of the Germans. How about you?"

Natalie's eyes flashed. "What can they do to me? I have an American passport. They don't know I'm a Jew."

"Well, don't tell them. I mean don't become all brave or defiant or anything, okay? The idea is just to get the hell out."

"I'm not an imbecile, Byron."

A Polish officer shouted, the gate opened, and the Americans began piling into the trucks. Some people were too old to climb up, some were trying to take extra luggage, the Polish drivers and officers were urgent and short-tempered, and nobody was in charge. Yelling, complaining, weeping, and fist-waving went on, but most of the people, hungry and uncomfortable though they were, felt so happy at starting out that they continued to sing and laugh. The trucks clanked off in single file. A black Chevrolet with American flags on its fenders brought up the rear, carrying Slote, his three highest-ranking assistants, and the wives of two of them. Ouside the gate the Polish secretaries stood and waved, tears running down their faces. Byron and Natalie jolted along in a truck, clasping each other's waists. Slote had offered her a place in the Chevrolet. She had shaken her head without a word.

The bombardment was going on as heavily as ever: the distant *HRUMP! HRUMP! HRUMP!* of the artillery, the blasting explosions of bombs from three small V's of German planes passing slowly in the hazy midday sky, and the popping and stuttering of the Polish antiaircraft guns. The convoy crawled, stopped, and crawled through the shattered streets, the canyons of yellow-patched structures, careening up on sidewalks to avoid holes and tank traps, once backing out of a boulevard blocked by a newly fallen building.

At the bridge across the Vistula truck convoys flying various embassy flags were converging. The bridge was jammed to a standstill with refugee trucks. There were more than two thousand neutral nationals in Warsaw, and every one of them evidently meant to get out. Byron kept glancing at his watch. The traffic started to move again, but so slowly that he feared they might not reach the departure point by one o'clock. German shells kept whistling by, and splashes like geysers boiled up in the river, sometimes showering the bridge and the trucks. The Germans clearly thought it all in the game if they killed nine-tenths of the neutrals on the bridge, fifteen minutes before the cease-fire.

The convoys ended in a stupendous pileup at the school-house with the stone goose. Colonel Rakowski and the Swedish ambassador stood together in the road, shouting instructions to each truckload of descending passengers and handing out mimeographed instruction sheets. With some pride of authorship, Byron noticed that whoever had traced his sketch on the stencil had faithfully copied it, even to his crude pictures of the three churches.

Guns in the woods all around the school were thundering away, but at five minutes to one the bombardment began to fade down. At one o'clock the guns fell silent. The loudest noise was the chattering of refugees in many languages along both sides of the road. Byron could hear birds, too, and the strumming of grasshoppers. It struck him that the noise of grasshoppers was the most peaceful sound on earth. A loudspeaker bawled final instructions in one language after another. Groups of neutrals, picking up their suitcases, began to walk down the sloping road. Finally came the English in a heavy Polish accent, *"Please keep together. Do not make wrong turns. The German command has stated it will accept no responsibility for anybody who is not at the Kantorovicz church by three o'clock. Therefore the Polish command can accept no such responsibility. It is an easy hour's walk even for an old person. The enemy will undoubtedly recommence hostilities at three. We will return the heaviest possible fire at the first shot. Please, therefore, hurry. Good luck to you all. Long live America. Long live Poland."*

At this, the Americans took up their luggage and walked into no-man's-land.

For two or three hundred yards it was no different than the rest of Praha, but then the asphalt road narrowed and trailed off into a dusty, rutted, one-lane cart track. They passed ruined houses. The barnyards had no animals, except for an occasional abandoned chicken wandering and clucking, and some slinking jumpy cats. The road entered woods where sunlight slanted down in green-yellow bars through the leaves. The leader of the Americans, a tall

gray Episcopalian minister in a black suit and turnaround
collar, checked Byron's sketch at each crossroad. This
strange slow walk between two silent enemy armies took a
full hour by Byron Henry's watch. As he remembered it
later, it was like a stroll in company in peacetime through
a fragrant autumnal forest. Many fall flowers, blue and
orange and white, dotted the dirt road and the woods; the
birds chirped and twittered; and the wonderful song of the
grasshoppers filled the air. He also remembered becoming
very dry-mouthed and thirsty from tension, so thirsty that
his legs felt weak. Two other memories stayed with him:
the diplomats' black cars going by, honking the walkers
out of the road, with Slote laughing in the front seat and
waving at him and Natalie; and then, near the end of the
trek, at the bend of the road where the Kantorovicz church
appeared, Mark Hartley coming up beside him, slipping his
hand through his elbow, and saying, "My name is Mark
Hartley, and oy, am I a good Christian!"—smiling at
Byron, his face dust-caked and terror-stricken.

All at once, there were the German guns and the German gun crews in the woods. The howitzers were bigger
than the Polish artillery pieces, with an appearance of
better, newer engineering. Watching the walkers, the soldiers stood quietly at their weapons, in their neat field
gray and formidable Wehrmacht helmets. Byron peered at
the German soldiers with immense curiosity. The helmets
gave them a beetling warrior look, but most of them were
young and had the same German faces he had seen in
Munich and Frankfurt. Many wore glasses. It was hard to
believe that these were the villains who had been pouring
flying steel and fire on Warsaw, setting pregnant women
aflame, blowing children's legs and hands off, and making
a general shambles of a handsome metropolis. They were
just young men in soldier suits and stern helmets, standing
around in the shady woods amid the pleasant noises of
birds and grasshoppers.

From the first, the Germans handled the refugees better
than the Poles had. A mule-drawn water cart—a large
olive-painted cylinder on wheels—stood by the road near
the church, and soldiers waited with tin cups to herd the
thirsty people into a queue. From the water tank, other
soldiers guided them toward new clean gray trucks, with

thick black deeply treaded tires, so different from the Poles' dirty deteriorated machines. Wehrmacht officers in tailored long military coats and high peaked caps were talking amiably, though with marked condescension, to the arriving diplomats near a table by the roadside. As each national group came to the trucks, its ambassador or chargé gave a typed roster to a bespectacled soldier behind the desk. He called off names, and one by one the people entered the vehicles, which unlike the Polish trucks had wooden seats. The Poles had not troubled with rosters. There was no bunching up, no disorder. Soldiers stood by with little stools to help up the elderly and to hand the few children to their mothers with a laugh and a playful little swing. At a field ambulance marked with a red cross medical orderlies gave restoratives. Two soldiers with movie and still cameras roamed the scene, recording all this good treatment of the neutrals. The loading was not quite over when the guns near the church all at once shot off a salvo that made the ground shake. Byron's watch read a minute past three o'clock.

"Poor Warsaw," Natalie said.

"Don't talk," Mark Hartley said in a low hoarse voice. "Don't say *anything* till we're out of this." They sat with Byron on the last bench of a truck, from which they could look out.

Natalie said, "Look at Slote, will you? Taking a cigarette from a German, for crying out loud, and *laughing!* It's just unbelievable. All these German officers with their long coats and pushed-up caps. There they are, just like their pictures."

"Are you afraid?" Byron said.

"Not any more, now that it's actually happening. I don't know why. It's sort of dreamlike."

"Some dream," Hartley said. "It should only be a dream. Jesus Christ. That officer with Slote is coming here." Hartley gripped a hand on Byron's knee.

The officer, a blond young man with a good-natured smile, came straight to Byron, speaking with a pleasant accent, slowly and precisely. "Your chargé tells me that your father is American naval attaché in Berlin."

"Yes, sir, he is."

"I am a Berliner. My father is in the foreign ministry."

The officer fingered the binoculars around his neck. His manner seemed not very military and rather self-conscious. Byron thought he might be feeling compunction of a sort, and he liked the German better for that. "I believe I had the pleasure of meeting your parents in August at the Belgian embassy, and of dancing with your mother. What on earth have you been doing in Warschau?"

"I was sightseeing."

"Well, you saw some unusual sights."

"That I did."

The officer laughed, and offered his hand to Byron. "Ernst Bayer," he said, putting his heels together.

"Byron Henry. Hi."

"Ah, yes. Henry. I remember the name. Well, you are comfortable? Can I offer you a ride in a staff car?"

"I'm fine. Where are we going?"

"Klovno. It's the nearest working railroad junction, and there you will all transfer to a special train for Königsberg. It's more than a three-hour trip. You might enjoy it more in an automobile."

"Well, I've been travelling with these folks, you know. I'll stay with them. Thanks a lot." Byron spoke cordially, though this polite chitchat with a German felt exceedingly strange after all his anger at them.

Slote said to Natalie, "We can still make room for you in the Chevy. That wooden slat's going to get kind of hard."

She shook her head, looking darkly at the German.

"Give my best to your mother," said the officer, with a casual glance at the girl and back at Byron. "She was really charming to me."

"I sure will."

Several guns fired in succession nearby, drowning out something the officer said. He grimaced, and smiled. "How are things in Warschau now? Very distressing?"

"Well, they seem to be hanging on pretty well."

Half-addressing Natalie as well as Byron, Bayer said, "A bad business! The Polish government was completely irresponsible, running off into Rumania and leaving the country without leadership. Warschau should have been declared an open city two weeks ago. This destruction is pointless. It will cost a lot to repair. The mayor is very

brave, and there is a lot of admiration here for him, but"
—he shrugged—"what is there to do but finish it off? This
will be over in a day or two."

"It may take longer than that," Byron said.

"You think so?" Bayer's pleasant smile faded. He
bowed slightly and walked off, toying with the glasses.
Slote shook his head at Byron and followed the officer.

"Why the hell did you get him mad?" Hartley whispered.

"Oh, Christ. Blaming the *Polish* government for the
siege!"

"He meant it," Natalie said, in a wondering tone. "The
man was absolutely sincere."

With some shouting in German, snorting of motors,
honking of horns, waving by the soldiers, the convoy departed from Kantorovicz, a hamlet of half a dozen wooden
houses around the church, intact but abandoned. Since
leaving the schoolhouse, the refugees had not seen a living
Pole, nor a dead one. The trucks wound along one-lane
dirt roads, passing burned-out barns, blown-apart houses,
overturned windmills, broken churches, schoolhouses without windows or roofs, and much torn-up, shell-plowed
ground and charred tree stumps. Still the scene was not at
all like battlegrounds in movies and books of the last war:
gray wastes of barren dead muck, tangles of barbed wire,
dark zigzagging trenches. These fields and woods were
green. Crops were still standing. Only the inhabitants were
eerily absent. It was almost as though H. G. Wells's invaders from Mars had passed through in their perambulating metal tripods, atomizing or eating the people and
leaving only slight trails of their transit. The first Poles who
came in sight, far behind the German lines, were an old
man and his wife working in a field in late sunshine; they
leaned on their implements and solemnly watched the trucks
go by. As the trucks travelled farther from Warsaw, more
peasants began to appear, going about their fieldwork or
repairing damaged houses, either ignoring the trucks or
watching their passage with blank faces. Nearly all were
old people or children. In this back country, Byron saw no
young men, and only two or three kerchiefed, skirted
figures that from their slimness and supple movements
might have been girls. Yet more striking, he saw not one

horse. The horse, and the vehicles it pulled, were the trademark, the very life, of rural Poland. On the way from Cracow to Warsaw, there had been thousands of horses, clogging the roads, working in the fields, carrying soldiers, dragging heavy loads in the cities. Behind the German lines this animal seemed extinct.

The ride was too bumpy for conversation, and the refugees were still tired, and perhaps frightened by the deepening awareness of being in the hands of the Germans. Hardly a word was spoken in the first hour or so. They came out on a tarred road, narrow and primitive enough, but by comparison with the cart tracks of the back country, a glassy highway. The convoy stopped at a knoll of smooth green lawns and flower gardens topped by a brick-walled convent, and the word passed for women passengers to dismount and "refresh themselves." The ladies happily went off, the men scattered among the trees or urinated by the roadside, and when the convoy rolled again everybody was much more cheerful.

Talk sprang up. Natalie brought back gossip from the ladies' room. All the neutrals, she said, would be offered a choice of flying to Stockholm, or else of taking German trains to Berlin, and thence going out via Belgium, Holland, or Switzerland.

"You know," the girl said, with a mild glint in her eye, "I'd sort of like to see Berlin myself."

"Are you crazy?" said Hartley. "Are you absolutely crazy? You must be kidding. You go to Stockholm, baby, and you just pray they *let* you go to Stockholm. This girl has a screw loose," Hartley said to Byron.

Byron said, "Berel's message to A.J. goes for you, too. *Lekh lekha.*"

"*Lekh lekha.*" She smiled. Byron had told her about this. "Get out, eh? Well, maybe."

"In the name of God," Hartley muttered, "stop with the Hebrew."

The ride stretched out to four and five hours of grinding through farmland and forests. All traces of war faded from the landscape. Houses, churches, whole towns were untouched. The inhabitants looked and acted as they had in the peacetime countryside. There were few young people, no horses, and very little cattle and poultry. In the towns

a red swastika flag flew over the main square, either on a
flagpole or from the town hall, and German soldiers stood
sentry or patrolled on foot or on motorcycles. But the conquered land was at peace. The absence of livestock and
young folks gave it a dead look, the peasants seemed
somewhat more dour and sullen, perhaps, but life was
going on exactly as before, except that the Germans were
in charge.

The sun sank behind the distant flat horizon in a brief
glow of pale orange. The trucks rolled on into the night.
The passengers quieted. Natalie Jastrow put her head on
Byron's shoulder and took his hand in hers. They both
dozed.

Commands shouted in German woke them. Lights
blazed. They were in a square before a wide railroad station, and people were streaming down out of the lined-up
trucks. The lower half-door of their truck was still closed,
but two helmeted Germans came along and opened it with
a clank. *"Bitte raus! Alle im Wartesaal!"* Their manner
was brisk, not hostile, and they stood by to help down the
women and old men. It was a cool moonlit night and
Byron was glad to see darkness and stars overhead once
more, instead of a smoke pall and a fiery glow.

The refugees gathered in a confused mass in the waiting
room, still blinking at the light. Double doors opened at
one end of the room, and soldiers shouting in German
shepherded them through, bearing along Byron and Natalie. Byron carried their suitcases and Hartley clung like
a child to his elbow. They entered a dining hall full of long
plank tables on trestles, laden with food.

It was the most dazzling banquet that Byron had seen in
his life—or so it seemed in the first thunderstruck seconds,
famished as he was after the long ride and the three weeks
of wretched food in besieged Warsaw. There were platters
of smoking sausages and sauerkraut, there were many
whole pink hams, there were mounds of boiled potatoes,
piles of fried chicken, stacked loaves of fresh bread, pitch-
ers of beer, immense whole yellow and orange cheeses. But
it seemed a mockery, a cruel Nazi trick, a Barmecide feast,
because the soldiers herded the neutrals along the walls
away from the tables. There they stood, hundreds of them,

staring at the distant food, and in the space between stood a few alert German soldiers with lowered tommy guns.

A voice spoke over a loudspeaker in clear conversational German: *"Welcome! The German people are your hosts. We welcome the citizens of the neutral countries in peace and friendship. The German people seek peace with all nations. Relations with Poland have now been normalized. The treacherous Smidgly-Rydz regime, having met its just punishment, has ceased to exist. A new Poland will rise from its ashes, cleaned up and law-abiding, where everybody will work hard, and irresponsible politicians will no longer provoke disastrous foreign adventures. The Führer can now seriously pursue a peaceful settlement of all outstanding questions with Great Britain and France, and afterward Europe will enter on a new order of unparalleled mutual prosperity. Now we ask you to sit down and eat. Hearty appetite!"*

A dozen smiling blonde girls in white waitress uniforms made their entrance, almost like a theatre chorus, carrying jugs of coffee and stacks of plates. The soldiers smiled and walked out of the space in front of the tables, making inviting hospitable motions with their lowered guns. There was an awkward, shocked moment. First one and then another refugee hesitantly stepped out of ranks to cross the space. Others followed them, a few sat on the low benches reaching for food, and a noisy break and rush began.

Like the rest, Byron, Natalie, and Hartley dived for places and gorged themselves on the richest, sweetest, most satisfying meal of their lives. Almost the best of it was the coffee—ersatz though it was—hot, all they wanted, poured again and again by willing cheery buxom girls. Over the loudspeaker, while they stuffed, came a cascade of brass band music—Strauss waltzes, marches, and jolly drinking songs. Many of the neutrals began singing, and even the watching soldiers joined in.

> *Du, du, liegst mir im Herzen,*
> *Du, du, liegst mir im Sinn—*

Byron himself, relaxed by the beer and carried away by the ecstasy of a full belly, the lift of the music, and the

outburst of relieved high spirits all around him, swung his
stein and sang:

> *Du, du, machst mir viel Schmerzen,*
> *Weisst nicht wie gut ich dir bin*
> *Ja, ja,*
> *Ja, ja!*
> *Weisst nicht wie gut ich dir bin,*

and Mark Hartley sang right along too, though his eyes
never ceased rolling at the German soldiers. Natalie, silent,
regarded them both with a satirical motherly look.

Returning to the waiting room, stuffed and dizzy after
this incredible, this visionary feast, they saw crudely lettered placards around the brown tile walls: BELGIEN,
BULGARIEN, KANADA, NIEDERLANDE. They went and stood
under the VEREINIGTE STAATEN sign. Laughing, chattering,
the refugees sorted themselves out, gay as though returning from a picnic. Men in black uniforms entered the waiting room. Conversation died among the Americans and
the cheery noise faded throughout the station.

Slote said soberly, "Listen, please, everybody. Those are
the SS. I'll do any talking to them that has to be done."

The men in black fanned out, one to each group of
neutrals. The one who headed for the Americans did not
appear sinister. Except for the operatic black costume,
with its silver double-lightning-flash insignia, he looked
like an American himself, perhaps a young insurance sales-
man one might sit next to on a train or plane. He carried
a black leather portfolio. Slote walked out to meet him.
"I'm Leslie Slote, first secretary of the United States embassy and acting chargé d'affaires."

The SS man bowed, heels together, both hands on the
case. "You have a gentleman named Byron Henry in your
party?" His English was smooth.

"This is Byron Henry," Slote said.

Byron took a step forward.

"Your father represents the American Navy in Berlin?"
Byron nodded.

"This message is forwarded to you via the foreign ministry." Byron put the yellow envelope in his breast pocket.
"You may read it now, of course."

"Thanks. I'll look at it later."

The SS man turned to Slote. "I am to collect the American passports." His tone was brisk and cool, his blue eyes distant, almost unfocussed on the Foreign Service man. "Let me have them, please."

Slote was very pale. "I'm reluctant to surrender them, for obvious reasons."

"I assure you it is quite routine. They are to be processed on the train. They will be returned to you before you arrive in Königsberg."

"Very well." At a motion from Slote, an assistant gave him a thick red portfolio, which he handed to the man in black.

"Thank you. Now your roster, please."

The assistant held out three clipped sheets. The SS man glanced through them, and then looked around. "No Negroes in your party, I see. How many Jews?"

Slote took a moment to reply. "I'm sorry, but in our passports we make no record of religious affiliation."

"But you do have Jews." The man spoke offhandedly, as though discussing doctors or carpenters.

"Even if there were Jews in the party, I would have to decline to answer. The policy of my country on religious groups is one of absolute equality of treatment."

"But nobody is suggesting that there will be inequality of treatment. Who are these Jews, please?" Slote looked silently at him, touching his tongue to his lips. The SS officer said, "You have mentioned your government's policy. We will respect it. The policy of my government is simply to maintain separate records where Jews are concerned. Nothing else is involved."

Byron, a couple of paces forward from the group, wanted to see how Natalie and Hartley were behaving, but he knew it would be disastrous to glance at them.

Slote did look around at the whole party in a glance of caution, appeal, and great nervousness. But he produced a calm professional tone when he spoke. "I'm sorry. I just don't know if anybody here is Jewish. I'm not personally interested, I haven't asked, and I don't have the information."

"My instructions are to separate out the Jews," said the officer, "and I must now do that." He turned to the Americans and said, "Form a double line, alphabetically, please." Nobody moved; they all looked to Slote. The SS man turned to him. "Your party is in the custody of the Wehrmacht, in a combat zone under strict martial law. I call this to your attention."

Slote glanced out toward the waiting room, his face harried. In front of several parties—the Swiss, the Rumanian, the Hungarian, the Dutch—a few miserable Jews already stood separated, heads bowed, with their suitcases. "Look here, for your purposes you can assume we're all Jews." His voice was starting to shake. "What next?"

Byron heard a shrill woman's voice behind him. "Now just a minute. What on earth do you mean by that, Mr. Slote? I'm certainly not a Jew and I won't be classified or treated as one."

Slote turned and said angrily, "I mean that we all must be treated alike, Mrs. Young, that's all. Please cooperate as I asked—"

"Nobody's putting me down for a Jew," said a man's voice from a different direction. "I'm just not buying that either, Leslie. Sorry."

Byron recognized both voices. He turned around as the SS officer addressed the woman: "Yes, madam. Who are you, please?"

"Clara Young of Chicago, Illinois, and I'm not Jewish, you can be darn sure of that." She was a dried-out little woman of sixty or so, a bookkeeper in the American movie distributor's office in Warsaw. She giggled, glancing here and there.

"Would you be kind enough to point out the Jews in your party, madam?"

"Oh, no, thank you, mister. That's your business, not mine."

Byron expected that. He was more worried by the man, a retired Army officer named Tom Stanley, who had been selling heavy machinery to the Polish government. Stanley was given to saying that Hitler was a great man and that the Jews had brought all their trouble on themselves.

The SS man asked for Stanley's name and then said to him in a cordial man-to-man way, "Who are the Jews here, please? Your party can't leave until I know. You seem to understand this matter better than your chargé."

Stanley, an old turkey-cock of a man with hanging jowls, a wattled throat, and a brush of gray hair, grew quite red and cleared his throat several times, thrusting his hands into the pockets of his loud green-and-brown sports jacket. All the Americans were staring at him. "Well, I'll tell you, friend, I'd like to cooperate, but so far as I know there aren't any. Not in this party."

The SS officer shrugged, ran his eyes over the group, and stopped at Mark Hartley. He flicked two fingers forward. "You. Yes, you, the one with the blue bow tie, step this way." Again he flicked the fingers.

"Stay where you are," Slote said to Hartley; then, to the officer, "I would like to have your name and rank. I protest this procedure, and I warn you that this incident will result in a written protest from my government if it continues."

The SS officer gestured around the waiting room, and said in a reasonable tone, "The officials of all the other governments are cooperating. You see for yourself. This is nothing to protest. This is a simple matter of conforming to local regulations. What is your name, you there?"

"Mark Hartley." The voice was steady enough, steadier than Slote's.

"Mark Hartley, I see." The SS man smiled a peculiar, chilling smile, his eyes wide and serious. It was the smile of the Polish soldier on the road to Warsaw, who had yanked the beard of the taxi driver. "*Hartley,*" he repeated. "And under what name were you born?"

"That name."

"Really! What were your parents?"

"Both Americans."

"Jews?"

Byron said, "I happen to know him, sir, we've been going to church together all the time in Warsaw. He's a Methodist like me."

The tall silver-haired minister, standing near Clara Young, ran his fingers inside his clerical collar. "I can vouch for that. I conducted services when Mr. Hartley was present. Mark is a devout Christian."

The SS officer, with a disagreeable, puzzled grin, said to Slote, "This one is certainly Jewish. I think a little physical examination would—"

Slote broke in, "I would report that as personal violence. In America circumcision at birth is routine."

"I'm circumcised," said Byron.

"So am I," said the old clergyman.

In the rest of the waiting room the process of sorting out the Jews was over. People were glancing at the Americans, pointing and whispering. The SS men were gathered at the entrance, all except a stout bald one with gold leaf in his black lapels, who now approached the American party, pulled aside the officer, and murmured with him, glancing at Hartley. The officer, without a word, pushed through to Hartley, took his suitcase, and undid the straps.

Slote said sharply, "Hold on, sir. This is not a customs point, and there's no reason to search personal belongings—" But the officer, down on one knee, already had the bag open and was rummaging in it, spilling its contents on the floor. He came on the New Testament, turned it over in his hands with an expression half-astounded, half-sneering, and brought it to his superior officer. The bald man examined it, handed it back, and threw his hands in the air. "So," he said in German, "in a hundred Americans, maybe not one. Why not? Any Jew would have been an idiot to come to Warsaw this summer. Come. The train is being delayed." He walked off.

The SS man tossed the black book with the gold cross in the open bag, and rudely gestured at Hartley to pick up his belongings, stepping over the pile as though it were garbage. Scanning the other faces in the group, he stepped up to Natalie Jastrow and gave her a long amused scrutiny.

"Well, what are you looking at?" she said, and Byron's heart sank.

"You're very pretty."

"Thank you."

"Rather dark. Your ancestry?"

"I'm Italian."

"What is your name?"

"Mona Lisa."

"I see. You step forward."

Natalie did not move.

The officer grunted and begun turning the pages of the roster.

Slote quickly said, "She's my fiancée. We'll be married next month."

The bald officer shouted from the entrance and waved at the SS man, who roughly handed the roster to Slote. "Very well. You love your Jews. Why do you refuse to take in ours? We have swarms." He turned to Byron. "You're the son of a naval officer, and yet you lie about a Jew! That fellow is a Jew."

"He's not, honestly," Byron said. "I think Mark sort of looks like Dr. Goebbels. You know short, dark, with a big nose."

"Dr. Goebbels? So." The SS man glared at Hartley and Natalie, broke into a nasty laugh, and walked off.

A loudspeaker called out in German, *"All Jews to the restaurant. Everybody else to track seven and board the train."*

The refugees went crowding out to the dark tracks. The Jews, a forlorn little group, straggled back to the dining room, with men in black surrounding them.

Soldiers halted the crowd at the train to allow diplomats aboard first.

Slote muttered to Byron, "I'll take a compartment. You'll see me at the window. Bring Natalie and Mark, and by all means Reverend Glenville and his wife."

Soon, through billowing steam, Byron could see the chargé waving from inside the dimly lit train. Byron came aboard with the four others, in a suffocating crush, and found the compartment.

"Thanks," Hartley whispered when they were all seated and Slote had slid shut the door. "A million thanks. Thanks to all of you. God bless you."

"Leslie Slote is the man," said the minister. "You did nobly, Leslie."

"Nobly," said Natalie.

Slote looked at her with a hangdog smile, as though not sure she was serious. "Well, I was on pretty good ground. They tried to get that information from me at Kantorovicz, you know, and couldn't. They got it from all the others. That's why the separation went so fast here. But why the devil did you make that Mona Lisa joke?"

"It was very risky," the minister said.

"Idiotic," Hartley said. They were talking in whispers,

though the corridor was buzzing with loud talk, the stationary train was hissing and clanging, and a public address system outside was bellowing in German.

"How about Byron and Dr. Goebbels?" Natalie said with a grin. "That was pretty neat, I thought."

"Neither of you seems to understand," Hartley said, "that these are murderers. Murderers. You're like kids, both of you."

Reverend Glenville said, "I'm not willing to believe that, Mr. Hartley. I know the German people. They have had a cruel, unjust system imposed on them, and one day they'll throw it off. At bottom they are good."

"Well, Stockholm ahoy," Natalie said. "I admit one thing. I've lost all curiosity about Berlin."

"You've got to get your passport back first," Hartley said. His jolly face was carved in a hundred lines and creases of tragic bitterness. He looked extraordinarily old, inhumanly old: the Wandering Jew, in an American sports jacket.

The train started with a wrenching clang. Byron now pulled out the yellow envelope. The message, on a Wehrmacht official form, had these few English words: GLAD YOU'RE OKAY. COME STRAIGHT TO BERLIN. DAD.

15

THE long string of cars squealed into the Friedrichstrasse terminal in clouds of white vapor, clanking, slowing. Rhoda clutched Victor Henry's arm and jumped up and down, to the amusement of the uniformed foreign ministry man who had escorted them to meet the train from Königsberg. Pug observed his smile. "We haven't seen our boy in over a year," he shouted above the train noise.

"Ah? Well, then this is a great moment."

The train stopped, and people came swarming out.

"My GOD!" exclaimed Rhoda. "Is THAT him coming down those steps? It CAN'T be him. He's a SKELETON."

"Where? Where?" Pug said.

"He disappeared. Somewhere over there. No, there he is!"

Byron's chestnut hair was very long and curly, almost matted; the bones stood out in his pale face and his eyes looked bright and enormous. He was laughing and waving, but at first blink his father almost failed to recognize this long-jawed sharp-chinned young man with the shabby clothes and raffish air.

"It's me. This is *me*," he heard Byron yell. "Don't you even know me, Dad?"

Pug plunged toward Byron, holding Rhoda's hand. Byron, smelling of wine, embraced him in a tight, fierce, long hug, scratching his father's face with a two-day growth of bristles. Then he hugged and kissed his mother.

"Gad, I'm reeling," he said, in a swooping note like Rhoda's but in a rough baritone voice. "They've been feeding us on this train like hogs going to market. I just finished a lunch with three different wines. Mom, you look beautiful. About twenty-five."

"Well, you look ghastly. Why the devil were you running around in Poland?"

The foreign ministry man pulled at Byron's elbow. "You do feel you have been treated well, Mr. Henry? Dr. Neustädter, foreign ministry," he said, with a click of heels and a crinkly smile.

"Oh, hi. Oh, irreproachably, sir, irreproachably," Byron said, laughing wildly. "That is, once we got out of Warsaw. In there it was kind of rough."

"Ah, well, that's war. We'd be pleased to have a little note from you about your treatment, at your convenience. My card."

Leslie Slote, ashen and distraught, came up with two hands full of documents and introduced himself to Victor Henry. "I'd like to call on you at the embassy tomorrow, sir," he said, "once I've straightened things out a bit."

"Come in any time," Pug Henry said.

"But let me tell you right now," Slote said over his shoulder as he left, "that Byron's been a real help."

Dr. Neustädter politely emphasized that Byron could go off in his father's custody now and pick up his documents some other time; or he himself could look after Byron's papers and drop them at Commander Henry's office. "After all," Neustädter said, "when it's a question of a son rejoining his parents, red tape becomes inhumane."

Rhoda sat beside her son as they drove to Grunewald, happily clutching his arm while complaining how awful he looked. He was her secret favorite. Rhoda had thought of the name Byron at her first glimpse of her baby in the hospital: a scrawny infant, blinking big blue eyes in a red triangular face; clearly a boy, even in the rolls of baby flesh. She thought the child had a manly romantic look. She had hoped he would be an author or an actor; she had even unclenched his tiny red fists to look for the "writer's triangles" which, she had read somewhere, one could see at birth in a baby's palm wrinkles. Byron hadn't turned out a writer, but he did actually have, she thought, a romantic streak. Secretly she sympathized with his refusal to consider a naval career, and even with his lazy school habits. She had never liked Pug's nickname for the boy, Briny, with its smell of the sea, and it was years before she would use it. Byron's switch to fine arts at Columbia, which had thrown Pug into black despondency, she had silently welcomed. Warren was a Henry: the plugger, the driver, the one who got things done, the A student, the one with his eye on flag rank and every step up toward it. Byron was like her, she thought, a person of fine quality, haunted and somewhat disabled by an unfulfilled dream.

She noticed the scar on his temple, touched it in alarm, and asked about it. He began narrating his odyssey from Cracow to Warsaw, interrupting himself now and then to exclaim at things he saw in the streets: red vertical swastika banners massed around a statue of Frederick the Great, a band of Hitler Youth marching past in their brown shirts, black neckerchiefs, and short black pants, nuns bicycling down the Friedrichstrasse, a band concert in a park, a turning merry-go-round. "It's so peaceful, isn't it? So goddamned peaceful! Dad, what's happening in the war? Has

Warsaw surrendered? Have the Allies gotten off their tails yet? The Germans are such liars, you never know."

"Warsaw's still holding out, but the war there is really over. There's a lot of talk about peace in the west, too."

"Honestly? Already? God, will you look at that café? Five hundred Berliners if there's one, eating pastry and drinking coffee, laughing, talking. Ah, to be a Berliner! Where was I? Oh yes. Well, anyway, at this point, see, the water pump gave out and the fan belt broke. The German planes never stopped going by overhead. The bride was having hysterics. We were twenty miles from the nearest town. There was a cluster of farmhouses about a mile down the road, but they'd been bombed to pieces, so—"

"Farmhouses?" Pug broke in alertly. "But the Germans keep claiming loud and clear that the Luftwaffe is attacking only military targets. That's a big boast of theirs."

Byron roared with laughter. "What? Dad, the military targets of the Germans include anything that moves, from a pig on up. I was a military target. There I was, above the ground and alive. I saw a thousand houses blown apart out in the countryside, far behind the front. The Luftwaffe is just practicing on them, getting ready for France and England."

"You want to be careful how you talk here," Rhoda said.

"We're in the car. That's safe, isn't it?"

"Sure it is. Go on," Pug said.

He was thinking that Byron's story might turn into an intelligence report. The Germans were indignantly complaining about Polish atrocities, and publishing revolting photographs of mutilated "ethnic Germans" and Wehrmacht officers. By contrast, they offered photographic proof of happy captured Polish soldiers eating, drinking, and doing folk dances; pictures of Jews being fed at soup kitchens, waving at the cameras and smiling; and many photographs of German guns and trucks rolling past farmhouses and through untouched towns, with jovial Polish peasants cheering them. Byron's tale cast an interesting light on all this.

On and on Byron talked. At the Grunewald house they went into the garden. "Hey, a tennis court! Great!" he exclaimed in the same manic tone. They sat in reclining

chairs, drinks in their hands, as he described the siege of
Warsaw with extraordinary clarity, picking out details that
made them see and hear and even smell the whole thing—
the dead horses on the streets, the tank traps and the
menacing sentries at the corners, the unflushed toilets at
the embassy when the water main broke, the gangs trying
to put out roaring fires in a whole block of buildings with
buckets of sand, the taste of horsemeat, the sound of artillery, the wounded piled in the hospital lobby, the façade
of a synagogue slowly sliding down into the street, the
embassy cellar with its rows of canvas cots, the eerie walk
across no-man's-land on a quiet dirt road dotted with
autumn wild flowers. The blue-gray Berlin evening drew
on, and still Byron talked, getting hoarse, drinking steadily,
and losing no coherence or clarity. It was an astonishing
performance. Again and again the parents looked at each
other.

"I get famished just talking about it," Byron said. He
was describing the startling feast laid out by the Germans
in the Klovno railroad station. "And there was another
spread just like it when we got to Königsberg. They've been
stuffing us ever since on the train. I don't know where it
all goes to. I think in Warsaw I must have digested the
marrow out of my bones. They got hollow and they're just
now filling up again. Anyway, when and where and how
do we eat?"

"You look like such a tramp, Byron," Rhoda said.
"Don't you have any other clothes?"

"A whole big bag full, Mom. It's in Warsaw, neatly
labelled with my name. Probably it's ashes by now."

They went to a small dark little restaurant off the
Kurfürstendamm. Byron laughed, pointing to the fly-
specked curling cardboard sign in the window: THIS RES-
TAURANT DOES NOT SERVE JEWS. "Are there any left in
Berlin to serve?"

"Well, you don't see them around much," Pug said.
"They're not allowed in the theatres and so forth. I guess
they're lying pretty low."

"Ah, to be a Berliner," Byron said. "Warsaw's alive
with Jews."

He stopped talking when the soup came. Apparently
his own voice had been keeping him awake, because be-

tween the soup and the meat course his head nodded and dropped on his chest. They had trouble rousing him.

"Let's get him home," Pug said, signalling to the waiter. "I was wondering how long he'd last."

"Wha? Less not go home," Byron said. "Less go to the theatre. The opera. Less have some civilized fun. Less do the town. Ah, to be a Berliner!"

Pug said, after they had put Byron to sleep and were strolling in the garden, "Quite a change in him."

"It's that girl," Rhoda said.

"He didn't say much about her."

"That's my point. He said nothing about her. Yet he went to Poland because of her, and got caught in Cracow on account of her. He lost his passport, for heaven's sake, protecting her relatives. Why, he was talking to her uncle when that synagogue all but fell on top of him. Seems to me he did almost everything in Poland but become a Jew." Pug looked coldly at her but she went on unheedingly, "Maybe you can find out something more about her from this man Slote. It's a strange business, and she must be some girl."

*   *   *

Topping the pile of letters on Pug's desk the following morning was a pale green envelope, almost square, engraved in one corner: THE WHITE HOUSE. Inside he found on a single sheet, similarly engraved, a slanted scrawl in heavy pencil.

You were dead right again, old top. Treasury just now informs me the ambassadors got hopping mad at the very idea of our offering to buy their ocean liners. Can I borrow your crystal ball? Ha ha! Write me a letter whenever you get a chance, about your life in Berlin—what you and your wife do for fun, who your German friends are, what the people and the newspapers are saying, how the food is in the restaurants, just anything and everything that occurs to you. What does a loaf of bread cost in Germany today? Washington is still incredibly hot and muggy, though the leaves have started turning.

FDR

Pug put all other mail aside, and stared at the curious communication from the curious man whom he had once soaked with salt water, who was now his Commander-in-Chief, the creator of the New Deal (of which Pug disapproved), the man with perhaps the best-known name and face on earth except Hitler's. The cheerful banal scribble was out of key with Roosevelt's stature, but it very much fitted the cocky young man who had bounced around on the *Davey* in a blazer and straw hat. He pulled a yellow pad toward him and listed points for an informal letter about his life in Berlin, for obedience and quick action were Navy habits soaked into his bones. The yeoman's buzzer rang. He flipped the key. "No calls, Whittle."

"Aye aye, sir. There's a Mister Slote asking to see you, but I can—"

"Slote? No, hold on. I'll see Slote. Let us have coffee."

The Foreign Service man looked rested and fit, if a bit gaunt, in his freshly pressed tweed jacket and flannel trousers. "Quite a view," Slote said. "Is that huge pink pile the new chancellery?"

"Yes. You can see them change the guard from here."

"I don't know that I'm interested in armed Germans on the move. I have the idea."

Both men laughed. Over the coffee the commander told Slote something of Byron's four-hour gush of narrative. The diplomat listened with a wary look, running his fingers repeatedly over the rim of his lit pipe. "Did he mention anything about that unfortunate business in Praha?" Henry looked puzzled. "When we had a girl in the car, and found ourselves under German shellfire?"

"I don't believe so. Was the girl Natalie Jastrow?"

"Yes. The incident involved the Swedish ambassador and an auto trip to the front lines."

Pug thought a moment. Slote watched his face intently. "No. Not a word."

With a heavy sigh, Slote brightened up. "Well, he exposed himself to direct enemy fire, while I had to take the girl out of the car and find shelter for her." Slote baldly narrated his version of the episode. Then he described Byron's water-hauling, his handiness in making repairs, his disregard of enemy planes and artillery shelling. "I'd be glad to put all this in a letter, if you wish," Slote said.

"Yes, I'd like that," Pug said with alacrity. "Now, tell me something about this Jastrow girl."

"What would you like to know?"

Victor Henry shrugged. "Anything. My wife and I are slightly curious about this young female who got our boy into such a jam. What the hell was she doing in Warsaw, with all of Europe mobilizing, and why was he with her?"

Slote laughed wryly. "She came to see me. We're old friends. I thought she was out of her mind to come. I did my best to stop her. This girl is a sort of lioness type, she does what she pleases and you just get out of the way. Her uncle didn't want her to travel alone, what with all the war talk. Byron volunteered to go along. That's as I understand it."

"He went with her to Poland as a courtesy to Dr. Jastrow? Is that the size of it?"

"Maybe you'd better ask Byron."

"Is she beautiful?"

Slote puffed thoughtfully, staring straight ahead. "In a way. Quite a brain, very educated." Abruptly he looked at his watch and stood up. "I'll write you that letter, and I'm going to mention your son in my official report."

"Good. I'll ask him about that incident in Praha."

"Oh, no, there's no need. It was just an instance of how he cooperated."

"You're not engaged to the Jastrow girl?"

"No, I'm not."

"Well, I hate to get personal, but you're much older than Byron, and quite different, and I can't picture a girl who bridges that gap." Slote looked at him and said nothing. Pug went on, "Where is she now?"

"She went to Stockholm with most of our people. Good-bye, Commander Henry."

Rhoda telephoned Pug around noon, breaking into his work on the letter to Roosevelt. "That boy's slept fourteen hours," she said. "I got worried and went in there, but he's breathing like an infant, with a hand tucked under his cheek."

"Well, let him sleep."

"Doesn't he have to report somewhere?"

"No. Sleep's the best thing for him."

Complying with the President's orders to write chattily,

Pug closed his letter with a short account of Byron's adventures in Poland. Plans were growing in his mind for official use of his son's experiences. He filed the letter for the diplomatic pouch, and went home uneasy at having bypassed the chain of command and wasted a workday. He did also feel vague pride in his direct contact with the President, but that was a human reaction. In his professional judgment, this contact was most likely a bad thing.

Byron was reclining in the garden, eating grapes from a bowl and reading a Superman comic book. Scattered on the grass beside him were perhaps two dozen more comic books, a patchwork of lurid covers. "Hi, Dad," he said. "How about this treasure? Franz collects them." (Franz was the butler.) "He says he's been panhandling or buying them from tourists for years."

Pug was stupefied at the sight. Comic books had been a cause of war in their household until Byron had gone off to Columbia. Pug had forbidden them, torn them up, burned them, fined Byron for possession of them. Nothing had helped. The boy had been like a dope fiend. With difficulty Pug refrained from saying something harsh. Byron was twenty-four. "How do you feel?"

"Hungry," Byron said. "God, this is a great Superman. It makes me homesick, reading these things."

Franz brought Pug a highball on a tray. Pug sat silently with it waiting for the butler to go. It took a while, because Franz wiped a glass-top table, cut some flowers, and fooled with a loose screen door to the tennis court. He had a way of lingering within earshot. Meanwhile, Byron read the Superman through, put it on the pile, and looked idly at his father.

Pug relaxed and sipped his drink. Franz was reentering the house. "Briny, that was quite a tale you told us yesterday."

The son laughed. "I guess I got kind of carried away, seeing you and Mom again. Also Berlin had a funny effect on me."

"You've had access to unusual information. I don't know if there's another American who went from Cracow to Warsaw after the war broke out."

"Oh, I guess it's all been in the papers and magazines."

"That's where you're wrong. There's a lot of arguing

between the Germans and the Poles—the few Poles who got away and can still argue—about who's committed what atrocities in Poland. An eyewitness account like yours would be an important document."

Byron shrugged, picking up another comic book. "Possibly."

"I want you to write it up. I'd like to forward your account to the Office of Naval Intelligence."

"Gosh, Dad, aren't you overestimating it?"

"No. I'd like you to get at it tonight."

"I don't have a typewriter," Byron said with a yawn.

"There's one in the library," Pug said.

"Oh, that's right, I saw it. Well, okay."

With such casual assents, Byron had often dodged his homework in the past. But his father let it go. He was clinging to a belief that Byron had matured under the German bombing.

"That fellow Slote came by today. Said you helped out a lot in Warsaw. Brought water to the embassy, and such."

"Well, yes. I got stuck with the water job."

"Also there was an incident at the front line with the Swedish ambassador. You climbed a tower under German fire, while Slote had to hide this Jastrow girl in a farmhouse. It seems to be very much on his mind."

Byron opened *Horror Comics,* with a cover picture of a grinning skeleton carrying a screaming half-naked girl up a stone staircase. "Oh yes. That was right before we crossed no-man's-land. I made a sketch of the road."

"Why does Slote dwell on it?"

"Well, it's about the last thing that happened before we left Warsaw, so I guess it remained in his mind."

"He intends to write me a letter of commendation about you."

"He does? That's fine. Has he got any word on Natalie?"

"Just that she's gone to Stockholm. You'll start on that report tonight?"

"Sure."

Byron left the house after dinner and returned at two in the morning. Pug was awake, working in the library and worrying about his son, who blithely told him he had gone with other Americans to the opera. Under his arm Byron carried a new copy of *Mein Kampf* in English. Next day

when Pug left the house Byron was up and dressed, lounging on the back porch in slacks and a sweater, drinking
coffee and reading *Mein Kampf*. At seven in the evening
the father found Byron in the same place, in the same
chair, drinking a highball. He was well into the thick tome,
which lay open on his lap. Rubbing bleary eyes, he gave
his father a listless wave.

Pug said, "Did you start on that report?"

"I'll get to it, Dad. Say, this is an interesting book. Did
you read it?"

"I did, but I didn't find it interesting. About fifty pages
of those ravings give you the picture. I thought I should
finish it, so I did, but it was like wading through mud."

Byron shook his head. "Really amazing," and turned
the page.

He went out again at night, returned late, and fell asleep
with his clothes on, an old habit that ground on Pug's
nerves. Byron woke around eleven, and found himself undressed and under the covers, his clothes draped on a
chair, with a note propped on them: WRITE THAT GOD-
DAMN REPORT.

.   .   .

He was idling along the Kurfürstendamm that afternoon,
with *Mein Kampf* under his arm, when Leslie Slote went
hurrying past him, halted, and turned. "Well, there you
are! That's luck. I've been trying to get hold of you. Are
you coming back to the States with us or not? Our transportation's set for Thursday."

"I'm not sure. How about some coffee and pastry? Let's
be a couple of Berliners."

Slote pursed his lips. "To tell the truth, I skipped lunch.
All right. What the devil are you reading that monstrosity
for?"

"I think it's great."

"Great! That's an unusual comment."

They sat at a table in an enormous sidewalk café, where
potted flowering bushes broke up the expanse of tables and
chairs, and a brass band played gay waltzes in the sunshine.

"God, this is the life," Byron said, as they gave orders

to a bowing, smiling waiter. "Look at all these nice, polite, cordial, joking, happy Berliners, will you? Did you ever see a nicer city? So clean! All those fine statues and baroque buildings, like that marvellous opera, and all the spanking new modern ones, and all the gardens and trees —why, I've never seen such a green, clean city! Berlin's almost like a city built in a forest. And all the canals, and the quaint little boats—did you see that tug that sort of tips its smokestack to get under the bridges? Completely charming. The only thing is, these pleasant folks have just been blowing the hell out of Poland, machine-gunning people from the sky—I've got the scar to prove it—pounding a city just as nice as Berlin to a horrible pulp. It's a puzzle, you might say."

Slote shook his head and smiled. "The contrast between the war front and the back area is always startling. No doubt Paris was as charming as ever while Napoleon was out doing his butcheries."

"Slote, you can't tell me the Germans aren't strange."

"Oh, yes, the Germans are strange."

"Well, that's why I've been reading this book, to try to figure them out. It's their leader's book. Now, it turns out this is the writing of an absolute nut. The Jews are secretly running the world, he says. That's his whole message. They're the capitalists, but they're the Bolsheviks too, and they're conspiring to destroy the German people, who by rights should *really* be running the world. Well, he's going to become dictator, see, wipe out the Jews, crush France, and carve off half of Bolshevist Russia for more German living space. Have I got it right so far?"

"A bit simplified, but yes—pretty much." Slote sounded amused but uneasy, glancing at the tables nearby.

"Okay. Now, all these nice Berliners *like* this guy. Right? They voted for him. They follow him. They salute him. They *cheer* him. Don't they? How is that? Isn't that very strange? How come he's their leader? Haven't they read this book? How come they didn't put him in a padded cell? Don't they have insane asylums? And who do they put in there, if not this guy?"

Slote, while stuffing his pipe, kept looking here and there at the people around them. Satisfied that nobody was eavesdropping, he said in a low tone, "Are you just discovering the phenomenon of Adolf Hitler?"

"I just got shot in the head by a German. That sort of called my attention to it."

"Well, you won't learn much from *Mein Kampf*. That's just froth on top of the kettle."

"Do *you* understand Hitler and the Germans?"

Slote lit his pipe and stared at the air for several seconds. Then he spoke, with a wry little smile of academic condescension. "I have an opinion, the result of a lot of study."

"Can I hear it? I'm interested."

"It's a terribly long story, Byron, and quite involved." Slote glanced around again. "Some other time and place I'll be glad to, but—"

"Would you give me the names of books to read, then?"

"Are you serious? You'd let yourself in for some dull plodding."

"I'll read anything you tell me to."

"Well, let me have your book."

On the flyleaf of *Mein Kampf,* Slote listed authors and titles all the way down the page, in a neat slanted hand, in purple Polish ink. Running his eye down the list, Byron felt his heart sink at the unfamiliar array of Teutonic authors, each name followed by a heavy book title, some by two:

... *Treitschke—Moeller van den Bruck—Fries—Menzel—Fichte—Schlegel—Arndt—Jahn—Rühs—Lagarde—Langbehn—Spengler* ...

Among them, like black raisins in much gray dough, a few names from his contemporary civilization course at Columbia caught his eye: *Luther—Kant—Hegel—Schopenhauer—Nietzsche.* He remembered that course as a nuisance and a nightmare. He had passed with a D minus, after frantic all-night cramming of smudgy lecture notes from the fraternity files. Slote drew a heavy line, and added more books with equally forbidding authors' names:

... *Santayana—Mann—Veblen—Renan—Heine—Kolnai—Rauschning* ...

"Below the line are critics and analysts," he remarked as he wrote. "Above are some German antecedents of Hitler. I think you must grasp these to grasp him."

Byron said dolefully, "Really? The philosophers too? Hegel and Schopenhauer? Why? And Martin Luther, for pity's sake?"

Contemplating the list with a certain arid satisfaction, Slote added a name or two as he pulled hard at his pipe, making the bowl hiss. "My view is that Hitler and the Nazis have grown out of the heart of German culture—a cancer, maybe, but a uniquely German phenomenon. Some very clever men have given me hell for holding this opinion. They insist the same thing could have happened anywhere, given the same conditions: defeat in a major war, a harsh peace treaty, ruinous inflation, mass unemployment, communism on the march, anarchy in the streets—all leading to the rise of a demagogue, and a reign of terror. But I—"

The waiter was approaching. Slote shut up and said not a word while they were being served. Watching the waiter until he went out of sight, the Foreign Service man drank coffee and ate cake. Then he started again, almost in an undertone.

"But I don't believe it. To me Nazism is unthinkable without its roots in German nineteenth-century thought: romanticism, idealism, nationalism, the whole outpouring. It's in those books. If you're not prepared to read every word of Hegel's *Philosophy of History,* for instance, give up. It's basic." He shoved the book back to Byron, open at the flyleaf. "Well, there you are, for a starter."

"Tacitus?" Byron said. "Why *Tacitus?* Isn't he a Roman historian?"

"Yes. Do you know about Arminius, and the Battle of the Teutoburger Forest?"

"No, I don't."

"Okay. In the year 9 A.D., Byron, a German war leader named Arminius stopped the Romans at the Rhine, once and for all, and so secured the barbarian sanctuary in the heart of Europe. It's a key event in world history. It led eventually to the fall of Rome. It's affected all European politics and war to this hour. So I believe, and therefore I think you should read Tacitus's account of the campaign. Either you go into these things, or you don't."

Byron kept nodding and nodding, his eyes narrowed and attentive. "You've read all these books? Every one?"

Slote regarded the younger man quizzically, gnawing his pipe. "I haven't retained them as well as I should, but, yes, I have."

"What you're actually trying to tell me, I imagine, is to go peddle my papers, that this is a subject for Rhodes Scholars."

"Not at all, but it is a hard subject. Now, Byron, I'm really overdue at the embassy. Are you or aren't you coming with us? We fly to Oslo Thursday, and from there to London. Then we just take our chances—destroyer, freighter, ocean liner, maybe an airplane trip via Lisbon—whatever turns up."

Byron said, "What are Natalie's plans? She got kind of snappish with me toward the end, and wouldn't talk much."

Slote looked at his watch. "She was disagreeable and vague with me, too. I really don't know." He hesitated. "I'll tell you something else. You may not like it. You may not believe it. But it's so, and possibly you'd be better off knowing it."

"Go ahead."

"I asked her about you, whether you planned to return to Siena. Her answer was, 'Well, I hope not. I sincerely hope I never see Byron Henry again, and if you ever get a chance, please tell him so with my compliments.'—You look surprised. Didn't you have an argument before she left? I was positive you had."

Byron, trying to compose his face, said, "Not exactly. She just seemed grouchy as hell."

Slote said, "She was in a gruesome mood. Said she had a bad backache from all the train riding, for one thing. Very likely she meant nothing by it. I know she felt grateful to you. As indeed I do."

Byron shook his head. "I can't say I've ever understood her."

Slote glanced at the check and said, tucking bright-colored marks under a saucer, "Well, look, Byron, there's no time to discuss Natalie Jastrow. I'll tell you this. I've had no peace of mind since the day I first met her two years ago, at a very stupid cocktail party on the Quai Voltaire."

"Why don't you marry her?" Byron said, as Slote started to rise.

The older man fell back in his chair, and looked at him for several seconds. "All right. I'm not at all sure I won't, Byron, if she'll have me."

"Oh, she'll have you. I'll tell you what. I guess I'll stay on here with my folks for a while. I won't go to Oslo."

Slote stood, holding out his hand. "I'll give your passport and so forth to your father's yeoman. Good luck."

Byron said, shaking hands and gesturing at *Mein Kampf,* "I appreciate the lecture and the list."

"Small return," Slote said, "for services rendered."

"Will you let me know," Byron said, "if you get word before you leave Berlin about where Natalie went?"

Knocking out his pipe against his palm, Slote said, "Certainly," and hurried off into the sidewalk crowd. Byron ordered more ersatz coffee and opened *Mein Kampf,* and the café band struck up a merry Austrian folk dance.

16

DURING Victor Henry's absence in the States, his wife had tangled herself in a romance; something she had not done in his much longer absences through almost twenty-five years. There was something liberating for her in the start of a war. She was forty-five. Suddenly the rules she had lived by so long seemed slightly out of date. The whole world was shaking itself loose from the past; why shouldn't she, just a wee bit? Rhoda Henry did not articulate this argument. She felt it in her bones and acted on it.

Being an ex-beauty, and remaining pretty, she had always drawn and enjoyed the attention of men, so she had not lacked opportunities for affairs. But she had been as faithful to Pug Henry as he had been to her. She liked to go to church, her hymn-singing and prayers were heartfelt,

she believed in God, she thought Jesus Christ was her
Savior—if she had never gone deeply into the matter—
and she was convinced in her soul that a married woman
ought to be true and good. In the old Navy-wife pastime
of ripping apart ladies who had not been true and good,
she wielded well-honed claws.

Setting aside a trivial kiss here and there, only one
episode in the dim past somewhat marred Rhoda's otherwise perfect record. After an officers' club dance in Manila,
where she had soaked up too much champagne—Pug being
out at sea in a fleet exercise—Kip Tollever had brought
her home and had managed to get her dress off. Madeline,
then a child troubled by bad dreams, had saved the situation by waking and starting to cry. By the time Madeline
was comforted, Rhoda had sobered up. Relieved to be
back from the brink, yet bearing Kip no malice, she had
donned a proper housecoat and had amiably shooed him
out of the house. That had been the end of it. No doubt
Kip the next morning had been just as grateful to Madeline. Victor Henry was practically the last man in the Navy
he wanted to risk angering.

Thereafter, Rhoda was always somewhat kittenish toward Tollever. Now and then she wondered what would
have happened had Madeline not awakened. Would she
really have gone through with it? How would she have
felt? But she would never know; she did not intend to get
that close to trouble again; the wine had been to blame.
Still, there had been something titillating about being undressed by a man other than old Pug. Rhoda preserved the
memory, though she buried it deep.

Dr. Palmer Kirby was a shy, serious, ugly man in his
middle-fifties. After the dinner party for him, discussing
the guests with Sally Forrest, Rhoda had dismissed him as
"one of these ghastly BRAINS." Just to be sociable, she had
vainly tried her usual coquettish babble on Kirby over the
cocktails. "Well, since friend husband's away, Dr. Kirby,
I've put you on my right, and we can make HAY while the
sun shines."

"Um. On your right. Thank you."

That had almost been the end of it. Rhoda detested such
heavy men. But he had happened to say at dinner that he
was going next day to a factory in Brandenburg. Rhoda

offered to drive him there, simply because she had long wanted to see the medieval town, and Kirby in a sense was her husband's guest.

On the way they had a dull, decorous lunch at an inn. Over a bottle of Moselle, Kirby warmed up and started to talk about himself and his work. At an alert question she asked him—living with Pug, Rhoda had learned to follow technical talk—Palmer Kirby suddenly smiled. It seemed to her that she had not seen him smile before. His teeth were big, and the smile showed his gums. It was a coarse male smile of knowledge and appetite, far from disagreeable, but startling in the saturnine engineer.

"Do you really care, Mrs. Henry?" said Dr. Kirby. "I'd be glad to explain the whole business, but I have a horror of boring a beautiful woman."

The smile, the words, the tone, all disclosed that the man had missed none of her coquetry; that on the contrary, he liked her. A bit flustered, she touched a hand to her hair, tucking the waves behind her small white ears. "I assure you, it all sounds fascinating. Just use words of one syllable as much as possible."

"Okay, but you brought this on yourself."

He told her all about magnetic amplifiers—"magamps," he called them—devices for precise control of voltages and currents, especially in high power. Asking one adroit question after another, Rhoda soon drew out the key facts about him. At the California Institute of Technology he had written his doctoral thesis on electromagnetism. At forty he had decided to manufacture magnetic amplifiers on his own, instead of settling for an executive post at General Electric or Westinghouse, and security for life. The long struggle for financing had all but sunk him; it was just now paying off. War industries demanded magamps in quantity, and he was first in the field. He had come to Germany because the Germans were ahead of the United States in the quality of some components. He was studying their techniques and buying their nickel-alloy cores.

She also learned that he was a widower and a grandfather. He talked about his dead wife, and then they exchanged long confidences about their children's faults and virtues. Like most men, Kirby loved to talk about himself, once over his shyness. His story of backbreaking money troubles and final big success so enthralled her that she forgot to be coy, and spoke pleasantly and to the point. Rhoda was most attractive, in fact, when she made the least effort to be. She was the kind of woman who can dazzle a man at first acquaintance by piling everything into the shop window: none of it forced or faked, but in sum nearly all she has to offer. Victor Henry had long since found that out. He had no complaints, though he had once imagined there must be much more. Palmer Kirby was hit hard by this maximum first impact. He ordered a second bottle of Moselle, and they got to Brandenburg almost an hour late. While he went about his business Rhoda strolled through the picturesque old town, guidebook in hand; and her mind unaccountably kept wandering to her little misconduct long ago with Kip Tollever. She was a bit dizzy from the Moselle, and it wore off slowly.

When they returned to Berlin toward evening, Kirby offered to take her to dinner and to the opera. It seemed quite natural to accept. Rhoda rushed home and began raking through her dresses and shoes, pushing her hair this way and that, wishing she could have gone to the hairdresser, hesitating over her perfumes. She was still at it when Kirby came to call for her. She kept him waiting for an hour. In girlhood she had always kept boys waiting. Pug had harshly cured her of the habit, for Navy social life began and ended by the clock, and he would not tolerate embarrassment by Rhoda. Keeping Palmer Kirby waiting while she fussed over herself was a delicious little nostalgic folly, a lovely childish self-indulgence, like eating a banana split. It almost made Rhoda feel nineteen again.

The mirror told her a different story, but even it seemed friendly to her that night: it showed shiny eyes, a pretty face, a firm figure in the sheer slip, and arms that were round and thin all the way up, instead of bagging above the elbow as so many women's did. She sailed into the living room wearing the pink suit with gold buttons that she had bought to please Hitler. Kirby sat reading one of Pug's technical journals. He took off big black-rimmed glasses and rose, exclaiming, "Well, don't you look grand!"

"I'm awful," she said, taking Kirby's arm, "dawdling so long, but you brought it on yourself, asking the old girl out after a hard day."

The opera was *La Traviata,* and they enjoyed discovering that they both had always loved it. Afterward, he proposed a glimpse of the notorious Berlin night life. It was nothing he'd ever do by himself, he said; still, Berlin night life was the talk of the world, and if it wouldn't offend Mrs. Henry, she might enjoy a peek at it.

Rhoda giggled at the notion. "Well, this seems to be my night to howl, doesn't it? Thank you very much for a disreputable suggestion, which I hasten to accept. Let's hope we don't run into any of my friends."

So it happened that when the telephone rang in the Henrys' home at two in the morning—the long-distance call from New York, via the U.S.S. *Marblehead* in Lisbon —there was nobody to answer. Rhoda was sipping champagne, watching a hefty blonde German girl fling her naked breasts about in blue smoky gloom, and glancing every now and then at Dr. Palmer Kirby's long solemn face in thick-rimmed glasses, as he smoked a long pipe and observed the hard-working sweaty dancer with faint distaste. Rhoda was aroused and deliciously shocked. She had never before seen a nude dancing woman, except in paintings.

After that, until her husband returned, she spent a lot of time with Kirby. They went to the less frequented restaurants. In her own vocabulary, she never "did anything." When Pug returned, the adventure stopped.

∎ ∎ ∎

A farewell lunch at Wannsee for Palmer Kirby was Rhoda's idea, but she got Sally Forrest to give the lunch, saying she had already sufficiently entertained this civilian visitor. If Sally Forrest detected an oddity in this she said nothing. With the end of the Polish war at hand—only Warsaw was still holding out—the two attachés felt able to take off some midday hours. Berlin wore a peacetime air, and there was even talk that rationing would soon be over. Byron drove them all out to the resort in an embassy car. Along the broad sandy beach on the Havel river, peo-

ple strolled in the sun or sat under broad gaily colored
umbrellas, and a number of gymnasts braved the fall
breezes to exercise in skimpy costumes.

In the luncheon the Forrests ordered, rationing was not
much in evidence. The pasty margarine tasted as usual like
axle grease, but they ate excellent turbot and good leg of
lamb. Midway during the lunch a loudspeaker crackled
and whined, and a voice spoke in firm clear German: *"Attention! In the next few minutes you will hear a report of
the highest importance to the fatherland."*

The identical words boomed all over the river resort.
People stopped on the promenade to listen. On the beach
the small figures of the gymnasts halted briefly in their
tumbling or running. An excited murmur rose all through
the elegant Kaiserpavillon restaurant.

"What do you suppose?" Sally Forrest said, as the
music resumed, thin gentle Schubert on strings.

"Warsaw, I'd guess," said her husband. "It must be
over."

Dr. Kirby said, "You don't suppose there's an armistice
coming up? I've been hearing armistice talk all week."

"Oh, wouldn't that be marvellous," Rhoda said, "and
put an end to this stupid war before it really gets going!"

Byron said, "It's been going."

"Oh, of course," said Rhoda with an apologetic smile,
"they'd have to make some decent settlement of that hideous Polish business."

"There'll be no armistice," said Pug.

The buzz of talk rose higher on the crowded terrace and
in the dining room. The Germans, eyes bright and gestures
animated, argued with each other, laughed, struck the
table, and called from all sides for champagne. When the
loudspeaker played the few bars of Liszt's music that
preceded big news, the noise began to die.

"Sondermeldung!" (Special bulletin!) At this announcement, an immediate total stillness blanketed the restaurant,
except for a clink here and there. The loudspeaker randomly crackled; then a baritone voice spoke solemn brief
words. *"From Supreme Headquarters of the Führer. Warsaw has fallen."*

The whole restaurant rang with applause and cheers.

Women jumped to their feet and danced. Men shook hands and hugged and kissed each other. Brass band music—first "Deutschland Über Alles," then the "Horst Wessel Lied"—came pouring out of the loudspeakers. To a man the diners in the Kaiserpavillon rose, all except the American party. On the beach, on the promenade, wherever the eye turned, the Germans stood still, most of them with arms thrust forward in the Nazi salute. In the dining room, about half were saluting and singing, a discordant swell of voices in the vulgar beery National Socialist anthem. Victor Henry's skin prickled as he looked around, and he felt at this moment that the Germans under Adolf Hitler would take some beating. He then noticed something he had not seen for many, many years. His son sat still, face frozen, lips pressed in a line, white-knuckled hands clasped on the table. Byron had almost always taken pain and punishment dry-eyed since the age of five, but now he was crying.

The American party, sitting in a restaurant full of people on their feet, was getting hostile glares.

"Do they expect us to stand?" Sally Forrest said.

"*I'm* not standing," Rhoda said.

Their waiter, a roly-poly man in black with very long straight blond hair, hitherto all genial expert service, stood bellowing with arm outstretched, visibly sneering at the Americans.

Byron saw none of this. Byron was seeing dead swollen horses in the gutter, yellow plywood patches on rows of broken buildings, a stone goose bordered with red flowers in a schoolyard, a little girl in a lilac dress taking a pen from him, orange starshells bursting in the night over church domes.

The song ended. The Germans applauded and cheered some more, and began toasting each other. The string orchestra switched to drinking songs, and the whole Kaiserpavillon went into a gay roar of

> *Du, du, liegst mir im Herzen,*
> *Du, du, liegst mir im Sinn—*

Byron cringed to hear it, and to recall that a full belly and a glass of beer had brought him to join German sol-

diers in this song, not six hours after he had escaped from
burning Warsaw.

> *Ja, ja,*
> *Ja, ja!*
> *Weisst nicht wie gut ich dir bin . . .*

At the Americans' table the waiter started removing
plates with a jerky clatter, spilling gravy and wine and
jostling them with his elbows.

"Watch what you're doing, please," Colonel Forrest
said.

The waiter went on with his brusque sloppy clearing.
Sally Forrest gave a little yelp as he struck her head with
a plate.

Pug said to him, "Look. Call your headwaiter, please."

"Headwaiter? I am the headwaiter. I am *your* head."
The man laughed and walked off. Dirty dishes remained
scattered on the table. Wet purple and brown messes
stained the cloth.

Forrest said to Henry, "It might be smart to leave."

"Oh, by all means," Sally Forrest said. "Just pay, Bill,
and we'll go." She picked up her purse.

"We haven't had our dessert," Pug Henry said.

"It might be an idea to knock that waiter on his behind,"
Dr. Kirby said, his face disagreeably contorted.

"I volunteer," said Byron, and he started to get up.

"For God's sake, boy!" Colonel Forrest pulled him
back. "An incident is just what he wants, and what we
can't have."

The waiter was striding past them to another table.
Henry called, "I asked you to bring your headwaiter."

"You're in a hurry, honorable sir?" the waiter jeered.
"Then you'd better leave. We're very busy in this restaurant." He turned a stout back on Henry and walked
away.

"*Stop! Turn around.*"

Pug did not shout or bark. He used a dry sharp tone of
command that cut through the restaurant gabble. The
waiter stopped and turned. "*Go call your headwaiter. Do
it immediately.*" He looked straight into the waiter's eyes,
his face serious and hard. The waiter's glance shifted, and

he walked off in another direction. The nearby diners were staring and muttering.

"I think we should go," Sally Forrest said. "This isn't worth the trouble."

The waiter soon approached, followed by a tall, bald, long-faced man in a frock coat, who said with a busy, unfriendly air, "Yes? You have a complaint?"

"We're a party of Americans, military attachés," Pug said. "We didn't rise for your anthem. We're neutrals. This waiter chose to take offense." He gestured at the table. "He's been deliberately clumsy and dirty. He's talked rudely. He's jostled the ladies. His conduct has been swinish. Tell him to behave himself, and be good enough to let us have a clean cloth for our dessert."

The expression of the headwaiter kept changing as Victor Henry rapped the sentences out. He hesitated under Henry's direct gaze, looked around at the other diners, and all at once burst out in a howl of abuse at the waiter, flinging both arms in the air, his face purpling. After a short fierce tantrum, he turned to Pug Henry, bowed from the waist, and said coldly, "You will be properly served. My apologies." And he bustled off.

Now a peculiar thing happened. The waiter reverted to his former manner without turning a hair, without a trace of surliness, resentment, or regret. The episode was obliterated; it had never happened. He cleared the dishes and spread a new cloth with deft speed. He smiled, he bowed, he made little jokes and considerate little noises. His face was blood red, otherwise he was in every respect the same charming, *gemütlich* German waiter who had first greeted them. He took their dessert orders with chuckles and nods, with arch jests about calories, with solicitous suggestions of wine and liqueurs. He backed away smiling and bowing, and hastened out of sight.

"I'll be damned," said Colonel Forrest.

"We hadn't had our dessert," Pug said.

"Well done," Kirby said to Pug Henry, with an odd glance at Rhoda. "Beautifully done."

"Oh, Pug has a way about him," Rhoda said, smiling brightly.

"Okay, Dad," Byron said. Victor Henry shot him a quick look. It was the one remark that gratified him.

The Americans rushed uneasily through their desserts: all but Victor Henry, who was very deliberate about eating his tart and drinking his coffee. He unwrapped a cigar. The waiter jumped to light it for him.

"Well, I guess we can shove off," he said, puffing out a cloud of smoke. "Time's a'wasting, and the colonel and I are cheating the U.S. Government."

. . .

That night after a late dinner, as they were having coffee on the terrace, Rhoda said, "I see you've brought home a pile of work. I thought we might see that new Emil Jannings movie. But I can get one of the girls to come along."

"Go ahead. I'm no fan of Emil Jannings."

Rhoda drank up her coffee and left the father and son sitting in the gloom.

"Briny, what about that report? How's it coming?"

"The report? Oh, yes, the report." Byron leaned forward in his chair, legs apart, elbows on knees, hands clasped. "Dad, I'd like to ask you something. What would you think of my joining the British navy? Or the RAF?"

Victor Henry blinked, and took a while to answer. "You want to fight the Germans, I take it?"

"I enjoyed myself in Warsaw. I felt useful."

"Well, this is one hell of a change, coming from you. I thought a military career was o-u-t out."

"This isn't a career."

Pug sat smoking and looking at his hands, crouching forward in his chair. Byron usually slouched back and extended his long legs, but now he was imitating his father. Their attitudes looked comically alike. "Briny, I don't think the Allies are going to make a deal with Hitler, but what if they do? A peace offensive's coming up, that's for sure. Suppose you join the British, possibly lose your citizenship—certainly create a peck of problems—and then the war's off? There you'll be, up to your neck in futile red tape. Why not hang on a while and see how the cat jumps?"

"I guess so." Byron sighed, and slouched back in his chair.

Pug said, "I don't like to discourage an admirable impulse. What might be a *good* idea right now is to ask for active duty in our Navy, and—"

"No, thanks."

"Now hear me out, dammit. You've got your commission. The reserves who go out to sea now will draw the best duty if and when the action starts. You'll have the jump on ninety-nine percent of the others. In wartime you'll be the equal of any Academy man."

"Meantime I'd be in for years. And *then* suppose the war ends?"

"You're not doing anything else."

"I wrote to Dr. Jastrow in Siena. I'm waiting to hear from him."

The father dropped the subject.

Rhoda went to see the Emil Jannings movie, but first she did something else. She picked up Dr. Palmer Kirby at his hotel and drove him to Tempelhof airport. This was not necessary; cabs were available in Berlin. But she had offered to do this and Kirby had accepted. Perhaps there would have been no harm in telling her husband that she was giving the visitor this last courtesy; but she didn't.

They hardly spoke in the car. She parked and went to the café lounge while he checked in. Had she encountered a friend, she would have needed an explanation on the spot and a story for her husband. But she had no such worry; she felt only a bittersweet excitement. What she was doing gave her not the slightest guilty feeling. She had no wrong intent. She liked Palmer Kirby. It was a long, long time since a man had seemed so attractive to her. He liked her, too. In fact, this was a genuine little wartime romance, so decorous as to be almost laughable; an unexpected flash of melancholy magic, which would soon be over forever. It was not in the least like her aborted drunken peccadillo with Kip Tollever.

"Well, I guess this is it," Kirby said, falling in the chair opposite her in the gangling way which always struck her as boyish, for all his grizzled head and sharply lined face. They sat looking at each other until the drinks came.

"Your happiness," he said.

"Oh, that. I've had that. It's all in the past." She sipped. "Did they give you the connection to Lisbon that you wanted?"

"Yes, but the Pan Am Clippers are jammed. I may be hung up in Lisbon for days."

"Well, I wish I had that in prospect. I hear that's becoming the gayest city in Europe."

"Come along."

"Oh, Palmer, don't tease me. Dear me, I was supposed to call you Fred, wasn't I? And now I find I've been thinking of you all along as Palmer. Fred—well, there are so many Freds. You don't strike me as Fred."

"That's very strange." He drank at his highball.

"What is?"

"Anne called me Palmer. She never would call me anything else."

Rhoda twirled the stem of her daiquiri glass. "I wish I had known your wife."

"You'd have become good friends."

"Palmer, what do you think of Pug?"

"Hm. That's a tough one." The engineer pushed his lips out ruefully. "My first impression was that he was a misplaced and—frankly—rather narrow-minded sea dog. But I don't know. He has a keen intellect. He's terrifically on the ball. That was quite a job he did on that waiter. He's a hard man to know, really."

Rhoda laughed. "How right you are. After all these years, I don't know him too well myself. But I suspect Pug's really something simple and almost obsolete, Palmer. He's a patriot. He's not the easiest person to live with. He's so goldarned single-minded."

"Is he a patriot, or is he a Navy career man? Those are two different things."

Rhoda tilted her head and smiled. "I'm not actually sure."

"Well, I've come to admire him, that much I know." Kirby frowned at his big hands, clasped around the drink on the table. "See here, Rhoda, I'm really a proper fellow, all in all. Let me just say this. You're a wonderful woman. I've been a sad dull man since Anne died, but you've made me feel very much alive again, and I'm grateful to you. Does this offend you?"

"Don't be a fool. It pleases me very much, and you know it does." Rhoda took a handkerchief from her purse.

"However, it's going to be a little hard on my contentment for a day or two. Oh, damn."

"Why? I should think it would add to your contentment."

"Oh, shut up, Palmer. Thanks for the drink. You'd better go to your plane."

"Look, don't be upset."

She smiled at him, her eyes tearful. "Why everything's fine, dear. You might write, just once in a while. Just a friendly little scribble, so I'll know you're alive and well. I'd like that."

"Of course I will. I'll write the day I get home."

"Will you really? That's fine." She touched her eyes with her handkerchief and stood. "Good-bye."

He said, getting to his feet, "They haven't called my plane."

"No? Well, my chauffeuring job is finished, and I'm leaving you here and now." They walked out of the lounge and shook hands in the quiet terminal. War had all but shut down the airport; most of the counters were dark. Rhoda squeezed Dr. Kirby's hand, and standing on tiptoe, kissed him once on the lips. This in a way was strangest of all, reaching up to kiss a man. She opened her mouth. After all, it was a farewell.

"Good-bye. Have a wonderful trip." She hurried away and turned a corner without looking back. She saw enough of the Emil Jannings movie to be able to talk about it to Pug.

. . .

Byron at last wrote the report on his adventures in Poland. Victor Henry, suppressing his annoyance over the five vapid pages, spent an afternoon dictating to his yeoman everything he remembered of Byron's tale. His son read the seventeen-page result next day with astonishment. "Ye gods, Dad, what a memory you have."

"Take that and fix it any way you want. Just make sure it's factually unchallengeable. Combine it with your thing and let me have it back by Friday."

Victor Henry forwarded the patched report to the Office of Naval Intelligence, but forgot his idea of sending a copy to the President. The cool autumn days went by and Berlin began taking on an almost peacetime look and mood. Byron lounged around the Grunewald house, knotting his forehead by the hour over one book after another from Leslie Slote's list. Three or four times a week he played tennis with his father; he was much the better player, but Pug, a steely plodder at first, wore him down and beat him. With food, exercise, and sun, however, Byron lost his famished look, regained strength, and started winning, which pleased Pug as much as it did him.

One morning he walked into his father's office at the embassy and saw sitting on the floor, carefully roped up and ticketed with a tag in his own handwriting, the large valise of suits, shoes, and shirts he had left behind in Warsaw. It was a shocking little clue to the efficiency of the Germans. But he was glad to have the clothes, for American styles were idolized in Germany. He blossomed out as a dandy. The German girls in the embassy looked after the slender young man whenever he walked down the hall, casually à la mode, with heavy red-glinting brown hair, a lean face, and large blue eyes that widened when he wistfully smiled. But he ignored their inviting glances. Byron pounced on the mail every morning, searching in vain for a letter from Siena.

When the Führer made his Reichstag speech offering peace to England and France, early in October, the propaganda ministry set aside a large block of seats in the Kroll Opera House for foreign diplomats, and Pug took his son along. Living through the siege of Warsaw, and then reading *Mein Kampf,* Byron had come to think of Adolf Hitler as a historic monster—a Caligula, a Genghis Khan, an Ivan the Terrible—and Hitler standing at the podium surprised him: just a medium-size pudgy individual in a plain gray coat and black trousers, carrying a red portfolio. The man seemed to Byron a diminutive actor, weakly impersonating the grandiose and gruesome history-maker.

Hitler spoke this time in a reasonable, pedestrian tone, like an elderly politician. In this sober style, the German leader began to utter such grotesque and laughable lies that Byron kept looking around for some amused reactions. But the Germans sat listening with serious faces.

Even the diplomats gave way only here and there to a mouth twitch that might have been ironic.

A powerful Poland had attacked Germany, the little man in the gray coat said, and had attempted to destroy her. The brave Wehrmacht had not been caught unawares and had justly punished this insolent aggression. A campaign strictly limited to attack of military targets had brought quick total victory. The civilian population of Poland, on his personal orders, had not been molested, and had suffered no loss or injury, except in Warsaw. There again on his orders, the German commanders had pleaded with the authorities to evacuate their civilians, offering them safe-conduct. The Poles with criminal folly had insisted on holding defenseless women and children within the city.

To Byron, the brazenness of this assertion was stupefying. All the neutral diplomats had made desperate efforts for weeks to negotiate the evacuation of Warsaw's women and children. The Germans had never even replied. It was not so much that Hitler was lying about this—Byron knew that the German nation was following a wild liar and had been for years, since *Mein Kampf* was full of obvious crazy lies—but that this lie was pointless, since the neutrals knew the facts and the world press had reported them. Why, then, was Hitler saying such vulnerable nonsense? The speech must be meant for the Germans; but in that case, he reflected—as Hitler went on to "offer an outstretched hand" to the British and the French—why was the speech so mild in style, and why were so many seats reserved for diplomats?

"Surely if forty-six million Englishmen can claim to rule over forty million square kilometers of the earth, then it cannot be wrong," Hitler said in a docile, placating tone, holding up both hands, palms outward, "for eighty-two million Germans to ask to be allowed to till in peace eight hundred thousand kilometers of soil that are historically their own." He was talking about his new order in central Europe, and the expanded Third Reich. The British and the French could have peace simply by accepting things as they now were, he said, adding a hint that it might be well if they also gave Germany back her old colonies. The Führer at the end fell into his old style, howling and sneering, shaking both fists in front of his face, pointing a fist and a finger straight upward, snapping his hands to his hips, as he pictured the horrors of a full-scale war, which he said he dreaded and which nobody could really win.

That night Pug Henry wrote in his intelligence report:

. . . Hitler looks very well. He obviously has first-rate powers of recuperation. Maybe licking Poland toned up his system a bit. Anyway, the haggardness is gone, his color is excellent, he isn't stooping, his voice is clear, not harsh, and—at least in this speech—very pleasant, and his walk is springy and quick. It would be a grave mistake to hope for a physical breakdown in this man.

The speech was a lot of the same old stuff, with some remarkable whoppers, even for the Führer, about who started the Polish war and about the sterling conduct of the Germans toward civilians. This tommyrot was certainly for internal consumption. His German listeners appeared to be swallowing it, though it's very hard to discern what Germans really think.

The radio tonight is making a great to-do about the "outstretched hand" peace proposal. We'll evidently be hearing "outstretched hand" from now on, possibly to the end of the war, even if it's ten years hence. The offer may have been authentic. If the Allies accept, Germany gets her half of Poland for the price of a quick cheap campaign, and also her pre–World War colonies, no doubt as a reward for the faultless chivalry of her armed forces. Hitler has never been bashful about making the most outrageous proposals. They've been accepted, too. So why not try another one?

At the very least, if he gets the truce and the conference he suggests, the British and French publics will undoubtedly relax and slack off. The Germans can use the breather to get their half-hearted industrial effort rolling for the showdown. On every count this was a clever speech by a leader who is riding high and seems to have the magic touch. The only fault I can find is a dull and boring delivery, but that too may have been calculated. Hitler today was the judicious European politician, not the roaring Aryan firebrand. Among his other talents he is a gifted vaudevillian.

Pug told Byron to write down his impressions of the speech. Byron handed him half a typewritten page:

My outstanding impression was the way Adolf Hitler follows out what he wrote in *Mein Kampf.* He says there, in his section on war propaganda, that the masses are "feminine," acting on feeling and sentiment, and that whatever you tell them must be addressed to the dullest ignoramus among them, in order to reach and convince the broadest possible audience. This speech was full of lies that ought to annoy a half-educated German boy of ten, and the peace proposals amounted to a total German grab. Maybe Hitler judges other countries by his own; otherwise I can't understand the speech. I realized only today what utter contempt Hitler has for the Germans. He regards them as bottomlessly naïve and stupid. They follow him and love him. Who am I to say he's wrong?

His father thought this was not bad, and included it in quotation marks as the comment of a youthful American spectator.

The din of the German radio and press in the next days was terrific. Italy and Japan had hailed the Führer as the greatest peacemaker of all time. A mighty popular surge for peace was sweeping the West and the United States. But "Churchillian" warmongers were trying to stamp out this warm response of the people to the Führer's outstretched hand. If they succeeded, the most ghastly bloodbath of all time would follow, and history would know whom to blame. Pug gathered from neutral intelligence in Berlin that some Frenchmen wanted to make a deal and call off the war, but not because they took seriously anything Hitler had said. It was just a question of yielding to the facts or fighting on.

Into this confusing noise came an electric shock of news. A U-boat had sneaked into the British fleet anchorage in Scapa Flow at the northern tip of Scotland, had sunk the battleship *Royal Oak,* and had returned home safe!

News pictures showed the solemn fat-faced Führer shaking the hand of Lieutenant Commander Prien, a nervous stiff young man with receding hair. The Nazi propaganda ministry foamed with ecstasy over the British Admiralty's report that sadly praised Prien's skill and daring. The writer was Churchill himself. Goebbels's broadcasters said the sinking of the *Royal Oak* would prove a great boon to peace, since the Führer's "outstretched hand" proposal would now receive more serious consideration.

A small reception was laid on for neutral military attachés to meet Prien. Victor Henry put his son's name on the list, with the rank *Ensign, USNR,* and Byron received a card. The Henrys dined before the reception at the apartment of Commander Grobke, a small dark walk-up flat on the fourth floor of an old house with bay windows. Heavy thick furniture so cluttered the rooms that there was hardly space to move. The meal was salt fish and potatoes, but it was well cooked and Byron enjoyed it. He found the Grobkes disconcertingly normal, though he was prepared to detest them. When the talk got around to Byron's experiences in Poland the woman listened with an unhappy, motherly look. "One never knows what to believe any more. Thank God it's over, at least. Let there only be peace, real peace. We don't want war. The last war ruined Germany. Another war will be the absolute end of our country."

Rhoda said, "It's so awful. Nobody in the world wants war, yet here we are in this mess."

Grobke said to Victor Henry, "What do you think? Are the Allies going to discuss the Führer's very reasonable offer?"

"Do you want me to be polite, or are you asking for information?"

"Don't be polite, Henry. Not with me."

"Okay. Germany can have peace if she gets rid of Hitler and his regime. You could even hang on to a lot of your gains. That gang has got to go."

Grobke and his wife looked at each other in the candlelight. "Then it's hopeless," he said, playing with his empty wineglass. "If your people won't understand one thing about Germany, we have to fight it out. You don't know what this country was like in the 1920's. I do. If the system had gone on another few years there would have been no navy, no economy, nothing. Germany would have fallen apart. This man stood up and put Germany back on the map. You have Roosevelt, we have him. Listen, Henry, I sat in a fancy club in New York and heard people call

Roosevelt an insane socialist cripple. There are millions who hate him. Right? Now I'm not a Nazi, I've never said the Führer is a thousand percent right. But he's a winner, damn it all. He gets things done, like Roosevelt. And you want us to get rid of him? First of all it isn't possible. You know what the regime is. And if it were possible we wouldn't do it. And yet there can be peace. It depends on one man, and he isn't our Führer."

"Who then?"

"Your President. The British and the French are beaten right now. Otherwise they'd have attacked in September. When will they ever have such a chance again? They're holding out for only one reason—they feel America's behind them. If your President says one word to them tomorrow—'I'm not helping you against Germany'—this world war will be over before it starts, and we'll all have a hundred years of prosperity. And I'll tell you one more thing. That's the only way your President can make sure Japan won't jump on your back."

It occurred to Victor Henry, not for the first time, that his meeting with Grobke on the *Bremen* had probably not been accidental. "I guess we'd better get on to that reception," he said.

Lieutenant Commander Prien looked surprised and interested when Byron's turn came in the reception line of floridly uniformed attachés. "You are young," he said in German, scrutinizing Byron's face and well-cut dark suit as they shook hands. "Are you a submariner?"

"No. Maybe I should be."

Prien said with a charming grin, and sudden wholehearted warmth, "Ach, it's the only service. But you have to be tough."

Blue-uniformed sailors lined up the chairs for a lecture. Pug Henry was flabbergasted by the candor of the U-boat captain's talk. It was no revelation that Prien had gone in on the surface at slack water, in the dark of the moon. That could be surmised. But Prien had no business exhibiting the Luftwaffe's aerial photographs of the entrances and analyzing the obstacles. It was handing the British their corrective measures on a silver platter. It also disclosed technical news about German reconnaissance photography—scary news, to be sure. This was urgent stuff for the next pouch.

Byron listened as intently as his father. What fascinated him was the living detail. Prien spoke a clear slow German. He could follow every word. He could see the northern lights shimmering in the black night, silhouetting the U-boat, reflecting in purple and green sparkles on the wet forecastle, and worrying the captain half to death. He was mentally dazzled by the automobile headlights on the shore that suddenly flashed out of the gloom and caught the captain square in the face. He saw the two dim gray battleships ahead, he heard the black chill waters of Scapa Flow lap on the U-boat hull as it slowed to fire four torpedoes. He almost shared the German's disappointment when only one hit.

The most amazing and inspiring part of the tale came after that. Instead of fleeing, Prien had made a big slow circle on the surface, inside the Royal Navy's main anchorage, to reload tubes; for the torpedo hit had failed to set off a general submarine alarm. It simply had not occurred to the British that there could be a U-boat inside Scapa Flow; on the *Royal Oak* they had taken the hit for an internal explosion. And so, by daring all, Prien had succeeded in shooting a second salvo of four torpedoes.

"We got three hits that time," Prien said. "The rest you know. We blew up the magazines, and the *Royal Oak* went down almost at once."

He did not gloat. Nor did he express regret over the nine hundred drowned British sailors. He had put his own life in hazard. The odds had been that he, and not they, would die in the night's work—tangled in the nets, impaled on rocks, or blown to bits by a mine. So Byron thought. He had sailed out, done his duty, and come home. Here he was, a serious, clean-cut professional, alive to tell the tale. This was not Warsaw, and this was not strafing horses and children on country roads.

Pug Henry and his son drove slowly home through deserted streets in the blue-lit blackout. They did not talk. Byron said as the car turned into their street, "Dad, didn't you ever consider submarines?"

The father shook his head. "They're a strange breed, those fellows. And once you're in the pigboats, you have a hell of a job ever getting out. This Prien's a lot like our own Navy submariners. Now and then I almost forgot there that he was talking German."

"Well, that's what I'd have picked, I think," Byron said, "if I'd gone in."

The car drew up to the house. Pug Henry leaned an elbow on the wheel, and looked at his son with an acid grin in the faint glow of the dashboard. "You don't get to sink a battleship every day."

Byron scowled, and said with unusual sharpness, "Is that what you think appeals to me?"

"Look here," Pug said, "the physical on submariners is a damn rigorous one, and they put you through a rough graduate school, but if you're actually interested—"

"No thanks, Dad." The young man laughed and tolerantly shook his head at his father's persistence.

Victor Henry often tried to start the topic of submarines again, but never drew another glint of interest.

He spent a week with Byron touring shipyards and factories. The German attaché in the United States had asked for such a tour, so a return of the courtesy was automatic. Pug Henry enjoyed travelling with his son. Byron put up with inconvenience, he never got angry, he joked in annoying moments, and he rose to sudden emergencies: a plane over-booked, a train missed, luggage vanished, hotel reservations lost. Pug considered himself fast on his feet, but Byron, by using a certain easygoing charm, could get out of holes, track things down, and persuade desk clerks and ticket agents to exert themselves, better than his father. During lunches with factory owners, plant managers, and yard superintendents, Byron could sit for two hours looking pleasant without talking, and reply when spoken to with something short and apt.

"You seem to be enjoying this," Pug remarked to Byron, as they drove back to the hotel in dark rain from a long tiring visit to the Krupp works in Essen.

"It's interesting. Much more so than the cathedrals and the schlosses and the folk costumes," Byron said. "This is the Germany to worry about."

Pug nodded. "Right. The German industrial plant is the pistol Hitler is pointing at the world's head. It bears study."

"Pretty sizable pistol," Byron said.

"Too sizable for comfort."

"How does it compare to the Allies', and to ours, Dad?"

A glass partition in the Krupp courtesy limousine separated them from the chauffeur, but Pug thought the man held his head at an attentive tilt.

"That's the question. We've got the biggest industrial plant in the world, no doubt of that, but Hitler isn't giving us a second thought right about now, because there's no national will to use it as a pistol. Germany with her industrial setup can run the world, if nobody argues. The means and the will exist. Macedonia wasn't very big when Alexander conquered the world. Brazil may be four times as big and have ten times the potential of Germany, but the payoff is on present capacity and will. On paper, as I keep insisting, the French and the British combined still have these people licked. But on paper Primo Carnera had Joe Louis licked. Hitler's gone to bat because he thinks he can take them. It's the ultimate way to match industrial systems, but a bit chancy."

"Then maybe this is what war is all about nowadays," Byron said. "Industrial capacity."

"Not entirely, but it's vital."

"Well, I'm certainly learning a lot."

Pug smiled. Byron was spending his hotel evenings doggedly reading Hegel, usually falling asleep in an hour or so over the open book.

"How are you coming along on that Hegel fellow?"

"It's just starting to clear up a bit. I can hardly believe it, but he seems crazier than Hitler. They taught me at Columbia that he's a great philosopher."

"Possibly he's too deep for you."

"Maybe so, but the trouble is, I think I understand him."

The gray, dignified chauffeur gave Byron a hideous look as he opened the door for them at the hotel. Byron ran over in his mind what he had said, and decided to be more careful about calling Hitler crazy. He didn't think the chauffeur was an offended Hegelian.

o   o   o

A letter arrived from Aaron Jastrow in a burst of air-mail from the outside a few days after the British and French, to the great rage of the German radio, rejected the Führer's outstretched hand. Mail to the embassy was supposed to be uncensored, but nobody believed that. The letters came in sudden sackfuls two or three weeks apart. The red and green Italian airmail envelope was rubber-stamped all over, purple and black and red. Dr. Jastrow was still typing with a worn-out ribbon, perhaps even the same one. He was too absentminded and, Byron suspected, too inept mechanically to change a ribbon, and unless someone did it for him he would use the old one until the words on the page looked like spirit typing. Byron had to put the letter under a strong light to make it out.

October 5th

Dear Byron:

Natalie is not here. I've had one letter from her, written in London. She'll try to come back to Siena, at least for a while. I'm selfishly glad of that, for I'm very much tied down without her.

Now about yourself. I can't encourage you to come back. I didn't discourage Natalie because I frankly need her. In her fashion she feels a responsibility for her bumbling uncle, which is a matter of blood ties, and very sweet and comforting. You have no such responsibility.

If you came here and I suddenly decided to leave, or were forced to go (and I must live with that possibility), think of all the useless motion and expense you'd have put yourself to! I would really like having you here, but I must husband my resources, so I couldn't pay for your trip from Berlin. Of course if you happened to come to Italy, though I can't think why you should, I would always be glad to see you and talk to you.

Meantime I must thank you for your inquiry. Just possibly it had some teeny connection with the other inquiry about Natalie's whereabouts, but I'm grateful for it anyway. I must recommend that for your own sake you forget about Siena, Constantine, and the Jastrows.

Thank you for all you did for my niece. I gather from her letter—not from your far too modest and bare note—that you

saved her from danger, perhaps from death. How glad I am
that you went!

My warmest regards to your parents. I briefly talked with
your father on the telephone. He sounded like a splendid man.

Faithfully yours,
Aaron Jastrow

When Byron got home that evening he took one look at
his father, sitting in a lounge chair on the porch facing the
garden, and backed away. Pug's head was thrust forward
and down, over a highball glass clenched in two hands.
Byron went to his room and plugged at Hegel and his
baffling "World Spirit" until dinner time.

Rhoda endured Victor Henry's glowering silence at the
table until the dessert came. "All right, Pug," she said,
digging into her ice cream, "what's it all about?"

Pug gave her a heavy-lidded look. "Didn't you read the
letter?"

Byron thought his mother's reaction was exceedingly
peculiar. Her face stiffened, her eyes widened, her back
straightened.

"Letter? What letter? From whom?"

"Get the letter on my dressing table for your mother,
please," Pug said to Byron.

"Well, goodness me," Rhoda gasped, as she saw Byron
trampling down the stairs with a pink envelope, "it's only
from Madeline."

"Who did you think it was from?"

"Well, good lord, how was I to know? The Gestapo or
somebody, from your manner. Honestly, Pug." She
scanned the letter. "So? What's wrong with this? That's
quite a raise, twenty dollars a week."

"Read the last page."

"I am. Well! I see what you mean."

"Nineteen years old," Pug said. "An apartment of her
own in New York! And I was the fusspot, about letting her
leave school."

"Pug, I merely said when you got here, that the thing
was done. She couldn't have enrolled any more."

"She damn well could have tried."

"Anyway, Madeline will be all right. She's a good girl.
She's as straitlaced as you."

"It's this war," Pug said. "The world's coming apart at the seams by the day. What can that girl do that's worth fifty-five dollars a week? That's what a senior grade lieutenant makes, after ten years in the service. It's absurd."

Rhoda said, "You've always babied Madeline. I think she's showed you up, and that's what really annoys you."

"I wish I were back there. I'd have a damn good look around."

Rhoda drummed the fingers of both hands on the table. "Do you want me to go home and be with her?"

"That would cost a fortune. It's one thing when you travel on government allowance, but—" Pug turned to Byron. "You'll be going back, won't you? Maybe you could find a job in New York."

"As a matter of fact, I wanted to talk about that. I got a letter too. From Dr. Jastrow. I'm going to Siena."

"You are?"

"Yes."

"Who says so?"

"I do."

Silence.

Rhoda said, "That's something we should all discuss, isn't it, Briny?"

"Is that girl there?" Pug said.

"No."

"She's gone back to the States?"

"No. She's trying to get there from England."

"How do you propose to go?"

"Train. They're running regularly to Milan and Florence."

"And what will you use for money?"

"I have enough to get there. I saved nearly all I made."

"And you'll do what? Literary research up in an Italian mountain town, with a war on?"

"If I get called to active duty, I'll go."

"That's damned bighearted, seeing that if you didn't, the Navy would track you down and put you in the brig for a few years. Well, I'm proud of you, Briny. Do as you please." Victor Henry coughed, rolled up his napkin, and left the table. Byron sat with his head thrust down and forward, his face white, the muscles in his jaw working.

Rhoda saw that talking to her son would be useless. She went upstairs to her dressing room, took out a letter she had put in a drawer beneath her underwear, read it once, then tore it into very small pieces.

*   *   *

17

Sitzkrieg

(from WORLD EMPIRE LOST)

The "Phony" War

The quiescent half year between the fall of Warsaw and the Norway episode became known in the West as the "phony" war, a phrase attributed to an American senator. We called it the *Sitzkrieg*, or "sitting war," a play on *Blitzkrieg*. On the British and French side the name was perhaps justified. During this lull they in fact did unbelievably little to improve their military posture, besides sit on their backsides and predict our collapse.

Early in this strange twilight period, the Führer delivered his "outstretched hand" peace speech to the Reichstag. Like most of his political moves, it was cleverly conceived. Had the Allies swallowed it, we might have achieved surprise in the west with a November attack, which Hitler had ordered when Warsaw fell, and which we were feverishly planning. But by now the Western statesmen had developed a certain wariness toward our Führer, and their response was disappointing. In the event this did not matter. A combination of bad weather and insoluble supply problems forced one postponement after another on the impatient Führer. The intent to attack France was never at issue, but the date and the strategy kept changing. In all, the attack day was postponed twenty-nine times. Meanwhile preparations went forward at an ever-mounting tempo.

Our staff's favorite comic reading as we worked on *Fall Gelb*—"Case Yellow," the attack on France—came to be the

285

long, learned articles in French newspapers and military journals, proving that we were about to cave in under economic pressure. In point of fact, for the first time our economy was really getting moving. Life in Paris, we gathered, was gayer and more relaxed than before the war. The British Prime Minister Chamberlain epitomized the Western frame of mind by stating, "Hitler has missed the bus." In this enforced half-year delay German industrial war production began to rise and—despite the never-ending confusion and interference in the Führer's headquarters—a new and excellent strategy for the assault on France was at last hammered out.

Distraction in Finland

The sitzkrieg lull was temporarily enlivened when the Soviet Union attacked Finland.

Stalin's unvarying policy after signing the Ribbentrop pact was to seize whatever territory he could, while we were at war with the democracies, to strengthen his position for an eventual showdown with us. Hitler had already given him huge concessions in the Baltic states and in Poland, to buy a free hand against the West. But like all Russian rulers, Czarist or Bolshevik, Stalin had a big appetite. This was his chance to take over the Karelian Isthmus and dominate the Gulf of Finland. When his emissaries failed to get these concessions from the proud Finns by threats, Stalin set out to take them by force. The rights of Finland were, as a matter of course, to be trampled upon.

But to the world's surprise, the Russian dictator got in trouble, for the attack went badly. The vaunted Red Army covered itself with disgrace, revealing itself in Finland as an ill-equipped, ill-trained, miserably led rabble, unable to crush a small well-drilled foe. Whether this was due to Stalin's purges of his officer force in the late thirties, or to the traditional Russian inefficiency added to the depressant effect of Bolshevism, or to the use of inferior troops, remained unclear. But from November 1939 to March 1940, Finland did bravely fight off the Slav horde. Nor did the Russians ever really defeat them militarily. In the classic manner of Russian combat, the handful of Finnish defenders was finally drowned in a rain of artillery shells and a bath of Slav blood. Thus Stalin's goal was achieved, at ruthless cost, of shaping up the Leningrad front by pushing back our Finnish friends on the Karelian Isthmus. This move, it must be confessed, probably saved Leningrad in 1941.

After the Finnish victory during Christmas—the classic battle of Suomussalmi in which nearly thirty thousand Russians were killed or frozen to death, at a cost of about nine hundred Finnish dead—it was impossible to regard the Soviet army as a competent modern adversary. Much later, Hermann Göring was to call the Finnish campaign "the greatest camouflage action in history," implying that the Russians in Finland had pretended to be weak in order to mask their potential. This was just an absurd excuse for the failures of his Luftwaffe in the east. In point of fact, Stalin's Russia in 1939 was militarily feeble. What happened between that time and our final debacle on the eastern front at Russian hands is the subject of a later section, but their performance in Finland certainly misled us in our planning.

Sitzkrieg Ends: Norway

Much vociferous propaganda went on in the Western democracies about the attack on Finland, and about sending the Finns military aid. In the end they did nothing. However, the opening of the Finnish front did force Hitler to face up to a genuine threat in the north: the British plot to seize Norway.

Of this we had hard intelligence. Unlike many of the "plots" and "conspiracies" of which our German armed forces were accused at the Nuremberg trials, this British plot certainly existed. Winston Churchill openly describes it in his memoirs. He acknowledges that the British invasion was laid on for a date ahead of ours, and then put off, so that we beat the British into Norway by the merest luck, by a matter of days.

The Russo-Finnish war made the problem of Norway acute, because England and France could use "aid to Finland" as a perfect pretext for landing in Norway and driving across Scandinavia. This would have been disastrous for us. The North Sea, bracketed by British bases on both sides, would have been closed to our U-boats, choking off our main thrust at sea. Even more important, the winter route for ships bringing us Swedish iron ore lay along the Norwegian coast.

Deprived of that iron ore, we could not have gone on fighting for long. When the High Command convinced Hitler of these risks, he issued the order for "Weser Exercise," the occupation of Norway, and postponed Case Yellow once again.

It is a sad commentary that Admiral Raeder, at the Nuremberg trials, was convicted of "a plot to occupy neutral Norway," when the British who sat in judgment had plotted the same thing themselves. Such paradoxes have enabled me to bear with honor my own experience at Nuremberg, and to regard it as not a disgrace at all, but rather as a political consequence of defeat. Had the war gone the other way, and had we hanged Churchill for plotting to occupy Norway, what would the world have said? Yet what is sauce for the goose should be sauce for the gander.

Our occupation of Norway, a surprise overwater move virtually under the guns of a highly superior British fleet, was a great success; not, however, because of Hitler's leadership, but in spite of it. We took heavy losses at sea, especially of destroyers that we sorely missed when the invasion of England was later planned. But the price was small compared to the gain. We forestalled the British, opened up a much wider coastline to counter the blockade, and secured the Swedish iron ore supply for the rest of the war.

Mistakes in Norway

Hitler's amateurishness showed up badly in Norway. It cropped up again and again in every campaign, tending only to get grosser as time went on.

The mark of the amateur in any field is to lose one's head when the going gets hard. What marks the professional is his competence in an emergency, and almost the whole art of the soldier is to make sound judgments in the fog of war. Hitler's propensity to lose his head took two forms: calling a panicky halt to operations when they were gathering momentum, and changing the objective in mid-campaign. Both these failings appeared in Weser Exercise. I give details in my Norway operational analysis, of his hysterical insistence day after day that we abandon Narvik, the real key to the position; his wild sudden scheme to capture the port of Trondheim with the luxury liner *Bremen*, and so forth. Why then was the occupation of Scandinavia a success? Simply because General Falkenhorst, once in Norway, ignored the Führer's interference, and did a fine professional job with good troops and a sound plan.

This interference from above, incidentally, was to haunt operations to the end. Adolf Hitler had used all his political shrewdness over many years to gain control of the armed forces, not stopping at strong-arm methods. There is no question that this man's lust for power was insatiable, and it is certainly regrettable that the German people did not understand his true nature until it was too late. The background of this usurpation will be sketched here, as it significantly affected the whole course of the six-year war.

How Hitler Usurped Control of the Army

In 1938, he and his Nazi minions did not scruple to frame grave charges of sexual misconduct against revered generals of the top command. Also, they took advantage of a few actual unfortunate lapses of this nature; the details need not be raked over in this account. Suffice it that the Nazis managed to topple the professional leadership in a bold underhanded coup based on such accusations. Hitler with sudden stunning arrogance then assumed supreme command himself! And he exacted an oath of loyalty to himself throughout the Wehrmacht, from foot soldier to general. In this act he showed his knowledge of the German character, which is the soul of honor, and takes such an oath as binding to the death.

Our staff, muted and disorganized by the disgusting revelations and pseudo-revelations about our honored leaders, offered no coherent resistance to this usurpation. So the strict independence of the German army from German politics, which for generations had kept the Wehrmacht a strong stabilizing force in the Fatherland, came to an end; and the drive wheel of the world's strongest military machine was grasped by an Austrian street agitator.

In itself this was not a catastrophic turn. Hitler was far from a military ignoramus. He had had four years in the field as a foot soldier, and there are worse ways to learn war. He was a voracious reader of history and of military writings. His memory for technical facts was unusual. Above all, he did have the ability to get to the root of a large problem.

He had almost a woman's intuition for the nub of a matter. This is a fine leadership trait in war, always providing that the politician listens to the soldiers for the execution of his ideas. The combination of a bold political adventurer, a Charles XII personality risen from the streets to weld Germany into a solid driving force, and our General Staff, the world's best military leadership, might well have brought us ultimate success.

But Hitler was incapable of listening to anybody. This undid him and ruined Germany. Grand strategy and incredibly petty detail were equally his preoccupations. The overruling axiom of our war effort was that Hitler gave the orders. In a brutal speech to our staff in November 1939, prompted by our efforts to discourage a premature attack on France, he warned us that he would ruthlessly crush any of us who opposed his will. Like so many of his other threats, he made this one good. By the end of the war most of our staff had been dismissed in disgrace. Many had been shot. All of us would have been shot sooner or later, had he not lost his nerve and shot himself first.

Thus it happened that the strength of the great German people, and the valor of the peerless German soldier, became passive tools in Hitler's amateur hands.

Hitler and Churchill: A Comparison

Winston Churchill, in a revealing passage of his memoirs on the functioning of his chiefs of staff, expresses his envy of Hitler, who could get his decisions acted upon without submitting them to the discouragement and pulling apart of hidebound professional soldiers. In fact, this was what saved England and won the war.

Churchill was exactly the kind of brilliant amateur meddler in military affairs that Hitler was. Both rose to power from the depths of political rejection. Both relied chiefly on oratory to sway the multitude. Both somehow expressed the spirit of their peoples, and so won loyalty that outlasted any number of mistakes, defeats, and disasters. Both thought in grandiose terms, knew little about economic and logistical realities, and cared less. Both were iron men in defeat. Above all, both men had overwhelming personalities that could silence rational opposition while they talked. Of this strange phenomenon,

I had ample and bitter experience with Hitler. The crucial difference was that in the end Churchill had to listen to the professionals, whereas the German people had committed itself to the fatal *Führerprinzip.*

Had Churchill possessed the power Adolf Hitler managed to arrogate to himself, the Allied armies would have bled to death in 1944, invading the "soft underbelly of the Axis," as Churchill called the fearful mountains and water obstacles of the Balkan peninsula. There we would have slaughtered them. The Italian campaign proved that. Only on the flat plains of Normandy did the Ford-production style of American warfare, using immense ¯masses of inferior, cheaply made machinery, have a chance of working. The Balkans would have been a colossal Thermopylae, won by the defenders. It would have been a Churchill defeat compared to which Gallipoli would have been a schoolboy picnic.

With a Führer's authority, Churchill would also have frittered away the Allied landing craft, always a critical supply problem, in witless attempts to recapture the Greek islands and to storm Rhodes. In 1944 he nagged Eisenhower and Roosevelt to commit these wild follies until they both stopped talking to him.

Churchill was a Hitler restrained by democracy. If the German nation ever rises again, let it remember the different ends of these two men. I am not arguing for the goose gabble of parliamentarians. By conviction I have always been a conservative monarchist. But whatever the civilian structure, let our people hereafter entrust military affairs to its trained generals, and insist that politicians keep hands off the war machine.

TRANSLATOR'S NOTE: *This very jarring and distorted comparison of Hitler and Churchill omits the crucial difference, of course. By the common verdict of historians, even most German ones, Hitler was a ruthless adventurer bent on conquest and plunder, while Churchill was a great defender of human liberty, dignity, and law. It is true that Churchill tended to interfere in military matters. Politicians find that temptation hard to resist.*

Roon's assertion about the British plan to land in Norway

is correct. His conclusions, again, are a different matter, showing how slippery the issues at Nuremberg were. England was the sole protector and hope of small neutral countries like Norway and Denmark. The purpose of a British landing would have been to defend Norway, not to occupy and dominate it. In a war, both sides may well try to take the same neutral objective for strategic reasons, which does not prove that both sides are equally guilty of aggression. That is the fallacy in Roon's argument. I would not recommend trying to persuade a German staff officer of this.—V.H.

*   *   *

18

WARREN HENRY and his fiancée Janice were set straight
about Russia's invasion of Finland by an unexpected
person: Madeline's new boyfriend, a trombone player and
student of public affairs named Sewell Bozeman. Early in
December the engaged couple came to New York and
visited Madeline in her new apartment. Finding the boyfriend there was a surprise.

The news of her move to her own apartment had enraged Pug Henry, but had he known her reason, he would
have been pleased. Madeline had come to despise the two
girls with whom she had shared a flat. Both were having
affairs—one with a joke writer, the other with an actor
working as a bellhop. Madeline had found herself being
asked to skulk around, stay out late, or remain in her
room while one or another pair copulated. The walls in
the shabby apartment were thin. She had no way of even
pretending unawareness.

She was disgusted. Both girls had good jobs, both
dressed with taste, both were college graduates. Yet they
behaved like sluts, as Madeline understood the word. She
was a Henry, with her father's outlook. Give or take a
few details of Methodist doctrine, Madeline believed in
what she had learned at home and at church. Unmarried
girls of good character didn't sleep with men; to her, that
was almost a law of nature. Men had more leeway; she
knew, for instance, that Warren had been something of a
hellion before his engagement. She liked Byron better
because he seemed, in this respect, more like her upright
father. To Madeline sex was a delightful matter of playing
with fire, but enjoying the blaze from a safe distance,
until she could leap into the hallowed white conflagration

of a bridal night. She was a middle-class good girl, and not in the least ashamed of it. She thought her roommates were gross fools. As soon as Hugh Cleveland gave her a raise, she got out.

"I don't know," she said, stirring a pot over a tiny stove behind a screen, "maybe this dinner was a mistake. We all could have gone to a restaurant."

She was addressing the boyfriend, Sewell Bozeman, called Bozey by the world. They had met at a party in September. Bozey was a thin, long, pale, tractable fellow with thick straight brown hair and thoughtful brown eyes that bulged behind rimless glasses. He always dressed in brown, to brown shoes, brown ties, and even brown shirts; he was always reading enormous brown books on economics and politics and had a generally brown outlook on life, believing that America was a doomed society, rapidly going under. Madeline found him a piquant and intriguing novelty. At the moment, he was setting her small dining table, wearing over his brown array the pink apron he had put on to peel onions for the stew.

"Well, it's not too late," he said. "You can save the stew for another night, and we can take your brother and his girl to Julio's."

"No, I told Warren I was cooking the dinner. That girl's rolling in money, she wouldn't like an Italian dive. And they have to rush off to the theatre." Madeline came out, patting her hot face with a handkerchief, and looked at the table. "That's fine. Thanks, Bozey. I'm going to change." She opened a closet door crusted with yellowing white paint and took out a dress and slip, glancing around the small room. With a three-sided bay window looking out on back yards and drying laundry, it was the whole apartment, except for the kitchenette and a tiny bath. Large pieces of blue cloth lay on the threadbare divan under yellow paper patterns. "Darn it. That divan is such a rat's nest. Maybe I'll have time to finish cutting that dress, if I hurry."

"I can finish cutting it," Bozey said.

"Nonsense, Bozey, you can't cut a dress. Don't try." A doorbell wheezily rang. "Well, the wine's here already. That's good." She went to open the door. Warren and Janice walked in and surprised the tall popeyed man in his pink apron, holding shears in one hand and a sleeve pattern in the other. What with the smell of the hot stew, and Madeline in a housecoat with a dress and a lacy slip on her arm, it was a strikingly domestic scene.

"Oh, hi. You're early. My gosh, Warren, you're tan!" Madeline was so sure of her own rectitude that it didn't occur to her to be embarrassed. "This is Sewell Bozeman, a friend of mine."

Bozey waved the shears feebly at them; he was embarrassed, and in his fluster he started to cut a ragged blue rayon sleeve.

Madeline said, "Bozey, *will* you stop cutting that dress!" She turned to Janice. "Imagine, he actually thinks he can do it."

"It's more than I can," Janice Lacouture said, staring incredulously at Bozeman. Bozey dropped the shears and took off his apron with a giggle.

Warren said just to say something and cover his stupefaction, "Your dinner smells great, Madeline."

After completing introductions, Madeline went off into what she called her boudoir, a grimy toilet about four feet square. "If you'd like to freshen up first—" she said to Janice as she opened the door, gesturing at the few cubic feet of yellow space crammed with rusty plumbing. "It's a bit cosy in there for two."

"Oh, no, no I'm just fine," Janice exclaimed. "Go ahead."

A halting conversation ensued while Bozey donned his jacket and tie. Soon Madeline put out her head and one naked shoulder and arm. "Bozey, I don't want that beef stew to boil over. Turn down the gas."

"Sure thing."

As he went behind the screen, Janice Lacouture and Warren exchanged appalled looks. "Do you play with the New York Philharmonic, Mr. Bozeman?" Janice raised her voice.

"No, I'm with Ziggy Frechtel's orchestra. We play the Feenamint Hour," he called back. "I'm working on getting up my own band." He returned and sat in an armchair, or rather lay in it, with his head propped against the back and the rest of him projecting forward and down, sloping to the floor. Warren, something of a sloucher himself, regarded this spectacular slouch by the limp long brown bulging-eyed trombonist with incredulity. In a way the strangest feature was his costume. Warren had never in his life seen a brown tie on a brown shirt. Madeline issued from the bathroom smoothing her dress. "Oh, come on, Bozey, mix some drinks," she carolled.

Bozey hauled himself erect and made drinks, talking on about the problems of assembling a band. A shy, awkward fellow, he honestly believed that the best way to put other people at their ease was to keep talking, and the one subject that usually occurred to him was himself. He disclosed that he was the son of a minister in Montana; that the local doctor had cured him of religion at sixteen, by feeding him the works of Ingersoll and Haeckel while treating him less successfully for thyroid trouble; and that in rebellion against his father he had taken up the trombone.

Soon he was on the topic of the war, which, he explained, was nothing but an imperialist struggle for markets. This was apropos of a remark by Warren that he was a naval fighter pilot in training. Bozey proceeded to set forth the Marxist analysis of war, beginning with the labor theory of value. Madeline meanwhile, finishing and serving up the dinner, was glad to let him entertain her company. She knew Bozey was talkative, but she found him interesting and she thought Warren and Janice might, too. They seemed oddly silent. Perhaps, she thought, they had just had a little spat.

Under capitalism, Bozey pointed out, workers never were paid what they really earned. The capitalist merely gave them the lowest wages possible. Since he owned the means of production, he had them at his mercy. Profit was the difference between what the worker produced and what he got. This had to lead to war sooner or later. In each country the capitalists piled up big surpluses because the workers weren't paid enough to buy back what they produced. The capitalists, to realize their profits, had to sell off those surpluses in other countries. This struggle for foreign markets, when it got hot enough, inevitably turned into war. That was what was happening now.

"But Hitler has no surpluses," Janice Lacouture mildly observed. An economics student, she knew these Marxist bromides, but was willing to let the boyfriend, or lover—she wasn't yet sure which—of Warren's sister run on for a while. "Germany's a land of shortages."

"The war is a struggle for foreign markets, all the same," Bozey insisted serenely, back in his deep slouch. "How about cameras, just at random? Germany still exports cameras."

Warren said, "As I understand you, then, the Germans invaded Poland to sell Leicas."

"Making jokes about economic laws is easy, but irrelevant." Bozey smiled.

"I'm fairly serious," Warren said. "Obviously Hitler's reason for attacking Poland was conquest and loot, as in most wars."

"Hitler is a figurehead," said Bozey comfortably. "Have you ever heard of Fritz Thyssen? He and the Krupps and a few other German capitalists put him in power. They could put someone else in tomorrow if they chose, by making a few telephone calls. Of course there's no reason why they should, he's a useful and obedient lackey in their struggle for foreign markets."

"What you're saying is the straight Communist line, you know," Janice said.

"Oh, Bozey's a Communist," Madeline said, emerging from behind the screen with a wooden bowl of salad. "Dinner's ready. Will you dress the salad, Bozey?"

"Sure thing." Bozey took the bowl to a rickety little side table, and made expert motions with oil, vinegar, and condiments.

"I'm not sure I've ever met a Communist before," Warren said, peering at the long brown man.

"My gosh, you haven't?" said Madeline. "Why, the radio business swarms with them."

"That's a slight exaggeration," Bozey said, rubbing garlic on the salad bowl, and filling the close, warm flat with the pungent aroma.

"Oh, come on, Bozey. Who isn't a Communist in our crowd?"

"Well, Peter isn't. I don't think Myra is. Anyway, that's just our gang." He added to Warren, "It dates from the Spanish Civil War days. We put on all kinds of shows for the benefit of the Loyalists." Bozey brought the salad bowl to the table, where the others were already seated. "Of course there's just a few of us left now. A lot of the crowd dropped away after Stalin made the pact with Hitler. They had no fundamental convictions."

"Didn't that pact bother you?" Warren said.

"Bother me? Why? It was a wise move. The capitalist powers want to snuff out socialism in the Soviet Union. If they bleed themselves white beforehand, fighting each other, the final attack on socialism will be that much weaker. Stalin's peace policy is very wise."

Warren said, "Suppose Hitler polishes off England and France in a one-front war, and then turns and smashes Russia? That may well happen. Stalin could have made a deal with the Allies, and all of them together would have had a far better chance of stopping the Nazis."

"But don't you see, there's no reason for a socialist country to take part in an imperialist struggle for foreign markets," Bozey patiently explained to the benighted naval aviator. "Socialism doesn't need foreign markets, since the worker gets all he creates."

"Bozey, will you bring the stew?" Madeline said.

"Sure thing."

Janice Lacouture said, speaking louder as he went behind the screen, "But surely you know that a Russian worker gets less than a worker in any capitalist country."

"Of course. There are two reasons for that. Socialism triumphed first in a feudal country," Bozey said, reappearing with the stew, "and had a big industrial gap to close. Also, because of the imperialist threat, socialism had to divert a lot of production to arms. When socialism triumphs everywhere, arms will become useless, and they'll all be thrown in the sea."

"But even if that happens, which I doubt, it seems to me," said Janice, "that when the state owns the means of production, the workers will get less than if capitalists own them. You know how inefficient and tyrannical government bureaucracies are."

"Yes," interjected Madeline, "but as soon as socialism triumphs everywhere the state will wither away, because nobody will need a central government any more. Then the workers will get it all. Pass the wine around, Bozey."

"Sure thing."

Warren said to his sister, narrowing his eyes at her, "Do you believe that?"

"Well, that's how the argument goes," Madeline said, giggling. "Wouldn't Dad die if he knew I'd made friends with Communists? For heaven's sake don't write and tell him."

"Have no fear." Warren turned to Bozey. "What about Finland?"

The Russian invasion of the tiny northern country was then about a week old, and already looking like a disaster.

"Okay. What about it?"

"Well, you know Russia claims that Finland attacked her, the way Hitler claimed Poland attacked Germany. Do you believe that?"

"It's ridiculous to think that Poland attacked Germany," Bozey said calmly, "but it's highly likely that Finland attacked the Soviet Union. It was probably a provocation engineered by others to embroil socialism in the imperialist war."

"The Soviet Union is fifty times as big as Finland," Janice Lacouture said.

"I'm not saying the Finns did something wise," said Bozey. "They were egged on into making a bad mistake. Anyway, Finland just used to be a duchy of Czarist Russia. It's not an invasion exactly, it's a rectification."

"Oh, come on, Bozey," Madeline said. "Stalin's simply making hay while the sun shines, slamming his way in there to improve his strategic position against Germany."

"Of course," Warren said, "and that's a damned prudent move in his situation, whatever the morality of it may be."

Bozey smiled cunningly, his eyes starting from his head. "Well, it's quite true he wasn't born yesterday. The imperialists all lift up their hands in holy horror when a socialist government does something realistic. They think that's their exclusive privilege."

"Why do you suppose the invasion's flopping on its face?" Warren said.

"Oh, do you believe the capitalist newspapers?" said Bozey, with a broad wink.

"You think the Russians are really winning?"

"Why, all this nonsense about the Finnish ski troops in

white uniforms makes me ill," Bozey said. "Don't you suppose the Russians have skis and white uniforms too? But catch the *New York Times* saying so."

"This is a lovely stew," Janice said.

"I used too many cloves," Madeline said. "Don't bite into one."

Warren and Janice left right after dinner to go to the theatre. He was on a seventy-two-hour pass from Pensacola, and Janice had come up from Washington to meet him; dinner with Madeline had been a last-minute arrangement by long-distance telephone. When they left, Madeline was cutting out her dress and Bozey was washing the dishes.

"What do I do now?" Warren said, out in the street. The theatre was only a few blocks away. It was snowing and cabs were unobtainable, so they walked. "Get myself a shotgun?"

"What for? To put Bozey out of his misery?"

"To get him to marry her, was my idea."

Janice laughed, and hugged his arm. "There's nothing doing between those two, honey."

"You don't think so?"

"Not a chance. That's quite a gal, your little sister."

"Jesus Christ, yes. The Red Flame of Manhattan. That's a hell of a note. And I wrote my folks I was going to visit her. Now what do I say?"

"You just write your parents that everything's peachy with her. Because it is."

They walked with heads bent, the snow whirling on the wind into their faces.

"Why are you so quiet?" said Janice. "Don't worry about your sister. Really, you don't have to."

"I'm thinking how this war's blown our family apart. I mean, we used to scatter here and there," Warren said. "We're a service family and we're used to that, but it's different now. I don't feel there's a base any more. And we're all changing. I don't know if we'll ever pull back together again."

"Sooner or later all families change and scatter," said Janice Lacouture, "and out of the pieces new families start up. That's how it goes, and a very lovely arrangement it is, too." She put her face to his for a moment, and snow-flakes fell on the two warm cheeks.

"The imperialist struggle for foreign markets," said Warren. "Jehosephat! I hope she's rid of *that* one by the time Dad gets back. Otherwise he'll lay waste to Radio City."

19

"BYRON!"

Dr. Jastrow gasped out the name and stared. He sat as usual on the terrace, the blue blanket over his legs, the gray shawl around his shoulders, the writing board and yellow pad on his lap. A cold breeze blowing across the valley from Siena fluttered Jastrow's pages. In the translucent air the red-walled town, with its black-and-white striped cathedral atop the vineyard-checkered hills, looked hauntingly like the medieval Siena in old frescoes.

"Hello, A.J."

"Dear me, Byron! I declare I'll be a week recovering from the start you've given me! We were talking about you only at breakfast. We were both absolutely certain you'd be in the States by now."

"She's here?"

"Of course. She's up in the library."

"Sir, will you excuse me?"

"Yes, go ahead, let me collect myself—oh, and Byron, tell Maria I'd like some strong tea right away."

Byron took the center hall steps three at a time and walked into the library. She stood at the desk in a gray sweater, a black skirt, pale and wide-eyed. "It is, by God! It *is* you. Nobody else galumphs up those stairs like that."

"It's me."

"Why the devil did you come back?"

"I have to make a living."

"You're an imbecile. Why didn't you let us know you were coming?"

"Well, I thought I'd better just come."

She approached him, stretched out a hand uncertainly, and put it to his face. The long fingers felt dry and cold. "Anyway, you look rested. You seem to have put on some weight." She backed off awkwardly and abruptly. "I owe you an apology. I was feeling beastly that day in Königsberg, and if I was rude to you I'm sorry." She walked away from him and sank into her desk chair. "Well, we can use you here, but surprises like this are never pleasant. Don't you know that yet?" As though he had returned from an errand in town, she resumed clattering at the typewriter.

That was all his welcome. Jastrow put him back to work, and within a few days the old routines were restored. It was as though the Polish experience had never occurred, as though neither of them had left the hilltop. The traces of the war in these quiet hills were few. Only sporadic shortages of gasoline created any difficulty. The Milan and Florence newspapers that reached them played down the war. Even on the BBC broadcasts there was little combat news. The Russian attack on Finland seemed as remote as a Chinese earthquake.

Because the buses had become unreliable, Dr. Jastrow gave Byron a lodging on the third floor of the villa: a cramped little maid's room with cracking plaster walls, and a stained ceiling that leaked in hard rains. Natalie lived directly below Byron in a second-floor bedroom looking out on Siena. Her peculiar manner to him persisted. At mealtimes, and generally in Jastrow's presence, she was distantly cordial. In the library she was almost uncivil, working away in long silences, and giving terse cool answers to questions. Byron had a modest opinion of himself and his attractions, and he took his treatment as probably his due, though he missed the comradeship of their days in Poland and wondered why she never talked about them. He thought he had probably annoyed her by following her here. He was with her again, and that was why he had come; so, for all the brusque treatment, he was as content as a dog reunited with an irritable master.

When Byron arrived in Siena, the Constantine book was on the shelf for the moment, in favor of an expanded magazine article, "The Last Palio," In describing the race, Jastrow had evoked a gloom-filled image of Europe plunging again toward war. A piece startling in its foresight, it had arrived on the editor's desk on the first of September, the day of the invasion. The magazine printed it, and Jastrow's publisher cabled him a frantic request to work it up into a short book, preferably containing a note of optimism (however slight) on the outcome of the war. The cable mentioned a large advance against royalties. This was the task in hand.

In this brief book, Jastrow was striking an Olympian, farseeing, forgiving note. The Germans would probably be beaten to the ground again, he wrote; and even if they gained the rule of the earth, they would in the end be tamed and subdued by their subject peoples, as their ancestors, the Goths and Vandals, had been tamed to turn Christian. Fanatic or barbaric despotism had only its hour. It was a recurring human fever fated to cool and pass. Reason and freedom were what all human history eternally moved toward.

The Germans were the bad children of Europe, Jastrow argued: egotistic, willful, romantic, always poised to break up faltering patterns of order. Arminius had set the ax to the *Pax Romana;* Martin Luther had broken the back of the universal Church; now Hitler was challenging Europe's unsteady regime of liberal capitalism, based on an obsolete patchwork structure of nations.

The "Palio" of Europe, wrote Jastrow, the contest of hot little nationalisms in a tiny crowded cockpit of a continent, a larger Siena with the sea for three walls and Asia for a fourth, was worn out. As Siena had only one water company and one power company, one telephone system and one mayor, instead of seventeen of these in the seventeen make-believe sovereignties called Goose, Caterpillar, Giraffe, and so forth, so Europe was ripe for the same commonsense unification. Hitler, a bad-boy genius, had perceived this. He was going about the breakup of the old order cruelly, wrongly, with Teutonic fury, but what mattered was that he was essentially correct. The Second World War was the last Palio. Europe would emerge less

colorful but more of a rational and solid structure, whichever side won the idiotic and gory horse race. Perhaps this
painful but healthy process would become global, and the
whole earth would be unified at last. As for Hitler, the
villain of the melodrama, he would either be hunted down
and bloodily destroyed like Macbeth, or he would have
his triumph and then he would fall or die. The stars would
remain, so would the earth, so would the human quest for
freedom, understanding, and love among brothers.

As he typed repeated drafts of these ideas, Byron wondered whether Jastrow would have written such a tolerant
and hopeful book had he spent September under bombardment in Warsaw, instead of in his villa overlooking Siena.
He thought "The Last Palio" was a lot of high-flown irrelevant gab. But he didn't say so.

*   *   *

Letters were coming to Natalie from Leslie Slote, one
or two a week. She seemed less excited over them than she
had been in the spring, when she would rush off to her bedroom to read them, and return looking sometimes radiant,
sometimes tearful. Now she casually skimmed the single-
space typed pages at her desk, then shoved them in a
drawer. One rainy day she was reading such a letter when
Byron, typing away at the Palio book, heard her say,
"Good God!"

He looked up. "Something the matter?"

"No, no," she said, very red in the face, waving an
agitated hand and flipping over a page. "Sorry. It's nothing
at all."

Byron resumed work, struggling with one of Jastrow's
bad sentences. The professor wrote in a spiky hurried
hand, often leaving out letters or words. He seldom closed
his *s*'s and *o*'s. It was anybody's guess what words some of
these strings of blue spikes represented. Natalie could puzzle them out, but Byron disliked her pained condescending
way of doing it.

"Well!" Natalie sat back in her chair with a thump,
staring at the letter. "Briny—"

"Yes?"

She hesitated, chewing her full lower lip. "Oh, hell, I

can't help it. I've got to tell someone, and you're handy. Guess what I hold here in my hot little hand?" She rustled the pages.

"I see what you're holding."

"You only think you do." She laughed in a wicked way. "I'm going to tell you. It's a proposal of marriage from a gentleman named Leslie Manson Slote, Rhodes Scholar, rising diplomat, and elusive bachelor. And what do you think of that, Byron Henry?"

"Congratulations," Byron said.

The buzzer on Natalie's desk rang. "Oh, lord. Briny, please go and see what A.J. wants. I'm in a fog." She tossed the letter on the desk and thrust long white hands in her hair.

Dr. Jastrow sat blanketed in the downstairs study on the chaise longue by the fire, his usual place in rainy weather. Facing him in an armchair, a fat pale Italian official, in a green and yellow uniform and black half-boots, was drinking coffee. Byron had never seen the man or the uniform before.

"Oh, Byron, ask Natalie for my resident status file, will you? She knows where it is." Jastrow turned to the official. "Will you want to see their papers too?"

"Not today, *professore*. Only yours."

Natalie looked up with an embarrassed grin from re-reading the letter. "Oh, hi. What's doing?"

Byron told her. Her face sobering, she took a key from her purse and unlocked a small steel file by the desk. "Here." She gave him a manila folder tied with red tape. "Does it look like trouble? Shall I come down?"

"Better wait till you're asked."

As he descended the stairs he heard laughter from the study, and rapid jovial talk. "Oh, thank you, Byron," Jastrow said, breaking into English as he entered, "just leave it here on the table." He resumed his anecdote in Italian about the donkey that had gotten into the grounds the previous week, laid waste to a vegetable patch, and chewed up a whole chapter of manuscript. The official's belted belly shook with laughter.

In the library Natalie was typing again. The Slote letter was out of sight.

"There doesn't seem to be much of a problem," Byron said.

"That's good," she said placidly.

At dinner that night Dr. Jastrow hardly spoke, ate less than usual, and drank two extra glasses of wine. In this household, where things were so monotonously the same day after day, night after night, the first extra glass was an event, the second a bombshell. Natalie finally said, "Aaron, what was that visit about today?"

Jastrow came out of an abstracted stare with a little headshake. "Strangely enough, Giuseppe again."

Giuseppe was the assistant gardener, whom he had recently discharged: a scrawny, lazy, stupid old drunkard with wiry black hairs on his big knobby purple nose. Giuseppe had left open the gate through which the donkey had entered. He was always committing such misdemeanors. Jastrow had lost his temper over the destroyed chapter and the ravaged vegetable beds, had been unable to write for two days, and had suffered bad indigestion.

"How does that officer know Giuseppe?" Byron said.

"That's the odd part. He's from the alien registration bureau in Florence, yet he mentioned Giuseppe's nine children, the difficulty of finding work nowadays, and so forth. When I said I'd rehire him, that ended it. He just handed me the registration papers with a victorious grin." Jastrow sighed and laid his napkin on the table. "I've put up with Giuseppe all these years, I really don't mind. I'm rather tired. Tell Maria I'll have my fruit and cheese in the study."

Natalie said when the professor was gone, "Let's bring the coffee to my room."

"Sure. Great."

Never before had she invited him there. Sometimes in his room above he could hear her moving about, a tantalizing, faint, lovely noise. He followed her upstairs with a jumping pulse.

"I live in a big candy box," she said with a self-conscious look, opening a heavy door. "Aaron bought the place furnished, you know, and left it just the way the lady of the house had it. Ridiculous for me, but—"

She snapped on a light. It was an enormous room, painted pink, with pink and gilt furniture, pink painted cupids on a blue and gold ceiling, pink silk draperies, and a huge double bed covered in frilly pink satin. Dark Natalie, in the old brown wool dress she wore on chilly evenings, looked decidedly odd in this Watteau setting. But Byron found the contrast as exciting as everything else about her. She lit the log fire in the marble fireplace carved with Roman figures, and they sat in facing armchairs, taking coffee from the low table between them.

"Why do you suppose Aaron's so upset?" Natalie said, settling comfortably in the large chair and pulling the long pleated skirt far down over her beautiful legs. "Giuseppe's an old story. Actually it was a mistake to fire him. He knows all about the water connections and the electric lines, much more than Tomaso. And he's really good at the topiary work, even if he is a dirty old drunk."

"A.J. was coerced, Natalie." She bit her lip, nodding. Byron added, "We're at the mercy of these people, A.J. even more than you and me. He owns property, he's stuck here."

"Oh, the Italians are all right. They're not Germans."

"Mussolini's no bargain. Berel gave A.J. the right advice. Get out!"

Natalie smiled. *"Lekh lekha.* My God, how far off that all seems. I wonder how he is." Her smile faded. "I've shut Warsaw from my mind. Or tried to."

"I don't blame you."

"How about you, Briny? Do you ever think about it?"

"Some. I keep dreaming about it."

"Oh, God, so do I. That hospital—I go round and round in it, night after night—"

"When Warsaw fell," Byron said, "it hit me hard." He told Natalie about the Wannsee episode. At his description of the waiter's sudden turnabout, she laughed bitterly. "Your father sounds superb."

"He's all right."

"He must think I'm a vampire who all but lured you to your death."

"We haven't talked about you."

Sudden gloom shadowed Natalie's face. She poured more coffee for both of them. "Stir the fire, Briny. I'm cold. Giuseppe's brought in green wood, as usual."

He made the fire flare, and threw on it a light log from

a blighted tree, which quickly blazed. "Ah, that's good!" She jumped up, turned off the electric chandelier, and stood by the fire, looking at the flames. "That moment in the railroad station," she nervously burst out, "when they took away the Jews! I still can't face it. That was one reason I was so nasty at Königsberg. I was in torture. I kept thinking that I could have done something. Suppose I'd stepped forward, said I was Jewish, forced the issue? Suppose we'd all created a scandal? It might have made a difference. But we calmly went to the train, and they trudged off the other way."

Byron said, "We might have lost you and Mark Hartley. The thing was touch and go."

"Yes, I know. Leslie prevented that. He stood his ground, at least, though he was shaking like a leaf. He did his plain duty. But those other ambassadors and chargés —well—"

Natalie had begun to pace. "And my family in Medzice! When I picture those kind, good people in the clutches of the Germans—but what's the use? It's futile, it's sickening, to dwell on that." She threw up her hand in a despairing gesture and dropped in her chair, sitting on her legs with her skirt spread over them. Nothing of her was visible in the firelight but her face and her tensely clasped hands. She stared at the fire. "Speaking of old Slote," she said after a long pause, in an entirely different tone, "what do you think of his proposal to make an honest woman of me?"

"I'm not surprised."

"You're not? I'm stunned. I never thought I'd live to see the day."

"He told me in Berlin he might marry you. He'd be crazy not to, if he could."

"Well, he's had that option open to him for a hell of a long time, dear." She poured coffee and sipped, looking darkly at him over the rim of the cup. "Had a big discussion about me in Berlin, you two gentlemen, did you?"

"Not a big discussion. He mentioned that you were just as surly to him that last day in Königsberg as you'd been to me."

"I was feeling absolutely horrible that day, Briny."

"Well, that's all right. I thought I might have offended you somehow, so I asked him."

"This is getting interesting. What else did Slote say about me?"

The low, vibrant voice, the amused glinting of her eyes in the firelight, stirred Byron. "That you were no girl for me to get involved with, and that he hadn't known an hour's peace of mind since he first laid eyes on you."

She uttered a low gloating laugh. "Two accurate statements, my pet. Tell me more."

"That's about it. It was the same conversation in which he gave me the reading list."

"Yes, and wasn't *that* pure Slote? Coming it over you with his book learning! An illuminating little incident, that. Didn't he really tell you all about us? About him and me?"

Byron shook his head.

Natalie said, "You wouldn't go and get us some brandy, would you? I think I'd like a little brandy."

He raced down the stairs and up again, returning with a bottle and two shimmering snifters. Swirling the brandy round and round in her hands, looking into the balloon glass and rarely raising her eyes at him, Natalie broke loose with a surprising rush of words about her affair with Leslie Slote. It took her a long time. Byron said little, interrupting only to throw more wood on the fire. It was a familiar tale of a clever older man having fun with a girl and getting snared into a real passion. Resolving to marry him, she had made his life a misery. He didn't want to marry her, she said, simply because she was Jewish and it would be awkward for his career. That was all his clouds of words had ever come to. At last, with this letter, after thirty months, she had him where she wanted him.

Byron hated every word of the story, yet he was fascinated, and grateful. The closemouthed girl was taking him into her life. These words, which couldn't be unsaid, were ending the strange tension between them since Warsaw, their own little phony war—the long hostile silences in the library, her holing up in her room, her odd snappish condescension. As she talked, they were growing intimate as they never had become in a month of adventuring through Poland.

Everything about this girl interested him. If it was the account of her affair with another man, let it be that! At least Byron was talking about Natalie Jastrow with Natalie

Jastrow, and this was what he had been starved for. He was hearing this sweet rough voice with its occasional New Yorkisms, and he could watch the play of her free gesturing hand in the firelight, the swoop and sudden stop in the air of flat palm and fingers, her visible signature.

Natalie Jastrow was the one person he had ever met who meant as much to him as his father did. In the same way, almost, he hungered to talk to his father, to listen to him, to be with him, even though he had to resist and withdraw, even though he knew that in almost every conversation he either offended or disappointed Victor Henry. His mother he took for granted, a warm presence, cloying in her affection, annoying in her kittenish changeability. His father was terrific, and in that way Natalie was terrific, entirely aside from being a tall dark girl whom he had hopelessly craved to seize in his arms since the first hour they had met.

"Well, there you have it," Natalie said. "This mess has been endless, but that's the general idea. How about some more of Aaron's brandy? Wouldn't you like some? It's awfully good brandy. Funny, I usually don't care for it."

Byron poured more for both of them, though his glass wasn't empty.

"What I've been puzzling about all day," she said after a sip, "is why Leslie is throwing in the towel now. The trouble is, I think I know."

"He's lonesome for you," Byron said.

Natalie shook her head. "Leslie Slote behaved disgustingly on the Praha road. I despised him for it, and I let him know I did. That was the turnaround. *He's* been chasing *me* ever since. I guess in a way I've been running, too. I haven't even answered half his letters."

Byron said, "You've always exaggerated that whole thing. All he did—"

"Shut up, Byron. Don't be mealymouthed with me. All he did was turn yellow and use me as an excuse. He hid behind my skirts. The Swedish ambassador all but laughed in his face." She tossed off most of her brandy. "Look, physical courage isn't something you can help. It isn't even important nowadays. You can be a world leader and a cringing sneak. That's what Hitler probably is. Still, it happened. *It happened.* I'm not saying I won't marry

Leslie Slote because shellfire made him panic. After all, he behaved well enough at the railroad station. But I do say that's why he's proposing to me. This is his way of apologizing and being a man. It's not quite the answer to my maidenly prayers."

"It's what you want."

"Well, I don't know. There are complications. There's my family. My parents had wild fits when I told them I was in love with a Christian. My father took to his bed for a week, though *that* bit of melodrama left me unmoved. Well, now there's that whole fight again. And Leslie's proposal is odd. It's not very specific as to time and place. If I wrote him back yes, he might well get on his bicycle again."

"If he's really that kind of fool, which I doubt very much," Byron said, "you could just let him bicycle away."

"Then there's Aaron."

"He's not your problem. He ought to get out of Italy in any case."

"He's very reluctant to go."

"Well, he survived while we were away."

"Oh, that's what you think. You should have seen the library and study when I got back. And he hadn't written anything in weeks. Aaron should have gotten married ages ago. He didn't, and he needs a lot of fussing and petting. He can't even sharpen a pencil properly."

Byron wondered whether Natalie's irritable garrulity was due to the brandy. She was gesturing broadly, talking breathlessly, and her eyes were wild. "And there's still another complication, you know. The biggest."

"What's that?"

She stared at him. "Don't you know what it is, Briny? Haven't you any idea? Not the faintest inkling? Come on now. *Stop* it."

He said or rather stammered, because the sudden penetrating sexuality in Natalie Jastrow's glance made him drunk, "I don't think I do."

"All right then, I'll tell you. You've done it, you devil, and you know it. You've done what you've wanted to do from the first day you came here. I'm in love with you." She peered at him, her eyes shining and enormous. "Ye gods, what a dumb stunned face. Don't you believe me?"

Very hoarsely he said, "I just hope it's true."

He got out of his chair, and went to her. She jumped up and they embraced. "Oh God," she said, clinging to him, and she kissed him and kissed him. "You have such a marvellous mouth," she muttered. She thrust her hands in his hair, she caressed his face. "Such a nice smile. Such fine hands. I love to watch your hands. I love the way you move. You're so sweet." It was like a hundred day-dreams Byron had had, but far more intense and confusing and delicious. She was rubbing against him in crude sensual delight, almost like a cat. The brown wool dress was scratchy in his hands. The perfume of her hair couldn't be daydreamed, nor the moist warm sweet breath of her mouth. Above all gleamed the inconceivable wonder that all this was happening. They stood embraced by the crackling flames, kissing, saying broken foolish sentences, whispering, laughing, kissing, and kissing again.

Natalie pulled away. She ran a few steps and faced him, her eyes blazing. "Well, all right. I had to do that or *die*. I've never felt anything like this in my life, Byron, this maddening pull to you. I've been fighting it off and fighting it off because it's no damn good, you know. You're a boy. I won't have it. Not a Christian. Not again. And besides—" she put both hands over her face. "Oh. Oh! Don't look at me like that, Briny! Go out of my bedroom." Byron turned to go, on legs almost caving under him. He wanted to please her.

She said in the next breath, "Christ, you're a gentleman. It's one of the unbelievable things about you. Would you rather stay? My darling, my love, I don't want to put you out, I want to talk some more, but I want to make some sense, that's all. And I don't want to make any false moves. I'll do anything you say. I absolutely adore you."

He looked at her standing in the firelight in the long wool dress with her arms crossed, one leg out to a side, one hip thrust out, a typical Natalie pose. He was dazed with happiness beyond imagining, and flooded with gratitude for being alive. "Listen—would you think of marrying me?" Byron said.

Natalie's eyes popped wide open and her mouth dropped. Byron could not help it; he burst out laughing at the comic change of her face, and that made her laugh crazily too. She came to him, almost flung herself at him, still laughing so uproariously that she could hardly manage to kiss him. "God in heaven," she gasped, twining him in her arms, "you're incredible. That's two proposals in one day for la Jastrow! It never rains but it pours, eh?"

"I'm serious," he said. "I don't know why we're laughing. I want to marry you. It's always seemed preposterous, but if you really do love me—"

"It *is* preposterous"—Natalie spoke with her lips to his cheek—"preposterous beyond words, but where you're concerned I appear to be quite mindless, and perhaps—well! Nobody can say you're a beardless boy, anyway! Quite sandpapery, aren't you?" She kissed him once more, hard, and loosened her arms. "The first idea was right. You leave. Good-night, darling. I know you're serious, and I'm terribly touched. One thing we've got in this godforsaken place is time, all the time in the world."

In the darkness, on his narrow bed in the tiny attic room, Byron lay wide awake. For a while he heard her moving about below, then the house was silent. He could still taste Natalie's lips. His hands smelled of her perfume. Outside in the valley donkeys hee-hawed to each other across the echoing slopes, a misguided rooster hailed a dawn hours away, and dogs barked. There came a rush of wind and a long drumming of rain on the tiles, and after a while water dripped into the pail near his bed, under the worst leak. The rain passed, moonlight shafted faint and blue through the little round window, the pattering in the pail ceased, and still Byron lay with open eyes, trying to believe it, trying to separate his dreams and fantasies of half a year from the real hour when Natalie Jastrow had overwhelmed him with endearments. Now his feverish mind ran on what he must do next. The window was turning violet when he fell asleep in a jumble of ideas and resolves, ranging from medical school and short-story writing to the banking business in Washington. Some distant cousins of his mother did control a bank.

⁕　　⁕　　⁕

"Hi, Natalie."

"Oh, hi there. Sleep well?"

It was almost eleven when he hurried into the library. Byron was a hardened slugabed, but he had not come down this late before. Three books lay open on Natalie's desk, and she was typing away. She gave him one ardent glance and went on with her work. Byron found on his desk a mass of first-draft pages heavily scribbled with Jastrow's corrections, to which was clipped a note in red crayon: *Let me have this material at lunch, please.*

"A.J. looked in here ten minutes ago," Natalie said, "and made vile noises."

Byron counted the pages. "He's going to make viler ones at lunch. I'm sorry, but I didn't close my eyes till dawn."

"Didn't you?" she said, with a secret little smile. "I slept exceedingly well."

With a quick shuffling of papers and carbon he began to type, straining his eyes at Jastrow's scrawl. A hand ran through his hair and rested warmly on his neck. "Let's see." She stood over him, looking down at him with affectionate amusement. Pinned on the old brown dress over her left breast was the gold brooch with purple stones from Warsaw. She had never before worn it. She glanced through the pages and took a few. "Poor Briny, why couldn't you sleep? Never mind, type your head off, and so will I."

They did not finish the work before lunch, but by then, as it turned out, Dr. Jastrow had other things on his mind. At noon, an enormous white Lancia rattled the gravel outside the villa. Byron and Natalie could hear the rich voice of Tom Searle and the warm hard laugh of his wife. Celebrated American actors, the Searles had been living off and on for fifteen years in a hilltop villa not far from Jastrow's. The woman painted and gardened, while the man built brick walls and did the cooking. Endlessly they read old plays, new plays, and novels that might become plays. Other celebrities came to Siena just to see them. Through them Jastrow had met and entertained Maugham, Berenson, Gertrude Lawrence, and Picasso. A retired college professor would have been a minnow among these big fish; but the success of *A Jew's Jesus* had put him fairly in their company. He loved being part of the celebrities' group, though he grumbled about the interference with his work. He often drove down to Florence with the Searles to meet their friends, and Natalie and Byron thought the actors might be passing by now to fetch him off. But coming down for lunch, they found A.J. alone in the drawing room, sneezing, red-nosed, and waving an emptied sherry glass. He complained that they were late. In fact they were a bit early.

"The Searles are leaving," he said when lunch was over, having sneezed and blown his nose all through the meal without uttering a word. "Just like that. They came to say good-bye."

"Oh? Are they doing a new play?" said Natalie.

"They're getting out. Lock, stock, and barrel. They're moving every stick back to the States."

"But doesn't their lease run for—how many more years? Five?"

"Seven. They're abandoning the lease. They can't afford to get stuck here, they say, if the war spreads." Jastrow morosely fingered his beard. "That's one difference between leasing and buying. You just walk away. You don't bother your head about what happens to the place. I must say they urged me to lease. I should have listened to them. But the purchase price was so cheap!"

Byron said, "Well, sir, if you think there's any danger, your skin comes first."

"I have no such fears. Neither have they. For them it's a matter of business. We'll have our coffee in the lemon house." With a peevish toss of his head, he lapsed into silence.

The lemon house, a long glassed-in structure with a dirt floor, full of small potted citrus trees, looked out on a grand panorama of the town and the rounded brown hills. Sheltered here from cold winds that swept up the ravine, the trees throve in the pouring sunlight, and all winter long blossomed and bore fruit. Jastrow believed, contrary to every medical opinion, that the sweet heavy scent of the orange and lemon blooms was good for the asthma that hit him when he was nervous or angry. Possibly because he believed this, it tended to work. His wheezing stopped while they drank their coffee. The warm sun cheered him up. He said, "I predict they'll sneak back in short order with their tails between their legs, and three vans of furniture toiling up the hill. They remind me of the people who used to go fleeing off Martha's Vineyard at the first news of a hurricane. I sat through four hurricanes and thoroughly enjoyed the spectacle."

Natalie said after he left, "He's badly shaken."

"I hope he gets shaken loose from here."

"Dear, this house will go to rack and ruin if A.J. leaves it."

"So what?"

"You've never owned anything, have you, Briny? Or saved any money. Once you have, you may understand."

"Look, Natalie, A.J. had a windfall late in life and got carried away and bought himself a big Italian villa for a song, in a lonesome mountain town. All right. Suppose he walks away now? If he offers it for sale he'll get something for it. Otherwise he can return after the war and put it back in shape. Or he can just forget it, and let it fall down. Easy come, easy go."

"You see things so simply," she said.

They were sitting side by side on a white wicker couch. He started to put his arm around her. "Stop that," she said, catching her breath and deflecting his arm. "That's too simple, too. Listen carefully, Byron. How old are you? Are you twenty-five yet? I'm twenty-seven."

"I'm old enough for you, Natalie."

"Old enough for what? To sleep with me? Don't talk rubbish. The question is, what are you doing with yourself? I can teach at a university anytime. I've got my M.A. thesis almost finished. What have you got? A smile that drives me mad and a handsome head of hair. You're brave, you're gentle, but you just drifted here. You only stayed because of me. You're killing time and you're trained for nothing."

"Natalie, how would you like to be married to a banker?"

"A what? A *banker?*"

He told her about his relatives and their bank in Washington. Hands folded in her lap, she beamed at him, her face aglow in the sunshine. "How does that sound?" he said.

"Oh, fine," she said. "You're really facing up to life at last. A stern, serious business, isn't it? Tell me one thing."

"What?"

"Tell me when you decided you liked me."

"Don't you want to discuss this bank idea?"

"Of course, dear. All in good time. When was it?"

"All right, I'll tell you. When you took off your sunglasses."

"My sunglasses? When was that?"

"Why, that first day, when we came into the villa with Slote. Don't you remember? You had these big dark glasses on in the car, but then you took them off, and I could see your eyes."

"So?"

"You asked me when I fell in love with you. I'm telling you."

"But it's so absurd. Like everything else you say and do. What did you know about me? Anyhow, my eyes must have been totally bloodshot. I'd been up till four, having one hellish row with Leslie. You struck me as nothing at all, dear, so I didn't give a damn. Now look, you don't really *want* to be a banker, do you?"

He said with an abashed grin, "Well, I did think of one other thing. But don't laugh at me."

"I won't."

"I thought of the Foreign Service. It's interesting and it's serving the country."

"You and Leslie in the same service," she said. "That would be a hot one." She took his hand in a maternal way that depressed Byron. "This isn't much fun for you, Briny dear, all this serious talk."

"That's okay," Byron said. "Let's go right on with it."

For a moment she sat pondering, holding his hand in her lap, as she had in the Swedish ambassador's limousine. "I'd better tell you what I really think. The trouble is you *are* trained for something. You're a naval officer."

"That's the one thing I'm not, and that I've made a career of not being."

"You already have a commission."

"I'm just a lowly reserve. That's nothing."

"If the war goes on, you'll be called up. You'll stay in for years. That's what you'll probably be in the end, from sheer inertia, and family custom, and the passing of time."

"I can resign my reserve commission tomorrow. Shall I?"

"But suppose we get in the war? What then? Would you fight?"

"There's nothing else to do then."

She put her hand in his hair, and yanked it. "Yes, that's how your mind works. Well, I love you for that, and for other things, but Byron, I'm not going to be the wife of a naval officer. I can't think of a more ridiculous and awful existence for me. I wouldn't marry a test pilot either, or an actor, don't you understand?"

"It's no issue, I tell you, I'll never be a naval officer— what the devil? Now what? Why are you crying?"

She dashed the sudden tears from her face with the back of her hand, smiling. "Oh, shut up. This is an insane conversation. The more I try to make sense, the wilder it all gets. All I know is that I'm crazy about you. If it's a dead end, who cares? I obviously thrive on dead ends. No, not now, love, really, no—" She gasped the last words as he firmly took her in his arms.

There was nobody in sight. Beyond the glass there was only the panorama of hills and town, and inside the lemon house silence and the heavy sweet scent of the blossoms. They kissed and kissed, touching and holding and gripping each other. Soon Natalie happened to glance up and there stood the gardener Giuseppe outside the glass, leaning on a wheelbarrow full of cuttings, watching. With a squinting inebriated leer, he wiped a sleeve of his sweater across his knobbed nose, and obscenely winked.

"Oh, Jesus Christ," she said, yanking angrily at her skirt. The gardener showed sparse foul teeth in a grin and trundled the wheelbarrow away. Byron sat flushed, dazed, and dishevelled, looking after him.

"Well, there goes our little secret, sweetheart. Kissing and smooching *under glass!* What's happened to me? This whole thing is a plain brute attraction between two people isolated together too long." She leaped to her feet and pulled at his hand. "But I love you. I can't help it. I don't *want* to help it. Oh, that son of a bitch Giuseppe! Come, let's get back to the rock pile. We must."

Jastrow called from his study as they came into the house, "Natalie, where is your letter? May I read it?"

"What letter, A.J.? I didn't get any mail."

"Are you sure? I have one from your mother. She says she's written you another and much longer one. Come read this. It's important."

He waved a flimsy airmail sheet as Byron went upstairs. There were only half a dozen lines in her mother's neat featureless writing, a Manhattan public school script:

Dear Aaron:

We would both appreciate it if you would urge Natalie to come home. Louis took that story of her trip to Poland very hard. The doctor even thinks that it may have been the cause of this attack. I've written Natalie all about it. You may as well read that letter, there's no sense in my repeating the whole terrible story. In retrospect, we were very lucky. Louis seems in no immediate danger, but that's all the doctor will tell us.

We're all wondering how long you yourself intend to stay on in Italy. Don't you feel it's dangerous? I know that you and Louis have been out of touch all these years, but still he does worry about you. You're his one brother.

Love,
Sophie and Louis

Natalie checked the mail piled on her desk in the library, but there was only one letter for her, from Slote. Looking up from his work, Byron saw her sombre expression. "What is it, Natalie?"

"It's my father. I may have to leave."

.   .   .

The letter from her mother arrived two days later. Meantime Natalie resumed a certain aloofness toward Byron, though she still wore the brooch, and looked at him with changed eyes.

She took the long and somewhat frantic account of her father's heart attack to Jastrow, who was having his tea by the fire in the study, wrapped in a shawl. He shook his head sympathetically over it and handed it back to her. Gazing at the fire and sipping tea, he said, "You had better go."

"Oh, I think so. I'm practically packed."

"What was Louis's trouble last time? Was it this bad?"

The brothers were deeply estranged—Natalie did not know exactly why—and this breaking of their long tacit silence about her father gave her an awkward, unpleasant sensation.

"No, not really. The trouble was my announcement that I was in love with Leslie. Papa got awfully weak and had breathing difficulty and a blackout episode. But he wasn't hospitalized that time."

Jastrow pensively fingered his beard. "He's only sixty-one. You know, it gets to be suspenseful, Natalie, this question of whose heredity you've got. Our mother's family mostly popped off in their fifties. But Father's two brothers both made it past ninety and he reached eighty-eight. My teeth are like my father's. I have excellent teeth. Louis always had a lot of trouble with his teeth, the way Mama did." Jastrow became aware of the girl's dark watchful regard. He made a little apologetic gesture with both hands. "You're thinking what a self-centered old horror A.J. is."

"But I wasn't thinking that at all."

Jastrow put on cotton gloves to poke at the fire and throw on a fresh log. He was vain about his small finely shaped hands. "You won't come back. I know that. Life will get difficult here. Possibly I could go to New Mexico or Arizona. But they're such dull, arid, zero-culture places! The thought of trying to write there!" He gave a deep sigh, almost a groan. "No doubt my books aren't that important. Still, the work is what keeps me going."

"Your books are important, A.J."

"Are they? Why?"

Natalie sat leaning her chin on a fist, groping for an honest and precise answer. She said after a pause, "Of course they're extremely readable, and often brilliant, but that's not their distinction. Their originality lies in the spirit. The books are very Jewish. In a creditable, unsentimental way, in substance and in attitude. They've made me, at least, realize how very much Christendom owes this bizarre little folk we belong to. It's surprising how much of that you've gotten even into the Constantine book."

Her words had a remarkable effect on Aaron Jastrow. He smiled tremulously, his eyes misted, and he all at once did look strikingly Jewish—the mouth, the nose, the expression, the soft white hand at his beard, were all features of a hatless little rabbi. He spoke in a soft shaky voice. "Of course you know exactly what to say to please me."

"That's what I think, Aaron."

"Well, bless you. I've evolved into a pagan, a materialist, and a hedonist—and I fell in love with the grandeur of Christianity and of Jesus long long ago—but none of that has made me less Jewish. Nobody else in the family will accept that, your father least of all. I'm so grateful that you can. I truly think that the books on Constantine and Luther will round out the picture. I want to get them done. In my way I'm bearing witness, as my rabbinic forebears did in theirs. Though no doubt they'd be horrified by me." He studied her face. He smiled, and his eyes began to twinkle. "How long after you left would Byron remain? He gives me such a secure feeling, just by being here."

"Give him a raise in salary. That'll convince him more than anything. He's never earned a penny before."

Jastrow pursed his lips, rounded his eyes, and tilted his head. Many years of living in Italy showed in the mannerism. "I have to watch my money now. We'll see. My strong impression is, actually, that you'll marry Leslie once you get back there, and—oh, stop blushing and looking so coy. Have I hit it?"

"Never mind, A.J."

"I'm sure if Byron were aware of that, he'd be more likely to stay on." Jastrow stroked his beard, smiling at her.

"Good God, Aaron! Do you expect me to tell Byron Henry I'm going to marry Slote, just to make him stay with you?"

"Why, my dear, whoever suggested such a thing? Wait —my point is—" Jastrow stretched out a hand and looked after her, utterly astonished at her abrupt walkout.

20

"HOLY COW!" Byron exclaimed. "There's my father, or his double."

"Where?" said Natalie. Her flight was delayed, and they were drinking coffee in the Rome airport at a table outside a little café; the same café where they had lunched before setting off for Warsaw.

"Inside that ring of carabinieri over there."

He pointed to a group of men leaving the terminal, escorted by six deferential police officers. Some of the party wore the green uniform of the foreign ministry; the rest were in civilian clothes. The military bearing of a short broad-shouldered man, in a pepper-and-salt suit and soft hat, had caught Byron's eye. He stood, saying, "Can it be him? But why the devil didn't he write or wire me that he was coming to Italy? I'll take a look."

"Briny!"

He was starting to lope away; he stopped short. "Yes?"

"If it is your father—I'm so tacky and sooty from that horrible train ride, and he's obviously busy." Natalie, usually so self-assured, suddenly looked confused and nervous, in an appealing, pathetic way. "I wasn't expecting this. I'd rather meet him another time."

"Well, let's see if it's him."

Victor Henry heard the voice behind him just as the party reached the exit doors. "Dad! *Dad!* Wait up!"

Recognizing the voice, Pug turned, waved, and asked his escort from the ministry to wait for him. *"D'accordo."* The Italian smiled and bowed, eyeing sharply the young man who was hurrying up. "I will see to your luggage, Commander, and meet you outside. There is plenty of time."

The father and son clasped hands. "Well, how about

322

this?" Victor Henry said, looking up at Byron's face, with affection he usually concealed when less surprised.

"What's up, Dad? Couldn't you let me know you were coming?"

"It happened sudden-like. I intended to ring you tonight. What are you doing down here in Rome?"

"Natalie's going home. Her father's sick."

"Oh? Has she left already?"

"No. That's her, sitting over there."

"That's the famous Natalie Jastrow? The one in gray?"

"No, further over, in black. With the big hat."

Victor Henry caught a new proprietary note in his son's voice. The listless, hangdog air of his Berlin days had given way to a confident glance and a straighter back. "You're looking mighty bright-eyed and bushy-tailed," Pug said.

"I feel marvellous."

"I'd like to meet that girl." The father suddenly strode toward her, so fast that Byron had to take a running step or two to catch up. There was no stopping him. They came and faced Natalie, who remained seated, hands clasped in her lap.

"Natalie, this is Dad."

With such a flat introduction these two people, the opposed poles in Byron's life, all at once confronted each other. Natalie offered her hand to Byron's father, looked him in the eye, and waited for him to speak. At first sight, Victor Henry was taken by this weary-looking travel-stained girl with the dark eyes and gaunt face. She was not the legendary adventurous Jewess he had built up in his imagination; she had an everyday American look; but withal there was a certain exotic aura, and a strong calm feminine presence. She must be feeling highly self-conscious, he thought, but there was no sign of it. In her slight smile as he took her hand, there was even a trace of reflected affection for Byron.

He said, "I'm sorry to hear about your father."

She nodded her thanks. "I don't know how bad it is. But they want me at home, and so I'm going." Her low voice was sweet, yet as firm as her look.

"Are you coming back?"

"I'm not sure. Dr. Jastrow may be returning to the States too, you see."

"He'd be well advised to do that, fairly fast."

Pug was looking keenly at her, and she was meeting his glance. When neither found more to say for the moment, it became a sort of staring contest. Soon Natalie smiled a broad, wry, puckish smile, as though to say—"*All right, you're his father and I don't blame you for trying to see what's there. How do you like it?*"

This disconcerted Victor Henry. He seldom lost such eye-to-eye confrontations, but this time he shifted his glance to Byron, who was watching with lively interest, struck by Natalie's swift recovery of her poise. "Well, Briny," he almost growled, "I ought to mosey along, and not keep that foreign ministry type waiting."

"Right, Dad."

Natalie said, "Byron told me that you became friendly with the Tudsburys in Berlin, Commander. I know Pamela."

"You do?" Pug managed a smile. She was actually trying to put him at his ease with small talk, and he liked that.

"Yes, in Paris she and I used to date two fellows who shared the same flat. She's lovely."

"I agree, and very devoted to her father. Maniacal driver, though."

"Oh, did you find that out? I once drove with her from Paris to Chartres, and almost walked back. She scared me senseless."

"I'd guess it would take more than that to scare you." Pug held out his hand. "I'm glad I met you, even in this accidental way, Natalie." Awkwardly, in almost a mumble, he added, "It explains a lot. Happy landings. Flying all the way?"

"I've got a seat on the Thursday Clipper out of Lisbon. I hope I don't get bumped."

"You shouldn't. Things are quiet now. But you're well out of this continent. Good-bye."

"Good-bye, Commander Henry."

Victor Henry abruptly walked off, with Byron hurrying at his elbow. "Briny, what about you, now? You're staying on in Siena?"

"For the time being."

"Do you know that Warren's engaged?"

"Oh, it's definite now?"

"Yes. They've set a date for May twentieth, after he finishes his carrier training. I hope you'll count on getting back by then. You won't see any more brothers' weddings. I'm working on a leave for myself."

"I'll certainly try. How's Mom?"

"Off her feed. Berlin's getting her down."

"I thought she liked it."

"It's becoming less likable." They stopped at the terminal's glass doors. "How long will you be in Rome?"

"If I can see you, Dad, I'll just stay on till you're free."

"Well, fine. Check in at the embassy with Captain Kirkwood. He's the naval attaché. Could be we'll dine together tonight."

"Great."

"That's some girl."

Byron smiled uncertainly. "Could you really tell anything?"

"What you never said is that she's so pretty."

"What? I honestly don't think she is. Not pretty, exactly. I'm nuts about her, as you well know, but—"

"She's got eyes you could drown in. She's stunning. However, what I wrote you about her long ago still goes. Even more so, now that I've seen her. She's a grown-up woman." He put his hand for a moment on Byron's shoulder. "No offense."

"I love her."

"Well, we won't settle that question here and now. Go back to her, she's sitting there all alone. And call Kirkwood about tonight."

"I will."

Natalie's face was tense and inquiring when Byron came back. He fell into the chair beside her. "Gad, that was a shock. I still can't quite believe it. It all went so fast. He looks tired."

"Do you know why he's here?"

Byron shook his head slowly.

She said, "I didn't picture him that way. He doesn't look severe; on the contrary, almost genial. But then when he talks he's scary."

"He fell for you."

"Byron, don't talk rot. Look at me. A soot-covered slattern."

"He said something sappy about your eyes."

"I don't believe it. What did he say?"

"I won't tell you. It's embarrassing. I never heard him say anything like it before. What luck! He likes you. Say, my brother's getting married."

"Oh? When?"

"In May. She's the daughter of a congressman. She doesn't seem all that concerned about marrying a naval officer! Let's make it a double wedding."

"Why not? You'll be manager of a bank by then, no doubt."

They were both smiling, but the unsettled questions between them put an edge in their tones. It was a relief when the droning loudspeaker announced her flight. Byron carried her hand luggage and some fragile gifts for her family into the mill of jabbering, weeping passengers and relatives at the gate. Natalie was clutching her ticket, and trying to understand the shouts of the uniformed attendants. He attempted to kiss her, but it wasn't much of a kiss.

"I love you, Natalie," he said.

She embraced him with one arm amid the jostling passengers, and spoke over the tumult. "It's as well that I'm going home just now, I think. Meantime I met your father! That was something. He did like me? Really?"

"You bowled him over, I tell you. And why not?"

The crowd was starting to push through the gate.

"How will I ever carry all this stuff? Load me up, sweetheart."

"Promise me you'll cable if you decide not to come back," Byron said, poking bundles into her arms and under them. "Because I'll take the next plane home."

"Yes, I'll cable."

"And promise that you'll make no other decisions, do nothing drastic, before you see me again."

"Oh, Byron, how young you are. All these damned words. Don't you know how I love you?"

"Promise!"

Her dark eyes wet and huge, her hands and arms piled, the green and yellow ticket sticking out of her fingers, she shrugged, laughed, and said, "Oh, hell. It's a promise, but you know what Lenin said. Promises like piecrusts are made to be broken. Good-bye, my darling, my sweet. Good-bye, Byron." Her voice rose as the press of passengers dragged her away.

＊ ＊ ＊

After a couple of hours of troubled sleep at the hotel, Commander Henry put on a freshly pressed uniform, with shoes gleaming like black mirrors, and walked to the embassy. Under a low gray sky, in the rows of tables and chairs along the Via Veneto, only a few people were braving the December chill. The gasoline shortage had almost emptied the broad boulevard of traffic. Like Berlin, this capital city exuded penury and gloom.

Captain Kirkwood had left for the day. His yeoman handed Pug a long lumpy envelope. Two small objects clattered to the desk when he ripped it open: silver eagles on pins, the collar insignia of a captain.

Captain William Kirkwood presents his compliments to *Captain* Victor Henry, and trusts he is free to dine at nine, at the Osteria dell' Orso.

P.S. You're out of uniform. Four stripes, please.

Clipped to the note was a strip of gold braid, and the Alnav letter listing newly selected captains, on which *Victor (none) Henry* was ringed in heavy red lines.

The yeoman's refreshing, freckled American face wore a wide grin. "Congratulations, Cap'n."

"Thank you. Did my son call?"

"Yes, suh. He's coming to dinner. That's all arranged. Ah've got fresh coffee going, suh, if you'd like a cup in the cap'n's office."

"That'll be fine."

Sitting in the attaché's swivel chair, Pug drank one cup after another of the rich Navy brew, delightful after months of the German ersatz stuff. He ranged on the desk before him the eagles, the Alnav, the strip of gold braid. His seamed pale face looked calm, almost bored, as he swung the chair idly, contemplating the tokens of his new rank; but he was stirred, exalted, and above all relieved.

He had long been dreading that the selection board, on this first round, might pass him over. Execs of battleships and cruisers, squadron commanders of submarines and destroyers, insiders in BuShips and BuOrd, could well crowd out an attaché. The big hurdle of the race for flag rank was early promotion to captain. The few officers who became admirals had to make captain on the wing. This early promotion, this small dry irrevocable statistic in the record, was his guerdon for a quarter of a century of getting things done. It was his first promotion in ten years, and it was the crucial one.

He wished he could share this cheering news at once with his restless wife. Perhaps when he got back to Berlin they could throw a wingding, he thought, for embassy people, correspondents, and friendly foreign attachés, and lighten the gloom lying heavy in the Jew's mansion in Grunewald.

Natalie Jastrow popped back into his mind, displacing even the promotion. Since the chance encounter, he kept thinking of her. In those few minutes he had sensed the powerful, perhaps unbreakable, bond between his son and the girl. Yet how could that be? Young women like Natalie Jastrow, if they went outside their natural age bracket, tended to marry a man almost his own age rather than to reach down and cradle-snatch a stripling like Byron. Natalie was more mature and accomplished than Janice, who was marrying Byron's older brother. It was mismatch enough for these reasons, and made him wonder about her sense and stability, but the Jewish problem loomed above all.

Victor Henry was no bigot, in his own best judgment. His narrowly bounded life had brought him into very little contact with Jews. He was an arid realist and the whole thing spelled trouble. If he were to have half-Jewish grandchildren, well, with a such a mother they would probably be handsome and bright. But he thought his son was not man enough to handle the complications and might never be. The coolness and courage he had displayed in Warsaw were fine traits for an athletic or military career, but in daily life they meant little, compared to ambition, industry, and common sense.

"Mr. Gianelli is here, sir." The yeoman's voice spoke through the squawk box.

"Very well." Victor Henry swept up the tokens and put them in a trouser pocket, not nearly as happy as he had once thought promotion to captain would make him.

The San Francisco banker had changed to an elegant double-breasted gray suit with bold chalk stripes and outsize British lapels. The interior of his green Rolls Royce smelled of a strong cologne. "I trust you enjoyed your nap as much as I did mine," he said, lighting a very long cigar. All his gestures had the repose, and all the details of his person—manicure, rings, shirt, tie—the sleekness, of secure wealth. Withal, he appeared stimulated and slightly nervous. "Now I've already spoken to the foreign minister. You've met Count Ciano?" Pug shook his head. "I've known him well for many years. He's definitely coming to the reception, and from there will take me to the Palazzo Venezia. Now, what about you? What are your instructions?"

"To consider myself your aide as long as you're in Italy and Germany, sir, and to make myself useful in any way you desire."

"Do you understand Italian?"

"Poorly, to say the least. I can grope through a newspaper if I have to."

"That's a pity." The banker smoked his cigar with calm relish, his drooping eyes sizing up Victor Henry. "Still, the President said there might be value in having you along at both interviews, if these heads of state will stand for it. Just another pair of eyes and ears. At Karinhall, of course, I can ask that you interpret for me. My German's a bit weak. I think we'll have to feel our way as we go. This whole errand is unusual and there's no protocol for it. Ordinarily I'd be accompanied by our ambassador."

"Suppose I just come along, then, as though it's the natural thing, unless they stop me?"

The banker's eyes closed for several seconds, then he nodded and opened them. "Ah, here's the Forum. You've been in Rome before? We're passing the Arch of Constantine. A lot of old history here! I suppose envoys came to Rome in those days on errands just as strange."

Pug said, "This reception now, is it at your apartment?"

"Oh no, I keep just a very small flat off the Via Veneto. My uncle and two cousins are bankers here. It is at their town house, and the reception is for me. Let us just see how this goes. If, when we're with Ciano, I touch my lapel so, you'll excuse yourself. Otherwise come along, in the way you suggest."

These arrangements proved needless because Mussolini himself dropped in on the party. About half an hour after the arrival of the Americans, a commotion started up at the doorway of the enormous marble-columned room, and Il Duce came walking bouncily in. He was not expected, judging by the excitement and confusion among the guests. Even Ciano, resplendent in green, white, and gold uniform, seemed taken aback. Mussolini was a surprisingly small man, shorter than Pug, dressed in a wrinkled tweed jacket, dark trousers, a sweater, and brown-and-white saddle shoes. It struck Pug at once that with this casual apparel Mussolini was underlining—perhaps for its eventual effect on the Germans—his contempt for Roosevelt's informal messenger. Mussolini went to the buffet table, ate fruit, drank tea, and chatted jauntily with guests who crowded around. He moved through the room with a teacup, talking to one person and another. He glanced once at Luigi Gianelli as he passed close by, but otherwise he ignored the two Americans. In this setting Mussolini hardly resembled the chin-jutting imperial bully with the demonic glare. His prominent eyes had an Italian softness, his smile was wide, ironical, very worldly, and it seemed to Victor Henry that here was a smart little fellow who had gotten himself into the saddle and loved it, but whose bellicosity was a comedy. There was no comparing him with the ferocious Hitler.

Mussolini left the room while Pug was clumsily making talk with the banker's aunt, a bejewelled, painted crone with a haughty manner, a peppermint breath and almost no hearing. Seeing the banker beckon to him and walk off after Ciano, Pug excused himself and followed. The three men went through tall carved wooden doors into a princely high-ceilinged library, lined with volumes bound in gold-stamped brown, scarlet, or blue leather. Tall windows looked out over the city, which appeared so different from blacked-out Berlin, with electric lights twinkling and blazing in long crisscrossing lines and scattered clusters. Mussolini with a regal gesture invited them to sit. The banker came to the sofa beside him, while Ciano and Victor Henry faced them in armchairs. Mussolini coldly stared at Henry and turned the stare to Gianelli.

The look at once changed Pug's impression of the Italian leader, and gave him a forcible sense that he was out of his depth and under suspicion. He felt junior and shaky, an ensign who had blundered into flag country. Ciano had given him no such feeling, and still didn't, sitting there gorgeous and wary, the son-in-law waiting for the powerful old man to talk. At this close range Pug could see how white Mussolini's fringe of hair was, how deep the creases of decision were folded in his face, how vivid were the large eyes, which now had an opaque glitter. This man could readily order a hundred murders, Pug decided, if he had to. He was an Italian ruler.

Pug could half follow the banker's clear, measured Italian as he rapidly explained that Franklin Roosevelt, his treasured friend, had appointed the Berlin naval attaché as an aide for his few days in Europe; also that Henry would be acting as interpreter with Hitler. He said Henry could now remain or withdraw at Il Duce's pleasure. Mussolini gave the attaché another glance, this time obviously weighing him as a Roosevelt appointee. His expression warmed.

"Do you speak Italian?" he said in good English, catching Henry unawares almost as though a statue had broken into speech.

"Excellency, I can follow it in a fashion. I can't speak it. But then, I have nothing to say."

Mussolini smiled, as Pug had seen him smile at people in the other room. "If we come to naval matters maybe we will talk English."

He looked expectantly at the banker.

"Bene, Luigi?"

The banker talked for about a quarter of an hour. Since Pug already knew the substance, the banker did not altogether lose him. After some compliments, Gianelli said he was no diplomat and had neither the credentials nor the skill to discuss matters of state. He had come to put one question informally to Il Duce, on behalf of the President. Mr. Roosevelt had sent a private citizen who knew Il Duce, so that a negative reply would not affect formal relations between the United States and Italy. The President was alarmed by the drift toward catastrophe in Europe. If full-scale war broke out in the spring, horrors that nobody could foresee might engulf the whole world. Was it possible to do something, even at this late hour? Mr. Roosevelt had in mind a formal, urgent mission by a high United States diplomat, somebody on the order of Sumner Welles (Ciano, drumming the tips of his fingers together, looked up at the mention of the name), to visit all the chiefs of the warring states, perhaps late in January, to explore the possible terms of a general European settlement. Il Duce himself had made a last-minute call for a similar exploration on August 31, in vain. But if he would join the President now in bringing about such a settlement, he would hold a place in history as a savior of mankind.

Mussolini deliberated for a minute or so, his face heavy, his shoulders bowed, his look withdrawn, one hand fiddling with his tweed lapels. Then he said—as nearly as Pug could follow him—that the foreign policy of Italy rested on the Pact of Steel, the unshakable tie with Germany. Any attempt, any maneuver, any trick designed to split off Italy from this alliance would fail. A settlement in Europe was always possible. No one would welcome it more than he. As Mr. Roosevelt acknowledged, he himself had tried to the last to preserve the peace. But Hitler had offered a very reasonable settlement in October, and the Allies had spurned it. The American government in recent years had been openly hostile to Germany and Italy. Italy too had serious demands that had to be part of any settlement. These were not matters in Luigi's province, Mussolini said, but he was stating them to clarify his very pessimistic feeling about a mission by Sumner Welles.

"You have put a question to me," he concluded. "Now, Luigi, I will put a question to you."

"Yes, Duce."

"Does this initiative come from President Roosevelt, or is he acting at the request of the Allies?"

"Duce, the President has told me this is his own initiative."

Ciano cleared his throat, leaned forward with his hands clasped, and said, "Do the British and French know and approve of this visit you are making?"

"No, Excellency. The President said that he would be making informal inquiries of the same nature, at this same time, in London and Paris."

Mussolini said, "The newspapers have no information on any of this, is that correct?"

"What I have told you, Duce, is known outside this room only to the President and his Secretary of State. My trip is a matter of private business, of no interest to the press, and so it will remain forever."

"I have stated my deep reservations," said Mussolini, speaking slowly, in an extremely formal tone. "I have very little hope that such a mission would be to any useful purpose, in view of the maniacal hostility of the British and French ruling circles to the resurgent German nation and its great Führer. But I share Mr. Roosevelt's sentiment about leaving no stone unturned." He took a long portentous pause, then spoke with a decisive nod. "If the President sends Sumner Welles on such a mission, I will receive him."

Gianelli's fixed smile gave way to a real one of delight and pride. He gushed over Mussolini's wise and great decision, and his joy at the prospect of Italy and the United States, his two mother countries, joining to rescue the world from tragedy. Mussolini nodded tolerantly, seeming to enjoy the flood of flattery, though he waved a deprecating hand to calm down the banker.

Victor Henry seized the first pause in the banker's speech to put in, "Duce, may I ask whether Signor Gianelli is permitted to tell the Führer this? That you have consented to receive a formal mission by Sumner Welles?"

Mussolini's eyes sparked, as sometimes an admiral's did when Victor Henry said something sharp. He looked to Ciano. The foreign minister said condescendingly in his perfect English, "The Führer will know long before you have a chance to tell him."

"Okay," said Henry.

Mussolini rose, took Gianelli's elbow, and led him out

through french doors to the balcony, letting a gust of cold air into the room.

Ciano smoothed his thick black hair with both white hands. "Well, Commander, what do you think of the great German naval victory in the south Atlantic?"

"I hadn't heard of one."

"Really? It will be on Rome radio at seven o'clock. The battleship *Graf Spee* has caught a group of British cruisers and destroyers off Montevideo. The British have lost four or five ships and all the rest have been damaged. It's a British disaster that changes the whole balance of force in the Atlantic."

Victor Henry was shocked, but skeptical. "What happened to *Graf Spee?*"

"Minor hits that will be repaired overnight. *Graf Spee* was much heavier than anything it faced."

"The British have acknowledged this?"

Count Ciano smiled. He was a good-looking young man, and obviously knew it; just a little too fat and proud, Pug thought, from living high on the hog. "No, but the British took a little while to acknowledge the sinking of the *Royal Oak.*"

* * *

The dinner celebrating Victor Henry's promotion began in gloom, because of the *Graf Spee* news. The two attachés sat talking over highballs, waiting for Byron to show up.

Captain Kirkwood asserted that he believed the story; that in the twenty years since the war, a deep rot had eaten out the heart of England. Kirkwood looked like an Englishman himself—long-jawed, ruddy, and big-toothed —but he had little use for Great Britain. The British politicians had stalled and cringed in the face of Hitler's rise, he declared, because they sensed their people no longer had a will to fight. The Limey navy was a shell. England and France were going to crumple under Hitler's onslaught in the spring.

"It's too bad, I suppose," Kirkwood said. "One's sentiments are with the Allies, naturally. But the world moves on. After all, Hitler halted communism in its tracks. And don't worry, once he takes the fight out of the Allies, he'll settle Stalin's hash. The Russians are putting on one stumblebum performance in Finland, aren't they? They'll be a walkover for the Wehrmacht. In the end we'll have to make a deal with Hitler, that's becoming obvious. He holds all the cards on this side of the water."

"Hi, Dad." Byron's sports jacket and slacks were decidedly out of place in this old luxurious restaurant, where half the people wore evening dress.

Henry introduced him to the attaché. "Where have you been? You're late."

"I saw a movie, and then went to the YMCA to flake out for a little while."

"Is that all you could find to do in Rome? See a movie? I wish I had a few free hours in this city."

"Well, see, I was tired." Byron appeared much more his old slack self.

The waiter now brought champagne and Kirkwood proposed a toast to *Captain* Victor Henry.

"Hey, Dad! Four stripes! Really?" Byron sprang to life, radiating surprised joy. He clasped his father's hand and lifted a brimming glass. "Well! I'm sure glad I came to Rome, just for this. Say, I know one doesn't mention such things, but the hell with it, doesn't this put you way out front, Dad?"

Captain Kirkwood said, "He's been out front all along. That's what this means."

"All it takes now is one false move," said Pug dryly, shaking his head, "one piece of bad luck, one mislaid dispatch, one helmsman doping off on the midwatch. You're never out front till you retire."

"What's your situation, by the way, Byron?" Kirkwood said.

The young man hesitated.

"He's ROTC," Pug quickly said. "He's got a yen for submarines. By the way, Briny, the New London sub school is doubling the enrollment in May and accepting any reserves that can pass the physical."

Kirkwood smiled, examining Byron with a shade of curiosity. "Now's the time to get in on the ground floor, Byron. How're your eyes? Got twenty-twenty vision?"

"My eyes are okay, but I have this job to do here."

"What sort of job?"

"Historical research."

Kirkwood's face wrinkled.

Pug said, "He's working for a famous author, Aaron Jastrow. You know, the one who wrote *A Jew's Jesus.*"

"Oh, Jastrow, yes. That fellow up in Siena. I had lunch with him at the embassy once. Brilliant fellow. Having some trouble getting back home, isn't he?"

Byron said, "He isn't having trouble, sir, he just doesn't want to leave."

Kirkwood rubbed his chin. "Are you sure? Seems to me that's why he was in Rome. There's a foul-up in his papers. He was born in Russia or Lithuania or somewhere, and—whatever it is, I guess something can be worked out. Taught at Yale, didn't he?"

"Yes, sir."

"Well, he ought to make tracks while he can. Those Germans are just over the Alps. Not to mention old Benito's anti-Jew laws."

Victor Henry was returning to Berlin that night by train, accompanying the banker. He said nothing about his mission in Rome to Kirkwood or his son, and they did not ask. After dinner Byron rode to the railroad station in the taxi with him, in a prolonged silence. Natalie Jastrow was a heavy invisible presence in the cab, and neither one would start the topic. Pug said as they drove into the brilliantly lit empty square before the terminal, "Briny, if the British really took that shellacking off Montevideo, we won't stay out much longer. We can't let the Germans close the Atlantic. That's 1917 again. Why don't you put in for sub school? It won't start till May. By then Jastrow'll be back in the States, if he isn't simpleminded."

"May's a long way off."

"Well, I'm not going to argue." Pug got out of the cab. "Write to your mother a little more often. She's not happy."

"Okay, Dad."

"Don't miss Warren's wedding."

"I'll try not to. Gosh, won't that be something, if this family finally gets together again?"

"That's why I want you there. It'll be the last time in God knows how many years. Good-bye."

"Good-bye. Listen, I'm real proud you made captain, Dad."

Pug Henry gave his son a gloomy half-smile through the cab window and walked off to the train. And still not a word more had passed between them about the Jewish girl.

21

So IRASCIBLY did Rhoda Henry greet her husband on his return that he began to think something might be wrong with her.

He had left her in a nervous slump. Everything was an aggravating mess, the fall weather in Berlin stank, life stank, she was bored, German efficiency was a fiction, nobody understood how to do anything right, and there was no service and no honesty anymore. She had "her pain," an untreatable affliction that during previous slumps had showed up in an arm and in her back, and now was behind an ear. She feared cancer, but it didn't really matter because everything good was all finished anyway. Rhoda had always come out of these sags before, and then could be contritely sweet. Pug had hoped when he suddenly left Berlin for Rome that he would find her better when he got back. She was worse.

She wanted to go with him to Karinhall. In his absence an invitation engraved in gold on creamy thick stationery, addressed to Commander Victor Henry, had been delivered by a Luftwaffe staff officer. Pug hadn't been home ten minutes when she brought it out, wanting to know why she hadn't been invited too. If he went to the Görings' party at Karinhall and left her behind, she said, she could never face anybody in Berlin again.

Pug could not disclose that he was going along for secret state purposes, as a flunkey to an international financier. He couldn't take her into the snow-covered garden to soothe her with hints of this; it was almost midnight, and she was wearing a cloudy blue negligee, in which, indeed, she looked very pretty.

"Listen, Rhoda, take my word for it that there are security reasons for all this."

"Ha. Security reasons. That old chestnut, whenever you want to do anything your way."

"I'd rather have you along. You know that."

"Prove it. Call the protocol officer at the air ministry tomorrow. Or if you're too bashful, I will."

Pug was conducting this conversation in the library, while glancing through piled-up mail. He put down the letters. After a minute of cold staring at his wife, he said, "Are you well?"

"I'm bored to death, otherwise I'm fine, why?"

"Have you been taking the iron pills?"

"Yes, but I don't need pills. What I need is a little fun. Maybe I should go on a bender."

"You're not calling the air ministry! I hope that's understood."

Rhoda made a mutinous noise, and sat pouting.

"Hullo. Here's a letter from that Kirby fellow. What's he got to say for himself?"

"Read it. It's as dull as he is. All about how glad he is to be home, and how good the skiing is around Denver, and how much he enjoyed our hospitality. Three pages of nothing."

Pug tossed the letter unread on the routine pile.

"Honestly, you're a riot, you're so predictable, Pug. For twenty-five years whenever you've come home you've gone straight for the mail. What are you expecting, a letter from a lost love?"

He laughed, and shoved the letters aside. "Right you are. Let's have a drink. Let's have a couple of drinks. You look wonderful."

"I do not. That goddamned hairdresser baked my hair into shredded wheat again. I'm tired. I've been waiting up to talk to you. You were two hours late."

"There was trouble at the passport office."

"I know. Well, I'm going to bed. Nothing to talk about, since Karinhall is out. I even bought a sensational dress. I was going to show it to you, but to hell with it. I'll send it back."

"Keep it. You might just find a use for it pretty soon."

"Oh? Expect to be invited to the Görings' again?" She went out without staying for an answer.

Pug prepared a couple of highballs to toast the news of his promotion. When he got upstairs, her light was out—an old unpleasant marital signal. He wanted very much to spend the night with his wife. Moreover, he had been saving the story of his encounter with Natalie Jastrow for their bedroom talk. He drank both highballs himself, and slept on the sofa in the library.

The next day was brightened for him by the German announcement that the *Graf Spee* had heroically scuttled itself after its historic victory, and that its commanding officer had then nobly shot himself in a hotel room. He heard over the BBC that three much lighter British vessels had in fact beaten the German warship in a running sea fight and sent it limping into port before the scuttling. The German people didn't hear a word of this, and they were baffled by the revelation that the victorious pocket battleship had elected to blow itself up. The Nazi propagandists did not bother to explain, smothering the story instead with a whooping account of a vast fictitious air victory; twenty-five British bombers shot down over Heligoland. Pug knew that the chances of his ever meeting Count Ciano again were remote, but he would have given much to chat with him again about the *Graf Spee*.

Also, when Rhoda learned of Pug's promotion she came out of her blues as though by shock. Not another peep did she utter about Karinhall. She proceeded to give him the honeymoon treatment, and they had a happy week or so. His account of Natalie Jastrow fascinated and appalled her. "Sounds to me as though our only hope is that she'll come to her senses and drop Briny," she said.

*   *   *

Karinhall looked like a federal penitentiary built in the style of a hunting lodge. It sat in a game preserve about two hours' drive from Berlin, a wilderness of small bare trees and green firs mantled in snow. Off the autobahn, the approach ran through heavy gates electrically controlled, steel and concrete fences jagged with icicles, and a gauntlet of machine-gun-bearing Luftwaffe sentinels whose breaths smoked as they shouted challenges. Just as the car turned a corner and they caught a glimpse of the grandiose timber and stone building, a deer with big frightened eyes bounded across the road. The San Francisco banker no longer wore his automatic smile. His mouth was tightly pursed, and the soft brown Italian eyes were open wide and darting here and there, rather like the deer's.

In the vaulted banquet room, amid a dazzling crush of uniformed Nazis and their white-shouldered women—some lovely, some grossly fat, all brilliantly gowned and heavily gemmed—Adolf Hitler was playing with the little Göring girl. A string orchestra lost in a corner of the marble-paved expanse was murmuring Mozart. Great logs flamed in a fireplace with a triangular stone pediment soaring to the ceiling, and on a carved heavy table stretching the entire length of the room an untouched banquet lay piled. Rich smells hung in the air: wood smoke, cigar smoke, roast meat, French perfume. The happy, excited crowd of eminent Germans were laughing, cooing, clapping hands, their eyes shining at their Leader in his plain field-gray coat and black trousers as he held the beautiful white-clad child in his arms, talking to her, teasing her with a cake. Göring and his statuesque wife, both ablaze in operatic finery and jewelry, the man more showy than the woman, stood near, beaming with soft affectionate pride. Suddenly the little girl kissed the Führer on his big pale nose, and he laughed and gave her the cake. A cheer went up, everybody applauded, and women wiped their eyes.

"The Führer is so wonderful," said the Luftwaffe officer accompanying the two Americans, a small dark aviator wearing the diamond-studded cross of the Condor Legion. "Ach, if he could only marry! He loves children."

And to Pug Henry, also, there was something appealing about Hitler: his shy smile acknowledging the applause, the jocular reluctance with which he handed the girl to her ecstatic mother, his wistful shrug as he slapped Göring's back, like any bachelor congratulating a luckier man. At this moment Hitler had a naïve, almost mushy charm.

The Görings escorted Hitler to the table, and this signalled a general swarming toward the buffet. A troop of lackeys in blue and gold livery marched in, setting up gilt tables and chairs, helping the guests to food, pouring the wine, bowing and bowing. Guided by the Luftwaffe officer, he and Gianelli landed at a table with a banker named Wolf Stöller, who hailed the American financier as an old acquaintance: a slight Teuton in his fifties, with sandy hair plastered close to his head. The wife, an ashen-haired beauty, had eyes that glittered clear blue like the large diamonds on her neck, her arms, her fingers, and her ears.

By chance, Victor Henry had just written a short report on Stöller and knew a lot about him. Stöller's bank was the chief conduit by which Göring was amassing his riches. Stöller's specialty was acquiring *Objekte,* the term in German business jargon for Jewish-owned companies forced to the wall.

In the queer Germany of 1939, which Victor Henry was just beginning to understand, there was much stress on legality in looting the Jews. Outright confiscation or violence were rare. New codes of law dating from 1936 simply made it hard for them to do business; and month by month rulings came out making it ever harder. Jewish firms couldn't get import or export licenses or raw materials. Their use of railroad and shipping was restricted. Conditions kept tightening until they had no course but to sell out. A market flourished in such *Objekte,* with many alert upper-class Germans bidding eagerly against each other. Wolf Stöller's technique was to find and unite all the buyers interested in an *Objekt,* and to make a single very low offer. The owners had the choice of taking it or going bankrupt. Stöller's group then divided up the firm in shares. Through Göring, Stöller had access to the Gestapo's records, and was usually first on the scent of a major Jewish firm buckling to its knees. The big prizes Göring bought up himself—metal, banking, textiles—or took a large participation. Stöller's bank got its broker's fees and also its own participations in the *Objekte.*

All this Pug had learned from the American radio commentator in Berlin, Fred Fearing, who had been at some

pains to dig it up. Fearing recounted it to him with deep
anger, the more so as he couldn't broadcast the story. The
Germans claimed that any report of unfair treatment of
the Jews was paid Allied propaganda. The Jewish laws
aimed simply at restricting this minority, they said, to its
due share in Germany's economy.

Pug had more or less shut his mind to the Jewish problem, so as to focus on the military judgments which were
his job. Jews had become all but invisible in Berlin, except
in their special shopping hours, when, pallid and harried,
they briefly filled the stores and then again faded from
sight. The oppression was not a highly visible affair; Pug
had never seen even the outside of a concentration camp.
He had observed the signs on benches and restaurants, the
white-faced worried wretches pulled off trains and airplanes, an occasional broken window or old charred synagogue, and once a bad business of a man beaten bloody
in the zoo by three boys in Hitler Youth uniforms, while
the man's wife wept and screamed and two policemen
stood by laughing. But Fearing's account was his first
technical insight into German anti-Semitism. At bottom its
purpose, in Fearing's view, was just robbery, which was
disgusting but at least rational. Pug felt a qualm when
Wolf Stöller with a cultured bow offered his hand, but of
course he took it; and soon there they sat eating together
and toasting each other in Moselle, Riesling, and champagne.

Stöller was a cordial, clever German, in every way indistinguishable from the hundreds that Victor Henry had
met in the military and industrial worlds and at social
gatherings. He spoke a fine English. His countenance was
open and hearty. He made bright jokes, including bold
pleasantries about Göring's corpulence and theatrical uniforms. He expressed deep regard for the United States (he
especially loved San Francisco) and melancholy regret that
its relations with Germany were not better. In fact, could
he not do something to improve them, he said, by inviting
Gianelli and the Henrys for a weekend at his estate? It was
no Karinhall, but he could promise them good company.
Captain Henry might have the luck to shoot a deer. Game
was outside the meat ration, and some venison might be
very welcome to Mrs. Henry! The banker's wife, touching

Pug's hand with her cool jewelled white fingers, crinkled her blue eyes at him in invitation. She had heard that Mrs. Henry was the most elegant and attractive wife in the American diplomatic mission, and she longed to meet her.

Gianelli declined; he had to start his return journey in the morning. Officially there was every reason for Victor Henry to accept. Part of his job was to penetrate influential levels of Germans. He had no stomach for Stöller, but it occurred to him that here was a chance to give Rhoda the kind of fun she complained of missing. There was no telling good Germans from bad Germans. Stöller conceivably might be working for Göring under duress, though his wife in consequence dripped diamonds. Pug said he would come. The look the Stöllers exchanged convinced him that none of this was casual. They were cultivating him.

Stöller took the two Americans on a tour of Karinhall. Again Pug had the feeling that Nazi grandeur usually woke in him: the Hollywood impression, the sense of ephemeral, flamboyant make-believe, which persisted no matter how vast and solid the structures, how high the ceilings, how elaborate the decorations, how costly the art. The corridors and rooms of Karinhall seemed to go on for miles. Glass cases by the dozens displayed solid gold objects crusted with gems—vases, crosses, maces, swords, busts, batons, medals, books, globes—tributes to the field marshal from steel corporations, cities, and foreign governments on his birthday, his wedding, the birth of a child, the return of the Condor Legion from Spain. Italian and Dutch old masters crowded the walls, interspersed with the vapid calendar nudes of living Nazi-approved painters. Other reception rooms with nobody in them, almost as vast and ornate as the banquet hall, were hung with tapestries and flags, walled in wood, filled with statuary and jewelled suits of armor. Yet it all might almost have been papier-mâché and canvas. Even the food on the banquet table had looked like a Cecil B. De Mille feast, and the pink meat inside the roast pig might instead have been wax or plaster. But Victor Henry well knew that he was looking at an immense treasure, mostly booty collected through Dr. Stöller. Moral considerations aside, the vulgar edifice disappointed Pug because Göring was supposed to stem from an aristocratic family. Even the admiring comments of Luigi Gianelli had a strong tinge of irony.

The Luftwaffe officer wearing the diamond cross caught up with them and whispered to Stöller.

"Ah, what a pity, now you must go," said the German banker. "And you haven't begun to see the wonders of Karinhall. Captain Henry, my office will make all the arrangements to bring you and your dear wife on Friday to Abendruh, though I fear it will look rather pitiful after this. We will telephone you tomorrow."

Stöller accompanied the two Americans through more rooms and corridors, stopped at double doors of dark wood heavily carved with hunting scenes, and opened them on a timbered room with log-and-plaster walls, hung with antlers, stuffed heads, and animal hides. The dusty smell of the dead creatures was strong in the air. On either side of a roaring fire sat Ribbentrop and Göring. Hitler was not in the room. A long, crudely made wooden table and two low benches took up most of the floor space. Pug thought at once that this must be the main room of the old hunting lodge, around which the field marshal had constructed the banal palace. Here was the heart of Karinhall. Except for the glow from the fire, the room was dank, dark, and cold.

Göring lolled on a settee with one thick white leather-booted leg off the floor, sipping coffee from a gold demitasse—part of a gold service on a low inlaid marble table. He nodded and smiled familiarly at Gianelli. Diamond rings bulged on three of the fingers that held the cup. Ribbentrop stared at the ceiling, hands interlaced across his stomach. The German banker introduced Victor Henry, backed out of the room, and closed the door.

"You will have exactly seven minutes of the Führer's time to state your business," said Ribbentrop in German.

Gianelli stammered, "Excellency, permit me to reply in English. I am here in a private capacity, and I regard that much time as an extraordinary courtesy to my country and my President."

Ribbentrop sat with a blank face, looking at the ceiling, so Victor Henry ventured to translate. The foreign minister cut him off with a snapped sentence in perfect Oxford accents, "I understand English."

Göring said to Gianelli, "You are welcome to Karinhall, Luigi. I have tried to invite you more than once. But this time you have come a long way for a short interview."

"May I say, Field Marshal," the banker answered in broken German, "that I have seen millions of money made and lost in a conference lasting a few minutes, and that world peace is worth any effort, however unpromising."

"I am in complete agreement with that." Göring motioned them to chairs placed near him.

Ribbentrop, seizing the arms of his chair and closing his eyes, burst out in high rapid tones, in German, "This peculiar visitation is another studied insult by your President to the German head of state. Whoever heard of sending a private citizen as an emissary in such matters? Between civilized countries the diplomatic structure is used. Germany did not withdraw its ambassador in Washington by choice. The United States first made the hostile gesture. The United States has allowed within its borders a boycott of German products and a campaign of hate propaganda against the German people. The United States has revised its so-called Neutrality Act in blatant favor of the aggressors in this conflict. Germany did not declare war on England and France. They declared war on Germany."

The foreign minister stopped talking and sat with his eyes closed, the long-jawed haggard face immobile, some strands of the graying blond hair falling over his face. The California banker looked first at Göring, then at Victor Henry, clearly shaken. Göring poured himself more coffee.

Concentrating with all his might, Victor Henry translated the foreign minister's tirade. Ribbentrop did not correct or interrupt him.

Gianelli started to talk, but Ribbentrop burst out again: "What purpose can be served by this maladroit approach, other than a further deliberate provocation, one more expression of your President's highly dangerous contempt for the leader of a powerful nation of eighty million people?"

With a trembling wave of his hand at Henry to indicate that he understood, Gianelli said, "May I respectfully reply that—"

The bright blue eyes of Ribbentrop opened, closed again, and he said in still louder tones, "The willingness of the Führer to give you a hearing in these circumstances is a testimony to his desire for peace that history will someday record. This is the sole value this peculiar interview possesses."

Göring said to the banker in a milder, but no more friendly tone, "What is your purpose here, Luigi?"

"Field Marshal, I am an informal messenger of my President to your Führer, and I have a single question to put to him, by my President's instructions. To ask it, and to answer it, should take very little time. But by God's grace it can lead to lasting historical results." Victor Henry put this into German.

"What is the question?" Göring said.

The banker's face was going yellow. "Field Marshal, by my President's order, the question is for the Führer," he said hoarsely in German.

"It is for the Führer to answer," Göring said, "but obviously we are going to hear it anyway. What is the question?" He raised his voice, fixing his gaze on the banker.

Gianelli turned away from Göring's eyes, which were lazily hard, licked his lips, and said to Henry, "Captain, I beg you to confirm my instructions to the great field marshal."

Victor Henry was rapidly calculating the situation, including the trace of physical danger which had shadowed his mind since passing through the outer fences of Karinhall. Göring, for all his gross jolly façade, was a tough and ugly brute. If this monstrously fat German, with the rouge-red face, thin scarlet lips, and small jewelled hands, wanted to harm them, diplomatic immunity was a frail shield here. But Pug judged that his talk was cat-and-mouse fooling to kill time. He translated the banker's answer under the straight stare of Göring, and added, "I confirm that the instructions are to put the question directly to the Führer, as Herr Gianelli already has done to his good friend Il Duce in Italy, where in my presence Il Duce gave him a favorable response."

"We know all that," Ribbentrop said. "We know the question, too." Göring blinked at Henry and the tension broke. The banker brushed his fingers across his brow. The silence lasted for perhaps a minute. Adolf Hitler, pulling a lock of hair across his forehead, came into the room through a side door hung with a tiger skin.

As quickly as the Americans, Göring and Ribbentrop rose, assuming very much the lackey look. Göring moved away from the comfortable settee to a chair, and Hitler took his place, gesturing to the others to sit. He did not shake hands. Seen at this close range the Führer looked healthy and calm, though too fat and puffy-eyed. His dark hair was clipped to the bone at the sides like a common soldier's. Except for the famed moustache he had an ordinary face, the face of any small man of fifty or so walking by on a German city street. Compared to this man of the people, the other two Nazis seemed bedizened grotesques. His gray coat with the single Iron Cross over his left breast contrasted remarkably with Ribbentrop's gold-braided dark blue uniform and the air marshal's extravaganza of colors, gems, and medals.

Folding one hand over the other in his lap, he took in the Americans with a grave glance.

"Luigi Gianelli, American banker. Captain Victor Henry, United States naval attaché in Berlin," said Ribbentrop, in a sarcastic tone emphasizing the unimportance of the visitors. "Extraordinary informal emissaries, *Mein Führer,* from the President of the United States."

The banker cleared his throat, attempted an expression of gratitude for the interview in German, made a flustered apology, and shifted to English. The Führer, his gaze steady on the banker while Henry translated, kept shifting in his chair and crossing and uncrossing his ankles. With the same prologue on world peace that he had addressed to Mussolini, Gianelli put to the Führer the question about Sumner Welles. As it came out in English, a contemptuous smile appeared on Ribbentrop's face. Upon Henry's translation Hitler and Göring looked at each other, the Führer impassive, Göring hoisting his shoulders, waving his thick-gemmed hands, and shaking his head, as though to say, "That's really it. Unbelievable!"

Hitler meditated. The glance of his sunken, pallid blue eyes was straight ahead and far away. A bitter little smile moved his moustache and his small mouth. He began to speak in quiet, very clear, Bavarian-accented German, "Your esteemed President, Herr Gianelli, seems to feel a remarkable sense of responsibility for the whole present course of world history. It is all the more remarkable in that only the United States, among the great powers, failed to join the League of Nations, and in that your Congress and your people have repeatedly indicated that they want no foreign entanglements.

"In my speech of April twenty-ninth, mainly addressed to your President, I acknowledged that your country has more than twice the population of our little land, more than fifteen times the living space, and infinitely more mineral resources. Perhaps therefore your President feels that he must approach me from time to time with stern fatherly admonitions. But of course I am giving my life for the renascence of my people, and I cannot help seeing everything from that limited point of view."

Victor Henry did his best to translate, his heart pounding, his mouth dry.

Hitler now began reminiscing garrulously about the Rhineland, Austria, Czechoslovakia, and Poland. He spoke at length and seemed to be enjoying himself, slowly waving his hands and using relaxed tones. The justifications were familiar stuff. He grew briefly loud and acid only over the British guarantee to Poland, which, he said, had encouraged a cruel reactionary regime to engage in atrocious measures against its German minority, in the illusion that it had become safe to do so. That was how the war had started. Since then England and France had over and over spurned his offers of a peace settlement and disarmament. What more could he do, as a responsible head of state, than arm his country to defend itself against these two great military empires, who between them controlled three-fifths of the habitable surface of the earth and almost half its population?

German political aims were simple, open, moderate, and unchanging, he went on. Five centuries before Columbus discovered America, there had been a German empire at the heart of Europe, its boundaries roughly fixed by geography and the reproductive vigor of the people. War had come over and over to this European heartland through the attempts of many powers to fragment the German folk. These attempts had often had temporary success. But the German nation, with its strong instinct for survival and growth, had time and again rallied and thrown off foreign encirclements and yokes. In this part of his talk Hitler made references to Bismarck, Napoleon, Frederick the Great, the War of the Spanish Succession, and the Thirty Years' War, which were beyond Victor Henry. He translated them word for word as best he could.

The Versailles Treaty, said the Führer, had simply been the latest of these foreign efforts to mutilate the German heartland. Because it had been historically unsound and unjust it was now dead. The Rhineland was German. So was Austria. So was the Sudetenland. So were Danzig and the Corridor. The manufactured monstrosity of Czechoslovakia, thrust like a spear into Germany's vitals, had now become once again the traditional Bohemian protectorate of the Reich. This restoration of normal Germany was now complete. He had done it almost without bloodshed. But for the absurd British guarantee, it would have all been finished in peace; the question of Danzig and the Corridor had been practically settled in July. Even now nothing substantial stood in the way of lasting peace. The other side simply had to recognize this restored normality in central Europe, and return to Germany her colonial territories. For the Reich, like other great modern states, had a natural right to the raw materials of the underdeveloped continents.

Victor Henry was deeply struck by Hitler's steady manner, by his apparent moral conviction, by his identification of himself with the German nation—". . . and so I restored the Rhineland to the Reich . . . and so I brought back Austria to its historical origins . . . and so I normalized the Bohemian plateau . . ."—and by his broad visions of history. The ranting demagogue of the Party rallies was obviously nothing but a public image, such as the Germans, in Hitler's estimate, wanted. He radiated the personal force that Captain Henry had seen in only two or three admirals. As for the journalistic picture—the carpet-chewing hysterical Charlie Chaplin politician—Pug now felt that it was a distortion of small minds which had led the world into disaster.

"I share the President's desire for peace," Hitler was saying. He was starting to gesture now as in his speeches, though less broadly. His eyes had brightened astonishingly; Henry thought it must be an illusion, but they seemed eerily to glow. "I hunger and yearn for peace. I was a simple soldier in the front lines for four years, while he, as a rich and well-born man, had the privilege of serving as an Assistant Secretary of the Navy in a Washington office. I know war. I was born to create, not to destroy, and who can say how many years of life are left to me to fulfill my tasks of construction? But the British and French leaders call for the destruction of '*Hitlerism*' "—he brought out the foreign term with contempt-filled sarcasm—"as their price for peace. I can almost understand their hatred for me. I have made Germany strong again, and that did not suit them. But this hate, if persisted in, will doom Europe, because I and the German people cannot be separated. We are one. This is a simple truth, though I fear the English will need a test of fire to prove it. I believe Germany has the strength to emerge victorious. If not, we will all go down together, and historical Europe as we know it will cease to exist."

He paused, his face tightened and changed, and the pitch of his voice all at once began to rise. "How can they be so blind to realities? I achieved air parity in 1937. Since then I have never stopped building planes, planes, *planes,* U-boats, U-boats, *U-boats!*" He was screaming now, clenching his fists and waving his stiff outstretched arms. "I have piled bombs, bombs, *bombs,* tanks, tanks, *tanks,* to the sky! It has been a wasteful, staggering burden on my people, but what other language have great states ever understood? It is out of a sense of strength that I have offered peace. I have been rejected and scorned, and as the price of peace they have asked for my head. The German people only laugh at such pathetic nonsense!"

On the shouted litany of "*planes . . . bombs . . . U-boats*" he swept both fists down again and again to strike the floor, bending far over so that the famous black lock of hair tumbled in his face, giving him his more usual newsreel look of the street agitator; and the red face and screeching tones had indeed something of the carpet chewer, after all. Suddenly, dramatically, as at a podium, he dropped into quiet controlled tones. "Let the test of fire come. I have done my utmost, and my conscience is clear before the bar of history."

Hitler fell silent, then stood with an air of dismissal, his eyes burning and distant, his mouth a down-curved line.

"Mein Führer," Göring said, lumbering to his feet, his boots creaking, "after this wonderfully clear presentation of the realities you offer no objection to this visit of Herr Sumner Welles, I take it, if the President persists."

Hitler hesitated, appeared perplexed, and gave an impatient shrug. "I have no wish to return discourtesy for discourtesy, and petty treatment for petty treatment. I would do anything for peace. But until the British will to destroy me is itself destroyed, the only road to peace is through German victory. Anything else is irrelevant. I will continue to hope with all my heart for a last-minute signal of sanity from the other side, before the holocaust explodes."

In a worked-up manner, with no gesture of farewell, he strode out through the carved double door. Victor Henry glanced at his wristwatch. The Führer had spent an hour and ten minutes with them, and so far as Henry knew, President Roosevelt's question remained unanswered. He could see on Gianelli's pale, baffled face the same impression.

Göring and Ribbentrop looked at each other. The fat man said, "President Roosevelt has his reply. The Führer sees no hope in the Welles mission, but in his unending quest for a just peace he will not reject it."

"That was not my understanding," said Ribbentrop in a quick, strained voice. "He called the mission irrelevant."

"If you want to press the Führer for clarification," Göring said satirically to him, gesturing at the double doors, "go ahead. I understood him very well, and I think I know him." He turned again to the banker and his voice moderated. "In informing your President of this meeting, tell him that I said the Führer will not refuse to receive Welles, but sees no hope in it—and neither do I—unless the British and the French drop their war aim of removing the Führer. That is no more possible than it is to move Mont Blanc. If they persist in it, the result will be a frightful battle in the West, ending in a total German victory after the death of millions."

"That will be the result in any case," said Ribbentrop, "and the die will be cast before Mr. Sumner Welles can arrange his papers and pack his belongings."

Göring took each of the two Americans by an elbow and

said with a total change to geniality that brought to Victor Henry's mind the waiter at Wannsee, "Well, I hope you are not leaving so soon? We will have dancing a little later, and a bite of supper, and then some fine entertainers from Prague, artistic dancers." He rolled his eyes in jocose suggestiveness.

"Your Excellency is marvellously hospitable," Gianelli replied. "But a plane is waiting in Berlin to take me to Lisbon and connect with the Clipper."

"Then I must let you go, but only if you promise to come to Karinhall again. I will walk out with you."

Ribbentrop stood with his back to them, looking at the fire. When the banker hesitantly spoke a word of farewell, he grunted and hitched a shoulder. Arm in arm with Göring, the Americans walked down the corridors of Karinhall. The air minister smelled of some strong bath oil. His hand lightly tapped Victor Henry's forearm. "Well, Captain Henry, you have been to Swinemünde and seen our U-boat setup. What is your opinion of our U-boat program?"

"Your industrial standards are as high as any in the world, Your Excellency. And with officers like Grobke and Prien you're in good shape. The U-boats are already making quite a record in the Atlantic."

"It's only the beginning," Göring said. "U-boats are coming off the ways now like sausages. I doubt that all of them will even see action. The air will decide this war fast. I hope your attaché for air, Colonel Powell, has been reporting the Luftwaffe's strength accurately to your President. We have been very open with Powell, on my orders."

"Indeed he has made reports. He's very impressed."

Göring looked pleased. "We have learned a lot from America. Curtis in particular has brilliant designers. Your Navy's dive-bombing was carefully studied by us and the Stuka was the result." He turned to the banker and speaking in slow, simple German, asked him questions about South American mining companies. They were walking through an empty ballroom with huge crystal-and-gilt chandeliers, and their clicking steps on the parquet floor echoed hollowly. The banker replied in easy German, which he had not displayed under pressure, and they talked finance all the way to the front doors. Guests walking in the halls stared at the sight of Göring between the two Americans. The banker's man-of-the-world smile reappeared and color returned to his face.

It was snowing outside, and Göring stopped in the doorway to shake hands. Gianelli had so far recovered that he came out with something Victor Henry considered absolutely vital. Henry was trying to think of a way to hint it to him, when the banker said, shaking hands with the air minister in a light whirl of snow, "Excellency, I will have to tell the President that your foreign minister does not welcome the Welles mission and has stated the Führer does not."

Göring's face toughened. "If Welles comes, the Führer will see him. That is official." Göring glanced up at the sky and walked through the snow with the two Americans to their car, as a Luftwaffe officer drove it up to the entrance. "Remember this. Germany is like all countries. Not everybody here wants peace. But I do."

. . .

Victor Henry sat up most of the night writing his report, so it could go back to the President in the banker's hands. It was a longhand account, poured out pell-mell. After a tale of the facts up to Göring's last words in the snow, Victor Henry wrote:

The key question is, of course, whether or not a peace mission by Sumner Welles is now expected in the Third Reich. It seems inconceivable that in an interview with Hitler, Göring, and Ribbentrop, your emissary got no clear-cut answer. I believe that Sumner Welles will be received by Hitler. But I don't think the mission will achieve anything, unless the Allies want to change their minds and accept some version of the "outstretched hand" formula.

None of the three men seemed to take the interview very seriously. They have bigger matters on their minds. We were a pair of nobodies. I would guess that Göring wanted it to take place, and that Hitler, being there in Karinhall anyway, didn't mind. I got the feeling that he enjoyed sounding off to a pair of Americans who would report directly to you. All three men acted as though the offensive in the west is ready to roll. I don't think they give a damn whether Welles comes or not. If the British are really as set on their terms as Hitler is on his, you'll have all-out war in the spring. The parties are too far apart.

Göring, it seems to me, is playing a side game by his peace talk. This man is the biggest thug in the Third Reich. He looks like a circus freak—the man is really disgustingly fat and dolled up—but he is the supreme realist in that crowd, and the unchallenged number two man. He has made a good thing out of Nazism, much more than the others. Mr. Gianelli will no doubt describe Karinhall to you. It's vulgar but stupendous. Göring may be smart enough, even though he's riding high, to figure that no string of luck lasts forever. If the offensive should happen to go sour, then the man who always wanted peace will be right there, weeping tears over the fallen Führer and happy to take on the job.

Ribbentrop can only be described—if you will forgive me, Mr. President—as the classic German son of a bitch. He is right out of the books with his arrogance, bad manners, obtuseness, obstinacy, and self-righteousness. I think this is his nature, but I also believe he echoes how Hitler feels. This is just the old Navy business of the commanding officer being the impressive "old man," while the exec is the mean crab doing his dirty work. Hitler unquestionably hates your guts and feels you've interfered and crossed him up far too much. He also feels fairly safe defying the USA, because he knows how public opinion is divided. All this Ribbentrop expressed for him in no uncertain terms, leaving the boss free to be the magnanimous German Napoleon and the savior of Europe.

Driving away from Karinhall, I had a reaction like coming out of a trance. I began to remember things about Hitler that I really forgot while I was listening to him and translating his words: the ravings in *Mein Kampf*, the way he has broken his word time after time, his wild lies, the fact that he started this war, the gruesome bombing of Warsaw, and his persecution of the Jews. It's a measure of his persuasiveness that I could forget such things for a while, facing the man who has done them. He's a spellbinder. For big crowds I've heard him do coarse belligerent yelling, but in a room with a couple of nervous foreigners he can be—if it suits him—the reasonable, charming world leader. They say he can also throw a foaming rage; we saw just a hint of that, and I certainly believe it. But the picture of him as a ludicrous nut is a false-hood.

He never sounded more confident than when he said that he and the Germans are one. He simply knows this to be the truth. Take away his moustache, and he sort of looks like all the Germans rolled into one. He isn't an aristocrat, or a businessman, or an intellectual, or anything whatever except the German man in the street, somehow inspired.

It's vital to understand this relationship between Hitler and the German people. The present aim of the Allies seems to be to pry the two apart. I have become convinced that it can't be done. For better or worse, the Allies still have the choice of knuckling under to Hitler or beating the Germans. They had the same choice in 1936, when beating the Germans would have been a cinch. Nothing has changed, except that the Germans may now be invincible.

The glimpse of cross-purposes at the top may have showed a weakness of the Nazi structure, but if so it's all internal politics, it has nothing to do with Hitler's hold on the Germans. That includes Göring and Ribbentrop. When he entered the room they stood and cringed.

If Hitler were the half-crazy, half-comical gangster we've been reading about, this war would be a pushover, because running a war takes brains, steadiness, strategic vision, and skill. Unfortunately for the Allies, he is a very able man.

22

RHODA hugged and kissed Pug when he told her about the weekend. He didn't mention Stöller's part in what Fred Fearing called robbing the Jews. It wasn't precisely that; it was a sort of legalized expropriation, and damned un-savory, but that was life in Nazi Germany. There was no point in making Rhoda share his uneasy feelings, when one reason for accepting Stöller's hospitality was to give her a good time.

The chauffeur sent by Stöller drove past the colonnaded entrance to Abendruh and dropped them at a back door, where a maid conducted them two flights up narrow servants' stairs. Pug wondered whether this was a calculated German insult. But the spacious, richly furnished bedroom and sitting room looked out on a fine snowy vista of lawn, firs, winding river, and thatched outbuildings; two servants came to help them dress; and the mystery of the back stairs cleared up when they went to dinner. The curving main staircase of Abendruh, two stories high, balustraded in red marble, had been entirely covered with a polished wooden slide. Guests in dinner clothes stood on the brink, the men laughing, the ladies giggling and shrieking. Down below other guests stood with the Stöllers, watching an elegantly dressed couple sliding down, the woman hysterical with laughter as her green silk dress pulled away from her gartered thighs.

"Oh my gawd, Pug, I'll DIE!" chortled Rhoda. "I can't POSSIBLY! I've practically NOTHING on underneath! Why don't they WARN a girl!" But of course she made the slide, screaming with embarrassed delight, exposing her legs— which were very shapely—clear up to her lacy underwear. She arrived at the bottom scarlet-faced and convulsed, amid cheers and congratulations, to be welcomed by the hosts and introduced to fellow weekenders. It was a sure icebreaker, Victor Henry thought, if a trifle gross. The Germans certainly had the touch for these things.

Next day when he woke he found a green leather hunting costume laid out for him, complete with feathered hat, belt, and dagger. The men were a varied crowd: Luftwaffe and Wehrmacht officers, other bankers, the president of an electrical works, a prominent actor. Pug was the only foreigner. The jolly group took him warmly into their horseplay and joking, and then into the serious business of the hunt. Pug liked duck-hunting, but killing deer had never appealed to him. General Armin von Roon was in the party, and Pug lagged behind with the hook-nosed general, who remarked that to see a deer shot made him feel ill. In this meeting Roon was more loquacious than before. The forest was dank and cold, and like the others he had been drinking schnapps. They talked first about the United States, where, as it turned out, Roon had attended the Army War College. Then the general discussed the Polish campaign, and the Ribbentrop-Molotov pact, which he surprisingly called a disaster, because of all the ground Stalin had gained without firing a shot. His grasp of the field operations was masterly. His estimate of Hitler, Victor Henry thought, was cold-blooded and honest. Roon scarcely veiled his contempt for the master race theories of the Nazis, or for the Party itself, but he was making out a strong case for Hitler as a German leader, when shots rang out and a nearby hullabaloo drew them to join the party, ringed around a small deer lying dead in blood-spattered snow. A ceremony ensued of horn-blowing and pushing a sprig of fir into the dead mouth over the bloody lolling tongue. Henry became separated from the general. That evening he looked for him before dinner, and was sorry to learn that Roon had been summoned back to Berlin.

After dinner, a string quartet played Beethoven in a cream-and-gold French music room, and a fat-bosomed famous soprano sang Schubert songs. The guests listened with more attention than Pug could muster; some, during the lieder, had tears in their eyes. Rhoda felt in her element, for in Washington she was a patroness of music. She sat beaming, whispering expert comments between numbers. Dancing followed, and one German after another danced with her. From the floor, she kept darting sparkling looks of gratitude at her husband, until Stöller took him in tow to a library, where the actor and Dr. Knopfmann, the head of the electrical works, sat over brandy.

As yet, on the weekend, Pug had not heard a word about the war. Conversation had stayed on personal chatter, business, or the arts.

"Ah, here is Captain Henry," said the actor in a rich ringing voice. "What better authority do you want? Let's put it to him." A gray-moustached man with thick hair, he played emperors, generals, and older men in love with young women. Pug had seen his famous King Lear at the Schauspielhaus. His face just now was purple-red over his stiff collar and buckling starched shirt.

"It might embarrass him," Dr. Knopfmann said.

"No war talk now. That's out," said Stöller. "This weekend is for pleasure."

"I don't mind," Pug said, accepting brandy and settling in a leather chair. "What's the question?"

"I create illusions for a living," rumbled the actor, "and I believe illusions should be confined to the stage. And I say it is an illusion to hope that the United States will ever allow England to go down."

"Oh, to hell with all that," said the banker.

Dr. Knopfmann, a twinkling-eyed, round-faced man like the captain of the *Bremen,* but much shorter and fatter, said, "And I maintain that it isn't 1917. The Americans pulled England's chestnuts out of the fire once, and what did they get for it? A bellyful of ingratitude and repudiation. The Americans will accept the *fait accompli.* They are realists. Once Europe is normalized, we can have a hundred years of a firm Atlantic peace."

"What do you say, Captain Henry?" the actor asked.

"The problem may never come up. You still have to lick England."

None of the three men looked very pleased. The actor said, "Oh, I think we can assume that's in the cards— providing the Americans don't step in. That's the whole argument."

Stöller said, "Your President doesn't try to hide his British sympathies, Victor, does he? Quite natural, in view of his Anglo-Dutch ancestry. But wouldn't you say the people are against him, or at least sharply split?"

"Yes, but America is a strange country, Dr. Stöller. Public opinion can shift fast. Nobody should forget that, in dealing with us."

The eyes of the Germans flickered at each other. Dr. Knopfmann said, "A shift in public opinion doesn't just happen. It's manufactured."

"There's the live nerve," Stöller said. "And that's what I've found difficult to convey even to the air marshal, who's usually so hardheaded. Germans who haven't been across the water are impossibly provincial about America. I'm sorry to say this goes for the Führer himself. I don't believe he yet truly grasps the vast power of the American Jews. It's a vital factor in the war picture."

"Don't exaggerate that factor," Henry said. "You fellows tend to, and it's a form of kidding yourselves."

"My dear Victor, I've been in the United States nine times and I lived for a year in San Francisco. Who's your Minister of the Treasury? The Jew Morgenthau. Who sits on your highest court, wielding the most influence? The Jew Frankfurter."

He proceeded to reel off a list of Jewish officials in Washington, stale and boring to Pug from endless repetition in Nazi propaganda; and he made the usual assertion that the Jews had American finance, communications, justice, and even the Presidency in their pockets. Stöller delivered all this calmly and pleasantly. He kept repeating *"der Jude, der Jude"* without a sneer. There was no glare in his eyes, such as Pug had now and then observed when Rhoda challenged some vocal anti-Semite. The banker presented his statements as though they were the day's stock market report.

"To begin with," Pug replied, a bit wearily, "the Treasury post in our country has little power. It's a minor political reward. Christians hold all the other cabinet posts. Financial power lies with the banks, the insurance companies, the oil, rail, lumber, shipping, steel, and auto industries, and such. They're wholly in Christian hands. Always have been."

"Lehman is a banker," said Dr. Knopfmann.

"Yes, he is. The famous exception." Pug went on with his stock answers to stock anti-Semitism: the all but solid Christian ownership of newspapers, magazines, and publishing houses, the Christian composition of Congress, the cabinet, and the executive branch, the eight Christian judges out of nine on the Supreme Court, the paramount White House influence of a Christian, Harry Hopkins, and the rest. On the faces of his hearers appeared the curious universal smirk of Germans when discussing Jews: condescending, facetious, and cold, with superior awareness of a very private inside joke.

Stöller said in a kindly tone, "That's always the Jewish line, you know, how unimportant they are."

"Would you recommend that we take away what businesses they do have? Make *Objekte* of them?"

Stöller looked surprised and laughed, not in the least

offended. "You're better informed than many Americans, Victor. It would be an excellent idea for the health of your economy. You'll come to it sooner or later."

"Is it your position," the actor said earnestly, "that the Jewish question really has no bearing on America's entry into the war?"

"I didn't say that. Americans do react sharply to injustice and suffering."

The smirk reappeared on the three faces, and Knopfmann said, "And your Negroes in the South?"

Pug paused, "It's bad, but it's improving, and we don't put them behind barbed wire."

The actor said in a lowered voice, "That's a political penalty. A Jew who behaves himself doesn't go to a camp."

Lighting a large cigar, his eyes on the match, Stöller said, "Victor speaks very diplomatically. But his connections are okay. One man who's really in the picture is Congressman Ike Lacouture of Florida. He fought a great battle against revising the Neutrality Act." With a sly glance at Pug, he added, "Practically in the family, isn't he?"

This caught Pug off guard, but he said calmly, "You're pretty well informed. That's not exactly public knowledge."

Stöller laughed. "The air minister knew about it. He told me. He admires Lacouture. What happened to the dance music? Ach, look at the time. How did it get to be half past one? There's a little supper on, gentlemen, nothing elaborate—" He rose, puffing on the cigar. "The American Jews will make the greatest possible mistake, Victor, to drag in the United States. Lacouture is their friend, if they'll only listen to him. You know what the Führer said in his January speech—if they start another world war, that will be the end of them. He was in deadly earnest, I assure you."

Aware that he was butting a stone wall, but unable to let these things pass, Pug said, "Peace or war isn't up to the Jews. And you grossly misunderstand Lacouture."

"Do I? But my dear Captain, what do you call the British guarantee to Poland? Politically and strategically it was frivolous, if not insane. All it did was bring in two big powers against Germany on the trivial issue of Danzig,

which was what the Jews wanted. Churchill is a notorious
Zionist. All this was clearly stated between the lines in
Lacouture's last speech. I tell you, men like him may still
manage to restore the peace and incidentally to save the
Jews from a very bad fate they seem determined to bring
on themselves. Well—how about an omelette and a glass
of champagne?"

*   *   *

On Christmas Eve, Victor Henry left the embassy early
to walk home. The weather was threatening, but he wanted
air and exercise. Berlin was having a lugubrious Yuletide.
The scrawny newspapers had no good war news, and the
Russian attack on Finland was bringing little joy to Germans. The shop windows offered colorful cornucopias of
appliances, clothing, toys, wines, and food, but people
hurried sullenly along the cold windy streets under dark
skies, hardly glancing at the mocking displays. None of
the stuff was actually for sale. As Pug walked, evening fell
and the blackout began. Hearing muffled Christmas songs
from behind curtained windows, he could picture the
Berliners sitting in dimly lit apartments in their overcoats
around tinsel-draped fir trees, trying to make merry on
watery beer, potatoes, and salt mackerel. At Abendruh,
the Henrys had almost forgotten that there was a war on,
if a dormant one, and that serious shortages existed. For
Wolf Stöller there were no shortages.

Yielding to Rhoda's urging, he had accepted an invitation to come back to Abendruh in January, though he had
not enjoyed himself there. More and more, especially since
his glimpse of the National Socialist leaders at Karinhall,
he thought of the Germans as people he would one day
have to fight. He felt hypocritical putting on the good fellow with them. But intelligence opportunities did exist at
Stöller's estate. Pug had sent home a five-page account just
of his talk with General von Roon. By pretending he agreed
at heart with Ike Lacouture—something Stöller already
believed, because he wanted to—he could increase those
opportunities. It meant being a liar, expressing ideas he
thought pernicious, and abusing a man's hospitality—a hell
of a way to serve one's country! But if Stöller was trying

games with the American naval attaché, he had to take the risks. Victor Henry was mulling over all this as he strode along, muffled to his eyes against a sleety rain that was starting to fall, when out of the darkness a stooped figure approached and touched his arm.

"Captain Henry?"

"Who are you?"

"Rosenthal. You are living in my house."

They were near a corner, and in the glow of the blue streetlight Pug saw that the Jew had lost a lot of weight; the skin of his face hung in folds, and his confident bearing had given way to a whipped and sickly look. It was a shocking change. Holding out his hand, Pug said, "Oh, yes. Hello."

"Forgive me. My wife and I are going to be sent to Poland soon. Or at least we have heard such a rumor and we want to prepare, in case it's true. We can't take our things, and we were just wondering whether there are any articles in our home you and Mrs. Henry would care to buy. You could have anything you wished, and I could make you a very reasonable price."

Pug had also heard vague stories of the "resettlement" of the Berlin Jews, a wholesale shipping-off to newly formed Polish ghettos, where conditions were, according to the reports you chose to believe, either moderately bad or fantastically horrible. It was disturbing to talk to a man actually menaced with this dark misty fate.

"You have a factory here," he said. "Can't your people keep an eye on your property until conditions get better?"

"The fact is I've sold my firm, so there's nobody." Rosenthal held up the frayed lapels of his coat against the cutting sleet and wind.

"Did you sell out to the Stöller bank?"

The Jew's face showed astonishment and timorous suspicion. "You know about these matters? Yes, the Stöller bank. I received a very fair price. Very fair." The Jew permitted himself a single ironic glance into Henry's eyes. "But the proceeds were tied up to settle other matters. My wife and I will be more comfortable in Poland with a little ready money. It always helps. So—perhaps the carpets— the plate, or some china?"

"Come along and talk it over with my wife. She makes all those decisions. Maybe you can have dinner with us."

Rosenthal sadly smiled. "I don't think so, but you're very kind."

Pug nodded, remembering his Gestapo-planted servants. "Herr Rosenthal, I have to repeat to you what I said when we rented your place. I don't want to take advantage of your misfortune."

"Captain Henry, you can't possibly do me and my wife a greater kindness. I hope you will buy something."

Rosenthal put a card in his hand and melted into the blackout. When Pug got home Rhoda was dressing for the chargé's dinner, so there was no chance to talk about the offer.

The embassy's Christmas party had none of the opulence of an Abendruh banquet, but it was good enough. Nearly all the Americans left in Berlin were there, chatting over eggnogs and then assembling at three long tables for a meal of roast goose, pumpkin pie, fruit, cheese, and cakes, all from Denmark. Diplomatic import privileges made this possible, and the guests grew merry over the unaccustomed abundance. Victor Henry loved being back among American faces, American talk, offhand open manners, laughter from the diaphragm and not from the face muscles; not a bow or a clicked pair of heels, not a woman's European smile, gleaming on and off like an electric sign.

But trouble broke out with Rhoda. He heard her raising her voice at Fred Fearing, who was sucking his corncob pipe and glaring at her far down the table. Pug called, "Hey, what's it about, Fred?"

"The Wolf Stöllers, Pug, the loveliest people your wife has ever met."

"I said the nicest Germans," Rhoda shrilled, "and it's quite true. You're blindly prejudiced."

"It's time you went home, Rhoda," Fearing said.

"And just what does that mean?" she snapped back, still much too loud. At Abendruh Rhoda had loosened up on her count of drinks, and tonight she appeared to be further along than usual. Her gestures were getting broad, she was holding her eyes half-closed, and her voice tones were going up into her nose.

"Well, kid, if you think people like Wolf Stöller and his wife are nice, you'll believe next that Hitler just wants to reunite the German folk peacefully. About that time you need to go back for a while on American chow and the *New York Times*."

"I just know that Germans are not monsters with horns and tails," said Rhoda, "but ordinary people, however misguided. Or did one of your fräuleins show up in bed with cloven hoofs, dear?"

The crude jibe caused a silence. Fearing was an ugly fellow, tall, long-faced, curly-headed, with a narrow foxy nose; upright, idealistic, full of rigid liberal ideas, and severe on injustice and political hypocrisy. But he had his human side. He had seduced the wife of his collaborator on a best seller about the Spanish Civil War. This lady he had recently parked in England with an infant daughter, and he was now—so the talk ran—making passes at every available German woman, and even some American wives. Rhoda had once half-seriously told Pug that she had had trouble with Freddy on the dance floor. All the same, Fred Fearing was a famous, able reporter. Because he detested the Nazis, he tried hard to be fair to them, and the propaganda ministry understood this. Most Americans got their picture of Nazi Germany at war from Fearing's broadcasts.

Victor Henry said, as amiably as he could, to break the silence, "It might be easier to navigate in this country, Rhoda, if the bad ones would sprout horns or grow hair in their palms or something."

"What Wolf Stöller has in his palms is blood, lots of it," Fearing said, with a swift whiskeyed-up pugnacity. "He acts unaware of it. You and Rhoda encourage this slight color blindness, Pug, by acting the same way."

"It's Pug's job to socialize with people like Stöller," said the chargé mildly, from the head of the table. "I propose a moratorium tonight on discussing the Germans."

Colonel Forrest was rubbing his broken nose, a mannerism that signalled an itch to argue, though his moon face remained placid. He put in, nasally, "Say, Freddy, I happen to think Hitler just wants to reorganize central Europe as a German sphere, peacefully if he can, and that he'll call off the war if the Allies will agree. Think I should go home, too?"

Fearing emitted a column of blue smoke and red sparks from his pipe. "What about *Mein Kampf,* Bill?"

"Campaign document of a thirty-year-old hothead," snapped the military attaché, "written eighteen years ago in jail. Now he's the head of state. He's never moved beyond his strength. *Mein Kampf*'s all about tearing off the southern half of Russia and making a German bread-basket of it. That's an old Vienna coffeehouse fantasy. It went out of the window once and for all with the pact. The Jewish business is bad, but the man's doing his job with the crude tools at hand. That unfortunately includes anti-Semitism. He didn't invent it. It was big on the German scene before he was born."

"Yes, time for you to go home," said Fearing, gulping Moselle.

"Well, what's your version?" Now plainly irritated, the military attaché put on an imitation of the broadcaster's voice. "That Adolf Hitler the mad house painter is out to conquer the world?"

"Oh, hell, Hitler's revolution doesn't know where it's going, Bill, any more than the French or Russian revolutions did," exclaimed Fearing, with an exasperated wave of his corncob. "It's just raging along the way those did and it'll keep going and spreading till it's stopped. Sure he moves peacefully where he can. Why not? Everywhere he's pushed in there have been welcoming groups of leading citizens, or traitors, you might say. In Poland they swarmed. Why, you know that France and England have parties ready right this second to cooperate with him. He just has to strike hard enough in the west to knock out the ins and bring in the outs. He's already got Stalin cravenly feeding him all the Russian oil and wheat he needs, in return for the few bones he threw him in the Baltic."

With swinging theatrical gestures of the smoking pipe, Fearing went on, "By 1942, the way things are going, you may see a world in which Germany will control the industries of Europe, the raw materials of the Soviet Union, and the navies of England and France. Why, the French fleet would go over to him tomorrow if the right admiral sneezed. He'll have a working deal with the Japs

for exploiting Asia and the East Indies and ruling the
Pacific and Indian oceans. Then what? Not to mention the
network of dictatorships in South America, already in the
Nazis' pocket. You know, of course, Bill, that the United
States Army is now two hundred thousand strong, and that
Congress intends to cut it."

"Well, I'm against that, of course," said Colonel Forrest.

"I daresay! A new bloody dark age is threatening to
engulf the whole world and Congress wants to cut down
the Army!"

"An interesting vision," smiled the chargé. "Slightly
melodramatic."

Rhoda Henry raised her wineglass, giggling noisily.
"Lawks a mercy me! I never heard such wild-eyed poppy-
cock. Freddy, you're the one who should go home. Merry
Christmas."

Fred Fearing's face reddened. He looked up and down
the table. "Pug Henry, I like you. I guess I'll go for a
walk."

As the broadcaster strode away from the table, the
chargé rose and hurried after him, but did not bring him
back. The Henrys went home early. Pug had to hold up
Rhoda as they left, because she was half-asleep, and
unsteady at the knees.

The next pouch of Navy mail contained an Alnav listing
changes of duty for most of the new captains. They were
becoming execs of battleships, commanding officers of
cruisers, chiefs of staff to admirals at sea. For Victor
Henry there were no orders. He stared out of the window
at Hitler's chancellery, at the black-clad SS men letting
snow pile on their helmets and shoulders like statues.
Suddenly, he had had enough. He told his yeoman not to
disturb him, and wrote three letters. The first expressed
regret to the Stöllers that, due to unforeseen official problems, he and Rhoda would not be coming back to Abendruh. The second, two formal paragraphs to the Bureau of
Personnel, requested transfer to sea duty. In the third, a
long handwritten letter to Vice-Admiral Preble, Pug
poured out his disgust with his assignment and his desire
to go back to sea. He ended up:

I've trained twenty-five years for combat at sea. I'm miserable, Admiral, and maybe for that reason my wife is miserable. She's falling apart here in Berlin. It's a nightmarish place. This isn't the Navy's concern, but it's mine. If I have been of any service to the Navy in my entire career, the only recompense I now ask, and beg, is a transfer to sea duty.

A few days later another White House envelope came with a scrawl in black, thick, slanting pencil. The postmark showed that it had crossed his letter.

Pug—
Your report is really grand, and gives me a helpful picture. Hitler is a strange one, isn't he? Everybody's reaction is a little different. I'm delighted that you are where you are, and I have told CNO that. He says you want to return briefly in May for a wedding. That will be arranged. Be sure to drop in on me when you can spare a moment.

FDR

Victor Henry bought two of Rosenthal's Oriental carpets, and a set of English china that Rhoda particularly loved, at the prices the man named. His main motive was to cheer her up, and it worked; she gloated over the bargains for weeks, and never tired of saying, truly enough, that the poor Jewish man's thankfulness to her had been overwhelming. Pug also wrote the Stöllers about this time that, if the invitation held, he and Rhoda would come back to Abendruh after all. If his job was intelligence, he decided, he had better get on with it; moreover, the moral gap between him and Stöller seemed to have narrowed. Notwithstanding Rosenthal's pathetic gratitude for the deal, his possessions were *Objekte*.

23

Briny dear—

I can't think of a better way to start 1940 than by writing to you. I'm home, typing away in my old bedroom, which seems one-tenth as large as I remembered it. The whole house seems so cramped and cluttered, and God, how that smell of insecticide wipes away the years.

Oh, my love, what a marvellous place the United States is! I had forgotten, completely forgotten.

When I reached New York, my father was already out of the hospital—I learned this by phoning home—so I blew two hundred of my hard-earned dollars on a 1934 Dodge coupe, and I drove to Florida! I really did. Via Washington. I wanted to see the Capitol dome and the Monument. Yes, I wanted to see Slote too. More of that later, but let me assure you that he got little comfort out of the meeting. But so help me, Briny, I mainly wanted to get the feel of the country again. Well, in dead of winter, in lousy weather, and despite the tragic Negro shantytowns that line the roads down South, the Atlantic states are beautiful, spacious, raw, clean, full of wilderness still, exploding with energy and life. I loved every billboard, every filling station. It's really the *New World*. The Old World's mighty pretty in its rococo fashion, but it's rotten-ripe and going insane. Thank God I'm out of it.

Take Miami Beach. I've always loathed this place, you know. It's a measure of my present frame of mind that I regard even Miami Beach with affection. I left here a raging anti-Semite. It jars me even now to see these sleek Jews without a care in the world, ambling about in their heavy tans and outlandish sun clothes—often wearing furs, or pearls and diamonds, my dear, with pink or orange shirts and shorts. The Miami Beachers don't believe in hiding what they've got. I think of Warsaw, and I get angry, but it passes. They're no different, in their obliviousness to the war, from the rest of the Americans.

The doctors say my father's coming along fine after a heart attack that all but did him in. I don't like his fragile look, and he doesn't do much but sit in the sun in the garden and listen to the news on the radio. He's terribly worried about Uncle Aaron. He never used to speak much of him (actually he used to avoid the subject) but now he goes on and on about Aaron. My father is terrified of Hitler. He thinks he's a sort of devil who's going to conquer the world and murder all the Jews.

But I guess you're waiting to hear about my little chat with Leslie Slote—eh, darling?

Well—he was definitely *not* expecting the answer I brought back to his proposal! When I told him I'd fallen head over ears in love with you, it literally staggered him. I mean he tottered to a chair and fell in it, pale as a ghost. Poor old Slote! A conversation ensued that went on for hours, in a bar, in a restaurant, in my car, in half a dozen circuits on foot around the Lincoln Memorial in a freezing wind, and finally in his apartment. Lord, did he carry on! But after all, I had to give him his say.

The main heads of the dialogue went something like this, round and round and round:

SLOTE: It's just that you were isolated with him for so long.

ME: I told Briny that myself. I said it's a triumph of propinquity. That doesn't change the fact that I love him now.

SLOTE: You can't intend to marry him. It would be the greatest possible mistake. I say this as a friend, and somebody who knows you better than anyone else.

ME: I told Byron that too. I said it would be ridiculous for me to marry him, and gave him all the reasons.

SLOTE: Well, then, what on earth have you in mind?

ME: I'm just reporting a fact to you. I haven't anything in mind.

SLOTE: You had better snap out of it. You're an intellectual and a grown woman. Byron Henry is a pleasant light-headed loafer, who managed to avoid getting an education even in a school like Columbia. There can't be anything substantial between you.

ME: I don't want to hurt you, dear, but—*(this is the way I walked on eggs for a while, but in the end I came flat out with it)* the thing between Byron Henry and me is damned substantial. In fact by comparison, just now, nothing else seems very substantial. *(Slote plunged in horrid gloom.)*

SLOTE *(he only asked this once)*: Have you slept with him?

ME: None of your business. *(Jastrow not giving Slote any cards to play that she can help. Slote sunk even deeper in gloom.)*

SLOTE: Well, *"la coeur a ses raisons,"* and all that, but I truly don't understand. He's a boy. He's very good-looking, or rather, charming-looking, and he is certainly courageous. Perhaps that's assumed an outsize importance for you.

ME *(ducking that sore topic; who needs trouble?)*: He has other nice qualities. He's a gentleman. I never knew the animal really existed outside of books any more.

SLOTE: I'm not a gentleman, then?

ME: I'm not saying you're a boor or a cad. I mean a gentleman in the old sense, not somebody who avoids bad manners.

SLOTE: You're talking like a shopgirl. You're obviously rationalizing a temporary physical infatuation. That's all right. But the words you're choosing are corny and embarrassing.

ME: All that may be. Meantime I can't marry you. *(Yawn.)* And I *must* go to sleep now. I want to drive four hundred miles tomorrow. *(Exit Jastrow, at long last.)*

All things considered, he took it well. He calmly says we're getting married once I'm over this nuttiness, and he's going ahead with his plans for it. He's remarkably sure of himself, to that extent he remains very much the old Slote. Physically he's like a stranger now. I never kissed him, and though we spent an hour in his apartment, very late, he never laid a hand on me. I wonder if the talk about gentlemen had anything to do with it? He never used to be like that, I assure you. (I daresay I've changed too!)

Maybe he's right about me and you. I choose not to look beyond the present moment, or more truly beyond the moment when we stood by the fire in my bedroom and you took me in your arms. I'm still overwhelmed, I still love you, I still long for you. Separated though we are, I've never been so happy in all my life. If only you were here right this minute!

I said you see things too simply, but on one point you were just plain right. Aaron should leave that stupid house, let it fall down and rot, and come back to this wonderful land to live out his days. His move there was stupid. His remaining there is imbecilic. If you can convince him of it—and I'm writing him a letter too—I'd feel a lot better about your coming back. But don't just abandon him, sweetheart. Not yet. Wait till my plans jell a bit.

Happy New Year, and I hope to God that 1940 brings the end of Hitler and this whole grisly nightmare, and brings us together again.

I adore you.
Natalie

Three letters came straggling in during the next few weeks. The first two were shallow awkward scrawls:

I'm the world's worst letter writer. . . . I sure miss you more than I can say . . . things are pretty dull around here now without you . . . sure wish I could have been there with you in Lisbon. . . . Well, got to get back to work now . . .

She read Byron's embarrassing banalities over and over. Here on paper was just the young featherweight sloucher she had first seen, propped against a red Siena wall in the noon sun. Even his handwriting fitted the picture: slanting, undistinguished, the letters small and flattened. The pathetically flourishing *B* of his signature stood out of the mediocre penmanship. All of Byron's frustrated yearning to amount to something, to measure up to his father's hopes, was in that extravagant *B*. All his inconsequence was in the trailed-off, crushed ". . . *yron.*" Poor Briny!

Yet Natalie found herself dwelling on the artless empty scribblings as though they were letters of George Bernard Shaw. She kept them under her pillow. They contrasted most cruelly with her other preoccupation, for to pass the time she had hauled out her master's thesis, already three-quarters written in French: "Contrasts in the Sociologismic Critique of War: Durkheim's Writings on Germany, 1915–1916, and Tolstoy's Second Epilogue to *War and Peace,* 1869." She was giving thought to translating it, and enrolling in Columbia or NYU in the fall to finish it off and get her degree. It was a good thesis. Even Slote had read sections with approval, if now and again with a thin Oxonian smile. She wanted not only to finish, but to revise it. She had started with the anti-French, pro-German bias of most American university opinion between the wars. Her experiences in Poland had inclined her to agree much more with Durkheim about Germany. These things were as far beyond the writer of the letters under her pillow as the general theory of relativity. It would give Briny a headache just to read her title. But she didn't care. She was in love.

Popular songs were sweetly stabbing her: songs about women infatuated with worthless men, whining cowboy laments about absent sweethearts. It was as though she had developed a craving for penny candy. She was ashamed of gratifying her fancy, but she couldn't get enough of these songs. She bought records and played them over and over. If Byron Henry wrote stupid letters, too bad. All judgments fell away before her remembrance of his eyes and his mouth and his arms, her delight at contemplating a few ill-written sentences because they came from his hand.

A much better letter came along: the answer to her first long one from Miami Beach, several pages typed with Byron's odd offhand clarity. He somehow never struck a wrong key in his quick rattling, and his pages looked like a stenographer's work.

Natalie darling:

Well, that's more like it. A real letter. God, I waited a long time.

I skipped all that stuff about the USA and Miami, to get to the Slote business, but then I went back and read it all. Nobody has to tell me how good the United States is, compared to Europe. I'm so homesick at this point, I could die. This is quite aside from my yearning for you, which remains as strong as if you were in the room downstairs. I'm beginning to understand how iron filings must feel around a magnet.

Sometimes, sitting in my room thinking about you, the pull gets so strong, I have the feeling if I let go of the arms of my chair I'd float out of the window and across France and over the Atlantic, straight to your house at 1316 Normandie Drive.

Natalie was enchanted with this imaginative little conceit, and read it over and over.

Slote only thinks he's going to marry you. He had his chance.

By the way, I'm more than one-third through Slote's list of tomes about the Germans. Some of them aren't available in English, but I'm slogging along with what I can get. There's not much else to do here. The one reward of my isolation in this godforsaken town is the one-man seminar that A.J. is conducting with me. His view is more or less like Slote's, and I'm getting the picture. The Germans have been the comers in Europe ever since Napoleon, because of their geographical place, their numbers, and their energy, but they're a strange dark people. All of these writers Slote listed eventually come out with the pedantic destructiveness, the scary sureness that they're right, that the Germans have been gypped for centuries, that the world's got to be made over on their terms. What it boils down to so far for me is that Hitler is, after all, the soul of present-day Germany—which is self-evident when you're there; that the Germans can't be allowed to rule Europe because they have some kind of mass mental distortion, despite their brilliance, and can't even rule themselves; and that when they try for mastery, somebody's got to beat the living daylights out of them or you'll have barbarism triumphant. A.J. adds his own notion about the "good Germany" of progressive liberals and the "bad Germany" of Slote's romantics and nationalists, all tied in with geographical location and the Catholic religion, which sort of loses me. (Wonder if any of this will get past the censors? I bet it will. The Italians fear and loathe the Germans. There's a word that passes around here about Mussolini. They say he's the monkey that opened the tiger's cage. Pretty good.)

Getting A.J. out of here seems to be a bit of a project, after all.

There was a minor technical foul-up in his naturalization,

way, way back. I don't know the details, but he never bothered to correct it. The new consul general in Rome is a sort of prissy bureaucrat, and he's creating difficulties. All this will straighten out, of course—they've said as much in Rome—but it's taking time.

So I won't abandon A.J. now. But even if your plans aren't clear by mid-April, I must come home then and I will, whether A.J. does or not. Aside from my brother's wedding, my father's on fire to get me into submarine school, where the next officer course starts May 27. The course lasts six months, and then there's a year of training in subs operating around Connecticut. So even in the unlikely event that I do enroll—I'll only do it if the war breaks wide open—we could be together a lot.

Siena's gotten real dumpy. The hills are brown, the vines are cut to black stumps. The people creep around the streets looking depressed. The Palio's off for 1940. It's cold. It rains a lot. But in the lemon house, anyway, the trees are still blooming, and A.J. and I still have our coffee there. I smell the blossoms and I think of you. I often go in there just to take a few breaths, and I close my eyes and there you are, for a moment. Natalie, there has to be a God or I wouldn't have found you, and He has to be the same God for both of us. There's only one God.

I love you.
Briny

"Well, well," Natalie said aloud, as tears sprang from her eyes and dropped on the flimsy airmail paper. "You miserable chestnut-haired devil." She kissed the pages, smearing them orange-red. Then she looked at the date again: February 10, and this was April 9—almost two months for an airmail letter! There was no point in answering, at that rate. He might be on his way back now. But she seized a pad and began writing. She couldn't help it.

Natalie's father was listening to the radio in the garden. They had just eaten lunch and her mother had gone off to a committee meeting. As Natalie poured loving words on paper, a news broadcast came drifting in on the warm air through the open window. The announcer, with rich dramatic doom in his voice, spoke words that arrested her pen:

"*The 'phony war' has ended. A fierce air, sea, and land battle is raging for Norway. NBC brings special bulletins from the war capitals that tell the story.*

"London. *In a lightning attack, without warning or provocation, Nazi Germany has invaded neutral Norway by sea and air, and German land forces have rolled into Denmark. Fierce resistance is reported by the Norwegian government at Oslo, Narvik, Trondheim, and other key points along the coast, but German reinforcements are continuing to pour in. The Royal Navy is moving rapidly to cut off the invasion. Winston Churchill, First Lord of the Admiralty, declared this morning, 'All German vessels entering the Skagerrak will be sunk.'*"

Putting aside the pad and pen, Natalie went to the window. Her father, sitting with his back to her in blazing sunshine, his grizzled head in a white cap tilted far to one side, was listening with motionless intensity to this shattering development.

"Paris. *In an official communiqué, the French government announced that the Allies would rally to the cause of democratic Norway, and would meet the German onslaught quote with cold steel unquote. Pessimistic commentators pointed out that the fall of Norway and Denmark would put more than a thousand additional miles of European coastline in German hands and that this would mean the collapse of the British blockade.*

"Berlin. *The propaganda ministry has issued the following bulletin. Forestalling a British plan to seize Scandinavia and deny Germany access to Swedish iron ore and other raw materials, the German armed forces have peaceably taken Denmark under their protection and have arrived in Norway by sea and air, where the populace has enthusiastically welcomed them. Oslo is already in German hands, and the life of the capital is returning to normal. Scattered resistance by small British-bribed units has been crushed. The Führer has sent the following message of congratulation to . . ."*

Natalie came out into the garden to talk to her father about the shocking news, and was surprised to find him sleeping through it, his head dropped on his chest. The radio was blaring; and her father usually hung on the news broadcasts. The shadow from his white linen cap obscured his face, but she could see a queer expression around his mouth. His upper teeth were protruding ludicrously over his lip. Natalie came to him, and touched his shoulder. "Pa?" He did not respond. He felt inert. She could see now that his upper plate had worked loose. *"Pa!"* As she shook him his head lolled and the cap fell off. She thrust her hand inside his loose flowered sport shirt; there was no heartbeat under the warm clammy skin. In the instant before she shrieked and ran inside to telephone the doctor, she saw on her dead father's face a strong resemblance to Aaron Jastrow that in his lifetime she had never observed.

She walked through the next weeks in a fog of shocked grief. Natalie had stopped taking her father seriously at about the age of twelve; he was just a businessman, a sweater manufacturer, a temple president, and she was then already a brash intellectual snob. Since then she had become more and more aware of how her father's sense of inferiority to Aaron Jastrow, and to his own daughter, permeated his life. Yet she was prostrated when he died. She could not eat. Even with drugs she could not sleep. Her mother, a conventional woman usually preoccupied with Hadassah meetings and charity fund-raising, for many years completely baffled by her daughter, pulled out of her own grief and tried in vain to comfort her. Natalie lay in her room on her bed, wailing and bawling, almost constantly at first, and in spells every day for weeks afterward. She suffered agonies of guilt for neglecting and despising her father. He had loved her and spoiled her. When she had told him she wanted to go to the Sorbonne for two years, that had been that. She had never even asked whether he could afford it. She had felled him with her bizarre misadventures and had experienced no remorse while he was alive. Now he was gone, and she was on her own, and it was too late. He was unreachable by love or regret.

The radio news—disaster on disaster in Norway, German drives succeeding, Allied landings failing, the remnants of the Norwegian army retreating into the mountains where the Germans were hunting them down—came to her as dim distant rumors. Reality was only her wet pillow, and the stream of middle-aged sunburned Jews paying condolence calls, and all the endless talk about money problems.

She was shocked back into her senses by two events, one on top of the other: Byron's return from Europe, and the German attack on France.

*　　*　　*

24
Case Yellow

(from WORLD EMPIRE LOST)

The Great Assault

Modern war is characterized by sudden swift changes on the grand scale. In the spring of 1940, seven days sufficed for our German armed forces to upset the world order. On May 10, the English and French were still the victors of Versailles, still masters of the seas and continents. By May 17 France was a beaten, almost helpless nation, and England was hanging on for her life.

On paper, the odds had been heavy against *Fall Gelb* ("Case Yellow"), our plan for attacking France. The figures of the opposing forces had certainly comforted the enemy and disturbed us. But put to the test, Case Yellow (revised) brought a big victory. Our soldiers man for man proved superior to the best the democracies had. Our High Command used well the lessons of massed armor and gasoline-engine mobility learned in the defeat of World War I at the hands of British tank battalions. The Anglo-French world hegemony stood unmasked as a mere historical husk. It still commanded the seas and the access to raw materials; its resources for a long war were superior to ours; but without the will to use them these advantages were meaningless. Persia had greater resources than Alexander the Great.

In judging Hitler, historians must recognize that he sensed this weakness of the other side, and that we of the General Staff erred. We assumed that our professional opponents were preparing with due urgency to wage war. But in fact their countrymen would not face realities, and their politicians would not tell the people unpleasant truths. Adolf Hitler gambled the future of Germany, and therefore of Europe, and therefore of the existing world order, on one heavy armed thrust. It succeeded beyond anybody's expectation, including his own.

Besides ordering the attack over the pessimistic objections of our staff, Hitler also, almost at the last minute, adopted the bold Manstein Plan for an armored strike in force through the bad Ardennes terrain, to turn the left flank of the Maginot Line. This departure from the classic Schlieffen Plan achieved total surprise, and led to Rundstedt's magnificent race across northern France to the sea. It split the Allies, sent the British fleeing across the Channel in an improvised flotilla of pleasure yachts, coal scows, and fishing boats, and ended the shaky French will to fight. Thereafter we marched south to Paris against fast-crumbling resistance. And so Germany achieved in a few weeks, under a former corporal, what it had failed to do in four years of desperate combat under Kaiser Wilhelm II.

The technical key to our victory in France was simply that we massed our armor into whole spearhead divisions, like iron cavalry, thus restoring speed and movement to the battle-fields of the industrial age, supposedly paralyzed forever into trench warfare by the strength and range of mechanical firepower. We learned this from the works of the English tactician Fuller and the French tactician de Gaulle, analyzing the lessons of World War I.

The French army, with armored strength superior to our own, ignored these Allied thinkers, and scattered thousands of tanks piecemeal among the infantry divisions. This question of how to use the new self-propelled armor had been much disputed between the wars. We took the right path of Fuller, de Gaulle, and our own Guderian. Our opponents took the wrong one. The coordination of dive-bombing with these new ground tactics hastened the victory.

The Maginot Line

The world was stunned. For months Western newspapers and magazines had been printing maps of Europe, showing imaginary battle lines for the coming campaign. The French commander-in-chief, Generalissimo Maurice Gamelin, "the world's foremost professional soldier," as the Western journalists called him, was supposed to have a masterly plan to beat us.

In modern war, according to this rumored "Gamelin Plan," industrial firepower gave the defense an advantage over the offense of ten or fifteen to one. France had spent one and a half million soldiers' lives in World War I proving that the massed infantry attacks of Napoleon no longer worked against machine guns and cannon. There would be no more Verduns. The new concept was to build in peacetime a great wall of linked fortresses with the strongest modern firepower. No matter how many millions of men a future enemy might hurl against this wall, they would all drown in their own blood.

On this theory, France had constructed a chain of fortresses united by underground tunnels, the Maginot Line. If we Germans did not attack, then between the land wall of the Maginot Line and the British sea blockade, the economic life would be choked out of us. Finally the Allied armies would sally forth from the Line to deliver the coup de grâce, if revolution did not topple Hitler first, and bring our generals crawling for peace terms, as we had in 1918. So ran the newspaper talk in the West during the sitzkrieg.

Informed military men had a question or two about this Maginot Line. It was indeed a marvel of engineering, but was it not too short? Beginning at the Swiss Alps, it ran along the French-German border for more than a hundred miles to a place called Longuyon. There it stopped. Between Longuyon and the English Channel, there still remained a hole of open level country, the boundary between France and Belgium, at least as long as the Line itself. In 1914, we bestial Germans had attacked through Belgium precisely because this hole offered such a flat fine road to Paris. Couldn't we just go around the famous Maginot Line and come down by that route again?

The proponents of the Gamelin Plan met such questions with ironic smiles. Yes, to run the Line straight through Belgium to the sea would have been very fine, they said. But that was up to the Belgians, who insisted on preserving their neutrality instead. As for completing the Line in French territory, it would have had to cut through a hundred thirty miles of important industrial areas. Moreover, at the time when it might have been done, a mood of economy had come over the government. The people wanted shorter hours and higher pay. The cost would have been astronomical. Also subsurface water in the area made a tunnel system difficult. Also, by then Hitler was in power, and extending the Line might have provoked the bellicose Führer to do something rash.

In short, the wisest military brains in France had decided not to finish the Maginot Line. Instead, there was the Gamelin Plan. If war came, the French and British armies would be poised along the unfortified Belgian border. If the Germans did try to come through there again, the Allies under Gamelin would leap forward and join the tough Belgian army of two hundred thousand men on a strong river line. Given the enormous advantage of the defense in modern warfare, a German attack on such a narrow front would bloodily collapse.

Outcome of the Plan

We did attack, though not exactly where the Plan called for us to do so. Five days later, Generalissimo Gamelin was fired. We were pouring around the north end of the Maginot Line through the supposedly "impassable" Ardennes country, and flooding westward across France. Thus we cut off the French and British armies which, following the Gamelin Plan, had duly leaped forward into Belgium. Our Eighteenth Army under Küchler was also coming at them from Holland to the north. They were trapped. On the morning of May 15, the Prime Minister of France telephoned his defense minister to ask what countermeasures Gamelin was proposing. The minister answered, according to history, "He has none."

At an urgent conference in Paris next day at the Quai d'Orsay, Winston Churchill, who had desperately flown over from London, asked Generalissimo Gamelin, "General, where is the reserve—the *masse de manoeuvre*—to bring up against the German breakthrough?"

The world's foremost professional soldier replied, according to Churchill's memoirs, "*Aucune.*" (There isn't any.)

General Weygand relieved him. We took the Maginot Line from behind with no trouble, since the guns pointed the other way; marched off to captivity the French armies found sitting inside the forts and tunnels; transferred all the cannon to the

English Channel for use against the British; took all the stored food and equipment in the labyrinth; and left a few light bulbs to illuminate the empty concrete passageways. So the Maginot Line remains to this day.

The French passed from the stage of historical greatness. Germany's implacable enemy of the centuries had at last come to grief. Strategically, they had guessed wrong on the use of industrial power in war, and had wasted their national energy and treasure on an enormous tragic joke in steel and concrete: half a wall. Tactically, when General Gamelin said, "*Aucune,*" the military history of France was over.

Shadows on the Victory

In the headquarters of the Supreme Command, the victory over France, while welcome and exhilarating, had its worrisome aspects. Some of us who were present at the signing of the armistice watched with heavy hearts as the Führer danced his little jig of triumph in the sunshine of Compiègne. We were torn between pride in this feat of German arms, this virile reversal of the 1918 defeat, and our inside knowledge of tragic errors the capering Dictator had made or tried to make. These were completely covered up for the world at large by the rosy glow of success. Germany in that hour was like a virgin at a military ball, all radiant with the blushes aroused in her by the admiring eyes of handsome officers, and all unaware of a fatal cancer budding inside her.

The cancer already afflicting Germany at that hour, unfelt by all but a handful in the innermost circle of command, was amateur military leadership. We had watched the symptoms crop up in the minor Norway operation. Our hope was that our inexperienced warlord, having been blooded in that victory, would steady down for the great assault in the west.

But, six days after the breakthrough, when Rundstedt was rolling to the sea, with Guderian's panzers in the van and all enemy forces in flight, Hitler had a bad fit of nerves, fearing a French counterattack from the south—no more likely at that moment than a Hottentot counterattack—and halted Rundstedt's army group for two precious days. Fortunately Guderian wangled permission for a "reconnaissance in force" westward. Thereupon he simply ignored the Führer and blitzed ahead to the coast.

Then followed an incredible tactical blunder. With the British expeditionary force helplessly retreating toward the sea, but far behind in the race and about to be cut off by Guderian's massed tanks, the Führer halted Guderian on the River Aa, *nine miles from Dunkirk, and forbade the tank divisions to advance for three days!* To this day nobody has factually ascertained why he did this. Theories are almost as abundant as military historians, but they add little to the facts. During these three days the British rescued their armies from the Dunkirk beaches. That is the long and short of the "miracle of Dunkirk."

Had Hitler not halted Guderian, the panzers would have beaten the foe to Dunkirk and cut him off. The British would have lost over three hundred thousand men and officers, the bulk of their trained land force, in the Flanders cauldron. I discuss in detail, under my section "Fantastic Halt at the River Aa," the preposterousness of the excuse that the terrain around Dunkirk was too marshy, and too crisscrossed by hedges and canals, for tank operations. The fact is that finally Guderian did advance, after seventy-two mortal hours in which the first golden chance for quick victory in World War II slipped from our grasp. Hermann Göring's Luftwaffe was supposed to take over from the halted armored divisions and finish off the British. Perhaps Hitler relished this notion of letting a Nazi air marshal in at the kill, instead of the distrusted Army General Staff. History records what Göring accomplished.

But if final victory was denied us, at least we had vanquished France; that much seemed indisputable. Yet on June 6 even this was momentarily cast in doubt when Hitler had another brainstorm. Paris, he suddenly declared, was not the objective; what our armies should do next was cut southeast in force and capture the Lorraine basin, so as to deny France its coal and armaments industries! Fortunately the momentum of operations was beyond even the Führer's power to meddle. We took Paris even while a number of divisions went wheeling needlessly into Lorraine.

His Worst Mistake

But worse than all these mistakes—so bad that history will forever stand amazed at the fact—the Wehrmacht arrived at the English Channel without any plan of what to do next! There we were at the sea, millions strong, armed to the teeth, flushed with victory, facing a beaten, disarmed, impotent enemy across a ditch forty miles wide; but our infallible Leader, who had all staff activities so firmly in his grip that nobody could make a move without his nod, had somehow overlooked the slight detail of how one got to England.

Here nevertheless was a moment for greatness, such as comes once in a thousand years. Alexander, Caesar, and Napoleon in their time had made mistakes as major as any of Hitler's. What they possessed to balance and outweigh these was *generalship:* the ability to divine and seize a favoring moment with the utmost speed and audacity. Yes, we had no plan for invading England, but had the British had a plan for crossing the Channel from Dunkirk in a scraped-together flotilla of cockleshells? Under the spur of necessity, despite the total disorganization of defeat, despite fierce Luftwaffe bombardment, they had moved three hundred thousand men across the water. Why then could not we, the strongest armed force on earth in the full tide of victory, do a "Dunkirk in reverse," and throw a force of armored divisions across the Channel to an undefended, helpless shore? There was nothing on the ground in England to oppose our march to London. The rescued expeditionary force was a disarmed rabble; all its equipment lay abandoned in Flanders. The Home Guard was a pathetic raggle-taggle of old men and boys.

Opposing our invasion would have been the Royal Air Force and the British fleet, two formidable fighting organizations. But had Hitler seized the first moment in June, using every available vessel afloat in western and northern Europe —there were thousands—to hurl an invasion body across the Channel, the fleet would have been caught by surprise, as it had been in the Norway operation. We would have been across before it could mass to counterattack. The aerial Battle of Britain would have been fought out in the skies over the Channel, under conditions vastly more favorable to the Luftwaffe.

Assuredly we would have taken heavy losses. The attack phase and the supply problem would have cost dearly. Again we would have been staking all on one throw. But in the hindsight of history, what else was there to do? I have several times requested in writing, from American and German archivists, a copy of a draft memorandum I wrote in June 1940, outlining for headquarters discussion a plan for exactly such an immediate cross-Channel assault. My requests have gone unanswered. The memorandum is only a curiosity, and I have no way of knowing whether it has actually survived. At the time Jodl returned it to me without a single word, and that was the end of it.

The Aborted Invasion

Seelöwe (Sea Lion), the invasion scheme scrambled together in the ensuing months, proved an exercise in leisurely futility. Forcing the Channel, once the British had caught their breath and fortified their coast, needed a complex buildup. Hitler never really pushed it. Against England he had lacked the greatness to dare all; and we gradually saw that he lacked the stomach to dare much. He merely allowed Göring to waste his Luftwaffe over the British aerodromes far inland, while the army and the navy frittered away weeks that stretched through the summer, disputing over the operation plan, and passing the buck back and forth. In the end, "Sea Lion" was abandoned. Germany certainly had the industrial plant and the military strength to mount the invasion, but not the leadership. When an ounce more of boldness in battle might have won a world, Hitler faltered; and the professional generals were all in impotent subjection to this amateur.

That was the real "triumph" of the *Führerprinzip* in the summer of 1940. In retrospect, the wrong leader danced the jig.

TRANSLATOR'S NOTE: *Roon's biting discussion of the Maginot Line and the French leadership leaves little more to be said.*

My friends in the Royal Navy stoutly deny that even in June the Germans could have made it across the Channel. They would have thrown in every last ship they had, of course, to drown the invaders. It is a moot point, but in my judgment Roon makes out a fair case. The U-boats, which he does not mention, would have wreaked havoc in the narrow Channel against a defensively positioned fleet. Roon is on weaker ground in blaming Hitler for the lack of staff plans for an invasion. Had they had a feasible one ready, he might have activated it, as he did the Manstein Plan. Apparently, there was in the files a sketchy naval staff study, and nothing more. The German General Staff in World War II had a strange tendency not to see beyond the next hill, or maybe they preferred not to look.—V.H.

*   *   *

25

BIG GERMAN BREAKTHROUGH IN BELGIUM!
Still Not Our Fight, Declares Lacouture

PASSING a newsstand on the corner of Fifth Avenue and Fifty-seventh Street, where a fresh stack of afternoon papers fluttered under a cobblestone, Janice Lacouture said to Madeline, "Oh gawd, there's Daddy again, sounding off. Won't your folks be impressed!" Madeline was helping her shop for her trousseau. Rhoda, Pug, and Byron were due at three o'clock in the Brooklyn Navy Yard, aboard the cruiser *Helena*. Janice's first encounter with Warren's mother was much on her mind, far more so than the bad war news.

A rough May wind swooped along the avenue, whipping the girls' skirts and hats. Madeline clutched a package with one hand and her hat with the other, peering at the two-column photograph of Congressman Isaac Lacouture on the Capitol steps, with three microphones thrust in his face. "He's handsome, you know," she said.

"I hope you'll like him. He's really an awfully smart man," Janice said, pitching her voice above the wind. "Actually the reporters have pushed him further than he ever intended to go. Now he's way out on a limb."

Madeline had redecorated the little flat. The walls were pale green, with cream-and-green flowered draperies. New Danish teak furniture, austere and slight, made the place seem roomier. Jonquils and irises in a bowl on the dining table touched the place with spring and youth, much as the two girls did when they walked in. It was not a flat where one expected to find a Communist boyfriend. Indeed

387

Madeline had long since discarded the poor popeyed trombone player in brown—something Janice had been relieved to learn. Her current boyfriend was a CBS lawyer, a staunch Roosevelt man and very bright, but going bald at twenty-six.

She called her telephone answering service, briskly jotted notes on a pad, and slammed the receiver down. "Rats. I can't go with you to meet my folks, Janice, after all. Isn't that a pain? Two of the amateurs have loused out. I have to spend the afternoon listening to replacements. Always something!" She was clearly quite pleased with herself at being kept so busy. "Now. Do you happen to know a man named Palmer Kirby? He's at the Waldorf and he says he's a friend of the family." Janice shook her head.

Madeline rang him and liked his voice with his first words; it had a warm humorous resonance. "You are Rhoda Henry's daughter? I saw your name in the book and took a chance."

"Yes, I am."

"Good. Your family was very hospitable to me in Berlin. Your mother wrote me they'd be arriving today. I just thought they might be tired and at a loose end, their first evening in New York. I'd like to take all of you to dinner."

"That's kind of you, but I don't know their plans. They won't arrive till one or so."

"I see. Well, suppose I make the dinner reservations? If your folks can come, I'll expect you all in my suite at six or so. If not, just give me a ring, or your mother can."

"I guess so, sure. Thank you. Warren's fiancée is visiting me, Mr. Kirby."

"Ike Lacouture's daughter? Excellent. By all means bring her."

Off Madeline went, brimming with zest for existence, while Janice changed into warmer clothes for the Navy Yard.

Madeline was now the "program coordinator" of *The Walter Field Amateur Hour*. Walter Field, an old ham actor, had stumbled into great radio popularity with the hackneyed vaudeville formula of amateur entertainment.

Suddenly made rich, he had gone into a whirl of big real estate deals, and just as suddenly dropped dead. Hugh Cleveland had stepped in as master of ceremonies. Madeline still fetched chicken sandwiches and coffee for him, but she now also interviewed the amateurs. She remained Cleveland's assistant for his morning show, and she was making more money than ever. For Madeline Henry, May 1940 was as jolly a month as she had ever lived.

In the Brooklyn Navy Yard the wind was stronger and colder. The cruiser was already tied up at the pier, fluttering a rainbow of signal flags strung down from the mast to stem and stern. Amid a swarm of waving, shouting relatives on the pier, war refugees were streaming off the gangway. Janice found her way to the customs shed, where Rhoda stood by a heap of luggage, blowing her nose. The tall young blonde in a green wool suit and toque caught Rhoda's eye.

"Well, isn't this Janice? I'm Rhoda Henry," she said, stepping forward. "The snapshots didn't do you justice at ALL."

"Oh, yes, Mrs. Henry! Hello!" Rhoda's willowy figure, modish straw hat, and fuchsia gloves and shoes surprised Janice. Warren's father had struck Janice, during their brief meeting in Pensacola, as a coarse-grained weather-beaten man. By contrast Mrs. Henry seemed youthful, elegant, even sexy. This was true despite the woman's reddened nose and frequent sneezing.

"Aren't you CLEVER to wear that suit. I dressed for spring and it's positively ARCTIC here," Rhoda said. "Where's Madeline? Is she all right?"

Quickly Janice explained why the daughter hadn't come.

"Well! Hasn't Mad turned into the little career girl! My dear, I want to kiss you, but I daren't. Don't come near me. I'm virulent! I've got the cold of the ages. They should quarantine me. I'll infect the nation. Well! How beautiful you are. You're ravishing. Lucky Warren! How is he, anyway?"

"All right, I hope. He's sweating out carrier landings, down off Puerto Rico somewhere."

Victor Henry, looking more impressive than Janice remembered in a gold-buttoned blue bridge coat and gold-encrusted cap, came through the crowd with a surly-looking customs inspector. After a brusque greeting to Janice and an inquiry about Madeline, he wanted to know where Byron had gotten off to.

"Briny disappeared. He had to make a phone call," the mother said.

As the inspector glanced through the luggage, Janice told the Henrys about Palmer Kirby's invitation. Between sneezes, Rhoda said, "Well, of all things. His factory's in Denver. What's he doing here? I don't think we can go, can we, Pug? Of course dinner at the Waldorf would be a lovely way to start life in the USA again. Take the taste of Berlin out of our mouths! Janice, you just can't picture what Germany is like now. It's gruesome. I'm cured. When I saw the Statue of Liberty I laughed and cried. Me for the USA hereafter, now and forever."

"Matter of fact, I have to talk to Fred Kirby," Pug said.

"Oh, Pug, it's impossible, I have this filthy cold—and my HAIR!" Rhoda said. "What could I wear to the Waldorf, anyhow? Everything's a mass of wrinkles, except what I'm standing up in. If I could only get my pink suit pressed—and if I could get to a hairdresser for a couple of hours—"

Byron came sauntering through the noisy crowd. "Hey, Janice! I'm Warren's brother. I thought you'd be here." He produced from his pocket a small box with a London label, and gave it to her.

Janice opened it, and there lay a Victorian pin, a little golden elephant with red stones for eyes. "Good heavens!"

"Anybody who marries one of us needs the patience of an elephant," said Byron.

"Ye gods, if that's not the truth," said Rhoda, laughing.

Janice gave Byron a slow female blink. He was even handsomer than Warren, she thought. His eyes had an eager aroused sparkle. She kissed him.

.   .   .

"*. . . I have nothing to offer,*" said the grainy strong singsong voice out of the radio, slurring the consonants almost like a drunken man, "*but blood, toil, tears, and sweat.*"

"Why, he's a genius!" Rhoda exclaimed. She sat on the edge of a frail gilt chair in Kirby's suite, champagne glass in hand, tears in her eyes. "Where has he been till now?"

Smearing caviar from a blue Russian-printed tin on a bit of toast, and carefully sprinkling onion shreds, Byron said, "He was running the British Navy when Prien got into Scapa Flow and sank the *Royal Oak*. And when the Germans crossed the Skagerrak to Norway."

"Shut up and listen," Victor Henry said.

Janice glanced from the son to the father, crossed her long legs, and sipped champagne. Palmer Kirby's eyes flickered appreciatively at her legs, which pleased her. He was an interesting-looking old dog.

"*. . . You ask, what is our policy? I will say, it is to wage war, by sea, land, and air, with all our might and all the strength that God can give us: to wage war against a monstrous tyranny, never surpassed in the dark, lamentable catalogue of human crime. That is our policy. You ask, what is our aim? I can answer in one word: Victory —victory at all costs, victory in spite of all terror . . . I take up my task with buoyancy and hope. I feel sure that our cause will not be suffered to fail among men . . .*"

The speech ended. An American voice said with a cough and tremor, "*You have just heard the newly appointed Prime Minister of Great Britain, Winston Churchill.*"

After a moment, Rhoda said, "That man will save civilization. We're going to get in now. The Germans overplayed their hand. We'll never let them conquer England. There's something strangely thick about the Germans, you know? One must observe them close up for a long time to understand that. Strangely thick."

Victor Henry said to Dr. Kirby, glancing at his watch, "Quite a speech. Can we talk now for a few minutes?"

Kirby got to his feet and Rhoda smiled at him. "Champagne, caviar, and business as usual. That's Pug."

"We're just waiting for Madeline," Pug said.

"Come along," Kirby said, walking into the bedroom.

"Say, Dad, I'm going to have to mosey along," Byron said. "There's this plane to Miami I have to catch. It leaves La Guardia in about an hour."

"What! Dr. Kirby thinks you're dining with him."

"Well, see, I made the reservation before I knew about this dinner."

"You're not waiting till Madeline comes? You haven't seen her in two years. She's taking us all to her show after dinner."

"I think I'd better go, Dad."

Abruptly, Pug left the room.

"Briny, you're impossible," his mother said. "Couldn't you have waited until tomorrow?"

"Mom, do you remember what it's like to be in love?"

Rhoda surprised him and Janice Lacouture by turning blood red. "Me? My goodness, Byron, what a thing to say! Of course not, I'm a million years old."

"Thank you for my marvellous pin." Janice touched the elephant on her shoulder. "That must be some girl, in Miami."

Byron's blank narrow-eyed look dissolved in a charming smile and an admiring glance at her. "She's all right."

"Bring her to the wedding with you. Don't forget."

As Byron went to the door, Rhoda said, "You have a real talent for disappointing your father."

"He'd be disappointed if I didn't disappoint him. Good-bye, Mom."

In the bedroom Dr. Kirby sat at a desk, checking off a stack of journals and mimeographed reports that Victor Henry had brought him from Germany. As he scribbled in a yellow notebook, the little desk shook and two reports slid to the floor. "They must rent this suite to midgets," he said, continuing to write.

Victor Henry said, "Fred, are you working on a uranium bomb?"

Kirby's hand paused. He turned, hanging one long loose arm over the back of his chair, and looked into Henry's eyes. The silence and the steady look between the men lasted a long time.

"You can just tell me it's none of my goddamn business, but"—Pug sat on the bed—"all that stuff there zeroes in on the uranium business. And some of the things I couldn't get, like the graphite figures, why, the Germans told me flatly that they were classified because of the secret bomb aspects. The Germans are fond of talking very loosely about this terrible ultra-bomb they're developing. That made me think there was nothing much to it. But that list of requests you sent gave me second thoughts."

Kirby knocked out his pipe, stuffed it, and lit it. The process took a couple of minutes, during which he didn't talk, but looked at Captain Henry. He said slowly, "I'm not a chemist, and this uranium thing is more or less a chemical engineering problem. Electricity does come into it for production techniques. A couple of months ago I was approached to be an industrial consultant."

"What's the status of the thing?"

"All theory. Years away from any serious effort."

"Do you mind telling me about it?"

"Why not? It's in the college physics books. Hell, it's been in *Time* magazine. There's this process, neutron bombardment. You expose one chemical substance and another to the emanations of radium, and see what happens. It's been going on for years, in Europe and here. Well, these two Germans tried it on uranium oxide last year, and they produced barium. Now that's transmutation of elements by atom-splitting. I guess you know about the fantastic charge of energy packed in the mass of the atom. You've heard about driving a steamship across the ocean on one lump of coal, if you could only harness the atomic energy in it, and so forth." Victor Henry nodded. "Well, Pug, this was a hint that it might really be done with uranium. It was an atom-splitting process that put out far more energy than they'd used to cause it. These Germans discovered *that* by weighing the masses involved. There'd been an appreciable loss of mass. They published their finding, and the whole scientific community's been in an uproar ever since.

"Okay, the next step is, there's this rare hot isotope of uranium, U-235. This substance may turn out to have gigantic explosive powers, through a chain reaction that gives you a huge release of energy from mass. A handful maybe can blow up a city, that sort of talk. The nuclear boys say it may be practicable right now, if industry will just come up with enough pure U-235."

Pug listened to all this with his mouth compressed, his

body tensed forward. "Uh-huh, uh-huh," he kept saying when Kirby puffed on his pipe. He pointed a stiff finger at the engineer. "Well, I follow all that. This is vital military intelligence."

Kirby shook his head. "Hardly. It's public knowledge. It may be a complete false alarm. These chemical engineers don't guarantee anything. And what they want will take one hell of a big industrial effort to deliver. Maybe the stuff will explode, maybe it won't. Maybe as soon as you have enough of it, it'll all fly apart. Nobody knows. Five minutes of scratch pad work shows that you're talking about an expenditure of many many millions of dollars. It could run up to a billion and then you could end up with a crock of horseshit. Congress is on an economy rampage. They've been refusing Roosevelt the money for a couple of hundred new airplanes."

"I'll ask you a couple of more questions. If I'm off base, tell me."

"Shoot."

"Where do you come into it?"

Kirby rubbed his pipe against his chin. "Okay, how do you separate out isotopes of a very rare metal in industrial quantities? One notion is to shoot it in the form of an ionized gas through a magnetic field. The lighter ions get deflected a tiny bit more, so you stream 'em out and catch them. The whole game depends on the magnetic field being kept stable, because any wavering jumbles up the ion stream. Precise control of voltages is my business."

"Uh-huh. Now. One last point. If an occasion arises, should I volunteer my valued opinion to the President that he should get off his ass about uranium?"

Kirby uttered a short baritone laugh. "The real question here is the Germans. How far along are they? This cuteness of theirs about pure graphite disturbs me. Graphite comes into the picture at a late stage. If Hitler gets uranium bombs first, Pug, and if they happen to work, that could prove disagreeable."

A doorbell rang.

"I guess that's your daughter," Kirby said. "Let's go down to dinner."

* * * *

Madeline arrived in a black tailored suit with a flaring jacket and a tight sheath skirt, dark hair swept up on her head. It was hard to think of her as only twenty. Possibly she was putting on the young career woman a bit, but she did have to leave the table in the Empire Room twice, when the headwaiter came and said with a bow that CBS was on the telephone. Victor Henry liked her confident, demure manner and her taciturnity. With alert eyes darting from face to face, she listened to the talk about Germany and about the wedding plans, and said almost nothing.

In the studio building, at the reception desk, a stiff, uniformed youngster awaited them. "Miss Henry's party? This way, please." He took them to a barren low-ceilinged green room where Hugh Cleveland and his staff sat around a table. Briskly cordial, Cleveland invited them to stay in the room till the show started. He was looking at cards, memorizing spontaneous jokes he would make later, and discussing them with his gagman. After a while he snapped a rubber band around the cards and slipped them in his pocket. "Well, five minutes to go," he said, turning to the visitors. "I hear this fellow Churchill gave a pretty good speech. Did you catch it?"

"Every word," Rhoda said. "It was shattering. That speech will go down in history."

"Quite a speech," Pug said.

Madeline said, "Darn, and I was so busy I missed it."

The show's producer, who looked forty-five and dressed like a college boy, put a manicured hand to the back of his head. "It was fair. It needed cutting and punching up. Too much tutti-frutti. There was one good line about blood and sweat."

"There was? How would that go with the butcher who plays the zither?" Cleveland said to the joke writer at his elbow, a melancholy young Jew who needed a haircut. "Could we throw in something about blood and sweat?"

The joke writer sadly shook his head. "Bad taste."

"Don't be silly, Herbie. Try to think of something. Captain Henry, how's the war going? Will the Gamelin Plan stop the Krauts?"

"I don't know what the Gamelin Plan is."

Madeline put her guests in privileged seats on the stage of the studio, near the table where Cleveland interviewed the amateurs before a huge cardboard display extolling Morning Smile pink laxative salts. She posted herself in the glassed control booth. A large audience, which to Victor Henry seemed composed entirely of imbeciles, applauded the stumbling amateurs and roared at Cleveland's jokes.

Cleveland ran the program with smooth foxy charm; Pug realized now that Madeline had latched herself to a comer. But the show disgusted him. One amateur identified himself as a line repairman. Cleveland remarked, "Well, haw haw, guess they could use you in France right about now."

"France, Mr. Cleveland?"

"Sure. On that Maginot Line."

He winked at the audience; they guffawed and clapped.

"Does this amuse you?" Pug said across Rhoda, in a low tone, to Palmer Kirby.

"I never listen to the radio," said the engineer. "It's interesting. Like a visit to a madhouse."

"That Cleveland's cute, though," Rhoda said.

Madeline came to them after the show, as the audience swarmed on stage around Hugh Cleveland seeking his autograph. "Damn, two of our best bits got cut off the air by news bulletins. They're so high-handed, those news people!"

"What's happening?" Victor Henry asked.

"Oh, it's the war, naturally. Just more of the same. The Germans have overrun some new town, and the French are collapsing, and so on. Nothing very unexpected. Hugh will have a fit when he hears they cut the butcher with the zither."

"Miss Henry?" A uniformed page approached her.

"Yes?"

"Urgent long-distance call, miss, in Mr. Cleveland's office, for Miss Lacouture. From Puerto Rico."

.   .   .

On the flying bridge of the fishing boat *Blue Bird*, rocking gently along at four knots in the Gulf Stream, Byron and Natalie lay in each other's arms in the sun. Below, the jowly sunburned skipper yawned at the wheel over a can of beer, and the ship-to-shore telephone dimly crackled and gabbled. From long poles fixed in sockets at the empty fighting chairs, lines trailed in the water. Sunburned, all but naked in swimming suits, the lovers had forgotten the fish, the lines, and the skipper. They had forgotten death and they had forgotten war. They lay at the center of a circle of dark blue calm water and light blue clear sky. It seemed the sun shone on them alone.

The deck echoed with loud rapping from below, four quick knocks like a Morse code *V*. "Hey, Mr. Henry! You awake?"

"Sure, what is it?" Byron called hoarsely, raising himself on an elbow.

"They're calling us from the beach. Your father wants you to come on in."

"My father? Wrong boat. He's in Washington."

"Wait one—Hello, hello, *Blue Bird* calling Bill Thomas—" They heard the squawking of the ship-to-shore again. "Hey, Mr. Henry. Your father—is he a naval officer, a captain?"

"That's right."

"Well, the office has your girl's mother on the telephone. Your father's at her house and the message is to get back there pronto."

Natalie sat up, her eyes wide and startled.

Byron called, "Okay, let's head back."

"What on earth?" Natalie exclaimed.

"I haven't the foggiest idea."

The boat, scoring a green-white circle on the dark sea, picked up speed and started to pitch. The wind tumbled Natalie's long free black hair. She pulled a mirror from a straw basket. "My God, look at me. Look at that mouth. I look gnawed. As though the rats had been at me!" She put the back of her hand to her lips. "Well, no use trying to patch up this Gorgon's head till we come in. What can your father want, Briny?"

"Why are you so alarmed? Probably he's here with my mother, and she wants a look at you. I can't blame her, the way I shot down here. If so, I'm going to tell them, Natalie."

Her face turned anxious. She took his hand. "Angel, there's some Jewish law about not getting married too soon after a parent dies. Possibly for as long as a year, and—good heavens! Don't make such a face! I'm not going to observe *that*. But I can't distress my mother at this point. I need some time to figure this out."

"I don't want you violating your religion, Natalie, but lord, that's a blow."

"Sweetie, I wasn't planning on marrying you until about an hour ago." She shook her head and ruefully laughed. "I feel weird. Almost disembodied. Too much sun, or maybe I'm just drunk on kisses. And now your father suddenly showing up! Isn't it all like a fever dream?"

He put his arm around her shoulders, holding her close as the boat pitched and rocked more. "Not to me. It's damned real, and the realest thing of all is that we're getting married. Reality just seems to be starting."

"Yes, no doubt. I certainly don't look forward to writing to Leslie—Jehosephat, that scowl again! You put it on and off like a Hallowe'en mask, it's unnerving— Briny, he came down to see me right after Papa died. He was remarkably helpful and kind. A new Slote, just a bit too late. He's been writing to his university friends to find me a teaching job. I *wish* I knew what your father wanted! Don't tell him about us, Byron. Not till I've talked to my mother."

"You'd better talk to her right away, then. My father has a way of getting at the facts."

"Oh! Oh!" She put both hands to her hair. "I'm so happy, and so confused, and so upset! I'm dizzy. I feel sixteen, which I'm not, God knows! Better for you if I were."

When the *Blue Bird* drew closer in, Byron got the binoculars and scanned the ragged row of skyscraper hotels along the beach. "I thought so. There he is, waiting on the pier."

Natalie, lounging in one of the chairs, sat bolt upright. "Oh, no. You're sure?"

"Right there, pacing back and forth. I know that walk."

She seized her basket and darted into the cabin, saying to the skipper, "Slow down, please."

"Right, miss." The bewhiskered man, with a grin, pulled back on the throttle.

She closed the little door to the forward cabin. Soon

she emerged in a cotton skirt and white blouse, her black hair brushed gleaming and loose to her shoulders. "I'm seasick," she said to Byron, wanly smiling. "Try putting on eyebrows and a mouth sometime in a rocking boat, in a hot little cabin. Whew! Am I green? I feel green."

"You look wonderful."

The boat was wallowing half a mile from the pier. Natalie could see the man in blue walking up and down. "Full steam ahead," she said shakily. "Damn the torpedoes."

Victor Henry, leaning down from the tar-smelling pier, held out a hand as the boat stopped. "Hello, Natalie. This is a helluva thing to do to you. Watch it, don't step on that nail."

Byron leaped ashore. "What's up, Dad? Is everybody all right?"

"Have you two had lunch?" Pug said.

They looked at each other, and Natalie nervously laughed. "I did pack sandwiches. They're in this basket. We, well, I don't know, we forgot."

An amused look came and went in Victor Henry's eyes, though his face remained stern. "Uh-huh. Well, the smells from that joint there"—he pointed with his thumb at a dilapidated clam bar on the pier—"have been driving me nuts, but I thought I'd wait for you. I haven't eaten yet today."

"Please come to my house. I'd love to fix you something."

"Your mother was kind enough to give me orange juice and coffee. D'you mind if we go in here? These waterfront places can be pretty good."

They sat in a tiny plywood booth painted bright red. Byron and his father ordered clam chowder. "I've never learned to like that stuff," Natalie said to the waiter. "Can I have a bacon and tomato sandwich?"

"Sure, miss."

Victor Henry looked oddly at her. "What's the matter?" she said.

"You're not fussy about what you eat."

She looked puzzled. "Oh. You mean the bacon? Not in the least, I'm afraid. Many Jews aren't."

"How about your mother?"

"Well, she has some vague and inconsistent scruples. I can never quite follow them."

"We had quite a chat. She's a clever woman, and holding up remarkably, after her loss. Well!" Pug put cigarettes and lighter on the table. "It looks like France is really folding, doesn't it? Have you heard the radio this morning? In Paris they're burning papers. The BEF is high-tailing it for the Channel, but it may already be too late. The Germans may actually bag the entire British regular army."

"Good God," Byron said. "If they do that the war's over! How could this happen in three days?"

"Well, it has. While I was waiting for you I heard the President on my car radio, making an emergency address to a joint session of Congress. He's asked them for fifty thousand airplanes a year."

"Fifty thousand a year?" exclaimed Natalie. *"Fifty thousand?* Why, that's just wild talk."

"He said we'd have to build the factories to turn 'em out, and then start making 'em. In the mood I saw in Washington yesterday, he's going to get the money, too. The panic is finally *on,* up there. They've come awake in a hurry."

Byron said, "None of this can help England or France."

"No. Not in this battle. What Congress is starting to think about is the prospect of us on our own, against Hitler and the Japanese. Now." Pug lit a cigarette, and began ticking off points against spread stiff fingers. "Warren's thirty-day leave has been cancelled. The wedding's been moved up. Warren and Janice are getting married tomorrow. They'll have a one-day honeymoon, and then he goes straight out to the Pacific Fleet. So. Number one: You've got to get to Pensacola by tomorrow at ten."

With a hesitant look at Natalie, who appeared dumbfounded, Byron said, "All right, I'll be there."

"Okay. Number two: If you want to get into that May 27 class at sub school, you've got to report to New London and take the physical by Saturday."

"Can't I take a physical at Pensacola?"

The father pursed his lips. "I never thought of that. Maybe I can get Red Tully to stretch a point. He's already doing that, holding this place open for you. The applications are piling up now for that school."

"May 27?" Natalie said to Byron. "That's eleven days from now! Are you going to submarine school in eleven days?"

"I don't know. It's a possibility."

She turned to his father. "How long is the school?"

"It's three months."

"What will become of him afterward?"

"My guess is he'll go straight out to the fleet, like Warren. The new subs are just starting to come on the line."

"Three months! And then you'll be gone!" Natalie exclaimed.

"Well, we'll talk about all that," Byron said. "Will you come with me to the wedding tomorrow?"

"Me? I don't know. I wasn't invited."

"Janice asked me to bring you."

"She did? When? You never told me that."

Byron turned to his father, "Look, when does the submarine course *after* this one begin?"

"I don't know. But the sooner you start, the better. It takes you thirteen more months at sea to get your dolphins. There's nothing tougher than qualifying in submarines, Briny. A flier has an easier job."

Byron took one of his father's cigarettes, lit it, inhaled deeply, and said as he exhaled a gray cloud, "Natalie and I are getting married."

With an appraising glance at Natalie, who was biting her lower lip, Victor Henry said, "I see. Well, that might or might not affect your admittance to the school. I hadn't checked that point, not knowing of this development. In general, unmarried candidates get the preference in such situations. Still, maybe the thing to do—"

Natalie broke in, "Captain Henry, I realize it creates many difficulties. We only decided this morning. I myself don't know when or how. It's a fearful tangle."

Looking at her from under his eyebrows as he ate, Pug nodded.

"There are no difficulties that can't be overcome," said Byron.

"Listen, darling," Natalie said, "the last thing I'll ever do is stop you from going to submarine school. My God, I was in Warsaw!"

Byron smoked, his face blank, his eyes narrowed at his father.

Victor Henry looked at his wristwatch and gathered up his cigarettes and lighter. "Well, that's that. Great chowder. Hits the spot. Say, there's a plane to Pensacola that I can still make this afternoon."

"Why didn't you just telephone all this?" Byron said. "It would have been simple enough. Why did you come here?"

Victor Henry waved the check and a ten-dollar bill at the waiter. "You took off like a rocket, Byron. I didn't know your plans or your state of mind. I wasn't even sure you'd agree to come to the wedding."

"Why, I wouldn't have heard of his staying away," Natalie said.

"Well, I didn't know that either. I thought I ought to be available to talk to both of you, and maybe answer questions, and use a little persuasion if necessary." He added to Natalie, "Janice and Warren do expect you. That I can tell you."

She put a hand to her forehead. "I just don't know if I can come."

"We'll be there," Byron said flatly. "Or at least I will. Does that take care of everything?"

Pug hesitated. "What about sub school? I told Red I'd call him today."

"If Captain Tully has to know today, then I'm out. All right?"

Natalie struck the table with her fist. "Damn it, Byron. Don't make decisions like that."

"I don't know any other way to make decisions."

"You can talk to me. I'm involved."

Victor Henry cleared his throat. "Well, I've spoken my piece and I'll shove off. We can pick this topic up tomorrow."

"Oh?" Byron's tone was acid. "Then you don't really have to call Captain Tully today, after all."

Victor Henry's face darkened. He leaned back in the hard seat. "See here, Byron. Hitler and the Germans are creating your problem. I'm not. I'm calling it to your attention."

"Well, all this bad news from Europe may be highly exaggerated, and in any case, no American submarine will ever fail to sail because I'm not in it."

"Oh, be quiet, Briny," Natalie said in a choked voice. "Let your father catch his plane."

"Just keep remembering I didn't start this war, Byron," Victor Henry said, in almost the tone he had used on the waiter in Wannsee, picking his white cap off a peg while looking his son in the face. "I think you'd make a good submariner. They're all a bunch of goofy individualists. On the other hand, I can't hate you for wanting to marry this brilliant and beautiful young lady. And now I'm getting the hell out of here." Victor Henry stood. "See you in church. Get there early, you'll be best man. Wear your dark suit.—Good-bye, Natalie. Sorry I broke up your day on the boat. Try to come to Pensacola."

"Yes, sir." A sad little smile lit her worried face. "Thank you."

When he went out, she turned to Byron. "I have always loathed the smell of cooking fish. Let's get out of here. I was half sick during all that. God knows how I've kept from shooting my cookies."

Natalie strode seaward along the wharf, taking deep gulps of air, her skirt fluttering on her swinging hips, the thin blouse wind-flattened on her breasts, her long hair flying. Byron hurried after her. She stopped short at the end of the wharf, where two ragged Negro boys sat fishing, and turned on him, her arms folded.

"Why the devil did you treat your father like that?"

"Like what? I know why he came here, that's all," Byron returned with equal sharpness. "He came to separate us." His voice rang and twanged much like Victor Henry's.

"Oh, take me home. Straight home. He was utterly right, you know. You're blaming *him* for the way the war is going. That's the essence of immaturity. I was embarrassed for you. I hated that feeling."

They walked back up the pier to her father's new blue Buick sedan, glittering and baking in the sun, giving off heat like a stove. "Open all the doors, please. Let some air blow through, or we'll die in there!"

Byron said as he went from door to door, "I have never

wanted anything before, not of life, not of him, not of anybody. Now I do."

"Even if it's true, you still have to look at reality, not throw tantrums."

"He did quite a job on you," said Byron. "He usually gets anything done that he intends to."

They climbed into the car.

"That's how much you know," she said harshly, slamming her door as he whirred the motor. "I'm coming to Pensacola with you. All right? I love you. Now shut up and drive me home."

26

WITH a groan, to the clatter of an old tin alarm clock, Lieutenant (jg) Warren Henry woke at seven on his wedding day. Until four he had been in the sweet arms of his bride-to-be in a bedroom of the Calder Arms Hotel, some twenty miles from Pensacola. He stumbled to the shower and turned on the cold water in a gush. As the needling shock brought him to, he wearily wondered whether spending such a night before his wedding morning hadn't been somewhat gross. Poor Janice had said she would have to start dressing and packing as soon as she got home. Yes, certainly gross, but ye gods! Warren laughed aloud, held up his face to the cold water, and started to sing. It was rough, after all—a rushed wedding, a one-night honeymoon, and then a separation of thousands of miles! Too much to ask of human nature. Anyway, it wasn't the first time.

Still—Warren was drying himself with a big rough towel, and cheering up by the minute—there was such a thing as propriety. Such doings on the wedding eve were ill-timed. But it was rotten luck to be torn away from her like this. It was just one of those things, and Hitler's invasion of France was the real cause, not any looseness in himself or Janice.

Truth to tell, the prospect of parting from Janice was not bothering Warren much. She would be coming along to Pearl Harbor in due course. The sudden orders to the Pacific had put him in an excited glow. Cramming in a premature night with Janice had been an impulse of this new bursting love of life he felt. He was rushing to fly a fighter plane from the U.S.S. *Enterprise,* because war threatened. It was a star-spangled destiny, a scary ride to the moon. For all his mental motions of regret at leaving Janice, and remorse at having enjoyed her a little too soon and a little too much, Warren's spirit was soaring. He called the mess steward, ordered double ham and eggs and a jug of coffee, and gaily set about dressing for his nuptials.

Byron, standing in the hall outside his brother's room, smiled at a crude cartoon tacked to the door: Father Neptune, a lump throbbing on his pate, wrathfully rising from the sea ahead of an aircraft carrier, brandishing his trident at an airplane with dripping wheels, out of which the pilot leaned, saluting and shouting, *"So sorry!"*

"Come in!" Warren called to his knock.

" 'Wet Wheels' Henry, I presume?" Byron quoted the cartoon caption.

"Briny! Hey! My Christ, how long has it been? Well, you look great! God, I'm glad you made it for the wedding." Warren ordered more breakfast for his brother. "Listen, you've got to tell me all about that wild trip of yours. I'm supposed to be the warrior, but Jesus, you're the one who's had the adventures. Why, you've been bombed and strafed by the Nazis! My buddies will sure want to talk to you."

"Nothing heroic about getting in the way of a war, Warren."

"Let's hear about it. Sit down, we have a lot to catch up on."

They talked over the food, over coffee, over cigars, and as Warren packed they kept talking, awkwardly at first, then loosening up. Each was taking the other's measure. Warren was older, heavier in the face, more confident, more than ever on top of the world and ahead of his brother: so Byron felt. Those new gold wings on his white dress uniform seemed to Byron to spread a foot. About flying Warren was relaxed, humorous, and hard. He had mastered the machines and the lingo, and the jokes about his mishaps didn't obscure the leap upward. He still spoke the words "naval aviator" with pride and awe. To Byron, his own close calls under fire had been stumblebum episodes, in no way comparable to Warren's disciplined rise to fighter pilot.

For his part, Warren had last seen Byron setting off to Europe, a hangdog slouching youngster with a bad school record and not a few pimples, already cooling off about a career in fine arts. Byron's skin now stretched brown and clear over a sharpened jaw; his eyes were deeper; he sat up straighter. Warren was used to the short haircuts and natural shoulder lines of the Navy. Byron's padded dark Italian suit and mop of reddish hair gave him a dashing appearance that went with his saga of roaming in Poland under German bombs with a beautiful Jewess. Warren had never before envied his younger brother anything. He envied the red stitch-marked scar on his temple—his own scar was a mishap, not a war wound—and he even somewhat envied him the Jewess, sight unseen.

"What about Natalie, Byron? Did she come?"

"Sure. I parked her at Janice's house. That was decent of Janice, telephoning her last night. Did Dad put her up to it?"

"He just said the girl wasn't sure she was expected. Say, that thing's serious, is it?" Warren paused, suitcase hanger in one hand and a uniform jacket in the other, and looked hard at his brother.

"We're getting married."

"You are? Good for you."

"Do you mean that?"

"Sure. She sounds like a marvellous girl."

"She is. I know the religious problem exists—"

Warren grinned and ducked his head to one side. "Ah, Byron, nowadays—does it really? If you wanted the ministry—or politics, say—you'd have to give it more thought. Christ, with the war on and the whole world coming apart, I say grab her. I look forward to meeting that girl. Isn't she a Ph.D. or something?"

"She was going for an M.A. at the Sorbonne."

"Brother! I'd be more scared of her than of a carrier landing at night in a line squall."

Byron's grin showed possessive pride. "I was around her six months, and never opened my mouth, hardly. Then she up and said she loved me. I'm still trying to believe it."

"Why not? You've gotten damned handsome, my lad. You've lost that string-bean look. You marrying up now, or after sub school?"

"Who the devil says I'm going to sub school? Don't start that. I get enough from Dad."

Warren deftly moved clothes from bureau to a foot locker. "But he's right, Byron. You don't want to wait till you get called up. If you do they'll shove you around, rush you through, and you may not even draw the duty you want. You can pick your spot now and get decent training. Say, have you given naval aviation any thought? Why do you want to go crawling around at four knots, three hundred feet underwater, when you can fly? I get claustrophobia just thinking about subs. You might make a great flier. One thing you are is relaxed."

"I got interested in subs." Byron described Prien's talk in Berlin on the sinking of the *Royal Oak*.

"That was a brave exploit," said Warren. "A real score. Even Churchill admitted that. Very romantic. I guess that's what attracts you. But this is an air war, Briny. Those Germans haven't got that much of an edge on the ground. The papers keep talking panzers, panzers, but the French have more and better tanks than the Germans. They're not using them. They've been panicked by those Stukas, which just use our own dive-bombing tactics."

"That's what got me, a Stuka," Byron said. "It didn't look that scary. Fixed wheels, single engine, medium size, kind of slow and awkward."

Tossing Byron a large gray book, Warren said with a grin, "Take a look through *The Flight Jacket*. I'm there in Squadron Five, tying on my solo flags. I've got to pay some bills, then we're off to church."

Byron was still looking through the yearbook when his brother returned.

"Holy cow, Warren, number one in ground school! How'd you do that and court Janice, too?"

"It took a toll." Warren made an exhausted face, and they both laughed. "Bookwork is never too tough when you organize it."

Byron held up the yearbook, pointing to a black-bordered page. "These fellows all got it?"

Warren's face sobered. "Yep. Frank Monahan was my instructor, and a great flier." He sighed and looked around the barren room, hands on hips. "Well, I'm not sorry to leave this room. Eleven months I've sweated in here."

Pensacola might look small and sleepy, Warren said as they drove into town, but it had perfect climate, great water sports, fine fishing, good golf and riding clubs, and up-and-coming industries. This was the real Florida, not that Brooklyn with palm trees called Miami. These rural western countries were the place to get a political start. Congressman Lacouture had had no competition. He had recently decided to run for the Senate in the fall, and his chances were considered excellent. Warren said he and Janice might well come back here one day.

"When you retire?" Byron said. "That's looking far ahead."

"Possibly before then." With a side glance, Warren took in Byron's astonishment. "Listen, Briny, the day I soloed, President Roosevelt fired the Commander-in-Chief of the United States Fleet. Some dispute over policy for the Asiatic Fleet. Made him ambassador to Turkestan, or something, but actually just kicked him out. CinCus himself! In the Navy you're just a hired man, my lad, right on up that big climb through the bureaus and the shore stations and the sea billets. Right to the top. Don't ever tell Dad I talked like this. Janice is an only child and the Lacouture firm does twenty million a year. Of course, as long as I can fly, that's all I want to do."

Inside the pink stone church topped by a square bell tower, two men in smocks were finishing up a huge flower display, and an unseen organist was rippling a Bach prelude. "Nobody can say I kept her waiting at the church," Warren said. "Almost an hour to go. Well, we can talk. It's cool in here."

They sat halfway down the rows of empty purple-cushioned pews. The music, the odor of the flowers, the unmistakable childhood smell of church, hit Byron hard. He felt again what it was like to be a reverent boy, sitting or standing beside his father, joining in the hymns, or trying to follow the minister's talk about the misty and wonderful Lord Jesus. Marrying Natalie, there would be no such wedding as this. What kind could they have? A church was altogether out of the question. What was it like to be married by a rabbi? They had not discussed that part at all. The two brothers sat side by side in a long silence. Warren was again regretting, in a fashion, last night's indulgence, and making halfhearted pious resolves. The feelings of a bridegroom were coming over him.

"Briny, say something. I'm getting nervous. Who knows when we'll have a chance to talk again?"

Byron wistfully smiled, and it struck Warren once more how good-looking his brother had become. "Long time since you and I went to church together."

"Yes. Janice likes to go. I guess if these walls aren't falling in on me now, there's still hope for me. You know, Briny, all this may work out pretty well. If you do get into subs, you can put in for duty at Pearl. Maybe the four of us will end up there together for a couple of years. Wouldn't that be fine?"

◦ ◦ ◦

Natalie had often visited the homes of wealthy college friends, but she was not prepared for the Lacouture mansion, a rambling stone house on the bay, in a private section guarded by a mossy stucco wall, an iron-fenced entrance, and an iron-faced gatekeeper. Gentility, seclusion, exclusion, were all around her. The rooms upon rooms of antique furniture, Persian rugs, grandfather clocks, large oil portraits, heavy worn draperies, ironwork, gilt-framed big mirrors, old-fashioned photographs—the whole place unsettled her. Janice scampered to meet her in a fluttery pink housecoat, her blonde hair tumbling to her shoulders.

"Hi! So sweet of you to come on this short notice. Look at me. I didn't sleep all night. I'm so tired I can't see. I'll never be ready. Let's get you some breakfast."

"Please, just put me in a corner somewhere till we go. I'm fine."

Janice scanned her with weary but keen big hazel eyes. This happy girl, all pink and gold, made Natalie the more conscious of her own dark eyes, dark hair, wrinkled linen suit, and sad dowdy look.

"No wonder Byron fell for you. My God, you're pretty. Come along."

Janice took her to a breakfast alcove facing the water, where a maid brought her eggs and tea in old blue-and-white china on a silver tray. She ate and felt better, if no more at home. Outside, sailboats tacked here and there in the sunshine. Clocks struck nine in the house, one after the other, bonging and chiming. She could hear excited voices upstairs.

She took the letter from her purse, where it had seemed a lump of lead all the way from Miami: five single-space pages so faintly typed that her eyes ached to read them. Obviously A.J. was not going to learn to change a type-writer ribbon till he died.

It was a long tale of woe. He had a fractured ankle. With a French art critic, an old friend, he had gone on a tour of cathedrals the week after Byron had left. At Orvieto, mounting a ladder to look at an inaccessible fresco, he had slipped and fallen to the stone floor. To make matters worse, there was his mixed-up citizenship problem, which for the first time he was taking seriously.

He had "derivative citizenship" from his father's naturalization around 1900; but because of his long residence out of the country, difficulties had arisen. There seemed to be conflicting records of his age at the time of his father's naturalization. The man in Rome, a decent enough person to talk to but an obsessive bureaucrat, had pressed searching questions and demanded more and more documents, and Aaron had left Rome in deep confusion. Aaron wrote:

I may have made a mistake at that point, but I decided to drop the whole thing. This was in December of last year. It seemed to me that I was like the fly blundering into a spider web; the more I'd struggle, the tighter I'd become enmeshed. I didn't really want to go home just then. I assumed that if I let the thing cool off and asked for the passport renewal later—especially if some other consul general were appointed meantime—I'd get it. It's a question of a purple stamp and a two-dollar fee. It seemed unthinkable to me then, and still does now, that I could actually be denied permission to return to my own country, where I am even listed in *Who's Who!*

During the spasm of alarm over Norway, he had once visited the Florence consulate. There a "shallow but seemingly affable crew-cut type" had conceded that these were all silly technicalities, that Dr. Jastrow was certainly an eminent and desirable person, and that the consular service would somehow solve the difficulty. Much relieved, Jastrow had gone off on the cathedral tour, fractured his ankle, and thus missed an appointment to return to the consulate two weeks later. The letter continued:

What comes next I still cannot understand. It was either incredible stupidity or incredible malevolence. Crew-cut wrote a letter to me. The tone was polite enough. The gist was that as a stateless person in wartime I faced serious complications, but he thought he had found a way out. Congress has recently passed a law admitting certain special classes of refugees. If I were to apply under that law, I probably would have no further trouble, being a prominent Jew. That was his recommendation.

Do you realize the full depth of the stupidity and the damage in his letter? I received it only five days ago. I'm still boiling. To begin with he wants me to abandon all claim to being an American—*which I am,* whether my papers are in order or not—and to enlist myself in the mob of clamoring Jewish refugees from Europe seeking admittance as hardship cases!

But that isn't the worst of it. *He put all this on paper and he put it in the mail.*

I cannot believe that even such a dullard doesn't know that a letter from the consular office to me would be opened and read by the Italians. I'll never know why Crew-cut did it, but I'm forced to suspect a trace of anti-Semitism. That bacillus is in the European air, and in certain personalities it lodges and flourishes. The Italian authorities now know my problem. That alarmingly increases my vulnerability here.

I've been sitting in the lovely sunshine of the terrace day after day, in a wheelchair, alone except for Italian servants, growing more and more perturbed. Finally I decided to write to you, and give the letter to my French friend to mail.

Natalie, I have certainly been heedless about a serious matter. I can only plead that before the war these things seemed of no consequence. To you I'm sure they still don't. You were born on American soil. I was born on the banks of the Vistula. I am getting a late lesson in the vast difference that makes, and in the philosophy of personal identity. I really should straighten my situation out.

Happily, there's no desperate urgency in it. Siena's tranquil, food's plentiful again, my ankle's healing, and the war is distant summer thunder. I am getting on with my work, but I had better clarify my right to go home. One can never know when or where the villain with the moustache will make his next move.

Now will you tell all this to Leslie Slote? There he sits in Washington, at the heart of things. A hangman's noose of red tape can be cut by one word spoken in the right place. If he still has a shred of regard for me, let him look into this. I could write him directly but I know we'll get faster action if you go to him. I beg you to do this.

Jastrow wrote a touching paragraph about Natalie's father. He blamed their estrangement on himself. The scholarly temperament was a self-absorbed one. He hoped that he could treat her as a daughter, though a father's place could never really be filled. Then came the passage about Byron which had prevented Natalie from showing him the letter.

Have you seen Byron yet? I miss him. He has a curiously charming presence—*triste,* humorous, reserved, virile. I've never known a more winning boy, and I've known hundreds. A young fellow in his twenties shouldn't seem a boy, but he does. An aureole of romance plays about him. Byron might be all right if he had any talent, or a vestige of drive.

Sometimes he shows doggedness: and he has a way of coming out with bright flashes. He said Hegel's World Spirit was just God minus Christianity. That's commonplace enough, but he added it was much easier to believe in God's sacrificing Himself for mankind, than in His groping to understand Himself through the unfolding of mankind's stupidities. I rather liked that. Unhappily it was the one good thing amid many banalities such as, "This Nietzsche was just some kind of a nut," and "Nobody would bother reading Fichte, if anybody could understand him." If I'd marked Byron for our seminar on the Slote Reading List, he'd have made a C minus.

Often I came upon him reading your letters over and over in the lemon house. The poor lad has a terrible crush on you. Are you at all aware of that? I hope you won't inadvertently hurt him, and I rather wonder at your writing him so often.

For all my troubles, I've been a reasonably good boy, and stand on manuscript page 847 of *Constantine*.

A clock chiming the half hour brought Natalie back with a start from the terrace in Siena—where in her mind's eye she could see A.J. sitting wrapped in his blue shawl, writing these words—to the Lacouture mansion on Pensacola Bay.

"Oh God," she muttered, "oh my God."

Feet trampled on a staircase; many voices called, laughed, chattered. The bride came sailing down the long dining room, wheat-colored hair beautifully coiffed and laced with pearls, cheeks pink with pleasure. "Well, I did it. Here we go."

Natalie jumped to her feet, cramming A.J.'s pages into her purse. "Oh, you're enchanting! You're the loveliest sight!"

Janice pirouetted clear around on a toe. "Bless you."

The white satin, clinging to flanks and breasts like creamy skin, rose demurely to cover her throat. She moved in a cloud of white lace. This blend of white chastity and crude fleshy allure was devastating; it shook Natalie with envy. The bride's eye had an ironic gleam. After her wild pre-wedding night, Janice Lacouture felt approximately as virginal as Catherine of Russia. It didn't bother her. Rather, it appealed to her sense of humor.

"Come," she said. "You'll ride with me." She took the Jewish girl's arm. "You know, if I weren't marrying Warren Henry, I'd give you a run for that little Briny. He's an Adonis, and so sweet. Those Henry men!"

Rhoda arrived at the hotel in a flurry, and frantically bathed and dressed, pulling cosmetics from one valise, underwear from another, her new Bergdorf Goodman frock from a third. Dr. Kirby had chartered a small plane and had flown down with her and Madeline. "He saved our LIVES!" trilled Rhoda, dashing about in a sheer green slip. "The last plane we could get from New York didn't leave us a MINUTE to finish shopping. Your daughter and I would have come to this wedding in OLD RAGS. This way, we had a whole extra afternoon and, Pug, you never SAW such fast shopping. Isn't this a cunning number?" She held the green frock against her bosom. "Found it at the last second. Honestly, a small plane is such FUN. I slept most of the way, but when I was awake it was GREAT. You really know you're flying."

"Damn nice of him," Pug said. "Is Fred that rich?"

"Well, of course, I wouldn't hear of it, but then he said it was all charged to his company. He's taking the plane on to Birmingham today. Anyway, I wasn't going to argue too much, dear. It was a deliverance. Fasten me up in back. Pug, did Briny really bring that Jewish girl here? Of all things. Why, I've never even laid eyes on her. She'll have to sit with us, and everybody'll think she's part of the family."

"Looks like she will be, Rhoda."

"I don't believe it. I just don't. Why, how much older is she? Four years? That Briny! Just enjoys giving us heart failure. Always has, the monster. Pug, what's taking you so long? My land, it's hot here."

"She's two years older, and terrifically attractive."

"Well, you've got me curious, I'll say that. I pictured her as one of these tough Brooklyn chickens who shove past you in the New York department stores. Oh, stop fumbling, I'll finish the top ones. Mercy, I'm roasting! I'm perspiring IN RIVERS. This dress will be black through before we get to church."

Natalie knew in thirty seconds that the handsome woman in green chiffon and rose-decorated white straw hat didn't like her. The polite handshake outside the church, the prim smile, told all. Pug presented Natalie to Madeline as "Byron's sidekick on the Polish jaunt," obviously trying with this clumsy jocularity to make up for his wife's freeze.

"Oh, yes, wow! Some adventure!" Madeline Henry smiled and looked Natalie over. Her pearl-gray shantung suit was the smartest outfit in sight. "I want to hear all about that, some time. I still haven't seen Briny, you know, and it's been more than two years."

"He shouldn't have rushed down to Miami the way he did," Natalie said, feeling her cheeks redden.

"Why not?" said Madeline, with a slow Byron-like grin. It was strange to see echoes of his traits in his family. Mrs. Henry held her head as Byron did, erect on a long neck. It made him seem more remote. He wasn't just himself any more, her young companion of Jastrow's library and of Poland, or even the son of a forbidding father, but part of a quite alien group.

The church was full. From the moment she went in, Natalie felt uncomfortable. Cathedrals gave her no uneasiness. They were just sights to see, and Roman Catholicism, though she could write a good paper about it, was like Mohammedanism, a complex closed-off structure. A Protestant church was the place of the other religion, the thing she would be if she weren't a Jew. Coming into one, she trod hostile territory. Rhoda didn't make quite enough room for her in the pew, and Natalie had to push her a little, murmuring an excuse, to step clear of the aisle.

All around, women wore bright or pastel colors. Officers and air cadets in white and gold abounded. And there Natalie stood at a May wedding in black linen, hastily selected out of a vague sense that she was still in mourning and didn't belong here. People peered at her and whispered. It wasn't her imagination: they did. How charming and fine the church was, with its dark carved wooden ceiling arching up from pink stone walls; and what stunning masses of flowers! How pleasant, comfortable, and normal

to be born an Episcopalian or a Methodist, and how perfect to be married this way! Perhaps A.J. was right, and
encouraging Byron had been irresponsible. Leslie Slote was
an arid bookish pagan like herself, and they had even
talked of being married by a judge.

The robed minister appeared, book in hand, and the
ceremony began.

As the bride paced down the aisle on the congressman's
arm, moving like a big beautiful cat, Rhoda started to cry.
Memories of Warren as a little boy, memories of her own
wedding, of other weddings, of young men who had wanted
to marry her, of herself—a mother before twenty of the
baby who had grown into this handsome groom—flooded
her mind; she bowed her head in the perky hat and brought
out the handkerchief. For the moment she lost her awareness of the melancholy Jewish girl in black beside her, and
even of Palmer Kirby towering above people three rows
back. When Victor Henry softly took her hand, she clasped
his and pressed it to her thigh. What fine sons they had,
standing up there together!

And Pug stood slightly hunched, almost at attention, his
face sombre and rigid, wondering at the speed with which
his life was going, and realizing again how little he allowed
himself to think about Warren, because he had such in-
ordinately high hopes for him.

Standing up beside his brother, Byron felt many eyes
measuring and comparing them. Warren's uniform, and the
other uniforms in the church, troubled him. His Italian
suit with its exaggerated lines, beside Warren's naturally
cut whites, seemed to Byron as soft and frivolous as a
woman's dress.

As Janice lifted her veil for the kiss, she and Warren
exchanged a deep, knowing, intimately amused glance.

"How are you doing?" he murmured.

"Oh, still standing up. God knows how, you dog."

And with the minister beaming on them, they embraced,
kissed, and laughed, there in the church in each other's
arms, over the war-born joke that would last their whole
lives and that nobody else would ever know.

.   .   .

Cars piled up in front of the beach club, only a few hundred yards from the Lacouture house, and a jocund crowd poured into the canopied entrance for the wedding brunch.

"I swear, I must be the only Jew in Pensacola," Natalie said, hanging back a little on Byron's arm. "When I walk through that door, I'm going to set off gongs."

He burst out laughing. "It's not quite that bad."

She looked pleased at making him laugh. "Maybe not. I do think your mother might be a wee bit happier if a wall had fallen on me in Warsaw."

At that moment, Rhoda, half a dozen paces behind them, was responding to a comment by a Washington cousin that Byron's girl looked striking. "Yes, doesn't she? So interesting. She might almost be an Armenian or an Arab. Byron met her in Italy."

Champagne glass in hand, Byron firmly took Natalie around the wedding party from room to room, introducing her. "Don't say I'm your fiancée," Natalie ordered him at the start. "Let them think what they please, but don't let's get into all that." She met Captain Henry's father, an engineer retired from the lumber trade, a short withered upright man with thick white hair, who had travelled in from California and who looked as though he had worked hard all his life; and his surprisingly fat brother, who ran a soft-drink business in Seattle; and other Henrys; and a knot of Rhoda's kin, Grovers of Washington. The clothes, the manners, the speech of the Washington relatives set them off not only from the California people, but even from Lacouture's Pensacola friends, who by comparison seemed a Babbitty lot.

Janice and Warren came and stayed, joking, eating, drinking, and dancing. Nobody would have blamed them, in view of their limited time, for vanishing after a round of handshakes, but they evinced no impatience for the joys of their new state.

Warren asked Natalie to dance, and as soon as they were out on the floor, he said, "I told Byron this morning that I'm for you. That was sight unseen."

"Do you always take such blind risks? A flier should be more prudent."

"I know about what you did in Warsaw. That's enough."

"You're cheering me up. I feel awfully out of place here."

"You shouldn't. Janice is as much for you as I am. Byron seems changed already," Warren said. "There's a lot to him, but nobody's ever pressed the right button. I've always hoped that someday a girl would, and I think you're the girl."

Rhoda Henry swooped past, champagne glass in hand, and gathered them up to join a large family table by the window. Possibly because of the wine, she was acting more cordial to Natalie. At the table Lacouture was declaring, with relish for his own pat phrases, that the President's request for fifty thousand airplanes a year was "politically hysterical, fiscally irresponsible, and industrially inconceivable." Even the German air force didn't have ten thousand planes all told; and it didn't have a single bomber that could fly as far as Scotland, let alone across the Atlantic. A billion dollars! The interventionist press was whooping it up, naturally, but if the debate in Congress could go on for more than a week, the appropriation would be licked. "We have three thousand miles of good green water between us and Europe," he said, "and that's better protection for us than half a million airplanes. Roosevelt just wants new planes in a hurry to give to England and France. But he'll never come out and *say* that. Our fearless leader is slightly deficient in candor."

"You're willing to see the British and French go down, then," Pug Henry said.

"That's how the question's usually put," said Lacouture. "Ask me if I'm willing to send three million American boys overseas against the Germans, so as to prop up the old status quo in Europe. Because that's what this is all about, and don't ever forget it."

Palmer Kirby put in, "The British navy's propping up our own status quo free of charge, Congressman. If the Nazis get hold of it, that'll extend Hitler's reach to Pensacola Bay."

Lacouture said jovially, "Yes, I can just see the *Rodney* and the *Nelson* right out there, flying the swastika and shelling our poor old beach club."

This raised a laugh among the assorted in-laws around the table, and Rhoda said, "What a charming thought."

Victor Henry said, "This isn't where they'll come."

"They're not coming at all," Lacouture said. "That's *New York Times* stuff. If the British get in a jam, they'll throw out Churchill and make a deal with Germany. But naturally they'll hang on as long as they think there's a chance that the Roosevelt administration, the British sympathizers, and the New York Jews will get us over there."

"I'm from Denver," said Kirby, "and I'm Irish." He and Victor Henry had glanced at Natalie when Lacouture mentioned the Jews.

"Well, error is contagious," said the congressman with great good nature, "and it knows no boundaries."

This easy amused war talk over turkey, roast beef, and champagne, by a broad picture window looking out at beach umbrellas, white sand, and heeling sailboats, had been irritating Natalie extremely. Lacouture's last sentence stung her to say in a loud voice, "I was in Warsaw during the siege."

Lacouture calmly said, "That's right, so you were. You and Byron. Pretty bad, was it?"

"The Germans bombed a defenseless city for three weeks. They knocked out all the hospitals but one, the one I worked in. The wounded were piled up in our entrance hall like logs. In one hospital a lot of pregnant women burned up."

The table became a hole of quiet in the boisterous party. The congressman spun an empty champagne glass between two fingers. "That sort of thing has been going on in Europe for centuries, my dear. It's exactly what I want to spare the American people."

"Say, I heard a good one yesterday," spoke up a jolly-faced man in steel-rimmed glasses, laughing. "Abey and his family, see, are driving down to Miami, and about Tampa they run out of gasoline. Well, they drive into this filling station, and this attendant says, 'Juice?' And old Abey he says, 'Vell, vot if ve are? Dunt ve get no gess?'"

The jolly man laughed again, and so did the others. Natalie could see he meant no harm; he was trying to ease the sober turn of the talk. Still she was very glad that Byron came up now and took her off to dance.

"How long does this go on?" she said. "Can we go outside? I don't want to dance."

"Good. I have to talk to you."

They sat on the low wall of the terrace in blazing sun, by stairs leading to the white sand, not far from the picture window, behind which Lacouture was still holding forth, shaking his white-thatched head and waving an arm.

Byron leaned forward, elbows on knees, fingers clasped together. "Darling, I think I'm getting organized here. I may as well fly up to New London today or tomorrow and take that physical, so that—what's the matter?"

A spasm had crossed her face. "Nothing, go on. You're flying to New London."

"Only if you agree. I'll do nothing that we both don't concur on, from now on and forever."

"All right."

"Well, I take the physical. I also check the situation, and make very sure that a married applicant has a chance, and that if he's admitted he gets to spend time with his wife. That takes care of our first few months, maybe our first year. I'll eventually go to one submarine base or another, if I get through, and you'll come along, the way Janice is doing. We all might end up at Pearl Harbor together. There's a university in Hawaii. You might even teach there."

"Goodness, you've been thinking with might and main, haven't you?"

Victor Henry came through the doors to the terrace. Byron glanced up, and said coolly and distantly, "Hi, looking for me?"

"Hi. I understand you're driving Madeline to the airport. Don't leave without me. I just talked to Washington and I've got to scoot back. Your mother's staying on."

"When's the plane?" Natalie said.

"One-forty."

"Can you lend me some money?" she said to Byron. "I think I'll go to Washington on that plane."

Pug said, "Oh? Glad to have your company," and went back into the club.

"You're going to Washington!" Byron said. "Why there, for crying out loud?"

She put a cupped palm to Byron's face. "Something about Uncle Aaron's citizenship. While you're in New

London, I can take care of it. My God, what's the matter? You look as though you've been shot."

"You're mistaken. I'll give you the fare."

"Byron, listen, I do have to go there, and it would be plain silly to fly down to Miami and then right back up to Washington. Can't you see that? It's for a day or two at most."

"I said I'd give you the fare."

Natalie sighed heavily. "Darling, listen, I'll show you Aaron's letter. He asked me to talk to Leslie Slote about his passport problem, it's beginning to worry him." She opened her purse.

"What's the point?" Byron stiffly stood up. "I believe you."

Warren insisted on coming to the airport, though Pug tried to protest that the bridegroom surely had better things to do with his scanty time. "How do I know when I'll see all of you again?" Warren kept saying. Rhoda and Janice got into the argument, and the upshot was that the Henrys plus the bride and Natalie all piled into Lacouture's Cadillac.

Rhoda on the way out had snatched a bottle of champagne and some glasses. "This family has been GYPPED by this miserable, stupid war," she declared, handing the glasses around as Byron started up the car. "The first time we're all together in how many years? And we can't even stay together for twelve hours! Well, I say, if it's going to be a short reunion it's damn well going to be a merry one. Somebody sing something!"

So they sang "Bell Bottom Trousers" and "She Wore a Yellow Ribbon" and "I've Got Sixpence" and "Auld Lang Syne" as the Cadillac rolled toward the airport. Natalie, crowded between Rhoda and Madeline, tried to join in, but "Auld Lang Syne" was the only song she knew. Rhoda pressed a glass on her, and filled it until wine foamed over the girl's fingers. "Oops, sorry, dear. Well, it's a mercy your suit's black," she said, mopping at Natalie's lap with her handkerchief. When the car drove through the airport entrance they were singing one Natalie had never even heard, a family favorite that Pug had brought from California:

> *Till we meet, till we meet*
> *Till we meet at Jesus' feet*
> *Till we meet, till we meet*
> *God be with you till we meet again*

and Rhoda Henry was crying into her champagne-soaked handkerchief, stating that these were tears of happiness over Warren's wonderful marriage.

PART TWO

Pamela

27

As FRANCE was caving in, people began at last to perceive that a main turn of mankind's destiny now hung on flying machines. Of these there were only a few thousand on the planet. The propeller warplanes of 1940 were modestly destructive, compared to aircraft men have built since. But they could shoot each other down, and unopposed, they could set fire to cities far behind battle lines. Massive bombing of cities from the air had, for some years after the First World War, been considered war's ultimate and unthinkable horror. But by 1940, the Germans had not only thought of it, but had twice done it: in the Spanish Civil War and in Poland. The Japanese, too, had bombed China's cities from the air. Evidently the ultimate horror was quite thinkable, though the civilized term for it, strategic bombing, was not yet in vogue. The leaders of England therefore had to face a bitter decision: whether to send their few precious planes to fight over France against the Germans, or hold them back to defend the homeland's cities and shores.

The French had even fewer planes. In the years before the war, instead of constructing an air fleet, the French had built their Maginot Line. Their military thinkers had argued that aircraft were the scouts and stinging insects of war, useful, annoying, hurtful, but incapable of forcing a decision. As the French state, under the punch of German dive bombers, flew to pieces like a Limoges vase hit by a bullet, its premier issued a sudden frantic public appeal to President Roosevelt to send "clouds of airplanes." But there were no clouds to send. Maybe the French premier did not know what a paltry air force America had, or that even then, no fighter plane in existence could travel more than a couple of hundred miles. The level of information among French politicians at the time was low.

Meantime, over the fields of Belgium and France, British pilots had learned something important. They could knock down German flying machines. They knocked down many; but many British planes fell too. As the Battle of France went on, the French implored their retreating allies to throw in all their aircraft. This the British did not do. Their air commander, Dowding, told Winston Churchill that twenty-five squadrons had to be kept intact to save England, and Churchill listened to him. The French collapse thus became foredoomed, if it had ever been anything else.

At the height of the debacle, on June 9, in a letter to old General Smuts, Winston Churchill explained himself. The military sage had reproved him for failing to observe a first principle of war: *Concentrate everything at the decisive point.* Churchill pointed out that with the short-ranged fighter planes then in the air on both sides, the side that fought nearer its airdromes had a big advantage.

"The classical principles are in this case modified by the actual quantitative data," he wrote. *"I see only one way through now, to wit, that Hitler should attack this country, and in so doing break his air weapon. If this happens, he will be left to face the winter with Europe writhing under his heel, and probably with the United States against him after the presidential election is over."*

Winston Churchill, today an idealized hero of history, was in his time variously considered a bombastic blunderer, an unstable politician, an intermittently inspired orator, a reckless self-dramatizer, a voluminous able writer in an old-fashioned vein, and a warmongering drunkard. Through most of his long life he cut an antic, brilliant, occasionally absurd figure in British affairs. He never won the trust of the people until 1940, when he was sixty-six years old, and before the war ended they dismissed him. But in his hour he grasped the nature of Hitler, and sensed the way to beat him: that is, by holding fast and pushing him to the assault of the whole world, the morbid German dream of rule or ruin, of dominion or *Götterdämmerung*. He read his man and he read the strategic situation, and

with the words of his mouth he inspired the British people
to share his vision. By keeping back the twenty-five squadrons from the lost Battle of France, he acted toughly, wisely, and ungallantly; and he turned the war to the course
that ended five long years later, when Hitler killed himself
and Nazi Germany fell apart. This deed put Winston
Churchill in the company of the rare saviors of countries,
and perhaps of civilizations.

With France and the Low Countries overrun, and the
Germans at the Channel, England now lay within range
of the Luftwaffe's fighter planes. The United States was
safe from air attack in 1940, but the onrolling conquest of
Europe by the Germans, combined with the growing menace of Japan, posed a danger to the future safety of the
United States. The question arose: if selling warplanes to
the British would enable them to go on knocking down
German aircraft, killing German pilots, and wrecking German bomber factories, might not that be, for American
security, the best possible use of the aging craft while new,
bigger, and stronger machines were built in the inaccessible
sanctuary across the ocean?

The answer, from the United States Navy, the Army, the
War Department, the Congress, the press, and the public,
was a roaring *NO!* Franklin Roosevelt wanted to help the
British, but he had to reckon with that great American
NO! Churchill, with the power of a wartime chief of state,
had not sent planes to France, because the survival of
England depended on them. Roosevelt, presiding over a
wealthy huge land at peace, could not even sell planes to
England without risking impeachment.

*   *   *

It was a shock for Victor Henry to see Franklin Roosevelt out from behind the desk in a wheelchair. The shirt-
sleeved President was massive and powerful-looking down
to the waist; below that, thin seersucker trousers hung
pitifully baggy and loose on his fleshless thigh bones and
slack lower legs. The crippled man was looking at a painting propped on a chair. Beside him stood the Vice Chief
of Naval Operations for Air, whom Victor Henry knew

well: a spare withered little naval aviator, one of the surviving pioneers, with a lipless mouth, a scarred red face,
and ferocious tangled white eyebrows.

"Hello there!" The President gave Victor Henry a hearty
handshake, his grip warm and damp. It was a steamy day,
and though the windows of the oval study were open, the
room was oppressively hot. "You know Captain Henry, of
course, Admiral? His boy's just gotten his wings at Pensacola. How about this picture, Pug? Like it?"

Inside the heavy ornate gold frame, a British man-o'-
war under full sail tossed on high seas beneath a storm-
wracked sky and a lurid moon. "It's fine, Mr. President. Of
course I'm a sucker for sea scenes."

"So am I, but d'you know he's got the rigging wrong?"
The President accurately pointed out the flaws, with great
relish for his own expertise. "Now how about that, Pug?
All the man had to do was paint a sailing ship—that was
his whole job—and he got the rigging wrong! It's positively
unbelievable what people will do wrong, given half a
chance. Well, that thing's not going to hang in here."

During all this, the admiral was training his eyebrows
like weapons at Victor Henry. Years ago, in the Bureau of
Ordnance, they had violently disagreed over the deck plating on the new carriers. Junior though he was, Henry had
carried his point, because of his knowledge of metallurgy.
The President now turned his chair away from the painting,
and glanced at a silver clock on his desk shaped like a
ship's wheel. "Admiral, what about it? Are we going to put
Pug Henry to work on that little thing? Will he do?"

"Well, if you assigned Pug Henry to paint a square-
rigger, Mr. President," the admiral replied nasally, with a
none too kind look at Pug, "you might not recognize it,
but he'd get the rigging right. As I say, a naval aviator
would be a far more logical choice, sir, but—" He gestured
reluctant submission, with an upward chop of a hand.

The President said, "We went through all that. Pug, I
assume somebody competent is tending shop for you in
Berlin?"

"Yes, sir."

Roosevelt gave the admiral a glance which was a command. Picking his white hat off a couch, the admiral said,
"Henry, see me at my office tomorrow at eight."

"Aye aye, sir."

Victor Henry was left alone with the President of the United States. Roosevelt sighed, smoothed his thin rumpled gray hair, and rolled himself to his desk. Victor Henry now noticed that the President did not use an ordinary invalid's wheelchair, but an odd piece of gear, a sort of kitchen chair on wheels, in and out of which he could easily slide himself. "Golly, the sun's going down, and it's still sweltering in here." Roosevelt sounded suddenly weary, as he contemplated papers piled on the desk. "Isn't it about time for a drink? Would you like a martini? I'm supposed to mix a passable martini."

"Nothing better, sir."

The President pressed a buzzer. A grizzled tall Negro in a gray gabardine jacket appeared and deftly gathered papers and folders out of various trays, while Roosevelt pulled wrinkled papers from one pocket and another, made quick pencilled notes, jabbed papers on a spike and threw others in a tray. "Let's go," he said to the valet. "Come along, Pug."

All down one long hall, and in the elevator, and down another hall, the President glanced at papers and scrawled notes, puffing at the cigarette holder in his teeth. His gusto for the work was evident, despite the heavy purple fatigue smudges under his eyes and the occasional deep coughs racking his chest. They arrived in a small dowdy sitting room hung with sea paintings. "That thing isn't going to end up in here either," said the President. "It's going in the cellar." He handed all the papers to the valet, who wheeled a chromium-stripped bar beside his chair and left.

"Well, how was the wedding, Pug? Did your boy get himself a pretty bride?" said the President in chatty and warm, if faintly lordly tones, measuring out gin and vermouth like an apothecary. Henry thought that perhaps the cultured accent made him sound more patronizing than he intended to be. Roosevelt wanted to know about the Lacouture house, and wryly laughed at Victor Henry's account of his argument with the congressman. "Well, that's what we're up against here. And Ike Lacouture's an intelligent man. Some of them are just contrary and obstinate fools. If we get Lacouture in the Senate, he'll give us real trouble."

A very tall woman in a blue-and-white dress came in, followed by a small black dog. "Just in time! Hello there, doggie!" exclaimed the President, scratching the Scottie's head as it trotted up to him and put its paws on the wheel-chair. "This is the famous Pug Henry, dear."

"Oh? What a pleasure." Mrs. Roosevelt looked worn but energetic: an imposing, rather ugly woman of middle age with fine skin, a wealth of soft hair, and a smile that was gentle and sweet, despite the protruding teeth stressed in all the caricatures. She firmly shook hands, surveying Pug with the astute cool eyes of a flag officer.

"The Secret Service has an unkind name for my dog," Roosevelt said, handing his wife a martini. "They call him The Informer. They say he gives away where I am. As though there were only one little black Scottie in the world. Eh, Fala?"

"What do you think of the way the war's going, Captain?" said Mrs. Roosevelt straight off, sitting in an arm-chair and holding the drink in her lap.

"It's very bad, ma'am, obviously."

Roosevelt said, "Are you surprised?"

Pug took a while to answer. "Well, sir, in Berlin they were mighty sure that the western campaign would be short. Way back in January, all their government war contracts had a terminal date of July first. They thought it would all be over by then and they'd be demobilizing."

Roosevelt's eyes widened. "That fact was never brought to my attention. That's extremely interesting."

Mrs. Roosevelt said, "Meantime, are they suffering hardships?"

Victor Henry described the "birthday present for the Führer" drive, collecting household tin, copper, and bronze; the newsreel of Göring adding busts of himself and Hitler to a mountain of pots, pans, and irons, and wash-tubs; the death penalty announced for collectors caught taking anything for their own use; the slogan, *One pan per house; ten thousand tons for the Führer*. He talked of snowbound Berlin, the lack of fuel, the food rationing, the rule that a spoiled frozen potato had to be bought with each good one. It was against the law, except for foreigners and sick people, to hail a taxi in Berlin. Russian food deliveries were coming in slowly, if at all, so the Nazis were wrapping butter from Czechoslovakia in Russian-printed packages to foster the feeling of Soviet support. The "wartime beer," a uniform brew reduced in hops and alcohol content, was undrinkable, but the Berliners drank it.

"They've got a 'wartime soap' too," Pug said. *"Einheitsseife.* When you get into a crowded German train it's not much in evidence."

Roosevelt burst out laughing. "Germans are getting a bit ripe, eh? I love that. *Einheitsseife!"*

Pug told jokes circulating in Berlin. In line with the war effort speedup, the Führer had announced that the period of pregnancy henceforth would be three months. Hitler and Göring, passing through conquered Poland, had stopped at a wayside shrine. Pointing to the crucified Christ, Hitler asked Göring whether he thought that would be their final fate. *"Mein Führer,* we are perfectly safe," Göring said. "When we are through there will be no wood or iron left in Germany."

Roosevelt guffawed at the jokes and said that there were far worse ones circulating about himself. He asked animated questions about Hitler's mannerisms in the meeting at Karinhall.

Mrs. Roosevelt interjected in a sharp serious tone, "Captain, do you think that Mr. Hitler is a madman?"

"Ma'am, he gave the clearest rundown on the history of central Europe I've ever heard. He did it off the cuff, just rambling along. You might think his version entirely cockeyed, but it all meshed together and ticked, like a watch."

"Or like a time bomb," said the President.

Pug smiled at the quick grim joke, and nodded. "This is an excellent martini, Mr. President. It sort of tastes like it isn't there. Just a cold cloud."

Roosevelt's eyebrows went up in pride and delight. "You've described the *perfect* martini! Thank you."

"You've made his evening," said Mrs. Roosevelt.

Roosevelt said, "Well, my dear, even the Republicans would agree that as a President, I'm a good bartender."

It wasn't much of a jape, but it was a presidential one, so Pug Henry laughed. The drink, the cosiness of the room, the presence of the wife and the dog, and the President's naïve pleasure in his trivial skill, made him feel strangely at home. The little black dog was the homiest touch; it sat worshipping the crippled President with a bright stare, now and then running a red tongue over its nose or shifting its look inquiringly to Pug.

Sipping his martini, his pose in the wheelchair as relaxed as before, but the patrician tones subtly hardening for business, Roosevelt said, "Do you think the British will hold out, Pug, if the French collapse?"

"I don't know much about the British, sir."

"Would you like to go there for a spell as a naval observer? Possibly after you've had a month or so back in Berlin?"

Hoping that Franklin Roosevelt was in as pleasant a mood as he seemed, Victor Henry took a plunge. "Mr. President, any chance of my not going back to Berlin?"

Roosevelt looked at the naval captain for an uncomfortable five or ten seconds, coughing hard. His face sobered into the tired gravity of the portraits that hung in post offices and naval stations.

"You go back there, Pug."

"Aye aye, sir."

"I know you're a seafaring man. You'll get your sea command."

"Yes, Mr. President."

"I'd be interested in your impressions of London."

"I'll go to London, sir, if that's your desire."

"How about another martini?"

"Thank you, sir, I'm fine."

"There's the whole question of helping the British, you see, Pug." The President rattled the frosty shaker and poured. "No sense sending them destroyers and planes if the Germans are going to end up using them against us."

Mrs. Roosevelt said with a silvery ring in her voice, "Franklin, you know you're going to help the British."

The President grinned and stroked the Scottie's head. Over his face came the look of complacent, devilish slyness with which he had suggested buying the Allied ocean liners—eyebrows raised, eyes looking sidewise at Pug, mouth corners pulled far up. "Captain Henry here doesn't know it yet, but he's going to be in charge of getting rid of those old, useless, surplus Navy dive bombers. We badly need a housecleaning there! No sense having a lot of extra planes cluttering up our training stations. Eh, Captain? Very untidy. Not shipshape."

"Is that definite at last? How wonderful," said Mrs. Roosevelt.

"Yes. Naturally the aviators didn't want a 'black shoe' to handle it." Roosevelt used the slang with self-conscious pleasure. "So naturally I picked one. Aviators all stick together and they don't like to part with planes. Pug will pry the machines loose. Of course it may be the end of me if word gets out. *That'll* solve the third-term question! Eh? What's your guess on that one, Pug? Is that man in the White House going to break George Washington's rule and try for a third term? Everybody seems to know the answer but me."

Victor Henry said, "Sir, what I know is that for the next four years this country is going to need a strong Commander-in-Chief."

Roosevelt's mobile pink face turned grave and tired again, and he coughed, glancing at his wife. He pressed a buzzer. "Somebody the people aren't bored with, Pug. A politician exhausts his welcome after a while. Like an actor who's been on too long. The good will ebbs away and he loses his audience." A Navy lieutenant in dress blues with gold shoulder loops appeared in the doorway. Roosevelt offered his hand to Victor Henry. "That Sumner Welles thing didn't come to anything, Pug, but our conscience is clear. We made the effort. You were very helpful."

"Aye aye, sir."

"Welles wasn't as impressed with Hitler as you evidently were."

"Sir, he's more used to being around great men."

A peculiar flash, not wholly pleasant, came and went in the President's tired eyes. "Good-bye, Pug."

•   •   •

A crashing thunderstorm, with thick rain hissing down from skies black as night, stopped Victor Henry from leaving the White House. He waited for a letup in a crowded open doorway marked PRESS, where a cool damp wind brought in a smell of rainy grass and flowers. All at once a heavy hand thwacked his shoulder.

"I say, Henry, you've got yourself another stripe!" Alistair Tudsbury, swelling in green gabardine, leaning on a cane, his moustached face purpler than before around the nose and on the cheeks, beamed down at him through thick glasses.

"Hello there, Tudsbury!"

"Why aren't you in Berlin, old cock? And how's that magnificent wife of yours?"

As he spoke, a small black British car pulled up to the entrance in the streaming rain and honked. "That's Pamela. What are you doing now? Why not come along with us? There's a little reception at the British embassy, just cocktails and such. You'll meet some chaps you ought to know."

"I haven't been asked."

"You just have been. What's the matter, don't you like Pam? There she sits. Come along now." Tudsbury propelled Henry by the elbow out into the rain.

"Of course I like Pamela," Henry managed to say as the father opened the car door and thrust him in.

"Pam, look who I bagged outside the press room!"

"Why, how wonderful." She took a hand off the wheel and clasped Pug's, smiling familiarly as though not a week had passed since their parting in Berlin. A small diamond sparkled on her left hand, which before had been bare of rings. "Tell me about your family," she said as she drove out of the White House grounds, raising her voice over the slap of the wipers and the drumming of the rain. "Is your wife well? And what happened to that boy of yours who was caught in Poland? Is he safe?"

"My wife's fine, and so's Byron. Did I mention to you the name of the girl he travelled with to Poland?"

"I don't believe you did."

"It's Natalie Jastrow."

"Natalie! Natalie *Jastrow*? Really?"

"Knows you, she says."

Pamela gave Henry a quizzical little glance. "Oh, yes. She was visiting a chap in your embassy in Warsaw, I should think. Leslie Slote."

"Exactly. She went to see this fellow Slote. Now she and my son intend to get married. Or so they say."

"Oh? Bless me. Well, Natalie's quite a girl," said Pamela, looking straight ahead.

"How do you mean that?"

"I mean she's extraordinary. Intelligence, looks." Pamela paused. "Willpower."

"A handful, you mean," Pug said, remembering that Tudsbury had used the word to describe Pamela.

"She's lovely, actually. And ten times more organized than I'll ever be."

"Leslie Slote's coming to this party," Tudsbury said.

"I know," Pamela said. "Phil Rule told me."

The conversation died there, in a sudden cold quiet. When the traffic halted at the next red light, Pamela shyly reached out two fingers to touch the shoulder board of Henry's white uniform. "What does one call you now? Commodore?"

"Captain, captain," boomed Tudsbury from the rear seat. "Four American stripes. Anybody knows that. And mind your protocol. This man's becoming the Colonel House of this war."

"Oh, sure," Pug said. "An embassy papershuffler, you mean. The lowest form of animal life. Or vegetable, more exactly."

Pamela drove skillfully through the swarming traffic of Connecticut and Massachusetts Avenues. As they came to the embassy, the rain was dwindling. Late sunlight shafted under the black clouds, lighting up the pink banks of blooming rhododendron, the line of wet automobiles, and the stream of guests mounting the steps. Pamela's streaking arrival and skidding halt drew glares from several Washington policemen, but nothing more.

"Well, well, sunshine after the storm," said Tudsbury. "A good omen for poor old England, eh? What's the news, Henry? Did you hear anything special at the White House? Jerry is really riding hell for leather to the sea, isn't he? The teletype says he's knocked the French Ninth Army apart. I do think he's going to cut the Allied line right in two. I told you in Berlin that the French wouldn't fight."

"They're supposed to be counterattacking around Soissons," Pug said.

Tudsbury made a skeptical face. As they went inside and fell into the long reception line extending up a majestic stairway, he said, "The bizarre thing to me is the lack of noise over Germany's invasion of Belgium and Holland. The world just yawns. This shows how far we've regressed in twenty-five years. Why, in the last war the rape of Belgium was an earth-shaking outrage. One now starts by assuming total infamy and barbarity in the Germans. That gives them quite an edge, you know. Our side doesn't have that freedom of action in the least."

At the head of the wide red-carpeted stairs, the guest of honor, a skinny, ruddy man of fifty or so, in a perfectly cut double-breasted black suit with huge lapels, stood with the ambassador, shaking people's hands under a large painting of the King and Queen, and now and then nervously touching his wavy blond hair.

"How are you, Pam? Hullo there, Talky," he said.

"Lord Burne-Wilke, Captain Victor Henry," Tudsbury said. Pamela walked on, disappearing into the crowd.

Duncan Burne-Wilke offered Pug a delicate-looking but hard hand, smoothing his hair with the other.

"Burne-Wilke is here to try to scare up any old useless aeroplanes you happen to have lying around," said Tudsbury.

"Yes, best prices offered," said the ruddy man, briefly smiling at the American, then shaking hands with somebody else.

Tudsbury limped with Pug through two large smoky reception rooms, introducing him to many people. In the second room, couples shuffled in a corner to the thin music of three musicians. The women at the party were elegantly clad, some were beautiful; men and women alike appeared merry. It struck Victor Henry as an incongruous scene, considering the war news. He said so to Tudsbury.

"Ah well, Henry, pulling long faces won't kill any Germans, you know. Making friends with the Americans may. Where's Pam? Let's sit for a moment, I've been on my feet for hours."

They came upon Pamela drinking at a large round table with Leslie Slote and Natalie Jastrow. Natalie wore the same black suit; so far as Pug knew she had come to Washington in the clothes she stood up in, with no luggage but a blue leather sack. She gave him a haggard smile, saying, "Small world."

Pamela said to her father, "Governor, this is Natalie Jastrow. The girl who went tootling around Poland with Captain Henry's son."

Slote said, rising and shaking hands with Tudsbury, "Talky, you may be the man to settle the argument. What do you think the chances are that Italy will jump into the war now?"

"It's too soon. Mussolini will wait until France has all but stopped twitching. Why do you ask?"

Natalie said, "I've got an old uncle in Siena, and somebody should go and fetch him out. There's nobody in the family but me to do it."

Slote said, "And I tell you, Aaron Jastrow's quite capable of getting himself out."

"Aaron Jastrow?" said Tudsbury with an inquisitive lilt. "*A Jew's Jesus?* Is he your uncle? What's the story?"

"Will you dance with me?" Pamela said to Pug, jumping up.

"Why, sure." Knowing how much she disliked dancing, he was puzzled, but he took her hand and they made their way through the jam toward the musicians.

She said as he took her in his arms, "Thanks. Phil Rule was coming to the table. I've had enough of him."

"Who is Phil Rule?"

"Oh—he was the man in my life for a long time. Far too long. I met him in Paris. He was rooming with Leslie Slote. He'd been at Oxford when Leslie was a Rhodes Scholar. Phil's a correspondent, and an excellent one, but a monster. They're much alike, a pair of regular rips."

"Really? Slote's the brainy quiet type, I thought."

Pamela's thin lips twisted in a smile. "Don't you know they can be the worst? They have pressure-cooker souls, those fellows." They danced in silence for a while; she was as clumsy as ever. She spoke up cheerily. "I'm engaged to be married."

"I noticed your ring."

"Well, it was a good job I didn't wait for that Navy flier son of yours, wasn't it?"

"You didn't give me any encouragement, or I might have worked on it."

Pamela laughed. "Fat lot of difference that would have made. And Natalie really has your other boy, has she? Well, that's the end of the available Henrys, then. I made my move in good time."

"Who is he, Pamela?"

"Let's see. Ted's rather hard to describe. Teddy Gallard. From an old Northamptonshire family. He's nice-looking and rather a lamb, and a bit mad. He's an actor, but he hadn't got too far when he joined the RAF. He's only twenty-eight. That makes him fairly ancient for flying. He's in France with a Hurricane squadron."

After another silence Pug said, "I thought you didn't like to dance. Especially with Americans."

"I don't. But you're so easy to dance with and so tolerant. The young ones are now doing an insane thing called the shag. One or two have got gold of me and fairly shagged my teeth loose."

"Well, my style is straight 1914."

"Possibly that was my year. Or should have been. Oh dear," she said, as the music changed tempo and some of the younger couples began hopping up and down, "here's a shag now."

They walked off the dance floor to a purple plush settee in the foyer, where they sat under a bright bad painting of Queen Mary. Pamela asked for a cigarette and took several puffs, leaning an elbow on her knee. Her low-cut dress of rust-colored lace partly showed a small smooth white bosom; her hair, which on the *Bremen* had been pulled back in a thick bun, hung to her shoulders now in glossy brown waves.

"I have a yen to go home and enlist in the WAAFs." He said nothing. She cocked her head sideways. "What do you think?"

"Me? I approve."

"Really? It's rank disloyalty, isn't it? Talky's doing a vital service to England here."

"He can get another secretary. Your lucky RAF man is there."

She colored at the word *lucky*. "It's not that simple. Talky's eyes do get tired. He likes to dictate and to have things read to him. He keeps weird hours, works in the bathtub, and so forth."

"Then he'll have to indulge his eccentricities a bit less."

"But is it right just to abandon him?"

"He's your father, Pamela, not your son."

Pamela's eyes glistened at him.

"Well, if I actually do it, we shall have Tudsbury in *Lear,* for a week or two. *'How sharper than a serpent's tooth it is, to have a thankless child!'*—I think the governor will rather enjoy throwing himself into the part, at that. Perhaps we should return to him now, Captain Henry."

He said as they stood and walked to the main reception room, "Why not call me Pug, by the way? Everybody does who knows me."

"Yes, I heard your wife call you that. What does it mean?"

"Well, at the Naval Academy, anybody named Henry usually gets called Patrick, the way a Rhodes gets labelled Dusty. But there was a 'Patrick' Henry in the class above me, and I was a freshman boxer, so I got tagged Pug."

"You boxed?" Her glance travelled across his shoulders and arms. "Do you still?"

He grinned. "Kind of strenuous. Tennis is my game, when I can get around to it."

"Oh? I play fair tennis."

"Well, good. If I ever get to London, maybe we can have a game."

"Are you—" She hesitated. "Is there any chance of your coming to London?"

"It's not impossible. There they are, way down there," Pug said. "Gosh, this room's mobbed."

"Natalie seems miserable," Pamela said.

Pug said, "She just lost her father."

"Oh? I didn't know that. Well, she's grown more attractive, that's sure. Definitely marrying your boy, is she?"

"It seems so. Maybe you can give *me* advice on that one. I feel she's too old for him, too smart for him, and just about everything else is wrong with it, except that they're crazy about each other. Which is something, but not everything."

"Maybe it won't come off. There's many a slip," Pamela said.

"You never have met Byron. You'd see in a minute what I mean, if you did. He's really still a baby."

She mischievously glanced at him and tapped his arm. "You do sound fatherly at that."

Tudsbury and Slote were in a lusty argument, with Natalie looking sombrely from one to the other.

"I'm not talking about anything he owes England. That's beside the point," Tudsbury said, striking his empty glass on the table. "It's his responsibility to the American people as their leader to ring the alarm and get them cracking, if they're to save their own hides."

"What about the Chicago quarantine speech?" Slote said. "That was over two years ago, and he's still trying to live down the warmonger charges. A leader can't dash ahead around the bend and out of sight. The people still haven't gotten over their disgust with the First World War. Now here's another one, brought on by stupid French and British policy. It's not the time for singing 'Over There,' Talky. It just won't work."

"And while Roosevelt watches his timing," said Tudsbury, "Hitler will take half the world. Pamela, be a love and get me another drink. My leg's killing me."

"All right." Pamela docilely walked to the bar.

Tudsbury turned to Henry, "You know the Nazis. Can Roosevelt afford to wait?"

"What choice has he? A few months ago Congress was fighting him just on selling you guns."

"A few months ago," Tudsbury said, "Hitler wasn't overrunning Belgium. Holland, and France, and directly facing you across the water."

"Lot of water," said Pug.

Slote slowly beat two fingers with one, like a professor. "Talky, let's review the ABC's. The old regimes are simply not competent for the industrial age. They're dead scripts, molted skins. Europe's made a start on replacing them by a lot of wholesale murder—the usual European approach to problems, and that's all the First World War was about—and then by resorting to tyrannies of the left or the right. France has simply stagnated and rotted. England's played its same old upper-crust butterfly comedy, while soothing the workers with gin and the dole. Meantime Roosevelt has absorbed the world revolt into legislation. He has made America the only viable modern free country. It was a stupendous achievement, a peaceful revolution that's gutted Marxian theory. Nobody wholly grasps that yet. They'll be writing books about it in the year 2000. Because of it, America's the power reserve of free mankind. Roosevelt knows that and moves slowly. It's the last reserve available, 'the last best hope.' "

Tudsbury was screwing all his heavy features into a mask of disagreement. "Wait, wait, *wait*. To begin with, none of the New Deal issued from this great revolutionary's brain. The ideas flooded into Washington with the new people when the administration changed. They were quite derivative ideas, mostly copied from us decadent butterflies. We were a good deal ahead of you in social legislation.— Ah, thank you, Pam.—Now this slow moving can be good politics, but in war it's a tactic of disaster. Fighting Germany one at a time, we'll just go down one at a time. Which would be a rather silly end to the English-speaking peoples."

"We have theatre tickets. Come and have dinner with us," Slote said, standing and stretching out a hand to Natalie, who rose too. "We're going to L'Escargot."

"Thank you. We're dining with Lord Burne-Wilke. And hoping to inveigle Pug Henry into joining us."

*   *   *

Slote bought Natalie as luxurious a dinner as Washington offered, with champagne; took her to a musical comedy at the National Theatre; and brought her back to his apartment, hoping for the best. In a common enough masculine way, he thought that if all went well he could win her back in one night. She had once been his slave; how could such a feeling disappear? At first she had seemed just another conquest. He had long planned a prudent marriage in his thirties to some girl of a rich or well-connected family, after he had had his fun. Natalie Jastrow now put him in a fever that burned up all prudent calculations. Leslie Slote had never wanted anything in his life as he wanted Natalie Jastrow. Her distracted lean look of the moment was peculiarly enticing. He was quite willing to marry her, or do anything else, to have her again.

He opened his apartment door and snapped on lights.

"Ye gods, a quarter to one. Long show. How about a drink?"

"I don't know. If I'm to search around tomorrow in New York courthouses for Aaron's documents, I'd better get to bed."

"Let me see his letter again, Natalie. You mix us a couple of shorties."

"All right."

Removing his shoes, jacket, and tie, Slote sank in an armchair, donned black-rimmed glasses, and studied the letter. He took one book after another from the wall— heavy green government tomes—and drank, and read. The ice in both drinks tinkled in the silence.

"Come here," he said.

Natalie sat on the arm of the couch, under the light. Slote showed her, in a book, State Department rules for naturalized citizens living abroad more than five years. They forfeited citizenship, but the book listed seven exceptions. Some seemed to fit Aaron Jastrow's case—as when health was a reason for staying abroad, or when a man past sixty and retired had maintained his ties with the United States.

"Aaron's in hot water on two counts," Slote said. "There's this joker about his father's naturalization. If Aaron actually wasn't a minor at the time, even by a week or a day, he isn't an American, technically, and never has been one. But even if he was, he has the five-year problem. I mentioned this to him once, you know. I said he should go back to the United States and stay a few months. I'd just seen too many passport messes crop up on this point, ever since the Nazis took over Germany." Slote picked up the glasses, went to his kitchenette, and mixed more drinks, continuing to talk. "Aaron's been a fool. But he's far from unique. It's unbelievable how careless and stupid Americans can be about citizenship. In Warsaw a dozen of these foul-ups turned up every week. The best thing now—by far—is to get the Secretary of State to drop a word to Rome. The day that word arrives Aaron will be in the clear." Padding to the couch in his stocking feet, he handed her a drink and sat beside her. "But trying to unravel any technical problem, however small, through channels scares me. There's a monumental jam of cases from Europe. It could take Aaron eighteen months. I therefore don't think there's much point in your digging around in Bronx courthouses for his alien registration and his father's naturalization records. Not yet. After all, Aaron's a distinguished man of letters. I'm hoping the Secretary will shake his head in amusement at the folly of absentminded professors, and shoot off a letter to Rome. I'll get on this first thing in the morning. He's a thorough gentleman. It ought to work."

Natalie stared at him.

He said, "What's the matter?"

"Oh, nothing." The girl drank off half her drink, all at once. "It certainly helps to know a man who knows a man, doesn't it? Well! If I'm to hang around Washington till the end of the week, we'll have to get me a hotel room, Leslie. I'm certainly not going to stay here after tonight. I feel damned odd even about that. I can still try a few of the hotels."

"Go ahead. I was on the phone for an hour. Washington in May is impossible. There are four conventions in town."

"If Byron finds out, God help me."

"Won't he believe that I slept on the couch?"

"He'll have to, if he finds out. Leslie, will you get me permission to go to Italy?"

He compressed his mouth and shook his head. "I told you, the Department's advising Americans to leave Italy."

"If I don't go, Aaron won't come home."

"Why? A broken ankle isn't disabling."

"He just will never pull himself together and leave. You know that. He'll dawdle and potter and hope for the best."

Slote said with a shrug, "I don't think you want to go there to help Aaron. Not really. You're just running away, Natalie. Running away, because you're in way over your head with your submarine boy, and shattered by losing your father, and actually don't know what on earth to do next with yourself."

"Aren't you clever!" Natalie clinked the half-full glass down on the table. "I leave in the morning, Slote, if I have to stay at the YWCA. But I'll make your breakfast first. Do you still eat your eggs turned over and fried to leather?"

"I've changed very little, altogether, darling."

"Good-night." She closed the bedroom door hard.

Half an hour later Slote, dressed in pajamas and a robe, tapped at the door.

"Yes?" Natalie's voice was not unfriendly.

"Open up."

Her faintly smiling face was pink and oily, and over a nightgown she had bought that afternoon she wore a floppy blue robe of his. "Hi. Something on your mind?"

"Care for a nightcap?"

She hesitated. "Oh, why not? I'm wide awake."

Humming happily, Leslie Slote went to the kitchen and emerged almost immediately with two very dark highballs. Natalie sat on the couch, arms folded, face shiny in the lamplight.

"Thanks. Sit down, Leslie. Stop pacing. That was a mean crack about Byron."

"Wasn't it the truth, Natalie?"

"All right. If we're playing the truth game, isn't it simpler today than it was a year ago for a Foreign Service officer to have a Jewish wife, since the Nazis are now beyond the pale?"

Slote's cheery look faded abruptly. "That never once occurred to me."

"It didn't have to occur to you. Now listen, dear. You can feed me stiff highballs, and play 'This Can't Be Love' on the phonograph, and all that, but do you really want me to invite you into the bedroom? Honestly, it would be a sluttish thing to do. I don't feel like it. I'm in love with somebody else."

He sighed and shook his head. "You're too damned explicit, Natalie. You always have been. It's coarse, in a girl."

"You said that the first time I proposed, sweetie." Natalie stood, sipping her highball. "My goodness, what a rich drink. I do believe you're nothing but a wolf." She was scanning the books. "What can I read? Ah, Graham Wallas. The very man. I'll be asleep in half an hour."

He stood and took her by the shoulders. "I love you, I'll love you forever, and I'll try every way I can to get you back."

"Fair enough. Leslie, I must go to Italy to get Aaron out. Honestly! I feel horrible about my father. He was worrying over Aaron the very day he died. Maybe this is irrational expiation, but I've got to bring Aaron home safe."

"I'll arrange it, if it's arrangeable."

"Now you're talking. Thanks. Good-night." She kissed him lightly, went to the bedroom, and closed the door. He did not rap again, though he read for a long time and had more drinks.

28

THE Vice Chief of Naval Operations for Air was drinking coffee with a blond man in a blue Royal Air Force uniform. It was Lord Burne-Wilke; he nodded at Victor Henry, with a faint smile. During their long convivial dinner with the Tudsburys, Burne-Wilke had said not a word to Pug about this meeting.

"Good morning, Henry. I understand you know the Air Commodore." The admiral worked his eyebrows at Pug.

"Yes, sir."

"Good. Have a cup of coffee." The wiry old man bounced away from his desk to a map of the United States on the wall. "And let's get at it. Here, here, and here"—his bony finger jumped to Pensacola, St. Louis, and Chicago—"we've got fifty-three old-type scout bombers, SBU-1's and 2's, that have been declared surplus. We want to get them back to Chance-Vought, in Stratford, Connecticut—that's the manufacturer—and get all U.S. Navy markings and special equipment removed. Our British friends will then pick 'em up as is, and fly 'em to a carrier that's standing by in Halifax. That's the picture. For obvious reasons"—the admiral contracted his brows fiercely at Pug—"involving the Neutrality Act, this is a touchy business. So the idea is to get this done without leaving a conspicuous trail of blood, guts, and feathers. You can have a plane to take you around and you should get at it today."

"Aye aye, sir."

"We have sixty pilots on hand and waiting," said Lord Burne-Wilke. "How soon d'you suppose you could have the planes, Captain Henry?"

Victor Henry studied the map, then turned to the Englishman, "Day after tomorrow, sir, late afternoon? Would that be convenient? It'll take some time to get off those markings."

The Englishman gave him a stare, and then smiled at the Vice Chief of Naval Operations. The admiral remained impassive. "Day after tomorrow?" said Lord Burne-Wilke.

"Yes, sir. The stragglers, if any, could come along on the deck of the next available cargo ship."

"Actually, we were thinking in terms of a week from now," said Lord Burne-Wilke. "We've given some of the fliers leave. It would require a bit of rounding up. How about Wednesday morning? That gives you and us four days."

"Very well, sir."

Burne-Wilke said to the admiral, "You do think that's feasible?"

"He says so."

"Well, then, I had better get right at this."

As the door closed, the admiral glared at Victor Henry, with a tinge of humor showing. "Day after tomorrow, hey?"

"Admiral, I didn't think those pilots were really on hand and waiting."

The two men exchanged a look of insiders' amusement. The foreigner had demanded fast action; the U.S. Navy had offered him faster action than he could handle; very satisfying, and needing no words. "Well, Wednesday's cutting it close enough. Let's have some fresh coffee, hey? Now, this whole thing is a subterfuge." The admiral pressed a buzzer. "I suppose you grasp that. The boss man wants it, so that's that. There are a few things you'd better understand, however."

Showing a new grudging cordiality toward Victor Henry,

the admiral explained that the President had elicited from the Attorney General—"probably by twisting his arm pretty damn hard"—the scheme and the ruling for selling these planes to England despite the Neutrality Act. First, the Navy was declaring the aircraft surplus. Second, Chance-Vought was accepting them for a trade-in on new F-4-U's, at a good high price. Chance-Vought could afford to do this, because it was turning around and selling the old planes to England at a profit. The catch was that the delivery of the F-4-U's lay far in the future. Undoubtedly President Roosevelt was evading the spirit of the Neutrality Law and the will of Congress, by allowing these planes out of the country now. The Army in particular would raise a howl. It was very short of aircraft, and had a standing request in to the Navy for surplus flying machines of any description.

"Now, Henry, there's no question here, and no hope, of concealment in the long run. But if it were announced in advance, there'd be a big storm on the front pages. It might not go through, which would be too bad. Any Germans that the Limeys knock down with those old SBU's we won't have to fight later. We're not going to stay out of this brawl. The boss man's idea is to get it done and then take what comes. The way the war news is breaking, it may not cause a whisper, after the fact. I hope not. However"—the admiral paused, squinting at Victor Henry over the rim of his coffee cup—"this does involve a chance of congressional investigation. Somebody like you could end up a goat. The President thought you could get the job done, and I concurred, but this is a volunteer job. Strictly volunteer."

"Aye aye, sir," said Pug. "I'd better get at it."

⋅　　⋅　　⋅

Briny, my love—

Brace yourself. When you receive this letter I ought to be in Lisbon. I'm flying to Italy to fetch Uncle Aaron out of there. With luck I'll be back in two months or less. It depends on the earliest boat passage I can get for us, and for that damned library and all those research files.

Sweetheart, don't be angry. It's good for both of us to catch our breaths. Your submarine school, and even Uncle Aaron's mess, are providential. Your father's visit to Miami was an alarm clock, and it rang just in time.

My ideas have altered, I must say, since my Radcliffe days when I started the Student Antiwar Committee! I never realized there were people like you, Warren, and your father. I'm sure the stereotyped military men do exist in droves, the hard-drinking narrow bigoted nincompoops. I've met a few of those. The new thing is the Henrys. You're peculiarly unobtrusive on the American scene, I don't know just why, but thank God you're there!

Darling—weren't you having sober second thoughts about me at Warren's wedding? Honestly, I saw your mother's viewpoint and quite sympathized with her. Why on earth should her little boy Briny want to marry this dusky old Jewess, with Rhine maidens like Janice Lacouture so abundant in the United States?

Now, mind you, I have not the slightest sense of inferiority. I value my intelligence and I know I'm a passably attractive Dark Lady. Being a Jew is an accident to me. It's left little trace on my ideas or my conduct. Too little, I guess; we live in a secular age, and I'm a product of it. The question remains, should you and I try to bridge a big gap of background and interests because of a random encounter and a fantastic physical pull?

I'm *not* backing out, Byron, *I love you.* But a couple of months to think it over is no hardship, it's a godsend.

Now let me quickly tell you what's been happening. I enclose the letter Aaron sent me that you didn't want to look at. You can ignore his silly words about us. The whole picture of his problem is very clear in it.

Leslie Slote has been absolutely marvellous. You mustn't be jealous of him, Briny. The way you behaved when I left Pensacola was very upsetting to me. I've rejected repeated, almost grovelling marriage proposals from this man. I've told him that I love you, that I've promised to marry you, and that he is *out.* He knows it. Still he dropped everything to work on Aaron's stupid mess. Never forget that. Word has gone out to Rome *from the Secretary's office* to expedite Aaron's return!

It's less than two hours to plane time. I'm dashing this off in the airport. I didn't go home. I stopped in New York for a day and bought enough things to see me through the trip. I'm travelling *very* light—one suitcase! You'll be admitted to that submarine school, I'm positive of that. I know your father wants it desperately, and I think deep down you do too. It's the right thing for you now. When I come back, if you still want me, I'm yours. Plain enough?

So courage, and wish me luck. Here I go.

Love you,
Natalie

* * *

Three days before the start of the submarine course, Byron was sitting in a squalid furnished room over a Chinese laundry in New London, looking through the formidable reading list, when the postman rang. Natalie's large hurried *Special Delivery* scrawl on the thick envelope promised bad news. Slumped in a ragged armchair amid smells of soap and hot starch from below, Byron read her shocking letter over and over. He was glancing through Aaron's faintly typed sheets when the telephone jarred him.

"Ensign Henry? Chief Schmidt, commandant's office. Your father's here. He's gone with Captain Tully to inspect the *Tambor* over at Electric Boat. If you want to join them they're at Pier Six, the commandant says."

"Thank you."

Sore at being followed even here by his father, hot to vent his anger and disappointment, Byron took ten minutes to dress and leave.

Victor Henry, meanwhile, walking through the new submarine with his classmate, was in high good humor, though red-eyed with lack of sleep. The scout bomber job was done. It had taken a lot of work and travel. A dozen aircraft had been in repair shops, the pilots had been scattered over the countryside, and there was no sense of urgency anywhere. Getting all-night work on the disabled planes, dragging those pilots out of their wives' arms or back from their fishing trips, had been a struggle. Some commandants had asked rough questions. Jiggs Parker at the Great Lakes Air Station, another classmate of his, had put up a fight to get a written record of the transfer, until

Pug had told an outright lie about new top-secret equipment to be tested on the planes, which might be expended in the process. Jiggs had eyed him for a long silent minute, and then given in. Well, white lies were part of security, Victor Henry thought, and Jiggs knew that.

Byron caught up with his father and the commandant in the forward torpedo room of the *Tambor,* inspecting the new firing mechanisms. "Hello, Dad. What brings you here?"

The harsh voice, the look on Byron's face, told Pug something serious was wrong. "Happened to be not far from here, so I thought I'd mosey over. You met Byron yet, Red?"

"Not yet. I know he passed the physical and he's in the new class." Captain Tully offered his hand. "Welcome aboard, Byron. You're in for a rough couple of months."

"I'll try to survive, sir."

At the almost contemptuous words, Red Tully's eyes shifted disapprovingly to the father. Byron followed along on the tour without another word, his countenance white and angry.

"Say, what the devil's the matter with you?" Victor Henry snapped as he and his son came out of the conning tower on the breezy slippery black deck, leaving Captain Tully below talking to the skipper. "You'd do well to watch your tone toward your superiors. You're in the Navy now."

"I know I'm in the Navy. Read this."

Pug saw Natalie's name on the envelope Byron thrust out. "Isn't it personal?"

Still Byron offered the letter. Victor Henry held the flapping pages in both hands and read them there on the submarine deck. His face was flushed as he handed them back to his son. "Quite a girl. I've said that before."

"If anything happens to her over there, I'll hold you responsible, Dad, and I'll never forget it."

Pug frowned at his son. "That's unreasonable. She's gone to Italy because of her uncle."

"No. You scared her off by saying I might not get admitted here if I were married. It wasn't true. A lot of the students are married men. If you hadn't come to Miami I might be one by now."

"Well, if I misled her, I'm sorry. I wasn't sure of the criteria, I thought that for hazardous duty they preferred single men, and for all I know, they do, and simply can't get enough. Anyway, this is what you should be doing. She's dead right about that, and I give her credit for realizing it. Possibly I should have butted out, but the decisions you're making now will shape your whole life, and I wanted to help."

It was a wordy speech for Victor Henry, and he spoke without his usual firmness, disturbed by his son's fixed hostile expression. He felt guilty, an unfamiliar sensation: guilty of interfering in his son's life and possibly of driving off the girl. Even if Natalie had been wrong for Byron, her sudden flight was a blow that he could feel almost as his son did. Suppose she had been the best thing in the world for the drifting youngster? Suppose, despite all good fatherly intentions, her being Jewish had made a difference?

Byron's answer was as sharp and short as his father's had been apologetic and strung-out. "Yes, you helped. She's gone. I'll never forget, Dad."

Red Tully emerged from the conning tower, looked around, and waved. "Hey, Pug? Ready to go ashore?"

Victor Henry said rapidly to his son, "You're in this now, Briny. It's the toughest school in the Navy. What's past is past."

Byron said, "Let's get off this thing," and he walked toward the gangway.

On a hot beautiful evening early in June, when the newspaper headlines were roaring of the British evacuation from Dunkirk, and Churchill on the radio was promising to fight to the end, on the beaches, in the streets, and in the hills, Victor Henry left for Europe. Rhoda stayed behind, because of the worsening of the war, to make a home for Madeline in New York. Pug had suggested this and Rhoda had rather enthusiastically agreed. Madeline, a busy and happy young woman, put up no objection.

Pug found it surprisingly easy to get a plane ticket at that time into the warring continent, as Natalie had. The hard thing was to get out.

29

NATALIE tried for five days to fly from Lisbon to Rome. She finally obtained a plane ticket, but at the last minute it was voided when a large party of boisterously laughing German army officers, obviously full of lunch and wine, streamed through the gate, leaving twenty excluded passengers looking at each other. This soured her on the airlines. Railroad passage across collapsing France was far too risky. She booked passage on a Greek freighter bound for Naples. The wretched voyage took a week. She shared a hot tiny cabin with a horde of black roaches and a withered Greek woman smelling of liniment; and she scarcely left it, horrid as it was, because on deck and in passageways the ship's officers and rough crewmen gave her disquieting looks. She could scarcely eat the food. The pitching and rolling kept her awake at night. En route, her portable radio squawked the BBC stories of the French government's flight from Paris, of Italy's jump into the war, and of Roosevelt's words, *"The hand that held the dagger has struck it into the back of its neighbor."* Natalie arrived in Italy nervous and exhausted, with a strong feeling that she had better get Aaron out of Siena at once, forgetting books, clothes, furniture—everything except the manuscript.

But once on dry land, after a decent meal or two with good wine, and a long luxurious night's sleep in a large soft hotel bed, she wondered at her own panic. Neither in Naples nor in Rome was there much sign that Italy was at war. The summer flowers spilled purple and red over stucco walls in bright sunshine, and in crowded streets the Italians went their lively ways as usual. Jocular, sunburned young soldiers had always abounded in Italian trains and cafés. They appeared as unbuttoned and placid as ever.

After the long, hot, filthy train ride to Siena, her first distant glimpse of the old town, rising out of the vine-covered round hills, gave her a stifled bored feeling, almost as Miami streets did. "God, who ever thought I'd come back here?" she said to herself. The hills outside the town already showed the veiled dusty green of midsummer. In Siena nothing had changed. The after-lunch deadness lay on the town; scarcely a dog moved in the empty red streets in the sun. It took her half an hour to find a working taxicab.

Aaron, in his broad-brimmed white hat and yellow Palm Beach summer suit, sat in his old place in the shade of the big elm, reading a book. Beyond him, over the ravine, the black-and-white cathedral towered above the red-roofed town. "Natalie! You made it! Splendid." He came stumping toward her on a cane, with one foot in a metal-framed cast. "I called and called for a taxicab, but when it was time for my nap none had come. I did have a wonderful nap.—Come inside, my dear, you'll want some refreshment. Giuseppe will see to your things."

The house looked the same, though the heavy foyer furniture now wore its green chintz slipcovers. In his study the pile of manuscript, the pile of notes, the array of reference books, were all in the same places. His writing board lay on the desk, with the yellow pages of his day's work clipped to it, awaiting morning revision.

"Why, Aaron, you haven't even begun to pack!"

"We'll talk about it over tea," he said, with an embarrassed smile. "I suppose you'd like to have a wash first?"

"But what's the situation, Uncle Aaron? Haven't you heard from Rome? Didn't word come from Washington?"

"Word came from Washington. That was fine of Leslie." He sank into a chair. "I really can't stand on this ankle yet for more than a few minutes. I stupidly fell again when it was almost healed. What a nuisance I am! But anyway, I reached page 967 today, and I do think it's goodish. Now go and have a wash, Natalie, you look positively boiled, and you're caked with dust."

. . .

The young consul in Florence received her affably, rising from behind a heavy carved black desk to escort her to a chair. The room reeked of the rum-flavored tobacco he was smoking in a curved rough briar pipe. The Sherlock Holmes prop looked odd in his small hand. He had a pink-and-white face, gentle bright blue eyes, and a childish thin mouth with the lower lip pulled in as though at some permanent grievance. His blond hair was thick, short, and straight. His gray silk suit, pinned white collar, and blue tie were elegant and neat. His desk nameplate read AUGUST VAN WINAKER II.

He said in a quavering voice, clearing it of hoarseness as he talked, "Well! The eminent author's niece, eh? What a pleasure. I'm sorry I couldn't see you this morning, but I was just up to my ears."

"Perfectly all right," Natalie said.

He waved his little hand loosely. "People have been scurrying home in droves, you see, and just dumping everything on the consulate. There's an awful lot of commerce still going on, and I'm stuck with the paperwork. I'm becoming a sort of broker and business agent for any number of American companies—unpaid, of course. I was in the most unbelievable snarl this morning over—of all things —a truckload of insecticide! Can you bear it? And, of course, there still are Americans in Florence. The screwier they are, the longer they stay." He giggled and rubbed his back hair. "The trouble I've been having with these two girls, room-mates, from California! I can't mention names, but one of them is from a rich Pasadena oil family. Well! She's gotten herself engaged to this slick little Florentine sheik, who calls himself an actor but actually is nothing but an overgrown grocery boy. Well, this oily charmer has gone and gotten her *room-mate* pregnant, my dear! The three of them have been having all-night brawls, the police have been in, and—oh, well. You don't get rich in this work, but there's never a dull moment." He poured water from a tall bottle into a heavy cut-glass goblet, and drank. "Excuse me. Would you like some Évian water?"

"No, thank you."

"I have to drink an awful lot of it. Some stupid kidney thing. Somehow it gets worse in the spring. I actually think Italian weather leaves a lot to be desired, don't you? Well!" His inquiring bland look seemed to add—*"What can I do for you?"*

Natalie told him about the new wrinkle in Jastrow's situation. The day Italy had entered the war, a man from the Italian security police had visited Jastrow and warned him that, as a stateless person of Polish origin, he was confined to Siena until further notice. She mentioned, as cordially as she could, that the OVRA undoubtedly knew this fact from intercepting Van Winaker's letter.

"Oh, my God, how perfectly awful," gasped the consul. "Is *that* what's happened? You're quite right, I didn't have my thinking cap on when I wrote that letter. Frankly, Natalie—if I may call you that—I was floored when your name came in today. I figured you'd have come and gone by now and taken your troublesome uncle home. He has been a trial, you know. Well! This is a pretty kettle of fish. I thought the visa solved everything and that I'd seen the last of the Jastrow case."

"What do we do now?" Natalie said.

"I'm blessed if I know, just offhand," said Van Winaker, running his fingers through his hair upward from the back of his neck.

"May I make a suggestion?" Natalie spoke softly and sweetly. "Just renew his passport, Mr. Van Winaker. That would stop the statelessness business. They couldn't hold him back then."

Van Winaker drank more Évian water. "Oh, Natalie, that's so easy to say! People don't see the screaming directives we get, warning us against abuse of the passport system. People don't see departmental circulars about consuls who've been recalled and whose careers have gone *poof!* because they were loose about these things. Congress makes the immigration laws, Natalie. The Consular Service doesn't. We're simply sworn to uphold them."

"Mr. Van Winaker, the Secretary of State himself wants Aaron cleared. You know that."

"Let's get one thing straight." Van Winaker held up a stiff finger, his round blue eyes gone sober. He puffed his pipe and waved it at her. "I have had no instructions from the Secretary. I'm extremely glad we're doing this face to face, Natalie, instead of on paper. He couldn't go on record as intervening for one individual against another in matters involving equal treatment under law." The eyes relaxed in a sly twinkle. "I *did* hear from Rome, between you and me, that his office asked us to expedite your uncle's departure. I was stretching way over backwards, honestly, issuing that visa, jumping him to the head of a list of *hundreds and hundreds* of names." Van Winaker knocked his pipe into a thick copper tray, and went on in a different, gossipy tone. "Actually, I think time will solve your uncle's problem. The French are already asking for an armistice. The British won't fight on very long. They'd be mad to try. If they do, the Luftwaffe will pound them to a jelly in short order. No, I fear me this round goes to Fritz. No doubt they'll have another go twenty years hence, when I devoutly hope to be out to pasture."

"But we can't count on the war ending," Natalie expostulated.

"Oh, I think you can. I expect peace by July first, if not sooner, Natalie. Then these wartime exit regulations will lapse and your uncle can just pick up and go home. Actually, this gives him the leisure to sort and crate his books. He seemed so concerned about his books."

"I want to take Uncle Aaron home tomorrow, and abandon books and everything. Please give him the passport."

"My dear, the contradiction in dates is right there in your uncle's expired book. It's incredible how those things used to slip through, but I've seen a hundred such cases if I've seen one. People used to be mighty careless! Now that it's been detected and made a matter of record, he has no more claim to American citizenship, technically speaking, than Hitler does. I couldn't be sorrier, but it's my duty to tell you the law."

This man was getting on Natalie's nerves. The use of Hitler's name disgusted her. "It strikes me that your duty is to help us, and that you're not really doing it."

He opened his eyes very wide, blinked, drank more Évian, and slowly stuffed his pipe, staring at the tobacco. "I have a suggestion. It's off the record, but I think it'll work."

"Tell me, by all means."

He pushed his hair straight up. "Just go."

She stared at him.

"I mean that! He's got his visa. You've got your passport. Hop a bus or train, or hire a car, and scoot to Naples. Ignore the confinement to Siena. The Italians are so sloppy! Get on the first boat and just leave. You won't be stopped. Nobody's watching your uncle."

"But won't they ask for an exit permit?"

"It's a trivial formality, dear. Say you lost it! Fumbling for it, you happen to take out a few thousand lire and put it on the table." He blinked humorously. "Customs of the country, you know."

Natalie felt her self-control giving way. Now the man was advising them to bribe an official, to risk arrest and imprisonment in a Fascist country. Her voice rose to shrillness. "I think I'd rather go to Rome and tell the Consul General that you're thwarting the desire of the Secretary of State."

The consul drew himself up, smoothed his hair with both hands, put them on the table, and said slowly and primly, "That is certainly your privilege. I'm prepared to take the consequences of that, but not of breaking the law. As it happens, I'm exceptionally busy, several other people are waiting, so—"

Natalie understood now how her uncle had fallen foul of this man. With a quick change to a placating smile, she said, "I'm sorry. I've been travelling for two straight weeks, I've just lost my father, and I'm not in the best of shape. My uncle's disabled and I'm very troubled about him."

At once the consul responded to the new manner. "I entirely understand, Natalie. Tell you what, I'll comb his file again. Maybe I'll come up with something. Believe me, I'd like nothing better than to see him go."

"You will try to find a way to give him a passport?"

"Or to get him out. That's all you want, isn't it?"

"Yes."

"I'll give it my serious attention. That's a promise. Come back in a week."

*　　*　　*

30

Eagle and Sea Lion

(from WORLD EMPIRE LOST)

The False Legend

The British have always been brilliant at war propaganda. Their portrayal of the so-called Battle of Britain was their supreme triumph of words. For uninformed people, their propaganda has hardened into history. A serious military discussion has to start by clearing away the fairy tales.

After the fall of France, Germany was incomparably stronger than England on the ground, about equally matched in the air, and gravely inferior at sea. Our surface navy was weak and meager; only the U-boat arm had real weight. The whole problem in the summer of 1940 was to force a decision across a sea barrier. In a set-piece invasion campaign, therefore, the British held the crucial advantage.

I have already stated, in my outline of Case Yellow, my belief that had we improvised a surprise crossing in June, when the disarmed British land forces were reeling home from Dunkirk, and their fleet was on far-flung stations, we might have conquered England in a short fierce campaign. But Hitler had passed up that chance. The resilient English had caught their breaths, instituted drastic anti-invasion measures, and marshalled their powerful navy to block a Channel crossing. At that point, Germany could only attack in the air, either to force a decision or to blast a path for invasion.

At the start one must compare the opposed air forces. Ninety-nine out of a hundred people, including Germans, still believe that a vast and powerful Luftwaffe was defeated by a

458

valorous handful of Thermopylae defenders in RAF uniforms
—or, in the words of the great phrasemaker, "Never in the
field of human conflict was so much owed by so many to so
few." In fact, both Germany and England had about a thousand fighter planes when the contest began. Germany's
bomber command was larger than England's, but the English
bombers, at least the newer ones, were heavier, longer-
ranged, and more powerfully armed.

Hitler and Göring, of course, voiced the most extravagant
boasts about the Luftwaffe, to induce the British to make
peace. Churchill, on the other hand, played up the fact that
England was outnumbered and alone, so as to pull the
United States into the war. As a result, the contest took on a
false aspect of David against Goliath.

British Advantages

Not only is the conventional picture distorted on the
comparison of forces; it takes no account of the handicaps
under which the Luftwaffe operated.

Most of the battle was fought over the British air bases.
Every German pilot shot down over land was lost, either dead
or a prisoner. But a downed British pilot, if he were unharmed, could soon take another plane into the skies. The
German pilot had only a few minutes of flying time in which
to do battle, for our fighters had a fuel limit of ninety minutes or so, most of which was consumed simply in getting to
the scene and returning to base. The British pilot, as soon as
he had climbed to combat altitude, could fight until he ran
out of bullets or gas.

Because of our fighter planes' short range, we could reach
only the southeast corner of England. The Luftwaffe was like
a tethered falcon, with London at the far end of the tether.
The rest of the United Kingdom was fairly safe from air attack, because unescorted bombers ran a high risk of annihila-
tion. The Royal Air Force could retire beyond range at will
for rest and repair; and far beyond the firing line could keep
fresh reserves and could rush the building of new planes.

Our fighters were further handicapped by orders to fly in
close formation with the bombers, like destroyers screening
battleships. No doubt this gave the bomber pilots a sense of
security, but it hobbled the fighters. In air combat, "seek out

and destroy" is the rule of rules. Fighter pilot teams should be free to roam the air space, spot the enemy, and strike first. Göring could never grasp this elementary point, though his fighter aces kept urging it on him. As our bomber losses climbed, he insisted more and more violently that the fighters should nursemaid the bombers, almost wingtip to wingtip. This seriously depressed pilot morale, already strained by prolonged combat and the death of many comrades.

Finally, the British in 1940 had one lucky scientific edge. They were first in the field with battleworthy radar and the fighter control it made possible. They could follow our incoming flights and speed their fighters straight at us. No fuel was wasted in patrol, nor were forces dispersed in search. If not for this factor alone, the Luftwaffe fighter command might have won a quick knockout victory. For in the end the Luftwaffe did all but shoot the Royal Air Force out of the skies. Churchill himself—and he is not interested in praising the German effort—states that in September the battle tilted against his fighter command.

Our attack at that point shifted to strategic bombing of London. Churchill asserts that it was Göring's fatal mistake. In truth, given the onset of bad weather, the provocative terror-bombing of our cities which required stern immediate retaliation, and the fact that invasion had to be tried before October 1 or not at all, the shift was almost mandatory. I discuss this point in detail in my day-by-day analysis of the campaign.

The Purpose of "Eagle Attack"

Adlerangriff, the Luftwaffe's "Eagle Attack" on England in the summer of 1940, was essentially a peacemaking gesture. It was a limited effort, intended to convince the British that to prolong the war would serve no purpose. The effort had to be made before the attack on Russia, to protect our rear to the westward. That it failed was of course a tragedy for Germany, since we were condemned to carry on this climactic world battle on two fronts. Historians are curiously slow to realize that it was more tragic for England.

Germany, after all, entered the war with little to lose, but in 1939 England was the world's first power. As a result of the war, though a supposed victor, she lost her world-girdling empire and shrank to the size of her home islands. Had the *Adlerangriff* induced her to make peace with Germany in 1940, that empire would almost surely still be hers, so it is hard to understand why the so-called Battle of Britain was her "finest hour." Her pilots performed with dash and valor, like their German racial cousins. But England threw away her last chance to prolong her world role, linked to a vigorous rising continental power; after that, she allied herself with Bolshevism to crush that power, Europe's last bastion against barbaric Asia; and she became as a result a weak withered satellite of the United States.

This debacle was all the work of the visionary adventurer Churchill, to whom the people had never before given supreme office. Churchill cast himself in the role of St. George saving the world from the horrible German dragon. He had the pen and the tongue to push this legend. He himself always believed it. The English believed it long enough to lose their empire, before becoming disillusioned and voting him out.

Hitler and England

Of all things, Hitler wanted no war with England. To this, I can personally testify. I do not need to, for it is written plainly in his turgid and propagandistic self-revelation, *Mein Kampf*. I saw his face at a staff conference on the day that England gave its strategically insane guarantee to Poland. I saw it again by chance in a corridor of the chancellery, on September 3, when contrary to Ribbentrop's assurances, England marched. That time, it was the face of a shattered man. It is impossible to understand what happened in 1940 without having this fact about Adolf Hitler firmly in mind, for from the start of the war to the end, German strategy, German tactics, and German foreign policy were never anything but this man's personal will.

No world-historical figure, when entering the scene, ever made his aims and his program clearer. By comparison, Alexander, Charles XII, and Napoleon were improvisers, moving where chance took them. In *Mein Kampf*, Hitler wrote in bombastic street-agitator language what he intended to do upon attaining power; and in the twelve years of his reign he did it. He wrote that the heart of German policy was to seize territory from Russia. That effort was the fulcrum of the Second World War, the sole goal of German arms. He also wrote that before this could be attempted, our traditional enemy France would have to be knocked out.

In discussing England, Hitler in *Mein Kampf* praises the valor of the race, its historical acumen, and its excellent imperial administration. Germany's grand aim, he says, must be a Nordic racial alliance in which England maintains its sea empire, while Germany as its equal partner takes first place on the continent and acquires new soil in the east.

From this conception Hitler never departed. When Churchill spurned his many peace offers, he felt a frustrated fury, which he vented on the Jews of Europe, since he felt that British Jewry was influencing Churchill's irrational policy. Almost to the hour of his suicide, Hitler hoped that England would see the light and would come to the only sensible arrangement of the world that was possible, short of abandoning one half to Bolshevism, and the other half to the dollar-obsessed Americans—the outcome the world must now live with.

In these considerations lies the secret of the failure of *Adlerangriff;* of our arrival at the coast, facing panicky England, without an operational plan for ending the war; and of the persistently unreal air about the Sea Lion plan, which, after elaborate and costly preparations, never came off. In the last analysis, the set-piece invasion did not sail because Hitler had no heart for beating England, and somehow our armed forces sensed this.

The Air Battle

The battle went in several stages. The Luftwaffe first attempted to make the British fight over the Channel, by attacking shipping. When the RAF would not come out and fight for the ships, Göring bombed the fighter bases. This forced the British fighter planes into the air. After knocking them about pretty badly, Göring—pushed by Hitler because of unconscionable British bombing of our civilians—sent in his bombers in the great Valhalla waves against London and other major cities, hoping to cause the people to depose Churchill and make peace. Hitler's July 19 speech, though perhaps a little blustery in language, had set forth very generous terms. But all was in vain, and the October rains and fogs closed gray curtains on the weary stalemate in the air. So ended the "Battle of Britain," with honors even, and England badly battered but gallantly hanging on.

Most military writers still blame Göring for our "defeat" over England. But this falls into the trap of the Churchillian legend that the Luftwaffe was beaten. That Germany's sparkling air force could do no better than fight a draw, I do, however, lay to Göring's charge. Despotic political control of an armed force, here as in Case Yellow, again meant amateurism in the saddle.

Herman Göring was a complicated mixture of good and bad qualities. He was clever and decisive, and before he sank into stuporous luxury, he had the brutality to enforce the hardest decisions. All this was to the good. But his vanity shut his mind to reason, and his obstinacy and greed crippled aircraft design and production. Until Speer came into the picture, the Luftwaffe was worse hit by bad management and supply on the ground than by any enemy in the air, including the Royal Air Force in 1940. Göring vetoed excellent designs for heavy bombers, and built a short-range air force as a ground support tool. Then in 1940 he threw the lightly built Luftwaffe into a strategic bombing mission beyond its capabilities, which nevertheless almost succeeded. As a ground support force, the Luftwaffe shone in Poland and France and in the opening attack on the Soviet Union. It fell off as our armies got further and further away from the air bases; but for quick knockout war on land, its achievements have yet to be surpassed.

In popular history—which is only Churchill's wartime rhetoric, frozen into historical error—Hitler the raging tiger sprang first on Poland, then insensately turned and tore France to death, then reached his blood-dripping claws toward England and recoiled snarling from a terrible blow between the eyes from the RAF. Maddened, blinded, balked at the water's edge, he turned from west to east and hurled himself against Russia to his doom.

In fact, from start to finish Hitler soberly and coolly— though with self-defeating amateurish mistakes in combat situations—followed out the political goals laid down in *Mein Kampf*, step by step. He yearned to come to terms with

England. No victorious conqueror ever tried harder to make peace. The failure to achieve this peace through the Eagle attack was of course a disappointment. It meant that our rear remained open to nuisance attack from England while we launched the main war in the east. It meant we had to divert precious limited resources to U-boats. Above all it meant the increasing intervention of America under Roosevelt.

The Final Tragedy

These nagging results of British obduracy festered in Adolf Hitler's spirit. He had in any case an unreasonable attitude toward the Jewish people. But the regrettable excesses which he at last permitted trace directly to this frustration in the west. A Germany allied with England—even with a benevolently neutral England—would never have drifted into those excesses. But our nation was beleaguered, cut off from civilization, and we became locked in a mortal combat with a primitive, giant Bolshevist country. Humane considerations went by the board. Behind the line, in conquered Poland and Russia, the neurotic extremists of the Nazi Party were free to give rein to their criminal tendencies. Hitler, enraged by the Churchillian opposition, was in no mood to stop them, as he could have with one word. When crossed, he was a formidable personality.

This was the most important result of the "Battle of Britain."

TRANSLATOR'S NOTE: Roon's discussion of the Battle of Britain is unacceptable. It is not a Teutonic trait to admit defeat gracefully. I have read most of the important German military books on the war, and few of them manage to digest this bitter pill. But Roon's far-fetched thesis that Winston Churchill's stubbornness caused the murder of the European Jews may be the low point in all this literature of self-extenuation.

His figures on the airplanes involved in the battle are unreliable. To be sure, few statistics of the war are harder to pin down. Depending on the date one takes as the start, the original balance of forces differs. Thereafter the figures change week by week due to combat losses and replacements. The fog of war at the time was dense, and both commands remained with tangled records. Still, no official source I have read calls it an equal match, as Roon calmly does.

His assertion that the attack was a "peacemaking gesture" is as ridiculous as his claim that the outcome was a draw. If there is ever another major war, I devoutly hope the United States armed forces will not fight such a "draw."

"Popular history" has it right. Göring tried to get daylight mastery of the air, the two fighter commands slugged it out, and he failed; then he tried to bomb the civilian population into quitting, first by day and then by night, and failed. The British fighter pilots turned the much larger Luftwaffe back, and saved the world from the Germans. The sea invasion never came off because Hitler's admirals and generals convinced him that the British would drown too many Germans on the way across, and in Churchill's words, "knock on the head the rest who crawled ashore." A navy remains a handy thing to have around when the going gets rough. I hope my countrymen will remember this.

There was no clear-cut moment of victory for the British. They really won when Sea Lion was called off, but this Hitler backdown was a secret. The Luftwaffe kept up heavy night raids on the cities, and this with the U-boat sinkings made the outlook for England darker and darker until Hitler attacked the Soviet Union. But the Luftwaffe never recovered from the Battle of Britain. This was one reason why the Germans failed to take Moscow in 1941. The blitzkrieg ran out of blitz in Russia because it had dropped too much of it on the fields of Kent and Surrey, and in the streets of London.—V.H.

*   *   *

31

SILVERY fat barrage balloons, shining in the cloudless sky ahead of the plane before land came in view, gave the approach to the British Isles a carnival touch. The land looked very peaceful in the fine August weather. Automobiles and lorries crawled on narrow roads, through rolling yellow-and-green patchwork fields marked off by dark hedgerows. Tiny sheep were grazing; farmers like little animated dolls were reaping corn. The plane passed over towns and cities clustered around gray spired cathedrals, and again over streams, woods, moors, and intensely green hedge-bounded fields, the pleasant England of the picture books, the paintings, and the poems.

This was the end of a tedious week-long journey for Pug via Zurich, Madrid, Lisbon, and Dublin. It had begun with the arrival in Berlin of a wax-sealed envelope in the pouch from Washington, hand-addressed in red ink: *Top Secret—Captain Victor Henry only*. Inside he had found a sealed letter from the White House.

Dear Pug:

Vice CNO says you are a longtime booster of "radar." The British are secretly reporting to us a big success in their air battle with something called "RDF." How about going there now for a look, as we discussed? You'll get dispatch orders, and our friends will be expecting you. London should be interesting now, if a bit warm. Let me know if you think it's too warm for us to give them fifty destroyers.

FDR

Pug had had mixed feelings about these chattily phrased instructions. Any excuse to leave Berlin was welcome. The red-ink blare and boasts in the meager newspapers were becoming intolerable; so were the happy triumphant Germans in government offices, chortling about the pleasant postwar life that would start in a mouth or so; so were the women strolling the tree-lined boulevards, looking slyly complacent in French silks and cosmetics. Pug even felt guilty eating the plunder in the improved restaurant menus: Polish hams, Danish butter, and French veal and wine. The gleeful voices of the radio announcers, claiming staggering destruction of British airplanes and almost no Luftwaffe losses, rasped his nerves as he sat alone in the evenings in the Grunewald mansion looted from a vanished Jew. An order to leave all this behind was a boon. But the letter dismayed him, too. He had not walked the deck of a ship now in the line of duty for more than four years, and this shore-bound status appeared to be hardening.

Walking home that afternoon he passed the rusting olive-painted Flakturm, and like nothing else it made him realize how glad he would be to get out of Berlin. People no longer gawked at the high tower bristling at the top with guns, as they had when the girder frame and the thick armor plates had been going up. Guesses and rumors about it had run fast and wild for weeks. Now the story was out. It was an A.A. platform for shooting at low-flying bombers. No high building could get in the lines of fire, for it rose far above the tallest rooftops in Berlin, a crude eyesore. So far the few English raiders had hugged maximum altitude, but the Germans seemed to think of everything. This gigantic drab iron growth, towering over the playing children and elderly strollers in the pretty Tiergarten, seemed to Victor Henry to epitomize the Nazi regime.

The lonely cavernous house got on his nerves that evening, as his quiet-stepping Gestapo butler served him pork chops from Denmark at one end of the long bare dining table. Pug decided that if he had to come back he would take a room at the Adlon. He packed suits and uniforms, the great weariness of an attaché's existence: morning coat, dress blues, dress whites, evening uniform, khakis, civilian street clothes, civilian dinner jacket. He wrote letters to Rhoda, Warren, and Byron, and went to sleep thinking of his wife, and thinking, too, that in London he would probably see Pamela Tudsbury.

Next day Pug's assistant attaché, a handsome commander who spoke perfect German, said he would be glad to take over his duties and appointments. He happened to be a relative of Wendell Willkie. Since the Republican convention, he had become popular with the Germans. "I guess I'll have to hang around this weekend, eh?" he said. "Too bad. I was going out to Abendruh with the Wolf Stöllers. They've been awfully kind to me lately. They said Göring might be there."

"Go by all means," said Pug. "You might pick up some dope about how the Luftwaffe's really doing. Tell your wife to take along a pair of heavy bloomers." He enjoyed leaving the attaché staring at him, mystified and vaguely offended.

And so he had departed from Berlin.

•   •   •   •

"How the devil do you keep looking so fit?" he said to Blinker Vance, the naval attaché who met him at the London airport. After a quarter of a century, Vance still batted his eyes as he talked, just as he had at Annapolis, putting the plebe Victor Henry on report for a smudged white shoe. Vance wore a fawn-colored sports jacket of London cut, and gray trousers. His face was dried and lined, but he still had the flat waist of a second classman.

"Well, Pug, it's pretty good tennis weather. I've been getting in a couple of hours every day."

"Really? Great war you've got here."

"Oh, the war. It's going on up there somewhere, mostly to the south." Vance vaguely waved a hand up at the pellucid heavens. "We do get some air raid warnings, but so far the Germans haven't dropped anything on London. You see contrails once in a while, then you know the fighters are mixing it up close by. Otherwise you just listen to the BBC for the knockdown reports. Damn strange war, a sort of airplane numbers game."

Having just toured bombed areas in France and the Low Countries, Henry was struck by the serene, wholly undamaged look of London, the density of the auto traffic, and the cheery briskness of the well-dressed sidewalk crowds. The endless shop windows crammed with good things surprised him. Berlin, even with its infusion of loot, was by comparison a bleak military compound.

Vance drove Victor Henry to a London apartment off Grosvenor Square, kept by the Navy for visiting senior officers: a dark flat on an areaway, with a kitchen full of empty beer and whiskey bottles, a dining room, a small sitting room, and three bedrooms along a hall. "I guess you'll be a bit crowded here," Vance said, glancing around at the luggage and scattered clothes of two other occupants in the apartment.

"Be glad of the company."

Blinker grimaced, winked his eyes, and said tentatively, "Pug, I didn't know you'd become one of these boffins."

"Boffins?"

"Scientific red-hots. That's what they call 'em here. The word is you came for a look-see at their newest stuff, with a green light from way high up."

Victor Henry said, unstrapping his bags, "Really?"

The attaché grinned at his taciturnity. "You'll hear from the Limeys next. This is the end of the line for me—until I can be of service to you, one way or another."

The loud coarse ring of a London telephone, quite different in rhythm and sound from the Berlin double buzz, startled Pug out of a nap. A slit of sunlight gleamed through drawn brown curtains.

"Captain Henry? Major-General Tillet here, Office of Military History." The voice was high, crisp, and very British. "I'm just driving down to Portsmouth tomorrow. Possibly drop in on a Chain Home station. You wouldn't care to come along?"

Pug had never heard the expression *Chain Home*. "That'll be fine, General. Thank you."

"Oh, really? Jolly good!" Tillet sounded delighted, as though he had suggested something boring and Pug had been unexpectedly gracious. "Suppose I pick you up at five, and we avoid the morning traffic? You might take along a shaving kit and a shirt."

Pug heard whiskeyish laughter in the next bedroom, the boom of a man and the tinkling of a young woman. It was six o'clock. He turned on the radio and dressed. A

mild Schubert trio ended, one he had often heard on the
Berlin station, and news came on. In a calm, almost
desultory voice, the broadcaster told of a massive air
battle that had been raging all afternoon. The RAF had
shot down more than a hundred German planes, and had
lost twenty-five. Half the British pilots had safely parachuted. The fight was continuing, the announcer said. If
there were any truth in this almost ludicrously understated
bulletin, Pug thought, an astonishing victory was shaping
up, high and invisible in the sky, while the Londoners
went about their business.

He found Pamela Tudsbury's number in the telephone
book and called her. A different girl answered, with a
charming voice that became more charming when Victor
Henry identified himself. Pamela was a WAAF now, she
told him, working at a headquarters outside London. She
gave him another number to call. He tried it, and there
Pamela was.

"Captain Henry! You're here! Oh, wonderful! Well, you
picked the right day to arrive, didn't you?"

"Is it really going well, Pam?"

"Haven't you heard the evening news?"

"I'm not used to believing the radio."

She gave an exhilarated laugh. "Oh, to be sure. The
Berlin radio. My God, it's nice to talk to you. Well, it's
all quite true. We've mauled them today. But they're still
coming. I have to go back on duty in an hour. I'm just
snatching a bite to eat. I heard one officer say it was the
turning point of the war. By the way, if inspection tours
are in order for you, you might bear in mind that I'm
working at Group Operations, Number Eleven Fighter
Group."

"Will do. How's your fiancé?"

"Oh, Ted? Fit as a flea. He's on the ground at the
moment. He's had a busy day! Poor fellow, old man of
the squadron, just turned twenty-nine. Look here, any
chance that we can see you? Ted's squadron gets its spell
off ops next week. We'll undoubtedly come down to
London together. How long will you be here?"

"Well, next week I should still be around."

"Oh, lovely. Let me have your number then, and I'll
call you. I'm so glad you're here."

He went out for a walk. London wore a golden light that evening, the light of a low sun shining through clear air. He zigzagged at random down crooked streets, along elegant rows of town houses, and through a green park where swans glided on calm water. He came to Trafalgar Square, and walked on through the Whitehall government buildings and along the Thames to Westminster Bridge. Out to the middle of the bridge he strolled, and stood there, looking at the untouched famous old city stretching on both sides of the river.

London's top-heavy red buses and scuttling black little taxis streamed across the bridge amid an abundant flow of private cars. Berlin's sparse traffic had been mostly government or army machines. London was a civilian city still, he thought, for all the uniforms. It had no Flakturm. The British seemed to have produced their navy and their RAF from the mere table scraps of the prosperity still visibly spread here. Now these table-scrap forces had to hold the line. His job was to make a guess whether they would; also, to see whether their new electronic stuff was really advanced. Looking at this pacific and rich scene, he doubted it.

He dined alone in a small restaurant, on good red roast beef such as one could only dream of in Berlin. The apartment was dark and silent when he returned. He went to bed after listening to the news. The claimed box score for the day was now a hundred thirty German planes down, forty-nine British. Could it be true?

　　　　　·　　　·　　　·

The small bald moustached general, in perfectly tailored khakis, smoked a stubby pipe as he drove, a severe look on his foxy much-wrinkled face. It had occurred to Victor Henry, after the phone conversation, that he might well be E. J. Tillet, the military author, whose books he greatly admired. And so he was; Tillet more or less resembled his book-jacket pictures, though in those the man had looked twenty years younger. Pug was not inclined to start a conversation with this forbidding pundit. Tillet said almost nothing as he spun his little Vauxhall along highways and down back roads. By the sun, Pug saw they were moving straight south. The further south they went, the more warlike the country looked. Signposts were gone, place names painted out, and some towns seemed deserted. Great loops of barbed steel rods over-arched the unmarked roads. Tillet said, pointing, "To stop glider landings," and shut up again. Victor Henry finally tired of the silence and the beautiful rolling scenery. He said, "I guess the Germans took a bad beating yesterday."

Tillet puffed until his pipe glowed and crackled. Victor Henry thought he wasn't going to reply. Then he burst out, "I *told* Hitler the range of the Messerschmitt 109 was far too short. He agreed with me, and said he'd take it up with Göring. But the thing got lost in the Luftwaffe bureaucracy. It's a great mistake to think dictators are all-powerful! They're hobbled by their paper shufflers, like all politicians. More so, in a way. Everybody lies to them, out of fear or sycophancy. Adolf Hitler walks in a web of flattery and phony figures. He does an amazing job, considering. He's got a nose for facts. That's his mark of genius. You've met him, of course?"

"Once or twice."

"I had several sessions with him. He's a great admirer of mine, or so he says. His grasp is quick and deep. The gifted amateur is often like that. I *said* Göring was making the same mistake with his fighter planes—designing them for ground support—that the French were making with their tanks. You don't have to give a ground support machine much range, because the fuel trucks are always close at hand to fill them up. Those French tanks were superb fighting machines, and they had thousands of them. But the wretched things could only run fifty, sixty miles at a crack. Guderian drove two hundred miles a day. Some difference! The French never could get it into their heads that tanks should mass and operate independently. God knows Fuller, de Gaulle, and I tried hard enough to explain it to them."

The car was bumping along a muddy detour past con-crete dragons' teeth and a stone wall, ringed in barbed wire, that blocked the highway. Masked workmen were raising clouds of gray dust with pneumatic hammers and drills.

"There's foolishness for you." Tillet pointed at the tank

trap with his pipe. "Intended to halt invaders. What this rubbish actually would do is reduce the maneuverability of our reserve to zero. Happily Brooke's taken charge now. He's cleaning all this out."

Pug said, "General Alan Brooke, is that?"

"Yes, our best man, a genius in the field. He managed the Dunkirk retreat. I was with his headquarters. I saw him demoralized only once. Headquarters was shifting from Armentières to Lille." Tillet knocked out his pipe in a dashboard tray and shifted his cold gray eyes to Pug. "The roads were crammed with refugees. Our command cars could hardly move. The Armentières lunatic asylum had been bombed. All the boobies had got out. There must have been two thousand of them all over the road, in loose brown corduroy pajamas, moping, drooling, and giggling. They swarmed around our car and looked into the windows, dripping saliva, making silly faces, waggling their hands. Alan turned to me. 'It's a rout, Ted,' he said. 'We're lost, you know, the whole BEF's lost. We've lost the damned war.' That's when I said, 'Never mind, Alan. There are a lot more lunatics on the German side of the hill, including the boss.' Well, that made him laugh, for the first time in days. After that he became himself again. A word in season, the Good Book says."

"Do you think Hitler's crazy?" Henry said.

Tillet chewed at his pipe, eyes on the road. "He's a split personality. Half the time he's a reasonable, astute politician. When he's beyond his depth he gets mystical, pompous, and silly. He informed me that the English Channel was just another river obstacle, and if he wanted to cross, why, the Luftwaffe would simply operate as artillery, and the navy as engineers. Childish. All in all, I rather like the fellow. There's an odd pathos about him. He seems sincere, and lonely. Of course, there's nothing for it now but to finish him off.—Hullo, we almost missed that turn. Let's have a look at the airfield."

This was Pug's first look at a scene in England that resembled beaten Poland and France. Bent blackened girders hung crazily over wrecked aircraft in the hangars. Burned-out planes stood in sooty skeletal rows on the field, where bulldozers were grinding around rubble heaps and cratered runways. "Jerry did quite a job here," said

Tillet cheerfully. "Caught us napping." The ruined airfield
lay amid grassy fields dotted with wild flowers, where
herds of brown cattle grazed and lowed. Away from the
burned buildings, the air smelled like a garden. Tillet said
as they drove off, "Göring's just starting to make sense,
going for the airfields and plane factories. He's wasted a
whole bloody month bombing harbors and pottering about
after convoys. He's only got till the equinox, the damned
fool—the Channel's impassable after about September the
fifteenth. His mission is mastery of the air, not blockade.
Define your mission!" he snapped at Victor Henry like a
schoolmaster. "Define your mission! And stick to it!"

Tillet cited Waterloo, lost for want of a few handfuls
of nails and a dozen hammers, because a general forgot his
mission. Marshal Ney's premature cavalry charge against
Wellington's center, he said, surprised and overran the
British batteries, gaining a golden chance to spike the
guns. But nobody had thought of bringing along hammers
and nails. "Had they spiked those guns," said Tillet
through his teeth—puffing angrily at his clenched pipe,
chopping a hand on the steering wheel, and getting very
worked up and red-faced—"had Marshal Ney remembered
what the *hell* his charge was all about, had one Frenchman among those five thousand thought about his mission,
we'd be living in a different world. With our artillery
silenced, the next cavalry charge would have broken Wellington's center. We'd have had a French-dominated
Europe for the next hundred and fifty years, instead
of a vacuum into which the German came boiling up. We
fought the Kaiser in 1914 and we're fighting Adolf right
now because that ass Ney forgot his mission at Waterloo
—if he ever knew it."

"For want of a nail the kingdom was lost," said Pug.

"Damned right!"

"I don't know much about Waterloo, but I never heard
that version. I just remember Blücher and his Prussians
showing up at sunset and saving the day."

"Wouldn't have been worth a tinker's dam if Ney had
fetched along his hammers and nails. By sunset Wellington would have been in full flight. Napoleon had routed
Blücher three days earlier. He'd have done it again with
ease."

The car went over the crest of a hill. Ahead, beyond green empty pastureland, lay the blue Channel, shining in the sun, and a hairline of French coast all along the horizon. They got out and stood amid high grass and red poppies blowing in a cool sea breeze. After an impressive silence, broken only by birdsong, Tillet said, "Well, there we are. You're looking at Hitler's France."

Turn by turn they scanned the coast through a telescope Tillet brought out of the car's trunk. Small images of houses and ships shimmered on the far shore.

"That's as close as Jerry's ever come," Tillet said. "Close enough, too."

"The Germans took all the neutral attachés on a tour of France not long ago," Pug said. "Brought us clear to the coast. The poppies are growing over there, too. We saw your chalk cliffs, and the Maginot Line guns they were pointing at you. Now I'm looking down the wrong end of those guns."

Tillet said, "They're no problem. They lob a few shells over for terror, but they fall in the fields. Nobody's terrorized."

Running westward along the coast, they passed through silent boarded-up villages, thickly tangled with barbed wire. Camouflaged pillboxes stood thick along the hills and in the towns. Pug saw a children's merry-go-round with the snouts of cannon peeking from under the platform of painted horses. Along the flat stony beaches, jagged iron rods spiked up, festooned with wire. As waves rose and fell, queerly shaped tangles of pipe poked above the water.

Pug said, "Well, you're not exactly unprepared."

"Yes. Adolf was decent enough to give us a breather, and we've used it. Those pipes out beyond the waterline are just the old Greek fire idea. We set the sea ablaze with petroleum, and fry the Germans we don't drown."

Barrage balloons came in sight over the hills to the west. "Ah. Here we are." Tillet pulled up under a spreading old tree. "Portsmouth has two possible restaurants, but the city's taken a pasting. They may be short of crockery. I have some sandwiches and coffee in the boot."

"Perfect."

Pug trotted up and down the road, restoring circulation

to his numb heavy legs, then sat beside Tillet under the tree. They ate the lunch wordlessly. Tillet appeared to have no small talk whatever. Pug did not mind, being more or less like that himself. "Look there," Tillet said, gesturing with the last of his sandwich. In the blue sky a patch of orange was flowering over the city, a barrage balloon on fire. "They're back today, after all. More coffee?"

"No thanks."

"Now, what's the damned fool doing hitting poor Portsmouth again? Yesterday he was going inland, where he should be." Tillet deftly packed the lunch things and got his binoculars. The air vibrated with the distant thump of A.A. firing and the hum of planes. "Shall we get along down there? I imagine it's a feint. It doesn't look like much of a show."

"Right."

Climbing in the car, Pug paused, and scanned the sky high to the east. "Look there, General."

Tillet squinted skyward, saw nothing, and used his binoculars. His eyes widened. "Yes. That's more like it." He passed the binoculars to Victor Henry. The binoculars resolved the gray moving dot into swarms of airplanes moving north in tight V's across the cloudless blue.

"Heinkels, a lot of 109's, and some 110's," Pug said. "More than a hundred of them."

"No Stukas? They're sitting birds. Our pilots say it's hardly sporting to go after them."

"I don't see any crooked wings up there. But they're pretty far off."

"Care to join our observer corps, Captain Henry?" Tillet's voice to him was slightly more cordial.

More barrage balloons over Portsmouth burst into flame and went writhing lazily down in black smoke. Fires were burning on the docks; white smoke trails crisscrossed the blue sky. The car passed a black plane nose down, burning in a grassy field, its markings hidden by flames. By the time they reached Portsmouth, fire fighters were streaming water on the blazes, and people were out in the streets gawking. Though buildings were smashed and burning and rubble heaps blocked many streets, the town did not look anything like Rotterdam, or even some of the badly hit French towns.

"Care to inspect the damage? You're welcome to, but it's a dreary sight. I'm thinking we might go straight on to the Chain Home station. Since Jerry does seem to be coming over today, you might find it interesting."

"Sure thing."

They had the ferry to themselves. The old wooden boat rolled nauseatingly on the little stretch of open water to the Isle of Wight.

"People forget how choppy this Channel is," said Tillet, clinging to a stanchion and raising his voice above the wind and the engine thump. "If the Germans do cross, they may arrive too seasick to fight. It's a factor."

An olive-painted military car awaited them at the landing. They drove across the bucolic island, passing one mansion after another shuttered and dead amid rolling wide lawns and shrubbery sprouting and flowering rankly. They saw no other car on their way to a cluster of iron and wooden huts around steel towers thrusting toward the sky, a grim blotch on the green holiday island.

A tubby man with a scarlet face, the group captain in charge of the station, offered them tea in his little office, chatting about the raid on Portsmouth. He also mentioned with some pride a large sea bass which he had hauled from the surf at dawn. "Well, shall we have a look at how things are going? There's rather a large attack been laid on today, I believe."

Victor Henry's first glimpse of British radar scopes at Ventnor, in a small stuffy room lit by one red light and foul with smoke, was a deep shock. He listened intently to the talk of the pale, slender man in gray tweed called Dr. Cantwell, a civilian scientist, as they inspected the scopes. But the sharp green pips were news enough. The British were miles ahead of the United States. They had mastered techniques that American experts had told him were twenty years off.

The RAF could measure the range and bearing of a ship down to a hundred yards or less, and read the result off a scope at sight. They could do the same to a single incoming airplane, or count a horde of airplanes, and give the altitude too. These instruments were marvels compared to the stuff that he had seen tested on the *New York* last year and that the Navy had ordered in large quantities. Pug Henry had two immediate thoughts: that the United States Navy had to get hold of this equipment; and that the British were far better prepared for war than the world knew. He admired the quiet sense of drama with which General Tillet had bowled him over. That was well done. But it all hung on the fact that they had these remarkable radars. Here was a moment of confrontation between America and England masked in a casual visit, in an offhand atmosphere, in a smoky, dim little room smelling of electric machinery, on a playground island deserted by the rich, facing the displaced Maginot Line guns.

"We have nothing like this," he said.

"Mm?" said Dr. Cantwell, lighting a cigarette. "Are you sure? They're pretty far along at MIT, we understand, with this sort of thing."

"I know what we've got." Pug saw on General Tillet's face, in the red light, the shadowy gleam that comes of drawing a good hand of cards: a deepening of lines, a brightening of eyes, nothing more. "How the devil do you obtain such a sharp beam? I pressed our boys on this. The answer was that it was a question of stepping down to shorter and shorter wavelengths. Beyond a certain point you can't do that, they say, and still get the power to shoot out the pulses to any distance."

The scientist nodded, his eyes almost shut, his face as blank as possible. But he too, Pug thought, was a happy man.

"Mm, yes, that's the problem, isn't it?" he mumbled. "But they'll certainly get around to the answer. It's a question of tube design, circuitry, and so forth. Our cavity magnetron does a pretty good job, at that. We're not entirely displeased with it."

"Cavity magnetron?"

"Yes. Cavity magnetron. One gets rid of the grid in a vacuum tube, you see, and one controls current flow with an external magnetic field. That allows for the more powerful pulses. It takes a bit of designing, but your people will certainly work it up in due course."

"No doubt. Got any cavity magnetrons for sale?"

Both Tillet and Dr. Cantwell burst out laughing, and even the enlisted men at their scopes turned around and smiled.

The scarlet-faced group captain peered at a scope where a boyish operator was chattering into a headphone. "Hullo, looks like we have another circus heading this way. Forming up over Le Havre again. A couple of dozen would you say, Stebbins?"

"Thirty-seven, sir."

Excitement thickened in the dark room as reports came in from several scopes. A young duty officer wearing headphones strolled from scope to scope, making notes on a clipboard, talking to the operators. To Pug Henry's eye this was smooth expert work, like the controlled tumult in a submarine conning tower during an attack run.

General Tillet said, "I take it you think rather well of our cavity magnetron."

"It's a major breakthrough, General."

"Hm. Yaas. Strange, isn't it, that warfare has come down to fencing with complicated toys that only a few seedy scholars can make or understand."

"Pretty useful toys," said Pug, watching the duty officer write down the ranges and bearings that the radar operators were barking. "Exact intelligence of the enemy's location and movements, without disclosing your own."

"Well, of course. We're damned grateful for our boffins. A few Englishmen did stay awake while our politicians kicked away air parity and all the rest of our military posture. Well, now that you've had a look, would you just as soon pop back to London? I thought we might have to stay here a day or two to see action, but Jerry's been obliging. We can break our trip overnight at some decent hotel, then whip up to London. A couple of people there would like a word with you."

·   ·   ·

Outside 10 Downing Street a single helmeted bobby paced in the morning sun, watched by a few sightseers on the opposite sidewalk. Remembering the grim arrays of SS men in front of Hitler's marble chancellery, Victor Henry smiled at this one unarmed Englishman guarding the Prime Minister's old row house. Tillet brought him in, introduced him to a male secretary in a morning coat, and left. The secretary led him up a wide stairway lined with portraits—

Pug recognized Disraeli, Gladstone, and Ramsay Mac-Donald—and left him waiting in a broad room full of beautiful old furniture and splendid paintings. Perched on a petit-point sofa, all alone, Pug had plenty of time to grow nervous before the secretary returned to fetch him.

In a small hot cluttered room that smelled of old books and dead cigars, the corpulent old Prime Minister stood near the window, one hand on his hip, looking down at a spread of photographs on his desk. He was very short and very stooped, with graceful little hands and feet; he bulged in the middle, and tapered upward and downward like Tweedledum. As he turned and went to meet Victor Henry, his walk was slow and heavy. With a word of welcome he shook hands and motioned Pug to a seat. The secretary left. Churchill sat in his armchair, put a hand on one arm, leaned back, and contemplated the American naval captain with filmy eyes. The big ruddy face, flecked and spotted with age, looked severe and suspicious. He puffed at the stump of his cigar, and slowly rumbled, "We're going to win, you know."

"I'm becoming convinced of that, Mr. Prime Minister," Victor Henry said, trying to control his constricted throat and bring out normal tones.

Churchill put on half-moon glasses, took up a paper and glanced at it, then peered over the rims at Henry. "Your post is naval attaché in Berlin. Your President has sent you here to have a look at our RDF, a subject in which you have special knowledge. He reposes much confidence in your judgment."

Churchill said this with a faint sarcastic note suggesting that he knew Pug was one more pair of eyes sent by Roosevelt to see how the British were taking the German air onslaught; also, that he did not mind the scrutiny a bit.

"Yes, sir. We call it radar."

"What do you think of my stuff, now that you've seen it?"

"The United States could use it."

Churchill uttered a pleased grunt. "Really? I haven't had an opinion quite like that from an American before. Yet some of your best people here have visited Chain Home stations."

"Maybe they don't know what we've got. I do."

"Well, then, I suggest you report to your President that we simple British have somehow got hold of something he can use."

"I've done so."

"Good! Now have a look at these."

From under the outspread pile of photographs, the Prime Minister drew several charts and passed them to the American. He dropped his gnawed stub into a shiny brass jar of sand, and lit a fresh cigar, which trembled in his mouth.

The colored curves and columns of the charts showed destroyer and merchant ship losses, the rate of new construction, the increase of Nazi-held European coastline, and the rising graph of U-boat sinkings. It was an alarming picture. Puffing clouds of blue and gray smoke, Churchill said that the fifty old destroyers were the only warships that he would ever ask of the President. His own new construction would fill the gap by March. It was a question of holding open the convoy lines and beating off invasion during these next eight months.

Every day danger mounted, he said, but the deal was bogging down. Roosevelt wanted to announce the lease of Caribbean naval bases on British islands as a trade for the destroyers. But Parliament would be touchy about bartering British soil for ships. Moreover, the President wanted a written guarantee that if the Nazis invaded and won, the British fleet would not yield to the Germans or scuttle itself, but would steam to American ports. "It is a possibility that I won't discuss, let alone publicly record," Churchill growled. "The German fleet has had considerable practice in scuttling and surrendering. We have had none."

Churchill added—with a crafty grin that reminded Pug a bit of Franklin Roosevelt—that giving fifty warships to one side in a war perhaps was not a wholly friendly act toward the other side. Some of the President's advisers feared Hitler might declare war on the United States. That was another difficulty.

"There's not much danger of that," Victor Henry said.

"No, not much hope of that," Churchill said, "I quite agree." His eyes under twisted brows looked impish as a comedian's. Victor Henry felt that the Prime Minister had paid him the compliment of stating his entire war policy in one wily joke.

"Here's that bad man's invasion fleet. Landing craft department," Churchill went on, scooping up and handing him a sheaf of photographs showing various oddly shaped boats, some viewed in clusters from the air, some photographed close on. "A raggle-taggle he's still scraping together. Mostly the prahms they use in inland waterways. Such cockleshells will ease the task of drowning Germans, as we devoutly hope to do to the lot of them. I should like you to tell your President that now is the time to get to work on landing craft. We shall have to go back to France and we shall need a lot of these. We have got some fairly advanced types, based on designs I made back in 1917. Look at them, while you're here. We shall want a real Henry Ford effort."

Victor Henry couldn't help staring in wonder at this slumping, smoke-wreathed puddle of an old man, fiddling with the thick gold chain across his big black-clad belly, who with three or four combat divisions, with almost no guns or tanks left after Dunkirk, with his back to the wall before a threatened onslaught of Hitler's hundred and twenty divisions, was talking of invading Europe.

Churchill stared back, his broad lower lip thrust out. "Oh, I assure you we shall do it. Bomber Command is growing by leaps and bounds. We shall one day bomb them till the rubble jumps, and invasion will administer the coup de grace. But we shall need those landing craft." He paused, threw his head back, and glared at Henry. "In fact, we are prepared now to raid Berlin in force, if he dares to bomb London. Should that occur while you're still here, and if you don't consider it foolhardy nonsense, you might go along to see how it's done." The pugnacious look faded, the wrinkled eyes blinked comically over the spectacles, and he spoke in slow jocular lisping rhythms. "Mind you, I don't suggest you return to your duty post by parachute. It would save time, but might be considered irregular by the Germans, who are sticklers for form."

Pug thought it was extremely foolhardy nonsense, but he said at once, "I'd be honored, of course."

"Well, well. Probably out of the question. But it would be fun, wouldn't it?" Churchill painfully pushed himself out of his chair, and Pug jumped up. "I trust General Tillet is taking good care of you? You are to see everything here that you've a mind to, good or bad."

"He's been perfect, sir."

"Tillet is very good. His views on Gallipoli I regard as slightly unsound, since he makes me out at once a Cyrano, a jackass, and a poltroon." He held out his hand. "I suppose you've seen a bit of Hitler. What do you think of him?"

"Very able, unfortunately."

"He is a most wicked man. The German badly wants tradition and authority, or this black face out of the forest appears. Had we restored the Hohenzollerns in 1919, Hitler might still be a ragged tramp, muttering to himself in a squalid Vienna doss house. Now, alas, we must be at considerable trouble to destroy him. And we shall." Churchill shook hands at the desk. "You were in War Plans and you may be again. I recommend that you obtain all our latest stuff on landing craft. Ask Tillet."

"Yes, sir."

"We shall require great swarms of the things. Great . . . *swarms!*" Churchill swept his arms wide, and Victor saw in his mind's eye thousands of landing craft crawling toward a beach in a gray dawn.

"Thank you, Mr. Prime Minister."

General Tillet was waiting in his car. They went to a room in the Admiralty where huge wall charts showed the disposition of the fleet. In the blue spaces of the Mediterranean, the Persian Gulf, and the Indian Ocean, the little colored pins looked sparse and lonesome, but the sowing around the home islands bristled thick. Pins in a thin line marked the great-circle convoy path across the Atlantic; Tillet traced this line with his pipe. "There's the problem. We breathe through that tube. If Jerry can cut it, we've bought it. Obviously we can use some old destroyers you've got lying around from the last war, not doing much of anything."

"Yes, so the Prime Minister said. But there's a political problem, General. Either Hitler's a menace to the United States, in which case we need everything we've got and a lot more—or he isn't, and in that case why should we let

you have part of our Navy to fight him? I'm just giving you
the isolationist argument."

"Mm, yaas. Of course we hope you'll think of common
traditions and all that, and the advantage of keeping us
alive, and the possibility that the Germans and Japanese,
dominating Europe and Asia and the oceans, might prove
more disagreeable over the years than we've been. Now I'm
still to show you those landing craft we've got up in Bristol,
and Fighter Command in Stanmore—"

"If I can, I'd also like to visit Group Operations, Number Eleven Fighter Group."

Tillet blinked at him. "Number Eleven? Jolly good idea.
Take a bit of arranging, but I believe we can lay it on."

32

VICTOR HENRY sat in the lobby of the Savoy, waiting for
Pamela and her fighter pilot. Uniforms thronged past, with
only a sprinking of dinner jackets on white-headed or bald
men. The young women, in colorful thin summer finery,
looked like a stream of excited amorous angels. On the
brink of being invaded by Hitler's hordes, England was the
gayest place he had ever seen.

This was nothing like the glum hedonism of the French
in May, going down with knives and forks in their hands.
Wherever the American had visited in a hard-driving week
—and by now this included shipyards, navy and air bases,
factories, government offices, and army maneuvers—he had
noted the resolute, cheerful spirit, borne out by the rise in
production figures. The British were beginning to turn out
tanks, planes, guns, and ships as never before. They now
claimed to be making airplanes faster than the Germans
were knocking them down. The problem was getting to be

fighter pilots. If the figures given him were true, they had
started with somewhat more than a thousand seasoned
men. Combat attrition was taking a steep toll, and to send
green replacements into the skies was fruitless. They could
kill no Germans and the Germans could kill them. England
had to sweat out 1940 with the fighter pilots on hand. But
how fast was the Luftwaffe losing its own trained pilots?
That was the key, Tillet said; and the hope was that
Göring was already throwing everything in. If so, and if
the British could hold on, there would come a crack in
Luftwaffe performance. The signal, said Tillet, might be a
shift to terror bombing of the cities.

"Here we are, late as hell," chirruped Pamela, floating
up to him in a mauve silk dress. Pamela's flier was short,
swarthy, broad-nosed, and rather stout, and his thick wavy
black hair badly needed cutting. Except for the creased
blue uniform, Flight Lieutenant Gallard looked like a
young lawyer or businessman rather than an actor, though
his brilliant blue eyes, sunken with fatigue, had a dramatic
sparkle.

Diamonds glittered in Pamela's ears. Her hair was done
up in a makeshift way. Pug thought she had probably
emerged from bed rather than a beauty parlor; and fair
enough, in the time and place! The notion gave him a pang
of desire to be young and in combat. Their table was waiting in the crowded grillroom. They ordered drinks.

"Orange squash," said Flight Lieutenant Gallard.

"Two dry martinis. One orange squash. *Very* good, sir,"
purred the silver-haired waiter, with a low bow.

Gallard gave Victor Henry a fetching grin, showing perfect teeth; it made him seem more of an actor. The fingers
of his left hand were beating a brisk tattoo on the starched
cloth. "That's the devil of an order, isn't it, in the Savoy?"

Pamela said to Pug, "I'm told he used to drink like a
proper sponge, but he went on orange squash the day we
declared war."

Pug said, "My son's a Navy flier. I wish he'd go on
orange squash."

"It's not a bad idea. This business up there"—Gallard
raised a thumb toward the ceiling—"happens fast. You've
got to look sharp so as to see the other fellow before he
sees you. You have to react fast when you do see him,

and then you have to make one quick decision after another. Things get mixed up and keep changing every second. You have to fly that plane for dear life. Now, some of the lads thrive on drink, they say it blows off their steam. I need all my steam for that work."

"There's a lot I'd like to ask you," said Victor Henry. "But probably this is your night to forget about the air war."

"Oh?" Gallard gave Pug a long inquiring look, then glanced at Pamela. "Not a bit. Fire away."

"How good are they?"

"The Jerries are fine pilots and ruddy good shots. Our newspaper talk about how easy they are makes us a little sick."

"And their planes?"

"The 109's a fine machine, but the Spitfire's a good match for it. The Hurricane's quite a bit slower; fortunately it's much more maneuverable. Their twin-engine 110 is an inferior machine, seems to handle very stiffly. The bombers of course are sitting birds, if you can get at them."

"How's RAF morale?"

Gallard flipped a cigarette in his mouth and lit it with swift gestures of one hand. "I'd say it's very high. But not the way the papers tell it. Not that dashing patriotic business. I can remember the first time I fought over England, when those dots appeared in the sky just where Fighter Control said they were, I had a bit of that feeling, I thought, 'Why, damn their eyes, they're really trying it, and what the hell are they doing flying over my country? Let's shoot the bloody bastards down!' But right away I became damn busy trying not to get shot down myself. That's how it's been ever since." He smoked in silence, his eyes wide and far away, his fingers dancing and dancing. He shifted in the chair, as though it were too hard. "It's a job, and we're trying to do our best. It's a lot more fighting than we had over France. You can tell your son, Captain, that fear's a big factor, especially as the thing goes on and on. The main thing is learning to live with it. Some chaps simply can't. We call it LMF, lack of moral fibre. The brute fact is that as range decreases, accuracy increases. You've *got* to close the range. There's nothing to do about that old truth of warfare. But there's always the chap who opens up and blazes away from afar, you know, and runs out of bullets and heads for home. And there's the one who somehow always loses the bird he's after in the clouds, or who never finds the foe and aborts the mission. One soon knows who they are. Nobody blames them. After a while they're posted out." He fell silent again, looking down at the smoking cigarette in his clasped hands, obviously absorbed in memory. He shifted in the chair again, and glanced up from Victor Henry to Pamela, who was watching his face tensely. "Well—the long and the short of it is, it's us against the Jerries, Captain Henry, and that's exciting. We're flying these machines that can cross all of England in half an hour. Excellent gun platforms. Best in the world. We're doing what very few men can do or ever have done. Or perhaps will ever do again." He looked around at the elegant grillroom full of well-dressed women and uniformed men, and said with an uncivilized grin, the whites showing around his eyeballs, "If excelling interests you, there it is"—he made the thumb gesture—"up there."

"Your orange squash, sir," said the waiter, bowing.

"And just in time," said Gallard. "I'm talking too much."

Pug raised his glass to Gallard. "Thanks. Good luck and good hunting."

Gallard grinned, drank, and moved restlessly in the chair. "I was an actor of sorts, you know. Give me a cue and I rant away. What does your son fly?"

"SBD, the Douglas Dauntless," said Pug. "He's a carrier pilot."

Gallard slowly nodded, increasing the speed of his finger tattoo. "Dive bomber."

"Yes."

"We still argue a lot about that. The Jerries copied it from your navy. Our command will have no part of it. The pilot's in trouble, we say, in that straight predictable path. Our chaps have got a lot of victories against the Stukas. But then again, providing they get all the way down, they do lay those bombs in just where they're supposed to go. Anyhow, my hat's off to those carrier fellows, landing on a tiny wobbly patch at sea. I come home to broad immovable mother earth, for whom I'm developing quite an affection."

"Ah, I have a rival," said Pamela. "I'm glad she's so old and so flat."

Gallard smiled at her, raising his eyebrows. "Yes, you've rather got her there, haven't you, Pam?"

During the meal, he described in detail to Victor Henry the way fighter tactics were evolving on both sides. Gallard got very caught up in this, swooping both palms to show maneuvers, pouring out a rapid fire of technical language. For the first time he seemed to relax, sitting easily in his chair, grinning with enthusiastic excitement. What he was saying was vital intelligence and Pug wanted to remember as much as possible; he drank very little of the Burgundy he had ordered with the roast beef. Pamela at last complained that she was drinking up the bottle by herself.

"I need all my steam, too," Pug said. "More than Ted does."

"I'm tired of abstemious heroes. I shall find myself a cowardly sot."

Gallard was having his second helping of roast beef and Yorkshire pudding—he was eating enormously, saying that he had lost almost a stone in three weeks and proposed to make it up in three days—when the headwaiter came to him with a written note. Gallard crumpled it up, wiped a napkin across his mouth, and excused himself. He returned in a few minutes, smiled at them, and resumed eating.

"Pam, there's been a change," he abruptly said when his plate was empty. "Our squadron's rest off ops is cancelled. We'll get it when the weather's a little cooler." He smiled at Victor Henry and drummed ten fingers on the table. "I don't mind. One gets fidgety, knowing the thing's still going on full blast and one's out of it."

In the silence at the little table, Victor Henry thought that the ominousness of this summons went much beyond the riskiness of recalling and sending up a fatigued, edgy pilot. It signalled that the RAF was coming to the end of its rope.

Pamela said, "When do you have to go back? Tomorrow?"

"Oh, I'm supposed to be on my way now, but I was damned well going to enjoy this company, and my beef."

"I shall drive you to Biggin Hill."

"Well, actually, they're digging the chaps out of various pubs and places of lesser repute, Pam. We'll be going up together. Those of us they can find." He glanced at his watch. "I'll be cracking off soon, but the evening's young. No reason for you not to go on to that Noel Coward show. I've heard it's very funny."

Quickly Pug said, "I think now's the time for me to leave you both."

The RAF pilot looked him straight in the eye. "Why? Don't you think you could bear Pamela's drunken chatter for another little while? Don't go. Here she is all tarted up for the first time in weeks."

"All right," Pug said. "I think I can bear it."

The pilot and the girl stood. Pamela said, "So soon? Well, we shall have a nice long stroll through the lobby."

As Pug got up and offered his hand, Ted Gallard said, "Good luck to you, Captain Henry, and to that son of yours in the Dauntless dive bomber. Tell him I recommend orange squash. Come and see us at Biggin Hill aerodrome."

Left alone at the table, Pug sat and wiped his right hand with a napkin. Gallard's palm had been very wet.

He did visit Ted Gallard's squadron, one afternoon a few days later. Biggin Hill lay southeast of London, squarely in the path of incoming German bombers from the nearest airfields across the Channel. The Luftwaffe was persisting in a fierce effort to knock out Biggin Hill, and the aerodrome was a melancholy scene: wrecked aircraft, burned-out roofless hangars, smashed runways, everywhere the inevitable stinks of burned wood, broken drains, blown-up earth, and smashed plaster. But bulldozers were snorting here and there, patching the runways, and a couple of planes landed as Pug arrived. On stubby fighters dispersed all over the field, mechanics in coveralls were climbing and tinkering, with much loud cheerful profanity. The aerodrome was very much in business.

Gallard looked very worn, yet happier than he had been in the Savoy Grill. In the dispersal hut he introduced Pug Henry to a dozen or so hollow-eyed, dishevelled lads in wrinkled uniforms, fleece-lined boots and yellow life jackets, lounging about on chairs and iron cots, either bare-headed or with narrow blue caps tilted over one eye. The arrival of an American Navy captain in mufti dried up the talk, and for a while the radio played jazz in the awkward silence. Then one pink-cheeked flier, who looked as though he had never shaved, offered Pug a mug of bitter tea, with a friendly insult about the uselessness of navies. He had been shot down by a British destroyer in the Channel, he said, and so might be slightly prejudiced. Pug said that speaking for the honor of navies, he regretted the idiocy; but as a friend of England, he approved the marksmanship. That brought a laugh, and they began talking about flying again, self-consciously for a while, but then forgetting the visitor. Some of the slang baffled him, but the picture was clear enough: everlasting alert, almost no sleep, too many airplanes lost in accidents as well as combat, far too many German fighters, and desperate, proud, nervous high spirits in the much reduced squadron. Pug gathered that almost half the pilots that had started the war were dead.

When the six o'clock news came on, the talk stopped and all huddled around the radio. It had been a day of minor combat, but again the Luftwaffe had come off second best in planes shot down, at a rate of about three to two. The fliers made thumbs-up gestures to each other, boyishly grinning.

"They're fine lads," Gallard said, walking Victor Henry back to his car. "Of course, for your benefit they cut the talk about girls. I'm the middle-aged man of the squadron, and I get left out of it too, pretty much. When they're not flying, these chaps have the most amazing experiences." He gave Pug a knowing grin. "One wonders how they manage to climb into their cockpits, but they do, they do."

"It's a good time to be alive and young," Pug said.

"Yes. You asked me about morale. Now you've seen it." At the car, as they shook hands, Gallard said diffidently, "I owe you thanks."

"You do? Whatever for?"

"Pamela's coming back to England. She told me that when they met you by chance in Washington, she was trying to make up her mind. She decided to ask you about it, and was much impressed by what you said."

"Well, I'm flattered. I believe I was right. I'm sure her father's surviving nicely without her."

"Talky? He'll survive us all."

. . .

"It's not going well," General Tillet said, maneuvering his car through a beetle-cluster of wet black taxicabs at Marble Arch. The weather had lapsed into rain and fog; pearl-gray murk veiled a warm, sticky, unwarlike London. Umbrella humps crowded the sidewalks. The tall red omnibuses glistened wetly; so did the rubber ponchos of the bobbies. The miraculous summer weather had given the air battle an exalting radiance, but today London wore a dreary peacetime morning face.

"The spirit at Biggin Hill is damned good," Pug said.

"Oh, were you there? Yes, no question about spirit! It's the arithmetic that's bad. Maybe the Fat Boy's getting low on fighter pilots, too. We are, that's flat. Perilously low. One doesn't know the situation on the other side of the hill. One hangs on and hopes."

The rain trailed off as they drove. After a while the sun hazily shone out on wet endless rows of identical grimy red houses, and sunlight shafted into the car. Tillet said, "Well, our meteorology blokes are on top of their job. They said the bad weather wouldn't hold, and that Jerry would probably be flying today. Strange, the only decent English summer in a century, and it comes along in the year the Hun attacks from the sky."

"Is that a good or bad break?"

"It's to his advantage for locating his target and dropping his bombs. But our interceptors have a better chance of finding him and shooting him down. Given the choice, our chaps would have asked for clear skies."

He talked of Napoleon's luck with weather, and cited battles of Charles XII and Wallenstein that had turned on freak storms. Pug enjoyed Tillet's erudition. He was in no position to challenge any of it, and wondered who was. Tillet appeared to have total knowledge of every battle ever fought, and he could get as annoyed with Xerxes or Caesar for tactical stupidity, as he was with Hermann Göring. About an hour later they came to a town, drove

along a canal of very dirty water, and turned off to a com-
pound of sooty buildings surrounded by a high wire fence.
A soldier at the gate saluted and let them pass. Pug said,
"Where are we?"

"Uxbridge. I believe you wanted to have a look at
Group Operations, Number Eleven Fighter Group," said
Tillet.

"Oh, yes." In three weeks, Tillet had never once mentioned the request and Victor Henry had never repeated
it.

A flight lieutenant with a pleasant chubby round face
met them. He was a lord, but Tillet clicked the long name
out too crisply for Pug to catch it. His lordship conducted
them out of the bright sunshine, down and down a long
turning stairway into the ground. "One rather expects to
encounter a white rabbit, doesn't one, Captain?" he fluted
in Oxonian tones. "Hurrying by consulting its pocket
watch, and all that. Nothing here that interesting, I'm
afraid."

They entered a shallow balcony in a small strange
theatre. In place of the stage and curtain stood a black
wall full of columns of electric bulbs, white except for a
single line of red lamps near the top. At the side of the
wall was a column of RAF terms for stages of readiness.
On the floor below, twenty or so girls in uniform, some
wearing headphones on long lines, worked around a large-
scale table map of southern England. On either wall, in
glassed boxes like radio control booths, men with headphones scrawled at desks. The place had an underground,
earth-and-cement smell, and it was quiet and cool.

"Burne-Wilke, here's your American visitor," said Tillet.

The blond officer sitting in the middle of the balcony
turned, smiling. "Hullo there! Frightfully glad to hear you
were coming. Here, sit by me, won't you?" He shook hands
with them. "Nothing much doing yet, but there will be
soon. The bad weather's drifting clear of the Channel, and
Jerry's getting airborne." Burne-Wilke rubbed his bony
pink chin with one hand, giving Pug a quizzical glance. "I
say, those aeroplanes you rounded up have proven ever so
useful."

"They can't play in this league," Pug said.

"They're excellent on patrol. They've done some smart

punishing of invasion barges. The pilots are keen on them."
Burne-Wilke looked him in the eye. "See here, *could* you
have produced those planes in two days?"

Pug only grinned.

Burne-Wilke shook his head and caressed his wavy hair.
"I was sorely tempted to take you up. But you struck me
as a chap who might just bring it off, and then we'd have
looked proper fools. Hullo, there's a mutual friend. Didn't
I first meet you with the Tudsburys, in a sweaty Washington receiving line?"

Pamela was walking in to take the place of another girl.
She looked up, threw Victor Henry a smile, then got to
work, and did not glance his way again.

"This is all fairly clear, isn't it?" said Burne-Wilke,
gesturing toward the map and the wall. "Fighter Command
at Stanmore is responsible for air defense, but it lets each
group run its own show. Our beat is southeast England. It's
the hot spot, closest to the Germans, and London's here."
He swept one lean arm toward the wall, straight up and
down. "Those six columns of lamps stand for our group's
six fighter control stations. Each vertical row of lights
stands for one fighter squadron. All in all, twenty-two
squadrons. In theory, we dispose of more than five hundred
fighter pilots." Burne-Wilke wrinkled his lips. "In *theory*.
Just now we're borrowing pilots from other groups. Even
so, we're way under. However . . ." He gestured toward
the bottom part of the black wall, where white lights
burned in a ragged pattern. "Going up the wall, you step
up in readiness, till you get to AIRBORNE, ENEMY IN SIGHT,
and of course ENGAGED. That's the red row of lamps. Our
six substations talk to us and to the pilots. Here we put
together the whole picture. If things warm up enough, the
air vice-marshal may come in and run the show.—Oh, yes.
Those poor devils under glass on the left collect reports
from our ground observer corps, on the right from our
anti-aircraft. So all the information about German planes
in our air will show up here fairly fast."

Pug was not quite as surprised as he had been at Ventnor. He knew of the system's existence; but this close view
awed him. "Sir, aren't you talking about a couple of hundred thousand miles of telephone cable? Thousands of

lines, a forest of equipment? When did all this spring into being?"

"Oh, we had the plan two years ago. The politicians were aghast at the money, and balked. Right after Munich we got our budget. It's an ill wind, eh? Hullo, here we go. I believe Jerry's on his way."

On the black wall, white lights were starting to jump upward. The young lord at Burne-Wilke's elbow gave him a telephone. Burne-Wilke talked brisk RAF abracadabra, his eyes moving from the wall to the map table. Then he handed back the telephone. "Yes. Chain Home at Ventnor now reports several attacks forming up or orbiting. Two of them are forty-plus, one sixty-plus."

Tillet said, "Göring's been an abysmal donkey, hasn't he, not to knock out our Chain Home stations? It will prove his historic mistake."

"Oh, he has tried," Burne-Wilke said. "It isn't so easy. Unless one hits a steel tower dead on and blows it to bits, it just whips about like a palm tree in a storm, then steadies down."

"Well, he should have gone on trying."

White lights kept moving up the board. An air of business was settling over the operations room, but nobody moved in an excited way, and the hum of voices was low. The air vice-marshal appeared, a spare stern sparse-moustached man, with a sort of family resemblance to General Tillet. He ignored the visitors for a while as he paced, then said hello to Tillet with a surprising warm smile that made him look kind and harmless.

The first lights that leaped to red were in the column of the Biggin Hill control station. Victor Henry saw Pamela glance up at these lights. On the table, where she busily continued to lay arrows and numbered discs with the other girls, a clear picture was forming of four flights of attackers, moving over southern England on different courses. The reports of the telephone talkers on the floor merged into a steady subdued buzz. There was not much chatting in the balcony. Henry sat overwhelmed with spectator-sport fascination, as one by one the red lamps began to come on. Within twenty minutes or so, half the squadrons on the board were blinking red.

"That's about it," Burne-Wilke said offhandedly, breaking away from giving rapid orders. "We've got almost two hundred planes engaged. The others stand by to cover, when these land to refuel and rearm."

"Have you ever had red lights across the board?"

Burne-Wilke wrinkled his mouth. "Now and then. It's not the situation of choice. We have to call on other fighter groups then to cover for us, and just now there's not much left in reserve."

Far away and high in the blue sky, thought Pug, forcing himself to picture it, planes were now darting and twisting in and out of clouds in a machine joust to the death of German kids and British kids, youngsters like Warren and Byron. Pamela's pudgy actor, cold sober on orange squash, was up there in his yellow life jacket, flying at several hundred miles an hour, watching his rearview mirror for a square white nose, or squirting his guns at an onrushing airplane with a black cross on it.

Two of the Biggin Hill lights moved up to white: RE-TURNING BASE.

"These things seldom last longer than an hour or so from the time Jerry starts," said Burne-Wilke. "He runs dry rather fast and has to head back. They keep falling in the sea like exhausted bats. Prisoners say that the Luft-waffe has given the Channel an impolite name—roughly equivalent to your American 'shit creek.' "

Within a few minutes, the red lights blinked off one by one. The air vice-marshal left. Below, the girls began clearing markers off the table. Lord Burne-Wilke spoke on the telephone, collecting reports. He put slender, hairy hands over his face and rubbed hard, then turned to Pug, his eyes reddened. "Wouldn't you like to say hello to Pamela Tudsbury?"

"Very much. How did it go?"

With a weary shrug, Burne-Wilke said, "One can't stop every bomber. I'm afraid quite a number got through and did their work. Often once the fires are out, things don't look so bad. We lost a number of planes. So did they. The count takes a day or so to firm up. I think we did all right."

As Pug went out with the young lord, leaving Tillet conversing with the slumped senior officer, he glanced back at the theatre. On the wall, all lights were burning at or near the bottom again. The room was very quiet, the earth

smell strong. The staircase to the surface seemed very long
and steep. Pug felt drained of energy, though he had done
nothing but sit and watch. He puffed and panted and was
glad to see the daylight. Pamela stood in the sun outside
in a blue uniform. "Well, you made it, but not on the best
day. Ted's down." Her voice was calm, even chatty, but
she gave his hand a nervous squeeze in two ice-cold hands.

"Are you sure?"

"Yes. He may have parachuted, but his plane dove into
the sea. Two of his squadron mates reported it. He's
down." She clung to his hand, looking into his face with
glistening eyes.

"Pam, as you've said, they often climb out of the water,
and go right back to work."

"Oh, certainly. Leave that to Ted. I've asked for a special pass. I think I shall come to London this evening.
Would you buy me a dinner?"

*   *   *

A week passed, and another, and Gallard did not return. Pamela came several times to London. Once Victor
Henry remarked that she appeared to be fighting the war
only when it suited her. "I am behaving shockingly," she
said, "using every trick I know, presuming on everybody's
sympathy and good nature, and pushing them all much too
far. I shall soon be confined to camp until further notice.
By then you'll be gone. Meantime you're here."

It became a settled thing among the Americans that Pug
Henry had found himself a young WAAF. To cheer her up,
he took her often to Fred Fearing's apartment on Belgrave
Square, the center for the partying American-British
crowd. Shortly after the Christmas night row with Rhoda,
the Germans had expelled Fearing for telling the truth
about some bomb damage in Hamburg. Fearing was having such a good time with the London girls that, as he put
it, he often arrived at the broadcasting studio on his hands
and knees. His thrilling and touching word pictures of England at war were stirring up so much sympathy in the
United States that isolationists were claiming he was obviously in the pay of the British.

The second time Victor Henry brought Pamela to the

apartment, Fearing remarked, catching Pug alone for a moment in the hallway, "Aren't you the sly one, Reverend Henry? She's small, but saucy."

"She's the daughter of a guy I know."

"Of course. Talky Tudsbury. Old pal of mine, too."

"Yes. That's who she is. Her fiancé's an RAF pilot missing in action."

Fearing's big knobby face lit in an innocent smile. "Just so. She might enjoy a little consolation."

Pug looked up at him. The correspondent was over six feet tall, and heavily built. "How would you enjoy getting knocked on your ass?"

Fearing's smile went away. "You mean it, Pug?"

"I mean it."

"Just asking. What do you hear from Rhoda?"

"She misses me, New York stinks, she's bored, and the weather is unbearably hot."

"Situation normal. Good old Rhoda."

The other men who drifted in and out of the apartment, usually with a woman, usually more or less drunk—observers from the Army and the Air Corps, correspondents, film actors, businessmen—danced or bantered with Pamela, but otherwise let her alone, assuming she was Victor Henry's doxy.

Once, early in September, when they were having a drink in her apartment and joking about this, Pug said, " 'Lechery, lechery—still wars and lechery—nothing else holds fashion.' "

She widened her eyes at him. "Why, bless me. He's a Shakespeare scholar, too."

"Aside from Western stories, Pamela, practically the only things I read for recreation are the Bible and Shakespeare," Pug said, rather solemnly. "It's always time well spent. You can get through a lot of Shakespeare in a Navy career."

"Well, there's precious little lechery around here," said Pamela. "If people only knew."

"Are you complaining, my girl?"

"Certainly not, you leathery old gentleman. I can't imagine how your wife endures you."

"Well, I'm good, patient, uncomplaining company."

"God love you, you are that."

At this point the air raid sirens started their eerie moaning and wailing—a heart-stopping noise no matter how often Pug heard it.

"My God!" said Pamela. "There they come! This is *it*. Where on earth is Fighter Command?" She stood with Victor Henry on the little balcony outside her living room, still holding her highball glass, staring at arrays of bombers in wide ragged V's as they sailed through a bright blue sky, starkly visible in yellowing late sunlight. Anti-aircraft bursts all around and through the formations looked like white and black powder puffs, and seemed to be having no more effect.

"Tangling with the fighter escort further south, I'd guess." Victor Henry's voice shook. The number of bombers staggered him. The mass of machines was coming on like the invaders in a futuristic movie, filling the air with a throbbing angry hum as of a billion bees. The pop and thump of scattered anti-aircraft guns made a pitiful counterpoint. One V-wave passed; in the azure distance several more appeared, swelling to unbelievable width and numbers as they drew over the city. The bombers were not very high, and the A.A. seemed to be exploding dead inside the V's, but on they thrummed. The muffled thunder of bomb hits boomed over the city, and pale flame and smoke began billowing up in the sunshine.

Pug said, "Looks like they're starting on the docks."

"Shall I get you another drink? I must, I *must* have one." She took his glass and hurried inside.

More bombers kept appearing from the southeast. Pug wondered whether General Tillet could be right; was this a sign of weakening, a play of Göring's last card? Some show of weakness! Yet a heavy toll of German fighter escorts must be paying for the incredibly serene overflight of these bomber waves. The British fighters could knock these big slow machines down like tin ducks. They had proved that long ago, yet on the bombers came, sailing unscathed across London's sky from horizon to horizon, an awesome pageant of flying machinery.

She brought the drinks and peered at the sky. "Why, God help us, there's *more* of them!"

She leaned against the rail, touching shoulders. He put

his arm around her and she nestled against him. So they stood together, watching the Luftwaffe start its effort to bomb London to its knees. It was the seventh of September.

Along the river more and bigger fires shot skyward in great billows of dirty smoke. Elsewhere in the city random small blazes were flaring up from badly aimed bombs. After the first shock, there was not much terror in the sight. The noise was far off, the patches of fires meager and dispersed in the red and gray expanse of untouched buildings. London was a very, very large city. The Fat Boy's big try was not making much of a dent after all. Only along the burning Thames embankment was there a look of damage. So it seemed, in the view from Pamela's balcony of the first all-out Valhalla attack.

So it seemed too in Soho, where they went to dine after the all clear. The Londoners thronging the sidewalk looked excited, undismayed, even elated. Strangers talked to each other, laughed, and pointed thumbs up. The traffic flowed thick as ever. There was no trace of damage on the street. Distant clangs of fire engines and a heavy smokiness overhead remained the only traces, in this part of town, of Göring's tremendous attempt. Queues even stood as usual outside the movie houses, and the stage box offices were briskly selling tickets too.

When they walked in twilight down toward the Thames, after an excellent Italian dinner, the picture began to change. The smell of smoke grew stronger; flickering red and yellow light gave the low clouds, thickened by ever-billowing smoke, a look of inferno. The crowds in the street grew denser. It became an effort to push through. The people here were more silent and grave. Henry and Pamela came to roped-off streets where amid noise and steam, shouting firemen dragged hoses toward blackened buildings and streamed water at tongues of fire licking out of the windows. Pamela skirted through alleys and side streets till they emerged on the riverbank into a mob of onlookers.

Here an oppressive stench of burning fouled the air, and the river breeze brought gusts of fiery heat in the warm summer night. A low moon shone dirty red through the rolling smoke. Reflections of the fires on the other bank flickered in the black water. The bridge was slowly disgorging a swarm of refugees, some with carts, baby carriages, and wheelchairs, a poor shabby lot for the most part, many workmen in caps, and a horde of ill-dressed children who alone kept their gaiety, running here and there as they came.

Victor Henry looked up at the sky. Above rifts in the smoke, the stars shimmered.

"It's a very clear night, you know," he said. "These fires are a beacon they can see for a hundred miles. They may come back."

Pamela said coldly and abruptly, "I must return to Uxbridge. I'm beginning to feel rotten." She looked down at her flimsy gray dress. "But I seem to be slightly out of uniform."

The sirens began their hideous screaming just as Pug and Pamela found a taxicab, many blocks from the river. "Come along," said the wizened little driver, touching his cap. "Business as usual, wot? And to 'ell with 'Itler!"

Victor Henry watched the start of the night raid from the balcony while she changed. His senses were sharpened by the destruction, the excitement, the peculiar beauty of the fire panorama and the swaying blue-white searchlight beams, the thick thrumming of the bomber motors, and the thump-thump of the anti-aircraft, which was just starting up. Pamela Tudsbury, coming out on the gloomy moonlit balcony in her WAAF uniform, appeared to him the most desirable young female on God's earth. She looked shorter because of the low-heeled shoes, but the severe garb made her small figure all the sweeter. So he thought.

"They're here?" she said.

"Arriving."

Again she leaned her shoulder to his. Again he held her with one encircling arm. "Damn, the bastards just can't miss," he said, "with those fires to guide them."

"Berlin can catch fire, too." Pamela suddenly looked about as ugly as she could: a grim, nasty face with hate scored on it in the red paint of her mouth.

New fires sprang up along the river, and spread and ran

into the big fire. More blazes flared out of the darkness far from the Thames. Still, most of the vast city remained black and still. A tiny bomber came toppling down through the smoky sky, burning like a candlewick, transfixed by two crossing searchlights.

"Oh God, they *got* him. They got one. Get more of them. Please."

And in short order two more bombers fell—one plunging straight down in a blaze like a meteor, the other circling and spiralling black smoke until it exploded in midair like a distant firecracker. In a moment they heard the sharp pop.

"Ah, lovely. Lovely!"

The telephone rang.

"Well!" she laughed harshly. "Uxbridge, no doubt, screaming for their little fugitive from duty. Possibly inviting me to a court-martial."

She returned after a moment with a puzzled face. "It seems to be for you."

"Who?"

"Wouldn't say. Sounded important and impatient."

General Tillet said, "Ah, Henry. Jolly good. Your friend Fearing suggested I try you here. Ah, you do recall, don't you, when you paid a little morning call a couple of weeks ago on a portly old gentleman, he mentioned that you might want to go along on a little expedition that was in the works? A trip to familiar foreign scenes?"

A tingle ran down Victor Henry's spine. "I remember."

"Well, the trip seems to be on. I'm to meet you tonight when this nuisance stops, to give you the details, if you're interested.—I say, are you there, Henry?"

"Yes, General. Will you be going on the trip?"

"Me? Good God, dear chap, no. I'm a timid old fellow, quite unsuited for the rigors of travel. Besides, I haven't been asked."

"When is the trip?"

"I gather they'll be leaving tomorrow, some time."

"Can I call you back?"

"I'm supposed to pass your answer along within the hour."

"I'll call you back very soon."

"Jolly good."

"Tell me this. Do you think I should go?"

"Why, since you ask, I think you'd be insane. Damned hot where they're going. Worst time of year. You have to be very fond of that kind of scenery. Can't say I am."

"Are you at the same number?"

"No." Tillet gave him another number. "I'm sitting here and waiting."

As he came out on the balcony, she turned to him, her face alight. "They've got two more. Our night fighters must be up. At least we're getting some of our own back."

Pug peered out at the fantastic show—the fires, the searchlight beams, the sky-climbing pillars of red and yellow smoke over the lampless city. "I gave you some good advice in Washington. Or you thought it was good advice."

"Yes, indeed." Her eyes searched his. "Who telephoned you?"

"Come inside. I'll take that drink now."

They sat in two armchairs near the open french windows to the balcony. He leaned forward, elbows on his knees, holding the glass in his cupped hands. "Pamela, the RAF will be bombing Berlin tomorrow night, and it seems I'm invited along as an observer."

The girl's face in the shadowy light went taut. She took her lower lip in her teeth, and looked at him so. It was not an attractive expression. Her eyes were round as an owl's. "I see. Shall you go?"

"That's what I'm wondering. I think it's a goddamned idiotic notion, and General Tillet agrees, but meantime he's reported the invitation. I've got to accept it or duck it."

"Strange they'd ask you. You're not Air Force."

"Your Prime Minister mentioned it in passing when I saw him. He apparently has a good memory."

"Do you want my opinion?"

"That's what I'm asking for."

"Decline. Quickly, firmly, and finally."

"All right, why?"

"It's not your business. It's especially not the business of America's naval attaché in Berlin."

"True."

"Your chances of returning are something like three out of five. It's miserably unfair to your wife."

"That was my first thought." Pug paused, looking out of the balcony doors. In the night the A.A. snapped and thumped, and searchlights swayed blue fingers across the blackness. "Still, your Prime Minister thinks there'd be some purpose in my going."

Pamela Tudsbury flipped her hand in a quick irritated gesture. "Oh, rot. Winnie is a perpetual undergraduate about combat. He probably wishes he could go himself, and imagines everyone's like him. He got himself unnecessarily captured in South Africa long ago. Why, in May and June he flew over to France time after time, got in the hair of the generals, and skittered around the front making a frightful nuisance of himself. He's a great man, but that's one of his many weaknesses."

Victor Henry lit a cigarette and took deep puffs, turning the match packet round and round in his fingers. "Well, I'm supposed to call General Tillet pretty damn quick. I'd better do that." He reached for the telephone.

She said quickly, "Wait a minute. What are you going to say?"

"I'm going to accept."

Pamela drew a sharp noisy breath, and said, "Why did you ask my opinion, then?"

"I thought you might voice a good objection that hadn't occurred to me."

"You gave the best objection yourself. It's idiotic."

"I'm not positive. My job is intelligence. This is an extraordinary opportunity. There's also a taunt in it, Pamela. The U.S. Navy's out of the war, and I'm here to see how you're taking it. Question, how will I take it? It's hard to duck that one."

"You're reading too much into it. What would your President say to this? Did he send you here to risk getting killed?"

"After the fact he'd congratulate me."

"If you returned to be congratulated."

As he reached for the telephone again, Pamela Tudsbury said, "I shall wind up with Fred Fearing. Or his equivalent." That stopped the motion of Pug's arm. She said, "I'm in dead earnest. I miss Ted horribly. I shall not be able to endure missing you. I'm *much* more attached to

you than you realize. And I'm not at all moral, you know.
You have very wrong ideas about me."

The seams in his face were sharp and deep as he peered
at the angry girl. The thumping of his heart made speech
difficult. "It isn't very moral to hit below the belt, I'll say
that."

"You don't understand me. Not in the least. On the
Bremen you took me for a schoolgirl, and you've never
really changed. Your wife has somehow kept you remarkably innocent for twenty-five years."

Victor Henry said, "Pam, I honestly don't think I was
born to be shot down over Berlin in a British bomber. I'll
see you when I get back."

He telephoned Tillet, while the girl stared at him with
wide angry eyes. "Ass!" she said. "*Ass!*"

33

A YOUNGSTER in greasy coveralls poked his head through
the open door. "Sir, the briefing's begun in B flight crew
room."

"Coming," said Pug, struggling with unfamiliar tubes,
clasps, and straps. The flying suit was too big. It had not
been laundered or otherwise cleaned in a long time, and
smelled of stale sweat, grease, and tobacco. Quickly Pug
pulled on three pairs of socks and thrust his feet into
fleece-lined boots, also too big.

"What do I do with these?" Pug gestured at the raincoat
and tweed suit he had folded on a chair.

"They'll be right there when you get back, sir."

Their eyes met. In that glance was complete mutual
recognition that, for no very good reason, Pug was going
out to risk death. The young man looked sorry for him,

and also wryly amused at the Yank officer's predicament. Pug said, "What's your name?"

"Aircraftsman Horton, sir."

"Well, Aircraftsman Horton, we seem to be about the same size. If I forget to pick up that suit or something, it's all yours."

"Why, thank you, sir." The young man's grin became broad and sincere. "That's very fine tweed."

Several dozen men in flying clothes slouched in the darkened room, their pallid faces attentive to the wing commander, who motioned the American to a chair. He was talking about the primary and secondary targets in Berlin, using a long pointer at a gray, grainy aerial picture of the German capital blown up on a large screen. Victor Henry had driven or walked past both targets often. One was a power plant, the other the main gasworks of Berlin. It made him feel decidedly odd to discern, in the Grunewald area, the lake beside which the Rosenthal house stood.

"All right, let's have the opposition map."

Another slide of Berlin flashed on the screen, marked with red and orange symbols, and the officer discussed anti-aircraft positions and searchlight belts. The fliers listened to the dull droning voice raptly.

"Lights."

Bare lamps in the ceiling blazed up. The bomber crews blinked and shifted in their chairs. Rolled up, the screen uncovered a green-and-brown map of Europe, and over it a sign in large red block letters: IT IS BETTER TO KEEP YOUR MOUTH SHUT AND LET PEOPLE THINK YOU'RE A FOOL, THAN TO OPEN IT AND REMOVE ALL DOUBT.

"All right, that's about it. Berlin will be on the alert after all the stuff they've been dumping on London, so look alive." The wing commander leaned his pointer against the wall, put hands on hips, and changed to an offhand tone: "Remember to be careful of the moon. Don't fly directly into it, you'll look like a cat on a Christmas card. When you've done your stuff, get your photographs, shove the nose down, and pedal home downhill as fast as you can. Keep Very pistols loaded and have those photoflash bombs handy. Work fast, the flak will be heavy. Incidentally, our American observer will be flying in F for

Freddie. He's Admiral Victor Henry, one of the least prudent officers in the United States Navy."

Faces turned to Pug, who cleared his throat. "Sir, maybe I'll be entitled to the field promotion when I get back, but I'm only Captain Henry."

"The promotion stands for this mission," said the wing commander with a laugh. "You deserve it!"

He went out. After a silence a boy's voice behind Pug piped, "Anybody who'd go on a ruddy mission like this when he ruddy well doesn't have to, should be in a ruddy loony bin."

A short skinny flier with heavy, crinkling black hair and bloodshot little eyes approached him, holding out a paper box crudely tied with red ribbon. "Admiral, a little token of welcome from the squadron."

Pug opened the box and took out a roll of toilet paper. He glanced around at the expectant white amused faces.

"I'm touched. But I don't think I'll be needing this, inasmuch as I'm already scared shitless."

He got a good laugh. The little flier offered his hand. "Come along with me, Admiral. I'm Peters, the sergeant navigator of F for Freddie." He took him to a row of lockers and gave the American his parachute, showing him how to clip it to his chest. He also handed him a paper sack with his ration.

"Now you don't wear your chute. That's a good chute. You just stow it where it'll be handy in a hurry. It's hard enough moving around inside the Wimpy, you'll find, without that thing on. Now you'll want to meet the pilots. They're Flight Lieutenant Killian and Sergeant Pilot Johnson. Tiny, we call the sergeant."

He conducted Victor Henry to a small room where the two pilots were studying and marking up maps of Berlin. The lieutenant, who had the furrowed brow and neat little moustache of an assistant bank manager, was using a magnifying glass. Sergeant Tiny Johnson, booted feet on the desk, was holding the map up and glaring at it. "Hullo! Brassed off, I am, Admiral," he said, when Peters introduced Victor Henry. "Ruddy well brassed off." He was a large fellow with a ham face and thick lips.

"Pack it up, Tiny," said the first pilot.

"Brassed off, I say. A nine-hour sweat just for us. While

those twerps in all the other squadrons go for a quick one on the Channel coast to hit the invasion barges, and then home for tea, mother. I've been over Berlin. I don't like it."

"You've never stopped boasting about being over Berlin," said the skipper, drawing lines on the map.

"Rottenest moment of my life," said the sergeant, with a rolling side glance at Victor Henry. "Ruddiest thickest flak you ever saw. Masses of searchlights turning the night into day." He got up yawning. "Brassed off, that's what I am, mates. Brassed off. You're a brave man, Admiral."

He went out.

"Tiny's a good pilot," said the first pilot in upper-class tones, tucking the map into a canvas pouch. "He does talk a lot."

The six men of the F for Freddie crew gathered under a naked light in a hallway for a last word from Flight Lieutenant Killian, reading notes on a clipboard. Aside from the theatrical-looking flying suits and life vests, they seemed like any half-dozen young men off any London street. The wireless operator was thin and somewhat ratty; the rear gunner was a fresh-faced boy—almost a child, Pug thought—on his first operational flight; the pimply front gunner vulgarly worked chewing gum in long jaws. Only their nervy, apprehensive, adventurous, and cheerful look was unusual.

The warm night was studded with summer stars: Vega, Deneb, Altair, Arcturus—the old navigation aids reliably twinkling away. The senior pilot went aboard the plane. The crew lounged on the grass nearby.

"F for Freddie," said the sergeant pilot, giving the fuselage a loud affectionate slap. "Been through many a long sweat, Admiral."

This was how Pug found out that a Wellington bomber had a skin of fabric. The slapped cloth sounded just like what it was. He was used to his Navy's metal aircraft. It had never occurred to him that the British could use fabric planes as attack bombers, and this piece of intelligence had not come his way, for he was not an aviator. Victor Henry could still have walked away from the flight, but he felt as compelled to enter this cloth plane and fly over Berlin as a murderer is to climb a gallows to be hanged. In the sweet-smelling quiet night, plaintive birdsongs rose here and there, richly warbling and rolling.

"Ever heard nightingales before?" said Tiny Johnson.

"No, I never have."

"Well, Admiral, you're hearing nightingales."

Far down the field, one plane after another coughed and began to roar, shooting out flames in the darkness. A truck rolled up to F for Freddie. A mechanic plugged a cable into its fuselage. The motors caught and turned over, spitting smoke and fire, as other planes trundled to a dimly lit runway and thundered up and away into gauzy blue moonlight. Soon only F for Freddie was left, its crew still lying on the grass, its spinning motors cherry red. All at once the engines shut off.

Pug heard nightingales again.

"Eh? What now?" said Tiny. "Don't tell me we've been scrubbed, due to some splendid, lovely engine trouble?"

Mechanics came trotting out and worked rapidly on one engine, with many a vile cheerful curse, their tools clanking musically in the open air. Twenty minutes after the other planes left, F for Freddie took off and flew out over the North Sea.

After what seemed a half hour of bumping through cold air in a dark shaking machine, Pug glanced at his watch. Only seven minutes had gone by. The crew did not talk. The intercom crackled and buzzed—the helmet, unlike the rest of his clothing, was too tight and hurt his ears—but once the plane left the coast on course, the pilots and navigator shut up. Victor Henry's perspiration from the heavy suit cooled and dried, chilling him. His watch crawled through twenty more minutes as he sat there. The lieutenant gestured to him to look through the plexiglass blister where the navigator had been taking star sights, and then to stretch out prone in the nose bubble, the bombardier position. Pug did these things, but there was nothing to see but black water, bright moon, and jewelled stars.

"Keep that light down, navigator," the lieutenant croaked.

The sergeant who had given Pug the toilet paper was marking a chart on a tiny fold-down wooden slat, and trying to squelch the dim beam of an amber flashlight with his fingers. Crouching beside him, watching him struggle with star tables, star sight forms, dividers, ruler, and flashlight, Pug wondered what kind of navigational fix he could possibly come up with. The youngster gave him a harried grin. Pug took the flashlight from his hands and shielded the beam to strike just the chart. Peters gestured his gratitude and Pug squatted there, cramped in the space behind the two pilots, until the navigator had finished his work. The American had imagined that the long-range British bomber would be as big as an airliner, with a control cabin offering ample elbow room. In fact five men sat crowded within inches of each other—the two pilots, the front gunner, the navigator, and the wireless operator. Pug could just see the gunner in the forward bubble, in faint moonlight. The others were faces floating in the glow of dials.

Stumbling, crouching, grasping at guy wires, Pug dragged his parachute down the black fuselage to the bubble where the rear gunner sat. The hatless boy, his bushy hair falling in his face, gave him a thumbs-up and a pathetic smile. This was a hell of a lonely, shaky, frigid place to be riding, Pug thought. The bomber's tail was whipping and bouncing badly. He tried to yell over the wind noise and motor roars, then made a hopeless gesture. The boy nodded, and proudly operated his power turret for him. Pug groped to a clear space in the fuselage, and squatted on his parachute, hugging his knees. There was nothing to do. It was getting colder and colder. He took something from his ration bag—when he put it in his mouth he tasted chocolate—and sucked it. He dozed.

Garbled voices in his ear woke him. His nose was numb, his cheeks felt frostbitten, and he was shivering. A hand in the dark tugged him forward. He stumbled after the vague figure toward the cockpit glow. Suddenly it was bright as day in the plane. The plane slanted and dived, and Pug Henry fell, bruising his forehead on a metal box. Rearing up on his hands and knees, he saw the bright light go out, come on and go out again as though snapped off. The plane made sickening turns one way and another while he crawled forward.

Tiny Johnson, gripping the controls, turned around, and Pug saw his lips move against the microphone. "Okay,

Admiral?" The voice gargled in the intercom. "Just passing the coast searchlight belt."

"Okay," Henry said.

The helmeted lieutenant threw a tight grim glance over his shoulder at Henry, then stared ahead into the night.

Tiny waved a gloved hand at a fixture labelled OXYGEN. "Plug in, and come and have a look."

Sucking on rubber-tasting enriched air, Pug crawled into the bombardier position.

Instead of sparkling sea he saw land grayed over by moonlight. The searchlight beams waved behind them. Straight below, tiny yellow lights winked. Red and orange balls came floating slowly and gently up from these lights, speeding and getting bigger as they rose. A few burst and showered red streaks and sparks. Several balls passed ahead of the plane and on either side of it, flashing upward in blurry streaks of color.

The voice of Tiny said, "Coast flak was heavier last time."

Just as he said this something purple-white and painfully brilliant exploded in Victor Henry's face. Blackness ensued, then a dance of green circles. Pug Henry lay with his face pressed to cold plexiglass, sucking on the oxygen tube, stunned and blind.

A hand grasped his. The voice of Peters, the navigator, rattled in his ear. "That was a magnesium flash shell. Ruddy close, Admiral. Are you all right?"

"I can't see."

"It'll take a while. Sit up, sir."

The plane ground ahead, the blindness persisted and persisted, then the green circles jerked in a brightening red mist. A picture gradually faded in like a movie scene: faces lit by dials and the gunner in moonlight. Until his vision returned, Victor Henry spent nasty minutes wondering whether it would. Ahead he saw clouds, the first of this trip, billowing up under the moon.

The navigator spoke. "Should be seeing beams and flak now."

"Nothing," said Lieutenant Killian. "Black night."

"I've got Berlin bearing dead ahead at thirty miles, sir."

"Something's wrong. Probably your wind drift again."

"D.F. bearings check out, sir."

"Well, damn it, Peters, that doesn't put Berlin up ahead." The skipper sounded annoyed but unworried. "It looks like solid forest down there, clear across the horizon. Featureless and black."

Tiny Johnson observed bitterly that on his last raid almost half of the planes had failed altogether to find Berlin, and that none of Bomber Command's official navigational procedures were worth a shit. He added that he was brassed off.

The piping voice of the rear gunner broke in to report searchlights far astern, off to the right. At almost the same moment, the pilots saw, and pointed out to Victor Henry, a large fire on the horizon ahead: a yellow blotch flickering on the moonlit plain. After some crisp talk on the intercom, Lieutenant Killian swung the plane around and headed for the searchlights; as for the fire, his guess was that another bomber had overshot the mark and then gone ahead and bombed the wrong target. *"That's* Berlin," he soon said, pointing a mittened hand at the lights. "All kinds of fireworks shooting off. Well done, Reynolds. How goes it back there?"

The high strained voice of the rear gunner replied, "Oh, I'm fine, sir. This operational stuff's the real thing, isn't it?"

As they neared Berlin, the nose gunner was silhouetted black by exploding balls and streaks of color, and fanning rays of blue light. Tiny's voice in the intercom rasped, "Those poor bastards who got there first are catching the heat blisters."

The lieutenant's voice came, easy and slow: "It looks worse than it is, Admiral. The stuff spreads apart once you're in it. The sky's a roomy place, actually."

F for Freddie went sailing into the beautiful, terrible display, and as the captain had said, it thinned out. The searchlight beams scattered and ran down to the left and right. The streaks and balls of flak left great holes of darkness through which the plane bored smoothly ahead. The captain and the navigator talked rapidly in fliers' jargon.

"See that fire off there, Admiral? Some other chaps have pretty well clobbered the primary target," said Killian.

"Or at least dropped a lot of bombs in the vicinity,"

Tiny said. "I can't make out a damned thing for the smoke."

The view below was half moonlit clouds, half black city flickering with anti-aircraft flashes. Pug Henry saw a peculiar high column of flickers—the Flakturm, that must be—and, in another direction, an irregular blob of fire and smoke enveloping buildings and smokestacks, near the river curling silver through Berlin. The black puffs and fiery streaks of the flak slid past F for Freddie, but the plane plowed ahead as though protected by a charm. The captain said, "Well, I'm going for secondary. Course, navigator."

Shortly thereafter the motor noise ceased. The nose of the plane dipped way down. The sudden quiet was a big surprise.

"Gliding approach, Admiral," the captain's voice gargled. "They control their lights and flak with listening devices. Navigator's got to take your place now."

The plane whiffled earthward. Pug made his way to the rear gunner, who was looking down with saucer eyes in a pallid baby face at the moonlit German capital, and at the anti-aircraft winking like fireflies. A rush of icy air and a roar followed the captain's order, "Open bomb bay." Into the plane a strong acrid smell poured, and Pug had a mental flash of gunnery exercises on a sunny blue sea near green islands. Off Manila or over Berlin, cordite smelled the same. The navigator kept talking in a drilled cheerful tone: "Left, left . . . too much . . . right . . . dead on . . . no, left, left . . . smack on. Smack on. Smack on. *There!*"

The plane jumped. Pug saw the bombs raggedly fall away behind them, a string of black tumbling sticks. The airplane slanted up, the motors came bellowing on, and they climbed.

Below, a string of small red explosions appeared alongside the buildings and the huge fat gas-storage tower. Pug thought the bombs had missed. Then, in the blink of an eye, yellow-white flame with a green core came blasting and billowing up from the ground, almost to the height of the climbing plane, but well behind. In the gigantic flare, the city of Berlin was suddenly starkly visible, spread out below like a picture postcard printed with too much yellow ink—the Kurfürstendamm, Unter den Linden, the Brandenburg Gate, the Tiergarten, the river, the bridges, the Flakturm, the chancellery, the Opera—clear, sharp, close, undamaged, peculiarly yellow.

The cheers in the intercom hurt his ears. He seized his microphone and gave a rebel yell.

As he did so, F for Freddie was transfixed by half a dozen searchlights that swung and stopped. In the gunner's bubble all was blue radiance. The boy looked horror-stricken at Pug and suddenly started to scream in fright, his eyes tight shut, his mouth wide open. There was so much noise that Pug could hardly hear him. It looked like a painted scream, and in the blue light the boy's tongue and gums were black. The plane seemed to have landed on a shining blue pyramid. The motors howled, the machine lurched, dived, sideslipped, but the pyramid stayed locked under it. Pug seized the gun mount with both arms to steady himself. The gunner fell against the mount, knocking the microphone away from his open mouth. His clamor ceased in the intercom, and Pug heard Lieutenant Killian and Tiny talking in brisk controlled voices. A mass of orange and red balls lazily left the ground and floated up directly at F for Freddie. They came faster. They burst all around, a shower of fire, a barrage of explosions. Pug felt a hard thump, heard the motor change sound, heard a fearful whistling. Icy air blasted at him. Fragments rattled all over the plane, and F for Freddie heeled over in a curving dive. Victor Henry believed that he was going to die. The plane shrieked and horribly shuddered, diving steeply. Both pilots were shouting now, not in panic but to make themselves heard, and through the frail plexiglass bubble Henry stared at the fabric wings, waiting for them to break off, flutter away, and signal the end of his life.

All at once the screeching, whistling blue pyramid turned black. The dizzying swoops and slips stopped, the plane flew straight. Pug caught a whiff of vomit. The gunner had fainted, and the puke was dribbling from his mouth in the moonlight and rolling down his chest: chocolate, coffee, bits of orange. The boy had eaten his whole ration. Out of the left leg of his flying suit black blood welled.

Pug tried the intercom, but the crackling in his ears had stopped. The system was dead. The stricken plane lurched on in a tumult of wind roars and howls. He went forward, clutching the guy ropes, and ran head-on into a figure who shouted that he was Peters. Pug screamed in his ear that Reynolds was wounded, and moved on to the cockpit, passing a ragged flapping hole in the starboard fuselage through which he could see the stars. Mechanically he noted the form of the Dipper. They were heading west, back to England.

In the cockpit the pilots sat as before, busy at their controls. Tiny shouted, "Ah, Admiral. We're going home to tea. To hell with ruddy pictures. You'll tell them you saw that gas plant go up, won't you?"

"Damn right I will. How's the airplane?"

"The port engine was hit, but it's still pulling. Heading back over land, in case we have to come down. Looks like we can make it, unless that engine completely packs up."

"Your rear gunner's got a leg wound. Navigator's back there with him."

The swinging searchlights of the outer belt loomed ahead, probing the clouds, but F for Freddie climbed into the overcast undetected. Tiny bellowed at Victor Henry, his big blue eyes rolling, both hands on the wheel, "Ruddy asinine way to make a living, isn't it, Admiral? Brassed off, I am. Should have joined the ruddy navy!"

Pulling off his helmet, Lieutenant Killian turned over control to Tiny, and wiped his face with a big white handkerchief no whiter than his skin. He gave the American a tired smile, his forehead a mass of wrinkled lines.

"It may be close at that, Admiral. We're having a bit of trouble holding altitude. How's your French?"

34

PAMELA had remained in London. She knew it was a night bombing mission and she knew the distances. It was not hard to calculate when Victor Henry would be getting back. At ten in the morning she went to his flat—it had no other occupant for the moment—and persuaded the charwoman to let her in. She sat in the dowdy living room, trying to read a newspaper, but actually only counting the minutes and praying that he was still alive.

Pug Henry had entered her life at a dark time. Her parents had been divorced before she was fourteen. Her mother had remarried, made a new life, and shut her out. Alistair Tudsbury had deposited her in schools while he travelled. She had grown up well-mannered, attractive, but almost wild, and had had several love affairs before she was out of her teens. In her early twenties she had met Philip Rule, a tall golden-haired newspaper correspondent, who had for a while shared Leslie Slote's flat in Paris. An ice-cold man with beguiling ways, a rich flow of clever talk, and corrupt tastes, Rule had bit by bit destroyed her ambition, her self-confidence, and almost her will to live. She had fought off suicidal depression by breaking off with him at last and going to work as her father's slave; and as such, she had encountered Victor and Rhoda Henry on the *Bremen*.

She had never met a man quite like Commander Henry: remote, taciturn, apparently an old-fashioned narrow professional, yet incisive and engaging. She had found him attractive from the start, and had come to like him more and more. Aboard ship, such attractions take on an unreal intensity, but usually fade fast on dry land. For Pamela the feeling had only grown stronger on seeing him again in Berlin. There she had sensed that Pug was beginning to like her, too. But the start of the war had broken their contact, except for the momentary encounter in Washington.

When Victor Henry arrived in London, Pamela had been quite ready to marry the fighter pilot; and this visit of the older man who had been something like a shipboard crush had not changed that. But since then Gallard had vanished, and she had had two weeks with Pug. In wartime, as on board ship, relationships deepen fast. Nothing had yet happened between them. He had awkwardly put an arm around her while watching the German bombers come in; that was all. But Pamela now thought that, whatever the views and scruples of this very married man, she could go to bed with him if she pleased, and when she pleased.

Still, Pam had no intention of enticing Captain Henry into what he termed a "shack-up." Blinker Vance, in Henry's disapproving view, was shacked up with Lady Maude Northwood, though the shack was one of the most elegant flats in Mayfair and Lady Maude, if somewhat horse-faced, was a clever and charming woman. Pamela didn't in the least believe in Victor Henry's morality. She thought it was a crust of cramping nonsense that stopped her from giving the lonely man and herself pleasure. But that was how he was. She was determined above all things not to upset or repel him; rather, to let matters take their course.

Almost exactly at noon the key turned in the lock.

As Pug let himself in, he could hear the noonday news broadcast echoing in the flat. He called, "Hello, who's here?"

Steps clicked in the living room. The girl struck him like a blue projectile. "Oh, my God, you came back."

"What the devil?" Victor Henry managed to say between kisses. "What are you doing here?"

"I'm absent without leave. I shall be court-martialled and shot. I should have sat here for a week. Your charwoman let me in. Ahhh!" With growls of pleasure, she kissed him again and again. Disorganized enough before this surprise, Pug dazedly kissed her back, not quite believing what was happening. Pam said, "Good heavens, Captain Henry, you do reek of rum."

"That's the debriefing. They give you a big breakfast and lots of rum and you talk." He had difficulty getting this out, because Pamela kept kissing him. Dead on his feet as he was, he nevertheless began on instinct to respond to this eager aroused girl clinging to him. He realized foggily, as he pulled her close and returned her kisses, that at this rate he was soon going to take her to bed. He was caught by surprise and had no impulse to stop, strange and dreamlike as it all was. He was hours away from a brush with death, and still numb and stunned. "Well, how about this?" he said hoarsely. "The conquering hero's reward, hey?"

She was covering his face with soft slow kisses. She leaned back in his arms, looking into his eyes. "Just so. Exactly."

"Well, I didn't do a goddamned thing except take up space, burn up gasoline, and get in everybody's way. However, thank you, Pam. You're beautiful and sweet, and this welcome makes me feel great."

His evident exhaustion, his clumsy moves, his comical indecisiveness about what to do next with this unfamiliar female body in his arms, caused a wave of deep tenderness to go through her. "You look absolutely drained," she said, stepping free. "Totally wrung out. Was it very bad?"

"It was long."

"Want a drink? Some food?"

"A drink, I guess. I feel okay, but I'd better get some sleep."

"So I figured." She led him to the darkened bedroom. The bed was turned down, his pajamas laid out. She took her time about mixing the drink, and when she came back to the bedroom he was asleep. On the floor, uncharacteristically dumped, lay the tweed suit that Aircraftsman Horton had missed out on.

The hand on his shoulder was gently persistent. "Captain Henry! It's five o'clock. You've had a call from the embassy."

He opened his eyes. "What? What embassy?"

It took him a few seconds to recollect where he was, and why Pamela Tudsbury was standing over him in uniform, with a smile so intimate and bright. In his dream he had been back in F for Freddie, fumbling and fumbling for a cloth to wipe the vomit off the poor rear gunner; the hallucinatory stench was still in his nostrils. He sat up and sniffed. A delicious odor of broiling meat floated through the open door, erasing the dream smell. "What's that?"

"I thought you'd be hungry by now."

"But where'd you get food? There's nothing in that icebox but beer and club soda."

"Went out and bought it."

He tried to shock himself awake with a cold shower, but still had a feeling, as he shaved and dressed, of stumbling through dreams within dreams. He could not get used to the wonder of being alive in normal circumstances. A dim recollection of Pamela's ardent welcome added to that wonder.

"What the Sam Hill!" he said. "Where and how did you get all this?"

The salads, the bowl of fruit, the long bread, and the bottle of red wine made an attractive clutter on the small table. She was humming in the kitchen. She said, entering with steaks on two plates, "Oh, I'm a London alley cat, I know where to forage. Sit down and get at this. The oven's really not very good, but I've done my best."

He cut into the meat and took a hot mouthful. The bread broke soft and crusty; the heavy wine was delicious. Pug Henry fell to with the gusto of a boy home from tobogganing. Pamela cut herself a piece of steak and ate it, not taking her eyes off Victor Henry as he wolfed the food. "Well," she said. "Rather hungry at that, weren't you?"

"Why, this is marvellous. It's the best meat, the best wine, the best bread I've ever eaten."

"You exaggerate, but I'm glad you're enjoying it. I'm trying to make up for the stupid way I acted before you left."

"Pam, I'm glad I went. That was the right decision."

"Oh, now that you're back, there's no argument. My apologies."

Victor Henry put down his knife and fork. All his senses were new-edged. To his eyes, Pamela Tudsbury's face radiated remarkable beauty and sweetness. He experienced a pleasant quake in all his nerves, remembering vividly their stunning kisses at the door.

"You're forgiven."

"Good." She drank wine, looking at him over the edge of the glass. "Do you know that I fell for you on the *Bremen*? Did you have any inkling of it? In Berlin I was hard put to it not to try my luck with you. But I knew it was impossible. You're so devoted to your wife."

"Yes indeed," Pug said. "Rock of Gibraltar. I guess I'm dumb, but I hadn't the slightest notion of that, Pamela."

"Well, it's true. I'd been in rotten shape for a couple of years. It did me good to be able to like a man so much. I proceeded to go mad over Ted shortly thereafter." A shadow of sadness flickered across her face. "When you opened the door a few hours ago, I came close to believing in God. There's strawberry tart for dessert."

"You're kidding."

"I'm not kidding. I passed a pastrycook's and the tarts looked good."

He reached out and took her slim wrist. Her skin felt as sweet to his blunt fingers as her lips had felt on his mouth. "Pam, I've developed a high regard for a London alley cat, myself."

"I'm glad. I should be sorry to think that my great passion was totally unrequited. If you'll unhand me, I'll serve your strawberry tart and coffee. It's getting on for six. Captain Vance was most insistent that you be at the embassy by six-thirty."

"What will you do? Go back to Uxbridge?"

"What will *you* do? That's what matters."

"First I have to find out what Blinker wants."

"Shall I wait for your call at my flat?"

"Yes, Pam. Please do that."

They parted on the sidewalk. He kept glancing back over his shoulder at the dwindling figure in blue, marching among the pedestrians with that odd swing he had first noticed on the *Bremen*—just another perky little WAAF among the thousands in London.

He felt reborn. He smiled at people he passed on the street, and they smiled back. The young girls appeared seductive as starlets; the older women were full of grace. The men were all great good fellows, the slope-shouldered pale clerks with briefcases and bowler hats no less than the passing soldiers, the withered gray men, and the purple-faced fat men in tweed. They all had the stuff that he had seen at the Biggin Hill dispersal hut and in F for Freddie. They were Englishmen, the happy breed. The sunlight dappling the leaves in Grosvenor Square was golden, the leaves were fresh green, and the sky was the blue of a WAAF uniform. What a world! What an idiocy in these Europeans to dump fire and explosives on each other's habitations, built with such hard work! All things were washed clean, or at least he was seeing them with a child's clear inquisitive eye—a shiny automobile, a shop-window dummy, a box of red geraniums on a windowsill. He noticed that the sidewalk gave off tiny sparkles in the late sunlight.

The American flag fluttering from the second story of the embassy struck Pug with a pang of pride. Its red, white, and blue seemed so rich, its slow waving so full of majesty, that a sixty-piece orchestra might have been playing "The Star-Spangled Banner"; but there was no orchestra in the square, only discordant loud traffic noise. He sat on a bench for a moment looking at the flag, suffused with zest for life and a burning wish to live a long time yet in this radiant world through which he had been walking blind as a bat. This grim stocky obscure American Navy captain sat bemused on a London park bench, undergoing an exaltation for which he finally found the name. At first he had thought his exhilarated mood was the snapback from the bombing mission, the plain joy of being alive after brushing death in a diving plane, in a whirl of blue cones and exploding colored balls. But it was something more. Nothing like this had happened to him in twenty-five years, and he had not expected it ever to happen again, so recognizing it had taken him this long. Nothing could be simpler. He had fallen in love.

A black Cadillac pulled up at the embassy door and discharged an admiral whom Pug recognized, two Army

generals, and Blinker Vance. Pug hastened across the
street.

"Hey, Pug!" Admiral Benton offered a fat hand. This
holy terror, his old boss at War Plans, was a short rotund
man with a shiny round face and a bald round head. Pug
liked him, despite his short temper, because he was a smart
and driving worker, wasted no words, admitted ignorance,
and took blame when the blame was his. He was a gunnery
expert too, the Navy's best. His weakness was opinionated
political theorizing; he thought the New Deal was a
Communist plot.

Blinker Vance brought the four men to a quiet second-
floor conference room panelled in cherry wood. He left.
They sat themselves at one end of a long polished table
lined with twenty chairs upholstered in blue leather.
Admiral Benton took the head, with the two generals on
either side of him and Pug below the younger-looking one.
"Now goddamn it, Pug," Benton began, "the ambassador
says if he'd known about this observer flight of yours,
he'd have stopped you. He's dead right. We don't want to
give the Army and its Air Corps"—he gestured at the
other men—"the idea that the Navy trains goofy dare-
devils." Benton sounded very pleased with Pug. "These
gentlemen and I have been waiting for you to get back
from that blamed fool excursion. This is General Anderson, and General Fitzgerald here is Army Air Corps."
Benton glanced at the others. "Well, shall we get at it?"

General Fitzgerald, who sat beside Pug, danced long
lean fingers together. He had wavy blond hair and a handsome thin face; he might have been an artist or an actor,
except for the stone-hard look in his pale blue eyes.
"Admiral, I'd like to hear about the captain's bomber ride
myself."

"So would I," said Anderson. Victor Henry now recognized him as Train Anderson, a West Point football star
of around 1910. Anderson was heavy and jowly, and his
thin hair was smoothed tight on a pink scalp.

Victor Henry narrated his bomber adventure in a matter-of-fact way.

"Great!" Benton burst out when Pug came to the
explosion of the gasworks.

The three senior officers listened tensely to the account

of his return trip in a damaged aircraft; the jettisoning of all removable weight to maintain altitude; the final thirty miles flown at a few hundred feet. When Pug finished, Train Anderson lit a cigar and leaned back on a thick elbow. "Quite a yarn, Captain. It amounted to a token bombing though, didn't it? Berlin sounds untouched, compared to this place. You've been to the docks, I presume?"

"Yes, sir."

"We toured them today. The Germans are making mincemeat of the area. At this rate, in a week London will cease to be a port. Then what happens? Famine? Plague?"

"That's a big dock area," Pug said. "Their repair and fire-fighting crews are good, General. Things look worse than they are."

The Air Corps general laced his fingers daintily together. "Have you been in the public shelters, Henry? We visited one during a raid. Nothing but a shallow cement hole. A hit would have killed everybody. All stinking of unwashed bodies and urine, all jammed with nervous, jittery old folks and crying kids. Big crayon scrawl on the ceiling, *This is a Jew War.* We visited the underground, too, last night. A mob of people sleeping on the tracks and the platforms, a sanitation nightmare, a setup for an outbreak of typhus."

"Sickness and casualties are running far under their estimates, sir," Pug said. "There are thousands of empty hospital beds."

"So this man Vance told us," put in Anderson. "Well, they'll fill 'em. Now, Captain Henry, you've been an observer here, and you've been sending optimistic reports to the President recommending all-out assistance."

"Not wholly optimistic, sir, but recommending full assistance, yes."

"Possibly you're a bit out of touch with what's happening on the other side of the water. So let me read you something. It's from the *St. Louis Post-Dispatch,* a red-hot New Deal paper." He took out his wallet, unfolded a neatly cut newspaper clipping, and intoned through his nose:

" 'Mr. Roosevelt today committed an act of war, turn-

ing over to a warring power a goodly portion of the United States Navy. We get in exchange leases on British possessions. What good will these leases be if Hitler should acquire title to these islands by right of conquest? Of all sucker real estate deals in history, this is the worst. If Mr. Roosevelt gets away with this, we may as well say goodbye to our liberties and make up our minds that henceforth we live under a dictatorship.' "

"That's a Roosevelt *supporter* talking," observed Anderson, puffing violently on the cigar. "Now, we're proceeding from here to a dinner at the Army and Navy Club, in half an hour or so, with some British generals and admirals. We already have the list of the war materials they want. It would strip our armed forces clean. We have to make cabled recommendations to the President within five days. He's already let them have—in addition to these fifty warships—virtually all our seventy-five-millimeter field guns, several squadrons of naval aircraft, half a million rifles, millions of rounds of ammunition—"

"He hasn't given 'em away, General," Benton observed. "The Limeys have paid cash on the barrelhead."

"Yes, luckily the Neutrality Act compels that, but still it was a goddamned lie to call the stuff surplus. Surplus! We don't have any surplus! You know that. Fifty destroyers! All this without any authorization from Congress. All things we're short of. And now Congress is passing a draft law. Our boys will be drilling with broomsticks! There's going to be an accounting one day, you know. If the British fold and this stuff winds up in German hands—a possibility to be reckoned with—the accounting will not be far off. All who have taken part in these transactions, or even advocated them"—here General Anderson turned a belligerent face at Victor Henry—"I warn you, stand a good chance of hanging from lamp posts on Constitution Avenue."

After a silence, Admiral Benton said mildly, folding his hands over his stomach, "Well, Pug, I've told these gentlemen that I know you, and that any dope you put out is reliable. We've got a big responsibility. We've been handed one hell of a hot potato. So get down to the short hairs. What makes you think the British will keep fighting, after the way the French folded? No horseshit now."

"All right, Admiral."

To begin with, Victor Henry said, the British had made better use than the French of the time between the wars. He described their scientific advances, the strength and disposition of the battle fleet, the fighter control system he had seen at Uxbridge, the figures of German and British plane losses, the morale of the fliers, the preparations along the invasion beaches, the Chain Home stations, the production of aircraft. Fitzgerald listened with his eyes closed, his head flung back, his fingers dancing. Benton stared gravely at Pug, pulling at an ear as he had done in a hundred War Plans meetings. Train Anderson, wreathing himself in smoke, also looked hard at Pug, though the glare was fading to a frigid calculating expression.

Pug gave as sober and clear an account as he could, but it was an effort. As he plodded through his military facts, Pamela Tudsbury shimmered in his mind's eye, shifting with afterimages of the flight over Berlin. He felt in an undisciplined mood and was hard put to it to keep a respectful tone.

"Now wait, Pug, this RDF you're so hot on," Benton interposed, "that's nothing but radar, isn't it? We've got radar. You were with me aboard the *New York* for the tests."

"We haven't got this kind of radar, sir." Victor Henry described in detail the cavity magnetron. The senior officers began glancing at each other. He added, "And they've even started installing the stuff in their night fighters."

General Fitzgerald sat straight up. *"Airborne* radar? What about the weight problem?"

"They've licked it."

"Then they've developed something new."

"They have, General."

Fitzgerald turned a serious gaze on Train Anderson, who stubbed out his cigar, observing to the admiral, "Well, I'll say this, your man makes out a case, at least. We've got to come across anyhow, since that's what Mr. Big wants. What we can do is exercise tight control item by item, and that by God we will do. And get trade-offs like that cavity thing, wherever possible." He regarded Henry through half-shut eyes. "Very well. Suppose they do hold out? Suppose Hitler doesn't invade? What's their future? What's their plan? What can they do against a man who controls all Europe?"

"Well, I can give you the official line," Victor Henry said. "I've heard it often enough. Hold him back in 1940. Pass him in air power in 1941, with British and American production. Shoot the Luftwaffe out of the skies in 1942 and 1943. Bomb their cities and factories to bits if they don't surrender. Invade and conquer in 1944."

"With what? Ten or fifteen divisions against two hundred?"

"Actually, General, I think the idea is simpler. Hang on till we get in."

"Now you're talking. But then what?"

General Fitzgerald said very quietly, "Why, then *we* pound Germany from the air, Train, with the bomber fleet we're building. A few months of that, and we land to accept the surrender, if anyone's alive to crawl out of the rubble."

Raising an eyebrow at Victor Henry, Admiral Benton said, "How's that sound, Pug?"

Victor Henry hesitated to answer.

"You're dubious?" General Fitzgerald observed amiably.

"General, I've just been out pounding Germany from the air. Twenty-four bombers went on the mission. Fifteen returned. Of those, four didn't bomb the right target. Navigation was off, they had operational troubles, there were German decoy fires, and so forth. Two didn't bomb *any* target. They got lost, wandered around in the dark, then dropped their bombs in the ocean and homed back on the BBC. In one mission they lost a third of the attacking force."

"This business is in its infancy," smiled Fitzgerald. "Twenty-four bombers. Suppose there'd been a thousand, with much heavier payloads? And at that, they did get the gasworks."

"Yes, sir. They got the gasworks."

"How do *you* think it's going to go?" General Anderson said brusquely to Henry.

"Sir, I think sooner or later a couple of million men will have to land in France and fight the German army."

With an unpleasant grunt, Train Anderson touched his

left shoulder. "Land in France, hey? I landed in France in 1918. I got a German bullet through my shoulder in the Argonne. I don't know what that accomplished. Do you?"

Victor Henry did not answer.

"Okay." Train Anderson rose. "Let's be on our way, gentlemen. Our British cousins await us."

"I'll be right along," Benton said. When the Army men were gone he slapped Victor Henry's shoulder. "Well done. These Limeys are holding the fort for us. We've got to help 'em. But Jesus God, they're not bashful in their requests! The big crunch comes when they run out of dollars. They can't even pay for this list of stuff, without selling their last holdings in America. What comes next? It beats me. The boss man will have to figure a way to give 'em the stuff. He's a slippery customer and I guess he will. Say, that reminds me—" He reached into a breast pocket and brought out a letter. *Victor Henry,* in his wife's small handwriting, was the only address on the envelope, which was much thicker than usual.

"Thank you, Admiral."

The admiral was fumbling in his pockets. "No, there's something else. Damn, I couldn't have—no, here we are. Whew! That's a relief."

It was a White House envelope. Pug slipped both letters into his pocket.

"Say, Pug, for a gunnery officer you've painted yourself into a peculiar corner. That screwball socialist in the White House thinks a lot of you, which may or may not be a good thing. I'd better mosey along. Rhoda sounded fine when I talked to her, only a little sad." Benton sighed and stood. "They have to put up with a lot, the gals. Good thing she didn't know about that bomber ride. Now that you're back I sort of envy you. But me, I'm absurdly fond of my ass, Pug. I'm not getting it shot off except in the line of duty. I commend that thought to you hereafter."

Blinker Vance took off big black-rimmed glasses and stepped out from behind his desk to throw an arm around Pug. "Say, I want to hear all about that joyride one of these days. How did it go with the big brass?"

"All right."

"Good. There's a dispatch here for you from BuPers."

He peeled a tissue off a clipboard hung on the wall, and handed it to Pug.

VICTOR HENRY DETACHED TEMPORARY DUTY LON-
DON X RETURN BERLIN UNTIL RELIEVED ON OR ABOUT
1 NOVEMBER X THEREUPON DETACHED TO PROCEED
WASHINGTON HIGHEST AIR PRIORITY X REPORT BUPERS
FOR FURTHER REASSIGNMENT X

Vance said, "Glad you'll be getting out of Berlin?"

"Overjoyed."

"Thought you'd be. Transportation tells me they've got a priority to Lisbon available on the fourteenth."

"Grab it."

"Right." With a knowing little smile, Vance added, "Say, maybe you and that nice little Tudsbury girl can have a farewell dinner with me and Lady Maude tomorrow night."

Several times Blinker had asked Victor Henry to join them for dinner. Pug knew and liked Blinker's wife and their six children. Avoiding a censorious tone, he had declined the invitations. Victor Henry knew how common-place these things were—*"Wars and lechery, nothing else holds fashion"*—but he had not felt like endorsing Blinker's shack-up. Vance now was renewing the bid, and his smile was reminding Pug that on telephoning the flat, he had found Pamela there.

"I'll let you know, Blinker. I'll call you later."

"Fine!" Vance's grin broadened at not being turned down. "Lady Maude will be charmed, and my God, Pug, she has a fabulous wine cellar."

Victor Henry returned to the bench in Grosvenor Square. The sun still shone, the flag still waved. But it was just a sticky London evening like any other. The strange brightness was out of the air.

The President's hasty pencilled scrawl was on a yellow legal sheet this time.

Pug—

Your bracing reports have been a grand tonic that I needed. The war news has been so bad, and now the Republicans have gone and put up a fine candidate in Wendell Willkie! Come

November, you just might be working for a new boss. Then you can slip the chain and get out to sea! Ha ha!

Thank you especially for alerting us on their advanced radar. The British are sending over a scientific mission in September, with all their "wizard war" stuff, as Churchill calls it. We'll be very sure to follow that up! There's something heartwarming about Churchill's interest in landing craft, isn't there? Actually he's right, and I've asked for a report from CNO. Get as much of their material as you can.

FDR

Pug stuffed the vigorous scrawl in his pocket like any other note, and opened his wife's letter. It was a strange one.

She had just turned on the radio, she wrote, heard an old record of "Three O'Clock in the Morning," and burst out crying. She reminisced about their honeymoon, when they had danced so often to that song; about his long absence in 1918; about their good times in Manila and in Panama. With Palmer Kirby, who now kept a small office in New York, she had just driven up to New London to visit Byron—a glorious two-day trip through the early autumn foliage of Connecticut. Red Tully had told her that Byron was lazy in his written work, but very good in the simulator and in submarine drills. She had asked Byron about the Jewish girl.

The way he changed the subject, I think maybe all that is over. He got a peculiar look on his face, but said nary a word. Wouldn't *that* be a relief!

You know that Janice is pregnant, don't you? You must have heard from them. Those kids didn't waste much time, hey? Like father like son, is all *I* can say! But the thought of being a GRANDMOTHER!!! In a way I'm happy, but in another way it seems like the end of the world! It would have helped a lot if you'd been here when I first got the news. It sure threw me into a spin. I'm not sure I've pulled out of it yet, but I'm trying.

Let me give you a piece of advice. The sooner you can come home, the better. I'm all right, but at the moment I could really use a HUSBAND around.

He walked to his flat and telephoned Pamela.

"Oh, my dear," she said, "I'm so glad you called. In another quarter of an hour I'd have been gone. I talked to Uxbridge. They're being very broad-minded. If I come back tonight, all is forgiven. They're short-handed and they expect heavy raids. I must, I really must go back right away."

"Of course you must. You're lucky you're not getting shot for desertion," Pug said, as lightly as he could.

"I'm not the first offender at Uxbridge," she laughed. "A WAAF has a certain emotional rope to use up, you know. But this time I've really done it."

He said, "I'm ever so grateful to you."

"*You're* grateful?" she said. "Oh, God, don't you know that you've pulled me through a very bad time? I shall get another special pass in a week, at most. Can we see each other then?"

"Pam, I'm leaving day after tomorrow. Going back to Berlin for about a month or six weeks, and then home. . . . Hello? Pamela?"

"I'm still here. You're going day after tomorrow?"

"My orders were waiting at the embassy."

After a long pause, in which he heard her breathing, she said, "You wouldn't want me to desert for two more days and take what comes. Would you? I'll do it."

"It's no way to win a war, Pam."

"No, it isn't, Captain. Well. This is an unexpected good-bye, then. But good-bye it is."

"Our paths will cross again."

"Oh, no doubt. But I firmly believe that Ted's alive and is coming back. I may well be a wife next time we meet. And that will be far more proper and easy all around. All the same, today was one of the happiest of my life, and that's unchangeable now."

Victor Henry was finding it difficult to go on talking. The sad, kind tones of this young voice he loved were choking his throat; and there were no words available to his rusty tongue to tell Pamela what he felt. "I'll never forget, Pamela," he said awkwardly, clearing his throat. "I'll never forget one minute of it."

"Won't you? Good. Neither will I. Some hours weigh against a whole lifetime, don't they? I think they do. Well!

Good-bye, Captain Henry, and safe journeyings. I hope you find all well at home."

"Good-bye, Pam. I hope Ted makes it."

Her voice broke a little. "Somebody's coming for me. Good-bye."

Fatigued but tensely awake, Victor Henry changed to civilian clothes and drifted to Fred Fearing's noisy airless hot apartment. A bomb bursting close by earlier in the week had blown in all the windows, which were blocked now with brown plywood. Fearing's broadcast, describing his feelings under a shower of glass, had been a great success.

"Where's la Tudsbury?" said Fearing, handing Victor Henry a cupful of punch made of gin and some purple canned juice.

"Fighting Germans."

"Good show!" The broadcaster did a vaudeville burlesque of the British accent.

Pug sat in a corner of a dusty plush sofa under a plywood panel, watching the drinking and dancing, and wondering why he had come here. He saw a tall young girl in a tailored red suit, with long black hair combed behind her ears, give him one glance, then another. With an uncertain smile, at once bold and wistful, the girl approached. "Hello there. Would you like more punch? You look important and lonesome."

"I couldn't be less important. I'd like company more than punch. Please join me."

The girl promptly sat and crossed magnificent silk-shod legs. She was prettier than Pamela, and no more than twenty. "Let me guess. You're a general. Air Corps. They tend to be younger."

"I'm just a Navy captain, a long, long way from home."

"I'm Lucy Somerville. My mother would spank me for speaking first to a strange man. But everything's different in the war, isn't it?"

"I'm Captain Victor Henry."

"Captain Victor Henry. Sounds so American." She looked at him with impudent eyes. "I like Americans."

"I guess you're meeting quite a few."

"Oh, heaps. One nicer than the other." She laughed. "The bombing's perfectly horrible, but it is exciting, isn't it? Life's never been so exciting. One never knows whether one will be able to get home at night. It makes things interesting. I know girls who take their makeup and pajamas along when they go out in the evening. And dear old Mums can't say a word!"

The girl's roguish, inviting glance told him that here probably was a random flare of passion for the taking. Wartime London was the place, he thought; *"nothing else holds fashion!"* But this girl was Madeline's age, and meant nothing to him; and he had just said a stodgy, cold, miserable good-bye to Pamela Tudsbury. He avoided her dancing eyes, and said something dull about the evening news. In a minute or so a strapping Army lieutenant approached and offered Lucy Somerville a drink, and she jumped up and was gone. Soon after, Pug left.

Alone in the flat, he listened to a Churchill speech and went to bed. The last thing he did before turning out the light was to reread Rhoda's nostalgic, sentimental, and troubled letter. Something shadowy and unpleasant was there between the lines. He guessed she might be having difficulties with Madeline, though the letter did not mention the daughter's name. There was no point in dwelling on it, he thought. He would be home in a couple of months. He fell asleep.

* * *

Rhoda had slept with Dr. Kirby on the trip to Connecticut. That was the shadowy and unpleasant thing Pug half discerned. Proverbially the cuckold is the last to know his disgrace; no suspicion crossed his mind, though Rhoda's words were incautious and revealing.

War not only forces intense new relationships; it puts old ones to the breaking stress. On the very day this paragon of faithfulness—as his Navy friends regarded him —had received his wife's letter, he had not made love to Pamela Tudsbury, mainly because the girl had decided not to bring him to it. Rhoda had fallen on the way back from New London. It had been unplanned and unforeseen. She would have recoiled from a cold-blooded copulation. The back windows of the little tourist house, where she and Kirby had stopped for tea, looked out on a charming pond where swans moved among pink lily pads in a gray drizzle. Except for the old lady who served them, they were alone in this quiet relaxing place. The visit to Byron had gone well and the countryside was beautiful. They intended to halt for an hour, then drive on to New York. They talked of their first lunch outside Berlin, of the farewell at Tempelhof Airport, of their mutual delight at seeing each other in the Waldorf. The time flowed by, their tone grew more intimate. Then Palmer Kirby said, "How wonderfully cosy this place is! Too bad we can't stay here."

And Rhoda Henry murmured, hardly believing that she was releasing the words from her mouth, "Maybe we could."

Maybe we could! Three words, and a life pattern and a character dissolved. The old lady gave them a bedroom, asking no questions. Everything followed: undressing with a stranger, casting aside with her underclothes her modesty and her much-treasured rectitude, yielding to a torrent of novel sensations. To be taken by this large demanding man left her throbbing with animal pleasure. All her thoughts since then went back to that point in time, and there halted. Like a declaration of war, it drew a line across the past and started another era. The oddest aspect of this new life was that it was so much like the old one. Rhoda felt she had not really changed. She even still loved Pug. She was trying to digest all this puzzlement when she wrote to her husband. She did have twinges of conscience, but she was surprised to find how bearable these were.

In New York, Rhoda and Kirby heard in bright afternoon sunshine the Churchill broadcast which Pug had listened to late at night. Rhoda had chosen well the apartment for Madeline and herself. It faced south, across low brownstones. Sunshine poured in all day through white-draped windows, into a broad living room furnished and decorated in white, peach, and apple green. Photographs of Victor Henry and the boys stood in green frames on a white piano. Few visitors failed to comment on the genteel cheerfulness of the place.

"He has lighted a fire which will burn with a steady and consuming flame, until the last vestiges of Nazi tyranny have been burnt out of Europe. . . ."

Puffing at his pipe, Kirby slouched in an armchair and stared at the radio. "Marvellous phrasemaker, that man."

"Do you think they'll actually hold off the Germans, Palmer?"

"What does Pug say?"

"He wrote a pessimistic letter when he first arrived there. He hasn't written again."

"Odd. He's been there a while."

"Well, I tell myself if anything had happened to him I'd have heard. I do worry."

"Naturally."

The speech ended. She saw him glance at the watch on his hairy wrist. "When does your plane go?"

"Oh, not for a couple of hours." He turned off the radio, strolled to the windows, and looked out. "This is not a bad view. Radio City, the Empire State Building. Pity that apartment house blocks out the river."

"I know what you'd like right now," she said.

"What?"

"Some tea. It's that time." Answering his sudden coarse grin with a half-coy, half-brazen smile, she hurriedly added, "I really mean *tea,* Mr. Palmer Kirby."

"My favorite drink, tea. Lately, anyway."

"Don't be horrible, you! Well? Shall I make some?"

"Of course. I'd love tea."

"I suppose I should swear off it, since it was my downfall. Of all things." She walked toward the kitchen with a sexy sway. "If only I could plead having been drunk, but I was sober as a minister's wife."

He came to the kitchen and watched her prepare the tea. Palmer Kirby liked to watch her move around, and his eyes on her made Rhoda feel young and fetching. They sat at a low table in the sunshine and she decorously poured tea and passed him buttered bread. The picture could not have been more placid and respectable.

"Almost as good as the tea at Mrs. Murchison's guesthouse," Kirby said. "Almost."

"Now never mind! How long will you be in Denver?"

"Only overnight. Then I have to come to Washington. Our board's going to meet with some British scientists. From the advance papers, they've got some remarkable stuff. I'm sure they're surprising the Germans."

"So! You'll be in Washington next."

"Yes. Got a good reason to go to Washington?"

"Oh, dear, Palmer, don't you realize I know everybody in that town? Absolutely everybody. And anybody I don't know, Pug knows."

He said after a glum pause, "It's not very satisfactory, is it? I don't see myself as a homewrecker. Especially of a military man serving abroad."

"Look, dear, I don't see myself as a scarlet woman. I've been to church both Sundays since. I don't feel guilty, but I do feel mighty CURIOUS, I'll tell you that." She poured more tea for him. "It must be the war, Palmer. I don't know. With Hitler bestriding Europe and London burning to the ground, all the old ideas seem, I don't know, TRIVIAL or something. I mean compared to what's real at the moment—the swans out in back at Mrs. Murchison's place—those sweet pink lily pads, the rain, the gray cat— the tea, those funny doughy cakes—and you and me. That's as far as I've gotten."

"I didn't tell you why I'm going to Denver."

"No."

"There's a buyer for my house. Wants to pay a tremendous price. I've told you about the house."

"Yes, it sounds heavenly. Do you really want to let it go?"

"I rattle around in it. I've been thinking, and it comes to this. Most of my friends are in Denver. The house is perfect to live in, to entertain in, to have my children and the grandchildren for visits. If I had a wife, I wouldn't sell it." He stopped, looking at her now with serious, large brown eyes filled with worried shyness. The look was itself a proposal of marriage. "What do you think, Rhoda?"

"Oh, Palmer! Oh, heavenly days!" Rhoda's eyes brimmed. She was not totally astonished, but the relief was beyond description. This resolved the puzzlement. It had not been a crazy slip, after all, like that foolishness with Kip Tollever, but a grand passion. Grand passions were different.

He said, "That can't really be news to you. We wouldn't have stayed at Mrs. Murchison's if I hadn't felt this way."

"Well! Oh, my lord. I'm proud and happy that you should think of me like that. Of course I am. But—*Palm-*

er!" She swept her hand almost gaily at the photographs on the piano.

"I have friends who've married again in their fifties, Rhoda. After divorces, some of them, and some are blissfully happy."

Rhoda sighed, dashed her fingers to her eyes, and smiled at him. "Is it that you want to make an honest woman of me? That's terribly gallant, but unnecessary."

Palmer Kirby leaned forward earnestly, tightening his large loose mouth. "Pug Henry is an admirable man. It didn't happen because you're a bad woman. There was a rift in your marriage before we met. There had to be."

In a very shaky voice, Rhoda said, "Before I ever knew him, Pug was a Navy fullback. I saw him play in two Army-Navy games. I had a boyfriend who loved those games—let me talk, Palmer, maybe I'll collect myself. He was an aggressive, exciting player, this husky little fellow darting all over the field. Then, my stars, he BURST on me in Washington. The actual Pug Henry, whose picture had been in the papers and all that. The war was on. He looked dashing in blue and gold, I must say! Well, great heavens, he courted the way he played football. And he was very funny in those days. Pug has a droll wit, you know, when he bothers to use it. Well, all the boys I went with were just from the old Washington crowd, all going to the same schools, all cut out by the same cookie cutter, you might say. Pug was something different. He still is. For one thing, he's a very serious Christian, and you can bet *that* took a lot of getting used to! I mean right from the start it was a complicated thing. I mean it didn't seem to interfere at all with his ROMANCING, if I make myself clear, and yet—well, Pug is altogether unusual and wonderful. I'll always say that. I must bore Pug. I know he loves me, but—the thing is he is so Navy! Why, that man left me standing at my wedding reception, Palmer, for half an hour, while he drove his commanding officer to catch a train back to Norfolk! That's Victor Henry for you. But in twenty-five years—oh dear, now for the very first time I suddenly feel very, very wretched."

Rhoda cried into her handkerchief, her shoulders shaking. He came and sat beside her. When she calmed down, she looked at him and said, "You go along to Denver, but ask yourself this. I've done this to Pug. Wouldn't you be thinking forever and a day, if by some wild chance you got what you're asking for, that I'd do it to you? Of course you would. Why not?"

He stood. "I'll keep that appointment in Denver, Rhoda. But I don't think I'll sell the house."

"Oh, sell it! As far as I'm concerned, you go right ahead and sell that house, Palmer. I only think you yourself might regret it one day."

"Good-bye, Rhoda. I'll telephone you from Washington. Sorry I missed Madeline this time. Give her my best." He said, glancing at the photographs on the piano, "I think your kids would like me. Even that strange Byron fellow."

"How could they fail to? That isn't the problem." She walked with him to the door. He kissed her like a husband going off on a trip.

35

SEPTEMBER was crisping the Berlin air and yellowing the leaves when Pug got back. Compared to London under the blitz, the city looked at peace. Fewer uniforms were in sight, and almost no trucks or tanks. After beating France, Hitler had partially demobilized to free workers for the farms and factories. His remaining soldiers were not loafing around Berlin. Either they were poised for invasion on the coast, or they garrisoned France and Poland, or they guarded a thin prudent line facing the Soviet Union. Only the air war showed its traces: round blue-gray snouts of flak guns poking above autumn leaves, flaxen-haired German children in a public square gawking at a downed Wellington. The sight of the forlorn British bomber—a twin of F for Freddie—with its red, white, and blue bull's-eye, gave Pug a sad twinge. He tried and failed to see the wrecked gasworks. Scowling Luftwaffe guards and wooden street barriers cordoned off the disaster. Göring had long ago announced that if a single British bomb ever fell on Berlin, the German people could call him Meyer. The evidence of Meyer's shortcomings was off limits.

But Pug wondered how many Germans would have gone there anyway to look. These were weird people. In Lisbon, when he boarded the Lufthansa plane, Germany had then and there smitten him: the spotless interior, the heel-clicking steward, the fast service of food and drink, the harsh barking loudspeaker, and his seatmate, a fat bespectacled blond doctor who clinked wineglasses with him and spoke warmly of the United States and of his sister in Milwaukee. The doctor expressed confidence that America and Germany would always be friends. Hitler and Roosevelt were equally great men and they both wanted peace. He deplored the ruthless murder of Berlin civilians by British bombers, as contrasted to the Luftwaffe's strict concentration on military targets. The RAF, he pointed out, painted the underside of their planes with a remarkable black varnish that rendered them invisible at night, and constantly changed altitude so that the A.A. batteries had trouble finding the range. That was how they had sneaked by. But these petty unfair tricks would avail them nothing. German science would find the answer in a week or two. The war was really over and won. The Luftwaffe was invincible. The British criminals responsible for dropping bombs on women and little children would soon have to face the bar of justice.

This man was exactly like a London music-hall burlesque German, complete to the squinting smile and the rolls of fat on his neck. Pug got tired of him. He said dryly that he had just come from London and that the Luftwaffe was getting beaten over England. The man at once froze, turned his back on Pug, and ostentatiously flourished an Italian newspaper with lurid pictures of London on fire.

Then when Pug first returned to the Grunewald house, the art museum director who lived next door, a vastly learned little dark man named Dr. Baltzer, rushed over, dragging a game leg, to offer his neighbor a drink and to chat about the imminent British collapse. Besides being obliging neighbors, the Baltzers had invited the Henrys to many interesting exhibitions and parties. Mrs. Baltzer had become Rhoda's closest German friend. Tactfully, Pug tried to tell his neighbor that the war wasn't going quite the way Goebbels's newspapers and broadcasters pictured it. At the first hint that the RAF was holding its own, the little art expert bristled and went limping out, forgetting his offer to give Pug a drink. And this was a man who had hinted many times that the Nazis were vulgar ruffians and that Hitler was a calamity.

This was what now made Berlin completely intolerable. The Germans had balled themselves into one tight fist. The little tramp had his "one Reich, one people, one leader," that he had so long screeched for. Victor Henry, a man of discipline, understood and admired the stiff obedient efficiency of these people, but their mindless shutting out of facts disgusted him. It was not only stupid, not only shameless; it was bad war-making. The "estimate of the situation"—a phrase borrowed by the Navy from Prussian military doctrine—had to start from the facts.

When Ernst Grobke telephoned to invite him to lunch shortly after his return, he accepted gladly. Grobke was one of the few German military men he knew who seemed to retain some common sense amid the Nazi delirium. In a restaurant crowded with uniformed Party officials and high military brass, the submariner griped openly about the war, especially the way Göring had botched the Battle of Britain. From time to time he narrowed his eyes and glanced over one shoulder and the other, an automatic gesture in Germany when talking war or politics.

"We'll still win," he said. "They'll try all the dumb alternatives and then they'll get around to it."

"To what?" Pug said.

"Blockade, of course. The old English weapon turned against them. They can't blockade *us*. We've got the whole European coast open from the Baltic all the way around to Turkey. Even Napoleon never had that. But England's got a negative balance of food and fuel that has to choke her to death. If Göring had just knocked out harbors this summer and sunk ships—adding that to the tremendous score our U-boat and magnetic mines have been piling up

—England would already be making approaches through the Swiss and the Swedes." He calmly lifted both hands upward. "No alternative! We're sinking them all across the Atlantic. They don't have the strength to convoy. If they did, our new tactics and torpedoes would still lick them. Mind you, we started way under strength on U-boats, Victor. But finally Dönitz convinced Raeder, and Raeder convinced the Führer. After Poland, when England turned down the peace offer, we started laying keels by the dozens. They begin coming off the ways next January. An improved type, a beauty. Then—four, five months, half a million tons sunk a month, and *phfff!*—Churchill *kaput*. You disagree?" Grobke grinned at him. The small U-boat man wore a well-tailored purplish tweed suit and a clashing yellow bow tie. His face glowed with sunburned, confident good health. "Come on. You don't have to sympathize. We all know your President's sentiments, hm? But you understand the sea and you know the situation."

Pug regarded Grobke wryly. He rather agreed with this estimate. "Well, if Göring really will switch to blockade, and if you do have a big new fleet of 'em coming along— but that's a couple of big if's."

"You doubt my word?"

"I wouldn't blame you for expanding a bit."

"You're all right, Victor." Grobke laughed. "Goddamn. But I don't have to expand. You'll see, beginning in January."

"Then it may get down to whether we come in."

The U-boat man stopped laughing. "Yes. That's the question. But now your President sneaks a few old airplanes and ships to England, and he can't even face your Congress with that. Do you think your people will go for sending out American warships to be sunk by U-boats? Roosevelt is a tough guy, but he is afraid of your people."

"Well! Ernst Grobke and Victor Henry! The two sea dogs, deciding the war."

The banker Wolf Stöller was bowing over them, thin sandy hair plastered down, cigarette holder sticking out of his smile. "Victor, that is a beautiful new suit. Savile Row?"

"Yes, as a matter of fact."

"Unmistakable. Well, it will be a pleasure to start ordering clothes there again. There are no tailors like the British. I say, how far along are you gentlemen? Come and join us. Just a few pleasant chaps at our table."

"No thank you, Herr Stöller," Pug said. "I must get back to my office quickly."

"Of course. I say, Ernst, did you tell Captain Henry you're coming to Abendruh this weekend? Victor's an old Abendruh visitor, you know. By Jove! Why don't you come along this time, Victor? Twice lately you've said no, but I'm not proud. You and your old friend Ernst can tell each other big sea lies all weekend! Do say yes. There will be just two or three other splendid fellows. And some lovely ladies, not all of them attached."

Under Victor Henry's quick glance, Grobke smiled unnaturally and said, "Well, that's not a bad idea, is it?"

"All right," said the American. It was quite clear to him now what was going on and why Grobke had called him. "Thank you very much."

"Grand. Ripping. See you on Friday," said the banker, clapping Victor Henry on the shoulder.

After this, the talk of the two naval officers was lame and sparse. Ernst Grobke busied himself with his food, not looking much at Pug.

That same afternoon, to Victor Henry's surprise, his yeoman rang him and said Natalie Jastrow was on the line from Siena.

"Jehosephat! Put her on."

"Hello? Hello? What happened? I was calling Captain Henry in Berlin." The girl's voice was muffled and burbling.

"Here I am, Natalie."

"Oh, *hello!* Is Byron all right?"

"He's fine."

"Oh, what a relief!" The interference on the line stopped. Natalie's voice came clear. "I haven't had a single letter from him since I left. I sent a cable and got no answer. I know how impossible the mail is nowadays, but still I've begun to worry."

"Natalie, he hasn't had any letters from you. He wrote me that. And I'm sure he didn't get your cable. But he's in good shape."

"Why, I've been writing once a week. How aggravating

that is! I miss him so. How's he doing in submarine school?"

Outside Victor Henry's window, the guard was changing at the chancellery, with rhythmic boot-thumpings and brisk German barks. Natalie's telephone voice stirred an ache in him. The New York accent was different from Pamela's, but it was a young low girlish voice like hers.

"Scraping by, I gather."

Her laugh, too, was much like Pamela's, husky and slightly mocking. "That sounds right."

"Natalie, he expected you back long before this."

"I know. There were problems, but they're straightening out. Be sure to tell him I'm fine. Siena's quite charming in wartime, and very peaceful. It's sort of sinking back into the Middle Ages. Byron's got three months to go, hasn't he?"

"He finishes in December, if they don't throw him out sooner."

Again the laugh. "They won't. Briny is actually very surefooted, you know. I'll be back by December. Please write and tell him that. Maybe a letter from you will get through."

"It will. I'll write today."

*   *   *

It was a small gathering at Abendruh, with no staircase slide. Pug was sorry that Ernst Grobke didn't see the crude elaborate joke, so much to the Teutonic taste. The submariner obviously was ill at ease, and could have used the icebreaker. The other men were a Luftwaffe general and a high official in the foreign ministry, company far above Grobke. The five pretty ladies were not wives. Mrs. Stöller was absent.

Victor Henry sized all this up as an orgy in the making, to get him to talk about the British. After dinner, somewhat to his surprise, they went to a wood-panelled room where musical instruments were ready, and Stöller, the Luftwaffe general, the man from the foreign ministry, and a redheaded lady played quartets. In Pug's previous visits, the banker had shown no musical skill, but Stöller played first violin quite well. The Luftwaffe general, a very tall dark cadaverous man with sickly hollow eyes, bowed and swayed over the cello, drawing forth luscious sounds. Pug had seen this man once before, at a distance at Karinhall in full uniform; he had looked far more formidable then than he did now in his dinner jacket and monocle. The musicians made mistakes, stopped a couple of times, joked swiftly, and took up the music once more. The foreign ministry man on the second violin, a roly-poly Bavarian with a drooping yellow moustache, was a superb fiddler. It was the best amateur music Pug had ever heard. Grobke sat with the submissiveness of most Germans in the presence of art, drinking a lot of brandy and stifling yawns. After a couple of hours of this, the ladies abruptly said good-night and left. If there had been a signal, Pug missed it.

"Perhaps we might have a nightcap outside," said the banker to Pug, putting his violin carefully in its case. "The evening is warm. Do you like the tone of my Stradivarius? I wish I were worthy to play it."

The broad stone terrace looked out on a formal garden, a darkly splashing fountain, and the river; beyond that, forest. A smudged orange moon in its last quarter was rising over the trees. In the light of reddish-yellow flares on long iron poles, shadows danced on the house and the flagstone floor. The five men sat, and a butler passed drinks. Melodious birds sang in the quiet night, reminding Pug of the nightingales at the British bomber base.

"Victor, if you care to talk about England," said Stöller from the depths of an easy chair, his face in black shadow, "we would of course be interested."

Pug forced a jocular tone. "You mean I have to admit I've been in England?"

The banker heavily took up the note. "Ha, ha. Unless you want to get our intelligence people in bad trouble, you'd better." After everybody else laughed, he said, "If you prefer, we'll drop the subject here and now for the weekend. Our hospitality hasn't got—how do you say it in English?"—he switched from the German they were all speaking—" 'strings tied to it.' But you're in an unusual position, having travelled between the capitals."

"Well, if you want me to say you've shot the RAF out

of the sky and the British will quit next week, it might be better to drop it now."

In a gloomy bass voice, the long shadowy form of the general spoke. "We know we haven't shot the RAF out of the sky."

"Speak freely. General Jagow is my oldest friend," said Stöller. "We were schoolboys together. And Dr. Meusse" —he waved an arm at the foreign ministry man, and a long skeletal shadow arm leaped on the wall—"goes back almost that far."

"We say in the Luftwaffe," put in the general, "the red flag is up. That means we all talk straight. We say what we think about the Führer, about Göring, about anything and anybody. And we say the goddamnedest things, I tell you."

"Okay, I like those ground rules," said Victor Henry. "Fire away."

"Would an invasion succeed?" spoke up Dr. Meusse.

"What invasion? Can your navy get you across?"

"Why not?" said General Jagow in calm professional tones. "Through a corridor barricaded on both sides by mine belts, and cordoned off by U-boats, under an umbrella of Luftwaffe? Is it so much to ask of the Grand Fleet?"

Pug glanced at Grobke, who sat glumly swirling brandy in a bell glass. "You've got a U-boat man here. Ask him about the cordons and the mine belts."

With an impatient gesture that flicked brandy into the air, Grobke said, in thick tones, "Very difficult, possibly suicidal, and worst of all, entirely unnecessary."

General Jagow leaned toward Grobke, his monocle glittering in the flare light, his face stiff with anger.

Pug exclaimed, "Red flag's up."

"So it is," Jagow said, with an unforgiving glare at the submariner, who slouched down in darkness.

"I agree with him," Pug said. "Part of a landing force might get through—not saying in what shape. There's still the invasion beaches—which I've seen close on. Which I personally would hate to approach from seaward."

"Clearing beach obstacles is a technical task," Jagow said, with a swift return to offhand tones. "We have special sappers well trained for that."

"General, our Marine Corps has been studying and rehearsing beach assaults intensively for years. It's the toughest attack problem in the book. I don't believe the Wehrmacht ever thought about it until a few weeks ago."

"German military ingenuity is not negligible," said Dr. Meusse.

"No argument," said Victor Henry.

Jagow said, "Of course we can't land without wastage. We would take big but endurable losses. Once we obtained a solid lodgment, you might see Churchill fall. The Luftwaffe would fight for the beachhead to the last plane. But I believe the RAF would run out of planes first."

Victor Henry made no comment.

"What is the bombing of London doing to British morale?" Stöller asked.

"You're making Churchill's job easier. They're fighting mad now. Knocking hell out of London won't win the war. Not in my judgment. Not to mention that bombers can fly east as well as west."

The general and the banker looked at each other. The general's voice was sepulchral. "Would it surprise you if some people here agreed with you?"

"Churchill cleverly provoked the Führer by bombing Berlin on the twenty-sixth," said Stöller. "We had to hit back, for morale reasons. The trick worked, but the British people must now pay. There's no political alternative but a big reprisal."

"Let's be honest," said Dr. Meusse. "Field Marshal Göring wanted to go after London and try to end it."

Jagow shook his head. "He knew it was too soon. We all did. It was those six days of bad weather that saved the RAF. We needed another week against those airfields. But in the long run it will all be the same."

Stöller said, "They're a brave people. I hate to see them prolong the agony."

"They don't seem to mind," Victor Henry said. "By and large, they're having a good time. They think they're going to win."

"There is the weakness," said Dr. Meusse, pulling on his moustache. "National megalomania. When a people loses touch with reality, it is finished."

Stöller lit a thick cigar. "Absolutely. The course of this

war is fixed now by statistics. That is my department. Would you care to hear them?"

"Gladly. Especially if you'll give away some secrets," said Victor Henry, evoking friendly laughter from all the Germans except Grobke. The submariner was sunk in gloom or sleep.

"No secrets," said Stöller. "The financial stuff may be a little new to you. But take my word for it, my figures are right."

"I'm sure of that."

"Good. England lives at the end of—how would you put it—a revolving bucket chain of ships. She always has. This time the buckets are being shot off the chain faster than she can replace them. She started the war with about twenty million tons of shipping. Her own, and what she could scrape up elsewhere. That tonnage is disappearing fast. The rate now is—what's the latest?" He spoke condescendingly to Grobke.

The submariner covered a yawn. "That figure is secret. Victor must have a damn good idea from what he heard in London."

Pug said, "I have."

"All right. Then you know the curve is upward. Nothing else matters in this war. England will soon run out of fuel and food, and that will be that. When her machines stop, and her planes are grounded, and her people are clamoring for food, Churchill will fall. There's no way out."

"Isn't there? My country has a lot of fuel and food—and steel and shipyards too—and we're open for business."

The banker coldly smiled. "Yes, but your Neutrality Act requires that England pay cash for everything. Cash and carry. That is the one sensible thing your people learned from the last war, when England repudiated her war debts. Roosevelt, Willkie, it doesn't matter now. There isn't a chance—you bear me out on this, Victor—that your Congress will ever make another war loan to England. Will they?"

"No."

"All right. Then she is *kaput*. She started the war with about five billions in foreign exchange. Our intelligence is she's already spent more than four. The planes and sup-

plies and ships she needs right now to keep going will wipe
out the last billion or so like a snowball on a hot stove. By
December the British Empire will be broke. Bankrupt!
You see, dear fellow, they got into a war they couldn't
fight and couldn't pay for. That is the simple fact. And it
was the political genius of the Führer, Victor—whatever
you think of him—to foresee this, through all the fog of
the future. Just as he foresaw that the French wouldn't
fight. Such leadership brings victory." Stöller leaned forward, with a disdainful hand-wave. "Yes, Churchill's
words are very eloquent, very touching, very spiritual. But
he was England's worst Chancellor of the Exchequer. He
hasn't the slightest notion of logistical or financial realities.
Never has had. His pretty literary soap bubbles are all
going to pop. Then there will be peace."

Dr. Meusse put in, "We are sinking ships now at a rate
we never reached until the best months of 1917. Do you
know that?"

"I know that," said Captain Henry. "And as I said to
Ernst the other day, that's when we came in."

The silence on the terrace lasted a long time. Then
Wolf Stöller said, "And that is the world tragedy that must
not occur now, Victor—Germany and America, the two
great anti-Bolshevik powers, going to war. The only victor
will be Stalin."

The voice of Grobke, coarse and fuddled, issued from
the depths of his chair. "It won't happen. It'll all be over
too fast. Wait till January, when we get ourselves some
U-boats."

The weekend proved cold, dull, rainy, and—for Pug—
very heavy on music and culture. The five ladies, all in
their thirties, all mechanically flirtatious, were available
for talks, for walks, for dancing; and when the rain briefly
stopped, for tennis. Pug assumed they were available for
the night, too. He had trouble telling them apart.

Ernst Grobke slept a lot and left early on Sunday. The
other three men had been indifferent to the submariner,
though markedly warm and agreeable to Victor Henry.
Obviously Grobke had served his purpose. Obviously his
telephone call and the encounter with Stöller in the restaurant had been arranged. These big shots were incapable of

carrying further a pretense of cordiality to a German four-striper.

Pug was asked, and he answered, many more questions about his trip to England. Except for one probe by the gaunt Luftwaffe man about the radar stations—which Pug answered with a blank, stupid look—there was no effort to pump hard intelligence out of him.

Rather, there seemed to be an effort to pump him full of German politics, philosophy, and poetry. These three old comrades were mightily fond of intellectual talk, and kept pressing on Henry books from Stöller's library that came up in conversation. He tried to read them at bedtime. After fifteen minutes, night after night, he fell into deep restful slumber. Germany's strange literature usually had that effect on Victor Henry. He had long since given up trying to understand the fantastic seriousness with which Germans took themselves, their "world-historical" position, and every twist and turn of their murky history since Charlemagne. From a military standpoint, all this river of ink about German destiny, German culture, German spirituality, Germanophilism, pan-Germanism, and the rest, kept underlining one fact. Here was an industrial people of eighty million that had spent a century uniting itself, talking to itself, rolling up its sleeves to lick the world, and convincing itself that God would hold Germany's coat and cheer it on. That was worth bearing in mind.

The sun broke through late Sunday when they were having cocktails on the terrace. Stöller offered to show Victor Henry his prize pigs, and walked him a long way down the river to the pens. Here amid a great stink, the host told Henry the pedigrees of several remarkably large hairy porkers, lying in muck and hungrily grunting. As they strolled back, the banker said, "Have you been badly bored, Victor?"

"Why, not in the least," Pug lied.

"I know it's been a different sort of weekend. Meusse and Jagow are very spiritual fellows. We have been pals forever. Jagow was my first real contact with Göring. Before that I was very close to von Papen, who as you know was the Nazis' biggest opponent, until he himself in 1933 saw where destiny was pointing. He actually made Hitler chancellor." Stöller idly struck at purple flowering thistles with his heavy black stick, knocking off their heads. The broken flowers gave off a fresh rank smell. "Jagow thinks the world of you."

"He plays a hell of a cello," said Pug, "for a fly-fly boy."

"Yes. He is brilliant. But he is not well. Victor, he especially appreciates your willingness to talk about England. Most friendly of you."

"I haven't revealed anything. Not intentionally."

Stöller laughed. "You're an honorable servant of your government. Still, your observations have been illuminating. What strikes all of us is your sense of honor. Honor is everything to a German."

Flattery made Pug Henry uncomfortable. He met it as usual with silence and a dulled look.

"If there's anything that General Jagow could do for you, I know it would give him pleasure."

"That's very kind, but not that I know of."

"Installations you might care to visit?"

"Well, our air attaché would jump at such an invitation."

"As you wish. Jagow would take a more personal interest in you."

"There's one thing, a bit out of the ordinary. An RAF pilot, a good friend of mine, went down in the Channel several weeks ago. Your people might have picked him up."

With a wave of the knobby stick, Stöller said, "That should be simple to find out. Give Jagow this pilot's name, rank, and so forth. You'll have your answer shortly."

"I'll be much obliged."

"If your friend is a prisoner, you might even be able to visit him."

"That would be great."

•   •   •

Wolf Stöller called him early in October, when Victor Henry had almost forgotten the strange weekend. "Your man is alive."

"Who is?"

Stöller reeled off Gallard's name, rank, and serial number. "He is in France, still in a hospital but in good condition. General Jagow invites you, as his personal guest, to visit Luftwaffe Headquarters close by. You are invited as a friend, not as an American attaché. This telephone call is the only communication there will be. No reciprocity is necessary."

After a moment Pug said, "Well, that's good news. The general is mighty kind."

"As I told you, you made a hit with him."

"I'll have to call you back."

"Of course."

The chargé d'affaires, when Pug told him about this, drooped his eyes almost shut, leaned back in his chair, and ran his thumb back and forth on his moustache. "The Luftwaffe man wants something of you."

"Naturally."

"Well, you have my approval. Why not jump at it? You might learn something, and you'll see this flier. Who is he?"

"Well—he's engaged to the daughter of a friend of mine." The chargé's eyes opened a little wider and he stroked his moustache. Pug felt pressed to add something. "Alistair Tudsbury's daughter, in fact."

"Oh, he's Pam's fiancé, is he? Lucky boy. Well, by all means go ahead and see how Pam Tudsbury's fiancé is," said the chargé, with a wisp of irony that did not escape, and that irritated, Victor Henry.

The weather was bad. Pug went to Lille by train. Rail travel was surprisingly back to normal in German-ruled Europe. The train left on time and roared through tranquil rainy autumn landscapes. Germany, Belgium, and northern France looked all alike in October mist and drizzle, one large flat plain of farms, evergreens, and yellowing trees. The cities looked alike too, hodgepodges of ornate venerable buildings at the center, rimmed by severe modern structures; some were untouched by the war, some were scarred and blotched with rubble. In the crowded restaurant car, amiably chatting Germans, Dutchmen, Frenchmen, Belgians, a few with wives, wined and dined amid rich good smells and a cheery clatter. Uniformed Wehrmacht officers, at a table apart, glanced with contempt at the civilians and gave the scurrying waiters curt commands. Otherwise it was business as usual under the New

Order, except for the absence of Jews. The Jews had been the busiest travellers in Europe, but on this train none were to be seen. In the Berlin-Lille express, the Third Reich looked a good bet to last a thousand years, by right of natural superiority and the ability to run things. Trains headed the other way, jammed with cheerful young troops, gave Victor Henry his first solid hint that the invasion—if it had ever been on—might be off.

An emissary of General Jagow, a rigid thin lieutenant with extra gold braid on a shoulder, a splotch of ribbons, and a twitching eye muscle, met the American naval officer at the station, drove him to a grimy stone building with a façade of wet statues in the middle of Lille, and left him in a cheerless, windowless little office containing an ink-stained desk and two chairs. The dusty yellow walls had clean squares and oblongs where pictures of French officials had been removed. Behind the desk was a bright new red, white, and black swastika flag, and the popular picture of Hitler scowling in his soldier's coat, cowlick falling over one eye, a photo crudely touched up to make him look younger. The room had the loudest-ticking pendulum wall clock Pug had ever heard; its face was green and faded with age.

The door opened. A helmeted German soldier with a submachine gun tramped in, wheeled at the desk, and crashed his boots to stiff attention. Gallard followed him, his right arm in a sling, his face puffy, discolored, and bandaged, and behind him came the lieutenant with the twitching eye. The pilot wore his flying suit, in which large rips were crudely patched up.

"Hello, Ted," said Victor Henry.

Gallard said, with a look of extreme surprise, "Hello there!" A dressing on his lower lip and chin muffled his speech.

In quick precise German, the lieutenant told Captain Henry that, since British airmen were honor bound by their orders to seize every chance to escape, General Jagow could not—to his regret—omit the precaution of an armed guard. There was no time limit. The soldier would not interfere. He had no knowledge of English. He was instructed to shoot at the first move to escape, so the lieutenant begged the gentlemen to avoid any gestures that might confuse him. As to the content of the interview, the general left it wholly to the honor of Captain Henry. If there were no questions, he would now withdraw.

"How do I let you know when we're through?" Pug jerked a thumb at the blank-faced soldier. "If I get up and walk toward the door, for instance, that might confuse him."

"Very true." The lieutenant inclined his head and his eye twitched. "Then kindly raise the telephone for a few moments and replace it in the cradle. I will then return. Permit me to mention that the general hopes you will join him for lunch at advance headquarters, a drive of forty kilometers from here."

As the door closed, Pug pulled out his cigarettes, and lit one for the pilot.

"Ah! God bless you." Gallard inhaled the smoke as a man emerging from under water gulps air. "Does Pam know? Did anybody see me parachute?"

"One of your mates claimed he had. She's sure you're alive."

"Good. Now you can tell her."

"That'll be a rare pleasure."

The wall clock ticked very loudly. Flicking the cigarette clumsily with his left hand, Gallard glanced at the guard, who stood like a post, machine gun slanted in his white-knuckled hands. The beetling line of the German helmet gave the farm-boy face a stern, statuesque look.

"Puts a bit of a chill on the small talk, eh?"

"He's rather a ripe one," Pug said.

The guard, staring straight ahead, was giving off a corrupt unwashed smell in the close little room, though his smooth-shaven face was clean enough.

"Rather. I say, this is the surprise of my life. I thought I was in for a rough grilling, or maybe for getting whisked off to Germany. They never told me a thing, except that I'd get shot if I misbehaved. You must have good friends in the Luftwaffe."

"What do you want me to tell Pamela?"

"Will you be seeing her?"

"I don't think so. I'm going back to Washington shortly. I can wire or write her."

"There's so much to tell. First of all, I'm all right, more

or less. Some burns around the face and neck." He lifted the slung arm. "Luckily the bullet only broke the bone, didn't shatter it. I can't fault the medical attention. The food's been bloody awful—moldy black bread, vile margarine with a petroleum aftertaste, soup full of rotten potatoes. The other day it mysteriously improved. Just in my ward. Last night we had a really passable stew, though it might have been Lille cats and dogs. Tasted good. I suppose all that was apropos of your little visit. I'm terribly grateful to you. Really, it's splendid that you've managed to do this, Captain Henry. How is Pam? Tell me about her. When did you last see her? How did she look?"

"I saw her several times after you disappeared. She'd come down to London, and I'd take her to dinner and to cheerful places. For a while she was peaky and wouldn't eat. But she was coming around. Practically the last thing she told me was that she expected you back. That she was going to wait for you and marry you."

The pilot's eyes grew moist. "She's a marvellous girl, Pamela." He looked around at the guard. "Say, he does smell bad, doesn't he?" Watching the soldier's dull unchanging face, he said in an offhand tone, "Will you look at that face? Explains a lot, doesn't it? Eighty million docile dangerous swine like this fellow. No wonder Hitler's their leader." There was not a flicker in the soldier's eyes. "I really don't think he understands English."

"Don't count on it," said Pug, dry and fast.

"Well, tell her I admit she was right. When I get back I'll take the headquarters job. That's where I belong." He shook his head. "Silly clot that I am. These Jerries were ahead of me and below, Me-110's, three sitters—a great chance. But I missed my shot, didn't pull up in time, dove right down between them, and next thing I knew I felt a slam on the shoulder, just like a very hard punch. My engine caught fire. I pulled back hard on my stick and by God it was loose as a broken neck. I looked around and saw I had no tail section. Shot clean off. Well, I released the hood and the harness pin, and crawled out of there. I don't even remember getting burned, but the flames got to my face, mostly around the mouth. I only felt it when the salt water stung." Gallard sighed and glanced around the room, his dejected eyes coming to rest on the rigid malodorous soldier. "And here I am. What's happening in the war? The Hun doctors say it's practically over. Of course that's a lie."

Victor Henry made his account as cheerful as possible. The pilot nodded and brightened. "That's more like it."

The clock ticked. The soldier startled them by contorting his face and sneezing twice. Tears ran down his face, but he stood rigid as before.

"Ruddy idiotic," said Gallard, "that you'll walk out of here to lunch with a Luftwaffe general, and I'll still be a prisoner at gunpoint. I suppose you'd better be cracking off."

"No hurry. Take a few cigarettes. I'd give you the pack, but Rosebud might think it was funny business and get confused."

"Ha! Rosebud is good. Damned thoughtful of you, sir." Gallard pulled out several cigarettes, and then impulsively extended the pack toward the soldier. The German's eyes shifted down and up, and he briefly shook his head like a horse driving off flies.

Gallard chain-lit a cigarette. "Look here, I don't know how you've managed this, but thank you. Thank you! It's helped more than you can guess."

"Well, it was mainly luck, but I'm glad I tracked you down."

With a distorted grin—the left side of Gallard's bandaged mouth seemed frozen—the pilot said, "Of course Pam thinks you can do anything."

Pug glanced up at the old clock. The numbers were too faded to read, but the hands were almost closed at noon. "I guess I'd better not keep the general waiting."

"Certainly not, sir." The pilot looked at the guard and added, "Anyway, while I'll never forget Rosebud, he's making me ill."

The clock pock-pocked a dozen times while Victor Henry held the telephone receiver up off the hook. He replaced it.

"Tell Pam I'll be seeing her," said Gallard, in firm tones implying an intention to escape.

"Be careful."

"Trust me for that. I've got a lot to live for, you know.

You're elected to be best man, if you're within a thousand miles."

"If I am, I'll come."

Driving through Lille, Pug marked again, as he had in the restaurant car, how German rule had serenely settled in. In the drizzly gray streets and boulevards of this large industrial town, the French were going about their business, directed by French policemen, driving French cars with French license plates, amid French shops and billboards. Only here and there an official poster in heavy black German type, a sign on a street or over a building entrance—often containing the word VERBOTEN—and the jarring sight of German soldiers cruising in army cars, reminded one that Hitler was the master of Lille. No doubt the city was being politely and methodically plundered. Pug had heard about the techniques: the worthless occupation currency with which the Germans bought up most things, and the meaningless custody receipts given by outright looters. But the process was nowhere visible. The busy pedestrians of Lille looked glum, but Victor Henry had never seen the French when they were not looking glum. Here, as on the train, the New Order appeared good for a thousand years.

In a tall Luftwaffe cap, shiny black boots, and a slick blue-gray military raincoat to his ankles, the cello player looked taller, leaner, and considerably fiercer. The lieutenant's slavish bows and heel clicks, the scrambling obsequiousness of everybody at headquarters, amply showed that Jagow was most high brass. He offered Victor Henry his choice of a decent lunch at a "rather comfortable" château nearby, commandeered by the Luftwaffe, or a mere bite here at the airfield. Nodding approval of Pug's preference, he doffed his raincoat, dropping it from his shoulders without looking around at the lieutenant who caught it.

On a cloth-covered table in an inner office, the general and his guest ate soup, trout, veal, cheese, and fruit, all served up in gold-trimmed china by gliding, smiling French waiters, with three superb wines. General Jagow picked at the food and hardly tasted the wine. Recognizing the cyanosed pallor of heart trouble, Victor Henry made no comment. He was hungry and dug in heartily while the general smoked cigarettes and talked, in a clipped exact German which his lieutenant evidently had been imitating. Often he interrupted himself to cover his mouth and cough carefully.

The United States Navy, Jagow said, was the only military machine in the world professionally comparable to the German army. He had visited it as an observer in the thirties, and had brought back to Göring the dive-bombing idea. So the Luftwaffe had developed the Stuka. "Whether you approve or not," he said with a tired smile, "the success of our blitzkrieg owes a sizable debt to your Navy."

"Well, maybe we'll take that bow after the war, General."

The American Army, Jagow went on with a wry nod at Pug's irony, was in no way comparable. The doctrine and practice, like that of all modern armies, derived from German General Staff concepts. But he had noticed an amateurishness, a lack of spirit in the maneuvers, and the numbers were pitiful. Essentially, the United States was a great sea power, he said, linking the two world oceans. The state of the armed forces reflected that geopolitical fact.

That started him on Spengler, who he said had failed, like all too many Germans, to understand the United States. That was the fallacy in *The Decline of the West*. The United States was white Christian Europe again, given a second chance on a rich virgin continent. America allied to a modernized orderly Europe could bring on a vast rebirth of the West, a new golden age. At least this was what Pug made out of the general's cloudy high-flown talk, so much like the evening conversations at Abendruh.

Over the coffee—terrible stuff tasting like burned walnut shells—Jagow said, "Would you care to have a look at the aerodrome? The weather is rather disagreeable."

"I'd like that very much, if one of your aides can spare the time."

The weary smile reappeared. "I finished my work on this campaign long ago. The rest is up to the field commanders. I am at your disposal."

They drove around the aerodrome in a small closed car, full of the sulphurous fumes of German gasoline. In wan sunlight, from holes of bright blue opening in the low overcast sky, stubby Messerschmitt 109's stood half-concealed in dispersal bunkers, their painted crosses and swastikas much the worse for wear. It was just like a British fighter base: repair shops, hangars, dispersal huts, crisscrossing air strips, set among peaceful farms, and rolling pastures where herds of cows grazed. Fading signs in French showed that this was an expanded base of the defeated French air force. Most of the buildings were raw new structures of wood or cement. Cracked old landing strips stood beside broad fresh ones like autobahns.

"You've done all this since June?" said Pug. "Pretty good."

Jagow for a moment looked like a flattered old man, showing his sparse teeth in a pleased soft grin. "You have the professional eye. The Western newspaper smart alecks want to know why the Luftwaffe waited six precious weeks before commencing the attack. What do they know about logistics?"

While Hitler left the operation of the air force strictly to Göring, said the general, he had insisted on one point which showed his military genius. After the conquest of the Low Countries and northern France, advanced air bases had had to be set up on his orders. Only then would he allow the Luftwaffe to strike at England. Advanced bases would double or triple German air power. The same plane could make two or three times as many attacks in the same number of hours, and on these shortened runs kilograms of bombs could replace kilograms of gasoline.

"The simplest strategic thinking," said Jagow, "and the soundest."

They visited a dispersal hut, where worn-looking German youngsters, strangely like the RAF fighter pilots, lounged in flying suits, ready to go. But when they saw Jagow they sprang to attention as the British pilots never had. The hut was more roughly built, and the plump simpering pinup girls on the wooden walls, next to mimeographed watch notices and regulations, offered doughy German sexiness rather than the bony Anglo-American variety. Otherwise it was all the same, including the mildewy smell of bedding and flying clothes.

As Jagow's car drove along the field, an air raid siren

went off. Pilots came scrambling out of their huts. "Stop the car," he said to the driver, adding to Victor Henry, "A nuisance raid, high level. A sound tactic, we must respond and it throws our pilots off balance. But the British pay with a lot of bombers. Flimsy planes, poorly armed. Shall we get out and watch?"

Messerschmitt after Messerschmitt wheeled into position and roared off, a steady stream of steep-climbing fighters.

"To me this is a depressing sight," said Jagow, hugging his lean body in the shiny long coat with both arms, as though chilled. "Germans fighting Englishmen. Diamond cut diamond. It is civil war in the West, plain suicidal foolishness. The English could have a decent honorable peace tomorrow. That bulldog Churchill is counting on one thing and one thing only—American help."

"General, he's counting on the courage of his people and the quality of his air force."

"Captain Henry, if Roosevelt cut off all help and told Churchill he wanted to mediate a peace, how long would this war go on?"

"But that's impossible."

"Very true, because your President is surrounded by Morgenthaus, Frankfurters, and Lehmans." General Jagow held up a long skinny hand in a long gray glove as Pug started to protest. "I am not a Nazi. I came into the Luftwaffe from the army. Don't ever think anti-Semitism is a German problem. All over Europe the attitude toward the Jews is exactly the same. The Führer has been realistic in spelling it out, that's all. Some of his Party followers have committed silly excesses. But you can't indict a whole people for the crudeness of a few. Those American Jews around Roosevelt make the same mistake that our Nazi fanatics do."

"General Jagow," Pug broke in earnestly, "you can't make a greater mistake than to believe that the Jews are behind our hostility to Hitler's regime." He was hoping to penetrate this hardened German obsession just once. Jagow was unusually intelligent. "A lot of our people deeply admire the Germans. I do. But some things Hitler has done are unforgivable to any American."

"Things Hitler has done!" Jagow sighed, his eyes heavy and sad. "Let me tell you something that may amaze you,

Captain. When we took Poland, *it was we Germans who stopped the Poles from murdering the Jews.* They took our arrival as a signal to let loose. It was like open season on Jews! The atrocities were unbelievable. Yes, our Wehrmacht had to step in and shield the Jews from the Poles." The general coughed hard. "I am not pretending we love the Jews. I don't claim they should love us. I actually understand the Morgenthaus. But they're tragically wrong. The United States must not allow a war to the death between England and Germany. We are all one civilization. We are the West. If we fight it out among ourselves we'll go down before Asiatic Bolshevism. There will be barbaric darkness for a thousand years."

Jagow fell silent, his hollow, somewhat feverish eyes boring at Pug. Then he put out a long stiff finger.

"If there were only a few strong advisers to give your President this viewpoint! But those advisers who aren't Jewish are of British descent. It's a damnable situation. We'll beat the British, Captain Henry. We have the power. We never intended to fight them. The Führer could have built a thousand submarines and strangled England in three months. He never emphasized U-boats. You know that. What do we gain by such a victory? We only crush our finest natural ally."

"Well, General, you attacked Poland when she was England's ally. You made the deal with Stalin. Those things are done."

"They were forced on us." Behind a gloved hand, Jagow coughed long and genteelly. "We are a strange people, Captain Henry, hard for others to understand. We are very serious, very naïve. Always we are reaching for the stars. To others we seem insensitive and arrogant. Our English cousins are every bit as arrogant, I assure you. Ah, but what a manner they cultivated! They despise their Jews. They keep them out of the clubs where power is concentrated, and the banks, and all vital positions. But they act politely to them. We admitted the Jews to all our very highest circles, until they swarmed in and threatened to take over entirely. But we showed our feelings. That's the difference. The German is all feeling, all Faustian striving. Appeal to his honor, and he will march or fly or sail to his death with a happy song. That is our naïveté,

yes, our primitivism. But it is a healthy thing. America too
has its own naïveté, the primitive realism of the frontier,
the cowboys.

"What does it all add up to? We need friends in the
United States to explain that there are two sides to this
war, and that the only solution is peace in the West, unity
in the West, an alliance in the West that can control the
world.—Ah, look there. The British marksmanship is
rather hard on the French livestock, but that's about all."

On a distant hill, huge inverted pyramids of dirt splashed
high in the air amid flame and smoke, and cows galloped
clumsily around. The general glanced at his watch. "I
have a little conference at headquarters. If you can stay
for dinner, there is a very pleasant restaurant in Lille—"

"I have to return to Berlin, General. I can't express my
gratitude, but—"

Up went the glove. "Please. To talk to an American, a
professional military man, who shows some understanding
of our situation, is literally good for my health."

Messerschmitts were landing in the rain when Jagow
turned Victor Henry over to his lieutenant at the entrance
to the headquarters building.

"If we can be of further service in the matter of Flight
Lieutenant Gallard, let us know," Jagow said, stripping off
a glove to offer a damp cold hand. *"Auf Wiedersehen,*
Captain Henry. If I have been of any small service, all I
ask is this. Wherever duty takes you, remember there are
two sides to the war, and that on both sides there are men
of honor."

* * *

The ornately molded and carved ceilings in Wolf Stöller's bank seemed forty feet high. It was after hours. A few
clerks worked silently behind the grilles. The footsteps of
the two men on the red marble floor echoed and re-echoed
under the high vault, like the tramp of a platoon. "It is a
little gloomy here now," said Stöller, "but very private.
This way, Victor."

They passed through a sizable conference room into a
small richly furnished office, with a blaze of paintings

crowding the walls; little though he knew, Henry recognized two Picassos and a Renoir.

"So, you go so soon," Stöller said, gesturing to a heavy maroon leather couch. "Did you expect this?"

"Well, I thought my relief would be along in a couple of weeks. But when I got back from Lille, here he was, waiting."

"Of course you are anxious to be reunited with your very beautiful wife."

Victor Henry said, with a glance at the larger Picasso, a gruesomely distorted woman in flaring colors, "I thought modern art was frowned on in the Third Reich."

Stöller smiled. "It has not gone down in value. The field marshal has one of the great collections of the world. He is a very civilized man. He knows these things will change."

"They will?"

"Most assuredly, once the war is over. We are a nation under siege, Victor. Nerves get frayed, a mood of extremism prevails. That will die away. Europe will be a wonderful place to live. Germany will be the pleasantest place of all. What do you say to a glass of sherry?"

"That'll be fine. Thanks."

Stöller poured from a heavy crystal decanter. "What do we drink to? I daresay you won't drink to the victory of Germany."

With a tart grin Pug said, "We're neutral, you know."

"Ah, yes. Ah, Victor, if only you were! How gladly we would settle for that! Well, to an honorable peace?"

"Sure. To an honorable peace."

They drank.

"Passable?"

"Fine. I'm no expert on wines."

"It's supposed to be the best sherry in Europe."

"It's certainly very good."

The banker settled in an armchair and lit a long cigar. In the light of the floor lamp his scalp glistened pink through his thin flat hair. "Your little trip to Lille was a success, hm?"

"Yes, I'm obliged to you and the general."

"Please. By the ordinary rules, such a thing would be not only unusual but utterly impossible. Among men of honor, there are special rules." Stöller heaved an audible sigh. "Well, Victor, I didn't ask you to give me some time just to offer you sherry."

"I didn't suppose so."

"You're a military man. There are special conversations that sometimes have to be forgotten, obliterated without a trace. In German we have a special phrase for these most delicate matters. 'Under four eyes.' "

"I've heard the phrase."

"What transpires next is under four eyes."

Victor Henry, intensely curious at this point, felt there was nothing to do but let the banker talk on. What might be coming next, he could not imagine; his best guess was a wispy peace feeler at second hand from Göring, to convey to the President.

"You had a conversation with Gregor Jagow about the course of the war. About the tragic absurdity of this fratricidal conflict between Germany and England."

Pug nodded.

"Did his ideas make sense to you?"

"Frankly, we don't study geopolitics in the Navy. At least we don't call it that. So I'm not up on Spengler and so forth."

"You're an American pragmatist," said Stöller with a smile.

"I'm a gunnery expert misplaced in diplomacy, and hoping the hell to get out of it."

"I believe you. The man of honor wants to serve in the field."

"I'd like to do what I'm trained for."

"You do agree that American help, and expectation of far greater help, is what is keeping England in the war?"

"Partly. They just don't feel like quitting. They think they'll win."

"With American help."

"Well, they think they'll get it."

"Then what stands between the whole Western world and an honorable peace—which you and I just drank to— is Churchill's reliance on help from Roosevelt."

Pug took a few moments to answer. "Maybe, but what's an honorable peace? Churchill would want to depose Hitler. Hitler would want to depose Churchill. Both those gentlemen are equally firmly in the saddle, and both really represent the national will. So there you are."

"You are going back to serve as naval aide to President Roosevelt." Stöller said this with a slight interrogative note.

Pug's face registered no surprise. "I'm going back to the Bureau of Personnel for reassignment."

The banker's smile was tolerant and assured. "Well, our intelligence usually gets these things right. Now, Victor, let me have my say, and don't break in until I've finished. That's all I ask. All right?"

"All right."

The banker puffed twice at his cigar. "Men of honor talk among themselves, Victor, in a special language. I'm addressing you now in that vocabulary. These are matters of incredible delicacy. In the end, beneath the words there must be a spiritual kinship. With you, Gregor Jagow and I have felt that kinship. You have been impeccably correct, but unlike so many people at the American embassy, you don't regard Germans as cannibals. You have treated us as human beings like yourself. So did your delightful and beautiful wife. It has been noticed, I assure you. That you sympathize with England is only natural. I do myself. I love England. I spent two years at Oxford.

"Now, you heard what Gregor said about the Jewish influence around your President. I know you have to deny it, but it is a very serious fact of this war. We must live with it and do what we can about it."

Pug tried to speak. Stöller held up a rigid palm. "You said you would hear me out, Victor. In the circumstances, we need friends in Washington. Not to use undue influence, as the Jews do so shamelessly. Simply to present the other side. Roosevelt is a man of very broad vision. He can be made to see that American interest requires a swift honorable peace in the West. For one thing, only such a development can free him to handle Japan. Do you suppose we give a damn about Japan? That new pact is all a comedy to keep the Russians worried and quiet.

"Now, Victor—and remember this is under four eyes— we do have such friends. Not many. A few. Patriotic Americans, who see the realities of the war instead of the propaganda of the Jews—and of Churchill, who is just an adventurous megalomaniac and has never been anything else. We hope you'll be another such friend."

Victor Henry regretted that he had drunk up the glass of sherry rather fast. The conversation was taking a turn which needed sharp handling. He leaned forward.

"Let me go on," said the banker, waving the cigar at him. "You know of my connection with Hermann Göring. To me he is a great figure of European history. His practical grasp of affairs and his energy still astound me. The Führer—well, the Führer is different, he operates on a plane above all of us, a plane of prophecy, of grand dreams. The engineer at the throttle is Göring. Nothing in Germany escapes him. Nothing happens that he does not approve and know about. You Americans with your Puritan bias think him a bit of a sultan. But we Germans love opera and opulence. It's a weakness. The field marshal knows that and plays to it. Of course, he thoroughly enjoys himself, too. Why not? His zest for life is Faustian, Rabelaisian.

"Victor, Hermann Göring has established in Switzerland some anonymous, untraceable bank accounts. His resources are enormous. These bank accounts, after the war, will be the rewards of Germany's honorable friends, who have said the right word in the right place for her when it mattered. It is nothing like espionage, where you pay some sneaking wretch for papers or information he hands over. This is simple gratitude among men of honor, a sharing of benefits in the day of victory. If our friends want the accounts, they will be there. If they don't—" Stöller shrugged and sat back. "I've said my piece, Victor. And after you've said yours, this conversation will be as if it never existed."

It was one of the few occasions in Victor Henry's life when he was taken totally by surprise.

"That's interesting," he said. "Extremely interesting." After a measurable pause he went on, "Well! First, please tell me, if you can, what made you, or General Jagow, or Field Marshal Göring, think that I might be receptive to this approach. That's highly important to me, and to this whole matter, I assure you."

"My dear chap, the Washington picture is vital, and you're en route to Washington. The day American supplies to England are shut off, we've won the war. We've got it won now, really, but England is just hanging on, hoping for she doesn't know what. She'll be flat broke in three or four months, and if your Neutrality Act holds, that's the end. Now Victor, the field marshal remembers your interesting visit with the banker Gianelli. His purpose now is exactly what Roosevelt's was then, to avoid further useless bloodshed. He thinks you can help, and General Jagow is confident that you will." Stöller gave Pug his most ingratiating smile, crinkling his eyes almost shut. "As for me, I know your exquisite wife is a very sympathetic and friendly woman. My guess is that she has always reflected your real feelings, more than your correct words. I trust I'm right."

Victor Henry nodded. "I see. That's a clear answer, Herr Stöller. Here's mine, under four eyes. Please tell Field Marshal Göring, for me, to stick his Swiss bank account up his fat ass."

Blue smoke wreathed around Stöller's shocked face. His eyes went wide and glassy, his face became dark red from his striped collar to his hair, and his scalp reddened too. His teeth showed in an ugly smile. "I remind you, Captain Henry," he said in a new slow singsong tone, "that you have not left the Third Reich yet. You are still in Berlin. Field Marshal Herman Göring is second here only to the Führer."

"I'm an officer in the United States Navy. Unless I misunderstood you, or you want to withdraw it"—Victor Henry's voice hardened almost to a bark—"you've asked me, in his name, to commit treason for money."

The banker's nasty smile faded. In a placating tone, with a soft look, spreading out his hands, he said, "My dear Victor, how *can* you take it in that way? I beg you, think! The highest officers in the American armed forces blatantly and openly advocate help for England all the time. What I asked of you was just to present both sides, when the occasion arose, for the sake of American security and for peace."

"Yes, as a man of honor. I heard you. I really believe you mean it. General Jagow said you Germans were a difficult people to understand. That is the truth. I'm giving up. My assignment here is over." Victor Henry knew he had hit too hard, but he had reacted as he did in a ball game, on instinct and impulse. He stood, and the banker got to his feet too.

"See here, old top," Stöller said gently, "we Germans are at war, surrounded by foes. If the United States is ever in such a situation—and history takes strange turns—you may one day make an approach like this to a man you respect, and find it as difficult as I have. I think your response has been naïve and wrong. Your phrasing was coarse. Still, the spiritual quality was there. It was an honorable reaction. I have absolutely no hard feelings. I trust you have none. I place a high value on your goodwill, Victor. And we did have good times at Abendruh, didn't we?"

Smiling, Stöller held out his smooth thin clean hand. Pug turned on his heel and walked out of the room. Out of the loudly echoing bank he walked, nodding at the door attendant's deep bow. In the warm sunlit Berlin evening, on the sidewalk outside, beautiful German children surrounded a one-legged man on a crutch, who was selling pink paper dolls that danced on strings. Victor Henry walked several blocks at a pace that made his heart pound. The first new thought that came to him was that, with his grossly insulting words and acts, he might have murdered Ted Gallard.

*   *   *

36

𝕿𝖍𝖊 𝕲𝖆𝖗𝖉𝖊𝖓 𝕳𝖔𝖘𝖊

(from WORLD EMPIRE LOST)

The Falling Crown

The winter and spring between the Battle of Britain and our attack on the Soviet Union stand in popular history as a breathing spell. Actually, in these eight months the axis of the war changed, for the British Empire as a reality left the stage of history.

In 1939, this momentous event lay shrouded in the future. A proper name for this war might well be "The War of the British Succession," for the real question that was fought out was this: after the collapse of the British Empire, which would drag with it all European colonialism, what shape was the new world order to take, and under whose rule?

This historic turn, and this momentous issue, Adolf Hitler foresaw. He inspired and mobilized Germany to rise and dare all to seize the falling crown. The feats that our nation performed against odds will someday be justly treated in history, when passions die and the stain of certain minor excesses can be seen in perspective. Meantime historians write as though only the struggles of the Allies were heroic, as though we Germans were a species of metal monster incapable of bleeding, freezing, or hungering, and therefore deserving of no credit for our vast victories. As Hitler said, the winning side writes the history. Yet, in their praise of their own arduous successes, the Allies despite themselves honor us, the nation that almost won the British succession, against a combination of all the industrial nations in the world except feeble Italy and far-off impoverished Japan.

566

For all of Hitler's military mistakes, and they were many and serious, my professional judgment remains that the German armed forces would have won the war, and world empire, but for one historical accident. His real opponent, produced by fate at this point in time, was an even craftier and more ruthless political genius, with more sober military judgment and greater material means for industrialized warfare: Franklin D. Roosevelt.

The nation this man led was in no way comparable to the German people in military valor, as test after test in the field eventually showed. But that did not matter. This great manipulator so managed the war that other nations bled themselves almost to death, so as to hand his country the rule of the earth on a silver platter.

The United States of America, today the troubled master of the world, lost fewer men in the entire war than Germany expended in any one of half a dozen campaigns. Almost twenty million soldiers, sailors, and airmen perished in the Second World War. Of these, America in four years of global war lost *about three hundred thousand on all fronts including her war with Japan!* For this almost bloodless conquest of the earth, which has no parallel in all history, the American people can thank that enigmatic, still shrouded figure, the Augustus of the industrial age, the Dutch-descended millionaire cripple, Roosevelt.

Franklin D. Roosevelt's world conquest still goes unrecognized. In the present historical writings on the war, he is granted nothing like the stature he will one day have. There is little doubt that he wanted it that way. The Augustan ruler, a recurring figure in history, seizes the realities of power under a mask of the humble, benign, humanitarian citizen. Nobody since the emperor Augustus ever managed this as Franklin Roosevelt did. Even Augustus was not as sanctimonious, for in those days the Christian vocabulary of humility and humaneness was not in vogue to lend such depths to hypocrisy.

Roosevelt's Feat

In his successful waging of the Second World War, Franklin Roosevelt made no major military mistakes. That is a record not matched by any world conqueror since Julius

Caesar. His slogan of "unconditional surrender" was widely called a blunder, by commentators as diverse as Goebbels and Eisenhower. I do not agree, and in its place, I will take up that stricture and challenge it.

Our propaganda office called him a tool of the Jews, but of course that was the silliest bosh. Roosevelt did nothing to save the Jews. He knew that any such action would annoy Congress and interfere with winning the war. Under his clever facade of a Christian humanitarian liberal, he was one of the coldest, most ruthless calculators in history. He sensed that the Americans liked the Jews no more than we did; and they amply confirmed this all through the war in their immigration policies, and at the Évian and Bermuda conferences, where they simply abandoned the Jews to their fate.

This author is no admirer of Roosevelt as a person, but the aim of my work is to set down the facts as military history should view them. On such a valuation, Franklin Roosevelt was the mastermind of the war. Even such a powerful, energetic, and brilliant figure as Adolf Hitler was in the end no more than a foil for him. Adventuristic conquerors often pave the way, in this fashion, for the dominion of their enemies. The adventurer sees the opportunity, and with meager means tries to capture it. He does the destroying and the bulldozing. His ice-blooded successor then crushes him and builds on the ruins. Napoleon in the last analysis merely put Wellington's England in the saddle for a century. Charles XII hardly has a place in history, except as a foil for Peter the Great. And the German people under Adolf Hitler accomplished nothing in the long run except to hand the British succession to the United States under Roosevelt.

Roosevelt's Difficulty

Franklin Roosevelt's problem was that at this great turning point in history he did not lead a warlike nation, whereas Adolf Hitler did. The American people are not cowardly. But, living in prosperous isolation, they have been the spoiled children of modern history. Spoiled children do not bear well the rigors of the field. Once they entered the war, the Americans fought with a logistic train of luxury and self-protection that to the warriors of Germany, the Soviet Union, and even England, was laughable. Nevertheless they had the riches and the will for this. The strong can fight any kind of fight they please.

The Americans have a tradition of militia-like fighting. Presented with a threat, they drop their pleasures, take up arms, and fight amateurishly but bravely to get the thing over with. They formed this pattern in their revolution, and confirmed it in their civil war and the First World War. Roosevelt understood this. He had to hold Germany at bay until he could present the chance for world conquest to his people in the guise of a threat to their safety. This, with a masterly exhibition of patient, spider-like waiting, he did. Meantime, he robbed Germany of two certain victories—over Great Britain and over the Soviet Union—by an inspired instrument of indirect war-making, a genuine new thing in military history, the so-called Lend-Lease Act.

A Cunning Trick

By the end of 1940, despite her narrow escapes at Dunkirk and in the air battle, Britain was sinking to her knees. She had only one recourse left on the planet to save her: the United States. But the Neutrality Act threatened to cut the English off from the American farms and factories that were keeping them alive. They were running out of dollars to pay even for grain and oil, let alone the ships, planes, guns, and bullets which they could no longer manufacture for themselves in the necessary quantities. For they lacked labor, materials, and plant, and they kept falling further behind under air attack.

The Neutrality Act forced belligerents to pay dollars for United States goods, and to come and fetch them. The Act posed more of a dilemma for Roosevelt than for the British. For them, a clear wise course lay open: negotiated peace with Germany. As this writer has often pointed out, had England made such a peace the British Empire would exist today. The Soviet Union would have been crushed in a one-front war, and instead of a rampant Bolshevism we would see in Russia at worst some pacific, disarmed form of social democracy. But none of this fitted in with Roosevelt's ideas. He had no intention of allowing Germany to gain ascendancy over the Euro-Asian heartland in a world-dominating partnership with the sea lords of Britannia.

And so, to circumvent the Neutrality Act, Franklin Roosevelt devised Lend-Lease, which was nothing more or less than a policy to give the British *free of charge*—and later the Russians too—all the war materials they needed to fight us! The audacity of the trick was breathtaking; the disguise was cunning. And while the record shows that Roosevelt's clever advisers did much to push this unprecedented proposal through the stunned, balky Congress, it also clearly shows that the revolutionary idea sprang, in the phrase of Sherwood, straight from Roosevelt's "forested mind."

Roosevelt sold this scheme to the simpleminded, inattentive American people with a typical bit of Augustan demagoguery, the famous comparison to a garden hose. When a neighbor's house is on fire, he said at a press conference, one does not bargain with him over the sale or renting of the garden hose he needs to put it out. One gladly lends him the hose, so as to keep the fire from one's own house. Once the fire is out, the neighbor returns the hose; or if he has damaged it, there is time enough then to settle the account.

This was, of course, shameless and hollow poppycock. Warships, warplanes, war materials are not garden hoses. To take Roosevelt's comparison at its face value, if your neighbor's house is on fire, what you really do is rush over there and fight the fire with him. You do not lend him your hose, and then stand idly by watching him try to cope with the flames. That this silly stuff was swallowed whole by the Americans simply shows how uncannily shrewd Roosevelt was in managing them. During his successful 1940 election campaign for an unprecedented third term, he had declared in a famous speech, *"I tell you again, and again, and again, your boys are not going to be sent into foreign wars."* He was eagerly awaiting a chance to go back on this clear pledge. Meantime he had to use tricks and guile to oppose Germany.

The Real Meaning of Lend-Lease

It was impossible for him—and this he knew—to present the case to his people in realistic terms. Otherwise he could have told them in effect, "My friends, this war is for the mastery of the world. Our aim should be to achieve that mastery ourselves, but with a minimum of blood. Let us encourage others to do our fighting for us. Let us give them all the stuff they need to keep fighting. What do we care? In developing the industries to produce this Lend-Lease stuff, we will be preparing ourselves, industrially and militarily, for world leadership. They will use up all our early models, our discardable stuff, killing Germans for us. Maybe they will do the whole job for us, but that is doubtful. We will have to step in at the end, but mopping up will be easy. We will have gained a world victory with the expenditure of a lot of hardware, which we can turn out faster, and in greater quantities, than all the world put together, without even feeling the pinch. The others will shed the blood, and we will take the rule."

That was what Lend-Lease meant and that was how it worked.

First the British, and then the Russians, were induced by Lend-Lease to keep on with extremely bloody, almost hopeless struggles, when the easier, safer, more profitable alternative of negotiated peace always lay open to them. There is reason to think that at Stalin's low point late in 1941, when his armies and his air force had virtually ceased to exist as coherent battle formations and we were smashing toward Moscow, that supreme realist would have proposed peace again, if not for the encouragement in words and supplies— not in lives—of the United States. As it was, the Russian people made sacrifices in blood never matched in all history, to transfer world hegemony from one Anglo-Saxon power to another.

And Franklin Roosevelt so maneuvered matters that the British had to beg for this bloodletting help! They were put in the position of being abjectly grateful for the chance to fight Roosevelt's battles. On December 8, 1940, Churchill wrote the American President a very long letter, which deserves a bolder place in history than it now holds. Churchill once said that he had not become Prime Minister to preside over the dissolution of the Empire, but with this letter he dissolved it. Churchill in this document frankly stated that England had come to the end of her rope, in the matter of ships, planes, materials, and dollars; and he asked the President to "find ways and means" to help England in the common cause. This was what Roosevelt had been icily waiting for in his wheelchair: this written confession by the British

Prime Minister that without American aid the Empire was finished. Within two weeks he had proposed Lend-Lease to his advisers, and within a month he had laid it before Congress.

Empire means rule, and sufficient armed power to enforce the rule. In Churchill's letter, he acknowledged that his country and his Empire had become powerless to enforce their rule, and begged for succor. Roosevelt leaped to comply. Even if England was finished as an imperial power, she remained a country of forty millions with a good navy and air force, at war with Roosevelt's archrival; a splendid island base just off the coast of Europe, moreover, from which to attack Germany in the future. The first order of business was to keep her fighting.

Bargain War-Making

Despite all the quack language in the act about lending and leasing, the transfer of American weapons and materials throughout the war was a gift. No formal accounting was even kept. The President asked, and the Congress granted him, power to send arms and war goods wherever he pleased, in whatever quantities he pleased. Certainly the Congress when they passed the law would have balked at including Bolshevist countries. But at that time the Soviet Union was supposedly Hitler's friend. Later, when war broke out on the eastern front, Roosevelt poured a flood of supplies to the Bolsheviks without consulting Congress. The Americans complain that the Russians have never shown proper gratitude. The attitude of the Russians is more realistic. Having spilled the blood of perhaps eleven million of their sons to help the United States to its present world position, they tend to feel that the tanks and planes were paid for.

The Yankees love a bargain. Lend-Lease was bargain war-making. For the big corporations, and for millions of workers, it merely meant a tremendous increase of prosperity. The price was painlessly postponed to the future by means of defense bonds. Others did the actual fighting and dying.

Roosevelt and his advisers did discuss the risk that Germany would take Lend-Lease as an act of war—*which it certainly was*—and would formally declare war on the United States. Since this was just what he wanted, he was prepared to run the risk. America would have responded with a militia-like surge. Little as Adolf Hitler understood the United States, he did understand that. He had no intention of taking on the United States until he had finished with the Soviet Union, an operation which was already in an advanced planning stage. So Germany swallowed Lend-Lease with some harsh words, and the "arsenal of democracy" tooled up to help British plutocracy and Russian Bolshevism destroy the Reich, the last bastion in Europe against the Red Slav tide.

TRANSLATOR'S NOTE: *Most broad statistics of the war are approximations, and the figures on total deaths vary widely from one source to another. The low rate of eventual American losses is a fact. We planned and fought that kind of war, expending money and machines instead of human lives where possible. Roon seems to think this indicates a deficiency in American valor. We had enough valor to beat the Germans wherever we took them on. That was all the valor we needed.—V.H.*

* * *

37

TRAVELLING to his new post in mid-January, Leslie Slote found himself stalled in Lisbon by a shortage of Lufthansa accommodations to Berlin. He checked into the Palace Hotel in Estoril, Lisbon's palm-lined seaside resort, where diplomats, wealthy refugees, Gestapo, and other foreign agents congregated. He thought he might pick up some information there while he waited for an air reservation to open up. Actually, he found Estoril in January an exceedingly chilly and boring place. The Germans abounded, but they kept in aloof clusters, regarding other people with supercilious eyes.

He sat in the crowded lobby of the hotel one afternoon gnawing at his pipe, and reading in a Swiss newspaper about British successes against the Italians in Abyssinia and North Africa, faint rays in the gloom. The neutral newspaper had been hard to come by. Fascist and Nazi journals now blanketed Portuguese newsstands, with a few scrawny, disgustingly servile periodicals from Vichy France. British and American publications had vanished. It was a fair barometric reading of the way the war was going, at least in the judgment of Portugal's rulers. A year ago, on Lisbon newsstands, papers of both sides had been equally available.

"*Meestair Slote! Meestair Leslie Slote!*"

He jumped up and followed the small pink-cheeked page to a telephone near the reception desk.

"Leslie? Hello, it's Bunky. How goes it by the old sea-side?"

Bunker Wendell Thurston, Jr., had attended the Foreign Service school with Slote, and now held the post of second secretary in the American legation in Lisbon.

"Mighty dull, Bunky. What's up?"

"Oh, nothing much." Thurston sounded amused. "It's just that you've spoken to me now and then, I believe, about a girl named Natalie Jastrow."

Slote said sharply, "Yes, I have. What about her?"

"A girl by that name is sitting across the desk from me."

"*Who* is? Natalie?"

"Like to talk to her? When I told her you were here she jumped a foot."

"Christ, yes."

Natalie came on the phone laughing, and Slote's heart throbbed at the familiar lovely sound. "Hello, old Slote," she said.

"Natalie! This is so staggering, and wonderful. What are you doing here?"

"Well, how about you?" Natalie said. "I'm as surprised as you are. Why aren't you in Moscow?"

"I got hung up, in Washington and then here. Is Aaron with you?"

"I wish he were. He's in Siena."

"What! Aren't you on your way back to the States?"

Natalie took a moment to answer. "Yes and no. Leslie, as long as you're here, can I see you for a while?"

"Naturally! Wonderful! Immediately! I'll come in to the legation."

"Wait, wait. You're at the Palace Hotel, aren't you? I'll come out and meet you. I'd rather do that."

Bunky Thurston came on the line. "Look, Leslie, I'll put her on the bus. She'll arrive in half an hour or so. If I may, I'll join you two in the Palace lobby at five."

She still had a fondness for big dark hats. He could see her through the dusty bus window, moving down the aisle in a jam of descending passengers. She ran to him, threw her arms around him, and kissed his cheek. "Hi! I'm freezing. I could have worn my ratty beaver coat, but who'd think it would be this cold and gray in Lisbon? Brrr! It's even colder out here by the sea, isn't it?" She clapped her hand to her hat as the wind flapped it. "Let's look at you. Well! No change. If anything, you look rested."

She said all this very fast, her eyes wide and shiny, her manner peculiarly excited. The old spell worked at once.

In the months since he had last seen Natalie, Slote had started up a romance with a girl from Kansas named Nora Jamison. Nora was tall, brunette, and dark-eyed like this one, but otherwise as different as a doe from a bobcat: even-tempered, affectionate, bright enough to be in her third year as a senator's secretary, and pretty enough to play leads with a semiprofessional Washington theatre group. Her father was a rich farmer; she drove a Buick convertible. She was altogether a find, and Slote was thinking seriously of marrying her on his return from Moscow. Nora worshipped him, and she was better looking than Natalie Jastrow and much easier to manage. But this Jewish girl in the big hat put her arm around him and brushed his face with her lips; he experienced a stabbing remembrance of what her love was like, and the snare closed on him again.

He said, "Well, you know how I admire you, but you do look slightly beat up."

"Do I ever! I've had hell's own time getting here. Let's get out of this wind. Where's the Palace Hotel? I've been to Estoril twice, but I forget."

He said, taking her arm and starting to walk, "It isn't far. What's the story? Why didn't Aaron come? What are you doing here?"

"Byron's arriving tomorrow on a submarine." He halted in astonishment. She looked up at him, hugged his arm, and laughed, her face alive with joy. "That's it. That's why I'm here."

"He made it through that school?"

"You sound surprised."

"I thought he might find it too much work."

"He squeaked by. This is his first long cruise. The sub's stopping here, just for a few days. I suppose you think I'm rattlebrained, but he wrote me to come and meet him, and here I am."

"Nothing you do really surprises me, sweetie. I'm the man you came to visit in Warsaw in August '39."

Again she squeezed his arm, laughing. "So I did. Quite an excursion *that* turned out to be, hey! My God, it's *cold* here! It's a wonder all these palm trees don't turn brown and die. You know, I've been through Lisbon twice before, Slote, and each time I've been utterly miserable. It feels very strange to be happy here."

He asked her about Aaron Jastrow's situation. Natalie said the impact of the note from the Secretary of State's office had somehow been frittered away. The fact that Jastrow's lapsed passport showed a questionable naturalization had fogged his case. Van Winaker, the young consul in Florence, had dawdled for almost a month, promising action and never getting around to it; then he had fallen ill and gone for a cure in France, and several more weeks had slipped by. Now Van Winaker was corresponding with the Department on how to deal with the matter. She had his firm promise that, one way or another, he would work it out. The worst of it was, she declared, that Aaron himself really was in no hurry to leave his villa, now that it seemed just a matter of unravelling a little more red tape. He half welcomed every new delay, though he went through the motions of being vexed. This was what was defeating her. He would not fight, would not put any pressure on the consul to settle the thing. He was writing serenely away at his Constantine book, keeping to all his little routines and rituals, drinking coffee in the lemon house, taking his walks at sunset, rising before dawn to sit blanketed on the terrace and watch the sun come up. He believed that the Battle of Britain had decided the war, that Hitler had made his bid and failed, and that a negotiated peace would soon emerge.

"I suppose I made a mistake, after all, going back to Italy," she said, as they walked into the hotel. "With me around he's perfectly comfortable and not inclined to budge."

Slote said, "I think you were right to return. He's in more danger than he realizes, and needs a hard push. Maybe you and I together can shake him free."

"But you're going to Moscow."

"I have thirty days, and I've only used up ten. Perhaps I'll go back to Rome with you. I know several people in that embassy."

"That would be marvellous!" Natalie halted in the middle of the pillared lobby. "Where's the bar?"

"It's down at that end and it's very dismal and beery.

It's virtually Gestapo headquarters. Why? Would you like a drink?"

"I'd just as lief have tea, Leslie." Her manner was oddly evasive. "I haven't eaten all day. I was just wondering where the bar was."

He took her to a long, narrow public room full of people in sofas and armchairs drinking tea or cocktails. Walking down the smoky room behind the headwaiter, they heard conversations in many languages: German was the commonest, and only one little group was talking English.

"League of Nations here," Natalie said, as the waiter bowed them into a dark corner with a sofa and two chairs, "except that so many look Jewish."

"A lot of them are," Slote said dolefully. "Too many of them are."

Natalie devoured a whole plate of sugared cakes with her tea. "I shouldn't do this, but I'm famished. I'm big as a house. I've gained ten pounds in six months at the villa. I just eat and eat."

"Possibly I'm prejudiced, but I think you look like the goddess of love, if a bit travel-worn."

"Yes, you mean these hefty Venus de Milo hips, hey?" She darted a pleased look at him. "I hope Byron likes hips. I've sure got 'em."

"I hadn't noticed your hips, but I assure you Byron will like them. Not that I really think you're worried. There's Bunky Thurston." Slote waved as a little man at the doorway far down the room came toward them. "Bunky's a prince of a fellow."

"He has the world's most impressive moustache," Natalie said.

"It's quite a moustache," Slote said.

The moustache approached, a heavy rounded tawny brush with every hair gleamingly in place, attached to a pleasant pink moon face set on a slight body dressed in natty gray flannel.

Slote said, "Hi, Bunky. You're late for tea, but just in time for a drink."

With a loud sigh, Thurston sat. "Thanks. I'll have a double Canadian Club and water. What foul weather. The chill gets in your bones. Natalie, here's that list I promised you." He handed her a folded mimeographed sheet. "I'm afraid you'll agree that it kills the notion. Now, I couldn't track down Commander Bathurst, but I left word everywhere. I'm sure he'll call me here within the hour."

Slote glanced inquisitively at the paper in Natalie's hand. It was a list of documents required for a marriage of foreigners in Portugal, and there were nine items. Avidly studying the sheet, Natalie drooped her shoulders and glanced from Slote to Thurston. "Why, getting all this stuff together would take months!"

"I've seen it done in one month," Thurston said, "but six to eight weeks is more usual. The Portuguese government doesn't especially want foreigners to get married here. I'm not sure why. In peacetime we send people over to Gibraltar, where you go through like greased lightning. But the Rock is shut up tight now."

"Thinking of getting married?" Slote said to Natalie.

She colored at the dry tone. "That was one of many things Byron wrote about. I thought I might as well check. It's obviously impossible, not that I thought it was such a hot idea anyway."

"Who's Commander Bathurst?" Slote said.

Thurston said, "Our naval attaché. He'll know exactly when the submarine's arriving." He tossed off half his whiskey when the waiter set it before him, and carefully smoothed down his moustache with two forefingers, looking around the room with a bitter expression. "God, Lisbon gives me the creeps. Forty thousand desperate people trying to get out of the net. I've seen most of the faces in this room at our legation." Thurston turned to Slote. "This isn't what you and I bargained for when we went to Foreign Service school."

"Bunky, you'd better get rid of that Quaker conscience, or you really will crack up. Remember that it isn't us who's doing it. It's the Germans."

"Not entirely. I never thought much about our immigration laws until this thing started. They're pernicious and idiotic." Bunky Thurston drank again and coughed, empurpling his face. "Forty thousand people. Forty thousand! Suppose we admitted them all? What difference would forty thousand people make, for God's sake, in the wastes of Montana or North Dakota? They'd be a blessing!"

"They wouldn't go there. They'd huddle in the big cities, where there's still an unemployment problem."

Thurston struck the table with a fist. "Now don't *you* give me that stale drivel, Leslie. It's enough that I have to parrot it all day myself. They'd go anywhere. You know that. They'd sign papers to live out their lives in Death Valley. Our law's inhuman. Wasn't America started as a sanctuary from European oppression?"

Slote took off his glasses, rubbed his eyes, and glanced warily at the people nearest them, four elderly men arguing in French. "Well, I'm not going to defend the law, but how do you draw the line? Or do you have unrestricted immigration? Do you let in everybody who wants to come? You'd empty southern and eastern Europe. They'd flood our economy, starve, ferment, and boil up in a revolution. What about the Orientals? Do you break the dike to the west? In ten years the United States would be a big Chinese suburb."

Natalie said with a gesture at the room, "He's talking about *these* few people in Lisbon who have escaped from the Germans. That's all."

"Tried to escape," said Thurston. "The Germans can take Portugal overnight."

"And I'm talking about the arguments that arise in Congress when you try to alter the law," Slote said, "especially in favor of Jews. Nobody wants any more competition from them, they're too energetic and smart. That's the fact of it, Natalie, like it or not."

"We could give refuge to all the Jews in Europe, all five million of them. We'd only be a lot better off," Thurston said. "Remember your Ruskin? 'Wealth is life,' he said. And if that's a bit too simple, it's certainly true that wealth is brains." He leaned toward Natalie, lowering his voice. "If you want to see the head of the Gestapo in Portugal, he's just walking in, and with him is the German ambassador. Charming man, the ambassador. My wife really likes him."

Natalie stared. "Is he the one with the scar?"

"No, I don't know who that one is, though I've seen him around. I'm sure he's Gestapo too. The ambassador's the one in the gray suit."

The three men sat not far from them, and the headwaiter fluttered and grinned eagerly, taking their orders.

"They look so ordinary," Natalie said.

"The Germans are quite ordinary," Slote said. "It's a little scary, in fact, how much like Americans they are."

Gloomily, Natalie said, "Those people at the table next to them are obviously Jews. Drinking and laughing, side by side with the Gestapo. Eerie."

Thurston said, "I know them. They bought their way out of Belgium, and they still don't believe they can't buy their way into the United States. Most of the Jews here have been stripped penniless, but there are a handful of those. They're in the casino night after night, whooping it up. Fish in the net, jumping and flopping, still enjoying the water while they can." Thurston finished his drink, smoothed his moustache, and waved his glass at the waiter. "I want another. I've had some awful interviews today. Lisbon is a very sad and horrible place right now. My request for a transfer is in. The question is whether I'll wait. I may just quit the service. I've never realized before how nice it is to have a wealthy father."

Slote said to Natalie, "Am I taking you to dinner?"

"Please, I'd love that."

"How about you, Bunky? Will you join us? Let's all go upstairs to my suite for a while. I want to change my shirt, and all that."

"No, I have a dinner appointment. I'll sit here and have my drink with Natalie. I left word for Bathurst to page me here."

Slote stood up. "Well, thanks for all you've done."

"I can do wonders for people who don't need help."

Slote told Natalie the number of his suite, and left. Later she found a pencilled note stuck in his doorjamb: *N— door's open.* She walked into a very large living room, looking out onto the purple sea beyond a long iron-railed balcony. Old heavy gilt and green furniture, gold cloth draperies, gilded mirrors, and large dark old paintings filled the room. Slote sang in a remote gushing shower. She yelled through an open bedroom door, "Hey! I'm here."

The water shut off, and he soon appeared in a plaid robe, towelling his head. "How about these digs? Fit for a

rajah, what? The legation had it reserved for some petroleum big shot and he didn't show. I've got it for a week."

"It's fine." She dropped heavily in a chair.

"What's the matter?"

"Bathurst finally called. Briny's sub has been re-routed
to Gibraltar. It won't come to Lisbon at all. No explanation, that's just how it is."

"I see. Well, too bad. Maybe you can get to see him at
Gibraltar."

"Thurston doesn't think so, but he's going to the British
embassy tomorrow morning, first thing, to find out. He's
being very kind. Especially since it's obvious he thinks I'm
a damned fool. No doubt you do, too." She looked up at
him with a defiant scowl that was familiar and beguiling,
took off her hat, and tossed her hair. "What had you told
him about Briny, anyway? And about me? He seemed to
know quite a bit."

"Oh, we had too much wine one night and I cried on
his shoulder about my tragic love life. I was very nice about
Byron, I assure you, considering."

She said with a trace of malice, "Yes, I'll bet. Say, this
is quite a layout at that. It'll bankrupt you."

"Not in the few days I'll be here."

"Me, I've dropped my bags in a flea trap back in town,
sharing a room with a poor old Jewish lady from Rotterdam, whose husband got pulled off the train in Paris. I
haven't had a shower since Sunday."

"Look, why not move in here? There's an extra room
for a maid. I'll sleep in there. Look at that bed. A football
field. It's yours."

"Nothing doing. Listen, Slote, if I can get to Gibraltar
I'll marry Byron. That's what he wants." Slote, combing his
hair at a mirror framed by trumpeting gilded cherubs,
stopped and gave her a pained skeptical look. She went on
nervously, "I know it sounds harum-scarum and wild."
Her eyes suddenly shone, and she laughed. "But in point
of fact, I want to do it myself."

"Well, I suppose I should congratulate you, Natalie.
God knows I wish you well."

"Oh, I know you do, Slote. Don't bother telling me how
bizarre all this is. Some things are just inevitable. I love
Byron."

"Well, the place is at your disposal, anyway. They eat dinner late here. Take a shower."

"And climb into the same old underwear?" Natalie shook her head, looking thoughtful. "I noticed a shop downstairs. Let me see what Lisbon can offer a big heifer like me."

She came back shortly, carrying a box and looking sly. "Did you mean that invitation? I bought a pile of stuff. Maybe it's my trousseau! A fast half hour of shopping. They had all these things from Seville, cheap and just yummy. Byron's eyes will pop out of his head, if he ever shows up."

"Are you low on money now?"

"My dear, I'm still rolling in it. That's one thing about sitting on that Siena hill, with nothing to spend it on! Aaron pays me like clockwork and it just accumulates. Really, may I stay? I hate the idea of going back to town tonight. That poor old woman gives me the horrors."

"I said the place is yours."

"I can't register."

"Don't worry."

"All right." She paused at the bedroom door and turned, holding the box in both arms. Her intense dark glance shook the diplomat. "People wouldn't understand about us, would they, Slote?"

"There's nothing to understand about me. You're the puzzle."

"You didn't used to think I was puzzling."

"I thought I had you figured out. I'm paying a steep price for oversimplifying."

"You were an egotistical fool. I am very fond of you."

"Thanks, Jastrow. Go take your goddamned shower."

＊　＊　＊

Next morning a buzzing at the suite door woke Slote. Tying on a robe, he came yawning out of the tiny maid's room, and blinked. There in a blaze of sunshine sat Natalie in a dazzling white wool dress with a broad red gold-buckled belt, watching a waiter fuss over a breakfast on a wheeled table. "Oh, hi," she said, smiling brightly and touching her carefully coiffed hair. "I didn't know whether you wanted to get up. I ordered eggs for you, just in case. Everything's so cheap and plentiful here!"

"I'll brush my teeth and join you. You're all spiffed up! How long have you been awake?"

"Hours and hours. I'm supposed to wait for Byron in the bar here at eleven o'clock today. That was the original plan."

Slote rubbed his eyes and peered at her. "What's the matter with you? His sub's en route to Gibraltar."

"That's what that man Bathurst said. Suppose he's mistaken?"

"Natalie, he's the naval attaché."

"I know that."

Shaking his head, Slote signed for the breakfast and left the room. Soon he returned in a shirt, slacks, and sandals, and found her eating with appetite. She grinned at him. "Forgive me for being a pig, dear. What a difference sunlight makes, and coffee! I feel marvellous."

He sat down and cut into a ripe Spanish melon. "Sweetie, do you honestly expect Byron Henry to materialize in the bar of this hotel at eleven o'clock? Just on your sheer willpower?"

"Well, Navy signals get crossed up like any others, don't they? *I'm* going to be there."

"It's just irrational, but suit yourself."

"Do you like my dress? I bought it yesterday, right out of the window of that shop."

"Very becoming."

She kept glancing at her watch. "Well, wish me luck," she said at last, dropping her napkin on the table. "I'm off."

"Do you intend to sit in the bar all day, like patience on a monument?"

"Don't be cross with me, Leslie."

"I'm not. I'd just like to plan the time."

"Well, obviously, if he hasn't showed by noon or thereabouts, the next thing is to find out how I get to Gibraltar."

"I'll call Bunky on that, and I'll come down at noon."

"Will you, please? Thanks, Leslie, thanks for everything. That bed's wonderful, I haven't slept so well in months."

She could not quite keep the mischief out of her face as

she said this and left with a nonchalant wave. Clearly, thought Slote, she was relishing his discomfiture. The tables were turned, and he had to endure it until he could turn them again.

He judged his chance was now at hand. Leslie Slote intended to take every possible advantage of this encounter. He could not understand Natalie's resolve to squander herself on Byron Henry. He had made a fearful mistake in his early treatment of this magnificent girl, and now he wanted to retrieve it. Slote knew how a divorced man must feel, finding himself thrown together with an ex-wife he still loved. Between them stood a barrier of old quarrels and new proprieties—it had effectively kept him out of the big bed last night—but beneath all that lay a deep bond. If it had not been for Natalie's fortuitous passion for the strange skinny Henry kid, he believed, they would by now be back together, very likely married. And he honestly thought he was more worthy of her and better suited to her.

Natalie might thrash about here in Lisbon for a while, he calculated; her willpower was formidable; but Gibraltar was probably impossible to get to. She would have to go back to Italy. He would accompany her to Siena, pry Aaron Jastrow loose, and send them both home. If necessary he would wire Washington for a travel time extension. If he could not win Natalie back during all this, he sadly overestimated himself and the tie between them. He had been her first lover, after all. Slote believed that no woman ever really forgot the first man who had had her, ever got him quite out of her system.

He finished his breakfast at leisure, then telephoned Thurston. "Morning, Bunky. What did you find out about Natalie's going to Gibraltar?"

"Forget it, Les. That submarine's here."

Slote had seldom heard worse news, but he suppressed any emotion in his voice. "It is? How come?"

"I don't know. It came in at dawn. It's tied up down at the river, near the customhouse."

"Then what on earth was Bathurst talking about?"

"He's mighty puzzled and he's going down there later to talk to the skipper. That submarine had orders to go to Gibraltar."

"How long will it be here?"

"The original schedule called for three days." Thurston's voice turned puckish. "Tough luck, Les. Fantastic girl. I'd sweat out the three days and then see."

In self-defense Slote said calmly, "Yes, she's all right, but she used to be a lot prettier." He dressed and hurried downstairs. In the dark bar there were only a handful of Germans, who turned suspicious faces to him. He went striding through the lobby.

"Here, Slote! Look behind you!" Natalie's voice rang like joyous bells.

Half screened by potted palms, she sat on a green plush sofa with Byron. Before them on a coffee table, beside an open dispatch case, lay a pile of documents. The girl's cheeks flamed, her eyes were gleaming, her whole face brilliantly animated. Byron Henry jumped up to shake hands. He appeared just the same, even to the tweed jacket in which Slote had seen him for the first time slouched against a wall in Siena.

Slote said, "Well, hello there! Did Natalie tell you we had some very wrong information?"

Byron laughed. "It wasn't wrong, exactly, but anyway, here we are." His glance swept the lobby. "Say, this place has a queer smell of Berlin. Isn't it full of Germans?"

"They swarm, darling. Don't say anything about anything." Excitedly shuffling the documents, Natalie pulled at Byron's hand. "I can't find your certificate of residence."

"It's clipped with yours."

"Then he's got everything," Natalie exclaimed to Slote. "Everything! All by the regulations, translated into Portuguese, notarized, and the notary seals authenticated by Portuguese consuls. The works." As Byron dropped beside her, she put her hand in his thick hair and gave his head a yank. "I thought you were lousy at paperwork, you devil. How in God's name did you manage this?"

Slote said, "Are you really sure everything's there? I've never seen regulations as tough as these. Suppose I check that stuff over for you."

"Oh, please, Leslie? Would you?" Natalie said, making room on the sofa and handing him the documents and the sheet Thurston had given her. Red ink check marks ran down the side of the page.

"How'd you assemble all this?" Slote said, starting to examine the papers.

Byron explained that as soon as he had learned of the scheduled cruise to Lisbon, he had obtained an emergency four-day pass, and had flown to Washington to find out at the Portuguese embassy what the marriage regulations were. The naval attaché there, Captain D'Esaguy, had turned out to be a friend of his from Berlin; the captain had been his tennis doubles partner for a while, playing against his father and the Swedish attaché. D'Esaguy had gone right to work. "It's surprising what those fellows can accomplish in a few days when they want to," Byron said. "I rounded up some of the papers, but the Portuguese consuls themselves did the hardest ones."

"That's the Foreign Service everywhere," said Slote, methodically turning over one paper after another and glancing at the check list. "The wheels either turn glacially, or so fast you can't see them whiz—well, Byron, I honestly think you, or this Portuguese navy captain, or both of you, did it. Everything seems to be here."

"What now?" Natalie said.

"Will you marry me?" Byron said, very solemnly.

Natalie said, "I sure will, by God."

They burst out laughing. With a melancholy chuckle, Slote slipped the papers into the folder which Byron had labelled in neat red block letters: MARRIAGE. "Suppose I telephone Thurston and ask him what you do next? Thurston's my friend here in the legation, Byron."

Byron Henry slowly, gratefully smiled, and Slote could not but see how appealing the smile was. "Thanks a lot. Will you? I'm not thinking too clearly at the moment."

"No? On the whole, I'd say you're doing all right."

Returning a few minutes later, he saw them holding hands on the sofa, looking adoringly at each other and both talking at once. He hesitated, then approached them. "Sorry. Problems."

Natalie looked up at him, startled and frowning. "What now?"

"Well, Bunky's bowled over by what you've done, Byron, just impressed as hell. He's at your service and wants to help. But he doesn't know what he can do about that twelve-day requirement for posting banns. Then there's the

Foreign Office's authentication of the consuls' signatures. He says that usually takes a week. So——" Slote shrugged, and dropped the folder on the table.

"Right, D'Esaguy mentioned both those points," Byron said. "He thought they could be gotten around. I stopped off at the navy ministry on the way here this morning and gave his uncle a letter. His uncle's a commodore, or something. He was awfully nice to me, but he only speaks Portuguese. I think he's working on those snags. I'm supposed to go back to the ministry at one o'clock. Could Mr. Thurston meet us there? That might be a real help."

Slote looked from Byron to Natalie, whose mouth was twitching with amusement. She still held Byron's hand in her lap. "I'll call back and ask him. You've certainly been forehanded."

"Well, I sort of wanted this to come off."

With some stupefaction, Bunker Thurston agreed over the telephone to meet them at the navy building at one. "Say, Leslie, I thought you called this ensign of hers a sluggard and a featherhead. He's organized this thing like a blitzkrieg."

"Surprised me."

"You have my sympathies."

"Oh, shut up, Bunky. I'll see you at one."

"You're coming too?"

"Yes, oh yes."

"You're a glutton for punishment."

A tall man in Navy dress blues leaned on the fender of an automobile outside the hotel, smoking a very black, very fat cigar. "Hey, Briny! Is the exercise on?"

"It's on." Byron introduced him to Natalie and Slote as Lieutenant Aster, his executive officer. Aster took in the girl with a keen, rather greedy glance of pale small blue eyes. He was broader and heavier than Byron, with thick wavy blond hair growing to a peak on his forehead, and a long face that looked genial because the corners of his mouth turned up. But it was a tight tough mouth. "Say, Natalie, that picture of you that Briny keeps mooning over doesn't do you justice. Hop in, everybody. I phoned the skipper, Briny, and told him you'd made contact. You're off the watch list while we're here."

"Great, Lady. Thanks."

Not sure she had heard this right, Natalie said, *"Lady?"*

The executive officer's smile was a bit weary. "That happened to me in my plebe year at the Academy. With a name like Aster, I guess it had to. My name's Carter, Natalie, and by all means use it."

Driving into the city, the two submariners described how the *S-45*, a hundred fifty miles out of Lisbon, had in fact been ordered to Gibraltar. The captain, who knew about Byron's plans, had expressed his regrets but altered course to the south. Within an hour reports came in to the captain that the number two main engine was down, the forward battery was throwing off excessive hydrogen, an evaporator had salted up, and a general plague of malfunctions was breaking out in the old boat, necessitating an emergency call in Lisbon for two or three days of alongside repairs. Aster, who brought in the reports, gave his opinion, which was backed by the Chief of the Boat, that it might be hazardous to proceed to Gibraltar. All this was done with a straight face, and with a straight face the captain accepted the executive officer's recommendation and turned back to Lisbon.

"How can you possibly get away with that?" said Slote. "Won't you all be court-martialled?"

"Nobody was lying." Aster said with an innocent smile. "We have the engine records to prove it. These old S-boats just gasp and flounder along, and at practically any moment you could justify an order to abandon ship. Coming into Lisbon was highly commendable prudence."

Natalie said to Byron, "And you submerge in an old wreck like that?"

"Well, the *S-45* has made four thousand, seven hundred and twenty-three dives, Natalie. It should be good for a few more."

"Diving is nothing," said Lady Aster. "You pull the plug and she goes down; you blow air and she pops up. It's going from one place to another that's kind of a strain on the old hulk. But we manage. By the way, everybody's invited aboard after the ceremony."

"Me? On a submarine?" Natalie tucked her skirt close around her thighs.

"The captain wants to congratulate you. He was pretty nice about coming in to Lisbon, you know."

"We'll see," Natalie said. "Slote! Are you trying to maim us all?"

"Sorry, that truck came out of nowhere," said Slote, pulling the car back on the bumpy road. He was driving too fast.

Shaking hands in the sunshine outside the navy ministry, Bunker Thurston gave Ensign Henry a prolonged curious scrutiny. "I'm glad to meet a fellow with such a knack for getting things done."

"This thing's not done yet, by a long shot, sir. Thanks for offering to help out."

"Well, come along, and let's see what happens. You've got some strong pull on your side. D'Esaguy seems to be something like a deputy chief of naval operations."

Judging by the number of anterooms and armed guards outside his office, the size of the room, the magnificence of the furniture, and the effulgence of his gold braid and combat ribbons, D'Esaguy certainly held some exalted post. He was a short dark man, with an elongated stern Latin face, and heavy hair graying at the sides. He held himself, and shook hands, and gestured as he welcomed them, with noble grace; and to Natalie he made a deep bow, his black eyes showing a spark of admiration. He turned businesslike and rattled rapidly to Thurston in Portuguese.

"He says these things take time," Thurston reported. "He would like to invite us all to lunch."

Byron glanced at Natalie, and said, "That's very cordial of him. Does he know we only have three days?"

"I'm not sure you ought to press him," Thurston muttered.

"Please tell him what I said."

"Okay."

The Portuguese officer listened gravely to Thurston. His eyes were on Byron. A wrinkle of his mouth, a flash of fun in the sombre face, acknowledged the impatience of a young lover. He turned and rapped an order to an assistant only slightly less crusted with gold braid than himself, who sat at a small desk. The assistant jumped up and went out.

After a minute of heavy silence he returned with a bouquet of red roses. He gave these to D'Esaguy, who handed them to Natalie Jastrow with a bow and a few charmingly spoken words.

Thurston translated, "The dew will not dry on these roses before you are married."

"Good God. How beautiful. Thank you!" Natalie's voice trembled. She stood holding the roses, looking around at the men, blushing. "You know, I'm beginning to believe it! For the very first time."

"The exercise is on, lady," said Lieutenant Aster. "Cancel now, if you're ever going to."

"Cancel?" She took Byron's arm. "Nonsense. Commence firing!"

"Hey, a Navy wife," said Lieutenant Aster.

D'Esaguy, trying alertly to follow this chatter, asked Thurston to translate. He burst out laughing, took Natalie's hand, and kissed it.

"Come," he said in English. "A leetle luncheon."

The lunch was long and excellent, in a restaurant with a lordly view, much like a San Francisco panorama, of the Lisbon hills and the broad sparkling river. The commodore seemed in no hurry at all. Thurston kept checking his watch, knowing that most government offices would shut by four-thirty or five. At three D'Esaguy said casually that perhaps they might see now how the little business was coming along. In an enormous black Mercedes limousine they commenced a whirling tour of office buildings. Thurston tried to explain what was happening, but after a while he gave up, because he wasn't sure. Sometimes the commodore descended for a few minutes by himself, sometimes he took the couple along to sign a ledger or a document, with Thurston accompanying them. An official invariably waited at the door to greet them and to lead them past crowded anterooms into dusty old inner offices, where fat pallid old department heads got awkwardly out of their chairs to bow to D'Esaguy.

About two hours later they arrived at an office familiar to Thurston, where civil marriages were registered. It was closed for the day and the blinds were drawn. As the black limousine came to a stop, one blind went up and the door opened. A huge old woman in a brown smock, with visible chin whiskers, led them through dark empty rooms to an inner office where a chandelier blazed. At an ancient desk, fussing with papers, sat a dark frog-faced man with gold-rimmed glasses, several gold teeth, and three thick gold rings. He smiled at them and spoke to Thurston in Portuguese. Thurston translated his questions; the man scratched with a blotchy pen on many of Byron's documents and kept stamping them. Natalie, Byron, and the two witnesses—Aster and Slote—signed and signed. After a while the man stood, and with a lewd gold-flecked smile held out his hand to Natalie and then to Byron, saying brokenly, "Good luck for you."

"What's this now?" Natalie said.

"Why, you're married," Thurston said. "Congratulations."

"We *are*? Already? When did we get married? I missed it."

"At one point there, where you both signed the green book. That was it."

"I haven't the faintest recollection."

Byron said, "Nor have I. However, I'll take your word for it. Let's have that ring, Lady."

Aster put it in his hand. He slipped the yellow band on Natalie's finger, swept her into his arms, and kissed her. Meantime Thurston told D'Esaguy how the couple had missed the moment of marriage, and the Portuguese officer laughed. He laughed again when Thurston explained the American custom of kissing the bride. Natalie said that D'Esaguy must kiss her first. With marked pleasure, the old aristocrat executed the privilege on her lips. Then he left, after courtly handshakes all around, as Byron gathered up his sheaf of documents and paid the fees.

Slote was the last to kiss her. Natalie hesitated, looking into his eyes, and said, "Well, old Slote, I seem to have done it, don't I? Wish me well."

"Oh, I do, I do, Jastrow. You know that."

She gave him a cool brief kiss on the mouth, putting her free hand on his neck.

When they emerged into the late golden sunshine, the black limousine was gone. The office door closed behind them and Slote felt something loose and grainy thrust in his hand. It was rice. Lieutenant Aster grinned a strange cold thin-lipped grin at him and winked a sharp blue eye. At a signal from Aster, the three men pelted the couple.

Natalie, brushing rice from her dress, wiped her eyes with a knuckle. "Well, *that* certainly makes it official! Now what happens?"

"If you don't know," said Lady Aster, "Byron's got a lot of fast explaining to do."

Natalie choked and turned brick red. "My God, Briny, who *is* this character?"

"Lady's spent too much time submerged," said Byron. "He has trouble raising his mind to sea level."

"Marriage is holy and beautiful," said Lady Aster. "But before you hop to it, how about visiting the old *S-45* for a minute? The skipper's sort of expecting us."

"Of course, of course," Natalie said hurriedly. "I want to see the *S-45*. I'm dying to. By all means."

"Have you any idea where you'll go after that?" Leslie Slote dryly put in.

Byron said, "Well, I figured there'd be a place—a hotel, something."

"Lisbon's jammed to bursting," said Slote.

"My God, so it is. I never gave it a thought," Natalie said.

"Why not take my place?" said Leslie Slote. "That's a honeymoon suite, if ever I saw one."

Natalie looked very surprised and glanced at Byron. "That's sweet of you, Slote, but I wouldn't dream of it."

"We'll find something," Byron said, shaking his head.

"Oh, but his place is out of the Arabian Nights," said Natalie, adding very casually, "I had a drink there last night. *Would* you do such a thing for us, old Slote?"

"Leslie can stay with me," Thurston said. "No problem at all. Pick me up at the legation, Les. I have to rush there now."

"It's all set," said Slote. "While you two visit the submarine, I'll go to the hotel and clear out."

"Bless you. Thank you. My bags," said Natalie distractedly, "they're in Mrs. Rosen's room. Maybe I should get them! No, I have things to throw in. I'll get 'em later.

Thanks, Slote. And you too, Bunky. Thanks for everything."

Slote signalled at a passing taxicab. "Good luck."

    •   •   •

Natalie was astonished at the small size of the submarine, at its ugliness, and at its rustiness. "Good heavens!" she shouted over the clanks and squeals of the crane moving overhead, as they got out of the cab. "Is *that* the S-45? Briny, honestly, don't you get claustrophobia when you dive in that thing?"

"He's never stayed awake long enough to find out," said Aster. They were walking toward a gangway that was only a couple of planks nailed together. Sailors lounged on the low flat black forecastle, staring at the girl in white with an armful of roses. "One day when we're submerged he'll open his eyes and begin screaming."

"I don't mind anything but the low company," said Byron, "and the body odors. It's especially marked among the senior officers. When I sleep I don't notice it."

A young tousle-headed sailor at the gangway, wearing a gun slung low on his hip, saluted Aster, gave Natalie a yearning respectful glance, and said, "Cap'n wants you-all to wait for him on the dock, sir."

"Very well."

Soon a figure in a blue uniform, with the gold stripes of a lieutenant, emerged from the rust-streaked black sail—the housing that rose amidships over the conning tower—and crossed the gangplank to the dock. The captain was shaped rather like his submarine, clumsily thick in the middle and tapering abruptly to either end. He had big brown eyes, a broad nose, and a surprisingly boyish face.

"Captain Caruso, this is my wife," said Byron, jolting Natalie with the word.

Caruso took her hand in a white fat paw. "Well, congratulations! Byron's a good lad, in his short conscious intervals."

"Do you really sleep that much?" Natalie laughed at Byron.

"It's pure slander. I seldom close my eyes on this boat,"

said Byron, "except to meditate on my folly in going to sub school. That I admit I do very frequently."

"Eighteen hours at a stretch, he can meditate," said Aster. "That's solid gold meditating."

Two sailors in dungarees came up out of an open hatch on the forecastle and crossed the gangway, one carrying a bottle of champagne in an ice bucket, the other a tray of water glasses.

"Ah, here we go. Navy Regs don't allow us to consume spirituous liquors on board, Mrs. Henry," said the captain, and again she felt the little joyous jolt. He popped the cork and ceremoniously poured as the sailor held out one glass after another.

"To your happiness," he shouted, as the crane went by overhead with a wild clanging.

"To you, God bless you," yelled Natalie, "for bringing him here."

"To number two engine," bellowed Lady Aster, "to the evaporators, the exhaust system, and the forward battery. Never has there been such a massive breakdown on a naval vessel."

Byron silently lifted his glass to his captain and executive officer.

They drank. The crane rumbled away.

"Captain," said Lady Aster, as Caruso refilled the glasses, "do you think that picture in Byron's room does Natalie justice?"

"Not in the least," said the captain, looking at her with liquid woman-loving Italian eyes. "It doesn't begin to."

"That's how I feel. Now that you've actually seen her, sir, don't you agree with me that what has to be done in Lisbon may take at least five days?"

"Three," snapped Captain Caruso, the dreamy look vanishing. "Exactly seventy-two hours."

"Aye aye, sir."

"And you'd better produce some damned convincing malfunction reports, Lady." The captain tossed off his wine and smiled at Natalie. "Now, can I offer you the hospitality of the boat for a little while?"

She followed the officers into the rusty sail and down a hatch. The ladder was cold and greasy, with narrow slippery rungs that caught at Natalie's high heels. She had to lower herself through a second round hatch and down another ladder into a tiny room full of machinery, strongly conscious of her exposed legs and glad that they were pretty and that her skirt was narrow.

"This is the control room," Byron said, helping her down. "Up above was the conning tower."

Natalie looked around at solemn-faced sailors in dungarees, and at the valves, knobs, dials, handles, big wheels, twisted cables, and panels of lights filling all the green-painted bulkheads. Despite a humming exhaust blower, the close, warm air smelled sourly of machinery, cooking, old cigars, and unwashed men. "Briny, do you really know what all these things are?"

"He's learning," said Lady Aster. "Between hibernations."

They stepped through an open watertight door to the tiny wardroom, where Natalie met two more young officers. On the table stood a heart-shaped white cake, iced in blue with a submarine, cupids, and *Mr. and Mrs. Byron Henry*. She squeezed herself into the place of honor at the head of the table, opposite the captain. Byron and Lady Aster sat crouched against the bulkhead, to avoid a bunk folded back over their heads.

Somebody produced a sword, Natalie cut up the cake, and the captain sent what was left to the crew's quarters. The two glasses of champagne were going to Natalie's head. She was half-dizzy anyway from the rush of events and the longing that blazed at her from the young men's eyes. Over the coffee and cake she laughed and laughed at Lady Aster's jokes, and decided that the old submarine, for all its cramped squalor, its reek of machinery and male bodies, was a mighty jolly vessel. Byron looked more desirable to her by the minute, and she kissed him often.

Before they left the *S-45*, Byron took his bride to a tiny cabin and showed her the narrow black aperture near the deck, beneath two other bunks, where he slept. "I ask you," he said, "would anybody spend extra time in that morgue slot through choice?"

"The alternative might be more frightful," said Lady Aster, over Natalie's shoulder. "Like staying awake."

When Natalie and Byron came out on deck into cool fresh air, crewmen on the forecastle waved and cheered.

Natalie waved back and some bold sailors whistled. The taxicab, called by the gangway watch for them, started off with a great clatter. The driver jammed on his brakes, jumped out, and soon Natalie and Byron heard him cursing in Portuguese as he threw aside shoes and tin cans. The crew laughed and yelled until the cab drove away.

"I daresay poor Slote's left the hotel by now." Natalie snuggled against her husband. "We'll collect my bags and go there, right? Wait till you see it. It was terrible of me to jump at it like that, but honestly, Briny, it's the royal suite."

In Natalie's room, in a boardinghouse on a side street, an old woman snored in an iron bed. "Well, Slote's place must be better than this," Byron whispered, glancing at the cracked ceiling and at the roaches on the peeling wallpaper, scurrying to hide from the electric light. Natalie swiftly gathered her things and left a note with her key on the table. At the door she turned to look at Mrs. Rosen, lying on her back, jaw hanging open, gray hair tumbled on the pillow. What kind of wedding night had Mrs. Rosen had, she thought, with the husband whose silver-framed face smiled brownly on her bedside table, her one memento of the wretched man dragged off a French train by Germans? Natalie shivered and closed the door.

The desk clerk at the Palace Hotel evidently had been informed and tipped by Slote, for he yielded up the key to Byron with a greasy grin. The newlyweds had to give him their passports. Natalie felt a touch of fear, handing over the maroon American booklet that set her off from Lisbon's forty thousand other Jews.

"I just thought of something," she said in the elevator. "How did you register?"

"Mr. and Mrs., naturally. Big thrill."

"I'm still Natalie Jastrow on that passport."

"So you are." The elevator stopped. He took her arm. "I wouldn't worry about it."

"But maybe you should go back and explain."

"Let them ask a question first."

As the bellboy opened the door to the suite, Natalie felt herself whisked off her feet. "Oh, Byron, stop this nonsense. I'm monstrously heavy. You'll slip a disk." But she clung to his neck with one hand and clutched her skirt with the other, excited by his surprising lean strength.

"Hey!" he said, carrying her inside, "I see what you meant. Royal suite is right."

When he put her down she darted ahead into the bedroom. Natalie had a slight nag of worry about the negligee she had left hanging in Slote's bathroom, and the new sexy underwear in a bureau drawer. It might take some explaining! But all the stuff was gone—where, she had no idea. She was puzzling over this when Byron appeared in the french window of the bedroom, on the balcony. "This is great out here, all right. Cold as hell, though. Fabulous string of lights along the water. Did you notice the champagne? And the lilies?"

"Lilies?"

"In there."

In a corner of the living room, beside champagne in a silver cooler on a marble table, stood a bouquet of red and white calla lilies, and beside them Slote's small white card, with no writing. The doorbell rang. A bellboy gave Natalie a box from the lingerie shop. She hurried into the bedroom and opened it. There lay the underclothes Slote had cleared out, a many-colored froth of silk and lace.

"What's that?" Byron said from the balcony.

"Oh, some stuff I bought in a lobby shop," Natalie said airily. "I guess Slote told them I'd be here." She picked up a peach nightgown, and with mock witchery draped it against her bosom. "Not bad for an academic type, hey?"

Then she saw a note in Slote's handwriting, lying under the silks. Byron started to come in. She ran for the french door and shut it on him. "Give me a minute. Open the champagne."

The note read: *Wear the gray, Jastrow. You always looked angelic in gray. Confidential communication, to be destroyed. Yours till death. Slote.*

The words brought a mist to Natalie's eyes. She tore the note to bits and dropped them in a wastebasket. In the next room she heard a cork pop. She pulled from the box the gray silk nightdress laced and trimmed in black, and quite forgot Leslie Slote, as she speedily showered and perfumed herself. She emerged from the bedroom brushing her long black hair down on her shoulders. Byron seized her. . . .

. . . Wine, lilies, and roses; the dark sea rolling beyond the windows under a round moon; young lovers separated for half a year, joined on a knife-edge of geography between war and peace, suddenly married, far from home; isolated, making love on a broad hospitable bed, performing secret rites as old as time, but forever fresh and sweet between young lovers, the best moments human existence offers—such was their wedding night. The human predicament sometimes seems a gloomy tapestry with an indistinct, baffling design that swirls around and inward to brilliant naked lovers. The Bible starts with this centerpiece. Most of the old stories end with the lovers married, retiring to their sacred nakedness. But for Byron and Natalie, their story was just beginning.

The lavish pulses and streams of love died into the warm deep sleep of exhausted lovers: Mr. and Mrs. Byron Henry, Americans, slumbering in wedlock in the Palace Hotel outside Lisbon, on a January night of 1941, one of the more than two thousand nights of the Second World War, when so much of mankind slept so badly.

38

Natalie opened her eyes, awakened by the warbling and chirping of birds. Byron sat beside her, smoking. A cool breeze was blowing from an open door to the balcony. In a pink-streaked sky, the wan moon and one star hung low over the choppy sea.

"Hi. Listen to those birds! How long have you been awake, Byron?"

"Not long, but I'm really wide awake. Wide awake and still trying to believe it."

She sat up. The bedclothes slipped from her breasts as she kissed him softly, sighing with satiated pleasure. "Gosh, that air's icy, isn't it?"

"I can close the door."

"No, no, the sea smell is lovely." She pulled the blanket to her neck, nestling beside him. After a silence she said, "Byron, how does a submarine work?"

He glanced down at her. His arm was around her, caressing her shoulder. "Are you kidding?"

"No. Is it hard to explain?"

"Not at all, but why talk about that?"

"Because I want to know."

"Well, it's a hell of a topic to take up with a beautiful naked girl, but okay. I'll tell you how a submarine works. To begin with, it's built so that it just about floats when ballasted. So when you flood the diving tanks with a few tons of seawater you go right down, and when you blow the water out with compressed air, you pop up again. You begin with marginal buoyancy, and by changing the water ballast you become a rock or a cork as desired. That's the general idea. The details are numerous and dull."

"Well, is it safe? How much have I got to worry about?"

"Less than if I were a New York traffic cop."

"You get hazardous duty pay."

"That's because civilians, like congressmen and you, yourself, have the illusion that it's scary and risky to dive a boat under the water. No submariner will ever argue Congress out of that."

"But when you go deep, isn't there quite a risk of being crushed?"

"No. A sub's just a long watertight steel tube, braced to hold off sea pressure. That's the inner hull. It's the real ship. The outside that you see is just a skin for tanks, open at the bottom. The water sloshes in and out. The inner hull has a test pressure depth. You never submerge near that. Nobody to this day knows how deep the old *S-45* can go. We ride on a thick cushion of safety."

"Submarines have been lost."

"So have ocean liners and sailing yachts. When men are

trapped in a hull on the ocean bottom, tapping out Morse code, it makes a good story, but it's only happened a couple of times. Even then there are ways of escaping, and we're all trained in them."

"But when you flood the boat to go down, can't the flooding get out of hand? Don't smile, darling. It's all a mystery to somebody like me."

"I smile because you ask good questions. But as I told you, the main tanks are outside the real hull. They're just stuck on. When they flood, you're awash, waterlogged. For diving there's a small sealed tank inside, the negative tank. It can hold about twelve tons of seawater. Flood negative and down you go fast. When you're at the depth you want, you blow negative, and there you are, hanging. You spread your bow planes, and you're sort of like a fat airplane, flying slowly through thick air. Submariners are picked men, and great guys, darling, and all seventy-five of them dearly want nothing to go wrong! There are no slobs on a submarine. That's the truth about submarines, and this is one peculiar conversation to be having in bed with a new wife."

Natalie yawned. "You're making me feel better. That rusty little boat scared me."

"The new fleet submarines are luxury liners compared to the *S-45*," Byron said. "I'll go to one of those next."

She yawned again, as a patch of pink light appeared on the wall. "Bless my soul, is that the sun? Where did the night go? Draw the curtains."

Byron walked naked to the windows and closed the heavy draperies. As he returned to her in the gloom, she thought with piercing pleasure how handsome he was—a sculptured male figure—alive, warm, and brown.

He settled beside her. She leaned over him and gave him a kiss. When the young husband strongly pulled her close she pretended for a moment to fight him off, but she couldn't choke down her welling joyous laughter. As the sun rose outside the screening curtains on another day of war, Byron and Natalie Henry went back to lovemaking.

They breakfasted at noon in the sunny sitting room, where the air was heavy with the scent of roses. Their breakfast was oysters, steak, and red wine; Natalie ordered it, saying it was precisely what she wanted, and Byron called it a perfect menu. They ate in dressing gowns, not talking much, looking deep in each other's eyes, sometimes laughing at a foolish word or at nothing at all. They were radiant with shared, gratified desire.

Then she said, "Byron, exactly how much time do we have?"

"Well, seventy-two hours from the time we came alongside would be half past two, Thursday."

Some of the pure gladness in her eyes dimmed. "Hm. That soon? Short honeymoon."

"This isn't our honeymoon. I'm entitled to twenty days' leave. I reported straight to the *S-45* from sub school. I'll take those twenty days once you're back home. When will that be?"

She leaned her head on her hand. "Oh, dear. Must I start thinking?"

"Look, Natalie. Why not send Aaron a wire that we're married, and go straight home?"

"I can't do that."

"I don't want you going back to Italy."

Natalie raised her eyebrows at his flat tone. "But I have to."

"No, you don't. Aaron's too cute," Byron said. "Here, let's finish this wine. As long as you or I or somebody will do the correspondence and dig in the library and keep after the kitchen, the gardeners, and the plumbers, he won't leave that house. It's that simple. He loves it, and he doesn't scare easily. He's a tough little bird, Uncle Aaron, under the helplessness and the head colds. What d'you suppose he'd do if you sent him that wire?"

Natalie hesitated, "Try to get me to change my mind. If that failed, make a real effort to leave."

"Then it's the best favor you can do him."

"No. He'd make a mess of it. He's not good with officials, and the stupider they are the worse he gets. He could really trap himself. Leslie Slote and I together can get him on his way in short order, and this time we'll do it."

"Slote? Slote's en route to Moscow."

"He's offered to stop off in Rome and Siena first. He's very devoted to Aaron."

"I know who he's devoted to."

Natalie said softly with a poignant look, "Jealous of Leslie Slote, Briny?"

"All right. Sixty days."

"What, dear?"

"Go back there for two months. No more. That should be plenty. If Aaron's not out by April first or before, it'll be his own doing, and you come home. Book your own transportation, right now."

Natalie's wide mouth curved wryly. "I see. Are you giving me orders, Byron?"

"Yes."

She rested her chin on her palm, contemplating him with surprised eyes. "You know, that feels pretty good, being ordered around. I can't say why. Possibly the delicious novelty will wear off. Anyway, lord and master, I'll do as you say. Sixty days."

"All right," Byron said. "Let's get dressed and see Lisbon."

"I've seen Lisbon," said Natalie, "but I'm all in favor of coming up for air."

Dropping the key at the desk, Byron asked for their passports. With a heavy-lidded look, the swarthy short clerk disappeared through a door.

"Look at those fellows," Byron said. Half a dozen Germans, in belted black raincoats despite the sunshine, were talking together near the lobby entrance, looking hard at everybody who came in and went out. "They might as well be wearing boots and swastikas. What is it about them? Those raincoats? The big brims on the hats? The bronze sunburns? How do they find time for sunbathing?"

"I recognize them with the back of my neck. It crawls," Natalie said.

The desk clerk emerged from the door, busily shuffling papers. "Sorry, passports not ready yet."

"I need mine!" Natalie's tone was strident.

The clerk barely lifted his eyes at her. "Maybe this afternoon, madame," he said, turning his back.

After the languors of the bedroom, the cold sunny outdoors felt bracing. Byron hired a taxi to drive them into and around Lisbon. The city was no Rome or Paris for sights, but the rows of pastel-colored houses—green, pink, blue—perched along the hills above a broad river made a pretty picture. Byron enjoyed himself, and he thought his bride was having fun too; she clung to his arm and smiled, saying little. The peculiar mixture of Moorish and Gothic styles in the churches, and in the great fortress commanding the city's highest hill, brought back to Byron his dead-and-gone fine arts drudgery. They left the cab to descend arm in arm the steep, narrow, extremely small streets of the Alfama, where ragged children swarmed in and out of cracking crazy houses hundreds of years old, and open shops the size of telephone booths sold fish, bread, and meat scraps. It was a long wandering walk.

"Where did the cab promise to meet us?" Natalie spoke up in a strained tone, as they traversed an alley where the stinks made them gasp.

"Everything all right?" he said.

She wearily smiled. "At the risk of sounding like every stupid woman tourist in the world, my feet hurt."

"Why, let's go back. I've had plenty of this."

"Do you mind?"

She said not a word as they drove along the river road back to the hotel. When he took her hand it was clammy. Entering the hotel, she pulled at his elbow. "Don't forget —passports."

It proved unnecessary. With the key, the desk clerk, showing large yellow false teeth in an empty grin, handed him two maroon booklets. Natalie snatched hers and riffled through it as they walked to the elevator.

"Okay?" he said.

"Seems to be. But I'll bet anything the Gestapo's photographed it, and yours too."

"Well, it's probably routine in this hotel. I don't think the Portuguese are denying the Germans much nowadays. But what do you care?"

When she went into the bedroom of the suite to put away her coat and hat, Byron followed, took her in his arms, and kissed her. She responded, she held him close, but her manner was apathetic. He leaned back with a questioning look.

"Sorry," she said. "I have a thundering headache. Burgundy for breakfast may not be just the thing, after all. Luckily I have some high-powered pills for this. Just let me take one."

Soon she came back from the bathroom smiling. "Okay. Proceed."

He said, "It couldn't work that fast."

"Oh, it will. Don't worry."

They kissed, they lay on the bed, Byron was on fire to make love and tried to please her, but it was as though a spring had broken in Natalie. She whispered endearments and tried to be loving. After a while he sat up, and gently raised her. "All right. What is it?"

She crouched against the head of the bed, hugging her knees. "Nothing, nothing! What am I doing wrong? Maybe I'm a little tired. The headache's not gone yet."

"Natalie." He took her hand, kissed it, and looked straight into her eyes.

"Oh, I guess nobody can experience such joy without paying. That's all. If you must know, I've been in a black hole all afternoon. It started when we didn't get our passports back, and those Germans were standing there in the lobby. I got this horrible sinking feeling. All the time we were sightseeing, I was having panicky fantasies. The hotel would keep stalling about my passport, and you'd sail away in the submarine, and here I'd be, just one more Jew stuck in Lisbon without papers."

"Natalie, you never turned a hair all through Poland. You've got your passport back now."

"I know. It's sheer nonsense, just nervous depletion, too many wonderful things happening too fast. I'll get over it."

He caressed her hair. "You fooled me. I thought you were enjoying Lisbon."

"I *loathe* Lisbon, Briny. I always have. I swear to God, whatever else happens, I'll regret to my dying day that we married and spent our wedding night here. It's a sad, painful city. You see it with different eyes, I know. You keep saying it looks like San Francisco. But San Francisco isn't full of Jews fleeing the Germans. The Inquisition didn't baptize Jews by force in San Francisco, and burn the ones who objected, and take away all the children to raise them as Christians. Do you know that little tidbit of history? It happened here."

Byron's face was serious, his eyes narrowed. "Maybe I read it once."

"Maybe? If you had, how could you forget? *Anybody's* blood should run cold at such cruelty. But somehow, what's happened to Jews in Europe over the centuries is just a matter of course. What was Bunky's pretty phrase? *Fish in a net.*"

Byron said, "Natalie, I'll do anything you want about the religion. I've always been prepared for that. Would you want me to become Jewish?"

"Are you *insane?*" She turned her head sharply to him and her eyes had an angry shine. She had looked like this in Königsberg, giving him a rude abrupt good-bye. "Why did you insist on getting married? *That's* what's eating at me. Just tell me that. We could have made love, you know that, all you wanted. I feel tied to you now with a rope of raw nerves. I don't know where you're going. I don't know when I'll ever see you again. I only know you're sailing away Thursday in that damned submarine. Why don't we tear up those Portuguese documents? Let everything be as it was. My God, if we ever find ourselves in a human situation, and if we still care, we can get properly married. This was a farce."

"No, it wasn't. It's the only thing I've wanted since I was born. Now I've got it. We're not tearing up any papers. You're my wife."

"But God in heaven, *why* have you gone to all this trouble? Why have you put yourself in this mess?"

"Well, it's like this, Natalie. Married officers get extra allowances."

She stared at him. Her taut face relaxed, she slowly, reluctantly smiled, and thrust both her hands in his hair. "I see! Well, that makes a lot of sense, Briny. You should have told me sooner. I can understand greed."

Mouth to mouth, they fell back on the bed, and the lovemaking started to go better, but the telephone rang. It rang and rang and rang, and the kisses had to stop. Byron sighed, "Could be the *S-45*," and picked up the receiver. "Yes? Oh, hello. Right. That's thoughtful of you. Nine o'clock? Wait." He covered the mouthpiece. "Thurston apologizes for intruding. He and Slote thought we might conceivably want to have dinner in a special place. Best food in Lisbon, best singer in Portugal."

"Good heavens. Old Slote is uncovering a masochistic streak."

"Yes or no?"

"As you wish."

Byron said, "They mean to be nice. Why not? We have to eat. Get away from the black raincoats."

He accepted, hung up, and took her in his arms.

. . .

The restaurant was a brick-walled low room, illuminated only by table candles and the logs blazing in an arched fireplace. Jews, many in sleek dinner clothes, filled half the tables. Two large British parties side by side made most of the noise in the sedate place. Directly in front of the fire a table for six stood empty, longingly eyed by customers clustering in a small bar. The four Americans sat at another favored table near the fire. Over Portuguese white wine, Bunky Thurston and the newlyweds soon grew merry. Not Slote; he drank a lot but hardly spoke or smiled. The firelight glittered on his square glasses, and even in that rosy light his face looked ashen.

"I don't know if you youngsters are interested in the war, by the way," Thurston said over the meat. "Remember the war? There's news."

"If the news is good I'm interested," Natalie said. "Only if it's good."

"Well, the British have captured Tobruk."

Natalie said, "Is Tobruk important?"

Byron exclaimed, "Important! It's the best harbor between Egypt and Tunis. That's mighty good news."

"Right," Thurston said. "They're really roaring across North Africa now. Makes the whole war look different."

Slote broke his silence to say hoarsely, "They're fighting Italians." He cleared his throat and went on, "Byron, did you actually read the list of books I gave you in Berlin? Natalie says you did."

"Whatever I could find in English, yes. Maybe seven or eight out of ten."

The diplomat shook his head. "Extraordinary heroism."

"I don't claim I understood them all," Byron said. "Sometimes my eyes just passed over words. But I plowed on through."

"What books?" Thurston said.

"My darling here became slightly curious about the Germans," said Natalie, "after a Luftwaffe pilot almost shot his head off. He wanted to know a little more about them. Slote gave him a general syllabus of German nineteenth-century romanticism, nationalism, and idealism."

"Never dreaming he'd do anything about it," Slote said, turning his blank firelit glasses toward her.

"I had all this time in Siena last year," Byron said. "And I was interested."

"What did you find out?" said Thurston, refilling Byron's glass. "You couldn't get me to read German philosophy if the alternative were a firing squad."

"Mainly that Hitler's always been in the German bloodstream," Byron said, "and sooner or later had to break out. That's what Leslie told me in Berlin. He gave me the list to back up his view. I think he pretty well proved it. I used to think the Nazis had swarmed up out of the sewers and were something novel. But all their ideas, all their slogans, and practically everything they're doing is in the old books. That thing's been brewing in Germany for a hundred years."

"For longer than that," Slote said. "You've done your homework well, Byron. A-plus."

"Oh, balderdash!" Natalie exclaimed. "A-plus for what? Repeating a tired cliché? It's only novel to Byron because American education is so shallow and because he probably didn't absorb any he got."

"Not much," Byron said. "Mostly I played cards and ping-pong."

"Well, it's very evident." His bride's tone was sharp. "Or you wouldn't have gone boring through that one-sided list of his like a blind bookworm, just to give him a chance to patronize you."

"I deny the patronizing and the one-sidedness," said Slote. "Not that it matters, Jastrow—I guess I'll have to call you Henry now—but I think I covered the field, and I admire your hubby for tackling the job so earnestly."

"The whole thesis is banal and phony," Natalie said, "this idea that the Nazis are a culmination of German thought and culture. Hitler got his racism from Gobineau, a Frenchman, his Teutonic superiority from Chamberlain, an Englishman, and his Jew-baiting from Lueger, a Viennese political thug. The only German thinker you can really link straight to Hitler is Richard Wagner. He was another mad Jew-hating socialist, and Wagner's writings are all over *Mein Kampf*. But Nietzsche broke with Wagner over that malignant foolishness. Nobody takes Wagner seriously as a thinker, anyway. His music disgusts me too, though that's neither here nor there. I know you've read more in this field than I have, Slote, and I can't imagine why you gave Byron such a dreary loaded list. Probably just to scare him off with big names. But as you ought to know, he doesn't scare."

"I'm aware of that," Slote said. Abruptly he splashed wine into his glass, filling it to the brim, and emptied it without pausing for breath.

"Your veal's getting cold," Byron said to his bride. This unexpected edgy clash between Natalie and her ex-lover was threatening to get out of hand.

She tossed her head at him and impatiently cut a bit of meat, talking as she ate. "*We* created Hitler, more than anybody. We Americans. Mainly by not joining the League, and then by passing the insane Smoot-Hawley tariff in 1930, during a deep depression, knocking over Europe's economy like a row of dominoes. After Smoot-Hawley the German banks closed right and left. The Germans were starving and rioting. Hitler promised them jobs, law and order, and revenge for the last war. And he promised to crush the Communists. The Germans swallowed his revolution to fend off a Communist one. He's kept his promises, and he's held the Germans in line with terror, and that's the long and short of it. Why, there isn't a German in a thousand who's read those books, Briny. It's all a thick cloud of university gas. Hitler's a product of American isolation and British and French cowardice, not of the ideas of Hegel and Nietzsche."

"University gas is good, my dear," Slote said, "and I'll accept it." He touched his spread fingertips together, slouched in his chair, regarding her with a peculiar smile at once superior and frustrated. "In the sense that in any time and place the writings of the philosophers are a kind of exhaust gas of the evolving social machinery—a point that Hegel more or less makes, and that Marx took and vulgarized. But you can recover from an analysis of the gas what the engine must be like and how it works. And the ideas may be powerful and true, no matter how produced. German romanticism is a terribly important and powerful critique of the way the West lives, Jastrow. It faces all the nasty weaknesses."

"Such as?" Her tone was mean and abrupt.

A rush of argument broke from Slote, as though he wanted to conquer her with words in Byron's presence, if he could do nothing else. He began stabbing one finger in the air, like exclamation points to his sentences. "Such as, my dear, that Christianity is dead and rotting since Galileo cut its throat. Such as, that the ideas of the French and American revolutions are thin fairy tales about human nature. Such as, that the author of the Declaration of Independence owned Negro slaves. Such as, that the champions of liberty, equality, and faternity ended up chopping off the heads of helpless women, and each other's heads. The German has a very clear eye for such points, Natalie. He saw through the rot of Imperial Rome and smashed it, he saw through the rot of the Catholic Church and broke its back, and now he thinks Christian industrial democracy is a rotting sham, and he proposes to take over by force. His teachers have been telling him for a century that his turn is coming, and that cruelty and bloodshed are God's footprints in history. That's what's in the books I listed for Byron, poured out in great detail. It's a valid list. There was another strain in Germany, to be sure, a commonsense liberal humanist tendency linked with the West. The 'good Germany!' I know all about it, Natalie. Most of its leaders went over to Bismarck, and nearly all the rest followed the Kaiser. When his time came, Hitler had a waltz. Now listen!"

In a solemn tone, like a priest chanting a mass, beating time in the air with a stiff finger, Slote quoted: " *'The German revolution will not prove any milder or gentler because it was preceded by the* Critique *of Kant, by the*

*Transcendental Idealism of Fichte. These doctrines served
to develop revolutionary forces that only await their time
to break forth. Christianity subdued the brutal warrior
passion of the Germans, but it could not quench it. When
the cross, that restraining talisman, falls to pieces, then
will break forth again the frantic Berserker rage. The old
stone gods will then arise from the forgotten ruins and
wipe from their eyes the dust of centuries. Thor with his
giant hammer will arise again, and he will shatter the
Gothic cathedrals.' "*

Slote made an awkward, weak gesture with a fist to
represent a hammerblow, and went on: " *'Smile not at the
dreamer who warns you against Kantians, Fichteans, and
the other philosophers. Smile not at the fantasy of one
who foresees in the region of reality the same outburst of
revolution that has taken place in the region of intellect.
The thought precedes the deed as the lightning the thunder.
German thunder is of true German character. It is not very
nimble, but rumbles along somewhat slowly. But come it
will, and when you hear a crashing such as never before
has been heard in the world's history, then know that at
last the German thunderbolt has fallen.'*

"Heine—the Jew who composed the greatest German
poetry, and who fell in love with German philosophy—
Heine wrote that," Slote said in a quieter tone. "He wrote
that a hundred and six years ago."

Behind him chairs rasped, and a party in evening
clothes, cheerily chattering in German, flanked by three
bobbing, ducking waiters, came to the big table by the
fire. Slote was jostled; glancing over his shoulder, he
looked straight into the face of the Gestapo chief, who
amiably smiled and bowed. With him was the man with
the scarred forehead they had seen in the hotel, and
another German with a shaved head, and three giggling
Portuguese women in bright evening dresses.

"End of philosophy seminar," muttered Bunky Thurston.

"Why?" said Byron.

"Because for one thing," Natalie snapped, "I'm bored
with it."

As the Germans sat down, conversation died throughout the restaurant. The Jews were looking warily toward

them. In the lull, only the boisterous and oblivious British parties sounded louder.

"Who are those English people?" Natalie said to Thurston.

"Expatriates, living here because it's cheap and there's no rationing. Also, I guess, because it's out of range of Luftwaffe bombs," Thurston said. "The British embassy staff isn't crazy about them."

"That's a remarkable quote from Heine," Byron said to Slote.

"I wrote a paper on Hegel and Heine at Oxford." Slote smiled thinly. "Heine was fascinated by Hegel for a long time, then repudiated him. I translated that passage for an epigraph. The rhetoric is rather purple. So is Jeremiah's. Jewish prophets have one vein."

As they were drinking coffee, a pink spotlight clove the dark room, striking a gray curtain on a little platform. Bunky Thurston said, "Here he comes. He's the best of the *fado* singers."

"The best of what?" Byron said. A pale dark-eyed young man, in a black cloak with thick fringes, stepped through the curtain holding an onion-shaped guitar.

"*Fado* singers. Fate songs. Very pathetic, very Portuguese."

At the first chords that the young man struck—strong sharp sad chords, in a hammering rhythm—the restaurant grew still. He sang in a clear high florid voice, looking around with his black eyes, his high bulging forehead pink in the spotlight. Natalie murmured to Thurston, "What song is that?"

"That's an old one, the *fado* of the students."

"What do the words mean?"

"Oh, the words never amount to anything. Just a sentence or two. That one says, 'Close your eyes. Life is simpler with your eyes closed.' "

The glance of the newlyweds met. Byron put his hand over Natalie's.

The young man sang several songs, with strange moments of speeding up, slowing down, sobbing, and trilling; these evidently were the essence of *fado,* because when he performed such flourishes in the middle of a song, the Portuguese in the room applauded and sometimes cheered.

"Lovely," Natalie murmured to Bunky Thurston when a song ended. "Thank you."

He smoothed his moustache with both hands. "I thought you'd find it agreeable. It's something different."

"Spieler! Können Sie 'O Sole Mio' singen?" The shaven-headed German was addressing the singer. He sat only a few feet from the platform.

Smiling uneasily, the singer replied in Portuguese, gesturing at his oddly shaped guitar, that he only performed *fado* songs. In a jolly tone, the German told him to sing "O Sole Mio" anyway. Again the young man made helpless gestures, shaking his head. The German pointed a smoking cigar at him, and shouted something in Portuguese that brought dead quiet in the restaurant, even among the British, and froze the faces of the three women at his table. With a piteous look around at the audience, the young performer began to do "O Sole Mio," very badly. The German leaned back, beating time in the air with his cigar. A thick pall fell in the restaurant.

Natalie said to Thurston, "Let's leave now."

"I'm for that."

The singer was still stumbling through the Italian song as they walked out. On the counter at the entrance, under a picture of him, phonograph records in paper slipcovers were piled. "If that first song is there," Natalie said to Byron, "buy me a record."

He bought two.

The streetlights outside were brighter than the illumination in the restaurant, and the wind was cutting. Leslie Slote, tying a muffler around his neck, said to Byron, "When do you leave?"

"Not till day after tomorrow."

"Years hence, the way I'm counting time," said Natalie with a note of defiance, hugging her husband's arm.

"Well, Natalie, shall I try to get us on a plane to Rome Saturday?"

"Oh, wait. Maybe he won't leave. I can always hope."

"Of course." Slote held out his hand to Byron. "If I don't see you again, congratulations, and good luck, and smooth sailing."

"Thanks. And thanks for that suite. It was brash of us to put you out of it."

"My dear fellow," said Slote, "it was quite wasted on me."

*   *   *

All her limbs jerking, Natalie woke from a nightmare of Gestapo men knocking at the door. She heard real knocking in the darkness. She lay still, hoping that a trace of the nightmare was hovering in her fogged brain, and that the knocking would stop. It did not. She looked at her luminous watch and touched Byron's warm hairy leg.

"Byron! Byron!"

He raised himself on an elbow, then sat up straight. "What time is it?"

"Quarter to two."

The knocking became faster and louder. Byron jumped from the bed and slipped into a robe.

"Briny, be careful about letting anyone in! First make sure who it is."

Natalie left the warm nest of the bed and was putting on a negligee, shivering in the chilly night air, when Byron opened the bedroom door. "It's only Aster, so don't be scared."

"What does he want?"

"That's what I'm finding out."

The door shut. Natalie went and leaned her ear against it, and heard Tobruk mentioned. Humiliated at having to eavesdrop, she rattled the knob and went in. The two young men rose from the sofa where they sat hunched in talk. Lieutenant Aster, in a blue and gold uniform and white peaked cap, was eating an apple.

"Hi, Natalie. This is one terrible thing to do, breaking in on honeymooners," he said cheerily. "Talk about extrahazardous duty!"

"What's the matter?"

Byron said, "Change of orders, nothing serious or urgent, no sweat."

"Right. Matter of fact I was just shoving off." Lieutenant Aster dropped the apple core in a tray. "I have to round up some crew members that had overnights. It's going to be an interesting tour of Estoril and Lisbon after dark. See you, Byron."

With a grin at her, and a brief tip of his rakishly tilted hat, the lieutenant left.

"Well? Tell me." Natalie confronted her husband, arms folded.

Byron went to the red marble fireplace and touched a match to papers under a pile of kindling and logs. "The *S-45* leaves this morning."

"This very morning, eh? Too bad. Where to?"

"I don't know. The fall of Tobruk has changed the mission—which to tell you the truth, I never exactly knew in the first place. Something about surveying submarine facilities in the Mediterranean."

"Well. All right. I guess I asked for this. My entire married life—as it may yet turn out—cut short by one-third."

"Natalie, our married life starts when you get back from Italy." He put his arm around her and they stood watching the fire brighten. "It's going to be very long, happy, and fruitful. I plan on six kids."

This made the young wife laugh through her gloom and put a hand to his face. "Oh lord. Six! I'll never last the course. Jiminy, that fire feels marvellous. Did we finish the wine before we went to sleep? Look and see." He brought a glass of wine and lit a cigarette for her. "Briny, one thing you should know. Back in November, Aaron was so sick he thought he might die. I had to take him to a specialist in Rome. It was a kidney stone. He lay in the Excelsior for two weeks, really in torture. Finally it cleared up, but one night, when he was very low, Aaron told me that he'd left everything he has to me. And he told me what it added up to. I was amazed." She smiled at him, sipping her wine. Byron looked at her with slitted eyes. "I guess he's sort of a miser, like most bachelors. That's one reason he moved to Italy. He can live handsomely there on very little. Aaron's actually kept nearly all the money he made on *A Jew's Jesus,* and it brings in more every year. The book on Paul earned quite a bit too. And before that he'd saved a lot of his professor's salary. Living in Italy, he hasn't even paid taxes. Aside from the value of his house, Aaron's worth more than a hundred thousand dollars. He lives just on his interest. The money is invested back in New York. I had no idea of any of this. Not the slightest. That he would leave anything to me never crossed my mind. Nevertheless, that's how things stand." Natalie took Byron's chin in her hand and pushed it this way and that. "What are you looking so grim about? I'm telling you you've married an heiress."

Byron poked a fallen red coal back into the fire. "Damn. He's really cute. Cuter than I thought."

"Are you being fair? Especially with your plan for six kids?"

"Possibly not." Byron shrugged. "Do you have enough money to get home with? You're coming home in two months, no matter what."

"I know. I agreed to that. I have plenty. Whew, that fire's beginning to scorch." She reclined on a couch before the blaze. The negligee fell away, and the light played warmly on her smooth legs. "Briny, does your family know you intended to get married?"

"No. No sense making trouble when I wasn't sure it would come off. I did write Warren."

"Is he still in Hawaii?"

"Yes. He and Janice love it. I think you and I may well land there. The Navy keeps beefing up the Pacific Fleet. Warren thinks we'll be fighting Japan soon. That's the feeling all through the Navy."

"Not Germany?"

"No. It may sound strange to you, sitting here, but our people still don't get excited about Hitler. A few newspapers and magazines froth around, but that's about it."

He sat on the floor at her feet, looking at the fire, resting his head against her soft uncovered thigh. She caressed his hair. "Exactly when do you leave, and how?"

"Lady's going to come back for me at six."

"Six? Why, that's hours and hours. Big big chunk of our marriage left to enjoy. Of course you have to pack."

"Ten minutes."

"Can I go with you to the boat?"

"I don't see why not."

With a deep sigh, Natalie said, "Why are you sitting on the floor? Come here."

There was no dawn. The sky turned paler and paler until it was light gray. Mist and drizzle hid the sea.

Lieutenant Aster picked them up in a rattling little French car; the back seat was packed with four glum sailors smelling of alcohol and vomit. He drove with one hand, leaning far out to work a broken windshield wiper, keeping the accelerator on the floor. The foggy road along the river was empty, and they reached Lisbon quickly.

The submarine was dwarfed by a very rusty tramp steamer berthed directly ahead, with an enormous Stars and Stripes painted on its side, an American flag flying, and the name *Yankee Belle* stencilled in great drippy white letters on bow and stern. Its grotesquely cut-up shape and crude rivetted plating looked foreign, and thirty or forty years old. It rode so high in the water that much of its propeller and mossy red bottom showed. Jews lined the quay in the drizzle, waiting quietly to go aboard, most of them with cardboard suitcases, cloth bundles, and frayed clothes. The children—there were quite a number —stood silent, clinging to their parents. At a table by the gangway, two uniformed Portuguese officials, under umbrellas held by assistants, were inspecting and stamping papers. Policemen in rubber capes paced up and down the queue. The rail of the ship was black with passengers staring at the quay and the Lisbon hills, as freed prisoners look back at the jail to savor their liberty.

"When did that ocean greyhound show up?" Byron said.

"Yesterday morning. It's an old Polish bucket, and the crew are mostly Greeks and Turks," Aster said. "I've tried talking to them. The pleasanter ones seem to be professional cutthroats. I gather the Jews will be packed in like sardines in five-decker bunks, for which they'll pay the price of deluxe suites on the *Queen Mary*. These fellows laughed like hell about that." He glanced at his wristwatch. "Well, we cast off at 0715. Good-bye, Natalie, and good luck. You were a beautiful bride, and now you're a beautiful Navy wife."

The exec stepped aboard, smartly returning the salute of the gangway watch. On the dock near the gangway, unmindful of the rain beginning to fall, a sailor was hugging and kissing a dumpy Portuguese trollop dressed in red satin. Byron held out his arms to his wife, with a glance at the sailor and a grin. She embraced him. "You fool. Your trouble is, you went and married the creature."

"I was drunk," Byron said. He kissed her again and again.

A boatswain's whistle blew on the submarine, and a loudspeaker croaked, *"Now station the special sea details."*

"Well, I guess this is it," he said. "So long."

Natalie was managing not to cry; she even smiled. "Getting married was the right idea, my love. I mean that. It was an inspiration, and I adore you for it. I feel very married. I love you and I'm happy."

"I love you."

Byron went aboard the submarine, saluting as he stepped on deck. In the thickening drizzle, her raincoat pulled close, her breath smoking in the damp frigid air, Natalie stood on the dock, smelling wharfside odors—tar, machinery, fish, the sea—hearing the bleak cry of the gulls, and feeling for the first time what she had gotten herself into. She was a Navy wife all right!

Three men in black trench coats and oversized fedora hats came strolling along the quay, calmly inspecting the refugees, who either tried to ignore them or peered at them in horror. Women pulled their children closer. The men halted near the gangway; one pulled papers from a black portfolio, and they all began talking to the officials at the table. Meanwhile on the submarine sailors in pea coats pulled in the gangplank. The boatswain's whistle blew; the loudspeaker squawked. Appearing on the narrow little bridge in foul-weather clothes, the captain and Lieutenant Aster waved. "Good-bye, Natalie," Captain Caruso called. She did not see Byron come out on the forecastle, but after a while noticed him standing near the anchor among the sailors, in a khaki uniform and a brown windbreaker, hands in his back pockets, trousers flapping in the breeze. It was the first time she had ever seen Byron in a uniform; it made him seem different, remote, and older. Aster was shouting orders through a megaphone. Colored signal flaps ran up. The sailors hauled in the lines. Byron walked along the forecastle and stood opposite his bride, almost close enough to reach out and clasp hands. She blew him a kiss. His face under the peaked khaki cap was business-like and calm. A foghorn blasted. The submarine fell away from the dock and black water opened between them.

"You come home, now," he shouted.

"I will. Oh, I swear I will."

"I'll be waiting. Two months!"

He went to his duty station. With a swish of water from the propellers, the low black submarine dimmed away into the drizzle.

Craaa! Craaa! Craaa! Mournfully screeching, the gulls wheeled and followed the fading wake.

Natalie hurried up the quay, past the Gestapo men, past the line of escaping Jews, whose eyes were all fixed in one direction—the gangway table they still had to pass, where the Portuguese officials and the three Germans were comparing papers and laughing together. Natalie's hand sweatily clutched the American passport in her pocket.

"Hello, old Slote," she said, when she found a telephone and managed to make the connection. "This is Mrs. Byron Henry. Are you interested in buying me a breakfast? I seem to be free. Then let's push on to Italy, dear, and get Aaron out. I have to go home."

39

IN Washington Victor Henry was reassigned to War Plans. He did not hear from Roosevelt at all. People said the President was unaccountable, and from firsthand knowledge, the naval captain was beginning to believe it. But he was untroubled by the assignment, though he had craved and expected sea duty.

More than anything else—more than the gray hairs beginning to show at his temples, more than the sharper lines on his forehead and around his mouth, more than his calmer pace on the tennis court—his contentment with still another desk job showed how Victor Henry was changing.

Washington in January 1941, after London and Berlin, struck him as a depressing panorama of arguments, parties, boozing, confusion, lethargy, and luxury, ominously like Paris before the fall. It took him a long time to get used to brilliantly lit streets, rivers of cars, rich overabundant food, and ignorant indifference to the war. The military men and their wives, when Pug talked to them, discussed only the hairline advantages that the distant explosions might bring in their own tiny lives. Navy classmates of his calibre were stepping into the major sea commands that led to flag rank. He knew he was regarded as a hard-luck guy, a comer sunk by bureaucratic mischance. But he had almost stopped caring. He cared about the war; and he cared about the future of the United States, which looked dark to him.

The Navy was as preoccupied as ever by Japan. Every decision of the President to strengthen the Atlantic Fleet caused angry buzzes and knowing headshakes in the Department, and at the Army and Navy Club. When he tried to talk about the Germans, his friends tended to regard him askance; a bypassed crank, their amused glances almost said, trying to inflate his importance by exaggerating minor matters he happened to know about. The roaring debate over Lend-Lease, in Congress and the newspapers, seemed to him a farrago of illogic and irrelevance. It suited Hitler's book at the moment not to declare war on the United States—that was all. It apparently suited the American people in turn to fake neutrality while commencing a sluggish, grudging effort on the British side, arguing every inch of the way. These two simple facts were being lost in the storm of words.

Pug Henry was content in the War Plans Division because here he worked in another world, a secret, very small world of hard-boiled reality. Early in January, with a few other officers in War Plans, he had begun "conversations" with British military men. In theory, Lord Burne-Wilke and his delegation were in Washington on vague missions of observing or purchase. Supposedly the talks were low-level explorations binding on nobody, and supposedly the President, the Army Chief of Staff, and the Chief of Naval Operations took no cognizance of them. In fact, by the first of March these conferences were finishing up a written war operations plan on a world scale. The assumption was that Japan would sooner or later attack, and the key decision of the agreement lay in two words: "Germany first." It heartened Victor Henry that the American Army and Air Corps planners concurred in this, and also, to his considerable surprise and pleasure, Admiral Benton and two other naval colleagues who had thought the war through—unlike the rest of the Navy, still rolling along in the greased grooves of the old drills and war games against "Orange," the code name for Japan.

It was clear to Pug Henry that if Japan entered the war, with her annual steel production of only a few million tons, she could not hold out long if Germany were beaten. But if the Germans knocked out the British and got the fleet, they could go on to conquer whole continents, getting stronger as they went, whatever happened to Japan. From his conversations at the Army and Navy Club he knew that this "Germany first" decision would, if it came out, create a fearsome howl. He was one of a handful of Americans—perhaps less than twenty, from the President downward—who knew about it. This was a peculiar way to run national affairs, perhaps; but to his amazement, which never quite faded, this was how things were going. To be part of this crucial anonymous work satisfied him.

It was passing strange to arrive in the morning at the drab little offices in a remote wing of the old Navy Building, and sit down with the British for another day of work on global combat plans, after reading in the morning papers, or hearing on the radio, yesterday's shrill Lend-Lease argument in Congress. Pug could not get over the cool dissembling of the few high officials who knew of the "conversations." He kept wondering about a form of government which required such deviousness in its chiefs, and such soothing, cajoling fibs to get its legislators to act sensibly. Once the planners, weary after a hammering day, sat in their shirt-sleeves around a radio, listening to General Marshall testify before a Senate committee. They heard this Army Chief of Staff, whose frosty remote uprightness made Henry think of George Washington, assure the senators that no intention existed for America to enter the war, and that at present there was no need for any large buildup of its armed forces. The planners had just been discussing an allocation of troops based on an American army of five million in 1943, a projection of which Marshall was well aware.

"I don't know," Pug remarked to Burne-Wilke, "maybe the only thing you can say for democracy is that all other forms of government are even worse."

"Worse for what?" was the air commodore's acid reply. "If other forms are better for winning wars, no other virtue counts."

Pug got along well with Burne-Wilke, who had fully grasped the landing craft problem. Among the planners, a labored joke was spreading about Captain Henry's girlfriend, "Elsie"; this was in fact a play on l.c. (landing craft), which he kept stressing as the limiting factor of operations in all theatres. Pug had worked up formulas converting any troop movement across water into types and quantities of landing craft, and these formulas threw cold water on many an ambitious and plausible plan. Somebody would usually say, "Pug's girl Elsie acting up again"; and Burne-Wilke always supported his insistence on this bottleneck.

Henry seldom encountered Pamela Tudsbury, whom the air commodore had brought along as his typist-aide. Tucked in an office in the British Purchasing Mission, she evidently worked like a dog, for her face was always haggard. A glad shock had coursed through him when he first saw Pamela, standing at Burne-Wilke's elbow, regarding him with glowing eyes. She had not written that she was coming. They met for a drink just once. Pug amplified all he could on his letter about the meeting with Ted Gallard. She looked extremely young to him; and his gust of infatuation with this girl after the bombing mission seemed, in the bustling Willard bar in Washington, a distant and hardly believable episode. Yet the hour with her was warmly pleasurable. Any day thereafter when he saw her was a good day for him. He left these encounters to chance. He did not telephone her, nor ask her to meet him again; and while she always acted glad to see him, she made no move to do so more often.

As a college boy thinks about fame, and an exile about going home, this Navy captain of forty-nine once in a while mused on what a romance with the young Englishwoman might be like; but it was the merest daydreaming. He remained devoted to his wife, in his fashion. Rhoda had received her husband back with a puzzling mixture of moods—demonstrative affection, and even lust, alternating with spells of heavy gloom, coldness, and loud irascibility over her move back to Washington from New York. She levelled off to a low-temperature detachment, busying herself with Bundles for Britain and her old-time music committees, and making numerous trips to New York for one reason or another. She sometimes mentioned Palmer Kirby, now one of the chairmen of Bundles for Britain, in a most casual way. Rhoda went to church with Pug, and sang the hymns, and relayed gossip about unfaithful Navy wives, all exactly as before. She was plainly disappointed when Pug went back to War Plans instead of getting a command at sea. But they settled back into their old routines, and Pug soon was too preoccupied to worry much about Rhoda's moods, which had always been jagged.

News about their children intermittently drew them together. Byron's offhand letter about his hasty marriage in Lisbon was a shock. They talked for days about it, worrying, agonizing, comforting each other, before resigning themselves to live with the fact. Warren as usual sent the good news. His wife was returning to Washington to have her baby, and he had been promoted to lieutenant.

Pug turned fifty on a Sunday early in March. He sat in church beside his wife, trying, as he listened to the choir sing "Holy, Holy, Holy," to shake off a sense that he had missed all the right turns in life. He counted his blessings. His wife was still beautiful, still capable of love; if she had failings, what woman didn't? His two sons were naval officers, his daughter was self-supporting and clever. Perhaps his career had gone off the rails, but he was serving in a post where he was doing some good. He could not really complain.

Rhoda, as she sat there beside him, was thinking mainly about the fact that her husband, for the first time since his return from abroad, would soon be meeting Palmer Kirby face to face.

* * *

A snowstorm clogged the capital on the night of Rhoda's dinner party. By quarter past seven her guests, including Kirby, had straggled in, brushing and stamping off snow, but the dinner was still stalled. Pug was missing.

In the cramped hot kitchen of an elegant little furnished house on Tracy Place, rented from a millionaire bachelor who was now the ambassador to Brazil, Rhoda made a last-minute check of the dinner and found all in order: soup hot, ducks tender, vegetables on the boil, cook snarling over the delay. She sailed out to her guests after a scowl in the hallway mirror and a touch at her hairdo. Rhoda wore a silvery dress molded to her figure; her color was high, her eyes bright with nervous excitement. In the living room, Kirby and Pamela Tudsbury were talking on the big couch, Madeline and Janice had their heads together in a corner, and on facing settees before a log fire, Alistair Tudsbury and Lord Burne-Wilke were chatting with the recently elected Senator Lacouture and his wife. It was a hodgepodge company, but since it was only for a hurried dinner before a Bundles for Britain concert, she was not too concerned. Pug's meeting with Kirby was the chief thing on her mind.

"We'll wait ten more minutes." Rhoda sat herself beside the scientist. "Then we'll have to eat. I'm on the committee."

"Where is Captain Henry?" Pamela said calmly. Her mauve dress came to a halter around her neck, leaving her slim shoulders naked; her tawny hair was piled high on her head. Rhoda remembered Pamela Tudsbury as a mousy girl, but this was no mouse; Rhoda recognized Kirby's expression of lazy genial appetite.

"I'm blessed if I can say. Military secrecy covers a multitude of sins, doesn't it?" Rhoda laughed. "Let's hope he's working on defense, and not a blonde."

"I very much doubt that it's a blonde," said Pamela. "Not Captain Henry."

"Oh, these goody-goody ones are the worst, my dear. That's a divine dress."

"Do you like it? Thank you." Pamela adjusted the skirt. "I feel all got up for a pantomime, almost. I've been in uniform day and night for weeks."

"Does Lord Burne-Wilke drive you that hard?"

"Oh no, Mrs. Henry. There really are masses of things to do. I feel so lucky at being in Washington, that I guess I work off my guilt with the late hours."

"The Waring Hotel then would be the best bet, Pamela?" Kirby's tone took up the conversation Rhoda had broken into.

"If they've repaired the bomb damage. By now, they should have. The Germans went after Buckingham Palace very hard, and the whole neighborhood took quite a beating, but that was back in October."

"I'll shoot a cable to the Waring tomorrow."

"Why, Palmer, are you going to London?" said Rhoda. Kirby turned to her, crossing his long legs. "It appears so."

"Isn't that something new?"

"It's been in the works for a while."

"London! How adventurous." Rhoda laughed, covering her surprise.

Mrs. Lacouture's voice rose above the talk. "Janice, should you be drinking all those martinis?"

"Oh, Mother," said Janice, as the white-coated old Filipino, a retired Navy steward hired by Rhoda for the evening, shakily filled the glass in her outstretched hand.

"That baby will be born with an olive in its mouth," remarked the senator. The two Englishmen laughed heartily, and Lacouture's pink face wrinkled up with self-satisfaction.

"So, you did see Byron," Janice said to Madeline. "When was this?"

"A couple of weeks ago. His submarine put in at the Brooklyn Navy Yard overnight. He took me to dinner."

"How was he?"

"He's—I don't know—more distant. Almost chilly. I don't think he likes the Navy much."

"Maybe he doesn't like being married much," Janice said. "I never heard of anything so peculiar! A couple of days of whoop-de-do in Lisbon, and back she goes to Italy, and off he chugs in his little S-boat. Why on earth did they bother to get married?"

"Well, possibly a Jewish girl would insist," Madeline said in arch tones.

Janice laughed shortly. "That may well be. I'll say this,

she's a mighty bright and pretty one." She grimaced, moving her large stomach under her flowing green gown, trying to get more comfortable. "Ugh, what a bloated cow I am. This is what it all leads to, honey. Never forget it. And how's your love life?"

"Oh dear. Well—" Madeline glanced toward her mother. "You remember that trombone player? With the big sad eyes, the one who dressed all in brown?"

"That Communist? Oh, Madeline, don't tell me—"

"Oh, no, no. Bozey was an utter drip. But I went with him to this peace rally at Madison Square Garden. It was really something, Jan! Packed, and this gigantic red, white, and blue sign stretching clear across the Garden—THE YANKS ARE NOT COMING"—Madeline waved her hands far apart—"and all these Loyalist Spain songs, and these mass chants they do, and novelists and poets and college professors making red-hot antiwar speeches and whatnot. Well, there was this other fellow in our box. He writes horror programs. He's very successful, he makes about five hundred dollars a week, and he's handsome, but he's another Communist." Madeline sneezed, blew her nose, and looked slyly at Janice. "What do you think would jolt my family more, Byron's Jewish girl or a Communist? Bob comes from Minnesota, he's a Swede at least. He's awfully nice."

Janice said, "What about that boss of yours?"

"Hugh Cleveland? What about him?"

The two young women regarded each other. Wry knowing wrinkles turned up the corners of Janice's mouth. Madeline colored under the rouge and powder on her pallid face. "Yes? Why the grin, Janice?" She drank most of her martini.

"Oh, I don't know. You keep taking up with one impossible fellow after another."

"If you mean am I lying in wait for Mr. Cleveland," Madeline said with her father's briskness, "you're about as wrong as you can be. He's a paunchy pink-haired freckled man, ten years older than I am, and personally I regard him as a snake."

"Snakes have the power to hypnotize, dear."

"Yes, rabbits and birds. I'm neither."

Rhoda went to a small Chinese Chippendale desk to

answer the telephone. "Oh, *hello* there," she said. "Where are you? . . . Oh, my gawd . . . of course . . . yes, naturally. Okay. I'll leave your ticket at the box office. Yes, yes, they've been here for hours. Right. Bye, dear."

She hung up, and fluttered her long pale hands at the company. "Well, let's drink up. Pug sends apologies. He's at the White House and he doesn't know when he can get away."

In Washington, when the absent diner is at the White House, the empty chair is not an embarrassment. Quite the contrary. Nobody asked what Victor Henry was doing at the executive mansion, or indeed commented on Rhoda's words. She put Burne-Wilke on her right and the senator on her left, saying, "After all these years protocol still baffles me. How do you choose between a United States Senator and a British lord? I'm favoring our foreign guest, Senator."

"Absolutely proper," said Lacouture.

Alistair Tudsbury said, "Lord Burne-Wilke will gladly yield you his seat on this occasion, Senator, if he can take yours when Lend-Lease comes to a vote."

"Oh, done, done," exclaimed the air commodore, whose bemedalled dress uniform dazzled Rhoda.

Everyone laughed, Tudsbury loudest of all. "Haw haw haw!" The correspondent's belly shook under a vast expanse of wrinkled waistcoat, spanned by an enormous suspension of gold chain. Rhoda said, "Well, what good spirits! I was half afraid our English friends would eat Senator Lacouture alive."

The senator wrinkled his eyes. "You British aren't that hard up for meat yet, are you?" He added after the laugh, "No, seriously, Rhoda, I'm glad you brought us together. Maybe I've convinced our friends that I'm not a Nazi-lover, but just one fellow out of ninety-six, with my own point of view. I certainly don't go for this talk of Senator Wheeler's, that Lend-Lease will plow under every fourth American boy. That's way out of bounds. But if Roosevelt wants to send England arms free of charge, why the devil doesn't he come out and *say* so, instead of giving us all this Lend-Lease baloney? It insults our intelligence."

"I went to a peace rally in New York," Madeline piped up. "One speaker told a good story. A tramp stops a rich man on the street. 'Please, mister, give me a quarter, I'm starving,' he says. The rich man says, 'My dear fellow, I can't *give* you a quarter. I can *lend* you or *lease* you a quarter.' "

Senator Lacouture burst out laughing. "By God, I'll work that into my next speech."

From across the table, Palmer Kirby said, "Are you sure you want to draw on a Communist source?"

"Was that one of those Commie meetings? Well, a story's a story."

"It's so crazy," said Janice. "I got stuck in a taxi on Pennsylvania Avenue this afternoon, in front of the White House. We just couldn't move. The newsreel people were there, taking pictures of the pickets. Communists with signs marching round and round in a circle, chanting, 'The Yanks are not coming,' and next to them a mob of women kneeling and praying right there on the sidewalk in the snow, The Christian Mothers of America. They'll pray there round the clock, my driver said, until Lend-Lease is defeated or vetoed. Honestly! Coming from Hawaii, I get the feeling the country's going mad."

"It just shows how broad the opposition to this thing is," said the senator. "Cuts across all lines."

"On the contrary," put in Kirby, "both extremes seem to be against helping England, while the mass in the middle is for it."

Senator Lacouture waved a flat hand in the air. "No, sir. I've been a middle-of-the-roader all my life. You should hear some of the quiet talk in the Senate dining room. I tell you, if they didn't have to worry about the big-city Jews—and I don't blame the Jews for feeling as they do, but this issue can't be decided on any parochial basis—there'd be twenty more votes on my side of the fence right now. I still think they'll end there. The nose count changes every day. If the ground swell continues for another week, we'll lick this thing."

The street door opened and closed. Victor Henry came into the dining room, brushing flakes of snow from his blue bridge coat. "Apologies to all hands," he said, doffing the coat. "No, no, don't get up, I'll just join you, and change my duds later."

But the men were all standing. Victor Henry walked

around the table for handshakes, and came last to Palmer Kirby. "Hello," he said. "It's been a long time."

"Sure has. Too long."

Only Rhoda knew the scientist well enough to note that his smile was awkward and artificial. At this moment, which she had been dreading for a couple of weeks, Rhoda had a surprising sensation—pleasure and pride that two such men loved her. She felt no trace of guilt as her lover clasped hands with her husband of twenty-five years. Kirby was more than a head taller than Captain Henry, and in the columnar black and white of full dress he was a magnificent fellow. Yet Pug was impressive too: erect, short, thickset, his tired eyes in deep sockets very shrewd and alive, his whole bearing charged with energy—her own husband, just back from the White House. Rhoda felt lucky, beautiful, desired, pleasantly confused, and quite safe. It was actually one of the nicest moments in her life, and it went off like a dream. Pug took his seat and began eating shrimp cocktail.

"Say, it's a bit late for this," he remarked to Kirby, "but I sure want to thank you for driving Rhoda up from New York last summer to see Byron at sub school. That was a long way."

Kirby spread his big hands. "Why, it was great to get a look at a submarine base. Your friend Captain Tully really gave us the ten-dollar tour."

"Red Tully is 4.0," Pug said. "I sort of suspect he nudged Byron through that school. However, I've asked no questions."

It was exciting as a play for Rhoda, that the two men were actually talking straight off about that fateful trip. She said gaily, "Oh, Pug, you're always selling poor Briny short. Red told us he was the champion of his class in the training tank. Caught on to the lung right away, and did his escape perfectly the first time cool as a fish. Why, when we were there they had him instructing in the tank."

"That's self-preservation, not work. Briny's always been good at that."

"That's a talent, too," said Pamela Tudsbury.

Pug looked at her with a trace of special warmth. "Well, Pamela, one can't get far without it, that's true. But it's the talent of a turtle."

"Honestly! Did you ever?" Rhoda said to Lord Burne-Wilke. "What a father."

Mrs. Lacouture uttered a little shriek. The old steward was offering soup to Lord Burne-Wilke, and distracted by the Englishman's medals, he was tilting the tray. The open soup tureen went slipping toward Rhoda, and her silver dress was seconds away from ruin. But as the tureen came sliding off the tray, Rhoda, who had a watchful eye for servants, plucked it out of the air, and with the quick controlled movements of a cat in trouble, set it on the table, not spilling a drop.

Pug called out over the gasps and laughter, "Well done."

"Self-preservation runs in the family," Rhoda said. Amid louder laughter, Alistair Tudsbury started a round of applause.

"By God! Never have I seen anything so neat," exclaimed Senator Lacouture.

Everybody had a joke or a compliment for Rhoda. She became exhilarated. Rhoda loved to entertain. She had the ability to nail down details beforehand, and then breeze airily through the evening. Rhoda told stories of mishaps at dinner parties in Berlin, and began to reminisce with sharp satire about the Nazis. Forgotten was her former friendliness to the Germans; she was now the Bundles for Britain lady, partisan to the core. Palmer Kirby, getting over his stiffness in Pug's presence, threw in his experiences at a Nuremberg *Parteitag*. Pug offered an account of the slide at Abendruh, making the women giggle. Then Lord Burne-Wilke gave jocular anecdotes about the arrogance of captured Luftwaffe pilots.

Senator Lacouture interrupted him. "Lord Burne-Wilke, were you people ever really in trouble last year?"

"Oh, rather." The air commodore told of the dwindling of planes and pilots through July and August, of the week in September when the count of pilots fell below the survival minimum, of the desperate pessimism in the RAF all through October, with London burning, civilians dying in large numbers, no night fighters available, and the Luftwaffe still coming on and on, setting fire to residential districts and bombing and spreading the fires, trying to break the city's spirit.

Lacouture probed with more questions, his pink face

growing sober. The RAF, the air commodore said, was anticipating a new, larger onslaught in the spring and summer. The submarine sinkings, at their present rate, might ground the British planes for lack of fuel. An invasion would then be in the cards. "Mind you, we hope to weather all this," he said, "but this time, Hitler may have the wherewithal. He's expanded his armed forces massively. We haven't been idle either. But unfortunately a lot of our stuff is ending up these days at the bottom of the Atlantic."

Lacouture's fingers were rolling little balls of bread. He looked straight at the air commodore. "Well," he said, "nobody's comparing the British and the Nazis as people, as civilizations. You people have been fine, and I'll tell you, possibly we should be hearing a bit more of this stuff up on the hill."

Lord Burne-Wilke, with a humble little bow that made the party laugh, said, "I'm available."

While the others had dessert, Victor Henry changed into his dress uniform. The guests were wrapping up to brave the snow when he rejoined them. He helped Pamela Tudsbury into her coat, scenting perfume that stirred his memory.

She said over her shoulder, "There's news of Ted."

For a moment Victor Henry didn't understand. On the *Bremen* she had slipped across the joke about Hitler in just that swift quiet way. "Oh? Really? Good or bad?"

"Won't you telephone me?"

"Yes."

"Do. Please do. Do."

The party separated into three cars, with Pug driving the British guests. He said to the air commodore, as they stopped on Massachusetts Avenue at a red light that made a cherry-colored halo in the falling snow, "You scored some points with Senator Lacouture."

"Words over wine," said the air commodore, shrugging.

＊　＊　＊

"Well! Nobody's seen Constitution Hall looking like this before," Rhoda said, "or ever will again, maybe. It's fantastic."

Every seat was filled. All the men in the orchestra, and many up the long side slopes wore full dress suits or gold-crusted military uniforms. The women made a sea of un-covered skin, bright colors, and winking gems. Great American and British flags draped the stage. Rhoda had taken for herself two boxes nearest to the President's. The Lacoutures with Janice, the air commodore, and Alistair Tudsbury were ensconced in the choicer one, and she and Pamela sat at the rail in the other, with Pug and Kirby behind them, and Madeline in the rear.

A commotion arose in the aisle behind them among police guards and latecomers. A murmur washed across the auditorium, and the Vice President and his wife stepped into the presidential box, into a blue-white spotlight. The audience stood and applauded. Henry Wallace responded with a self-conscious smile and a brief wave. He looked like an intelligent farmer, unhappily wearing full dress for some anniversary. The orchestra struck up "The Star-Spangled Banner," and then "God Save the King." The British anthem, with the nearness of Pamela Tudsbury's bare white shoulders, awakened the London days and nights in Victor Henry's mind. As the audience settled in its seats and the violins began the slow introduction of a Haydn symphony, Pug's thoughts wandered through the blitz, the bombing run over Berlin, the German capital showing yellow in the night under the flare of the explod-ing gas, Pamela flinging herself at him as he came into his apartment. The music broke into a dancing allegro and brought him back to the present. Pug studied the profile of his wife, sitting in her usual concertgoing pose—back straight, hands folded in lap, head tilted to suggest at-tentive pleasure. He thought how charming she could be and how splendidly she had carried off the dinner. A wisp of guilt touched him for the affection he felt for Pamela Tudsbury. Victor Henry was inexpert at self-excuse, having done too few things in his life of which he disapproved.

Rhoda herself couldn't have been more at ease. The music of Haydn delighted her. She loved being highly visible in her new silver dress in a box so near the Vice President. She was pleased that the concert was a sellout. She looked forward to the supper-dance afterward. All this splendid fun was actually work in the noblest of causes, and her name stood high on the committee list. How could things be better? Only Palmer Kirby's news that he was going to England troubled her a bit. She meant to ask him more questions about *that*.

No doubt Dr. Kirby had his thoughts, and Pamela hers. The two intruders on the long marriage, with the husband and wife, looked much like dozens of other foursomes in boxes along both sides of the cavernous hall: attractive people, elegantly clad, calmly listening to music. Kirby was sitting behind Rhoda, Pug in back of Pamela Tudsbury. A stranger might have guessed that the tall people were one pair, the short ones another, except that the smaller woman seemed young for the naval officer with the weathered face and heavy eyebrows.

During the intermission crush, Victor Henry and Dr. Kirby were left together by the ladies in an overheated lobby foul with smoke. Pug said, "How's for a breath of air? Looks like the snow's stopped."

"You're on."

Chauffeurs were stamping by their limousines on the fresh snow. It was bitter cold. A few young music lovers from the rearmost seats, in sweaters and parkas, chatted with smoking breaths on the slushy steps of the hall.

Pug said, "Anything very new on uranium?"

The scientist looked at him with head aslant. "What's uranium?"

"Are you that far along?" Pug grinned.

Kirby slowly shook his head, making a discouraged mouth.

"Are the Germans going to beat us to it?"

The answer was a shrug.

"As you know, I'm in War Plans," Victor Henry said curtly. "I'm pushing you on this because we ought to have the dope, and we can't get it. If this other thing is really in the works, maybe we're just playing tic-tac-toe in our shop."

Kirby stuffed his pipe and lit it. "You're not playing tic-tac-toe. It's not that close. Not on our side."

"Could we be doing more about it?"

"One hell of a lot more. I'm going to England on this. They're apparently far ahead of us."

"They've been ahead on other things," Pug said. "That's

something nobody mentions in this brainless Lend-Lease dogfight. We have to be goddamned glad we've got the British scientists on our side, and we better break our necks to keep them there."

"I tend to agree. But we're ahead of them in many things too." Kirby puffed his pipe, squinting at Pug. "Are you happy to be home?"

"Happy?" Pug scooped up snow and packed a snowball. The crunching snow in his warm hands always gave him an agreeable flash of childhood. "I'm too busy to think about it. Yes, I guess I'm happy." He pegged the snowball over the cars into the empty street. "Rhoda was sick of Berlin, and being there by myself was certainly grim."

"She's a superb hostess, Rhoda," said Kirby. "I've never attended better dinner parties than hers. That was something, the way she rescued that tureen." The pipe in his teeth, Kirby uttered a harsh laugh. "Really something."

"Among her other talents," said Pug, "Rhoda's always been a born juggler."

Kirby wrinkled his whole face. "It's pretty sharp out here at that, eh? Let's go back."

At the top of the stairs they encountered Madeline hurrying out, her white fox coat wrapped close around her long dress, a red shawl on her hair tied under her chin.

"Where are you off to?" her father said.

"I told Mom I wouldn't be able to stay through. Mr. Cleveland's back from Quantico. I have to see him."

"Will you come to the dance afterward?"

Madeline sneezed. "I'm not sure, Dad."

"Take care of that cold. You look fierce."

The two men went inside. Madeline clung to the wooden rail, hastening down the slippery steps.

·   ·   ·

A waiter with a sandwich and a double martini on a tray was knocking at the door of Hugh Cleveland's suite when Madeline got there. The rich familiar voice sounded peevish. "It's open, it's open, come on in."

Her employer, wearing an unbecoming purple silk robe, sat with his stocking feet up on an imitation antique desk, talking into a telephone and making pencil notes on a racing form. "What about Hialeah?" he was saying. "Got anything good there for tomorrow?" He waved at her, putting his hand for a moment over the mouthpiece. "Hey Matty! I thought you weren't going to make it. Sign that. Give him a buck."

The waiter, a small dull-eyed youngster, hovered in the room, staring with a vacuous grin as Cleveland talked to the bookmaker. "Mr. Cleveland, I just want to tell you I'm a big fan of yours," he blurted when Cleveland hung up. "I really think you're terrific. So does my whole family. We never miss the amateur hour."

"Thanks," Cleveland rumbled with a heavy-lidded look, fingering his sandy hair. "Want anything, Matty?"

"A drink, thanks. I've got a cold."

"Bring her another double," said Cleveland, with a sudden charming smile at the waiter. "And get me three Havana cigars. Monte Cristos, if there are any. See how fast you can do it."

"Yes, *sir,* Mr. Cleveland."

"How was Quantico?" Madeline threw her coat on a chair and sat down, blowing her nose.

"The stage'll work fine. The commandant's all excited. He thinks it's a wonderful recruiting stunt." Yawning, Cleveland lit a cigar and explained the arrangements for the broadcast that he had made with the commandant. "He showed me all over the camp. I saw a real combat exercise. Jesus, those marines shoot live ammunition over each other's heads! I'll be deaf for a week," he said, rubbing his ears. "I guess they won't put you through that."

"Me? Am I going there?"

"Sure. Tomorrow."

"What for?"

"Screen the performers, get the personal stuff on them, and all that. They've already got an amateur thing going there, it turns out. They call it the Happy Hour."

Madeline said, "The Happy Hour's an old custom all through the service."

"Really? It was news to me. Anyhow, that makes it a cinch." He described the arrangements for her interview at Quantico.

The doorbell rang. Blowing her nose, Madeline went to

answer it. "I think I've got a fever. I don't want to go and interview a lot of marines."

A girl with dyed black hair stood simpering in the doorway, in a yellow coat and yellow snow boots, showing stained teeth in a thickly painted mouth. Her smile faded when Madeline opened the door.

"I was looking for Mr. Hugh Cleveland."

"Right here, baby," he called.

The girl came into the suite with uncertain steps, peering from Cleveland to Madeline.

"What is this?" she said.

"Wait in there," he said, indicating the bedroom with his thumb. "I'll be along."

The girl closed the bedroom door behind her. Ignoring Cleveland's embarrassed grin, Madeline snatched her coat and jerked on one sleeve and the other. "Good-night. I'll talk to you tomorrow."

"You've got a drink coming."

"I don't want it. I want to get to bed. I'm shivering."

Cleveland came padding to her in stocking feet and put his hand on her forehead. She pushed it away.

"You have no fever."

"Don't touch me, please."

"What's the matter?"

"I just don't like to be touched."

The waiter knocked at the door and came in. "Double martini, sir, and the Monte Cristos."

"Great. Thanks." Cleveland offered the tray to Madeline when the waiter left. "Here. Take off your coat and drink up."

Both hands jammed in her coat pockets, Madeline said, "It's not fair to keep a prostitute waiting. All she has to sell is time."

Hugh Cleveland slowly grinned, putting down the tray. "Why, Madeline Henry."

"I'm sorry. I feel extremely lousy. Good-night."

Cleveland strode to the bedroom. A murmur of voices, and the girl, tucking money in a shiny yellow purse, emerged from the room. She gave Madeline a tough unpleasant sad glance, and left the suite.

"Sit down and have your drink. Here's all the dope on Quantico"—he flourished a manila envelope—"and who to see, and the list of the performers. If you're still not feeling well tomorrow just call me, and I'll have Nat or Arnold come down and take over."

"Oh, I guess I'll manage." Madeline sat, throwing her coat back on her shoulders, and drank.

"How are your folks?"

"Fine."

"Any interesting guests at dinner?"

"Alistair Tudsbury, for one."

"Tudsbury! Say, there's genius. There's a man I'd like to meet. He's got style, Tudsbury, and a superb radio voice. But he'd never come on *Who's in Town*. Who else?"

"Air Commodore Burne-Wilke, of the RAF."

"Is an air commodore somebody?"

"From what my father says, he more or less ran the Battle of Britain."

Wrinkling his nose, Cleveland put his feet on the desk again. "Hmmm. Not bad. The Battle of Britain's awfully tired, though, isn't it? I don't know if he'd mean anything today, Matty. The audience has had the Battle of Britain, up to here."

"I wouldn't dream of asking him."

"I would." Hands clasped, two fingers pressed judiciously to his chin, Cleveland shook his head. "No. Dated. I say balls to the Battle of Britain."

"There was Senator Lacouture."

Her employer's thick sandy eyebrows rose. "Now, *he's* hot. That's right, isn't he an in-law of yours, or something?"

"His daughter married my brother."

"The one on the submarine?"

"No. The aviator."

"What do you think? Would Lacouture come to New York?"

"For the chance to attack Lend-Lease, I think he'd go to Seattle."

"Well, Lend-Lease is front-page. Not that one person in forty knows what it's all about. Let's get Lacouture. Do you mind talking to him?"

"No." Madeline finished her drink and stood.

"Fine. Set him up for Monday if you can. We're kind of blah on Monday."

Madeline tapped the envelope in her hand, regarding it absently. The drink was making her feel better. "There are Happy Hours at all the Navy bases, you know," she said. "Practically on every ship. Probably in the Army camps, too. Couldn't you do another show like this every now and then? It's something different."

Cleveland shook his head. "It's a one-shot, Matty. Just a novelty. The regular amateurs are the meat and potatoes."

"If we get in the war," Madeline said, "they'll start drafting talented people, won't they? There'll be camps all over the country."

"Well, could be." With his most engaging smile, he waved a thumb at the bedroom door. "Sorry about her, kid. I thought you weren't coming tonight."

"It doesn't make the slightest difference to me, I assure you."

"You really disapprove of me. I know you do. The way my wife does. You've had a good upbringing."

"I hope so."

"Well, see, I wasn't that fortunate."

"Good-night, Hugh."

"Say, listen." With an amused genial squint, Cleveland scratched his head. "There might be something in that Happy Hour thing at that, if we do get in the war. It might be a series in itself. Start a file on Wartime Ideas, Matty. Type up a memo on that and stash it away."

"All right."

"Your father's an insider. Does he think we'll get in the war?"

"He thinks we're in it."

Cleveland stretched and yawned. "Really? But the war's sort of petering out, isn't it? Nothing's happening, except for the messing around in Greece and Africa."

"The Germans are sinking a couple of hundred thousand tons a month in the Atlantic."

"Is that a lot? It's all relative, I'd imagine. I guess Hitler's got it won, though." Cleveland yawned again. "All right, Matty. See you back in New York."

When the girl had gone, Cleveland picked up the telephone, yawning and yawning. "Bell captain . . . Cleveland. Oh, is that you, Eddy? Fine. Listen, Eddy, she looked all right but I was busy. I sent her down to the bar for a while. Black hair, yellow coat, yellow purse. Thanks, Eddy."

      •   •   •

The slow movement of a Brahms symphony was putting Victor Henry in a doze, when a tap and a whisper roused him, "Captain Henry?" The girl usher appeared excited and awed. "The White House is on the telephone for you."

He spoke a few words in his wife's ear and departed. During applause after the symphony, Rhoda said, looking around at his still empty chair, "Pug's evidently gone back to the White House."

"Man's life isn't his own, is it?" Kirby said.

"When has it ever been?"

Pamela said, "Will he rejoin you at the dance?"

Rhoda made a helpless gesture.

An hour or so later, Victor Henry stood at the entrance to the grand ballroom of the Shoreham, glumly surveying the scene: the brilliantly dressed dancers crowding the floor; the stage festooned with American flags and Union Jacks; the huge spangled letters, BUNDLES FOR BRITAIN, arching over the brassy orchestra; and the long jolly queues at two enormous buffets laden with meats, salads, cheeses, and cakes. The naval aide at the White House had just told him, among other things, of thirty thousand tons sunk in the North Atlantic in the past two days.

Alistair Tudsbury came capering past him, with a blonde lady of forty or so quite naked from the bosom up except for a diamond necklace. The correspondent's gold-chained paunch kept the lady at some distance, but her spirits seemed no less hilarious for that. He dragged his bad leg a bit as he danced, obviously determined to ignore it.

"Ah, there, Pug! You're glaring like Savonarola, dear boy."

"I'm looking for Rhoda."

"She's down at the other end. You know Irina Balsey?"

"Hello, Irina." The blonde lady giggled, waving fingers at Henry. "Did Pamela come to the dance?"

"She went back to the office. The little prig's doing the overworked patriot."

Tudsbury twirled the blonde away with vigor ill-suited to his size and lameness. Crossing the dance floor, Victor Henry saw his wife at a little round side table with Palmer Kirby.

"Hello, dear!" she called. "So you escaped! Get yourself a plate and join us. The veal is marvellous."

"I'll bring you some," said Kirby, hastily rising. "Sit down, Pug,"

"No, no, Fred. I have to run along."

"Oh, dear," Rhoda said. "You're not staying at all?"

"No. I just came to tell you I'll be gone overnight, and possibly longer. I'm heading home to pack a bag, and then I'll be off."

Palmer Kirby said to him with a stiff smile, "Sorry you can't stay. It's a fine party."

"Make the best of it. You won't find such living in London."

"Oh, damn," Rhoda said.

Pug bent over his wife and kissed her cheek. "Sorry, darling. Enjoy the dance." The figure in blue disappeared among the dancers.

Rhoda and Palmer Kirby sat without speaking. The music jazzily blared. Dancers moved past them, sometimes calling to Rhoda, "Lovely party, dear. Marvellous." She was smiling and waving in response when Kirby pushed aside his half-full plate of cooling food. "Well, I leave for New York at seven tomorrow, myself. I'd better turn in. It was an excellent dinner, and a fine concert. Thanks, Rhoda."

"Palmer, I just have to stay another half hour or so." Kirby's face was set, his large brown eyes distant and melancholy. Rhoda said, "Well, will I see you again before you go to London?"

"I'm afraid not."

With an alert searching look at him, she deliberately wiped her mouth with a napkin. "I'll walk out with you."

In the crowded lobby, Rhoda stopped at a full-length mirror. Primping her hair, glancing at Kirby now and then in the glass, she spoke in a tone of the most careless chit-chat. "I'm sorry. I meant to tell Pug as soon as he got back. But he had so much to do, with his new job. And he was so relieved to be home. I just couldn't, that's all."

Kirby nodded, with a cold expression.

She went on, "All right. Then along came this awful jolt, Byron marrying this girl in Lisbon. It took both of us days and days to simmer down. And hard upon *that* Janice arrived, all pregnant and whatnot. I mean, this close prospect of becoming grandparents, for the first time— you've just got to let me pick my moment, dear. It won't be easy at best."

"Rhoda, you and Pug have many things that bind you together. I fully realize it."

She turned and looked in his eyes, then went back to her primping. "Don't we?"

He said, frowning at her image in the mirror, "I've been very uncomfortable tonight. I really want to get married again, Rhoda. I've never felt that more strongly than I did at your dinner table."

"Palmer, don't give me an ultimatum, for heaven's sake. I can't be rushed." Rhoda faced him, speaking rapidly, shifting her eyes around the lobby, and smiling at a woman who swished by in trailing orange satin. "Or rather, do just as you please, dear. Bring back an English wife, why don't you? You'll find dozens of fine women there eager to adore you, and delighted to come to America."

"I won't bring home an English wife." He took her hand, glancing up and down her body with a sudden smile. "My God, how pretty you look tonight! And what a fine dinner you put on, and what a grand success this dance is! You're quite a manager. My guess is I won't get back till May. That should be plenty of time, Rhoda. You know it should be. Good-bye."

Rhoda went back to the dance, much relieved. That last moment had cleared the air. At least until May, she could go on juggling.

*   *   *

Wearing owlish black-rimmed spectacles, Pamela Tudsbury clattered away at a typewriter, in her mauve evening dress and fancy hairdo. A desk lamp lit the machine; the rest of the shabby, windowless little office was in half-darkness. A knock came on the door.

"Bless my soul, that was quick!" She opened the door to

Victor Henry, in a brown felt hat and brown topcoat, carrying a canvas overnight bag. She walked to a silex steaming on a small table amid piled papers, pamphlets, and technical books. "Black you drink it, with sugar, as I recall."

"Good memory."

She poured two cups of coffee and settled into the swivel chair by the typewriter. They sipped, regarding each other in the lamplight.

"You look absurd," Pug Henry said.

"Oh, I know, but he wants it by eight in the morning." She took off the glasses and rubbed her eyes. "It was either get up at five, or finish it tonight. I wasn't sleepy, and I hadn't the faintest desire either to dance or to stuff myself."

"What are you working on?"

She hesitated, then smiled. "I daresay you know a lot more about it than I do. The annex on landing craft."

"Oh, yes. *That* one. Quite a document, eh?"

"It seems like sheer fantasy. Can the United States really develop all those designs and build those thousands of machines by 1943?"

"We can, but I have no reason to think we will. That isn't an operation order. It's a plan."

He relished being alone with her in this tiny, dreary, dimly lit office. Pamela's formal half-nudity had a keener if incongruous sweetness here: a bunch of violets, as it were, on a pile of mimeographed memoranda. He said gruffly, "Well, what's the dope on Ted Gallard?"

"I received a letter from his squadron commander only yesterday. It's quite a long story. The nub of it is that three RAF prisoners in his hospital escaped, made their way to the coast, and got picked up and brought home. Teddy was supposed to break out with them. But after your visit he got a room of his own and special surveillance. So he couldn't. They think that by now he's been shipped to Germany and put in a camp for RAF prisoners. That's the story. He'll be well treated, simply because we're holding so many Luftwaffe pilots. Still, you can see why I've no particular desire just now to go to posh supper-dances."

Victor Henry glanced at the wall clock. "It was my doing, then, that he couldn't get out."

"That's ridiculous."

"No, it's a fact. I hesitated before talking to the Luft-waffe about him, you know. I figured it would call attention to him and give him a special status. I wasn't sure whether that would be good or bad. Sometimes it's best to leave things as they fall."

"But I asked you to find out what you could about him."

"Yes, you did."

"You relieved me of a couple of months of agonizing."

He said, "Anyway, it's done. And now you know he's still alive. That's something. I'm very glad to hear it, Pam. Well—I guess I'll go along."

"Where to?"

With a surprised grin, he said, "You know better than that."

"You can always just shut me up. You're not leaving the country?"

He pointed at the small suitcase. "Hardly."

"Because we're finishing up here very soon," she said, "and in that case I might not see you for a long while."

Pug leaned forward, elbows on knees, clasping his hands. He felt little hesitation in confiding to her things he never told his wife. Pamela was, after all, almost as much of an insider as he was. "The President's had a bad sinus condition for weeks, Pam. Lately he's been running a fever. This Lend-Lease hubbub isn't helping any. He's taking the train to Hyde Park to rest up for a few days, strictly on the q.t. I'm to ride with him. It's a big surprise. I thought, and sort of hoped, he'd forgotten me."

She laughed. "You're not very forgettable. You're a legend in Bomber Command, you know. The American naval officer who rode a Wellington into the Berlin flak for the fun of it."

"That's a laugh," said Pug. "I was crouching on the deck the whole time with my eyes tight shut and my fingers in my ears. I still shudder to think what would have happened if I'd been shot down and survived. The U.S. naval attaché to Berlin, riding over Germany in a British bomber! Lord almighty, you were angry at me for going."

"I certainly was."

Pug stood, buttoning his coat. "Thanks for the coffee.

I've been yearning for coffee ever since I had to skip it to put on my monkey suit."

"It was a splendid dinner. Your wife's wonderful, Victor. She manages things so well. The way she picked that bowl out of the air, like a conjurer! And she's so beautiful."

"Rhoda's all right. Nobody has to sell Rhoda to me."

Pamela put on her glasses and ran a sheet of paper into the typewriter.

"Good-bye, then," Pug said, adding awkwardly, "and maybe I'll see you before you go back home."

"That would be nice." She was peering at scribbled papers beside the typewriter. "I've missed you terribly, you know. More so here than in London."

Pamela slipped these words out in the quiet manner peculiar to her. Victor Henry had his hand on the doorknob. He paused, and cleared his throat. "Well—that's Rhoda's complaint. I get buried in what I'm doing."

"Oh, I realize that." She looked up at him with eyes glistening roundly through the lenses. "Well? You don't want to keep the President waiting, Captain Henry."

40

IN the dark quiet railroad station, two Secret Service men lifted the President from the limousine and set him on his feet. He towered over them in a velvet-collared coat, his big-brimmed soft gray hat pulled low on his head and flapping in the icy wind. Holding one man's arm, leaning on a cane, he lurched and hobbled toward a railed ramp, where he drew on gloves and hauled himself up into the rear car, jerking his legs along. Victor Henry, many yards away, could see the huge shoulders heaving under the overcoat.

A tall woman with a nodding brown feather in her hat and a fluttering paper in her hand scampered up and touched Victor Henry's arm. "You're to go in the President's car, Captain."

Climbing the ramp, Pug realized why the President had put on gloves. The steel rails were so cold, the skin of his hands stuck to them. A steward led Victor Henry past a pantry where another steward was rattling ice in a cocktail shaker. "You be stayin' in heah, suh. When you ready, de President invite you join him."

The room was an ordinary Pullman sleeper compartment. The strong train smell was the same. The green upholstery was dusty and worn. Victor Henry hung coat and cap in a tiny closet, brushed his hair, cleaned his nails, and gave a flick of a paper towel to his highly polished shoes. The train started in a slow glide, with no jolt and no noise.

"Sit down, sit down, Pug!" The President waved from a lounge chair. "What'll you have? Whiskey sours are on the menu, because Harry drinks them all night long, but we can fix up almost anything."

"Whiskey sour will be fine, Mr. President. Thank you."

Harry Hopkins, slouching on a green sofa, said, "Hello, Captain."

Though Roosevelt was supposed to be ill, Hopkins looked the worse of the two: lean, sunken-chested, gray of skin. The President's color was high, perhaps feverish, his black-rimmed eyes were very bright, and a perky red bow tie went well with the gay relaxed look of his massive face. He bulked huge in the chair, though his legs showed so pitifully skeletal through the trousers. It crossed Pug's mind that Washington and Lincoln too had been oversized men.

"How are you on poetry, Pug?" said the President, in the cultured accents that always sounded a bit affected to the Navy man. "Do you know that poem that ends, 'There isn't a train I wouldn't take, no matter where it's going'? Golly, that's the way I feel. Just getting on this train has made me feel one hundred percent better." The President put the back of his hand to his mouth, and harshly coughed. "Well, ninety percent. If this were a ship, it would be one hundred percent."

"I prefer a ship too, sir."

"The old grievance, eh, sailor?"

"No, sir, truly not. I'm quite happy in War Plans."

"Are you? Well, I'm glad to hear it. Of course, I haven't the faintest notion of what you're cooking up with those British fellows."

"So I understand, sir."

Eyebrows mischievously arched, the President went on, "No, not the foggiest. When your draft that the Secretary of War got yesterday bounces back to Lord Burne-Wilke, and he sees corrections in what looks like my handwriting, that will be an *accidental* resemblance."

"I'll remember that."

"Yes, indeed. On the very first page of the forwarding letter, if you recall, there's a sentence that begins, *'When the United States enters the war.'* Somebody, with a handwriting just like mine, has crossed out that perfectly terrible clause, and written instead, *'In the event that the United States is compelled to enter the war.'* Small but important change!" A steward passed a tray of drinks. The President took a tall glass of orange juice. "Doctor's orders. Lots and lots of fruit juice. Harry, do you have that thing with you?"

"Right here, Mr. President."

"Well, let's get at it. I want to have a snack, and then try to sleep a little. How do you sleep on trains, Pug?"

"Fine, sir, if I can just get the heat right. Usually I roast or freeze."

The President threw his head back. "Ha, ha! By George, I'll tell you a state secret—the President of the United States has the same trouble! They're building a special armored car for me now. I *told* them, I said, I don't care about anything else, but that heating system had better work! Harry, let's get in our order for a snack." He glanced at his watch. "Are you hungry, Pug? I am. I'll tell you another state secret. The food at the White House leaves something to be desired. Tell them I want sturgeon and eggs, Harry. I've been thinking of sturgeon and eggs for days."

Hopkins went forward.

The President's car, so far as Pug could tell, was a regular

Pullman lounge car, rearranged to look like a living room. He had expected something more imposing. Roosevelt leaned one elbow on the chair arm, and rested a hand on his knee, looking out of the window in a calm majestic manner. "I really am feeling better by the minute. I can't tell you how I love being away from the telephone. How are your boys? The naval aviator, and that young sub-mariner?"

Victor Henry knew that Roosevelt liked to display his memory, but it still surprised and impressed him. "They're fine, sir, but how do you remember?"

The President said with almost boyish gratification, "Oh, a politician has to borrow the virtues of the elephant, Pug. The memory, the thick hide, and of course that long inquisitive nose! Ha ha ha!"

Hopkins returned to the sofa, stooping with fatigue, zipped open his portfolio, and handed Captain Henry a document three pages long with one dark facsimile page attached. "Take a look at this."

Pug read the first page with skepticism that shifted to amazement while the train wheels gently clack-clacked. He leafed through the sheets and looked from Hopkins to the President, not inclined to speak first. What he held in his hands was a summary from Army intelligence sources of a startling German operation order, purportedly slipped to a civilian in the American embassy in Berlin by anti-Nazi Wehrmacht officers. Pug knew the man well, but his intelligence function was a complete surprise.

Franklin Roosevelt said, "Think it's genuine?"

"Well, sir, that photostat of the first page does look like the German military documents I've seen. The headings are right, the look of the typeface, the paragraphing, and so forth."

"What about the content?"

"Well, if that's genuine, Mr. President, it's one incredible intelligence break."

The President smiled, with fatigued tolerance for a minor person's naïveté. *"If* is the longest two-letter word in the language."

Hopkins said hoarsely, "Do the contents seem authentic to you?"

"I can't say, sir. I don't know Russian geography that well, to begin with."

"Our Army people find it plausible," Hopkins said. "Why would anybody fake a staggering document like that, Captain? A complete operation order for the invasion of the Soviet Union, in such massive detail?"

Pug thought it over, and spoke carefully. "Well, sir, for one thing they might be hoping to prod the Soviet Union to mobilize, and so kick off a two-front war. In that case the army might depose or kill Hitler. Then again, it could be a plant by German intelligence, to see how much we pass on to the Russians. The possibilities are many."

"That's the trouble," said the President, yawning. "Our ambassador in Russia has begged us not to transmit this thing. He says Moscow is flooded with such stuff. The Russians assume it all emanates from British intelligence to start trouble between Stalin and Hitler, so as to get the Germans off England's back." The President coughed heavily for almost a minute. He sat back in his chair, catching his breath, looking out at streetlamps of a small town sliding past. He suddenly appeared very bored.

Harry Hopkins leaned forward, balancing the drink in both hands. "There's a question about giving this document to the Russian ambassador here in Washington, Pug. Any comment?"

Pug hesitated; a political problem like this was not in his reach. President Roosevelt said, with a trace of annoyance, "Come on, Pug."

"I'm for doing it."

"Why?" said Hopkins.

"What's there to lose, sir? If this thing turns out to be the McCoy, we'll have scored a big point with the Russkis. If it's a phony, well, so what? They can't be any more suspicious of us than they are."

The weary tension of Harry Hopkins's face dissolved in a warm, gentle smile. "I think that's a remarkably astute answer," he said, "since it's what I said myself." He took the document from Pug and zipped it into the briefcase.

"I'm more than ready to eat that sturgeon and eggs," said Franklin Roosevelt, "if it's cooked."

"Let me go and check, Mr. President." Hopkins jumped to his feet.

Tossing on the narrow bunk, Pug sweated and froze in the compartment for an hour or so, fiddling with the heat controls in vain. He settled down to freeze, since he slept better in cold air. The slow, even motion of the train began to lull him.

Rap, rap. "Suh? The President like to speak to you. You want a robe, suh? The President say not to bother dressing. Just come to his room."

"Thanks, I have one."

Pug passed shivering from his cold compartment to the President's bedroom, which was far too hot. The famous big-chinned face of Franklin Roosevelt, with the pince-nez glasses and jaunty cigarette holder, looked very strange on a slumped large body in blue pajamas and coffee-stained gray sweater. The President's thin hair was rumpled, his eyes bleary. He looked like so many old men look in bed: defenseless, shabby, and sad, his personality and dignity stripped from him. There was a smell of medicine in the room. The picture disturbed Victor Henry because the President appeared so vulnerable, unwell, and unimportant; and also because he was only seven or eight years older than Pug, yet seemed decrepit. The blue blanket was piled with papers. He was making pencil notes on a sheaf in his hand.

"Pug, did I break in on your beauty rest?"

"Not at all, sir."

"Sit down for a moment, old top." The President removed his glasses with a pinch of two fingers, and vigorously massaged his eyes. On the bedside table several medicine bottles tinkled as the train clacked over a bumpy rail. "Lord, how my eyes itch," he said. "Do yours? Nothing seems to help. And it's always worse when I get these sinus attacks." He clipped papers and dropped them on the blanket. "Something I've promised myself to do— if I ever find the time, Pug—is to write out a memorandum of the things that come to me in just one day. Any day at random, any twenty-four-hour period. You'd be amazed." He slapped at the papers. "It would be a valuable sidelight on history, wouldn't it? For instance.

Just take tonight's laundry that I've been doing. Vichy France seems about to sign a full alliance with Hitler. Threaten to cut off their food and starve them out? That's what the British advise. Give them even more food, bribe them to hold out against Hitler? Our ambassador's idea. But when we send the French more food, the Germans simply swallow up more of what the French produce. So where are you?—Now. Here." He picked up a clipped document. "The Japanese foreign minister is meeting with Hitler. You've read about that. What are they up to? Shall we move the Asiatic fleet from Manila to Singapore, to make them think twice about jumping on the French and Dutch East Indies? That's the British idea. Or shall we pull everything in the Pacific all the way back to the west coast, for prudence's sake? That's what my Chief of Naval Operations wants. I'd like your opinion on *that*, by the way. Here's another touchy item—the Azores. Grab them before Hitler invades Portugal and takes them himself? Or if we grab them, will that *make* him invade Portugal?"

The President flipped through more papers as though they were butcher and grocer bills. "Oh yes. Selective Service. *This* is bad. From Stimson. The authorizing bill will run out in a few months. We have to start new legislation rolling now. But after the Lend-Lease battle, Congress will be in no mood to extend the draft. And if they don't we'll be militarily helpless.—Morgenthau. Treasury is bedevilling me to freeze all the funds of Germany and Italy here, but State says no, we've got four times as much invested in those countries as they've got with us.—Morgenthau again. The British agreed to sell all their investments here to give us their remaining dollars, and Morgenthau told Congress they would, and now the British are dragging their feet. There's ever so much more. That's part of one day's basketful, old chap. I mean, a historian would certainly find a cross section like that interesting, wouldn't he? I had a check made on the papers of Wilson and Lincoln. Nothing like it ever turned up. I am definitely going to do it one day."

Roosevelt coughed long and hard, closing his eyes, wincing, and putting a hand to his back. The gesture threw him off balance in the swaying train, and the large body began to topple over like a tipped barrel. Victor Henry jumped to steady his shoulder, but the President's long powerful arm had caught an edge of the bed. "Thanks, Pug. This train isn't supposed to go more than thirty-five miles an hour. They're shading it up there." He rubbed his back. "I get a stabbing pain when I cough, but Doc McIntyre assures me it's a pulled muscle. Just so it isn't pleurisy! I really can't afford pleurisy right now. I'd better have more of that cough medicine. Would you hand me that spoon and that bottle with the red stuff? Thank you, old fellow." The President took a spoonful of the medicine, making a face. Tilting his large head to one side in the way all the nightclub clowns imitated, Roosevelt fixed the Navy captain with a sharp look from bloodshot eyes. "Pug, the U-boats keep working westward with this new wolfpack tactic. The sinkings are outrunning the combined capacity of our yards plus the British yards to build new bottoms. You're aware of all that."

"I've been hearing plenty about it at our conferences, sir."

"You accept the British figures of sinkings?"

"Oh, yes, Mr. President."

"So do I. The minute Lend-Lease passes, we'll be sending out a vast shipment of stuff. Now, none of that stuff must land on the ocean floor instead of in England. That's terribly important."

Roosevelt's offhand remark about Lend-Lease surprised Victor Henry, who was deeply worried, as the British were, about the violent debate in the Senate. "You think Lend-Lease will pass, sir?"

"Oh, the bill will pass," said the President absently. "But then what? Seventy ships are standing by now to be loaded. This shipment simply cannot be scattered and sunk by the U-boats, Pug. The British need the stuff. They need even more the morale boost of seeing it arrive. The problem is getting it through as far as Iceland. From there the British can convoy them, but not from here to Iceland. They're simply stretched to the breaking point. Well? What do we do?"

Victor Henry said uncomfortably, under the President's questioning gaze, "Convoy, sir?"

The President heavily shook his head. "You know the answer on that, Pug, as of this moment."

In the Lend-Lease fight, the issue of convoying was red-hot. The Lacouture group was screaming that if Lend-Lease passed, the warmongers would next demand to convoy the ships that carried the supplies, and that convoy meant immediate war with Germany. The President was publicly insisting that American policy would not change in the Atlantic: "neutrality patrol," *not* convoy.

Roosevelt's grim flushed face creased in the sly mischievous look that was becoming familiar to Pug. "I've been thinking, however. Suppose a squadron of destroyers went out on an exercise? Not convoying, you understand. Not convoying at all. Just practicing convoy *procedures*. Just professional drill, you might say. The Navy is always drilling, isn't it? That's your job. Well, suppose they chose to travel with these vessels—strictly for drill purposes, you understand—just this once? And to avoid difficulties and complications, suppose all this were done highly informally, with no written orders or records? Don't you suppose the U-boats might be a bit discouraged to see sixteen or so Benson-class United States destroyers out there screening those ships?"

"Discouraged, yes. Still, what happens will depend on their instructions, Mr. President."

"They've got instructions not to tangle with our warships," Roosevelt said, sounding and looking very hard. "That's obvious."

Victor Henry's pulse was quickening. "They've never encountered our destroyers in a convoy screen, sir. Suppose a U-boat closes and fires a torpedo?"

"I don't believe it will happen," Roosevelt said shortly. "The ships may never even be sighted by the Germans before the British take over the convoy. The North Atlantic weather's atrocious now. And most of the U-boat action is still on the other side of Iceland." He was fitting a cigarette in his holder as he spoke. Victor Henry swiftly snapped his lighter and offered a flame. "Thanks. This is against doctor's orders, but I need a smoke. Pug, I want this thing done, and I'm thinking you might handle it and go out with the destroyers."

Captain Henry swallowed his astonishment and said, "Aye aye, sir."

"It's very much like that airplane transfer, which you

handled so well. Everything depends on doing it in the calmest, quietest, most unobtrusive way. The point is to make no records, and above all no history, but simply to get those ships silent and safe as far as Iceland. Can it be done?"

The Navy captain sat hunched for perhaps a minute, looking at the President. "Yes, sir."

"With an absolute minimum of people in the know? I haven't even discussed this thing with Harry Hopkins."

"Admiral Stark and Admiral King would have to know, of course, sir. And Commander, Support Force, and the officer in tactical command of the screen. Everybody else in the exercise will just obey orders."

Roosevelt laughed and puffed at his cigarette. "Well! If you can keep it down to three admirals and one other officer, that will be swell. But a lot of personnel will take part in this exercise. There'll be talk."

Victor Henry said stonily, "Not very much." Franklin Roosevelt raised his bushy eyebrows. "Mr. President, what do we do if a U-boat does attack? I agree it's unlikely. But suppose it happens?"

Roosevelt regarded him through wreathing cigarette smoke. "This is a gamble that it won't happen."

"I know that, sir."

"You understand that a combat incident destroys the whole purpose," the President said, "and you know the other implications."

"Yes, sir."

"Now tell me," said the President, in a much milder manner, "what do you honestly think of the idea? It's my own. If you think it's bad, say so, but tell me why."

Sitting forward hunched, elbows on his knees, ticking off points with an index finger against his other hand, Victor Henry said, "Well, sir—to begin with, those U-boat fellows may never see us, as you say. If they do, they'll be surprised. They'll radio for instructions. We may run into a trigger-happy type, but I doubt it. I know those German submariners. They're excellent professional officers. This is a policy decision that will have to go up to Hitler. That'll take time. I think the ships will get through without incident, Mr. President."

"Grand!"

"But it'll only work once. It's a policy surprise. It's too risky to repeat."

Roosevelt sighed and nodded. "That's it. The whole situation is terrible, and some kind of risk has to be taken. The British say that before the next big convoy goes, they'll have many damaged destroyers back in action. We're also giving the Canadians some coast guard cutters —in confidence, Pug—to help close this gap to Iceland. It's this first Lend-Lease shipment that is crucial." The President gathered up the papers stacked around on his blanket. "Would you put these in that case?"

As Victor Henry was closing the dispatch case the President said through a yawn, using both arms to ease himself down into the bed, "How have those conferences with the British been going?"

"Excellently, on the whole, Mr. President."

The President yawned again. "It was so important to start this pattern of joint staff work. I'm very happy about it." He snapped off his bed lamp, leaving the room dimly lit by recessed lights in the walls. "They've been giving you some trouble about Singapore, haven't they?"

"Actually we just put that issue aside, sir. There was no resolving it."

"You can turn out the lights, Pug. The button's by the door."

"Yes, sir."

One blue light, and the President's cigarette end, still glowed in the darkness. His voice came weary and muffled from the bed. "We'll run into that time and again. They want to hold on to their Empire, naturally. But the job is to beat Hitler. Those are different undertakings. They'll insist to the end that they're one and the same. Well— we'll chat again about that *exercise* in the morning, Pug." The President used his tricky word with sardonic relish.

"Aye aye, sir."

"And when you come back from that little sea jaunt— which you ought to enjoy, for a change—I want you and your wife and family to come to dinner with us. Just a little quiet dinner. Mrs. Roosevelt often speaks of you."

"Thank you, Mr. President. I'm very honored."

"Good-night, old top."

The red cigarette end went out in an ashtray. As Victor

Henry put his hand on the doorknob, the President suddenly said, "Pug, the best men I have around me keep urging me to declare war. They say it's inevitable, and that it's the only way to unite the people and get them to put their backs into the war effort. I suppose you agree with them?"

The Navy captain said after a pause, looking at the bulky shadow in blue light, "Yes, Mr. President, I do."

"It's a bad thing to go to war," said the President. "A very bad thing. If the moment is coming, it isn't here. Meantime I shall just have to go on being called a warmonger, a coward, and a shillyshallyer, all rolled in one. That's how I earn my salary. Get a good rest, Pug."

*   *   *

41

The Negative Front

(from *WORLD EMPIRE LOST*)

Provocation in the Atlantic

As our U-boat campaign in 1941 began to show better results, Franklin Roosevelt stepped up his countermoves. Each month brought a new story, undramatic to the newspaper reader but ominous to our staff, of bolder and bolder moves by Roosevelt to deny us freedom of the seas. He occupied Greenland, putting the United States Navy astride the convoy routes in the gap between Canadian escorting and British escorting, just where our U-boats were making their best scores. The American admiral, King, arrogantly declared that the "Western hemisphere began at the twenty-sixth line of western longitude." This line took in all the best hunting grounds of the U-boats, including the Bahamas, the Caribbean, and the Azores. The American Navy, in addition to its "neutrality patrol," did some surreptitious convoying, relying on German forbearance and congressional ignorance to get away with such flagrant acts of war. Finally in May the President proclaimed "an unlimited national emergency," coming out with sly hints that if things kept going so badly, his countrymen might actually have to shed a little blood. This was his public justification for the ever increasing interference on the side of England.

But long before that, in January, full-scale military staff conferences of the British and United States forces, exceeding in scope anything between Germany and Italy, had already taken place in Washington, in great secrecy. There it was agreed that when global war broke out, "Germany first" would be the policy. Such was American neutrality in 1941, and such was Roosevelt's candor with his countrymen. All that time he kept flooding them with assurances that they would not have to fight, if only England received enough help. Churchill abetted this deception with the famous speech ending, "Give us the tools, and we will finish the job," a completely empty and fatuous boast, as he well knew.

The American President's worst interference at this time, however, was in the Balkans. The Balkan campaign of 1941 need never have occurred. Winston Churchill and Franklin Roosevelt fanned a manageable political problem into a cruel armed conflict.

Yugoslavia's Treachery: The Donovan Mission

It is well known that Roosevelt often used informal emissaries to bypass established diplomatic channels and regular government structures. In this way he could perform machinations without responsibility if they miscarried, and without leaving a trail of records. He could also make probes and inquiries without committing himself. The most celebrated of these emissaries was, of course, Harry Hopkins, who helped to form the fateful policy of all-out aid to the Bolsheviks. Lesser known was Colonel William Donovan, who later in the war created the notorious OSS spy ring. In March 1941, Donovan paid a visit to Yugoslavia that brought disaster to that country. For an American President to meddle in Balkan politics when war was flaming in Greece, in order to pull other countries into the conflict against Germany, was nothing but a war crime. Yet that was Donovan's mission, and it was successful.

The war in Greece was not of our doing; it was a miscarried adventure of our cardboard ally, Benito Mussolini. During the summer of 1940, Mussolini had ordered his Libyan troops to invade Egypt, for England was fighting for her life at home, and he thought Italy could grab off her Mediterranean empire cheaply. In October he had also laid on an invasion of Greece, and with typical theatricality he scheduled it for a day when he met with Adolf Hitler in Florence. He told Hitler nothing about this in advance. Mussolini itched to show the Führer that he was not just a hanger-on, but another daring military conqueror.

Unfortunately for him, within a few weeks the small Greek army routed the Italians, chased them into Albania, and captured their army base at Port Edda. With this politico-military disaster, Hitler's fellow dictator stood exposed as an incompetent loudmouthed fool. The English in Egypt took heart and also fought back, and at the first hint of British pluck, Mussolini's "indomitable legions" either ran away with unbelievable speed, or surrendered in the finest of holiday spirits. It was a disgraceful display seldom seen in modern warfare. The Italian army plainly had no heart for the war and counted for nothing. Most of the Italian navy had already been knocked out at anchor in Taranto, back in November. (This fine surprise attack by torpedo planes from British aircraft carriers was successfully imitated later by the Japanese at Pearl Harbor.) Our southern flank therefore stood exposed.

Hitler was deeply loyal to Mussolini, his one real ally, and for political reasons he felt the Italian had to be shored up. Also, with our invasion of the Soviet Union imminent, the neutralizing of the Balkans on our southern flank was important. The Führer embarked on skillful political moves to keep the conflagration in Greece localized, planning to snuff it out with a few good German divisions. He wisely seized the Rumanian oil fields and forced an accommodation with Hungary. He also dictated friendly pacts with Bulgaria and Yugoslavia, and despite Russian complaints, he moved troops into Bulgaria for the Greek action. All was in readiness for the pacification of the Balkans, when Roosevelt's emissary came to Belgrade.

The Simovic Cabal

Winston Churchill had a farfetched vision of drawing neutral Yugoslavia and Turkey into the Greek mess, thus creating a major Balkan front against us, where as usual other people would fight and die for England. Donovan had tried in January to interest the Yugoslav government in Churchill's scheme, but the Prince Regent Paul had shrugged off the American meddler. Donovan had managed, however, to make contact with a conspiracy of Serbian military men, led by an air force general, one Simovic. A patchwork creation of the Versailles settlement, Yugoslavia was torn by antagonism between the Croats, who were friendly to the

Reich, and the Serbians, our fierce enemies. These Serbian officers were quite receptive to the harebrained Churchill plan; it was Serbian hotheads, it will be recalled, who touched off the First World War at Sarajevo.

On his visit in March, Donovan found the British scheme in collapse; for, under severe pressure from the Führer, Yugoslavia was joining the Axis. Roosevelt now sent a stiff message to the Yugoslav government, which history records: *"The United States is looking not merely to the present but to the future, and any nation which tamely submits on the grounds of being quickly overrun would receive less sympathy from the world than a nation which resists, even if this resistance continues for only a few weeks."*

Here, in effect, was a command to Yugoslavia from the American President, almost five thousand miles away, to embroil itself in war with Germany, on pain of being punished at some future peace treaty if it did not! There are few instances of more callous effrontery in the chronicles of mankind. The government returned a noble negative reply to the American ambassador, through Prince Paul: *"You big nations are hard. You talk of our honor, but you are far away."*

Now came the turn of the Simovic cabal, provoked and encouraged by American promises. It ramified throughout the Yugoslav armed forces like a cancer, and in an overnight bloodless revolution the conspirators deposed the government, seized control of the state, and repudiated the pact with the Axis. Joyous street demonstrations of Serbians followed, and there was much satisfaction and praise for the "heroic Yugoslavs" in the Western newspapers.

"Operation Punishment"

But all this was short-lived. Adolf Hitler ordered the swift and merciless destruction of Yugoslavia. He could do no less. Successful defiance of the Reich by a Balkan cabal would have led to bloody revolts throughout our tranquil New Order in Europe. A fierce bombardment, "Operation Punishment," levelled Belgrade on April 6. The Wehrmacht conquered Yugoslavia in eleven days, at the same time commencing operations in Greece. Hitler partitioned Yugoslavia up among Germany, Italy, and the Balkan allies, and the country as such ceased to exist (though a Bolshevik partisan movement in the mountains remained a nuisance). The unfortunate Yugoslav people thus paid with wholesale deaths, a surrendered army, and national destruction, for the scheming of Churchill and Roosevelt.

From a technical viewpoint, the Yugoslavia campaign was admirable. Quick victories always look easy; but the terrain is mountainous, and the Yugoslavs had an army of over a million tough men. The Wehrmacht triumphed through the decisiveness of the Führer and the swiftness of the blow. The campaign had to be worked up in Wehrmacht Supreme Headquarters in a single sleepless night, for, unlike our previous land operations, no planned attack on Yugoslavia lay ready in our files. Still, it was executed to perfection; and incredibly, our casualties were less than six hundred soldiers.

Possibly the most banal cliché about the Second World War is that Hitler lost it by giving vent to personal rage against Yugoslavia, thus delaying the attack against the Soviet Union for three to five precious weeks, in order to wreak vengeance on a small harmless neighbor. In point of fact, Hitler's decision was absolutely forced. In planning an attack on Russia, a hostile front in the Balkans on the southern flank, so close to the Rumanian oil fields, could not be tolerated. As for his anger, it was the Führer's way of making his generals exert themselves. Though it was uncomfortable to be a target of such displays, the technique worked. The argument about lost time is nugatory, since weather and ground conditions governed our timetable against Russia.

Germany would have been better off, it must be conceded, had Italy never entered the war. There are advantages in keeping one's flanks secured by belts of neutral countries. All Mussolini did was add the two huge Italian and Balkan peninsulas to our negative front. In the end, the decision was fought out on the classical battleground of Europe, the great northern plain between the Volga and the English Channel, where we fatally missed all the vast strength we dissipated southward.

The Mediterranean Strategy

Still, since the flame of war had despite us jumped south, some of our highest leaders, including Hermann Göring and

Admiral Raeder, urged the Führer early in 1941 to strike at England in the Mediterranean by seizing Gibraltar, North Africa, and the Suez Canal. The British were helpless to stop such an attack in force; they were stretched too thin. In this way we could have sealed the southern flank with the impenetrable Sahara Desert. The British sea lines to Africa and Asia would have been cut. The shock to the British morale and supply system might well have brought on the fall of Churchill, and the peace that both we and the British needed.

Hitler was tempted. But when the Spanish dictator Franco treacherously refused to join us in attacking the British—after Germany had won his civil war for him—the Führer lost interest. His heart lay in the invasion of Russia. He acted, however, with energy and dispatch as events confronted him in North Africa, Yugoslavia, and Greece, while the crucial assault on the Soviet Union was being mashalled. Our armed forces triumphed in short order wherever they went, and the history of the time records nothing but glorious German victories, one after the other.

Churchill's Disastrous Folly

Winston Churchill helped our cause with a display of strategic ineptness equal to Mussolini's. When we entered Greece, the British in Africa were sweeping through Libya, Eritrea, and Abyssinia, with the Italians everywhere fleeing or giving up. Here was England's chance to wrap up North Africa and secure her Mediterranean lifeline before we could mount an attack. Churchill, however, writes that, though he knew that the British lacked the strength to oppose Germany for long on the Greek peninsula, he felt "honor bound" to help the Greeks. He pulled vital troops out of his triumphant African forces, killing the momentum of their drive, and threw them into Crete and Greece, whence he soon had to withdraw them, crushed and bloodied, in a "little Dunkirk," for here they were not fighting Italians. The survivors who got back to Africa found themselves once more confronting Germans, since meantime Rommel had consolidated a landing in Tripoli with his famous Afrika Korps. That spelled the end of the merry British romping in Africa. The Americans had to bail them out there, as everywhere else.

"Honor" had nothing to do with Churchill's maladroit move.

He had an obsession about the Balkans, deriving from his fiasco at Gallipoli in World War I. Later in the war this obsession was to estrange him from Roosevelt and reduce him to a pathetic hanger-on at the war conferences, fussing vainly at the Russians and Americans about the Balkans, while they coldly went ahead with plans to finish the war on sound strategic lines in the plains of the north.

Had Churchill left the Balkans alone and allowed his generals to finish off their African campaign early in 1941, the destruction of Yugoslavia, and the subsequent Allied landings in Morocco, Sicily, and Italy, might all have been unnecessary. The war might have been shortened by two years, sparing both sides much horror and bloodshed. But it was not to be.

——————————

TRANSLATOR'S NOTE: *Roon puts an unlikely construction on Colonel Donovan's visits to Yugoslavia. The Simovic revolution was a popular one. Most Yugoslavs were willing to risk Hitler's anger, they paid the price, and they earned the respect of the United States and all the world. Communist Yugoslavia's unique friendly relationship with America today stems from that gallant stand in 1941. But even if Roon's assertions about Donovan were factual, it seems unusually obtuse to blame the destruction of Yugoslavia on Roosevelt and Churchill, while overlooking the little fact that it was the Germans who firebombed Belgrade to ashes, invaded the land, and killed the people.*

It is true that President Roosevelt made occasional use of informal emissaries, but their importance is overrated in melodramatic films and books, as well as in some military history. These men usually performed minor donkeywork, which for reasons of speed or security could not be done as well through regular channels. To class Harry Hopkins or even Colonel Donovan with these anonymous small-bore persons is inaccurate.—V.H.

*　　*　　*

42

LEND-LEASE passed the Senate by sixty votes to thirty-one. Few Americans followed the debate more keenly than Pug Henry. In the visitors' gallery of the Senate, hand cupped to his ear because of the bad acoustics, he absorbed a new knowledge of how his own government worked. More and more he admired Franklin Roosevelt's ability to drive this balky team. After weeks of wild controversy, the vote itself went smooth as oil. The last excitement lay in the crushing of trick amendments. Two to one, the Senate voted in Lend-Lease, while the country and the press hardly paid attention. The debate had bored them into indifference.

Yet this vote struck Pug Henry as the key world event since Hitler's smash into Poland. Here in the yeas of sixty elderly voices the tide might be starting to turn. The President at last had the means to put the United States on a war footing, long before the people were ready to fight. The new factories that must now rise to make Lend-Lease planes and guns, would in time arm the American forces that so far existed only on paper.

That same day he was ordered to fly down to the Norfolk Navy Yard and report to Admiral Ernest King, a dragon he had not met before. King had his flag in the *Texas*.

Texas was the first battleship to which Pug had ever reported, shortly after the World War, on just such a raw and blowy March day as this, in this same Navy Yard, and possibly at this same pier. With one stack gone, and tripod instead of basket mast, *Texas* looked much different than in the old coal-burning days. Pug noted in the paint and bright work topside an arid sepulchral cleanliness. The gangway watch, and the sailors working around the old gun turrets, were starched and scrubbed as surgeons. Outside the four-starred door to flag quarters a glittery-eyed marine presented arms like a clock striking.

King sat behind a desk, showing blue sleeves stiff to the elbow with gold. The bare office was warmed only by a framed picture of Admiral Mayo on the bulkhead. King had a long, thin, deeply scored red face with high cheekbones, a narrow shiny pate, and a sharp nose. Behind him hung a chart of the Atlantic, with bold black letters in one corner, COMMANDER-IN-CHIEF, ATLANTIC FLEET. He motioned Victor Henry to a seat, tilted back his chin, and eyed him.

"I received a telephone call from the Chief of Naval Operations yesterday," he commenced in a sandy voice, "that one Captain Victor Henry of War Plans would report to me directly from the President of the United States."

Henry bobbed his head as though he were an ensign.

Silence, and the hum of ventilators. "Well? State your business."

The captain told Admiral King what Franklin Roosevelt desired. The admiral calmly smoked a cigarette in a holder, eyes boring at Henry. Then Pug described his plan for executing the President's desires. He talked for six or seven minutes. King's long, weathered face remained immobile and faintly incredulous.

"So! You're prepared to get the United States of America into this war all by yourself, are you, Captain?" said Ernest King at last, with frigid sarcasm. "Well, that's one way for an obscure person to go down in history."

"Admiral, it's the President's judgment that this exercise will go off without incident."

"So you said. Well, suppose his judgment's wrong? Suppose a U-boat fires a fish at you? What then?"

"If we're fired on, sir, why, I propose to fire back. That won't start a war unless Hitler wants war."

Ernest King nodded peevishly. "Hell, we're in this war, anyway. It doesn't matter too much when or how the whistle blows. The Japanese are going to kick off against us when it suits them and the Germans. Probably when it least suits us. I agree with Mr. Roosevelt that it very likely won't happen now. But how about the battle cruisers? Hey? Thought about them? The *Scharnhorst* and the *Gneisenau?* They've picked off more than a hundred thousand tons in the past month."

"Yes, sir. I hope the Catalinas will warn us if they're around, so we can evade."

Admiral King said, "That's a big ocean out there. The air patrol can easily miss them."

"Well, then, the cruisers can miss us too, Admiral."

After another pause, looking Victor Henry over like a dog he was considering buying, King picked up the telephone. "Get me Admiral Bristol.—Henry, you have nothing in writing?"

"No, sir."

"Very well. You will discontinue *all* references to the President."

"Aye aye, sir."

"Hello? Admiral, I'm sending to your office"—King glanced at a scrap of paper on his desk—"Captain Victor Henry, a special observer from War Plans. Captain Henry will visit Desron Eight and conduct surprise drills, inspections, and maneuvers, to test combat readiness. He is to be regarded as my assistant chief of staff, with appropriate authority. . . . Affirmative. He will be in your office within the hour. Thank you."

Hanging up, King folded bony hands over his flat stomach and, staring at Victor Henry, he spoke in a formal drone. "Captain, I desire that you now form out of Desron Eight an antisubmarine screen, and proceed to sea to conduct realistic tests and drills. This includes forming up screens on cooperative merchant vessels which you may encounter. You will of course avoid provoking belligerent vessels that may sight you. I desire you to keep security at a maximum and paperwork at a minimum. For that reason my instructions are verbal. You'll conduct yourself similarly."

"Understood, Admiral."

A chilly smile moved one side of Ernest King's mouth, and he reverted to his natural voice. "Perfect horseshit, but that's the story. In the event of an incident, it will be a hanging party for all hands. That will be all."

· · ·

Even in the North Atlantic in March, even in a destroyer, even on such risky and peculiar business, going back to sea was a tonic. Pug paced the bridge of U.S.S. *Plunkett* all day, a happy man, and slept in the sea cabin by the chart house.

On clear nights, no matter how cold the wind and how rough the sea, he spent hours after dinner alone on the flying bridge. The broad dark ocean, the streaming pure air, the crowded stars arching overhead, always made him feel what the Bible called the spirit of God hovering on the face of the waters. Down the years even more than his childhood Bible training, this religious awe inspired by nights at sea had kept Captain Henry a believer. He spoke of this to nobody, not to ministers who were his old friends; he would have felt embarrassed and mawkish, for he was not sure how seriously even they took the Lord. On this voyage, the Almighty was there for Victor Henry as always in the black starry universe, a presence actual and lovable, if disturbingly unpredictable.

Officially Pug was an observer of the "exercise," and he kept to that role, leaving operations to the commander of the destroyer screen. He interfered once. On the second day after the join-up off Newfoundland, the long ragged columns of merchant ships, stretching across the horizon, plowed into a snowstorm. Lookouts were coming down off their posts almost too stiff to move, and covered with icicles. Plunging up and down over huge black waves, ships a mile apart were losing sight of each other. After several reports of minor collisions and near-misses in the zigzags, Pug called into his sea cabin Commander Baldwin, who headed the screen, and the British liaison officer.

"I've been figuring," he said, pointing to a chart, and hanging on to his gyrating chair. "We can gain an advance of half a day by proceeding on a straight course. Now maybe there are U-boats out there in all that stuff, and then again maybe there aren't. If they're going to try to penetrate a screen of fifteen American destroyers, well, with seventy-one juicy crawling targets, zigzagging won't help much. Let's head straight for Point Baker, turn over this hot potato, and skedaddle."

Mopping snow from red eyebrows under an iced-up

parka hood, Commander Baldwin grinned. "Concur, Captain."

Pug said to the British signal officer, a little quiet man who had come in from the stormy bridge smoking a pipe upside down, "Give your commodore a flag hoist: DISCONTINUE ZIGZAGGING."

"Aye aye, sir," said the Englishman, managing to look delighted with a small tightening of his mouth around the pipe.

Day after day, Victor Henry and Commander Baldwin ate breakfast from trays in the sea cabin, reviewing courses of action in case of a German attack. Each morning the screen conducted combat drills, in a ragged style that enraged Pug. He was tempted to take over and work these units hard; but to maintain the dull calm of the operation was paramount, so he did nothing. Unmolested, the first Lend-Lease convoy steamed straight eastward. About half the time bad weather shrouded the ships. On the crystalline days and bright moonlit nights Victor Henry remained clothed and awake, drank gallons of coffee, and smoked his throat raw, now and then dozing in the captain's chair. Whether U-boats saw the convoy and laid low because of the American destroyers fanned ahead of it, or whether it got through undetected, Victor Henry never knew. They arrived at Point Baker, a dot of latitude and longitude on the wide empty sea, without a single episode of alarm.

A feeble yellow sun was just rising. The convoy began steaming in a pattern ten miles square, in a ring of desolate ice-flecked black water and pearly sky, waiting for the British. Victor Henry stood on the flying bridge peering eastward, hoping that the *Plunkett*'s navigator knew his job. Since the return from Berlin, he had never felt so well. He had read a lot of Shakespeare in his mildewed seagoing volume, and had caught up on a footlocker full of paperwork, and slept and slept, his body responding in the old way to the rocking of a destroyer. After three hours, the first hulls began to show above the horizon, due east: old American four-pipers. As the motley British screen of destroyers, frigates, and corvettes came on, the leading ship began to blink a yellow light. A signalman rushed up

to the flying bridge, bringing a pencilled scrawl: THANKS
YANKS X CUPBOARD IS BARE.

Pug grunted. "Send him EAT HEARTY—X-RAY—MORE
COMING—X-RAY—and sign it MOTHER HUBBARD."

The grinning sailor said, "Aye aye, sir," and trampled
down the ladder.

"As an observer," Pug called to Commander Baldwin on
the bridge below, "I would now be pleased to observe
how fast your signal gang can hoist REVERSE COURSE,
MAKE 32 KNOTS."

●   ●   ●

When the *Plunkett* tied up in the Norfolk Navy Yard,
Victor Henry went straight to flag quarters on the *Texas*.
Admiral King listened to his report with the face of a
scrawny sandstone pharaoh, showing a human reaction
only when Pug mentioned the poor performance of the
destroyers. The pharaoh face then became slightly more
unpleasant. "I am aware of the low level of preparedness
in the fleet, and have instituted corrective programs. Now
then. On what basis, Captain, did the President choose
you for this mission?"

"When I was naval attaché in Germany, sir, he happened to use me on jobs involving high security. I suppose
this fell in that category."

"Will you report back to him?"

"Yes, sir." Victor Henry jumped to his feet as the
admiral walked to a map of the world, newly hung on the
bulkhead opposite his desk in place of the photograph of
Admiral Mayo.

"I suppose while out at sea you've gotten the news?
You know that the Germans blitzed Yugoslavia in one
week? That Greece has surrendered"—the admiral ran a
bony finger along Adriatic and Mediterranean coastlines
hatched in angry fresh red ink—"that this fellow Rommel
has knocked the British clear back into Egypt, and is
massing to drive on the Suez Canal? That the big British
force trapped in Greece will be lucky to pull off another
Dunkirk? That the Arabs are rising to throw the British
out of the Middle East? That Iraq's already ordered them
out and asked the Germans in?"

"Yes, sir. We got most of that. It's been a bad few weeks."

"Depends on the viewpoint. For the Germans it's been a fine few weeks. In a month or so, they've tipped the world balance. My considered judgment is that this war's almost over. There seems to be very little awareness of that here. When the Germans take the canal, master the Middle East, and close the Mediterranean, the British Empire lines will be severed. That's the ball game. There will be no viable military force left in all of Asia between Hitler and the Japs. India and China will fall to them." Admiral King swept bony fingers across the Eurasian land-mass. "Solid dictator-ruled, from Antwerp to Tokyo, and from the Arctic Circle to the equator. Did you hear about that neutrality deal between the Soviets and the Japs?"

"No, sir. I missed that one."

"Well, they signed a pact—oh, a couple of weeks ago, this was—agreeing to lay off each other for the time being. The press here almost ignored it, but that's terrific news. It secures the Jap rear"—he waved toward Siberia—"and turns them loose to pick up all these big marbles." The gnarled hand jumped south and ran over Indo-China, the East Indies, Malaya, and the Philippines; it paused, and one stiff finger glided to the Hawaiian Islands.

Admiral King stared sourly from the map to Victor Henry and strode back to his desk. "Now, of course the President has to make the political judgments. He's an outstanding politician and a great Navy President. Possibly his judgment is correct, that *politically* he can't do any more now than extend our patrol area. Maybe *politically* he has to chop hairs about 'patrolling' versus 'convoying.' But it's just as belligerent for us to patrol, and broadcast the positions of German U-boats and raiders, as it is to convoy. Just as belligerent, but weak and futile. The British haven't enough ships as it is to keep the Mediterranean open and cut this fellow Rommel's supply lines. If we took over convoying, they might have a chance to stay in the game. My opinion hasn't been asked by the President. You seem to be in his entourage. You might find a moment to make these points." Ernest King sat, hands folded on the desk, and looked at the captain for a silent minute. "That might be, by sheer accident, the best contribution you ever make to the security of the United States."

.   .   .

"Henry! Hey, Henry!"

Byron groaned, went rigid as a stretching cat, and opened one eye. Lieutenant Caruso and the other officers on the *S-45* were used to this waking pattern of Ensign Henry. Until he went rigid there was no rousing him. It sometimes took violent shaking of the limp form.

"Huh?"

"Your father is here."

"What?" Byron fluttered his eyes and reared up on an elbow. He now occupied the middle bunk of three. "You're kidding, skipper. My father?"

"He's in the wardroom. Care to join us?"

In his underwear, unshaven, mussed, and blinking, Byron stumbled to the doorway of the tiny wardroom. "Holy cow. You really are here."

"You heard your commanding officer say I was." Immaculate in dress blues, Victor Henry frowned at his son over a coffee cup.

"They'll tell me anything on this boat to get me out of my bunk. They're all fiends."

"What the devil are you doing in the sack at noon?"

"I had the midwatch. Excuse me, sir, for coming out like this. Be right back." Byron quickly reappeared in a freshly starched khaki uniform, groomed and shaved. Victor Henry was alone. "Gosh, Dad, it's good to see you."

"Briny, a midwatch isn't major surgery. You're not supposed to take to your bed to recover."

"Sir, I had it two nights in a row." He poured coffee for his father and himself. "Say, this is a real surprise. Mom said you were somewhere at sea. Have you been detached from War Plans, Dad?"

"No, this was a temporary thing. I'm heading back now. I was visiting the *Texas*. I saw the *S-45* on the yard roster and thought I'd look in." Victor Henry scanned his son's thin face. "Well? How goes it?"

"Oh, first-rate. Swell bunch of guys on this boat. The

skipper is 4.0, and the exec, I'd really like you to meet him. Lieutenant Aster. He was a witness at my wedding." Byron grinned the old half-melancholy, half-amused grin that never failed to charm Pug Henry, and most other people. "I'm glad to see you. I'm lonesome."

"What's your wife's situation? Is she on her way home yet?"

Byron gave his father a veiled glance that hinted at his standing grudge about Natalie. But he was in a good mood and responded amiably. "I don't know. We got in this morning from maneuvers. The yeoman just went for the mail."

Pug put down his cup. "Incidentally, will your boat be in port on the twenty-sixth?"

"I can find out. Why?"

"Nothing much. Just if you are, and if you can get overnight leave, you're invited to dinner at the White House."

Byron's deep-set eyes opened wide. "Cut it out, Dad."

"Your mother and Madeline, too. I don't guess Warren can fly in from Pearl Harbor. But if you're around, you might as well come. Something to tell your children about."

"Dad, how do we rate?"

Victor Henry shrugged. "Oh, a carrot for the donkey. Your mother doesn't know about it yet."

"No? Dinner at the White House! Mom will go clear through the overhead."

Lieutenant Aster, carrying a basket of mail, poked his head into the wardroom. "Briny, Carson's got a fistful of letters for you at the gangway."

"Hey. Good enough. This is my exec, Dad, Lieutenant Carter Aster. Be right back." Byron vanished.

Seating himself at the narrow wardroom table and slitting envelopes with an Indian paper cutter, Aster said, "Excuse me, sir. Priority mail."

"Go ahead." Victor Henry studied the blond officer as he attacked the letters. One could sometimes guess, by the way a young man went at papers or a book, the kind of officer he was. Aster traversed the pile fast, scribbling a note here and a checkmark there. He looked good. He pushed the basket aside and poured coffee for himself when Henry held up a hand to decline.

"Lieutenant, you were a witness at Briny's wedding?"

"Yes, sir. She's a wonderful girl."

"How's Briny doing?"

Aster's jolly reminiscent smile disappeared. The wide mouth became a slash of tight lips. "In his work?"

"Yes, let me have it straight."

"Well, we all like him. There's something about Briny, I guess you know that. But for submarines . . . don't get the idea that he can't measure up. He can, but he won't bother. Briny just slides along the bottom edge of tolerable performance."

Victor Henry was not surprised; still, the words hurt. "People run true to form, I guess."

"He's way behind on his officer qualification book. Now he knows his way around the boat, sir, he knows the engines, the compressed air system, the batteries, all that. He stands a good diving watch. He has a knack for trimming the boat and keeping her at the depth the captain wants. But when it comes to writing reports on time, or even logs, keeping track of records and dispatches and the crew's training books—an officer's main work—forget it." Aster looked Byron's father in the eye. "The skipper sometimes talks of beaching him."

Victor Henry said sadly, "That bad?"

"In a way he's kind of nuts, too."

"How, nuts?"

"Well, like last week, we had this surprise inspector aboard. We fired this dummy torpedo and surfaced to recover it. We hadn't tried a recovery for a long time. It was a rough sea, raining, cold as hell. The torpedo detail was out there trying to retrieve the thing. It was bobbing up and down, banging and crashing against the hull, and we were rolling like mad, and the sailors were slipping around with lifelines tied to them. It was awful. They messed about for an hour and couldn't hook that fish. I was sure somebody would get drowned or crushed. The inspector got tired and went below. The skipper was exploding. The deck gang was soaked and frozen and falling all over itself. Well, as you know, a dummy warhead's hollow, and the fish floats straight up and down. Briny was the officer on that detail. Suddenly he took the hook, stuck it in his lifeline, and by Christ if he didn't go and jump on that torpedo! He timed it so right, it looked easy. He hung on, with these icy waves breaking over him, riding that yellow steel dummy head like a goddamn bronco. He secured the hook and then got knocked off. Well, we hauled him in half-dead and then we hoisted the fish aboard. The skipper filled him full of medicinal brandy. He slept eighteen hours and was fine."

Victor Henry said, clearing his throat, "He took a stupid chance."

"Sir, I'd like to have him on any boat I ever command. But I'd expect to wear out two pairs of heavy shoes, kicking his ass for him."

"If the occasion arises, let me buy you the brogans, Lieutenant," said Pug.

"She's pregnant!" Byron catapulted into the little wardroom, arresting himself by grabbing the doorway. "Natalie's pregnant, Dad." He brandished torn-open letters. "How about that? Hey, Lady, how about that? Boy, I feel strange."

"Fast work," said Aster. "You better get that gal home for sure, now. Pleasure to meet you, Captain. Excuse me."

The executive officer slid out from behind the table with his mail basket.

"Any news on her coming home?" Victor Henry asked.

"She says Leslie Slote really built a fire under the consuls this time. She and Jastrow should be on their way by—well, maybe by now! She'd better be, or I'll desert and go fetch her, Dad. My kid's going to be born in the United States."

"That's great news, Briny. Great." Victor Henry stood, putting a hand on his son's shoulder. "I've got a plane to catch. You'll find out about the twenty-sixth, won't you? And let me know."

"The what? Oh, yes." Byron was sitting with his chin on both fists, reading a closely written airmail sheet, his face lit up with happiness. "That dinner. Yes, sir, I'll telephone you or something."

"I'm sure you have a load of paperwork, after your maneuvers. Get at it, boy."

"Oh, sure," said Byron. "So long, Dad."

"I'm happy about your wife, Byron."

Again the veiled glance, again the amiable tone. "Thanks."

＊　　＊　　＊

Rhoda was in bad turmoil. Palmer Kirby had returned from England in April, while Pug was at sea. The cherry blossoms were early that year; and in Virginia and North Carolina, where they went on a four-day drive like a honeymoon, the countryside was flooded with fragrant blossoms. Rhoda came back to Washington committed in the strongest terms to leave her husband and to marry Kirby.

The decision seemed clear, simple, and natural to Rhoda in the bedrooms of wayside hotels, and on long walks amid the peach and plum blossoms of the southland. But when Kirby went happily off to Denver to put the big old house in order for a new life, leaving her in a home full of Henry photographs and mementos, the simplicity of the vision, and some of its charm, started to fade.

Rhoda's inexperience was misleading her. An investment of more than twenty-five years of love and intimacy— even if it has gone slightly sour—usually should not be liquidated. Its equivalent in romance, in thrills, or even money, can seldom be recovered. So hardheaded bad women tend to decide. Rhoda's trouble was that, in her own mind, she was still a good woman, caught up in a grand passion which consumed all moral law. One misstep during her husband's long absence in Germany—at an age when many men and women make missteps—had led to another and another. Her desire to keep her good opinion of herself had completed her confusion.

She still liked—perhaps loved—and also feared Pug, but his career was a growing disappointment. For a while she had hoped that his "in" with President Roosevelt might lead to big things, but that was not happening. Some of her friends were preening over their husbands' new commands: battleships, destroyer flotillas, cruisers. The rivalry of Digger Brown, Paul Munson, and Harry Warendorf was exactly paralleled among their ladies. Rhoda Henry was becoming the wife of a man bogged in twilit shore jobs after more than twenty years of racing along with the front-runners. Evidently Pug didn't have it. This was bitter medicine for Rhoda. She had always hoped that he would someday become at least a Deputy Chief of Naval Operations. After all, she had preferred him to fellows who had since gone on to careers like bank president, steel executive, army general. (These men had not necessarily proposed; if she had dated and kissed them, she considered them possibilities sacrificed for Pug.) Now it seemed he might not even make rear admiral! Certainly that limited goal was receding with every month he spent in a Navy Department cubicle while his competitors accumulated command time at sea. With such thoughts Rhoda Henry was working herself up to tell Pug that she had fallen in love with another man. But she did not look forward with dewy pleasure to this, and she teetered, ready to be pushed either way.

She missed his return from the convoy trip. He had not telephoned from Norfolk, for he knew that she liked to sleep late. Arriving by airplane in Washington, he found the house empty, cook off, Rhoda out, mail overflowing his desk, no coffee. He couldn't blame anybody, but it was a cold homecoming.

At the War Plans office, by chance, he encountered Pamela Tudsbury. She had not gone back to England with Burne-Wilke. Secretaries cleared for Very Secret were rare, so the British Purchasing Council had requisitioned her for a while. Spry, springy, refreshingly unmilitary in a yellow and green cotton frock, Pamela greeted him with the warmth he had not found at home. He asked her to lunch with him in the Navy cafeteria. During the quarter hour it took to bolt a sandwich, pie, and coffee, Pamela spoke of her unhappiness at being left behind by Burne-Wilke. "I want to be there now," she said, eyes somewhat moist. "Not that I really think the end is at hand, as some do. But in the wee hours, one does begin to picture how one accommodates to German military police and street signs. It's a nightmare that now and then gets terribly real." She shook her head and smiled. "Of course it's darkest before the dawn. You poor man. You've got a splendid color. The sea so obviously agrees with you. You look ten years younger. I hope it lasts, or that you get back to sea."

"Well, I've tried to walk a lot and play tennis. It isn't the same."

"Of course not."

He asked her for further news of Ted Gallard, but there was none. They parted with a casual good-bye. All the rest of the day, plowing through the mound of accumulated paper, Victor Henry felt much better.

Rhoda was waiting for him at home in a bright red dress, with ice and drink mixes ready, and cheese and crackers out. Her manner and conversation struck him as strange. She gabbled about houses. She was so eager to talk, so voluble, that he had no chance at first to tell her of the White House invitation. Early that afternoon, finding Pug's note on her dressing table, she had rushed out with an agent and visited three. All her suppressed guilt feelings focussed on the house business. If only she could convince Pug that she had been diligently looking at houses, she felt her tracks would be covered. This made no sense. She was planning to break the news to him. She acted on nervous instinct, triggered by the short scrawl in Pug's handwriting: *He's back. Man the bar.*

Pug was uninterested in a verbose account of faults in houses he had never seen. But he put up with it. Next, Rhoda chattered on that sore topic, recent promotions: that utter fool, chaser, and drunk, Chipper Pennington, had gotten the *Helena;* and did Pug know that even Bill Foley was now commanding a destroyer squadron at Pearl Harbor? Pug broke in on Rhoda's flow of words—this was at dinner, over the meat—to tell her of the President's invitation. Her mouth fell open. "Pug! *Really?*" She asked many questions, worried out loud over what she would wear, and gloated about how Annette Pennington and Tammy Foley would feel when they heard *this!*

It was a bad performance. He was seeing her at her very worst—worse than her worst, for she had never been quite so demoralized, though she looked extremely pretty and her wonderful skin glowed smooth as ever. Pug found himself looking at his wife detachedly, as he judged professional matters. Few wives in their forties can weather such a scrutiny.

That night Victor Henry recognized familiar signals that he was not, for the time being, welcome in her bedroom.

He did not know why; but he had long ago decided that Rhoda was entitled to these spells, physical or mental, though it seemed too bad after his six weeks at sea. It took him a long time to fall asleep. He kept thinking of the callous happy-go-lucky mood he had found in the capital, the sense that by passing the Lend-Lease Bill, America had done its bit to stamp out Nazism. Nobody appeared to care how much stuff was actually being produced and shipped. The figures at War Plans had appalled him. Conflicting boards and agencies, contradictory directives, overlapping demands by the Air Corps, the Navy, the Army, and the British had overwhelmed the program. Under an amazing welter of meetings, talks, and mimeographed releases, Lend-Lease was paralyzed.

He kept thinking, too, of the contrasts between his wife and the English girl. At last he got up and swallowed a stiff drink of bourbon like a pill.

* * *

Pug cheered up later in the week, as most people did, when Hitler's deputy Führer, the black-browed fanatic Rudolf Hess, made a solo flight to Scotland, landed by parachute, and demanded to see Winston Churchill. For a day or two it seemed that Germany might be cracking. But the Nazis at once announced that Hess, through heroic overwork, had gone off his head. The British said little publicly. Pug heard from Pamela, who had it from the embassy, that in fact Hess, mad as a hatter, was shut up in a sanatorium, drivelling peace plans.

Certainly in the war news there was no sign of German weakness. They were bagging hordes of British prisoners and mountains of arms in Greece, sinking ships in the Atlantic at a great rate, showering London and Liverpool with fire-bombings worse than any during the 1940 blitz, laying siege to Tobruk, and launching a breathtaking airborne invasion of Crete, over the heads of the British Mediterranean fleet. This outpouring of military energy to all points of the compass, this lava flow of violence, was awesome. In the face of it, Vichy France was folding up and negotiating a deal with the Nazis that would hand over North Africa to them, and perhaps the strong French fleet too. This was a brutal bloody nose for American diplomats trying to hold France neutral, and keep the Germans out of the African bulge at French Dakar, which dominated the whole south Atlantic.

The Nazis appeared unstoppable. The entrenched, heavily armed British on Crete claimed to be butchering the sky invaders. But floating to earth dead or alive in their parachute harnesses, crashing in gliders, on the airborne multitudes came. The confident British communiqués grew vaguer. Somehow, they conceded, the Germans at incredible cost had managed to capture one airfield; then one more. It soon became clear that Hitler was doing a new thing in Crete, taking a strong island from the air without sea power, in fact in the teeth of sea power. This was threatening news for England. Aside from the heavy defeat itself, Crete began to look like a dress rehearsal for the end.

And still the United States did nothing. In the inner War Plans circles, a split was widening between the Army and the Navy. Victor Henry's section wanted strong fast moves in the North Atlantic to save England: convoys, the occupation of Iceland, shipment of all possible arms. But the Army, which now gave England only three months before collapse, preferred a move into Brazil and the Azores, to face the expected Nazi thrust in the south Atlantic from Dakar. Between these two plans, the President was stalling and hesitating.

Then came the scarifying news that the *Bismarck,* a new German battleship, had blown up England's mighty war vessel, the *Hood,* off Greenland, with a single salvo at thirteen miles, and vanished into the north Atlantic mists! This jolted the country out of its Maytime languor. The President announced a major radio address. Speculations about the speech filled the press and radio. Would he proclaim the start of convoying? Would he ask Congress to declare war? The brawny feat of the *Bismarck* seemed to show Hitler achieving mastery of the oceans as well as the land and the air. The shift of the power balance in the Atlantic was suddenly self-evident and frightful.

Rhoda's reaction to all this heavy news was loud frantic fretting that the White House would call off the dinner invitation, after she had told all her friends about it. FDR was probably getting ready to go to war. How could he bother with a social dinner, especially with unimportant people like themselves? Victor Henry, to secure some peace, checked with the President's naval aide. The invitation to the White House stood.

"What do you think, Dad? Will the Limeys get the *Bismarck?*"

Perched on the edge of the bathtub, Byron observed that Victor Henry still liked to rest one leg on the tub as he shaved. Nor had Pug's shaving motions ever changed, the successive scrape of cheeks, chin, and neck, then the scowl to stretch his upper lip. Byron had sat exactly so as a child countless times, talking to his dad.

"Well, Briny, they claim the *Prince of Wales* winged her off Greenland there. But those Germans have fine damage control. I've been aboard the *Bismarck*. She's a floating steel honeycomb. If they were hit, they probably just buttoned up the flooded compartments and lit out for home. The British are throwing everything into their search. To hell with convoys, to hell with the Mediterranean! They know where she's heading—the French coast, as fast as she can skedaddle—and they know the speed she can make. Aircraft ought to find her. Unless"—he rinsed his razor and shook it—"unless the *Bismarck* is undamaged. In which case heaven keep any convoys she runs across. With that fire control she displayed, she'll pick off forty ships in half an hour."

"I wish I were out there," said Byron, "in that search."

"Do you?" Pug gave his son a pleased look. Where Byron saw much the same father, Victor Henry saw a pallid, melancholy, thin-faced little boy transformed into a spruce six-foot ensign in blue and gold. Pug wiped his face with a wet towel. "What time is it? Let's make tracks."

Byron followed him into his dressing room. "Say, Dad, you're pretty close to the President, aren't you?"

Buttoning his dress shirt, Pug said, "Close? Nobody's really close to Mr. Roosevelt, that I can see. Except maybe this Harry Hopkins."

Byron crouched on a stool, watching his father dress. "I got two more letters from Natalie yesterday. She's stuck, after all."

Pug frowned at the mirror over his bureau. "Now what?"

"Same thing, Dad, this balled-up foolishness about when her uncle's father was naturalized. He just can't get that passport renewed. One official makes promises, and the next one fudges on them. The thing goes round and round."

"Tell your wife to come home, and let him sweat it out."

"Let me finish, Dad." Byron waved both hands. "It was all set, they'd even bought steamship tickets. Some formality of approval from Washington just never came through. Natalie had to turn back the boat tickets. Dad, they're ringed by Germans now. Germans in France, Yugoslavia, Greece, North Africa, and for that matter all through Italy. They're a couple of Jews."

"I'm aware of that," said Victor Henry.

Rhoda's voice called from the bedroom, "Pug, will you come here? I'm going out of my MIND."

He found her glaring at the full-length closet mirror, in a tight blue silk dress, the back of which hung open, displaying underwear and an expanse of rosy skin. "Hook me up. Look how my stomach is bulging," she said. "Now why is that? The stupid dress didn't look the least bit like this in the store. It looked fine."

"You're not bulging," said Victor Henry, trying to fix the snaps despite the poor light on her back. "You look very pretty."

"Oh, Pug, for God's sake. I'm bulging a FOOT. I look six months pregnant. I'm horrible. And I'm wearing my tightest girdle. Oh, what'll I do?"

Her husband finished closing the snaps and left her. Rhoda looked much the same as always, and was making much the usual evening-dress noises. Her laments and queries were rhetorical, and best ignored.

Byron still crouched on the stool. "Dad, I thought you might mention this thing to the President."

Victor Henry's response was quick and curt. "That's an unreasonable notion."

Heavy silence. Byron slumped down, elbows on knees, hands clasped. Pug was jarred by the hostility, almost the hatred, on his son's face.

"Byron, I don't think your wife's uncle's citizenship mess

is a suitable problem to submit to the President of the United States. That's all."

"Oh, I knew you wouldn't do it. You're sore at me for marrying a Jew, you always have been, and you don't care what happens to her."

Rhoda marched in, pulling on gloves. "For heaven's sake, what are you two jawing about? Pug, will you put on your jacket and come along?"

On the Pennsylvania Avenue side of the White House, the Henrys passed several dozen pickets, marching with antiwar signs in a ragged oval, and chanting, *"The Yanks are not coming!"* Near them a handful of men sauntered in sandwich boards that read: THE AMERICAN PEACE MOBILIZATION IS A COMMUNIST FRONT. Two yawning policemen kept watch on this tranquil agitation.

"Good evening."

A tall Negro in a colorful uniform opened the door, sounding—at least to Rhoda—like the basso in *The Magic Flute*. The Henrys stepped from a warm May night, sweet with the scent of the White House lawns and flowers, into a broad dazzling marble-floored foyer. A middle-aged man in a dinner jacket stood by the presidential seal inlaid in brass in the floor. He introduced himself as the chief usher. "Mrs. Henry, you will be sitting on the President's left," he said, glancing at a large card. "You see, Crown Princess Marta of Norway is a houseguest. She will sit on his right."

"Oh, yes, yes, oh my. Princess Marta? Well, she ranks me all right," said Rhoda with a nervous giggle.

"I guess we're early," Victor Henry said.

"Not at all. Please come this way." He left them in the large public room called the Red Room, saying they would go upstairs soon.

"Oh, dear, think of Warren missing all this!" Rhoda peered at the paintings of Presidents hung near the high ceilings, and the elegant red-upholstered furniture. "Him, with his love of American history."

"That's just it," Madeline said, looking around with bright snapping eyes. She wore a long-sleeved black silk dress buttoned to the throat, quite a contrast to her mother's bared arms and bosom. "It's like walking into a history book."

"I wonder if it's okay to smoke," Byron said.

"No, no, don't," his mother said.

Pug said, "Why not? There are ashtrays all around. This is a house. You know what the White House is really like?" He too was nervous, and talking to cover it. "Commandant's quarters on a base. The big fancy house with stewards that the boss man gets to live in. This one is the biggest and fanciest. Just the cumshaw of becoming Number One."

"But the thought of actually keeping house here!" said Rhoda. Despite themselves they were all speaking in unnatural voices, hushed or too loud. "Even with an army of servants, I'd go mad. I can't imagine how she does it, especially traipsing around the country the way she does. Byron, watch those ashes, for heaven's sake."

"May I present Mr. Sumner Welles?" The chief usher led in a bald lean gloomy man. "And I believe we can go upstairs now," he added, as the Undersecretary of State shook hands with the Henrys.

An elevator took them up. Behind his desk at one end of an enormous yellow room hung with sea paintings sat the President, rattling a cocktail shaker.

"Hello there, just in time for the first round!" he called, a big grin lighting up the jowly pink face. His voice had a clear virile ring. He wore a black tie and dinner jacket with a soft white shirt; and when Pug leaned across the desk to take drinks, he noticed the brown trousers of a business suit. "I hope Mrs. Henry likes Orange Blossoms, Pug. That's what I'm mixing. Good evening, Sumner."

The President gave all the Henrys firm moist handshakes, cold from the shaker. "How about you, Sumner? Would you prefer something else? I make a fair martini, you know."

"Thank you, sir. That looks just right."

In the center of the room at the mantel, Eleanor Roosevelt stood drinking cocktails with a tall black-haired woman and a sharp-faced, aged little man. On either side of them warm breezes stirred the lace curtains of open windows, bringing in a heavy sweet smell of flowers. The usher introduced the Henrys to Mrs. Roosevelt, to Princess Marta, and to Mr. Somerset Maugham. When Rhoda heard the author's name, her stiff manner broke. "Oh my!

Mr. Maugham! What a surprise. This may be very bad form, but I've read all your books and I love them."

The author exhaled cigarette smoke and stammered, "Tha—that's charming of you," moving only his thin scowling lips, his aged filmy eyes remaining cold and steady.

"Well, we're all here. Why don't we sit?" The President's wife moved a chair near the desk, and the men at once did the same, all except for Somerset Maugham, who sat in a chair Byron put down.

"Anything very new on the *Bismarck*, Sumner?" said the President.

"Not since about five o'clock, sir."

"Oh, I've talked to Averell in London since then. The connection was abominable, but I gathered there was no real news. What do you say, Pug? Will they get her?"

"It's a tough exercise, Mr. President. Mighty big ocean, mighty bad weather."

"You should know," said Franklin Roosevelt slyly.

"But if they winged her, as they claim," Pug went on, "they ought to catch her."

"Oh, they hit the *Bismarck*. Their cruisers followed a trail of oil far into the fog. That's straight from Churchill. Harriman's his houseguest."

Rhoda was trying not to stare at Crown Princess Marta, who, she thought, held a cocktail glass like a sceptre. Unconsciously imitating her posture, Rhoda decided that her skin was almost as good as Marta's, though the princess was younger and had such rich black hair, done up in a funny way. Contemplating royalty, she lost track of the war talk, and was a little startled when everybody rose. They left the President and followed Mrs. Roosevelt to the elevator. When they arrived in the dining room, there sat Franklin Roosevelt, already whisked to his place at the head of the table. Here too, strong flower scent drifted through the open windows, mingling with the smell of a big silver bowl of carnations, the table centerpiece.

"Well, I had a good day!" the President exclaimed as they sat down, with the obvious intent of putting everybody at ease. "The Ford Company finally promised Bill Knudsen to make Liberators in their huge new plant. We've been sweating over that one. The business people seem to be waking up at last." He started on his soup, and everyone else began to eat. "We want to put out five hundred heavy bombers a month by next fall, and this will do it. Mr. Maugham, there's good news to pass on! By next fall, we'll be making five hundred heavy bombers a month. That's hard intelligence."

"Mr. President, the—hard intelligence is"—Maugham's stammer caught everybody's attention, so they hung on his words—"that you *s-say* you'll be making them."

The President was smiling before the author got the words out; then he roared with laughter. This houseguest was privileged to make jokes, Pug saw.

"Mr. Maugham was a British spy in the last war, Pug," Roosevelt said across the table. "Why, he even wrote a spy novel. *Ashenden*. Watch out what you say here. It'll get right back to Churchill."

"M-Mr. President, you know a houseguest would never do that. I am not a f-f-ferret now, I assure you, but a lower form of life. A-a-a sponge."

Mrs. Roosevelt said cheerily, amid the laughter, "What else happened, Franklin, to make it a good day?"

"Why, the fellows finally finished the umteenth draft of my big speech. It looks pretty good, pretty good. So I let them have coffee and sandwiches, and now they're locked up downstairs doing draft umteen-plus-one. What's the betting now, Sumner? Am I going to ask for war, or proclaim convoying, or what? Why, the suspense is even getting me." The President laughed and added, "Mr. Maugham, as a great writer have you no ideas for my speech? War? Convoy? Or some real new inspiration?"

"Mr. President, you r-remember your Oliver Twist? 'Please, sir, I w-want some more'?"

"Of course," said the President, his close-set, clever eyes twinkling in anticipation of a joke.

"Well, p-please, sir," said the author with a dead serious face, "I w-want some w-war."

The whole table broke into laughter. "Ha ha ha! Spoken like a true British agent!" said the President, gaining another general laugh.

Uniformed waiters cleared the table for the next course. Franklin Roosevelt took obvious pleasure in slicing the saddle of lamb. Rhoda Henry ventured to remark, "My goodness, I wish Pug could carve like that!"

"Oh, I'm sure he can." Arching his thick grizzled eyebrows with self-satisfaction, the President swept the knife artistically through the meat. "I do like a *slice* of lamb, though, don't you, Rhoda? Not a steak, and not a shaving, either. The secret is a sharp knife and a firm hand."

Victor Henry was answering Mrs. Roosevelt's questions about Nazi Germany, raising his voice because she had said she was rather deaf.

"What's that, Pug?" the President said, cocking an ear as he sliced meat. "Am I missing something good?"

"I was saying, sir, that when I left Germany, their industrial effort was just getting into high gear."

"You don't say. They scored pretty well in low gear, then."

"Well, Mr. President, as it turned out, the others had been doing even less."

Roosevelt faced Maugham, on the other side of the crown princess. "Captain Henry was in the intelligence business too, Willie. He was naval attaché in Berlin. He predicted that pact between Hitler and Stalin before it happened. All the clever diplomats, generals, and columnists were caught flat-footed, but not Pug. What's your prediction now, Pug? How about all that massing of troops in the east? Will Hitler attack Russia?" The President's quick wily glance told Pug that he was thinking of the document they had discussed on the train.

"Mr. President, after that piece of luck, I hocked my crystal ball and threw away the ticket."

Maugham wagged a knobby tobacco-stained finger. "C-captain, don't ever admit to luck, in our r-racket."

"What do you think, Sumner?" the President said.

"If one studies *Mein Kampf*," said Welles in undertaker tones, "the attack is inevitable, sooner or later."

"How long ago did he write that book? Twenty years ago?" said Franklin Roosevelt, his powerful voice reminding Rhoda very strongly of his radio manner. "I'd hate to be bound by anything I said or wrote way back then."

Mrs. Roosevelt said, "Mr. Maugham—if Germany attacks the Soviet Union, will England help Russia, or leave Stalin to stew in his own juice?"

The author looked at the President's wife for several seconds. A heavy silence enveloped the table. "I-I can't really say."

"You know, Willie," said the President, "a lot of folks here don't believe the story that Rudolf Hess is crazy. They say that he was sent over to advise your people of the coming attack on Russia, and to get a hands-off agreement, in return for a promise to help you keep the Empire."

"That very plan is in *Mein Kampf*." Mrs. Roosevelt spoke out like a schoolteacher.

Somerset Maugham, caught in the cross-fire of crisp words from the President and his wife, spread his hands, crouching in his chair, looking small, old, and tired.

"Sumner, do you suppose we could explain it to the American people," said Roosevelt, "if the British did not help Russia?"

"I think that would finish off aid to England, Mr. President," said Sumner Welles. "If Hitler is a menace to mankind, that's one thing. If he's just a menace to the British Empire, that's something very different."

With a brief look at the British author, the President said in a much lighter tone, "Well! Shall I slice some more lamb?"

"I will thank you for some, Mr. President," spoke up the crown princess. "Of course, Hitler may be massing his troops in the east precisely because he intends to invade England." The princess talked precise English with a Scandinavian lilt. She was making a tactful cover, Pug thought, for the awkward moment with Maugham. She had not previously said anything. "You know, every time Hitler starts a new campaign, Stalin pinches off something here and something there. This may be a show of force to keep him out of the Rumanian oil fields."

"That, too, is possible," said Sumner Welles.

"European politics can be such a miserable tangle," said Mrs. Roosevelt.

"But it all boils down to Hitler's impulses nowadays," said the President. "Pity we must live in the same century with that strange creature. Say, we have here two men who talked at length face to face with the fellow. Let's take a Gallup poll. Sumner, do you think Hitler is a mad-man?"

"I looked hard for such evidence, Mr. President. But as I reported, I found him a cool, very knowledgeable, very skilled advocate, with great dignity and—I'm afraid—considerable charm."

"How about you, Pug?"

"Mr. President, don't misunderstand me. But to me, so far, all heads of state are more alike than they are different."

Roosevelt looked taken aback, then he threw his head back and guffawed, and so the others laughed. "Well! That's something! At my own table, I've been compared to Hitler! Pug, you'd better talk your way out of that one fast."

"But it's the truth. He has a very powerful presence, sir, face to face—though I hate to admit it—with an incredible memory, and a remarkable ability to marshal a lot of facts as he talks. In his public speeches he often raves like a complete nut. But I think when he does that, he's just giving the Germans what they want. That impressed me, too. His ability to act such different parts."

Roosevelt was slightly smiling now. "Yes, Pug, that would be part of the job. The fellow *is* able, of course. Or he wouldn't be giving us all this trouble."

Rhoda blurted, "Pug, when on earth did you have a talk with Hitler? That's news to me." The artless injured-wife tone made the President laugh, and laughter swept the table. She turned on Roosevelt. "Honestly, he's always been closemouthed, but to keep something like that from me!"

"You didn't need to know," Pug said across the table.

"C-captain Henry," said Somerset Maugham, leaning forward, "I bow to a p-p-professional."

The conversation broke into little amused colloquies. Roosevelt said to Rhoda Henry, "My dear, you couldn't have paid your husband a handsomer compliment in public."

"I didn't intend to. Imagine! He's just a sphinx, that man." She darted a tender look at Pug. She was feeling very kindly toward him, and indeed to all the world, having enjoyed a moment of spontaneous success at the presidential table.

"Pug is a fine officer," said the President, "and I expect great things of him."

Rhoda felt warm excitement. "I always have, Mr. President."

"Not everybody deserves such a beautiful wife," Roosevelt said, with a decidedly human glance at her that took in her décolletage, "but he does, Rhoda."

With the oldest instinct in the world, blushing, Rhoda Henry looked toward Mrs. Roosevelt, who was deep in conversation with Sumner Welles. It flashed through Rhoda's mind that there was a tall woman who had married a very tall man. But Pug at least could walk. Life balanced out in strange ways, Rhoda thought; the heady situation was making her philosophical.

Madeline and Byron sat on opposite sides of the table, she between Maugham and Welles, Byron between the crown princess and a deaf, very old lady in purple named Delano. This lady had said nothing all evening; a relative, obviously, living at the White House and interested mainly in the food. Madeline was speaking first to the Undersecretary of State and then to the famous author, her face alive, flushed, and gay, her gestures quick. Maugham offered to come on Cleveland's interview program, when she told him what she did. He said candidly that his mission was British propaganda, so why not? She was entranced.

Byron throughout the dinner sat silent, collected, withdrawn. Victor Henry saw Roosevelt looking quizzically at him. The President loved to charm everybody and to have only cheerful faces around him. Pug kept glancing at his son, hoping to catch his eye and signal him to perk up.

Over the ice cream, the President said in a moment's lull, "We haven't heard from our submariner here. Byron, you're a natural for the silent service. Ha ha." The young officer gave him a melancholy smile. "How's the morale in your outfit?"

"Good, Mr. President."

"Are you ready to go to war, as Mr. Maugham seems to desire?"

"Personally, sir, I'm more than ready."

"Well, that's the spirit."

Victor Henry interposed, "Byron was visiting a friend in Poland when the war began. He was strafed by a Luftwaffe plane and wounded."

"I see," said the President, giving Byron an attentive stare. "Well, you have a motive then for wanting to fight Germans."

"That's not it so much, Mr. President. The thing is that my wife is trapped in Italy."

Franklin Roosevelt appeared startled. "Trapped? How, trapped?" The rich voice went flat.

Everybody at the table looked at Byron. The atmosphere was thick with curiosity.

"Her uncle is Dr. Aaron Jastrow, Mr. President, the author of *A Jew's Jesus*. He's had some trouble about his passport. He can't come home. He's old and not well, and she won't abandon him." Byron spoke as flatly as the President, getting out each word very distinctly.

Mrs. Roosevelt put in with a smile, "Why, Franklin, we both read *A Jew's Jesus*. Don't you remember? You liked it very much indeed."

"Dr. Jastrow taught at Yale for years, Mrs. Roosevelt," Byron said. "He's lived here almost all his life. It's just some crazy red tape. Meantime there they are."

"*A Jew's Jesus* is a good book," said the President, bored and stern. "Sumner, couldn't you have somebody look into this?"

"Certainly, Mr. President."

"And let me know what you find out."

"I will, sir."

Franklin Roosevelt resumed eating his ice cream. Nobody spoke. Perhaps eight or ten seconds ticked by, but at that table, in that company, it was a long time. Everybody appeared bent on eating dessert, and the spoons clinked and scraped.

"Speaking of that book," the President's wife said with a bright smile, looking up, "I have just been reading the most extraordinary little volume—"

The door to the hallway opened, and a pale moustached Navy commander entered, carrying a brown envelope. "I beg your pardon, Mr. President."

"Yes, yes. Let me have it." The commander went out.

The tearing envelope made a noisy rasp. Yellow strips like telegram tape were pasted on the white sheet the President unfolded.

"Well!" Franklin Roosevelt looked around, his face all at once charged with teasing relish. "May I relay a bit of news?" He took a dramatic pause. "It seems they've got the *Bismarck!*"

"Ah!" The crown princess bounced in her chair, clapping like a girl, amid an excited babble.

The President raised his hand. "Wait, wait. I don't want to be overoptimistic or premature. What it says is, airplanes from the *Ark Royal* have caught up with her and put several torpedoes in her. They must have hit her steering gear, because when night fell she was trailing thick oil and steaming slowly *west*—the wrong way. The entire fleet is closing in and some units now have her in sight."

"Does it give a position, Mr. President?" said Victor Henry.

The President read off a latitude and longitude.

"Okay. That's a thousand miles from Brest," said Pug. "Well outside the Luftwaffe air umbrella. They've got her."

President Roosevelt turned to a servant. "Fill the glasses, please."

Several waiters sprang to obey him. Silence enveloped the table.

The President lifted his glass. "The British Navy," he said.

"The British Navy," the company said in chorus, and all drank.

Somerset Maugham blinked his lizard eyes many times.

.   .   .

Next morning, long after Victor Henry had gone to work, when the maid came to remove the breakfast things, Rhoda asked her for pen and paper. She wrote a short note in bed:

Palmer, dear—
You have a kindly heart that understands without explanations. I can't do it. I realize we can't see each other for a long while, but I hope we will be friends forever. My love

and everlasting thanks for offering me more than I deserve
and can accept. I'll never forget.

Forgive me.

Rhoda

She sealed it up at once, dressed quickly, and went out
in the rain and mailed it herself.

That same dark and muggy morning, shortly before
noon, a buzzer sounded on the desk of Victor Henry's office. He sat in his shirt-sleeves working by electric light.

"Yes?" he growled into the intercom. He had left word
that he would take no calls. The head of War Plans wanted,
by the end of the week, a study of merchant shipping
requirements for the next four years.

"Excuse me, sir. The office of Mr. Sumner Welles is
calling, sir."

"Sumner Welles, hey? Okay, I'll talk to Sumner Welles."

Welles's secretary had a sweet sexy Southern voice. "Oh,
Captain Henry. Oh, suh, the Undersecretary is most anxious to see you today, if you happen to be free."

Glancing at his desk clock and deciding to skip lunch,
Pug said, "I can come over right now."

"Oh, that will be fahn, suh, just fahn. In about fifteen
minutes?"

When he arrived at Welles's office, the warm sexy voice
turned out to belong to a fat old fright, sixty or so, in a
seersucker dress.

"Mah, you got here fast, Captain. Now, the Undersecretary is with Secretary Hull just now. He says do you
mind talking to Mr. Whitman? Mr. Whitman has all the
details."

"Yes, I'll talk to Mr. Whitman."

She led him from the spacious and splendid offices of
Sumner Welles to a much smaller and more ordinary
office without a window. The projecting sign over the doorway indicated a minor official in European Affairs. Aloy-
sius R. Whitman was a thick-haired man in his late forties,
indistinguishable from ten thousand other denizens of
Washington offices, except for his somewhat horsy clothes,
an unusually florid face, and an unusually bright smile.
Several prints of horses livened the walls of the small
office. "The Undersecretary sends his thanks to you, Cap-

tain, for interrupting a busy schedule to come over." He
gestured at a chair. "Cigarette?"

"Thanks."

The two men smoked and regarded each other.

"Wretched weather," said Whitman.

"The worst," said Pug.

"Well, now. The business of Dr. Aaron Jastrow's passport," Whitman said genially. "It's no problem whatever,
as it turns out. The authorization was sent out a while ago.
It may have been delayed en route, the way things often are
nowadays. At any rate it's all set. We double-checked by
cable with Rome. Dr. Jastrow can have his passport any
time he'll come down from Siena to pick it up, and has
been so informed. It's all locked up."

"Good. That was fast work."

"As I say, there was no work to do. It had already been
taken care of."

"Well, my son will be mighty glad to hear about this."

"Oh yes. About your son." Whitman uttered a little
laugh. He rose, hands jammed in the patch pockets of his
green and brown jacket, and leaned casually on the edge
of his desk near Pug, as though to make the chat less official. "I hope you'll take this in the right spirit. The Undersecretary was disconcerted to have this thing raised at the
President's dinner table."

"Naturally. I was mighty jarred myself. So was my wife.
I chewed Byron out afterward, gave him holy hell, but the
thing was done."

"I'm awfully glad you feel that way. Suppose you just
drop a little note to the President, sort of apologizing for
your son's rather touching gaffe, and mentioning that
you've learned the matter was all taken care of long ago?"

"An unsolicited letter from me to the President?"

"You're on very good terms with the President. You
just dined with him."

"But he asked for a report from Mr. Welles."

The captain and the State Department man looked each
other in the eye. Whitman gave him the brightest of smiles
and paced the little office. "We went to a rather dramatic
effort this morning, Captain, just to make sure young Mrs.
Henry could get home. Literally thousands of these cases
of Jewish refugees come to us, all the time. The pressure is

enormous. It's absolutely unbelievable. Now the problem in your family is settled. We hoped you'd be more appreciative."

Rightly or wrongly, Henry sensed an unpleasant nuance in the way the man said "your family," and he broke in, "Natalie and her uncle aren't Jewish refugees, they're a couple of Americans."

"There was some question, Captain—apparently a very serious question—as to whether Aaron Jastrow was technically an American. Now we've cleared it up. In return I really think you should write that letter."

"I'd like to oblige you, but as I say, I wasn't asked to address the President on this subject." Pug got to his feet. "Is there something else?"

Whitman confronted him, hands in jacket pockets. "Let me be frank. The Undersecretary wants a report from me, for him to forward to the President. But just a word from you would conclude the matter. So—"

"I'll tell you, Mr. Whitman, I might even write it, if I could find out why a distinguished man like Jastrow got stopped by a technicality when he wanted to come home. That's certainly what the President wants to know. But I can't give him the answer. Can you?" Whitman looked at Victor Henry with a blank face. "Okay. Maybe somebody in your section can. Whoever was responsible had better try to explain."

"Captain Henry, the Undersecretary of State may find your refusal hard to understand."

"Why should he? He's not asking me to write this letter. You are."

Pulling hairy hands from his pockets, Whitman chopped both of them in the air with a gesture that was both a plea and a threat. He suddenly looked weary and disagreeable. "It's a direct suggestion of the State Department."

"I work for the Navy Department," said Pug. "And I have to get back on the job. Many thanks."

He walked out, telephoned the Norfolk Navy Yard from a booth in the lobby, and sent a message to Byron on the *S-45*. His son called him at his office late in the afternoon.

"*Eeyow!*" shouted Byron, hurting his father's ear. "No kidding, Dad! Do you believe it this time?"

"Yes."

"God, how marvellous. Now if she can only get on a plane or a boat! But she'll do it. She can do anything. Dad, I'm so happy! Hey! Be honest now. Was I right to talk to the President, or was I wrong? She's coming home, Dad!"

"You had one hell of a nerve. Now I'm goddamned busy and I hope you are. Get back to work."

43

". . . Therefore I have tonight issued a proclamation that an UNLIMITED national emergency exists, and requires the strengthening of our defenses to the extreme limit of our national power and authority . . ."

"Okay!" exclaimed Pug Henry, sitting up, striking a fist into a palm, and staring at the radio. "There he goes!"

Roosevelt's rich voice, which in broadcasting always took on a theatrical ring and swing, rose now to a note of passion.

"I repeat the words of the signers of the Declaration of Independence—that little band of patriots, fighting long ago against overwhelming odds, but certain, as we are, of ultimate victory: 'With a firm reliance on the protection of Divine Providence, we mutually pledge to each other our lives, our fortunes, and our sacred honor.' "

After a moment of crackling static, the announcer sounded awed: *"You have been listening to an address by the President of the United States, speaking from the East Room of the White House in Washington."*

"That's terrific! It's far more than I expected." Pug snapped the radio off. "He finally did it!"

Rhoda said, "He did? Funny. I thought he just pussy-footed around."

"Pussyfooted! Weren't you listening? 'We are placing our armed forces in position . . . we will use them to repel attack . . . an *unlimited* national emergency exists . . .' "

"What does all that mean?" Rhoda yawned and stretched on the chaise longue, kicking her legs. One pink-feathered mule dropped off her naked foot. "Is it the same as war?"

"Next thing to it. We convoy right away. And that's just for starters."

"Makes me wonder," said Rhoda, flipping the negligee over her legs, "whether we should pursue those houses any further."

"Why not?"

"They'll surely give you a sea command if we go to war, Pug."

"Who knows? In any case, we need a place to hang our hats."

"I suppose so. Have you thought any more about which house you'd want?"

Pug grimaced. Here was an old dilemma. Twice before they had bought a bigger house in Washington than he could afford, with Rhoda's money.

"I like the N Street house."

"But, dear, that means no guest room, and precious little entertaining."

"Look, if your heart is set on Foxhall Road, okay."

"We'll see, honey. I'll look again at both of them." Rhoda rose, stretching and smiling. "It's that time. Coming to bed?"

"Be right up." Pug opened a briefcase.

Rhoda swished out, purring, "Bring me a bourbon-and-water when you come."

Pug did not know why he was back in her good graces, or why he had fallen out in the first place. He was too pre-occupied to dwell on that. His arithmetic on merchant shipping was obsolete if the United States was about to convoy. Transfers of ownership and other roundabout tricks could be dropped. It was a whole new situation now, and Pug thought the decision to convoy would galvanize the country. He made two bourbon-and-waters, nice and rich, and went upstairs humming.

*   *   *

The yeoman's voice on the intercom was apologetic. "Sir, beg your pardon. Will you talk to Mr. Alistair Tudsbury?" Victor Henry, sweating in shirt-sleeves over papers laid out on every inch of his desk, was trying—at the urgent demand of the office of the Chief of Naval Operations—to bring up to date before nightfall the operation plan filed months earlier, for combined American and British convoying.

"What? Yes, put him on. . . . Hello? Henry speaking."

"Am I disturbing you, dear boy? That's quite a bark."

"No, not at all. What's up?"

"What do you make of the President's press conference?"

"I didn't know he'd had one."

"You *are* busy. Ask your office to get you the afternoon papers."

"Wait a minute. They should be here."

Pug's yeoman brought in two newspapers smelling of fresh ink. The headlines were huge:

NO CONVOYS—FDR

and

PRESIDENT TO PRESS:
SPEECH DIDN'T MEAN CONVOYS
"Unlimited Emergency" Merely a Warning;
No Policy Changes

Skimming the stories, Pug saw that Franklin Roosevelt had blandly taken back his whole radio speech, claiming the reporters had misunderstood it. There would be no stepped-up United States action in the Atlantic, north or south. He had never suggested that. Patrolling, not convoying, would go on as before. No Army troops or marines would be sent to Iceland or anywhere else. All he had been trying to do was warn the nation that great danger existed.

Tudsbury, who could hear the pages turning, said, "Well? Tell me something encouraging."

"I thought I understood Franklin Roosevelt," Pug Henry muttered.

Tudsbury said, "What's that? Victor, our people have been ringing church bells and dancing in the streets over last night's speech. Now I have to broadcast and tell about this press conference."

"I don't envy you."

"Can you come over for a drink?"

"I'm afraid not."

"Please try. Pam's leaving."

"What?"

"She's going home, leaving on a boat tonight. She's been pestering them for weeks to let her return to Blighty."

"Let me call you back."

He told his yeoman to telephone an old shipmate of his, Captain Feller, at the office of the Chief of Naval Operations.

"Hello, Soapy? Pug. Say, have you seen the papers about that press conference? . . . Yes, I quite agree. Well, now, next question. This Convoy Annex Four. Do you still want it by tonight? . . . Now, Soapy, that's a rude suggestion, and it's an awfully bulky annex. Moreover I hope we'll use it one day. . . . Okay. Thanks."

Pug hit the buzzer. "Call Tudsbury. I'm coming over."

"The funny part is," Pug said to Tudsbury, "Rhoda said he pussyfooted around. I was taken in."

"Maybe it needs a woman to follow that devious mind," said the correspondent. "Pam, where are your manners? Pug's here to say good-bye to you. Come in and have your drink."

"In a minute. My things are all in a slop." They could see Pamela moving in the corridor, carrying clothes, books, and valises here and there. They sat in the small living room of Tudsbury's apartment off Connecticut Avenue, hot and airless despite open windows through which afternoon traffic noise and sunlight came streaming.

Tudsbury, sprawling on a sofa in a massively wrinkled Palm Beach suit, with one thick leg up, heaved a sign. "I shall be alone again. There's a girl who is all self, self, self."

"Family trait," called the dulcet voice from out of sight.

"Shut up. Please, Pug, give me something comforting to say in this bloody broadcast."

"I can't think of a thing."

Tudsbury took a large drink of neat whiskey and heavily shook his head. "What's happened to Franklin Roosevelt? The Atlantic convoy route is the jugular vein of civilization. The Huns are sawing at it with a razor. He *knows* the tonnage figures of the past three months. He *knows* that with Crete and the Balkans mopped up, the Luftwaffe will come back at us, double its size of last year and howling with victory. What the devil?"

"I'll have my drink now," said Pamela, striding in. "Don't you think you should be going, governor?"

He held his tumbler out to her. "One more. I have never been more reluctant to face a microphone. I have stage fright. My tongue will cleave to the roof of my mouth."

"Oh yes. Just as it's doing now." Pamela took his glass and Pug's to the small wheeled bar.

"Put in more ice. I've caught that decadent American habit. Pug, the Empire's finished. We're nothing but an outpost of forty millions, with a strong navy and a plucky air force. Why, man, we're your Hawaii in the Atlantic, many times as big and powerful and crucial. Oh, I could make one hell of a broadcast about how preposterous your policy is!"

"Thanks, Pam," Pug said. "I agree with you, Tudsbury. So does the Secretary of the Army. So does Harry Hopkins. They've both made speeches urging convoy now. I have no defense of the President's policy. It's a disaster. Cheers."

"Cheers. Yes, and it's *your* disaster. This is a contest now between Germany and the United States. If you lose, God help you and all mankind. We were too slow, too stupid, and too late. But in the end we did our best. You're doing nothing, in the last inning." He swallowed his drink and pulled himself to his feet. "We expected more from the United States Navy, anyhow. I'll tell you that."

"The United States Navy is ready," Pug shot back. "I've

been working like a bastard all day on a general operation order for convoy. When I saw those headlines, it was like my desk blowing up in my face."

"Good God, man, can I say that? Can I say that the Navy, before this press conference, was preparing to start convoying?"

"Are you crazy? I'll shoot you if you do."

"I don't have to quote you. Please."

Pug shook his head.

"Can I say your Navy is ready to go over to convoy on a twenty-four hours' notice? Is that true?"

"Why, of course it's true. We're out there now. We've got the depth charges on ready. All we have to do is uncover and train out the guns."

Tudsbury's bulging eyes were alive now and agleam. "Pug, I want to say that."

"Say what?"

"That the United States Navy is ready to go over to convoy and expects to do it soon."

Pug hesitated only a second or two. "Oh, what the hell. Sure, say it! You can hear that from anybody in the service from CNO down. Who doesn't know that?"

"The British, that's who. You've saved me." Tudsbury rounded on his daughter. "And you told me not to telephone him, you stupid baggage! Blazes, I'm late." The fat man lumbered out.

Pug said to Pamela, "That isn't news."

"Oh, he has to work himself up. He'll make it sound like something. He's rather clutching at straws."

She sat with her back to the window. The sun in her brown hair made an aureole around her pallid sad face.

"Why did you tell him not to phone me?"

She looked embarrassed. "I know how hard you're working."

"Not that hard."

"I meant to ring you before I left." She glanced down at her intertwined fingers, and reached him a mimeographed document from the coffee table. "Have you seen this?"

It was the British War Office's instructions to civilians for dealing with German invaders. Pug said, leafing through it, "I read a lot of this stuff last fall. It's pretty nightmarish, when you start picturing the Germans driving through

Kent and marching up Trafalgar Square. It won't happen, though."

"Are you sure? After that press conference?"

Pug turned up both hands.

Pamela said, "They've updated that manual since last year. It's calmer, and a lot more realistic. And therefore somehow more depressing. I can just see it all happening. After Crete, I really do think it may."

"You're brave to go back, then."

"Not in the least. I can't stand it here. I choke on your steaks and your ice cream. I feel so bloody guilty." Pamela wrung her fingers in her lap. "I just can't wait to go. There's this girl in the office—would you like another drink? no?—well, the fool's gone dotty over a married man. An American. And she has a fiancé in the RAF. She has nobody to talk to. She pours it all out to me. I have to live with all this maudlin agonizing, day in, day out. It's wearing me down."

"What does this American do?"

"That would be telling." With a little twist of her mouth she added, "He's a civilian. I can't imagine what she sees in him. I once met him. A big thin flabby chap with glasses, a paunch, and a high giggle."

They sat in silence. Pug rattled the ice in his glass, round and round.

"Funny, there's this fellow I know," he spoke up. "Navy fellow. Take him, now. He's been married for a quarter of a century, fine grown family, all that. Well, over in Europe he ran into this girl. On the boat actually, and a few times after that. He can't get her out of his mind. He never does anything about it. His wife is all right, there's nothing wrong with her. Still, he keeps dreaming about this girl. All he does is dream. He wouldn't hurt his wife for the world. He loves his grown kids. Look at him, and you'd call him the soberest of sober citizens. He has never had anything to do with another woman since he got married. He wouldn't know how to go about it, and isn't about to try. And that's the story of this fellow. Just as silly as this girlfriend of yours, except that he doesn't talk about it. There are millions of such people."

Pamela Tudsbury said, "A naval officer, you say?"

"Yes, he's a naval officer."

"Sounds like somebody I might like." The girl's voice was grainy and kind.

Through the automobile noises outside, a vague sweeter sound drew nearer, and defined itself as a hand organ. "Oh listen!" Pam jumped up and went to the window. "When did you last hear one of those?"

"A few of them wander around Washington all the time." He was at her side, looking down five stories to the organ grinder, who was almost hidden in a crowding circle of children. She slipped her hand in his and leaned her head against his shoulder. "Let's go down and watch the monkey. There must be one."

"Sure."

"First let me kiss you good-bye. On the street, I can't."

She put her thin arms around him and kissed his mouth. Far below, the music of the hurdy-gurdy thumped and jangled. "What is that song?" she said, the breath of her mouth warm on his lips. "I don't recognize it. It's a little like Handel's *Messiah*."

"It's called 'Yes, We Have No Bananas.'"

"How moving."

"I love you," said Victor Henry, considerably surprising himself.

She caressed his face, her eyes looking deep into his. "I love you. Come."

On the street, in the hot late sunshine, the children were squealing and shouting as a monkey on the end of a light chain, with a red hat stuck fast on its head, turned somersaults. The hurdy-gurdy was still grinding the same song. The animal ran to Victor Henry, and balancing itself with its long curled tail, took off the hat and held it out. He dropped in a quarter. Taking the coin and biting it, the monkey tipped the hat, somersaulted back to his master, and dropped the coin in a box. It sat on the organ, grinning, chattering, and rapidly tipping the hat.

"If that critter could be taught to salute," said Victor Henry, "he might have a hell of a naval career."

Pamela looked up in his face and seized his hand. "You're doing as much as anybody I know—anybody, *anybody*—about this accursed war."

"Well, Pam, have a safe trip home." He kissed her hand and walked rapidly off, leaving her among the laughing children. Behind him the barrel organ wheezily started again on "Yes, We Have No Bananas."

*   *   *

A couple of days later, Victor Henry received an order to escort to the Memorial Day parade the oldest naval survivor of the Civil War. This struck him as strange, but he pushed aside a mound of work to obey. He picked the man up at a veterans' home, and drove with him to the reviewing stand on Pennsylvania Avenue. The man wore a threadbare uniform like an old play costume, and the dim eyes in his bony, withered, caved-in face were cunningly alert.

President Roosevelt's white linen suit and white straw hat glared in the bright sun, as he sat in his open car beside the stand. He gave the tottering ancient a strong handshake and bellowed at the box of his hearing aid, "Well, well! You look better than I do, old top. I bet you feel better."

"I don't have your worries," quavered the veteran. The President threw his head back and laughed.

"How would you like to watch the parade with me?"

"Better than—hee hee—marching in it."

"Come along. Come on, Pug, you sit with me too."

The veteran soon fell asleep in the sunshine, and not even the booming and crashing of the brass bands could wake him. Roosevelt saluted, waved, put his straw hat over his heart when a flag went by, and smiled obligingly for the newsreel men and photographers crowding around the slumbering veteran beside the President.

"The Navy's my favorite," he said to Victor Henry, as blue Annapolis ranks swung by with set young faces under the tall hats. "They march better than those West Point cadets. Don't ever tell any Army men I said so! Say, Pug, incidentally, whom can I send over to London to head up our convoy command?" Pug sat dumbstruck. Ever since the press conference, the President had been sticking firmly to his no-convoy stance. "Well? Don't you know of anybody? We'll call him a 'special naval observer,' of course, or something, until we get things started."

The President's voice did not carry over the blaring

brasses to the chauffeur, nor to his naval aide in front, nor to the Secret Service men flanking the automobile.

"Sir, *are* we going to convoy?"

"You know perfectly well we will. We've got to."

"*When,* Mr. President?"

The President smiled wearily at Pug's bitter emphasis. He fumbled in his pocket. "I had an interesting chat with General Marshall this morning. This was the upshot."

He showed Victor Henry a chit of paper scrawled with his own handwriting:

Combat Readiness, June 1, 1941

Army Ground Forces — 13%
(Major shortages all types arms; rapid expansion; incomplete training; Selective Service Act expiring)
Army Air Corps — 0%
(All units involved in training and expansion)

Victor Henry read these frustrating figures while American flags streamed past him and the marine band blared out "The Stars and Stripes Forever." Meanwhile Roosevelt was searching through more chits. He handed another to Pug, while taking the salute of the marine formation as it stalked splendidly past. This was in another handwriting, in green ink, with the last line ringed in red:

Public Attitude Toward War, 28 May 1941

For getting in if "no other way to win" — 75%
Think we'll eventually get in — 80%
(Against our getting in now — 82%)

"I'll take that," Roosevelt said, retrieving the chit. "Those are the figures, Pug, for the day *after* my speech."

"Convoying would be a Navy job, sir. We're all ready."

"If we get into war," said the President through a broad smile and a wave at schoolchildren cheering him "—and convoying might just do it—Hitler will at once walk into French West Africa. He'll have the Luftwaffe at Dakar, where they can jump over to Brazil. He'll put new submarine pens there, too. The Azores will be in his palm. The people who are screaming for convoy now just ignore these things. Also the brute fact that eighty-two percent, *eighty-two* percent of our people don't want to go to war. *Eighty-two percent.*"

The Navy veteran was sitting up now, blinking, and working his bony jaws and loose sunken mouth. "My, this is a fine parade. I still remember marching past President Lincoln," he said reedily. "There he stood, the President himself, all in black." The old man peered at the President. "And you're all in white. And you're sitting, hee hee."

Victor Henry shrank with embarrassment. Roosevelt laughed gaily, "Well, there you are. Every President does things a little differently." He lit a cigarette in his long holder, and puffed. Boy Scouts in a brown mass went stepping by, with heads and bright eyes turned toward the President. He waved his hat at them. "So far this year, Pug, we've produced twenty percent more automobiles than we made last year. And Congress wouldn't dream of giving me the power to stop it. Well? What about London? You didn't suggest anybody."

Victor Henry diffidently named three well-known rear admirals.

"I know them," the President nodded. "The fact is, I was thinking of you."

"It wouldn't work, Mr. President. Our man's opposite number in the Royal Navy will have flag rank."

"Oh, that could be fixed up. We could make you an admiral temporarily."

From the surprise, and perhaps a little from the beating sun overhead, Pug felt dizzy. "Mr. President, as you know, I just go where I'm ordered."

"Now, Pug, none of that. Frankly, I like you right where you are. Deciding who gets what weapons and supplies is a big job. I'm glad you're working on it, because you have sense. But think about London."

"Aye aye, sir."

Pug returned the veteran to his nursing home, and went back to a piled-up desk. He got through a high heap of work and walked home, to give himself a chance to think. The city lay in holiday quiet. Connecticut Avenue was almost empty, the evening air was sweet and clear.

Think about London!

Young couples on the benches in Dupont Circle turned and laughed, looking after the stocky man in Navy whites, striding along and humming a tune that had been popular before some of them were born.

"Hey, what the Sam Hill?" Pug exclaimed, as he entered the living room. "Champagne? And why are you gussied up like that? Whose birthday is it?"

"Whose birthday, you old fool?" Rhoda stood, splendid in a pink silk frock, her eyes glittering with tears. "Don't you know? Can't you guess?"

"I suppose I'm fouled up on my dates."

"It's Victor Henry's birthday, that's whose birthday it is."

"Are you potted? Mine's in March."

"Oh, God, how dense the man is. Pug, at four o'clock this afternoon, Janice had a boy! You're a grandfather, you poor man, and his name is Victor Henry. And I'm a doddering old grandmother. And I love it. I love it! Oh, Pug!"

Rhoda threw herself in his arms.

They talked about the great event over the champagne, downing a whole bottle much too fast. Janice and her baby were in fine shape. The little elephant weighed nine and a half whole pounds! Rhoda had raced up to the naval hospital for a look at him in the glass cage. "He's the image of you, Pug," she said. "A small pink copy."

"Poor kid," said Pug. "He'll have no luck with the women."

"I like that!" exclaimed Rhoda, archly giggling. "Didn't you have marvellous luck? Anyway, Janice and the baby are coming to stay with us. She doesn't want to take him back to Hawaii for a while. So that makes the house decision urgent. Now, Pug, just today I got that old lady in Foxhall Road to come down another five thousand! I say let's grab it. That glorious lawn, those fine old elms!

Sweetie, let's enjoy these coming years, let's wither in style, side by side, Grandma and Grandpa Henry. And let's always have lots of spare room for the grandchildren. Don't you think so?"

Victor Henry stared at his wife for such a long time that she began to feel odd. He heaved a deep sigh and made a curious upward gesture with both palms.

"Well, I'll tell you, Grandma. I couldn't agree with you more. The time has come. Let's go to Foxhall Road by all means. And there we'll wither, side by side. Well said."

"Oh, how marvellous! I love you. I'll call the Charleroi Agency in the morning. Now let me see what's happened to the dinner." She hurried out, slim silky hips swaying.

Pug Henry upended the champagne bottle over his glass, but only a drop or two ran out, as he sang softly:

> But yes, we have no bananas,
> We have no bananas today.

*

Three weeks later the Germans invaded the Soviet Union.

PART THREE

The Winds Rise

44

Barbarossa

(from WORLD EMPIRE LOST)

TRANSLATOR'S NOTE: *The world still wonders, a quarter of a century later, why Adolf Hitler turned east in June 1941, when he had England hanging on the ropes from disastrous defeats in Africa and the Balkans, and from losses to U-boats, and when the United States was impotent to stop the knockout. It appeared then that Hitler had the Second World War all but won. With England mopped up, he could have proceeded to take on the Soviet Union in a one-front war, after digesting his amazing gains. Instead, sparing England, he turned east, unloosed the biggest and longest bloodbath in history, left his rear open to the Normandy landing, and destroyed himself and Germany.*

Why?

On this question, it seems to me that General von Roon, from the other side of the hill, sheds a lot of light. Since the American reader is more interested in operations in the west, I have greatly abridged this material. But I have tried to preserve the main thread of Roon's analysis.—V.H.

The Turn East

Hitler's invasion of the Soviet Union is widely regarded as his great blunder, perhaps the greatest blunder in world history. For this view, there are two reasons. The first is, that people are as yet unable to think clearly about Adolf Hitler, an enigmatic and fearsome personality. The second and more important reason is that, in judging a military situation, laymen (and too many military men as well) seldom bother to get at facts. Such judgment always begins by looking at a map. People are bored and confused by maps. Yet the key to Hitler's turn east in June 1941 lies in cartography.

One has to look at a map of Europe, preferably a terrain map that clearly shows rivers and the raised areas of mountains.

And one has to bear in mind certain simple unchanging facts about war. War is a violent clash of energies. The energies are of three kinds: animal, mechanical, and chemical, as in the destructive process of fire. Until the seventeenth century, the animal energies of horses and men were decisive, although machines like catapults and crossbows were of some use. With the chemical energy of exploding gunpowder, a new factor was added. The American Civil War first reflected the industrial revolution, chiefly in the massive gain of troop mobility through railroads exploiting the chemical energies of a fossil fuel, coal; and also in guns with new ranges and accuracy, thanks to advanced metallurgy and design.

Industrial war came fully into its own in 1914—18. The German people, operating on interior lines, on a grid of railroads brilliantly designed by Moltke for the swift shuttling of armies, with an industrial plant planned and built for war, all but beat a coalition that included nearly the whole world. In 1918, the revolutionary possibilities of a new use of fossil energy, the petroleum engine, were disclosed by the British tanks at Amiens, and by air combat among flimsy scout planes. A few military men grasped these possibilities; but only one postwar politician really understood them, and that man was an obscure ex-foot soldier, Adolf Hitler.

Hitler saw that the British and French, the supposed victors, were so exhausted that world empire lay open to their successor; and that even a small nation, with massive bold use of the petroleum engine, especially in combined operations on the ground and in the air, could gain the prize.

The Situation on the Map

The drawback of horses in war is that they must have hay; Napoleon faltered at Borodino partly from a shortage of fodder. Similarly, a petroleum engine must have petroleum to burn. Adolf Hitler could never forget this simple fact, no matter how many armchair strategists and shallow-clever journalists did.

There was only one filling station available for the German war effort on the European continent, and that was the oil under Rumania. We could get no oil by sea. All of Hitler's Balkan maneuvers and campaigns of 1940—41 therefore revolved around the Ploesti oil field. The war could not be won in the Balkans, but Germany might have lost it there.

A glance at the map shows that Ploesti, in the great plain drained by the Danube, lies dangerously near the Soviet border. Ploesti is a clear flat march from the Prut River of less than a hundred miles. But it is *six hundred miles* from Germany, and the Carpathian Mountains bar the way.

For this reason, when war between Hungary and Rumania threatened in July of 1940, Hitler acted fast to force a settlement. The Soviet Union did not like this. Russia, whether Czarist or Communist, has always stretched its bear claws toward the Balkan peninsula, and at the time Russia was sending vague threatening notes to Rumania. Hitler could not worry about Russian sensibilities, however, where his supply of petroleum was concerned. Without oil, the entire German war machine was but a mountain of dead iron.

But Russia's conduct gave him pause. His pact with Stalin was just a truce. He so regarded it, and he had to assume that a ruthless butcher like Stalin so regarded it. The question was, when would Russia move? This, Hitler could only guess from Russia's actions. In the Balkans, in the summer of 1940, while we were completing our brilliant campaign in France, the Soviet Union moved into Bessarabia, bringing the Red Army to the banks of the Prut, an advance averaging one hundred miles along a broad front toward our oil. Bulgaria, with a border only fifty miles from Ploesti, began at the same time to make territorial demands and military threats. In these gestures of Bulgaria against Rumania, we possessed hard intelligence that Russian intrigue was at work.

These ominous moves took place during the so-called "Battle of Britain." Western newspapers and broadcasters virtually ignored them. Western historians still ignore them. Balkan politics have always confused and bored Westerners, especially Americans. Yet this tense obscure maneuvering around Rumanian petroleum was much more crucial than all the romantically headlined dogfights in the English skies. Authors who chew over and over the Battle of Britain invariably wonder at Adolf Hitler's marked lack of interest in it. None of them seem to know enough military chronology and cartography to appreciate that the Führer had his eye, all during that inconclusive air skirmish, on the vital lowlands of the Danube.

Late in July, with the "Battle of Britain" barely started, Hitler ordered General Jodl to begin staff work on an invasion of the Soviet Union, to be set for late 1940 or the spring of 1941. Western writers often cite this move as conclusive proof of the German leader's "perfidy." But this comes of not looking at maps or studying chronology. Had Hitler not taken this precaution after Russia's tightening squeeze play on Ploesti, he would have been guilty of criminal neglect of his nation's interests.

The Grand Strategy Picture

Hitler's world view was Hegelian. Nations, empires, cultures, all have their season in history, the great Hegel taught us. They come, and they go. Not one is permanent, but in each age one dominates and gives the theme. In this succession of world dominions, we recognize the evolving will of the God of history, the World Spirit. God therefore expresses and reveals himself in the will of those world-historical individuals, like Caesar, Alexander, and Napoleon, who lead their states to world empire. Conventional morality cannot apply to the deeds of such men, for it is they who create the new modes and themes of morality in each age.

This Hegelian world view is, of course, at the other pole from the petit bourgeois morality which expects great nations to behave like well-brought-up young ladies in a finishing school, and would hold a mighty armed people no different, in the rules applicable to its conduct, than some pale shoe clerk. The big bourgeois powers like France, England, and America built their strength and expanded their territory by actions indistinguishable from armed robbery. Having achieved their "manifest destiny," they found it easy, of course, to scold a young vigorous Germany seeking to play its world role in turn. Adolf Hitler was not, however, a personality much impressed by such preachments.

In his program, the attack on Russia was the doorway through which Germany would enter world dominion. *Russia was our India, to be conquered and exploited in British style.* Germany had the will, the strength, the sense of destiny. She lacked only the food, the living space, and the petroleum. These things she had to take. Hitler's view was that once rule of the European continent was firmly in Germany's grasp, the Anglo-Saxon sea powers would perforce change their governments, choosing politicians who could get along with the new German world imperium.

The Center of Gravity

Clausewitz says, "We may . . . establish it as a principle that if we conquer all our enemies by conquering one of them, the defeat of that one must be the aim of the war, because in that one we hit the common center of gravity of the whole war."

The attack on Russia, which aimed for control of the central landmass of the earth with its limitless manpower and natural resources, was the true strike at the center of gravity.

Much specious argument is offered that England was "really" the center of gravity, because she could raise another coalition to combat Germany. This is the writing of men obsessed by Napoleonic analogies. England was neutralized, and virtually out of the war, in the spring of 1941, except for the minor nuisance of her air raids. She no longer ruled the seas. Japan and America both surpassed her. They presented no immediate problem to Germany, though a reckoning with the United States always lay in the future.

If militarily England was through, why was she not surrendering? Obviously, because she hoped for deliverance from the Soviet Union, or the United States, or both. America was far off and almost unarmed. Russia, on the other hand, was rapidly rearming, at our very borders, and openly threatening the lifeblood of Germany at Ploesti. True, she was attempting to mollify us, in the usual crude fashion of Russian diplomacy, by sending wheat and oil; but in return she was receiving machinery for arming herself against us. To be dependent for long in this fashion on a Stalin was intolerable.

Our bid for world empire was always a race against time. Germany was much smaller than its two great rivals, the Soviet Union and the United States of America. Its advantage lay only in its unity of purpose, its discipline, and the forceful leadership of Hitler. By 1941 it was clear that Franklin Roosevelt intended to get into the battle as soon as he could convert his industries to war, and delude his unwilling countrymen into following him; and it was equally clear that Stalin was only seeking a safe cowardly way to cut Germany's throat at Ploesti. Hitler put the case plainly in a frank and eloquent letter to Mussolini, on the eve of June 22: *"Soviet Russia and England are equally interested in a Europe . . . rendered prostrate by a long war. . . . Behind these two countries stands the North American Union, goading them on. . . . I have therefore, after constantly racking my brains, finally reached the conclusion to cut the noose before it can be drawn tight."*

Was Barbarossa Sound?

The argument that Hitler should have finished off England first has no realistic basis.

Hitler resembled Caesar in his determination to take, wherever it could be found, the lands and the resources his nation wanted. He was like Alexander in his broad vision of a new peaceful world order. But in his strategy he was Napoleonic, for like Napoleon his central problem was that he was surrounded by enemies. The Napoleonic solution was to use speed, energy, surprise, and extreme concentration of his forces at the attack point, in order to knock off his foes one at a time. This was what Hitler did. He always had a brilliant if somewhat adventurous sense of grand strategy; only his dilettantish interference in tactical operations, and his inability to be soldierly in the clutch, were ruinous.

In May of 1940 he had allotted a mere two dozen divisions in the east to confront the more than *two hundred* divisions of the Red Army, while he finished France and drove the disarmed British remnant off the continent. It was a fantastic gamble, but a perspicacious one. Stalin, who might have taken Berlin, proved only too happy to let Germany destroy France, while he grabbed land in the Baltic and the Balkans.

In 1941 the Soviet Union had grown much stronger. It had

moved within a hundred miles of Ploesti. It had gained control of the Baltic Sea. It had massed on its borders, confronting Germany and its conquered Polish territory, more than three million soldiers. And it was demanding a free hand in the Dardanelles, Bulgaria, and Finland. These demands, brought by Molotov in November 1940, were the last straw.

Hitler felt he really had only three choices. He could shoot himself, leaving the German people to negotiate a surrender; he could attempt the inconclusive task of subjugating England with the carnage of a Channel crossing, opening himself meantime to a treacherous assault from the east; or he could ignore neutralized, prostrate England, and attempt to realize his entire historic aim, in the hour of his greatest strength, in one devastating blow. Barbarossa was the solution: a one-front Napoleonic thrust, not the opening of a true two-front war.

Unprejudiced military historians of the future will never be able to fault Hitler for turning east. From the start he was playing against odds. He lost his well-calculated risk through a combination of operational errors and misfortunes, and the historic accident that at this hour he was opposed by a ruthless, spidery genius of the same mettle—Franklin Roosevelt.

The Role of Roosevelt

Roosevelt's essential problem in 1941 was timing. He was playing from temporary weakness against an opponent playing from top strength. The weakness of the American President was both internal and external. Where the German people were united behind their leader, the American people, confused and nonplussed by Roosevelt's supercilious and untrustworthy personality, were divided. Where Hitler disposed of the greatest armed forces on earth, at their peak of strength and fighting trim, Roosevelt had no Army, no Air Force, and a dispersed, ill-trained Navy. How then could the American President bring any weight to bear?

Yet he did it. He was well trained in the devices of impotence, having won the presidency in a wheelchair.

The first thing he had to do was strengthen Churchill's hand. Only Churchill, the amateur military adventurer with his obsessive hatred of Hitler, could keep England in the war. Churchill was having a wonderful time playing general and admiral, as his memoirs relate. However, under his leadership the Empire was going down the drain. England's one chance to save it lay in getting rid of its grand-talking Prime Minister, and electing a responsible politician to make peace with Germany. Had this occurred, the present world map would look unguessably different, but the pink areas of the British Empire would still stretch around the globe. Roosevelt's masterstroke of Lend-Lease kept Churchill in power. The Americans sent the British precious little in 1941. But Lend-Lease gave this brave, beaten people hope, and wars are fought with hope.

Hope was also the main commodity Franklin Roosevelt sent the Soviet Union in 1941, though supplies started to trickle through in November and December. Stalin knew the gargantuan industrial potential of America. That knowledge, and Roosevelt's pledges of help, stiffened him to fight. He sensed that while Roosevelt would never sacrifice much American blood to save the Soviet Union, he would probably send the Russians all kinds of arms, so that Slav bravery and self-sacrifice could fight the American battle for world hegemony.

The Convoy Decision

Roosevelt's instinct for subtle and breathtaking chicanery on a world scale was never better displayed than in his conduct on the question of the Atlantic convoys.

Most Americans were indifferent to the European war in May 1941. The soundest people were against intervening. Roosevelt managed to find an unpleasant name for them: "isolationists." However, in the circles around him, his sycophants kept urging him to initiate convoying of American ships to England. Indeed, it made very little sense to keep loading up English ships, only to have America's food and arms go to the ocean bottom.

Roosevelt obstinately refused to convoy. He had already received intelligence of the coming attack on Russia. In fact the whole world seemed to know it was coming, except Stalin. The last thing he wanted to do was interfere. He saw in it the inevitable slaughter of vast numbers of Germans. This prospect warmed his heart.

But an outbreak of war in the Atlantic could have halted Barbarossa. Hitler could have countermanded the orders until dawn on June 22. An order to stand down from Barbarossa would have been obeyed with great relief by the German General Staff.

Franklin Roosevelt understood what not too many other politicians of the time could grasp—that even Hitler in the last analysis depended on public opinion. The German people were united behind him and ready for any sacrifice, but they were not ready to commit plain suicide. News of war with the United States would have taken all the spiritual steam out of the drive on Russia. The German public had no understanding of America's military weakness. Despite Goebbels's propaganda, they remembered only that America's entry into the last war had spelled defeat.

Roosevelt was ready for war with Germany, he ardently desired it, but not until we were embroiled with the tough gigantic hordes of Stalin. So he kept his own counsel, put off his advisers, and kept twisting and turning under the probes of the press about convoying. His one course to ensure war between Germany and Russia was to hold off the convoying decision. That was what he did. He baffled and dismayed everybody around him, including his own wife. But he gained his grisly aim on June 22, when Hitler turned east.

TRANSLATOR'S NOTE: *Roon's defense of Barbarossa is unusual; most other German military writers do condemn it as the fatal opening of a two-front war. It seems Roon either played a part in designing the operation, or that the plan submitted by the Army Staff agreed with his own study made at Supreme Headquarters. Every man cherishes his own ideas, particularly military men.*

The argument about the key role of the Ploesti oil fields is not emphasized in many other military histories. Hitler began planning to attack Russia as far back as July 1940. The nonaggression pact was then less than a year old, and Stalin was punctiliously delivering vast quantities of war materials, including oil, to Germany. Hitler's act does look a bit like bad faith, if faith can be said to exist between two master criminals. The usual extenuation in German writings is that the Soviet troop buildups showed Stalin's intent to attack, and that Hitler merely forestalled him. But most German historians now concede that the Russian buildup was defensive. Hitler always regarded the attack on Russia to gain Lebensraum as his chief policy. It was natural for him to start planning it in July 1940, when his huge land armies were at maximum strength, with no other place to go. This was the big picture, and the oil supply problem may have been a detail. Nevertheless, Roon's discussion illuminates Hitler's problems.—V.H.

* * *

45

The players in our drama were now scattered around the earth. Their stage had become the planet, turning in the solar spotlight that illumined half the scene at a time, and that moved always from east to west.

At the first paling of dawn, six hundred miles to the west of Moscow, at exactly 3:15 A.M. by myriads of German wristwatches, German cannon began to flash and roar along a line a thousand miles long, from the icy Baltic to the warm Black Sea. At the same moment fleets of German planes, which had taken off some time earlier, crossed the borders and started bombing Soviet airfields, smashing up aircraft on the ground by the hundreds. The morning stars still twinkled over the roads, the rail lines, and the fragrant fields, when the armored columns and infantry divisions—multitudes upon multitudes of young healthy helmeted Teutons in gray battle rig—came rolling or walking toward the orange-streaked dark east, on the flat Polish plains that stretched toward Moscow, Leningrad, and Kiev.

A sad and shaken German ambassador told Foreign Minister Molotov in Moscow, shortly after sunrise, that since Russia was obviously about to attack Germany, the Leader had wisely ordered the Wehrmacht to strike first in self-defense. The oval gray slab of Molotov's face, we are told, showed a very rare emotion—surprise. History also records that Molotov said, "Did we deserve this?" The German ambassador, his message delivered, slunk out of the room. He had worked all his life to restore the spirit of Rapallo, the firm alliance of Russia and Germany. Eventually Hitler had him shot.

Molotov's surprise at the invasion was not unique. Stalin

was surprised. Since his was the only word or attitude in Russia that mattered, the Red Army and the entire nation were surprised. The attack was an unprecedented tactical success, on a scale never approached before or since. Three and a half million armed men surprised four and a half million armed men. The Pearl Harbor surprise attack six months later involved, by contrast, only some thousands of combatants on each side.

Communist historians use events to prove their dogmas. This makes for good propaganda but bad record-keeping. Facts that are hard to fit into the Party theories tend to slide into oblivion. Many facts of this most gigantic of land wars, which the Russians call *Velikaya Otechestvennaya Voina,* "The Great Patriotic War"—"Second World War" is not a phrase they favor—may never be known. The Communist historians assert that Stalin was to blame for neglecting intelligence warnings, and that is why the German surprise attack was successful. It is a very simple way to look at the amazing occurrence. So far as it goes, it is true.

*   *   *

Sunlight touched the red Kremlin towers, visible from the windows of Leslie Slote's flat, and fell on an opened letter from Natalie Henry in Rome, lying on his desk by the window.

Slote had gone to bed very late and he was still asleep. Natalie had sent him a joyous screed, for suddenly Aaron Jastrow had received his passport! He actually had it in hand and they were getting ready to leave on a Finnish freighter sailing early in July; and going by ship would even enable Aaron to retrieve much of his library. Knowing nothing of Byron's action at the White House, Natalie had written to thank Slote in effervescent pages. The news astonished the Foreign Service man, for in Italy he had felt he was encountering the cotton-padded stone wall that was a State Department specialty. In his answer, which lay unfinished beside her letter, he took modest credit for the success, and then explained at length why he thought the rumored impending invasion of Russia was a false alarm, and why he was sure the Red Army would crush a German attack if by chance one came. Trying to find gracious words about Natalie's pregnancy, he had given up and gone to bed. By the time his alarm clock woke him, his letter was out of date; but he did not yet know it.

Peering out of the window, he saw the usual morning sights of Moscow: a hazy blue sky, men in caps and young women in shawls walking to work, a crowded rusty bus wobbling up a hill, old women standing in line at the milk store, more old women queueing at a bread store. The Kremlin loomed across the river, huge, massive, still, the walls dark red in the morning sun, the multiple gold domes gleaming on the cathedrals. There were no air raid alarms. There were as yet no loudspeaker or radio reports. It was a scene of tranquil peace. Stalin and Molotov were waiting a while before sharing their astonishment with the people they had led into this catastrophe. But at the front, several million Red Army men were already sharing it and trying to recover from it before the Germans could kill them all.

Knowing nothing of this, Slote went to the embassy with a light heart, hoping to dispose of some overdue work on this quiet Sunday. He found the building in a most unsabbathlike turmoil; and there he learned, with a qualm in his gut, that once again the Germans were coming.

The sunrise slid westward to Minsk. Its first rays along a broad silent street fell on a clean-shaven workingman in a cloth cap and a loose worn suit dusted all over with flour. Had Natalie Henry been walking this street, she could not possibly have recognized her relative, Berel Jastrow. Shorn of a beard, the broad flat Slavic face with its knobby peasant nose gave him a nondescript East European look, as did the shoddy clothing. He might have been a Pole, a Hungarian, or a Russian, and he knew the three languages well enough to pass as any of these. Though over fifty, Berel always walked fast, and this morning he walked faster. At the bakery, on a German shortwave radio he kept behind flour sacks, he had heard Dr. Goebbels from Berlin announce the attack, and in the distance, just after leaving work, he had heard a familiar noise: the thump of bombs. He was concerned, but not frightened.

Natalie Henry had encountered Berel as a devout prosperous merchant, the happy father of a bridegroom. Berel had another side. He had served on the eastern front in the

Austrian army in the last war. He had been captured by the Russians, had escaped from a prison camp, and had made his way back through the forests to Austrian lines. In the turmoils of 1916 he had landed in a mixed German and Austrian unit. Early in his army service he had learned to bake and to cook, so as to avoid eating forbidden foods. He had lived for months on bread, or roasted potatoes, or boiled cabbage, while cooking savory soups and stews which he would not touch. He knew army life, he could survive in a forest, and he knew how to get along with Germans, Russians, and a dozen minor Danubian nationalities. Anti-Semitism was the normal state of things to Berel Jastrow. It frightened him no more than war and he was just as practiced in dealing with it.

He turned off the main paved avenue, and walked a crooked way through dirt streets and alleys, past one-story wooden houses, to a courtyard where chickens strutted clucking in the mire, amid smells of breakfast, woodsmoke, and barnyard.

"You've finished work early," said his daughter-in-law, stirring a pot on a wood-burning oven while holding a crying baby on one arm. She was visibly pregnant again; and with a kerchief on her cropped hair, and her face pinched and irritable, the bride of a year and a half looked fifteen years older. In a corner, her husband in a cap and sheepskin jacket murmured over a battered Talmud volume. His beard too was gone, and his hair cut short. Three beds, a table, three chairs, and a crib filled the tiny hot room. All four dwelled there. Berel's wife and daughter had died in the winter of 1939 of the spotted fever that had swept bombed-out Warsaw. At that time the Germans had not gotten around to walling up the Jews; and using much of his stored money for bribes, Berel Jastrow had bought himself, his son, and his daughter-in-law out of the city, and had joined the trickle of refugees heading eastward to the Soviet Union through back roads and forests. The Russians were taking in these people and treating them better than the Germans had, though most had to go to lonely camps beyond the Urals. With this remnant of his family Berel had made his way to Minsk, where some relatives lived. Nearly all of the city's bakers were off in the army, so the Minsk bureau for aliens had let him stay.

"I'm home early because the Germans are coming again." Accepting a cup of tea from the daughter-in-law, Berel sank into a chair and smiled sadly at her stricken expression. "Didn't you hear the bombs?"

"Bombs? What bombs?" His son closed the book and looked up with fright on his pale bony face. "We heard nothing. You mean they're fighting the Russians now?"

"It just started. I heard it on the radio. The bombs must have come from airplanes. I suppose the Germans were bombing the railroad. The front is very far away."

The woman said wearily, shushing the wailing baby as it pounded her with a little fist, "They won't beat the Red Army so fast."

The son stood. "Let's leave in the clothes we're wearing."

"And go where?" his father said.

"East."

Berel said, "Once we do, we may not be able to stop till we're in Siberia."

"Then let it be Siberia."

"*Siberia!* God Almighty, Mendel, I don't want to go to Siberia," said the wife, patting the peevish baby.

"Do you remember how the Germans acted in Warsaw?" Mendel said. "They're wild animals."

"That was the first few weeks. They calmed down. We kept out of the way and we were all right, weren't we?" the father said calmly. "Give me more tea, please. Everybody expected to be murdered. So? The typhus and the cold were worse than the Germans."

"They killed a lot of people."

"People who didn't follow the rules. With the Germans, you have to follow the rules. And keep out of their sight."

"Let's leave today."

"Let's wait a week," said the father. "They're three hundred kilometers away. Maybe the Red Army will give them a good slap in the face. I know the manager in the railroad ticket office. If we want to, we can get out in a few hours. Siberia is far off, and it's no place for a Jew."

"You don't think we should leave today?" said the son.

"No."

"All right." Mendel sat down and opened his book.

"I'm putting food on the table," said his wife.

"Give me a cup of tea," said her husband. "I'm not hungry. And make that baby stop crying, please."

Clever though he was, Berel Jastrow was making a serious mistake. The Germans were jumping off nearer Minsk than any other Soviet city, bringing another surprise, compared with which even their invasion of Russia has since paled in the judgment of men.

Bright morning sunshine bathed the columns of soldiers that crawled like long gray worms on the broad green earth of Soviet-occupied Poland. Behind the advancing soldiers, out of range of the fire flashes and smoke of the cannonading, certain small squads travelled, in different uniforms and under different orders. They were called *Einsatzgruppen,* Special Action Units, and they were something unparalleled in the experience of the human race. To place and understand these Special Action Units, one needs a brief clear picture of the invasion.

Much of the European continent in that area is a low-lying, soggy saucer almost like everglades, spreading over thousands of square miles. This big swamp, the Pripet Marshes, has always confronted western invaders of Russia. They have had to go south or north of it. Adolf Hitler's generals, intending to break the Soviet state with one sharp blow in a few summer weeks, were hitting north and south of the great swamp at the same time.

But the Special Action Units had no military purpose. Their mission concerned the Jews. From the time of Catherine the Great, Russia had compelled its millions of Jews to live in the "Pale," a borderland to the west, made up of districts taken in war from Poland and Turkey. The revolution had ended the Pale, but most of the Jews, impoverished and used to their towns and villages, had stayed where they were.

The border defense belt held by the Red Army, from the Baltic to the Black Sea, was therefore precisely where most of the Soviet Union's Jews lived. The Special Action Units were travelling executioners, and their orders were to kill Russia's Jews without warning and without regard to age or sex. These orders were unwritten; they came down from Adolf Hitler through Göring and Heydrich to the "Security Service," Germany's federal police, which organized the units. These squads had collateral orders to shoot summarily all commissars—political officers—of the Red Army. But these later orders were on paper.

There were four Special Action Units in all, placed to follow close on the three giant prongs of the German assault.

Army Group South, composed of Germans and Rumanians, was striking into the Ukraine, south of the marshes and along the Black Sea into the Crimea. With them came two Special Action Units, for here the Jewish settlement was dense.

Army Group Center was setting forth on the straight short road Napoleon took—Minsk, Smolensk, Vyazma, Borodino, Moscow. This road points north of the great swamp like an arrow for the capital. It passes between the headwaters of two rivers, one flowing north and the other south, the Dvina and the Dnieper. Military men call it the dry route and greatly favor it. With this main central thrust travelled another Special Action Unit.

Army Group North was driving up along the Baltic toward Leningrad, and a Special Action Unit followed close behind.

Counting officers and men, there were about three thousand of these travelling executioners all told in the four units. They were setting out to kill between three and four million people, which figured out to more than ten thousand murders for each man. It was clearly beyond them. The plan was to start the process, and then recruit native anti-Semites and German soldiers to complete the gruesome, unheard-of, but entirely real job they were setting out to do.

The Germans in the ranks of the Special Action Units were recruited mainly from the civil services: policemen, detectives, clerks, and the like. There were no lunatics or criminals among them. The officers were mostly lawyers, doctors, or businessmen, who through age or disability could not fight in the army. Many had high university degrees; one officer had been a theologian. Officers and men alike were good Germans, the sort of men who did not drive past red traffic lights, who liked opera and concerts, who read books, who wore ties and jackets, who had wives and children, who for the most part went to church and sang hymns, and who worked in little weekend gardens. Obedience was a German virtue. They had been recruited and ordered to kill these people. They had been told that the Jews were Germany's enemies, and that the only way to deal with them was to kill every last one of them, down to the babes in arms and their mothers. This word came from above. A prime German virtue was to accept such words from above and carry them out.

Strangely, the Jews already in German hands, in the territories stretching west from the invasion line to the Atlantic Ocean, were not yet being killed en masse. Nor was a program even under way to kill them. A mistaken idea exists that the Germans began killing Jews as soon as Hitler took power in 1933. That is untrue. They robbed the Jews, as they later robbed all the peoples they conquered, but the extortion was usually done under legal expropriation rules. Jews were often insulted, sometimes beaten, sometimes tortured, sometimes done to death or worked to death. But as late as June 22, 1941, only a few concentration camps existed, and most of the inmates were German opponents of Hitler. The existence of the camps filled the Jews with terror, but the Germans themselves were terrorized, too.

By June 1941 the European Jews were living a vile life and were yielding the last scraps of their property to the squeeze of German law. But they were living. "One can live under any law," a German Jewish newspaper put it.

So it happened that a Jew was safer behind the German lines, just then, than ahead of them. The Warsaw Jews, for instance, had reorganized themselves under the draconic Nazi rules. Though overwork, starvation, and disease were taking a toll, they were in the main managing to survive. At this point the Jastrows would have been somewhat better off not to have left Warsaw.

But Berel Jastrow, astute as he was and schooled in living with anti-Semitism, had not anticipated the Special Action Units. They were something new.

Adolf Hitler had given the order for the *Einsatzgruppen* back in March, so they may not have been much in his mind on June 22. He was following the progress of the invasion in a map room, where the light remained cool and gray long after sunrise. Disliking sunshine, the Führer had ordered his eastern campaign headquarters, which he dubbed *Wolfsschanze,* to be built facing north. A rail spur in a forest of east Prussia, not far from the jump-off line of Army Group North, led to this "Wolf's Lair," a compound of concrete bunkers and wooden huts surrounded by barbed wire, watchtowers, and minefields. *Wolfsschanze,* in fact, singularly resembled a concentration camp.

At the elbow of General Jodl stood one of the youngest and newest of German generals, Armin von Roon. Hitler did not like Roon and showed his dislike by abruptness. Roon came from a titled family, and spoke a polished Berlin German that contrasted sharply with Hitler's folksy, coarse Bavarian speech. His uniform, faultlessly tailored, contrasted too with Hitler's oversize, baggy soldier's coat. Above all, Roon had a beaked nose that looked a bit Jewish. But as a colonel in Operations, he had taken part in three elaborate Barbarossa war games. His memory was unusual; he knew to the hour the projected advances and had the picture of the thousand-mile-wide battlefield by heart. The Soviet Union was for Roon rather like a table model, spectacularly larger than the ones used in the games. The troops were men, instead of pinned and numbered flags, but the principles and the scenario were the same, at least to start with. (At the Nuremberg trials, Roon denied knowledge of the Special Action Units, until confronted with the order to kill the commissars, countersigned by him for the Operations Section. Then he recalled it, but pleaded ignorance of the *Einsatzgruppen*'s other purpose. The tribunal judged this farfetched, like some other points in Roon's defense.)

Until three hours after sunup of the invasion day, Roon dodged the Leader's harsh nagging questions about the trend of ground operations. Then he gave his judgment that things were going better than planned in the north; much better in the center; worse in the south. It proved an accurate estimate, and for a long period thereafter Hitler warmed to the beak-nosed general.

Here then was the laying down of the first cards in the giant poker hand. Hitler and his staff had guessed that the Russians would mass most strongly in the center, north of the Pripet River bogs, to shield their capital. But whoever had disposed of the Russian forces—Stalin, or the generals to whom he listened—had bet that the Germans would make their main drive south, to seize the Ukrainian farmlands and the Caucasus oil fields. Perhaps this judgment had come from reading *Mein Kampf*, in which Hitler openly called this seizure his life's aim. At any rate, the largest mass of Russian defenders lay south of the marsh. Thus the battle line was unbalanced. The Germans found themselves slowed in the south, but punching through with surprising ease toward Moscow. The first big Russian city in their path was Minsk.

When the sun rose in Rome, Aaron Jastrow was already working at his desk, in his suite in the Hotel Excelsior. By now Dr. Jastrow's book on Constantine needed only four or five more chapters, and he was very happy with it. At precisely eight as usual, the unchanging waiter brought the unchanging breakfast. Jastrow finished it and was settling back at his desk when a bedroom door opened noisily, and Natalie waddled in, wearing a pink bathrobe. Pregnancy, besides making her shapeless, had hollowed her cheeks and her eyes, and exaggerated her full mouth. "My God, have you heard the latest?"

"Has something good happened?"

"That depends. The Germans have invaded Russia."

"What! Are you sure?"

"It was just on the eight o'clock news."

"Bless me." Jastrow took off his glasses and rubbed them with a handkerchief. "Why, when did it start?"

"At dawn today."

"Well, I declare! The villain with the moustache is really throwing himself into his part, isn't he? A two-front war again!"

Natalie walked to the serving table on wheels that bore the breakfast remnants. "Would this coffee still be hot?"

"Yes, help yourself."

"The doctor told me not to eat or drink before he examined me, but I can't help it. I'm ravenous." Natalie began to wolf a sweet roll with coffee. "You'd better call the ambassador."

"I suppose so. But Russia's very far off, and what difference can it make to us? It's pleasant, really, to think of Hitler dwindling off into Russia. Shades of Napoleon, let us hope."

"If Finland gets dragged in, the *Vaasa* won't sail."

"Dear me, yes. You're completely right. Any news about Finland?"

"Not that I heard." Dropping heavily into a chair, Natalie glanced around at the broad room, furnished with maroon plush chairs and sofas, gilt mirrors, and marble statues. "God, this suite is oppressive. Just to get out of it will be so marvellous!"

"My dear, it's spacious, and we've got it for the price of two small rooms."

"I know, I know, but why not? The hotel's empty, except for Germans. It's giving me the creeps."

"I imagine they're in every hotel."

Natalie said with a gloomy look, "No doubt. Yesterday I recognized a Gestapo man on the elevator. Byron and I saw him in Lisbon. I know he's the same one. He has an odd scar like this"—she made an *L* in the air with one finger—"on his forehead."

"Surely that's a coincidence. Did he recognize you?"

"He gave me quite a stare."

"I wouldn't worry about it. Those men stare for a living. What did the doctor say yesterday, by the way? Everything normal?"

"Oh, yes." She sounded uncertain. "He just wanted to see me once more. I'm going to bed now for a while."

"To bed again?"

"He wants me to rest a lot. My appointment's not till noon."

"Well, all right. I do have this chapter just about ready for smooth copy."

"Aaron"—Natalie paused, chewing her underlip—"he doesn't want me to type for a while. It tires my back. Just until this fatigue clears up."

"I see." Jastrow sighed, and glanced around the room. "I agree, this place is *not* very cheerful. When I think of my lovely house standing empty . . . Natalie, do you suppose this Russian war changes things at all? I mean—"

"Jesus Christ, Aaron," Natalie snapped most disagreeably, "are you going to suggest you might still remain on the same continent with the Germans?"

"My dear"—Jastrow made a very Jewish gesture, a hunching of shoulders and an upward wave of both hands —"don't be impatient with me. You were a baby in the last war, but to me so little time has elapsed between them! It's just a continuation after a truce. Well, the talk we had then of the Huns spearing Belgian babies on bayonets and cutting off the breasts of nuns! And then I spent a year in Munich with some truly wonderful people. There are Germans, and Germans—oh, gracious, did I tell you that there's a letter from Byron?"

"What? *Where?*"

"The waiter left it in the hall, I think."

She ran heavily out of the room, snatched the white envelope, took it to her bedroom, and read it panting. It was a dully written letter, with no news except that he had been detached from the *S-45,* to go to a new fleet submarine, the *Tuna,* in the Pacific, and that Lieutenant Aster had been ordered to an older boat, the *Devilfish.* But the words of love and loneliness were plentiful, if banal. She undressed, got into bed, and greedily read and reread the pages until the sentences lost meaning.

The Italian doctor had told her that the blood stains, only two or three small ones, might mean nothing, but that she had to rest, to be sure of keeping the baby. Natalie intended to spend the next two weeks in bed.

The line between night and day glided across the Atlantic Ocean, for the most part passing over fluffy cloud and empty wrinkling blue water; very rarely, over specks in orderly rows, and other specks randomly scattered. The orderly specks were convoys; the random specks, German submarines trying to hunt them down or American ships trying to spot the submarines and warn the convoys. Bringing light and warmth indifferently to the hunters and the hunted in this far-flung three-way game, which the participants called the Battle of the Atlantic, the sunrise slid onto the next landmass, the New World.

Soon the windows of the CBS building in New York flamed with morning sun, but in the tomblike broadcasting floors there was only the same timeless electric light. The corridors and cubicles of the CBS news section, despite the early hour, were swarming and bustling. Hugh Cleveland, badly in need of a shave, sat at his old desk, scrawling on a yellow pad and puffing at a long cigar. He had not quit the *Who's in Town* program, despite the popularity of the amateur hour. The news feature show would still be his bread and butter, he liked to say, when the amateur fad was forgotten. Out of the portable radio on his desk came the sonorous accents of Winston Churchill:

"No one has been a more consistent opponent of Communism than I have . . . I will unsay no word that I have spoken about it. But all this fades away before the spectacle which is now unfolding. . . . I see the ten thousand villages of Russia, where maidens laugh and children play. I see advancing upon all this in hideous onslaught . . . the dull, drilled, docile, brutish masses of the Hun soldiery, plodding on like a swarm of crawling locusts . . ."

His telephone began to ring. He tried to ignore it, then snatched it and snarled, "Goddamn it, I'm listening to Churchill. . . . Oh! Sorry, Chet. Listen, if you're near a radio, turn the guy on. He is sensational!" Leaning back in his swivel chair, he cocked one ear toward the radio, holding the phone to the other.

"Behind all this glare, behind all this storm, I see that small group of villainous men who plan, organize, and launch this cataract of horrors upon mankind . . ."

"Chet, of course I thought of it. The minute the news broke, I sent a wire to the Russian consulate here. Naturally, I couldn't get through on the telephone. About an hour ago, they finally called me. Madeline Henry's gone over there, and they've promised they'll send somebody back with her. No, I don't know who, not yet. Hell, this morning their scrubwoman would be news!"

"Can you doubt what our policy will be? We have but one aim and one single, irrevocable purpose. We are resolved to destroy Hitler and every vestige of the Nazi regime. From this nothing will turn us—nothing. . . . Any man or state who fights against Nazidom will have our aid. Any man or state who marches with Hitler is our foe . . .

"The Russian danger is our danger, and the danger of the United States . . ."

Madeline scampered into the office, red-faced and shiny-eyed, and wildly pantomimed at her boss.

"Hang on, Chet, she's here." Hand over the receiver, Cleveland said, "What luck?"

"I got the ambassador. He's here in New York, and I got him."

"Holy Jesus! Are you kidding? The *ambassador?* What's his name, Ouskinsky?"

"Oumansky." She nodded excitedly. "He's coming here at ten to nine. The consul's bringing him."

"Hey, Chet, listen, will you? That girl has got Ambassador Oumansky. I swear to Christ! Oumansky! Listen, I've got to get ready for him. Sure, sure. Thanks." He slammed down the receiver. "How'd you do that, Madeline? Why isn't he in Washington?" Churchill's voice was rising in peroration. Cleveland snapped off the radio.

"Hugh, I asked to see the consul and told this beefy girl at the desk that I was from the *Who's in Town* program. That's all. Next thing I knew I was in this big office, with a huge picture of Lenin staring down at me, and there was Ambassador Oumansky, and he said he'd come on the show. He's a nice man, with wonderful manners."

"Fantastic! Terrific! Marry me!" Cleveland looked at his watch and passed a hand over his bristly face. "Christ! The Bolshie ambassador himself! What luck!" He jumped up, pulled the small girl into his arms, and gave her a kiss.

Madeline broke free, blushing darkly, glancing over her shoulder at the open door, and straightening her dress.

"You're a doll, Madeline. Now listen. While I clean up, how about drafting an intro and some questions and bringing them to me in the dressing room?"

The ambassador arrived promptly. Hugh Cleveland had not met a Russian Communist in his life, and he was amazed at Oumansky's excellent clothes, natural bearing, and smooth English. The consul was even smoother. The two Russians settled themselves, perfectly at ease, at the microphones.

"Mr. Ambassador, it is a privilege for me, and for *Who's in Town*, to welcome you at this historic moment—" Cleveland began, and got no further.

"Thank you very much. Since our two countries are now in a common struggle," Oumansky said, "I welcome the opportunity to give the American people the assurance of my country's fighting spirit on your popular program, *Who's in Town.* Allow me to read from Mr. Molotov's broadcast."

The consul handed Oumansky a typewritten document, to the horror of Cleveland, whose iron rule it was to cut off prepared statements.

"Well, Mr. Ambassador, if I may simply say—"

"Thank you. For brevity I have abridged the speech, but here are significant portions of Foreign Minister Molotov's exact words: *'Without any claim having been presented to the Soviet Union, without a declaration of war, German troops attacked our country, and bombed from their airplanes our cities . . .'* "

Cleveland held up a hand and tried to speak, but the ambassador rolled right on: " *'This unheard-of attack on our country is perfidy unparalleled in the history of civilized nations. It was perpetrated despite a treaty on non-aggression between the USSR and Germany, which the Soviet government has most faithfully abided by . . .'* "

"Mr. Ambassador, about that treaty, if I may ask just one—"

"Excuse me, I shall continue, and perhaps if time permits we can have a discussion too," Oumansky said with unruffled charm, and he went on reading sentences and paragraphs neatly underlined in purple ink. Cleveland made two more vain efforts to interrupt, which the ambassador pleasantly ignored, proceeding to the last lines on the last page:

" *'The entire responsibility for this predatory attack on the Soviet Union falls on the German Fascist rulers . . .*

" *'The Soviet government has ordered our troops to drive the German troops from the territory of our country . . .*

" *'Ours is a righteous cause. The enemy shall be defeated. Victory will be ours.'*

"To these eloquent words," said Oumansky, "I have little to add. I must return to my many official duties, and I thank you for this opportunity."

He passed the paper to the consul, smiled at Cleveland, and moved as though to rise. Desperately, Cleveland struck in, "Mr. Ambassador, I know how pressed you are in this tragic hour. I won't detain you. Just tell me this. How will the American Communists react to the news? They've been violently advocating neutrality, you know. They campaigned tooth and nail against Lend-Lease. Are they going to make a fast about-face now?"

Oumansky sat back placidly. "Most certainly not. As you know, the working class all over the world is in its nature peace-loving. It has nothing to gain from war, and everything to lose. The war began as a struggle between imperialistic powers, so the workers—as, for instance, the American Communist Party, as you just mentioned—opposed the war. But the Soviet Union has no empire and no colonies. It is simply a country of peasants and workers who want peace. In attacking us, the German Fascists threw off their mask and revealed themselves as the brutish common enemy of mankind. Therefore all peoples will now unite in solidarity to crush the German Fascist beasts. The American people too are a peace-loving people. The Soviet people will count on their support of our righteous battle."

"Mr. Ambassador—"

"In this connection," said Oumansky, "the historic British pledge of full support, which Mr. Churchill has just given, will be of decisive influence, since Winston Churchill is so justly admired in the United States for his heroic stand against Hitlerism. Good morning, and thank you very much."

As Madeline escorted the Russians out of the studio, Cleveland was saying, looking after them with exasperation, *"Who's in Town* has just brought you the exclusive first broadcast of the Russian ambassador to the United States, Mr. Constantine Oumansky, on the German invasion of the Soviet Union." His voice shifted from dramatic resonance to oleaginous good cheer. "Well, folks, it's sort of a big jump from invasions to the amazing new improved Fome-Brite, isn't it? But life does go on. If dirt invades your kitchen, the new improved Fome-Brite is the modern way to fight back—"

The sunrise, coming to Chicago, was invisible; a thunderstorm was blanketing the city. Through dark pelting rain, Palmer Kirby was riding in a taxicab to a secret meeting of the President's Uranium Committee, which was interviewing engineers from all over the country. The pur-

pose of the committee was to find out, from the practical
men who had to do it, whether enough U-235 could be
produced within the predictable time span of the war—
which was set at four or five more years—to make atomic
bombs or power plants. Dr. Lawrence's letter had asked
him to bring a feasibility report on manufacturing certain
giant electromagnets. The men were old friends; over the
years Kirby had supplied the Nobel Prize winner with
much specially built equipment for his cyclotron work.

Palmer Kirby worked on the borderline where commerce
exploited science; he always referred to himself as a money-
maker, but he had some scientific standing, because of his
early work at the California Institute of Technology. Kirby
knew what the giant electromagnets were for. His opinion
on producing uranium for military purposes was definite.
Not only could it be done; Kirby thought the Germans
were well along to doing it. The invasion of Russia struck
him as a scary corroboration of this.

Ordinary uranium looks like nickel. Chemically it is
lively, but nothing can make it blow up. Its strange radio-
activity will fog photographic plates; it may feel warmish;
and very long exposure to it may give a human being slight
burns. For better or worse, in the matter scattered through
the universe, there is also a tiny trace of the stuff, chemically the same, but different in atomic structure: the explosive isotope U-235. We know all about this now, but in
1941 scientists only guessed that a U-235 bomb might
work. It was all theory. The problem was first, to find out
whether a controlled chain reaction of uranium fission was
possible, or whether some unknown fact of nature would
stop it; second—if the first answer was yes—to get enough
pure uranium 235 to try exploding it; and third, if that
worked, to produce enough of the stuff to cow the world.
When he heard the news of Hitler's attack on Russia, Kirby
decided that *the Germans must have succeeded at least
with the first step*.

From his narrow vantage point, he saw the entire war
as a race between Germans and Americans to make
uranium 235 explode. Everything else—submarine sinkings, land campaigns, air battles—more and more looked
to him like vain blood-spillings, inconclusive obsolete
gestures before this one big showdown. Hitler's plunge into

Russia, opening a second front and releasing England from near doom, struck him as a madman's mistake—unless the Germans had successfully created a controlled chain reaction. If Hitler had uranium bombs or could count on having them within a year or two, the war was decided, and the Germans were simply making a gigantic slave raid in Russia, preparatory to assuming the rule of the earth.

From the information Kirby had, this appeared likely. It was the Germans who had discovered uranium fission. In 1939 they had set aside the whole Kaiser Wilhelm Institut to work on military use of the discovery. In conquered Norway, intelligence reported, they were making large amounts of heavy water. There was only one possible military use for heavy water, the queer substance with the doubled hydrogen nucleus—as a neutron slower in uranium fission.

The United States had no nuclear reactors, no technique for building one, no scientist who was sure a chain reaction could be created. In the whole country there were not forty pounds of uranium suitable for experiments; there was no setup for producing ordinary uranium in quantity, let alone the very rare isotope 235 that might blow up; and for all the meetings of the Uranium Committee and the whisperings among scientists, the government had not yet spent on this project *one hundred thousand dollars in cash.* Kirby estimated that by now the Germans, in their massive try for world empire, might have already spent, in the same effort, something like a billion dollars.

The Uranium Committee sat in a drab seminar room, warm and smoky despite the open windows and the continuing thunderstorm outside. Elementary equations from an undergraduate course were chalked on the small dusty blackboard. Kirby knew everybody who sat around the table except for two uniformed military visitors: an Army colonel and a Navy captain. The scientists were in shirtsleeves, some with ties off and sleeves rolled up. Lyman Briggs, director of the National Bureau of Standards, was still chairman, and this further depressed Kirby. Briggs was a pleasant gray-haired bureau head to whom a thousand dollars was a spectacular Federal expenditure. He wore his coat and tie.

Dr. Lawrence gave Kirby a friendly wave and turned to the military men sitting beside him. "This is Dr. Kirby, president of Denver Electric Works—Colonel Thomas and Captain Kelleher."

Kirby passed out copies of a mimeographed document and read the paper aloud, sometimes pausing for thunder crashes. The committee listened with narrow-eyed attention —all but Captain Kelleher, a bald chain smoker with a big double chin, who stared straight ahead in a slump, now and then scratching through his blue and gold uniform at one place on his chest. The Army colonel, a studious-looking small man with a bad cough, kept eating lozenges from a paper box, while he made shorthand notes on the margins of Kirby's paper.

Kirby was replying to questions posed to him by Lawrence in the letter: could he manufacture these giant electric magnets, and if so, what would be the probable costs and production time? Lawrence's idea—which he was pushing with the peculiar force and single-mindedness that made him loved or hated by other scientists—was to produce uranium 235 by separating a stream of ionized molecules of uranium in a magnetic field; a method Kirby had once described to Victor Henry. There already existed a laboratory tool, the mass spectrograph, that worked this way. Lawrence wanted to make giant mass spectrographs to get uranium 235 in sufficient quantities for war use. Nothing like it had ever been done. The whole notion required—among other things—monster electromagnets which would keep an unwavering field. The slightest voltage change would wash out the infinitesimal difference in the molecule paths of U-238 and U-235, on which the whole idea hung.

When Kirby named a feasible date for delivering the first magnets, and the range of prices he would charge, the committeemen started glancing at each other. He finished with a warning about supply problems requiring high priorities, and sat down. Lawrence was beaming at him through his round glasses.

"Well, that's encouraging," Lyman Briggs said mildly,

fingering his tie. "Of course, the price figures are still in the realm of pure fantasy."

The Navy captain put in, "Dr. Kirby, we've had fellows from General Electric and Westinghouse report on this. They project twice as much time, more than twice as much money, and they shade those performance characteristics considerably."

Palmer Kirby shrugged. "Could well be."

"Why should we take your word on feasibility against theirs?" Colonel Thomas said hoarsely, shaking a lozenge out of his box.

Kirby said, "Colonel, I once worked at Westinghouse. They make everything that uses an electric current. I make custom-designed equipment, and I specialize in electromagnets. It's a narrow specialty, but it's mine. The Germans were way ahead of us at one point. I went to Germany. I studied their components and imported their nickel alloy cores. Westinghouse and General Electric don't know that area of technology as I do. They don't have to. For special jobs in electromagnetics I can outperform them. At least I'm claiming that I can, and I'm prepared to bid in these terms."

When Palmer Kirby mentioned Germany, the glances went again around the table. The Navy captain spoke up in a peevish voice. "Are the Germans still ahead of us?"

"On what, sir?"

"On anything. On making these bombs, to get down to the short hairs."

Kirby puffed at his pipe. "Well, the self-confidence they've just showed isn't encouraging."

"I agree. Well, why don't we get going, then? All this committee seems to do is palaver." Kelleher sat up straight, glowering. "I'm not a scientist, and I can't say I've taken much stock in these futuristic weapons, but by Christ if there's anything in them let's get cracking. Let's go straight to the President and howl for money and action. I can assure you the Navy will back the committee."

Holding up a thin hand in dismay, Briggs said, "The President has more immediate things, Captain, requiring money and action."

"I don't agree," Thomas said. "More immediate than these bombs?"

Briggs retorted, "It's all pure theory, Colonel, years away from any possible practical result."

Captain Kelleher slapped his hand on the table. "Look, let me ask a real dumb question. What's Kirby talking about here? Is it the diffusion business, or the spectrograph business? Maybe I ought to know, but I don't."

"The spectrograph business," Lawrence said in a fatherly tone.

"All right. Then, why don't you just shoot the works on that? You've got a Nobel Prize. Why don't you send the President a red-hot plain-language memo that he can grasp? Why do you keep fudging around on these other approaches?"

"Because if we guess wrong on the basic approach," another scientist mildly observed, "we may lose several years."

Kirby could not resist saying, "Or lose the whole race to the Germans."

The discussion halted. The heavy drumming of the rain for a moment or two was the only sound. Briggs said, "Well! These things are still very iffy, as the President likes to say. We can't be going off half-cocked in this business, that much is certain. In any case"—he turned to Kirby with an agreeable smile—"I don't think we need detain you. Your report has been very useful. Many thanks."

Gathering up his papers, Kirby said, "Will you need me again, or do I go back to Denver?"

"Don't rush off, Fred," Lawrence said.

"Right. I'll be at the Stevens."

Kirby passed the morning in his hotel suite, listening to the radio bulletins and special reports on the invasion of Russia, and growing gloomier and gloomier. The incessant rain, with the sporadic lightning and thunder, reinforced his dark mood. He had not drunk before lunch in a long time, but he sent for a bottle of Scotch, and had it almost a third emptied when Lawrence called in high spirits. "Fred, you shone this morning. I thought we might manage lunch, but the committee's sending out for coffee and sandwiches, and working straight on through. Meantime something has come up. Do you have a minute?"

"I'm just sitting here, listening to CBS broadcast the end of the world."

Lawrence laughed. "It won't end. We'll beat the Germans to U-235, and that's the key to this war. Their industrial base is far inferior to ours. But the committee will certainly have to change its ways. The procedure is incredibly cumbersome. This business right now, for instance. Intolerable! One interview at a time, for secrecy, tying all of us up for days on end! We need one knowledgeable man in constant liaison with business and industry, and we need him right away." Lawrence paused, and added, "We've just been talking about you."

"Me? No *thanks.*"

"Fred, you're an engineer, you know business, and your grasp of theory is adequate. That's the desired combination, and it's rare. Unfortunately, no job in the world is more important right now, and you know that."

"But ye gods, who would I work for? And report to? Not the National Bureau of Standards, for God's sake!"

"That point is wide open. For secrecy, you might just get a consultant post in the Navy. Captain Kelleher is full of fire to get going, which rather amuses me. Years ago, Fermi came to the Navy with this entire project outlined. They turned him away as a crackpot. The Navy turned away Enrico Fermi! Well, Fred? Will you serve?"

After a pause Kirby said, "Where would I be posted?"

"It would have to be in Washington." Kirby was silent so long that Lawrence added, "Something wrong with going to Washington?"

"I didn't say that, but if you want those electromagnets built—"

"That's a year away, even assuming the approach is approved and the money appropriated. This must be done now. What do you say?"

This was Lawrence in his urgent and imperious vein, which Kirby knew well. He considered Lawrence possibly the most brilliant man alive. Kirby was several years older than the Nobel Prize winner. He had given up a straight scientific career and gone into industry after getting his Ph.D., largely because of his encounters with Lawrence and a few other men much younger than himself and unreachably more brilliant. They had made him feel outclassed and deflated. To be urged now by this man to take on a task of this importance was irresistible.

"I hope to hell I'm not offered the job," he said. "If I am, I'll accept."

By the time the sun rose over San Francisco, the line between night and day had travelled halfway around the earth, and the invasion of the Soviet Union was half a day old. Masses of men had been killed, most of them Russians, and the Soviet air force had lost hundreds of airplanes—or perhaps more than a thousand; the disaster was already beyond precise documenting.

In the officers' club at the Mare Island Navy Yard, at a window table in the sunshine, several submarine skippers were chatting about the invasion over ham and eggs. There was little dispute over the outcome. All agreed that the Soviet Union would be crushed; some gave the Red Army as long as six weeks, others foresaw the end in three weeks or ten days. These young professional officers were not a narrow-minded or prejudiced handful; their view was held in the armed forces of the United States right to the top. The wretched showing of the Red Army against Finland had confirmed the judgment that Communism, and Stalin's bloody purges, had reduced Russia to a nation of no military account. American war plans, in June 1941, ignored the Soviet Union in estimating the world strategic picture. The submariners at Mare Island, peacefully gossiping at breakfast about the spread of the holocaust on the other side of the world, were expressing only what the service as a whole believed.

The main topic of discussion was whether or not the Japanese would now strike; and if so, where. These few lieutenant commanders inclined to agree that so long as the President kept up his suicidal policy of letting them buy more and more oil and scrap iron, the Japs would probably hold off. But the consensus lasted only until Branch Hoban of the *Devilfish* challenged it.

No skipper in the squadron had more prestige. Hoban's high standing in his class, his chilling air of competence, his sharp bridge game, his golf shooting in the seventies, his ability to hold liquor, his beautiful wife, his own magazine-cover good looks, all added up to an almost suspiciously glamorous façade. But the façade was backed by performance. Under his command the *Devilfish* had earned three E's in engineering and gunnery, and in fleet maneuvers in May he had sneaked the *Devilfish* inside a destroyer screen and hypothetically sunk a battleship. He was clearly a comer headed for flag rank. When Lieutenant Commander Hoban talked, others listened.

Hoban argued that the world situation was like a football game, and that in Asia, the Russian Siberian army was the player facing Japan. With this latest move, Hitler had sucked the Russian man back toward the other wing, to be held as Stalin's last reserve. This was Japan's big chance. The Nips now had a clear field to run the ball from China south to Singapore, the Celebes, and Java, cleaning up all the rich European possessions. If only they moved fast enough, they could go over the line before the United States could pull itself together and interfere. He broke off elaborating this favorite metaphor of servicemen and left the breakfast table when he saw his new executive officer motioning to him from the doorway.

Lieutenant Aster handed him a dispatch from Commander, Submarines Pacific: DEVILFISH OVERHAUL CANCELLED EXCEPTION REPAIRS VITAL OPERATIONAL READINESS X REPORT EARLIEST POSSIBLE DATE UNDERWAY MANILA.

"Well, well, back to base!" Hoban grinned, with a trace of high-strung eagerness. "Very well! So ComSubPac expects the kickoff too. Let's see, today's the twenty-second, eh? There's that compressor and number four torpedo tube that have to be buttoned up. Obviously we don't get the new motor generator, and all the job orders will have to wait till we get alongside in Manila. But that's okay." Holding the dispatch against the wall, he pencilled in neat print, *Underway twenty-fourth 0700,* and handed it to Aster. "Send that off operational priority."

"Can we do it, sir?"

"Make the Captain of the Yard an information addressee. He'll damn well get us out of here."

"Aye aye, sir. We'll be short an officer. Ensign Bulotti's hospitalized for two weeks."

"Damnation. *That* I forgot. Well, we sail with four officers, then. Stand watch-and-watch till we get to Pearl, and try to hook us a fresh ensign out of the sub pool there."

"Captain, do you know anybody in ComSubPac Personnel?"

"Yes. Why?"

"Well enough to swipe an ensign off new construction?"

To Aster's saucy grin, Hoban returned a droll grimace. "Got someone in mind?"

"There's this ensign, a shipmate of mine off the *S-45* who's just reported aboard the *Tuna*. It's two whole months away from shakedown."

"Is he a good officer?"

"Well, unfortunately he's a sack rat and goof-off."

"Then what do we want him for?"

"I can make him deliver. In a pinch he's resourceful and courageous. His father's a captain in War Plans, and his brother flies an SBD off the *Enterprise*."

"That doesn't sound too bad. What class is he?"

"He's a reserve. Look, Captain," Aster exclaimed, at Hoban's wry expression, "the officer pool will be full of reserves. You're not going to keep a whole wardroom of regulars. Not on the *Devilfish*. Byron stands a good watch, and I know him."

"Byron?"

"His name's Byron Henry. Briny, they call him."

"Okay, maybe I'll telephone Pearl. Kind of a dirty trick to play on this Briny, though, isn't it? New construction, based in Pearl, is a lot better duty than going to Manila in the *Devilfish*."

"Tough titty."

Hoban looked curiously at his executive officer. He did not yet have Aster sized up. "Don't you like him, Lady?"

Aster shrugged. "We're short a watch stander."

The Pacific showed no combative specks to the westward-moving sunrise. Early sunlight slanted into the hangar deck of the *Enterprise*, moored to buoys in Pearl Harbor, on disembowelled airplanes, half-assembled torpedoes, and all the vast clutter of the floating machine shop that this deck was in peacetime. Sailors in greasy dungarees and officers in khakis were at work everywhere. Through the steel hollow, smelling as all carriers do of gasoline, rubber, metal, and sea air, a boatswain's pipe reverberated above the workaday noise, followed by a Southern voice on the loudspeaker: *"Now hear this. Meeting of all officers in the wardroom in ten minutes."*

Warren Henry climbed out of the cockpit of an SBD, wiping his hands on a greasy cloth. He put on his khaki cap, saying to the sailors working with him, "That's me. Wish me luck."

When he arrived in the wardroom, officers in khaki shirts and black ties already filled the chairs and lined the sides. Amidships, against the forward bulkhead, stood the movie screen, and on the green baize of a nearby table a slide projector rested. The captain, a chubby man with thick prematurely gray hair, rose and strode before the screen as soon as he saw Warren. "Gentlemen, I guess you've all heard the news. I've been keeping track on the shortwave, and it seems clear already that Der Führer has caught Joe Stalin with his hammer and sickle down." The officers tittered formally at the captain's pleasantry. "Personally I feel sorry for the Russian people, saddled with such lousy leadership. The few times I've encountered their navy officers, I've found them friendly and quite professional, though somewhat odd in their ways.

"The question is, how does this affect the mission of the *Enterprise?*

"Now, as many of us know, Lieutenant Henry of Scouter Squadron Six is something of a red-hot on military history. I've asked him to give us a short fill-in here, before we get on with the day's work, so that—attention on deck!"

Rear Admiral Colton appeared through a doorway, and with the noisy scrape of scores of chairs, all the officers stood up. He was a barrel-chested man with a plump purplish face scarred by plane crashes, a naval aviator dating back to the *Langley,* now ComAirPac's chief of staff. The captain conducted him to a leather armchair hastily vacated by his exec. Lighting an enormous black cigar, the admiral motioned at the officers to take their seats.

Standing before the screen, Warren started in the modest monotone of most Navy instructors, hands on hips, legs slightly apart. He made the conventional deprecatory joke about his ignorance, then went straight at the topic.

"Okay. Now, naturally, our concern is the Japanese. In

theory, there should be no battle problem here. We're so much stronger than Japan in military potential that any Jap move to start a war looks suicidal. So you hear civilians say we'll blow the little yellow bastards off the map in two weeks, and all that poppycock." Some of the young officers were smiling; their smiles faded. Warren hooked a blue and yellow Hydrographic Office chart over the movie screen, and took up a pointer. "Here's a chart of the Pacific. People shouldn't talk about blowing anybody off the map without a map in front of them." Warren's pointer circled the French, Dutch, and British possessions in southeast Asia. "Oil, rubber, tin, rice—you name what Japan needs to be a leading world power, and there it sits. With what's happened to the armed forces of the European empires since 1939, it's almost up for grabs. And the first thing to notice is that it's all in the Jap back yard. We have to steam for days, far past Japan, just to get there. The territory in dispute, in any Pacific war, will be ten thousand miles or more from San Francisco, and at some points only eight hundred miles from Tokyo.

"Well, so our government's been trying to keep the Japs quiet by letting them buy from us all the steel, scrap iron, and oil they want, though of course the stuff goes straight into the stockpile they need to fight a war against us. Now, I have no opinion of that policy—"

"*I* sure have," came a sarcastic gravelly growl from the admiral. The officers laughed and applauded. Colton went on, "It's not fit for tender ears. Sooner or later they'll come steaming east, burning Texaco oil and shooting pieces of old Buicks at us. Some policy! Go ahead, Lieutenant. Sorry."

Quiet ensued as Warren took away the chart. A pallid slide flashed on the screen, a situation map of the Russo-Japanese war.

"Okay, a little ancient history now. Here's Port Arthur," Warren pointed, "tucked far into the Yellow Sea, behind Korea. Jap back yard again. Here's where the Japs beat the Russians in 1905. Without a declaration of war, they made a sneak attack on the Czar's navy, a night torpedo attack. The Russkis never recovered. The Nips landed and besieged this key ice-free port. When Port Arthur finally fell, that was it. The Czar accepted a negotiated peace with a

primitive country, one-sixtieth the size of his own! It was
as great a victory for the Japs as the American Revolution
was for us.

"Now I personally think our history books don't give
that war enough play. That's where modern Japanese history starts. Maybe that's where all modern history starts.
Because that's where the colored man for the first time
took on the white man and beat him."

In one corner, near the serving pantry, the white-coated
steward's mates, all Filipino or Negro, were gathered.
When the topic was not secret, they had the privilege of
listening to officer lectures. Glances now wandered to them
from all over the wardroom, in a sudden stillness. The
Filipino faces were blank masks. The Negroes' expressions
were various and enigmatic; some of the younger ones
tartly smiled. This awkward moment caught Warren unawares. The presence of the steward's mates had been a
matter of course to him, hardly noticed. He shook off the
embarrassment and plowed on.

"Well, this was a hell of a feat, only half a century after
Perry opened up the country. The Japs learned fast. They
traded silk and art objects to the British for a modern
steam navy. They hired the Germans to train them an army.
Then they crossed to the mainland and licked Russia.

"But remember, Moscow was a whole continent away
from Port Arthur. The only link was a railroad. Long
supply lines licked the Czar. Long supply lines licked
Cornwallis, and long supply lines licked Napoleon in Russia. The further you have to go to fight, the more you thin
out your strength just getting there and coming back.

"Incidentally, at the Naval War College, war games
often start with a sneak attack by the Japs on us, right
here in Pearl Harbor. That derives from the Port Arthur
attack. The way the Jap mind works, why shouldn't they
repeat a trick on the white devils that once paid off so
well?

"Well, of course 1941 isn't 1905. We've got search
planes and radar. This time the Japs could get themselves
royally clobbered. Still, the nature of this enemy is strange.
You can't rule that possibility out.

"But always remember his objective. When the Japs
took on the Czar in 1904, they had no intention of march-

ing to Moscow. Their objective was to grab off territory in their own back yard and hold it. That's what they did, and they still hold it.

"If war breaks out in the Pacific, the Japs are not going to set forth to occupy Washington, D.C., and my guess is they won't even menace Hawaii. They couldn't care less. They'll strike south for the big grab, and then they'll dare us to come on, across a supply line ten thousand miles long, through their triple chain of fortified island airfields—the Gilberts, the Marshalls, the Marianas—and their surface and submarine fleets, operating close to home under an umbrella of land-based air.

"So I don't exactly see us blowing them off the map in two weeks."

Warren looked around at the more than a hundred sombre young faces.

"Peace in the Pacific once rested on a rickety three-legged stool. One leg was American naval power; the second, the European forces in southeast Asia; and the third, the Russian land power in Siberia.

"The European leg of the stool got knocked out in 1940 by the Germans. Yesterday, the Germans knocked out the Russian leg. Stalin's not going into any Asian war —not now. So it's all up to us, and with two legs out of the stool, I would say peace in the Pacific has fallen on its ass."

Warren had been talking along very solemnly, flourishing his pointer. The joke brought surprised chuckles.

"As to Captain Nugent's question, what does Hitler's move mean to us, the answer therefore comes out loud and clear, when you look at the map. Der Führer has sounded general quarters for the *Enterprise*."

Rear Admiral Colton was first on his feet to lead the applause. Clenching the cigar in his teeth, he pumped Warren's hand.

Gliding across an imaginary line that splits the Pacific Ocean from the north to the south polar caps, the sunrise acquired a new label, June 23. Behind that line, June 22 had just dawned. This murky international convention, amid world chaos, still stood. For the globe still turned as always in the light of the sun, ninety million miles away in black space, and the tiny dwellers on the globe still had to agree, as they went about their mutual butcheries, on a way to tell the time.

The daylight slipped westward over the waters, over charming green island chains, once German colonies, all entrusted to Japan under her pledge not to fortify them—all fortified. Endeavoring to emulate the white man, Japan had studied European history in the matter of keeping such pledges.

Day came to the city of Tokyo, dotted with charming parks and temples and an imperial palace, but otherwise a flat sprawling slum of matchbox shacks and shabby Western buildings. Catching up with the white man in two generations had impoverished the Japanese; four years of the "China Incident" had drained them dry. Obedient to their leaders, they were bending to their tasks, eating prison fare, building war machines by borrowed blueprints with borrowed metals under borrowed technical advisers, desperately trading silk, cameras, and toys for oil to make the machines go. Ninety million of them toiled on four quake-ridden rocky islands full of slumbering volcanoes, an area no larger than California. Their chief natural resource was willpower. The rest of the world knew little more about them than what could be learned from Gilbert and Sullivan's *Mikado*.

They were puzzling people. Their Foreign Minister, a little moustached man named Matsuoka, American-educated and much travelled in Europe, gave the impression of being a lunatic, with his voluble, self-contradictory chatter, and his wild giggling, grinning, and hissing, so different from the expected deportment of the Oriental. White diplomats guessed that his strange ways must be part of the Japanese character. Only later did it turn out that the Japanese also thought he was demented. Why the militarist cabinet entrusted him with mortally serious matters at this time remains a historical mystery, like the willingness of the Germans to follow Hitler, who in his writings and speeches always appeared to people of other countries an obvious maniac. It is not clear just how crazy Stalin was at this time, though most historians agree he later went stark mad. In any case, the deranged Matsuoka was in charge of Japan's relations with the world, when the deranged Hitler attacked the deranged Stalin.

Japanese historians recount that Matsuoka obtained an urgent audience with the emperor and begged him to invade Siberia right away. But the army and navy leaders were cool to the idea. In 1939, the army had had a nasty unpublicized tangle with Stalin's Siberian army, taking losses in the tens of thousands. They wanted to go south, where the Vichy French were impotent, the Dutch were cut off from home, and the beleaguered English could spare little force. Warren Henry's amateur analysis on the *Enterprise's* hangar deck had not been wrong on these main alternatives.

But Matsuoka insisted that by signing the Tripartite Pact with Germany and Italy, Japan had pledged to help them if they were attacked; and the German invasion clearly had taken place to fend off a Russian attack. Morality therefore required Japan to invade Siberia at once. As for the nonaggression pact with Russia—which he had himself negotiated—Russia never kept pacts anyway. To attack right now was vital, before Russia collapsed, in order for the onslaught to appear honorable, and not just picking up pieces. Matsuoka called this position "moral diplomacy."

One high-placed official is supposed to have commented quite seriously at this time that the foreign minister was insane; to which an elder statesman replied that insanity in Matsuoka would be an improvement. So much one can sift from the Japanese record.

The official secret decision was to "let the persimmon ripen on the tree"—that is, not to attack the Soviet Union until its defeat looked like more of a sure thing. For the China war went on and on, an endless bog, and the Japanese leaders were not eager to take on heavy new land operations. The thrust south looked like the easier option, if they had to fight. Planning for this was to proceed. Matsuoka was dismayed, and he soon fell from office.

At the time of sunrise in Tokyo, the sun had already been traversing Siberia for over three hours, starting at Bering Strait. Before bringing a second sunrise to the battlefront, it had eight more hours to travel, for the Soviet Union stretches halfway around the globe.

Amid the invasion rumors of May and June, a bitter story had swept through Europe, crossing the frontiers between German-held and free territory. A Berlin actress, the story went, resting after lovemaking with a Wehrmacht general, persuaded him to tell her about the coming invasion of Russia. He obligingly took down an atlas of the world and began, but she soon interrupted him:

"*Liebchen,* but what is that great big green space there all across the map?"

"Why that, *Liebchen,* as I told you, is the Soviet Union."

"*Ach so.* And where did you say Germany was?"

The general showed her the narrow black blob in mid-Europe.

"*Liebchen,*" the actress said pensively, "has the Führer seen this map?"

It was a good joke. But the nerve center of the Soviet Union was not in Vladivostok, at the far eastern end of the green space. The sunrise of June 23, passing west of the Russian capital, shone out within the hour on German columns, twenty-five miles advanced toward Minsk and Moscow in one day, through the massed forces of the Red Army and its heaviest border defenses.

46

PURPLE lightning cracked down the black sky, forking behind the Washington Monument in jagged streams. July on the Potomac was going out, as usual, in choking heat and wild thunderstorms. "There goes my walk home," Victor Henry said. Through the open window, a tongue of cool air licked into the stifling, humid office, scattering heavy raindrops on the wall charts. It began to pour in the street, a thick hissing shower.

"Maybe it'll break the heat wave," Julius said. Julius was a chief yeoman who had worked with him in the Bureau of Ordnance, a fat placid man of fifty with a remarkable head for statistics.

"No such luck. The steam will be denser, that's all." Pug looked at his watch. "Hey, it's after six. Ring my house, will you? Tell the cook dinner at seven."

"Aye aye, sir."

Tightening his tie and slipping into a seersucker jacket, Pug scooped up papers from the desk. "I want to study these figures some more. They're kind of incredible, Julius."

With a shrug and wave of both hands, Julius said, "They're as good as the premises you gave me to work from."

"Jehosephat, if it comes to that many landing craft for the two oceans, how can we build anything else for the next three years?"

Julius gave him the slightly superior smile of an underling who, on a narrow topic, knows more than the boss. "We produce sixty million tons of steel a year, sir. But making all those hair dryers and refrigerators and forty different models of cars too—that's the problem."

Pug dove through the rain to a taxicab that drew up at the Navy Building. A very tall man got out, pulling a soft hat low on his head. "All yours—why, hello there."

"Well, hi!" Pug pulled out his wallet and gave the taxi driver a bill saying, "Wait, please. —How long have you been in Washington, Kirby?"

"About a month."

"Come home with me for a drink. Better yet, join me for dinner."

"Thanks, but I don't think I can."

"I'm alone," said Victor Henry.

Kirby hesitated. "Where's your wife?"

"Spending my money in New York. She saw off our daughter-in-law and grandson on a plane to Hawaii. Now she's shopping for furniture and stuff. We bought a house."

"Oh? Did she get the one on Foxhall Road?"

"That's the one. How'd you know about it?"

"Well—I ran into Rhoda when she was house-hunting. You were out at sea, I guess. We had lunch and she showed me the place. I was all for it."

"Got much to do?" Pug insisted. "I'll wait for you."

"As a matter of fact," Kirby said abruptly, "I only have to pick up some papers. Let me dash in here for a minute. I'll be glad to have that drink with you."

Soon they sat together in the cab, moving slowly in the clogged rush-hour traffic of Constitution Avenue, in torrents of rain. "What are you doing in this dismal town?" Pug said.

"Oh, this and that."

"U know what?" grinned Pug, stressing *U* for uranium. Kirby glanced at the bald round head and red ears of the driver.

"Driver, turn on your radio," Pug said. "Let's catch the news."

But the driver could only get jazz, buzzing with static.

"I don't know what you hope to hear," Kirby said. "Except that the Germans are another fifty miles nearer Moscow."

"Our department's getting edgy about the Japs."

"I can't figure out the President's order," Kirby said. "Neither can the papers, it seems. Okay, he froze their credits. Does it or doesn't it cut off their oil?"

"Sure it does. They can't pay."

"Doesn't that force them to go to war?"

"Maybe. The President had to do something about this Vichy deal that puts Jap airfields and armies in Indo-China. Saigon's a mighty handy jump-off point for Malaya and Java—and Australia, for that matter."

Kirby deliberately packed his pipe. "How is Rhoda?"

"Snappish about various foul-ups in the new house. Otherwise fine."

Through puffs of blue smoke, the scientist said, "What do we actually want of the Japs now?"

"To cease their aggression. Back up out of Indo-China. Get off the Chinese mainland. Call off that Manchukuo farce, and free Manchuria."

"In other words," said Kirby, "give up all hope of becoming a major power, and accept a military defeat which nobody's inflicted on them."

"We can lick them at sea."

"Do we have an army to drive them out of Asia?"

"No."

"Then don't we have our gall, ordering them out?"

Pug looked at Kirby under thick eyebrows, his head down on his chest. The humidity was giving him a headache, and he was very tired. "Look, militarist fanatics have taken charge there, Kirby. You know that. Slant-eyed samurais with industrial armaments. If they ever break loose and win southeast Asia, you'll have a yellow Germany in the Pacific, with unlimited manpower, and most of the oil and rubber in the world. We have to maneuver while we can, and fight if we must. The President's freezing order is a maneuver. Maybe he'll work out some deal with them."

"Appeasement," Kirby said.

"Exactly, appeasement. We've been appeasing them right along with the oil shipments. So far they haven't attacked south and they haven't hit Russia in the back. I think the President's just feeling his way, day by day and week by week."

"Why doesn't he declare war on Germany?" Kirby said. "Why this interminable pussyfooting about convoys? Once Russia collapses, the last chance to stop Hitler will be gone."

"I can tell you why Roosevelt doesn't declare war on Germany, mister," spoke up the taxi driver in a rough, good-humored Southern voice, not looking around.

"Oh? Why?" said Kirby.

"Because he'd be impeached if he tried, that's why, mister. He knows goddamned well that the American people aren't going to war to save the Jews." He glanced over his shoulder. Blue eyes twinkled in a friendly fat face, smiling jovially. "I have no prejudices. I'm not prejudiced against the Jews. But I'm not prejudiced for them, either. Not enough to send American boys to die for them. That's not unreasonable, is it?"

"Maybe you'd better look where you're driving," said Pug.

The cabbie subsided.

"It's a nice spot," Kirby said. They were on the back porch and Pug was pouring martinis. The house stood on a little knoll, topping a smooth lawn and a ravine of wild woods. A fresh breeze smelling of wet leaves and earth cooled the porch.

"Rhoda likes it."

They drank in silence.

"How about that cabbie?" said Kirby.

"Well, he said it straight out. It's been said on the Senate floor often, in double-talk."

Kirby emptied his glass, and Pug at once refilled it.

"Thanks, Pug. I'm having unusual feelings these days. I'm starting to suspect that the human race, as we know it, may not make it through the industrial revolution."

"I've had a bad day myself," Pug said, as the scientist lit his pipe.

"No," Kirby said, slowly waving out the thick wooden match, "let me try to put this into words. It's occurred to me that our human values, our ideas of right and wrong, good and bad, evolved in simpler times, before there were machines. Possibly the Germans and the Japanese are really adapting better to the new environment. Their successes suggest that. Also the way their opponents keep stumbling and crumbling. We may be having a Darwinian change in society. Authoritarian rule may be best suited to urban machine life—armed bosses indifferent to mercy or probity, keeping order by terror, and ready to lie and kill as routine policy. After all, most of the machines aren't a hundred years old. The airplane isn't forty years old. And democracy's still a fragile experiment." Kirby paused to drain his glass. "You called the Japanese industrial samurais. That rang the bell. They've starved themselves, stripped their country, to build or buy machines, and they've jumped out of nowhere to center stage of history. The Nazi or samurai idea may just make more sense in a changed world, Pug. Is this merely martini talk, and is there any left in that jug?"

"There's plenty," said Pug, pouring, "and more where it came from. I'm feeling better by the minute. It's nice on this porch."

"It's marvellous," said Palmer Kirby.

"Why don't you stay for dinner?" Pug said. "What else do you have to do?"

"I don't like to impose on you."

"I'm having chops, potatoes, and a salad. It's just putting on a couple more chops. Let me tell the cook."

"All right, Pug. Thanks. I've done a lot of eating alone lately."

"Be back in a minute," said Victor Henry, taking the jug. He brought it back full and tinkling.

"I put off dinner," he said. "Give us a chance to relax."

"Suits me," said Kirby, "though from the mood I'm in and the size of that jug, you may have to lead me to the dining room."

"It's not far," Pug said, "and the furniture has few sharp edges."

Kirby laughed. "You know, about the first thing your very sweet wife Rhoda said to me was that I drank too much. At the dinner she gave me in Berlin. You remember, when you had to fly back to see the President. I was in a bad mood, and I did swill a lot of wine fast. She brought me up short."

"That was rude. The amount a man drinks is his own business," said Pug. "Not to mention that on occasion my proud beauty has sort of a hollow leg herself."

"Say, you mix a hell of a good martini, Pug."

"Kirby, what you were saying before, you know, is only this wave-of-the-future stuff that the Lindberghs have been peddling."

"Well, Lindy's the type of the new man, isn't he? Flying an ocean by himself in a single-motor plane! He pointed the way to much that's happened since."

"He's not a liar and murderer."

"Only the bosses need be, Henry. The rest, including the scientific and mechanical geniuses like Lindy, and the wheelhorses like me, merely have to obey. That's obviously what's been happening in Germany."

"I'll tell you, Kirby," Pug said, swirling his glass and feeling very profound, "there's nothing new about such leaders. Napoleon was one. He had his propaganda line, too, that weakened the foe before he fired a shot. Why, he was bringing liberty, equality, fraternity to all Europeans. So, he laid the continent waste and made it run with blood for a dozen years or so, until they got wise to him and caught him and marooned him on a rock."

"You think that'll happen to Hitler?"

"I hope so."

"There's a difference. Napoleon had no machines. If he had had airplanes, telephones, tanks, trucks, machine guns —the whole industrial apparatus—don't you think he might have clamped a lasting tyranny on Europe?"

"I'm not sure. I happen to have a low opinion of Napoleon. Napoleon sold Jefferson nearly a million square miles of prime land, you know—our whole Middle West, from Louisiana to the Rockies and the Canadian border—for fifteen million dollars. Fifteen million! It figured out to four cents an acre for real estate like Iowa and Nebraska. And Minnesota, with all that iron ore. Colorado with its gold and silver. Oklahoma with its oil. I don't see how anybody, even a Frenchman, can figure Napoleon as a genius. He was a bloodthirsty ass. If he'd sent just one of his smaller armies over here to protect that territory—just a couple of divisions to hold the Louisiana territory, instead of wandering around Europe slaughtering and looting—and a few thousand Frenchmen to colonize the land, there's little doubt that France would be the world's greatest power today. Instead of what she is, a raped old bag."

"I can't say that has occurred to me before," Kirby said, smiling at the phrase. "It's probably fallacious."

"What's happening with uranium?" Victor Henry said.

Kirby's smile turned wary. "Is that why you're plying me with martinis?"

"If martinis can loosen you up about uranium, Kirby, let it happen first with an officer in War Plans, and thereafter don't drink martinis."

"Doesn't War Plans have any information?"

"No. It's still Jules Verne talk to us."

"Unfortunately, it's more than that."

The rain was starting again, with a whistle of wind, a rumble of thunder, and a whoosh of raindrops through the porch screen. Pug dropped a canvas flap on the windward side, fastening it down as Kirby talked.

"The best present judgment, Pug, is that the bomb can be built. It might take, with an all-out effort, two years or fifty years. Those are the brackets. But we're not making an all-out effort. We're making a good effort on the theory end, that's all. Tremendous brains are at work, some of them driven from Europe by the Germans, for which we owe them cordial thanks. The big question is, how far ahead are the Germans by now? We aren't even started. There's no money available and no plan. Making uranium bombs will go in several stages, and some of us fear that the Germans have cracked stage one, which is to get enough of the isotope to start a controlled chain reaction."

"What kind of weapon are we talking about here?" said Pug. "How powerful an explosive?"

"Again, the answer is X. The power may be too much altogether. That is, the bomb may blow itself apart before it can really work. In theory one bomb might level New York City. Or even an area like Rhode Island. You're dealing here with very large unknowns. There's talk that it could start a process that could blow up the earth. The best men don't take that too seriously. I frankly don't know enough to be sure."

"You're talking about a pretty good bomb," said Victor Henry.

"Hellooo!"

Rhoda Henry's voice rang through the spacious house, and they heard heels clicking on the parquet floor. "Surprise! Anybody home? I'm DRENCHED. I'm a drowned RAT."

"Hi! I'm out here," Pug called, "and we've got company."

"We have?"

"Hello, Rhoda," said Kirby, standing.

"Oh my GAWD!" She froze in the doorway, staring. Rhoda's purple hat dripped, she carried a sodden paper bundle, and her flowered silk dress clung wetly to her shoulders and bosom. Her face glistened with rain. Her eye makeup was blurred, her lipstick blotchy on pale lips. Wet strands of hair hung down her forehead and neck.

Pug said, "You finished up sort of fast in New York, didn't you? I asked Fred Kirby in for a drink, because we happened—"

Rhoda vanished. Her scampering footsteps dwindled into the house and up a staircase.

"Dad, what a place! It's a mansion!" Madeline walked through the doorway, as wet as her mother, shaking rain from her hair and laughing.

"Well, Matty! You too?"

"Look at me! Christ, did we catch it! No cabs in sight, and—hello, Dr. Kirby."

"You'll both get the flu," Pug Henry said.

"If somebody gave me a martini," said Madeline, eyeing the jug, "I might fight the infection off." She explained, as her father poured the drink, that Hugh Cleveland had business at the War Department next morning. Rhoda had decided to come back to Washington with them. The girl took a quick practiced pull at the cocktail.

"Where's your luggage?" Pug said. "Go put on dry clothes."

"I dropped my stuff at the Willard, Dad."

"What? Why? Here's a whole big house at your disposal." .

"Yes. I came to have a look at it. Then I'll go back to the hotel and change."

"But why the devil are you staying at the hotel?"

"Oh, it's simpler." She glanced at her watch. "Christ, almost seven o'clock."

Pug wrinkled his nose at his daughter, not caring much for her brassiness. But she looked pretty, despite her wet hair and wrinkled pink linen suit. Rhoda's fear that Madeline would turn plain at twenty-one was proving flat wrong. "What's the rush?"

"We're having dinner with a big Army wheel, Dad, to try to sell him on a new program idea. Hugh visits a different military installation every week. We put on amateurs from the service, and do a tour of the base, and a pitch about preparedness. I suggested the idea, even the name. *The Happy Hour*. The network is wild about it." She looked at the two middle-aged men, her eyes very bright, and held out her glass. "Can I have a little more? I'll own stock in this thing if it goes through! Imagine! I actually will. Hugh Cleveland's going to form a corporation and give me some stock. He promised me. How about that? Maybe I'll be rich! Well, Dad?" she added with an arch giggle. "You look kind of sour."

"To begin with," Pug said, "come September we may not have an army. Don't you read the papers?"

Madeline's face fell. "You mean about the draft?"

"Yes. Right now it's fifty-fifty or worse that Congress won't vote for renewal."

"But that's insane. Why, by September Hitler will probably have beaten Russia. How far is he from Moscow now? A hundred miles, or something?"

"I'm not saying the politicians make sense. I'm telling you the fact."

"Christ, that would blow *The Happy* Hour sky high, wouldn't it? Oh, well. We'll see." She stood, shaking out her skirt. "Ugh. I have rain trickling around inside, in odd little places. I'll take a fast gander at the house. Then I'll tool off."

"I'll show you around," Pug said. "How about it, Kirby? Want to join the tour?"

"I guess I'll leave," said Kirby. "Rhoda's back, and I don't want to intrude, and besides I have a lot of—"

"You sit right down," Victor Henry said, pushing Palmer Kirby into a wicker armchair. "Houses bore me too. Have one more shortie, and I'll be joining you."

"I've had plenty," Kirby said, reaching for the jug.

Madeline went from room to room with her father, exclaiming with pleasure at what she saw. "Christ, look at the moldings in this dining room . . . Oh, Christ, what a stunning fireplace . . . Christ, look at the size of these closets!"

"Say, I'm no prude," Pug remarked at last, "but what's this 'Christ, Christ,' business? You sound like a deckhand."

Rhoda called from her dressing room, "That's right, Pug, tell her! I've never heard anything like it. You get more Christs from her in five minutes than in a church sermon an hour long. It's so vulgar."

Madeline said, "Sorry, it's a habit I've caught from Hugh."

"Oh, Pug"—Rhoda's voice again, loudly casual—"where did you dig up Palmer Kirby? Did he telephone?"

"Just ran into him. He's staying for dinner. Is that all right?"

"Why not? Madeline, you're not really staying at the Willard, are you? It looks so PECULIAR, dear. Please go and bring your bags home."

"Never mind, Mother. Bye-bye."

Pug said, walking down the stairs with her, "We bought a big place just so you kids could stay here when you're in town."

She put a hand lightly on his arm and smiled. The condescension embarrassed him. "Really, Dad, I know what I'm doing. We'll be up very late with the writers tonight."

"This fellow Cleveland," said Victor Henry with difficulty. "Is he okay?"

Her secure womanly smile broadened. "Daddy, if there were any hanky-panky going on, I'd be a lot sneakier, wouldn't I? Honestly. Give me some credit."

"Well, you're grown-up. I know that. It just came on kind of fast."

"Everything's fine. I'm having the time of my life, and one day you'll be real proud of me."

"I'll call a cab for you," Pug muttered, but as he reached for the telephone in the marble-floored hallway, it rang. "Hello? Yes, speaking . . . *yes*, Admiral." Madeline saw her father's face settle into tough alert lines. "Aye aye, sir. Yes, will do. Good-bye, sir."

Pug dialled Rhoda's room on the intercom line. "Are you almost dressed?"

"Five minutes. Why?"

"I'll tell you when you come down."

He called for a taxicab. Madeline was used to asking no questions when Victor Henry's face took on that look and he spoke in those tones. They returned to the porch, where Kirby lolled in the wicker armchair, smoking his pipe. Rhoda appeared almost at once in a swishy green dress, her hair smartly combed and curled, her face made up as for a dance.

"Well! Quick-change artistry," Pug said.

"I hope so. When I got here I looked like the witch in *Snow White*."

"Rhoda, I just got a call from Admiral King. He's at the Department. I'll ride downtown with Madeline. You go ahead and give Fred his dinner. Maybe I'll get back in time for coffee, or something. Anyway, I'll call you when I know what it's all about."

The taxi honked outside. Kirby offered to leave too. Victor Henry wouldn't hear of it. He liked the scientist. He had invited him home partly for company, partly to pump him about uranium. Pug Henry no more imagined anything between this man and Rhoda than he suspected his wife of cannibalism. He prevailed on Kirby to stay, and left with his daughter.

When the outside door closed, Rhoda said brightly, "Well! How long has it been, Palmer? An age."

Kirby sat forward, hands on his knees. "Pug doesn't know he's put you in a spot. I'll be going."

Rhoda sat composed, legs crossed, arms folded, head atilt. "You'll waste some good double lamb chops. Can't you smell them? Dinner's about ready."

"Rhoda, I really believe you don't feel in the least awkward."

"Oh, Palmer, I take things as they come. I'm very glad to see you, actually. What brings you to Washington anyway?"

"A defense job, about which I can tell you nothing except that it's going very badly."

"You mean you're living here?"

"I have an apartment in the Wardman Park."

"Well, well. What about your factory?"

"I have excellent managers and foremen. I fly to Denver every two weeks or so. I just got back." With a sarcastic, one-sided grin he added, "It's disturbing how well things go on without me."

"And how is that house of yours?"

"Fine. I didn't sell it, and now I won't."

"Oh? And now, here you are. Funny."

" 'Funny' isn't the word I would choose."

Rhoda dropped her voice to a soft, intimate note. "Was my letter so very upsetting?"

"It was the worst blow I've had since my wife died."

Rhoda blinked at his rough tone, and sighed. "I'm sorry." She sat clasping and unclasping her fingers in her lap. Then she tossed her head. "I'm trying to think how to tell this so I don't come out a flibbertigibbet, but to hell with that. I sat next to the President at that White House dinner. He was nice to me. He liked me. He said wonderful things about Pug, about his future career. A divorced man is very handicapped in the service, especially when he's in sight of flag rank. I'm very aware of that. I've seen how it works. And—well, so I did what I did. I've slept badly ever since, Palmer, and I've been an awful crab. But I've stuck to him, and I don't intend to apologize."

"Dinner, Miz Henry." A gray-haired colored woman in a white smock appeared in the doorway, looking sad and reproachful.

"Oh dear. Oh yes. What time is it, Barbara?"

"It's half past eight now, Miz Henry."

"That's awful. I never intended for you to remain this late. Palmer, you're staying, of course. Just put it on the table, will you, Barbara? Then you can go."

By the time Rhoda Henry and Palmer Kirby had finished off the thick chops, a salad, and a bottle of wine, the tension between them was gone, and he was laughing at her droll stories of troubles with the new house. She was laughing too, though, as she said, at the time the mishaps had put her in wild rages.

"What would you say to another glass of St. Julien with the cheese, Palmer?"

"Rhoda, if he comes home and finds us cracking a second bottle, those eyebrows will go way up, so."

"Oh, pshaw." She began clearing dishes. "Many's the second bottle he and I have cracked. And third ones, on occasion." She paused, holding a stack of dishes. "I can't tell you how good I feel. This couldn't possibly have been planned. But there's a great weight off my mind."

Rhoda brought the coffee, and the second bottle, out to the back porch. The rain was over. Beyond the dim trees, in July twilight fading into darkness, a few stars showed.

"Ah! Isn't this pleasant?" she said. "I think this porch is the reason I wanted the place. It makes me think of the house we had in Berlin."

"This is like a Berlin summer evening," Kirby said. "The light that lingers on, the fresh smell of rained-on trees—"

She said, "You remember?"

"I have an excellent memory. A little too good."

"I have a very handy one, Palmer. It tends to remember the good and forget the bad."

"That is a female memory." Dr. Kirby gulped his wine with an abrupt motion. "Now let me ask you something, Rhoda. This may really sound offensive. But we may never talk like this again. I've had a lot to drink. Much too much, no doubt. Your letter was a bad shock. I've thought and thought about this thing ever since. You told me that until I came along there had been no one else. I believed you. I still do. But I have a question to ask you. How come?" After a marked silence, broken only by the chirping of birds, he said, "I've made you angry."

"No." Rhoda's voice was throaty and calm. "Of course I know the answer you want—that you were irresistible and there'd never been anyone remotely like you. That's true enough. Still. I've had plenty of chances, dear. And I don't just mean drunken passes at the officers' club. There have been times . . . but to be absolutely honest, these men have all been naval officers like Pug. That's the circle I move in. Not one has measured up to him, or even come very close." She was silent for a space. "Don't take this wrong. I'm not blaming Pug for what happened this time. That would be too low. But he does shut me out so much! And from the moment the war started, that got much worse. Pug's a fanatic, you know. Not about religion, or politics. About getting things done."

"That's an American trait," said Palmer Kirby. "I'm the same kind of fanatic."

"Ah, but in Berlin, whether you knew it or not, you were courting me. When Pug courted me, I fell in love with him, too." She uttered a low chuckle, and added, "Let me say one thing more. Though you, of all people, might give me the horselaugh. I'm a good woman. At least I think I am. So, with one thing and another, there's been no one else. Nor will there be. I'm a quiet grandma now. That's that."

They did not speak for a long time. In the darkness, they were two shadowy shapes, visible only by the dim reflection of unseen streetlamps on the leaves.

"Pug's never called," said Rhoda quietly.

The shape of Kirby emerged from the wicker chair, looming tall. "I'll go now. The dinner was a success. I feel remarkably better. Thanks."

She said, "Will I see you again?"

"Washington's a pretty small town. Look at the way I bumped into Pug."

"Can you find your way out, dear?"

"Certainly."

"I don't mean to be rude, but to be frank, at the moment my eyes are messy."

Palmer Kirby came to her, bowed over her hand, and

kissed it. She put her other hand over his and gave it a soft lingering pressure.

"My," she said. "So continental. And very sweet. Straight through the living room, darling, and turn left to the front door."

47

A WEEK later, Victor Henry lay in the upper bunk of an officer's cabin in the heavy cruiser *Tuscaloosa,* above a gently snoring colonel of the Army War Plans Division. A hand on his shoulder and a whisper, "Captain Henry?" brought him awake. In the red glow from the corridor, he saw a sailor offering a dispatch board. Pug switched on his dim bunk light.

DESIRE CAPTAIN VICTOR HENRY TRANSFER WITH ALL
GEAR TO AUGUSTA PRIOR TO 0500 TODAY FOR FORTH-
COMING EXERCISE X

KING

"What time is it?" Pug muttered, scribbling his initials on the flimsy sheet.

"0430, and the OOD says the captain's gig is standing by for you, sir."

Pug tried to pack quietly, but a squeaky metal drawer woke the colonel. "Hey, skipper, leaving me? Where are you off to?"

"The *Augusta.*"

"What?" The colonel yawned, and snuggled under his blanket. Even in midsummer, the morning air was cool in Nantucket Bay. "I thought that boat's only for big brass and the President."

"I guess the admiral decided he needs another typist."

"Would that be Admiral King? The one who shaves with a blowtorch?"

Henry laughed politely. "Yes, that's the one."

"Well, good luck."

A brisk wind was tumbling and scattering the fog in the twilit anchorage, and the choppy water tossed the slow-moving gig so that the bell clanged randomly and Henry had to brace himself on the dank leather seat. After a dull rocky ride the *Augusta* loomed ahead through the mist, a long dark unlit shape. The cruiser was not even showing anchor lights, a serious and strange peacetime violation. In the breaking fog, the President's yacht and the dunes of Martha's Vineyard were barely visible. As Captain Henry mounted the cruiser's ladder, a faint pink glow was appearing in the east. The cleanliness of the old vessel, the fresh smooth paint, the pale gleam of brightwork, the tense quiet gait of sailors in spotless uniforms, marked it as King's flagship. Peculiar long ramps on the decks, and freshly welded handrails, were obvious special fittings for the crippled President.

Admiral King in starchy whites, lean legs crossed, sat in his high bridge chair querying the captain of the *Augusta* about arrangements for Roosevelt. He took no notice whatever of Henry's arrival. The captain, a classmate of Pug, was answering up like a midshipman at an examination. When King dismissed him, he ventured a subdued "Hi, Pug," before leaving his bridge.

"Henry, the President will want a word with you when he comes aboard." Fitting a cigarette into a black filter holder, King turned cold eyes on Pug. "I just learned that, hence this transfer. We'll be under way before you can get back to the *Tuscaloosa*. I trust you're prepared with any reports or information he may desire."

"I have my work papers here, Admiral." Pug touched the dispatch case which, in the transit between cruisers, had not left his hand.

King, with chin high, looked down at Victor Henry through half-closed eyes, puffing at the cigarette. "As I told you last week, the President asked to have you along on this exercise. He didn't mention that he wanted you at his beck and call, however. Are you by any chance a distant relative or an old family friend of Mr. Roosevelt?"

"No, Admiral."

"Well—you might remember, when occasion offers, that you work for the United States Navy."

"Aye aye, sir."

Virtually nobody saw the crippled man hoisted aboard. The ship's company in dress whites was mustered on the long forecastle at attention under the main battery guns. No band played, no guns saluted. The yacht *Potomac* came along the port side, out of sight of Martha's Vineyard. Sharp commands rang out, a boatswain's pipe squealed, the *Potomac* churned away, and the President appeared in his wheelchair, pushed by a Navy captain, with an impressive following of civilians, admirals, and Army generals. As on a theatrical cue, the sun at that moment came out and sunlight shafted down the decks, illuminating the grinning, waving President. The white suit and floppy white hat, the high-spirited gestures, the cigarette holder cocked upward in the massive bespectacled face, were almost too Rooseveltian to be real. An actor would have come on so, and Pug thought FDR actually was putting on a little show for the crew, perhaps responding to the burst of sunshine. The wheelchair and its entourage passed across the forecastle and went out of sight.

At once the two cruisers weighed anchor and steamed out to sea, with a destroyer division screening ahead of them. The morning sun disappeared behind the clouds. In dreary gray North Atlantic weather, the formation plunged northeast at twenty-two knots, cutting across main ship lanes. Victor Henry walked the main deck for hours relishing the sea wind, the tall black waves, and the slow roll of iron plates under his feet. No summons came from the President. That scarcely surprised him. His chief in the War Plans Division was aboard the *Tuscaloosa;* they had intended to do a lot of work en route. Now when the two cruisers reached the rendezvous, they would need an all-night conference. The separation was probably pointless, but the President's whim had to be endured.

He was finishing bacon and eggs next morning in the flag mess, when a steward's mate handed him a sealed note on yellow scratch paper:

If you're not standing watch, old man, you might look in about ten or so.

The Skipper

He folded the note carefully away in his pocket. Pug was preserving all these communications, trivial or not, for his grandchildren. At the stroke of ten he went to flag quarters. A rugged frozen-eyed marine came to robot attention outside the President's suite.

"Hello there, Pug! Just in time for the news!" Roosevelt sat alone in an armchair at a green baize-covered table, on which a small portable radio was gabbling a commercial. Dark fatigue pockets under Roosevelt's eyes showed through the pince-nez glasses, but the open shirt collar outside an old gray sweater gave him a relaxed look. He had cut himself shaving; a gash clotted with blood marred the big chin. His color was good, and he was snuffing with relish the wind that blew in through a scoop and mussed his thin gray hair.

He shook his head sadly at a Moscow admission that the Germans had driven far past Smolensk. Then the announcer said that President Roosevelt's whereabouts were no longer a secret, and he perked up. FDR was vacationing aboard the *Potomac,* the announcer went on. Reporters had seen him on the afterdeck of the yacht at eight o'clock last evening, passing through the Cape Cod Canal. Roosevelt's eyes darted cunningly at Captain Henry. His smile curved up, self-satisfied and wise. "Ha ha. And here I was at eight o'clock, out on the high seas. How d'you suppose I worked that one, Pug?"

"Pretty good deception, sir. Somebody in disguise on the yacht?"

"Darn right! Tom Wilson, the engineer. We got him a white suit and white hat. Well, that's just grand. It worked!" He tuned down another commercial. "We didn't want U-boats out gunning for Churchill and me. But I admit I get a kick out of giving the press the slip, Pug. They do make my life a misery." Roosevelt was searching through piles of paper on the desk. "Ah. Here we are. Look this over, old fellow." The typewritten document was headed "For The President—Top Secret, Two Copies Only."

Turning up the radio again, the President slumped in his chair, and the mobile face went weary and grave as the announcer described a newspaper poll of the House of Representatives on the extension of the draft, predicting defeat of the bill by six to eight votes. "That is wrong," the President interjected, his heavy black-ringed eyes on the radio, as though arguing with the announcer. In the next item, the German propaganda ministry ridiculed an accusation by world Jewish leaders of massacres of Jews taking place in German-held parts of the Soviet Union. The Jews were spreading Allied atrocity propaganda, the ministry said, and the Red Cross was free to come in at any time to verify the facts. "There's another lie," the President said, turning off the radio with a disgusted gesture. "Those Nazis are the most outrageous liars, really. The Red Cross can't get in there at all. I think, and I certainly hope, those stories are terribly exaggerated. Our intelligence says they are. Still, where there's smoke—" He took off his pince-nez, and rubbed his eyes hard with thumb and forefinger. "Pug, did your daughter-in-law ever get home with her uncle?"

"I understand they're on their way, sir."

"Good. Very good." Roosevelt puffed out a long breath. "Quite a lad, that submariner of yours."

"A presumptuous pup, I'm afraid." Victor Henry was trying to read the document, which was explosive, while chatting with Roosevelt. It was hard because the pages were full of figures.

"I also have a son who's an ensign, Pug. He's aboard, and I want you to meet him."

"My pleasure, sir."

Roosevelt lit a cigarette, coughing. "I received a copy of that Jewish statement. A delegation of some old good friends brought it to me. The way the Jews stick together is remarkable, Pug. But what's one to do? Scolding the Germans is so humiliating, and so *futile*. I've exhausted that line long ago. We've tried to get around the immigration laws, with this device and that, and we've had some luck, actually. But when I've got a Congress that's ready to disband the Army, can you imagine my going to them with a bill to admit more Jews? I think we'll beat them on the draft, but it'll be close at best."

While he was saying this, Franklin Roosevelt cleared a space on the table, took up two decks of cards, and meticulously laid out a complex solitaire game. He moved cards around in silence for a while, then said in a new cheerful tone, as the ship took a long roll, "By George, Pug, doesn't it feel wonderful to be at sea again?"

"It sure does, Mr. President."

"Many's the time I've sailed in these waters. I could navigate this ship for them, honor bright!" He observed Pug turning over the last page. "Well? What do you think?"

"This is something for my chief, Mr. President."

"Yes, but Kelly Turner's over on the *Tuscaloosa*. Anyway, another squabble between the service heads is just what I *don't* want." The President smiled at him with flattering warmth. "Pug, you have a feeling for facts, and when you talk I understand you. Those are two uncommon virtues. So let's have it. Take your time."

"Yes, Mr. President."

Pug flipped through the document again, making quick notes on a pad. The President, chain-lighting a cigarette, carefully put down card on card.

Nothing in the document surprised Henry. He had heard it all before, in arguments with Army war planners. But here the Army was taking its case to the President, either through Marshall, or by some devious route which the President in his usual fashion kept open. The document was a scorcher indeed; if it leaked to isolationist senators, it might well end Lend-Lease, kill Selective Service, and even start an impeachment drive. Hence he was taken aback to see that it existed at all.

Roosevelt had called for the preparation of a "Victory Program," a fresh start to unlock the paralysis of Lend-Lease and war production. Half a dozen agencies had tangled themselves and the big industries into impotence— the Army and Navy Munitions Board, the War Resources Board, the Office of Emergency Management, the National Defense Advisory Commission, the Office of Production Management. Their heads were jockeying for presidential favor; all Washington was bewildered by the flood of new initials; shortages and bottlenecks were mounting; and actual munitions were being produced in a feeble trickle. To break this up, Roosevelt had ordered the armed forces to list everything they needed to win a global war, and to work out new priorities from this master list.

For weeks planners like Victor Henry had been calculating possible American invasions of France, Africa, Germany, Italy, China, and Honshu, air strikes against industrial cities, and joint operations with the British and even the Russians. The Army and the Navy, not particularly trusting each other, were hardly communicating about the program. Each had prepared a draft, and each had of course called for the greatest possible share of manpower and industrial output. They had been at the greatest pains to keep the Victory Program secret and the papers few. The document now in Victor Henry's hands was a sharp critique by the Army of the Navy's demands.

"How about some orange juice?" the President said, as a steward entered with a pitcher on a tray. "Wouldn't you like that? Felipe squeezes it fresh. He's gotten hold of some glorious oranges."

"Thank you, sir." Pug sipped at a glass of foaming juice. "This thing needs a paper just as long in reply, Mr. President. Essentially, the Navy and the Army are just using two different crystal balls. That's inevitable. The Army's the big service, and it's ultimately responsible for the security of the United States. No argument there. They figure they may have to fight the Axis single-handed, after Russia and England fold. That's why they demand so much. They arrive at the army of nine million men by working backward from the total manpower of the United States. It's the biggest force our country can field."

"And we may well need it," said the President.

"Yes, sir. It's mainly on Lend-Lease that we see the thing differently. The Army says we want to give away too many arms and machines which the Germans may capture and use against us. But our contention is that even if the Soviet Union does go down soon, and the British too, a hell of a lot of Germans will have to die first to lick them. And every German who dies is one less German who'll be shooting at us one day."

"I agree," the President said, very flatly.

"Well, then, Mr. President, shouldn't we at any cost

strengthen these people who are killing Germans right now? We can rebuild and replace lost matériel pretty fast, but it takes twenty years to raise a live Boche to replace a dead one."

The President observed with a slight grin, "Well said. But Lend-Lease isn't the only bone of contention here. I notice the Navy wants a pretty hefty share of our total steel production."

"Mr. President"—Pug leaned forward, elbows on knees, hands outstretched, talking as forcefully as he could—"Hitler didn't beat England last year because he couldn't land the strongest army in the world on a coast a few miles away. He had all the ships he needed to carry them across. But he couldn't dock them on the other side. Assault from the sea is a tough battle problem, Mr. President. They don't come much tougher. It's easy to put your men ashore, one place or another, but then how do you keep the defenders from wiping you out? Your men are stranded. The defenders have all the mobility, the numerical superiority, and the firepower. They can concentrate and crush you." As Pug talked, the President was nodding, cigarette holder drooping between his teeth, eyes piercingly attentive. "Well, sir, the answer is special craft that can hit an open beach in large numbers. You throw a large force ashore, and keep it supplied and reinforced until it captures a harbor. Then you can pile in with your regular transports, your luxury liners too—if you've got 'em—and your invasion's on. But those landing craft, you need swarms of them, sir, of many different designs. This analysis has been assigned to me. It looks as though we're going to have to manufacture something like a hundred thousand, all told."

"*A hundred thousand!*" The President tossed his big head. "Why, all the shipyards in the United States couldn't do that in ten years, Pug, even if they stopped doing everything else. You're talking sheer nonsense. Everybody exaggerates his little specialty." But Roosevelt was smiling in an excited way and his eyes were lighting up. He spoke of landing boats the Navy had used in the last war, when he was Assistant Secretary, and of the disastrous British landing at Gallipoli. Victor Henry took from his briefcase pictures of German invasion craft and of new British models, and some designs for American boats. The President scanned these with zest. Different craft would perform different missions, Pug said, from a big landing ship to cross the ocean with a great load of tanks and trucks in its belly, to little amphibious tanks that could crawl out on land, chug back into the water, and maybe even submerge. Roosevelt obviously loved all this. Under the spread of pictures and sketches lay his solitaire game, scattered and forgotten.

"Say, have you fellows ever thought of this?" The President seized a yellow ruled pad and sketched with crude black pencil strokes as he talked. "It's an idea I had back in 1917, studying the Gallipoli reports. I sent it to BuShips, sketches and all, and never heard another word. I still say it has merit, though it hadn't crossed my mind again until this minute. Look here, Pug."

The drawing showed an oblong, flat-bottomed craft. Amidships on an arching frame, over the heads of crouched soldiers, an airplane engine whirled its big propeller in a screened housing. "I know there's a stability question, with all that weight so high, but with a broad enough beam, and if you used aluminum—you see that boat could go right up on the beach, Pug, through marshes, anywhere. Underwater obstacles would be meaningless." The President grinned down at his handiwork with approval, then scrawled at the bottom, *FDR—on board USS Augusta, en route to meet Churchill, 7 August 1941.* "Here. Don't bury it the way BuShips did! Look into it. Maybe it's just a wild notion, but—Well! Will you look at Old Man Sunshine, pouring through that porthole at last!"

The President put on the white hat, and smoothly slid into his wheeled kitchen chair, pressing his hands on the table with almost simian strength to lift and move himself. Victor Henry opened a door to the sun deck. Roosevelt wheeled himself briskly across the gray-painted wooden ramps over the coaming. "Ah! Doesn't this feel swell! Warm sun and ocean air. Just what the doctor ordered. Give me a hand, Pug." The President eased himself into a blue leather reclining chair, in an angle of the deck structure sheltered from the wind. They were looking aft at the long gray guns and the foaming wake of the gently pitching cruiser. "I still say you'll never find the shipyard or Navy Yard space for those landing craft, Pug. There are the merchant ships to build, the destroyer escorts, the carriers. You're going to have to use factories wherever you can find them—on rivers and inland waterways—hundreds of little factories." President Roosevelt cocked his head, staring out at the sea. "You know? This program could be a godsend to small business. Congress has given us all *kinds* of trouble about that. There's a real thought. Money going out to small factories in many states—" The President lit a cigarette, deftly cupping the match against the breeze. "Very good. Let me have your notes on that Army paper, Pug. Just write them up yourself, and give them to me today."

"Yes, Mr. President."

"Now I'm extremely interested in that landing craft problem, but I don't want you getting bogged down in it. Once the Victory Program is finished, let's detach you from War Plans, and send you out to sea. You're overdue."

Victor Henry saw that he had scored with Roosevelt and that the moment was favorable. He said, "Well, Mr. President, for a long time I've been yearning for a battleship."

"You think you can command one?"

Trying hard not to show emotion in face or voice, realizing that a lifetime might hang on the next few words, Henry said, "I think I can, sir."

"Well, you've been delayed on the beach by unrewarding jobs. The Commander-in-Chief ought to have a little say in this. Let's get you command of a battleship."

The President spoke lightly. But the ring in his cultured voice, the self-satisfied tilt of his head, the regal way he held the arms of his chair and smiled at Captain Henry, showed his relish for power and his satisfaction in bestowing largesse.

"Thank you, Mr. President."

"Now, Pug, you'll find Chief Yeoman Terry in the flag office. Will you tell him to come here?"

Dazed by the last turn of the conversation, Victor Henry walked back into the President's suite, and interrupted a chat between General Marshall, Admiral King, Admiral

Stark, and General Watson, sitting relaxed on a couch and armchairs in splendid uniforms. The four elderly awesome heads turned at him. Admiral King gave him a puzzled scowl. Pug crossed the room as fast as he could without running, and went out.

It was for this chat, lasting less than an hour, that Franklin Roosevelt had evidently summoned Victor Henry to the *Augusta*. Except at a distance, the Navy captain did not see the President again all the way to Newfoundland.

Pug no longer tried to fathom the President's purposes. He did not feel flattered when Roosevelt summoned him, or put out when the President forgot he was alive. He was under no illusion that he held a high place in the President's esteem, or that anything he said or did influenced the course of history. The President used other obscure men. The identities and missions of some were fogged in secrecy. He himself knew of a marine colonel who ran presidential errands in Japan, China, and India; and an elderly Oregon lumberman, a friend of his own father, whose specialty was buying up scarce war materials in South America, to deny them to the Germans. Pug counted himself among these small fry, and took the President's use of him as the result of random impulse. Roosevelt liked him because he was knowledgeable, got things done, and kept his mouth shut. A lucky guess about the Nazi-Soviet pact had earned him more credit for acumen than he deserved. There was also the odd phrase Roosevelt had used: "When you talk, I understand you."

Still, the President's promise of a battleship command gave Victor Henry sleepless nights. Only two of his classmates had battleships. He went to the flag office and checked the Navy Register, to narrow down the possibilities. Of course, new construction—the *North Carolina* class, or the *Indiana* class giants—was out of the question for him. He would get a modernized old ship. The deadline for delivering the Victory Program was less than a month off. Scanning the records, he noted that places might open up within a couple of months in the *California* or the *West Virginia*. This was heady business for Captain Victor Henry, after thirty years in the Navy, checking over the battleship roster to guess which one he might soon command!

He tried to crush down his elation. Henry admired the President, and had moments when he almost loved the gallant cripple with the big grin and the boundless appetite for work. But he did not understand Roosevelt or trust him; and he did not in the least share the unlimited devotion to this man of people like Harry Hopkins. Behind the warm jolly aristocratic surface, there loomed a grim illdefined personality of distant visions and hard purpose, a tough son of a bitch to whom nobody meant very much, except perhaps his family; and maybe not they, either. It might be that Roosevelt would remember to get him a battleship command. It was equally likely that some new job would put the promise off until it faded. Roosevelt had taught Victor Henry what a great man was like; the captain thought time and again of the Bible's warning, that the clay pot should keep its distance from the iron kettle.

■   ■   ■

Gray peace pervaded the wilderness-ringed Argentia Bay in Newfoundland, where the American ships anchored to await the arrival of Winston Churchill. Haze and mist blended all into gray: gray water, gray sky, gray air, gray hills with a tint of green. The monstrously shaped graypainted iron ships, queer intruders from the twentieth century into the land of the Indians, floated in the haze like an ugly phantom vision of the future. Sailors and officers went about their chores as usual on these ships, amid pipings and loudspeaker squawks. But a primeval hush lay heavy in Argentia Bay, just outside the range of the normal ships' noises.

At nine o'clock, three gray destroyers steamed into view, ahead of a battleship camouflaged in swirls and splotches of color like snakeskin. This was H.M.S. *Prince of Wales,* bigger than any other ship in sight, bearing the guns that had hit the *Bismarck.* As it steamed past the *Augusta,* a brass band on its decks shattered the hush with "The Star-Spangled Banner." Quiet fell. The band on the quarterdeck of the *Augusta* struck up "God Save the King."

Pug Henry stood near the President, under the awning rigged at number-one turret, with admirals, generals, and august civilians like Averell Harriman and Sumner Welles. Churchill was plain to see not five hundred yards away, in an odd blue costume, gesturing with a big cigar. The President towered over everybody, stiff on braced legs, in a neat brown suit, one hand holding his hat on his heart, the other clutching the arm of his son, an Air Corps officer who strongly resembled him. Roosevelt's large pink face was self-consciously grave.

At this grand moment Pug Henry's thoughts were prosaic. BuShips experts were disputing over camouflage patterns. Some liked this British tropical splashing, some preferred plain gray or blue horizontal bands. Pug had seen the mottled battleship through the mist before espying monochrome destroyers that were a mile closer. He intended to report this.

"God Save the King" ended. The President's face relaxed. "Well! I've never heard 'My Country 'Tis of Thee' played better." The men around him laughed politely at the presidential joke, and Roosevelt laughed too. The squeal of boatswains' pipes broke up the dress parade on the cruiser's deck.

Admiral King beckoned to Pug. "Take my barge over to the *Prince of Wales,* and put yourself at Mr. Harry Hopkins's service. The President desires to talk with him before Churchill comes to call, so expedite."

"Aye aye, sir."

Passing from the *Augusta* to the *Prince of Wales* in King's barge, over a few hundred yards of still water, Victor Henry went from America to England and from peace to war. It was a shocking jump. King's spick-and-span flagship belonged to a different world than the storm-whipped British vessel, where the accommodation ladder was salt-crusted, the camouflage paint was peeling, and even the main battery guns looked pitted and rusty. Pug was aghast to see cigarette butts and wastepaper in the scuppers, though droves of bluejackets were doing an animated scrub-down. On the superstructure raw steel patches were welded here and there—sticking plaster for wounds from the *Bismarck*'s salvos.

The officer of the deck had a neatly trimmed brown beard, hollow cheeks, and a charming smile. Pug envied the green tarnish on the gold braid of his cap. "Ah, yes, Captain Henry," he said, smartly returning the salute in the different British palm-out style, "Mr. Hopkins has received the signal and is waiting for you in his cabin. The quartermaster will escort you."

Victor Henry followed the quartermaster through passageways hauntingly like those in American battleships, yet different in countless details: the signs, the fittings, the fire extinguishers, the shape of the watertight doors.

"Hello there, Pug." Hopkins spoke as though he had not seen the Navy captain for a day or two, though their last encounter had been on the train to Hyde Park early in March, and meantime Hopkins had travelled to London and Moscow in a blaze of worldwide newspaper attention. "Am I riding over with you?"

"Yes, sir."

"How's the President feeling?" Hopkins had two bags open on his bunk in a small cabin off the wardroom. In one he carefully placed papers, folders, and books; in the other he threw clothes, medicine bottles, and shoes as they came to hand. Hopkins looked thinner than before, a bent scarecrow with a gray double-breasted suit flapping loosely on him. In the long, curved, emaciated face, the clever, rather feminine eyes appeared enormous as a lemur's. The sea voyage showed in his fresh color and bouncy movements.

"He's having the time of his life, sir."

"I can imagine. So's Churchill. Churchill's like a boy going on his first date. Well, it's quite a historic moment, at that." Hopkins pulled dirty shirts from a drawer and crammed them in the suitcase. "Almost forgot these. I left a few in the Kremlin and had to scrounge more in London."

"Mr. Hopkins, what about the Russians? Will they hold?"

Hopkins paused, a stack of papers in his hand, and pursed his mouth before speaking decisively. "The Russians will hold. But it'll be a near thing. They'll need help." He resumed his hurried packing. "When you fly from Archangel to Moscow, Pug, it takes hours and hours, over solid green forests and brown swamps. Often you don't see a village from horizon to horizon. Hitler's bitten off a big bite this time." He was struggling with the clasps on his suitcase, and Pug gave him a hand. "Ah, thanks. What do you suppose Stalin wants from us most of all, Pug?"

"Airplanes," Victor Henry said promptly. " 'Clouds of airplanes.' Same as the French were yelling for last year."

"Aluminum," said Harry Hopkins. "Aluminum to *build* airplanes with. Well, let me correct that—his number one item was anti-aircraft guns. Next comes aluminum. Wants a lot of Army trucks, too. Stalin isn't planning to get beaten in three weeks, or six weeks, or three years." Hopkins tidied the papers in the smaller case, and closed it. "Let's go."

The way led through the wardroom, stretching grandly the width of the vessel, furnished like a London club, with dark panelling, easy chairs, rows of novels and encyclopedias, and a bar. When the door to the Prime Minister's cabin was opened by his valet, a strange sight greeted them. Winston Churchill, barefoot, was contemplating himself in a mirror in morning coat, tie, and yellow silk underdrawers. "Hello there, Harry." He ignored Captain Henry, slewing a long cigar around in his mouth. "I'm not aware that His Majesty's First Minister has ever before paid a call on the President of the United States at sea. I saw the President wearing a plain brown lounge suit. But he is the head of state. I am only a minister." Churchill's fat aged face was lit with puckish relish of the unique historical problem. "This looks odd, I know. My man of protocol wants me to wear the same old brass-buttoned jacket and cap. But it's such an informal dress."

"Prime Minister," Hopkins said, "you do look more like a Former Naval Person in it."

Churchill grinned at the whimsical name he used in messages to Roosevelt. He said to the valet, "Very well. The Trinity House uniform again."

"This is Captain Victor Henry, Prime Minister, of Navy War Plans."

Pulling down his eyebrows, Churchill said, "Hello there. Have you done anything about those landing craft?"

The eyes of Hopkins and Victor Henry met, and Churchill's wide mouth wrinkled with gratification. Pug said, "I'm amazed that you remember me, Mr. Prime Minister. That's part of my job now. The other day I talked with the President at length about landing craft."

"Well? Is the United States going to build enough of them? A very large number will be called for."

"We will, sir."

"Have our people given you everything you've requested?"

"Their cooperation has been outstanding."

"I think you'll find," Churchill rasped, as the valet helped him into enormous blue trousers, "that we simple islanders have hit on a design or two that may prove usable." Churchill spoke slowly, lisping on his *s*'s, in a tone that was almost a growl.

Hopkins said a word of farewell to Churchill, and they left. In the passageway, with an incredulous grin, Hopkins remarked, "We've been having ceremonial rehearsals for days, and yet he's fussing to the last minute about what to wear! A very, very great man, all the same."

As Hopkins shakily stepped aboard King's barge from the accommodation ladder, the stern rose high on a swell, then dropped away from under him. He lost his balance and toppled into the arms of the coxswain, who said, "Ooops-a-daisy, sir."

"Pug, I'll never be a sailor." Hopkins staggered inside, settling with a sigh on the cushions. "I flopped on my face boarding the seaplane that flew me to the Soviet Union. That nearly ended my mission right there." He glanced around at the flawlessly appointed barge. "Well, well. America! Peacetime! So—you're still in War Plans. You'll attend the staff meetings, then."

"Some of them, yes, sir."

"You might bear in mind what our friends will be after. It's fairly clear to me, after five days at sea with the Prime Minister." Hopkins held out one wasted hand and ticked off points on skeletal fingers. He seemed to be using Victor Henry as a sounding board to refresh his own mind for his meeting with the President, for he talked half to himself. "First they'll press for an immediate declaration of war on Germany. They know they won't get that. But it softens the ground for the second demand, the real reason Winston Churchill has crossed the ocean. They want a warning by the United States to Japan that any move against the British in Asia means war with us. Their empire is mighty rickety at this point. They hope such a warning will shore it up. And they'll press for big war supplies to their people in Egypt and the Middle East. Because if Hitler pokes down there and closes the canal, the Empire strangles. They'll also try, subtly but hard— and I would too, in their place—for an understanding that in getting American aid they come ahead of Russia. Now is the time to bomb the hell out of Germany from the west, they'll say, and build up for the final assault. Stuff we give Russia, it will be hinted, may be turned around and pointed against us in a few weeks."

Victor Henry said, "The President isn't thinking that way."

"I hope not. If Hitler wins in Russia, he wins the world. If he loses in Russia he's finished, even if the Japanese move. The fight over there is of inconceivable magnitude. There must be seven million men shooting at each other, Pug. Seven million, or more." Hopkins spoke the figures slowly, stretching out the wasted fingers of both hands. "The Russians have taken a shellacking so far, but they're unafraid. They want to throw the Germans out. That's the war now. That's where the stuff should go now."

"Then this conference is almost pointless," said Pug. The barge was slowing and clanging as it drew near the *Augusta*.

"No, it's a triumph," Hopkins said. "The President of the United States and the British Prime Minister are meeting face to face to discuss beating the Germans. The world will know that. That's achievement enough for now." Hopkins gave Victor Henry a sad smile, and a brilliantly intelligent light came into his large eyes. He pulled himself to his feet in the rocking boat. "Also, Pug, this is the changing of the guard."

Winston Churchill came to the *Augusta* at eleven o'clock. Among the staff members with him, Captain

Henry saw Lord Burne-Wilke, and a hallucinatory remembrance of Pamela Tudsbury in her blue WAAF uniform distracted him from the dramatic handshake of Roosevelt and Churchill at the gangway. They prolonged the clasp for the photographers, exchanging smiling words.

All morning, recollections of England and Pamela had been stirring Pug. The OOD's very British greeting at the *Prince of Wales* ladder, the glimpses of London magazines in the wardroom, Winston Churchill's voice with its thick *s*'s, had wakened his memory like a song or a perfume. Göring's 1940 air blitz on London already seemed part of another era, almost another war. Standing well back in the rank of King's staff officers, this short unknown Navy captain, whose face would be lost in the photographs, tried to shake irrelevancies from his brain and pay attention.

In an odd way the two leaders diminished each other. They were both Number One Men. But that was impossible. Who, then, was Number One? Roosevelt stood a full head taller, but he was pathetically braced on lifeless leg frames, clinging to his son's arm, his full trousers drooped and flapping. Churchill, a bent Pickwick in blue uniform, looked up at him with majestic good humor, much older, more dignified, more assured. Yet there was a trace of deference about the Prime Minister. By a shade of a shade, Roosevelt looked like Number One. Maybe that was what Hopkins had meant by "the changing of the guard."

The picture-taking stopped at an unseen signal, the handshake ended, and a wheelchair appeared. The erect front-page President became the cripple more familiar to Pug, hobbling a step or two and sinking with relief into the chair. The great men and their military chiefs left the quarterdeck.

The staffs got right to business and conferred all day. Victor Henry worked with the planners, on the level below the chiefs of staff and their deputies where Burne-Wilke operated, and of course far below the summit of the President, the Prime Minister, and their advisers. Familiar problems came up at once: excessive and contradictory requests from the British services, unreal plans, unfilled contracts, jumbled priorities, fouled communications. One cardinal point the planners hammered out fast. Building new ships to replace U-boat sinkings came first. No war matériel could be used against Hitler until it had crossed the ocean. This plain truth, so simple once agreed on, ran a red line across every request, every program, every projection. Steel, aluminum, rubber, valves, motors, machine tools, copper wire, all the thousand things of war, would go first to ships. This simple yardstick rapidly disclosed the poverty of the "arsenal of democracy," and dictated—as a matter of frightening urgency—a gigantic job of building new steel mills, and plants to turn the steel into combat machines and tools.

Through all the talk of grand hypothetical plans—hundreds of ships, tens of thousands of airplanes and tanks, millions of men—one pathetic item kept recurring: an immediate need for a hundred fifty thousand rifles. If Russia collapsed, Hitler might try to wrap up the war with a Crete-like invasion of England from the air. Rifles for defending British airfields were lacking. The stupendous matériel figures for future joint invasions of North Africa or the French coast contrasted sadly with this plea for a hundred fifty thousand rifles now.

Next morning, boats from all over the sparkling bay came clustering to the *Prince of Wales* for church services. On the surrounding hills, in sunlight that seemed almost blinding after days of gray mist, the forests of larch and fir glowed a rich green.

An American destroyer slowly nosed its bridge alongside the battleship, exactly level with the main deck, and a gangplank was thrown across. Leaning on his son's arm and on a cane, Franklin Roosevelt, in a blue suit and gray hat, lurched out on the gangplank, laboriously hitching one leg forward from the hip, then the other. The bay was calm, but both ships were moving on long swells. With each step, the tall President tottered and swayed. Victor Henry, like all the Americans crowding the destroyer bridge, hardly breathed as Roosevelt painfully hobbled across the narrow unsteady planks. Photographers waiting on the *Prince of Wales* quarterdeck were staring at the President, but Pug observed that not one of them was shooting this momentous crippled walk.

He thought of Franklin Roosevelt as he had first known

him—the young Assistant Secretary of the Navy, the athletic cocksure dandy, the obvious charmer and lady-killer, full of himself, on top of the world, bounding up and down a destroyer's ladders and spouting salty lingo. The years had made of him this half-disabled gray man, heaving himself one agonized step at a time over a gangplank a few feet long; but here was enough willpower displayed, Pug thought, to win a world war. A ramp could have been jury-rigged and laid across with ease. Franklin Roosevelt might have wheeled over in comfort and with dignity. But in his piteous fashion he could walk; and to board a British battleship, at Winston Churchill's invitation for church parade, he was walking.

His foot touched the deck of the *Prince of Wales*. Churchill saluted him and offered his hand. The brass band burst forth with "The Star-Spangled Banner." Roosevelt stood at attention, his chest heaving, his face stiff with strain. Then, escorted by Churchill, the President hitched and hobbled all the way across the deck, and sat. No wheelchair ever appeared.

As the sailors massed in ranks around the afterdeck sang "O God, Our Help in Ages Past" and "Onward Christian Soldiers," Winston Churchill kept wiping his eyes. The old hymns, roared by a thousand young male voices in the open air under the long guns, brought prickles to Victor Henry's spine and tears to his eyes. Yet this exalting service made him uneasy, too.

Here they were, men of the American and the British navies, praying as comrades-in-arms. But it was a phony picture. The English were fighting, the Americans were not. The Prime Minister, with this church parade under the guns, was ingeniously working on the President's feelings. Here was diamond cut diamond, will against will! Churchill was using everything he could, including Roosevelt's supposed religious tendency, to move him. If Franklin Roosevelt could come away from this experience without giving a promise to declare war on Germany, or at least to lay down an ultimatum to Japan, he was a hard man; and the weeping old fat politician beside him was playing a damned hard game himself, for which Victor Henry admired him.

The British chaplain, his white and crimson vestments

flapping in the wind, his thick gray hair blowing wildly, read the closing Royal Navy prayer: "... *Preserve us from the dangers of the sea, and from the violence of the enemy; that we may be a security for such as pass upon the sea upon their lawful occasions ... and that we may return in safety to enjoy the blessings of the land, with the fruits of our labors ... and to praise and glorify Thy Holy Name; through Jesus Christ our Lord ...*"

A few British sailors cautiously moved out of ranks. One, then another, sneaked cameras from their blouses. When nobody stopped them, and the two leaders smiled and waved, a rush began. Cameras appeared by the dozens. The sailors swarmed into a laughing, cheering ring around the two men. Pug Henry, watching this unwonted disorder on a warship with mixed feelings of amusement and outrage, felt a touch on his elbow. It was Lord Burne-Wilke. "Hello there, my dear fellow. A word with you?"

Either the British worried less about fire than the Americans, or they had found a good way to fake wood panels. Burne-Wilke's cabin had the dark, warm, comfortable look of a library den. "I say, Henry, what is your position on shipboard drinking? I have a fair bottle of sherry here."

"I'm for it."

"Good. You're dry as a bone in your service, aren't you? Yet last night the President served us an excellent wine."

"The President is the source of all Navy regulations, sir, and can tailor them to his desires."

"Ah? Jolly convenient." Burne-Wilke lit a cigar, and they both sipped wine. "I suppose you know that this ship crossed the ocean without escort," the air commodore resumed. "Our first night out of England, we ran into a whole gale. Our destroyers couldn't maintain speed, so we zigzagged on alone."

"Sir, I was appalled to hear about it."

"Really? Rather sporting of the British Prime Minister, don't you think, to give the Hun a fair shot at him on the open sea? Three thousand miles without air cover or surface escort, straight through the entire submarine fleet?"

"You had your good angels escorting you. That's all I can say."

"Oh, well, at any rate here we are. But it might be prudent not to overwork those good angels, what? Don't you agree? On our way back, every U-boat in the Atlantic will certainly be on battle alert. We shall have to run the gamut." Burne-Wilke paused, studying the ash on his cigar. "We're stretched thin for escorts, you know. We've rounded up four destroyers. Admiral Pound would be happier with six."

Victor Henry quickly said, "I'll talk to Admiral King."

"You understand that this cannot be a request from us. The Prime Minister would be downright annoyed. He's hoping we'll meet the *Tirpitz* and get into a running gun fight."

"Let me start on this now, sir." Pug drank up his sherry, and rose to his feet.

"Oh? Would you?" Burne-Wilke opened the cabin door. "Thanks awfully."

On the afterdeck, the photographing was still going on. Officers with cameras were now shouldering sailors aside, as the two politicians cheerfully chatted. Behind them stood their glum chiefs of staff and civilian advisers. Hopkins, squinting out at the sunny water, wore a pained expression. The military men were talking together, except for Admiral King, who stood woodenly apart, his long nose pointing seaward, his face congealed in disapproval. Pug walked up to him, saluted, and in the fewest possible words recounted his talk with Burne-Wilke. The lines along King's lean jaws deepened. He nodded twice and strolled away, without a word. He did not go anywhere. It was just a gesture of dismissal, and a convincing one.

Amid much wining and dining, the conference went on for two more days. One night Churchill took the floor in the *Augusta* wardroom after dinner, and delivered a rolling, rich, apocalyptic word picture of how the war would go. Blockade, ever-growing air bombardment, and subversion would in time weaken the grip of Nazi claws on Europe. Russia and England would "close a ring" and slowly, inexorably tighten it. If the United States became a full-fledged ally, it would all go much faster, of course. No big invasion or long land campaign would be needed in the west. Landings of a few armored columns in the occupied countries would bring mass uprisings. Hitler's black empire would suddenly collapse in rubble, blood, and flame. Franklin Roosevelt listened with bright-eyed smiling attention, saying nothing, and applauding heartily with the rest.

On the last day of the conference, just before lunch, Admiral King sent for Pug. He found the admiral in undershirt and trousers in his cabin, drying face and ears with a towel. "Task Unit 26 point 3 point 1, consisting of two destroyers, the *Mayrant* and the *Rhind*, has been formed," King said without a greeting. "It will escort the *Prince of Wales* to Iceland. You will embark in the *Prince of Wales* as liaison officer, disembark in Iceland, and return with our task unit."

"Aye aye, sir."

"You'll have no written orders. But we're not in the kind of spot we were in last time. In confidence, we'll soon be convoying all ships to Iceland. Maybe by next week. Hell, our own marines are occupying the place now. The President's even sending a young officer along as a naval aide to Churchill while he tours our Iceland base. Ensign Franklin D. Roosevelt, Junior." King spoke the name with an expressionless face.

"Yes, sir."

"Now, Henry, how are you at languages?"

"It's a long time since I tried a new one, Admiral."

"Well, a military supply mission will go to the Soviet Union in September. If Russia's still in the war by then, that is. Mr. Hopkins has brought up your name. He appears impressed, and the President too, by your expertise on landing craft and so forth. Now your service record has been checked, and it seems you claim a 'poor to fair' knowledge of Russian. Hey? How is that? That's very unusual."

"Admiral, I put that down when I entered the Academy in 1911. It was true then. I don't remember ten words now." Henry explained the circumstances that had given him Russian-speaking chums in his Sonoma County boyhood.

"I see. Well, it's there on the record. Upon returning from Iceland you will be detached from War Plans to prepare yourself, with an intensive refresher course in Russian, for a possible trip to the Soviet Union on special detached duty. You'll have interpreters. But with even a smattering, your intelligence value will be greater."

"Aye aye, sir."

King put on his uniform jacket, stared at Victor Henry, and for the first time that Henry could recall, favored him with a smile. "On the record, incidentally, I see you used to be a fair gunnery officer, too."

"My one hope is to get back to that."

"Have you heard that extension of the draft passed the House of Representatives an hour ago?"

"It did? Thank God."

"By one vote."

"What! *One* vote, sir?"

"One vote."

"Whew! That's not going to encourage the British, Admiral."

"No, nor the President, but it's how the American people feel right now. It may be suicidal, but there it is. Our job is to keep going anyway. Incidentally, Henry, I'll soon be needing an operations officer on my staff. After your Russian errand, if it comes off, that's an assignment you may get."

Victor Henry kept his face rigid. "It would be an honor, Admiral."

"I thought you might like it. I believe you'll measure up," King said, with an awkward trace of warmth.

Compared to a battleship command, it was a crushing prospect. Desperation forced Pug to say, "President Roosevelt may have other ideas. I just never know."

"I mentioned this to the President. He said it sounded like the perfect spot for you."

A verse from Psalms knifed into Pug's mind: *"Put not your trust in princes."*

"Thank you, Admiral."

Within the hour, as Victor Henry was packing, a summons came from the President. The interview this time took but a minute or two. Roosevelt appeared fatigued and preoccupied, making quick pencilled notes on one document after another at the baize-covered table. Harry Hopkins was in the room, and beside him a tall handsome ensign, with a strong resemblance to the Assistant Secretary who in 1917 had bounded around the destroyer *Davey*.

The President introduced Franklin D. Roosevelt, Junior, to Pug, saying "You gentlemen will be travelling together. You should know each other." As the ensign shook hands, the President gave Captain Henry a poignant man-to-man glance, as much as to say—*"Keep an eye on him, and talk to him."*

This human touch half dissolved Victor Henry's hard knot of mistrust for the President. Perhaps Roosevelt had turned off King with a pleasantry and still meant to give him the battleship. The President's bland manner in dismissing him was, as always, unfathomable.

To brass band anthems and booming gun salutes, in a brisk breeze smelling of green hills and gunpowder, the *Prince of Wales* left Argentia Bay. The great conference was over.

In the wardroom of the *Prince of Wales,* Victor Henry could sense the subtle gloom hanging over the ship. What the conference had accomplished to increase help for England remained undisclosed; and in itself this clearly struck the battleship's officers as a bad sign. These men, veterans of two combat years, of air attacks and gun fights, had a subdued dismal air, despite the grandeur of their ship and the stuffy luxury of their wardroom. The predicament of England seemed soaked in their bones. They could not believe that Winston Churchill had risked the best ship in their strained navy, and his own life, only to return empty-handed. That wasn't Winnie's style. But vague hope, rather than real confidence, was the note in their conversation. Sitting in the lounge over a glass of port after dinner, Pug felt quite out of things, despite their politeness to him. It struck him that his presence embarrassed them. He went to bed early. Next day he toured the *Prince of Wales* from flying bridge to engine rooms, noting contrasts with American ships, above all the slovenly, overburdened, tense crew, so different from the scrubbed happy-go-lucky *Augusta* sailors.

Major-General Tillet came up to him after dinner that evening, and laid a lean hand on his shoulder. "Like to have a look at the submarine sightings chart, Henry? The Prime Minister thought you might. Quite a reception committee gathering out there."

Pug had seen the forbidding old military historian here and there at the conference. Two nights ago, at a wardroom party for the American visitors, some junior British officers had started what they called a "rag," marching in dressed in kilts or colored towels, bizarre wigs, and not much else; skirling bagpipes, setting off firecrackers, and goose-stepping over chairs and tables. After a while Major-General Tillet had stood up unsmiling—Pug thought, to put a stop to the horseplay—and had broken into a long, wild jig on a table, as the bagpipers marched around him and the whole mess applauded. Now he was as stiff as ever.

Red secrecy warnings blazed on the steel door that Tillet opened. Dressed in a one-piece garment like a mechanic's coveralls, stooped and heavy-eyed, Churchill pondered a map of the Russian front all across one bulkhead. Opposite hung a chart of the Atlantic. Young officers worked over dispatches at a table in the middle of the room, in air thick with tobacco smoke.

"There," said the Prime Minister to Tillet and Pug Henry, gesturing at the map of the Soviet Union with his cigar, "*there* is an awful unfolding picture."

The crimson line of the front east of Smolensk showed two fresh bulges toward Moscow. Churchill coughed, and glanced at Henry. "Your President warned Stalin. I warned him even more explicitly, basing myself on very exact intelligence. Surely no government ever had less excuse to be surprised. In an evil hour, the heroic, unfortunate Russian people were led by a pack of outwitted bungling scoundrels." The Prime Minister turned and walked to the other bulkhead, with the tottering step Victor Henry had observed in his London office. At Argentia, Churchill had appeared strong, ruddy, springy, and altogether ten years younger. Now his cheeks were ashy, with red patches.

"Hullo. Don't we have a development here?"

Little black coffin-shaped markers dotted the wide blue spaces, and an officer was putting up several more, in a cluster close to the battleship's projected course. Farther on stood large clusters of red pins, with a few blue pins.

"This new U-boat group was sighted by an American patrol plane at twilight, sir," said the officer.

"Ah, yes. So Admiral Pound advised me. I suppose we are evading?"

"We have altered course to north, sir."

"Convoy H-67 is almost home, I see."

"We will be pulling those pins tonight, Mr. Prime Minister."

"That will be happy news." Churchill harshly coughed, puffing at his cigar, and said to Pug Henry, "Well. We may have some sport for you yet. It won't be as lively as a bomber ride over Berlin. Eh? Did you enjoy that, Captain?"

"It was a rare privilege, Mr. Prime Minister."

"Any time. Any time at all."

"Too much honor, sir. Once was plenty."

Churchill uttered a hoarse chuckle. "I daresay. What is the film tonight, General Tillet?"

"Prime Minister, I believe it is Stan Laurel and Oliver Hardy, in *Saps at Sea*."

"*Saps at Sea*, eh? Not inappropriate! The Surgeon-General has ordered me to remain in bed. He has also ordered me not to smoke. I shall attend *Saps at Sea*, and bring my cigars."

Pug Henry's enjoyment of *Saps at Sea* was shadowed by an awareness that at any moment the battleship might run into a U-boat pack. German skippers were adept at sneaking past destroyer screens. But the film spun to the end uninterrupted. "A gay but inconsequent entertainment," the Prime Minister remarked in a heavy, rheumy voice, as he plodded out.

Clement Attlee's broadcast the next day packed the wardroom. Every officer not on watch, and all staff officers and war planners, gathered in the wardroom around one singularly ancient, crack-voiced radio. The battleship, plowing through a wild storm, rolled and pitched with slow long groans. For the American guest, it was a bad half hour. He saw perplexed looks, lengthening faces, and headshakes, as Attlee read off the "Atlantic Charter." The high-flown language bespoke not a shred of increased American commitment. Abuse of Nazi tyranny, praise of "four freedoms," dedication to a future of world peace and brotherhood, yes; more combat help for the British, flat zero. Some sentences about free trade and independence for all peoples meant the end of the British Empire, if they meant anything.

Franklin Roosevelt was indeed a tough customer, thought Captain Henry, not especially surprised.

"Umph!" grunted Major-General Tillet in the silence after the radio was shut off. "I'd venture there was more to it than that. How about it, Henry?"

All eyes turned on the American.

Pug saw no virtue in equivocating. "No, sir, I'd guess that was it."

"Your President has now pledged in a joint communiqué to destroy Nazi tyranny," Tillet said. "Doesn't that mean you're coming in, one way or another?"

"It means Lend-Lease," Pug said.

Questions shot at him from all sides.

"You're not going to stand with us against Japan?"

"Not now."

"But isn't the Pacific your fight, pure and simple?"

"The President won't give a war warning to Japan. He can't, without Congress behind him."

"What's the matter with your Congress?"

"That's a good question, but day before yesterday it came within one vote of practically dissolving the United States Army."

"Don't the congressmen know what's happening in the world?"

"They vote their political hunches to protect their political hides."

"Then what's the matter with your people?"

"Our people are about where yours were at the time of the Munich pact."

That caused a silence.

Tillet said, "We're paying the price."

"We'll have to pay the price."

"We had Chamberlain then for a leader, sir," said a fresh-faced lieutenant. "You have Roosevelt."

"The American people don't want to fight Hitler, gentlemen," said Pug. "It's that simple, and Roosevelt can't help that. They don't want to fight anybody. Life is pleasant. The war's a ball game they can watch. You're the home team, because you talk our language. Hence Lend-Lease, and this Atlantic Charter. Lend-Lease is no sweat, it just means more jobs and money for everybody."

An unusually steep roll brought a crash of crockery in the galley. The crossfire stopped. Victor Henry went to his cabin. Before disembarking in Iceland, he did not talk much more to the British officers.

48

THE Atlantic Charter, like the elephant, resembled a tree, a snake, a wall, or a rope, depending on where the blind took hold of it.

Axis propaganda jeered at its gassy rhetoric about freedom, cited enslaved India and Malaya, noted the cowardice of the degenerate Americans in evading any combat commitment, and concluded that it was all a big empty bluff, tricked out with the usual pious Anglo-Saxon hypocrisy, to cover impotent hatred of the triumphant New World Order, which a thousand Atlantic Charters could no longer roll back.

In the United States, a howl went up that Roosevelt had secretly committed the country to go to war on England's side. A cheer went up—not nearly so loud—for the most glorious document in man's struggle toward the light since the Magna Carta.

British newspapers implied that much more than this fine charter had been wrought at Argentia Bay; but for the moment the rest had to be hushed up.

The Russians hailed the meeting of Roosevelt and Churchill on a battleship at sea as a triumph for all peace-loving peoples everywhere; hinting that, as was well known, a second front in Europe now was crucial, and the Atlantic Charter, failing to mention a plan for this, was somewhat disappointing.

No reaction was stronger or blinder than the one that swept the immured Jews in Minsk.

The Germans had confiscated their radios. The penalty for possessing one was death. A sixteen-year-old boy had heard the Russian broadcast imperfectly on a tiny receiving set rigged in his attic. He had joyously spread the story that Roosevelt had met Churchill, and that the United States was declaring war on Germany! The effect on the ghetto of this lie was so wonderful, so life-giving, that one may wonder whether falsehood may not sometimes be a necessary anodyne for souls in torment.

The spirit of the Minsk Jews had recently been shattered. They had resigned themselves, with the coming of the Germans, to be herded into a few square blocks, to be forced to register for work, to be arrested and maltreated, to endure hooligan raids and perhaps even shootings. This was a pogrom time. German pogroms could be expected to be very bad. But Jewry survived pogroms.

Then one night gray trucks had swarmed into the ghetto, and squads of Germans in unfamiliar dark uniforms had cleared out the dwellers along two main streets, house by house, loading the people into the vans—for resettlement, they announced. Some of the Germans were brutal, some polite, as they pushed and urged the people into the trucks. In other streets, behind barred doors, other Jews wondered and shivered. What had happened afterward—according to reports brought by partisans who haunted the woods—was so hideous and unbelievable that the Minsk Jews were still trying numbly to come to grips with it. The gray vans had driven five miles away, to the woods outside a village. There in a moonlit ravine the Germans had ordered the people out of the trucks, had lined them up in groups, and had shot every last one—including the babies and the old people—and then had thrown them in a big hole already dug, and shovelled them over with sand.

Peasants who had dug the huge sandy hole had seen this horror with their own eyes; so the partisan report went. The Germans had rounded them up for the job, then had ordered them to go home, and not to linger or to talk about the excavation, on pain of being shot. A few had sneaked back through the trees, all the same, to see what the

Germans were up to; and they had recounted to the partisans the massacre of the "Zhids" from the gray trucks.

To the Jews trapped in Minsk, three hundred miles behind the German armies approaching Moscow, this story was an unimaginable shock. The Germans were already shooting people for small offenses, after swift crude trials. Bloated smelly bodies of such victims, and of captured partisans, hung in the public squares. Such things could be expected in wartime. But the sudden murder, evidently at random, of all the people who lived in two long streets—children, women, old people, everybody —exceeded their deepest fears of what even Germans could do. Either the story was a hysterical exaggeration, or if it were true—and the reports as they trickled in began to seem overwhelming—then the Germans were far worse than the most frightful rumors had ever pictured them.

Yet next day Minsk looked much the same, the sun-flowers bloomed, the sun shone in a blue sky. Some buildings were ruined by bombs or fire, but most stood as before; German soldiers cruised the streets, already a common sight in their gray trucks and tanks marked with swastikas. The soldiers themselves looked entirely ordinary and human, lounging with their guns and squinting in the sunshine. Some even made jokes with passersby. Russians still walked everywhere, old neighbors of the Jews, and the same bells rang at the same hours. These streets were the scenes of the Jews' lives, as familiar as faces at home. Only now all the houses in two streets stood quiet and empty.

Into this stunned moment, the news broke that Roosevelt and Churchill had met at sea and that America was entering the war. The word flew from house to house. People cried, laughed, caught up their children and danced them on their shoulders, kissed each other, and found wine or vodka to drink to President Roosevelt. One fact was graven in Europe's memory: last time, the coming of the Americans had won the war. Happy arguments broke out. Would it take three months? Six months? However long it might take, there would be no more insane occurrences like the emptying of those two streets. The Germans would not dare now! The Germans were bad when they were on top, but how humble they could be when things turned around! They were all cowards. Now they would probably start being nice to the Jews, to avoid punishment by the Americans.

Berel Jastrow did not try to contradict the rumor, though he knew that it was untrue. At the bakery, he still kept his shortwave radio concealed. His papers allowed him to pass the ghetto boundaries, for the Germans needed bread and the Minsk bakers were fighting hundreds of miles away. At the underground meeting of Jewish leaders that night, in the boiler room of the hospital, Berel did report the accurate broadcast he had heard from Sweden. But he was a foreigner, and he was telling the committee what it did not want to hear. Somebody cut him short with the observation that he had probably been listening to the German-controlled Norwegian radio; and the excited planning continued for the armed uprising that would take place in Minsk, in cooperation with the partisans, as soon as the Americans landed in France.

A few days later Jastrow and his son, with the wife and baby, disappeared. They went silently in the night, asking nobody in the ghetto for permission or help, or for passwords to contact the partisans in the woods. The Jewish Board had some trouble with the Gestapo about the vanished Polish baker. But they pleaded that the Jastrows were refugees, for whom they couldn't be responsible. The Germans had themselves issued Jastrow his special papers.

The three Polish Jews with their infant did not come back to Minsk. The ghetto people assumed they had been shot right away by the Wehrmacht forest patrols, as most Jews were who tried to slip from the town without partisan guidance. It was the German custom to throw fresh bodies from the forest into Jubilee Square, as a warning to the other Jews. But nobody saw, in these gruesome stiff piles of dead unburied friends, the bodies of the Jastrows. That was the one reason for believing the Jastrows might still be alive somewhere.

∎ ∎ ∎

In Rome the Germans were conducting themselves very well, at least within the purview of Natalie and her uncle.

A certain arrogance toward the Italians had perhaps inten-
sified with all the conquests, but that had always been the
German demeanor. Ghastly rumors of Nazi treatment of
Jews had been flying around Europe for years. To these
were now added stories of the vilest atrocities against the
captured hordes of Slav soldiers. Yet when Aaron Jastrow
and his heavily pregnant niece dined in the hotel, or at
some fine Roman restaurant, there would very likely be
Germans at table on either side of them. Enough wine
might spark a bit of Teutonic boisterousness; but to
ascribe a capacity for mass murder to these well-dressed,
careful-mannered, good-looking people—so very much like
Americans in some ways—passed all belief.

Jastrow at last was eager to go home. He had finished
the first draft of his book on Constantine; he yearned to
show it to his publisher, and then finish up the revisions in
the Harvard Library's Byzantine section. The Vatican
Library was better, of course, and he had made charming
friends there. But as shortages multiplied, Rome was getting drearier. Hitler's triumphs in the Soviet Union were
sending earthquake tremors through Italy and sinking the
Italians in gloom. There was no real gladness even in the
Fascist press, but rather some traces of alarm at these giant
strides of the Führer over the last unsubdued reaches of
Europe.

At any price, even in the best restaurants, Roman food
was bad now, and getting worse. The heavy chalky bread
was quite inedible; the new brown spaghetti tasted rather
like mud; each month the cheese grew more rubbery; the
cooking and salad oils left a loathsome aftertaste; and a
bottle of decent table wine was hard to come by. Natalie
obtained proper milk occasionally at the embassy; Italian
expectant mothers had to drink the same blue slimy fluid
that sad shrugging waiters served with the fake coffee.

So Dr. Jastrow was ready to go; but he was not scared.
He had read so much history that the events of the hour
seemed a banal repetition of old games. He had delayed
and delayed leaving Italy, almost welcoming the difficulties
with his papers, because in his heart he had thought the
war was going to end soon. Even if the villain with the
moustache (as he loved to call Hitler) won, it might not

matter so much, providing the Nazis did not march into Italy. And why should they invade a grovelling satellite?

Germany might well be the new Byzantium, he liked to say over wine: a stable well-run tyranny, geared to run a thousand years, just as Hitler boasted. Byzantium had lasted almost that long, waxing and waning through the centuries as rivals grew strong or weak, pushing its borders out and shrinking them back much like Germany; but always hanging on, and often triumphing, with its military advantages of tyranny, centrality, and interior lines. A nation's history was formed by its geography, as another villainous tyrant, Napoleon, had long ago pointed out; and autocracy was the form of government most congenial to Europe anyway. As a Jew, Jastrow of course detested Hitler. But as a philosophical historian, he could place him, and even give him good marks for willpower and political skill. He quite disbelieved the atrocity stories; warmed-over British propaganda, he said, which he still remembered well from the last war.

Natalie, however, was getting scared. Ever since Finland's entry into the war had stopped the freighter from sailing, she had sought another way out. They were still quite free to go. But now she had to deal with the Italian railroads, airlines, and emigration offices. Altogether, they made a soft fuzzy paralyzing snarl. The thought of confinement far from home, of feeding a newborn infant the rations of pinched Italy, began to alarm her as nothing had before. President Roosevelt was intervening more and more openly in the Atlantic; a sudden declaration of war by Hitler would undoubtedly drag along Mussolini, and she and her uncle would be interned as enemy aliens!

The worst stumbling block at this stage was a thing called an exit permit. Formerly it had given her no trouble at all. The yellow card stamped in purple cost a few lire, and could be purchased as soon as one had ship, train, or air tickets to show. But now an application caused hemming, hawing, and mighty searchings of bureaucratic hearts. Once, after several disappointments, Natalie did get hold of two plane seats to Lisbon, and rushed them to the emigration office. An official took the tickets and the passports from her, telling her to come back in four days. On her return, the same stout and amiable official, breathing clouds of garlic, handed the passports back to her with a sigh. The military had requisitioned the two places on the airplane. The exit permits were therefore not granted, he said, but in due course the fare money would be refunded.

The very next day she heard the first exultant BBC broadcast about the meeting in Newfoundland. The entry of the United States into the war sounded like an accomplished fact. Out of sheer despair she at once concocted a reckless scheme. She would play the card most likely to touch the Italian heart: her pregnancy. She was really having intermittent bleeding. The Americans she knew were sarcastic and skeptical about Roman doctors. They had told her of an obstetrician in Zurich, one Dr. Wundt, the best man outside the Nazi reach in Europe. She decided to request permission from Swiss authorities for a short medical visit: two weeks, ten days, whatever she could get. Pleading her bad condition, she would take her uncle along and so get exit permits. Once in Switzerland, they would by hook or by crook stay there until they obtained passage to the United States. Aaron Jastrow had a publisher in Zurich, and she knew Bunky Thurston had been transferred there from Lisbon. Once she thought of it, the idea seemed brilliant.

To her delight, Aaron after some argument agreed to play his part. He would leave his travelling library, his luggage, and all his work papers at the hotel; everything except the typed book itself, which he would carry in one small valise with his clothing. If challenged, he would say he intended to work on the inky interlineated pages during the brief Zurich visit. If the Italians did not want Jastrow to leave for good—something Natalie now half-suspected —such a casual departure might deceive them. The Atlantic Charter broadcast had given Jastrow, too, a flicker of concern; that was why he consented.

The dodge worked like a charm. Natalie booked passage to Zurich and got the exit permits. A week later she and Dr. Jastrow flew to Switzerland. Everything was in order, except that he did not have formal permission from the Swiss, as she did, to stay for ten days. The document issued to him simply stated that he was accompanying an invalid for her safety en route. When Natalie telephoned

Bunky Thurston in Zurich about this, he said they had better leave it on that basis, and not push their luck further. He could take care of Aaron once they arrived.

The Zurich terminal was startling with its bustle, its clean glitter, its open shops crammed with splendid clothing, watches, porcelain, and jewelry, its heaped boxes of chocolates, exquisite pastries, and fresh fruits. Natalie ate a big yellow pear as she walked to Thurston's car, uttering little moans of delight.

"Ah, this pear. This pear! My God," she said, "what a filthy thing Fascism is. What a foul idiocy war is! Europe's a rich continent. Why do the bloody fools lay it waste time after time? The Swiss are the only smart Europeans."

"Yes, the Swiss are smart," Thurston sighed, stroking the enormous moustache, which was as sleek and perfect as ever. The rest of his face had paled and aged as though he were ill. "How's your submariner?"

"Who knows? Dashing around the Pacific. Have you ever witnessed a crazier wedding?" Natalie turned to Jastrow, her eyes all at once gone from dulled suffering to the old bright puckish gleam. "Bunky signed the marriage document. Do you like Zurich better than Lisbon, Bunky?"

"I don't like to think of eighty million Germans seething just beyond the Alps. But at least they're nice high Alps.—Here we are, the red Citroen.—The tragic refugee thing goes on here too, Natalie, but less visibly, less acutely. In Lisbon it was just too horrible."

Aaron Jastrow said as they drove down the highway, "Will they send our passports to you at the consulate?"

"Maybe you'll just pick them up when you go back."

"But we're not going back, darling," Natalie said. "Aaron, give me your handkerchief, my face is all pear juice. I wish I could bathe in pear juice."

"It's my only handkerchief," Jastrow said.

Thurston pulled a handkerchief from his breast pocket and passed it to her. "What do you mean, you're not going back?"

"My uncle and I intend to hop the first train, plane, or goat cart out of here, so long as it heads for the good old

USA. I couldn't tell you that over the telephone, Bunky, obviously. But it's the whole point of this trip."

"Natalie, it won't work."

"Why on earth not?"

"Aaron got through Swiss immigration on my parole. I must return him there. He has no transit visa."

After a silence Dr. Jastrow said from the back seat, in a low sad voice, "I thought it was going too easily."

"Bunky, wild horses can't get me back to Rome," Natalie said cheerfully. "I won't have my baby there. That's that. You have to figure out some way to clear Aaron, too. He's here now. His passport is good as gold. I know you can solve this."

Thurston ran a careful hand over the moustache as he drove. "Well, you've caught me unawares. Give me a little time."

"I've got ten days," Natalie said.

"There aren't too many ways to travel out of Zurich now," said Thurston. "I'll look into this a bit."

He left them outside Dr. Herman Wundt's office, which was in an old four-story house decked with flower-filled window boxes, and took their suitcases off to the hotel. Jastrow dozed in an anteroom while Wundt examined Natalie.

After asking a few questions and noting the answers on a card, the bald freckled doctor, a gnome not as tall as her uncle, with big ears and darting little brown eyes, probed, palpated, took specimens, and submitted Natalie to the usual indignities, and a couple of new painful ones with strange implements, all the while smiling and chatting in French. She lay on the table panting and exhausted under a sheet, her face sweating, all her lower body in an ache. The breeze brought a delicious scent of sweet peas from the window boxes.

"Very well, take a little rest."

She heard him washing his hands. He returned with a notebook and sat beside her.

"You're as strong as a horse, and you're carrying that baby perfectly."

"I had three bleeding episodes."

"Yes. You mentioned that. When was the last one?"

"Let's see. A month ago. Maybe a little more."

"Well, you can wait around a day or so for the result of the smear, and the urine test, and so forth. I'm almost sure they'll be negative, and Dr. Carona will deliver a fine baby for you. I know him well. He's the best man in Rome."

"Dr. Wundt, unless I go back to the States, I'd rather stay and have the baby here. I don't want to return to Rome."

"So? Why?"

"Because of the war. If the United States becomes involved, I'll find myself on enemy soil with a newborn baby."

"You say your husband is an American naval officer, in the Pacific Ocean?"

"Yes."

"You're too far away from him."

Natalie sadly laughed. "I agree, but that's done now."

"What kind of name is that—Henry?"

"Oh, I guess it's Scotch. Scotch-English."

"And your maiden name is Jastrow, you said? Is that Scotch-English too?"

"It's Polish." After a pause, as the little brown eyes stared at her, she added, "Polish-Jewish."

"And that gentleman outside, your uncle? Is he Polish-Jewish?"

"He's a famous American writer."

"Really? How exciting. Is he a Polish Jew?"

"He was born in Poland."

"You can get dressed now. Then come into the other room, please."

Dr. Wundt sat hunched in a swivel chair in his tiny office, smoking a cigar. The smoke wreathed up over wrinkled yellow diplomas on the walls, and a dusty engraving of the wounded lion of Lucerne. He rested the cigar in an onyx tray, pressed his fingertips together, and put them to his mouth. The brown-patched old face stared blankly at her.

"Mrs. Henry, in the past few years—I have to be frank with you—pregnancy has been used and abused to death here to solve passport difficulties. The immigration authorities have become very hard. I am an alien myself, and my license can easily be revoked. Do I make myself clear?"

"But I'm having no passport difficulties," Natalie replied calmly. "None at all. Do you think I can safely travel back to the United States? That's all I want to know."

The doctor hunched his shoulders, pursed his lips, and cocked his head like a bright dog, his eyes never leaving her. "By what means of transportation?"

"Airplane, I suppose."

"What was Dr. Carona's opinion?"

"I didn't ask him. Despite what you say, I don't have much confidence in him. That's why I want to stay here if I can't fly home."

The old doctor's eyes sparked and he spread his hands. "And that's precisely where I can't help you. The authorities will demand from me a written certificate that you're unable to travel. Otherwise they won't extend your stay. You're quite able to fly back to Rome. About flying to the United States"—he cocked his head again—"that is bound to be a rough long journey."

Natalie kept an unruffled manner. "You mean I might lose the baby?"

"Not necessarily, but an expectant mother with a first baby should avoid such a strain. Your pregnancy history already is not one hundred percent."

"Then why make me go back to Rome? The milk and the food are abominable. I don't like the doctor there. He mishandled my bleeding."

With a cold edge in his voice, the little doctor said, "Mrs. Henry, a flight to Rome is no problem for you, nothing to justify an extension of your stay. I'm very sorry. The authorities will ask me about your health, not about Roman milk or Dr. Carona." He flipped open an appointment book and peered into it. "I will see you tomorrow at a quarter past five, and we will discuss your tests."

At dinner with Thurston and her uncle that night, Natalie was quite blithe. The buoyant excitement of being out of Rome, and in a city at peace, overbore Wundt's sourness; and she was cheered by the examination results. She was "strong as a horse," the infant was kicking lustily inside her, and they had escaped from Fascist Italy. The rest would work out, she thought, especially since Thurston seemed in an optimistic mood. She decided not to quiz him, but let him talk when he was ready.

Meantime her common ground with him was Leslie Slote. She told droll anecdotes of her wretched Paris flat: the tiny stairwell elevator in which Slote got stuck and slept all one night, her Algerian landlord's efforts to keep her from cooking, the one-eyed homosexual sculptor on the floor above who pestered Slote to pose for him. Aaron Jastrow had not heard these yarns of young love on the Left Bank. What with the richly satisfying dinner, the fine wine, and the view from the open-air terrace restaurant of Zurich ablaze with lights, his spirits also rose. He accepted a cigar from Thurston, though he had a bad cough.

"My lord. Havana!" Dr. Jastrow rolled the smoke on his tongue. "This takes me back ten years to the commons room. How gracious and easy and pleasant life seemed! Yet all the time the villain with the moustache was piling up his tanks and his cannon. Ah, me. You're very merry, Natalie."

"I know. The wine, no doubt, and the lights. The lights! Bunky, electric light is the strongest enchantment there is. Live in a blackout for a few months and you'll see! You know what Zurich reminds me of? Luna Park in Coney Island, when I was a little girl. You walked in a blaze of lights, millions and millions of yellow bulbs. The lights were more exciting than the rides and games. Switzerland's amazing, isn't it? A little dry diving bell of freedom in an ocean of horror. What an experience! I'll never forget this."

"You can understand why the Swiss have to be very, very careful," Thurston said. "Otherwise they'd be swamped with refugees."

Natalie and her uncle sobered at that last word, listening for what he would say next.

The consul smoothed his moustache with both palms. "Don't forget there are more than four million Jews caught in Hitler's Europe. And in all of Switzerland there are only four million people. So the Swiss have become almost as sticky about Jews as our own State Department, but with infinitely more reason. They've got sixteen thousand square miles of land, much of it bare rock and snow. We've got three and a half million square miles. Compare population densities, and we're a vast empty wilderness. We're supposed to be the land of the free, the haven of outcasts. The Swiss make no such claim. Who should be taking in the Jews? Yet they are doing it, but carefully, and within limits. Moreover the Swiss depend on the Germans for fuel, for iron, for all trade, in and out. They're in a closed ring. They're free only as long as it suits the Nazis. I can't take a high moral tone with the Swiss authorities about you. As an American official, I'm in a hell of a lousy position for moral tone."

Jastrow said, "One can see that."

"Nothing's been decided in your case, you understand," the consul said. "I've just been making inquiries. A favorable solution is possible. Natalie, could you endure a long train trip?"

"I'm not sure. Why?"

"The only airline operating from Zurich to Lisbon now is Lufthansa."

Natalie felt a pang of alarm, but her tone was matter-of-fact. "I see. What about that Spanish flight?"

"You were misinformed. It shut down back in May. Lufthansa flies once a week, starting from Berlin and making every stop in between—Marseilles, Barcelona, Madrid. It's a rotten flight. I've taken it going the other way. It's usually crowded with Axis hotshots. Do you want to separate from your uncle and try Lufthansa? Your passport doesn't say you're Jewish. You're Mrs. Byron Henry. Even the Germans have some tenderness for pregnant women. But, of course, for twenty hours or so you'd be in Nazi hands."

"What's the alternative?"

"Train via Lyons, Nîmes, and Perpignan, sliding down the French coast, crossing the Pyrenees to Barcelona, and then, heaven help you, clear across Spain and Portugal to Lisbon. Mountains, tunnels, awful roadbeds, and God knows how many breakdowns, delays, and changes, with a long stretch through Vichy France. Maybe three, maybe six days en route."

Natalie said, "I don't think I should risk that."

"I wouldn't mind trying Lufthansa," said Jastrow in a far-off voice, rolling the cigar in his fingers. "I still don't believe, I truly don't, that the Germans would molest me."

Thurston shook his head. "Dr. Jastrow, she's the wife of a Gentile naval officer. I think she'd be all right. Don't you go on Lufthansa!"

"What I have to decide, then," Natalie said, "is whether I chance Lufthansa alone, or take the train with Aaron."

"You don't have to decide anything yet. I'm telling you some of the things to think about."

Natalie and her uncle killed the next day looking in shop windows, buying clothes, eating cream cakes, drinking real coffee, riding around in cabs, and luxuriating in the rich freedom of Switzerland, only a few hours by air from brown melancholy Rome. Toward evening she saw Dr. Wundt again. With a sad shrug, he told her that all her tests were negative.

"That's all right. I may be able to stay, anyway," she said. "My consul's looking into it."

"Ah, so?" the little doctor's face brightened. "Perfect! Nothing would please me more. Let me book your lying-in right away, Mrs. Henry. The hospitals are crowded."

"I'll let you know in a day or two."

"Excellent."

In the morning she found a white hotel envelope slipped under the door: *Hi. Things are cooking. Meet me at the lake front, both of you, four o'clock, at Zurich Pleasure Boats. Bunky.*

When they arrived at the dock, the consul had already hired an open boat with an outboard motor, and was sitting in it, waiting. Without a word he helped them in, started the engine, and went puttering off from the shore. About a mile out he killed the motor, and they could hear a German waltz thumping brassily over the blue water from the band of an approaching excursion steamer.

"I've got quite a report for you," Thurston said, and Natalie's heart leaped at his happy grin. "I thought we'd better be by ourselves while we talk it out."

"Is it all arranged?" Jastrow said, with an eagerness that struck his niece as childish.

Thurston smoothed a palm over his moustache. "Well, we're not in bad shape." The consul's eyes twinkled at Natalie. "Say, I've been on the telephone and teletype to Rome. Your Byron outdid his Lisbon feat, didn't he? Talking to President Roosevelt about your uncle's passport! What sheer nerve! Sight unseen, nobody in Rome likes him."

"I can imagine."

"Yes, but your uncle's file carries a big *'presidential'* flag on it now, and that's just fine. Now, Natalie, you're set. I've put you on the waiting list at Lufthansa. The next two flights are booked, but you've got a reservation on the third. Immigration will extend your stay till then."

"But by then I'll be in my eighth month—"

Holding up a hand, Thurston said, "Lufthansa is sure you'll get out sooner. Maybe next week. There are always cancellations, and you're high on the list, because of your pregnancy."

"What about Aaron?"

"Well, that's a different story."

"She's the important one," Jastrow said dramatically, "and what happens to me couldn't matter less. I've lived my life."

"Hold on, hold on." Thurston smiled. "Good lord, Dr. Jastrow! Everything's all right. You just can't stay on in Switzerland with her. That's out of the question. But you're set, too. Rome's in a big boil about you now. The ambassador is outraged. He says that if he has to, he'll appoint you to his staff and send you home on a diplomatic priority. You're returning to Rome, but he'll assume responsibility for dealing with the Italians. We have a lot of Italian bigwigs in the States, Dr. Jastrow, and I promise you there will be no more trouble with your exit permit."

"You do think that's better for me than taking the train to Lisbon?" Jastrow's question was rhetorical. He sounded pleased and relieved. "I'm quite willing to attempt that."

"Great heavens, Dr. Jastrow. I wouldn't do that myself. It's a gruelling schedule, and I'm not even sure the connections are still available. But the main objection is, you'd

of guilt about you at least as large as that baby you've got there. Someday you'll know the measure of my gratitude." He put his weak, bony little hand on hers. "You've earned yourself—as our fathers quaintly put it—a large share in the world to come. If only it existed!"

So Aaron Jastrow went back docilely to Rome. His niece heard nothing for ten days, ten dreary days in which the comforts and rich food of the Swiss rapidly palled. Even an albatross around one's neck, Natalie began to think, was company of a sort. She was terribly lonely. Bunky Thurston, carrying on a romance with the daughter of a refugee French novelist, had little time for her. The Swiss treated her, as they did all foreigners, with cool paid courtesy, as though the whole country were the grounds of a huge Class A hotel. The sad-eyed Jews in the shops, the streets, the excursion trains and boats, depressed her. A letter came at last, sprinkled with special-delivery stamps and censors' markings.

I assume this will be read, but it makes no difference. You and I are *in the clear* with the Italian authorities! I now have in my possession, Natalie, *two* air tickets, *and* properly dated exit permits, *and* Portuguese transit visas, *and* Pan Am connections, *and* highest diplomatic priority stickers. The works! They're lying on the desk before me, and I've never seen a more glorious sight.

Thurston sparked an explosion in this embassy, my dear. A fine chap. It was high time! The ambassador used all his available channels, including the Vatican—where, as you know, I have many friends. I should have tried long ago myself to throw my weight around, but it seemed so infra dig to plead my literary distinction, such as it is!

Now to cases.

The date of the tickets is December fifteenth. It's awfully far off, I know, but Pan Am's the bottleneck. No sense going to Lisbon and sitting there for months! And this transportation is *sure*. Of course it does mean having your baby here, after all. That decision is up to you.

I enclose a note from the ambassador's charming and quite bright wife. If you don't want to languish in Zurich, waiting for a chance to ride out with the gallant Huns, her invitation may be welcome.

I await your orders. I feel twenty years younger. Are you well? I worry about you day and night.

Love
Aaron.

The ambassador's wife had written in an ornate finishing-school hand in green ink, with little circles over the *i*'s:

Dear Natalie:

I sent my daughter home three months ago to have her baby. Her room is empty, her husband works in the embassy, and all of us miss her so much!

If you can get home from Switzerland, nothing could be better. Otherwise, please consider coming here, where at least you would eat well, and the baby would be born on American "soil," so to speak, among your friends. We would love to have you.

On this same morning, Bunky Thurston telephoned. Lufthansa had come across with an early reservation, as a special courtesy to him: one seat to Lisbon, September 17, four days off. No opening existed on Pan Am, he said, but they had put her high on the long Lisbon waiting list, and she would get any early vacancy.

"I'd suggest you go straight to the Lufthansa office on the Bahnhofstrasse, just two blocks down from the hotel, and grab yourself this ticket," Thurston said. "There are various forms to fill out, which I can't do for you, otherwise—"

"Wait, Bunky, wait." Natalie was having trouble following him. She had awakened with a sore throat and a fever of over a hundred; she was groggy from the aspirins and depressed by her uncle's letter, which had thrown her into a vortex of indecision. "I have a letter from Aaron. Can you spare a moment?"

"Shoot."

She read him the letter.

"Well! They really got hot, didn't they? Natalie, I can't presume to make your decision. I know what Leslie Slote would say. Byron too."

"I know. Play it safe, go straight back to Rome."

"Exactly."

"You're wrong about Byron. Byron would tell me to get on Lufthansa."

"Really? You know him better than I do. Whatever you decide, let me know if there's any way I can help you," Thurston said. "I hear Françoise honking. We're spending a day in the country."

Of all things, Natalie did not want to go back to Rome. It was the fixed idea she clung to. Heavily, dizzily, she dressed herself and set out to walk to Lufthansa. She kept swallowing, her throat rasping like sandpaper despite the aspirins. All the airline offices were in the same block. Air France, Pan American, and BOAC were closed and shuttered, the paint of their signs fading. The gilt of Lufthansa's eagle, perched on a wreathed swastika, shone bright in the sun. The swastika made Natalie hesitate outside. Through the window she saw behind a bare counter in a hospital-clean office a tanned blonde girl in an azure and gold uniform, perfectly groomed, laughing with very white teeth. A tanned man in a checked sports jacket was laughing with her. Wall posters showed castles on river bluffs, and girls in Bavarian costume, and fat men drinking beer, and busts of Beethoven and Wagner hovering over a baroque opera house.

They saw her looking in at them, stopped laughing, and stared. Shivering a little from the fever, Natalie entered the Lufthansa office.

"Grüss Gott," said the girl.

"Good afternoon," Natalie said hoarsely. "The American consul, Bunker Thurston, has made a reservation for me to fly to Lisbon on the seventeenth."

"Oh? Are you Mrs. Byron Henry?" The girl switched smoothly to clear English.

"Yes."

"Fine. Your passport?"

"Do you have the reservation?"

"Yes. Let me have your passport, please."

The girl held out a manicured, scrubbed hand. Natalie gave her the passport, and the girl handed her a long form printed on coarse green paper. "Fill this out, please."

Natalie scanned the form. "My goodness. What a lot of questions for an airplane ride."

"Wartime security regulations, Mrs. Henry. Both sides, please."

The first page asked for a detailed accounting of the passenger's travels in the past year. Natalie turned over the form. The first question at the top of the page was

GLAUBUNG *(Foi) (Religion)* . . . .
  Vater (Père) (Father) . . . .
  Mutter (Mère) (Mother) . . . .

A nerve spasm swept her. She wondered why Thurston had not warned her of this risky snag. Here was a quick decision to make! It was simple enough to write in *"Methodist";* they had her mother's maiden name in the passport, but "Greengold" wasn't necessarily Jewish. How could they check? Yet, after Aaron's troubles, what lists might she not be on? How could she be sure that the Königsberg incident had not been recorded? And what had happened to those Jewish neutrals at Königsberg whom the Germans had marched off? As these thoughts raced in her fevered mind, the baby gave a little jolt inside her.

The street outside seemed far away and inviting. Natalie's head swam and her throat seemed to be choking shut with bits of gravel. She dropped the green form on the counter. The Lufthansa girl was starting to write a ticket, copying data from the passport. Natalie saw her glance in puzzlement at the form, then at the man in the sports jacket, who reached into a pocket and said to Natalie in German, "Do you need a pen?"

"Give me my passport, please," she said.

The girl's eyebrows arched. "Is something wrong?"

Too rattled to think of a deft answer, Natalie blurted. "Americans don't ask people's religion for travel purposes, and don't give their own."

The man and the girl exchanged a knowing look. The man said, "If you want to leave that blank, it is up to you. It is quite all right, Mrs. Henry."

They both smiled slow queer smiles, the smile of the SS officer in Königsberg.

"I'll take my passport, please."

"I have started to write your ticket," said the girl. "It is very hard to get passage to Lisbon, Mrs. Henry."

"My passport."

The girl tossed the maroon booklet on the counter, and turned her back.

Natalie left. Three doors down, the Swissair office was open. She went in, and booked a flight to Rome the following morning. It was as Aaron Jastrow had said. Going back was as easy as descending a greased slope.

*   *   *

49

𝕿𝖍𝖊 𝕸𝖆𝖗𝖈𝖍 𝖔𝖓 𝕸𝖔𝖘𝖈𝖔𝖜

(from WORLD EMPIRE LOST)

The Geography of Barbarossa

In war the event is all, and Germany lost the war. This has obscured her victories in the field. Her enemies never won such victories; they overwhelmed her in the end with numbers, and a cataract of machines.

Defeat also, quite naturally, casts doubt on the conduct of the war by the loser. Thus we have wide agreement among military historians, regrettably including noted German generals like Guderian, Manstein, and Warlimont, that our plan for the invasion of Russia was "vague" or "patched-up" or "without a strategic objective." What is accomplished by this historical fouling of our own nest, except self-exculpation which should be beneath a soldier's dignity? It is bad enough that we lost the war, and world empire, by a heartbreakingly slender margin. There is no reason to describe ourselves, in our greatest national effort, as unprofessional dolts into the bargain. Such lickspittle writing, catering to the prejudices of the victors, does honor to nobody and violates history.

I myself was detailed to temporary service on the planning staff of General Marcks, which in the fall and winter of 1940 worked out the original war games of the invasion of the Soviet Union and then drafted an operational proposal. I was therefore in the picture from the start. It was a bold conception, for the factors of space and time, for the numbers of men and quantities of supplies, and for the grandeur of the political stakes. In detail Barbarossa was almost too complicated to be grasped by any one human intelligence. Yet in overall vision, it was a simple plan. In this lay its merit and its strength. It was firmly rooted in geographic, economic, and military realities. Within the limits of risk inherent in all war, it was sound.

Let the reader spend a moment or two studying the very simplified map I have prepared. Further on, in my operational narrative, there are more than forty situation maps from the archives. Here is the picture of the Barbarossa assault in a nutshell.

Line A was our main effort, or jump-off line in Poland. It was about five hundred miles long, running north and south from the Baltic Sea to the Carpathian Mountains. (There was also a holding action out of Rumania, intended to safeguard the Ploesti oil fields.)

Line C was our goal. Almost two thousand miles long, it ran from Archangel, on the White Sea, south to Kazan and then along the Volga to the Caspian Sea. Its farthest objectives were about twelve hundred miles from the starting point.

Line B was as far as we got in December 1941. The line runs from Leningrad on the Gulf of Finland, down through Moscow to the Crimea on the Black Sea, falling just short of Rostov on the Don. It is nearly twelve hundred miles long, and more than six hundred miles from where we started. We were apparently stopped by the Russians, therefore, about halfway. But that is not really so. We were halted at the last moment, in the last ditch.

The Attack Concept

During the spring of 1941, our intelligence reported that the Red Army was massing in the west, near the line cutting Poland in two. This menacing pileup of armed Slavs threatened to inundate Europe with Bolshevism. It was a main reason for the Führer's decision to launch his preventive war, and certainly justified all our earlier planning.

This menacing disposition of Stalin's forces nevertheless pleased us, because he was giving up the great Russian advantage of maneuvering space, and crowding the Red Army within reach of a quick knockout blow. Stalin was superior both in numbers and equipment. Our best information was that we would be marching with about one hundred fifty divisions against perhaps two hundred, with about thirty-two hundred tanks against as many as ten thousand, and with an unknown disadvantage in aircraft. Obviously, then, our hope lay in superior training, leadership, soldiers, and machines, and in the swift decisive exploitation of surprise. After Finland, this seemed a reasonable risk.

The strategic aim of Barbarossa was to shatter the Soviet state in one colossal summer stroke, and to reduce its fragments to disarmed socialist provinces garrisoned and ruled by Germany, from the Polish border to the Volga. The primitive land east of the Volga, the frozen Siberian deserts and the empty forests beyond the Urals, could then be cordoned off or taken at leisure. From those remote areas no existing bomber could reach Germany, a vital factor to consider.

Operationally, we expected to break through the thick crust at the western border with three huge simultaneous lightning attacks—two to the north of the marshland, one to the south—and encircle and mop up the broken forces within a couple of weeks. Thus, the main bulk of the Red Army would cease to exist almost at the outset.

This we estimated we could do; but we knew that would not be the end. We realized the enemy would maintain heavy reserve forces between the borders and Moscow, and that at some point these forces would dig in. We also knew that the stolid Slav fights best in defense of his fatherland. We therefore expected, and planned for, a second big central campaign during the first part of July, probably in the region behind the Dnieper-Dvina line, to round up and destroy these reserve forces. Finally, we expected that as we penetrated to the line Leningrad-Moscow-Sevastopol, we would encounter a last-ditch surge of Russian resistance (as we did), including a *levée en masse* of the populations of the capital and the other big industrial cities lying along this spinal column of the Soviet Union. Once we broke that spine, nothing lay beyond, in our judgment, to the Archangel-Volga line which was our goal, except for a gigantic mop-up of a panic-stricken population, with perhaps some minor partisan warfare.

This was, of course, a difficult undertaking, a gamble against odds. The battlefield was Soviet Russia itself, a funnel-shaped landmass five hundred miles wide at one end, seventeen hundred miles wide at the other. The northward slope of the funnel lay along the Baltic and the White seas; the southward slope, along the Carpathian Mountains and the Black Sea. Our forces had to fan out into the vast level monotony of the Russian plain, stretching our lines of communication and thinning our front as we went. This we expected, but we were surprised by the primitiveness of the roads and the wildness of the countryside. Here our intelligence was faulty. This was not terrain suited for blitzkrieg. In fact, the very inefficiency and low standards of Communist Russia proved a formidable defensive factor. They had not troubled to build decent highways, and their railroad beds were defective and—deliberately, of course—of a different gauge than ours.

TRANSLATOR'S NOTE: *In Roon's view, German staff plans for attacks on other countries are always defensive and hypothetical; but the other fellow always does something stupid or evil that triggers off the plan. Historians still debate Stalin's intentions in 1941, but it seems he had no offensive plans. The Soviets were frightened to death of the Germans, and did everything possible, to the last moment, to appease them and keep them from attacking.—V.H.*

Cutting the Pie

Barbarossa clicked from the start, despite various problems. All along the front, we achieved surprise. This will remain a supreme wonder in the annals of warfare. Guderian records how German artillerymen around Brest-Litovsk, poised to start a barrage on the unsuspecting Bolsheviks before dawn, watched the last Russian supply train chug faithfully out of the Soviet Union into our sector of Poland. Nothing could show more clearly how Stalin and his henchmen were fooled by the Führer's adroit politics. Western writers now call this a "perfidious attack," as though, at the outset of a struggle to the death, Germany could afford parlor-game niceties.

With this advantage in hand, Barbarossa proceeded according to plan. The Luftwaffe caught the enormous frontline Red air force on the ground and wiped it out in a few hours. In the center and in the north our armored pincers advanced by timetable, with the infantry rolling forward in their support. Six days saw us in Minsk and at the Dvina, bagging nearly half a million prisoners and thousands of guns and tanks. Only in the south did Rundstedt encounter some real resistance. Elsewhere, the Red Army was like a huge thrashing body without a head. Stalin was invisible and silent, paralyzed in the throes of melancholia.

Two more weeks, and a second vast armored encirclement had closed around Smolensk, two-thirds of the way along the main Moscow road. In the north we had overrun the Baltic states, turning the Baltic into a German lake, and were rapidly approaching Leningrad through wild terrain. Rundstedt's drive in the south had picked up steam and was nearing Kiev. We had rounded up several hundred thousand more prisoners. The Russians fought bravely and stubbornly in little pockets, but operationally we were no longer encountering the organized resistance of a national force. According to all reports from the field and the picture developing at Supreme Headquarters, we had once again won a war—or, more exactly, a grand police action—in three weeks, and were engaged in mop-up: Poland, France, and now the Soviet Union.

Of course, such a massive advance had taken its toll of men, supplies, and wear and tear on machines. A pause for consolidation ensued, lasting to mid-August. Some writers claim this was a "fatal display of irresolution," but they obviously know nothing of logistics. This pause was part of our original timetable. Far from being irresolute, the Wehrmacht, triumphant from the Baltic to the Black Sea, regrouped and tooled up in a flush of victorious excitement, which can still make the blood tingle in old soldiers who remember.

As the staff man familiar with the smallest details of Barbarossa, I was present at the famous conference at the Wolf's Lair Headquarters on July 16, when Hitler, sweeping both hands over his table map, exultantly told Göring, Rosenberg, Bormann, and other high Party brass, "Essentially, the point now is to slice up this gigantic pie for our purposes, in order to be able:

First, to dominate it,

Second, to administer it, and

Third, to exploit it!"

I can still see the radiant smile on Hitler's puffy, unhealthy face as he held up fingers to count, and the touch of hectic red that victory had brought to his wan cheeks. After the conference ended, he talked informally of disbanding forty divisions in September, in order to send the men back to the factories. He wanted to reduce tank and gun production, in favor of a swift air and sea building program for the final crushing of England and the end of the war. All this made plain common sense, and not one voice was raised in objection. From the visible facts in the field, the eastern campaign had been won.

The Critiques

Armchair strategists have the advantage not only of hindsight, but of being irresponsible. Nobody really cares what they think. The contest is over, and nothing hinges on their opinions. They are just consuming ink and paper, which are cheap. Before the event, however, every decision in war involves the lives of soldiers, perhaps the national existence itself. It is unwise to dismiss out of hand, long afterward, the judgments of the men in the field who had to do the job. But this caution is seldom exercised in critiques of Barbarossa.

Three fallacious objections to our campaign crop up over and over. They contradict each other, but that does not stop the critics from using one, or two, or all three. It is alleged:

First, that our invasion of the Soviet Union was doomed to fail, no matter how many military victories were won, because a small patch of Europe like Germany, with eighty million inhabitants, could not hope to hold down vast Russia with close to two hundred millions;

Second, that Hitler's harsh treatment of the Russian inhabitants was fatuous, because they would otherwise have welcomed us with open arms and helped to overthrow the hated Communist regime. In this connection, the old story of village women coming to greet the German invaders with flowers, or with bread and salt, is invariably trotted out;

Third, that the plan made the classic error of seeking territorial or economic objectives, instead of concentrating on destroying the enemy's armed forces.

Very well. To the first point, I reply that a glance at the world map shows that a tiny island like England, peopled by thirty or forty million, could not possibly have ruled South Africa, India, Canada, and Australia, with almost half a billion inhabitants. Nevertheless, for a long time, England did. Moreover, these subject lands were not contiguous, but thousands of miles away, at the end of thread-thin lines of sea communication. The Soviet Union, on the other hand, was in land communication with Germany, directly under our guns.

These critics forget that the Soviet Union in the first instance was the creation of a small extremist party of Bolsheviks, who overthrew the regime and seized control of a population ten thousand times as numerous as themselves, a conglomerate of many nationalities. Or that a small ferocious Mongolian invader, the Golden Horde, actually did rule the Slav masses for more than a century. In short, these critics know nothing of the history of conquest, or the techniques of military administration, especially with modern communications and equipment. Had we conquered the Soviet Union, we would have administered it. We did quite well in the provinces we held for years.

The second contention of course contradicts the first. If we could not hold down the Russians in any case, what would we have gained by an easy policy toward them? It would only have hastened the day of our overthrow. But this criticism rests on an absurd misconception of the entire nature of the war between Germany and the Soviet Union. This was, in the strictest sense, a war to the death.

History had come to a turn. There were two strong industrial powers left on the Eurasian landmass, and only two. They faced each other. They were dedicated to totally different revolutionary ideologies. If Bolshevism were to triumph, Germany as we knew it had to die. If German National Socialism prevailed, there was no room on this heartland for an independent, armed, menacing Bolshevik nation far bigger than the Reich.

The Green Folder

Much has been made of "The Green Folder," the master policy directive for the economic exploitation of conquered Russia, prepared by Economic Staff East under Göring. At the Nuremberg trials, I established that I had no part in drawing up this administrative plan, since my responsibilities were operational.

The proposals of the Green Folder were, without question, draconic. They meant the death by starvation of tens of millions of Russians. Göring admitted as much, and the documents are spread on the record, so denying this is absurd. Nor would there be either sense or profit in attempting to prove the "morality" of the Green Folder. However, certain observations of a military nature may be in order.

The Green Folder scheme rested on a plain geographic

fact. The fertile "black belt" region of southern Russia feeds not only itself and its own industries, but the whole industrial complex to the north. Northern Russia has always been a scrubby, impoverished area, where bad weather and bad soil combine to create a permanent deficit of foodstuffs. The Green Folder proposed a drastic levy on the corn, meats, coal, oil, fats, hides, and factory products of the south, for the purposes of maintaining our armies in the field and our strained German folk at home. The plan was to feed the southern Slavs a minimum caloric intake, so that they could keep up production. But Germany's need for so much of Russia's produce would naturally create a food shortage on a large scale. A serious wastage of the northern Russian population had to be accepted as a result.

Perhaps our administrative plan for Russia was less "moral" than the Americans' extirpation of the red race and the seizure from them of the richest lands on earth. Perhaps it lacked the religious high-mindedness with which the Spaniards sacked Mexico and South America and destroyed the fascinating Inca and Aztec civilizations. And possibly, in some way not very clear to this writer, the British subjugation of India, or the commercial spoliation of China by all the European colonialists plus the United States, were nicer and more moral programs than the proposals in the Green Folder. But the unprejudiced reader must never forget that in the German world-philosophical view, *Russia was our India.*

We Germans have always lacked the singular Anglo-Saxon gift for cloaking self-interest in pious moral attitudes. We honestly say what we think, and thus invariably shock the tender sensibilities of Western politicians and writers. Adolf Hitler was a world-historical individual; that much is now a settled fact. He presented the German nation with a world-historical goal. World-historical changes are, as Hegel taught, far beyond the petty limits of morality. They are revelations of God's will. Perhaps in the vast effort and the vast tragedy of Germany, Providence had a dark design that will become clear to later generations. The Green Folder was an integral part of that effort. By world-philosophical considerations, it was the just act of a people seeking to strike out new paths in mankind's endless Faustian journey.

In the light of these ideas, the argument that we should

have treated the Ukrainians and other Slavs nicely, so that they would help us overthrow their Communist rulers, becomes clearly ridiculous. Germany, a nation as poor as It was powerful, could not continue the war without confiscating the food of southern Russia. Was it to be expected that the Slavs would accept impoverishment, forced labor, and the death of millions by starvation, without a really serious revolt, unless their spirit had been broken from the start, and unless they had seen nothing in prospect but an iron fist and the firing squad if they did not labor and obey? Adolf Hitler said that the only way to administer southern Russia was to shoot anybody who made a wry face. He had a harsh way of putting things sometimes, but what he said in such matters seldom lacked realism.

Finally, it must be pointed out that the Green Folder administration scheme never became a reality, since we failed to conquer the Soviet Union. It was a hypothetical plan that could not be put into practice. The stress placed on it at the Nuremberg trials therefore seems highly excessive and distorted.

TRANSLATOR'S NOTE: *Roon's philosophical defense of the Green Folder—possibly the cruelest set of administrative plans ever put on paper—will no doubt be indigestible to the average reader in the United States. However, it was when I read this passage that I decided to translate* World Empire Lost.*—V.H.*

The Turn South

Basing themselves largely upon Guderian, many writers further maintain that Hitler lost the war in mid-July, after our amazing three-week advance to Smolensk—two-thirds of the way to Moscow—by ordering Guderian's panzer armies southward to help Rundstedt close the Kiev pocket, instead of allowing him to drive on. The contention is that precious weeks were thereby lost and the armored equipment became excessively worn, so that the punch was taken out of the final assault on the capital.

There are several gaping holes in this "Turn South" critique.

First of all, the closing of the Kiev pocket east of the Dnieper was the greatest military land victory in the history of mankind. At a blow, Germany killed or captured armed forces and equipment equal to almost half the entire Wehrmacht force with which she began the invasion of the Soviet Union! It is a little hard to dismiss such a mighty triumph as a "tactical diversion." With this victory, we won secure possession of the riches of southern Russia, which alone enabled us to fight on in the years ahead and to come close to winning. We secured the breadbasket, the industrial basin, and the fuel reserve, which Germany had sought for so long, and which was the whole pivot of Adolf Hitler's politics.

True, Clausewitz says the destruction of the enemy's armed forces, not the winning of territorial or economic objectives, is the chief aim of warfare. But the much-criticized "Turn South" achieved a big destruction of enemy armed forces.

Suppose that vast southern army had escaped and flanked us? Even if we had destroyed the armies in front of Moscow and occupied the capital, would we have been any better off than Napoleon? Napoleon essentially followed a Guderian strategy, striking for the "center of gravity" in Moscow. The trouble was, once he got there, that he could not feed his men or his horses, he was threatened on the left and right flanks, and after a while there was nothing to do but retreat to fathomless catastrophe.

We who planned Barbarossa, and watched it unfold, were seldom without a copy of Caulaincourt's Memoirs in hand! If the Wehrmacht held fast during the frightful winter of 1941, one very good reason was that we did not repeat Napoleon's mistake. We at least seized the south, which supported us and gave us hope to fight another day. When Hitler told Guderian, who came to Wolf's Lair to protest against the "Turn South," that generals know nothing about the economics of war, he spoke the cold truth. They are like pampered athletes who let some other fellow worry about the playing fields, the crowds, and the money; their only interest is in displaying their prowess. Such was Guderian, an opinionated if brilliant prima donna.

The contention that the drive through the center was weakened is itself rather weakened by the plain fact that after finishing his assigned duties in the south, Guderian returned north and jumped off for our spectacular September and October victories. There was nothing particularly enfeebled in that performance!

I have not hesitated to point out Adolf Hitler's amateurish errors in other situations; some of these were disastrous, but the turn south was a sound, necessary, and successful move.

To the Towers of the Kremlin

The remnants of the Red Army in the north and center, beaten and broken once again, went staggering back into the enormous spaces of Russia. Hordes were captured, but more hordes abandoned tanks and guns to slip through our encirclements in the night. In the north all our objectives were achieved except the actual taking of Leningrad. The city was laid under siege which lasted nine hundred days, in which it withered into helplessness and almost perished. The Baltic coast was ours, so that we could supply our northern forces by sea. We were in operational touch with our Finnish allies. In the south we invested the Crimea and were racing for the Caucasus oil fields. And in the center, giant armored pincers closed on Moscow from north and south, actually penetrating the suburbs. Bock's indomitable infantry, marching up the road from Smolensk with amazing speed, was smashing forward in a frontal thrust toward the Bolshevik capital. Panic seized Moscow. October 16 is known to this day in Russian war literature as the date of the "Great Skedaddle," when the foreign diplomats, many government departments, and a large number of Soviet big shots, together with a huge throng of civilians, abandoned the city and scuttled east for the safety of the Urals.

Stalin stayed behind in Moscow, making desperate speeches, and ordering women and children out to dig trenches in the path of our oncoming armies. On the central Russian plain it was just beginning to snow. The *Rasputitza* had already begun in September—the autumn mud time. God knows it was hard to advance under such conditions, but we advanced. Never has an armed force shown greater energy and spirit under greater difficulties. A remarkable élan glowed alike in the highest general and the humblest foot soldier. The end of the long road, the incredible nine-year march of the German nation under the Führer, was in view across muddy, snowy wild plains, on the misty Russian horizon lit by a low cold red sun. Our advance patrols saw the towers of the Kremlin. World empire at last lay within the German grasp.

TRANSLATOR'S NOTE: *General von Roon is tolerant throughout of Hitler's Barbarossa performance, perhaps because he took part in the planning and was in Hitler's favor at the time. Other historians contend that the armies caught in the Kiev pocket were rabble. The hard nut of Russian resistance lay around Moscow, they say, and destruction of these forces in October would have ended the war. The land campaigns in the Soviet Union are not in my field of competence, though I spent time there. The full truth about that front may never be known.—V.H.*

*   *   *

50

A SLIM dark-haired girl walked out on the stage of the open-air theatre at the Pearl Harbor Naval Base, taking off sunglasses and blinking in the white glare of morning sun. The swish of her ice-cream pink dress, displaying silk-sheathed legs, brought glad whistles from the soldiers and sailors who filled every seat in the theatre and most of the folding chairs before the stage. Directly up front sat the governor of Hawaii, the admirals, the generals, and their ladies, and photographers were still blinking feeble blue flashes at them. It was just before eleven o'clock, somewhat early for staged fun, but this first *Happy Hour* broadcast was being aimed at the big night-time audiences along the Atlantic seaboard. Beyond the low stage, where the Navy band sat with brass instruments glinting in the sun, several moored battleships were visible towering in a gray double row.

At the microphone, the girl stood smiling till the good-humored commotion subsided. Then she held up a varnished board lettered in black: APPLAUSE. The audience responded with a heavy round of handclapping.

"Thank you, and hello. I'm Mr. Cleveland's assistant, Madeline Henry." A lone piercing wolf whistle sliced down from the topmost row, and laughter swept the stands. She wagged a finger. "And you watch yourself up there! I have two brothers sitting out here, a naval aviator and a submariner, and they're both big and strong." This brought more laughter and applause.

The audience was in a lively expectant mood. This debut of a major new radio program at the naval base had been stirring the somnolent territory for days. The island's good white families, a bored lotus-eating little clique, had been vying to entertain Hugh Cleveland, and people had flown in from other islands to Oahu just to attend the parties. The Navy had even postponed a fleet drill simulating an enemy surprise attack, since it conflicted with the broadcast time. Front-page headlines in Honolulu papers about the show quite overshadowed the news of the German encirclement of several Russian armies around Kiev.

In an awkward, halting manner that had a certain shy charm, Madeline described the rules of the new show. Only genuine fighting men could take part in the amateur contest. Every participant would receive a five-hundred-dollar defense bond. The performer winning the most applause would get an extra prize: the sponsor would fly in his girl or his parents to visit him for a week. "Mr. Cleveland just hopes there won't be too many winners with girls in Cape Town or Calcutta," she said, drawing a laugh. "Well, I guess that's about it. Now here's the man you're all waiting for—the star of the famous *Amateur Hour* and now of our new *Happy Hour*—my nice boss, Mr. Hugh Cleveland." Walking to a seat near the band she demurely sat down, tucking her skirt close to her legs.

Cheers greeted Cleveland as he walked to the microphone. "Okeybe-bedokey," he drawled. This phrase, delivered in a cowboy twang, had become a sort of trademark for him, and it brought applause. "Maybe I ought to just let Madeline Henry keep going. I've got the job, but she's sure got the lines." He wagged his eyebrows, and the audience laughed. "I'd better introduce her brothers, so you'll see just how big and strong they are. The naval aviator is Lieutenant Warren Henry of the *Enterprise*. Where are you, Warren?"

"Oh, Christ," Warren said. "No. No." He cringed down in his chair in a middle row.

"Stand up, you fool," Janice hissed.

Warren got grimly to his feet, a long lean figure in white, and dropped at once, sinking far down.

"Welcome, Warren. And now here's Byron Henry, of the *Devilfish*."

Byron half rose, then sat down with an unpleasant mutter.

"Hi, Byron! Their father's a battleship man, folks, so the family's pretty well got the sea covered—the surface, the air, and the deeps. That's the Henry family, and one reason our country remains strong and safe is that we have plenty of Henry families." The governor and the admirals joined heartily in the handclapping. Slumped low, Byron made a gagging sound in his throat.

The first *Happy Hour* delighted the audience, and promised great popular success. Cleveland had been all over the United States; he could make folksy knowledgeable jokes about out-of-the-way places. Working without a script, holding prepared gags in his memory, he created the illusion of an easy, bright, small-town wit. What emerged above all was the reticent homesickness of the soldiers and sailors who performed. Their little acts resembled church social entertainment; the band played patriotic marches; it was an hour of sentimental Americana. Madeline's awkwardness, as she introduced the acts and took some joshing, fitted the homey atmosphere.

Byron was not amused. He sat through the show in a slouch, his arms folded, looking vacantly at his shoe tips. Once Janice nudged her husband, narrowing her eyes and tilting her head at Byron. Warren pantomimed the bulge of a pregnant woman's stomach.

After the show the stage was so crowded with the governor, his entourage, and the high brass, all ringing Cleveland, that the Henrys couldn't mount the steps.

"Wouldn't you know," Byron said, "Branch Hoban's right in there." The handsome skipper of his submarine, standing between two admirals, was shaking Cleveland's hand, talking to him like an old friend.

"You having trouble with Branch Hoban?" Warren said. "He's an okay guy, Briny."

"He's having trouble with me."

"Hey, the big strong brothers! Come on up." Cleveland saw them and beckoned, laughing. "Gad, Madeline's one girl whose honor is safe, hey? Janice, the governor here has just invited me to lunch, and I've just turned him down. Told him you're expecting me."

Janice gasped, "No, please, you mustn't do that."

"You're dead right about that," Madeline laughed.

The governor smiled at her. "It's all right. Hugh's coming to Washington Place later. I didn't realize Senator

Lacouture's daughter was lurking in our midst. We must have you to dinner soon."

Janice took a bold chance. "Won't you join us for lunch, Governor? We're just having steaks and beer on the lawn, nothing much, but we'd love to have you."

"Say, steaks and beer on the lawn sounds pretty good. Let me find my lady."

Warren and Branch Hoban were exchanging cheerful insults about their nonexistent paunches, and about how old and married they both looked. Byron stood by with blank face and dull eyes. He broke in, "Excuse me, Captain. My sister-in-law's invited me to lunch. May I go?"

Warren said, "Hey! Don't tell me junior's in hack."

"Oh, Briny and I have had a leetle disagreement. Sure, Briny, you have your lunch with Janice and Warren. Report aboard at fifteen hundred."

"Aye aye, sir. Thank you, sir." At Byron's uncivil tone, Warren slightly shook his head.

Janice rode home in the governor's limousine; Madeline and Byron went in Warren's old station wagon. The double lei of pink and yellow flowers around the sister's neck perfumed the air in the car. She said, gaily, "Well, well, just the three of us. When did this last happen?"

"Listen, Briny," Warren said, "Branch Hoban's an old pal of mine. What's the beef? Maybe I can help."

"I drew a sketch of an air compressor for my officers' course book. He didn't like it. He wants me to do it over. I won't. I'm in hack until I do."

"That's ridiculous."

"I think so myself."

"I mean you're being ridiculous."

"Warren, on our way from San Francisco, an air compressor conked out because the oil pump froze. The chief was sick. I stripped down that compressor and got it going."

"Three cheers, but did you draw a good sketch?"

"It was a lousy sketch, but I fixed that compressor."

"That's beside the point."

"It's the whole point."

"No, the whole point is that Branch Hoban decides whether or not to recommend you for your dolphins."

"I don't care about getting dolphins."

"The hell you don't," Warren said.

"Look, Warren, I was shanghaied aboard the *Devilfish*. I had orders to new construction, the *Tuna,* but my exec and Hoban pulled a fast one at ComSubPac. Moreover, it wasn't my idea to go to submarine school in the first place. Dad shoved me in, mostly to keep me from marrying Natalie. That's why she went to Italy. That's why she's still stuck there. My life is snafued beyond all measure because I went to sub school. God knows when I'll see my wife again. And my baby, if I've got one. She's having it on the other side of the world. That's what's on my mind, not dolphins."

"You're in the Navy now. Do you want to get beached?"

"Why not? The hours are better and the mail is more reliable."

"Oh, horseshit. Pardon me, Mad."

"Shucks, this is like old times. Anyhow, you should hear Hugh talk. Yikes!" she squealed, as Warren bounced off the highway onto grass, avoiding a rusty old green Buick cutting in front of him.

Warren said calmly, "These Kanaka drivers give you gray hairs."

"There's another fellow who leaves me cold, that Cleveland," Byron said. "How did you get mixed up with him, Matty?"

"I'm not mixed up with him," Madeline rapped out. "I work for him."

Byron gave her an affectionate smile. "I know, sis."

"He does a good job," Warren said. "That show goes over."

Byron said, "What? Why, the whole thing is so phony! He doesn't make up those jokes, he's got them memorized."

"You're dead right about that," Madeline laughed.

"It's obvious. He just puts on a big smooth empty act. He reminds me of Branch Hoban."

"Branch is no phony," said Warren. "He has a remarkable record, Briny. And you'd better make up your mind that he's boss man on that submarine."

"Sure he's boss man, and sure he's got a great record, and sure I'm in hack, but hell will freeze over before he gets another sketch of that air compressor. When I found out that Natalie had gone back to Italy to have her baby, I put in a request for transfer to the Atlantic. Our subs operate in and out of the Med, and I might have a chance to see her, and maybe even to get her out. I told him all this. He lectured me about subordinating my personal life to the Navy! Well, I said I was putting the request in anyhow. He forwarded it—he had to forward it—'*not recommending approval.*' "

Warren said, his eyes on the road, "You've been aboard that boat three months. The usual tour is two years."

"The usual ensign doesn't have a pregnant wife stuck in Italy."

"Don't get me wrong, but that's not the Navy's fault."

"I'm not blaming the Navy. I'm telling you why I'm not on fire to please Branch Hoban."

Madeline struck into this curt exchange with a laugh. "Say, do you guys know that Dad is studying Russian again, of all things?"

"Russian!" Warren exclaimed. "What for?"

"He's going there. I don't know when or how." Madeline laughed. "Mom's fit to be tied. He's taking a crash course, ten hours a day. She never sees him. She sits around that big new house by herself, except when somebody shows up to play tennis with her or go to a movie."

"Dad had better step on it," Warren said, "if he wants to beat the Germans into Moscow."

Byron took Madeline's lei and put it around his neck. "Boy, these are strong frangipani. God knows when we three will ever be together again like this. I'm in a rotten mood, but I love you both. How's the booze situation at your house, Warren?"

"Ninety-seven percent. We just topped off."

"Great. I intend to burn you down to fifty percent."

"By all means."

Byron came on the latest airmail *Time* at Warren's house, and read it in a deck chair among the multiple roots of a banyan tree, while Warren, Janice, and their guests grew gay on hors d'oeuvres and rum drinks. At sea for two weeks, he had heard only fragmentary news.

When the party reached the stage of hula dancing to the guitar music of the grinning houseboy, Warren began broiling steaks in billows of fragrant smoke. Meantime Hugh

Cleveland and Madeline did a barefoot hula while the Navy people and islanders clapped and laughed, and a photographer from the society page snapped pictures. Byron sourly watched his sister's white feet writhe in the grass, and her pink-sheathed bottom gyrate; and he wondered who was mad—he or this playful group. According to *Time*, the Germans were rolling through Russia exactly as they had through Poland two years before. It was the same month, September. The cheery German claims, backed by combat photographs, were most convincing. The pictures showed villages afire, skies aswarm with Luftwaffe, roads through cornfields jammed with refugees, and unshaven Russian prisoners behind barbed wire in sullen hordes. The scenes brought vividly back to Byron's mind the days when he and Natalie had drawn together: the flight in the old automobile from Cracow to Warsaw, his wound, the child on the road crying over her mother's smashed face, the orange flares, the whistling bombs, Natalie in the malodorous jammed hospital, the song of grasshoppers in no-man's-land.

Carrying two plates of sliced steak and french fries, Warren came and sat down beside him on the grass. "Eat hearty, my lad."

Byron said, "Thanks. Pretty grim issue of *Time*."

"Hell, Briny, you knew the Germans would take the Russkis, didn't you? The Russian's a hardy soldier, but that Bolshevik government's just a mess of crackpot politicians. Stalin shot half his officers in '38, including all the professionals left from the Czarist days. You can't fight a war without career officers. That's where the Germans have us all licked. That General Staff of theirs has been going for a hundred years. The day they lost the last war, why, they just started collecting maps and dope for fighting this one. That's a savvy outfit. How about some wine? California Burgundy gets here in pretty fair shape."

"Sure."

Returning with a big purple bottle, Warren said, "Well, there's one good thing. If Hitler does take Moscow, the Japs will jump north to grab their end of Siberia. That'll give us a breather. Otherwise they're a cinch to come south soon. Every day they're getting lower on oil. We're sure as hell not ready for them. We need a year just to harden the Philippines to where we can hold."

Byron slapped the copy of *Time*. "Incidentally, did you read about your father-in-law's latest speech? He wants us to explore making a deal with the Germans."

"I know. Well, he's way off base on that. Hitler's not making any deals, not while he's winning so big. But eventually, Briny, the Krauts may be easier to come to terms with than the Japs. They're white people."

"True, except for starters we'd have to shoot our Jews."

Warren slowly turned his bronzed face at his brother. An embarrassed smile played on his thin lips. "Even the Germans aren't shooting their Jews, guy. I think their policy is disgusting, but—"

"You don't know what they're doing. I run into a stone wall when I try to tell people here what the Germans are like. Branch Hoban thinks this war is Saxon civilization against the rising tide of Asia, and the Russians count as Asia, and we and the British should wise up and make common cause with the Nazis in a hurry, because they're fighting our battle, and it's the white race's last chance. He gets all this out of books by a nut called Homer Lea. He reads those books to pieces. *The Valor of Ignorance* is the main one, and *The Day of the Saxon.*"

"I've read Homer Lea," said Warren, looking at his watch. "He's a screwball, but pretty interesting—well, our friend Vic's due for a bottle, but it's a cinch Jan's not going to abandon the governor."

"I'll feed the baby."

"Do you like babies, or something?"

"I like this one."

While Victor lay on his uncle's lap drinking milk, Byron drank California Burgundy. Each finished his bottle at about the same time. He tucked the baby away in his side-porch crib, and returned to the lawn. The breeze had died, and it was very hot. The scent from the lemon trees filled Byron with melancholy. He lay face down under the banyan tree and fell asleep. When he woke, Lieutenant Aster, drink in hand, was shaking him.

"Blazes," Byron said, sitting up, a stale taste of wine in his mouth, "I was supposed to report in at three, wasn't I? Are you here to take me back in irons?"

"Amnesty. You're out of hack," Aster grinned, "and you've got twenty-four hours' leave. This just came in on the harbor circuit from Rome, forwarded via Lisbon, Washington, and San Francisco."

He handed a dispatch to Byron, who read it sitting cross-legged on the grass.

ENSIGN BYRON HENRY, USS DEVILFISH X CAN YOU THINK OF A GOOD NAME FOR A SEVEN-POUND BOY X BOTH FINE BOTH LOVE YOU X NATALIE AND WHOSIS HENRY

Byron bowed his head and put a hand over his face. Like his father, he had a simple religious streak; he muttered a prayer of thanks for the miracle of a boy, born from the wild lovemaking in Lisbon that had briefly joined two bodies, now almost as far apart as they could be on the planet. After a moment he looked up with a slow smile, his eyes glistening.

"How about that, Lady?"

"Congratulations, Briny."

Byron got to his feet, looking around dazedly at the party. The radio was pouring out "Lovely Hula Hands," Janice was wiggling barefoot with the captain of the *Enterprise,* the governor was dancing with Madeline, evincing pop-eyed pleasure at the play of her hips, and Hugh Cleveland was singing an obscene parody that brought barks of male laughter and delighted shrieks from the women. "I guess I'll tell my brother and sister."

Aster strolled beside him, rattling the ice in his glass. "Quite a wingding here. Isn't that the governor? Your sister-in-law is sure nice. I hardly had my foot inside the door when she handed me a planter's punch."

"Janice is okay."

"Is that her name, Janice? Pretty name. She's about the best-looking white woman I've seen on this godforsaken island."

"Easy, Lady."

"Why, Briny, I admire her like a sunset, or the Washington Monument."

"Say, Madeline—"

Hurrying past him toward the house behind Cleveland

and the Hawaiian houseboy, Madeline flipped a hand at him. "Long-distance call from New York, honey. Our sponsor. Imagine!"

Byron told the news to Warren and Janice. Before he could stop her, Janice made a delighted announcement. The guests ringed him with alcoholic jokes, congratulations, and questions, exclaiming over the odd fact that his wife was away off in Italy. The society columnist of the Honolulu *Star,* a bony hawk-faced blonde named Petsy Peters, stood at Byron's elbow, scribbling notes.

He went into the house after Madeline. He wanted to be the first to tell her. The telephone lay in its rack on a table in the hall. He heard a chuckle, and glancing down the zigzagging halls to the side porch where the baby lay asleep, he saw Hugh Cleveland embracing Madeline, out of sight of the lawn. Cleveland was holding Byron's sister with both hands by the rump. Her pink skirt was pulled up in back, exposing her thighs and underwear. She was clinging to him with obscene intimacy. Byron walked out of the house into the sunlight.

"I guess I'll get back to the *Devilfish,*" he said to Warren.

"Why? I thought Branch gave you a twenty-four."

"I want to write Natalie and the folks. Maybe shoot off a cable or two."

"Briny, the governor's just invited the whole crowd over to Washington Place for cocktails with Cleveland."

"Cleveland's in the house there kissing Madeline. I mean kissing her, and she's going right along with it."

"Is she?" the aviator said with a crooked grin. "I guess their sponsor liked the broadcast."

Madeline came hurrying out of the house, her face alight, her hair disorderly, and ran to her brothers. Behind her Cleveland emerged, wiping his mouth with a handkerchief. "Hey, guess what, fellows?" Madeline chirruped. "He talked to me, too. He said I sounded fine! But that's nothing. We had a spot check rating of 23.5. That's only four points less than Fred Allen—and on our very first show!"

Byron took the dispatch from his breast pocket and showed it to his sister.

"Oh my! More good news! Say, Hugh, what do you know? Briny's wife had her baby."

"Hey! Congrats, papa!" He put out a hand that Byron ignored, but he took no offense. "Come on, Madeline, let's tell the governor what Chet Fenton said."

Byron, arms folded, glowered at their departing backs.

"Look, Briny," his brother said, "you're not going to make trouble, are you? You'll embarrass Janice."

"The grinning son of a bitch," muttered Byron.

"Come off it. She's over twenty-one."

"He's a married man. I'll talk to Madeline, if you won't. Depending on what she says, I may tell the bastard to keep his distance from her, if he doesn't want the shit beaten out of him."

Warren sized up his brother with amusement. "He's got the weight on you, and he looks in good shape."

"That's just fine," Byron said.

The radio began blaring the news signal. It was four o'clock, and the governor had turned up the volume of the little portable sitting on the outdoor bar.

"Berlin. German Supreme Headquarters announces the capture of Kiev and claims the greatest victory in the war, and perhaps in the history of the world. According to German sources, four entire Russian armies, numbering almost a million men, have been surrounded and cut to pieces, and with the fall of Kiev all organized resistance in the vast pocket has come to an end. Radio Berlin proclaimed at midnight that, quote, 'The Soviet Union no longer has a military capability, and the end of hostilities on the eastern front is in sight.' More news in a moment. Now a word about Pepsi-Cola."

The governor said, swishing his rum drink as merry girlish voices burst into a jingle, "Well, well. The Russkis would really seem to be on the run, hey?"

"Where is Kiev, Governor?" said Petsy Peters. "Is that where caviar comes from? I hope this doesn't mean no more cavvy. There's always the Persian, but that's so expensive."

"Kiev is in the north, I think," the governor said. "Frankly my Russian geography is not so hot."

The Pepsi-Cola commercial ended. The announcer came on with drama in his voice:

"We interrupt this newscast for an urgent announcement by the Joint Army-Navy Command of the Hawaiian Islands. SURPRISE ENEMY ATTACK ON HAWAII! This is a DRILL. A hostile fleet of battleships and aircraft carriers has been located approximately four hundred and fifty miles northwest of Oahu. This is a DRILL."

"Oh no!" Petsy Peters said. "Not again. Four o'clock on a Sunday afternoon! What a misery! Are they going to keep us off the streets again for hours and hours?"

The governor put his finger to his lips.

"All leaves and liberties are cancelled, and all military personnel will return to their units at once. This is a DRILL. We repeat, this a DRILL. Surprise enemy attack on Hawaii! All military personnel return to their units at once. Special permission is granted to the players of the baseball game between the Air Command and the Battleship Force to complete the ninth inning, and for spectators to remain at the game until then. Restrictions on civilian travel are not, repeat, not in force."

"Well, thank goodness for that, at least," said Petsy Peters.

"All ships in the area will report to force commanders readiness to sortie, but will not, repeat not, leave anchorages or moorings unless ordered. At 1830 target planes towing sleeves will simulate attack on Pearl Harbor. All ships and shore batteries will conduct tracking and aiming exercises but will not, repeat not, fire ammunition. Vessels in dry dock or alongside for repairs will proceed with maintenance work and are excused from this exercise. We repeat. Surprise attack on Hawaii. This is a DRILL. This announcement will be repeated."

The governor snapped off the radio. "I wasn't sure they'd still try to get it in today. It was originally scheduled for ten this morning, Hugh, but *The Happy Hour* conflicted."

"Yes, sir, that was a real courtesy. My sponsor is writing letters of appreciation to the Army and the Navy."

"That's a fine idea."

The general invitation for cocktails at Washington Place, the governor's mansion, was called off. The party rapidly broke up. Soon only Cleveland, Madeline, Janice, and the two submariners remained on the lawn amid the party debris, with the governor and his wife. Aster and Byron were in no hurry to leave because the *Devilfish* was in dry dock.

"Why not join us at Washington Place for a drink, Janice?" said the governor. "Hugh and Madeline are coming along."

"Oh, not without a man, thank you, Governor," Janice said.

"There's an old Navy rule against sticking one's neck out, Janice," Lieutenant Aster spoke up, with a fetching grin. "But I don't know when I'll get another chance to see the inside of that mansion. I volunteer."

Janice laughed. "Why, you're on, Lieutenant. Give me three minutes, Governor."

Byron separated Madeline from the others, saying he wanted to talk to her and would take her to Washington Place in Warren's car.

"It's wonderful news about your baby, Briny," Madeline remarked, as they drove off.

Byron said, looking straight ahead at the road, "I went into the house before, looking for you. I saw you and Cleveland."

After a pause filled with engine noise he glanced at her. Her brows were contracted over wide dark eyes in a scowl, and she looked lovely, but tough. She very much resembled their father. "Is *this* why you offered to drive me to the governor's place? To lecture me? Thanks, dear."

"That's a married man, Madeline. Mom and Dad would be damned upset at what I saw."

"Don't talk to me about upsetting Mom and Dad. I have yet to marry a Jew."

Those were the last words spoken in the car until it drew up at Washington Place. Madeline opened the door. "I'm sorry, Briny. That was nasty. But didn't you deserve it, accusing me of God knows what? I have nothing against Natalie. I like her."

Byron reached across her legs and slammed the door shut. The glare on his white face was frightening. "One minute. You tell Hugh Cleveland—you be sure to tell him, Madeline—that if I ever find out he's done anything to you, I'll come after him and I'll put him in a hospital."

The girl's eyes filled with tears. "Oh, how dare you?

You're cruel, and you have a dirty mind. Do you actually think I'd play around with a married man? Why, *The Happy Hour* was my idea. I was so excited when Mr. Fenton told us about the rating, I'd have kissed anybody who was handy. You're being horrible, Byron." She took a handkerchief from her purse and wiped her eyes.

"All right. I didn't want to make you cry."

"Don't you believe me?" Madeline spoke in soft and wistful tones, tearfully smiling. "My God, I thought we knew each other so well. We used to. I admit Hugh *would* sleep with me if he could. He'll sleep with anybody, and I find that disgusting. He's nothing but a whoremaster, and his wife's the most miserable woman alive. I appreciate your concern for my honor. You're very old-fashioned and sweet, like Dad. But don't you worry about Madeline. Forgive me for that mean crack, darling. I'm awfully happy about the baby." She kissed his cheek. He felt the tears on her skin. She got out of the car, twinkled her fingers at him, and ran into Washington Place.

When Byron got back to the naval base, target planes were coming in high over the harbor, towing long fluttery red sleeves, and on all the ships the gun crews were shouting, and slanting their weapons skyward; but there were no sounds of firing, and the excitement seemed forced and silly. The *Devilfish,* sitting high and dry on blocks, was deserted except for yard workmen and the watch. Byron took out of his desk drawer a writing pad, and the record of the *fado* song that he and Natalie had heard together in Lisbon. He put the record on the wardroom phonograph, and started to write:

My darling,
The news about the baby just came and—

The hissing of the bad needle gave way to the guitar chords that opened the song. He put his head down on his arms. He wanted to picture his wife and the new baby, a boy who perhaps looked like Victor. But when he closed his eyes, what he saw was his sister's uncovered thighs and garters.

Byron stopped the record and spent the next hour drawing a sketch of an air compressor. Working from memory, using different colored crayons and inks, he produced a picture accurate and clear enough to be printed in a manual. To this he clipped a letter he typed in the abandoned mildewy-smelling yeoman's cubicle, formally requesting transfer to Atlantic duty. He added a scrawled pencil note on a chit:

Captain—I deeply appreciate the amnesty and the leave. The only thing I want in the world now is to see my wife and baby, and try to get them out of Europe. I'm sure you will understand.

Next morning Branch Hoban congratulated Byron on his sketch, explained with regret that he couldn't spare an officer from the watch list, declared his conviction that Natalie and her baby were quite safe in Rome, and said he would forward the request, not recommending approval.

51

RHODA was startled by the bulk of the wax-sealed envelope from the State Department. Inside she found another fat envelope with pale blue Russian printing on the flap. The eleven-page typewritten letter it contained was much struck-over with pen and ink. Clipped to it, on a small sheet headed MEMORANDUM FROM ALISTAIR TUDSBURY, was a red-pencilled note in Pug's firm slanted hand:

> 3 Oct.
> Moscow (and still can't
> believe it!)

Hi—
    Don't get scared—guess I haven't written a letter this

long since you've known me—haven't had many experiences like this.

Kremlin banquet was another incredible business— that's for next letter, this one has to go off pronto—

Regards from Tudsburys. I've used his typewriter and stationery. Letter explains. He's fatter than ever, daughter's a wraith—

Love
Pug

Hotel National, Moscow
Oct. 2, 1941

Dearest Rhoda—

Three hours from now I'll be dining in the Kremlin. How about that? It's God's truth. And the rest of this trip has been every bit as fantastic.

Now that we've got ourselves two grandsons (and how about *that*, Granny?) I'm beginning to feel I should record some of these things I'm going through, while they're fresh in my mind. I'm no writer, but just the bare record of the facts should interest those infants one day. So don't think I'm becoming a garrulous old fud if I start sending you occasional batches of these pages. After you've read them, tuck them away for the babies.

I'm somewhat punchy; haven't had a real night's sleep since I left London. The trip to Archangel in a British destroyer could have been restful, but for night conferences, and GQ alarms all day long. That is a hot hot run; you're in Luftwaffe range almost all the way. The convoys on this route take quite a shellacking. Luckily we had fog covering us about half the time.

I'm making all these typing mistakes because Tudsbury's typewriter is cranky, and there's nobody in the Soviet Union who can fix a British typewriter—or who wants to, you're never sure which. I've been cadging embassy typewriters for my work, but they're swamped today getting out the final conference documents. The Tudsburys occupy the best quarters in the National. Naturally! Leave that to Talky. His suite faces out on Red Square, and I can see the Kremlin through a drizzle from where I sit. Lenin stayed in this suite, they say; now here I am. It's all maroon plush and gold chandeliers and alabaster statues, with a Persian rug about an acre big, and this room even has a rosewood grand piano, almost lost in a corner. (The piano's out of tune.) Me, I'm lodged in a back room on the top floor about five feet by ten, with bare yellow plaster walls.

Tudsbury's here right now, dictating to Pamela his broadcast for tonight. Leave it to Talky to show up where the action is! He got the War Information Office to requisition Pamela for him; his stories and broadcasts are considered ace propaganda, and he pleaded failing eyesight. She's on extended leave from the RAF and seems miserable about it. Her flier has been a German prisoner for over a year, and she hasn't had word of him in months.

Like all the correspondents here, Tudsbury's trying to make bricks without straw. He bent my ear for two hours last night about how tough it is. The Russians keep the reporters in Moscow, and every other day or so just call them in and give them some phony handout. Most of them think the war's going very badly, but they don't have much to go on besides Moscow rumors and Berlin shortwave broadcasts. It seems the Russians have been more or less admitting all the German claims, but two or three weeks late. The pessimists here—and there are plenty—think Moscow may fall in a week! I don't, nor does Tudsbury; but our embassy people are nervous as hell, some of them, about Harriman being captured by the Nazis. They'll be mighty relieved tomorrow when the mission flies out.

Well, as to the trip—the sea approach to Russia reminded me of Newfoundland. Up north the world is still mostly conifer forest and white water, Rhoda. It may be that man in his jackass fashion will devastate the temperate and tropical zones, and civilization will make a scrubby new start at the top of the globe.

The first surprise and shock comes at Archangel. It's a harbor town in the wilds all built of wood. Piers, warehouses, sawmills, factories, churches, crane towers—wood. Stacks of lumber, billions of board feet, wherever you look. God knows how many trees were cut down to build that town and pile that lumber, yet the forests around Archangel look untouched. There's an Alaskan look about Archangel, like pictures of the Klondike.

The first honest-to-God Russian I saw was the harbor pilot. He came abroad well down channel, and that was another surprise, because he was a woman. Sheepskin coat, pants, boots, and a healthy, pretty face. I was on the bridge and watched her bring us in, and she was quite a seaman, or sea-woman. She eased us alongside very handily. Then she shook hands with the skipper and left, and all that time she hadn't cracked a smile. Russians smile only when they're amused, never to be pleasant. It makes them seem distant and surly. I guess we strike them as grinning monkeys. This epitomizes the job of communicating with Russians. Language aside, we just have different natures and ways.

Mr. Hopkins told me about the forests of Russia, but I still was amazed. You remember when we drove west in midsummer, I think in '35, and didn't get out of cornfields for three days? The north Russian woods are like that. We flew to Moscow at treetop height. Those green branches rushed by below our wings for hours and hours and hours, and then all at once we climbed, and ahead of us was a tremendous sprawl from horizon to horizon of houses and factories. Moscow is flat and gray. From a distance it could be Boston or Philadel-phia. But as you get closer in and see the onion-top churches, and the dark red Kremlin by the river, with a cluster of churches inside, you realize you're coming to a peculiar place. The pilot flew a circle around Moscow before landing, maybe as a special courtesy, and we got a good look. Incidentally, the takeoffs and landings are expert, but by our standards hairy. The Russian pilot jumps off the ground and zooms, or he dives in and slams down.

Well, since we got to Moscow we've been in the meat grinder. It's been round-the-clock. Our orders literally are to work through the night. When we aren't conferring we've been eating and drinking. The standard fare for visitors seems to be a dozen different kinds of cold fish and caviar, then two soups, then fowl, then roasts, with wine going all the time. Each man also has his own carafe of vodka. It's a hell of a way to do business, but on the other hand the Russians may be wise. The alcohol loosens things up. The feeling of getting drunk is evidently the same for a Bolshevik or a capitalist, so there at least you strike some common ground.

I think this conference has been an historic breakthrough. When have Americans and Russians sat down before to talk about military problems, however cagily? It's all most peculiar and new. The Russians don't tell hard facts of their military production, or of the battlefield situation. Considering that the Germans three short months ago were sitting where we and the British sit now, I don't exactly blame them. The Russians have been a hard-luck people. You can't forget that when you talk to them. This is a point that our interpreter, Leslie Slote, keeps making.

I'm not revealing secrets when I tell you the British are yielding some Lend-Lease priorities and even undertaking to send the Russians tanks. It'll all be in the papers. They were stripped bare at Dunkirk, so this is decent and courageous. Of course, they can't use the tanks on the Germans now, and the Russians can. Still, Churchill can't be sure Hitler and Stalin won't make a deal again, so the Germans may suddenly turn and throw everything into a Channel crossing. I don't think it'll happen. The growing hate here for the Germans is something savage; you only have to see the gruesome newsreels of villages they've been driven out of to understand why. Children strung up, women raped to death, and all that. Still, Hitler and Stalin seem to have mercury for blood. Nothing they do is too predictable or human, and I give the British lots of points for agreeing to send the Russians tanks.

Some of us Americans feel peculiar at this meeting, damn peculiar. The British, in danger themselves, are willing to help the Russians, while our Congress yells about sending the Russians anything. We sit between men of two countries that are fighting the Germans for their lives, while we represent a land that won't let its President lift a finger to help, not without outcries from coast to coast.

Do you remember Slote? He's the second secretary here now. He looked me up in Berlin, you remember, with a lot of praise for Briny's conduct under fire in Poland. He's the man Natalie went to visit. He still seems to think she's the finest girl alive, and I don't know why he didn't marry her when he had the chance. Right now he's trying to romance Talky's daughter. Since she's one of the few unattached Western girls—I almost said white girls—in Moscow, Slote has competition.

(Incidentally, my remark about white girls is ridiculous. After two days in Moscow, trying to put my finger on what was so different here, I said to Slote there were two things: no advertisements, and no colored people. It made him laugh.

Still, it's so. Moscow has a real American feel in the informality and equality of the people, but you don't find such a sea of white faces in any big city in America. All in all I like these Russians and the way they go about their business with determination and calm, the way the Londoners did.)

Now I have a story for you, and for our grandsons to read one day—especially Byron's boy. It's a grim one, and I'm still not sure what to make of it, but I want to write it down. Yesterday between the last afternoon conference and the official dinner at the Metropole Hotel, I went to Slote's apartment for a while with Tudsbury and Pam. Talky engineered this little party. He wanted to pump me about the conference, but there wasn't much I could disclose.

Anyway, I was having a drink with them—if you get this tired you have to keep up an alcohol level in your bloodstream, it's a sort of emergency gasoline—when a knock came on the door, and in walked a fellow in worn-out boots, a cap, a heavy shabby coat, and it was a Jewish merchant from Warsaw, Jochanan Jastrow, Natalie's uncle! The one they call Berel. Briny and Natalie went to his son's wedding in south Poland, you recall, and that's how they got caught in the invasion. He's clean-shaven, and speaks Russian and German with ease, and he doesn't seem Jewish, though Slote remarked that in Warsaw he wore a beard and looked like a rabbi.

This fellow's escape from Warsaw with the remnants of his family is a saga. They landed in Minsk and got caught there when the Germans blitzed White Russia. He gave us only bare details of how he got himself and his family out of Minsk through the woods, but obviously this is quite a guy for maneuvering and surviving.

Here comes the incredible part. Jastrow says that late one night, about a month after the capture of Minsk, the Germans came into the Jewish ghetto they had set up, with a caravan of trucks. They cleaned out two of the most heavily populated streets, jamming everybody into these trucks: men, women, children, babies, old folks who couldn't walk. Several thousand people, at least. They drove them to a ravine in the forest a few miles out of town, and there they shot them, every single one, and buried them in a huge freshly dug ditch. Jastrow says the Germans had rounded up a gang of Russians earlier to dig the ditch, and then had trucked them out of the area. A few of them sneaked back through the woods to see what would happen, and that was how the story got out. One of them had a camera and took pictures. Jastrow produced three prints. This occurrence, whatever it was, took place at dawn. In one of them you see a line of gun flashes. In another you see this distant shadowy crowd of people. In the third, which is the brightest, you just see men in German helmets shovelling. Jastrow also gave Slote two documents in Russian, one handwritten and one typed, that purported to be eyewitness accounts.

Jastrow says he decided to get to Moscow and give some American diplomat the story of the massacre in Minsk. I don't know how he got Slote's address. He's a resourceful man, but naïve. He believed, and evidently still believes, that once President Roosevelt found out this story and told the American people, the United States would immediately declare war on Germany.

Jastrow turned over these materials to Slote, and said he'd risked his life to get that stuff to Moscow, and that a lot of women and children had been murdered, so would he please guard those pictures and documents with care. He and I talked a bit about the kids; his eyes filled up when I told him Byron and Natalie'd had a boy.

After he left, Slote offered the stuff to Tudsbury. He said, "There's your broadcast for you. You'll hit all the front pages in the United States." To our surprise, Tudsbury said he wouldn't touch the story. He worked in British propaganda after he was wounded in the last war, and helped concoct and plant atrocity yarns. He claims the British invented the business of the Germans making soap out of the bodies of soldiers. Maybe this Minsk massacre happened, but to him Jastrow looked like an NKVD plant. It was too coincidental that a distant Polish relative of mine by marriage—a freakish connection to begin with—should suddenly pop up of his own free will in Moscow with this yarn and these documents.

A heated argument ensued, and Tudsbury finally said that even if he knew the story were true, he wouldn't use it. This thing could backfire and keep America out of the war, he claimed, just as Hitler's Jewish policy worked for years to paralyze the British. *"Nobody wants to fight a war to save the Jews,"* he kept insisting while banging the table, and Hitler still has a lot of people convinced that anyone who fights Germany is really spilling blood just for the Jews. Talky says this is one of the great war propaganda ideas of all time, and that this story about the Minsk Jews would play into German hands.

Well, I've just set down the bald facts of this. I didn't mean to get so long-winded, but it's been haunting me. If there's even an element of truth in Jastrow's yarn, then the Germans really have run amuck, and among other things Natalie and her infant, unless they're out of Italy by now, are in grave hazard. Mussolini apes whatever Hitler does. But I assume they did get out; Slote tells me it was all set before her confinement.

Rhoda, when I think about Jastrow's story my head spins and it seems to me the world I grew up in is dissolving. Even if it's an exaggeration, just hearing such a story makes me think we're entering some new dark age. It's all too much for me, and the worst of it is I found it hard not to believe Jastrow. The man has a keen and dignified manner; not a man I mind having for a relative, strange as it felt to look on him as such.

It's five minutes to six. I have to wrap this up and get on to the banquet.

This war has sure played hell with our family, hasn't it? The days in Manila, with all three kids in school, and that house with a tennis court where I taught them all to play, seem a far-off dream. Those were the best days. And now here I am in Moscow. I hope you're keeping up that weekly doubles game with Fred Kirby and the Vances. You always feel better when you get exercise. Give my best to Blinker and Ann, also to Fred, and tell him I hope Foggy Bottom isn't getting him down.

I miss you, busy as I am, but you sure wouldn't care for Soviet Russia, darling, in war or peace. Pamela Tudsbury says there isn't a hairdresser in Moscow she'd go to. She cleans her own suits and dresses with gasoline.

You know, I've now met Hitler, Churchill, Roosevelt, and tonight I may shake hands with Stalin. Considering that I'm nobody much, that's something! My career's taken a decidedly freakish turn. For my grandsons' information (you already know this) I'd have preferred an entry in my record showing I'd been at sea these past two years. But there's no changing that, and in a way I guess it's been an education. Only at this point I've had my bellyful, and so help me God, I would gladly

trade dinner in the Kremlin for one honest-to-God whiff of
Navy stack gas.

Till the next time, with lots of love—

Pug

* * *

Victor Henry had arrived with the Harriman-Beaver-
brook mission just as the Germans were starting their
autumn smash toward Moscow. The panzer armies were
breaking through less than a hundred miles away, but the
Russians wined and dined their visitors, whirled them
about the city in black limousines, took them to the ballet,
and carried on long committee meetings, with no hint that
anything was going wrong; though they did appear a bit
brisk in laying on a farewell banquet less than a week after
the guests had got there.

The Americans and the British understood that the Germans had been stopped east of Smolensk more than a
month earlier in their central push, and had been pinned
down there on the defensive ever since. In Moscow this
halting of the Nazi hordes in the center was still talked of
as a great feat of Soviet arms, a new "Miracle of the
Marne." Just as the French had stopped the Huns thirty
miles from Paris in 1914 and snatched away their chance
of quickly winning the war, so the Red Army had halted
Hitler's marauders, the assertion went, in their drive to
seize Moscow before the winter set in. The Russians had
even taken foreign correspondents to this central front,
showing them recaptured villages, smashed Nazi tanks,
and dead and captured Germans. Now the Germans
claimed the march toward Moscow was rolling again, and
the Russians were denying it. The fog of war effectively
hid what was really happening.

Contrary to a notion popular at the time—a notion
which has never quite died—the Wehrmacht was not a
giant solid phalanx of tanks and armored cars, spitting
flame and death as it clanked through whole nations. Hitler
had a horse-drawn army. It was larger than Napoleon's,
but mainly it advanced into Russia as the Grande Armée
had, by animal power and the march of men's feet. He
also had some armored divisions, spaced on the flanks of

the three big groups invading the Soviet Union. The blitzkrieg worked so: the armored forces, the panzers, chugged
ahead on either side of each attack front, slicing into the
enemy lines, counting on surprise, terror, and punch to
soften or panic the foe. The infantry came along between
these two swathes as fast as it could, killing or capturing
the forces which the panzer divisions had broken into or
thinly encircled.

These armored divisions were a big success, and no
doubt Hitler would have been glad to employ more of
them. But he had started his war—as his generals had
feebly grumbled—much too soon, only six years after he
took power. He had not come near arming Germany to the
full, though he had made frightening noises exactly as if
he had, and Europe had believed him. He was therefore
very low on panzer divisions, considering the vastness of
the front.

In August, when his three-pronged attack had jabbed
far into the Soviet Union, Hitler diverted the thin armored
layers of the central formation north and south, to help
wrap up the war on the flanks by taking Kiev and investing
Leningrad. This done, the panzers were to come back on
station and start driving again with the Center Group for
the knockout blow on the capital. It was a move that
military writers still argue about; but in any case, with the
central armor thus peeled away, the infantry and horse-
drawn artillery in the center perforce had to halt and dig
in, to await the return of the panzers, the steel cutting
edges, from their side excursions. This was the new "Miracle of the Marne." The Russians were at first surprised,
then immensely heartened, at this sudden stop of the huge
force advancing on their capital; and disorganized though
they were, they went over to counterattacks and won minor
gains. The "Miracle" ceased at the end of September, when
the panzer armies, back in their positions, and properly
overhauled and gassed up, went slashing toward Moscow
again, in two wide curving paths. That was when Harriman
and Beaverbrook arrived, with the obscure Captain Henry
in their train.

52

THE knot of Leslie Slote's tie came lopsided twice in his shaky hurrying hands. He flung the tie in a corner, pulled another from his dresser, and managed a passable knot. He put on his jacket and sat in a heavy brown leather armchair to calm himself with a cigarette, flinging long legs on the ottoman. A German correspondent had abandoned this apartment on June 15, making a hasty deal with him. For Moscow, these were splendid digs: three rooms, a kitchen, a bathroom, solid German furniture. Pamela Tudsbury liked the place and had cooked many a dinner here for Slote and some of their friends.

The English-speaking embassy people and correspondents—an isolated, gossipy little band—assumed that the British girl and the American Foreign Service officer were having an affair. So did Slote's thickset Russian maid, Valya, who beamed on them and tiptoed about when Pamela was visiting. Slote yearned for such an affair. He had not gotten over the marriage of Natalie Jastrow, and nothing closed such an ego wound like a new romance. But Pam Tudsbury, whom he remembered from Paris as the warm-blooded girlfriend of Philip Rule—wild in her ways, candidly sensual, freshest and gayest when the dawn came up—brushed off his passes. She was in a gloomy state; she was being true, she said, to her fiancé, a missing RAF pilot. Pam's skin was fair as in the Paris days, her heart-shaped face with its thin bow of a mouth still a flower of English prettiness. She wore tailored wool suits, flat shoes, and glasses; but inside that secretarial uniform glowed the girl who had whipped off her stockings and splashed barefoot in the fountain on a midsummer night with Phil Rule, holding her red silk dress at mid-thigh. She still owned that dress, and sometimes wore it.

Slote had patiently been taking Pamela's company on her terms, biding his chances to improve them. But the arrival of Captain Victor Henry deprived him of Pamela on any terms. When he glimpsed Pam with Henry, Slote knew at once he was looking at a woman in love. So much for fidelity to the missing airman! As for Captain Henry, this stumpy, sallow, tired-looking fellow of fifty or so seemed to the Foreign Service officer almost a caricature of the anonymous military man: short on small talk, quick on professional matters, poker-faced, firm, and colorless. One couldn't even tell whether Henry liked Pamela Tudsbury. He made no visible return of her unguarded deep glances. Slote failed to fathom the attraction this middle-aged dullard held for the young Englishwoman, and he had never understood Natalie Jastrow's infatuation with the man's son, either.

Fate had served him a strange, indigestible dish, Leslie Slote thought—to be beaten out first by the son and then by the father; neither of them, in his own judgment, a worthy rival. Byron Henry at least was a handsome young devil, and had much changed Slote's ideas of the susceptibility of clever women to surface charms. But there was nothing charming on the surface of Byron's father. The best one could say for the man was that he still had his hair, thick and dark, and that his waist showed an effort to stay trim. But his age was evident in the weary wrinkled eyes, the gnarled hands, the seamed mouth, the deliberate movements.

Slote was about to meet Admiral Standley and Captain Henry at the Hotel National; he was going to interpret for them at the Kremlin banquet. This privilege did not, in prospect, make him happy. He was in a state of panicky foreboding.

During the first weeks of the invasion, Slote's physical cowardice, which he lived with as other people live with hay fever or high blood pressure, had not acted up. Slote was an admirer of Soviet Russia. He believed the news on the loudspeakers and argued that the German victory claims were propaganda. Six hundred miles, more than a hundred million Russians, and above all the great Red

Army lay between him and the Germans. It was too far even for the Luftwaffe to fly. The barometer of his timidity read the Moscow climate as sunny and fair. The Muscovites—a peaceable, good-natured, rather shabby swarm of workingmen in caps, workingwomen in shawls, boys and girls in scarlet Young Communist neckerchiefs, all with flat calm Russian faces so much alike that they appeared to be one family of several million first cousins—placidly piled sandbags, taped windows, held anti-incendiary drills for air raids that didn't come, and otherwise went about their business as before under blue skies, in warm sparkling weather. Silver barrage balloons bobbed at their winches in open squares. Snouts of anti-aircraft guns appeared on the roofs of hotels and museums. Strapping red-cheeked young men wearing new uniforms and fine leather boots streamed to the railroad stations. Tanks, multi-wheeled trucks, and motor-driven big guns thumped and clanked along the boulevards day and night, all heading west. The theatres and cinemas stayed open. The ice cream of the street vendors was as rich as ever. The summer circus was playing to great crowds, for this year there was a dancing elephant as well as the bears. If one could trust one's eyes and ears in Moscow, the Soviet Union had met the onslaught at its distant borders and dealt the Nazis their first big defeat, exactly as Radio Moscow claimed.

Then Minsk fell, then Smolensk, then Kiev—each Russian acknowledgment lagging a week or more behind the German crows of victory. Air raids started; the Luftwaffe had come into range. Nobody else in the embassy became as alarmed as Slote, because nobody else had counted much on the Russians. Moreover, nobody else had undergone the ordeal of Warsaw. Since May, the ambassador had been storing food, fuel, and supplies in a large house thirty miles from the city, to sit out the coming siege. A few of the Americans, rubbed raw by the Russians' difficult ways, even looked forward to seeing the Wehrmacht march into Red Square. At least, after a few drinks, they said so.

Slote had stopped arguing, having been proved so wrong about the Red Army. But he thought the complacency and indifference of the other Americans was almost insane. The air raids were getting worse as the Germans drew nearer.

Moscow's amazingly thick anti-aircraft barrage provided a comforting canopy of green, red, and yellow fireworks, mounting past searchlight beams in the black night. Yet bombs did fall. The terror of the siege guns was still to come. Even if he survived the siege, thought Slote, how safe would he be? By then Roosevelt's blatant help to Nazism's enemies might have provoked a triumphant Hitler to declare war. If Moscow fell, the Americans might all be taken to a ravine and shot like the Jews in Minsk. Then Adolf Hitler could apologize for the mistake, or deny that it had happened, or say the Russians had done it.

Berel Jastrow's story filled Slote with horror. He had read the books about Germany on the list he had given Byron Henry, and many more. The Germans, in their naïve passion for obedience, their streaks of coarseness and brutality, their energy, their intelligence, their obsessive self-centeredness, their eternal grievance that the world was against them and doing them injustice, their romantic yearnings for new extremes of experience—this last trait bubbling up ad nauseam in the romantic philosophers, and nailed down by Goethe once and for all in the Faust image—these eighty million strangers in Europe seemed to Leslie Slote capable, once they abandoned their strict and docile conventions, of slaughtering any number of innocent people upon orders, cheerfully and with no sense of guilt, not in the least aware that they were "committing atrocities." There was no striking bottom in the German spirit. That was the strange and fearful thing about them. They were like remote cold children, as docile and as cruel. Hitler's dread secret was that he understood them. Other nations at war could be counted on to observe such rules as exchanging besieged or captured diplomats. In Slote's frightened view, such diplomats could perhaps count on Hitler's Germans not to eat them—little more.

The red light of the setting sun was fading outside his window. It was time to go and accompany Victor Henry to a night of sitting in the bull's eye of the Moscow air target.

Not surprisingly, he found Captain Henry in Tudsbury's suite. Despite the chill in the room, the naval officer lolled on a couch in his shirt-sleeves, smoking a cigar. Pamela was sewing at a crumpled blue coat with gold stripes, in the light of a red-shaded lamp atop an alabaster Venus.

"Hi there," Henry said.

Pamela said, "Loose brass buttons. We don't want them bouncing all over the Kremlin parquet floor. Have some Scotch and tap water, Leslie. Beaverbrook gave the governor a bottle."

Glancing at his wristwatch, Slote sat himself on the edge of a chair. "No thanks. I hope you haven't had much, Captain. When you start on a Russian dinner, the last thing you want in your system is alcohol."

Henry grunted. "You're telling me! I haven't touched it."

Pamela sewed, Victor Henry smoked, and the Foreign Service man felt he was very superfluous in the room. He looked at his watch once, twice, and coughed. "I said I'd meet the admiral in the lobby at six. It's ten of. Suppose I look for him now. You'll join us, Captain?"

"Sure," Henry said.

"You seem so calm, Leslie," Pam said. "If I were actually going into the Kremlin, I'd be vibrating."

"Captain Henry seems pretty calm," Slote said.

"Oh, him," Pamela said. "He's a robot. A mechanical man. Chug-chug! Choomp-choomp! Clank!"

"I need new batteries," Henry said. "And possibly a valve job."

The intimate teasing made Slote feel even more superfluous. "Well, in ten minutes then," he said.

Pamela said, "Just two more buttons. Damn! That's twice I've pricked my finger. I never could sew."

Clumsy black limousines clustered before the hotel, a rare sight. Since the start of the war, the sparse auto traffic on Moscow's wide boulevards and squares had been dwindling to nothing. Muscovites, taking evening strolls in their usual large numbers, glanced inquisitively at the machines, but did not stop to gawk. Chauffeurs and escorts in black caps and black leather jackets stood by the cars. The Americans called them "the YMCA boys"; they were secret police, and the people seemed loath to linger near them. But as the cars began to fill with well-dressed foreigners thronging out of the National's narrow entrance, the pedestrians did form lines of quiet onlookers, peering with round friendly eyes at the clothes, faces, and shoes.

"How did you make out on those harbor charts?" said Admiral Standley to Henry, settling into the back seat and adjusting his hearing aid. He had once been Chief of Naval Operations, and the President had called him out of retirement for this mission. Slote could never make this shrivelled, leathery, bespectacled man, whose uniform displayed four rows of campaign ribbons, stop talking near NKVD agents, who undoubtedly knew English, though they never spoke it.

"I got nowhere," Henry said. "As for operating codes and signals, forget it. Their fellow told me with a straight face that they had no such things, that they just communicated by Morse or flashing light, in plain language."

"What tripe! Did you give them our stuff?"

"Well, I showed them our General Signal Book, and a few strip ciphers. I almost got into a wrestling match with this rear admiral, the small fat one. He started to put them away in his briefcase, but I retrieved them. I said no tickee no shirtee."

"No! Did you really?" said the admiral. "Why, you may hang for that, Pug. We're supposed to give, give, give, here. Why, you should just have handed over all our Navy's code channels, and shaken hands, and toasted eternal brotherhood in vodka. I'm ashamed of you, Captain Henry, and goddamn glad you're along."

"We're getting a quid pro quo for all we're giving the Soviets," Slote said. "They're killing Germans for us."

"They're killing Germans so as not to get killed by Germans," said the admiral. "They're not doing it for us."

Pug said to Slote, "Look here, Leslie, if we're going to plan for convoys to Murmansk and Archangel, and for possible joint operations, we've *got* to swap hydrographic dope and operational codes. Hell, we're not asking for secret combat channels. This is the stuff we need for seamanship and piloting."

"Russians are obsessed with secrecy," Slote said. "Be persistent and patient."

The cars, having made a wide circuit of streets around the Kremlin, were stopping at a tall gateway under a red stone tower topped by a star.

"That won't help," said the admiral. "I think these birds just haven't gotten the green light from Mr. Big, and until they do, no dice."

At this stream of slang, the NKVD escort turned and squinted narrow Tartar eyes at the admiral, before saying to Slote in Russian, with a polite smile, that they would stay in the car on passing through the gate. The limousines, checked one at a time by big, fierce-looking, gun-bearing sentries in faultless uniform, drove into the citadel, stopped at an inner gate for another check, then passed among bizarre old churches to a long building with a majestic stone façade.

The visitors, with Russian officers mingling among them, left the cars, mounted the steps, and stood talking outside the great closed doors, their breaths smoking in the chilly air. A light blue sky, puffy with pink sunset clouds, arched from wall to wall of the fortress. Suddenly the palace doors opened, and the foreigners were blinking at dazzling light from globed chandeliers in a very long high-ceilinged hall, ending in a cascade of vermilion carpet on a far-off white marble staircase. As they walked in, warm air enveloped them, a novelty in Moscow, where all building heat had been forbidden until mid-October. Inside, a musty smell of old stone walls and old furnishings was mixed with an almost flowery odor. White-gloved attendants in military livery helped the visitors off with their coats and hats. Along the mirrored walls, on dark tables, dozens of combs and brushes were neatly laid out.

"Thoughtful touch, this," Victor Henry said to Slote, as they stood side by side, brushing their hair. "Say, what did the ambassador think of that stuff from Minsk? Did you get it to him?"

Slote nodded at Pug's mirror image. "I wanted it to go to Secretary Hull, high priority. The ambassador quashed that. The stuff's to be forwarded through channels to our east European desk."

Pug wrinkled his nose. "That'll be the end of it. Your department always drags its feet on the Jews. Better show the papers to some American newspaperman here."

"The boss directly ordered me not to, in case it's evaluated as fake atrocity propaganda."

Young army officers, handsome clear-eyed giants in

brown uniforms with scarlet collar tabs, appeared through side doors, and began shepherding the visitors toward the staircase. Walking beside Slote, Pug said, "Suppose you have Fred Fearing up for a drink, and he accidentally on purpose reads the material? A reporter will steal a scoop from his old blind grandmother, you know."

"Are you suggesting that I disobey orders?"

"I don't think that story should get buried."

The admiral came and hooked elbows with them on the staircase, cackling, "Say, how's this for socialist austerity? Can't you just see ghosts of Czarist nobles and their beautiful ladies on this red carpet? This is right out of the movies."

The company passed through a bleak modernist room full of desks with microphones, and the army officers explained that here the Supreme Soviet met. They straggled through one vast room after another, apparently unaltered since Czarist days, richly furnished in French or Italian or English styles, crammed with paintings and statuary, with no visible purpose except to overawe. The effect mounted of wasteful magnificence displayed helter-skelter with a heavy hand. In one room grander and richer than the rest, pillared in marble, with a vaulted gilt ceiling and red damask-covered walls, the company of about eighty men halted. The chamber seemed not at all crowded by them.

Mirrored doors opened and a party of Russian civilians came in, wearing unpressed flopping trousers and ill-fitting double-breasted jackets. Slote at once recognized several faces that lined Lenin's tomb at the May Day parades: Molotov, Kaganovitch, Suslov, Mikoyan.

"Look at those guys come on, will you?" Victor Henry said. "They make you feel like the revolution happened last week."

Slote gave him a quick glance. The apparition of these inelegant Communist bosses in the gorgeous Grand Palace had jarred him too, and the Navy man had crystallized this feeling in one sentence. Henry was sizing up the approaching Communists through half-closed eyes, as though he were peering at a horizon.

"That's the Politburo, Captain," Slote said. "Very big cheeses."

Henry nodded. "They don't look like big cheeses, do they?"

"Well, it's those terrible clothes," Slote said.

Introductions began. Liveried waiters passed with trays of vodka in little tulip-shaped glasses and plates of pastry sticks. Slote ate a stick, for research purposes; it was far too sugary. A little man walked alone into the room, smoking a cigarette. No ceremony was made of it, nobody stopped conversing, but the grand state chamber and all the people in it polarized toward this man, for he was Stalin. It was a matter of side-glances, of shoulders and faces turned, of small moves in the crowd, of a rounding of eyes. So Leslie Slote saw for the first time in the flesh the man whose busts, photographs, statues, and paintings filled the Soviet Union like images of Christ in a Catholic land.

The Communist dictator, a surprisingly short man with a small paunch, moved through the room shaking hands and chatting. The subtle focus travelled with him like a spotlight. He came to the two American naval officers, put out his hand to the admiral, and said, "Stalyin." He looked like his pictures, except that his pallid skin was very coarse and pitted, as though he had once had bad acne. His slanted eyes, thick back-swept grizzled hair, and arching moustache and eyebrows, gave him a genial leonine look. Unlike the other Communists, he wore a uniform of simple beige cloth superbly tailored, with sharply creased trousers tucked into soft gleaming brown boots.

Leslie Slote made introductions. Captain Henry said in slow Russian, with a bad American accent, "Sir, I will tell this story to my grandchildren."

Raising a thick eyebrow, Stalin said in a low pleasant voice, "Yes? Do you have any?"

"Two boys."

"And your children? Do you have sons?" The dictator appeared diverted by Victor Henry's slow, carefully drilled, mechanical speech.

"I have two, Mr. Chairman. My older son flies for the Navy. My younger one is in a submarine."

Stalin looked at Victor Henry through cigarette smoke with vague interest.

Pug said, "Forgive my poor Russian. I had Russian playmates once. But that was long ago."

"Where did you have Russian playmates?"

"I was born near the Russian River, in California. Some of those early families still remain there."

Stalin smiled a real smile, showing tobacco-stained teeth. "Ah, yes, yes. Fort Ross. Not many people know that we Russians settled California before you did. Maybe it's time we claimed California back."

"They say your policy is to fight on one front at a time, Comrade Chairman."

With a smiling grunt, Stalin said, *"Ha! Ochen horosho!"* ("Very good"), struck Henry lightly on his shoulder, and walked on.

"Now what the hell was all that about California, Pug?" The admiral had been listening with a baffled look. "By thunder, you've really picked up that lingo."

Victor Henry recounted the chat, and the admiral laughed out loud. "By God, write down every word of that, Pug. You hear? I intend to put it in my report. One fighting front at a time! Well done."

"I must compliment you," Slote said. "You spoke with presence of mind, and he enjoyed it."

"He puts you at your ease," Pug said. "I knew I was murdering the grammar, but he never let on. Did you see his hands? Beautifully manicured."

"Say, I didn't notice that," said the admiral. "How about that, Slote? Lots of us decadent capitalists don't bother with manicures, but the Head Red does. Makes you stop and think, hey?"

Slote hadn't noticed the manicure, and was vexed at having missed the detail.

Soon the large company was moving again, this time into a stupendous banquet hall of white marble, red tapestries, and shiny parquet, where silver, gold, and glass glittered on the white cloths of many tables set amid green stone columns. One table on a dais stretched the length of the room, perhaps a hundred feet; the others stood perpendicular to the dais. Light flooded from the myriad frosted globes of two gigantic baroque gilt chandeliers, hanging from a high ceiling of vermilion and gold. More light blazed on the walls, in ornate gold sconces.

"Wow!" Pug said.

Leslie Slote stared around at the walls and ceiling. "It's the Catherine the Great Room. I've seen it in paintings. There's her crest, in those big medallions. She got some French or Italian architect in to gut this part of the palace, I believe, and do it over. It was her throne room."

"Well, if this is their style of living, by God," said the admiral, "they'll make a Communist of me yet."

"I wouldn't be too surprised," Slote replied, "if this is the first time the room has been used since the revolution."

The menu, printed in Russian and English on thick creamy paper with a hammer and sickle gold crest, listed fish, soups, game, fowls, and roast meats, down the entire long page. Attendants began to bring the courses, while more attendants stood around with bottles of wine and vodka, springing to pour. The splendid great room, the massive array of brilliantly set tables, the multicolored uniforms of generals and admirals of three countries, the line of powerful men on the dais, with Stalin at a sharp focus even here, chatting left and right with Beaverbrook and Harriman, the lavish service, the river of wine, the gobs of caviar, the parade of rich fat foods on Czarist gold plate—all this overwhelmed Victor Henry with a reassuring sense of Russian resources, Russian strength, Russian largesse, Russian hospitality, and Russian self-confidence.

Slote had a different reaction. No doubt the Communist leaders were enjoying themselves and being hospitable, but in this vulgar outpouring, this choke of luxury, he sensed a note of crude Slav irony. Silent, unspoken, yet almost thunderous, was this message—*"Very well, you of the West, these are the things that seem to make you happy, opulence and pleasure sweated out of others. See how well we do it too, if we choose! See how our old Russian regime did it, before we kicked them out! Can you match them? Tomorrow we'll go back to the simple life we prefer, but since you come from the decadent West, fine, let's all get drunk together and gorge and swill. We Russians know how to live as well as you, and for the fun of it, we'll even go you one better tonight. Let's see who slides under the table first. VASHE ZDOROVYE!"*

Vashe zdorovye! Toasts kept flaring up. Anybody apparently had the license to stand, hammer at a glass with his knife for attention, and bawl a toast. Men would leave their seats and cross the room to clink glasses when a toast complimented or pleased them. Stalin kept trotting here and there, glass in hand. It was all marvellously interesting to Slote, but it was rushing by too fast, and he was missing too much, interpreting between the American admiral and the short fat Russian admiral who had tried to keep the Navy codes. Sweat shining on his bright red face, the old Russian kept groaning, as he tossed down vodka and wine, that he was a very sick man, had not much time to live, and might as well enjoy himself. The American admiral said at one point, "What the hell, Slote, tell him he looks a lot better than I do, he looks fine."

"Ah, but you see, tell him I am like the capitalistic system," groaned the little admiral. "Healthy on the outside, rotten inside."

Slote enjoyed translating this remark; but most of the admirals' talk was vague maundering about their families. He envied Victor Henry, quietly observing the scene and using all the tricks not to drink much. Slote's ears began to hurt from the shouting of the two admirals over the rising noise of the feast. He was trying to eat a succulent roast quail in sour cream, served with a fine cold Crimean white wine, but the sharpening exchange kept him too busy. Why, the Russian insisted, why wouldn't the mighty American Navy at least convoy Lend-Lease goods to England? Were they afraid of a few tin-plated U-boats? It was idiotic—his slamming fist made glasses jump—*idiotic* to manufacture war goods and ship them out just as target practice for Hitler's torpedoes.

"Tell him we'll be convoying any day," snapped the American, "but unless he loosens up with some harbor data and operation signals, hell will freeze over before we convoy to Murmansk."

The old Russian glared at the old American as Slote translated. Both officers gulped glasses of vodka and stopped talking. This respite allowed Slote to look around at the banquet, which was becoming very convivial indeed, with several heads down on tables, and one bald Russian general staggering out, held up at the elbows by two attendants. The cessation of the shouts in his ears enabled

him to hear another noise: muffled harsh thumps in an irregular pattern. *Bu bromp! Bromp, bromp!* His stomach
suddenly felt cold. His eyes met Victor Henry's.

"Gunfire," he started to say, but the word stuck in his
throat. He coughed. "Gunfire. Air raid."

Henry nodded. "I'll bet they have the heaviest A.A. in
the world right on these grounds. Listen to that, through
all those thick walls! Unreconstructed hell's breaking
loose."

"The Germans would do very well," Slote said with a
little laugh, "if they scored a bomb hit here tonight."

The thump of the guns came louder and thicker, and
some banqueters were glancing uneasily at the walls. The
old Russian admiral, slumped in his seat, scarlet face
resting on his chest, was shooting ill-natured glances at the
Americans. Now he pushed himself to his feet, clinked
furiously at a water glass until he got some attention,
then held up a brimming glass of yellow vodka. "If you
please! I am sitting with representatives of the United
States Navy, the most powerful Navy in the world. These
brave men must be very unhappy that while all humanity
is in mortal danger their ships ride at anchor gathering
barnacles"—he turned to the American admiral with a
sarcastic grin—"so I drink to the day when this strong
Navy will get in the scrap and help destroy the Hitlerite
rats, the common enemy of mankind."

The toast left a silence. Slote translated it in a low rapid
mutter. Military and civilian Russians at nearby tables
shook their heads and exchanged troubled looks. The old
man dropped heavily in his seat, glaring around with self-
satisfaction.

The American admiral's voice shook as he said to Slote,
"If I reply you'll have an international incident on your
hands."

Victor Henry said at once, "Admiral, shall I give it a
try, with my lousy Russian?"

"It's all yours, Pug."

Leslie Slote reached to touch Henry's arm. "See here,
the other Russians didn't like what he said, either—just
a drop of vodka too much—"

"Okay." Victor Henry rose, glass in hand. The subdued
talk in the room faded down. The whumping of the anti-

aircraft guns sounded louder, and glasses vibrated and tinkled with the concussions. The men at the head table, including Stalin, fastened intent eyes on the American. Henry brought out his response in slow, stumbling, painful phrases, in bad grammar:

"My chief tells me to respond for the United States Navy. It is true we are not fighting. I drink first to the wise peace policy of Marshal Stalin, who did not lead your country into the great war before you were attacked, and so gained time to prepare." Slote was startled by the barbed aptness of the retort. *"The wise peace policy of Comrade Stalin"* was the Communist cliché for Stalin's deal with Hitler. Henry went on, with groping pauses for words that left tense silence in the vast hall: "That is the policy of our President. If we are attacked we will fight. I hope as well as your people are fighting. Now as for"—he stopped to ask Slote for the Russian word—*"barnacles.* Any barnacles that get on our ships nowadays are barnacles that can swim very fast. Our ships are on the move. We don't announce everything we do. Secrecy is another wise policy of both our countries. But let's not keep so many secrets from each other that we can't work together."

"Now, our Navy needs some"—again Henry asked Slote for a word—"some harbor data, weather codes, and so forth from you. We need them before we leave. Since this is a farewell banquet, I also drink to some fast action. Finally, I was a naval attaché in Berlin. I have now travelled from Hitler's chancellery to the inside of the Kremlin. That is something Hitler will never do, and above all I drink to that."

There was loud applause, a general raising of glasses, and shouts of "Your health! Fast action!" Slote reached up to stop Pug from drinking, and pointed. Josef Stalin, glass in hand, was leaving his seat.

"Holy smoke, what's the etiquette on this?" Henry said.

"I don't know," Slote said. "Don't drink yet. By God, Captain Henry, that was rising to an occasion."

Pug strode toward Stalin, with Slote hurrying behind him. The dictator said with an amiable grin, as they met near the dais and clinked glasses amid smiles and handclapping, "I thank you for that fine toast, and in response, you can keep California."

"Thank you, Mr. Chairman," Pug said, and they both drank. "That's a good start, and can you do anything else for us?"

"Certainly. Fast action," said Stalin, linking his arm in Pug's. They were so close that Pug caught an odor of fish on Stalin's breath. "American style. We Russians can sometimes do it too." He walked toward the two admirals, and the old red-faced Russian stumbled to his feet and stood very erect. Stalin spoke to him in low rapid sentences. Slote, behind Victor Henry, caught only a few words, but the pop-eyed look of the admiral and Stalin's tones were self-translating. The dictator turned to Victor Henry, beaming again. "Well, it is arranged about the weather codes and so forth. Tell your chief that we Russians do not intentionally embarrass our guests. Tell him I feel the American Navy will do historic things in this struggle, and will rule the ocean when peace comes."

As Slote quickly translated, Admiral Standley stood, his thin withered lips quivering, and grasped the dictator's hand. Stalin went back to the head table. The incident seemed to stay in his mind, because when he rose to make the last toast of the evening, to President Roosevelt, he returned to the theme. The interpreter was Oumansky, the ambassador to the United States, whose well-cut blue suit marked him off from the other Russians. His English was extremely smooth. "Comrade Stalin says President Roosevelt has the very difficult task of leading a country which is nonbelligerent, yet wants to do all it can to help the two great democracies of Europe in their fight against Fascism. Comrade Stalin says"—Oumansky paused and looked all around the wide room, in a silence no longer marred by gunfire—"*may God help him in his most difficult task.*"

This religious phrase brought a surprised stillness, then a surge of all the banqueters, glasses in hand, to their feet, cheering, drinking, and applauding. Harriman heartily shook Stalin's hand; the plethoric little Russian admiral grasped the hands of Slote, Henry, and Standley; and all over the room the banquet dissolved in great handshaking, backslapping, and embracing.

But the evening was not over. The Russians marched their guests through more empty splendid rooms to a movie theatre with about fifty soft low armchairs, each with a small table where attendants served cakes, fruits, sweets, and champagne. Here they showed a war movie and then a long musical, and Slote did something he would never have believed possible: in the heart of the Kremlin, he fell asleep. A swelling of finale music woke him seconds before the lights came on. He saw others starting awake in the glare, furtively rubbing their eyes. Stalin walked out springily with Beaverbrook and Harriman, both of whom had red eyes and suffering expressions. In a grand hall, under a vast painting of a battle in snow, he shook hands with all the guests, one by one.

Outside the Grand Palace the night was black, without stars, and the wind was cold and biting. The NKVD agents, leather collars turned up to their ears, blue flashlights in hand, looked sleepy, chilled, and bored, sorting the guests into their limousines.

"Say, how the devil can he drive so fast in this black-out?" the admiral protested, as their car passed through the outer gate and speeded into an inky void. "Can Russians see like cats?" The car stopped in blackness, the escort guided the three Americans to a doorway, they passed inside, and found themselves in the small cold foyer of the Hotel National, where one dim lamp burned at the reception desk. The porter who had opened the door was muffled in a fur coat. The elevator stood open, dark, and abandoned. The admiral bade them good-night and plodded to the staircase.

"Come up for a minute," Henry said to Leslie Slote.

"No thanks. I'll grope my way to my apartment. It's not far."

Pug insisted, and Slote followed Henry up the gloomy staircase to his squalid little room on an areaway. "I don't rate like Tudsbury," he said.

"Tudsbury's about the best propagandist the Soviet Union's got," Slote said, "and I guess they know it."

Pug unlocked a suitcase, took a narrow dispatch case out, unlocked that, and glanced through papers.

"I hope you understand," Slote said, "that those locks are meaningless. All the contents of that case have been photographed."

"Yes," Victor Henry said absently. He slipped a letter

into his pocket. "Would you like a snooze? Please stick around for a while. Something may be doing."

"Oh?" Out of his new and growing respect for Henry, Slote asked no questions, but stretched out on the hard narrow bed to a twang and squeak of springs. His head still reeled from the champagne that shadowy attendants had kept pouring at the movie. Next thing he knew, knocking woke him. Victor Henry was talking at the door to a man in a black leather coat. *"Horosho, my gotovy,"* he said in his atrocious accent. *"Odnu minutu."* He closed the door. "Want to wash up or anything, Leslie? I'd like you to come with me."

"Where to?"

"Back to the Kremlin. I have a letter from Harry Hopkins for the big cheese. I didn't think I was going to get to hand it over in person, but maybe I am."

"Good lord, does the ambassador know about this?"

"Yes. Admiral Standley brought him a note about it from the President. I gather he was annoyed, but he knows."

Slote sat up. "Annoyed! I should think so. Mr. Hopkins has a way of doing these things. This is very outlandish, Captain Henry. Nobody should ever, ever see a head of state without going directly through the ambassador. How have you arranged this?"

"Me? I had nothing to do with it. I'm an errand boy. Hopkins wanted this letter to go to Stalin informally and privately or not at all. In my place you don't argue with Harry Hopkins. I understand he talked to Oumansky. If it puts you in a false position, I guess I'll go alone. There'll be an interpreter."

Calculating the angles in this astonishing business— mainly the angle of his own professional self-preservation —Slote began combing his hair at a yellowed wall mirror. "I'll have to file a written report with the ambassador."

"Sure."

* * *

In a long, high-ceilinged, bleakly lit room lined with wall maps, Stalin sat at one end of a polished conference table, with many papers piled on a strip of green cloth before him. A stone ashtray at the dictator's elbow brimmed with cigarette butts, suggesting that he had been steadily at work since the departure of the banquet guests. He now wore a rough khaki uniform which sagged and bulged, and he looked very weary. Pavlov, his usual English interpreter, sat beside him, a thin, pale, dark-haired young man with a clever, anxiously servile expression. There was nobody else in the big room. As the uniformed protocol officer ushered in the two Americans, Stalin rose, shook hands, with a silent gracious gesture waved them to chairs, and then sat down with an inquiring look at Captain Henry.

Henry handed him the letter and a round box wrapped in shiny blue paper. "Mr. Chairman, I'd better not inflict my bad Russian on you any longer," he said in English, as Stalin carefully opened the White House envelope with a paper knife. Slote translated and Stalin replied in Russian, slightly inclining his head, "As you wish." He passed to Pavlov the single handwritten pale green sheet, on which THE WHITE HOUSE was printed in an upper corner.

Pug said, as Stalin unwrapped the box, "And that is the special Virginia pipe tobacco Mr. Hopkins told you about, that his son likes so much." Pavlov translated this, and everything the American captain said thereafter, sometimes conveying Henry's tone as well as a quick exact version of his words. Slote sat silent, nodding from time to time.

Stalin turned the round blue tin in his hands. "Mr. Hopkins is very thoughtful to remember our casual chat about pipe tobacco. Of course, we have plenty of good pipe tobacco in the Soviet Union." He twisted open the tin with a quick wrench of strong hands and curiously inspected the heavy lead foil seal, before slashing it with a polished thumbnail and pulling a pipe from his pocket. "Now you can tell Mr. Hopkins that I tried his son's tobacco." Pug understood Stalin's Russian in this small talk, but could not follow him after that.

Stalin stuffed the pipe, put a thick wooden match to it, and puffed fragrant blue smoke while Pavlov translated Hopkins's letter aloud. After a meditative silence, the dictator turned veiled cold eyes on Victor Henry and proceeded to speak, pausing to let Pavlov catch up in English after three or four sentences. "That is a strange letter from Mr. Hopkins. We all know the United States manufactures millions of automobiles per year of many different models and types, including big, luxurious, complicated machines such as Cadillacs and so forth. What is the problem with landing craft, then? Landing craft are armored lighters with small simple engines. Surely you can produce as many as you want to. Surely the British have plenty already. I cannot see this as a real obstacle to a second front in Europe now, as Mr. Hopkins states."

Pug Henry pulled from his dispatch case sketches and production tables of landing craft. "Different types must be designed from scratch and manufactured, Mr. Chairman, to land against a solidly fortified coast. We expect mass production in mid-1942, at the latest. These papers may be of interest."

Unexpectedly, in mid-translation, Stalin uttered a short harsh laugh and began to talk fast in Russian, straight at Victor Henry. Slote and Pavlov made quick notes, and when the dictator paused, Pavlov took over and spoke with much of Stalin's hard sarcastic tone. "That is very fine! Mid-1942. Unfortunately, this is October 1941. If Mr. Hitler would only halt operations until mid-1942! But perhaps we cannot count on that. And what will happen meantime? I regard Mr. Harry Hopkins"—Stalin said *Gospodin Garry Gopkins*—"as a friend and a clever man. Doesn't he know that any operation that the British can mount now—just a reconnaissance in force of a few divisions, if they can do no better—might decide the course of this war? The Germans have only very weak reserves, mere token forces, on the French coast. They are throwing everything into the battle on our front. Any action in the west might make them pause, and draw off just the decisive margin of strength here."

Stalin doodled in red ink on a gray unlined pad during the interpretation, drawing a wolf.

Victor Henry said, "Mr. Chairman, I am instructed to answer any questions about the landing craft problem."

Stalin used the back of his hand to shove aside the papers Pug Henry had laid before him. "Landing craft? But it is a question of will, not of landing craft. However, we will study the matter of landing craft. Of course, we have such machines too, for landing on defended coasts. Perhaps we can lend-lease some to the British. In 1915, when war equipment was more primitive than today, Mr. Churchill managed to put a big force ashore in Gallipoli, thousands of miles from England. Possibly he found the experience discouraging. But the Japanese have in recent years put ashore more than a million soldiers in China. Those men surely did not swim across, in such cold waters. So it is obviously a question of will, not of landing craft. I hope Mr. Hopkins will use his great influence to establish a second front now in Europe, because the outcome of the war against the Hitlerites may turn on that. I can say no more."

The dictator finished the wolf in rapid strokes during the translation, and started another with bared fangs and a hanging tongue. He looked up at Henry with the oddly genial expression common in his photographs, and changed his tone. "Have you enjoyed your stay? Is there anything we can do for you?"

Victor Henry said, "Mr. Chairman, I have been a war-time military observer in Germany and in England. Mr. Hopkins asked me to go to the front here, if an opportunity arose, so as to bring him an eyewitness report."

At the word "front," Stalin shook his head. "No, no. We are obliged to guarantee the safety of our guests. That we cannot do, in the present stage of fighting. Mr. Hopkins would not forgive us if some misfortune befell you."

"Mr. Hopkins has been unsparing of his own health, sir. It is wartime."

An opaque wild look, almost the look in a gorilla's eyes, came into Stalin's gaze. "Well, you should understand that things are bad at the front. The Germans are breaking through again in force. We may soon see the worst hours for Russia since 1812. You will hear all the news tomorrow. That is why a second front now would earn for England the friendship of my people until the end of time." He went back to work on the wolf.

Pug said soberly, "In view of this news, Mr. Chairman, I admire your cheerfulness of spirit at the banquet tonight."

Stalin shrugged his broad sagging shoulders. "Wars are not won by gloom, nor by bad hospitality. Well, if Mr. Hopkins wants you at the front, he must have good reasons. We will see what we can do. Give him my thanks for the letter and the tobacco. It is not bad tobacco, though I am used to my Russian tobacco. Please tell him my feelings about the second front. Perhaps your trip to our front could bring home the urgency. Mr. Hopkins is a good adviser to your great President, and as you are an emissary from him, I wish you well."

Leaving the Kremlin and driving through the blackout, the two Americans said not a word. When the car stopped, Pug Henry spoke: "Well, I'll talk to you tomorrow. I guess these fellows will take you home."

"No, I'll get out." On the sidewalk, Slote touched Pug's arm as the limousine drove off. "Let's talk here. I was utterly shocked by this business of going to the front. If Mr. Hopkins knew of the catastrophic situation Stalin just admitted to"—the diplomat's voice wavered and he cleared his throat—"he would surely withdraw those instructions."

The night was ending, and though the icy street was still black, Pug could just see Slote's pale face under his fur hat.

"I don't agree with you on that. He's a pretty tough customer, Hopkins."

Slote persisted, "You won't really get to the front, you know. They've just given some correspondents a tour. They kept them far behind the lines, feeding them caviar, quails, and champagne. Still, the Luftwaffe pulled an air raid on a village and almost nailed them."

"Right, but that could happen to us here in Moscow, too."

"But why go, for God's sake?" Slote broke out in a ragged shrill tone. He lowered his voice. "At best you'll see one tiny sector for a few hours. It's foolhardy sightseeing. It'll create endless trouble at the embassy, as well as for the Russians."

Victor Henry chain-lit a cigarette. "Listen, if you can watch ten men under fire, you'll learn a lot about an army's morale in a few hours. Mr. Hopkins likes to call himself a glorified messenger boy. That's an exaggeration, but I'm an unglorified one. Doing this job might give me the illusion that I'm earning my salary. Come upstairs for a nightcap. I have some good Scotch."

"No, thank you. I'm going to write my report, and then try to get an hour's sleep."

"Well, cheer up. My own impression was that the big cheese was being affable, but that I won't get to go."

"That's what I hope. No foreign military attaché has yet gone to the front, or near it. Good morning."

During the talk the sky had turned violet, and Slote could see his way on the dead quiet streets. This was a relief, for he had more than once banged into lamp posts and fallen off curbs in the Moscow blackout. He had also been challenged at pistol-point by patrolmen. One walked toward him now in the gray dawn and gave him a suspicious squint, then passed on without a word.

In his flat Slote brewed coffee on the gas ring, and rapidly typed a long account of the banquet and the meeting with Stalin. When he had finished, he threw back the blackout curtains. The sun was shining. Staggering, bleary, he took a loose-leaf diary from a drawer and wrote briefly in it, ending with these words:

But the official report which I've just rattled off describes the meeting with Stalin in sufficient detail; and I'll keep a copy in my files.

As for the Henrys, father and son, the puzzle is simply enough resolved after all. I saw the answer in the past few hours. They both have an instinct for action, and the presence of mind that goes with it. Byron displayed these traits in moments of physical danger. His father probably would too. But I've just seen him act in more sophisticated and subtle situations, requiring quick thinking, hardihood, and tact. It is not easy to keep one's head in confronting a personage like Stalin, who has an aura like a large lump of radium, powerful, invisible, and poisonous. Victor Henry managed.

On reflection, I can understand why the ladies like such men. The man of action protects, feeds—and presumably fecundates, QED—more vigorously and reliably than the man of thought.

Possibly one can't change one's nature. Still one can perhaps learn and grow. Captain Henry suggested that I disregard orders and expose the Minsk documents to Fred Fearing or some newspaperman. Such an act goes entirely against my grain; and entirely for that reason, I intend to do it.

53

TALKY TUDSBURY was having five o'clock tea alone in his hotel suite that day, with some light refreshment of sprats, cheese, sturgeon, black bread, and honey cakes, when Victor Henry came in and told him that he was going to the front. The correspondent got so excited that he stopped eating. "Good God, man, you *are?* With the Germans swarming in all over the place? It's impossible. It's just talk. Dear Christ, these Russians are good at putting you off with talk. You'll never go." He brushed up his moustaches and reached for more food.

"Well, maybe," Pug said, sinking into a chair, and laying on his lap the briefcase stuffed with codes and harbor charts, which he had just collected at the navy ministry. He had had five or six hours' broken sleep in four days. The room was jerking back and forth in his vision as he strove to stay awake. "But my clearance has just come in from pretty high up."

Tudsbury was putting a chunk of bread heaped with sardines to his mouth. The morsel stopped in midair. He peered at Henry through his bottle-glass spectacles, and spoke in low quiet tones. "I'll go with you."

"The hell you will."

"Victor, the correspondents went to the central front two weeks ago, when the Russians were counterattacking. The day they left, I had flu, with a sizzling temperature." Tudsbury threw down the food, seized his cane, limped rapidly across the room, and began to put on a fur-lined coat and a fur hat. "Who's handling this, Lozovsky? Can't I just tell him you said I could come? I know them all and they love me. It's up to you."

873

Victor Henry did not want Tudsbury along, but he was exhausted and he was sure the Russians would refuse. "Okay."

"God bless you, dear fellow. Stay and finish my tea. Tell Pam I'll be back before six, and she's to retype my broadcast."

"Where is she?"

"A letter came for her in the Foreign Office pouch. She went to get it."

Pug fell asleep in the armchair where he sat.

Cold fingers brushing his cheek woke him. "Hello there. Wouldn't you rather lie down?" Pam stood over him, her face rosy from the frost, her eyes shining, wisps of brown hair showing under her gray lambskin hat.

"What? Oh!" He blinked and stretched. "What am I doing here? I guess I walked in and collapsed."

"Where's Talky?" She was taking off her hat and gloves. "Why did he leave his tea? That's not like him."

Sleep cleared from his brain like fog; he remembered his conversation with Tudsbury, and told her. Her face went stiff and strained. "The front? They'll never let him go, but *you?* Victor, are you serious? Have you heard the BBC, or the Swedish Radio?"

"Yes."

"Well, I know better than to argue, but—I can tell you this, our embassy's getting ready to be moved to the Urals or somewhere. By the bye, Ted's all right." She went to the desk, still in her fur coat, and picked up typed yellow sheets. "Oh, drat, another revision. Such niggling!"

By now Pug was used to her casual bombshells, but she dropped this one so swiftly that he wasn't sure he had heard aright. "Pamela, what's this? What about Ted?"

"He's fine. Or safe, anyhow."

"But where is he?"

"Oh, back in Blighty. Hardly the worse for wear, according to him. It seems he finally managed to escape—he and four French aviators—from a prison camp outside Strasbourg. He did have quite a few adventures in France and Belgium, straight out of the films. But he made it. I rather thought he would, sooner or later." She sat down and took the cover off the typewriter.

"Good God, girl, that's tremendous news."

"Yes, isn't it? You must read his letter. Seven pages, written on both sides, and quite amusing. He's lost three stone, and he still has a bullet in his thigh—or, more accurately, in his behind. He's quite chastened, he'll take the desk job now—as soon as he can sit at a desk, he adds rather ruefully! And that means I'm to come straight home and marry him, of course."

Pamela broke her offhand manner with a long glance at Victor Henry. She put on black-rimmed glasses. "I'd better get at this. And you obviously need some sleep."

"No use. The mission's leaving soon. I have to see them off. Pam, that's splendid about Ted. I'm very glad and relieved."

Rubbing her hands and blowing on them, she said, "Lord, it would be a relief at that, wouldn't it? I mean to get away from Talky's handwriting, and his optimistic drivel."

Tudsbury burst in on them a little later, his face aflame, his nose empurpled by the cold, just as Henry was putting on his bridge coat.

"*Mojet byt!* Qualified yes, by God! They'll confirm it tomorrow, but Victor, I believe I'm going with you!— Pam, have you finished yet? It's getting near that time. —The Narkomindel's in mad confusion, Victor, the news from the front must be really bad, but God Almighty, that clearance you've got, whatever it is, certainly is the secret password! Of course they adore me, and they know I'm entitled to a trip, but the look that came over Lozovsky's face, when I said *you* insisted that I accompany you!"

"Oh, Talky!" Pamela stopped typing, and glared at him. "Victor didn't insist at all. He couldn't have."

"Pam, one has to bludgeon these people." Tudsbury's face creased in a tricky grin. "I said you two were old friends, in fact, and that Victor rather liked you and wanted to oblige me. So please back my story if occasion arises."

"You unscrupulous old horror," Pamela said, her face mantling pink.

"Well, that's true enough, as far as it goes," Victor Henry said. "I have to get on to the airport now. Pamela's got some great news, Talky."

The instrusion of Tudsbury snagged the trip. The Narkomindel, the Foreign Office, hemmed, hawed, and stalled. Days went by. Pug remained stuck in Moscow with nothing to do. The ambassador and the attachés acted cool and distant, for Victor Henry was that plague of the Foreign Service, an interloper from Washington. Once he dropped in on Slote's office and found the diplomat pale, harassed, and given to pointless giggling.

"Say, what's my daughter-in-law doing on your desk?" Pug said. Natalie smiled from a silver frame, looking younger and fatter, with her hair in an unbecoming knot.

"Oh! Yes, that's Natalie." Slote laughed. "D'you suppose Byron would mind? She gave it to me ages ago, and I'm still fond of her. What's happened to your trip? You won't have far to go, at the rate the Germans are coming on, hee hee."

"God knows," Pug said, thinking that this man was in bad shape. "Maybe it's all off."

The main trouble, it turned out, was Pamela. Her father had asked to bring her along, claiming helplessness without her. He had since withdrawn the request. But the Narkomindel had fed the three names into the great obscure machine that handled the matter, and there was no starting over. Lozovsky began to lose his genial humor when Pug appeared or telephoned. "My dear Captain Henry, you will hear when you will hear. There are other equally pressing problems in the Soviet Union just now."

So Pug wandered the streets, observing the changes in Moscow. New red-and-black posters blazed appeals for volunteers, in the crude bold socialist imagery of muscular young workmen and peasant women brandishing bayonets at spiders, snakes, or hyenas with Hitler faces. Labor battalions shouldering spades and picks marched raggedly here and there; big trucks crammed with children crisscrossed the city; long queues stood at food shops, despite the heavy rain that persisted day after day. Soldiers and horse-drawn carts vanished from the streets. Under the sodden caps and wet shawls of street crowds, the swarm of white high-cheekboned faces wore a different look. The Slavic phlegm was giving way to knotted brows, inquiring glances, and a hurrying pace; Victor Henry thought that the approach of the Germans made the Muscovites look more like New Yorkers.

Lozovsky finally telephoned him at the hotel, his voice ringing cheerily. "Well, Captain, will tomorrow at dawn suit you? Kindly come here to the Narkomindel, wear warm clothing, a raincoat, and good boots, and be prepared to be out three or four days."

"Right. Is the girl coming too?"

"Of course." The Russian sounded surprised and a bit offended. "That was the problem. Really it was not easy to clear, though we wanted to make the exact arrangements you desired. Our Russian girls face combat conditions as a matter of course, but we know that foreign ladies are much less hardy. Still we all know Miss Tudsbury, she is attractive, and one understands such a devoted friendship. It is arranged."

Victor Henry decided to ignore the jollying, even ribald tone, and not to try to rewrite this record. "I'm grateful, and I'll be there."

⁕　⁕　⁕

They drove southward from Moscow in the rain, and all morning ground along in a thunderous parade of army trucks, stopping only for a visit to an amazingly well camouflaged airfield for interceptors, in the woods just outside the capital. The little black automobile, a Russian M-1 that looked and sounded much like a 1930 Ford, made cramped quarters, especially with unexplained packages and boxes lining the floor. When they had gone about a hundred miles, their guide, a mild-faced, bespectacled tank colonel, with the odd name of Porphyry Amphiteatrov, suggested that they stop to eat lunch and stretch their legs. That was when they first heard the German guns.

The driver, a burly silent soldier with a close-trimmed red beard, turned off to a side road lined with old trees. They wound among cleared fields and copses of birch, glimpsing two large white country houses in the distance, and entered a gloomy lane that came to a dead end in wild woods. Here they got out, and the colonel led them along a footpath to a small grassy mound under the trees where garlands of fresh flowers lay.

"Well, this was Tolstoy's country estate, you know," said Amphiteatrov. "It is called Yasnaya Polyana, and there is his grave. Since it was on the way, I thought you might be interested."

Tudsbury stared at the low mound and spoke in a hushed way not usual to him. "The grave of Tolstoy? No tomb? No stone?"

"He ordered it so. 'Put me in the earth,' he said, 'in the woods where I played Green Stick with my brother Nicholas when we were boys . . .'" Amphiteatrov's bass voice sounded coarse and loud over the dripping of water through the yellow leaves.

Victor Henry cocked his head and glanced at the colonel, for he heard a new noise: soft irregular thumps, faint as the plop of the rain on the grass. The colonel nodded. "Well, when the wind is right, the sound carries quite far."

"Ah, guns?" said Tudsbury, with a show of great calm.

"Yes, guns. Well, shall we have a bite? The house where he worked is interesting, but it is not open nowadays."

The bearded driver brought the lunch to benches out of sight of the burial spot. They ate black bread, very garlicky sausages, and raw cucumbers, washed down with warm beer. Nobody spoke. The rain dripped, the army trucks murmured on the highway, and the distant guns thumped faintly. Pamela broke the silence. "Who put the flowers there?"

"The caretakers, I suppose," said the colonel.

"The Germans must never get this far," she said.

"Well, that's a spiritual thought," the colonel said. "I don't think they will, but Yasnaya Polyana is not a strong point, and so the great Tolstoy must now take his chances with the rest of the Russians." He smiled, suddenly showing red gums, and not looking mild at all. "Anyway, the Germans can't kill him."

Tudsbury said, "They should have read him a little more carefully."

"We still have to prove that. But we will."

The sun momentarily broke through and birds began to sing. Victor Henry and Pamela Tudsbury sat together on a bench, and light shafted theatrically through the yellow leaves, full on the girl. She wore gray slacks tucked into white fur snowboots, and a gray lamb coat and hat.

"Why are you staring at me, Victor?"

"Pam, I've never visited Tolstoy's grave before, certainly not with you, but I swear I remember all this, and most of all the nice way you've got that hat tilted." As her hand went up to her hat he added, "And I could have told you you'd lift that hand, and the sun would make your ring sparkle."

She held out her fingers stiffly, looking at the diamond. "Ted and I had a bit of a spat about *that*. When he produced it, I wasn't quite ready to wear it."

The colonel called, "Well, Captain, I think we go on?"

Edging into the thickening traffic stream on the main road, the little black automobile rolled in the direction of the gunfire. Trucks filled the highway, one line moving toward the front, one returning. Whiskered men and stout sunburned women, working in fields between stretches of birch forest, paid no attention to the traffic. Children playing near the highway ignored the war vehicles too. In tiny villages, washing hung outside the log cabins and the wooden houses with gaily painted window frames. One odd observation forced itself on Victor Henry: the further one got from Moscow, the nearer to the front, the more normal and peaceful Russia appeared. The capital behind them was one vast apprehensive scurry. Directly outside it, battalions of women, boys, and scrawny men with glasses—clerks, journalists, and schoolteachers—had been frantically digging antitank ditches and planting concrete and steel obstacles in myriads. Beyond that belt of defense began tranquil forests and fields, with fall colors splashing the stretches of green conifer. Mainly the air raid shelters for trucks along the highway—cleared spaces in the woods, masked with cut evergreen boughs—showed there was an invasion on.

Toward evening the car rolled into a small town and stopped at a yellow frame house on a muddy square. Here red-cheeked children lined up at a pump with pails; smoke was rising from chimneys; other children were driving in goats and cows from broad fields, stretching far and flat under a purpling cloudy sky; and three burly old men were hammering and sawing at the raw frame of a new unfinished house. This was the strangest thing Pug saw all that day—these Russian ancients, building a house in the twilight, within earshot of German artillery, much louder here than at the Tolstoy estate, with yellow flashes flickering like summer lightning on the western horizon.

"Well, this is their home," the tank colonel replied, when Victor Henry remarked on the sight, as they climbed stiffly out of the car. "Where should they go? We have the Germans stopped here. Of course, we took out the pregnant women and the mothers with babies long ago."

In the warm little dining room of the house, now a regiment headquarters, the visitors crowded around the table with the tank colonel, four officers of the regiment, and a General Yevlenko, who wore three khaki stars on his thick wide shoulders. He was the chief of staff of the army group in that sector, and Colonel Amphiteatrov told Victor Henry that he had just happened to be passing through the town. This huge man with fair hair, a bulbous peasant nose, and big smooth pink jaws, appeared to fill one end of the narrow smoky room. Much taken with Pamela, Yevlenko kept passing gallant compliments and urging food and drink on her. His fleshy face at moments settled into an abstracted, stony, deeply sad and tired look; then it would kindle with jollity, though the eyes remained filmed by fatigue in sunken purple sockets.

A feast almost in Kremlin style appeared, on the rough yellow cloth, course by course, brought by soldiers: champagne, caviar, smoked fish, soup, fowls, steaks, and cream cakes. The mystery of this magnificent stunt was cleared up when Pug Henry glanced into the kitchen as one of the soldier-waiters opened and closed the door. The red-bearded driver of the M-1 automobile was sweating over the stove in a white apron. Pug had seen him carrying boxes from the car into the house. Evidently he was really a cook, and a superb one.

The general talked freely about the war, and the colonel translated. His army group was outnumbered in this sector and had far fewer tanks and guns than the Nazis. Still, they might yet surprise Fritz. They had to hold a line much too long for their strength, according to doctrine; but a good doctrine, like a good regiment, sometimes had to stretch. The Germans were taking fearful losses. He reeled off many figures of tanks destroyed, guns captured, men killed. Any army could advance if its commanders were willing to leave blood smeared on each yard of earth gained. The Germans were getting white as turnips with the bloodletting. This drive was their last big effort to win the war before winter came.

"Will they take Moscow?" Tudsbury asked.

"Not from this direction," retorted the general, "nor do I think they will from any other. But if they do take it, well, we'll drive them out of Moscow, and then we'll drive them out of our land. We are going to beat them. The Germans have no strategic policy. Their idea of a strategic policy is to kill, to loot, and to take slaves. In this day and age that is not a strategic policy. Furthermore, their resources are basically inferior to ours. Germany is a poor country. Finally, they overestimated themselves and they underrated us. According to V. I. Lenin, that is a very dangerous mistake in war. It is very dangerous in war, Lenin said, to think too much of yourself and too little of your opponent. The result can only be inaccurate plans and very unpleasant surprises, as, for example, defeat."

Pamela said, "Still, they have come so far."

The general turned a suddenly menacing, brutally tough, piteously exhausted, angry big face to her. His expression dissolved into a flirtatious smirk. "Yes, my dear girl, and I see that you mean that remark well and do not like what has happened any more than we do. Yes, the Nazis, through unparalleled perfidy, did achieve surprise. And there is another thing. They are cocky. Their tails are up. They are professional winners, having already won several campaigns, and driven the indomitable British into the sea, and so forth. They believe they are unbeatable. However, as they watch their comrades die like flies in Russia, I think they are starting to wonder. At first they would advance in column down our highways, not even bothering to guard their flanks. Lately they've grown more careful. Yes, Hitler trained them to maraud, kill, and loot, and those are old Teutonic customs, so they are good at it. We are a peace-loving people, and I suppose in a mental sense we were caught unprepared. So, as you say, they have come far. Now we have two jobs: to keep them from coming farther, and then to send them back where they came from, the ones we haven't squashed into our mud." He turned to Henry and Tudsbury. "We will do the job faster, naturally, if you help us with supplies, for we have lost a lot. But most of all, the opening of a front in western Europe can lead to the quick destruction of these rats. The English might be surprised to find they could march straight to Berlin once they set foot in France. I believe every German who can shoot a gun straight has been shipped here for this attack."

"I never broadcast without advocating a second front now," Tudsbury said.

The general nodded. "You are well known and esteemed as a friend of the Soviet people." He glanced at Victor Henry. "Well, and what are you interested in seeing, Captain? Unfortunately, this far inland, we cannot show you very good naval maneuvers."

"General, suppose—of course this is absurd, but—suppose my President could visit your front, in a cloak of invisibility from the fairy tales."

"We have such stories," Yevlenko said, "but unfortunately no such cloaks."

"What would you like him to see?"

The general glanced at the four officers sitting elbow to elbow at the table across from the visitors, smoking continuously, four kinky-haired pale Russians with shrewd weary eyes, who looked like quadruplets in their identical brown tunics. None of them had as yet uttered a word. Now he addressed them, and a colloquy in rapid Russian broke out. He turned back to Henry. "You put that well. It will be arranged. As the situation is a bit fluid, I suggest you make a start at dawn." He said to Pamela, gesturing upward, "A bedroom has been cleared for you. The gentlemen will bunk with these officers."

"Good heavens, a bedroom? I counted on sleeping on the floor or on the ground in my clothes," Pamela said. "Anyway, I'm not at all sleepy yet."

As the colonel translated, Yevlenko's face lit up. "So? You talk like one of our Russian girls, not like a delicate Englishwoman." Offering her his arm, he led them into the next room, where worn, inked-over maps hung on the walls, and the fusty house furniture was jumbled in with desks, stools, typewriters, and black twisting telephone cables. Soldiers pushed furniture, screeching here and there to clear a space around a shabby upright piano with bare wooden keys. An officer sat, cigarette dangling from his mouth, and thumped out "There'll Always Bc an England." Pamela laughed when she recognized the tune, and stood and sang it. The general led applause and called for more champagne. The pianist began stumbling through "Alexander's Ragtime Band." With an elegant low bow, General Yevlenko invited Pamela to dance. He towered head and shoulders above her, so they made a grotesque pair, two-stepping stiffly round and round the narrow clear space in heavy muddy boots, but his face shone with enjoyment. She danced with other officers, then with the general again, as the pianist ran through the few American tunes he knew and started over on "Alexander's Ragtime Band." Everybody in the room quaffed much champagne and vodka. In the doorway soldiers crowded, watching with round gay eyes the foreign lady in gray pants dancing and drinking with the officers. Pug knew that she hated to dance, especially with strangers; he recalled almost the first words he had heard Pamela utter, on the *Bremen* in the dim far past of peacetime: "I shall get myself a cane and a white wig." But she made a game show.

The pianist began playing Russian music—which he did much better—and Pamela sank into a chair while the officers danced alone or with each other. The laughing and the handclapping grew louder. One handsome young soldier with a week's growth of beard burst into the room and did a bravura solo, bounding, squatting, pirouetting, then acknowledging applause with the bow of a professional ballet artist. The general lumbered to his feet and began to dance by himself; he too twirled, jumped, then folded his arms and squatted, kicking his feet and hoarsely shouting, "*Skoreye! Skoreye!* Faster! Faster!" His heavy steps shook the floor. The soldiers broke into the room to ring him and to cheer; the room reeked of men's dirty bodies, of smoke, of alcohol, yet pressed beside Pamela, Victor Henry could faintly smell her carnation perfume too. When General Yevlenko finished with a shout and jumped up panting, the men roared and clapped, and Pamela came and kissed his perspiring big red face, and he heartily kissed her mouth, causing laughter and more roars; and that was the end. The general left. The soldiers pushed the furniture back as it had been. The visitors went to sleep.

54

AT DAWN, it was raining hard. Children and animals floundered in the dim violet light all over the square, and trucks splashed, skidded, and spun their wheels, throwing up curtains of muck. The back seat of the car was roomier, since many of the packages had been eaten or drunk up. Victor Henry thought of complimenting the master chef at the wheel, but decided against it. Pamela, squeezed between her father and Pug, had managed a touch of lipstick and eye makeup. In these surroundings she looked like a movie star visiting the troops, Pug thought.

"Well, we go," said Colonel Amphiteatrov. "In this weather we will go slower, and not so far." The car bumped and slid about a hundred yards, then sank and stalled.

"Well, I hope we will go farther than this," said the colonel. Soldiers in greatcoats surrounded the car. With shouting and shoving they got it to move. The wheels hit solider ground, and the car went splashing, rocking, and slewing out of the town. After a run on asphalted highway through the fields, they took a narrow mud road into a forest. The chef drove well (or the chauffeur cooked well—Pug never did find out the truth), and he kept the car going through terrible ruts, mounds, and holes, for perhaps twenty minutes. Then the car stopped dead. Pug got out with the driver and the colonel. The hubs of the rear wheels were buried in ropy red mud. It was still raining heavily. They were stuck in wild woods, so quiet that rain hitting the hot hood made a hiss.

"I suppose he has a shovel," Pug said.

"Yes, I suppose so." The colonel was looking around. He walked off into the woods some yards ahead—to relieve himself, Pug imagined, before getting to work. Pug heard voices, then hoarse engine snorts. The bushes began to move. Out of the shrubbery a light tank appeared, covered with boughs, its cannon pointed at Pug. Behind it walked the colonel and three muddy men in greatcoats. The American had been looking straight at the mottled, camouflaged cannon, yet had not noticed it until it started toward him. The tank chugged out of the trees, swerved, and backed on the road. Soldiers quickly attached a chain and the car was pulled loose in a moment, with the passengers inside. Then the bough-festooned turret opened, and two bristly, boyish Slav heads poked out. Pamela jumped from the car, splashed and stumbled to the tank, and kissed the tankists, to their embarrassed pleasure. The turret closed, the tank backed into the wood to its former place, and the black automobile went lurching on into the forest. Thus they were bogged and rescued several times, and so discovered that the wet silent forest was swarming with the Red Army.

They arrived at a washout that severed the road like a creek in flood. The gully's sides bore gouge marks of caterpillar treads and thick truck tires, but obviously the auto could not struggle across. Here soldiers emerged from the woods and laid split logs across the gash, smooth side up, lashing them together into a shaky but adequate bridge. This was a sizable crew, and their leader, a fat squinting lieutenant, invited the party to stop and refresh themselves. There was no way of telling him from his men, except that he gave the orders and they obeyed. They were all dressed alike and they were all a red earth color. He led the visitors through the trees and down into an icy, mucky dugout roofed with timbers, and so masked by brush and shrubs that Victor Henry did not see an entrance until the officer began to sink into the earth. The dugout was an underground cabin of tarred logs, crisscrossed with telephone cables, lit by an oil lamp and heated by an old open iron stove burning chopped branches. The officer, squinting proudly at a brass samovar on the raw plank table, offered them tea. While water boiled, a soldier conducted the men to a latrine so primitive and foul—though Tudsbury and the Russians happily used it—that Pug went stumbling off into the trees, only to be halted by a sentry who appeared like a forest spirit. While the American attended to nature, the soldier stood guard, observing with some interest how a foreigner did it. Returning to the dugout, Pug encountered three big blank-faced Russians, marching with fixed bayonets around Pamela, who looked vaguely embarrassed and amused.

Before they left, the lieutenant showed Pug and Tudsbury through the soldiers' dugouts, obviously proud of his men's workmanship. These freshly dug puddle-filled holes in the damp earth, smelling like graves, did have heavy timbered roofs that might survive a shell hit, and the mud-caked, unshaven soldiers, crouched in their greatcoats in the gloom, appeared content enough to smoke and talk and wait for orders here. Pug saw some feeding themselves with torn chunks of gray bread and dollops of stew from a muddy tureen lugged by two muddy soldiers. Munching on their bread, dragging at their cigarettes, these men placidly stared at the visitors, and slowly moved their heads to watch them walk through the trenches. Healthy-looking, well-nourished, they seemed as much at home in the red earth as earthworms, and they seemed almost as tough, abundant, and simple a form of life. Here Victor Henry first got an ineradicable feeling that Yevlenko had told the truth: that the Germans might gain the biggest victories, but that the Red Army would in time drive them out.

"Ye gods," Tudsbury managed to mutter on the way back to the car, "Belgium in 1915 was nothing like this. They live like animals."

"They can," Henry replied, and said no more, for Amphiteatrov's eye was on them in these brief asides.

"Well, we are not really far from our destination," the Russian said, wiping rain from his face and helping Pamela into the back seat. "If not for the mud, we would have been there now."

The car bumped and slopped out of the woods. Cleared fields stretched for miles ahead, flat as a table, under gray low clouds. "There's where we're going." Amphiteatrov pointed straight ahead to a distant line of forest. They came to a crossroads of mud churned up like water at a boil, and though the road ahead looked good, the driver slithered the car sharp right.

"Why don't we drive straight on?" Pamela said. "Doesn't the road go through?"

"Oh, yes. It goes through. It's mined. This whole area"

—the colonel's arm swept around the quiet stubbly fields—
"is mined."

Pug said, somewhat chilled, "Nice to know these things
when you start out."

Amphiteatrov gave him his infrequent, wolfish, red-
gummed smile, and wiped a clear drop from his thin bluish
nose. "Well, yes, Captain. Your Intourist guide in these
parts should really know what is what. Otherwise your
health could be affected."

They jolted along the soupy track in rain that made it
soupier, but in time the car sank with all four wheels into
the mire, and halted amid long rows of yellow stubble
stretching out of sight. No rescuers appeared; they could
not have, without rising from the earth, but Pug half
thought they might. The driver shovelled the wheels clear
and laid planks to the back tires. When the passengers got
out to lighten the car, Amphiteatrov warned them to stay
in the road, for mines were planted everywhere under the
stubble. Showering muck and splinters all over them, the
car lurched free. On they went.

Pug gave up trying to guess the direction. They never
passed a road marker or signpost. The low gray clouds
showed no sun patch. In the forest of the earthworm soldiers, the artillery thumps had been fainter than in the
village. Here they were considerably louder. But zigzags in
the front line could cause that. Obviously they had stopped
going west, because westward were the Germans. The car
appeared to be meandering five miles or so behind the fire
zone.

"Here we will go a bit out of the way," the tank colonel
said at another crossroads, "but you will see something
interesting." They entered fields where tall yellow-green
stalks of grain stood unharvested and rotting. After a mile
or so Amphiteatrov told the driver to stop. "Perhaps you
won't mind stretching your legs," he said. "You all have
nice thick boots." He gave Pamela an odd look. "But you
might find this walk boring. Perhaps you will stay with the
driver here?"

"I'll come, unless you tell me to stay."

"Very well. Come."

They went pushing in among the stalks. The wet quiet
field of overripe grain smelled sweet, almost like an or-

chard. But the visitors, squelching along behind Amphiteatrov in a file, soon glanced at each other in revulsion as a
rotten stench hit their noses. They broke into a clear space
and saw why. They were looking at a battlefield.

In every direction, the grain was crushed flat in great
crisscrossing swathes of brown muck. Random patches of
stalks still stood; and amid the long brown slashes and the
green-yellow clumps, damaged tanks lay scattered on their
sides, or turned clear over, or canted, their camouflage
paint blistered and burned black, their caterpillar tracks
torn, their armor plate blown open. Seven of the tanks bore
German markings; two were light Russian T-26 tanks,
such as Pug had often seen moving through Moscow. The
stink rose from German corpses, sprawled in green uniforms here and there on the ground, and others slumped
in blown-open tanks. Their dead purple faces were bloated
disgustingly and covered with fat black flies, but one could
see they had been youngsters. Pamela turned pale and
clapped a handkerchief to her face.

"Well, I am sorry," said the colonel, an ugly gleam lighting his face. "This happened only day before yesterday.
These Fritzes were probing and got caught. Their comrades went away from here and wouldn't stop to dig proper
graves, being in a slight hurry."

Helmets, papers, and broken bottles were littered among
the tanks and the corpses, and the oddest sight was a mess
of women's underwear—pink, blue, and white drawers and
petticoats—heaped soiled and sodden in the mud near an
overturned tank. Pamela, eyebrows rising over the handkerchief, pointed to these.

"Well, funny, isn't it? I suppose Fritz stole those from a
village. The Germans steal everything they can lay their
hands on. That is why they have come into our country,
after all—to steal. We had a tough tank fight around
Vyazma a month ago. One tank we blew up had a large
fine marble clock in it, and also a dead pig. The fire ruined
that pig. That was a pity. It was a very good pig. Well, I
thought this might interest you."

Pictures of knocked-out panzers were common in Moscow, but before this Victor Henry had seen actual German
tanks only in Berlin, clanking down boulevards lined with
red swastika flags, to the blare of brass-band marches over

the loudspeakers and the hurrahs of crowds giving Nazi salutes; or else massed factory-fresh on trains of flat cars, chugging to the front. Seeing a few broken and overturned in a desolate Russian cornfield two thousand miles from Berlin, with their crewmen rotting beside them in the mud, was a hard jolt. He said to the tank colonel, "Aren't these Mark Threes? How could your T-26's knock them out? They don't fire a shell that can penetrate the Mark Three."

Amphiteatrov grinned. "Well, very good. For a seaman you know a bit about tank warfare. But you had better ask the battalion commander who won this battle, so let us be on our way."

They backtracked to the crossroads, headed toward the forest, and arrived at what looked like an open-air machine shop for tank repairs, in a village of a dozen or so thatched log cabins straggling along the road through wild woods. Detached caterpillar tracks stretched long and straight on the ground under the trees; bogie wheels were off; guns were off; and on every side men in black or blue coveralls hammered, filed, greased, and welded, shouting in Russian and laughing at each other. Strolling down the street in an olive-colored greatcoat too large for him, a short, hook-nosed, swarthy officer broke into a trot when he saw the black automobile. He saluted the colonel, then the two embraced and kissed. Introducing the visitors, Amphiteatrov said, "Major Kaplan, I showed our friends those busted German tanks out there. Our American Navy friend asked a real tankist's question. He asked, how could T-26's knock out Panzer Mark Threes?"

The battalion commander grinned from ear to ear, clapped Victor Henry on the back, and said in Russian, "Good, come this way." Beyond the last cabin, he led them into the woods, past two lines of light tanks ranged under the trees and draped with camouflage netting over their own green-and-sand blotches. "Here we are," he said proudly. "This is how we knocked out the Mark Threes."

Dispersed in the thickets, all but invisible under branches and nets, five armored monsters thrust heavy square turrets with giant guns high in the air. Tudsbury's mouth fell open, as he stared up at them. He nervously brushed his moustaches with a knuckle. "My God! What are these things?"

"Our newest Russian tank," said Amphiteatrov. "General Yevlenko thought it might interest President Roosevelt."

"Fantastic!" said Talky. "Why, I'd heard you had these monsters, but—What do they weigh? A hundred tons? *Look* at that gun!"

The Russians smiled at each other. Amphiteatrov said, "It's a good tank."

Tudsbury asked if they might climb inside one and to Pug's surprise the colonel agreed. Young tankists helped the lame fat Englishman to the hatch, as Pug scrambled up. Inside the command turret, despite the clutter of machinery and instruments and the bulky gun breech, there was a lot of elbowroom. The machine smelled startlingly like a new car; Pug guessed this came from the heavy leather seats for the gunner and the commander. He knew very little about tanks, but the workmanship of the raw metal interior seemed good, despite some crude instrument brackets and wiring. The dials, valves, and controls had an old-fashioned German look.

"Great God, Henry, it's a land battleship," Tudsbury said. "When I think of the tiny tin cans we rode in! Why, the best German tanks today are eggshells to this. Bloody eggshells! What a surprise!"

When they climbed out, soldiers were clustering around the tank, perhaps a hundred or more, with others coming through the trees. On the flat hull stood Pamela, embarrassed and amused under the male stares. Bundled in mud-caked lambskin, Pamela was not a glamorous object, but her presence seemed to thrill and hypnotize the tankists. A pale moonfaced officer with glasses and long yellow teeth stood beside her. Major Kaplan introduced him as the political officer. "The commissar would like to present all of you to the troops," said Amphiteatrov to Victor Henry, "as he feels this visit is a serious occasion that can be used to bolster their fighting spirit."

"By all means," Victor Henry said.

He could understand only fragments of the strident, quick-tumbling harangue of the moonfaced commissar, but the earnest tones, the waving fist, the Communist slogans, the innocent, attentive faces of the handsome young tankists, made a clear enough picture. The commissar's speech was half a revivalist sermon and half a football coach's pep talk. Suddenly the soldiers applauded, and Amphiteatrov began to translate, in bursts of three or four sentences at a time, during which the moon face beamed at him:

"In the name of the Red Army, I now welcome the American naval captain, Genry, the British war correspondent, Tudsbury, and especially the brave English newspaperwoman, Pamela, to our front. It is always good for a fighting man's morale to see a pretty face." *(Laughter among the men.)* "But we have no evil thoughts, Miss Tudsbury, we think only of our own little sweethearts back home, naturally. Besides, your father has wisely come along to protect you from the romantic and virile young Russian tankists." *(Laughter and handclaps.)* "You have showed us that the British and American peoples have not forgotten us in our struggle against the Fascist hyenas.

"Comrade Stalin has said that the side which has more petroleum engines will win this war. Why is the petroleum engine so important? Because petroleum is the biggest source of energy today, and energy wins wars. We tankists know that! Hitler and the Germans thought they would make a lot of petroleum engines in a hurry, put them in tanks and aircraft, and steal a march on the world. Hitler even hoped that certain ruling circles in America and England would help him once he decided to attack the peaceful Soviet people. Well, he miscalculated. These two great nations have formed an unshakable front with the Soviet peoples. That is what the presence of our visitors shows us. We three countries possess many more petroleum engines than the Germans, and since we can manufacture still more engines faster than they can, because we have much larger industries, we will win this war.

"We will win it faster if our friends will hasten to send us plentiful war supplies, because the Nazi bandits will not quit until we have killed a great many of them. Above all, we will win much faster if our British allies will open a second front at once and kill some German soldiers too. Certain people think it is impossible to beat Germans. So let me ask this battalion: have you fought Germans?"

Twilight had fallen during the harangue, and Pug could barely see the nearest soldiers' faces. A roar came from the darkness: *"DA!"*

"Have you beaten them?"

"*DA!*"

"Are you afraid of Germans?"

"*NYET!*"—and barking male laughter.

"Do you think the British should be afraid to open a second front against them?"

"*NYET!*"—and more laughter, and another bellow, like a college cheer, in Russian, "*Second front now! Second front now!*"

"Thank you, my comrades. And now to dinner, and then back to our tanks, in which we have won many victories and will win more, for our socialist motherland, our sweethearts, our mothers, our wives, and our children, and for Comrade Stalin!"

A tremendous college cheer in the gloom: "*WE SERVE THE SOVIET UNION!*"

"The meeting is over," hoarsely cried the commissar, as the moon rose over the trees.

.   .   .

Pug came awake from restless sleep on a straw pallet, on the dirt floor of a log cabin. Beside him in blackness Talky Tudsbury liquidly snored. Groping for a cigarette and lighting it, he saw Pamela as the match flared upright on the only bed, her back to the plastered log wall, her eyes glittering. "Pam?"

"Hello there. I still feel as though we're bumping and sliding in mud. D'you suppose if I stepped outside, a sentry would shoot me?"

"Let's try. I'll step out first. If I get shot, you go back to bed."

"Oh, that's a fine plan. Thank you."

Pug pulled on the cigarette, and in the red glow Pamela came over and clasped hands. Moving along the rough wall, Pug found the door and opened a blue rectangle in the dark. "I'll be damned. Moon. Stars."

A high moon, partly veiled by swift-rolling clouds, dusted the thatched huts and the rutted empty road bluegray. Across the road in the woods, soldiers were sadly singing to an accordion. Victor Henry and Pamela Tudsbury sat down on a rough bench, hands clasped, huddling close in the frigid wind which blew straight up the road. Underfoot the mud was ridged hard.

"Dear God," Pamela said, "it's a long long way to Tipperary, isn't it?"

"Washington, D.C.'s even further."

"Thanks for bringing me out, Victor. I was sitting there not daring to move. I love the smell of the countryside, but lord, that wind cuts you!"

Yellow flashes ran along the sky and loud thumps followed fast. Pamela winced against him, with a little gasp. "Oh, oh! Look at that. Talky was a pig to drag me out here, wasn't he? Of course it suits him. He dictated two hours by candlelight tonight, and he couldn't have written a line himself. It's quite a story, I'll say that. Are those tanks as startling as he claims? He says in his last sentence that if the Soviet Union can mass-produce them, the war's as good as over."

"Well, that's journalism. Size isn't everything. Any tank, no matter how big, can be an incinerator for crews if it's built wrong. How maneuverable is it? How vulnerable is it? The Germans'll find the weak spots. They'll rush out a new gun that can penetrate these things. They're good at that. Still, it's quite a tank."

"Count on you!" Pamela laughed. "I think that was why I couldn't sleep. I had this vision of the war coming to a sudden end. It was such a weird, dazzling idea! The Germans beaten, Hitler dead or locked up, the lights going on again in London, the big cleanup, and then life continuing the way it used to be! All because of these monster tanks rolling by the thousands to Berlin—my God, those guns do sound close."

"It's a pipe dream," Victor Henry said. "The Germans are winning. We're pretty close to Moscow here, Pam."

After a silence she said, looking up at the moon and stars and then at Pug's shadowy face, "When you just said those tanks couldn't end the war, do you know what? I felt relieved. Relieved! What kind of mad reaction was that?"

"Well, the war's something different, while it lasts." Victor Henry gestured at the angry yellow flare-ups on the black western clouds. "The expensive fireworks—the travel to strange places—"

"The interesting company," Pamela said.

"Yes, Pam. The interesting company."

The accordion was playing alone now, a plaintive tune like a lullaby, half drowned by the cracking and sighing of trees in the wind.

"What is that sensation of sudden remembering supposed to mean?" she said. "The sort of thing you felt yesterday at the Tolstoy place?"

Pug said, "Isn't it a kind of short circuit in the brain? Some irrelevant stimulus triggers off the sense of recognition when it shouldn't. So I once read."

"On the *Bremen,* the second day out," said Pamela, "I was walking the deck in the morning. And so were you, going the other way. We passed each other twice. It was getting silly. I decided to ask you, next time we passed, to walk with me. And I suddenly knew you'd ask me. I knew the exact words you'd use. You used them. I made a remark about your wife as though I were acting a play, and your answer came like the next line in the play, all old and familiar. I've never forgotten that."

A tall soldier, muffled in his greatcoat, trudged by with smoking breath, the unsheathed bayonet of his rifle glinting in the moonlight. He stopped to glance at them, and passed on.

"Where are we heading tomorrow, Victor?"

"I'm going into the front line. You and Talky will stay in a town several miles back. Up front one sometimes has to make a dash for it, the colonel says, and of course Talky can't do that."

"Why must you go?"

"Well, Amphiteatrov offered. It'll be informative."

"This is the flight to Berlin again."

"No. I'll be on the ground all the way, on friendly territory. Quite a difference."

"How long will you be gone from us?"

"Just a few hours."

A green radiance blinded them, a sudden blaze filling the heavens. Pamela uttered a cry. As their pupils adjusted to the shock, they saw four smoky green lights floating very slowly down below the thickening clouds, and heard the thrum of engines. The sentry had darted off the road. The village showed no sign of life: a tiny sleeping Russian hamlet of thatched huts in the woods on a mud road, like a hundred others, with a stage-setting appearance in the artificial glare. All the tanks under repair had been camouflaged.

"You look ghastly," Pam said.

"You should see yourself. They're searching for this tank battalion."

The lights sank earthward. One turned orange and went out. The airplane sounds faded away. Pug glanced at his watch. "I used to think the Russians were nutty on camouflage, but it has its points." He stiffly rose and opened the cabin door. "We'd better try to sleep."

Pamela put a hand out, palm up to the black sky. The clouds were blotting out the moon and stars. "I thought I felt something." She held her hand toward Pug. In the light of the last falling flare he could see, melting on her palm, a fat snowflake.

55

THE car crossed a white bare plain in a steady snowfall in leaden light. Pug could see no road by which the driver guided the jolting, sliding, shaking machine. What about mines? Trusting that Amphiteatrov had no more appetite than he to get blown up, Pug said nothing. In about an hour an onion-top belfry of yellow brick loomed ahead through the veil of snow. They entered a town where soldiers milled and army trucks lurched on mud streets between unpainted wood houses. From some trucks the livid, bloody, bandaged faces of soldiers peered sadly. Villagers, mostly snow-flecked old women and boys, stood in front of the houses, dourly watching the traffic go by.

At the steps of the yellow brick church, Pug parted company with the others. A political officer in a belted white leather coat, with the slanted eyes of a Tartar and a little beard like Lenin's, came to take him off in a small British jeep. Talky Tudsbury happily said in Russian, pointing to the trademark, "Ah, so British aid has reached the front at last!" The political officer replied in ragged English that it required men and gunfire, not automobiles, to stop Germans, and that the British vehicles were not strong enough for heavy duty.

Pamela gave Victor Henry a serious wide-eyed stare. Despite the wear and soil of travel she looked charming, and the lambskin hat was tilted jauntily on her head. "Watch yourself," was all she said.

The jeep went west, out of the tumultuous town and into a snow-laden quiet forest. They appeared to be heading straight for the front, yet the only gunfire thumps came from the left, to the south. Pug thought the snow might be muffling the sound up ahead. He saw many newly splintered trees, and bomb craters lined with fresh snow. The Germans had been shelling the day before, the commissar said, trying in vain to draw the fire of Russian batteries hidden in the woods. The jeep bounced past some of these batteries: big horse-drawn howitzers, tended by weary-looking bewhiskered soldiers amid evergreens and piles of shells at the ready.

They came to a line of crude trenches through the smashed fallen trees, with high earthworks sugared by snow. These were dummy dugouts, the commissar said, deliberately made highly visible. They had taken much of the shellfire yesterday. The real trenches, a couple of hundred yards further on, had escaped. Dug along a riverbank, their log tops level with the ground and snowed over, the actual trenches were totally invisible. The commissar parked the jeep among trees, and he and Victor Henry crawled the rest of the way through the brush. "The less movement the Fritzes can observe, the better," said the Russian.

Here, down in a deep muddy hole—a machine-gun post manned by three soldiers—Victor Henry peered through a gun slit piled with sandbags and saw Germans. They were working in plain view across the river with earth-moving machines, pontoons, rubber boats, and trucks.

Some dug with shovels; some patrolled with light machine guns in hand. Unlike the Russians, concealed like wild creatures in the earth, the Germans were making no effort to hide themselves or what they were doing. Except for the helmets, guns, and long gray coats, they might have been a big crew on a peacetime construction job. Through binoculars handed him by a soldier—German binoculars—Victor Henry could see the eyeglasses and frost-purpled cheeks and noses of Hitler's chilled men. "You could shoot them like birds," he said in Russian. It was as close as he could come to the American idiom, "they're sitting ducks."

The soldier grunted. "Yes, and give away our position, and start them shelling us! No thanks, Gospodin American."

"If they ever get that bridge finished," said the commissar, "and start coming across, that'll be time enough to shoot a big dose down their throats."

"That's what we're waiting for," said a pipe-smoking soldier with heavy drooping moustaches, who appeared to be in command of this hole in the ground.

Pug said, "Do you really think you can hold out if they get across?"

The three soldiers rolled their eyes at each other, weighing this question asked in bad Russian by a foreigner. Their mouths set sourly. Here, for the first time, in sight of the Germans, Victor Henry detected fear on Red Army faces. "Well, if it comes to that," said the pipe smoker, "every man has his time. A Russian soldier knows how to die."

The political officer said briskly, "A soldier's duty is to live, comrade, not to die—to live and fight. They won't get across. Our big guns are trained on this crossing, and as soon as they've wasted all the time it takes to build a bridge, and they start across, we'll blast these Hitlerite rats! Eh, Polikov? How about it?"

"That's right," said a bristle-faced soldier with a runny nose, crouched on the earth in a corner blowing on his red hands. "That's exactly right, Comrade Political Officer."

Crawling through bushes or darting from tree to tree, Victor Henry and the commissar made their way along the dugouts, pillboxes, trenches, and one-man posts of the thinly held line. A battalion of nine hundred men was covering five miles of the river here, the commissar said, to deny the Germans access to an important road. "This campaign is simply a race," he panted, as they crawled between dugouts. "The Germans are trying to beat Father Frost into Moscow. That's the plain fact of it. They are pouring out their lifeblood to do it. But never fear, Father Frost is an old friend of Russia. He'll freeze them dead in the ice. You'll see, they'll never make it."

The commissar was evidently on a morale-stiffening mission. Here and there, where they found a jolly leader in a trench, the men seemed ready for the fight, but elsewhere fatalism darkened their eyes, slumped their shoulders, and showed in dirty weapons, disarrayed uniforms, and garbage-strewn holes. The commissar harangued them, exploiting the strange presence of an American to buck them up, but for the most part the hairy-faced Slavs stared at Henry with sarcastic incredulity as though to say—*"If you're really an American, why are you so stupid as to come here yourself? We have no choice, worse luck."*

The Germans were in view all along the river, methodically and calmly preparing to cross. Their businesslike air was more intimidating, Pug thought, than volleys of bullets. Their numbers were alarming, too; where did they all come from?

The commissar and Victor Henry emerged from one of the largest dugouts and lay on their elbows in the snow. "Well, I have finished my tour of this part of the line, Captain. Perhaps you will rejoin your party now."

"I'm ready."

With a grim little smile, the commissar stumbled to his feet. "Keep in the shadows of the trees."

When they got back to the jeep, Pug said, "How far are we from Moscow here?"

"Oh, quite far enough." The commissar whirred the noisy engine. "I hope you saw what you wanted to see."

"I saw a lot," Victor Henry said.

The commissar turned his Lenin-like face at the American, appraising him with suspicious eyes. "It is not easy to understand the front just by looking at it."

"I understand that you need a second front."

The commissar uttered a brutal grunt. "Then you understand the main thing. But even without the second front, if we must, Captain Genry, we ourselves will smash this plague of German cockroaches."

By the time they reached the central square of the town, the snowfall had stopped and patches of fast-moving blue showed through the clouds. The wind was bitter cold. The tangle of trucks, wagons, horses, and soldiers was worse than before. Vehement Russian cursing and arguing filled the air. The old women and the wrinkle-faced boys still watched the disorder with round sad eyes. In a big jam of vehicles around two fallen horses and an overturned ammunition wagon, the jeep encountered the black automobile. Talky Tudsbury, in great spirits, stood near forty yelling soldiers and officers, watching the horses kick and struggle in tangled traces, while other soldiers gathered up long coppery shells that had spilled from burst boxes and lay softly gleaming in the snow. "Hello there! Back already? What a mess! It's a wonder the whole wagon didn't go up with a bang, what? And leave a hole a hundred feet across."

"Where's Pamela?"

Tudsbury flipped a thumb over his shoulder. "Back at the church. An artillery spotter is stationed in the belfry. There's supposed to be a great view, but I couldn't climb the damned tower. She's up there making some notes. How are things at the front? You've got to give me the whole picture. Brrr! What frost, eh? Do you suppose Jerry is starting to feel it in his balls a bit? Hullo, they've got the horses up."

Amphiteatrov said he was taking Tudsbury to see a downed Junker 88 in the nearby field. Pug told him that he had seen plenty of Junker 88's; he would join Pam in the church and wait for them. Amphiteatrov made an annoyed face. "All right, but please remain there, Captain. We'll come back in twenty minutes or less."

Pug said good-bye to the bearded commissar, who was sitting at the wheel of the jeep, bellowing at a scrawny soldier who clutched a live white goose. The soldier was coarsely shouting back, and the goose turned its orange beak and little eyes from one to the other as though trying to learn its fate. Making his way around the traffic tangle, Pug walked to the church on crunching squeaking dry snow. Freedom from the escort—even for a few minutes—felt strange and good. Inside the church, a strong unchurchlike miasma of medicine and disinfectant filled the air; peeling frescoes of blue big-eyed saints looked down from grimy walls, at bandaged soldiers who lay on straw mats smoking, talking to each other, or sadly staring. The narrow stone staircase spiralling up the inside of the belfry with no handholds made Pug queasy, but up he went, edging along the rough wall, to a wooden platform level with big rusty bells, where wind gusted through four open brick arches. Here he caught his breath, and mounted a shaky wooden ladder.

"Victor!" As he emerged on the topmost brick walk, Pam waved and called to him.

Seen this close, the bulging onion dome was a crude job of tin sheets nailed rustily on a curving frame. Squared around it was a yellow brick walk and parapet, where Pamela crouched in a corner, out of the whistling wind. The artillery spotter, shapeless and faceless in an ankle-length brown coat, mittens, goggles, and fastened-down thick earflaps, manned giant binoculars on a tripod, pointed west. A fat black tomcat beside Pamela crouched over a bowl of soup, lapping, shaking its big head in distaste, and lapping again. Pamela and the spotter were laughing at the cat. "Too much pepper, kitty?" Pamela's gay flirtatious look showed she clearly was enjoying herself. Below, the bare plain stretched far east and south to distant forests, and west and north to the black wriggling river and sparse woods. Straight downward the town, a clot of life, made thin noise in an empty white flat world.

"*Vy Amerikanski offitzer?*" The spotter showed fine teeth in the hairy uncovered patch of his face.

"*Da.*"

"*Posmotritye?*" The mittened hand tapped the binoculars.

"*Videte nemtzi?*" Pug said. ("Can you see Germans?")

"*Slishkom m'nogo.*" ("Too many.")

"*Odin slishkom m'nogo,*" Pug said. ("One is too many!")

With a grim nod and chuckle the spotter stepped away from the binoculars. Pug's eyes were watering from the wind; he put them to the eyepieces and the Germans on the riverbank leaped into sight, blurry and small, still at the same work.

"Doesn't it give you an eerie feeling?" Pam said, stroking the cat. "They're so calm about it."

Victor Henry went to a corner of the brick parapet and surveyed the snowy vista through all points of the compass, hands jammed in his blue coat. The spotter, turning the binoculars from south to north, made a slow sweep along the river, talking into a battered telephone on a long black wire that dangled over the parapet.

"Kitty, don't forget behind the ears." The cat was washing itself, and Pamela scratched its head.

Pug told her about his trip, meanwhile scanning the horizon round and round as though he were on a flying bridge. An odd movement in the distant snowy forest caught his notice. With his back to the spotter, he peered intently eastward, shielding his eyes with one chapped red hand. "Pass me those." She handed him small field glasses, in an open case beside the binocular stand. One quick look, and Pug tapped the spotter's shoulder and pointed. Swinging the large binoculars halfway round on the tripod, the spotter started with surprise, pulled off goggles and cap, and looked again. He had a lot of curly blond hair and freckles, and he was only eighteen or twenty. Snatching up the telephone, he jiggled the hook, talked, jiggled some more, and gestured anger at no answer. Pulling on his cap, he went trampling down the ladder.

"What is it?" Pamela said.

"Take a look."

Pamela saw through the big eyepieces of the spotter's instrument a column of machines coming out of the woods.

"Tanks?"

"Some are trucks and armored personnel cars. But yes, it's a tank unit." Victor Henry, glasses to his eyes, talked as though he were watching a parade.

"Aren't they Russians?"

"No."

"But that's the direction we came from."

"Yes."

They looked each other in the eyes. Her red-cheeked face showed fear, but also a trace of nervous gaiety. "Then aren't we in a pickle? Shouldn't we get down out of here and find Amphiteatrov?"

To the naked eye the armored column was like a tiny black worm on the broad white earth, five or six miles away. Pug stared eastward, thinking. The possibilities of this sudden turn were too disagreeable to be put into words. He felt a flash of anger at Tudsbury's selfish dragging of his daughter into hazard. Of course, nobody had planned on being surprised in the rear by Germans; but there they were! If the worst came to the worst, he felt he could handle himself with German captors, though there might be ugly moments with soldiers before he could talk to an officer. But the Tudsburys were enemies.

"I'll tell you, Pam," he said, watching the worm pull clear of the forest and move sluggishly toward the town, leaving a black trail behind, "the colonel knows where we are now. Let's stick here for a while."

"All right. How in God's name did the Germans get around back there?"

"Amphiteatrov said there was trouble to the south. They must have broken across the river and hooked through the woods. It's not a large unit, it's a probe."

The top of the ladder danced and banged under a heavy tread. The blond youngster came up, seized a stadimeter, pointed it at the Germans, and slid a vernier back and forth. Hastily flattening out a small black and white grid map on one knee, he barked numbers into the telephone: "Five point six! One two four! R seven M twelve! That's right! That's right!" Animated and cheery now, he grinned at the visitors. "Our batteries are training on them. When they're good and close, we'll blow them to bits. So maybe you'll see something yet." He put on his goggles, changing back from a bright-eyed boy into a faceless grim spotter.

Victor Henry said, "They're watching across the river for your batteries to fire."

The spotter clumsily waved both heavy-clad arms. "Good, but we can't let those bastards take the town from the rear, can we?"

"I hear airplanes." Pug turned his glasses westward to the sky. *"Samalyutti!"*

"Da!" Swivelling and tilting the binoculars upward, the spotter began to shout into the phone.

"Airplanes too?" Pamela's voice trembled. "Well, I'm more used to them."

"That's the German drill," said Victor Henry. "Tanks and planes together."

The oncoming planes, three Stukas, were growing bigger in Pug's glasses. The spotter switched his binoculars to the tanks again, and began cheering. Pug looked in that direction. "Holy cow! Now I call this military observing, Pam." Tanks in another column were coming out of the woods about halfway between the Germans and the town, moving on a course almost at right angles to the panzer track. He handed her the glasses and squinted toward the airplanes.

"Oh! Oh!" Pamela exclaimed. "Ours?"

"*Da!*" cried the spotter, grinning at her. "*Nashi! Nashi!*"

A hand struck her shoulder and knocked her to her hands and knees. "They're starting their dive," Victor Henry said. "Crawl up close to the dome and lie still." He was on his knees beside her. His cap had fallen off and rolled away, and he brushed black hair from his eyes to watch the planes. They tilted over and dove. When they were not much higher than the belfry, bombs fell out of them. With a mingled engine roar and wind screech, they zoomed by. Pug could see the black crosses, the swastikas, the yellowish plexiglass cockpits. All around the church the bombs began exploding. The belfry shook. Flame, dirt, and smoke roared up beyond the parapet, but Pug remained clearheaded enough to note that the flying was ragged. The three ungainly black machines almost collided as they climbed and turned to dive again in a reckless tangle. The Luftwaffe had either lost most of its veteran pilots by now, he thought, or they were not flying on this sector of the front. Anti-aircraft guns were starting to pop and rattle in the town.

Pamela's hand sought his. She was crouched behind him, against the dome.

"Just lie low, this will be over soon." As Pug said this he saw one of the Stukas separating from the others and diving straight for the belfry. He shouted to the spotter, but the airplane noise, the chatter of A.A. guns, the clamor and cries from the town below, and the roar of the wind, quite drowned his voice. Tracers made a red dotted line to the belfry across the gray sky. The tin dome began to sing to rhythmically striking bullets. Victor Henry roughly pushed Pamela flat and threw himself on top of her. The plane stretched into a sizable black machine approaching through the air. Watching over his shoulder to the last, Victor Henry saw the pilot dimly behind his plexiglass, an unhelmeted young blond fellow with a toothy grin. He thought the youngster was going to crash into the dome, and as he winced, he felt something rip at his left shoulder. The airplane scream and roar and whiz mounted, went past, and diminished. The zinging and rattling of bullets stopped.

Pug stood, feeling his shoulder. His sleeve was torn open at the very top and the shoulder board was dangling, but there was no blood. The spotter was lying on the bricks beside the overturned binoculars. Bombs were exploding below; the other two planes were still whistling and roaring over the town; one plane was smoking badly. Blood was pooling under the spotter's head, and with horror Pug perceived white broken bone of the skull showing through the torn shot-away cap, under blond hair and thick-moving red and gray ooze. Pug went to the spotter and cautiously moved his goggles. The blue eyes were open, fixed and empty. The head wound was catastrophic. Picking up the telephone, Pug jiggled the hook till somebody answered. He shouted in Russian, "I am the American visitor up here. You understand?"

He saw the smoking plane, which was trying to climb, burst into flames and fall. *"Da!* Where is Konstantin?" The voice sounded exhilarated.

"Airplane killed him."

"All right. Somebody else will come."

Pamela had crawled beside the spotter and was looking at the dead face and smashed head. "Oh, my God, my God," she sobbed, head in hand.

The two surviving planes were climbing out of sight. Smoke rose from fires in the town, smelling of burning hay. To the east, the two tank unit tracks had almost joined in a black V, miles long, across the plain. Pug righted the binoculars. Through smoke billowing in the line of vision, he saw the tanks milling in a wild little yellow-flashing vortex on the broad white plain. Five of the KV monsters bulged among lighter Russian tanks. Several German tanks were on fire and their crewmen were running here and there in the snow like ants. Some German tanks and trucks were heading back to the woods. Pug saw only one light Russian tank giving off black smoke. But even as he watched, a KV burst into violent, beautiful purple-orange flame, casting a vivid pool of color on the snow. Meantime the rest of the German tanks began turning away.

"Kitty! Oh, Christ, Christ, no, stop it!"

Pam snatched up the cat, which was crouching over the dead man. She came to Pug, her tearstained face gaunt and stunned, holding the creature in her arms. Its nose and whiskers were bloody and its tongue flickered. "It's not the animal's fault," she choked.

"The Russians are winning out there," Victor Henry said.

She was staring at him with blank shocked round eyes, clutching the black cat close to her. Her hand went to the rip at his shoulder. "Dearest, are you hurt?"

"No. Not at all. It went right on through."

"Thank God! Thank God!"

The ladder jumped and rapped, and Colonel Amphiteatrov's face, excited and red, showed at the top. "Well, you're all right. Well, I'm glad. Many people killed. Quick! Both of you. Come along, please." Then his eye fell on the body lying in blood. "*Agh!*"

"We were strafed," Pug said. "He's dead."

The colonel shook his head and sank out of sight, saying, "Well, please, come quickly."

"Go first, Pam."

Pamela looked at the dead spotter lying on the bricks in snow and blood, and then at the tin dome, and out at the tank fight, and the black V gouged in the landscape. "It seems I've been up here for a week. I can't get down the ladder with the cat. We mustn't leave it here."

"Give the cat to me."

Tucking the animal inside his bridge coat, steadying it with one arm, Victor Henry awkwardly followed her down the ladder and the spiral stairs. Once the cat squirmed, bit, and scratched, and he almost fell. He turned the cat loose outside the church, but the clanking vehicles or the rolling smoke alarmed the animal and it ran back in and vanished among the wounded.

Through the open door of the black automobile Tudsbury waved his cane at them. "Hello! There's a monstrous tank battle going on just outside the town! They say there's at least a hundred tanks swirling around, an utter inferno, happening right this minute! Hello, you've torn your coat, do you know that?"

"Yes, I know." Though drained of spirit, Victor Henry was able to smile at the gap between journalism and war, as he detached his shoulder board and dropped it in his pocket. The reality of the two small groups of tanks banging away out there on the snowy plain seemed so pale and small-scale compared to Tudsbury's description.

"We had a view of it," he said. Pamela got into the car and sank into a corner of the back seat, closing her eyes.

"Did you? Well, Pam ought to be a help on this story! I say, Pam, you're all right, aren't you?"

"I'm splendid, Talky, thank you," Pam said, faintly but clearly.

Pug said to the colonel, "We saw the Germans starting to run."

"Good. Well, Kaplan's battalion got the word from down south. That is a good battalion." Amphiteatrov slammed the car door. "Make yourselves comfortable please. We are going to drive straight back to Moscow now."

"Oh no!" Tudsbury's fat face wrinkled up like an infant's. "I want to have a look when the fight's over. I want to interview the tank crews."

Amphiteatrov turned and faced them, and showed his gums and teeth without smiling. Behind him through the frosted windshield they could vaguely see on the main street of the town smoke, fire, a plunging horse, soldiers running, and green army trucks in a slow-moving jam. "Well, there has been a very big breakthrough in the north. Moscow is in danger. Well, all foreign missions will be evacuated to the Caucasus. We must skedaddle." He brought out the awkward slang word humorlessly, and turned to the driver. *"Nu, skoro!"*

Under the blanket stretched across the passengers' legs,

Pamela Tudsbury's gloved hand groped to Victor Henry's hand. She pulled off her glove, twined her cold fingers in his, and pressed her face against the torn shoulder of his bridge coat. His chapped hand tightened on hers.

56

LESLIE SLOTE heard footfalls in the dark, as he sat in an overcoat and fur hat, working by the light of a kerosene lamp. His desk overflowing with papers and reports stood directly under the grand unlit chandelier in the marble-pillared great hall of Spaso House, the ambassador's Moscow residence.

"Who's there?" The nervous strident words reverberated in the empty halls. He recognized the white Navy cap, white scarf, and brass buttons, before he could make out the face. "Ye gods, Captain Henry, why didn't they take you straight to the Kazan Station? Maybe you can still make it. You've got to get out of Moscow tonight!"

"I've been to the station. The train to Kuibyshev had left." Pug brushed snow from his shoulders. "The air raid held us up outside the city."

Slote looked at his wristwatch in great agitation. "But—that's terrible! God knows when there'll be another train to Kuibyshev—if ever. Don't you know that one German armored column's already passed by to the north and is cutting down behind the city? And they say another pincer is heading up from Kaluga. One doesn't know what to believe any more, but it's at least conceivable that in the next twenty-four hours we may be entirely surrounded. It begins to smell like Warsaw all over again." Slote gaily laughed. "Sorry there are no chairs, a party of mad

Georgian workmen came in and covered and stacked all the furniture—oh, there's a stool after all, do sit down—"

Pug said, "That's more than I know, about the German pincers, and I've just come from the Narkomindel." He sat down without opening his coat. It was almost as cold and dark in Spaso House as in the snowstorm outside.

"Did you suppose they'd tell you anything? I got this straight from the Swedish ambassador, I assure you, at nine o'clock tonight in the dining room at the Kazan Station, when I was seeing off the staff. My God, that station was a spectacle to remember! One bomb hit would have wiped out all the foreign correspondents and nine-tenths of the diplomats in Russia—and a healthy chunk of the Soviet bureaucracy too."

"Have all the typewriters been stowed? I have to write a report."

"There are typewriters in Colonel Yeaton's office. I have a skeleton staff, and we're to keep things going somehow until the chargé gets organized in Kuibyshev." Slote gave this answer with absentminded calm, then jumped at a muffled sound from outside. "Was that a bomb? You have no time to write reports, Captain. It's really my responsibility to see that you leave Moscow at once, and I must insist that somehow—"

Pug held up a hand. "The Nark's making arrangements. There are other stragglers like me. I have to check back in at eleven in the morning."

"Oh! Well, if the Narkomindel's assumed responsibility, that's that," Slote giggled.

Victor Henry looked narrowly at him. "How come you got stuck with this duty again? It seems kind of thick, after Warsaw."

"I volunteered. You look skeptical. I truly did. After all, I've been through the drill. I wasn't too proud of the job I did in Warsaw and I thought perhaps I could redeem myself this time."

"Why, Byron told me you did a helluva job in Warsaw, Leslie."

"Did he? Byron's a gentleman. A knight, almost. Which reminds me, an enormous pouch came in from Stockholm the day you left. There was stuff from Rome. Would you like to see a picture of your new grandson?" Fussing through papers on his desk, he pulled a photograph from a wrinkled envelope. "There he is. Don't you think he's handsome?"

The lamplight carved deep black marks in the naval officer's face as he read the writing on the back of the snapshot, *For old Slote—Louis Henry, aged 11 days, with circus fat lady,* then contemplated the photograph. A plump, hollow-eyed Natalie in a loose robe held a baby that looked startlingly like Byron as an infant. The triangular face, the large serious eyes, the comically determined look, the fine blond hair—they were the same; Louis was another print of the template that had molded his son. He was much more of a Henry than Janice's boy. Victor Henry cleared his choked-up throat. "Not bad. Natalie's right, she's gotten fat."

"Hasn't she though? Too much bed rest, she says. I'll bet the baby will be as clever as it's handsome. It looks clever." Victor Henry sat starting at the snapshot. Slote added, "Would you care to keep that?"

Henry at once extended it to him. "No, certainly not. She sent it to you."

"I'll only lose it, Captain Henry. I have a better picture of Natalie."

"Are you sure? All right." Victor Henry tried to express in an awkward smile the gratitude for which he could find no words. Carefully he put the print in an inner pocket.

"What about the Tudsburys?" Slote asked. "Are they stuck in Moscow too?"

"I left Talky trying to wangle a ride to Archangel for himself and Pam. The Russians are flying out some RAF pilot instructors. I'm sure he'll get on that plane."

"Good. Did you run into any trouble at the front? What an idiocy, dragging a girl out there!"

"Well, we heard some firing, and saw some Germans. I'd better get at this report. If Talky does fly out, I want to give him a copy to forward via London."

"Let me have a copy too, won't you? And another to go in the next pouch. *If* there is one."

"You're a pessimist, Slote."

"I'm a realist. I was in Warsaw. I know what the Germans can do."

"Do you know what the Russians can do?"

"I thought I did. I was the Red Army's biggest booster in the embassy, until—" Slote shrugged and turned to his desk, blowing his nose. "The only thing that really gets me is this stink of burning paper. My God, how it brings back Warsaw! The embassy absolutely reeks. We were burning and burning today, until the minute they all left. And there's still a ton that I've somehow got to get burned in the morning."

"All Moscow stinks of it," Pug said. "It's the damnedest thing to drive through a snowstorm and smell burned paper. The city's one unholy mess, Slote. Have you seen all the barbed wire and tangled steel girders blocking the bridges? And good Lord, the mob at that railway station! The traffic jams heading east with headlights blazing, blackout be damned! I didn't know there were that many trucks and cars in the whole Soviet Union. All piled with mattresses and old people and babies and what-all. And with those blue A.A. searchlights still swinging overhead— God knows why—and the snow and the wind, I tell you it's a real end-of-the-world feeling."

Slote chuckled. "Yes, isn't it? This exodus began the day you left. It's been snowballing. A convoy of government big shots left yesterday in a line of honking black limousines. Gad, you should have seen the faces of the people along the streets! I'm sure that triggered this panic. However, I give Stalin credit. He's staying on to the last, and that takes courage, because when Hitler catches Stalin he'll just hang him like a dog in Red Square. And he'll drag Lenin's mummy out of the tomb too, and string it up alongside to crumble in the wind. Oh, there'll be stirring things to see and record here, for whoever survives to tell it all."

Victor Henry rose. "Do you know there's no sentry at the door? I just walked in."

"That's impossible. We're guarded night and day by a soldier assigned by the Narkomindel."

"There's nobody there."

Slote opened and closed his mouth twice. "Are you positive? Why, we could be sacked by looters! It's getting near the end when soldiers leave their posts. I must call the Narkomindel. If I can get the operator to answer!" He jumped up and disappeared into the gloom.

Victor Henry groped to the military attaché's office. There he struck matches, and found and lit two kerosene lamps. In their bleak yellow-green glow he surveyed the office. Bits of black ash flecked the floor and every surface. BURN—URGENT was scrawled in red crayon on manila folders topping heaps of reports, files, and loose papers piled on the floor and in the leather armchair. Emptied drawers and files stood open; a swivel chair was overturned; the place looked as though it had been robbed. On the desk, on a typewriter with bunched tangled keys, a message was propped, printed in block letters on torn cardboard: IMPERATIVE—BURN TONIGHT CONTENTS SECOND BROWN LOCKED FILE. (L. SLOTE HAS COMBINATION.) Pug cleared the desk, untangled the typewriter keys and stood the lamps on either side of the machine. He found paper, carbons, and onionskin paper in a drawer.

Spaso House
October 16, 1941

THE MOSCOW FRONT—EYEWITNESS REPORT

His cold stiff fingers struck wrong keys. Typing in a bridge coat was clumsy and difficult. The slow clicks of the machine echoed hollowly in the deserted embassy. One lamp began to smoke. He fiddled with the wick until it burned clear.

This report attempts a description of a visit to the fighting front west of Moscow, from which I have just returned.

Tonight, twenty miles outside the city, our car halted because of an air raid on Moscow. At a distance this was quite a spectacle: the fanning searchlights, the A.A. like an umbrella of colored fireworks over one patch of the horizon, blazing away for half an hour straight. Whatever the Russian deficiencies, they seem to have an infinite supply of A.A. ammunition, and when the Luftwaffe ventures over the capital, they blow it skyward in huge displays. This beats anything I saw in Berlin or London.

However, this brave show is not being matched on the ground in Moscow tonight. The town is getting ready for a siege. It has an abnormal look, and the fainthearted are fleeing in a heavy snow. The Communist government is either unable or unwilling to stop the panic. I am told there is already a slang name for this mass exodus—*Bolshoi Drap*, the Big Scram. The foreign diplomats and newspapermen have been sent to Kuibyshev on the Volga, five hundred miles further east, and many government agencies are departing for the same haven en masse. Heavy vehicular and foot traffic eastward gives an undeniable aspect of rats leaving a sinking ship. However, it is reported that Stalin is staying on.

I believe this panic is premature, that Moscow has a fair chance of holding, and that even if it falls, the war may not end. I bring back many impressions from the front, but the outstanding one is that the Russians, though they are back on about their nine-yard line, are not beaten. The American leadership must guess whether Russia will stand or fall, and lay its bets accordingly in Lend-Lease shipments. An eyewitness account of the front, however fragmentary, may therefore be pertinent.

The typewriter was clicking fast now. It was almost one o'clock. Victor Henry still had to return to the hotel and pack. He chewed another "polar bear," the Russian chocolate candy, for energy, and began banging out the tale of his journey. Electricity all at once lit up the room, but he left the kerosene lamps burning and typed on. In about half an hour the lights flickered, burned orange, dimmed, and pulsed, and went out. Still he typed ahead. He was describing the interior of the KV tank when Slote came in, saying, "You're really going at it."

"You're working late yourself."

"I'm getting to the bottom of the pile." Slote dropped on the desk a brown envelope sealed with wax. "By the way, that came in the pouch, too. Care for some coffee?"

"You bet. Thanks."

Pug stretched and walked up and down the room, beating his arms and stamping his feet, before he broke the seal of the envelope. There were two letters inside, one from the White House and one from the Bureau of Personnel. He hesitated, then opened the White House letter; a few sentences in Harry Hopkins's dashed-off slanting hand filled a page:

My dear Pug—

I want to congratulate you on your new assignment, and to convey the Boss's good wishes. He is very preoccupied with the Japanese, who are beginning to get ugly, and of course we are all watching the Russian struggle with anxiety. I still think —and pray—they'll hold. I hope my letter reached Stalin. He's a land crab, and he's got to be convinced that the Channel crossing is a major task, otherwise bad faith accusations will start to fly, to Hitler's delight. There's been an unfortunate upturn in submarine sinkings in the Atlantic, and the Germans are cutting loose in Africa, too. All in all the good cause seems to be heading into the storm. You'll be missed in the gray fraternity of office boys.

Harry H.

The other envelope contained a Navy letter form in telegraphic style:

MAILGRAM
FROM: THE CHIEF OF PERSONNEL.
TO: VICTOR (NONE) HENRY, CAPTAIN, U.S.N.
DETACHED ONE NOVEMBER PRESENT DUTY X PROCEED FASTEST AVAILABLE TRANSPORTATION PEARL HARBOR X REPORT CALIFORNIA (BB 64) RELIEVE CO X SUBMIT VOUCHERS OF TRAVEL EXPENSES COMBAT FOR PEARL

In bald trite Navy jargon on a flimsy yellow sheet, here was command of a battleship. And what a battleship! The *California,* the old Prune Barge, a ship in which he had served twice, as an ensign and as a lieutenant commander, which he knew well and loved; the ship named for his own home state, launched in 1919 and completely modernized.

Captain of the *California!*

Pug Henry's first reaction was orderly and calculating. Evidently Admiral King's staff was a trap he had escaped. In his class only Warendorf, Munson, and Brown had battleships, and Robinson had the *Saratoga.* His strange "gray office boy" service to the President had proved a career shortcut after all, and flag rank was suddenly and brightly back in sight.

He thought of Rhoda, because she had sweated out with him the twenty-seven-year wait for this bit of yellow tissue paper; and of Pamela, because he wanted to share his excitement right now. But he was not even sure that he would see her again in Moscow. They had parted at the railroad station with a strong handclasp, as Talky Tudsbury pleaded with the RAF pilots to take him along and simultaneously blustered at a Narkomindel man who was trying to lead him off.

Leslie Slote walked in, carrying two glass tumblers of black coffee. "Anything good?"

"New orders. Command of the *California*."

"Oh? What is that?"

"A battleship."

"A battleship?" Slote sipped coffee, looking doubtful. "Is that what you wanted next?"

"Well, it's a change."

"I should think you'd find it somewhat confining and —well, routine, after the sort of thing you've been doing. Not many naval officers—in fact not many Americans— have talked to Stalin face to face."

"Leslie, I'm not entirely unhappy with these orders."

"Oh! Well, then, I gather congratulations are in order. How are you coming with that report? I'm almost ready to turn in."

"Couple of hours to go."

"You won't get much sleep." Slote went out shaking his head.

Victor Henry sat drinking coffee, meditating on this little rectangle of yellow paper, the sudden irreversible verdict on his life. He could ask for no better judgment. This was the blue ribbon, the A-plus, the gold medal of naval service. Yet a nag in his spirit shadowed the marvellous news. What was it? Between sips of coffee, probing his own heart, Pug found out something surprising about himself.

After more than twenty-five years, he had slightly outgrown his career drive. He was interested in the war. At War Plans, he had been waging a vigilant fight to keep priorities high for the landing craft program. "Pug's girlfriend Elsie" was no joke; but now he could no longer carry on that fight. Mike Drayton would take over. Mike was an excellent officer, a commander with a solid background in BuShips and an extraordinary knowledge of the country's industries. But he was not pugnacious and he lacked rank. "Elsie" was going to lose ground.

That could not last. One day the crunch would come— Henry was sure of this from his operational studies—and landing craft would shoot to the top of the priority list, and a frantic scramble would ensue to get them made. The war effort might suffer; conceivably a marginal landing operation would fail, with bad loss of life. But it was absurd, Pug thought, to feel the weight of the war on his shoulders, and to become as obsessed by "Elsie" as he had once been by his own career. That was swinging to the other extreme. The war was bigger than anybody; he was a small replaceable cog. One way or another, sooner or later, the United States would produce enough landing craft to beat Hitler. Meantime he had to go to his battleship.

Taking a lamp to a globe standing in the corner, he used thumb and forefinger to step off the distance from Moscow to Pearl Harbor. He found it made surprisingly little difference whether he travelled west or east; the two places were at opposite ends of the earth. But which direction would offer less delay and hazard? Westward lay all the good fast transportation, across the Atlantic and the United States, and then the Pan Am hop from San Francisco to Honolulu. Duck soup! Unfortunately, in that direction the fiery barrier of the war now made Europe impassable from Spitzbergen to Sicily, and from Moscow to the English Channel. Tenuous lanes through the fire remained: the North Sea convoy run, and a chancy air connection between Stockholm and London. In theory, if he could get to Stockholm, he could even pass via Berlin and Madrid to Lisbon; but Captain Victor Henry had no intention of setting foot in Germany or German-dominated soil on his way to take command of the *California*. His coarsely insulting last remark to Wolf Stöller about Goring undoubtedly was on the record. The Germans, now so close to world victory, might enjoy laying hands on Victor Henry.

Well then, eastward? Slow uncertain Russian trains, jammed already with fugitives from the German attack; occasional, even more uncertain Russian planes. But the way was peaceful and a bit shorter, especially from Kuibyshev, five hundred miles nearer Pearl Harbor. Yes, he thought, he had better start arranging now with the distraught Russians to make his way around the world eastward.

"You look like a mad conqueror," he heard Slote say.

"Huh?"

"Gloating over the globe by lamplight. You just need the little black moustache." The Foreign Service officer leaned in the doorway, running a finger along his smoking pipe. "We have a visitor out here."

By the desk under the chandelier, a Russian soldier stood slapping snow from his long khaki coat. He took off his peaked army cap to shake it by an earflap, and Pug was startled to recognize Jochanan Jastrow. The man's hair was clipped short now; he had a scraggly growth of brown beard flecked with gray, and he looked very coarse and dirty. He explained in German, answering Slote's questions, that in order to get warm clothes and some legal papers, he had passed himself off as a soldier from a routed unit. The Moscow authorities were collecting such refugees and stragglers and forming them into emergency work battalions, with few questions asked. He had had a set of false papers; a police inspector in an air raid shelter had queried him and picked them up, but he had managed to escape from the man. More forged papers could be bought—there was a regular market for them— but he preferred army identification right now.

"In this country, sir," he said, "a person who doesn't have papers is worse off than a dog or a pig. A dog or a pig can eat and sleep without papers. A man can't. After a while maybe there will be a change for the better in the war, and I can find my family."

"Where are they?" Slote said.

"With the partisans, near Smolensk. My son's wife got sick and I left them there."

Pug said, "You're not planning to go back through the German lines?"

Natalie's relative gave him a strange crooked smile. One side of the bearded mouth curled upward, uncovering white teeth, while the other side remained fixed and grim. "Russia is a very big country, Captain Henry, full of woods. For their own safety the Germans stick close to the main roads. I have already passed through the lines. Thousands of people have done it." He turned to Leslie Slote. "So. But I heard all the foreigners are leaving Moscow. I wanted to find out what happened to the documents I gave you."

The Foreign Service officer and Victor Henry looked at each other, with much the same expressions of hesitation and embarrassment. "Well, I showed the documents to an important American newspaperman," Slote said. "He sent a long story to the United States, but I'm afraid it ended up as a little item in the back pages. You see, there have been so many stories of German atrocities!"

"Stories like this?" exclaimed Jastrow, his bristly face showing anger and disappointment. "Children, mothers, old people? In their homes, not doing anything, taken out in the middle of the night to a hole dug in the woods and shot to death?"

"Most horrible. Perhaps the army commander in the Minsk area was an insanely fanatical Nazi."

"But the shooters were not soldiers. I told you that. They had different uniforms. And here in Moscow, people from the Ukraine and from up north are telling the same stories. This thing is happening all over, sir, not just in Minsk. Please forgive me, but why did you not give those documents to your ambassador? I am sure he would have sent them to President Roosevelt."

"I did bring your papers to his attention. I'm sorry to say that our intelligence people questioned their authenticity."

"What? But sir, that is incredible! I can bring you ten people tomorrow who will tell such stories, and give affidavits. Some of them are eyewitnesses who escaped from the very trucks the Germans used, and—"

In a tone of driven exasperation, Slote broke in, "Look here, my dear chap, I'm one man almost alone now"—he gestured at his piled-up desk—"responsible for all my country's affairs in Moscow. I really think I have done my best for you. In showing your documents to a newspaperman after our intelligence people had questioned them, I violated instructions. I received a serious reprimand. In fact, I took this dirty job of staying on in Moscow mainly to put myself right. Your story is ghastly, and I myself am unhappily inclined to believe it, but it's only a small part of this hideous war. Moscow may fall in the next seventy-two hours, and that's my main business now. I'm sorry."

Jastrow took the outburst without blinking and answered in a quiet, dogged tone, "I am very sorry about the reprimand. However, if President Roosevelt could only find out about this crazy slaughter of innocent people, he would put a stop to it. He is the only man in the whole world who can do it." Jastrow turned to Victor Henry. "Do you know of any other way, Captain, that the story could possibly be told to President Roosevelt?"

Pug was already picturing himself writing a letter to the President. He had seen several stories like Jastrow's in print, and even more gruesome official reports about German slaughter of Russian partisans and villagers. Such a letter would be futile; worse than futile—unprofessional. It would be nagging the President about things he suspected or knew. He, Victor Henry, was a naval officer, on temporary detached duty in the Soviet Union for Lend-Lease matters. Such a letter would be the sort of impertinence Byron had offered at the President's table; but Byron at least had been a youngster concerned about his own wife.

Victor Henry answered Jastrow by turning his hands upward.

With a melancholy nod, Jastrow said, "Naturally, it is outside your province. Have you had news of Natalie? Have she and Aaron gone home yet?"

Pug pulled the snapshot from his breast pocket. "This picture was taken several weeks ago. Maybe by now they're out. I expect so."

Holding the picture to the light, Jastrow's face broke into an incongruously warm and gentle beam. "Why, it is a small Byron. God bless him and keep him safe from harm." Peering at Victor Henry, whose eyes misted at these few sentimental words in German, he handed back the photograph. "Well, you gentlemen have been gracious to me. I have done the best I could to tell you what happened in Minsk. Maybe my documents will reach the right person one day. They are true, and I pray God somebody soon finds a way to tell President Roosevelt what is happening.

He must rescue the Jews out of the Germans' claws. Only he can do it."

With this Jochanan Jastrow gave them his mirthless crooked smile and faded into the darkness outside the small glow of the kerosene lamp.

* * * *

When his alarm clock woke him after an hour or two of exhausted slumber, Pug scarcely remembered writing the letter which lay on the desk beside the clock, scrawled on two sheets of Hotel National paper. The tiny barren room was freezing cold, though the windows were sealed shut. He threw on a heavy woollen bathrobe he had bought in London, and an extra pair of warm socks, and sat at the desk to reread the letter.

My dear Mr. President:

Command of the *California* fulfills my life's ambitions. I can only try to serve in a way that will justify this trust.

Mr. Hopkins is receiving a report on a visit I made at his request to the front outside Moscow. I put in all the trivial details which might not be worthy of your attention. My basic impression was confirmed that the Russians will probably hold the Germans and in time drive them out. But the cost will be terrible. Meantime they need and deserve all the aid we can send them, as quickly as possible. For our own selfish purposes, we can't make better use of arms, because they are killing large numbers of Germans. I saw many of the dead ones.

I also take the liberty to mention that the embassy here has recently received documentary evidence of an almost incredible mass slaying of Jews outside the city of Minsk by some German paramilitary units. I remember your saying on the *Augusta* that scolding Hitler any further would be humiliating and futile. But in Europe, America is regarded as the last bastion of humanity; and you, Mr. President, are to these people the voice of the righteous God on earth. It's a heavy burden, but nevertheless that is the fact.

I venture to suggest that you ask to see this material about Minsk yourself. The Germans will think twice about proceeding with such outrages if you denounce them to the world and back up your condemnation with documentary evidence. Also, world opinion might be turned once and for all against the Hitler government.

> Respectfully yours,
> Victor Henry, Captain, U.S.N.

In this fresh look after a sleep, the letter struck him most forcibly as an ill-considered communication, for which the right place was the wastebasket. The first two paragraphs were innocuous; but the President's sharp eye would at once detect that they were padding. The rest, the meat of the letter, was superfluous and even offensive. He was advising the President to go over the heads of everybody in the State Department, including his own ambassador in the Soviet Union, to demand a look at some documents. The odds against Roosevelt's actually doing this were prohibitive; and his opinion of Victor Henry would certainly drop. He would at once recall that Henry had a Jewish daughter-in-law, about whom there had been trouble. And Pug did not even know that the documents were authentic. Jastrow might have been sent by the NKVD, as Tudsbury thought, to plant the material for American consumption. The man seemed genuine, but that proved nothing.

In his career Henry had drafted dozens of wrongly conceived letters to get a problem out of his system, and then had discarded the letters. He had a hard editorial eye, and an unerring sense of professional self-preservation. He threw the letter face down on the desk as a heavy rapping came at the door. There stood Alistair Tudsbury, leaning on his cane in the doorway, enormous and red-faced in an astrakhan hat and a long brown fur coat. "Thank God you're here, old friend." The correspondent limped to an armchair and sat in a dusty shaft of sunlight, stretching out his bad leg. "Sorry to crash in on you like this, but—I say, you're all right, aren't you?"

"Oh yes. I'm just great." Pug was rubbing his face hard with both hands. "I was up all night writing a report. What's doing?"

The correspondent's bulging eyes probed at him. "This is going to be difficult, but here it is straight. Are you and Pamela lovers?"

"What!" Pug was too startled, and too tired, to be either angry or amused. "Why, no! Of course not."

"Well, funnily enough, I didn't think you were. That makes it all the more awkward and baffling. Pamela has just told me flatly that she's not returning to London unless you're going there! If you're off to Kuibyshev, she means to tag along and work for the British embassy or something. Now this is wild nonsense!" Tudsbury burst out, banging the cane on the floor. "To begin with, I know the Nark won't have it. But she's turned to stone. There's no reasoning with her. And those RAF fellows are flying off at noon, and they've got space for both of us."

"Where is she now?"

"Why, she's gone out for a stroll in Red Square, of all things! Can you imagine? Won't even pack, you see. Victor, I'm not coming the indignant father on you, you do realize that, don't you?" Talky Tudsbury appeared in a manic state of verbosity, even for him. "That would be a most absurd stance for me to take. Hell, I've done exactly as I pleased in these little matters myself all my life. She'd laugh in my face if I tried to talk morality to her. But what about common sense? You don't want her trailing after you, a happily married man, do you? It's so embarrassing! In any case, what about Ted Gallard? Why, she told me to tell him it was all off! When I said I'd do nothing of the sort, she sat down and scribbled a letter for him and threw it in my bag. I tell you I'm having the devil of a time with Pam."

Putting a hand to his brow, Victor Henry said in weary tones, yet with a glad surge at heart, "Well, take my word for it, I'm utterly amazed."

"I was sure you would be. I've told her till I'm blue in the face that it's no go, that you're a straitlaced old-fashioned man, the soul of honor, devoted to your wife, and all that sort of thing. Well, the minx simply agrees and says that's why she likes you. Quite unreachable! Victor, surely it's dangerous and silly for a British girl to go rattling aimlessly around in Moscow, with the Huns closing in on all sides."

"Yes, it is. Why don't you go to Kuibyshev with her, Talky? Every foreign correspondent in Russia was on that train, except you."

"They're all idiots. Getting news right here in Moscow

was hard enough. What the devil will they find to write about in that mudhole on the Volga? They'll just drink themselves into cirrhosis of the liver and play poker until their eyes give out. Mine are bad enough. I'm skedaddling. If the Russkis hold Moscow, I'll come back. I hope and believe they will, but if they don't, it's all over. England's at the end of her rope, you know that. We'll all throw in our hands. It'll be the great world shift, and your FDR with his brilliant sense of timing can then face a whole globe armed against him."

Victor Henry stumbled to the yellowed mirror and rubbed his bristly chin. "I'd better talk to Pamela."

"Please, dear fellow, please. And hurry!"

* * *

Pug came outside to fresh snow, bright sunshine, and a ragged burst of Russian song by male voices. A formation of old men and boys, shouldering picks and shovels and lustily shouting a marching tune, was following an army sergeant down Maneznaya Square. The rest of the Muscovites appeared to be trudging normally about their business, bundled up and shawled as usual, but the sidewalk crowds were much thinner. Perhaps, thought Pug, all the rats had now left and these were the real people of Moscow.

He walked up to Red Square, past an enormous poster of the embattled motherland, embodied as a shouting robust woman brandishing a sword and a red flag, and smaller posters of rats, spiders, and snakes with Hitler faces being bayonetted by angry handsome Russian soldiers or squashed under Red Army tanks. The square was deserted; white thick snow almost unmarked by footprints carpeted the great expanse. In front of the Lenin tomb outside the Kremlin wall, its red marble hidden by layers of snow-crusted sandbags, two soldiers stood as usual like clothed statues, but there was no line of visitors. Far on the other side, Victor Henry saw a small bulky figure in gray walking alone past Saint Basil's Cathedral. Even at this distance he recognized the swingy gait of the *Bremen* deck and the way she moved her arms. He headed toward her, his overshoes sinking deep in snow speckled black with paper ash. She saw him and waved. Hurrying to meet him across the snow, she threw herself in his arms and kissed him as she had on his return from the flight to Berlin. Her breath was fragrant and warm. "Damn! The governor went and told you."

"That's right."

"Are you exhausted? I know you were up all night. There are benches by the cathedral. What are your plans? Are you all set for Kuibyshev? Or will you go to London?"

They were walking arm in arm, fingers clasped. "Neither. Sudden change. I've gotten orders, Pam. They were waiting for me here. I'm going to command a battleship, the *California*."

She stopped and pulled on his elbow to swing him toward her, clasped both his arms, and looked in his face with wide glistening eyes. "Command a *battleship!*"

"Not bad, eh!" he said like a schoolboy.

"My God, smashing! You're bound to be an admiral after that, aren't you? Oh, how happy your wife will be!" Pamela said this with unselfconscious pleasure and resumed walking. "I wish we had a bottle of that sticky Georgian champagne, right here and now. Well! That's absolutely wonderful. Where's the *California* based? Do you know?"

"Pearl Harbor." She glanced inquiringly at him. "Oahu. The Hawaiian Islands."

"Oh. Hawaii. All right. We'll start plotting to get me to Hawaii. No doubt there's a British consulate there, or some kind of military liaison. There has to be."

"Aren't you on leave from the Air Force? Won't you have to go back on duty if Talky returns to London?"

"My love, let me take care of all that. I'm very, *very* good at getting what I want."

"I believe that."

She laughed. They brushed snow from a bench outside the rail of the bizarre cathedral. Its colored domes shaped like onions and pineapples were half-hidden, like the red stars on the Kremlin towers, under drapings of thick gray canvas. "When do you leave for Hawaii, and how do you get there?"

"I'll leave as soon as I can, and go via Siberia, Japan, and the Philippines." He clasped her hands as they sat down. "Now, Pam, listen—"

"Are you going to lecture me? Don't bother, please, Victor. It won't work."

"You mentioned my wife. She'll probably come to Pearl."

"I should think she would."

"Then what have you in mind, exactly?"

"Why, love, since you ask me, I have in mind that you and I deceive her, decently, carefully, and kindly, until you're tired of me. Then I will go home."

This blunt declaration shook Victor Henry. It was so novel, so outside the set rules of his existence, that he only replied with clumsy stiffness, "I don't understand that kind of arrangement."

"I know, darling, I know it must seem shocking and immoral to you. You're a dear nice man. Nevertheless I don't know what else to propose. I love you. That is unchangeable. I'm happy with you, and not happy otherwise. I *don't* propose to be separated from you any more for long stretches of time. Not until you yourself dismiss me. So you'll have to put up with this bargain. It's not a bad one, really."

"No, it isn't a bad bargain, but you won't keep it."

Pamela's face showed surprise; then into her eyes came an amused glow, and her lips curved in a mature clever smile. "You're not so dumb."

"I'm not in the least dumb, Pamela. The Navy doesn't give battleships to dumbbells."

A line of olive-painted trucks marked with large red stars came roaring up into the square, rolling past the red brick museum and the shuttered GUM building, and pulled up side by side facing the Lenin tomb.

"We're in a time bind here," Pug went on, raising his voice. "For the moment I'll put Rhoda aside, and just talk about you—"

She interrupted him. "Victor, love, I know you're faithful to your wife. I've always feared you'd think me a pushing slut. But what else can I do? The time has come, that's all. Ever since I was forced to tell Talky this morning, I've been flooded with joy."

Henry sat leaning forward, his elbows on his knees, his hands clasped, his eyes half closed in the sun glare off the snow, looking at her. Soldiers began piling out of the trucks. Obviously new recruits, they were lining up in ragged ranks in the snow under the barking of sergeants in ankle-length coats, while rifles were passed and handed out. After a long pause Henry said, in a matter-of-fact way, "I know this kind of chance won't roll around again in my life."

"It won't, Victor. It won't!" Her face shone with excitement. "People to whom it happens even once are very lucky. That's why I must go with you. It's a mischance that you can't marry me, but we must accept that and go on from there."

"I didn't say I can't marry you," Henry said. She looked astounded. "Let's be clear. If I love you enough to have an affair with you behind my wife's back, then I love you enough to ask her for a divorce. To me the injury is the same. I don't understand the decent kindly deception you talked about. There's a right name for that, and I don't like it. But all this is breaking too fast, Pam, and meantime you have to leave Moscow. The only place to go is London. That's common sense."

"I won't marry Ted. Don't argue," she said in a hardened tone as he started to talk, "I know it's a beastly decision, but it's taken. That's flat. I didn't know about your battleship. That's thrilling and grand, though it complicates things. I can't make you take me along across Siberia, of course, but you had better forbid me right now, or I'll manage to get to Hawaii myself—and much sooner than you'd believe possible."

"Doesn't it even bother you that you're needed in England?"

"Now you listen to *me*, Victor. There's no angle of this that I haven't contemplated very, very thoroughly and long. I wasn't thinking of much else on that four-day auto ride, if you want to know. If I leave old England in the lurch, it will be because something stronger calls me, and I'll do it."

This was direct language that Victor Henry understood. Pamela's gray coat collar and gray wool hat half hid her face, which was pink with cold; her nose was red. She was just another shapelessly bundled-up young woman, but all at once Victor Henry felt a stab of sexual hunger for her, and a pulse of hope that there might conceivably be a new life in store for him with this young woman, and her alone, in all the world. He was overwhelmed, at least for the moment, by the way she had pitched everything on this one toss.

"Okay. Then let's get down to realities," he said gently, glancing at his watch. "You've got to make a move today, in a couple of hours. And I have to attend to this little matter of going around to the other side of the world to take command of my ship."

Pamela smiled beautifully, after listening with a formidable frown. "What a nuisance I must be, suddenly draping myself around your neck at this moment of your life. Do you really love me?"

"Yes, I love you," Pug said without difficulty and quite sincerely, since it was the fact of the matter.

"You're sure, are you? Say it just once more."

"I love you."

Pamela heaved a thoughtful sigh, looking down at her hands. "Well! All right. What move shall I make today, then?"

"Go back with Talky to London. You have no choice, so go quietly. I'll write you or cable you."

"When?"

"When I can. When I know."

They sat in silence. The Kremlin wall, painted to look like a row of apartment houses, echoed the shouts of the sergeants and the metallic clash of rifle bolts, as the recruits clumsily did some elementary drill.

"Well, that will be a communication to look forward to," Pamela said lightly. "Can't you give me some hint of its contents now?"

"No."

For some reason this pleased her, or seemed to. She put a hand to his face and smiled at him, her eyes full of naked love. "Okay. I'll wait." Her hand slipped down to the ripped shoulder of his coat. "Oh, I wanted to mend that. What time is it?"

"It's after ten, Pam."

"Then I must get cracking. Oh dear, I honestly don't want to travel away from you again." They rose and began walking arm in arm. Among the recruits they were walking past stood Berel Jastrow, newly shaved. He looked older so, with his scraped skin hanging in reddened folds. He saw Victor Henry, and for a moment put his right hand over his heart. The naval officer took off his hat as though to wipe his brow, and put it back on.

"Who is he?" Pamela said, alertly watching. "Oh! Isn't that the man who burst into Slote's dinner?"

"Yes," Victor Henry said. "My relative from Minsk. That's him. Don't look around at him or anything."

In the unlit hallway outside her suite, Pamela unbuttoned her own coat and then unbuttoned Victor Henry's bridge coat, looking into his eye. She pressed herself hard to him, and they embraced and kissed. She whispered, "You'd better write me or cable me to come. Oh God, how I love you! Will you drive with us to the airport? Will you stay with me every second to the last?"

"Yes, of course I'll stay with you."

She dashed tears from her face with the back of her hand, then wiped her eyes with a handkerchief. "Oh, how glad I am that I dug in my nasty little hoofs!"

Tudsbury came limping eagerly toward the door as she opened it. "Well? Well? What's the verdict?"

"I was being silly," Pamela said. "I'm going home with you."

Tudsbury looked from her face to Henry's, for the tone was sharply ironic.

"Is she going with me, Victor?"

"She just said she was."

"Gad, what a relief! Well, all's well that ends well, and say, I was about to come looking for you. The RAF lads are being flown out half an hour earlier. There's a rumor that a German column's breaking through toward the airport and that it may be under shellfire soon. The Nark says it's a damned lie, but the boys had rather not take a chance."

"I can pack in ten minutes." Pamela strode toward her room, adding to Pug, "Come with me, love."

Victor Henry saw Tudsbury's eyes flash and a lewd smile curl the thick lips under his moustache. Well, Pamela was human, Pug thought, for all her strength. She couldn't resist exploding the possessive endearment like a firecracker in her father's face. He said, "Wait. There's a report Talky must take to London for me. I'll be right back."

"What do you think, Talky?" Pug heard her say gaily as he went out. "Victor's got himself a battleship command, no less, and he's off to Pearl Harbor. That's in Hawaii!"

He returned shortly, breathing hard from the run up and down the hotel staircase, and handed a manila envelope, stapled shut, to Tudsbury. "Give this to Captain Kyser, the naval attaché at our embassy, hand to hand. All right?"

"Of course. Top secret?" Tudsbury asked with relish.

"Well—be careful with it. It's for the next Washington pouch."

"When I travel, this case never leaves my hand," Tudsbury said, "not even when I sleep. So rest easy."

He slipped into a brown leather dispatch case Pug's envelope, which contained two other envelopes, sealed. One was the long typed report for Harry Hopkins, and the other was the letter to the President about the Jews of Minsk.

* * *

57

The Pearl Harbor Catastrophe

(from WORLD EMPIRE LOST)

The Bouleversement

One week in May 1940 sufficed to upset a balance of power in Europe that had lasted for centuries; and one week in December 1941 sufficed to decide the outcome of World War II and the future global balance of power.

On December 4, our Army Group Center was driving through blizzards into the outskirts of Moscow, and from Leningrad to the Crimea Bolshevik Russia was tottering. The French Empire was long since finished. The British Empire too was finished, though the British Isles still hung feebly on, more and more starved by our ever-expanding U-boat arm. No other power stood between us and world empire except America, which was too weakened by soft living and internal strife to make war. Its industrial plant, half paralyzed by strikes, was still geared to producing luxuries and fripperies. Its military strength lay in an obsolescent navy centered around battleships, riskily based in Hawaii in order to overawe the Japanese, and quite impotent to affect the world-historical German victory that loomed.

Seven days later, on December 11, we were at war with an America transformed into an aggressive military dictatorship, united with one will under a fanatical enemy of the Reich, converting its entire industry on a crash basis to war, and conscripting a vast fresh army and air force in order to crush us. The Red Army on the Moscow front, stiffened with Anglo-American supplies and fresh, primitive, hard-fighting

Siberian divisions, had swung over to the counterattack. Elsewhere Soviet troops were forcing us to retreat from Rostov—the first German retreat since Adolf Hitler had risen to lead us in 1933.

One step from the pinnacle of world empire on December 4, the German people on December 11 found themselves plunged into a total two-front war, fighting for their lives, menaced from the east and from the west by two industrial giants with five times our population and twenty times our territory.

History offers no parallel for this gigantic military bouleversement. The chief cause of it was the Japanese attack on Pearl Harbor. Sir Winston Churchill records frankly that when he got the news of this attack, he shed tears of thankful joy, for he knew then and there that the war was won. He wasted no tears, of course, on the American sailors caught by surprise and slaughtered.

———————

TRANSLATOR'S NOTE: *Here is the passage in Churchill: "No American will think it wrong of me if I proclaim that to have the United States at our side was to me the greatest joy. I could not foretell the course of events. I do not pretend to have measured accurately the martial might of Japan, but now at this very moment I knew the United States was in the war, up to the neck and in to the death. So we had won after all!"*

No tears are mentioned. As previously noted, General von Roon is not dispassionate in his references to Winston Churchill.—V.H.

———————

The Japanese Blunder

The Japanese attack was of course quite justified, but it was a hideous strategic mistake.

The fall of French and British power had left the far eastern European colonies almost undefended. Japan was the natural heir of this wealth. She needed it to fight her war against China to a finish. The Europeans had come halfway round the earth a few generations earlier to subjugate East

Asia and plunder its resources. But now all that was over. Japan was the only strong presence in East Asia. It was far more moral for this Asiatic people to take over administration of this rich sphere, than for a few drunken white civil servants of defunct European empires to continue their pukka-sahib parasitism. Adolf Hitler had sought only friendly ties with this clever hard-working people of destiny. In the General Staff we assumed that Japan would march at the time best suited to her. We approved of this on every basis of world philosophy.

The Japanese attack on Pearl Harbor was tactically an excellent operation, comparable in many ways to Barbarossa. In both cases a small poor nation caught a big wealthy nation off guard, despite a tense war atmosphere and all manner of advance warnings and indications. In both cases surprise was exploited to destroy on a great scale the enemy's first-line forces. The Barbarossa surprise depended on the nonaggression treaty, then in force with Soviet Russia, to lull the enemy. The Japanese went us one better by attacking in the middle of peace parleys.

At the time of both attacks, of course, there were loud outcries of "infamy" and "treachery," as though these terms of private morality had any relevance to historical events. A poor nation seeking to supplant a rich one must use the best means it can find; moreover Thucydides said long ago that men by a natural law always rule where they are strongest. In history what is moral is what works. The will of God, Hegel taught, reveals itself only in historical outcomes. So viewed, Barbarossa and Pearl Harbor were both idealistic thrusts toward a heroic new world order.

The difference was that Barbarossa was strategically impeccable and would have resulted in victory if not for unlucky and unforeseen factors—including this very Japanese attack five and a half months later, which, contrariwise, was such a strategic miscalculation that for once Churchill speaks no more than the truth in calling it suicidal madness.

One violation of a cardinal rule is enough to invalidate a strategic plan. The Japanese surprise attack violated two.

The two iron laws of warfare that Japan disregarded were:

1. *Strike for the heart.*
2. *Know your enemy.*

"Strike for the Heart"

The rule *"Strike for the heart"* is only a corollary of the first principle of warfare, the Concentration of Force. This was what Japan's military leaders overlooked.

From the moment they correctly decided that the war in Europe was their big chance to take East Asia, a hard choice confronted them: should they first move north against the Soviet Union by invading Siberia; or south, to scoop up the weakly held treasures of the European colonies? The move south was the more tempting, of course. But in warfare one must not be misled by mere easy loot or the line of least resistance.

The stakes of the war comprised nothing less than political redistribution of the world's landmasses. It was a radical global conflict, the first true World War. The lineup was classical: the rich against the poor, gold against iron. Germany was the only first-class power on the ascendant side, the side that was seeking to draw a new world map, and her attack on the Soviet Union was her great bid. Once master of Russia, Germany would have been invincible. It followed that the Japanese should have moved to help Germany crush the Soviet Union. With Germany triumphant, Japan could have taken and held anything in East Asia she wanted. But with Germany beaten, Japan had small hope of keeping even the vastest gains.

Had Japan invaded Siberia in 1941, the German drive to Moscow would have succeeded. The Russian counterattacks in December would not have been mounted. The Bolshevik regime would either have fallen or made a second peace of Brest-Litovsk. For what saved Moscow in December was only Stalin's desperate denuding of the Siberian front for reserves to throw into the battle, tipping the scales at the last second by a hair.

Moreover, if Napoleon's maxim holds that the moral is to the physical in warfare as three to one, the mere fact of a Japanese assault on Siberia in the autumn might have brought on a Russian collapse. In mid-October panic gripped the Bolsheviks to the highest levels of government, with whole departments fleeing Moscow in disgraceful tumult, and the frightened dictator issuing shrill orders for a *levée en masse* to save the city. There is even an unconfirmed story that Stalin himself secretly fled, secretly returned when the panic subsided, and had everybody shot who knew of his disgraceful act. Russian rulers operate inside a Byzantine maze, and there is no way of checking this episode.

In any case, this was surely the psychological moment of World War II, the once-in-a-thousand-years opportunity for the Japanese nation. Its irresolute leaders, poorly trained in military thinking and subject to the strange Oriental character mixture of excessive rashness, caution, and emotion, let the moment slip through their fingers to all eternity. History, like a woman, must be firmly taken when she is ready. Otherwise she scorns the fumbler, never forgives him, and never offers him another chance.

"Know Your Enemy"

The first mistake, then, was to go south instead of north, and to snatch booty instead of striking at the heart. But the Axis might still have won the war, despite this dispersion of effort, had Japan not compounded the blunder with a second one that verged on true insanity.

Granted the southward strategy, the obvious course was to move into the East Indies with maximum speed and force, consolidate rapidly, and prepare to defeat any American countermove. The Americans might not have moved at all. Tremendous opposition existed in the United States to sending American boys to die for the pukka sahibs in Asia. Roosevelt might have just sputtered harsh words, as he had after all of Adolf Hitler's triumphs. *Roosevelt never moved one visible step beyond the range of public opinion. This was the master key to the nature of the enemy.* Japan was oblivious to it, because of the distortions of Oriental thinking.

Even if Roosevelt had sent his Navy, defying half his public, against the entrenched Japanese in East Asia, this fleet would have fought its showdown battle at the end of a long supply line, in enemy waters, within range of Japan's land-based air force. It would have been another Battle of Tsushima Strait, with air power added. This humiliating slaughter in an unpopular cause might have brought on the impeachment of the none too popular Machiavellian in the White House.

But even this was not the worst aspect of the Japanese blunder.

America had the largest and most advanced industrial plant on earth. This mercenary nation, devoted to the almighty dollar and blessed with wonderful mineral resources stolen from the Indians, had reared an immense plant capacity for making toys and trifles. But it was a capacity readily convertible to munitions manufacture on the most fantastic imaginable scale. *The whole hope of Axis victory in World War II lay in keeping America divided and soft until the time came to deal with her as an isolated unit without allies.*

This prospect was in sight. Half of America would have rejoiced at a German victory over the Soviet Union. The Lend-Lease program was bogged down in red tape and inertia the day before the Pearl Harbor attack, reflecting the discord and confusion in the people.

For this, great credit goes to Adolf Hitler. He was a narrow-minded man, appallingly ignorant of the United States. But his almost female intuition warned him that he must give his blood enemy, Roosevelt, no chance to unite the Americans against him. That is why the Führer swallowed all the President's scurrilous public abuse and compelled the U-boat arm to endure appalling provocation.

This wise strategy of the Führer was blown to smithereens by Pearl Harbor. Overnight a hundred thirty million quarrelsome, uncertain, divided Americans became one angry mass thirsting for battle. Roosevelt rammed through Congress gigantic war plans and expenditures which a few days earlier would have been utterly inconceivable. The Congress, which in August had extended a mild draft law by a single vote after weeks of debate, now unanimously passed fierce declarations of war, and all Roosevelt's long-plotted stupendous war program, in a matter of hours.

This was the chief result of Pearl Harbor, for the fleet was soon repaired and expanded. In one week Germany passed from the strategic offensive, with world empire in her grasp, to the strategic defensive, with no long-range prospect but to be crushed unless our enemies did something just as stupid and self-destructive.

Nonexistent "Axis"

If one asks, "How did Germany permit such a catastrophe to occur?" the answer is that we were not consulted. We found out that Pearl Harbor was the target when the Americans did—when the torpedoes and bombs exploded.

The "Axis" of Germany, Japan, and Italy never existed as a military reality. It was a ferocious-looking rubber balloon blown up by propaganda. Its purpose was bluff. The three nations went their own ways throughout the war, and usually did not even inform their partners in advance about attacks, invasions, and strategic decisions.

Thus, when Hitler attacked Poland, Mussolini suddenly declined to fight and did not jump in until France was toppling. The Italian dictator invaded Greece without notifying Hitler. Hitler did not inform Il Duce of the attack on Russia until just before the event. But for this he had good reason. Our intelligence had advised us that anything Mussolini knew went straight to the British via the Italian royal family.

Not once did real staff talks take place among the "Axis" armed forces. England and America were having such conferences *a year before* Pearl Harbor! They followed a combined strategy throughout in close cooperation with the Bolsheviks. Now they can reflect at leisure on the wisdom of helping Stalin destroy us, and loosing the Slav flood to the Elbe. But Allied operations were a model of combined strategy, while "Axis" strategy was a nullity. It was every man for himself, and unhappy Germany was tied to second-rate partners who made rash wild plunges that ruined her.

Yamamoto's Role

Why did Japan take this aberrant, foredoomed course?

She had burst into modern history with the sneak attack on the Russian navy at Port Arthur in 1904, and perhaps was obsessed with this way for yellow men to beat white men. The Japanese Naval Staff favored the right move: a seizure of the Indies, and a showdown with the United States Navy— if one should occur—in Japanese waters. But Pearl Harbor was conceived by one Admiral Yamamoto, the commander-in-chief of the fleet, who forced it on his navy and government by threats to resign. Yamamoto opposed the war with the United States entirely, on the grounds that against an enemy with an industrial superiority of seven to one, the attempt was hopeless. But he insisted that if he had to fight, he wanted to knock out the American fleet at the outset. To the broader effects of the attack, he was blind. The Naval Staff considered the attack too risky a gamble, but Yamamoto prevailed. Tactically, of course, he was vindicated. As long as men read and write, "Pearl Harbor" will be a synonym for successful surprise attack. It is as much a part of world language as "Waterloo."

How, indeed, could the Japanese fleet assemble, steam across the Pacific to within two hundred miles of Hawaii, elude all United States intelligence efforts and all its sea and air patrols, and catch its Army and Navy by surprise? This mystery is doubled and tripled by the postwar revelation that the United States had broken Japan's codes and was reading her secret diplomatic cables! The record of the Pearl Harbor investigation by the American Congress runs to millions of words. Still the mystery remains.

As a German staff officer, I look upon Pearl Harbor as an abstract battle problem like Salamis or Trafalgar. Yamamoto's operation surprised the Americans precisely because it was such a foolish thing to do, such an outrageous gamble, such bad strategy, such muddled politics, and such unsound psychology. Even if it succeeded, it was just about the worst move the Japanese could try. Therefore the Americans made the mistake of shutting it from their minds. The Japanese irrationally went ahead and did it, and it happened to work.

A little-noted passage in the hearings, from the interrogation of the cashiered Admiral Kimmel, may provide a key to the mystery. Aerial torpedoes in those days needed to be dropped in deep water in order to straighten out and make their run. The minimum depth, according to American technical opinion, was about seventy-five feet. Pearl Harbor is thirty feet deep. The danger of a torpedo plane attack on the battle fleet was therefore called "negligible," and no torpedo nets were rigged. On December 7, aerial torpedoes hit seven battleships and wreaked vast havoc in Pearl Harbor. For the Japanese had devised a torpedo that could be launched in less than thirty feet, and their pilots had practiced shallow launchings from May to December! This sums up the mental difference in 1941 between the two nations.

Did Roosevelt Plan It?

The historical suspicion arose, and still lingers, that Roosevelt and his top aides conspired to cause the Pearl Harbor defeat. On this theory, they concealed from the Hawaiian command their certain knowledge that Japan was about to strike, obtained from decoded diplomatic telegrams, so as to keep the armed forces there unprepared for the blow. Roosevelt, on this view, decided that getting America solidly into the war was more important militarily than the loss of his battleships. This conjecture originated with the military leaders who were caught napping. They and their supporters maintain it to this day.

Roosevelt was, of course, capable of this dastardly action. He was capable of anything. But the record shows that the Pearl Harbor command, and all the United States forces in the Pacific, certainly knew that war was imminent. Indeed, all they had to do was read the newspapers. In any case, there is no acceptable excuse for professional military leaders ever to be surprised, even under the most lulling and peaceful of circumstances. It happens, but it is not excusable.

No evidence has turned up, in exhaustive investigations, that Roosevelt knew where the blow would fall. The Japanese kept the secret of the intended target perfectly. Their own top diplomats did not know it. Our Supreme Headquarters did not know it. It was never entrusted to a coded cable.

The American military men were surprised because, like the Red Army in June, they were psychologically unprepared for war. On the eve of the attack, the officers at Pearl Harbor no doubt observed the sacred American Saturday night ritual of getting stinking drunk, as did most of their men, and so when the first bombs fell, they were incapable of manning their numerous planes and A.A. guns to defend themselves. Here the rule *"Know the enemy"* definitely helped the Japanese. If American forces, wherever stationed, are ever attacked again, the proper time will always be Sunday morning. National character changes very slowly.

Roosevelt would have been far better served by a victory at Pearl Harbor than by a disaster. Success in repelling the blow would have raised the martial spirit higher. The Americans were a long time recovering mentally from the Pearl Harbor defeat. Roosevelt was not an imbecile, and only an imbecile would have forgone a chance to countersurprise the oncoming exposed Japanese fleet and sink it. Roosevelt did not warn the Pearl Harbor command of an imminent air strike because he, like everybody else, did not know and could not guess that the Japanese would act as grotesquely as they did. The conspiracy theory of Pearl Harbor is a trivial excuse for professional failure.

It is of course absolutely the case that by cutting off Japan's oil supply and then brusquely demanding, as the price of restoring it, that the Japanese make peace in China and stay out of East Asia, Franklin Roosevelt forced Japan to attack. There was no other honorable escape for this proud warlike nation from the corner into which he squeezed them. But these global political maneuvers, at which he was a grand master, he performed openly. The newspapers were full of the diplomatic exchanges, so talk of conspiracy is silly. Roosevelt probably hoped to the last that he could bully and bluff this smaller, weaker nation into obeying him without war. Hitler would have played that situation exactly the same way. However, there was this difference: the German armed forces would not have let him down by being surprised, as Roosevelt's did. We were soldiers.

TRANSLATOR'S NOTE: *Roon's professional acumen is most striking when German conduct is not in the picture. With his appraisal of the Pearl Harbor surprise, I unhappily concur. He neglects the real bungling and stupidity that went on in Washington during those days, as well as in Hawaii; but his conclusion must be accepted that there is never an excuse for commanders in the field to be surprised. A similar failure by our armed services in the nuclear age will spell the end of American history. There will be no margin for recovery next time.—V.H.*

*   *   *

58

A SENSE of lost time haunted Victor Henry as he sat on the back lawn of the Army and Navy Club in Manila at three o'clock in the morning, listening to a broadcast of a football game going on eleven thousand miles away. Overhead, as always on Army-Navy game night, Orion sprawled brilliantly across half the heavens. On the roads outside Moscow the constellation had blazed brightly, too, but far down toward the southern horizon.

Pug sat on the grass amid a crowd of officers from both services, and a sprinkling of their Filipino girlfriends. Wives had long since been sent home. The old smells of Army-Navy night—fresh-cut lawn grass, frangipani, rum, women's perfume, and the rank smell of harbor water—the paper lanterns, too, the heat, the sweaty feeling even in a cotton shirt and slacks, the old interservice jokes and insults, all pulled him back in spirit a dozen years. Life in Manila was amazingly unchanged. The jumpy overwrought embassy people in Tokyo had been speculating that there might be no Army-Navy game, that either the Japanese would go to war by Thanksgiving, or at least the American armed forces would be on full alert. Yet there stood the same old display board, with the flat white football that would slide back and forth on a string across the painted gridiron. There were the mascot animals—Army mule in a brown blanket, Navy goat in a blue one—tethered and waiting for the comic moments. It might just as well be sleepy 1928, Pug thought. Only the floodlights blazing across the bay at the Cavite Navy Yard for all-night repair work suggested that it was November 1941, and that the Navy was slightly bestirring itself for an emergency.

The loudspeakers bellowed above the chatter on the lawn, and the radio reception tonight was better than in some years. This game still had its old ritual fascination for Pug; he was following it tensely, smoking a cigar. Once his nostalgia had been keen for the tough youthful combat on the grass, the slamming of bodies, the tricky well-drilled plays, above all for the rare moments of breaking free and sprinting down the field, dodging one man and another with the stands around him a roaring sea of voices. Nothing in his life had since been quite like it. But long ago that nostalgia had departed; those grooves of memory had worn out. To think that lads much younger than his own two sons were out on that chilly field in Philadelphia now, made Victor Henry feel that he had led a very long, multilayered existence, and was now almost a living mummy.

"Pug! I heard you were here." A hand lightly struck his shoulder. His classmate Walter Tully, bald as an egg and deeply tanned, smiled down at him; Tully had left the submarine school to take command of the undersea squadron at Manila. He gestured at a crowded table near the display board. "Come and sit with us."

"Maybe at the half, Red." It was decidedly an anachronism, but everybody still used the nickname. "It's more like the old days, sitting on the grass."

"You're dead right. Well, I'll join you."

"Now you're talking. Sit you down."

Tully had played Academy football too, and he listened to the broadcast as intently as Pug. After a while the white football slid all the way for an Army run to a touchdown. Amid yells, cheers, and groans, a young lieutenant unloosed the mule, jumped on its back, and galloped around the lawn.

"Oh, hell," Pug exclaimed.

Tully shook his head. "We're going to lose this one, old buddy. They've got a fine backfield. We could use Pug Henry in there."

"Ha! Fifteen-yard penalty for illegal use of wheelchairs. Say, Red, you're the original Simon Legree, aren't you?"

"How do you mean?"

"I mean sending the *Devilfish* out on exercises the night of the Army-Navy game. What's the matter, you think there's a war threatening or something?"

Tully grinned at the heavily ironic tone. "It was Branch Hoban's idea. They're going alongside for two weeks start-

ing today—they're due in at noon—and he wanted to get
in some drills. You'll scc plenty of Byron."

"I'll only be here till the Clipper leaves."

"Yes, I hear tell you've got the *California*. That's just
great, Pug."

The game resumed. After some dull skirmishing the
white ball-shape shot far across the board; Navy had in-
tercepted a pass and run it deep into Army territory. Pug
and Tully got to their feet and joined in the Navy yells of
"Beat Army! Goal! Goal!" while an ensign happily pa-
raded the goat around. The half ended right after the touchdown. Cheerily Red Tully ordered drinks from a passing
steward. "Let's stay here on the grass, Pug. Tell me about
Rooshia."

His happy grin changed to a tough sober look as Victor
Henry described the tank battle he had observed and the
October 16 panic in Moscow. "Jesus, you've really been
in there! I envy you. And here we sit, fat, dumb, and
happy. They told me you flew here via Tokyo."

"That's right."

"What's the straight dope, Pug? Are those bastards
really going to fight? We're getting some scary alerts here,
but at this point we're kind of numb."

"Well, our people there are worried. The ambassador
talked to me at length about Japanese psychology. They're
a very strange nation, he said, and hara-kiri is a way of life
to them. The odds don't matter much. They're capable of
executing a suicidal plan suddenly, and he fears they will."

Tully glanced around at the nearby couples on the grass
or on folding chairs, and dropped his voice. "That checks
out. Admiral Hart received a straight war warning today,
Pug. But we've been hearing nervous chatter from Washington, on and off, all summer and fall. In July when they
landed in Indo-China and Roosevelt shut off their oil, we
all thought, *here goes!* The squadron ran dawn and dusk
GQ's for a week, till it got kind of silly. Should I start that
up again?"

Pug gestured his puzzlement with turned-up palms.
"Look, I talked to some businessmen one night at a dinner
party in the embassy, Americans, British, and one Jap, a
big-time shipbuilder. The Jap said the straight word, right
from the Imperial Court, is that war with the USA is

unthinkable. Everybody there agreed. So—you pays your money and you takes your choice."

"Well, all I know is, if they do go, we're in trouble. The state of readiness in the Philippines is appalling. The people themselves don't want to fight the Japs. That's *my* opinion. The submarine force is so short of everything—torpedoes, spare parts, watch officers, what have you—that it's simply pitiful. Speaking of which, when did you see Byron last?"

"I guess about six months ago. Why?"

"Well, he has more damn brass! He walked into my office the other day and asked for a transfer to the Atlantic command. His own skipper had turned him down and Byron was trying to go over his head. I sure ate him out about that. I told him, Pug—I said this, word for word—that if he weren't your son I'd have kicked his ass out of my office."

Victor Henry said with forced calm, "His wife and baby are in Italy. He's worried about them."

"We're all separated from our kinfolk, Pug. It just isn't in the cards to transfer him. I'm trying to comb submarine officers out of tenders and destroyers. I'd do anything within reason for a son of yours, but—"

"Don't put it that way. Byron's just another officer. If you can't do it, you can't."

"Okay. I'm glad you said that."

"Still, his family problem is serious. If it's possible, transfer him."

"There's this little problem of the Japs, too."

"No argument." Victor Henry was taking some pains to keep his tone light and friendly. A crowd roar poured from the loudspeakers, and he said with relief, "Okay! Second half."

When the game ended, many people were stretched out asleep on the grass, under a paling sky streaked with red. White-coated boys were still passing drinks and huddled Navy officers were bawling "Anchors Aweigh," for their team had won. Pug declined Captain Tully's invitation to breakfast and went up to his room for a nap.

He had stayed in a room like it—perhaps in this very one—on first reporting to Manila, before Rhoda had arrived with the children to set up housekeeping. High-ceilinged, dingy, dusty, with featureless old club furniture and a big perpetually turning and droning fan, the room hit Pug again with a strong sense of lost time and vanished days. He turned the fan up high, stripped to undershorts, opened the french windows looking out over the bay, and sat smoking cigarette after cigarette, watching the day brighten over the broad blue harbor and the busy traffic of ships. He was not sleepy. He sat so for more than an hour, scarcely moving, while gathering sweat trickled down his naked skin.

Thinking of what?

Seeing pictures generated by his return to Manila. Pictures of himself and Byron under a poinciana tree at the white house on Harrison Boulevard, working on French verbs; the boy's thin face wrinkling, silent tears falling at his father's roared exasperation. Of Warren winning a history medal, an English medal, and a baseball award at the high school; of Madeline, fairylike in a gossamer white frock, wearing a gold paper crown at her eighth birthday party.

Pictures of Rhoda crabbing about the heat and the boredom, getting drunk night after night in this club, falling on her face at the Christmas dance; of the quarrel that put an end to her drinking, when he coldly talked divorce. The smell of the club's lawns and halls, and of the spicy Manila air, gave him the illusion that all this was going on now, instead of belonging to a past more than a dozen years dead.

Pictures of Pamela Tudsbury in Red Square. Of the dreary mud streets of Kuibyshev, the all-night poker games, the visits to farm communes, the stagnant slow passing of time while he waited for train tickets; then the two-week rail ride across Siberia; the beautiful Siberian girls selling fruits, flat circular bread, sausage, and hot chickpeas at tiny wooden stations; the single track of the railroad stretching backward from the last car, a dark straight line through a pink snow desert, pointing straight at a setting sun that flattened like a football as it sank to the horizon; the long stops, the wooden benches in the "hard" coach, the onion breaths and body smells of the local travellers, some white, some Mongol, in queer fur hats; the awesome three-day forest stretches; the ugly miles on miles of huts in Tokyo; the wretchedness of the Japanese, the hate you could feel in the back of your neck on the street, the war weariness and poverty so much worse even than Berlin; the half-dozen letters to Pamela Tudsbury he had drafted and torn up.

Through all these strange scenes Victor Henry had preserved a happy sense that he was moving toward a new life, a fulfilled life he had almost despaired of, a life delayed, postponed, almost lost, but now within grasp. When he thought of Rhoda it was usually as the effervescent Washington girl he had courted. He could understand falling in love with that girl and marrying her. The present-day Rhoda he pictured with detachment, almost as though she were somebody else's wife, with all her faults and all her charms seen clear. To divorce her would be cruel and shocking. How had she offended? She had been giving him an arid, half-empty existence—he now knew that—but she had been doing her best. Yet the decision evidently lay between being kind to Rhoda and seizing this new life.

He had written the letters to Pamela as he had written the one about the Minsk massacre—to get a problem on paper for a clear look at it. By the time he arrived in Tokyo, he had decided that letters were too wordy and too slow-travelling. He had to send one of two cables—COME, or DON'T COME. Pamela needed no more than that. And he had concluded that Pamela was wiser than he, that the first step should indeed be a love affair in which they could test out this passion or infatuation before wounding Rhoda; for it might never come to that. In bald fact the prescription was a shackup. Victor Henry had to face the novel notion —for him—that in some circumstances a shackup might be the best of several difficult courses.

In Tokyo he had actually hesitated outside a cable office, on the point of cabling: COME. But he had walked away. Even if it were the best course, he could not yet picture himself bringing it off; could not imagine conducting a hole-in-corner affair, even if with Pamela it did not seem a squalid or immoral idea. It was not his style. He would botch it, he felt, and weaken or tarnish his work as the new captain of the *California*. So he had arrived still undecided in Manila.

And in Manila, for the first time since his talk with Pamela Tudsbury in Red Square, an awareness of his wife

Rhoda began to overtake him and the reality of Pamela to fade. Manila was saturated with Rhoda, the good memories and the bad memories alike, and with his own hardened identity. Red Tully, his classmate, a bald commander of all the submarines of the Asiatic Fleet; the Army-Navy game, in which he had last played twenty-eight years ago, when Pamela had been an infant a few months old; the dozens of young Navy lieutenants on the club lawn, with girlfriends Pamela's age—these were the realities now. The wild Siberian scenery was a fading patchwork of mental snapshots. So was the incandescent half hour on Red Square.

Was it really in the cards for him to start over, to have new babies learning to talk, little boys playing on grass, a little girl twining arms around his neck? Manila above all recalled to Pug the pleasure he had taken in his children. Those days he looked back on as the sweetest and best in his life. To do it all once again with Pamela would be a resurrection, a true second life. But could a rigid, crusty man like himself do it? He had been hard enough on his kids in his thirties.

He was very tired, and sleep at last overtook him in the chair, as it had in the Tudsburys' suite in the Hotel National. But this time no cold caressing fingers woke him. His inner clock, which seldom failed, snapped him awake in time to drive out to Cavite and watch the *Devilfish* arrive.

Byron was standing on the forecastle with the anchor detail, in khakis and a lifejacket, but Pug failed to recognize him. Byron sang out, as the *Devilfish* nosed alongside the pier, "Holy smoke, it's my father. You Dad! *Dad!*" Then Pug perceived that the slim figure with both hands in his back pockets had a familiar stance, and that his son's voice was issuing from the lean face with the curly red beard. Byron leaped to the dock while the vessel was still warping in, threw his arms around Victor Henry, and hugged him hard. Kissing that scratchy hairy face was a bizarre sensation for Pug.

"Hi, Briny. Why the foliage?"

"Captain Hoban can't stand beards. I plan to grow one to my knees. God, this is a monumental surprise, Dad."

From the bridge an officer shouted impatiently through a megaphone. Jumping back on the moving forecastle like a goat, Byron called to his father, "I'll spend the day with you. Hey, Mom wrote me you're going to command the *California!* That's fabulous!"

When the vessel was secured alongside, the *Devilfish* officers warmly invited Victor Henry to lunch at a house in the suburbs which they had rented. Pug caught a discouraging look from Byron, and declined.

"I live aboard the submarine," Byron said. They were driving back to Manila in the gray Navy car Pug had drawn from the pool. "I'm not in that setup."

"Why not? Sounds like a good thing."

"Oh, neat. Cook, butler, two houseboys, gardener, five acres, a swimming pool, and all for peanuts when they split up the cost. I've been there for dinner. They have these girls come in, you know, and stay overnight—different ones, secretaries, nurses, and whatnot—and whoop it up and all that."

"Well? Just the deal for a young stud, I should think."

"What did you do, Dad, when you were away from Mom?"

"Think I'd tell you?" Pug glanced at Byron. The bearded face was serious. "Well, I did a lot of agonized looking, Briny. But don't act holier-than-thou, whatever you do."

"I don't feel holier than thou. My wife's in Italy. That's that. They can do as they please."

"What's the latest word on her?"

"She's flying to Lisbon on the fifteenth. I've got a picture of the kid. Wait till you see him! It's incredible how much he looks like my baby pictures."

Pug had been poring over the snapshot in his wallet for two months, but he decided not to mention it. The inscription to Slote was an awkward detail.

"God, it's rotten, being this far apart," Byron exclaimed. "Can you picture it, Dad? Your wife with a baby you've never even seen, on the other side of the earth—no telephone, a letter now and then getting through by luck? It's hell. And the worst of it is, she almost got out through Switzerland. She panicked at taking a German airplane. She was sick, and alone, and I can't blame her. But she'd be home by now, if there'd been any other way to go. The

Germans! The goddamned Germans." After a silence he said with self-conscious chattiness, "Hot here, isn't it?"

"I'd forgotten how hot, Briny."

"I guess it was pretty cold in Russia."

"Well, it's freezing in Tokyo, too."

"Say, what's Tokyo like? Quaint and pretty, and all that?"

"Ugliest city in the world," Pug said, glad for a distracting subject. "Pathetic. A flat shantytown stretching as far as the eye can see. Downtown a few tall modern buildings and electric signs, and crowds of little Japanese running around. Most of the people wear Western clothes, but the cloth looks to be made of old blotters. You see a few women dressed Japanese doll–style, and some temples and pagodas, sort of like in San Francisco's Chinatown. It's not especially Oriental, it's poor and shabby, and it smells from end to end of sewage and bad fish. Biggest disappointment of all my travelling years, Tokyo. Moreover, the hostility to white men is thick enough to cut with a knife."

"D'you think they'll start a war?"

"Well, that's the big question." Victor Henry's fingers drummed the steering wheel. "I have a book on their Shinto religion you'd better read. It's an eye-opener. The ambassador gave it to me. Here are people, Briny, who in the twentieth century believe—at least some do—that their king's descended from a sun god, and that their empire goes straight back two thousand six hundred years. Before the continents broke apart, the story goes, Japan was the highest point on earth. So she's the center of the world, the divine nation, and her mission is to bring world peace by conquering everybody else—you're smiling, but you'd better read this book, boy. Under the religious gibberish it's exactly like Nazi or Communist propaganda, this idea of one crowd destined to take over the world by force. God knows why this idea has broken out in different forms and keeps spreading. It's like a mental leprosy. Say, how hungry are you? Let's look at the old house before lunch."

Byron's smile, framed in the neatly trimmed red beard, looked odd but no less charming. "Why, sure, Dad. I've never done that. I don't know why."

As they drove along Harrison Boulevard and approached the house, Byron exclaimed, "Ye gods, is that it? Someone went and painted it yellow."

"That's it." Pug parked the car across the street and they got out. The unpleasant mustardy color surprised him too. It was all over the low stone wall and the wrought-iron fence, as well as the house—a sun-faded old paint job, already peeling. On the lawn lay a tumbled-over tricycle, a big red ball, a baby carriage, and plastic toys.

"But the trees are so much taller and thicker," Byron said, peering through the fence, "yet the house seems to have shrunk. See, here's where Warren threw the can of red paint at me. How about that? There's still a mark." Byron rubbed his shoe over the dim red splash on the paving stone. "I had a bad time here, all in all. Warren laying my head open, and then the jaundice—"

"Yes, and that truck hitting you on your bicycle. I wouldn't think you'd remember it pleasantly."

Byron pointed. "That's where we used to sit, right there under that tree, when you'd tutor me. Remember, Dad? Look how thick that trunk is now!"

"Oh, you recall that? I wouldn't think that would be a pleasant memory either."

"What not? I missed all that school. You had to do it."

"But I was a lousy tutor. Maybe your mother should have taken it on. But in the morning she liked to sleep late, and in the afternoon, well, she was either shopping, or getting her hair done, you know, or fixing herself up for some party. For all the times I lost my temper, I apologize."

Byron gave his father a peculiar glance through half-closed eyes and scratched his beard. "I didn't mind."

"Sometimes you cried. Yet you didn't cry when you got hit by the truck. Pain never made you cry."

"Well, when you put on that angry voice, it scared me. But it was all right. I liked studying with you. I understood you."

"Anyway, you got good marks that year."

"Best I ever got."

They looked through the fence without talking for a couple of long minutes. "Well, now we've seen the place," Pug said. "How about lunch?"

"You know something?" Byron's gaze was still on the house. "Except for the three days I had in Lisbon with

Natalie, I was happier here than I've ever been in my life, before or since. I loved this house."

"That's the worst of a service career," Pug said. "You never strike roots. You raise a family of tumbleweeds."

The crab cocktail at the Army and Navy Club was still served with the same bland red sauce in the same long-stemmed cups, with one purposeless green leaf sticking up in the crabmeat. The roast beef from the steam table was lukewarm and overdone, much as it had been in 1928. Even the faces of the people eating lunch seemed the same —all but Byron's. The thin little boy who had eaten with such exasperating slowness was now a bearded tall young man. He still ate too slowly; Pug finished his meat first, though he was doing nearly all the talking.

He wanted to probe Byron a bit about Pamela, and about Jochanan Jastrow. He described Jastrow's sudden incursion into Slote's Moscow flat, and his spectral reappearance in Spaso House out of a snowstorm. Byron exploded in anger when his father mentioned Tudsbury's refusal to use the Minsk documents, and his guess that Jastrow might be an NKVD emissary. "What? Was he serious? Why, he's either a hypocrite or an idiot! What he said about people not wanting to help the Jews is true, God knows. Hitler paralyzed the world for years by playing on that chord. But nobody can talk to Berel for five minutes without realizing that he's a remarkable man. And dead on the level, too."

"You believe the story about the massacre?"

"Why not? Aren't the Germans capable of it? If Hitler gave the order, then it happened."

"I wasn't that sure myself, Byron, but I wrote to the President about it."

Byron stared openmouthed, then spoke in a low incredulous tone. "You did *what*, Dad?"

"Well, those documents got shunted aside in the embassy as probable fakes. I thought they deserved more investigation than that. It was an impulse—probably a stupid one—but I did it."

Byron Henry reached out, covered his father's hand, and pressed it. The bearded face took on an affectionate glow. "All I can say is, well done."

"No. I believe it was a futile gesture, and those are

never well done. But it's past. Incidentally, have you ever met Tudsbury's daughter? Natalie mentioned in the Rome airport that she knew her."

"You mean Pamela? I met her once in Washington. Why?"

"Well, the Tudsburys and I travelled in the combat area together. She struck me as an unusually brave and hardy sort. She endured a lot and always remained agreeable and well-groomed. Never whined or crabbed."

"Oh, Pam Tudsbury's the original endurer, from what Natalie says. They're not too unlike in that way, but otherwise they sure are. Natalie told me a lot about her. In Paris Pamela was a hellion."

"Really?"

"Yes, she had this Hemingwayish boyfriend who used to room with Leslie Slote. She and this character raised Cain all over Gay Paree. Then he dropped her and she went into a bad spin. I'm ready for some dessert, Dad. You too?"

"Sure." Victor Henry could not help persisting. "How— a spin?"

"Oh, can't you imagine? Sleeping around, trying to drink up all the wine in Paris, driving like a maniac. She wrapped a car around a tree outside Marseilles and almost killed this French writer she was with. What's the matter? You look upset."

"That's an upsetting story. She seems a fine girl. I'll be here a week," Pug said abruptly, "unless the Clipper changes its schedule. Can we get in some tennis?"

"Sure, but I'm not in shape, the way I was in Berlin."

"Nor am I."

They played early in the mornings to dodge the heat, and after showering they would breakfast together. Victor Henry did not mention Pamela again. At night, lying awake in warm humid darkness under the moaning fan, he would think of ways to reopen the subject. But facing his son at the breakfast table, he couldn't do it. He could guess what Byron would think of a romance between his staid father and Pamela Tudsbury. It would strike the youngster as a pure middle-aged aberration—disconcerting, shabby, and pathetic. Victor Henry now had spells of seeing it the same way.

One day Branch Hoban prevailed upon him to visit the house in Pasay for lunch. Byron mulishly would not join them. Pug took a long swim in a pool ringed by flowering trees, and enjoyed a superb curry lunch; and after a nap he beat Lieutenant Aster at tennis. It was altogether a satisfying afternoon. Before he left, over rum drinks on a terrace looking out on the garden, Hoban and Aster talked reassuringly about Byron. They both considered him a natural submarine man; only the military bone, they said, seemed to be missing in him. Transfer to the Atlantic was his obsession, but Hoban tolerantly pointed out to the father that it was impossible. The squadron was far under complement now, and the *Devilfish* could not put to sea if it lost one watch office. Byron had to make up his mind that the *Devilfish* was his ship.

Victor Henry brought up this topic at what he hoped was a good time—just before breakfast next morning after their game and shower, when they were having coffee on the lawn. On other days Byron had been in the highest spirits over this early cup of coffee. As casually as possible, Pug remarked, "Incidentally, Byron, you said Natalie's flying to Lisbon—when? The fifteenth of this month?"

"That's right, the fifteenth."

"Do you think she'll make it this time?"

"God, yes. She'd better! They've got every possible official assurance and high priority."

"Well now, the fifteenth isn't very far off, is it? This transfer request of yours—" Victor Henry hesitated, for a look came over Byron's face which he knew only too well: sullen, vacuous, remote, and introverted. "Isn't it something you can table, at least until then?"

"Table it? It's tabled, don't worry. I've been turned down by Hoban, Tully, and Admiral Hart's personnel officer. What more do you want?"

"I mean in your own mind, Briny."

"Listen, I'm *assuming* she'll get home with the baby. Otherwise I'd probably desert and go fetch her out. But I still want to be transferred. I want to see them. I want to be near them. I've never seen my own son! I've spent the sum total of three days with my wife since we got married."

"There's another side to it. Your squadron is desperate for watch officers, we're in a war alert, and—"

Byron broke in, "Look, what is this, Dad? I haven't asked you to go to Tully and use your influence with him, have I?"

"I'm sure glad you haven't. Red Tully can't do the impossible, Byron. He stretched a point, taking you into that May class, but that was different—"

Byron broke in, "Jesus, yes, and I'm eternally grateful to both of you. That's why my son was born in Italy, and that's why I'm separated from my wife by the whole wide earth."

"Maybe we'd better drop it," said Victor Henry.

"That's a fine idea, Dad."

Byron turned genial again over the bacon and eggs, but Victor Henry felt that in the short bitter exchange he had lost all the ground he had been gaining with his son.

Yet Byron could not have been more amiable when he saw his father off on the Clipper next day. On the pier he threw his arms around Pug. Impulsively Pug said, as the beard scratched his lips, "Is Natalie going to like all this shrubbery?"

It was a pleasure to hear Byron laugh. "Don't worry. The day I leave the *Devilfish,* off it comes."

"Well, then—I guess this is it, Byron."

"The tumbleweeds blowing apart," Byron said.

"That's exactly right. The tumbleweeds blowing apart."

"Well, you'll be seeing Warren and Janice in a few days, anyhow. That's great. Give them my love."

The loudspeaker called for passengers to board the huge flying boat.

Victor Henry looked in his son's eyes and said with great difficulty, "Look, I pray for Natalie and your boy."

Byron's eyes were steady and inscrutable.

"I'm sure you do, Dad. Thanks."

When the Clipper wheeled away for the long takeoff the son still stood on the pier, hands thrust in his back pockets, watching.

*

The Japanese fleet at that moment was well on its way to Hawaii.

The Kurile Islands, a chain of volcanic rocks more than

seven hundred miles long, loosely linking Japan and Siberia, had made a good secret rendezvous. Japan's six aircraft carriers had met in a setting of black snow-patched island crags, flecked with the gnarled vegetation that can survive in high winds and long freezes. Through rain and sleet, their fliers had practiced shallow torpedo runs while battleships, cruisers, oilers, and supply ships came straggling in. Nobody knew of this gathering armada except the men in the ships and a few of Japan's leaders. When the force set out eastward, only a few flag officers had been told where they were going, and why.

They had no set day or hour to attack. They were not sure the attack would go. The fleet was sailing in case the Washington talks broke down. Japanese peace envoys were trying to work out a *modus vivendi,* a "way of living," a sort of cease-fire in the Pacific before the guns could go off. The Japanese *modus vivendi* called for the United States to resume sending oil and scrap iron, and to recognize Japan's right to rule East Asia and colonize China. If the Americans granted this, the fleet on signal would turn back.

But the *modus vivendi* of the United States called for the Japanese to abandon the Chinese war and get off the southeast Asian mainland, in return for normal economic relations. The Japanese leaders had already decided that if this was the last word, they would fight. In that case, on signal, the timing of an enormous simultaneous assault, planned to burst out of Japan like red rays all over the South Pacific, would be locked on to one irrevocably appointed hour: the time for a surprise air strike against Hawaii.

The three strong points held by the white race in the South Pacific were Pearl Harbor, Manila, and Singapore. The plan was to knock out United States air and sea power at Pearl Harbor from the air; to capture Singapore by seaborne assault; to land troops in the Philippines and take Manila, and then to sweep up the chips in the East Indies; and thereafter to use these new resources for a strong drive to finish China, while beating off Anglo-American counterattacks. The ultimate gamble was that Germany would either win the big fratricidal white man's war that was giving Japan her chance, or would so use up American and British strength that Japan would in the end keep what she had seized, no matter what happened to Germany.

The Japanese leaders, including the emperor, doubted that this risky plan would come off, but they thought they had no choice. Japan's predicament was much like Germany's before the attack on the Soviet Union. Both countries, in the hands of their militarists, had started wars they couldn't finish. As time ran out and supplies dwindled, both turned to strike elsewhere, hoping to mend their fortunes.

Three reasons were forcing the Japanese to a showdown now. Their oil was running out. The weather would soon turn bad for military operations. And the white men, alarmed at last, were strengthening their three bastions every week with more and more planes, warships, anti-aircraft guns, tanks, and fortifications. Japan's temporary advantage in the South Pacific and East Asia was melting away. Unless President Roosevelt suddenly relented in Washington, she had to go, or give up her drive for empire.

And so, on the day before the Army-Navy game, the armada had sortied into the black stormy waters off the Kuriles, and set out for Hawaii.

And as the Japanese task force steamed east, a much smaller American task force sortied from Pearl Harbor, headed west. Admiral William Halsey was taking twelve marine fighter planes to Wake Island in the *Enterprise*. Japan had long since illegally fortified every island and atoll it held on trust in the Pacific. Time after time, President Roosevelt had failed to get money out of Congress for counter-fortifying American islands. Now, at the end of November 1941, the funds had come through. The work was being wildly rushed. At Wake it was half finished, but the atoll still had no air defense.

The second day out, on a sunny crystalline morning, Warren Henry returned from the dawn search and came slanting around to land on the *Enterprise*. The deck rose up at Warren, the hook caught the number two cable, his stomach thrust hard against the safety belt, and he was down and stopped among deck force sailors in brilliant red, green, and yellow jumpers, doing their frantic gesticulating dance around landed planes. Warm sea air eddied in from his rear gunner's open canopy. Disconnecting belts and cables, gathering up his charts and log sheets, Warren awkwardly climbed out into the brisk wind over the deck, as another scout plane roared in and jerked to a stop.

The landing officer shouted at him, holding his paddles on either side of his mouth, "Hi. All pilots to Scouting Six ready room at 0900."

"What's up?"

"The old man wants a word with you all."

"The captain?"

"Halsey."

"Christ."

In the ready room the deep comfortable chairs were already full, and pilots in khakis, or flying suits and yellow lifejackets, lined the bulkheads. Halsey entered with the ship's captain and the squadron commanders, and stood in front of the scored plexiglass panels up forward, where orange grease marks showed search patterns and assignments. Warren was only a few feet from him. Seen this close, Halsey's face looked patchy and aged, and now and then he grimaced, showing his teeth in a nervous tic.

The squadron commander waved a green mimeographed sheet. "Okay, now all you fellows received and discussed this yesterday, but the admiral has asked me to read it again, out loud.

"BATTLE ORDER NUMBER 1.

1. *The* Enterprise *is now operating under war conditions.*
2. *At any time, day or night, we must be ready for instant action.*
3. *Hostile submarines may be encountered.*
   . . . 'Steady nerves and stout hearts are needed now.'

> *Commanding Officer,*
> *U.S.S.* Enterprise.

> *Approved: W. F. Halsey*
> *Vice Admiral, U.S. Navy*
> *Commander Aircraft, Battle Force."*

The captain stepped back among the squadron commanders behind the admiral. Halsey squinted around the room, contracting his flaring gray eyebrows. "Thank you, skipper. I'm told there were questions yesterday. I'm here to accommodate you, gentlemen."

Not a word or a raised hand.

Admiral Halsey involuntarily grimaced, glancing over his shoulder at the ship's captain and the squadron commanders. He addressed the pilots again. "Cat got your tongue?" This raised an uneasy titter. "I'm reliably informed that someone said this paper gave every one of you carte blanche to put the United States of America into the world war. Now would the brave soul who said that care to stand?"

Warren Henry took a step forward from the bulkhead. Faces turned to him.

"What's your name?"

"Lieutenant Warren Henry, sir."

"Henry?" Hasley looked a shade less grim. "Are you related to Captain Victor Henry?"

"He's my father, sir."

"Well, *he's* a fine officer. Now then. You think this order permits you to plunge the country into war, do you?"

"Sir, I added yesterday that I was all for it."

"You're all for it, hey? Why? What are you, one of these bloodthirsty killer types?" The admiral raised his outthrust jaw.

"Admiral, I think we're in the war now, but fighting with both hands tied behind us."

Halsey's face twitched and he motioned Warren to step back. Clasping his hands behind his back, the admiral said in harsh tones: "Gentlemen, this force stripped for action weeks ago. There's nothing loose, dispensable, or inflammable left aboard the *Enterprise* that I know about, except the wardroom piano. I made that exception myself. Now, our mission is secret. There will be no vessels of the United States or of friendly powers in our path. They have been warned away. Ships we encounter will belong to the enemy. Unless we shoot first, we may never have a chance to shoot. Therefore, this force will shoot first and argue afterwards. The responsibility is mine—Questions?"

He slowly looked around at the young sober faces. "Good day, then, and good hunting."

Later, Warren's wing mate, lying naked on the top bunk, said, "Well, give him one thing. He's a fighting son of a bitch."

"Or a trigger-happy old nut," said Warren, rinsing lather from his razor. "Depending on events."

On the day that the Japanese steaming east and Halsey's ships steaming west made their closest approach, Warren Henry flew the northern search pattern, more than two hundred miles straight toward the Japanese fleet. The Japanese routinely sent a scout plane due south about the same distance. But in the broad Pacific Ocean the game was still blindman's buff. Hundreds of unsearched miles of water stretched between the two scouting planes at their far reach, and the two forces passed in peace.

■   ■   ■

The light was failing over Guam. From the window of the descending Clipper, Victor Henry glimpsed in the sunset glow the island's mountain ridges and broken sea cliffs to the south, levelling northward to a jungle checkered with terraced fields. The shadowy light flattened perspectives; Guam was like a painted island on a Japanese screen. Sharp on the red horizon jutted the black lump of Rota, an island held by the Japanese.

The passengers were standing in a sweaty weary cluster outside the immigration shed in the twilight, when a gray car drove up, fluttering on its front fenders an American flag and a starry blue jack.

"Captain Henry?" The white-clad marine officer saluted and handed him an envelope, confidently picking out the Navy four-striper in a seersucker suit from among the ferry pilots and civilians. "Compliments of the governor, sir."

The note was scrawled on cream-colored stationery crested in gold:

THE GOVERNOR OF GUAM
Clifton Norbert Tollever, Jr., Captain, U.S.N.

Hi, Pug—
Greetings to the world's worst hearts player, and as long as it's

not Sunday, how's for coming around for drinks, dinner, and a game?

Kip

Pug smiled at the tired joke about his minor Sabbath abstinence. "NG, Lieutenant. Sorry. By the time I check through here, go to the hotel, and get cleaned up and whatnot, it'll be way past the governor's dinner hour."

"No, sir. Let me expedite this. The governor said I'm to bring you out to the palace, bags and all. He'll give you a room to freshen up in."

The gold loops on the starchy white shoulder of the governor's aide conjured away difficulties. Victor Henry was entering the governor's car within five minutes, leaving the other Clipper passengers behind, enviously staring.

Driving across the island in gathering darkness on a narrow winding tarred road, the lieutenant skillfully avoided some potholes but struck others with bone-jarring jolts.

"You folks short of road repair equipment?" Pug asked.

"Sir, the governor's been cadging money from public works for gun emplacements and pillboxes. He says maybe he'll hang for it, but his first duty is not to patch roads but to defend this island. Insofar as it can be defended."

The headlights shone on green jungle and a few tilled fields most of the way. "Well, here's the metropolis at last, sir."

The car passed down a paved block of shuttered shops, and dimly lit bars with names like Sloppy Joe's and The Bucket of Blood. Here lonesome-looking sailors meandered on the sidewalk, some with giggling brown girls in flimsy dresses. The car emerged on a broad, handsomely gardened square, formed by four stone structures in antique Spanish style: a cathedral, a long barracks, an immense jail, and an ornate building that the lieutenant called the Governor's Palace.

Kip Tollever waved as Victor Henry mounted a broad staircase to the palace terrace. Wearing stiffly starched whites, he sat in a large carved Spanish armchair, in yellow light cast by a wrought-iron chandelier. Natives in shirt-sleeves and trousers stood before him.

"Sit you down, Pug!" He motioned at a chair beside

him. "Welcome aboard. This won't take long. Go ahead, Salas. What about the schoolchildren? Have they been drilling every day?"

It was a conference on defense preparations. Tollever addressed the Guamanians in English or Spanish, with condescending kindness. One or two spoke a queer dialect that the others translated. The men were taller than Filipinos, and very good-looking.

"Well, Pug Henry!" The governor lightly slapped his guest's knee as the natives bowed and went off down the stairs. "Quite a surprise, seeing *your* name on the Clipper passenger list! That's always the big news item on this island, you know. Kate used to fall on the list like a love letter twice a week, when she was still here. Well! What's your pleasure? A drink, then a shower? Come on, let's have just one. Where have you been? What brings you to our island paradise?"

They drank excellent rum punches there on the terrace, in tall curiously carved green glasses, and Pug talked about his travels. Tollever seemed far more interested in the Russian war than in Japan. His response to Pug's remark that he had spent four days in Tokyo was, "Oh, really? Say, incidentally, you'll stay overnight, won't you? I'll assign a boy to look after you. You'll be very comfortable."

"Well, Kip, thanks. I'd better bed down in the Pan Am Hotel. Takeoff depends on weather, and I don't want to get left by that Clipper."

"No problem." Kip's voice rang with magisterial authority. "They won't leave without you. I'll see to that."

Pug found the palace depressing, for all the handsomely tiled spaces and rich dark furniture. Under the slow-turning fan the bed in his room was covered in gold-and-silver brocade. New nickel plumbing in the vast bathroom gushed wonderful hot water. But the silence! The Guamanian stewards in their snowy mess jackets stole around like spirits. He and the governor seemed to be the only white men here, for the marine lieutenant had driven off to the bars. From the other end of the palace, Pug could hear the clink of silver and china as he dressed.

In a sombrely magnificent Spanish dining room, at one end of a long gleaming black table, the two Americans ate a dinner made up wholly of frozen or canned stores from home. Kip Tollever maintained his gubernatorial dignity through the first course or two, asking polite questions about his old friends in Berlin and about the situation in Manila. But as he drank glass after glass of wine, the façade cracked, then fell apart. Soon he was expressing friendly envy of Pug and admitting that his assignment was dismal. The younger officers could go to The Bucket of Blood, or drink and play cards at the club. The governor had to sit it out alone in the palace. He slept badly. He missed his wife. But of course the women had had to go. If the Japs moved, Guam could not be held for a week. At Saipan and Tinian, a half hour away by air, Jap bombers lined the new air strips and big troop transports swung to their anchors. Guam had no military airfield.

As dessert was being served, four young officers in white appeared, led by the marine aide-de-camp.

"Well, well, here's company," said the governor. "These tender lads come in every night after dinner, Pug, and I educate them in the subtler mysteries of hearts. What do you say? Care for a game, or would you rather just shoot the breeze?"

Pug saw the youngsters' faces light up at the mention of an alternative. Shading his voice toward lack of enthusiasm, he said, "Why, let's play, I guess."

The governor of Guam looked irresolutely from his visitor to the young officers. He held himself very straight, talking to his juniors; the thick gray hair, lean long-jawed face, and bright blue eyes should have made him formidable. Yet he seemed only tired and sad, hesitating over this small choice between habit and courtesy. The hearts game evidently was the high moment in the governor's isolated days.

"Oh, what the hell," Tollever said. "I don't get to see a classmate very often, especially such a distinguished one. You young studs run along and amuse yourselves. See you tomorrow, same time."

"Aye aye, sir," said the marine officer, trying to sound disappointed. The four young officers vanished in a rapid tattoo of heels on tile.

Captain Tollever and Captain Henry sat long over brandy. What did Pug really think, Kip asked; would the

Japs go, or was this buildup at Saipan just a bluff for the Washington talks? He had once served as attaché in Tokyo, but the Japs were an enigma to him. The wrong people had gotten in the saddle, that was the trouble. The army had gained the power to confirm or veto the minister of war. That meant the army brass could overthrow any cabinet it didn't like. Ever since then Japan had been going hell-bent for conquest; but would they really attack the United States? Some Japanese he had known had been the finest imaginable people, friendly to the United States and very worried about their militarists; on the other hand, Clipper travellers had been telling him blood-freezing stories of Japanese cruelties in China, especially toward white people who fell into their hands.

"And have you ever read about what the Jap army did, Pug, when they captured Nanking in '37? We were so steamed up about their sinking the *Panay,* we hardly paid attention. Why, they ran amuck. They raped twenty thousand Chinese women, so help me, and butchered most of 'em afterward. I mean *butchered*—just that. Women's thighs, heads, and *tits,* for God's sake, were strewn in the streets! This is the truth, Pug. And they tied Chinamen together by the hundreds and mowed 'em down with machine guns. They hunted kids in the street and shot 'em like rabbits. They murdered maybe two hundred thousand civilians in a few days. All this is in official reports, Pug. It *happened.* I've had occasion to check into the facts, being somewhat personally interested, as you might say. And here I sit," he went on, sloshing his fourth or fifth brandy into a shimmering balloon glass and rolling white eyeballs at his old classmate, "here I sit, with no aircraft, no warships, no ground troops, just a few sailors and a few marines. The Navy should order me to evacuate, but oh no, the politicians wouldn't stand for *that!* The same politicians who refused to vote the money to fortify the island. No, here we'll sit till they come. The fleet will never get here in time to save us.

"Pug, remember what the Lucky Bag said about me when we graduated? *'Any one of Kip Tollever's class-mates would like to be in his shoes today, and even more, thirty years from today.'* Funny, isn't it? Isn't that the biggest laugh of all time? Come on, let's have one more and listen to the midnight news from Tokyo."

In the wood-panelled library, the governor manipulated the dials of a Navy receiver: a big black machine seven feet high that winked red, green, and yellow lights and emitted whistles and moans. A Japanese woman's voice came through clearly. After recounting gigantic German victories around Moscow and predicting the early surrender of the Soviet Union, the voice went on in tones of glee to report a great uproar in the United States over the unmasking of Franklin Roosevelt's secret war plans. The *Chicago Tribune* had obtained a document known as the Victory Program—Victor Henry sat up as the dulcet voice drawled *"Vic-to-ly Plo-glam"*—calling for an army of eight million men, a defensive war against Japan, and an all-out air attack on Germany from bases in England, to be followed by invasion of Europe in 1943. The newspaper, she announced, had patriotically printed the whole plan!

Roosevelt's devilish schemes to drag America into war on the side of the colonialist plutocracies were now exposed; so the woman said. The American people were rising in anger. Congressmen were calling for impeachment of the White House deceiver. The White House was maintaining shameful silence, but the fairness and peaceful intent of the latest Japanese proposals—especially in the light of this secret warmongering Roosevelt plot—were being hailed throughout the United States. On and on the woman went, reading whole passages of the document from the *Tribune*. Pug recognized them. Some sentences were his own.

"What do you make of that, Pug? It's a lot of poppycock, isn't it?" Tollever yawned. "Some reporter got hold of a contingency staff study maybe, and blew it way up."

"Sure. What else?"

Pug felt sick to the heart. If this could happen, the United States was infected bone-deep with decay. The Japs could grab the East Indies, even the Philippines; America would not fight. This betrayal of the highest national secret in a newspaper was a collapse of honor, it seemed to him, unlike anything in history. The only relieving aspect was that so bald and amazing was the treason, the Germans and the Japanese could probably not bring themselves to believe it, though of course they would make heavy propaganda of it.

"Time for me to go to bed." Victor Henry shook his head and stood up.

"Hell, no, Pug. Sit down. How about an omelette, or something? My chef makes fine omelettes. In a half hour we'll get the 8 A.M. news from San Francisco. This beast picks it up like it was next door. Let's see if there's anything to all this *Chicago Tribune* business. It's always fun, checking Tokyo against San Francisco."

Pug insisted on going back to the Pan American Hotel. The sense of doom enveloping him was thick enough without the added black misery emanating like a smell from the trapped governor of Guam, the faded hotshot of his Naval Academy class, maundering over his brandy. Tollever ordered up the omelettes all the same, and kept Victor Henry for another hour, talking about the old days in Manila when they had been next-door neighbors. His dread of loneliness was stark and terrible.

Sadly Tollever went at last to a telephone and summoned the marine officer, who arrived in the car in a few minutes. Four Guamanian stewards busied themselves with Pug's valise and two handbags.

From the top of the palace stairway, Kip raised his voice. "Say, how about giving Kate a ring from Pearl? She's back in our house in La Jolla. Tell her you saw me and that everything's fine. She's very interested in the Guam schools, you know. Tell her the enrollment's way up for next term. And, you know, tell her I love her and all that stuff."

"I sure will, Kip."

"And say, you give my love to Rhoda, too. Will you? Of all the Navy wives I knew, she was the prettiest and the best—excepting my Kate, naturally."

"I'll tell her you said that, Kip," Pug replied, chilled by Tollever's use of the past tense about himself.

"Good hunting with the *California,* Pug." Tollever stood watching as the car left, a white straight mark in the warm night.

The Clipper took off from Guam at dawn.

59

On the day that Victor Henry left Manila, the Japanese embassy in Rome gave an unexpected party for Japanese and American newspaper correspondents. The purpose seemed to be a show of cordiality to counteract all the war talk. A *New York Times* man asked Natalie to come along. She had never before left her baby in the evening; none of her clothes fitted her; and she did not like the man much. But she accepted, and hastily got a seamstress to let out her largest dress. On leaving the hotel she gave to a motherly chambermaid an enormous list of written instructions for bathing and feeding him, which made the woman smile. The rumors of war in the Pacific were eating away Natalie's nerves, and she hoped to learn something concrete at the party.

She came back with a strange tale. Among the American guests had been Herb Rose, a film distributor who maintained his office in Rome. Herb had somewhat enlivened the cold, stiff, pointless party by speaking Japanese; it turned out that he had managed a similar office in Tokyo. Herb was a tall good-looking California Jew, who used the best Roman tailors, conversed easily in Italian, and seemed a most urbane man until he started talking English. Then he sounded all show business: wise-cracking, sharp, and a bit crude.

This Herb Rose, who was booked to leave for Lisbon on the same plane as Natalie and her uncle, had approached her at the party and walked her off to a corner. In a few quiet nervous sentences, he had told her to go to Saint Peter's with her uncle the following morning at nine o'clock, and stand near Michelangelo's *Pietà* statue. They would be offered a chance to get out of Italy fast, he said, via Palestine. War between America and Japan was coming in days or hours, Herb believed; he was departing that way himself and forgoing the Lisbon plane ticket. He would tell her no more. He begged her to drop the subject and not to discuss it inside the walls of the hotel. When she returned from the party she recounted all this to her uncle, while walking on the Via Veneto in a cold drizzle. Aaron's reaction was skeptical, but he agreed that they had better go to Saint Peter's.

He was in a testy mood next morning. He liked to rise at dawn and work till eleven. Sleep put an edge on his mind, he claimed, that lasted only a few hours, and to spend a morning on such a farfetched errand was a great waste. Also, the chill damp in the unheated hotel had given him a fresh cold. Hands jammed in his overcoat pockets, blue muffler wound around his neck, head drooping in a rain-stiffened old gray felt hat, he walked draggily beside his niece down the Via Veneto to the taxi stand, like a child being marched to school. "Palestine!" he grumbled. "Why, that's a more dangerous place than Italy."

"Not according to Herb. He says the thing is to get out of here at once, by hook or by crook. Herb thinks the whole world will be at war practically overnight, and then we'll never get out."

"But Herbert's leaving illegally, isn't he? His exit visa is for Lisbon, not Palestine. Now *that's* risky. When you're in a touch-and-go situation like this, the first principle is not to give the authorities the slightest excuse"—Jastrow waved a stiff admonitory finger—"to act against you. Obey orders, keep your papers straight, your head down, your spirits up, and your money in cash. That is our old race wisdom. And above all, *stay within the law.*" He sneezed several times, and wiped his nose and eyes. "I have always abominated the weather of Rome. I think this is a wild goose chase. Palestine! You'd be getting even further from Byron, and I from civilization. It's a hellhole, Natalie, a desert full of flies, Arabs, and disease. *Angry* Arabs, who periodically riot and murder. I planned a trip there when I was writing the Paul book. But I cancelled out once I'd made a few inquiries. I went to Greece instead."

There was a long queue at the taxi stand, and few taxis; they did not reach Saint Peter's until after nine. As they hurried out of the sunshine into the cathedral, the temperature dropped several degrees. Jastrow sneezed, wound the muffler tighter around his neck, and turned up his collar. Saint Peter's was quiet, almost empty, and very gloomy. Here and there black-shawled women prayed by pale flickering candles, groups of schoolchildren followed vergers, and tourist parties listened to guides, but these were all lost in the grand expanse.

"My least favorite among Italian cathedrals," said Jastrow. "The Empire State Building of the Renaissance, intended to overpower and stupefy. Well, but there's the *Pietà,* and that *is* lovely."

They walked to the statue. A German female guide stood beside it, earnestly lecturing to a dozen or so camera-bearing Teutons, most of whom were reading guidebooks as she talked instead of looking at the *Pietà,* as though to make sure the woman was giving them full value.

"Ah, but what a lovely work this is after all, Natalie," Jastrow said, as the Germans moved on, "this poor dead adolescent Christ, draped on the knees of a Madonna hardly older than himself. Both of them are so soft, so fluid, so young in flesh! How did he do it with stone? Of course it's not the *Moses,* is it? Nothing touches that. We must go and look at the *Moses* again before we leave Rome. Don't let me forget."

"Would you call that a Jew's Jesus, Dr. Jastrow?" said a voice in German. The man who spoke was of medium height, rather stout, about thirty, wearing an old tweed jacket over a red sweater, with a Leica dangling from his neck. He had been in the group with the guide and he was lingering behind. He took a book from under his arm, an old British edition of *A Jew's Jesus* in a tattered dust jacket. With a grin he showed Jastrow the author's photograph on the back.

"Please," said Jastrow, peering curiously at the man. "That picture gives me the horrors. I've since disintegrated beyond recognition."

"Obviously not, since I recognized you from it. I'm Avram Rabinovitz. Mrs. Henry, how do you do?" He spoke clear English now, in an unfamiliar, somewhat harsh accent. Natalie nervously nodded at him. He went on, "I'm glad you've come. I asked Mr. Rose what other

American Jews were left in Rome. It was a great surprise to learn that Dr. Aaron Jastrow was here."

"Where did you pick up that copy?" Jastrow's tone was arch. Any hint of admiration warmed him.

"Here in a secondhand store for foreign books. I'd read the work long ago. It's outstanding. Come, let's walk around the cathedral, shall we? I've never seen it. I'm sailing from Naples on the flood tide tomorrow at four. Are you coming?"

"*You're* sailing? Are you a ship's captain?" Natalie asked.

The man momentarily smiled, but looked serious again as he spoke, and rather formidable. His pudgy face was Slavic rather than Semitic, with clever narrow eyes and thick curly fair hair growing low on his forehead. "Not exactly. I have chartered the vessel. This won't be a Cunard voyage. The ship is an old one, and it's small, and it's been transporting hides, fats, horses, and such things along the Mediterranean coast. So the smell is interesting. But it'll take us there."

Natalie said, "How long a voyage will it be?"

"Well, that depends. The quota for the year was used up long ago, so the way may be roundabout."

"What quota?" Jastrow said.

The question seemed to surprise Rabinovitz. "Why, the British allow only a very small number of Jews into Palestine every year, Professor, so as not to get the Arabs too angry. Didn't you know that? So it creates a problem. I want to be frank about that. Depending on the current situation, we may sail straight to Palestine anyway, or we may go to Turkey, and then proceed overland—Syria, the Lebanon, and through the mountains into the Galilee."

"You're talking about an illegal entry, then." Jastrow sounded severe.

"If it can be illegal for a Jew to go home, yes. We don't think so. In any case, there's no choice for my passengers. They're refugees from the Germans, and all other countries have barred the doors to them, including your United States. They can't just lie down and die."

"That isn't our situation," Jastrow said, "and what you're proposing is unsafe."

"Professor, you're not safe here."

"What organization are you with? And what would you charge?"

"My organization? That's a long story. We move Jews out of Europe. As for paying—well, one can talk about that. You can ask Mr. Rose. That's secondary, though we can always use money. I came to Rome in fact for money. That's how I met Mr. Rose."

"And once we get to Palestine—then what?"

Rabinovitz gave him a warm, agreeable look. "Well, why not just stay? We would be honored to have a great Jewish historian among us."

Natalie put in, "I have a two-month-old infant."

"Yes, so Mr. Rose said."

"Could a small baby make that trip?"

Halting at the main altar, Rabinovitz stared in admiration at the twisted pillars. "This cathedral is so rich and beautiful. It's overwhelming, isn't it? Such a gigantic human effort, just to honor one poor Jew executed by the Romans. And now this building dominates all Rome. I guess we should feel flattered." He looked straight in Natalie's eyes in a forceful way. "Well, Mrs. Henry, haven't you heard the stories coming from Poland and Russia? Maybe you should take some risk to get your baby out of Europe."

Aaron Jastrow said benignly, "One hears all kinds of stories in wartime."

"Mr. Rabinovitz, we're leaving in less than two weeks," Natalie said. "We have all our tickets, all our documents. We were at tremendous pains to get them. We're flying home."

Rabinovitz put a hand to his face and his head swayed.

"Are you all right?" Natalie touched his arm.

He uncovered a knotted brow, and smiled painfully. "I have a headache, but that is all right. Look, Mr. Herbert Rose had an airplane ticket too, and he's coming to Naples with me. If you join us, you'll be welcome. What more can I say?"

"Even if we did want to consider this drastic move, we couldn't get our exit visas changed," Jastrow said.

"Nobody will have an exit visa. You will just come aboard to pay a visit. The ship will leave, and you will forget to go ashore."

"If one thing went wrong, we'd never get out of Italy," Jastrow persisted, "until the war ended."

Rabinovitz glanced at his watch. "Let's be honest. I'm not sure you will get out anyway, Dr. Jastrow. Mr. Rose told me about the difficulties you've been having. I don't think they're accidental. I'm afraid you're what some people call a 'blue chip' "—he used the American slang haltingly—"and that's your real problem. The Italians can trade you someday for a lot of 'white chips,' so something can always go wrong at the last minute when it's time to leave. Well, meeting you was a great honor. If you come along we'll talk some more. I have many questions about your book. Your Jesus had very little to do with this, did he?" He swung both his hands around at the cathedral.

"He's a Jew's Jesus," said Jastrow. "That was my point."

"Then tell me one thing," said Rabinovitz. "These Europeans worship a poor murdered Jew, the young Talmud scholar you wrote about so well—to them he's the Lord God—and yet they go right on murdering Jews. How does a historian explain that?"

In a comfortable, ironic, classroom tone, most incongruous in the circumstances, Jastrow replied, "Well, you must remember they're still mostly Norse and Latin pagans at heart. They've always chafed under their Jewish Lord's Talmudic morals, and possibly they take out their irritation on his coreligionists."

"Now that explanation hadn't occurred to me," Rabinovitz said. "It's a theory you should write up. Well, let us leave it this way. You want to think it over, I'm sure. Mr. Rose will telephone you tonight at six o'clock and ask you whether you want the tickets for the opera. Tell him yes or no, and that will be that."

"Good," Natalie said. "We're deeply grateful to you."

"For what? My job is moving Jews to Palestine. Is your baby a girl or a boy?"

"Boy. But he's only half-Jewish."

With his crafty grin, and an abrupt handwave of farewell, Rabinovitz said, "Never mind, we'll take him. We need boys," and he walked rapidly away. As his plump figure merged into a tourist group leaving Saint Peter's, Natalie and her uncle looked at each other in puzzlement.

"It's freezing in here," said Dr. Jastrow, "and very depressing. Let's go outside."

They strolled in the sunshine of the great piazza for a while, talking the thing over. Aaron tended to dismiss the idea out of hand, but Natalie wanted to give it thought and perhaps discuss it with Rose. The fact that he was going troubled her. Jastrow pointed out that Rose was not as secure as they were. If war should break out between the United States and Italy—and that was the threat in the Japanese crisis—they had the ambassador's promise of seats on the diplomatic train, with the newspaper correspondents and the embassy staff. Rose had no such assurance. Earlier in the year, the embassy had given him warning after warning to leave. He had chosen to stay at his own risk, and now he had to face the consequences. If he wanted to chance an illegal exit, that did not mean they needed to.

At the hotel, Natalie found the baby awake and fretful. He seemed a frail small creature indeed to expose to a sea voyage uncertain even in its desination, let alone its legalities; a voyage in a crowded old tub—no doubt with marginal food, water, sanitation, and medical service—that might lead to a rough trip through mountains; the goal, a primitive and unstable land. One look at her baby, in fact, settled Natalie's mind.

Rose called promptly at six. "Well, do you want the opera tickets?" His voice on the telephone was friendly and, it seemed, anxious.

Natalie said, "I think we'll skip it, Herb. But thank your friend who offered them."

"You're making a mistake, Natalie," Rose said. "I think this is the last performance. You're sure?"

"Positive."

"Good luck, kid. I'm certainly going."

*　　*　　*

Janice Henry left her house and drove toward Pearl City in a cool morning echoing with distant church bells. Vic had wakened her at seven o'clock, coughing fearfully; he had a fever of almost 105. Yawning on the telephone, the doctor had prescribed an alcohol rub to bring the baby's temperature down, but there was no rubbing alcohol in the house. So she had given the fiery, sweat-soaked little boy his cough medicine, and set out for town, leaving him with the Chinese maid.

From the crest of the hill, under a white sun just climbing up from the ocean rim, the harbor wore a Sabbath look. The fleet was in, and ranged at its moorings in the morning mist: a scattering of cruisers, oilers, and tenders, clusters of gray destroyers and minesweepers, nests of black submarines. Off Ford Island the battleships stood in two majestic lines with white sun-awnings already rigged; and on the airfield nearby dozens of planes touched wings in still rows. Scarcely anybody was moving on the ships, the docks, or the airfield. Nor was any large vessel under way to ruffle the glassy harbor. Only a few church party boats, with tiny sailors in whites, cut little foamy V's on the green still water.

Janice got out of the car to look for her husband's ship. To her disappointment, the *Enterprise* was not only absent from the harbor, it was nowhere in sight on the sea. She had been counting on a Sunday morning return. She took binoculars from the glove compartment and scanned the horizon. Nothing: just one old four-piper poking around, hull down. Tuesday would be two weeks that Warren had been gone; and now here she was with a sick baby on her hands, and a hangover. What a life! What a bore!

She had gone to the Officers' Club dance the night before out of loneliness and boredom, accepting the invitation of a lieutenant she had dated long ago, a Pensacola washout who now served on Cincpac's staff. Vic had had a cough for days, but his temperature had remained normal. Of course she would never have stayed out until after three, cavorting and boozing, had she known he would turn so sick. Still she felt guilty, irritated, and bored to the bone with this idiotic existence.

Since her return from Washington, she had been growing more and more bored, realizing that she had married not a dashing rake after all, but a professional Navy fanatic, who made marvellous love to her now and then and otherwise almost ignored her. Lovemaking at best took up very little time. What an end for Janice Lacouture—at twenty-three, a Navy baby-sitter! She had taken a half-day coding job at Cincpac to avoid being evacuated with the service wives, but that was dull drudgery too. Janice had spells of deep rebellion, but so far she had said nothing to Warren. She was afraid of him. But sooner or later, Janice meant to have it out, even if divorce ensued.

A small general store in a green wooden shack at a crossroads stood open, with two fat Japanese children playing on the rickety porch. That was lucky; it stocked a strange jumble of things, and she might not have to drive clear into town. As she went in, she heard gunfire pop over the harbor, as it had been popping for months off and on in target practice.

The storekeeper, a black-haired little Japanese in a flowered sport shirt, stood behind his counter drinking tea. On shelves within reach of his arms, goods were neatly stacked: canned food, drugs, pans, brooms, candy, toys, soda pop, and magazines. He bobbed his head, smiling, under hanging strips of dried fish. "Lubbing acoho? Ess, ma'am." He went through the green curtain behind him. The gunfire sounded heavier and louder, and planes thrummed overhead. A funny time for a drill, she thought, Sunday morning before colors; but maybe that was the idea.

Going to the doorway, Janice spotted the planes flying quite high, lots of them, in close order toward the harbor, amid a very heavy peppering of black puffs. She went to her car for the binoculars. At first she saw only blue sky and clouds of black smoke, then three planes flew into the field of vision in a shining silvery triangle. On their wings were solid orange-red circles. Stupefied, she followed their flight with the glasses.

"Ess, ma'am? Many pranes! Big, big drir!" The storekeeper stood beside her, offering her the package with a toothy smile that almost shut his eyes. His children stood behind him on the porch, pointing at the sky and chattering in shrill Japanese.

Janice stared at him. Nearly everybody in the Navy disliked the Hawaiian Japanese and assumed they were spies. She had caught the feeling. Now here was this Jap grinning at her, and overhead Jap planes were actually flying! Flying over Hawaii! What could it mean? The nerve of these Japs! She took the package and abruptly, rudely offered him the binoculars. The man bobbed his head and peered upward at the planes, now beginning to peel off and dive, one by one, glinting silver amid the thickening black puffs. With a queer noise in his throat, he pulled himself erect and held out the binoculars to her, regarding her with a blank face, his slant eyes like black glass. More than the unreal, startling sight of the orange-marked planes, the look on his face told Janice Henry what was happening in Pearl Harbor. She snatched the binoculars, jumped into her car, slammed the door, and whirred the ignition. He hammered on the door, holding out his hand, palm up, and shouting. She had not paid him.

Janice was an honest young lady, but now with a pulse of pleasurable childish excitement she shouted harshly—using the sailor epithet for the first time in her life—*"Fuck you!"* and shot off up the road.

That was how the war came to Janice Henry, and that was the story she told down the years after a few drinks in suitable company, usually to laughter and applause.

Accelerator to the floor, she careered and screeched uphill and around curves to the top of the ridge, jammed on the brakes, and leaped out into roadside grass. She was all alone here. Below, silver planes were flitting and diving about the peaceful Navy base, where the morning mist still lay pearly pink around the ships. Columns of water were shooting up, a couple of ships were on fire, and here and there guns were flashing pale yellow. But it still looked much more like a drill than like war.

Then she saw a very strange and shocking sight. A battleship vanished! One instant the vessel stood in the outer row and the next second nothing was there but a big red ball surrounded by black and yellow smoke. A cracking explosion hit and hurt her ears; the pressure wave struck her face like an errant warm breeze; and the ball of smoke and red fire climbed high into the air on a pillar of lighter smoke, and exploded again, in a beautiful giant burst of orange and purple, with another delayed *BOOM!* The vanished battleship dimly appeared again in the binoculars, a vast broken twisted wreck all on fire, sinking at a slant. Men were running around and jumping overboard, and some with their white suits on fire were moving in and out of the smoke, silently screaming. It looked like a movie, exciting and unreal, but now Janice Henry began to grow horrified. Here was one battleship actually sinking before her eyes, and the whole thing had scarcely been going on ten minutes! She saw more planes coming in overhead. Bombs began to explode in the hills. Remembering her baby, she ran to the car, backed it squealing onto the road, and raced home.

The Chinese maid sat in an armchair, dressed for church, hat on her knee, glumly leafing through the missal. "The baby's asleep," she said in clear English; she was island-born and convent-raised. "The Gillettes never even came. They forgot me. So I'll have to go to ten o'clock mass. Please telephone Mrs. Fenney."

"Anna May, don't you know that the Japanese are attacking us?"

"What?"

"Yes! Can't you hear the guns, the explosions?" Janice gestured nervously toward the window. "Turn on the radio. You'll hear plenty! Jap planes are all over the harbor. They've already hit a battleship."

Victor lay on his back, still doped by the cough syrup, breathing loud and fast. Janice stripped the hot, flushed little body. From the radio came the sliding twangs of Hawaiian guitars and a woman's voice singing "Lovely Hula Hands." As Janice sponged the infant an announcer gibbered cheerfully about Cashmere Bouquet Soap, and another Hawaiian melody began. The maid came to the doorway. "You sure about the war, 'Mis' Henry? There's nothing on the radio. I think maybe you just saw a drill."

"Oh, for heaven's *sake!* A drill! How stupid do you think I am? I saw a battleship blow up, I tell you! I saw a *hundred* Jap planes, maybe more! They're all asleep or out of their minds at that radio station. Here—please give him the aspirin. He feels a lot cooler. I'll try to call the Fenneys."

But the line was dead. She jiggled and jiggled the hook to no avail.

"Sheep dip—the tar that causes tobacco harshness. Lucky Strike is the only cigarette from which every trace of sheep dip has been removed," said a rich, happy male voice. *"Smoke Luckies, they're kind to your throat—"*

Janice spun the dial to another station and got organ music. "Good God! What's the matter with them?"

The maid leaned with arms crossed in the doorway, regarding Janice with quizzical slanted eyes as she twisted the dial, hunting in vain for news.

"Why, they're all *insane!* Sailors are burning up and drowning out there! What's that? Who's there? Is that the Gillettes?" She heard tires rattling the driveway gravel. A fist banged at the door and the bell chimed. The maid stared at her mistress, unmoving. Janice ran to the door and opened it. Bloody-faced, Warren Henry stumbled inside, in heavy flying boots, a zipper suit, and a bloodied yellow lifejacket. "Hi, have you got twenty bucks?"

"My *God,* Warren!"

"Go ahead, pay off the cab, Jan." His voice was hoarse and tight. "Anna May, get out some bandages, will you?"

The taxi driver, a hatchet-faced old white man, said, "Lady, I'm entitled to fifty. I heard the Japs have already landed at Kahuku Point. I got my own family to worry about—"

She gave him two bills. "Twenty is what my husband said."

"I'm getting on the first boat out of here," said the driver, pocketing the bills, "if I have to shoot my way aboard. Every white person in Hawaii will be butchered. That's Roosevelt for you."

In the kitchen, Warren sat bare-chested. The maid was dabbing antiseptic on his blood-dripping upper left arm. "I'll do that," Janice said, taking the sponge and bottle. "Make sure Victor's all right."

Warren gritted his teeth as Janice worked on a raw wound two inches long. "Jan, what's wrong with Vic?"

"Oh, a fever. A cough. Darling, what in God's name happened to you?"

"I got shot down. Those bastards killed my radioman. Light me a cigarette, will you? Our squadron flew patrol ahead of the *Enterprise* and ran into them—hey, easy with the iodine, that's plenty—How *about* these goddamned Japs?"

"Honey, you've got to go to the hospital. This has to be stitched up."

"No, no. The hospital will be jammed. That's one reason

I came *here*. And I wanted to be sure you and Vic were okay. I'm going to Ford Island, find out what's happening, and maybe get a plane. Those Jap carriers haven't gone far. We'll be counterattacking, that's for sure, and I'm not missing that. Just bandage it up, Jan, and then dress this nick in my ear. That's what's dripped most of this gore all over me."

Janice was dizzied to have Warren suddenly back, literally fallen out of the sky, half-naked, bloody, returned from battle. She felt deep happy stirrings as she rubbed his skin, smelled his sweat and blood, and bound up his wounds. He talked on at a great rate, all charged up. "God, it was weird—I thought those A.A. bursts were target practice, of course. We could see them forty miles away. There was a hell of a lot of smoke coming off the island, too. I talked to my wing mate about it. We both figured they were burning sugarcane. We never did spot the Japs until six of them jumped us out of the sun. That was the last I saw of Bill Plantz. I still don't know what happened to him, all I was doing from then on was trying to stay alive. The way those fellows came diving—zowie—"

"Hold still, honey."

"Sorry. I tell you, it was rough, Jan. The SBD's a good dive bomber, but these Jap Zeroes! The speed they've got, the maneuverability! They can turn inside you—whoosh! It's no contest. They do acrobatics like birds. You can't shake them and you can't hold them in your sights. The pilots are hot, let me tell you. I don't know if the F4F's a match for them, but one thing's sure, an SBD against Zeroes is simply a dead pigeon. All I could do was keep turning and turning to evade. They got De Lashmutt right away. He almost broke my eardrums with a horrible scream on the intercom. And then he yelled, 'Mr. Henry, I'm pouring blood, I'm dying,' and he moaned and that was all. There was nothing I could do. They kept coming at me. They were so eager, one of them finally overshot and hung for a second or two, in my sights, turning. I let go with my fifties and I could swear he started smoking, but I can't claim anything. I lost sight of him. Tracers started from three sides, right past my windows, these big pink streaks, *zing, zing, zing*—and then, goddamn it, our own A.A. opened up! Why the hell they shot at *me* I'll never know, the silly sons of bitches—maybe they were gunning for the Japs and missing—but the flak was bursting all around me. I still don't know whether they got me, or one of the Japs did. All I know is my gas tank caught fire. Poor De Lashmutt, I yelled and yelled at him, till the flames were coming up around the cockpit, but he didn't answer, he certainly was dead. So I popped the canopy and jumped. I didn't even see where I was until the parachute opened, I just saw water. I was out over Honolulu Harbor, but the wind took me inshore. I almost got hung up in a palm tree in a little park off Dillingham Boulevard; then I cleared it and got down. I grabbed that cab, but I had a time with that fellow. He *saw* the chute draped all over the tree, he saw me unbuckling—he stopped to watch—and he *still* wanted fifty dollars to take me home. A patriot, that one!"

"I've got the bleeding sort of under control, sweetie. Just sit quiet, will you?"

"Good girl. One thing I want to do before this day's out is get at a typewriter. I may file the first combat report of this war on Zeroes. Hey? How about that? . . . You should see the sights downtown!" Warren crookedly grinned at his wife. "People out in pajamas, nightgowns, or less, yelling, running around gawking at the sky. Old people, kids, mothers with babies. Damn fools, when A.A. shrapnel was raining all over the place! The only safe place was inside. I saw this beautiful Chinese girl—Anna May reminds me of her—go galloping across Dillingham Boulevard in nothing but a bra and pink panties, and I mean small transparent panties—really a sight—"

"You would notice something like that," said Janice. "No doubt you'd notice it if your arm had been shot clean off." With his good arm, Warren gave her a rough intimate caress, and she slapped his hand. "All right! I've got this wound plastered down. Maybe it'll hold for a while. Your ear is all right too. I still think you should see a doctor at the Naval Air Station."

"If there's time, if there's time." Grimacing as he moved the arm, Warren put on his shirt and sweater and zipped up the suit. "I'll have a look at Vic. Get out the car."

He emerged from the house a few moments later and opened the car door. "Why, the son of a gun's sleeping peacefully. He feels cool and he looks like he's grown twice as big."

"Maybe the fever broke." Janice paused, hand on the gearshift. The car radio was broadcasting an appeal from the governor to keep calm, with assurances that fleet damage was slight and that the attackers had all been driven off. "Warren, that cab driver said the Japs were landing at Kahuku. Do you suppose there's any danger of that, and—"

"No, no, get started. Landing? How the hell could they keep a beachhead supplied from four thousand miles away? You'll hear all kinds of crazy scuttlebutt. This was a hit-and-run raid. Christ, the high brass on this rock must be cutting their collective throats about now. Of all the sucker plays, a Sunday morning sneak attack! Why, it's been a routine battle problem for years."

On the ridge sightseers stood in the grass beside parked cars, chattering and pointing. Heavy black smoke boiled up out of the anchorage and mushroomed over the sky, darkening the sun to a pale ball. Janice stopped the car. Through the windshield, Warren swept the harbor with the binoculars.

"Good God, Jan, Ford Island's a junkyard! I don't see one undamaged plane. But there must be many left in the hangars. Lord, and there's a battlewagon *capsized*. I'll bet a thousand guys are caught inside that—hey! Jesus Christ! Are they coming *back?*"

All over the harbor guns began rattling and flaming, and black A.A. balls blossomed again in the blue. Warren peered skyward. "I'll be goddamned. There they are. How about that? Those sons of bitching Japs are sure betting everything on this one, Janice! Well, that means the carriers are still in range anyway, waiting to recover them. Great! Move over. I'm driving."

Speeding made Janice nervous when she wasn't at the wheel, and Warren knew it, but he whistled down to Pearl City like an escaping bank bandit. After a few moments of fright his wife began to enjoy the breakneck ride. Everything was different on this side of time, the side after the Japs attacked; more adventurous, almost more fun. How handsome Warren looked, how competent, how desirable, handling the wheel with a relaxed touch of his unhurt arm, puffing a cigarette in his taut mouth, watching the road through narrow eyes! Her boredom and irritability were gone and forgotten. The black puffballs were far thicker than before, and through the windshield they saw one Japanese plane after another burst into flames and fall. Each time Warren cheered.

The fleet landing was a mess and a horror. Sailors with blistered faces and hands, with skin hanging in yellow or black scorched pieces from bloody flesh, were being helped out of whaleboats or lifted off in stretchers and loaded onto hospital trucks by men in red-smeared whites. Wounded and unwounded alike were bawling obscenities, unmindful of the women crowding the landing and gnawing their fingers as they scanned the faces of the hurt men; unmindful too of the children who played and joked around the women's skirts—those not old enough to stare with round eyes at the burned sailors. The coxswain of a whaleboat full of sheeted bodies was trying to come alongside, and a fat old chief in khaki kept cursing at him and waving him off. Over all this noise rolled the massive thumping and cracking of guns, the wail of sirens, the blasts of ships' horns, and the roar of airplanes, for the second attack was now in full swing. There was a heavy smell of firecrackers in the air, mingled with a sour stink from the black oil burning on the water all around Ford Island and sending up clouds of thick smoke. Hands on hips, cigarette dangling from his mouth, Warren Henry calmly surveyed the terrible and spectacular scene.

Janice said, in shaken tones, "I don't know how you'll ever get across."

He nodded absently, then strode to the end of the landing to a long canopied boat. Janice hurried after him. "Coxswain, whose barge is this?"

The immaculate sailor at the tiller flipped a hand to a white hat perfectly squared on his close-cropped head. Big-jawed, bronzed, and tall, he eyed Warren's gory life-jacket curiously, and drawled, "Suh, this is Admiral Radburn's barge."

"Is the admiral on the beach?"

"Yes, suh."

"Do you know how long he'll be?"

"Negative, suh, he just told me to wait."

Glancing back at the milling boats along the landing, Warren said, "Well, look, here's how it is. I'm Lieutenant Henry, off the *Enterprise*. I'm a dive bomber pilot."

"Yes, suh?"

"I flew in this morning, just when the attack started. The Japs shot me down. I have to find another plane and get into this fight, so how's for taking me over to Ford Island?"

The coxswain hesitated, then straightened up and saluted. "Come aboard, suh. The important thing is to get those sons of bitches. Excuse me, ma'am."

"Oh, quite all right," Janice laughed. "I want him to get those sons of bitches too."

Hair stirring in the wind, bloody lifejacket dangling open, Warren stood in the stern sheets, hands on hips, smiling at her as the barge pulled away.

"Get them!" she called. "And come back to me."

"Roger. Don't drive back till these bastards quit, or you may get strafed. Be seeing you."

He ducked as a red and yellow Japanese plane passed right over his head, not twenty feet in the air, its motor noisily coughing and missing; then it turned sharply and flew away across the channel, over the capsized crimson hull of a battleship. Warren straightened, still grinning. Janice watched the admiral's beautiful barge, all new gray paint, shiny brass, snowy curtains and cordwork, carry her bloodstained husband away to the flaming smoky mid-harbor island that was the Navy's airfield. He waved and she wildly waved back. She was horror-stricken by what she had seen at the fleet landing; yet never had she felt so aroused, so full of life, so plain damn good, and so much in love.

An Army spokesman came on the automobile radio as she drove home, urging calm, warning against sabotage, and assuring the people that the second attack had been turned back with little further damage to the fleet, and at fearful cost to the Japanese. All-clear sirens were wailing over the island. She found the maid in an armchair listening to the radio, which was playing Hawaiian music again.

"Victor's been very quiet, Missus Henry," she said. "Not a sound. Isn't it terrible about the war? But we'll beat them."

"Sheep dip—the tar that causes tobacco harshness," said the jolly voice. *"Lucky Strike is the only cigarette from which every trace of sheep dip—"*

In his bedroom Victor coughed, a deep harsh cough like a man. "Why, there he goes now," Janice said.

"The very first time, ma'am, since he got his medicine. I've been listening."

Janice's watch read eight minutes to ten. "Well, it's been about two hours. I guess that's all the medicine's good for. I'll give him more." The baby still felt cool. He took the spoonful of brown syrup without opening his eyes, sighed, and turned over. Janice sank in a chair, perspiring and spent, thinking that a war had begun and the Pacific fleet had been smashed between her baby's two doses of cough medicine.

60

THE sun poked up over the horizon, painting a red flush on the Clipper's wing. Wide awake, Victor Henry watched the brightening disk rise free of the ocean. The flying boat's engines changed pitch, rasping at his nerves. Since he had said good-bye to Pamela Tudsbury in Red Square in the snow, he had been shaken up in trains, planes, boats, trucks, jeeps, sleighs, and even oxcarts. He thought his bones would vibrate aboard the *California* for a month. Forty-eight hours, two more fifteen-hundred-mile hops, and if nothing went wrong the trek halfway round the earth would be over.

The sun moved sidewise. The turn was so shallow that he felt no tilt in his seat. A pink ray shot across his lap from the opposite side of the plane. Pug left his seat and walked forward into the galley, where the steward was scrambling eggs. "I'd like to talk to Ed Connelly, if he's free."

The steward smiled, gesturing at the door marked FLIGHT DECK. The naval officer and the Clipper captain had been eating meals together and sharing rooms at the island hotels. In the dial-filled cockpit the engines sounded much louder, and beyond the plexiglass the void purple sea and clear blue sky stretched all around. The captain, a beefy freckled man in shirt-sleeves and headphones, looked oddly at Pug Henry.

"Morning, Ed. Why are we heading back?"

Connelly passed him a radio message, hand-printed in red ink on a yellow form.

CINCPAC HARBOR CIRCUIT GENERAL PLAIN LANGUAGE MESSAGE QUOTE AIR RAID ON PEARL HARBOR X THIS IS NO DRILL UNQUOTE X HEAVY GUNFIRE IN ANCHOR- AGE X RECOMMEND YOU RETURN WAKE TILL SITUA- TION CLARIFIES

"How about that?" The captain removed the sponge- rubber headphones and rubbed his curly red hair. "Do you suppose it's for real?"

"I wouldn't doubt it," said Victor Henry.

"I'm damned. I honestly never thought they'd go. At- tacking Pearl! They'll get creamed."

"Let's hope so. But what's the point of turning back, Ed?"

"I guess they might be hitting Midway, too."

"Well, they might be hitting Wake, for that matter."

"I've talked to Wake. All quiet."

Victor Henry returned to his seat, agitated though far from astonished. Here it was at last, he thought: an attempted sneak attack on Pearl, in the midst of a war scare. The uninventive Asiatics had elected to try the Port Arthur trick again, after all. But surely this time they were running their heads into a noose! The United States in 1941 wasn't Czarist Russia in 1904. One phrase in Cincpac's message nagged at him: *This is no drill.* That was silly, to a fleet on war alert! Some low-level com- municator must have tacked that one on.

A calm sunburned marine in a jeep, naked except for shorts, socks, and boots, waited for him at the landing. The marine commander had put his forces on combat alert and wanted to see Captain Henry. They drove along the beach road in blazing sunlight and choking coral dust, then turned off into the brush. Combat alert had not changed the look of Wake in the past hours: three flat sandy peaceful islands in a horseshoe shape around emerald shallows, ringed by the wide sea, alive with myriads of birds—for it had been a sanctuary—and bustling with the bulldozers and trucks of civilian construction gangs. The queer hump-backed island rats hopped like tiny kangaroos out of the jeep's path, and brilliantly colored birds rose from the brush in chirping clouds.

Perfectly camouflaged by scrub, the command post was sunk far down in coral sand. When Victor Henry faced the marine colonel in this deep timbered hole, saw the radio gear and crude furniture and smelled perking coffee and freshly dug soil, the war with Japan became a fact for him. The dugout did not have the graveyard-muck odor of the Russian trenches; it was roasting hot and dry, not freezing cold and wet; the men frantically working on the telephone lines and the overhead beams were not frost-bitten, pale, bundled-up Slavs, but sunburned, heavily sweating Americans in shorts. Yet here, where the roar of the Pacific dimly sounded, these Americans—like the Russians outside Moscow—were going into the ground to await attack. The United States was in.

The colonel, a mild-faced scrawny man with whom Pug had dined the night before, gave him an envelope to take to Cincpac. "Put it in the admiral's hand yourself, Captain. Please! It's a list of my worst shortages. We can make a fight of it here. Maybe we can hold out till we're relieved, if he'll send us that stuff. Radar gear for Wake is sitting right now on the dock in Hawaii. It's been there for a month. For God's sake, ask him to put it on a destroyer or better yet a bomber, and rush it here. I'm blind without radar. I can't send fighters on patrols, I have too few. I'm twenty feet above the ocean at my highest point, and I only gain a few more feet with my water tower. We'll probably end up eating fish and rice behind barbed wire anyway, but at least we can make the bastards work to take the place."

Pug got back to the hotel just ahead of a rain squall. The Clipper passengers were sitting down to lunch when blasts shook the floor, rattled the dishes, and sent broken window-panes clinking to the tiles. Amid shouts and cries the passengers jumped for the windows. Fat cigar-shaped air-planes, with orange circles painted on their flamboyant jungle camouflage, were flashing past in the rain; Pug noted their twin engines and twin tails. Smoke and fire were already rising from the airfield across the lagoon, and more explosions, bigger flames, heavier smoke came fast. Pug had often seen bombing, but this attack, destroy-ing an American installation with impunity, still outraged and numbed him.

The marauding bombers, blurry in the rain, kept criss-crossing the islands and the lagoon with thunderous engine roars, meeting only meager bursts of fire. Soon a line of bombers came winging straight for the Pan American com-pound, and this was what Victor Henry was fearing. An attack on the Clipper might strand him and paralyze his war career before it started. There was no way off Wake Island, except aboard that huge inviting silvery target.

Savage explosions and crashes burst around them as the planes bombed and machine-gunned the hotel, the Pan Am repair shops, the dock, and the radio tower. A gasoline dump close by went up in a colossal sheet of white flame, climbing to the sky with a terrific howl. The passengers dove under tables or huddled in corners, but Victor Henry still crouched at the window beside the pilot, watching. They saw spurts of water approach the flying boat. They saw pieces of the Clipper go flying.

When the bomber sounds faded, Pug followed the pilot out onto the pier at a run. Like a clothed ape, Ed Connelly clambered over the slippery flying boat in the rain, making it rock and slosh. "Pug, so help me God, I think we can still fly! They didn't hole the tanks or the engines. At least I don't think they did. I'm hauling my passengers the hell out of here now, and I'll argue with Hawaii later."

The passengers eagerly scrambled aboard. The Clipper took off, and it flew. Below, smashed airplanes flamed and all three islands poured smoke. Pug could see little figures looking up at the departing Clipper. Some waved.

Even in the dead of night, nine hours later, Midway was not hard to find. The pilot called Victor Henry to the cockpit to show him the star of flame far ahead on the black sea. "Christ, these Japs had the thing all lined up, didn't they?" he said. "They hit everywhere at once. I heard over the radio they're already in Malaya, Thailand, Hong Kong, they're bombing Singapore—"

"Can we land, Ed?"

"We've got to try. I can't raise them. All the navigation lights are out. Midway has a lot of underground tanks. And if we can just get down, we can fuel. Soooo—here goes."

The flying boat dropped low over dark waters, lit only by the glare from blazing hangars and buildings. On slapping into the sea, it hit something solid with a frightening clang, but slowed and floated undamaged. The airfields of Midway, they soon learned, had been shelled by a Japanese cruiser and a destroyer. An exhilarated mob of almost naked fire fighters was flooding the blazes with chemicals and water, generating giant billows of acrid red smoke. Victor Henry found his way to the commandant's office and tried to get news of the Pearl Harbor attack. The lieutenant on duty was obsequious and vague. The commandant was out inspecting the island's air defenses, he said, and he had no authority to show top secret dispatches, but he could tell the captain that the Navy had shot down a mess of Japanese planes.

"How about the *California*? I'm going there to take command of her."

The lieutenant looked impressed. "Oh, really, sir? The *California*? I'm sure she's all right, sir. I don't recall any word about the *California*."

This news enabled Victor Henry to sleep a little, though he tossed and muttered all night and got up well before dawn to pace the cool hotel veranda. The goony birds of Midway, big hook-beaked creatures which he had heard about but never seen, were out by the dozens, walking the gray dunes. He saw them clumsily fly, and land, and tumble on their heads. He watched a pair do a ridiculous mating dance on the beach as the sun came up, plopping their feet like a drunken old farm couple. Ordinarily Victor Henry would have seized the chance to inspect Midway, for it was a big installation, but today nothing could draw him out of sight of the flying boat, rising and falling on the swells and bumping the dock with dull booms.

The four hours to Hawaii seemed like forty. Instead of melting away at its usual rate, time froze. Pug asked the steward for cards and played solitaire, but forgot he was playing. He just sat, enduring the passage of time like the grind of a dentist's drill, until at last the steward came and spoke to him, smiling. "Captain Connelly would like you to come up forward, sir."

Ahead, through the plexiglass, the green sunny humps of the Hawaiian Islands were showing over the horizon.

"Nice?" said the pilot.

"Prettiest sight I've seen," said Pug, "since my wife had a girl baby."

"Stick around, and we'll take a look at the fleet."

Nobody aboard the Clipper knew what to expect. The rumors on Midway had varied from disaster to victory, with graphic details both ways. The Clipper came in from the north over the harbor and hooked around to descend. In these two passes, Victor Henry was struck sick by what his disbelieving eyes saw. All along the east side of Ford Island the battleships of the Pacific Fleet lay careened, broken, overturned, in the disorder of a child's toys in a bath. Hickam Field and the Navy's air base were broad dumps of blackened airplane fragments and collapsed burned hangar skeletons. Some dry docks held shattered tumbled-over ships. Pug desperately tried to pick out the *California* in the hideous smoky panorama. But at this altitude the ships with basket masts looked alike. Some of the inboard vessels appeared just slightly damaged. If only one was the *California!*

"My God," Connelly said, looking around at Pug, his face drawn, "what a shambles!"

Speechless, Victor Henry nodded and sat on a folding seat, as the flying boat swooped low past a smashed gutted battleship with tripod masts, sunk to the level of its guns and resting on the bottom at a crazy angle. The Clipper threw up a curtain of spray that wiped out the heart-rending sight.

Journey's end.

Passing several clanging, speeding Navy ambulances, Pug went from the customs shed at the Pan Am landing straight to the Cincpac building, where officers and sailors busily swarmed. They all wore unsure scared expressions, like people after a bad earthquake. A very handsome ensign in whites, at a desk that barred access to Cincpac's inner offices, looked incredulously at Pug, who wore wrinkled slacks and a seersucker jacket. "The admiral? You mean Cincpac, sir? Admiral *Kimmel?*"

"That's right," Pug said.

"Sir, you don't really expect to see Admiral Kimmel *today*, do you? Shall I try his Assistant Chief of Staff?"

"Give the admiral a message, please. I'm Captain Victor Henry. I've just come in on the Clipper with a personal letter for him from the marine commandant on Wake Island."

The very handsome ensign gestured wearily at a chair and picked up a telephone. "You may have to wait all day, or a week, sir. You know what the situation is."

"I have the general picture."

A minute or so later, a pretty woman in a tailored blue suit looked through the double doors. "Captain Henry? This way, sir."

The ensign stared at Victor Henry walking past him, as though the captain had sprouted another head. Along the corridor, the offices of Cincpac's senior staff stood open, and the sound of excited talk and typewriter clatter drifted out. A marine rigidly saluted before high doors decorated with four gold stars and a Navy seal, and labelled in gold COMMANDER-IN-CHIEF, PACIFIC FLEET. They passed into a wood-panelled anteroom. The woman opened a heavy polished mahogany door.

"Admiral, here's Captain Henry."

"Hey, Pug! Great day, how long has it been?" Kimmel waved cheerily from the window, where he stood gazing out at the anchorage. He was dressed in faultless gold-buttoned whites, and looked tanned, fit, and altogether splendid, though much older and quite bald. "Have I seen you since you worked for me on the *Maryland?*"

"I don't think so, sir."

"Well, the years are dealing kindly with you! Sit you down, sit you down. Been flying high, haven't you? Observing in Roosia, and all that, eh?" They shook hands. Kimmel's voice was as hearty and winning as ever. This was an outstanding officer, Pug thought, who had been marked for success all the way and had gone all the way. Now, after twenty years of war exercises and drills against Orange, the fleet he commanded lay in sight beyond the window, wrecked in port by the Orange team in one quick real action. He appeared remarkably chipper, but for his eyes, which were reddened and somewhat unfocussed.

"I know how little time you have, sir." Pug drew out of his breast pocket the letter from Wake Island.

"Not at all. It's nice to see an old familiar face. You were a good gunnery officer, Pug. A good officer all around. Cigarette?" Kimmel offered him the pack, and lit one for himself. "Let's see. Don't you have a couple of boys in the service now?"

"Yes sir. One flies an SBD off the *Enterprise,* and—"

"Well fine! They didn't get the *Enterprise* or any other carrier, Pug, because the carriers at least followed my orders and were on one hundred percent alert. And the other lad?"

"He's aboard the *Devilfish* in Manila."

"Manila, eh? They haven't hit the fleet at Manila yet, though I understand they've bombed the airfields. Tommy Hart's got some warning now, and *he'll* have no excuse. I only hope the Army Air people in Manila aren't as totally asleep as they were here! The Army was and is *completely* responsible for the safety of these islands *and* of this anchorage, Pug, including the definite responsibility of air patrol and radar search. Nothing on God's earth could be clearer than the way that is spelled out in the islands' defense instructions. The documents leave no doubt about *that,* fortunately. Well—you have something from Wake, don't you? Let's have a look-see. Were you there when they hit?"

"Yes, sir."

"How bad was it? As bad as this?"

"Well, I'd say about two dozen bombers worked us over.

Mainly they went after planes and air installations, Admiral. No ships were there to get bombed."

Cincpac shot a glance at Victor Henry, as though suspecting irony in his words. "Say, weren't you supposed to relieve Chip Wallenstone in the *California?*"

"Yes, sir."

Kimmel shook his head, and started to read the letter.

Pug ventured to say, "How did the *California* make out, Admiral?"

"Why, don't you know?"

"No, sir. I came straight here from the Clipper."

Not looking up, in the brisk tone of a report, Kimmel said, "She took two torpedoes to port and several bomb hits and near misses. One bomb penetrated below decks and the explosion started a big fire. She's down by the bow, Pug, and sinking. They're still counterflooding, so she may not capsize. She's electric drive, and the preliminary estimate"—he pulled toward him a sheet on his desk, and peered at it—"a year and a half out of action, possibly two. That's top secret of course. We're releasing no damage information."

Cincpac finished the letter from Wake in a heavy silence, and tossed it on the desk.

Victor Henry's voice trembled and he swallowed in mid-sentence. "Admiral, if I broke a lot of asses, including my own—ah, is there a chance I could put her back on the line in six months?"

"Go out and see for yourself. It's hopeless, Pug. A salvage officer will relieve Chip." The tone was sympathetic, but Victor Henry felt it did Cincpac good to give someone else catastrophic news.

"Well, that's that, then, I guess."

"You'll get another command."

"The only thing is, Admiral, there aren't that many available battleships. Not any more."

Again, the quick suspicious glance. It was hard to say anything in this context without seeming to needle the commander of the Pacific Fleet. Kimmel made a curt gesture at the letter Pug had brought. "Now there's a problem for you. Do we relieve Wake or not? It means exposing a carrier. We can't go in without air cover. He's asking for a pile of things I can't give him, for the simple reason that the Russians and the British have got the stuff. Mr. Roosevelt was a great Navy President until that European fracas started, Pug, but at that point he took his eye off the ball. Our real enemy's always been right here, *here* in the Pacific. This ocean is our nation's number one security problem. *That's* what he forgot. We never had the wherewithal to conduct proper patrols. I didn't want to rely on the Army, God knows, but equipment only has so much life in it, and what would we have had to fight the war with if we'd used up our planes in patrolling? Washington's been crying wolf about the Japs for a year. We've had so many full alerts and air raid drills and surprise attack exercises and all, nobody can count them, but—well, the milk is spilled, the horse is stolen, but I think it's pretty clear that the President got too damned interested in the wrong enemy, the wrong ocean, and the wrong war."

It gave Victor Henry a strange sensation, after Berlin and London and Moscow, and now this staggering personal disappointment, to hear from Admiral Kimmel the old unchanged Navy verbiage about the importance of the Pacific. "Well, Admiral, I know how busy you are," he said, though in fact he was struck by the quiet at the heart of the cataclysm, and by Kimmel's willingness to chat with a mere captain he did not know very well. Cincpac acted almost as lonesome as Kip Tollever had.

"Yes, well, I do have a thing or two on my mind, and you've got to go about your business too. Nice seeing you, Pug," said Admiral Kimmel, in a sudden tone of dismissal.

Janice answered Pug's telephone call and warmly urged him to come and stay at the house. Pug wanted a place where he could drop his bags, and get into uniform to go to the *California.* He drove out in a Navy car, took suitable if brief delight in his grandson, and accepted Janice's commiseration over his ship with a grunt. She offered to get his whites quickly pressed by the maid. In the spare room he opened his suitcase to pull out the crumpled uniform, and his letter to Pamela Tudsbury fell to the floor.

In a dressing gown he glanced through the letter, which

he had written during the long hop from Guam to Wake Island. It embarrassed him as one of his old love letters to Rhoda might have. There wasn't much love in this one, mostly a reasoned and accurate case for his living out his life as it was. The whole business with the English girl—romance, flirtation, love affair, whatever it had been—had begun to seem so far away after his stops in Manila and Guam, so dated, so unlike him, so utterly outside realities and possibilities! Pamela was a beautiful young woman, but odd. The best proof of her oddness was her very infatuation with him, a grizzled United States Navy workhorse with whom she had been thrown together a few times. Dour and repressed though he was, she had ignited a flash of romance in him in those last turbulent hours in Moscow. He had allowed himself to hope for a new life, and to half believe in it, in his elation over his orders to the *California*.

And now—how finished it all was! *California*, Pamela, the Pacific Fleet, the honor of the United States, and —God alone knew—any hope for the civilized world.

A knock at the door; the voice of the Chinese maid: "Your uniform, Captain?"

"Thank you. Ah, that's a fine job. I appreciate it."

He did not tear the letter up. He did not think he could write a better one. The situation of a man past fifty declining a young woman's love was awkward and ridiculous, and no words could help much. He slipped the envelope into his pocket. When he passed a mailbox on his way to the Navy Yard, he stopped and mailed it. The clank of the box was a sad sound in a sad day for Captain Victor Henry.

Sadder yet was the trip to the *California*, through foul-smelling water so coated with black oil that the motor launch cut no wake, but chugged slimily along in smoky air, thumping like an icebreaker through a floating mass of black-smeared garbage and debris. The launch passed all along Battleship Row, for the *California* lay nearest the channel entrance. One by one Pug contemplated these gargantuan gray vessels he knew so well—he had served in several—fire-blackened, bomb-blasted, down by the head, down by the stern, sitting on the bottom, listing, or turned turtle. Grief and pain tore at him.

He was a battleship man. Long, long ago he had passed up flight school. Navy air had seemed to him fine for reconnaissance, bombing support, and torpedo attacks, but not for the main striking arm. He had argued with the fly-fly boys that when war came, the thin-skinned carriers would lurk far from the action and would fuss at each other with bombings and dogfights, while the battleships with their big rifles came to grips and slugged it out for command of the sea. The fliers had asserted that one aerial bomb or torpedo could sink a battleship. He had retorted that a sixteen-inch steel plate wasn't exactly porcelain, and that a hundred guns firing at once might slightly mar the aim of a pilot flying a little tin crate.

His natural conservative streak had been reinforced by his football experience. To him, carriers had been the fancy-Dan team with tricky runners and razzle-dazzle passers; battlewagons, the heavy solid team of chargers, who piled up the yardage straight through the line. These tough ground gainers usually became the champions. So he had thought—making the mistake of his life. He had been as wrong as a man could be, in the one crucial judgment of his profession.

Other battleship men might still find excuses for these tragic slaughtered dinosaurs that the launch was passing. For Pug Henry, facts governed. Each of these vessels was a giant engineering marvel, a floating colossus as cunningly put together as a lady's watch, capable of pulverizing a city. All true, all true. But if caught unawares, they could be knocked out by little tin flying crates. The evidence was before his eyes. The twenty-year argument was over.

The setting sun cast a rosy glow on the canted superstructure of the *California*. She listed about seven degrees to port, spouting thick streams of filthy water in rhythmic pumped spurts. The smoke-streaked, flame-blistered, oil-smeared steel wall, leaning far over Pug's head as the motor launch drew up to the accommodation ladder, gave him a dizzy, doomed feeling. The climb up the canted and partly submerged ladder was dizzying too.

What an arrival! In bad moments in Kuibyshev, on Siberian trains, in Tokyo streets, in the Manila Club, Pug had cheered himself with pictures of his reception aboard this ship: side boys in white saluting, honor guard on parade, boatswain's pipe trilling, commanding officers shaking hands at the gangway, a sweet triumphant tour of a great ship shined up to holiday beauty and brilliance for the eye of a new captain. Often he had played a minor part in such rituals. But to be the star, the center, the incoming "old man"! It was worth a lifetime of the toughest drudgery.

And now this!

A vile corrupt stink hit Victor Henry in the face as he stepped on the sloping quarterdeck of the *California,* and said, "Request permission to come aboard, sir."

"Permission granted, sir." The OOD's salute was smart, his sunburned boyish face attractive. He wore grease-streaked khakis, with gloves and a spyglass. Five corpses lay on the quarterdeck, under sheets stained with water and oil, their soggy black shoes projecting, their noses poking up the cloth, water trickling from them down the slanted deck toward the OOD's stand. The smell came partly from them, but it was a compound of reeks— seeping smoke, gasoline fumes from the pumps, burnt oil, burnt wood, burnt paper, burnt flesh, rotted food, broken waste lines; a rancid mildewy effluvium of disaster, of a great machine built to house human beings, broken and disintegrating. Unshaven sailors and officers in dirty clothing wandered about. Above the filth and mess and tangled hoses and scattered shells and ammo boxes on the main deck, the superstructure jutted into the sunset sky, massive, clean, and undamaged. The long fourteen-inch guns were trained neatly fore and aft, newly and smoothly painted gray, tampions in place, turrets unscathed. The ship bristled with A.A. guns. The old Prune Barge was tantalizingly alive and afloat—wounded, but still mighty, still grandiose.

"I'm Captain Victor Henry."

"Yes, sir? Oh! Yes, *sir!* Captain Wallenstone's been expecting you for quite a while." He snapped his fingers at a messenger in whites, and said with a winning sad grin, "It's awful that you should find the ship like this, sir. Benson, tell the C.O. that Captain Henry is here."

"One moment. Where's your C.O.?"

"Sir, he's with the salvage officers down in the forward engine room."

"I know the way."

Walking familiar decks and passageways that were weird in their fixed slant, climbing down tipped ladders, choking on smoke, gasoline, and oil fumes, and a gruesome smell of rotting meat, penetrating ever deeper into gloom and stench, realizing that these fume-filled spaces were explosive traps, Victor Henry got himself down to the forward engine room, where four officers huddled on a high catwalk, playing powerful hand lights on a sheet of oil-covered water. By an optical illusion, the water half-drowning the engines appeared slanted, rather than the listing bulkheads.

With little ceremony, Victor Henry joined in the engineering talk about saving the ship. The quantity of water flooding through the torpedo holes was more than the pumps could throw out, so the ship was slowly settling. It was that simple. Pug asked about more pumps, about pumping by tugs and auxiliary vessels; but all over the anchorage the cry was for pumps. No more pumping was to be had, not in time to keep the battleship off the mud. Captain Wallenstone, haggard and untidy in greasy khakis and looking about sixty years old, reeled off sad answers to Pug's other ideas. Patching the holes would take months of underwater work. They stretched over a dozen frames. Sealing off the damaged spaces by sending in divers and closing them off one by one could not be done in time. In short, the *California,* though not yet on the bottom, was done for. The talk was about cofferdams and cement patches, about a complete refitting in the States, about return to service in 1943 or 1944.

Wallenstone took Victor Henry up to his cabin. It was a blessed thing to smell fresh air again streaming in through windward portholes, and to see the evening star bright in the apple-green sky. The commanding officer's quarters were intact, spacious, shipshape, glamorous, and beautiful, on this battleship sinking uncontrollably to the bottom. A Filipino steward brought them coffee, which they had to hold on their laps, for it would have slid off the tilted tables. Mournfully, the captain told Pug his experiences of the Japanese attack. Pug had never encountered this officer before, but Wallenstone appeared to know a lot about him. He asked Victor Henry what President Roosevelt was really like, and whether he thought the Russians could hold out much longer against the Germans.

"Oh, by the way," he said, as he started to accompany Pug out, "quite a bit of mail accumulated here for you. I'm not sure that"—he opened and closed desk drawers—"yes, here it is, all together."

Victor Henry tucked the bulky envelope under his arm and picked his way with the captain across the cluttered, stinking main deck in the twilight.

"You wouldn't believe what this ship looked like two days ago." The captain shook his head sadly, pitching his voice above the whine and thud of the pumps and the metallic hammering everywhere. "We had the word from Manila to expect you. I ran off a captain's inspection on Saturday. I was at it for five hours. What a job they'd done! You could have eaten your dinner off the engine room deck. It gleamed. She was the smartest ship in this man's Navy, Henry, and she had the finest crew that ever —oh well, what's the use? What's the use?"

At the quarterdeck the bodies were gone. The captain looked around and said, "Well, they took those poor devils away. That's the worst of it. At the last muster forty-seven were still missing. They're down below, Henry, all drowned. Oh, God! These salvage fellows say this ship will come back and fight one day, but God knows! And God knows where I'll be then! Who would think the sons of bitches could sneak all the way to Hawaii undetected? Who'd think they'd be screwy enough to try? *Where* was our air cover?"

"Is that the *Enterprise?*" Pug pointed at a black rectangular shape moving down channel, showing no lights.

Wallenstone peered at the silhouette. "Yes. Thank Christ *she* wasn't in port Sunday morning."

"My son's a flier on board her. Maybe I'll get to see him. First time in a long while."

"Say! That should cheer you up some. If anything can. I know how you must feel. All I can say is, I'm sorry, Henry. Sorry as a human being can be."

Captain Wallenstone held out his hand. Victor Henry hesitated.

In that tiny pause, he thought that if this man had been wiser than all the rest, had held the ship in readiness condition Zed or even Yoke—after all, he too had received a war warning—and had ordered a dawn air alert, the *California* might be the most famous battleship in the Navy now, afloat and ready to fight. Wallenstone then would be a national hero with a clear red carpet to the office of Chief of Naval Operations, and he would be turning over a fighting command to his relief. Instead, he was one of eight battleship captains conferring with salvage officers and saying how unfortunate it all was; and he was offering a handshake to the man who would never relieve him, because he had let the enemy sink his ship.

But could he, Pug Henry, have done any better? A battleship captain who roused his crew for dawn general quarters in port, while half a dozen other battleships slept, would have been a ridiculous eccentric. The entire fleet from Cincpac down had been dreaming. That was the main and forever unchangeable fact of history. The sinking of the *California* was a tiny footnote nobody would ever pay attention to.

He shook Wallenstone's hand, saluted the colors, and made his way down the ladder—which leaned nauseatingly over the water—to the luxurious and unharmed captain's gig that the OOD had summoned. The gig ran darkened to the landing. In the dim dashboard light of the car, Pug glanced over the envelopes of his piled-up mail; official stuff for the most part, with a couple of letters from Rhoda and one from Madeline. He did not open any of them.

"Dad!" Warren not only was at home, he had already changed into slacks and a flowered loose-hanging shirt. He came lunging into the living room, and threw an arm around his father, holding the other stiff at his side. One ear was plastered with surgical tape. "Well, you finally made it! Some haul, clear from Moscow! How are you, Dad?"

"I've just visited the *California*."

"Oh, Jesus. Bourbon and water?"

"Not that much water, and damned rich on the bourbon. What happened to your arm?"

"Jan told you about how I ran into those Japs, didn't she?"

"She didn't tell me you were wounded."

"It's just a few stitches. I'm still flying, that's the main thing. Come, it's cooler out here, Dad."

In the shadowy screened porch, Pug bitterly described the *California*'s state. Warren was scornful. The battleship Navy had been a lot of sleepy fat cats primed for defeat, he said; obsessed by promotions and competition scores, ignorant of the air, and forever drilling to fight the Battle of Jutland against the Japs. But the Japs had grasped naval aviation and had made a slick opening play. "We'll get 'em," he said, "but it'll be a long hard pull, and the naval aviators'll do it. Not the battlewagons, Dad."

"Seems to me a few airplanes got caught on the ground," Pug growled, feeling the bourbon comforting and radiant inside him.

"Sure, I admit that. This whole base was all unbuttoned. Dad, I'll tell you one thing, if Halsey had been Cincpac, none of it would have happened. He's been so ready and eager for war, his tongue's been hanging out. He'd have kept this goddamn fleet in condition Zed, and on dawn and dusk GQ's for a year. He'd have run patrols till the planes fell apart. He'd have been the most hated son of a bitch in Hawaii, but by God, when they came he'd have been waiting for 'em! Why, we stripped ship in November. We've run darkened ever since, with warheads in our torpedoes, and bombs in the planes, and depth charges on ready. Of course he does go galloping about like an old mule with a bee up its ass."

Warren described Halsey's futile dart south of Oahu looking for Japanese carriers. The direction had seemed dead wrong to Warren Henry and the other fliers. The only place for the Japs to be lurking was north, where they could dash straight for home after the strike. But Halsey—so they later learned—had received a direction-finder report of heavy radio signalling to the south, so southward he had roared, launching all his torpedo planes and dive bombers. For hours the planes had scoured over empty seas, till the *Enterprise* had sheepishly summoned them back. The report had been the commonest of direction-finder errors, a reciprocal bearing. The Japs had lain in the exact opposite direction—north. By then, of course, catching up with them had been hopeless.

His father grunted incredulously. "Is that what happened? God Almighty, that's nearly as stupid as the battleship performance."

"Well, yes, somebody on that big staff should have thought of the reciprocal bearing. But nobody's head was too clear, and I don't know—it was one carrier against four or five, anyway. Maybe it was for the best. At least he did try to find a fight. Listen, Dad, our own A.A. shot down many of our planes, and they sure peppered me. It was just a historic snafu all around. Tell me, how's Briny? Did you see him in Manila?"

The bourbon helped Victor Henry's sickened spirit, but talking to Warren was better medicine. Slanting light from the living room on his son showed him changed: older, more relaxed, rather hard-bitten, the dangling cigarette almost a part of his features. He had fought with the enemy and survived. That edge was in his bearing, though he deferred carefully to Pug.

"I'll tell you, Dad," he said, bringing him a refill from the other room, "I'm not saying this wasn't a defeat. It was the worst defeat in our history. The Navy will be a hundred years living down the shame of it. But by God, the Congress voted for war today with one dissenting vote! Only one! Think—what else could have accomplished that? The Japs were stupid not to move south and dare Roosevelt to come on. He'd have been in trouble." Warren took a deep drink of bourbon. "What's more, operationally they blew this attack. They had us flattened with the first wave. All they did the second time was paste the wagons some more and bomb a few smaller ships. What good was that? Our oil farm was sitting behind the sub base, wide open. Dozens of fat round juicy targets you couldn't miss with your hat. Why, if they'd gotten the oil—and nothing could have stopped them—we'd be evacuating Hawaii right now. The fleet couldn't have operated from here. We'd be staging a Dunkirk across two thousand five hundred miles of ocean. Moreover, they never hit the subs. They'll regret that! They never touched our repair shops—"

"I'm convinced," Pug said. "I'm sure that Jap admiral is

committing hara-kiri right now over his disgraceful failure."

"I said it was a defeat, Dad." Warren, unoffended, came back sharply but pleasantly. "I say they achieved surprise at high political cost, and then failed to exploit it. Say, it's another quarter of an hour to dinner. How about one more shortie?"

Pug wanted to examine his mail, but Warren's acumen was rejoicing his heavy heart, and the strong drink was working wonders. "Well, very short."

He told Warren about his meeting with Admiral Kimmel. The young aviator flipped a hand at the complaint of too much war material going to Europe. "Jesus, him too? Just a feeble excuse. It's got to cost several million lives to stop the Germans. Whose lives? Could be ours! The Russians made one deal with Hitler, and they could make another one. The Communists signed a separate peace in 1917, you know. It was the first thing Lenin did on taking over. The whole game here is to keep the Soviet Union fighting. That's so obvious!"

"You know, you ought to go over in your spare time, Warren, and straighten out Cincpac."

"I'd be glad to, but I'll have to move fast to catch him while he's Cincpac."

"Oh? You got some inside scoop?"

"Dad, the President isn't going to resign, and somebody's head's got to roll."

"Dinner, fellas," Janice's voice called.

"The only thing is," Warren said, as they walked in, "those Russians are going to exact payment for all those lives one day. They'll get to annex Poland, or Czechoslovakia, or some damn thing. But that's fair enough, maybe. Russia keeps swallowing and then puking up Poland every half century or so. What was it like in Moscow anyway, Dad? What are the Russkis like? How much did you see?"

Pug talked straight through dinner about his adventures in Russia. Janice had provided several bottles of red wine. It wasn't very good wine, and he wasn't much of a wine drinker, but tonight he poured down glass after glass, thinking that red wine was really remarkably fine stuff. Continuous talking, another unusual thing for him, eased his heart.

Janice asked questions about Pam Tudsbury, which led him to relate his experiences in England too, and his flight over Berlin. Warren pressed his father for details of the bomb racks and release mechanisms, but Pug could tell him nothing. Warren interrupted Pug's flow of words to describe his run-in with the Bureau of Ordnance over the bombing assembly of his plane, and the improved rack he had manufactured in the shipfitter's shop, which the Bureau was now grudgingly examining for possible use in all planes. Pug tried to keep surprise and pride out of his face, saying, "You'll get no thanks from anybody, boy. Especially if it works! Just a reputation as a trouble-maker."

"I'll get what I want—bombs that fall straight and hit."

Over brandy, back on the dark screened porch, Pug, now fairly close to being drunk, asked his son what he thought he should do, with the *California* command gone. It was an honest question. His son impressed him, and he thought Warren might give him good advice.

Warren laughed and said, "Dad, learn to fly."

"Don't think I haven't thought of it."

"Well, seriously, you'd better go back to Cincpac's staff tomorrow and pound desks till you get a command. They probably believe that you draw a lot of water with the President. You'll get what you ask for. But you have to move fast. If Mr. Roosevelt remembers that you're on the loose again, he'll send you on some other mission. Although I don't know, it must be very interesting work, at that."

"Warren, I hope you believe me—thanks, thanks, boy, just a little more, this is damn good brandy—nearly everything I've been doing in the past two has given me a swift pain in the ass. I don't know why Mr. Roosevelt chose in his wisdom to make a sort of high-octane errand boy out of me. I've talked to great men face to face, and that's a privilege, sure. If I were planning to write a book or go into politics, or something along that line, it would be dandy. But the bloom soon comes off the rose. You're a zero to these people. It's in their manner. You have to watch every sentence you utter and keep your eyes and ears peeled for every move, every word, every tone of some bird who may go down in history, but he's just another man, basically, and maybe even a big criminal, like Stalin or Hitler. I think you have to have a taste for associating with great men. There are people who do, God knows, who crave it, but I'm not one of them. I never want to get out of sight of ships and the water again, and I never want to see the inside of another embassy."

"How did it ever start, Dad? Here, have some more."

"No, no, Warren, I'm feeling no pain at all as it is. Well, okay, just wet the bottom of the glass—thanks, boy. How did it start? Well—"

Pug recounted his prediction of the Nazi-Soviet pact, his visits to the President, his assembling of the planes for England, and his reports from Berlin. He felt he was getting loose-tongued. "Well, that's the idea. I've never discussed these things before with anybody, Warren. Not even your mother. You strike me now as a thoroughgoing professional officer. It does my heart good and it gives me pleasure to confide a little in you. Also, I'm drunk as a fiddler."

Warren grinned. "Ha! You haven't told me a thing. That story about the planes for England cropped up in *Time* a couple of months ago."

"I'm well aware of that," said his father, "but I wasn't the one who spilled the beans. You didn't see *my* name in that story."

"I sure didn't. Dad, don't you know why the President likes you? You've a keen mind, you get things done, you don't talk—a rare enough combination—and added to all that, you don't want the job. He must be up to his nates in these people you describe who keep shoving to get near him. He must find you refreshing as well as useful. There can't be many patriots in Washington."

"Well, that's an interesting thought. I don't know why you're buttering me up, but thanks for calling me a patriot with a keen mind. I do try to be as keen as the next guy, Warren. Possibly I was a wee bit mistaken in that small dispute about carriers versus battleships. If I'd been ordered to the *Enterprise*, for instance, instead of the *California*—which might well have been, had I ever learned to fly—I would have a command right now, instead of a skinful of booze. Thanks, Warren. Thanks for everything, and God bless you. Sorry I did so much talking. Tomorrow I want to hear all about your tangle with the Zeroes. Now if my legs will support me, I think I'll go to bed."

He did not stir till noon. Janice was out on the back lawn, playing with the baby on a blanket, when her father-in-law emerged yawning on the screen porch in a white silk kimono, carrying a manila envelope.

"Hi, Dad," she called. "How about some breakfast?"

He sat in a wicker chair. "You mean lunch. No thanks, I'm still off schedule from the travelling. Your maid's making me coffee. I'll have a look at my mail, then mosey on down to Cincpac."

A few minutes later Janice heard a loud clink. Victor Henry sat upright staring at a letter in his lap, his hands still on the coffee cup he had set down so hard.

"What's the matter, Dad?"

"Eh? What? Nothing."

"Bad news from home?"

"That coffee's mighty hot. I burned my tongue. It's nothing. Where's Warren, by the way?"

"Went to the ship. He expects to be back for dinner, but I guess we can never be sure about anything any more."

"That's exactly right."

His voice and his manner were strained and queer, she thought. Covertly she watched him read and reread two handwritten letters, looking from one to the other, leaving a pile of office mail unopened.

"Say, Jan." He stood, stuffing the mail back in the big envelope.

"Yes, Dad. You're sure you won't eat something?"

"No, no. I don't want to eat. I'm a little tireder than I figured. I may even crawl back in the sack for a bit."

When night fell, his bedroom door was still shut. Warren came home after seven. Janice told him what had been happening. He cautiously rapped at his father's door. "Dad?"

Rapping louder, he tried the knob and went into the black room. Soon he came out with an empty brandy bottle. The cork and foil lay in his palm. "It was a fresh bottle, Janice. He opened it and drank it all."

"Is he all right?"

"He's just out. Out cold."

"Maybe you should look at his mail."

Warren gave her a frigid glare, lighting a cigarette.

"Listen," she said with mixed timidity and desperation, "those letters, whatever they were, upset him. You'd better find out what the trouble is."

"If he wants me to know, he'll tell me."

"What are you going to do?"

"Eat my dinner."

Warren did not speak again until he finished his meat. He sat silent, looking straight ahead when food was not before him. "Dad's taking the *California* thing hard," he finally said. "That's the whole trouble."

"Well, I hope that's all."

He said, "Did you listen to the evening news?"

"No."

"Big air strike on Manila. They made a mess of the Cavite Navy Yard. That's all the news Washington put out. But the communicator on the *Enterprise* told me two submarines were bombed, and one was sunk. That one was the *Devilfish*."

"Oh God, no!"

"And there's no word on survivors."

"Maybe it's a mistaken report."

"Maybe."

"Warren, I feel in my bones that Byron is all right."

His chilly grim face looked much like his father's. "That's comforting. Till we get some more definite information."

61

To military specialists, "Clark Field" is the name of a United States defeat as grave as Pearl Harbor. With this catastrophe at the main Army airfield on Luzon, the Philippines lost their air cover; the Asiatic Fleet had to flee south; and the rich south sea islands and archipelagoes were laid bare at a stroke for conquest. There has never been a rational explanation for what happened there. Yet Congress did not investigate it. Nobody was relieved. History still ignores Clark Field, and remembers Pearl Harbor. Clark Field was half a day late for immortality. Two great disasters five thousand miles apart in one day are boring, and like any good editor, history has cut the repetition.

Clark Field occurred half a day later than Pearl Harbor because the Japanese could not, for all their clever planning, arrange for the dawn to come up everywhere at once. They gave up hope of surprising the Philippines, for the sunrise took five hours to traverse the bulge of ocean from Hawaii. Their bombers waited for good weather in starting from Formosa, and droned straight in over the main island of Luzon just before high noon, expecting alert and violent opposition. The ground observers, on a war footing after the Pearl Harbor news, sent a spate of reports to the command center, tracking the attackers from the coast all the way to their objective. They got there unopposed, nevertheless, and found the fighters and bombers of the Far East Air Force—a formidable armada, built up in recent weeks as the hard core of resistance to Japan—lined up on the ground. This ignominious occurrence remains unaccounted for. It was the Japanese, this time, who were surprised, very pleasantly so. They laid utter waste to General Douglas MacArthur's air force, and flew away. Thus ended, in a quarter of an hour, any hope of stopping the Japanese in the south seas. No course remained for the American forces there but last-ditch stands and surrenders.

The Japanese at once set about to cash in on this startling success. Step one was to make Manila Bay uninhabitable for the United States Navy. Two days after Clark Field a horde of bombers came in and carefully, painstakingly destroyed the Cavite Naval Base at their leisure, having no air defenders to worry about. The *Devilfish* and Byron Henry were at dead center of this attack.

When the attack actually began, Byron was ashore with a working party, drawing torpedoes. The terrifying wail of the siren broke out not far from the big open shed of the torpedo shop. The overhead crane clattered to a halt. The echoing clanks and squeals of repair machinery quieted down. Chiefs, torpedomen, and machinists' mates in greasy dungarees trotted away from their benches and lathes to take battle stations.

Byron's party had four torpedoes in the truck. He decided to load two more before leaving. His orders called for six, and false alarms had been plentiful ever since Clark Field. But with the overhead crane shut down, it was slow work moving an assembled Mark 14 torpedo, a ton and a half of steel cylinder packed with explosives, propellant, and motor. The sweating *Devilfish* sailors were rigging one to the guy chains of a small cherry-picker crane when Byron's leading torpedoman glanced out at the sky. "Mr. Henry, here they come."

Hansen had the best eyes on the *Devilfish*. It took Byron half a minute to discern the neat V of silvery specks shining in the blue, far higher than the German planes he had seen over Poland. The old Warsaw feeling overwhelmed him—the fear, the exhilaration, the call to look sharp and act fast.

"God, yes, fifty or sixty of 'em," he said.

"I counted fifty-seven. They're headed this way, sir. Target angle zero."

"So I see. Well, let's hurry."

The sailor at the wheel of the cherry picker began gunning the motor, tightening the chains on the torpedo. "Hold it!" Byron exclaimed, hearing a distant explosion. More *CRUMPS!* sounded closer. The cement floor trembled. Now for the first time since Warsaw Byron's ears caught a familiar noise—a high whistle ascending in pitch and getting louder.

"Take cover!"

The sailors dove under the truck and a heavy worktable nearby. An explosion blasted close to the shed, then a cataract of noise burst all around, the floor shook and heaved, and Byron too threw himself under the table onto rough cement coated with sandy grease. Quarters were narrow here and his face was jammed against somebody's scratchy dungarees. Byron had never endured a bombing like this. Over and over he winced and gritted his teeth at the cracking blasts that shook the ground. It seemed to

him a fifty-fifty chance that he would get killed in the
next minute. But at last the noise lessened as the bombing
moved along to another part of the base. He crawled free
and ran outside. Flame and smoke were billowing all
around and walls were starting to crash down. The serene
blue sky was flecked with A.A. bursting impotently far
below the bombers, which were quite visible through the
smoke. The *Devilfish* sailors came huddling around Byron,
brushing themselves off and staring at the fires.

"Hey, Mr. Henry, it looks kind of bad, don't it?"

"Are we going back aboard?"

"Should we finish loading the fish?"

"Wait."

Byron hurried through the smoky shed to see the
situation on the other side. Hansen came with him. Hansen
was an old able submariner, a fat Swede from Oregon,
more than six feet tall, with a bushy blond beard and a
belt pulled tight under a bulging paunch. Hansen had
failed to make chief because once in Honolulu he had
resisted arrest by three marine shore patrol men, had given
one a brain concussion, and had broken another's arm.
He liked Byron and had taught him a lot without seeming
to; and Byron had grown his beard partly in sympathy with
Hansen, because the captain had been harrying the stubborn Swede to trim it or remove it.

On the other side of the torpedo shop, large fires also
roared and crackled, fanned by a sea wind. In the street
a bomb had blown a large crater; water was shooting up
out of a broken main, and fat blue sparks were flashing
among the torn and twisted underground cables. Three
heavy Navy trucks stood halted by the smoking pit, and
their Filipino drivers, chattering in Tagalog, were peering
down into the hole.

Byron shouted above the chaotic din, "Looks like we're
stuck, maybe, Hansen. What do you think?"

"I don't know, Mr. Henry. If these trucks would move
clear we could probably get out by doubling back around
the Commandancia."

One of the drivers called to Byron, "Say, can we drive
through this shop? There a way through to the wharf?"

Byron shook his head and raised his voice over the
shrieking siren and the yells of fire fighters dragging hoses

along the street. "All blocked on that side! Solid fire, and some walls down!"

Squinting up at the wind-driven smoke and flame, Hansen said, "Mr. Henry, the fire's gonna spread to this shop and all these fish are gonna go." Byron understood the pain in the torpedoman's voice. Without torpedoes, what good was a submarine squadron? The shortage was already well known and acute.

He said, "Well, if you could operate that overhead crane, maybe we could still pull out a few."

Hansen scratched his balding head. "Mr. Henry, I'm not a crane man."

Standing by the flooding crater was a lean civilian in overalls and a brown hard hat. He said, "I'm a crane operator. What's your problem?"

Byron turned to the Filipino driver. "Will you guys give us a hand? We want to move some torpedoes out of here."

After a rapid exchange in Tagalog with the other drivers, the Filipino exclaimed, "Okay! Where we go?"

"Come on," Byron said to the civilian. "In this shop. It's an overhead crane."

"I know, sonny."

In the bay off Sangley Point, meanwhile, a gray speedboat swooped alongside the *Devilfish,* which was under way, fleeing the Navy Yard and heading for the submarine base at Bataan. It was Red Tully's speedboat, and he was bringing the skipper of the *Devilfish* back from the base. Branch Hoban jumped from the speedboat to the forecastle of his vessel, as Captain Tully yelled up at the bridge through a megaphone, "Ahoy the *Devilfish!* What about *Seadragon* and *Sealion?*"

Lieutenant Aster cupped his hands around his mouth. "They were all right when we left, sir. But they're stuck alongside. No power."

"Oh, Christ. Tell Branch to lie off here. I'll go have a look."

"Shall we pull the plug, sir?"

"Not unless you're attacked."

Hoban arrived on the bridge as the speedboat thrummed away. "Lady, what about Briny and the working party?"

Aster gestured back toward the Navy Yard, which

appeared solidly afire under towering pillars of smoke. "They never showed. I figured I'd better get away from alongside, Captain."

"Damn right. Glad one of us was aboard."

In a short time the speedboat returned. The coxswain swerved it alongside and Tully came aboard the *Devilfish* white-faced and hoarse. "Bad business. They got straddled with bombs. I think the *Sealion*'s a goner—she's on fire, her after engine room's flooded, and she's sinking fast."

"Ye gods," Hoban said. "We were outboard of her."

"I know. Damn lucky."

"The *Pigeon*'s trying to tow the *Seadragon* clear. Better go back in there, Branch, and see if you can help."

"Aye aye, sir."

A sooty motor whaleboat was puttering toward the *Devilfish*. "Who's this now?" Tully said.

Hoban shaded his eyes. "Say, Lady, is that Pierce?"

"Yes, it's Pierce, sir," Lieutenant Aster said, glancing through binoculars.

Sailors ran out on the forecastle to help the young seaman scramble aboard. He came to the bridge, his eyes showing white and his mouth red as a minstrel's in a soot-covered face. "Captain, Mr. Henry sent me to tell you the working party's all right."

"Well, thank God! Where are they?"

"They're taking torpedoes out of the shop."

Tully exclaimed, "The *torpedo* shop? You mean it's still standing?"

"Yes, sir. The fire sort of blew away in another direction, so Mr. Henry and Hansen got these trucks and—"

"You come with me," Tully said. "Branch, I'm going back in there."

But when the squadron commander and the sailor reached the blazing Navy Yard, there was no way to get to the torpedo shop. Fallen buildings and smoking debris blocked every route into the wharf area. Tully circled in vain through drifting smoke in a commandeered jeep, avoiding bomb craters, rubble, and careering, screaming ambulances. "Captain Tully, sir, I think I see them trucks," said Pierce. He pointed to a grassy area on the other side of a small bridge crowded with cars, ambulances, and foot traffic. "See? Over there by the water tower."

"The big gray ones?"

"Yes, sir. I think that's them, sir."

Tully pulled the jeep out of the road and shouldered his way over the bridge. He found Byron Henry sitting on top of heaped torpedoes in a truck, drinking a Coca-Cola. Byron was almost unrecognizable, for his hands, face, and beard were sooty. The three trucks were full of torpedoes, and two cherry-picker crane trucks held more. A small Army truck was piled high with stencilled crates and boxes. The Filipino drivers sat on the grass, eating sandwiches and cracking jokes in Tagalog. The *Devilfish* working party lay sprawled in exhausted attitudes, all except Hansen, who sat smoking a pipe with his back to a huge tire of the truck on which Byron perched.

"Hello there, Byron," Tully called.

Byron turned around and tried to jump up, but it was hard to do on the heap of long cylinders. "Oh, good afternoon, sir."

"How many did you get?"

"Twenty-six, sir. Then we had to leave. The fire was closing in."

"I see you scooped up a truckload of spare parts, too."

"That was Hansen's idea, sir."

"Who's Hansen?"

Byron indicated the torpedoman, who had leaped to his feet on recognizing Captain Tully.

"What's your rating?"

"Torpedoman first class, sir."

"That's where you're wrong. You're a *chief* torpedoman."

Hansen's beard opened in an ecstatic smile, and his eyes gleamed at Ensign Henry. Tully looked around at the trove of rescued torpedoes. "You got exploders?"

"Yes, sir."

"Well, good. Suppose you drive this haul around to Mariveles."

"Aye aye, sir."

"I'll want a report on this, Byron, with the names and ratings of your working party and of these drivers."

"Yes, sir."

"Any chance of getting more fish out of there?"

"Depends on what the fire leaves, sir. The shop hadn't caught when we left, but now—I don't know."

"All right. I'll see about that. You get going."

Next morning Byron presented himself to Captain Tully. The squadron commander was working at a desk in a Quonset hut on the beach at Mariveles Harbor, a deep cove in the mountainous Bataan peninsula. Behind Tully's tanned hairless pate a large blue and yellow chart of Manila Bay covered most of the plasterboard wall. Byron handed him a two-page report. Tully glanced through it and said, "Pretty skimpy document."

"It has the facts, Captain, and all the names and ratings."

Tully nodded and dropped the sheets in a basket. "Branch told me you're allergic to paperwork."

"It's not my strong point, sir. I'm sorry."

"Now, did he tell you what I want you for?"

"Just something about salvage, sir."

"Byron, the Japs are bound to land soon. We probably can't hold Manila, but as long as MacArthur hangs on to Bataan, the squadron can go on operating out of Mariveles. This is a hell of a lot closer to Japan than any other sub base we've got now, or will have for a good long while." Tully stood, and gestured at the wall. "So—the idea is to clean out Cavite, what's left of it, *and* Manila, of every single item we can use, and fetch it here. You seem to have a sort of scavenger instinct." Tully laughed, and Byron responded with a polite smile. "You'll work on this until the *Devilfish* goes out on operations. Lieutenant Commander Percifield is in charge, and you'll report to him now over at Admiral Hart's headquarters in Manila. He's expecting you."

"Aye aye, sir."

"While you're there, look in on Admiral Hart. He's an old submariner, you know. I told him about those torpedoes. He appreciated it, and is writing a letter of commendation."

"Yes, Captain."

"Oh, and incidentally, I've written your father about your exploit, though Lord knows when and how it'll catch up with him." Tully irresolutely took off his glasses, looked at the erect impassive ensign, and swivelled to and fro. "Now, Byron. Do you *still* want to go to the Atlantic? With all hell busting loose out here?"

"Yes, sir. I do want that."

"You do? When there's only our squadron now to oppose the Japs on the sea? When this is where the fighting is?"

Byron did not reply.

"As for your wife and baby in Italy—that's unfortunate, but you know, she'll be an enemy alien now."

"Sir, we're not at war with Italy. Not yet."

"Oh, that's inevitable. Hitler's scheduled to make this big speech today, you know. Everybody expects him to declare war, and old Musso will just follow suit, p.d.q. Your wife will be interned, but that's no cause for alarm. After a while she'll be exchanged. The Italians are civilized people. I'm sure she'll be all right."

"Captain Tully, my wife's Jewish."

The squadron commander looked surprised, and turned a bit red. He avoided Byron's eye. "Well now, *that* I didn't know."

"My captain knows. I've told him. The Italians—and what's more to the point, the Germans—will class my baby son as Jewish, too."

Blowing out a long audible breath, Tully said, "Okay. That's a problem. I still don't see what you can do about it. Our submarine operations in the Atlantic will be minor for a long, long time. Here's where we need you." He looked up at the ensign, who stood at attention, blankfaced. "However, Byron, I'm going to send a dispatch, recommending your transfer to Submarine Force Atlantic —as and when the *Devilfish* gets a replacement for you. Not before."

Byron Henry showed no sign of the relief that filled him. "Thank you, Captain Tully."

The squadron commander opened a desk drawer. "One more thing. Your commanding officer concurs in this, so congratulations."

He laid on the desk before Byron a gold pin, the dolphins of a submariner.

*   *   *

62

War with the United States

(from WORLD EMPIRE LOST)

Hitler's Blowup

On December 11, the final calamity occurred. Adolf Hitler—after pausing for four days in which History herself must have held her breath—summoned the Reichstag and declared war upon the United States.

Franklin Roosevelt, in his war speech to Congress on December 8, had not so much as mentioned Germany. And with good reason! The surge of war spirit in his country was directed one hundred percent against "infamous" Japan. As usual, the wily President did not stick his neck out one inch beyond the stretch of public opinion.

For four anxious days it appeared to some of our staff that the Pearl Harbor attack might prove the great break of the war for us. Conceivably America might turn its back entirely on Europe to cope with Japan; the hysterical war pressure built up by Roosevelt would all vent itself into the Pacific Ocean, drying up Lend-Lease; and we would at last have the breathing space in which to strangle England and knock out the Soviet Union, after which we could deal with the USA in our own time and fashion.

However, the Führer was under violent Japanese pressure to "honor" the so-called Tripartite Pact.

A Pact Becomes a Trap

This pact was mainly a propaganda sham, like the Pact of Steel between Germany and Italy. Japan joined the

Pact of Steel in 1940, and so it became the Tripartite Pact, and the chimera of the worldwide "Axis" was born. It was a hollow bluff. Italy of course was a zero. Japan wanted to threaten the Americans with Germany, and Hitler wanted to threaten them with Japan. By uniting in a pact, the two poor nations hoped to paralyze into inactivity the rich nation that lay between them.

But the earth is round, and another powerful nation lay between them in the other direction—the Soviet Union. This was a different matter! Germany and Russia were linked by Ribbentrop's nonaggression pact. Therefore our diplomats had written a clause into the Tripartite Pact, saying that relations with the Soviet Union would not be affected by the new treaty.

When we began operations against Russia, the Japanese found this clause of ours a very lucky escape hatch. They politely cited it and the neutrality pact they had meantime signed with Russia, and declined to march. They might do so later when conditions permitted, they said—meaning, when Germany had done all the fighting and bleeding, and the winnings were about to be raked in. But with Pearl Harbor, global conditions suddenly reversed; and now Japan demanded that Germany come to her aid against America, though she had failed Germany against Russia!

It is self-evident that Adolf Hitler owed the Japanese nothing. The pact obliged the partners to assist each other only if one was attacked by a third party. To call Pearl Harbor an "attack" by America on Japan was stretching language, even in Oriental rhetoric. Hitler certainly had the right to demand at least that Japan should now as a quid pro quo declare war on the Soviet Union. The news of such a Japanese act would have raised the spirits of our snowbound troops in Russia beyond all measure. It might have changed the whole picture.

But Hitler never made the demand. He allowed Japan to stay on neutral terms with Russia, while he plunged the German people into war with America. With this one mystifying blowup, the Führer threw away his historic gains and the future of the Reich.

Why?

I myself was on an inspection tour by air of the Moscow front when the Führer journeyed to Berlin to declare war.

When I saw him again at Wolf's Lair in mid-December, he was very unconcerned and airy-fairy about the United States. In dinner table talk one evening when I was present, he called America a mongrel nation, half Jewified and half Negrified, incapable of making serious war. The United States would have its hands full just with Japan, he crowed, and would probably be defeated. There was no chance that it could intervene in Europe. So he said; but I believed then, and still do, that this was cheerful blather for his subordinates, or narcotic self-deception. Unlike the Japanese leaders, Hitler knew at heart the one crucial military fact about America: that nothing must be done to awaken and unite that confused, quarrelsome, luxury-rotted titan. Pearl Harbor had done it.

This war was at bottom a chess game with men and nations played between two wills and two world views, which had been competing since 1933—between Adolf Hitler and Franklin D. Roosevelt. Hitler started with a handicap of rook and two pawns, as it were, in industrial plant, population, allies, and natural resources. These odds compelled his flamboyant and desperate style. The man in the wheelchair could afford a slow, cautious game, waiting for his opponent to defeat himself by unsound gambles.

Hitler appeared to outplay Roosevelt brilliantly, year after year. His bloodless victories before 1939, his swift conquest of Poland and western Europe, and his breathtaking seizure of European Russia in 1941, turned the game heavily in his favor. Adolf Hitler was within sight of checkmate, when Japan attacked Pearl Harbor. That was the break Roosevelt had been waiting for.

I am well aware of the conventional explanation that Hitler felt we had a *de facto* war going with America anyway in the Atlantic, and wanted to beat Roosevelt to the punch with his declaration, for reasons of prestige. It is even contended that declaring war on America was a clever move to boost our morale, by taking the public mind off our halts and setbacks on the Eastern Front. But these conjectures ignore the fatal failure to demand Japanese action against Russia, and also the text of the actual war declaration. This unstatesmanlike document is one long scream of despair and rage, all directed against Roosevelt. My judgment will always be that Hitler saw the game unexpectedly go glimmering, and in anger kicked over the board.

Finis Germaniae

Other writers follow Churchill and place the turning point of the war a year later, in the triple cluster of events —Stalingrad, El Alamein, and the North African landings— when the turn became visible in the field. But the true turn was Pearl Harbor.

We scored our greatest successes, without question, and expanded our short-lived German empire to its amazing farthest reach only in 1942, long after Pearl Harbor and the halt at Moscow. Our U-boats almost mastered the Atlantic, sending whole fleets of British and American ships to the bottom. Our armies marched to the Caucasus Mountains, the Caspian Sea, and the Nile. Our energetic ally, Japan, captured her East Asian empire in swift blazing victories.

But one memory haunted me during all those victories: the airplane trip I had made to the Moscow front right after Pearl Harbor. From the air I saw German tanks, trucks, and gun carriages straggled over hundreds of miles of desolate plains, frozen in mud or bogged in snow under the gloomy low Russian sun. I saw dead horses lying in the snow, and our soldiers hacking at their frozen carcasses for meat to eat. We landed often among men and boys shivering in ragged green-gray summer uniforms, building fires under their vehicles to keep the radiators from bursting and the oil from getting too viscous to flow. Endless were the complaints I heard then about the lack of boots, heavy socks, gloves, antifreeze, and the salve that was supposed to free the tanks' telescopic sights. When the telescopes froze stuck without the salve, the tankists could not see to maneuver and protect themselves. Pathetic were the shivering soldiers wearing ladies' fur coats and boas, collected by Goebbels and sent to the front.

My trip took me within sight of Moscow's barrage balloons and anti-aircraft flashes. There I tasted the full bitterness of that tantalizing halt, and there I first heard that we were at war again with America. In my heart I knew that spelled, once and for all, *finis Germaniae.*

Germany after 1941 was like a charging elephant with a bullet in its brain, trampling and killing its tormentors with its last momentum before falling. The bullet was Pearl Harbor.

World Empire Lost

With these comments, I conclude Volume I of my operational analysis of the Second World War, and a word of summary is in order.

General George Marshall, in his 1945 victory report, called Germany, Japan, and Italy "three criminal nations bent on easy loot." But if we had won, as we almost did, the leaders who would have hung would have been Stalin, Churchill, Roosevelt, and Mr. Marshall. The criminal nations would have been the Allies, who tried to keep their plutocratic loot of previous centuries by murdering German and Japanese women and children from the air. Hitler did not order Hiroshima and Dresden!

There is no morality in world history. There are only tides of change borne on violence and death. The victors write the history, pass the judgments, and hang or shoot the losers. In truth history is an endless chain of hegemony shifts, based on the decay of old political structures and the rise of new ones. Wars are the fever crises of those shifts. Wars are inevitable; there will always be wars; and the one war crime is to lose. That is the reality, and the rest is sentimental nonsense.

We went on following Adolf Hitler to the last, to unbelievable triumphs and unparalleled disasters, from Pearl Harbor to the fall of Berlin, because he was our national destiny. A romantic idealist, an inspiring leader, dreaming grand dreams of new heights and depths of human possibilities, and at the same time an icy calculator with iron willpower, he was the soul of Germany. We are a romantic people, and Hitler was German Romance incarnate. No truthful history of our nation will ever be written which does not face that fact. He had his faults, including a definite taste for cruelty, a certain ingrained petit bourgeois vulgarity, an exaggerated opinion of his military acumen, and the well-known, regrettable tendency to anti-Semitism. Such were the blemishes of this world-historical individual, but no human being is perfect.

TRANSLATOR'S NOTE: *Armin von Roon properly breaks his two-part operational analysis of the Second World War at Pearl Harbor. In the period covered by* World Empire Lost, *a European war like World War I raged, with much the same lineup; for that reason Winston Churchill called it a continuation after a truce, and both conflicts together a new Thirty Years' War. But all that time, the United States was out of it. After Pearl Harbor, we were in it up to our necks, and it became the first global war. That is another story.*

Roon's summaries from his second volume have recently appeared in Germany under the title World Holocaust. *Analyzing mainly Germany's defeats and downfall, it has not been much of a success.*

His concluding estimate of Hitler overlooks one or two small points. This able and resolute homicidal maniac, using modern Germany as his murder instrument, directly caused between twenty-five and thirty-five million human deaths; the exact figure will never be known. To stop him cost the world billions, maybe trillions, of dollars. Had the German people shut this strange individual away in an insane asylum, instead of setting him up as their adored leader and throwing their full strength behind him for twelve years, these deaths and this waste would not have occurred.

On the historical record Adolf Hitler was certainly the worst liar, doublecrosser, destroyer, and mass murderer in the world's annals. Roon might have mentioned these facts among Hitler's blemishes.—V.H.

* * *

63

THE door stood open to Natalie's bedroom, and Hitler's screeching woke the baby. In the sitting room Natalie had the radio turned low, but at the Führer's sudden shriek —*"ROOSEVELT!"*—she and Aaron looked at each other in alarm, and Louis began sobbing.

"He is a maniac, after all." Slumped in an armchair in a bathrobe and muffler, his sunken red-shadowed eyes watering, Aaron Jastrow shook his head and lifted a trembling teacup to his mouth, as Hitler went on with his hoarse bellows, sneers, whispers, and yells. "Extremely clever, persuasive, and forceful, but a maniac. I confess I never grasped it before. I thought he playacted."

With a faintly contemptuous glance at her uncle, Natalie went to the baby.

The Führer's speech, starting with the usual complaints of injustices endured by Germany and himself, had worked up to the naming of the one supreme war criminal responsible for all the bloodshed and misery that he, the Führer, had worked so hard to avert, the insane hypocrite who had sold out his country and himself to the Jews, thwarted Germany at every turn, and loosed destruction on mankind. After a strangely long pause, came the wild scream that woke the child: *"Rooo-ss-felt!"*

And this bitter hate-filled animal cry somehow woke Aaron Jastrow, too.

In recent years, Jastrow had listened to few Hitler speeches. They bored him. He was a historian, and history's pages were crowded with such flamboyant tyrants who had strutted their brief seasons, done their damage, built their grandiose monuments, and passed away. So it would be with Hitler, he had once written after a visit to

Germany, in a cool meditative essay in *Harper's* entitled "Der Führer: Thoughts Before Midnight."

In this essay, Jastrow had pigeonholed the Nazi boilup with other brief violent mass upheavals which through the ages had come and gone. Sometimes they changed the order of things, like the Crusades and the French Revolution; sometimes they left only destruction, like the flashflood massacres of Alaric and Tamerlane. Perhaps this weirdly glorified little beggar had something to contribute to the world. His call for a new unified order in Europe made a certain sense. He might start a world war; he might win it or he might lose it; but in any case he would at last die, and the world would wag on.

God—Jastrow used the term with arch irony to denote the blind drift of events—like a good roadside juggler, did his act with whatever objects came to his hand. If Hitler triumphed and brought a tyrannic German unity to Europe, or even to the whole earth, lasting a century or two, perhaps that meant he had been needed at this time on our tiny earth. What happened, after all, was only what had to happen. There were no dice in heaven. The human spirit in its unending quest for freedom would either soften and tame its Teuton masters at last, or would crack the prison of tyranny, as a grass blade cracks a concrete pavement.

Having thus boxed the German dictator away in some neat paragraphs, Aaron Jastrow had mentally shelved the man. Hitler broke from Aaron Jastrow's mental box on this day, with his scream of Roosevelt's name.

As the dictator went on with his long, almost raving, yet mordant comparison between Roosevelt and himself—he the poor son of struggling parents, Roosevelt the pampered only child of a millionaire; he the common soldier of the First World War, enduring rain and gunfire and muck for four years, Roosevelt the highborn insider, enjoying a safe cushy desk job in the Navy Department; he the gassed veteran, lying penniless in a hospital, Roosevelt the tricky postwar financial speculator doubling his inherited wealth; he the restorer and rebuilder of a defeated, prostrate nation, Roosevelt the economic tinkerer, the wrecker of a rich country with his crackpot New Deal schemes; he the valiant righter of old wrongs, the messianic unifier of Europe, Roosevelt the master war criminal, seeking to stave off the future and preserve the world hegemony of the Jews—listening to this ferocious, crazed, queerly coherent fantasy, Aaron Jastrow wavered in his philosophic stance, and finally became scared.

The Italians had already cancelled the exit visas of Americans. The chargé had told Jastrow that this was just a precautionary move, and that they should still plan to leave on the fifteenth if meantime war was not declared. For days Jastrow had slept and eaten little. Now Hitler's speech, as he listened, seemed to be clanging shut an iron door.

"Well?" Natalie said, carrying in the blanket-wrapped squalling baby. "Is there any hope?"

"He hasn't declared war yet. Not in so many words."

In an absent practiced way, without much effort at modesty, she opened her sweater, suit jacket, and blouse, flashed a white breast, and drew the brown sweater over the baby. "Why is it so much colder in this room? It's icy, and the more—"

Jastrow put a finger to his lips. Hitler was whipping himself up to a crescendo. His audience, hushed for a long time, broke out in applause, cheers, and roars of *"Sieg Heil!"*

"Now what was that, Aaron?"

Jastrow raised his voice over the raucous noises of the crowd. "I'm afraid that was it. He said he's called in the United States diplomats and given them their papers. That started the cheering."

"Well, all I can say is, I couldn't be less surprised." Natalie stroked the baby's cheek with a finger, and dolefully smiled as it quieted and began sucking. "You're just hungry, monkey, aren't you?"

Her uncle said, "Mussolini still has to talk. We'll know in another hour or so."

"Oh, Aaron, what choice has he?"

He shut off the radio. "Well, that's that. I believe I'll have a glass of sherry. You, too?"

"No, no. I'd better keep my wits about me today, what's left of them."

Jastrow poured and gulped a glassful, then took another, and shrank in his armchair, sipping it, looking vacantly around at the high long frigid room piled with suitcases and wooden boxes. The hotel was silent and the street outside was silent.

"Don't despair, Natalie. In 1939 Il Duce did manage to squirm out of it, you know. He's no use to Hitler militarily. The Italians are sick and sour and beaten. If he declares war against the United States, he might be assassinated, and Hitler surely doesn't want that. Besides, he's wily. He may well find some weaseling formula, and we may yet be on that plane on the fifteenth."

"Oh, Aaron, quit it, for God's sake. He'll declare war."

Jastrow sighed heavily. "I suppose so. Natalie, I'm sorry, deeply and tragically sorry."

She held up a hand, palm out. "No, no. Don't. What's the use?"

"Let me have my say. I simply can't bear the way I've involved you and your baby. I've never—"

"Aaron, I did it myself. Don't rake it over now. *Don't.* I can't stand that."

A long silence, except for the baby making loud sucking noises. Jastrow sipped the sherry, glancing at his niece with a hangdog expression. "I might telephone the embassy, my dear, and ask if there are any plans afoot for the diplomatic train."

"That's a good idea, if you can get through. Otherwise we'd better go there."

"I'm planning to," Jastrow said, "in any case." He made the call, but the embassy lines were busy. Pouring more sherry, he spoke slowly, coughing now and then. "One thing wrong with being a historian is the way it distorts one's view of the present. I seem to see current events through the wrong end of a telescope. The figures look small and comical. The happenings seem so trivial, so repetitious, so banal! I can read the past fairly well, I think, and I also have some clarity about the future. Only in the present am I so dense. Hitler and Mussolini don't have the resources to last, my dear. This gaudy shabby militaristic madhouse in central Europe will fall. Russia and America are awesome, and between them they will crush Nazism. The only question is how soon. Well, I'd better dress."

"Yes, do that, Aaron."

"I'll just finish my wine first."

Natalie impatiently arose and took the baby into the bedroom to avoid a row with her uncle. She had no store of kindness left for this garrulous, vain, cranky old man, whose Olympian irony and willfully blinkered optimism had mired her and her baby in this peril; though in the end—she always came back to this—she herself was most responsible.

Natalie Henry had thought and thought about her predicament until she could no longer bear the self-probing. Where had she committed the fatal stupidity? In coming back? In marrying Byron? In not taking the German plane out of Zurich? In not following Herb Rose to the Palestine ship? No, something deep was wrong with her; she was in some ultimate sense, for all her apparent cleverness, a terrible fool. She was nothing and nobody; she had no real identity; all her life she had been floating like dandelion fuzz on the wind. She was "Jewish," but the label meant nothing to her beyond the trouble it caused. She had had her first love affair with an intellectual heathen Gentile. She had married a Christian without giving the clash of backgrounds much thought; his youth and lack of learning had bothered her more. What a queer, random, disjointed chain of happenings had created this sleepy blue-eyed little living thing at her breast!

In the past weeks, Natalie had started dreaming at night that none of it had happened. In these dreams time reeled back, sometimes to Paris, sometimes to college, most often to her childhood on Long Island. Relief and joy would fill her in her sleep at finding that she was out of the nightmare; cold sinking sadness would follow when she woke to discover that the wrong side of the dream-line was the real side. But at least on this side the baby dwelled.

The baby was becoming her anchor to life. At the moment the most real thing on earth was the warm little mouth at her chest: alive, sweet, and sublimely good. Beyond it—in the hotel suite, in Rome, in Europe—all was squalor, danger, uncertainty, and darkening horizons. The diplomatic train was the very last chance. Natalie tucked the infant away when he dropped asleep, and dressed to go to the embassy.

"Ah, my dear, you look very well." In the sitting room Aaron now reclined rather grandly on a couch, in the handsome blue cape that the Searles had given him for his sixty-second birthday, his best dark suit, and a large bow tie. He was still drinking sherry.

"Balderdash. If I ever get home safe, one of my first orders of business will be to burn this damned dress, and I'll never wear brown again."

Waving his half-full glass at her with stiff jauntiness, Aaron laughed merrily. "It's grand that you've kept your sense of humor," he said, although Natalie had been quite serious. "Sit down, my dear. Don't pace."

"Aren't we going to the embassy?" She perched on the arm of a couch.

"Tell me, Natalie, did you ever meet Father Enrico Spanelli?"

"That Vatican librarian? No."

He gave her the squinting teasing smile that appeared in late evenings when he had taken too much brandy. "But I thought we all had dinner one evening together."

"We were supposed to. Louis got sick."

"Oh yes. I remember now. Well, Enrico is coming in a little while to drive us to the Piazza Venezia. He knows all the newspapermen, and we'll hear and see Mussolini from the press section."

"What! Good Lord, I don't want to go there with the baby in that Fascist mob! What about—"

Jastrow held up a cautionary hand and began scrawling on a pad, talking at the same time. "Well, my dear, it's visible history. Since we're in a tight spot, we may as well have the good of it."

The sheet he passed to her read: *If it's war he'll take us straight to the embassy. That's the idea. We'll be out of the hotel, where we might be picked up.*

She wrote underneath, *Why do you trust him?* They did not know for certain that microphones had been planted in their suite, but they sometimes wrote notes as a precaution.

Jastrow blinked at her, took off his glasses, and polished them with a handkerchief. This was his unconscious signal, long familiar to Natalie, of a harangue. Softly he said, "Natalie, do you know that I am a Catholic?"

"What! What do you mean?"

"Ah, then you don't know. I thought perhaps you were being tactful, all these years. Well, it's quite true."

Aaron often made odd remarks over brandy or wine, but he had never said anything this strange. Puzzled and disconcerted, Natalie shrugged, "What am I supposed to say? Are you serious?"

"Oh, very. It's the family skeleton, my dear. I'm a bit surprised that they never told you. I converted when I was twenty-three." He gave her a red-eyed, twisted, sheepish grin, scratching his beard. "It never took. I fear I'm the wrong blood type for that or any religion. At the time the act was sincere."

Aaron now told her about a Radcliffe girl whom he had tutored in history and aesthetics, a girl of a wealthy Catholic family. After a stormy year and a half the love affair had collapsed. He had left Cambridge and finished up his doctorate at Yale, to put behind him the girl and his memories.

His conversion had been a very private matter. He had been discreet and stealthy about taking instruction, for many Jewish friends in Boston had been kind to him and he did not want to upset or argue with them. By the time he departed from Harvard, he had decided that the conversion was a mistake, having painfully worked his way to the skeptical naturalism that was his settled view. Thereafter, whenever the question of his religion came up, he had mentioned his self-evident Jewish origin and said no more. He had done nothing further about the Catholic episode; he had simply let it lapse from his life.

But he had made one bad mistake, very early in the affair. He had discussed it with his family. "That I've always regretted," he said gloomily. "It probably shortened my father's life—my mother by then was dead—and your parents certainly never got over the shock. We were estranged for good, though I once told your father that that phase was over, that I considered myself a non-practicing Jew and nothing else. It didn't help. They dropped me.

"When the Book-of-the-Month Club chose *A Jew's Jesus,* Louis did write me a stiff letter. His rabbi wanted me to come and lecture at his temple. He phrased it so that I could hardly accept. I thought his letter was cruel. I replied very warmly, but I declined. That was that. I never saw either of them again. I've only discussed this with one other person besides yourself in more than thirty years, Natalie, and that other person is Enrico Spanelli.

"I told him in September, when I was turned back from Switzerland. I thought it might prove useful. He's an excellent fellow and a fine classical scholar, though rather weak on early Byzantium. Well, he has been marvellously sympathetic. He never argued my religious position, but simply wrote to the United States for verification. He's got the documents, and I have copies. So—we have friends in the Vatican, my dear, I hope we won't need them, but it is a sort of insurance."

Natalie, who could think only of the possible effect on her baby, was pleased and amazed. This was like finding a forgotten rusty key to a dungeon cell. Aaron's youthful religious flip-flops were his own business; but the technicality might indeed bring help and refuge, or even escape in an emergency! This disclosure also explained, at long last, her parents' peculiarly strained and glum attitude about Aaron. Deep down, she herself felt a small involuntary stirring of disdain for her uncle.

She said, "Why, Aaron, I'm gasping a bit, but I think it's most amazingly clever of you to have stopped being a Jew more than forty years ago. What foresight!"

"Oh, I'm still a Jew. Don't make that mistake. So was Paul after his conversion, you know. You're not disgusted with me, then, as your parents were? How nice."

A satirical smile wrinkled her mouth. "A *Jew's* Jesus, indeed. You fraud."

"He was a Jew's Jesus." Aaron Jastrow straightened up inside the heavy cape and raised a bearded proud chin. "I insist on that. The book is the fruit of a bitter wrestle with myself. I was frankly swept away by the whole opulent Christian structure of thought and art that I discovered in college, all built on what that Palestinian fellow called a murdered Jew. We Jews pretend that structure doesn't exist, Natalie—that is, Jews like your parents and mine do —but that won't wash, you know. It's there. In the end I probed past the religious metaphors and came to grips with Jesus as he was, trying to grasp the historical reality. That was the essence of my wrestle for a year. I found an extraordinarily winning and magnetic personality, a talented and tragic poor relative of mine, who lived in Palestine in olden days. So the book really—"

The telephone rang. "Ah," Jastrow said, pushing himself out of his chair, "that's bound to be Enrico. Get the baby, dear."

Natalie hesitated, then said, "All right. Let's go."

At the wheel of a rusty, faded little car outside the hotel, a man wearing a clerical hat, and an overcoat with a ratty fur collar, waved a smoking cigarette at them in a thick peasant hand. *"Professore!"* The librarian-priest had a face strangely like Mussolini's—prominent brown eyes, big curved jaw, and wide fleshy mouth. But rimless glasses and a sweet placid expression under the flat black hat, as well as his indoor pallor, much reduced the ominous resemblance. "You look tired, Professore," he said, after greeting Natalie in charming Roman Italian, and admiring the heavily wrapped, almost invisible baby. The car started with rheumatic wheezings.

"I've not slept well."

The priest's glance was mild and kind. "I understand. As you requested, I've made inquiries about your taking refuge in the Vatican. It's not impossible, but the concordat pathetically limits our freedom of action. I would offer you one word of caution. Such exceptional expedients can have negative results. One calls attention to oneself. One becomes a special case." He drove carefully down the almost deserted boulevard and turned into a street where people were crowding toward the Piazza Venezia, with placards swaying above their heads.

"The trouble is," said Jastrow, "I already am one."

The priest pursed his lips and tilted his head in a most Italian way. "True. Well, your cloudy nationality might be an advantage. If you are actually stateless, then clearly you are not an enemy alien." Spanelli glanced around at Natalie with drooping eyes. "This is not true of your niece, naturally. One assumes your embassy will somehow provide for her—"

"Father, pardon me. Whoever gives me refuge must take her in too."

The priest pursed his lips again and was silent. The crowd thickened as they neared the piazza: quiet sad-looking people in shabby winter clothes. The blackshirts carrying the placards were trying to hold up their chins and glare like Il Duce.

"These signs are viler than usual," Jastrow said. Beside the car, a fat red-faced blackshirt marched with a crude cartoon of Mrs. Roosevelt sitting on a chamber pot, squawking obscenities about her husband. Ahead of the car, on another sign, a bag of money with a Roosevelt grin walked on crutches, smoking a cigarette in an uptilted holder.

"When the pot boils, the scum comes to the surface," said the priest.

He slipped the car through narrow side streets, parked in a rubbish-filled archway, and guided them down an alley into the Piazza Venezia. The thronged square was surprisingly still. People stood around saying nothing, or chatting in low tones. The sky was gray, the wind strong and cold. Flag-bearing schoolchildren were huddled in front of the balcony in a docile mass, not laughing or playing pranks, just holding their flapping flags up and fidgeting.

The priest brought Jastrow and Natalie into a roped-off section near the balcony, where photographers clustered with reporters, including a few Americans, as well as the grinning happy Japanese correspondents Natalie had met at the party. Somebody produced a folding chair for her. She sat holding the sleeping baby tightly in her lap, now and then shuddering, though she wore a heavy sweater under her coat. The raw wind seemed to cut through to her skin.

They waited a long time before Mussolini suddenly stepped out on the balcony and raised a hand in salute. A crowd roar cascaded and re-echoed in the square: *"Duce! Duce! Duce!"* It was a strange effect, since all the people were looking up silently, with blank or hostile faces, at the tubby figure in the gold-eagled, tasselled black hat, and the black and gold jacket, a get-up more like an opera costume than a uniform. Under the balcony, a few blackshirts were diligently manufacturing the cheers, huddled around microphones. A tall man in the uniform of the German Foreign Service appeared next, with a Japanese in a cutaway coat and high hat. They flanked the dictator, who was even smaller than the Oriental; and Mussolini looked as though he were between guards come to arrest him. The blackshirts quit their noise and turned their oval, sallow faces up at the balcony; a pack of waiters and barbers, Natalie thought, in sloppy pseudomilitary masquerade.

The brief speech was belligerent, the tone was belligerent, the gestures were very familiar and very belligerent, but it all came out ridiculous. The sound did not fit the gestures. Mussolini flailed his fist when he dropped his voice, and shouted fiercely some innocuous prepositions and conjunctions, and at the most inappropriate points he grinned. The old puffy dictator, already defeated in Greece and shorn of much of his North African empire, seemed to be having a highly irrelevant good time, as he declared war on the United States of America. While the blackshirts at random moments cheered and shouted *"Doo-chay!"* the crowd began to leave. Mussolini bellowed his last sentences at thousands of departing backs—an incredible sight in this dictatorship—an old ham actor scorned by the audience: *"Italians, once more arise and be worthy of this historic hour. We shall WIN!"* And again he smiled.

To blackshirt cheers, the three figures on the balcony withdrew; Mussolini came out twice to bow, but the mob was dispersing as though a cloudburst had started.

The little knot of Americans stayed together, talking excitedly in low tense tones. Though the thing was no surprise, it felt strange now that it had happened; they stood on the soil of an enemy country. The debate among the correspondents, who kept glancing at policemen hovering nearby, was whether to go to their offices to clear out their desks, or head straight for the embassy. Several decided for the office first, arguing that once in the embassy they might be holed up for a long time, perhaps even until the diplomatic train left.

This put Aaron Jastrow in mind of his manuscript. He asked Father Spanelli to take them to the hotel before going on to the embassy. The priest was agreeable, and Natalie did not argue. She was in a shocked state. The baby was beginning to cry, and she thought of picking up some diapers and supplies for him. They returned to the car and drove to the Excelsior, but the priest suddenly braked, a block from the hotel; and he pointed through the windshield at two police cars pulled into the entrance driveway.

Turning large, moist, worried brown eyes at Aaron Jastrow, he said, "Of course the manuscript is precious, Professore. Still, all things considered, had you not better go to your embassy first? If the worst comes to the worst, I can get your manuscript for you."

"The embassy, the embassy," Natalie said. "He's right. The embassy."

Jastrow nodded sadly.

But again, a couple of blocks from the embassy, Spanelli halted the car. A cordon of police and soldiers stood in front of the building. Across the street a small crowd of spectators stood waiting for some melodramatic occurrence. At the moment, from this distance, all looked quiet.

"Let us walk," said the priest. "You should pass through that line with no trouble, but let us see."

Natalie was sitting in back of the car. Jastrow turned to her and put a comforting hand over hers. His face was settling into a stony, weary, defiant expression. "Come, my dear. There's not much choice now."

They walked up the side of the street where the spectators were standing. On the edge of the crowd they encountered the *Times* man who had taken Natalie to the Japanese party. He was frightened and bitter; he urged them not to try to crash the cordon. The United Press correspondent had just attempted it, not five minutes earlier; he had been stopped at the gate, and after some argument a police car had appeared and had carried him off.

"But how can that be? That is not civilized, that is senseless," exclaimed Father Spanelli. "We have many correspondents in the United States. It is idiotic behavior. It will be corrected."

"When?" said the *Times* man. "And what will happen to Phil meantime? I've heard disagreeable things about your secret service."

Holding her baby close, fighting off a feeling of sinking in black waters, a feeling like the worst of bad dreams, Natalie said, "What now, Aaron?"

"We must try to go through. What else is there?" He turned to the priest. "Or—Enrico, can we go to the Vatican now? Is there any point to that?"

The priest spread his hands. "No, no, not now. Don't think of it. Nothing is arranged. It might be the worst of things to do. Given some time, something may be worked out. Surely not now."

"Jesus Christ, there you are," said a coarse American voice. "We're all in big trouble, kids, and you'd better come with me."

Natalie looked around into the worried, handsome, very Jewish face of Herbert Rose.

For a long while after that, the overpowering actuality was the smell of fish in the truck that was taking them to Naples, so strong that Natalie breathed in little gasps. The two drivers were Neapolitans whose business was bringing fresh fish to Rome. Rabinovitz had hired the truck to transport a replacement part for the ship's old generator; a burnt-out armature had delayed the sailing.

Gray-faced wtih migraine, the stocky Palestinian now crouched swaying on the floor of the truck beside the burlap-wrapped armature, eyes closed, knees hugged in his arms. He had spent two days and nights hunting for the armature in Naples and Salerno, and then had tracked down a used one in Rome. He had brought Herbert Rose along to help him bargain for it. When Rose had first brought Jastrow and Natalie to the truck, parked on a side street near the embassy, the Palestinian had talked volubly, though he had since lapsed into this stupor; and the story he had then told had convinced Natalie to climb into the truck with her baby. After a few last agonized words with Father Spanelli about the manuscript, Aaron had followed her.

This was the Palestinian's story. He had gone to the Excelsior at Herb Rose's urging, to offer Jastrow and Natalie a last chance to join them. There in Aaron Jastrow's suite he had found two Germans waiting. Well-dressed, well-spoken men, they had invited him inside and closed the door. When asked about Dr. Jastrow they had begun questioning him in a tough manner, without identifying themselves. Rabinovitz had backed out as soon as he could, and to his relief they had simply let him go.

During the first hour or so of the bouncing, rattling ride in this dark, malodorous truck, Jastrow vainly talked over all the possible benign explanations for the presence of Germans in his hotel suite. It was almost a monologue, for

Natalie was still dumb with alarm, Rabinovitz appeared sunk in pain, and Herbert Rose was bored. Obviously the men were Gestapo agents, Rose said, come to pick up the "blue chip," and there was nothing more to discuss. But Dr. Jastrow was having second thoughts about this precipitate decision to go with Rabinovitz, and he was having them aloud. Finally, diffidently, he mentioned the diplomatic train as a possibility that still existed. This roused Natalie to say, "You can go back to Rome, Aaron, and try to get on that train. I won't. Good luck." Then Jastrow gave up, curled himself in a corner in his thick cape, and went to sleep.

The fish truck was not halted on the way to Naples. A familiar sight on the highway, it was a perfect cover for these enemy fugitives. When it reached the port city, night had fallen. As it slowly made its way through blacked-out streets toward the waterfront, policemen repeatedly challenged the drivers, but a word or two brought laughter and permission to go on. Natalie heard all this through a fog of tension and fatigue. The sense of everyday reality had quite left her. She was riding the whirlwind.

The truck stopped. A sharp rapping scared her, and one of the drivers said in hoarse Neapolitan accents, "Wake up, friends. We're here."

They descended from the truck to a wharf, where the sea breeze was an intensely sweet relief. In the cloudy night, the vessel alongside the wharf was a shadowy shape, where shadowy people walked back and forth. It appeared no larger to Natalie than a New York harbor sightseeing boat.

Dr. Jastrow said to Rabinovitz, "When will you sail? Immediately?"

With a grunt, Rabinovitz said, "No such luck. We must install this unit and test it. That'll take time. Come aboard, and we'll find a comfortable place for you." He gestured at the narrow railed gangway.

"What's the name of this boat?" Natalie asked.

"Oh, it has had many names. It's old. Now it's called the *Redeemer*. It's Turkish registry, and once you're aboard you will be secure. The harbor master and the Turkish consul here have an excellent understanding."

Holding her baby close, Natalie said to Aaron Jastrow, "I'm beginning to feel like a Jew."

He smiled sourly. "Oh? And I've never stopped feeling like one. I thought I'd gotten away from it. Obviously I haven't. Come along, this is the way now." Aaron set foot on the gangway first. She followed him, clutching her baby son in both arms, and Rabinovitz plodded up behind them.

As Natalie set foot on the deck, the Palestinian touched her arm. In the gloom she could see him wearily smile. "Well, relax now, Mrs. Henry. You're in Turkey. That's a start."

64

JANICE was awakened by the sound of a shower starting full force. Her luminous bed clock read five minutes past five. She showered too, put on a housecoat, and combed her hair. In the living room Victor Henry sat buttoned up in white and gold, reading Navy correspondence by lamplight. His close-shaved face was ashen, which she more or less expected, after his dispatching a quart of brandy and passing sixteen hours in a stupor. Pencilling a note on a letter, he cleared his throat and said placidly, "Good morning, Jan. Did I disturb you? Sorry."

"Morning, Dad. No, Vic often gets me up around now. Is it too early for some bacon and eggs?"

"Matter of fact, that sounds pretty good. Warren get back last night?"

"Yes. He's in there." Janice wanted to tell him about the loss of the *Devilfish,* but he scared her, sitting there livid and cool in his starched uniform. He would find out, she thought, soon enough. She made coffee, fed the baby, and started breakfast. As usual, the smell of frying bacon brought Warren out, humming and brushing his hair, dressed in a khaki uniform. He grinned at his father, and Janice realized that he was putting on an act and would not disclose the *Devilfish* news. "Hi, Dad. How're you doing?"

"Not badly—all things considered." Brushing a fist against his forehead, Pug smiled ruefully. "I seem to have slept around the clock."

"Yes. Well, travel will do that to a fellow."

"Exactly. Funny effect travel has. Did I empty the bottle?"

Warren laughed. "Bone dry."

"I only remember drinking the first half."

"Dad, it was just what the doctor ordered. How about a hair of the dog?"

Pug raised a hand. "That's the road to perdition. This coffee's excellent."

Pouring himself a cup. Warren said, "You picked a good day to sleep through. Lots of news, none of it good."

"For instance?"

"Hitler and Mussolini declared war on us."

"They did? Then the lineup's complete. They're fools, making it easier for the President. Is that the worst of it?"

"Before you sacked out, had you heard about the *Prince of Wales* and the *Repulse?* The Japs got them both off Singapore."

"What!"

"Air attack. Battleships verus airplanes again, Dad, and they sank 'em both."

"God in heaven, Warren, they got the *Prince of Wales?* Did the British confirm that?"

"And the *Repulse.* Churchill admitted it. The Limeys are through in this ocean, right at the start. Australia's naked. Looks like it's all up to us out here."

Victor Henry half buried his face in a hand. That great ship in its splashy camouflage, he thought, that dark elegant wardroom, those tired, gallant officers and sailors, that deck where Winston Churchill and Franklin Roosevelt had sung hymns under the guns—gone, gone, sunk in the far Pacific! He said in a low mournful tone, "The changing of the guard."

"That's about the size of it."

"Have they hit the Philippines yet?"

Warren took a moment to sip coffee. He knew little about Clark Field; the American command in Luzon was muffling information that might panic the people. Even the official account of the Cavite raid had been skimpy. He had picked up the *Devilfish* news from a secret dispatch, and he was hoping the report might prove wrong; or if not, that a later dispatch would at least show Byron among the survivors.

"Well, they sort of plastered Cavite."

"Oh, they did?"

"Yes."

Staring at his son, Pug said, "Any dope?"

"Not much. They apparently went for the shore installations."

"The *Devilfish* was alongside."

"So you told me."

Warren was relieved when Janice called them to the table. Pug picked at the food. It was embarrassing, with his son and daughter-in-law eating heartily, but his throat was almost shut, and he had to force down the mouthfuls he ate.

"What's the plan of the day, Dad?" Warren said, as the lack of talk grew awkward.

"Huh? Oh, I thought I might scare up a tennis game at the club."

"*Tennis?* Are you serious?"

"Why not? Start getting back in some kind of shape."

"What about going down to Cincpac Personnel?"

"Well, I'll tell you, Warren, I've been wondering about that. At this point a thousand officers are looking for new assignments. Every Tom, Dick, and Harry of the battleship force must be warming chairs down at Personnel. The Navy will find work for me in due course, and maybe at this point I'd just better take what comes."

"You're dead wrong." In his life Warren had never heard his father talk this way, and he reacted immediately and forcibly. "You've had a bad break, but you're not Tom, Dick, or Harry. You're entitled to the best ship command they've got left in this fleet. You've already lost a day. The Navy's not going to come looking for you, Dad.

You play tennis for a few days and you'll end up back in War Plans. Is that what you want?"

Warren's energetic tone and thinking, so much like his own younger self, drew a smile from Pug. "Jan, hand me the Cincpac roster. It's there on top of that pile of mail." She passed him the mimeographed sheets and he leafed through them. "Hm. Interesting. *'Personnel Section—Captain Theodore Prentice Larkin, II.'* "

"Know him?" Warren asked.

"Jocko Larkin? Biggest boozer in my Academy class. I pulled him out of the Severn once when he fell off a sailboat dead drunk. Quite a wingding—Thanksgiving, I think —and I was the only sober one aboard. I didn't drink then."

"Dad, our squadron's got an officers' meeting at 0700. I'll drop you off at Cincpac. Let's go."

"Well, okay. Jocko sure won't throw me out."

At the overlook point where Janice had watched the Japanese onslaught, Warren halted the car. The sun had not yet risen. In the grayish-pink morning light far down in the harbor, there lay the incredible picture: seven United States battleships in a double row, canted, sunk, or turned turtle. Smoke rising from the wrecks still drifted heavily over the black flat oily water.

Bitterly Victor Henry muttered, looking out through the windshield, "The game board after the game."

"After the first move," Warren retorted. "Have you heard what Halsey said when they told him aboard the *Enterprise* about the attack? *'Before we're through with them, the Japanese language will be spoken only in hell!'* "

With a cynical grunt, Pug asked, "Did that impress you?"

"It gave the crew a big charge. Everyone was quoting it."

"Yes. Good talk for sailors. Beating the Japanese now is a tough battle problem. Especially with a bigger war on our hands in Europe."

"Dad, we ought to do it handily, with the stuff we've got building."

Pug said, "Maybe. Meantime we're in for a rugged couple of years. How much stomach do the people back home have for defeat? Because they're going to take plenty in this ocean. Maybe they'll pressure the President to quit and make a deal. They don't really give a damn about Asia, they never have."

Warren started the car. His father's low mood disturbed him. "They won't quit. Not now. Not after this. Let's get you down to Cincpac."

He drove in his usual breakneck fashion. His father appeared to take no notice. Neither spoke. In this lame silence they arrived at the Cincpac building and pulled into a parking space.

"Well!" Pug Henry roused himself from a listless abstraction. "Here we are. Now, what about you? Will I be seeing you again?"

"Why, I hope so. Sometime during this war."

"I mean tonight."

"It's hard to say. We were supposed to sortie yesterday. Maybe we will today. There's a rather headless feeling in this fleet."

"I completely understand. I feel sort of headless myself."

"It's still there on your shoulders, Dad."

"Well, I wouldn't want to give an emphatic nod."

This made Warren laugh. It was more like his father. "Don't take no from Captain Larkin, now. Better keep these car keys, in case I do leave."

"Right. And in case you do—good luck and good hunting, Warren."

The father and son looked each other in the face, and parted without more words. Victor Henry went straight to the Cincpac communications office and looked through the dispatches. In the long garbled battle report of the evening before about Cavite, he saw the *Devilfish* listed as sunk.

He went to Jocko Larkin's office to wait. It was a quarter to seven, and nobody was there yet, not even the yeoman. Pug unceremoniously took a lounge chair in the inner office; Larkin would have done the same in an office of his. The large wide-windowed room had a panoramic view—the sunny sugarcane slopes, the blue ocean beyond the anchorage, and the hideous black-coated harbor, with its grotesque fringe of defeat and damage.

Victor Henry felt ill: nauseous, chilly, yet greasily perspiring. Consuming a bottle of brandy in a few hours had

done this, of course; but after the letters from Rhoda and
Madeline, the only safe immediate recourse had been
oblivion. The news that the *Devilfish* was lost had struck
an almost numb man, scarcely surprising him. As soon as
he had heard of the Cavite attack, he had half expected
evil tidings about his son. When things went bad, his long
experience told him, they went very bad; and he seemed
to be falling into a gulf of bad luck without a bottom.

But there was always a bottom to hit; meantime, he
groggily thought, the main thing was to hold himself together. He did not know, after all, that Byron was really
dead or injured. The *Devilfish* might not even be sunk. An
excited first report was unreliable. The idea was to brace
himself and hang on to hope until the straight word came.

On his wife and his daughter, however, the straight
word was in. Rhoda wanted to divorce him and marry
Fred Kirby; and his daughter had entangled herself with
her employer, had probably been committing adultery, and
it all might be in the newspapers any day. These were unchangeable facts, however hard to grasp. He had to absorb
them and somehow act on them.

Far from harboring any relieved notion that he might be
free for Pamela Tudsbury, Pug now first understood how
hopeless his romance with the English girl had been, and
what a strong bond tied him to his wife. That Rhoda did
not feel this tie too—that she could write and mail such a
letter with her usual breezy exclamation marks and under-
linings, cheerily blaming herself and her long dislike of a
Navy wife's existence, praising Pug up almost as a saint,
yet telling him that after more than twenty-five years she
wanted out, to go to another man—this was a stab from
which it would be difficult to recover. He felt it in his gut,
a throbbing, weakening wound. Rhoda's letter was coy
about the big question: exactly what had been going on
between her and Fred Kirby? Here Victor Henry was torn
two ways: by his hard good judgment, which told him that
of course his wife had been opening naked thighs to the
other man, probably for a long time; and by his love for
his wife and his own self-love, which protested that such
a thing was impossible. He clung to the dim fact—it *was*
a fact—that Rhoda hadn't said it in so many words.

Because what Victor Henry now wanted was to get her

back. He felt himself desperately in love with Rhoda. Much
of this was injured ego—he well understood that—but not
all. She was half of him, for better or worse; the weld was
a quarter of a century old; she was irreplaceable in his
life, with her arms, her mouth, her eyes, her sweet particular graces and ways; she was beautiful, desirable, and
above all capable of surprising him. It had taken a nasty
shock to drive these blunt truths home. He would have to
court this woman again! He could not greatly blame her
for the affair; he had already decided that in a brandy-
soaked fog before passing out. How close had he not come
to writing exactly the same kind of letter? Nor, strangely,
did he have strong feelings about Fred Kirby. The thing
had happened to those two people, much as it had to him
and Pamela; only Rhoda had gone over the edge. The pictures in his mind made him sick with revulsion; but in cold
honesty he had to look at the event in this rational way.

Rage at Madeline's boss perhaps did him some good.
One reason for surmounting this crisis was to seek out and
confront Hugh Cleveland. Regret cut at Pug for his softness in letting her stay in New York. At least he could
have tried to order her back to Washington; she might
have gone. Now this celebrated swine's wife was threatening to sue him for divorce, naming his twenty-one-year-old
assistant—unjustly, Madeline swore in a long vehement
paragraph, but that was hard to swallow. Unlike Rhoda's
letter, Madeline's was no bombshell. What could have been
more predictable for a girl adrift alone in New York; if
not with Cleveland, then with some other man? Madeline
had been shot down like a dove flying over a rifle range.

"Pug! I tried all yesterday afternoon to find you. Where
the hell were you hiding!"

Jocko Larkin came striding in, a scarlet-faced freckled
fat four-striper indistinguishable from twenty others. He
closed his door, tossed his cap on a hook, and said into his
squawk box, "No calls, Amory."

"Aye aye, sir."

"Well!" Larkin sat back in his swivel chair, fat hands
locked behind his head, surveying his classmate with a
penetrating eye. "Good to see you. That's hell about the
California. She'd have had a great skipper."

"Well, Jocko, I'd say my misfortune's lost in the shuffle."

"Pug, who gave you my message? I left it at half a dozen places."

"What message? Nobody. I came here to see you."

"What about?"

"Orders."

"That's what I wanted to see *you* about." Larkin looked over his shoulder, though nobody else was in the room, and turned off his intercom. "Pug, Admiral Kimmel is going to be relieved. At his own request." Jocko almost whispered this, adding with a sarcastic little grin, "Like Louis the Sixteenth had himself shortened by a head, at his own request. His successor will be Admiral Pye—for how long, we don't know, but Pye wants to start shaking up the staff. Let's face it, something smells here. Luckily, the personnel section has nothing to do with war alerts. It didn't happen on *my* watch. But it happened. Admiral Pye wants you for Operations—now hold it, Pug!" Jocko Larkin held up a hand as Victor Henry violently shook his head. "Let me give you my judgment. This is as great a break as a man in our class can have. Just remember there are six *Iowa* class battleships building now, due for commissioning in twelve to twenty months. The greatest warships in the world. You'll probably get one after this."

"Jocko, give me a ship."

"I'm telling you, you'll undoubtedly get one."

"Now. Not in 1943."

"No can do, Pug. Listen to me. *You don't say no to Cincpac!* Operations is a marvellous opening for you."

"Where's Admiral Pye's office?" Henry got to his feet.

"Sit down, Pug." Larkin rose too, and they stood glaring at each other. Larkin said, "You son of a bitch, you never could play football *or* tennis, and you can't think straight, either."

"I can swim pretty good."

Larkin looked nonplussed, then he burst out laughing. "Oh, sit down, Pug."

"Do I get a ship?"

"Sit down."

Pug sat.

"What's the matter, Pug? You look green around the gills, and you don't act right. Is everything okay?"

"I drank too much brandy last night."

"You did? *You?*"

"I didn't like losing the *California.*"

"I see. How's Rhoda?"

"Just fine." Victor Henry thought he brought the words out calmly, but Larkin raised his eyebrows. Folding fat fingers over his white-clad paunch, Larkin stared thoughtfully at Henry.

"Let's see. You have a boy on the *Enterprise,* don't you? Is he all right?"

"He's fine. I have a submariner, too. He's on the *Devilfish.* Or was."

"The *Devilfish,* eh?" Larkin's calm tone was very forced.

"Yes."

Opening a folder on his desk, Larkin studied several sheets clipped inside. "The *Northampton* might conceivably be available. I say *might.* Most likely not."

"The *Northampton?* God love you, Jocko, that's about the heaviest thing we've got left here."

"Pug, I don't care. A cruiser command doesn't compare to Cincpac's Deputy Chief for Operations. You know that! Tim Saunders came out of that job last year with two stars, junior as hell. Even if I could get you the *Northampton,* you'd be making the mistake of your life."

"You don't know the mistakes I've made. Now you listen to me, Jocko. I've shuffled all the high-strategy paper I ever want to in this Navy. Four years in War Plans, nearly three years in Europe. I'm not bucking for two stars, not any more. I'm a sailor and a gunner, and there's a war on." Victor Henry swept an arm at the window and the shattered battle fleet. "If you can't find me anything else, I'll take a squadron of minesweepers. Okay? *I want to go to sea.*"

"I hear you, loud and clear." Heaving a sigh that turned into a groan, Jocko Larkin said, "One more flap I'll have with the admiral, that's all."

"The hell with that. I want him to know this is my doing. Where is he?"

"Listen, Pug, if you talk to the admiral the way you've been talking to me, you'll get sent to the States on a medical. You look like death warmed over, and you're acting shell-shocked. I'll see what I can do here. Get some sleep, lay off the brandy, and whatever's bothering you, put it on ice. I'll try to find something."

"Thanks, Jocko. If you want to call me, I'll be at my son's house." He gave Larkin the number.

As they shook hands over the table, Captain Larkin said with odd softness, "When you write Rhoda, give her my love."

> Naval Officers Club
> Pearl Harbor
> 12 December, 1941

Dear Rhoda:

I'm somewhat stymied by the problem of answering your astounding letter, but putting it off won't give me any inspiration. I don't think I should waste your time setting down my feelings on paper. Anyway, I'm not sure I can do it, not being very good at that sort of thing, at best.

If I really believed this move would make you happy, maybe I could endure it better. However, it strikes me as a calamity for you as well as for me; and I am expressing this opinion though it hasn't been asked for.

I know I'm no Don Juan, and in fact have been pretty much of a pickle-face around you a good part of the time. The reasons for this are complicated, and it might not be too helpful to go into them now. The basic point is that, taking the rough with the smooth, you and I have made it this far. I still love you—a lot more than I've showed, perhaps—and in your letter you've managed to say a few kind things about me.

I'm compelled to believe that at the moment you're "lovesick as a schoolgirl," and that you can't help it, and all that part. I guess these things will happen, though one's always caught unawares when the roof falls in. Still, you're not really a schoolgirl, are you? Getting used to anybody new at our age is a very hard job. If you're a widow, that's different. Then you have no choice. But here I am still.

The life we've been leading in recent years has put a strain on our marriage. I recognize that, and I've certainly felt the strain myself. In Manila I said to Byron that we've become a family of tumbleweeds. That's the truth, and lately the winds of war have been blowing us all around the world. Right now it strikes me that those same winds are starting to flatten civilization. All the more reason for us to hang on to what we have—mainly each other, and our family—and to love each other to the end. That's the way I've worked it out. I hope that on further thought you will, too.

I'll probably be at sea most of the time for the next year or two; so I can't make the immediate effort to mend matters that seems urgently called for. Here's how I'm compelled to leave it. I'm ready to forget—or try to—that you ever wrote the letter; or to talk it over with you on my next Stateside leave; or, if you're absolutely certain you want to go ahead with it, to sign the papers and do what you wish. But I'll put up a helluva fight first about that. I have no intention of simply letting you go. In plain words I want two things, Rhoda: first, your happiness; second, if at all possible, that we go on together.

I've seen a bit of Warren. He's turned into a splendid officer. He has everything. His future is limitless. He has the brains, drive, acuteness, toughness, and sheer ability to become Chief of Naval Operations. Byron has come along too. We've been fortunate in our sons. I know they're facing hazards, but the whole world's in hazard, and at least my boys are serving.

I don't know what went wrong with Madeline. I'm kind of sick about that, and don't propose to dwell on it. If the fellow wants to marry her, that may clean the mess up as much as anything can. If not, he'll be hearing from me.

You were right to say that your news would hurt less because of my orders to the *California*. In a peculiar fashion it's working out that way. Ever since I flew into Pearl Harbor on the Clipper, after seeing Wake and Midway in flames, I've been living on a straight diet of disaster. Your letter almost fitted in as something normal. Almost.

I'm a family man, and a one-woman man, Rhoda. You know all that. Maybe I'm a kind of fossil, a form that's outlived its time. Even so, I can only act by my lights while I last. My impression was, and remains, that Fred Kirby—despite what's happened—is much the same sort of fellow. If I'm right about that, this thing will not work out for you in the long run, and you had better extricate yourself now. That's as honest a judgment as I can give you.

Victor is a handsome baby, and Janice is a good mother and very pretty. Our other grandson looks unbelievably like Briny as an infant. I'm enclosing a snapshot I picked up in Moscow from Natalie's old friend Slote. I hate to part with it but you'll want to see it, I know. Let's hope to God she got herself and that kid safely out of Italy before Mussolini declared war.

Jocko Larkin sends his love. He's fat and sleek.

That's about it. Now I'm going to start earning my salary— I trust—by fighting a war.

Love,
Pug

It was nearly lunchtime when Victor Henry finished writing this letter, and the officers' club lounge was becoming crowded and noisy. He read the letter twice, thinking how meager and stiff it was, but he decided against rewriting it. The substance was there. One could revise some letters a hundred times without improving them. The letter he had posted to Pamela Tudsbury (how long ago that seemed!) had been more clumsy and barren than most of the discarded ones. He sealed the envelope.

"Say, Pug!" Jocko Larkin, walking past with three younger officers, halted, and told them to go ahead and secure a table. "I've been trying to call you. Do you know about the *Devilfish?*"

"No." Pug's heart thumped heavily. "What about it?"

"Well, it was the *Sealion* that was sunk at Cavite. The follow-up report came in a little while ago. The *Devilfish* was undamaged."

"Really?" Pug had to clear his throat twice. "That's definite, now?"

"Couldn't be more definite. The dispatch says the *Devilfish* report was erroneous."

"I see. I'm sorry about the *Sealion,* but you're a bearer of good news. Thanks."

"My other news isn't so hot, Pug. The thing we talked about—I'm trying but that looks like a pipe dream."

"Well, you warned me. It's all right."

"I'm still scratching around for something, though. Join us for lunch."

"Another time, Jocko."

Dropping the letter in the club mailbox, Pug went out into the sunshine. A stone had rolled off his heart; Byron was all right! And one way or another, Jocko would get him out to sea. Strolling aimlessly through the Navy Yard, digesting these sharp turns of fortune, he arrived at the waterfront. There alongside the fuel dock, with thick oil hoses pulsing, was the *Northampton.*

On leaving Larkin's office, Pug had fought off a temptation to visit the cruiser, deciding that it might be a jinx to set foot on board before knowing his orders. Now it didn't matter. He thought of mounting the gangway and having a look around. But what for? He had served a year and a half in a sister ship, the *Chester.* These were handsome vessels, he thought, strolling along the dock beside the bustling *Northampton,* which was loading ammunition and frozen food stores as well as fuel for battle patrol—handsome vessels, but half-breed bastards, spawned by a sickly cross of politics and warship-building.

The Washington Treaty, which Pug considered a preposterous folly, had bound the United States back in 1922 to limit its cruisers to less than ten thousand tons, and to guns of eight-inch caliber. There had been no limit on length. These hybrids were the result—overblown destroyers, with the length of battleships but a quarter the weight of metal, with slender beams, light armor, and medium punch. Their mission was to act as scouts and merchant raiders, and to fight enemy cruisers. Any one of Japan's ten battleships could blow the *Northampton* out of the water; nor could she survive a torpedoing, except with perfect damage control. After the *California,* the *Northampton* was a relatively shrunken affair.

Still, Pug thought, he would have been glad enough to get her. It was exciting to see the cruiser taking on beans, bullets, and oil for a combat mission. Jocko was right, Operations was the inside track. But, for the good of his soul right now, Pug felt he needed to be loading beans, bullets, and oil on his own ship.

He drove back to the house. On the desk in his bedroom, a handwritten note was clipped to a wrinkled Western Union cable:

From: Janice.
To: Dad-in-law.
Subject: Miscellaneous.
1. In case anything comes up, am at the Gillettes with Vic Home for dinner.

2. Warren phoned. Won't be back. They sortie at dawn.
3. Yeoman from *California* delivered the attached. Says it's been kicking around the base for days, and just came to their office on the beach.
4. Love.

He opened the cable.

DEAREST JUST THIS INSTANT HEARD ON THE RADIO OF JAPANESE ATTACK AM UTTERLY HORRIFIED FRIGHTFULLY WORRIED ABOUT YOU DESPERATELY ASHAMED OF THAT RIDICULOUS IDIOTIC LETTER WORST POSSIBLE TIMING FORGET IT PLEASE PLEASE AND FORGIVE HOPE YOURE SAFE AND WELL CABLE ME LOVE RHO

He sat nodding grimly as he read it. Rhoda to the life! He could hear her telephoning it: "Am UTTERLY horrified, FRIGHTFULLY worried about you, DESPERATELY ashamed of that RIDICULOUS, IDIOTIC letter. Worst POSSIBLE timing . . ." Pug suspected it was a bone to the dog. He knew Rhoda's bursts of contrition. She was never so sweet as immediately after some disgusting behavior. This saving grace had gotten her over many rough spots; and her impulse in sending the cable might well have been sincere. But the process of repair would be long, if indeed it was even beginning. Their marriage now was a salvage job like the *California*. He did not know what to reply, so he tossed the cable into the desk drawer, beside the letter for which it apologized.

That night at dinner Pug drank a lot of wine, and a lot of brandy afterward; Janice kept pouring, and he gratefully accepted. He knew he would not sleep otherwise. The alcohol worked; he scarcely remembered turning in. At four in the morning, he snapped wide awake, and it occurred to him that he might as well watch the sortie of the *Enterprise*. He dressed quietly, closed the outside door without a sound, and drove to the overlook point.

The darkness was merciful to Pearl Harbor. The smashed battleships were invisible. Overhead a clear starry black sky arched, with Orion setting in the west, and Venus sparkling in the east, high above a narrow streak of red.

Only the faintest smell of smoke on the sea breeze hinted at the gigantic scene of disaster below. But the dawn brightened, light stole over the harbor, and soon the destruction and the shame were unveiled once more. At first the battleships were merely vague shapes; but even before all the stars were gone, one could see the Pacific Battle Force, a crazy dim double line of sunken hulks along Ford Island—and first in the line, the U.S.S. *California.*

Victor Henry turned his face from the hideous sight to the indigo arch of the sky, where Venus and the brightest stars still burned: Sirius, Capella, Procyon, the old navigation aids. The familiar religious awe came over him, the sense of a Presence above this pitiful little earth. He could almost picture God the Father looking down with sad wonder at this mischief. In a world so rich and lovely, could his children find nothing better to do than to dig iron from the ground and work it into vast grotesque engines for blowing each other up? Yet this madness was the way of the world. He had given all his working years to it. Now he was about to risk his very life at it. Why?

Because the others did it, he thought. Because Abel's next-door neighbor was Cain. Because with all its rotten spots, the United States of America was not only his homeland but the hope of the world. Because if America's enemies dug up iron and made deadly engines of it, America had to do the same, and do it better, or die. Maybe the vicious circle would end with this first real world war. Maybe it would end with Christ's second coming. Maybe it would never end.

But he was living in 1941. Below in the brightening dawn lay his own sunken ship and his own destroyed fleet. The professional sailors and fliers who had done this thing, and done a damned smart job of it, had obeyed orders of politicians working with Hitler. Until the life was beaten out of that monster, the world could not move an inch toward a more sane existence. There was nothing to do now but win the war. So Victor Henry meditated as the *Enterprise* moved down channel in the sunrise and out to sea under the escort of destroyers and cruisers, taking his firstborn son into battle.

Back at the house, he found Janice all dressed. "Hi.

Going somewhere?" he said. "I thought you'd still be asleep."

"Oh, it's Vic's cough. It hangs on and on. I'm taking him to the clinic down at the base for a checkup. You just missed a call from Captain Larkin."

"Jocko? This early?"

"Yes. He left a message for you. He said, 'She's all yours.' "

Victor Henry dropped in a chair, with a blankly startled look.

"Good news, I hope?" Janice asked. "He said you'd understand."

" *'She's all yours'*? That's the whole message?"

"That's it. He said he wouldn't be in his office till noon, but he thought you'd want to know right away."

"I see. Well, it's pretty fair news. Is the coffee on?"

"Yes. Anna May will make you breakfast."

"No, no, coffee's all I want, thanks. Look, Janice, you'll be passing by Western Union. Can you send Rhoda a cable for me?"

"Sure."

Victor Henry reached for the memo pad by the telephone, and scrawled: LETTER COMING AM FINE HAVE JUST BEGUN TO FIGHT.

Glancing at the little sheet he handed her, Janice curved her mouth in an indulgent female grin.

"What's the matter with that?" Pug said.

"How about *'Love'*?"

"By all means. Thanks, Jan. You add that."

When she left with the baby, he was on the telephone, trying to reach Commander, Cruisers Pacific. He responded to her farewell wave with a bleak preoccupied smile. Janice thought, closing the door on him, that nothing could be more like her austere, remote father-in-law than the little business of the cable. You had to remind this man that he loved his wife.

1964–1971